PS 3511 .A86 A6 1994
Novels 1942-1954
Faulkner, William
196571

DATE DUE

BRODART Cat. No. 23-221

WILLIAM FAULKNER

William Faulkner

NOVELS 1942–1954

Go Down, Moses
Intruder in the Dust
Requiem for a Nun
A Fable

THE LIBRARY OF AMERICA

Volume compilation, notes, and chronology copyright © 1994 by
Literary Classics of the United States, Inc., New York, N.Y.
All rights reserved.
No part of this book may be reproduced commercially
by offset-lithographic or equivalent copying devices without
the permission of the publisher.

Go Down, Moses copyright © 1942 by William Faulkner; copyright
renewed 1970 by Estelle Faulkner and Jill Faulkner Summers.
Intruder in the Dust copyright © 1948 by Random House, Inc.;
copyright renewed 1975 by Jill Faulkner Summers. *Requiem for a Nun*
copyright © 1950, 1951 by William Faulkner; copyright renewed 1978,
1979 by Jill Faulkner Summers. *A Fable* copyright © 1950, 1954 by
William Faulkner; copyright renewed 1978, 1982 by Jill Faulkner
Summers. Published by arrangement with Random House, Inc.

The paper used in this publication meets the
minimum requirements of the American National Standard for
Information Sciences—Permanence of Paper for Printed
Library Materials, ANSI Z39.48—1984.

Distributed to the trade in the United States
by Penguin Books USA Inc
and in Canada by Penguin Books Canada Ltd.

Library of Congress Catalog Number: 94–2942
For cataloging information, see end of Notes.
ISBN 0–940450–85–2

First Printing
The Library of America–73

Manufactured in the United States of America

Joseph Blotner and Noel Polk
wrote the notes and edited the texts
for this volume

The publishers wish to thank Mrs. Paul D. Summers, Jr.,
and the Alderman Library of the University of Virginia
for use of archival materials, and
Lieutenant Colonel John D. Hart, of the Faulkner Concordance
Project at the United States Military Academy, and the
University of Southern Mississippi for technical assistance.

The texts of Go Down Moses, Intruder in the Dust,
Requiem for a Nun, and A Fable have been established by
Noel Polk.

Contents

GO DOWN, MOSES

To Mammy

CAROLINE BARR

Mississippi

[1840–1940]

Who was born in slavery and who gave to my family a fidelity without stint or calculation of recompense and to my childhood an immeasurable devotion and love.

Contents

Was

1.

ISAAC McCASLIN, 'Uncle Ike', past seventy and nearer eighty than he ever corroborated anymore, a widower now and uncle to half a county and father to no one

this was not something participated in or even seen by himself, but by his elder cousin, McCaslin Edmonds, grandson of Isaac's father's sister and so descended by the distaff, yet notwithstanding the inheritor, and in his time the bequestor, of that which some had thought then and some still thought should have been Isaac's, since his was the name in which the title to the land had first been granted from the Indian patent and which some of the descendants of his father's slaves still bore in the land. But Isaac was not one of these:—a widower these twenty years, who in all his life had owned but one object more than he could wear and carry in his pockets and his hands at one time, and this was the narrow iron cot and the stained lean mattress which he used camping in the woods for deer and bear or for fishing or simply because he loved the woods; who owned no property and never desired to since the earth was no man's but all men's, as light and air and weather were; who lived still in the cheap frame bungalow in Jefferson which his wife's father gave them on their marriage and which his wife had willed to him at her death and which he had pretended to accept, acquiesce to, to humor her, ease her going but which was not his, will or not, chancery dying wishes mortmain possession or whatever, himself merely holding it for his wife's sister and her children who had lived in it with him since his wife's death, holding himself welcome to live in one room of it as he had during his wife's time or she during her time or the sister-in-law and her children during the rest of his and after

not something he had participated in or even remembered except from the hearing, the listening, come to him through and from his cousin McCaslin born in 1850 and sixteen years his senior and hence, his own father being near seventy when Isaac, an only child, was born, rather his brother than cousin and rather his father than either, out of the old time, the old days

2.

When he and Uncle Buck ran back to the house from discovering that Tomey's Turl had run again, they heard Uncle Buddy cursing and bellowing in the kitchen, then the fox and the dogs came out of the kitchen and crossed the hall into the dogs' room and they heard them run through the dogs' room into his and Uncle Buck's room then they saw them cross the hall again into Uncle Buddy's room and heard them run through Uncle Buddy's room into the kitchen again and this time it sounded like the whole kitchen chimney had come down and Uncle Buddy bellowing like a steamboat blowing and this time the fox and the dogs and five or six sticks of firewood all came out of the kitchen together with Uncle Buddy in the middle of them hitting at everything in sight with another stick. It was a good race.

When he and Uncle Buck ran into their room to get Uncle Buck's necktie, the fox had treed behind the clock on the mantel. Uncle Buck got the necktie from the drawer and kicked the dogs off and lifted the fox down by the scruff of the neck and shoved it back into the crate under the bed and they went to the kitchen, where Uncle Buddy was picking the breakfast up out of the ashes and wiping it off with his apron. "What in damn's hell do you mean," he said. "Turning that damn fox out with the dogs all loose in the house?"

"Damn the fox," Uncle Buck said. "Tomey's Turl has broke out again. Give me and Cass some breakfast quick. We might just barely catch him before he gets there."

Because they knew exactly where Tomey's Turl had gone; he went there every time he could slip off, which was about twice a year. He was heading for Mr Hubert Beauchamp's place just over the edge of the next county, that Mr Hubert's sister, Miss Sophonsiba (Mr Hubert was a bachelor too, like Uncle Buck and Uncle Buddy) was still trying to make people call Warwick after the place in England that she said Mr

Hubert was probably the true earl of only he never even had enough pride, not to mention energy, to take the trouble to establish his just rights. Tomey's Turl would go there to hang around Mr Hubert's girl, Tennie, until somebody came and got him. They couldn't keep him at home by buying Tennie from Mr Hubert because Uncle Buck said he and Uncle Buddy had so many niggers already that they could hardly walk around on their own land for them, and they couldn't sell Tomey's Turl to Mr Hubert because Mr Hubert said he not only wouldn't buy Tomey's Turl, he wouldn't have that damn white half-McCaslin on his place even as a free gift, not even if Uncle Buck and Uncle Buddy were to pay board and keep for him. And if somebody didn't go and get Tomey's Turl right away, Mr Hubert would fetch him back himself, bringing Miss Sophonsiba, and they would stay for a week or longer, Miss Sophonsiba living in Uncle Buddy's room and Uncle Buddy moved clean out of the house, sleeping in one of the cabins in the quarters where the niggers used to live in his great-grandfather's time until his great-grandfather died and Uncle Buck and Uncle Buddy moved all the niggers into the big house which his great-grandfather had not had time to finish, and not even doing the cooking while they were there and not even coming to the house anymore except to sit on the front gallery after supper, sitting in the darkness between Mr Hubert and Uncle Buck until after a while even Mr Hubert would give up telling how many more head of niggers and acres of land he would add to what he would give Miss Sophonsiba when she married, and go to bed. And one midnight last summer Uncle Buddy just happened by accident to be awake and hear Mr Hubert drive out of the lot and by the time he waked them and they got Miss Sophonsiba up and dressed and the team put to the wagon and caught Mr Hubert, it was almost daylight. So it was always he and Uncle Buck who went to fetch Tomey's Turl because Uncle Buddy never went anywhere, not even to town and not even to fetch Tomey's Turl from Mr Hubert's, even though they all knew that Uncle Buddy could have risked it ten times as much as Uncle Buck could have dared.

They ate breakfast fast. Uncle Buck put on his necktie while they were running toward the lot to catch the horses. The only time he wore the necktie was on Tomey's Turl's account and he hadn't even had it out of the drawer since that night last summer when Uncle Buddy had waked them in the dark and said, "Get up out of that bed and damn quick." Uncle Buddy didn't own a necktie at all; Uncle Buck said Uncle Buddy wouldn't take that chance even in a section like theirs, where ladies were so damn seldom thank God that a man could ride for days in a straight line without having to dodge a single one. His grandmother (she was Uncle Buck's and Uncle Buddy's sister; she had raised him following his mother's death. That was where he had got his christian name: McCaslin, Carothers McCaslin Edmonds) said that Uncle Buck and Uncle Buddy both used the necktie just as another way of daring people to say they looked like twins, because even at sixty they would still fight anyone who claimed he could not tell them apart; whereupon his father had answered that any man who ever played poker once with Uncle Buddy would never mistake him again for Uncle Buck or anybody else.

Jonas had the two horses saddled and waiting. Uncle Buck didn't mount a horse like he was any sixty years old either, lean and active as a cat, with his round, close-cropped white head and his hard little gray eyes and his white-stubbled jaw, his foot in the iron and the horse already moving, already running at the open gate when Uncle Buck came into the seat. He scrabbled up too, onto the shorter pony, before Jonas could boost him up, clapping the pony with his heels into its own stiff, short-coupled canter, out the gate after Uncle Buck, when Uncle Buddy (he hadn't even noticed him) stepped out from the gate and caught the bitt. "Watch him," Uncle Buddy said. "Watch Theophilus. The minute anything begins to look wrong, you ride to hell back here and get me. You hear?"

"Yes, sir," he said. "Lemme go now. I wont even ketch Uncle Buck, let alone Tomey's Turl——"

Uncle Buck was riding Black John, because if they could just catch sight of Tomey's Turl at least one mile from Mr Hubert's gate, Black John would ride him down in two minutes. So when they came out on the long flat about three miles from Mr Hubert's, sure enough, there was Tomey's Turl on the Jake mule about a mile ahead. Uncle Buck flung his arm out and back, reining in, crouched on the big horse, his little round head and his gnarled neck thrust forward like a cooter's. "Stole away!" he whispered. "You stay back where he wont see you and flush. I'll circle him through the woods and we will bay him at the creek ford."

He waited until Uncle Buck had vanished into the woods. Then he went on. But Tomey's Turl saw him. He closed in too fast; maybe he was afraid he wouldn't be there in time to see him when he treed. It was the best race he had ever seen. He had never seen old Jake go that fast, and nobody had ever known Tomey's Turl to go faster than his natural walk, even riding a mule. Uncle Buck whooped once from the woods, running on sight, then Black John came out of the trees, driving, soupled out flat and level as a hawk, with Uncle Buck right up behind his ears now and yelling so that they looked exactly like a big black hawk with a sparrow riding it, across the field and over the ditch and across the next field, and he was running too; the mare went out before he even knew she was ready, and he was yelling too. Because, being a nigger, Tomey's Turl should have jumped down and run for it afoot as soon as he saw them. But he didn't; maybe Tomey's Turl had been running off from Uncle Buck for so long that he had even got used to running away like a white man would do it. And it was like he and old Jake had added Tomey's Turl's natural walking speed to the best that old Jake had ever done in his life, and it was just exactly enough to beat Uncle Buck to the ford. Because when he and the pony arrived, Black John was blown and lathered and Uncle Buck was down, leading him around in a circle to slow him down, and they could already hear Mr Hubert's dinner horn a mile away.

Only, for a while Tomey's Turl didn't seem to be at Mr Hubert's either. The boy was still sitting on the gate-post, blowing the horn—there was no gate there; just two posts and a nigger boy about his size sitting on one of them, blowing a fox-horn; this was what Miss Sophonsiba was still reminding people was named Warwick even when they had already known for a long time that's what she aimed to have it called, until when they wouldn't call it Warwick she wouldn't even seem to know what they were talking about and it would sound like she and Mr Hubert owned two separate plantations covering the same area of ground, one on top of the other. Mr Hubert was sitting in the spring-house with his boots off and his feet in the water, drinking a toddy. But nobody there had seen Tomey's Turl; for a time it looked like Mr Hubert couldn't even place who Uncle Buck was talking about. "Oh, that nigger," he said at last. "We'll find him after dinner."

Only it didn't seem like they were going to eat either. Mr Hubert and Uncle Buck had a toddy, then Mr Hubert finally sent to tell the boy on the gate-post he could quit blowing, and he and Uncle Buck had another toddy and Uncle Buck still saying, "I just want my nigger. Then we got to get on back toward home."

"After dinner," Mr Hubert said. "If we dont start him somewhere around the kitchen, we'll put the dogs on him. They'll find him if it's in the power of mortal Walker dogs to do it."

But at last a hand began waving a handkerchief or something white through the broken place in an upstairs shutter. They went to the house, crossing the back gallery, Mr Hubert warning them again, as he always did, to watch out for the rotted floor-board he hadn't got around to having fixed yet. Then they stood in the hall, until presently there was a jangling and swishing noise and they began to smell the perfume, and Miss Sophonsiba came down the stairs. Her hair was roached under a lace cap; she had on her Sunday dress and beads and a red ribbon around her throat and a little nigger girl carrying her fan and he stood quietly a little behind Uncle Buck, watching her lips until they opened and he could see the roan tooth. He had never known anyone before with a roan tooth and he remembered how one time his grandmother and his father were talking about Uncle Buddy and Uncle Buck and his grandmother said that Miss Sophonsiba had matured into a fine-looking woman once. Maybe she had. He didn't know. He wasn't but nine.

"Why, Mister Theophilus," she said. "And McCaslin," she said. She had never looked at him and she wasn't talking to him and he knew it, although he was prepared and balanced to drag his foot when Uncle Buck did. "Welcome to Warwick."

He and Uncle Buck dragged their foot. "I just come to get

my nigger," Uncle Buck said. "Then we got to get on back home."

Then Miss Sophonsiba said something about a bumblebee, but he couldn't remember that. It was too fast and there was too much of it, the ear-rings and beads clashing and jingling like little trace chains on a toy mule trotting and the perfume stronger too, like the ear-rings and beads sprayed it out each time they moved and he watched the roan-colored tooth flick and glint between her lips; something about Uncle Buck was a bee sipping from flower to flower and not staying long anywhere and all that stored sweetness to be wasted on Uncle Buddy's desert air, calling Uncle Buddy Mister Amodeus like she called Uncle Buck Mister Theophilus, or maybe the honey was being stored up against the advent of a queen and who was the lucky queen and when? "Ma'am?" Uncle Buck said. Then Mr Hubert said:

"Hah. A buck bee. I reckon that nigger's going to think he's a buck hornet, once he lays hands on him. But I reckon what Buck's thinking about sipping right now is some meat gravy and biscuit and a cup of coffee. And so am I."

They went in to the diningroom and ate and Miss Sophonsiba said how seriously now neighbors just a half day's ride apart ought not to go so long as Uncle Buck did, and Uncle Buck said Yessum, and Miss Sophonsiba said Uncle Buck was just a confirmed roving bachelor from the cradle born and this time Uncle Buck even quit chewing and looked and said, Yes ma'am, he sure was, and born too late at it to ever change now but at least he could thank God no lady would ever have to suffer the misery of living with him and Uncle Buddy, and Miss Sophonsiba said ah, that maybe Uncle Buck just aint met the woman yet who would not only accept what Uncle Buck was pleased to call misery, but who would make Uncle Buck consider even his freedom a small price to pay, and Uncle Buck said, "Nome. Not yet."

Then he and Mr Hubert and Uncle Buck went out to the front gallery and sat down. Mr Hubert hadn't even got done taking his shoes off again and inviting Uncle Buck to take his off, when Miss Sophonsiba came out the door carrying a tray with another toddy on it. "Damnit, Sibbey," Mr Hubert said. "He's just et. He dont want to drink that now." But Miss

Sophonsiba didn't seem to hear him at all. She stood there, the roan tooth not flicking now but fixed because she wasn't talking now, handing the toddy to Uncle Buck until after a while she said how her papa always said nothing sweetened a Missippi toddy like the hand of a Missippi lady and would Uncle Buck like to see how she used to sweeten her papa's toddy for him? She lifted the toddy and took a sip of it and handed it again to Uncle Buck and this time Uncle Buck took it. He dragged his foot again and drank the toddy and said if Mr Hubert was going to lay down, he would lay down a while too, since from the way things looked Tomey's Turl was fixing to give them a long hard race unless Mr Hubert's dogs were a considerable better than they used to be.

Mr Hubert and Uncle Buck went into the house. After a while he got up too and went around to the back yard to wait for them. The first thing he saw was Tomey's Turl's head slipping along above the lane fence. But when he cut across the yard to turn him, Tomey's Turl wasn't even running. He was squatting behind a bush, watching the house, peering around the bush at the back door and the upstairs windows, not whispering exactly but not talking loud either: "Whut they doing now?"

"They're taking a nap now," he said. "But never mind that; they're going to put the dogs on you when they get up."

"Hah," Tomey's Turl said. "And nem you mind that neither. I got protection now. All I needs to do is to keep old Buck from ketching me unto I gets the word."

"What word?" he said. "Word from who? Is Mr Hubert going to buy you from Uncle Buck?"

"Huh," Tomey's Turl said again. "I got more protection than whut Mr Hubert got even." He rose to his feet. "I gonter tell you something to remember: anytime you wants to git something done, from hoeing out a crop to getting married, just get the womenfolks to working at it. Then all you needs to do is set down and wait. You member that."

Then Tomey's Turl was gone. And after a while he went back to the house. But there wasn't anything but the snoring coming out of the room where Uncle Buck and Mr Hubert were, and some more light-sounding snoring coming from upstairs. He went to the spring-house and sat with his feet in the water as Mr Hubert had been doing, because soon now it would be cool enough for a race. And sure enough, after a while Mr Hubert and Uncle Buck came out onto the back gallery, with Miss Sophonsiba right behind them with the toddy tray only this time Uncle Buck drank his before Miss Sophonsiba had time to sweeten it, and Miss Sophonsiba told them to get back early, that all Uncle Buck knew of Warwick was just dogs and niggers and now that she had him, she wanted to show him her garden that Mr Hubert and nobody else had any sayso in. "Yessum," Uncle Buck said. "I just want to catch my nigger. Then we got to get on back home."

Four or five niggers brought up the three horses. They could already hear the dogs waiting still coupled in the lane, and they mounted and went on down the lane, toward the quarters, with Uncle Buck already out in front of even the dogs. So he never did know just when and where they jumped Tomey's Turl, whether he flushed out of one of the cabins or not. Uncle Buck was away out in front on Black John and they hadn't even cast the dogs yet when Uncle Buck roared, "Gone away! I godfrey, he broke cover then!" and Black John's feet clapped four times like pistol shots while he was gathering to go out, then he and Uncle Buck vanished over the hill like they had run at the blank edge of the world itself. Mr Hubert was roaring too: "Gone away! Cast them!" and they all piled over the crest of the hill just in time to see Tomey's Turl away out across the flat, almost to the woods, and the dogs streaking down the hill and out onto the flat. They just tongued once and when they came boiling up around Tomey's Turl it looked like they were trying to jump up and lick him in the face until even Tomey's Turl slowed down and he and the dogs all went into the woods together, walking, like they were going home from a rabbit hunt. And when they caught up with Uncle Buck in the woods, there was no Tomey's Turl and no dogs either, nothing but old Jake about a half an hour later, hitched in a clump of bushes with Tomey's Turl's coat tied on him for a saddle and near a half bushel of Mr Hubert's oats scattered around on the ground that old Jake never even had enough appetite left to nuzzle up and spit back out again. It wasn't any race at all.

"We'll get him tonight though," Mr Hubert said. "We'll

bait for him. We'll throw a picquet of niggers and dogs around Tennie's house about midnight, and we'll get him."

"Tonight, hell," Uncle Buck said. "Me and Cass and that nigger all three are going to be half way home by dark. Aint one of your niggers got a fyce or something that will trail them hounds?"

"And fool around here in the woods for half the night too?" Mr Hubert said. "When I'll bet you five hundred dollars that all you got to do to catch that nigger is to walk up to Tennie's cabin after dark and call him?"

"Five hundred dollars?" Uncle Buck said. "Done! Because me and him neither one are going to be anywhere near Tennie's house by dark. Five hundred dollars!" He and Mr Hubert glared at one another.

"Done!" Mr Hubert said.

So they waited while Mr Hubert sent one of the niggers back to the house on old Jake and in about a half an hour the nigger came back with a little bob-tailed black fyce and a new bottle of whisky. Then he rode up to Uncle Buck and held something out to him wrapped in a piece of paper. "What?" Uncle Buck said.

"It's for you," the nigger said. Then Uncle Buck took it and unwrapped it. It was the piece of red ribbon that had been on Miss Sophonsiba's neck and Uncle Buck sat there on Black John, holding the ribbon like it was a little water moccasin only he wasn't going to let anybody see he was afraid of it, batting his eyes fast at the nigger. Then he stopped batting his eyes.

"What for?" he said.

"She just sont hit to you," the nigger said. "She say to tell you 'success'."

"She said what?" Uncle Buck said.

"I dont know, sir," the nigger said. "She just say 'success'."

"Oh," Uncle Buck said. And the fyce found the hounds. They heard them first, from a considerable distance. It was just before sundown and they were not trailing, they were making the noise dogs make when they want to get out of something. They found what that was too. It was a ten-foot-square cottonhouse in a field about two miles from Mr Hubert's house and all eleven of the dogs were inside it and the door wedged with a chunk of wood. They watched the dogs come boiling out when the nigger opened the door, Mr Hubert sitting his horse and looking at the back of Uncle Buck's neck.

"Well, well," Mr Hubert said. "That's something, anyway. You can use them again now. They dont seem to have no more trouble with your nigger than he seems to have with them."

"Not enough," Uncle Buck said. "That means both of them. I'll stick to the fyce."

"All right," Mr Hubert said. Then he said, "Hell, 'Filus, come on. Let's go eat supper. I tell you, all you got to do to catch that nigger is——"

"Five hundred dollars," Uncle Buck said.

"What?" Mr Hubert said. He and Uncle Buck looked at one another. They were not glaring now. They were not joking each other either. They sat there in the beginning of twilight, looking at each other, just blinking a little. "What five hundred dollars?" Mr Hubert said. "That you wont catch that nigger in Tennie's cabin at midnight tonight?"

"That me or that nigger neither aint going to be nowhere near nobody's house but mine at midnight tonight." Now they did glare at one another.

"Five hundred dollars," Mr Hubert said. "Done."

"Done," Uncle Buck said.

"Done," Mr Hubert said.

"Done," Uncle Buck said.

So Mr Hubert took the dogs and some of the niggers and went back to the house. Then he and Uncle Buck and the nigger with the fyce went on, the nigger leading old Jake with one hand and holding the fyce's leash (it was a piece of gnawed plowline) with the other. Now Uncle Buck let the fyce smell Tomey's Turl's coat; it was like for the first time now the fyce found out what they were after and they would have let him off the leash and kept up with him on the horses, only about that time the nigger boy began blowing the fox-horn for supper at the house and they didn't dare risk it.

Then it was full dark. And then—he didn't know how much later nor where they were, how far from the house, except that it was a good piece and it had been dark for a good while and they were still going on, with Uncle Buck leaning down from time to time to let the fyce have another smell of Tomey's Turl's coat while Uncle Buck took another drink from the whisky bottle—they found that Tomey's Turl had doubled and was making a long swing back toward the house. "I godfrey, we've got him," Uncle Buck said. "He's going to earth. We'll cut back to the house and head him before he can den." So they left the nigger to cast the fyce and follow him on old Jake, and he and Uncle Buck rode for Mr Hubert's, stopping on the hills to blow the horses and listen to the fyce down in the creek bottom where Tomey's Turl was still making his swing.

But they never caught him. They reached the dark quarters; they could see lights still burning in Mr Hubert's house and somebody was blowing the fox-horn again and it wasn't any boy and he had never heard a fox-horn sound mad before either, and he and Uncle Buck scattered out on the slope below Tennie's cabin. Then they heard the fyce, not trailing now but yapping, about a mile away, then the nigger whooped and they knew the fyce had faulted. It was at the creek. They hunted the banks both ways for more than an hour, but they couldn't straighten Tomey's Turl out. At last even Uncle Buck gave up and they started back toward the house, the fyce riding too now, in front of the nigger on the mule. They were just coming up the lane to the quarters; they could see on along the ridge to where Mr Hubert's house was all dark now, when all of a sudden the fyce gave a yelp and jumped down from old Jake and hit the ground running and yelling every jump, and Uncle Buck was down too and had snatched him off the pony almost before he could clear his feet from the irons, and they ran too, on past the dark cabins toward the one where the fyce had treed. "We got him!" Uncle Buck said. "Run around to the back. Dont holler; just grab up a stick and knock on the back door, loud."

Afterward, Uncle Buck admitted that it was his own mistake, that he had forgotten when even a little child should have known: not to ever stand right in front of or right behind a nigger when you scare him; but to always stand to one side of him. Uncle Buck forgot that. He was standing facing the front door and right in front of it, with the fyce right in front of him yelling fire and murder every time it could draw a new breath; he said the first he knew was when the fyce gave a shriek and whirled and Tomey's Turl was right behind it. Uncle Buck said he never even saw the door open; that the fyce just screamed once and ran between his legs and then Tomey's Turl ran right clean over him. He never even bobbled; he knocked Uncle Buck down and then caught him before he fell without even stopping, snatched him up under one arm, still running, and carried him along for about ten feet, saying, "Look out of here, old Buck. Look out of here, old Buck," before he threw him away and went on. By that time they couldn't even hear the fyce anymore at all.

Uncle Buck wasn't hurt; it was only the wind knocked out of him where Tomey's Turl had thrown him down on his back. But he had been carrying the whisky bottle in his back pocket, saving the last drink until Tomey's Turl was captured, and he refused to move until he knew for certain if it was just whisky and not blood. So Uncle Buck laid over on his side easy, and he knelt behind him and raked the broken glass out of his pocket. Then they went on to the house. They walked. The nigger came up with the horses, but nobody said anything to Uncle Buck about riding again. They couldn't hear the fyce at all now. "He was going fast, all right," Uncle Buck said. "But I dont believe that even he will catch that fyce. I godfrey, what a night."

"We'll catch him tomorrow," he said.

"Tomorrow, hell," Uncle Buck said. "We'll be at home tomorrow. And the first time Hubert Beauchamp or that nigger either one set foot on my land, I'm going to have them arrested for trespass and vagrancy."

The house was dark. They could hear Mr Hubert snoring good now, as if he had settled down to road-gaiting at it. But they couldn't hear anything from upstairs, even when they were inside the dark hall, at the foot of the stairs. "Likely hers will be at the back," Uncle Buck said. "Where she can holler down to the kitchen without having to get up. Besides, an unmarried lady will sholy have her door locked with strangers in the house." So Uncle Buck eased himself down onto the bottom step, and he knelt and drew Uncle Buck's boots off. Then he removed his own and set them against the wall, and he and Uncle Buck mounted the stairs, feeling their way up and into the upper hall. It was dark too, and still there was no sound anywhere except Mr Hubert snoring below, so they felt their way along the hall toward the front of the house, until they felt a door. They could hear nothing beyond the door, and when Uncle Buck tried the knob, it opened. "All right," Uncle Buck whispered. "Be quiet." They could see a little now, enough to see the shape of the bed and the mosquito-bar. Uncle Buck threw down his suspenders and unbuttoned his trousers and went to the bed and eased himself carefully down onto the edge of it, and he knelt again and drew Uncle Buck's trousers off and he was just removing his own when Uncle Buck lifted the mosquito-bar and raised his feet and rolled into the bed. That was when Miss Sophonsiba sat up on the other side of Uncle Buck and gave the first scream.

3.

When he reached home just before dinner time the next day, he was just about worn out. He was too tired to eat, even if Uncle Buddy had waited to eat dinner first; he couldn't have stayed on the pony another mile without going to sleep. In fact, he must have gone to sleep while he was telling Uncle Buddy, because the next thing he knew it was late afternoon and he was lying on some hay in the jolting wagon-bed, with Uncle Buddy sitting on the seat above him exactly the same way he sat a horse or sat in his rocking chair before the kitchen hearth while he was cooking, holding the whip exactly as he held the spoon or fork he stirred and tasted with. Uncle Buddy had some cold bread and meat and a jug of buttermilk wrapped in damp towsacks waiting when he waked up. He ate, sitting in the wagon in almost the last of the afternoon. They must have come fast, because they were not more than two miles from Mr Hubert's. Uncle Buddy waited for him to eat. Then he said, "Tell me again," and he told it again: how he and Uncle Buck finally found a room without anybody in it, and Uncle Buck sitting on the side of the bed saying, "O godfrey, Cass. O godfrey, Cass," and then they heard Mr Hubert's feet on the stairs and watched the light come down the hall and Mr Hubert came in, in his nightshirt, and walked over and set the candle on the table and stood looking at Uncle Buck.

"Well, 'Filus," he said. "She's got you at last."

"It was an accident," Uncle Buck said. "I swear to godfrey——"

"Hah," Mr Hubert said. "Dont tell me. Tell her that."

"I did," Uncle Buck said. "I did tell her. I swear to god——"

"Sholy," Mr Hubert said. "And just listen." They listened a minute. He had been hearing her all the time. She was nowhere near as loud as at first; she was just steady. "Dont you want to go back in there and tell her again it was an accident, that you never meant nothing and to just excuse you and forget about it? All right."

"All right what?" Uncle Buck said.

"Go back in there and tell her again," Mr Hubert said. Uncle Buck looked at Mr Hubert for a minute. He batted his eyes fast.

"Then what will I come back and tell you?" he said.

"To me?" Mr Hubert said. "I would call that a horse of another color. Wouldn't you?"

Uncle Buck looked at Mr Hubert. He batted his eyes fast again. Then he stopped again. "Wait," he said. "Be reasonable. Say I did walk into a lady's bedroom, even Miss Sophonsiba's; say, just for the sake of the argument, there wasn't no other lady in the world but her and so I walked into hers and tried to get in bed with her, would I have took a nine-year-old boy with me?"

"Reasonable is just what I'm being," Mr Hubert said. "You come into bear-country of your own free will and accord. All right; you were a grown man and you knew it was bear-country and you knew the way back out like you knew the way in and you had your chance to take it. But no. You had to crawl into the den and lay down by the bear. And whether you did or didn't know the bear was in it dont make any difference. So if you got back out of that den without even a claw-mark on you, I would not only be unreasonable, I'd be a damned fool. After all, I'd like a little peace and quiet and freedom myself, now I got a chance for it. Yes sir. She's got you, 'Filus, and you know it. You run a hard race and you run a good one, but you skun the hen-house one time too many."

"Yes," Uncle Buck said. He drew his breath in and let it out again, slow and not loud. But you could hear it. "Well," he said. "So I reckon I'll have to take the chance then."

"You already took it," Mr Hubert said. "You did that when you came back here." Then he stopped too. Then he batted his eyes, but only about six times. Then he stopped and looked at Uncle Buck for more than a minute. "What chance?" he said.

"That five hundred dollars," Uncle Buck said.

"What five hundred dollars?" Mr Hubert said. He and Uncle Buck looked at one another. Now it was Mr Hubert that batted his eyes again and then stopped again. "I thought you said you found him in Tennie's cabin."

"I did," Uncle Buck said. "What you bet me was I would catch him there. If there had been ten of me standing in front of that door, we wouldn't have caught him." Mr Hubert blinked at Uncle Buck, slow and steady.

"So you aim to hold me to that fool bet," he said.

"You took your chance too," Uncle Buck said. Mr Hubert blinked at Uncle Buck. Then he stopped. Then he went and took the candle from the table and went out. They sat on the edge of the bed and watched the light go down the hall and heard Mr Hubert's feet on the stairs. After a while they began to see the light again and they heard Mr Hubert's feet coming back up the stairs. Then Mr Hubert entered and went to the table and set the candle down and laid a deck of cards by it.

"One hand," he said. "Draw. You shuffle, I cut, this boy deals. Five hundred dollars against Sibbey. And we'll settle this nigger business once and for all too. If you win, you buy Tennie; if I win, I buy that boy of yours. The price will be the same for each one: three hundred dollars."

"Win?" Uncle Buck said. "The one that wins buys the niggers?"

"Wins Sibbey, damn it!" Mr Hubert said. "Wins Sibbey! What the hell else are we setting up till midnight arguing about? The lowest hand wins Sibbey and buys the niggers."

"All right," Uncle Buck said. "I'll buy the damn girl then and we'll call the rest of this foolishness off."

"Hah," Mr Hubert said again. "This is the most serious foolishness you ever took part in in your life. No. You said you wanted your chance, and now you've got it. Here it is, right here on this table, waiting on you."

So Uncle Buck shuffled the cards and Mr Hubert cut them. Then he took up the deck and dealt in turn until Uncle Buck and Mr Hubert had five. And Uncle Buck looked at his hand a long time and then said two cards and he gave them to him, and Mr Hubert looked at his hand quick and said one card and he gave it to him and Mr Hubert flipped his discard onto the two which Uncle Buck had discarded and slid the new card into his hand and opened it out and looked at it quick again and closed it and looked at Uncle Buck and said, "Well? Did you help them threes?"

"No," Uncle Buck said.

"Well I did," Mr Hubert said. He shot his hand across the table so that the cards fell face-up in front of Uncle Buck and they were three kings and two fives, and said, "By God, Buck McCaslin, you have met your match at last."

"And that was all?" Uncle Buddy said. It was late then, near sunset; they would be at Mr Hubert's in another fifteen minutes.

"Yes, sir," he said, telling that too: how Uncle Buck waked him at daylight and he climbed out a window and got the pony and left, and how Uncle Buck said that if they pushed him too close in the meantime, he would climb down the gutter too and hide in the woods until Uncle Buddy arrived.

"Hah," Uncle Buddy said. "Was Tomey's Turl there?"

"Yes, sir," he said. "He was waiting in the stable when I got the pony. He said, 'Aint they settled it yet?' "

"And what did you say?" Uncle Buddy said.

"I said, 'Uncle Buck looks like he's settled. But Uncle Buddy aint got here yet.' "

"Hah," Uncle Buddy said.

And that was about all. They reached the house. Maybe Uncle Buck was watching them, but if he was, he never showed himself, never came out of the woods. Miss Sophonsiba was nowhere in sight either, so at least Uncle Buck hadn't quite given up; at least he hadn't asked her yet. And he and Uncle Buddy and Mr Hubert ate supper and they came in from the kitchen and cleared the table, leaving only the lamp on it and the deck of cards. Then it was just like last night, except that Uncle Buddy had no necktie and Mr Hubert wore clothes now instead of a nightshirt and it was a shaded lamp on the table instead of a candle, and Mr Hubert sitting at his end of the table with the deck in his hands, riffling the edges with his thumb and looking at Uncle Buddy. Then he tapped the edges even and set the deck out in the middle of the table, under the lamp, and folded his arms on the edge of the table and leaned forward a little on the table, looking at Uncle Buddy, who was sitting at his end of the table with his hands in his lap, all one gray color, like an old gray rock or a stump with gray moss on it, that still, with his round white head like Uncle Buck's but he didn't blink like Uncle Buck and he was a little thicker than Uncle Buck, as if from sitting down so much watching food cook, as if the things he cooked had made him a little thicker than he would have been and the things he cooked with, the flour and such, had made him all one same quiet color.

"Little toddy before we start?" Mr Hubert said.

"I dont drink," Uncle Buddy said.

"That's right," Mr Hubert said. "I knew there was something else besides just being woman-weak that makes 'Filus seem human. But no matter." He batted his eyes twice at Uncle Buddy. "Buck McCaslin against the land and niggers you have heard me promise as Sophonsiba's dowry on the day she marries. If I beat you, 'Filus marries Sibbey without any dowry. If you beat me, you get 'Filus. But I still get the three hundred dollars 'Filus owes me for Tennie. Is that correct?"

"That's correct," Uncle Buddy said.

"Stud," Mr Hubert said. "One hand. You to shuffle, me to cut, this boy to deal."

"No," Uncle Buddy said. "Not Cass. He's too young. I dont want him mixed up in any gambling."

"Hah," Mr Hubert said. "It's said that a man playing cards with Amodeus McCaslin aint gambling. But no matter." But he was still looking at Uncle Buddy; he never even turned his head when he spoke: "Go to the back door and holler. Bring the first creature that answers, animal mule or human, that can deal ten cards."

So he went to the back door. But he didn't have to call because Tomey's Turl was squatting against the wall just outside the door, and they returned to the dining-room where Mr Hubert still sat with his arms folded on his side of the table and Uncle Buddy sat with his hands in his lap on his side and the deck of cards face-down under the lamp between them. Neither of them even looked up when he and Tomey's Turl entered. "Shuffle," Mr Hubert said. Uncle Buddy shuffled and set the cards back under the lamp and put his hands back into his lap and Mr Hubert cut the deck and folded his arms back onto the table-edge. "Deal," he said. Still neither he nor Uncle Buddy looked up. They just sat there while Tomey's Turl's saddle-colored hands came into the light and took up the deck and dealt, one card face-down to Mr Hubert and one face-down to Uncle Buddy, and one face-up to Mr Hubert and it was a king, and one face-up to Uncle Buddy and it was a six.

"Buck McCaslin against Sibbey's dowry," Mr Hubert said. "Deal." And the hand dealt Mr Hubert a card and it was a three, and Uncle Buddy a card and it was a two. Mr Hubert looked at Uncle Buddy. Uncle Buddy rapped once with his knuckles on the table.

"Deal," Mr Hubert said. And the hand dealt Mr Hubert a card and it was another three, and Uncle Buddy a card and it was a four. Mr Hubert looked at Uncle Buddy's cards. Then he looked at Uncle Buddy and Uncle Buddy rapped on the table again with his knuckles.

"Deal," Mr Hubert said, and the hand dealt him an ace and Uncle Buddy a five and now Mr Hubert just sat still. He didn't look at anything or move for a whole minute; he just sat there and watched Uncle Buddy put one hand onto the table for the first time since he shuffled and pinch up one corner of his face-down card and look at it and then put his hand back into his lap. "Check," Mr Hubert said.

"I'll bet you them two niggers," Uncle Buddy said. He didn't move either. He sat there just like he sat in the wagon or on a horse or in the rocking chair he cooked from.

"Against what?" Mr Hubert said.

"Against the three hundred dollars Theophilus owes you for Tennie, and the three hundred you and Theophilus agreed on for Tomey's Turl," Uncle Buddy said.

"Hah," Mr Hubert said, only it wasn't loud at all this time, nor even short. Then he said "Hah. Hah. Hah" and not loud either. Then he said, "Well." Then he said, "Well, well." Then he said: "We'll check up for a minute. If I win, you take Sibbey without dowry and the two niggers, and I dont owe 'Filus anything. If you win——"

"—Theophilus is free. And you owe him the three hundred dollars for Tomey's Turl," Uncle Buddy said.

"That's just if I call you," Mr Hubert said. "If I dont call you, 'Filus wont owe me nothing and I wont owe 'Filus nothing, unless I take that nigger which I have been trying to explain to you and him both for years that I wont have on my place. We will be right back where all this foolishness started from, except for that. So what it comes down to is, I either got to give a nigger away, or risk buying one that you done already admitted you cant keep at home." Then he stopped talking. For about a minute it was like he and Uncle Buddy had both gone to sleep. Then Mr Hubert picked up his face-down card and turned it over. It was another three, and Mr Hubert sat there without looking at anything at all, his fingers beating a tattoo, slow and steady and not very loud, on the table. "H'm," he said. "And you need a trey and there aint but four of them and I already got three. And you just shuffled. And I cut afterward. And if I call you, I will have to buy that nigger. Who dealt these cards, Amodeus?" Only he didn't wait to be answered. He reached out and tilted the lamp-shade, the light moving up Tomey's Turl's arms that were supposed to be black but were not quite white, up his Sunday shirt that was supposed to be white but wasn't quite either, that he put on every time he ran away just as Uncle Buck put on the necktie each time he went to bring him back, and on to his face; and Mr Hubert sat there, holding the lamp-shade and looking at Tomey's Turl. Then he tilted the shade back down and took up his cards and turned them face-down and pushed them toward the middle of the table. "I pass, Amodeus," he said.

4.

He was still too worn out for sleep to sit on a horse, so this time he and Uncle Buddy and Tennie all three rode in the wagon, while Tomey's Turl led the pony from old Jake. And when they got home just after daylight, this time Uncle Buddy never even had time to get breakfast started and the fox never even got out of the crate, because the dogs were right there in the room. Old Moses went right into the crate with the fox, so that both of them went right on through the back end of it. That is the fox went through, because when Uncle Buddy opened the door to come in, old Moses was still wearing most of the crate around his neck until Uncle Buddy kicked it off of him. So they just made one run, across the front gallery and around the house and they could hear the fox's claws when he went scrabbling up the lean-pole, onto the roof—a fine race while it lasted, but the tree was too quick.

"What in damn's hell do you mean," Uncle Buddy said, "casting that damn thing with all the dogs right in the same room?"

"Damn the fox," Uncle Buck said. "Go on and start breakfast. It seems to me I've been away from home a whole damn month."

The Fire and the Hearth

I

1.

FIRST, in order to take care of George Wilkins once and for all, he had to hide his own still. And not only that, he had to do it singlehanded—dismantle it in the dark and transport it without help to some place far enough away and secret enough to escape the subsequent uproar and excitement and there conceal it. It was the prospect of this which had enraged him, compounding in advance the physical weariness and exhaustion which would be the night's aftermath. It was not the temporary interruption of business; the business had been interfered with once before about five years ago and he had dealt with that crisis as promptly and efficiently as he was dealing with this present one—and since which time that other competitor, whose example George Wilkins might quite possibly follow provided Carothers Edmonds were as correctly informed about his intentions as he professed to be about his bank account, had been plowing and chopping and picking cotton which was not his on the State penal farm at Parchman.

And it was not the loss of revenue which the interruption entailed. He was sixty-seven years old; he already had more money in the bank now than he would ever spend, more than Carothers Edmonds himself provided a man believed Carothers Edmonds when he tried to draw anything extra in the way of cash or supplies from the commissary. It was the fact that he must do it all himself, singlehanded; had to come up from the field after a long day in the dead middle of planting time and stable and feed Edmonds' mules and eat his own supper and then put his own mare to the single wagon and drive three miles to the still and dismantle it by touch in the dark and carry it another mile to the best place he could think of where it would be reasonably safe after the excitement started, probably getting back home with hardly enough of the night left to make it worth while going to bed before time to return to the field until the time would be ripe to speak the one word to Edmonds;—all this alone and unassisted because the two people from whom he might reasonably and logically have not only expected but demanded help were completely interdict: his wife who was too old and frail for such, even if he could have trusted not her fidelity but her discretion; and as for his daughter, to let her get any inkling of what he was about, he might just as well have asked George Wilkins himself to help him hide the still. It was not that he had anything against George personally, despite the mental exasperation and the physical travail he was having to undergo when he should have been at home in bed asleep. If George had just stuck to farming the land which Edmonds had allotted him he would just as soon Nat married George as anyone else, sooner than most of the nigger bucks he knew. But he was not going to let George Wilkins or anyone else move not only into the section where he had lived for going on seventy years but onto the very place he had been born on and set up competition in a business which he had established and nursed carefully and discreetly for twenty of them, ever since he had fired up for his first run not a mile from Zack Edmonds' kitchen door;—secretly indeed, for no man needed to tell him what Zack Edmonds or his son, Carothers (or Old Cass Edmonds either, for that matter), would do about it if they ever found it out. He wasn't afraid that George would cut into his established trade, his old regular clientele, with the hog swill which George had begun to turn out two months ago and call whisky. But George Wilkins was a fool innocent of discretion, who sooner or later would be caught, whereupon for the next ten years every bush on the Edmonds place would have a deputy sheriff squatting behind it from sundown to sunup every night. And he not only didn't want a fool for a son-in-law, he didn't intend to have a fool living on the same place he lived on. If George had to go to jail to alleviate that condition, that was between George and Roth Edmonds.

But it was about over now. Another hour or so and he would be back home, getting whatever little of sleep there might be left of the night before time to return to the field to pass the day until the right moment to speak to Edmonds. Probably the outrage would be gone by then, and he would have only the weariness to contend with. But it was his own field, though he neither owned it nor wanted to nor even needed to. He had been cultivating it for forty-five years, since before Carothers Edmonds was born even, plowing and planting and working it when and how he saw fit (or maybe not even doing that, maybe sitting through a whole morning on his front gallery, looking at it and thinking if that's what he felt like doing), with Edmonds riding up on his mare maybe three times a week to look at the field, and maybe once during the season stopping long enough to give him advice about it which he completely ignored, ignoring not only the advice but the very voice which gave it, as though the other had not spoken even, whereupon Edmonds would ride on and he would continue with whatever he had been doing, the incident already forgotten condoned and forgiven, the necessity and the time having been served. So the day would pass at last. Then he would approach Edmonds and speak his word and it would be like dropping the nickel into the slot machine and pulling the lever: all he would have to do then would be just to watch it.

He knew exactly where he intended to go, even in the darkness. He had been born on this land, twenty-five years before the Edmonds who now owned it. He had worked on it ever since he got big enough to hold a plow straight; he had hunted over every foot of it during his childhood and youth and his manhood too, up to the time when he stopped hunting, not because he could no longer walk a day's or a night's hunt, but because he felt that the pursuit of rabbits and possums for meat was no longer commensurate with his status as not only the oldest man but the oldest living person on the Edmonds plantation, the oldest McCaslin descendant even though in the world's eye he descended not from McCaslins but from McCaslin slaves, almost as old as old Isaac McCaslin who lived in town, supported by what Roth Edmonds chose to give him, who would own the land and all on it if his just rights were only known, if people just knew how old Cass Edmonds, this one's grandfather, had beat him out of his patrimony; almost as old as old Isaac, almost, as old Isaac was, coeval with old Buck and Buddy McCaslin who had been alive when their father, Carothers McCaslin, got the land from the Indians back in the old time when men black and white were men.

He was in the creek bottom now. Curiously enough, visibility seemed to have increased, as if the rank sunless jungle of cypress and willow and brier, instead of increasing obscurity, had solidified it into the concrete components of trunk and branch, leaving the air, space, free of it and in comparison lighter, penetrable to vision, to the mare's sight anyway, enabling her to see-saw back and forth among the trunks and the impassable thickets. Then he saw the place he sought—a squat, flat-topped, almost symmetrical mound rising without reason from the floor-like flatness of the valley. The white people called it an Indian mound. One day five or six years ago a group of white men, including two women, most of them wearing spectacles and all wearing khaki clothes which had patently lain folded on a store shelf twenty-four hours ago, came with picks and shovels and jars and phials of insect repellant and spent a day digging about it while most of the people, men women and children, came at some time during the day and looked quietly on; later—within the next two or three days, in fact—he was to remember with almost horrified amazement the cold and contemptuous curiosity with which he himself had watched them.

But that would come later. Now he was merely busy. He could not see his watch-face, but he knew it was almost midnight. He stopped the wagon beside the mound and unloaded the still—the copper-lined kettle which had cost him more than he still liked to think about despite his ingrained lifelong scorn of inferior tools—and the worm and his pick and shovel. The spot he sought was a slight overhang on one face of the mound; in a sense one side of his excavation was already dug for him, needing only to be enlarged a little, the earth working easily under the invisible pick, whispering easily and steadily to the invisible shovel until the orifice was deep enough for the worm and kettle to fit into it, when—and it was probably only a sigh but it sounded to him louder than an avalanche, as though the whole mound had stooped roaring down at him—the entire overhang sloughed. It drummed on the hollow kettle, covering it and the worm, and boiled about his feet and, as he leaped backward and tripped and fell, about his body too, hurling clods and dirt at him, striking him a final blow squarely in the face with something larger than a clod—a blow not vicious so much as merely heavy-handed, a sort of final admonitory pat from the spirit of darkness and solitude, the old earth, perhaps the old ancestors themselves. Because, sitting up, getting his breath again at last, gasping and blinking at the apparently unchanged shape of the mound which seemed to loom poised above him in a long roaring wave of silence like a burst of jeering and prolonged laughter, his hand found the object which had struck him and learned it in the blind dark—a fragment of an earthenware vessel which, intact, must have been as big as a churn and which even as he lifted it crumbled again and deposited in his palm, as though it had been handed to him, a single coin.

He could not have said how he knew it was gold. But he didn't even need to strike a match. He dared risk no light at all as, his brain boiling with all the images of buried money he had ever listened to or heard of, for the next five hours he crawled on hands and knees among the loose earth, hunting through the collapsed and now quiet dirt almost grain by grain, pausing from time to time to gauge by the stars how much remained of the rapid and shortening spring night, then probing again in the dry insensate dust which had yawned for an instant and vouchsafed him one blinding glimpse of the absolute and then closed.

When the east began to pale he stopped and straightened up, kneeling, stretching his cramped and painful muscles into something approximating erectness for the first time since midnight. He had found nothing more. He had not even found any other fragments of the churn or crock. That meant that the rest of it might be scattered anywhere beneath the cave-in. He would have to dig for it, coin by coin, with pick and shovel. That meant time, but more than that, solitude. Obviously there must no longer be even the remotest possibility of sheriffs and law men prying about the place hunting whisky stills. So George Wilkins was reprieved without knowing his luck just as he had been in jeopardy without knowing his danger. For an instant, remembering the tremendous power which three hours ago had hurled him onto his back without even actually touching him, he even thought of taking George into partnership on a minor share basis to do the actual digging; indeed, not only to do the actual work but as a sort of justice, balance, libation to Chance and Fortune, since if it had not been for George, he would not have found the single coin. But he dismissed that before it even had time to become an idea. He, Lucas Beauchamp, the oldest living McCaslin descendant still living on the hereditary land, who actually remembered old Buck and Buddy in the living flesh, older than Zack Edmonds even if Zack were still alive, almost as old as old Isaac who in a sense, say what a man would, had turned apostate to his name and lineage by weakly relinquishing the land which was rightfully his to live in town on the charity of his great-nephew;—he, to share one jot, one penny of the money which old Buck and Buddy had buried almost a hundred years ago, with an interloper without forbears and sprung from nowhere and whose very name was unknown in the country twenty-five years ago—a jimber-jawed clown who could not even learn how to make whisky, who had not only attempted to interfere with and jeopardise his business and disrupt his family, but had given him a week of alternating raging anxiety and exasperated outrage culminating in tonight—or last night now—and not even finished yet, since he still had the worm and kettle to conceal. Never. Let George take for his recompense the fact that he would not have to go to the penitentiary to which Roth Edmonds would probably have sent him even if the Law did not.

The light had increased; he could see now. The slide had covered the still. All necessary would be a few branches piled against it so that the recent earth would not be too apparent to a chance passer. He rose to his feet. But he still could not straighten up completely. With one hand pressed to his back and still bent over a little he began to walk stiffly and painfully toward a clump of sapling cottonwoods about fifty feet away, when something crashed into flight within or beyond it and rushed on, the sound fading and already beginning to curve away toward the edge of the jungle while he stood for perhaps ten seconds, slackjawed with amazed and incredulous comprehension, his head turning to pace the invisible running. Then he whirled and leaped, not toward the sound but running parallel with it, leaping with incredible agility and speed among the trees and undergrowth, breaking out of the jungle in time to see, in the wan light of the accelerating dawn, the quarry fleeing like a deer across a field and into the still night-bound woods beyond.

He knew who it was, even before he returned to the thicket where it had flushed, to stand looking down at the print of his daughter's naked feet where she had squatted in the mud, knowing that print as he would have known those of his mare or his dog, standing over it for a while and looking down at it but no longer seeing it at all. So that was that. In a way, it even simplified things. Even if there had been time (another hour and every field along the creek would have a negro and a mule in it), even if he could hope to obliterate all trace and sign of disturbed earth about the mound, it would do no good to move his still to another hiding-place. Because when they came to the mound to dig they must not only find something, they must find it quick and at once and something the discovery and exhumation of which would cause them to desist and go away—say, only partly buried, and with just enough brush in front of it that they couldn't help but find it even before they got the brush dragged off. Because it was a matter open to, admitting, no controversy, not even discussion. George Wilkins must go. He must be on his way before another night had passed.

2.

He shoved his chair back from the supper table and stood up. He gave his daughter's lowered, secret face a single look, not grim but cold. But he addressed neither her nor his wife directly. He might have been speaking to either of them or both or to neither: "Going down the road."

"Where you going this time of night?" his wife said. "Messing around up yonder in the bottom all last night! Getting back home just in time to hitch up and get to the field a good hour after sunup! You needs to be in bed if you going to get that creek piece broke like Mister Roth——"

Then he was out of the house and didn't need to hear her any longer. It was night again. The dirt lane ran pale and dim beneath the moonless sky of corn-planting time. Presently it ran along beside the very field which he was getting ready to plant his cotton in when the whippoorwills began. If it had not been for George Wilkins, he would have had it all broken and bedded and ready now. But that was about over now. Another ten minutes and it would be like dropping the nickel into the slot machine, not ringing down a golden shower about him, he didn't ask that, need that; he would attend to the jackpot himself, but giving him peace and solitude in which to do so. That, the labor even at night and without help, even if he had to move half the mound, did not bother him. He was only sixty-seven, a better man still than some men half his age; ten years younger and he could still have done both, the night-work and the day. But now he wouldn't try it. In a way, he was a little sorry to give up farming. He had liked it; he approved of his fields and liked to work them, taking a solid pride in having good tools to use and using them well, scorning both inferior equipment and shoddy work just as he had bought the best kettle he could find when he set up his still—that copper-lined kettle the cost of which he liked less than ever to remember now that he was not only about to lose it but was himself deliberately giving it away. He had even planned the very phrases, dialogue, in which, after the first matter was attended to, he would inform Edmonds that he had decided to quit farming, was old enough to retire, and for Edmonds to allot his land to someone else to finish the crop. "All right," Edmonds would say. "But you cant expect me to furnish a house and wood and water to a family that aint working any land." And he would say, if it really came to that—and it probably would, since he, Lucas, would affirm to his death that Zack Edmonds had been as much better a man than his son as old Cass Edmonds had been than both of them together: "All right. I'll rent the house from you. Name your price and I will pay you every Saturday night as long as I decide to stay here."

But that would take care of itself. The other matter was first and prime. At first, on his return home this morning, his plan had been to notify the sheriff himself, so that there would be absolutely no slip-up, lest Edmonds should be content with merely destroying George's still and cache and just running George off the place. In that case, George would continue to hang around the place, merely keeping out of Edmonds' sight; whereupon, without even any farm work, let alone the still, to keep him occupied, he would be idle all day and therefore up and out all night long and would constitute more of a menace than ever. The report would have to come from Edmonds, the white man, because to the sheriff Lucas was just another nigger and both the sheriff and Lucas knew it, although only one of them knew that to Lucas the sheriff was a redneck without any reason for pride in his forbears nor hope for it in his descendants. And if Edmonds should decide to handle the matter privately, without recourse to the law, there would be someone in Jefferson whom Lucas could inform that not only he and George Wilkins knew of a still on Carothers Edmonds' place, but Carothers Edmonds knew it too.

He entered the wide carriage gate from which the drive curved mounting to the oak and cedar knoll where he could already see, brighter than any kerosene, the gleam of electricity in the house where the better men than this one had been content with lamps or even candles. There was a tractor under the mule-shed which Zack Edmonds would not have allowed on the place too, and an automobile in a house built especially for it which old Cass would not even have put his foot in. But they were the old days, the old time, and better men than these; Lucas himself made one, himself and old Cass coevals in more than spirit even, the analogy only the closer for its paradox:—old Cass a McCaslin only on his mother's side and so bearing his father's name though he possessed the land and its benefits and responsibilities; Lucas a McCaslin on his father's side though bearing his mother's name and possessing the use and benefit of the land with none of the responsibilities. Better men:—old Cass, a McCaslin only by the distaff yet having enough of old Carothers McCaslin in his veins to take the land from the true heir simply because he wanted it and knew he could use it better and was strong enough, ruthless enough, old Carothers McCaslin enough; even Zack, who was not the man his father had been but whom Lucas, the man McCaslin, had accepted as his peer to the extent of intending to kill him, right up to the point when, his affairs all set in order like those of a man preparing for death, he stood over the sleeping white man that morning forty-three years ago with the naked razor in his hand.

He approached the house—the two log wings which Carothers McCaslin had built and which had sufficed old Buck and Buddy, connected by the open hallway which, as his pride's monument and epitaph, old Cass Edmonds had enclosed and superposed with a second storey of white clapboards and faced with a portico. He didn't go around to the back, the kitchen door. He had done that only one time since the present Edmonds was born; he would never do it again as long as he lived. Neither did he mount the steps. Instead he stopped in the darkness beside the gallery and rapped with his knuckles on the edge of it until the white man came up the hall and peered out the front door. "Well?" Edmonds said. "What is it?"

"It's me," Lucas said.

"Well, come in," the other said. "What are you standing out there for?"

"You come out here," Lucas said. "For all you or me either know, George may be laying out yonder right now, listening."

"George?" Edmonds said. "George Wilkins?" He came out onto the gallery—a young man still, a bachelor, forty-three years old last March. Lucas did not need to remember that. He would never forget it—that night of early spring following ten days of such rain that even the old people remembered nothing to compare it with, and the white man's wife's time upon her and the creek out of banks until the whole valley resembled a river choked with down timber and drowned livestock until not even a horse could have crossed it in the darkness to reach a telephone and fetch the doctor back. And Molly, a young woman then and nursing their own first child, wakened at midnight by the white man himself and they followed the white man through the streaming darkness to his house and Lucas waited in the kitchen, keeping the fire going in the stove, and Molly delivered the white child with none to help but Edmonds and then they knew that the doctor had to be fetched. So even before daylight he was in the water and crossed it, how he never knew, and was back by dark with the doctor, emerging from that death (At one time he had believed himself gone, done for, both himself and the mule soon to be two more white-eyed and slack-jawed pieces of flotsam, to be located by the circling of buzzards, swollen and no longer identifiable, a month hence when the water went down.) which he had entered not for his own sake but for that of old Carothers McCaslin who had sired him and Zack Edmonds both, to find the white man's wife dead and his own wife already established in the white man's house. It was as though on that louring and driving day he had crossed and then recrossed a kind of Lethe, emerging, being permitted to escape, buying as the price of life a world outwardly the same yet subtly and irrevocably altered.

It was as though the white woman had not only never quitted the house, she had never existed—the object which they buried in the orchard two days later (they still could not cross the valley to reach the churchyard) a thing of no moment, unsanctified, nothing; his own wife, the black woman, keeping his baby in the white man's house and he now living alone in the house which old Cass had built for them when they married, keeping alive on the hearth the fire he had lit there on their wedding day and which had burned ever since though there was little enough cooking done on it now;—thus, until almost half a year had passed and one day he went to Zack Edmonds and said, "I wants my wife. I needs her at home." Then—and he hadn't intended to say this. But there had been that half-year almost and himself alone keeping alive the fire which was to burn on the hearth until neither he nor Molly were left to feed it, himself sitting before it night after night through that spring and summer until one night he caught himself standing over it, furious, bursting, blind, the cedar water bucket already poised until he caught himself and set the bucket back on the shelf, still shaking, unable to remember taking the bucket up even.—then he said: "I reckon you thought I wouldn't take her back, didn't you?"

The white man was sitting down. In age he and Lucas could have been brothers, almost twins too. He leaned slowly back in the chair, looking at Lucas. "Well, by God," he said quietly. "So that's what you think. What kind of a man do you think I am? What kind of a man do you call yourself?"

"I'm a nigger," Lucas said. "But I'm a man too. I'm more than just a man. The same thing made my pappy that made your grandmaw. I'm going to take her back."

"By God," Edmonds said, "I never thought to ever pass my oath to a nigger. But I will swear——" Lucas had turned, already walking away. He whirled. The other was standing now. They faced one another, though for the instant Lucas couldn't even see him.

"Not to me!" Lucas said. "I wants her in my house tonight. You understand?" He went back to the field, to the plow standing in midfurrow where he had left it when he discovered suddenly that he was going now, this moment, to the commissary or the house or wherever the white man would be, into his bedroom if necessary, and confront him. He had tied the mule under a tree, the gear still on it. He put the mule back to the plow and plowed again. When he turned at the end of each furrow he could have seen his house. But he never looked toward it, not even when he knew that she was in it again, home again, not even when fresh woodsmoke began to rise from the chimney as it had not risen in the middle of the morning in almost half a year; not even when at noon she came along the fence, carrying a pail and a covered pan and stood looking at him for a moment before she set the pail and pan down and went back. Then the plantation bell rang for noon, the flat, musical, deliberate clangs. He took the mule out and watered and fed it and only then went to the fence-corner and there it was—the pan of still-warm biscuit, the lard pail half full of milk, the tin worn and polished with scouring and long use until it had a patina like old silver—just as it had used to be.

Then the afternoon was done too. He stabled and fed Edmonds' mule and hung the gear on its appointed peg against tomorrow. Then in the lane, in the green middle-dusk of summer while the fireflies winked and drifted and the whippoorwills quired back and forth and the frogs thumped and grunted along the creek, he looked at his house for the first time, at the thin plume of supper smoke windless above the chimney, his breathing harder and harder and deeper and deeper until his faded shirt strained at the buttons on his chest. Maybe when he got old he would become resigned to it. But he knew he would never, not even if he got to be a hundred and forgot her face and name and the white man's and his too. *I will have to kill him*, he thought, *or I will have to take her and go away.* For an instant he thought of going to the white man and telling him they were leaving, now, tonight, at once. *Only if I were to see him again right now, I might kill him*, he thought. *I think I have decided which I am going to do, but if I was to see him, meet him now, my mind might change.—And that's a man!* he thought. *He keeps her in the house with him six months and I dont do nothing: he sends her back to me and I kills him. It would be like I had done said aloud to the whole world that he never sent her back because I told him to but he give her back to me because he was tired of her.*

He entered the gate in the paling fence which he had built himself when old Cass gave them the house, as he had hauled and laid the field stone path across the grassless yard which his wife had used to sweep every morning with a broom of bound willow twigs, sweeping the clean dust into curving intricate patterns among the flower-beds outlined with broken brick and bottles and shards of china and colored glass. She had returned from time to time during the spring to work the flower-beds so that they bloomed as usual—the hardy, blatant blooms loved of her and his race: prince's feather and sunflower, canna and hollyhock—but until today the paths among them had not been swept since last year. *Yes*, he thought. *I got to kill him or I got to leave here.*

He entered the hall, then the room where he had lit the fire two years ago which was to have outlasted both of them. He could not always remember afterward what he had said but he never forgot the amazed and incredulous rage with which he thought, *Why she aint even knowed unto right now that I ever even suspected.* She was sitting before the hearth where the supper was cooking, holding the child, shielding its face from the light and heat with her hand—a small woman even then, years before her flesh, her very bones apparently, had begun to wither and shrink inward upon themselves, and he standing over her, looking down not at his own child but at the face of the white one nuzzling into the dark swell of her breast—not Edmonds' wife but his own who had been lost; not his son but the white man's who had been restored to him, his voice loud, his clawed hand darting toward the child as her hand sprang and caught his wrist.

"Whar's ourn?" he cried. "Whar's mine?"

"Right yonder on the bed, sleeping!" she said. "Go and look at him!" He didn't move, standing over her, locked hand and wrist with her. "I couldn't leave him! You know I couldn't! I had to bring him!"

"Dont lie to me!" he said. "Dont tell me Zack Edmonds know where he is."

"He does know! I told him!" He broke his wrist free, flinging her hand and arm back; he heard the faint click of her teeth when the back of her hand struck her chin and he watched her start to raise her hand to her mouth, then let it fall again.

"That's right," he said. "It aint none of your blood that's trying to break out and run!"

"You fool!" she cried. "Oh God," she said. "Oh God. All right. I'll take him back. I aimed to anyway. Aunt Thisbe can fix him a sugar-tit——"

"Not you," he said. "And not me even. Do you think Zack Edmonds is going to stay in that house yonder when he gets back and finds out he is gone? No!" he said. "I went to Zack Edmonds' house and asked him for my wife. Let him come to my house and ask me for his son!"

He waited on the gallery. He could see, across the valley, the gleam of light in the other house. *He just aint got home yet*, he thought. He breathed slow and steady. *It aint no hurry. He will do something and then I will do something and it will be all over. It will be all right*. Then the light disappeared. He began to say quietly, aloud: "Now. Now. He will have to have time to walk over here." He continued to say it long after he knew the other had had time to walk back and forth between the two houses ten times over. It seemed to him then that he had known all the time the other was not coming, as if he were in the house where the white man waited, watching his, Lucas', house in his turn. Then he knew that the other was not even waiting, and it was as if he stood already in the bedroom itself, above the slow respirations of sleep, the undefended and oblivious throat, the naked razor already in his hand.

He re-entered the house, the room where his wife and the

two children were asleep on the bed. The supper which had been cooking on the hearth when he entered at dusk had not even been taken up, what was left of it long since charred and simmered away and probably almost cool now among the fading embers. He set the skillet and coffee pot aside and with a stick of wood he raked the ashes from one corner of the fireplace, exposing the bricks, and touched one of them with his wet finger. It was hot, not scorching, searing, but possessing a slow, deep solidity of heat, a condensation of the two years during which the fire had burned constantly above it, a condensation not of fire but of time, as though not the fire's dying and not even water would cool it but only time would. He prised the brick up with his knife blade and scraped away the warm dirt under it and lifted out a small metal dispatch box which his white grandfather, Carothers McCaslin himself, had owned almost a hundred years ago, and took from it the knotted rag tight and solid with the coins, some of which dated back almost to Carothers McCaslin's time, which he had begun to save before he was ten years old. His wife had removed only her shoes (he recognised them too. They had belonged to the white woman who had not died, who had not even ever existed.) before lying down. He put the knotted rag into one of them and went to the walnut bureau which Isaac McCaslin had given him for a wedding present and took his razor from the drawer.

He was waiting for daylight. He could not have said why. He squatted against a tree halfway between the carriage gate and the white man's house, motionless as the windless obscurity itself while the constellations wheeled and the whippoorwills quired faster and faster and ceased and the first cocks crowed and the false dawn came and faded and the birds began and the night was over. In the first of light he mounted the white man's front steps and entered the unlocked front door and traversed the silent hall and entered the bedroom which it seemed to him he had already entered and that only an instant before, standing with the open razor above the breathing, the undefended and defenseless throat, facing again the act which it seemed to him he had already performed. Then he found the eyes of the face on the pillow looking quietly up at him and he knew then why he had had to wait until daylight. "Because you are a McCaslin too," he said. "Even if you was woman-made to it. Maybe that's the reason. Maybe that's why you done it: because what you and your pa got from old Carothers had to come to you through a woman—a critter not responsible like men are responsible, not to be held like men are held. So maybe I have even already forgive you, except I cant forgive you because you can forgive only them that injure you; even the Book itself dont ask a man to forgive them he is fixing to harm because even Jesus found out at last that was too much to ask a man."

"Put the razor down and I will talk to you," Edmonds said.

"You knowed I wasn't afraid, because you knowed I was a McCaslin too and a man-made one. And you never thought that, because I am a McCaslin too, I wouldn't. You never even thought that, because I am a nigger too, I wouldn't dare. No. You thought that because I am a nigger I wouldn't even mind. I never figured on the razor neither. But I gave you your chance. Maybe I didn't know what I might have done when you walked in my door, but I knowed what I wanted to do, what I believed I was going to do, what Carothers McCaslin would have wanted me to do. But you didn't come. You never even gave me the chance to do what old Carothers would have told me to do. You tried to beat me. And you wont never, not even when I am hanging dead from the limb this time tomorrow with the coal oil still burning, you wont never."

"Put down the razor, Lucas," Edmonds said.

"What razor?" Lucas said. He raised his hand and looked at the razor as if he did not know he had it, had never seen it before, and in the same motion flung it toward the open window, the naked blade whirling almost blood-colored into the first copper ray of the sun before it vanished. "I dont need no razor. My nekkid hands will do. Now get the pistol under your pillow."

Still the other didn't move, not even to draw his hands from under the sheet. "It's not under the pillow. It's in that drawer yonder where it always is and you know it. Go and look. I'm not going to run. I couldn't."

"I know you aint," Lucas said. "And you know you aint. Because you know that's all I needs, all I wants, is for you to try to run, to turn your back on me and run. I know you aint going to. Because all you got to beat is me. I got to beat old Carothers. Get your pistol."

"No," the other said. "Go home. Get out of here. Tonight I will come to your house——"

"After this?" Lucas said. "Me and you, in the same country, breathing the same air even? No matter what you could say, what you could even prove so I would have to believe it, after this? Get the pistol."

The other drew his hands out from under the sheet and placed them on top of it. "All right," he said. "Stand over there against the wall until I get it."

"Hah," Lucas said. "Hah."

The other put his hands back under the sheet. "Then go and get your razor," he said.

Lucas began to pant, to indraw short breaths without expiration between. The white man could see his foreshortened chest, the worn faded shirt straining across it. "When you just watched me throw it away?" Lucas said. "When you know that if I left this room now, I wouldn't come back?" He went to the wall and stood with his back against it, still facing the bed. "Because I done already beat you," he said. "It's old Carothers. Get your pistol, white man." He stood panting in the rapid inhalations until it seemed that his lungs could not possibly hold more of it. He watched the other rise from the bed and grasp the foot of it and swing it out from the wall until it could be approached from either side; he watched the white man cross to the bureau and take the pistol from the drawer. Still Lucas didn't move. He stood pressed against the wall and watched the white man cross to the door and close it and turn the key and return to the bed and toss the pistol onto it and only then look toward him. Lucas began to tremble. "No," he said.

"You on one side, me on the other," the white man said. "We'll kneel down and grip hands. We wont need to count."

"No!" Lucas said in a strangling voice. "For the last time. Take your pistol. I'm coming."

"Come on then. Do you think I'm any less a McCaslin just because I was what you call woman-made to it? Or maybe you aint even a woman-made McCaslin but just a nigger that's got out of hand?"

Then Lucas was beside the bed. He didn't remember moving at all. He was kneeling, their hands gripped, facing across the bed and the pistol the man whom he had known from infancy, with whom he had lived until they were both grown almost as brothers lived. They had fished and hunted together, they had learned to swim in the same water, they had eaten at the same table in the white boy's kitchen and in the cabin of the negro's mother; they had slept under the same blanket before a fire in the woods.

"For the last time," Lucas said. "I tell you——" Then he cried, and not to the white man and the white man knew it; he saw the whites of the negro's eyes rush suddenly with red like the eyes of a bayed animal—a bear, a fox: "I tell you! Dont ask too much of me!" *I was wrong*, the white man thought. *I have gone too far*. But it was too late. Even as he tried to snatch his hand free Lucas' hand closed on it. He darted his left hand toward the pistol but Lucas caught that wrist too. Then they did not move save their forearms, their gripped hands turning gradually until the white man's hand was pressed back-downward on the pistol. Motionless, locked, incapable of moving, the white man stared at the spent and frantic face opposite his. "I give you your chance," Lucas said. "Then you laid here asleep with your door unlocked and give me mine. Then I throwed the razor away and give it back. And then you throwed it back at me. That's right, aint it?"

"Yes," the white man said.

"Hah!" Lucas said. He flung the white man's left hand and arm away, striking the other backward from the bed as his own right hand wrenched free; he had the pistol in the same motion, springing up and back as the white man rose too, the bed between them. He broke the pistol's breech and glanced quickly at the cylinder and turned it until the empty chamber under the hammer was at the bottom, so that a live cartridge would come beneath the hammer regardless of which direction the cylinder rotated. "Because I'll need two of them," he said. He snapped the breech shut and faced the white man. Again the white man saw his eyes rush until there was neither cornea nor iris. *This is it*, the white man thought, with that rapid and even unamazed clarity, gathering himself as much as he dared. Lucas didn't seem to notice. *He cant even see me right now*, the white man thought. But that was too late too. Lucas was looking at him now. "You thought I wouldn't, didn't you?" Lucas said. "You knowed I could beat you, so you thought to beat me with old Carothers, like Cass Edmonds done Isaac: used old Carothers to make Isaac give up the land that was his because Cass Edmonds was the woman-made McCaslin, the woman-branch, the sister, and old Carothers would have told Isaac to give in to the woman-kin that couldn't fend for herself. And you thought I'd do that too, didn't you? You thought I'd do it quick, quicker than Isaac since it aint any land I would give up. I aint got any fine big McCaslin farm to give up. All I got to give up is McCaslin blood that rightfully aint even mine or at least aint worth much since old Carothers never seemed to miss much what he give to Tomey that night that made my father. And if this is what that McCaslin blood has brought me, I dont want it neither. And if the running of it into my black blood never hurt him any more than the running of it out is going to hurt me, it wont even be old Carothers that had the most pleasure.—Or no," he cried. *He cant see me again*, the white man thought. *Now*. "No!" Lucas cried; "say I dont even use this first bullet at all, say I just uses the last one and beat you and old Carothers both, leave you something to think about now and then when you aint too busy to try to think up what to tell old Carothers when you get where he's done already gone, tomorrow and the one after that and the one after that as long as tomorrow——" The white man sprang, hurling himself across the bed, grasping at the pistol and the hand which held it. Lucas sprang too; they met over the center of the bed where Lucas clasped the other with his left arm almost like an embrace and jammed the pistol against the white man's side and pulled the trigger and flung the white man from him all in one motion, hearing as he did so the light, dry, incredibly loud click of the miss-fire.

That had been a good year, though late in beginning after the rains and flood: the year of the long summer. He would make more this year than he had made in a long time, even though and in August some of his corn had not had its last plowing. He was doing that now, following the single mule between the rows of strong, waist-high stalks and the rich, dark, flashing blades, pausing at the end of each row to back the plow out and swing it and the yawing mule around into the next one, until at last the dinner smoke stood weightless in the bright air above his chimney and then at the old time she came along the fence with the covered pan and the pail. He did not look at her. He plowed on until the plantation bell rang for noon. He watered and fed the mule and himself ate—the milk, the still-warm biscuit—and rested in the shade until the bell rang again. Then, not rising yet, he took the cartridge from his pocket and looked at it again, musing—the live cartridge, not even stained, not corroded, the mark of the firing-pin dented sharp and deep into the unexploded cap—the dull little brass cylinder less long than a match, not much larger than a pencil, not much heavier, yet large enough to contain two lives. Have contained, that is. *Because I wouldn't have used the second one*, he thought. *I would have paid. I would have waited for the rope, even the coal oil. I would have paid. So I reckon I aint got old Carothers' blood for nothing, after all. Old Carothers*, he thought. *I needed him and he come and spoke for me*. He plowed again. Presently she came back along the fence and got the pan and pail herself instead of letting him bring them home when he came. But she would be busy today; and it seemed to him still early in the afternoon when he saw the supper smoke—the supper which she would leave on the hearth for him when she went back to the big house with the children. When he reached home in the dusk, she was just departing. But she didn't wear the white woman's shoes now and her dress was the same shapeless faded calico she had worn in the morning. "Your supper's ready," she said. "I aint had time to milk yet. You'll have to."

"If I can wait on that milk, I reckon the cow can too," he said. "Can you tote them both all right?"

"I reckon I can. I been taking care of both of them a good while now without no man-help." She didn't look back. "I'll come back out when I gets them to sleep."

"I reckon you better put your time on them," he said gruffly. "Since that's what you started out to do." She went on, neither answering nor looking back, impervious, tranquil, somehow serene. Nor was he any longer watching her. He breathed slow and quiet. *Women,* he thought. *Women. I wont never know. I dont want to. I ruther never to know than to find out later I have been fooled.* He turned toward the room where the fire was, where his supper waited. This time he spoke aloud: "How to God," he said, "can a black man ask a white man to please not lay down with his black wife? And even if he could ask it, how to God can the white man promise he wont?"

3.

"George Wilkins?" Edmonds said. He came to the edge of the gallery—a young man still, yet possessing already something of that almost choleric shortness of temper which Lucas remembered in old Cass Edmonds but which had skipped Zack. In age he could have been Lucas' son, but actually was the lesser man for more reason than that, since it was not Lucas who paid taxes insurance and interest or owned anything which had to be kept ditched drained fenced and fertilised or gambled anything save his sweat, and that only as he saw fit, against God for his yearly sustenance. "What in hell has George Wilkins——"

Without changing the inflection of his voice and apparently without effort or even design Lucas became not Negro but nigger, not secret so much as impenetrable, not servile and not effacing, but enveloping himself in an aura of timeless and stupid impassivity almost like a smell. "He's running a kettle in that gully behind the Old West field. If you want the whisky too, look under his kitchen floor."

"A still?" Edmonds said. "On my land?" He began to roar. "Haven't I told and told every man woman and child on this place what I would do the first drop of white mule whisky I found on my land?"

"You didn't need to tell me," Lucas said. "I've lived on this place since I was born, since before your pa was. And you or him or old Cass either aint never heard of me having truck with any kind of whisky except that bottle of town whisky you and him give Molly Christmas."

"I know it," Edmonds said. "And I would have thought George Wilkins——" He ceased. He said, "Hah. Have I or haven't I heard something about George wanting to marry that girl of yours?"

For just an instant Lucas didn't answer. Then he said, "That's right."

"Hah," Edmonds said again. "And so you thought that by telling me on George before he got caught himself, I would be satisfied to make him chop up his kettle and pour out his whisky and then forget about it."

"I didn't know," Lucas said.

"Well, you know now," Edmonds said. "And George will too when the sheriff——" He went back into the house. Lucas listened to the hard, rapid, angry clapping of his heels on the floor, then to the prolonged violent grinding of the telephone crank. Then he stopped listening, standing motionless in the half-darkness, blinking a little. He thought, *All that worrying. I never even thought of that*. Edmonds returned. "All right," he said. "You can go on home now. Go to bed. I know it wont do a damn bit of good to mention it, but I would like to see your south creek piece planted by tomorrow night. You doped around in it today like you hadn't been to bed for a week. I dont know what you do at night, but you are too old to be tomcatting around the country whether you think so or not."

He went back home. Now that it was all over, done, he realised how tired he actually was. It was as if the alternating waves of alarm and outrage and anger and fear of the past ten days, culminating in last night's frantic activity and the past thirty-six hours during which he had not even taken off his clothes, had narcotised him, deadened the very weariness itself. But it was all right now. If a little physical exhaustion, even another ten days or two weeks of it, was all required of him in return for that moment last night, he would not complain. Then he remembered that he had not told Edmonds of his decision to quit farming, for Edmonds to arrange to rent the land he had been working to someone else to finish his crop. But perhaps that was just as well too; perhaps even a single night would suffice to find the rest of the money which a churn that size must have contained, and he would keep the land, the crop, from old habit, for something to occupy him.—*Provided I dont need to keep it for a better reason still*, he thought grimly. *Since I probably aint even made a scratch yet on the kind of luck that can wait unto I am sixty-seven years old, almost too old to even want it, to make me rich.*

The house was dark except for a faint glow from the hearth in his and his wife's room. The room across the hallway where his daughter slept was dark too. It would be empty too. He had expected that. *I reckon George Wilkins is entitled to one more night of female company,* he thought. *From what I have heard, he wont find none of it where he's going tomorrow.*

When he got into bed his wife said without waking, "Whar you been? Walking the roads all last night. Walking the roads all tonight, with the ground crying to get planted. You just wait unto Mister Roth——" and then stopped talking without waking either. Sometime later, he waked. It was after midnight. He lay beneath the quilt on the shuck mattress. It would be happening about now. He knew how they did it—the white sheriff and revenue officers and deputies creeping and crawling among the bushes with drawn pistols, surrounding the kettle, sniffing and whiffing like hunting dogs at every stump and disfiguration of earth until every jug and keg was found and carried back to where the car waited; maybe they would even take a sup or two to ward off the night's chill before returning to the still to squat until George walked innocently in. He was neither triumphant nor vindictive. He even felt something personal toward George now. *He is young yet,* he thought. *They wont keep him down there forever.* In fact, as far as he, Lucas, was concerned, two weeks would be enough. *He can afford to give a year or two at it. And maybe when they lets him out it will be a lesson to him about whose daughter to fool with next time.*

Then his wife was leaning over the bed, shaking him and screaming. It was just after dawn. In his shirt and drawers he ran behind her, out onto the back gallery. Sitting on the ground before it was George Wilkins' patched and battered still; on the gallery itself was an assortment of fruit jars and stoneware jugs and a keg or so and one rusted five-gallon oilcan which, to Lucas' horrified and sleep-dulled eyes, appeared capable of holding enough liquid to fill a ten-foot horse trough. He could even see it in the glass jars—a pale, colorless fluid in which still floated the shreds of corn-husks which George's tenth-hand still had not removed. "Whar was Nat last night?" he cried. He grasped his wife by the shoulder, shaking her. "Whar was Nat, old woman?"

"She left right behind you!" his wife cried. "She followed you again, like night before last! Didn't you know it?"

"I knows it now," Lucas said. "Get the axe!" he said. "Bust it! We aint got time to get it away." But there was not time for that either. Neither of them had yet moved when the sheriff of the county, followed by a deputy, came around the corner of the house—a tremendous man, fat, who obviously had been up all night and obviously still did not like it.

"Damn it, Lucas," he said. "I thought you had better sense that this."

"This aint none of mine," Lucas said. "You know it aint. Even if it was, would I have had it here? George Wilkins——"

"Never you mind about George Wilkins," the sheriff said. "I've got him too. He's out there in the car, with that girl of yours. Go get your pants on. We're going to town."

Two hours later he was in the commissioner's office in the federal courthouse in Jefferson. He was still inscrutable of face, blinking a little, listening to George Wilkins breathing hard beside him and to the voices of the white men.

"Confound it, Carothers," the commissioner said, "what the hell kind of Senegambian Montague and Capulet is this anyhow?"

"Ask them!" Edmonds said violently. "Ask them! Wilkins and that girl of Lucas' want to get married. Lucas wouldn't hear of it for some reason—I just seem to be finding out now why. So last night Lucas came to my house and told me George was running a still on my land because—" without even a pause to draw a fresh breath Edmonds began to roar again "—he knew damn well what I would do because I have been telling every nigger on my place for years just what I would do if I ever found one drop of that damn wildcat——"

"Yes, yes," the commissioner said; "all right, all right. So you telephoned the sheriff——"

"And we got the message——" it was one of the deputies, a plump man though nowhere as big as the sheriff, voluble, muddy about the lower legs and a little strained and weary in the face too "—and we went out there and Mr Roth told us where to look. But there aint no kettle in the gully where he said, so we set down and thought about just where would we hide a still if we was one of Mr Roth's niggers and we went and looked there and sho enough there it was, neat and careful as you please, all took to pieces and about half buried and covered with brush against a kind of mound in the creek bottom. Only it was getting toward daybreak then, so we decided to come on back to George's house and look under the kitchen floor like Mr Roth said, and then have a little talk with George. So we come on back to George's house, only there aint any George or nobody else in it and nothing under the kitchen floor neither and so we are coming on back toward Mr Roth's house to ask him if maybe he aint got the wrong house in mind maybe; it's just about full daylight now and we are about a hundred yards from Lucas's house when what do we see but George and the gal legging it up the hill toward Lucas's cabin with a gallon jug in each hand, only George busted the jugs on a root before we could get to them. And about that time Lucas's wife starts to yelling in the house and we run around to the back and there is another still setting in Lucas's back yard and about forty gallons of whisky setting on his back gallery like he was fixing to hold a auction sale and Lucas standing there in his drawers and shirt-tail, hollering, 'Git the axe and bust it! Git the axe and bust it!' "

"Yes," the commissioner said. "But who do you charge? You went out there to catch George, but all your evidence is against Lucas."

"There was two stills," the deputy said. "And George and that gal both swear Lucas has been making and selling whisky right there in Edmonds' back yard for twenty years." For an instant Lucas looked up and met Edmonds' glare, not of reproach and no longer even of surprise, but of grim and furious outrage. Then he looked away, blinking, listening to George Wilkins breathing hard beside him like a man in the profoundest depths of sleep, and to the voices.

"But you cant make his own daughter testify against him," the commissioner said.

"George can, though," the deputy said. "George aint any

kin to him. Not to mention being in a fix where George has got to think up something good to say and think of it quick."

"Let the court settle all that, Tom," the sheriff said. "I was up all last night and I haven't even had my breakfast yet. I've brought you a prisoner and thirty or forty gallons of evidence and two witnesses. Let's get done with this."

"I think you've brought two prisoners," the commissioner said. He began to write on the paper before him. Lucas watched the moving hand, blinking. "I'm going to commit them both. George can testify against Lucas, and that girl can testify against George. She aint any kin to George either."

He could have posted his and George's appearance bonds without altering the first figure of his bank balance. When Edmonds had drawn his own check to cover them, they returned to Edmonds' car. This time George drove it, with Nat in front with him. It was seventeen miles back home. For those seventeen miles he sat beside the grim and seething white man in the back seat, with nothing to look at but those two heads—that of his daughter where she shrank as far as possible from George, into her corner, never once looking back; that of George, the ruined panama hat raked above his right ear, who still seemed to swagger even sitting down. *Leastways his face aint all full of teeth now like it used to be whenever it found anybody looking at it*, he thought viciously. But never mind that either, right now. So he sat in the car when it stopped at the carriage gate and watched Nat spring out and run like a frightened deer up the lane toward his house, still without looking back, never once looking at him. Then they drove on to the mule lot, the stable, and he and George got out and again he could hear George breathing behind him while Edmonds, behind the wheel now, leaned his elbow in the window and glared at them both.

"Get your mules!" Edmonds said. "What in hell are you waiting for?"

"I thought you were fixing to say something," Lucas said. "So a man's kinfolks cant tell on him in court."

"Never you mind about that!" Edmonds said. "George can tell plenty, and he aint any kin to you. And if he should begin to forget, Nat aint any kin to George and she can tell plenty. I know what you are thinking about. But you have waited too late. If George and Nat tried to buy a wedding license now, they would probably hang you and George both. Besides, damn that. I'm going to take you both to the penitentiary myself as soon as you are laid-by. Now you get on down to your south creek piece. By God, this is one time you will take advice from me. And here it is: dont come out until you have finished it. If dark catches you, dont let it worry you. I'll send somebody down there with a lantern."

He was done with the south creek piece before dark; he had intended to finish it today anyhow. He was back at the stable, his mules watered and rubbed down and stalled and fed while George was still unharnessing. Then he entered the lane and in the beginning of twilight walked toward his house above whose chimney the windless supper smoke stood. He didn't walk fast, neither did he look back when he spoke. "George Wilkins," he said.

"Sir," George said behind him. They walked on in single file and almost step for step, about five feet apart.

"Just what was your idea?"

"I dont rightly know, sir," George said. "It uz mostly Nat's. We never aimed to get you into no trouble. She say maybe ifn we took and fotch that kettle from whar you and Mister Roth told them shurfs it was and you would find it settin on yo back porch, maybe when we offered to help you git shet of it fo they got here, yo mind might change about loandin us the money to——I mean to leffen us get married."

"Hah," Lucas said. They walked on. Now he could smell the cooking meat. He reached the gate and turned. George stopped too, lean, wasp-waisted, foppish even in faded overalls below the swaggering rake of the hat. "There's more folks than just me in that trouble."

"Yes sir," George said. "Hit look like it is. I hope it gonter be a lesson to me."

"I hope so too," Lucas said. "When they get done sending you to Parchman you'll have plenty of time between working cotton and corn you aint going to get no third and fourth of even, to study it." They looked at one another.

"Yes sir," George said. "Especially wid you there to help me worry hit out."

"Hah," Lucas said. He didn't move; he hardly raised his voice even: "Nat." He didn't even look toward the house then as the girl came down the path, barefoot, in a clean, faded calico dress and a bright headrag. Her face was swollen from crying, but her voice was defiant, not hysterical.

"It wasn't me that told Mister Roth to telefoam them shurfs!" she cried. He looked at her for the first time. He looked at her until even the defiance began to fade, to be replaced by something alert and speculative. He saw her glance flick past his shoulder to where George stood and return.

"My mind done changed," he said. "I'm going to let you and George get married." She stared at him. Again he watched her glance flick to George and return.

"It changed quick," she said. She stared at him. Her hand, the long, limber, narrow, light-palmed hand of her race, rose and touched for an instant the bright cotton which bound her head. Her inflection, the very tone and pitch of her voice had changed. "Me, marry George Wilkins and go to live in a house whar the whole back porch is done already fell off and whar I got to walk a half a mile and back from the spring to fetch water? He aint even got no stove!"

"My chimbley cooks good," George said. "And I can prop up the porch."

"And I can get used to walking a mile for two lard buckets full of water," she said. "I dont wants no propped-up porch. I wants a new porch on George's house and a cook-stove and a well. And how you gonter get um? What you gonter pay for no stove with, and a new porch, and somebody to help you dig a well?" Yet it was still Lucas she stared at, ceasing with no dying fall of her high, clear soprano voice, watching her father's face as if they were engaged with foils. His face was not grim and neither cold nor angry. It was absolutely expressionless, impenetrable. He might have been asleep standing, as a horse sleeps. When he spoke, he might have been speaking to himself.

"A cook-stove," he said. "The back porch fixed. A well."

"A new back porch," she said. He might not have even heard her. She might not have spoken even.

"The back porch fixed," he said. Then she was not looking

at him. Again the hand rose, slender and delicate and markless of any labor, and touched the back of her head-kerchief. Lucas moved. "George Wilkins," he said.

"Sir," George said.

"Come into the house," Lucas said.

And so, in its own good time, the other day came at last. In their Sunday clothes he and Nat and George stood beside the carriage gate while the car came up and stopped. "Morning, Nat," Edmonds said. "When did you get home?"

"I got home yistiddy, Mister Roth."

"You stayed in Vicksburg a good while. I didn't know you were going until Aunt Molly told me you were already gone."

"Yassuh," she said. "I lef the next day after them shurfs was here.—I didn't know it neither," she said. "I never much wanted to go. It was pappy's idea for me to go and see my aunt——"

"Hush, and get in the car," Lucas said. "If I'm going to finish my crop in this county or finish somebody else's crop in Parchman county, I would like to know it soon as I can."

"Yes," Edmonds said. He spoke to Nat again. "You and George go on a minute. I want to talk to Lucas." Nat and George went on. Lucas stood beside the car while Edmonds looked at him. It was the first time Edmonds had spoken to him since that morning three weeks ago, as though it had required those three weeks for his rage to consume itself, or die down at least. Now the white man leaned in the window, looking at the impenetrable face with its definite strain of white blood, the same blood which ran in his own veins, which had not only come to the negro through male descent while it had come to him from a woman, but had reached the negro a generation sooner—a face composed, inscrutable, even a little haughty, shaped even in expression in the pattern of his great-grandfather McCaslin's face. "I reckon you know what's going to happen to you," he said. "When that federal lawyer gets through with Nat, and Nat gets through with George, and George gets through with you and Judge Gowan gets through with all of you. You have been on this place all your life, almost twice as long as I have. You knew all the McCaslins and Edmonds both that ever lived here, except old

Carothers. Was that still and that whisky in your back yard yours?"

"You know it wasn't," Lucas said.

"All right," Edmonds said. "Was that still they found in the creek bottom yours?"

They looked at each other. "I aint being tried for that one," Lucas said.

"Was that still yours, Lucas?" Edmonds said. They looked at one another. Yet still the face which Edmonds saw was absolutely blank, impenetrable. Even the eyes appeared to have nothing behind them. He thought, and not for the first time: *I am not only looking at a face older than mine and which has seen and winnowed more, but at a man most of whose blood was pure ten thousand years when my own anonymous beginnings became mixed enough to produce me.*

"Do you want me to answer that?" Lucas said.

"No!" Edmonds said violently. "Get in the car!"

When they reached town, the streets leading into it and the Square itself were crowded with cars and wagons; the flag rippled and flew in the bright May weather above the federal courthouse. Following Edmonds, he and Nat and George crossed the thronged pavement, walking in a narrow lane of faces they knew—other people from their place, people from other places along the creek and in the neighborhood, come the seventeen miles also with no hope of getting into the courtroom itself but just to wait on the street and see them pass—and faces they only knew by hearsay: the rich white lawyers and judges and marshals talking to one another around their proud cigars, the haught and powerful of the earth. They entered the marble foyer, crowded too and sonorous with voices, where George began to walk gingerly on the hard heels of his Sunday shoes. Then Lucas took from his coat the thick, soiled, folded document which had lain hidden under the loose brick in his fireplace for three weeks now and touched Edmonds' arm with it—the paper thick enough and soiled enough yet which of its own accord apparently fell open at a touch, stiffly but easily too along the old hand-smudged folds, exposing, presenting among the meaningless and unread lettering between salutation and seal the three phrases in the cramped script of whatever nameless clerk which alone of the whole mass of it Lucas at least had bothered to read: *George Wilkins* and *Nathalie Beauchamp* and a date in October of last year.

"Do you mean," Edmonds said, "that you have had this all the time? All these three weeks?" But still the face he glared at was impenetrable, almost sleepy looking.

"You hand it to Judge Gowan," Lucas said.

He and Nat and George sat quietly on a hard wooden bench in a small office, where an oldish white man—Lucas knew him though not particularly that he was a deputy marshal—chewed a toothpick and read a Memphis newspaper. Then a young, brisk, slightly harried white man in glasses opened the door and glinted his glasses an instant and vanished; then, following the old white man they crossed the foyer again, the marble cavern murmurously resonant with the constant slow feet and the voices, the faces watching them again as they mounted the stairs. They crossed the empty courtroom without pausing and entered another office but larger, finer, quieter. There was an angry-looking man whom Lucas did not know—the United States Attorney, who had moved to Jefferson only after the administration changed eight years ago, after Lucas had stopped coming to town very often anymore. But Edmonds was there, and behind the table sat a man whom Lucas did know, who had used to come out in old Cass' time forty and fifty years ago and stay for weeks during the quail season, shooting with Zack, with Lucas to hold the horses while they got down to shoot when the dogs pointed. It took hardly any time at all.

"Lucas Beauchamp?" the judge said. "With thirty gallons of whisky and a still sitting on his back porch in broad daylight? Nonsense."

"Then there you are," the angry man said, flinging out his hands. "I didn't know anything about this either until Edmonds——" But the judge was not even listening to him. He was looking at Nat.

"Come here, girl," he said. Nat moved forward and stopped. Lucas could see her trembling. She looked small, thin as a lath, young; she was their youngest and last—seventeen, born into his wife's old age and, it sometimes seemed to him, into his too. She was too young to be married and face all the troubles which married people had to get through in order to become old and find out for themselves the taste and savor of peace. Just a stove and a new back porch and a well were not enough. "You're Lucas's girl?" the judge said.

"Yassuh," Nat said in her high, sweet, chanting soprano. "I'm name Nat. Nat Wilkins, Gawge Wilkins' wife. There the paper fer hit in yo hand."

"I see it is," the judge said. "It's dated last October."

"Yes sir, Judge," George said. "We been had it since I sold my cotton last fall. We uz married then, only she wont come to live in my house unto Mister Lu—I mean I gots a stove and the porch fixed and a well dug."

"Have you got that now?"

"Yes sir, Judge," George said. "I got the money for hit now and I'm just fo gittin the rest of it, soon as I gits around to the hammerin and the diggin."

"I see," the judge said. "Henry," he said to the other old man, the one with the toothpick, "have you got that whisky where you can pour it out?"

"Yes, Judge," the other said.

"And both those stills where you can chop them to pieces, destroy them good?"

"Yes, Judge."

"Then clear my office. Get them out of here. Get that jimber-jawed clown out of here at least."

"He's talking about you, George Wilkins," Lucas murmured.

"Yes sir," George said. "Sound like he is."

4.

At first he thought that two or three days at the outside would suffice—or nights, that is, since George would have to be in his crop during the day, let alone getting himself and Nat settled for marriage in their house. But a week passed, and though Nat would come back home at least once during the day, usually to borrow something, he had not seen George at all. He comprehended the root of his impatience—the mound and its secret which someone, anyone else, might stumble upon by chance as he had, the rapid and daily shortening of the allotted span in which he had not only to find the treasure but to get any benefit and pleasure from it, all in abeyance until he could complete the petty business which had intervened, and nothing with which to pass the period of waiting—the good year, the good early season, and cotton and corn springing up almost in the planter's wheel-print, so that there was now nothing to do but lean on the fence and watch it grow;—on the one hand, that which he wanted to do and could not; on the other, that which he could have done and no need for. But at last, in the second week, when he knew that in one more day his patience would be completely gone, he stood just inside his kitchen door and watched George enter and cross the lot in the dusk and enter the stable and emerge with his mare and put her to the wagon and drive away. So the next morning he went no further than his first patch and leaned on the fence in the bright dew looking at his cotton until his wife began to shout at him from the house.

When he entered, Nat was sitting in his chair beside the hearth, bent forward, her long narrow hands dangling limp between her knees, her face swollen and puffed again with crying. "Yawl and your George Wilkins!" Molly said. "Go on and tell him."

"He aint started on the well or nothing," Nat said. "He aint even propped up the back porch. With all that money you give him, he aint even started. And I axed him and he just say he aint got around to it yet, and I waited and I axed him again and he still just say he aint got around to it yet. Unto I told him at last that ifn he didn't get started like he promised, my mind gonter change about whatall I seed that night them shurfs come out here and so last night he say he gwine up the road a piece and do I wants to come back home and stay because he mought not get back unto late and I say I can bar the door because I thought he was going to fix to start on the well. And when I seed him catch up pappy's mare and wagon, I knowed that was it. And it aint unto almost daylight when he got back, and he aint got nothing. Not nothing to dig with and no boards to fix the porch, and he had done spent the money pappy give him. And I told him what I was gonter do and I was waiting at the house soon as Mister Roth got up and I told Mister Roth my mind done changed about what I seed that night and Mister Roth started in to cussing and say I done waited too late because I'm Gawge's wife now and the Law wont listen to me and for me to come and tell you and Gawge both to be offen his place by sundown."

"There now!" Molly cried. "There's your George Wilkins!" Lucas was already moving toward the door. "Whar you gwine?" she said. "Whar we gonter move to?"

"You wait to start worrying about where we will move to when Roth Edmonds starts to worrying about why we aint gone," Lucas said.

The sun was well up now. It was going to be hot today; it was going to make cotton and corn both before the sun went down. When he reached George's house, George stood quietly out from behind the corner of it. Lucas crossed the grassless and sunglared yard, the light dust swept into the intricate and curving patterns which Molly had taught Nat. "Where is it?" Lucas said.

"I hid hit in that gully where mine use to be," George said. "Since them shurfs never found nothing there the yuther time, they'll think hit aint no use to look there no more."

"You fool," Lucas said. "Dont you know a week aint going to pass from now to the next election without one of them looking in that gully just because Roth Edmonds told them there was a still in it once? And when they catch you this time, you aint going to have any witness you have already been married to since last fall."

"They aint going to catch me this time," George said. "I done had my lesson. I'm gonter run this one the way you tells me to."

"You better had," Lucas said. "As soon as dark falls you take that wagon and get that thing out of that gully. I'll show you where to put it. Hah," he said. "And I reckon this one looks enough like the one that was in that gully before not to even been moved at all."

"No sir," George said. "This is a good one. The worm in hit is almost brand-new. That's how come I couldn't git him down on the price he axed. That porch and well money liked two dollars of being enough, but I just made that up myself, without needing to bother you. But it aint worrying about gittin caught that troubles my mind. What I cant keep from studying about is what we gonter tell Nat about that back porch and that well."

"What *we* is?" Lucas said.

"What I is, then," George said. Lucas looked at him for a moment.

"George Wilkins," he said.

"Sir," George said.

"I dont give no man advice about his wife," Lucas said.

II

I.

ABOUT a hundred yards before they reached the commissary, Lucas spoke over his shoulder without stopping. "You wait here," he said.

"No, no," the salesman said. "I'll talk to him myself. If I cant sell it to him, there aint a——" He stopped. He recoiled actually; another step and he would have walked full tilt into Lucas. He was young, not yet thirty, with the assurance, the slightly soiled snap and dash, of his calling, and a white man. Yet he even stopped talking and looked at the negro in battered overalls who stood looking down at him not only with dignity but with command.

"You wait here," Lucas said. So the salesman leaned against the fence in the bright August morning, while Lucas went on to the commissary. He mounted the steps, beside which a bright-coated young mare with a blaze and three stockings stood under a wide plantation saddle, and entered the long room with its ranked shelves of tinned food and tobacco and patent medicines, its hooks pendant with trace chains and collars and hames. Edmonds sat at a roll-top desk beside the front window, writing in a ledger. Lucas stood quietly looking at the back of Edmonds' neck until the other turned. "He's come," Lucas said.

Edmonds swivelled the chair around, back-tilted. He was already glaring before the chair stopped moving; he said with astonishing violence: "No!"

"Yes," Lucas said.

"No!"

"He brought it with him," Lucas said. "I saw with my own eyes——"

"Do you mean to tell me you wrote him to come down here after I told you I wouldn't advance you three hundred dollars nor three hundred cents nor even three cents——"

"I saw it, I tell you," Lucas said. "I saw it work with my own eyes. I buried a dollar in my back yard this morning and that machine went right straight to where it was and found it.

We are going to find that money tonight and I will pay you back in the morning."

"Good!" Edmonds said. "Fine! You've got over three thousand dollars in the bank. Advance yourself the money. Then you wont even have to pay it back." Lucas looked at him. He didn't even blink. "Hah," Edmonds said. "And because why? Because you know damn well just like I know damn well that there aint any money buried around here. You've been here sixty-seven years. Did you ever hear of anybody in this country with enough money to bury? Can you imagine anybody in this country burying anything worth as much as two bits that some of his kinfolks or his friends or his neighbors aint dug up and spent before he could even get back home and put his shovel away?"

"You're wrong," Lucas said. "Folks find it. Didn't I tell you about them two strange white men that come in here after dark that night three or four years ago and dug up twenty-two thousand dollars in a old churn and got out again before anybody even laid eyes on them? I saw the hole where they filled it up again. And the churn."

"Yes," Edmonds said. "You told me. And you didn't believe it then either. But now you've changed your mind. Is that it?"

"They found it," Lucas said. "Got clean away before anybody even knowed it, knowed they was here even."

"Then how do you know it was twenty-two thousand dollars?" But Lucas merely looked at him. It was not stubbornness but an infinite, almost Jehovah-like patience, as if he were contemplating the antics of a lunatic child.

"Your father would have lent me three hundred dollars if he was here," he said.

"But I aint," Edmonds said. "And if I could keep you from spending any of your money on a damn machine to hunt buried gold with, I would do that too. But then, you aint going to use your money, are you? That's why you came to me. You've got better sense. You just hoped I didn't have. Didn't you?"

"It looks like I'm going to have to use mine," Lucas said. "I'm going to ask you one more time——"

"No!" Edmonds said. Lucas looked at him for a good minute this time. He did not sigh.

"All right," he said.

When he emerged from the commissary, he saw George too, the soiled gleam of the ruined panama hat where George and the salesman now squatted in the shade of a tree, squatting on their heels without any other support. *Hah*, he thought, *He mought talk like a city man and he mought even think he is one. But I know now where he was born at*. The salesman looked up as Lucas approached. He gave Lucas one rapid, hard look and rose, already moving toward the commissary. "Hell," he said, "I told you all the time to let me talk to him."

"No," Lucas said. "You stay out of there."

"Then what are you going to do?" the salesman said. "Here I've come all the way from Memphis——And how you ever persuaded them up there in Saint Louis to send this machine out without any downpayment in the first place, I still dont see. And I'll tell you right now, if I've got to take it back, turn in an expense account for this trip and not one damn thing to show for it, something is——"

"We aint doing any good standing here, at least," Lucas said. He went on, the others following him, back to the gate, the road where the salesman's car waited. The divining machine sat on the back seat and Lucas stood in the open door, looking at it—an oblong metal box with a handle for carrying at each end, compact and solid, efficient and business-like and complex with knobs and dials. He didn't touch it. He just leaned in the door and stood over it, blinking, bemused. He spoke to no one. "And I watched it work," he said. "I watched it with my own eyes."

"What did you expect?" the salesman said. "That's what it's supposed to do. That's why we want three hundred dollars for it. Well?" he said. "What are you going to do? I've got to know, so I can know what to do myself. Aint you got three hundred dollars? What about some of your kinfolks? Hasn't your wife got three hundred dollars hid under the mattress somewhere?" Lucas mused on the machine. He did not look up yet.

"We will find that money tonight," he said. "You put in the machine and I'll show you where to look, and we'll go halves in it."

"Ha, ha, ha," the salesman said harshly, with no muscle of his face moving save the ones which parted his lips. "Now I'll tell one." Lucas mused above the box.

"We bound to find hit, captain," George said suddenly. "Two white men slipped in here three years ago and dug up twenty-two thousand dollars in a old churn one night and got clean away fo daylight."

"You bet," the salesman said. "And you knew it was exactly twenty-two grand because you found where they had throwed away the odd cents they never wanted to bother with."

"Naw sir," George said. "Hit mought a been more than twenty-two thousand dollars. Hit wuz a big churn."

"George Wilkins," Lucas said. He was still half way inside the car. He didn't even turn his head.

"Sir," George said.

"Hush," Lucas said. He withdrew his head and upper body and turned and looked at the salesman. Again the young white man saw a face absolutely impenetrable, even a little cold. "I'll swap you a mule for it," Lucas said.

"A mule?"

"When we find that money tonight, I'll buy the mule back from you for the three hundred dollars." George drew in his breath with a faint hissing sound. The salesman glanced quickly at him, at the raked hat, the rapid batting of his eyes. Then the salesman looked back at Lucas. They looked at one another—the shrewd, suddenly sober, suddenly attentive face of the young white man, the absolutely expressionless one of the negro.

"Do you own the mule?"

"How could I swap it to you if I didn't?" Lucas said.

"Let's go see it," the salesman said.

"George Wilkins," Lucas said.

"Sir," George said.

"Go to my stable and get my halter."

2.

Edmonds found the mule was missing as soon as the lot-men, Dan and Oscar, brought the drove in from pasture that evening. She was a three-year-old, eleven-hundred-pound mare mule named Alice Ben Bolt, and he had refused three hundred dollars for her in the spring. He didn't even curse. He merely surrendered the mare to Dan and waited beside the lot fence while the rapid beat of the mare's feet died away in the dusk and then returned and Dan sprang down and handed him his flashlight and pistol. Then, himself on the mare and the two negroes on saddleless mules, they went back across the pasture, fording the creek, to the gap in the fence through which the mule had been led. From there they followed the tracks of the mule and the man in the soft earth along the edge of a cotton field, to the road. And here too they could follow them, Dan walking now and carrying the flashlight, where the man had led the unshod mule in the soft dirt which bordered the gravel. "That's Alice's foot," Dan said. "I'd know it anywhere."

Later Edmonds would realise that both the negroes had recognised the man's footprints too. But at the time his very fury and concern had short-circuited his normal sensitivity to negro behavior. They would not have told him who made the tracks even if he had demanded to know, but the realization that they knew would have enabled him to make the correct divination and so save himself the four or five hours of mental turmoil and physical effort which he was about to enter.

They lost the tracks. He expected to find the marks where the mule had been loaded into a waiting truck; whereupon he would return home and telephone to the sheriff in Jefferson and to the Memphis police to watch the horse-and-mule markets tomorrow. There were no such marks. It took them almost an hour to find where the tracks had disappeared onto the gravel, crossing it, descending through the opposite roadside weeds, to reappear in another field three hundred yards away. Supperless, raging, the mare which had been under saddle all day unfed too, he followed the two shadowy mules, cursing Alice and the darkness and the single puny light on which they were forced to depend.

Two hours later they were in the creek bottom four miles from the house. He was walking too now, lest he dash his brains out against a limb, stumbling and thrashing among briers and undergrowth and rotting logs and tree-tops, leading the mare with one hand and fending his face with the other arm and trying to watch his feet, so that he walked into one of the mules, instinctively leaping in the right direction as it lashed viciously back at him with one hoof, before he discovered that the negroes had stopped. Then, cursing aloud now and leaping quickly again to avoid the invisible second mule which would be somewhere on that side, he realised that the flashlight was off now and he too saw the faint, smoky glare of a lightwood torch among the trees ahead. It was moving. "That's right," he said quickly. "Keep the light off." He called Oscar's name. "Give the mules to Dan and come back here and take the mare." He waited, watching the light, until the negro's hand fumbled at his. He relinquished the reins and moved around the mules, drawing the pistol and still watching the moving light. "Hand me the flashlight," he said. "You and Oscar wait here."

"I better come with you," Dan said.

"All right," Edmonds said, watching the light. "Let Oscar hold the mules." He went on without waiting, though he presently heard the negro close behind him, both of them moving as rapidly as they dared. The rage was not cold now. It was hot, and there was an eagerness upon him, a kind of vindictive exultation as he plunged on, heedless of underbrush or log, the flashlight in his left hand and the pistol in his right, gaining rapidly on the torch.

"It's the Old Injun's mound," Dan murmured behind him. "That's how come that light looked so high up. Him and George Wilkins ought to be pretty nigh through it by now."

"Him and George Wilkins?" Edmonds said. He stopped dead in his tracks. He whirled. He was not only about to perceive the whole situation in its complete and instantaneous entirety, as when the photographer's bulb explodes, but he knew now that he had seen it all the while and had refused to believe it purely and simply because he knew that when he did accept it, his brain would burst. "Lucas and George?"

"Digging down that mound," Dan said. "They been at it every night since Uncle Lucas found that thousand-dollar gold piece in it last spring."

"And you knew about it?"

"We all knowed about it. We been watching them. A thousand-dollar gold piece Uncle Lucas found that night when he was trying to hide his——" The voice died away. Edmonds couldn't hear it anymore, drowned by a rushing in his skull which, had he been a few years older, would have been apoplexy. He could neither breathe nor see for a moment. Then he whirled again. He said something in a hoarse strangled voice and sprang on, crashing at last from the undergrowth into the glade where the squat mound lifted the gaping yawn of its gutted flank like a photographer's backdrop before which the two arrested figures gaped at him—the one carrying before him what Edmonds might have taken for a receptacle containing feed except that he now knew neither of these had taken time to feed Alice or any other mule since darkness fell, the other holding the smoking pine-knot high above the ruined rake of the panama hat.

"You, Lucas!" he shouted. George flung the torch away, but Edmonds' flashlight already held them spitted. Then he saw the white man, the salesman, for the first time, snap-brim hat, necktie and all, just rising from beside a tree, his trousers rolled to his knees and his feet invisible in caked mud. "That's right," Edmonds said. "Go on, George. Run. I believe I can hit that hat without even touching you." He approached, the flashlight's beam contracting onto the metal box which Lucas held, gleaming and glinting among the knobs and dials. "So that's it," he said. "Three hundred dollars. I wish somebody would come into this country with a seed that had to be worked every day from New Year's right on through Christmas. As soon as you niggers are laid-by, trouble starts. But never mind that. Because I aint going to worry about Alice tonight. And if you and George want to spend the rest of it walking around with that damn machine, that's your business. But that mule is going to be in her stall in my stable at sunup. Do you hear?" Now the salesman appeared suddenly at Lucas' elbow. Edmonds had forgotten about him.

"What mule is that?" he said. Edmonds turned the light on him for a moment.

"My mule, sir," he said.

"Is that so," the other said. "I've got a bill of sale for that mule. Signed by Lucas here."

"Have you now," Edmonds said. "You can make pipe lighters out of it when you get home."

"Is that so? Look here, Mister What's-your-name——" But Edmonds had already turned the light back to Lucas, who still held the divining machine before him as if it were some object symbolical and sanctified for a ceremony, a ritual.

"On second thought," Edmonds said, "I aint going to worry about that mule at all. I told you this morning what I thought about this business. But you are a grown man; if you want to fool with it, I cant stop you. By God, I dont even want to. But if that mule aint in her stall by sunup tomorrow, I'm going to telephone the sheriff. Do you hear me?"

"I hear you," Lucas said sullenly. Now the salesman spoke again.

"All right, big boy," he said. "If that mule is moved from where she's at until I'm ready to load her up and move out of here, I'm going to telephone the sheriff. Do you hear that too?" This time Edmonds jumped, flung, the light beam at the salesman's face.

"Were you talking to me, sir?" he said.

"No," the salesman said. "I'm talking to him. And he heard me." For a moment longer Edmonds held the beam on the other. Then he dropped it, so that only their legs and feet showed, planted in the pool and its refraction as if they stood in water. He put the pistol back into his pocket.

"Well, you and Lucas have got till daylight to settle that. Because that mule is going to be back in my stable at sunup." He turned. Lucas watched him go back to where Dan waited at the edge of the glade. Then the two of them went on, the light swinging and flicking on among the trees, the brush. Presently it vanished.

"George Wilkins," Lucas said.

"Sir," George said.

"Find the pine-knot and light it again." George did so; once more the red glare streamed and stank away in thick smoke, upward against the August stars of more than midnight. Lucas put the divining machine down and took the torch. "Grab holt of that thing," he said. "I got to find it now."

But when day broke they had not found it. The torch paled in the wan, dew-heavy light. The salesman was asleep on the wet ground now, drawn into a ball against the dawn's wet chill, unshaven, the dashing city hat crumpled beneath his cheek, his necktie wrenched sideways in the collar of his soiled white shirt, his muddy trousers rolled to his knees, the brightly-polished shoes of yesterday now two shapeless lumps of caked mud. When they waked him at last he sat up cursing. But he knew at once where he was and why. "All right now," he said. "If that mule moves one foot from that cottonhouse where we left her, I'm going to get the sheriff."

"I just want one more night," Lucas said. "That money is here."

"Take one more," the salesman said. "Take a hundred. Spend the rest of your life here if you want to. Just tell me first what about that fellow that claims he owns that mule?"

"I'll tend to him," Lucas said. "I'll tend to him this morning. You dont need to worry about that. Besides, if you try to move the mule yourself today, that sheriff will take her away from you. You just leave her where she is and stop worrying yourself and me too. Let me have just one more night with this thing and I'll fix everything."

"All right," the salesman said. "But do you know what one more night is going to cost you? It's going to cost you exactly twenty-five dollars more. Now I'm going to town and go to bed."

They returned to the salesman's car. He put the divining machine back into the trunk of the car and locked it. He let Lucas and George out at Lucas' gate. The car went on down the road, already going fast. George batted his eyes rapidly after it. "Now whut we gonter do?" he said.

"Eat your breakfast quick as you can and get back here," Lucas said. "You are going to town and back by noon."

"I needs to go to bed too," George said. "I'm bad off to sleep too."

"You can sleep tomorrow," Lucas said. "Maybe most of tonight."

"I could have rid in and come back with him, if you had just said so sooner," George said.

"Hah," Lucas said. "But I didn't. You eat your breakfast quick as you can. Or if you think maybe you cant catch a ride to town, maybe you better start now without waiting for breakfast. Because it will be thirty-four miles to walk, and you are going to be back here by noon." When George reached Lucas' gate ten minutes later, Lucas met him, the check already filled out in his laborious, cramped, though quite legible hand. It was for fifty dollars. "Get it in silver dollars," Lucas said. "And be back here by noon."

It was just dusk when the salesman's car stopped again at Lucas' gate, where Lucas and George waited. George carried a pick and a long-handled shovel. The salesman was freshly shaven and his face looked rested; the snap-brim hat had been brushed and his shirt was clean. But he wore now a pair of cotton khaki pants still bearing the manufacturer's stitched label and still showing the creases where they had lain folded on the store's shelf when it opened for business that morning. He gave Lucas a hard, jeering stare as Lucas and George approached. "I aint going to ask if my mule's all right," he said. "Because I dont need to. Do I?"

"It's all right," Lucas said. He and George got into the back seat. The divining machine now sat on the front seat beside the salesman. George stopped halfway in and blinked rapidly at it.

"I just happened to think how rich I'd be if I just knowed what hit knows," he said. "All of us would be. We wouldn't need to be wasting no night after night hunting buried money then, would we?" He addressed the salesman now, affable, deferential, chatty: "Then you and Mister Lucas neither wouldn't care who owned no mule, nor even if there was ere mule to own, would you?"

"Hush, and get in the car," Lucas said. The salesman put the car into gear, but it did not move yet. He sat half-turned, looking back at Lucas.

"Well?" he said. "Where do you want to take your walk tonight? Same place?"

"Not there," Lucas said. "I'll show you where. We were looking in the wrong place. I misread the paper."

"You bet," the salesman said. "It's worth that extra twenty-five bucks to have found that out——" He had started the car. Now he stopped it so suddenly that Lucas and George, sitting gingerly on the edge of the seat, were flung forward against the back of the front one. "What did you say?" the salesman said. "You did what to the paper?"

"I misread it," Lucas said.

"Misread what?"

"The paper."

"You mean you've got a letter or something that tells where it was buried?"

"That's right," Lucas said. "I misread it yesterday."

"Where is it?"

"It's put away in my house."

"Go get it."

"Never mind," Lucas said. "We wont need it. I read it right this time." For a moment longer the salesman looked at Lucas over his shoulder. Then he turned his head and put his hand to the gear lever, but the car was already in gear.

"All right," he said. "Where's the place?"

"Drive on," Lucas said. "I'll show you."

It took them almost two hours to reach it, the road not even a road but a gullied overgrown path winding through hills, the place they sought not in the bottom but on a hill overlooking the creek—a clump of ragged cedars, the ruins of old cementless chimneys, a depression which was once a well or a cistern, the old wornout brier- and sedge-choked fields spreading away and a few snaggled trees of what had been an orchard, shadowy and dim beneath the moonless sky where the fierce stars of late summer swam. "It's in the orchard," Lucas said. "It's divided, buried in two separate places. One of them's in the orchard."

"Provided the fellow that wrote you the letter aint come back and joined them together again," the salesman said. "What are we waiting on? Here, Jack," he said to George, "grab that thing out of there." George lifted the divining machine from the car. The salesman had a flashlight now, quite new, thrust into his hip pocket, though he didn't put it on at once. He looked around at the dark horizon of other hills, visible even in the darkness for miles. "By God, you better find it first pop this time. There probably aint a man in ten miles that can walk that wont be up here inside of an hour, watching us."

"Dont tell me that," Lucas said. "Tell it to this three-hundred-and-twenty-five-dollar talking box I done bought that dont seem to know how to say nothing but No."

"You aint bought this box yet, big boy," the salesman said. "You say one of the places is in them trees there. All right. Where?"

Lucas, carrying the shovel, entered the orchard. The others followed. The salesman watched Lucas pause, squinting at the trees and sky to orient himself, moving on again. At last he stopped. "We can start here," he said. The salesman snapped on the flashlight, cupping the beam with his hand onto the box in George's hands.

"All right, Jack," he said. "Get going."

"I better tote it," Lucas said.

"No," the salesman said. "You're too old. I dont know yet that you can even keep up with us."

"I did last night," Lucas said.

"This aint last night," the salesman said. "Get on, Jack!" he said sharply. They moved on, George in the middle, carrying the machine, while all three of them watched the small cryptic dials in the flashlight's contracted beam as they worked back and forth across the orchard in parallel traverses, all three watching when the needles jerked into life and gyrated and spun for a moment, then stopped, quivering. Then Lucas held the box and watched George spading into the light's concentrated pool and saw the rusted can come up at last and the bright cascade of silver dollars glint and rush about the salesman's hands and heard the salesman's voice: "Well, by God. Well, by God." Lucas squatted also. He and the salesman squatted opposite one another across the pit.

"Well, I done found this much of it, anyhow," Lucas said. The salesman, one hand spread upon the scattered coins, made a slashing blow with the other as if Lucas had reached for the money. Squatting, he laughed harshly and steadily at Lucas.

"*You* found? This machine dont belong to you, old man."

"I bought it from you," Lucas said.

"With what?"

"A mule," Lucas said. The other laughed at him across the pit, harsh and steady. "I give you a billy sale for it," Lucas said.

"Which never was worth a damn," the salesman said. "It's in my car yonder. Go and get it whenever you want to. It was so worthless I never even bothered to tear it up." He scrabbled the coins back into the can. The flashlight lay on the ground where he had dropped it, flung it, still burning. He rose quickly out of the light until only his lower legs showed, in the new creased cotton trousers, the low black shoes which had not been polished again but merely washed. "All right," he said. "This aint hardly any of it. You said it was divided, buried in two separate places. Where's the other one?"

"Ask your finding machine," Lucas said. "Aint it supposed to know? Aint that why you want three hundred dollars for it?" They faced one another in the darkness, two shadows, faceless. Lucas moved. "Then I reckon we can go home," he said. "George Wilkins."

"Sir," George said.

"Wait," the salesman said. Lucas paused. They faced one another again, invisible. "There wasn't over a hundred here," the salesman said. "Most of it is in the other place. I'll give you ten percent."

"It was my letter," Lucas said. "That aint enough."

"Twenty," the salesman said. "And that's all."

"I want half," Lucas said.

"Half?"

"And that mule paper back, and another paper saying that that machine is mine."

"Ha ha," the salesman said. "And ha ha ha. You say that letter said in the orchard. The orchard aint very big. And most of the night left, not to mention tomor——"

"I said it said some of it was in the orchard," Lucas said. They faced one another in the darkness.

"Tomorrow," the salesman said.

"Now," Lucas said.

"Tomorrow."

"Now," Lucas said. The invisible face stared at his own invisible face. Both he and George seemed to feel the windless summer air moving to the white man's trembling.

"Jack," the salesman said, "how much did you say them other fellows found?" But Lucas answered before George could speak.

"Twenty-two thousand dollars."

"Hit mought er been more than twenty-two thousand," George said. "Hit was a big——"

"All right," the salesman said. "I'll give you a bill of sale for it as soon as we finish."

"I want it now," Lucas said. They returned to the car. Lucas held the flashlight. They watched the salesman rip open his patent brief case and jerk out of it and fling toward Lucas the bill of sale for the mule. Then they watched his jerking hand fill in the long printed form with its carbon duplicates and sign it and rip out one of the duplicates.

"You get possession tomorrow morning," he said. "It belongs to me until then." He sprang out of the car. "Come on."

"And half it finds is mine," Lucas said.

"How in hell is it going to be any half or any nothing, with you standing there running your mouth?" the salesman said. "Come on." But Lucas didn't move.

"What about them fifty dollars we done already found then?" he said. "Dont I get half of them?" This time the salesman merely stood laughing at him, harsh and steady and without mirth. Then he was gone. He hadn't even closed the brief case. He snatched the machine from George and the flashlight from Lucas and ran back toward the orchard, the light jerking and leaping as he ran. "George Wilkins," Lucas said.

"Sir," George said.

"Take that mule back where you got it. Then go tell Roth Edmonds he can quit worrying folks about it."

3.

He mounted the gnawed steps beside which the bright mare stood under the wide saddle, and entered the long room with its ranked shelves of tinned food, the hooks from which hung collars and traces and hames and plowlines, its smell of molasses and cheese and leather and kerosene. Edmonds swivelled the chair around from the desk. "Where've you been?" he said. "I sent word to you two days ago I wanted to see you. Why didn't you come?"

"I was in bed, I reckon," Lucas said. "I been up all night long for the last three nights. I cant stand it anymore like when I was a young man. You wont neither when you are my age."

"And I've got better sense at half your age than to try it. And maybe when you get twice mine, you'll have too. But that's not what I wanted. I want to know about that damn Saint Louis drummer. Dan says he's still here. What's he doing?"

"Hunting buried money," Lucas said.

For a moment Edmonds didn't speak. Then he said, "What? Hunting what? What did you say?"

"Hunting buried money," Lucas said. He let himself go easily back against the edge of the counter. He took from his vest pocket a small tin of snuff and uncapped it and filled the cap carefully and exactly with snuff and drew his lower lip outward between thumb and finger and tilted the snuff into it and capped the tin and put it back in his vest pocket. "Using my finding box. He rents it from me by the night. That's why I've been having to stay up all night, to see I got the box back. But last night he never turned up, so I got a good night's sleep for a change. So I reckon he's done gone back wherever it was he come from."

Edmonds sat in the swivel chair and stared at Lucas. "Rents it from you? The same machine you stole my——that you ——the same machine——"

"For twenty-five dollars a night," Lucas said. "That's what he charged me to use it one night. So I reckon that's the regular rent on them. He sells them; he ought to know. Leastways, that's what I charges." Edmonds put his hands on the chair arms, but he didn't move yet. He sat perfectly still, leaning forward a little, staring at the negro leaning against the counter, in whom only the slight shrinkage of the jaws revealed the old man, in threadbare mohair trousers such as Grover Cleveland or President Taft might have worn in the summertime, a white stiff-bosomed collarless shirt beneath a pique vest yellow with age and looped across by a heavy gold watchchain, and the sixty-dollar handmade beaver hat which Edmonds' grandfather had given him fifty years ago above the face which was not sober and not grave but wore no expression at all. "Because he was looking in the wrong place," he said. "He was hunting up there on that hill. That money is buried down yonder by the creek somewhere. Them two white men that slipped in here that night four years ago and got clean away with twenty-two thousand dollars——" Now Edmonds got himself out of the chair and onto his feet. He drew a long deep breath and began to walk steadily toward Lucas. "And now we done got shut of him, me and George Wilkins——" Walking steadily toward him, Edmonds expelled his breath. He had believed it would be a shout but it was not much more than a whisper.

"Get out of here," he said. "Go home. And dont come back. Dont ever come back. When you need supplies, send Aunt Molly after them."

III

WHEN Edmonds glanced up from the ledger and saw the old woman coming up the road, he did not recognise her. He returned to the ledger and it was not until he heard her toiling up the steps and saw her enter the commissary itself, that he knew who it was. Because for something like four or five years now he had never seen her outside her own gate. He would pass the house on his mare while riding his crops and see her sitting on the gallery, her shrunken face collapsed about the reed stem of a clay pipe, or moving about the washing-pot and clothes-line in the back yard, moving slowly and painfully, as the very old move, appearing to be much older even to Edmonds, when he thought about it at all, than Edmonds certainly knew her to be. And regularly once a month he would get down and tie the mare to the fence and enter the house with a tin of tobacco and a small sack of the soft cheap candy which she loved, and visit with her for a half hour. He called it a libation to his luck, as the centurion spilled first a little of the wine he drank, though actually it was to his ancestors and to the conscience which he would have probably affirmed he did not possess, in the form, the person, of the negro woman who had been the only mother he ever knew, who had not only delivered him on that night of rain and flood when her husband had very nearly lost his life fetching the doctor who arrived too late, but moved into the very house, bringing her own child, the white child and the black one sleeping in the same room with her so she could suckle them both until he was weaned, and never out of the house very long at a time until he went off to school at twelve—a small woman, almost tiny, who in the succeeding forty years seemed to have grown even smaller, in the same clean white headcloth and apron which he first remembered, whom he knew to be actually younger than Lucas but who looked much older, incredibly old, who during the last few years had begun to call him by his father's name, or even by the title by which the older negroes referred to his grandfather.

"Good Lord," he said. "What are you doing away over here? Why didn't you send Lucas? He ought to know better than to let you——"

"He's in bed asleep now," she said. She was panting a little from the walk. "That's how I had a chance to come. I dont want nothing. I come to talk to you." She turned a little toward the window. Then he saw the myriad-wrinkled face.

"Why, what is it?" he said. He rose from the swivel chair and drew the other one, a straight chair with wire-braced legs, out from behind the desk. "Here," he said. But she only looked from him to the chair with the same blind look until he took her by the arm which, beneath the two or three layers of clothing beneath the faded, perfectly clean dress, felt no larger than the reed stem of the pipe she smoked. He led her to the chair and lowered her into it, the voluminous layer on layer of her skirts and underskirts spreading. Immediately she bowed her head and turned it aside and raised one gnarled hand like a tiny clump of dried and blackened roots, before her eyes.

"The light hurts them," she said. He helped her up and turned the chair until its back was toward the window. This time she found it herself and sat down. Edmonds returned to the swivel chair.

"All right," he said. "What is it?"

"I want to leave Lucas," she said. "I want one of them. . . . . one of them. . . . . ." Edmonds sat perfectly motionless, staring at the face which now he could not distinctly see.

"You what?" he said. "A divorce? After forty-five years, at your age? What will you do? How will you get along without somebody——"

"I can work. I will——"

"Damn that," Edmonds said. "You know I didn't mean that. Even if father hadn't fixed it in his will to take care of you for the rest of your life. I mean what will you do? Leave the house that belongs to you and Lucas and go live with Nat and George?"

"That will be just as bad," she said. "I got to go clean away. Because he's crazy. Ever since he got that machine, he's done went crazy. Him and—and. . . . ." Even though he had just spoken it, he realised that she couldn't even think of George's name. She spoke again, immobile, looking at nothing as far as he could tell, her hands like two cramped ink-splashes on the lap of the immaculate apron: "—stays out all night long every night with it, hunting that buried money. He dont even take care of his own stock right no more. I feeds the mare and the hogs and milks, tries to. But that's all right. I can do that. I'm glad to do that when he is sick in the body. But he's sick in the mind now. Bad sick. He dont even get up to go to church on Sunday no more. He's bad sick, marster. He's doing a thing the Lord aint meant for folks to do. And I'm afraid."

"Afraid of what?" Edmonds said. "Lucas is strong as a horse. He's a better man than I am, right now. He's all laid-by now, with nothing to do until his crop makes. It wont hurt him to stay up all night walking up and down that creek with George for a while. He'll have to quit next month to pick his cotton."

"It aint that I'm afraid of."

"Then what?" he said. "What is it?"

"I'm afraid he's going to find it."

Again Edmonds sat in his chair, looking at her. "Afraid he's going to find it?" Still she looked at nothing that he could see, motionless, tiny, like a doll, an ornament.

"Because God say, 'What's rendered to My earth, it belong to Me unto I resurrect it. And let him or her touch it, and beware'. And I'm afraid. I got to go. I got to be free of him."

"There aint any buried money in this country," Edmonds said. "Hasn't he been poking around in the bottom ever since last spring, hunting for it? And that machine aint going to find it either. I tried my best to keep him from buying it. I did everything I knew except have that damn agent arrested for trespass. I wish now I had done that. If I had just foreseen—— But that wouldn't have done any good. Lucas would just have met him down the road somewhere and bought it. But he aint going to find any more buried money with it than he found walking up and down the creek, making George Wilkins dig where he thought it ought to be. Even he'll believe that soon. He'll quit. Then he'll be all right."

"No," she said. "Lucas is an old man. He dont look it, but he's sixty-seven years old. And when a man that old takes up money-hunting, it's like when he takes up gambling or whisky or women. He aint going to have time to quit. And then he's gonter be lost, lost. . . ." She ceased. She did not move on the hard chair, not even the depthless splotches of her knotted hands against the apron's blanched spread. *Damn, damn, damn*, Edmonds thought.

"I could tell you how to cure him in two days," he said. "If you were twenty years younger. But you couldn't do it now."

"Tell me. I can do it."

"No," he said. "You are too old now."

"Tell me. I can do it."

"Wait till he comes in with that thing tomorrow morning, then take it yourself and go down to the creek and hunt buried money. Do it the next morning, and the one after that. Let him find out that's what you are doing—using his machine while he is asleep, all the time he is asleep and cant watch it, cant hunt himself. Let him come in and find there's no breakfast ready for him, wake up and find there's no supper ready because you're still down in the creek bottom, hunting buried money with his machine. That'll cure him. But you're too old. You couldn't stand it. You go back home and when Lucas wakes up, you and he— No, that's too far for you to walk twice in one day. Tell him I said to wait there for me. I'll come after supper and talk to him."

"Talking wont change him. I couldn't. And you cant. All I can do is to go clean away from him."

"Maybe it cant," Edmonds said. "But I can damn sure try it. And he will damn sure listen. I'll be there after supper. You tell him to wait."

She rose then. He watched her toil back down the road toward home, tiny, almost like a doll. It was not just concern, and, if he had told himself the truth, not concern for her at all. He was raging—an abrupt boiling-over of an accumulation of floutings and outrages covering not only his span but his father's lifetime too, back into the time of his grandfather McCaslin Edmonds. Lucas was not only the oldest person living on the place, older even than Edmonds' father would have been, there was that quarter strain not only of white blood and not even Edmonds blood, but of old Carothers McCaslin himself, from whom Lucas was descended not only by a male line but in only two generations, while Edmonds was descended by a female line and five generations back; even as a child the boy remarked how Lucas always referred to his father as Mr Edmonds, never as Mister Zack, as the other negroes did, and how with a cold and deliberate calculation he evaded having to address the white man by any name whatever when speaking to him.

Yet it was not that Lucas made capital of his white or even his McCaslin blood, but the contrary. It was as if he were not only impervious to that blood, he was indifferent to it. He didn't even need to strive with it. He didn't even have to bother to defy it. He resisted it simply by being the composite of the two races which made him, simply by possessing it. Instead of being at once the battleground and victim of the two strains, he was a vessel, durable, ancestryless, nonconductive, in which the toxin and its anti stalemated one another, seetheless, unrumored in the outside air. There had been three of them once: James, then a sister named Fonsiba, then Lucas, children of Aunt Tomey's Turl, old Carothers McCaslin's son, and Tennie Beauchamp, whom Edmonds' great-uncle Amodeus McCaslin won from a neighbor in a poker game in 1859. Fonsiba married and went to Arkansas to live and never returned, though Lucas continued to hear from her until her death. But James, the eldest, ran away before he became of age and didn't stop until he had crossed the Ohio River and they never heard from or of him again at all— that is, that his white kindred ever knew. It was as though he had not only (as his sister was later to do) put running water between himself and the land of his grandmother's betrayal and his father's nameless birth, but he had interposed latitude and geography too, shaking from his feet forever the very dust of the land where his white ancestor could acknowledge or repudiate him from one day to another, according to his whim, but where he dared not even repudiate the white ancestor save when it met the white man's humor of the moment.

But Lucas remained. He didn't have to stay. Of the three children, he not only had no material shackles (nor, as Carothers Edmonds began to comprehend later, moral ones either) holding him to the place, he alone was equipped beforehand with financial independence to have departed forever at any time after his twenty-first birthday. It was known father to son to son among the Edmondses until it came to Carothers in his turn, how when in the early fifties old Carothers McCaslin's twin sons, Amodeus and Theophilus, first put into operation their scheme for the manumission of their father's slaves, there was made an especial provision (hence a formal acknowledgment, even though only by inference and only from his white half-brothers) for their father's negro son. It was a sum of money, with the accumulated interest, to become the negro son's on his verbal demand but which Tomey's Turl, who elected to remain even after his constitutional liberation, never availed himself of. And he died, and old Carothers McCaslin was dead more than fifty years then, and Amodeus and Theophilus were dead too, at seventy and better, in the same year as they had been born in the same year, and McCaslin Edmonds now had the land, the plantation, in fee and title both, relinquished to him by Isaac McCaslin, Theophilus' son, for what reason, what consideration other than the pension which McCaslin and his son Zachary and his son Carothers still paid to Isaac in his little jerry-built bungalow in Jefferson, no man certainly knew. But relinquished it certainly was, somehow and somewhere back in that dark time in Mississippi when a man had to be hard and ruthless to get a patrimony to leave behind himself and strong and hard to keep it until he could bequeath it;—relinquished, repudiated even, by its true heir (Isaac, 'Uncle Ike', childless, a widower now, living in his dead wife's house the title to which he likewise declined to assume, born into his father's old age and himself born old and became steadily younger and younger until, past seventy himself and at least that many years nearer eighty than he ever admitted anymore, he had acquired something of a young boy's high and selfless innocence) who had retained of the patrimony, and by his own request, only the trusteeship of the legacy which his negro uncle still could not quite seem to comprehend was his for the asking.

He never asked for it. He died. Then his first son, James, fled, quitted the cabin he had been born in, the plantation, Mississippi itself, by night and with nothing save the clothes he walked in. When Isaac McCaslin heard about it in town he drew a third of the money, the legacy, with its accumulated interest, in cash and departed also and was gone a week and returned and put the money back into the bank. Then the daughter, Fonsiba, married and moved to Arkansas. This time Isaac went with them and transferred a third of the legacy to a local Arkansas bank and arranged for Fonsiba to draw three dollars of it each week, no more and no less, and returned home. Then one morning Isaac was at home, looking at a newspaper, not reading it, looking at it, when he realised what it was and why. It was the date. *It's somebody's birthday,* he thought. He said aloud, "It's Lucas's. He's twenty-one today," as his wife entered. She was a young woman then; they had been married only a few years but he had already come to know the expression which her face wore, looking at it always as he did now: peacefully and with pity for her and regret too, for her, for both of them, knowing the tense bitter indomitable voice as well as he did the expression:

"Lucas Beauchamp is in the kitchen. He wants to see you. Maybe your cousin has sent you word he has decided to stop even that fifty dollars a month he swapped you for your father's farm." But it was all right. It didn't matter. He could ask her forgiveness as loudly thus as if he had shouted, express his pity and grief; husband and wife did not need to speak words to one another, not just from the old habit of living together but because in that one long-ago instant at least out of the long and shabby stretch of their human lives, even though they knew at the time it wouldn't and couldn't last, they had touched and become as God when they voluntarily and in advance forgave one another for all that each knew the other could never be. Then Lucas was in the room, standing just inside the door, his hat in one hand against his leg—the face the color of a used saddle, the features Syriac, not in a racial sense but as the heir to ten centuries of desert horsemen. It was not at all the face of their grandfather, Carothers McCaslin. It was the face of the generation which had just preceded them: the composite tintype face of ten thousand undefeated Confederate soldiers almost indistinguishably caricatured, composed, cold, colder than his, more ruthless than his, with more bottom than he had.

"Many happy returns!" Isaac said. "I godfrey, I was just about——"

"Yes," Lucas said. "The rest of that money. I wants it."

"Money?" Isaac said. "Money?"

"That Old Marster left for pappy. If it's still ourn. If you're going to give it to us."

"It's not mine to give or withhold either. It was your father's. All any of you had to do was to ask for it. I tried to find Jim after he——"

"I'm asking now," Lucas said.

"All of it? Half of it is Jim's."

"I can keep it for him same as you been doing."

"Yes," Isaac said. "You're going too," he said. "You're leaving too."

"I aint decided yet," Lucas said. "I might. I'm a man now. I can do what I want. I want to know I can go when I decide to."

"You could have done that at any time. Even if grandpa hadn't left money for Tomey's Turl. All you, any of you, would have had to do would be to come to me. . . . ." His voice died. He thought, *Fifty dollars a month. He knows that's all. That I reneged, cried calf-rope, sold my birthright, betrayed my blood, for what he too calls not peace but obliteration, and a little food.* "It's in the bank," he said. "We'll go and get it."

Only Zachary Edmonds and, in his time, his son Carothers knew that part of it. But what followed most of the town of Jefferson knew, so that the anecdote not only took its place in the Edmonds family annals, but in the minor annals of the town too:—how the white and the negro cousins went side by side to the bank that morning and Lucas said, "Wait. It's a heap of money."

"It's too much," the white man said. "Too much to keep hidden under a brick in a hearth. Let me keep it for you. Let me keep it."

"Wait," Lucas said. "Will the bank keep it for a black man same as for a white?"

"Yes," the white man said. "I will ask them to."

"How can I get it back?" Lucas said. The white man explained about the check. "All right," Lucas said. They stood side by side at the window while the white man had the account transferred and the new pass-book filled out; again Lucas said "Wait" and then they stood side by side at the ink-splashed wooden shelf while Lucas wrote out the check, writing it steadily under the white man's direction in the cramped though quite legible hand which the white man's mother had taught him and his brother and sister too. Then they stood again at the grille while the teller cashed the check and Lucas, still blocking the single window, counted the money tediously and deliberately through twice and pushed it back to the teller beyond the grille. "Now you can put it back," he said. "And gimme my paper."

But he didn't leave. Within the year he married, not a country woman, a farm woman, but a town woman, and McCaslin Edmonds built a house for them and allotted Lucas a specific acreage to be farmed as he saw fit as long as he lived or remained on the place. Then McCaslin Edmonds died and his son married and on that spring night of flood and isolation the boy Carothers was born. Still in infancy, he had already accepted the black man as an adjunct to the woman who was the only mother he would remember, as simply as he accepted his black foster-brother, as simply as he accepted his father as an adjunct to his existence. Even before he was out of infancy, the two houses had become interchangeable: himself and his foster-brother sleeping on the same pallet in the white man's house or in the same bed in the negro's and eating of the same food at the same table in either, actually preferring the negro house, the hearth on which even in summer a little fire always burned, centering the life in it, to his own. It did not even need to come to him as a part of his family's chronicle that his white father and his foster-brother's black one had done the same; it never even occurred to him that they in their turn and simultaneously had not had the first of remembering projected upon a single woman whose skin was likewise dark. One day he knew, without wondering or remembering when or how he had learned that either, that the black woman was not his mother, and did not regret it; he knew that his own mother was dead and did not grieve. There was still the black woman, constant, steadfast, and the black man of whom he saw as much as and even more than of his own father, and the negro's house, the strong warm negro smell, the night-time hearth and the fire even in summer on it, which he still preferred to his own. And besides, he was no longer an infant. He and his foster-brother rode the plantation horses and mules, they had a pack of small hounds to hunt with and promise of a gun in another year or so; they were sufficient, complete, wanting, as all children do, not to be understood, leaping in mutual embattlement before any threat to privacy, but only to love, to question and examine unchallenged, and to be let alone.

Then one day the old curse of his fathers, the old haught ancestral pride based not on any value but on an accident of geography, stemmed not from courage and honor but from wrong and shame, descended to him. He did not recognise it then. He and his foster-brother, Henry, were seven years old. They had finished supper at Henry's house and Molly was just sending them to bed in the room across the hall where they slept when there, when suddenly he said, "I'm going home."

"Les stay here," Henry said. "I thought we was going to get up when pappy did and go hunting."

"You can," he said. He was already moving toward the door. "I'm going home."

"All right," Henry said, following him. And he remembered how they walked that half mile to his house in the first summer dark, himself walking just fast enough that the negro boy never quite came up beside him, entering the house in single file and up the stairs and into the room with the bed and the pallet on the floor which they slept on when they passed the night here, and how he undressed just slow enough for Henry to beat him to the pallet and lie down. Then he went to the bed and lay down on it, rigid, staring up at the dark ceiling even after he heard Henry raise onto one elbow, looking toward the bed with slow and equable astonishment. "Are you going to sleep up there?" Henry said. "Well, all right. This here pallet sleeps all right to me, but I reckon I just as lief to if you wants to," and rose and approached the bed and stood over the white boy, waiting for him to move over and make room until the boy said, harsh and violent though not loud:

"No!"

Henry didn't move. "You mean you dont want me to sleep in the bed?" Nor did the boy move. He didn't answer, rigid on his back, staring upward. "All right," Henry said quietly and went back to the pallet and lay down again. The boy heard him, listened to him; he couldn't help it, lying clenched and rigid and open-eyed, hearing the slow equable voice: "I reckon on a hot night like tonight we will sleep cooler if we——"

"Shut up!" the boy said. "How'm I or you neither going to sleep if you keep on talking?" Henry hushed then. But the boy didn't sleep, long after Henry's quiet and untroubled breathing had begun, lying in a rigid fury of the grief he could not explain, the shame he would not admit. Then he slept and it seemed to him he was still awake, waked and did not know he had slept until he saw in the gray of dawn the empty pallet on the floor. They did not hunt that morning. They never slept in the same room again and never again ate at the same table because he admitted to himself it was shame now and he did not go to Henry's house and for a month he only saw Henry at a distance, with Lucas in the field, walking beside his father and holding the reins of the team while Lucas plowed. Then one day he knew it was grief and was ready to admit it was shame also, wanted to admit it only it was too late then, forever and forever too late. He went to Molly's house. It was already late afternoon; Henry and Lucas would be coming up from the field at any time now. Molly was there, looking at him from the kitchen door as he crossed the yard. There was nothing in her face; he said it the best he could for that moment, because later he would be able to say it all right, say it once and forever so that it would be gone forever, facing her before he entered her house yet, stopping, his feet slightly apart, trembling a little, lordly, peremptory: "I'm going to eat supper with you all tonight."

It was all right. There was nothing in her face. He could say it almost any time now, when the time came. "Course you is," she said. "I'll cook you a chicken."

Then it was as if it had never happened at all. Henry came almost at once; he must have seen him from the field, and he and Henry killed and dressed the chicken. Then Lucas came and he went to the barn with Henry and Lucas while Henry milked. Then they were busy in the yard in the dusk, smelling the cooking chicken, until Molly called Henry and then a little later himself, the voice as it had always been, peaceful and steadfast: "Come and eat your supper."

But it was too late. The table was set in the kitchen where it always was and Molly stood at the stove drawing the biscuit out as she always stood, but Lucas was not there and there was just one chair, one plate, his glass of milk beside it, the platter heaped with untouched chicken, and even as he sprang back, gasping, for an instant blind as the room rushed and swam, Henry was turning toward the door to go out of it.

"Are you ashamed to eat when I eat?" he cried.

Henry paused, turning his head a little to speak in the voice slow and without heat: "I aint shamed of nobody," he said peacefully. "Not even me."

So he entered his heritage. He ate its bitter fruit. He listened as Lucas referred to his father as Mr Edmonds, never as Mister Zack; he watched him avoid having to address the white man directly by any name at all with a calculation so coldly and constantly alert, a finesse so deliberate and unflagging, that for a time he could not tell if even his father knew that the negro was refusing to call him mister. At last he spoke to his father about it. The other listened gravely, with something in his face which the boy could not read and which at the moment he paid little attention to since he was still young then, still a child; he had not yet divined that there was something between his father and Lucas, something more than difference in race could account for since it did not exist between Lucas and any other white man, something more than the white blood, even the McCaslin blood, could account for since it was not there between his uncle Isaac McCaslin and Lucas. "You think that because Lucas is older than I am, old enough even to remember Uncle Buck and Uncle Buddy a little, and is a descendant of the people who lived on this place where we Edmonds are usurpers, yesterday's mushrooms, is not reason enough for him not to want to say mister to me?" his father said. "We grew up together, we ate and slept together and hunted and fished together, like you and Henry. We did it until we were grown men. Except that I always beat him shooting except one time. And as it turned out, I even beat him then. You think that's not reason enough?"

"We're not usurpers," the boy said, cried almost. "Our grandmother McCaslin was as much kin to old Carothers as Uncle Buck and Buddy. Uncle Isaac himself gave—Uncle Isaac himself says. . . . . ." He ceased. His father watched him. "No, sir," he said harshly. "That's not enough."

"Ah," his father said. Then the boy could read what was in his face. He had seen it before, as all children had—that moment when, enveloped and surrounded still by the warmth and confidence, he discovers that the reserve which he had thought to have passed had merely retreated and set up a new barrier, still impregnable;—that instant when the child realises with both grief and outrage that the parent antedates it, has experienced things, shames and triumphs both, in which it can have no part. "I'll make a trade with you. You let me and Lucas settle how he is to treat me, and I'll let you and him settle how he is to treat you."

Then, in adolescence, he knew what he had seen in his father's face that morning, what shadow, what stain, what mark—something which had happened between Lucas and his father, which nobody but they knew and would ever know if the telling depended on them—something which had happened because they were themselves, men, not stemming from any difference of race nor because one blood strain ran in them both. Then, in his late teens, almost a man, he even knew what it had been. *It was a woman*, he thought. *My father and a nigger, over a woman. My father and a nigger man over a nigger woman*, because he simply declined even to realise that he had even refused to think *a white woman*. He didn't even think Molly's name. That didn't matter. *And by God Lucas beat him*, he thought. *Edmonds*, he thought, harshly and viciously. *Edmonds. Even a nigger McCaslin is a better man, better than all of us. Old Carothers got his nigger bastards right in his back yard and I would like to have seen the husband or anybody else that said him nay.—Yes, Lucas beat him, else Lucas wouldn't be here. If father had beat Lucas, he couldn't have let Lucas stay here even to forgive him. It will only be Lucas who could have stayed because Lucas is impervious to anybody, even to forgiving them, even to having to harm them.*

Impervious to time too. Zachary Edmonds died, and in his turn he inherited the plantation the true heir to which, by male descent and certainly morally and, if the truth were known, probably legally too, was still alive, living on the doled pittance which his great-nephew now in his turn sent him each month. For twenty years now he had run it, tried to even with the changed times, as his father and grandfather and great-grandfather had done before him. Yet when he looked back over those twenty years, they seemed to him one long and unbroken course of outrageous trouble and conflict, not with the land or weather (or even lately, with the federal government) but with the old negro who in his case did not even bother to remember not to call him mister, who called him Mr Edmonds and Mister Carothers or Carothers or Roth or son or spoke to him in a group of younger negroes, lumping them all together, as 'you boys'. There were the years during which Lucas had continued to farm his acreage in the same clumsy old fashion which Carothers McCaslin himself had probably followed, declining advice, refusing to use improved implements, refusing to let a tractor so much as cross the land which his McCaslin forbears had given him without recourse for life, refusing even to allow the pilot who dusted the rest of the cotton with weevil poison even fly his laden aeroplane through the air above it, yet drawing supplies from the commissary as if he farmed, and at an outrageous and incredible profit, a thousand acres, having on the commissary books an account dating thirty years back which Edmonds knew he would never pay for the good and simple reason that Lucas would not only outlive the present Edmonds as he had outlived the two preceding him, but would probably outlast the very ledgers which held the account. Then the still which Lucas had run almost in his, Edmonds', back yard for at least twenty years, according to his daughter, until his own avarice exposed him, and the three-hundred-dollar mule which he had stolen from not only his business partner and guarantor but actually from his own blood relation and swapped for a machine for divining the hiding-place of buried money; and now this: breaking up after forty-five years the home of the woman who had been the only mother he, Edmonds, ever knew, who had raised him, fed him from her own breast as she was actually doing her own child, who had surrounded him always with care for his physical body and for his spirit too, teaching him his manners, behavior—to be gentle with his inferiors, honorable with his equals, generous to the weak and considerate of the aged, courteous, truthful and brave to all—who had given him, the motherless, without stint or expectation of reward that constant and abiding devotion and love which existed nowhere else in this world for him;—breaking up her home who had no other kin save an old brother in Jefferson whom she had not even seen in ten years, and the eighteen-year-old married daughter with whom she would doubtless refuse to live since the daughter's husband likewise had lain himself liable to the curse which she believed her own husband had incurred.

Impervious to time too. It seemed to Edmonds, sitting at his solitary supper which he couldn't eat, that he could actually see Lucas standing there in the room before him—the face which at sixty-seven looked actually younger than his own at forty-three, showed less of the ravages of passions and thought and satieties and frustrations than his own—the face which was not at all a replica even in caricature of his grandfather McCaslin's but which had heired and now reproduced with absolute and shocking fidelity the old ancestor's entire generation and thought—the face which, as old Isaac McCaslin had seen it that morning forty-five years ago, was a composite of a whole generation of fierce and undefeated young Confederate soldiers, embalmed and slightly mummified—and he thought with amazement and something very like horror: *He's more like old Carothers than all the rest of us put together, including old Carothers. He is both heir and prototype simultaneously of all the geography and climate and biology which sired old Carothers and all the rest of us and our kind, myriad, countless, faceless, even nameless now except himself who fathered himself, intact and complete, contemptuous, as old Carothers must have been, of all blood black white yellow or red, including his own.*

2.

It was full dark when he tied the mare to Lucas' fence and walked up the rock path neatly bordered with broken brick and upended bottles and such set into the earth, and mounted the steps and entered. Lucas was waiting, standing in the door with his hat on, in silhouette against the firelight on the hearth. The old woman did not rise. She sat as in the commissary that afternoon, motionless, only bent a little forward, her tiny gnarled hands immobile again on the white apron, the shrunken and tragic mask touched here and there into highlight by the fire, and for the first time in his memory he was seeing her in or about the house without the clay pipe in her mouth. Lucas drew up a chair for him. But Lucas did not sit down. He went and stood at the other side of the hearth, the firelight touching him too—the broad sweep of the handmade beaver hat which Edmonds' grandfather had given him fifty years ago, the faintly Syriac features, the heavy gold watch-chain looped across the unbuttoned vest. "Now what's all this?" Edmonds said.

"She wants a voce," Lucas said. "All right."

"All right?" Edmonds said. "All right?"

"Yes. What's it going to cost me?"

"I see," Edmonds said. "If you got to pay out money for it, she cant have one. Well, this is one thing you aint going to swangdangle anybody out of. You aint buying or selling a gold-finding machine either now, old man. She dont want any mule."

"She can have it," Lucas said. "I just want to know how much it will cost me. Why cant you declare us voced like you done Oscar and that yellow slut he fotched out here from Memphis last summer? You not only declared them voced, you took her back to town yourself and bought her a railroad ticket back to Memphis."

"Because they were not married very hard," Edmonds said. "And sooner or later she was going to take a lick at him with that razor she carried. And if she had ever missed or fumbled, Oscar would have torn her head off. He was just waiting for a chance to. That's why I did it. But you aint Oscar. This is different. Listen to me, Lucas. You are an older man than me; I admit that. You may have more money than I've got, which I think you have, and you may have more sense than I've got, as you think you have. But you cant do this."

"Dont tell me," Lucas said. "Tell her. This aint my doing. I'm satisfied like this."

"Yes. Sure. As long as you can do like you want to—spend

all the time you aint sleeping and eating making George Wilkins walk up and down that creek bottom, toting that damn—that damn——" Then he stopped and started over, holding his voice not down only but back too, for a while yet at least: "I've told you and told you there aint any money buried around here. That you are just wasting your time. But that's all right. You and George Wilkins both could walk around down there until you drop, for all of me. But Aunt Molly——"

"I'm a man," Lucas said. "I'm the man here. I'm the one to say in my house, like you and your paw and his paw were the ones to say in his. You aint got any complaints about the way I farm my land and make my crop, have you?"

"No complaints?" Edmonds said. "No complaints?" The other didn't even pause.

"Long as I do that, I'm the one to say about my private business, and your father would be the first to tell you so if he was here. Besides, I will have to quit hunting every night soon now, to get my cotton picked. Then I'll just hunt Saturday and Sunday night." Up to now he had been speaking to the ceiling apparently. Now he looked at Edmonds. "But them two nights is mine. On them two nights I dont farm nobody's land, I dont care who he is that claims to own it."

"Well," Edmonds said. "Two nights a week. You'll have to start that next week, because some of your cotton is ready." He turned to the old woman. "There, Aunt Molly," he said. "Two nights a week, and he's bound, even Lucas, to come to his senses soon——"

"I dont axes him to stop hunting but two nights a week," she said. She hadn't moved, speaking in a monotonous singsong, looking at neither of them. "I dont axes him to stop hunting for it at all. Because it's too late now. He cant help himself now. And I gots to be free."

Edmonds looked up again at the impassive, the impenetrable face under the broad, old-fashioned hat. "Do you want her to go?" he said. "Is that it?"

"I'm going to be the man in this house," Lucas said. It was not stubborn. It was quiet: final. His stare was as steady as Edmonds' was, and immeasurably colder.

"Listen," Edmonds said. "You're getting along. You aint

got a lot more time here. You said something about father a minute ago. All right. But when his time came and he laid down to die, he laid down in peace. Because he never *had anything* Jesus, he had almost said it aloud. *Damn damn damn* he thought *had anything about his wife in her old age to have to say God forgive me for doing that.* Almost aloud; he just caught it. "And your time's coming to want to lay down in peace, and you dont know when."

"Nor does you."

"That's correct. But I'm forty-three. You are sixty-seven." They stared at one another. Still the face beneath the hat was impassive, impenetrable. Then Lucas moved. He turned and spat neatly into the fire.

"All right," he said quietly. "I want to lay down in peace too. I'll get shut of the machine. I'll give it to George Wilkins——" That was when the old woman moved. When Edmonds looked around she was trying to rise from the chair, trying to thrust herself up with one hand, the other arm outstretched, not to ward Lucas off but toward him, Edmonds.

"No!" she cried. "Mister Zack! Cant you see? Not that he would keep on using it just the same as if he had kept it, but he would fotch onto Nat, my last one and least one, the curse of God that's gonter destroy him or her that touches what's done been rendered back to Him? I wants him to keep it! That's why I got to go, so he can keep it and not have to even think about giving it to George! Dont you see?"

Edmonds had risen too, his chair crashing over backward. He was trembling, glaring at Lucas. "So you'll try your tricks on me too. On me," he said in a shaking voice. "All right. You're not going to get any divorce. And you're going to get rid of that machine. You bring that thing up to my house the first thing in the morning. You hear me?"

He returned home, or to the stable. There was a moon now, blanched upon the open cotton almost ready for picking. The curse of God. He knew what she meant, what she had been fumbling toward. Granted the almost unbelievable circumstance that there should be as much as a thousand dollars buried and forgotten somewhere within Lucas' radius, and granted the even more impossible circumstance that Lucas should find it: what it might do to him, even to a man sixty-seven years old, who had, as Edmonds knew, three times that sum in a Jefferson bank; even a thousand dollars on which there was no sweat, at least none of his own. And to George, the daughter's husband, who had not a dollar anywhere, who was not yet twenty-five and with an eighteen-year-old wife expecting a child next spring.

There was no one to take the mare; he had told Dan not to wait. He unsaddled himself and rubbed her down and opened the gate to the pasture lane and slipped the bridle and slapped her moon-bright rump as she rushed suddenly away, cantering, curvetting, her three stockings and the blaze glinting moonward for an instant as she turned. "God damn it," he said, "I wish to hell either me or Lucas Beauchamp was a horse. Or a mule."

Lucas did not appear the next morning with the divining machine. When Edmonds himself departed at nine oclock (it was Sunday) he still had not appeared. Edmonds was driving his car now; for a moment he thought of going to Lucas' house, stopping there on his way. But it was Sunday; it seemed to him that he had been worrying and stewing over Lucas' affairs for six days a week since last May and very likely he would resume stewing and fretting over them at sunup tomorrow, and since Lucas himself had stated that beginning next week he would devote only Saturdays and Sundays to the machine, possibly until that time he would consider himself under his own dispensation to refrain from it on those two days. So he went on. He was gone all that day—to church five miles away, then to Sunday dinner with some friends three miles further on, where he spent the afternoon looking at other men's cotton and adding his voice to the curses at governmental interference with the raising and marketing of it. So it was after dark when he reached his own gate again and remembered Lucas and Molly and the divining machine once more. Lucas would not have left it at the empty house in his absence, so he turned and drove on to Lucas' cabin. It was dark; when he shouted there was no answer. So he drove on the quarter-mile to George's and Nat's, but it was dark too, no answer there to his voice. *Maybe it's all right now*, he thought. *Maybe they've all gone to church. Anyway, it'll be tomorrow in another twelve hours. I'll have to start in worrying about Lucas and something and so it might as well be this, something at least I am familiar with, accustomed to.*

Then the next morning, Monday, he had been in the stable for almost an hour and neither Dan nor Oscar had appeared. He had opened the stalls himself and turned the mule drove into the lane to the pasture and was just coming out of the mare's stall with the feed basket as Oscar came into the hallway, not running but trotting wearily and steadily. Then Edmonds saw that he still wore his Sunday clothes—a bright shirt and a tie, serge trousers with a long tear in one leg and splashed to the knees with mud. "It's Aunt Molly Beauchamp," Oscar said. "She been missing since yestiddy sometime. We been hunting her all night. We found where she went down to the creek and we been tracking her. Only she so little and light she dont hardly make a foot on the ground. Uncle Luke and George and Nat and Dan and some others are still hunting."

"I'll saddle the mare," Edmonds said. "I've turned the mules out; you'll have to go to the pasture and catch one. Hurry."

The mules, free in the big pasture, were hard to catch; it was almost an hour before Oscar returned bareback on one of them. And it was two hours more before they overtook Lucas and George and Nat and Dan and another man where they followed and lost and hunted and found and followed again the faint, light prints of the old woman's feet as they seemed to wander without purpose among the jungle of brier and rotted logs along the creek. It was almost noon when they found her, lying on her face in the mud, the once immaculate apron and the clean faded skirts stained and torn, one hand still grasping the handle of the divining-machine as she had fallen with it. She was not dead. When Oscar picked her up she opened her eyes, looking at no one, at nothing, and closed them again. "Run," Edmonds told Dan. "Take the mare. Go back for the car and go get Doctor Rideout. Hurry. —Can you carry her?"

"I can tote her," Oscar said. "She dont weigh hardly nothing. Not nigh as much as that finding-box."

"I'll tote her," George said. "Bein as she's Nat's——" Edmonds turned on him, on Lucas too.

"You tote that box," he said. "Both of you tote it. Hope it finds something between here and the house. Because if those needles ever move on my place afterward, neither of you all will be looking at them.—I'm going to see about that divorce," he said to Lucas. "Before she kills herself. Before you and that machine kill her between you. By God, I'm glad I aint walking in your shoes right now. I'm glad I aint going to lie in your bed tonight, thinking about what you're going to think about."

The day came. The cotton was all in and ginned and baled and frost had fallen, completing the firing of the corn which was being gathered and measured into the cribs. With Lucas and Molly in the back seat, he drove in to Jefferson and stopped before the county courthouse where the Chancellor was sitting. "You dont need to come in," he told Lucas. "They probably wouldn't let you in. But you be around close. I'm not going to wait for you. And remember. Aunt Molly gets the house, and half your crop this year and half of it every year as long as you stay on my place."

"You mean every year I keep on farming my land."

"I mean every damned year you stay on my place. Just what I said."

"Cass Edmonds give me that land to be mine long as I——"

"You heard me," Edmonds said. Lucas looked at him. He blinked.

"Do you want me to move off of it?" he said.

"Why?" Edmonds said. "What for? When you are going to be on it all night long every night, hunting buried money? You might as well sleep on it all day too. Besides, you'll have to stay on it to make Aunt Molly's half-crop. And I dont mean just this year. I mean every——"

"She can have all of it," Lucas said. "I'll raise it all right. And she can have all of it. I got them three thousand dollars old Carothers left me, right there in that bank yonder. They'll last me out my time—unless you done decided to give half of them to somebody. And when me and George Wilkins find that money——"

"Get out of the car," Edmonds said. "Go on. Get out of it."

The Chancellor was sitting in his office—a small detached building beside the courthouse proper. As they walked toward it Edmonds suddenly had to take the old woman's arm, catching her just in time, feeling again the thin, almost fleshless arm beneath the layers of sleeve, dry and light and brittle and frail as a rotted stick. He stopped, holding her up. "Aunt Molly," he said, "do you still want to do this? You dont have to. I'll take that thing away from him. By God, I——"

She tried to go on, tugging at his hand. "I got to," she said. "He'll get another one. Then he'll give that one to George the first thing to keep you from taking it. And they'll find it some day and maybe I'll be gone then and cant help. And Nat was my least and my last one. I wont never see the others before I die."

"Come on," Edmonds said. "Come on then."

There were a few people going in and out of the office; a few inside, not many. They waited quietly at the back of the room until their turn came. Then he found that he actually was holding her up. He led her forward, still supporting her, believing that if he released her for an instant even she would collapse into a bundle of dried and lifeless sticks, covered by the old, faded, perfectly clean garments, at his feet. "Ah, Mr Edmonds," the Chancellor said. "This is the plaintiff?"

"Yes, sir," Edmonds said. The Chancellor (he was quite old) slanted his head to look at Molly above his spectacles. Then he shifted them up his nose and looked at her through them. He made a clucking sound. "After forty-five years. You cant do anything about it?"

"No, sir," Edmonds said. "I tried. I. . . . ." The Chancellor made the clucking sound again. He looked down at the bill which the clerk laid before him.

"She will be provided for, of course."

"Yes, sir. I'll see to that."

The Chancellor mused upon the bill. "There's no contest, I suppose."

"No, sir," Edmonds said. And then—and he did not even know Lucas had followed them until he saw the Chancellor slant his head again and look past them this time across the spectacles, and saw the clerk glance up and heard him say, "You, nigger! Take off your hat!"——then Lucas thrust Molly aside and came to the table, removing his hat as he did so.

"We aint gonter have no contest or no voce neither," he said.

"You what?" the Chancellor said. "What's this?" Lucas had not once looked at Edmonds. As far as Edmonds could tell, he was not looking at the Chancellor either. Edmonds thought idiotically how it must have been years since he had seen Lucas uncovered; in fact, he could not remember at all being aware previously that Lucas' hair was gray.

"We dont want no voce," Lucas said. "I done changed my mind."

"Are you the husband?" the Chancellor said.

"That's right," Lucas said.

"Say sir to the court!" the clerk said. Lucas glanced at the clerk.

"What?" he said. "I dont want no court. I done changed my——"

"Why, you uppity——" the clerk began.

"Wait," the Chancellor said. He looked at Lucas. "You have waited too late. This bill has been presented in due form and order. I am about to pronounce on it."

"Not now," Lucas said. "We dont want no voce. Roth Edmonds knows what I mean."

"What? Who does?"

"Why, the uppity——" the clerk said. "Your Honor——" Again the Chancellor raised his hand slightly toward the clerk. He still looked at Lucas.

"Mister Roth Edmonds," Lucas said. Edmonds moved forward quickly, still holding the old woman's arm. The Chancellor looked at him.

"Yes, Mr Edmonds?"

"Yes, sir," Edmonds said. "That's right. We dont want it now."

"You wish to withdraw the bill?"

"Yes, sir. If you please, sir."

"Ah," the Chancellor said. He folded the bill and handed it to the clerk. "Strike this off the docket, Mr Hulett," he said.

When they were out of the office, he was almost carrying her, though she was trying to walk. "Here," he said, almost roughly, "it's all right now. Didn't you hear the judge? Didn't you hear Lucas tell the judge that Roth Edmonds knows what he means?"

He lifted her into the car almost bodily, Lucas just behind them. But instead of getting in, Lucas said, "Wait a minute."

"Wait a minute?" Edmonds said. "Hah!" he said. "You've

bankrupted your waiting. You've already spent——" But Lucas had gone on. And Edmonds waited. He stood beside the car and watched Lucas cross the Square, toward the stores, erect beneath the old, fine, well-cared-for hat, walking with that unswerving and dignified deliberation which every now and then, and with something sharp at the heart, Edmonds recognised as having come from his own ancestry too as the hat had come. He was not gone long. He returned, unhurried, and got into the car. He was carrying a small sack—obviously candy, a nickel's worth. He put it into Molly's hand.

"Here," he said. "You aint got no teeth left but you can still gum it."

3.

It was cool that night. He had a little fire, and for supper the first ham from the smokehouse, and he was sitting at his solitary meal, eating with more appetite than it seemed to him he had had in months, when he heard the knocking from the front of the house—the rapping of knuckles on the edge of the veranda, not loud, not hurried, merely peremptory. He spoke to the cook through the kitchen door: "Tell him to come in here," he said. He went on eating. He was eating when Lucas entered and passed him and set the divining machine on the other end of the table. It was clean of mud now; it looked as though it had been polished, at once compact and complex and efficient-looking with its bright cryptic dials and gleaming knobs. Lucas stood looking down at it for a moment. Then he turned away. Until he left the room he did not once look toward it again. "There it is," he said. "Get rid of it."

"All right. I'll put it away in the attic. Maybe by next spring Aunt Molly will forget about it and you can——"

"No. Get rid of it."

"For good?"

"Yes. Clean off this place, where I wont never see it again. Just dont tell me where. Sell it if you can and keep the money. But sell it a far piece away, where I wont never see it nor hear tell of it again."

"Well," Edmonds said. "Well." He thrust his chair back

from the table and sat looking up at the other, at the old man who had emerged out of the tragic complexity of his motherless childhood as the husband of the woman who had been the only mother he ever knew, who had never once said 'sir' to his white skin and whom he knew even called him Roth behind his back, let alone to his face. "Look here," he said. "You dont have to do that. Aunt Molly's old, and she's got some curious notions. But what she dont know—— Because you aint going to find any money, buried or not, around here or anywhere else. And if you want to take that damn thing out now and then, say once or twice a month, and spend the night walking up and down that damn creek——"

"No," Lucas said. "Get rid of it. I dont want to never see it again. Man has got three score and ten years on this earth, the Book says. He can want a heap in that time and a heap of what he can want is due to come to him, if he just starts in soon enough. I done waited too late to start. That money's there. Them two white men that slipped in here that night three years ago and dug up twenty-two thousand dollars and got clean away with it before anybody saw them. I know. I saw the hole where they filled it up again, and the churn it was buried in. But I am near to the end of my three score and ten, and I reckon to find that money aint for me."

Pantaloon in Black

I.

HE STOOD in the worn, faded clean overalls which Mannie herself had washed only a week ago, and heard the first clod strike the pine box. Soon he had one of the shovels himself, which in his hands (he was better than six feet and weighed better than two hundred pounds) resembled the toy shovel a child plays with at the shore, its half cubic foot of flung dirt no more than the light gout of sand the child's shovel would have flung. Another member of his sawmill gang touched his arm and said, "Lemme have hit, Rider." He didn't even falter. He released one hand in midstroke and flung it backward, striking the other across the chest, jolting him back a step, and restored the hand to the moving shovel, flinging the dirt with that effortless fury so that the mound seemed to be rising of its own volition, not built up from above but thrusting visibly upward out of the earth itself, until at last the grave, save for its rawness, resembled any other marked off without order about the barren plot by shards of pottery and broken bottles and old brick and other objects insignificant to sight but actually of a profound meaning and fatal to touch, which no white man could have read. Then he straightened up and with one hand flung the shovel quivering upright in the mound like a javelin and turned and began to walk away, walking on even when an old woman came out of the meagre clump of his kin and friends and a few old people who had known him and his dead wife both since they were born, and grasped his forearm. She was his aunt. She had raised him. He could not remember his parents at all.

"Whar you gwine?" she said.

"Ah'm goan home," he said.

"You dont wants ter go back dar by yoself," she said. "You needs to eat. You come on home and eat."

"Ah'm goan home," he repeated, walking out from under her hand, his forearm like iron, as if the weight on it were no more than that of a fly, the other members of the mill gang whose head he was giving way quietly to let him pass. But before he reached the fence one of them overtook him; he did not need to be told it was his aunt's messenger.

"Wait, Rider," the other said. "We gots a jug in de bushes——" Then the other said what he had not intended to say, what he had never conceived of himself saying in circumstances like these, even though everybody knew it—the dead who either will not or cannot quit the earth yet although the flesh they once lived in has been returned to it, let the preachers tell and reiterate and affirm how they left it not only without regret but with joy, mounting toward glory: "You dont wants ter go back dar. She be wawkin yit."

He didn't pause, glancing down at the other, his eyes red at the inner corners in his high, slightly backtilted head. "Lemme lone, Acey," he said. "Doan mess wid me now," and went on, stepping over the three-strand wire fence without even breaking his stride, and crossed the road and entered the woods. It was middle dusk when he emerged from them and crossed the last field, stepping over that fence too in one stride, into the lane. It was empty at this hour of Sunday evening—no family in wagon, no rider, no walkers churchward to speak to him and carefully refrain from looking after him when he had passed—the pale, powder-light, powder-dry dust of August from which the long week's marks of hoof and wheel had been blotted by the strolling and unhurried Sunday shoes, with somewhere beneath them, vanished but not gone, fixed and held in the annealing dust, the narrow, splay-toed prints of his wife's bare feet where on Saturday afternoons she would walk to the commissary to buy their next week's supplies while he took his bath; himself, his own prints, setting the period now as he strode on, moving almost as fast as a smaller man could have trotted, his body breasting the air her body had vacated, his eyes touching the objects—post and tree and field and house and hill—her eyes had lost.

The house was the last one in the lane, not his but rented from Carothers Edmonds, the local white landowner. But the rent was paid promptly in advance, and even in just six months he had refloored the porch and rebuilt and roofed the kitchen, doing the work himself on Saturday afternoon and

Sunday with his wife helping him, and bought the stove. Because he made good money: sawmilling ever since he began to get his growth at fifteen and sixteen and now, at twenty-four, head of the timber gang itself because the gang he headed moved a third again as much timber between sunup and sundown as any other moved, handling himself at times out of the vanity of his own strength logs which ordinarily two men would have handled with cant-hooks; never without work even in the old days when he had not actually needed the money, when a lot of what he wanted, needed perhaps, didn't cost money—the women bright and dark and for all purposes nameless he didn't need to buy and it didn't matter to him what he wore and there was always food for him at any hour of day or night in the house of his aunt who didn't even want to take the two dollars he gave her each Saturday—so there had been only the Saturday and Sunday dice and whiskey that had to be paid for until that day six months ago when he saw Mannie, whom he had known all his life, for the first time and said to himself: "Ah'm thu wid all dat," and they married and he rented the cabin from Carothers Edmonds and built a fire on the hearth on their wedding night as the tale told how Uncle Lucas Beauchamp, Edmonds' oldest tenant, had done on his forty-five years ago and which had burned ever since; and he would rise and dress and eat his breakfast by lamplight to walk the four miles to the mill by sunup, and exactly one hour after sundown he would enter the house again, five days a week, until Saturday. Then the first hour would not have passed noon when he would mount the steps and knock, not on post or doorframe but on the underside of the gallery roof itself, and enter and ring the bright cascade of silver dollars onto the scrubbed table in the kitchen where his dinner simmered on the stove and the galvanised tub of hot water and the baking powder can of soft soap and the towel made of scalded flour sacks sewn together and his clean overalls and shirt waited, and Mannie would gather up the money and walk the half-mile to the commissary and buy their next week's supplies and bank the rest of the money in Edmonds' safe and return and they would eat once again without haste or hurry after five days—the sidemeat, the greens, the cornbread, the buttermilk from the well-house, the cake which she baked every Saturday now that she had a stove to bake in.

But when he put his hand on the gate it seemed to him suddenly that there was nothing beyond it. The house had never been his anyway, but now even the new planks and sills and shingles, the hearth and stove and bed, were all a part of the memory of somebody else, so that he stopped in the half-open gate and said aloud, as though he had gone to sleep in one place and then waked suddenly to find himself in another: "Whut's Ah doin hyar?" before he went on. Then he saw the dog. He had forgotten it. He remembered neither seeing nor hearing it since it began to howl just before dawn yesterday—a big dog, a hound with a strain of mastiff from somewhere (he had told Mannie a month after they married: "Ah needs a big dawg. You's de onliest least thing whut ever kep up wid me one day, leff alone fo weeks.") coming out from beneath the gallery and approaching, not running but seeming rather to drift across the dusk until it stood lightly against his leg, its head raised until the tips of his fingers just touched it, facing the house and making no sound; whereupon, as if the animal controlled it, had lain guardian before it during his absence and only this instant relinquished, the shell of planks and shingles facing him solidified, filled, and for the moment he believed that he could not possibly enter it. "But Ah needs to eat," he said. "Us bofe needs to eat," he said, moving on though the dog did not follow until he turned and cursed it. "Come on hyar!" he said. "Whut you skeered of? She lacked you too, same as me," and they mounted the steps and crossed the porch and entered the house—the dusk-filled single room where all those six months were now crammed and crowded into one instant of time until there was no space left for air to breathe, crammed and crowded about the hearth where the fire which was to have lasted to the end of them, before which in the days before he was able to buy the stove he would enter after his four-mile walk from the mill and find her, the shape of her narrow back and haunches squatting, one narrow spread hand shielding her face from the blaze over which the other hand held the skillet, had already fallen to a dry, light soilure of dead ashes when the sun rose yesterday—and himself standing there while the last of light died about the strong and indomitable beating of his heart and the deep steady arch and collapse of his chest which walking fast over the rough going of woods and fields had not increased and standing still in the quiet and fading room had not slowed down.

Then the dog left him. The light pressure went off his flank; he heard the click and hiss of its claws on the wooden floor as it surged away and he thought at first that it was fleeing. But it stopped just outside the front door, where he could see it now, and the upfling of its head as the howl began; and then he saw her too. She was standing in the kitchen door, looking at him. He didn't move. He didn't breathe nor speak until he knew his voice would be all right, his face fixed too not to alarm her. "Mannie," he said. "Hit's awright. Ah aint afraid." Then he took a step toward her, slow, not even raising his hand yet, and stopped. Then he took another step. But this time as soon as he moved she began to fade. He stopped at once, not breathing again, motionless, willing his eyes to see that she had stopped too. But she had not stopped. She was fading, going. "Wait," he said, talking as sweet as he had ever heard his voice speak to a woman: "Den lemme go wid you, honey." But she was going. She was going fast now; he could actually feel between them the insuperable barrier of that very strength which could handle alone a log which would have taken any two other men to handle, of the blood and bones and flesh too strong, invincible for life, having learned at least once with his own eyes how tough, even in sudden and violent death, not a young man's bones and flesh perhaps but the will of that bone and flesh to remain alive, actually was.

Then she was gone. He walked through the door where she had been standing, and went to the stove. He did not light the lamp. He needed no light. He had set the stove up himself and built the shelves for the dishes, from among which he took two plates by feel and from the pot sitting cold on the cold stove he ladled onto the plates the food which his aunt had brought yesterday and of which he had eaten yesterday though now he did not remember when he had eaten it nor what it was, and carried the plates to the scrubbed bare table beneath the single small fading window and drew two chairs up and sat down, waiting again until he knew his voice would be what he wanted it to be. "Come on hyar, now," he said roughly. "Come on hyar and eat yo supper. Ah aint gonter have no——" and ceased, looking down at his plate, breathing the strong, deep pants, his chest arching and collapsing until he stopped it presently and held himself motionless for perhaps a half minute, and raised a spoonful of the cold and glutinous pease to his mouth. The congealed and lifeless mass seemed to bounce on contact with his lips. Not even warmed from mouth-heat, pease and spoon spattered and rang upon the plate; his chair crashed backward and he was standing, feeling the muscles of his jaw beginning to drag his mouth open, tugging upward the top half of his head. But he stopped that too before it became sound, holding himself again while he rapidly scraped the food from his plate onto the other and took it up and left the kitchen, crossed the other room and the gallery and set the plate on the bottom step and went on toward the gate.

The dog was not there, but it overtook him within the first half mile. There was a moon then, their two shadows flitting broken and intermittent among the trees or slanted long and intact across the slope of pasture or old abandoned fields upon the hills, the man moving almost as fast as a horse could have moved over that ground, altering his course each time a lighted window came in sight, the dog trotting at heel while their shadows shortened to the moon's curve until at last they trod them and the last far lamp had vanished and the shadows began to lengthen on the other hand, keeping to heel even when a rabbit burst from almost beneath the man's foot, then lying in the gray of dawn beside the man's prone body, beside the labored heave and collapse of the chest, the loud harsh snoring which sounded not like groans of pain but like someone engaged without arms in prolonged single combat.

When he reached the mill there was nobody there but the fireman—an older man just turning from the woodpile, watching quietly as he crossed the clearing, striding as if he were going to walk not only through the boiler shed but through (or over) the boiler too, the overalls which had been clean yesterday now draggled and soiled and drenched to the knees with dew, the cloth cap flung onto the side of his head, hanging peak downward over his ear as he always wore it, the whites of his eyes rimmed with red and with something urgent and strained about them. "Whar yo bucket?" he said. But before the fireman could answer he had stepped past him and lifted the polished lard pail down from a nail in a post. "Ah just wants a biscuit," he said.

"Eat hit all," the fireman said. "Ah'll eat outen de yuthers' buckets at dinner. Den you gawn home and go to bed. You dont looks good."

"Ah aint come hyar to look," he said, sitting on the ground, his back against the post, the open pail between his knees, cramming the food into his mouth with his hands, wolfing it—pease again, also gelid and cold, a fragment of yesterday's Sunday fried chicken, a few rough chunks of this morning's fried sidemeat, a biscuit the size of a child's cap—indiscriminate, tasteless. The rest of the crew was gathering now, with voices and sounds of movement outside the boiler shed; presently the white foreman rode into the clearing on a horse. He did not look up, setting the empty pail aside, rising, looking at no one, and went to the branch and lay on his stomach and lowered his face to the water, drawing the water into himself with the same deep, strong, troubled inhalations that he had snored with, or as when he had stood in the empty house at dusk yesterday, trying to get air.

Then the trucks were rolling. The air pulsed with the rapid beating of the exhaust and the whine and clang of the saw, the trucks rolling one by one up to the skidway, he mounting the trucks in turn, to stand balanced on the load he freed, knocking the chocks out and casting loose the shackle chains and with his cant-hook squaring the sticks of cypress and gum and oak one by one to the incline and holding them until the next two men of his gang were ready to receive and guide them, until the discharge of each truck became one long rumbling roar punctuated by grunting shouts and, as the morning grew and the sweat came, chanted phrases of song tossed back and forth. He did not sing with them. He rarely ever did, and this morning might have been no different from any other—himself man-height again above the heads which carefully refrained from looking at him, stripped to the waist now, the shirt removed and the overalls knotted about his hips by the suspender straps, his upper body bare except for the handkerchief about his neck and the cap clapped and clinging somehow over his right ear, the mounting sun sweat-glinted steel-blue on the midnight-colored bunch and slip of muscles until the whistle blew for noon and he said to the two men at the head of the skidway: "Look out. Git out de way," and rode the log down the incline, balanced erect upon it in short rapid backward-running steps above the headlong thunder.

His aunt's husband was waiting for him—an old man, as tall as he was, but lean, almost frail, carrying a tin pail in one hand and a covered plate in the other; they too sat in the shade beside the branch a short distance from where the others were opening their dinner pails. The bucket contained a fruit jar of buttermilk packed in a clean damp towsack. The covered dish was a peach pie, still warm. "She baked hit fer you dis mawnin," the uncle said. "She say fer you to come home." He didn't answer, bent forward a little, his elbows on his knees, holding the pie in both hands, wolfing at it, the syrupy filling smearing and trickling down his chin, blinking rapidly as he chewed, the whites of his eyes covered a little more by the creeping red. "Ah went to yo house last night, but you want dar. She sont me. She wants you to come on home. She kept de lamp burnin all last night fer you."

"Ah'm awright," he said.

"You aint awright. De Lawd guv, and He tuck away. Put yo faith and trust in Him. And she kin help you."

"Whut faith and trust?" he said. "Whut Mannie ever done ter Him? Whut He wanter come messin wid me and——"

"Hush!" the old man said. "Hush!"

Then the trucks were rolling again. Then he could stop needing to invent to himself reasons for his breathing, until after a while he began to believe he had forgot about breathing since now he could not hear it himself above the steady thunder of the rolling logs; whereupon as soon as he found himself believing he had forgotten it, he knew that he had not, so that instead of tipping the final log onto the skidway he stood up and cast his cant-hook away as if it were a burnt match and in the dying reverberation of the last log's rumbling descent he vaulted down between the two slanted tracks of the skid, facing the log which still lay on the truck. He had done it before—taken a log from the truck onto his hands, balanced, and turned with it and tossed it onto the skidway, but never with a stick of this size, so that in a complete cessation of all sound save the pulse of the exhaust and the light free-running whine of the disengaged saw since every eye there, even that of the white foreman, was upon him, he nudged the log to the edge of the truck-frame and squatted and set his palms against the underside of it. For a time there was no movement at all. It was as if the unrational and inanimate wood had invested, mesmerised the man with some of its own primal inertia. Then a voice said quietly: "He got hit. Hit's off de truck," and they saw the crack and gap of air, watching the infinitesimal straightening of the braced legs until the knees locked, the movement mounting infinitesimally through the belly's insuck, the arch of the chest, the neck cords, lifting the lip from the white clench of teeth in passing, drawing the whole head backward and only the bloodshot fixity of the eyes impervious to it, moving on up the arms and the straightening elbows until the balanced log was higher than his head. "Only he aint gonter turn wid dat un," the same voice said. "And when he try to put hit back on de truck, hit gonter kill him." But none of them moved. Then—there was no gathering of supreme effort—the log seemed to leap suddenly backward over his head of its own volition, spinning, crashing and thundering down the incline; he turned and stepped over the slanting track in one stride and walked through them as they gave way and went on across the clearing toward the woods even though the foreman called after him: "Rider!" and again: "You, Rider!"

At sundown he and the dog were in the river swamp four miles away—another clearing, itself not much larger than a room, a hut, a hovel partly of planks and partly of canvas, an unshaven white man standing in the door beside which a shotgun leaned, watching him as he approached, his hand extended with four silver dollars on the palm. "Ah wants a jug," he said.

"A jug?" the white man said. "You mean a pint. This is Monday. Aint you all running this week?"

"Ah laid off," he said. "Whar's my jug?" waiting, looking at nothing apparently, blinking his bloodshot eyes rapidly in his high, slightly back-tilted head, then turning, the jug hanging from his crooked middle finger against his leg, at which moment the white man looked suddenly and sharply at his eyes as though seeing them for the first time—the eyes which had been strained and urgent this morning and which now seemed to be without vision too and in which no white showed at all—and said,

"Here. Gimme that jug. You dont need no gallon. I'm going to give you that pint, give it to you. Then you get out of here and stay out. Dont come back until——" Then the white man reached and grasped the jug, whereupon the other swung it behind him, sweeping his other arm up and out so that it struck the white man across the chest.

"Look out, white folks," he said. "Hit's mine. Ah done paid you."

The white man cursed him. "No you aint. Here's your money. Put that jug down, nigger."

"Hit's mine," he said, his voice quiet, gentle even, his face quiet save for the rapid blinking of the red eyes. "Ah done paid for hit," turning on, turning his back on the man and the gun both, and recrossed the clearing to where the dog waited beside the path to come to heel again. They moved rapidly on between the close walls of impenetrable cane-stalks which gave a sort of blondness to the twilight and possessed something of that oppression, that lack of room to breathe in, which the walls of his house had had. But this time, instead of fleeing it, he stopped and raised the jug and drew the cob stopper from the fierce duskreek of uncured alcohol and drank, gulping the liquid solid and cold as ice water, without either taste or heat until he lowered the jug and the air got in. "Hah," he said. "Dat's right. Try me. Try me, big boy. Ah gots something hyar now dat kin whup you."

And, once free of the bottom's unbreathing blackness, there was the moon again, his long shadow and that of the lifted jug slanting away as he drank and then held the jug poised, gulping the silver air into his throat until he could breathe again, speaking to the jug: "Come on now. You always claim you's a better man den me. Come on now. Prove it." He drank again, swallowing the chill liquid tamed of taste or heat either while the swallowing lasted, feeling it flow solid and cold with fire, past then enveloping the strong steady panting of his lungs until they too ran suddenly free as his moving body ran in the silver solid wall of air he breasted. And he was all right, his striding shadow and the trotting one of the dog travelling swift as those of two clouds along the hill; the long cast of his motionless shadow and that of the lifted jug slanting across the slope as he watched the frail figure of his aunt's husband toiling up the hill.

"Dey tole me at de mill you was gone," the old man said. "Ah knowed whar to look. Come home, son. Dat ar cant help you."

"Hit done awready hope me," he said. "Ah'm awready home. Ah'm snakebit now and pizen cant hawm me."

"Den stop and see her. Leff her look at you. Dat's all she axes: just leff her look at you——" But he was already moving. "Wait!" the old man cried. "Wait!"

"You cant keep up," he said, speaking into the silver air, breasting aside the silver solid air which began to flow past him almost as fast as it would have flowed past a moving horse. The faint frail voice was already lost in the night's infinitude, his shadow and that of the dog scudding the free miles, the deep strong panting of his chest running free as air now because he was all right.

Then, drinking, he discovered suddenly that no more of the liquid was entering his mouth. Swallowing, it was no longer passing down his throat, his throat and mouth filled now with a solid and unmoving column which without reflex or revulsion sprang, columnar and intact and still retaining the mold of his gullet, outward glinting in the moonlight, splintering, vanishing into the myriad murmur of the dewed grass. He drank again. Again his throat merely filled solidly until two icy rills ran from his mouth-corners; again the intact column sprang silvering, glinting, shivering, while he panted the chill of air into his throat, the jug poised before his mouth while he spoke to it: "Awright. Ah'm ghy try you again. Soon as you makes up yo mind to stay whar I puts you, Ah'll leff you alone." He drank, filling his gullet for the third time and lowered the jug one instant ahead of the bright intact repetition, panting, indrawing the cool of air until he could breathe. He stoppered the cob carefully back into the jug and stood, panting, blinking, the long cast of his solitary shadow slanting away across the hill and beyond, across the mazy infinitude of all the night-bound earth. "Awright," he said. "Ah just misread de sign wrong. Hit's done done me all de help Ah needs. Ah'm awright now. Ah doan needs no mo of hit."

He could see the lamp in the window as he crossed the pasture, passing the black-and-silver yawn of the sandy ditch where he had played as a boy with empty snuff-tins and rusted harness-buckles and fragments of trace-chains and now and then an actual wheel, passing the garden patch where he had hoed in the spring days while his aunt stood sentry over him from the kitchen window, crossing the grassless yard in whose dust he had sprawled and crept before he learned to walk. He entered the house, the room, the light itself, and stopped in the door, his head back-tilted a little as if he could not see, the jug hanging from his crooked finger, against his leg. "Unc Alec say you wanter see me," he said.

"Not just to see you," his aunt said. "To come home, whar we kin help you."

"Ah'm awright," he said. "Ah doan needs no help."

"No," she said. She rose from the chair and came and grasped his arm as she had grasped it yesterday at the grave. Again, as on yesterday, the forearm was like iron under her hand. "No! When Alec come back and tole me how you had wawked off de mill and de sun not half down, Ah knowed why and whar. And dat cant help you."

"Hit done awready hope me. Ah'm awright now."

"Dont lie to me," she said. "You aint never lied to me. Dont lie to me now."

Then he said it. It was his own voice, without either grief or amazement, speaking quietly out of the tremendous panting of his chest which in a moment now would begin to strain at the walls of this room too. But he would be gone in a moment.

"Nome," he said. "Hit aint done me no good."

"And hit cant! Cant nothing help you but Him! Ax Him! Tole Him about hit! He wants to hyar you and help you!"

"Efn He God, Ah dont needs to tole Him. Efn He God,

He awready know hit. Awright. Hyar Ah is. Leff Him come down hyar and do me some good."

"On yo knees!" she cried. "On yo knees and ax Him!" But it was not his knees on the floor, it was his feet. And for a space he could hear her feet too on the planks of the hall behind him and her voice crying after him from the door: "Spoot! Spoot!"—crying after him across the moon-dappled yard the name he had gone by in his childhood and adolescence, before the men he worked with and the bright dark nameless women he had taken in course and forgotten until he saw Mannie that day and said, "Ah'm thu wid all dat," began to call him Rider.

It was just after midnight when he reached the mill. The dog was gone now. This time he could not remember when nor where. At first he seemed to remember hurling the empty jug at it. But later the jug was still in his hand and it was not empty, although each time he drank now the two icy runnels streamed from his mouth-corners, sopping his shirt and overalls until he walked constantly in the fierce chill of the liquid tamed now of flavor and heat and odor too even when the swallowing ceased. "Sides that," he said, "Ah wouldn't thow nothin at him. Ah mout kick him efn he needed hit and was close enough. But Ah wouldn't ruint no dog chunkin hit."

The jug was still in his hand when he entered the clearing and paused among the mute soaring of the moon-blond lumber-stacks. He stood in the middle now of the unimpeded shadow which he was treading again as he had trod it last night, swaying a little, blinking about at the stacked lumber, the skidway, the piled logs waiting for tomorrow, the boiler shed all quiet and blanched in the moon. And then it was all right. He was moving again. But he was not moving, he was drinking, the liquid cold and swift and tasteless and requiring no swallowing, so that he could not tell if it were going down inside or outside. But it was all right. And now he was moving, the jug gone now and he didn't know the when or where of that either. He crossed the clearing and entered the boiler shed and went on through it, crossing the junctureless backloop of time's trepan, to the door of the tool-room, the faint glow of the lantern beyond the plank-joints, the surge and fall of living shadow, the mutter of voices, the mute click and scutter of the dice, his hand loud on the barred door, his voice loud too: "Open hit. Hit's me. Ah'm snakebit and bound to die."

Then he was through the door and inside the tool-room. They were the same faces—three members of his timber gang, three or four others of the mill crew, the white night-watchman with the heavy pistol in his hip pocket and the small heap of coins and worn bills on the floor before him, one who was called Rider and was Rider standing above the squatting circle, swaying a little, blinking, the dead muscles of his face shaped into smiling while the white man stared up at him. "Make room, gamblers," he said. "Make room. Ah'm snakebit and de pizen cant hawm me."

"You're drunk," the white man said. "Get out of here. One of you niggers open the door and get him out of here."

"Dass awright, boss-man," he said, his voice equable, his face still fixed in the faint rigid smiling beneath the blinking of the red eyes; "Ah aint drunk. Ah just cant wawk straight fer dis yar money weighin me down."

Now he was kneeling too, the other six dollars of his last week's pay on the floor before him, blinking, still smiling at the face of the white man opposite, then, still smiling, he watched the dice pass from hand to hand around the circle as the white man covered the bets, watching the soiled and palm-worn money in front of the white man gradually and steadily increase, watching the white man cast and win two doubled bets in succession then lose one for twenty-five cents, the dice coming to him at last, the cupped snug clicking of them in his fist. He spun a coin into the center.

"Shoots a dollar," he said, and cast, and watched the white man pick up the dice and flip them back to him. "Ah lets hit lay," he said. "Ah'm snakebit. Ah kin pass wid anything," and cast, and this time one of the negroes flipped the dice back. "Ah lets hit lay," he said, and cast, and moved as the white man moved, catching the white man's wrist before his hand reached the dice, the two of them squatting, facing each other above the dice and the money, his left hand grasping the white man's wrist, his face still fixed in the rigid and deadened smiling, his voice equable, almost deferential: "Ah kin pass even wid miss-outs. But dese hyar yuther boys——" until the white man's hand sprang open and the second pair of dice clattered onto the floor beside the first two and the white man wrenched free and sprang up and back and reached the hand backward toward the pocket where the pistol was.

The razor hung between his shoulder-blades from a loop of cotton string round his neck inside his shirt. The same motion of the hand which brought the razor forward over his shoulder flipped the blade open and freed it from the cord, the blade opening on until the back edge of it lay across the knuckles of his fist, his thumb pressing the handle into his closing fingers, so that in the second before the half-drawn pistol exploded he actually struck at the white man's throat not with the blade but with a sweeping blow of his fist, following through in the same motion so that not even the first jet of blood touched his hand or arm.

2.

After it was over—it didn't take long; they found the prisoner on the following day, hanging from the bell-rope in a negro schoolhouse about two miles from the sawmill, and the coroner had pronounced his verdict of death at the hands of a person or persons unknown and surrendered the body to its next of kin all within five minutes—the sheriff's deputy who had been officially in charge of the business was telling his wife about it. They were in the kitchen. His wife was cooking supper. The deputy had been out of bed and in motion ever since the jail delivery shortly before midnight of yesterday and had covered considerable ground since, and he was spent now from lack of sleep and hurried food at hurried and curious hours and, sitting in a chair beside the stove, a little hysterical too.

"Them damn niggers," he said. "I swear to godfrey, it's a wonder we have as little trouble with them as we do. Because why? Because they aint human. They look like a man and they walk on their hind legs like a man, and they can talk and you can understand them and you think they are understanding you, at least now and then. But when it comes to the normal human feelings and sentiments of human beings, they might just as well be a damn herd of wild buffaloes. Now you take this one today——"

"I wish you would," his wife said harshly. She was a stout woman, handsome once, graying now and with a neck definitely too short, who looked not harried at all but composed in fact, only choleric. Also, she had attended a club rook-party that afternoon and had won the first, the fifty-cent, prize until another member had insisted on a recount of the scores and the ultimate throwing out of one entire game. "Take him out of my kitchen, anyway. You sheriffs! Sitting around that courthouse all day long, talking. It's no wonder two or three men can walk in and take prisoners out from under your very noses. They would take your chairs and desks and window sills too if you ever got your feet and backsides off of them that long."

"It's more of them Birdsongs than just two or three," the deputy said. "There's forty-two active votes in that connection. Me and Maydew taken the poll-list and counted them one day. But listen——" The wife turned from the stove, carrying a dish. The deputy snatched his feet rapidly out of the way as she passed him, passed almost over him, and went into the dining room. The deputy raised his voice a little to carry the increased distance: "His wife dies on him. All right. But does he grieve? He's the biggest and busiest man at the funeral. Grabs a shovel before they even got the box into the grave they tell me, and starts throwing dirt onto her faster than a slip scraper could have done it. But that's all right——" His wife came back. He moved his feet again and altered his voice again to the altered range: "—maybe that's how he felt about her. There aint any law against a man rushing his wife into the ground, provided he never had nothing to do with rushing her to the cemetery too. But here the next day he's the first man back at work except the fireman, getting back to the mill before the fireman had his fire going, let alone steam up; five minutes earlier and he could even have helped the fireman wake Birdsong up so Birdsong could go home and go back to bed again, or he could even have cut Birdsong's throat then and saved everybody trouble.

"So he comes to work, the first man on the job, when

McAndrews and everybody else expected him to take the day off since even a nigger couldn't want no better excuse for a holiday than he had just buried his wife, when a white man would have took the day off out of pure respect no matter how he felt about his wife, when even a little child would have had sense enough to take a day off when he would still get paid for it too. But not him. The first man there, jumping from one log truck to another before the starting whistle quit blowing even, snatching up ten-foot cypress logs by himself and throwing them around like matches. And then, when everybody had finally decided that that's the way to take him, the way he wants to be took, he walks off the job in the middle of the afternoon without by-your-leave or much obliged or goodbye to McAndrews or nobody else, gets himself a whole gallon of bust-skull white-mule whisky, comes straight back to the mill and to the same crap game where Birdsong has been running crooked dice on them mill niggers for fifteen years, goes straight to the same game where he has been peacefully losing a probably steady average ninety-nine percent of his pay ever since he got big enough to read the spots on them miss-out dice, and cuts Birdsong's throat clean to the neckbone five minutes later." The wife passed him again and went to the dining room. Again he drew his feet back and raised his voice:

"So me and Maydew go out there. Not that we expected to do any good, as he had probably passed Jackson, Tennessee, about daylight; and besides, the simplest way to find him would be just to stay close behind them Birdsong boys. Of course there wouldn't be nothing hardly worth bringing back to town after they did find him, but it would close the case. So it's just by the merest chance that we go by his house; I dont even remember why we went now, but we did; and there he is. Sitting behind the barred front door with a open razor on one knee and a loaded shotgun on the other? No. He was asleep. A big pot of field pease et clean empty on the stove, and him laying in the back yard asleep in the broad sun with just his head under the edge of the porch in the shade and a dog that looked like a cross between a bear and a Polled Angus steer yelling fire and murder from the back door. And we wake him and he sets up and says, 'Awright, white folks. Ah done it. Jest dont lock me up,' and Maydew says, 'Mr Birdsong's kinfolks aint going to lock you up neither. You'll have plenty of fresh air when they get hold of you,' and he says, 'Ah done it. Jest dont lock me up'—advising, instructing the sheriff not to lock him up; he done it all right and it's too bad but it aint convenient for him to be cut off from the fresh air at the moment. So we loaded him into the car, when here come the old woman—his ma or aunt or something—panting up the road at a dog-trot, wanting to come with us too, and Maydew trying to explain to her what would maybe happen to her too if them Birdsong kin catches us before we can get him locked up, only she is coming anyway, and like Maydew says, her being in the car too might be a good thing if the Birdsongs did happen to run into us, because after all interference with the law cant be condoned even if the Birdsong connection did carry that beat for Maydew last summer.

"So we brought her along too and got him to town and into the jail all right and turned him over to Ketcham and Ketcham taken him on up stairs and the old woman coming too, right on up to the cell, telling Ketcham, 'Ah tried to raise him right. He was a good boy. He aint never been in no trouble till now. He will suffer for what he done. But dont let the white folks get him,' until Ketcham says, 'You and him ought to thought of that before he started barbering white men without using no lather first.' So he locked them both up in the cell because he felt like Maydew did, that her being in there with him might be a good influence on the Birdsong boys if anything started if he should happen to be running for sheriff or something when Maydew's term was up. So Ketcham come on back down stairs and pretty soon the chain gang come in and went on up to the bull pen and he thought things had settled down for a while when all of a sudden he begun to hear the yelling, not howling: yelling, though there wasn't no words in it, and he grabbed his pistol and run back up stairs to the bull pen where the chain gang was and Ketcham could see into the cell where the old woman was kind of squinched down in one corner and where that nigger had done tore that iron cot clean out of the floor it was bolted to and was standing in the middle of the cell, holding the cot over his head like it was a baby's cradle, yelling, and says to the old woman, 'Ah aint goan hurt you,' and throws the cot against the wall and comes and grabs holt of that steel barred door and rips it out of the wall, bricks hinges and all, and walks out of the cell toting the door over his head like it was a gauze window-screen, hollering, 'It's awright. It's awright. Ah aint trying to git away.'

"Of course Ketcham could have shot him right there, but like he said, if it wasn't going to be the law, then them Birdsong boys ought to have the first lick at him. So Ketcham dont shoot. Instead, he jumps in behind where them chain gang niggers was kind of backed off from that steel door, hollering, 'Grab him! Throw him down!' except the niggers hung back at first too until Ketcham gets in where he can kick the ones he can reach, batting at the others with the flat of the pistol until they rush him. And Ketcham says that for a full minute that nigger would grab them as they come in and fling them clean across the room like they was rag dolls, saying, 'Ah aint tryin to git out. Ah aint tryin to git out,' until at last they pulled him down—a big mass of nigger heads and arms and legs boiling around on the floor and even then Ketcham says every now and then a nigger would come flying out and go sailing through the air across the room, spraddled out like a flying squirrel and with his eyes sticking out like car headlights, until at last they had him down and Ketcham went in and begun peeling away niggers until he could see him laying there under the pile of them, laughing, with tears big as glass marbles running across his face and down past his ears and making a kind of popping sound on the floor like somebody dropping bird eggs, laughing and laughing and saying, 'Hit look lack Ah just cant quit thinking. Look lack Ah just cant quit.' And what do you think of that?"

"I think if you eat any supper in this house you'll do it in the next five minutes," his wife said from the dining room. "I'm going to clear this table then and I'm going to the picture show."

The Old People

I.

AT FIRST there was nothing. There was the faint, cold, steady rain, the gray and constant light of the late November dawn, with the voices of the hounds converging somewhere in it and toward them. Then Sam Fathers, standing just behind the boy as he had been standing when the boy shot his first running rabbit with his first gun and almost with the first load it ever carried, touched his shoulder and he began to shake, not with any cold. Then the buck was there. He did not come into sight; he was just there, looking not like a ghost but as if all of light were condensed in him and he were the source of it, not only moving in it but disseminating it, already running, seen first as you always see the deer, in that split second after he has already seen you, already slanting away in that first soaring bound, the antlers even in that dim light looking like a small rocking-chair balanced on his head.

"Now," Sam Fathers said, "shoot quick, and slow."

The boy did not remember that shot at all. He would live to be eighty, as his father and his father's twin brother and their father in his turn had lived to be, but he would never hear that shot nor remember even the shock of the gun-butt. He didn't even remember what he did with the gun afterward. He was running. Then he was standing over the buck where it lay on the wet earth still in the attitude of speed and not looking at all dead, standing over it shaking and jerking, with Sam Fathers beside him again, extending the knife. "Dont walk up to him in front," Sam said. "If he aint dead, he will cut you all to pieces with his feet. Walk up to him from behind and take him by the horn first, so you can hold his head down until you can jump away. Then slip your other hand down and hook your fingers in his nostrils."

The boy did that—drew the head back and the throat taut and drew Sam Fathers' knife across the throat and Sam stooped and dipped his hands in the hot smoking blood and wiped them back and forth across the boy's face. Then Sam's horn rang in the wet gray woods and again and again; there was a boiling wave of dogs about them, with Tennie's Jim and Boon Hogganbeck whipping them back after each had had a taste of the blood, then the men, the true hunters—Walter Ewell whose rifle never missed, and Major de Spain and old General Compson and the boy's cousin, McCaslin Edmonds, grandson of his father's sister, sixteen years his senior and, since both he and McCaslin were only children and the boy's father had been nearing seventy when he was born, more his brother than his cousin and more his father than either—sitting their horses and looking down at them: at the old man of seventy who had been a negro for two generations now but whose face and bearing were still those of the Chickasaw chief who had been his father; and the white boy of twelve with the prints of the bloody hands on his face, who had nothing to do now but stand straight and not let the trembling show.

"Did he do all right, Sam?" his cousin McCaslin said.

"He done all right," Sam Fathers said.

They were the white boy, marked forever, and the old dark man sired on both sides by savage kings, who had marked him, whose bloody hands had merely formally consecrated him to that which, under the man's tutelage, he had already accepted, humbly and joyfully, with abnegation and with pride too; the hands, the touch, the first worthy blood which he had been found at last worthy to draw, joining him and the man forever, so that the man would continue to live past the boy's seventy years and then eighty years, long after the man himself had entered the earth as chiefs and kings entered it;—the child, not yet a man, whose grandfather had lived in the same country and in almost the same manner as the boy himself would grow up to live, leaving his descendants in the land in his turn as his grandfather had done, and the old man past seventy whose grandfathers had owned the land long before the white men ever saw it and who had vanished from it now with all their kind, what of blood they left behind them running now in another race and for a while even in bondage and now drawing toward the end of its alien and irrevocable course, barren, since Sam Fathers had no children.

His father was Ikkemotubbe himself, who had named himself Doom. Sam told the boy about that—how Ikkemotubbe, old Issetibbeha's sister's son, had run away to New Orleans in his youth and returned seven years later with a French companion calling himself the Chevalier Soeur-Blonde de Vitry, who must have been the Ikkemotubbe of his family too and who was already addressing Ikkemotubbe as *Du Homme*;—returned, came home again, with his foreign Aramis and the quadroon slave woman who was to be Sam's mother, and a gold-laced hat and coat and a wicker wine-hamper containing a litter of month-old puppies and a gold snuff-box filled with a white powder resembling fine sugar. And how he was met at the River landing by three or four companions of his bachelor youth, and while the light of a smoking torch gleamed on the glittering braid of the hat and coat Doom squatted in the mud of the landing and took one of the puppies from the hamper and put a pinch of the white powder on its tongue and the puppy died before the one who was holding it could cast it away. And how they returned to the Plantation where Issetibbeha, dead now, had been succeeded by his son, Doom's fat cousin Moketubbe, and the next day Moketubbe's eight-year-old son died suddenly and that afternoon, in the presence of Moketubbe and most of the others (the People, Sam Fathers called them) Doom produced another puppy from the wine-hamper and put a pinch of the white powder on its tongue and Moketubbe abdicated and Doom became in fact The Man which his French friend already called him. And how on the day after that, during the ceremony of accession, Doom pronounced a marriage between the pregnant quadroon and one of the slave men which he had just inherited (that was how Sam Fathers got his name, which in Chickasaw had been Had-Two-Fathers) and two years later sold the man and woman and the child who was his own son to his white neighbor, Carothers McCaslin.

That was seventy years ago. The Sam Fathers whom the boy knew was already sixty—a man not tall, squat rather, almost sedentary, flabby-looking though he actually was not, with hair like a horse's mane which even at seventy showed no trace of white and a face which showed no age until he smiled, whose only visible trace of negro blood was a slight dullness of the hair and the fingernails, and something else which you did notice about the eyes, which you noticed because it was not always there, only in repose and not always then—something not in their shape nor pigment but in their expression, and the boy's cousin McCaslin told him what that was: not the heritage of Ham, not the mark of servitude but of bondage; the knowledge that for a while that part of his blood had been the blood of slaves. "Like an old lion or a bear in a cage," McCaslin said. "He was born in the cage and has been in it all his life; he knows nothing else. Then he smells something. It might be anything, any breeze blowing past anything and then into his nostrils. But there for a second was the hot sand or the cane-brake that he never even saw himself, might not even know if he did see it and probably does know he couldn't hold his own with it if he got back to it. But that's not what he smells then. It was the cage he smelled. He hadn't smelled the cage until that minute. Then the hot sand or the brake blew into his nostrils and blew away, and all he could smell was the cage. That's what makes his eyes look like that."

"Then let him go!" the boy cried. "Let him go!"

His cousin laughed shortly. Then he stopped laughing, making the sound that is. It had never been laughing. "His cage aint McCaslins," he said. "He was a wild man. When he was born, all his blood on both sides, except the little white part, knew things that had been tamed out of our blood so long ago that we have not only forgotten them, we have to live together in herds to protect ourselves from our own sources. He was the direct son not only of a warrior but of a chief. Then he grew up and began to learn things, and all of a sudden one day he found out that he had been betrayed, the blood of the warriors and chiefs had been betrayed. Not by his father," he added quickly. "He probably never held it against old Doom for selling him and his mother into slavery, because he probably believed the damage was already done before then and it was the same warriors' and chiefs' blood in him and Doom both that was betrayed through the black blood which his mother gave him. Not betrayed by the black blood and not wilfully betrayed by his mother, but betrayed by her all the same, who had bequeathed him not only the blood of slaves but even a little of the very blood which had enslaved it; himself his own battleground, the scene of his own vanquishment and the mausoleum of his defeat. His cage aint us," McCaslin said. "Did you ever know anybody yet, even your father and Uncle Buddy, that ever told him to do or not do anything that he ever paid any attention to?"

That was true. The boy first remembered him as sitting in the door of the plantation blacksmith-shop, where he sharpened plow-points and mended tools and even did rough carpenter-work when he was not in the woods. And sometimes, even when the woods had not drawn him, even with the shop cluttered with work which the farm waited on, Sam would sit there, doing nothing at all for half a day or a whole one, and no man, neither the boy's father and twin uncle in their day nor his cousin McCaslin after he became practical though not yet titular master, ever to say to him, "I want this finished by sundown" or "why wasn't this done yesterday?" And once each year, in the late fall, in November, the boy would watch the wagon, the hooped canvas top erected now, being loaded—the food, hams and sausage from the smokehouse, coffee and flour and molasses from the commissary, a whole beef killed just last night for the dogs until there would be meat in camp, the crate containing the dogs themselves, then the bedding, the guns, the horns and lanterns and axes, and his cousin McCaslin and Sam Fathers in their hunting clothes would mount to the seat and with Tennie's Jim sitting on the dog-crate they would drive away to Jefferson, to join Major de Spain and General Compson and Boon Hogganbeck and Walter Ewell and go on into the big bottom of the Tallahatchie where the deer and bear were, to be gone two weeks. But before the wagon was even loaded the boy would find that he could watch no longer. He would go away, running almost, to stand behind the corner where he could not see the wagon and nobody could see him, not crying, holding himself rigid except for the trembling, whispering to himself: "Soon now. Soon now. Just three more years" (or two more or one more) "and I will be ten. Then Cass said I can go."

White man's work, when Sam did work. Because he did nothing else: farmed no allotted acres of his own, as the other ex-slaves of old Carothers McCaslin did, performed no field-work for daily wages as the younger and newer negroes did—

and the boy never knew just how that had been settled between Sam and old Carothers, or perhaps with old Carothers' twin sons after him. For, although Sam lived among the negroes, in a cabin among the other cabins in the quarters, and consorted with negroes (what of consorting with anyone Sam did after the boy got big enough to walk alone from the house to the blacksmith-shop and then to carry a gun) and dressed like them and talked like them and even went with them to the negro church now and then, he was still the son of that Chickasaw chief and the negroes knew it. And, it seemed to the boy, not only negroes. Boon Hogganbeck's grandmother had been a Chickasaw woman too, and although the blood had run white since and Boon was a white man, it was not chief's blood. To the boy at least, the difference was apparent immediately you saw Boon and Sam together, and even Boon seemed to know it was there—even Boon, to whom in his tradition it had never occurred that anyone might be better born than himself. A man might be smarter, he admitted that, or richer (luckier, he called it) but not better born. Boon was a mastiff, absolutely faithful, dividing his fidelity equally between Major de Spain and the boy's cousin McCaslin, absolutely dependent for his very bread and dividing that impartially too between Major de Spain and McCaslin, hardy, generous, courageous enough, a slave to all the appetites and almost unratiocinative. In the boy's eyes at least it was Sam Fathers, the negro, who bore himself not only toward his cousin McCaslin and Major de Spain but toward all white men, with gravity and dignity and without servility or recourse to that impenetrable wall of ready and easy mirth which negroes sustain between themselves and white men, bearing himself toward his cousin McCaslin not only as one man to another but as an older man to a younger.

He taught the boy the woods, to hunt, when to shoot and when not to shoot, when to kill and when not to kill, and better, what to do with it afterward. Then he would talk to the boy, the two of them sitting beneath the close fierce stars on a summer hilltop while they waited for the hounds to bring the fox back within hearing, or beside a fire in the November or December woods while the dogs worked out a coon's trail along the creek, or fireless in the pitch dark and heavy dew of April mornings while they squatted beneath a turkey-roost. The boy would never question him; Sam did not react to questions. The boy would just wait and then listen and Sam would begin, talking about the old days and the People whom he had not had time to ever know and so could not remember (he did not remember ever having seen his father's face), and in place of whom the other race into which his blood had run supplied him with no substitute.

And as he talked about those old times and those dead and vanished men of another race from either that the boy knew, gradually to the boy those old times would cease to be old times and would become a part of the boy's present, not only as if they had happened yesterday but as if they were still happening, the men who walked through them actually walking in breath and air and casting an actual shadow on the earth they had not quitted. And more: as if some of them had not happened yet but would occur tomorrow, until at last it would seem to the boy that he himself had not come into existence yet, that none of his race nor the other subject race which his people had brought with them into the land had come here yet; that although it had been his grandfather's and then his father's and uncle's and was now his cousin's and someday would be his own land which he and Sam hunted over, their hold upon it actually was as trivial and without reality as the now faded and archaic script in the chancery book in Jefferson which allocated it to them and that it was he, the boy, who was the guest here and Sam Fathers' voice the mouthpiece of the host.

Until three years ago there had been two of them, the other a full-blood Chickasaw, in a sense even more incredibly lost than Sam Fathers. He called himself Jobaker, as if it were one word. Nobody knew his history at all. He was a hermit, living in a foul little shack at the forks of the creek five miles from the plantation and about that far from any other habitation. He was a market hunter and fisherman and he consorted with nobody, black or white; no negro would even cross his path and no man dared approach his hut except Sam. And perhaps once a month the boy would find them in Sam's shop—two old men squatting on their heels on the dirt floor, talking in a mixture of negroid English and flat hill dialect and now and then a phrase of that old tongue which as time went on and the boy squatted there too listening, he began to learn. Then Jobaker died. That is, nobody had seen him in some time. Then one morning Sam was missing, nobody, not even the boy, knew when nor where, until that night when some negroes hunting in the creek bottom saw the sudden burst of flame and approached. It was Jobaker's hut, but before they got anywhere near it, someone shot at them from the shadows beyond it. It was Sam who fired, but nobody ever found Jobaker's grave.

The next morning, sitting at breakfast with his cousin, the boy saw Sam pass the diningroom window and he remembered then that never in his life before had he seen Sam nearer the house than the blacksmith-shop. He stopped eating even; he sat there and he and his cousin both heard the voices from beyond the pantry door, then the door opened and Sam entered, carrying his hat in his hand but without knocking as anyone else on the place except a house servant would have done, entered just far enough for the door to close behind him and stood looking at neither of them—the Indian face above the nigger clothes, looking at something over their heads or at something not even in the room.

"I want to go," he said. "I want to go to the Big Bottom to live."

"To live?" the boy's cousin said.

"At Major de Spain's and your camp, where you go to hunt," Sam said. "I could take care of it for you all while you aint there. I will build me a little house in the woods, if you rather I didn't stay in the big one."

"What about Isaac here?" his cousin said. "How will you get away from him? Are you going to take him with you?" But still Sam looked at neither of them, standing just inside the room with that face which showed nothing, which showed that he was an old man only when it smiled.

"I want to go," he said. "Let me go."

"Yes," the cousin said quietly. "Of course. I'll fix it with Major de Spain. You want to go soon?"

"I'm going now," Sam said. He went out. And that was all. The boy was nine then; it seemed perfectly natural that nobody, not even his cousin McCaslin, should argue with Sam. Also, since he was nine now, he could understand that Sam could leave him and their days and nights in the woods together without any wrench. He believed that he and Sam both knew that this was not only temporary but that the exigencies of his maturing, of that for which Sam had been training him all his life to some day dedicate himself, required it. They had settled that one night last summer while they listened to the hounds bringing a fox back up the creek valley; now the boy discerned in that very talk under the high, fierce August stars a presage, a warning, of this moment today. "I done taught you all there is of this settled country," Sam said. "You can hunt it good as I can now. You are ready for the Big Bottom now, for bear and deer. Hunter's meat," he said. "Next year you will be ten. You will write your age in two numbers and you will be ready to become a man. Your pa" (Sam always referred to the boy's cousin as his father, establishing even before the boy's orphanhood did that relation between them not of the ward to his guardian and kinsman and chief and head of his blood, but of the child to the man who sired his flesh and his thinking too.) "promised you can go with us then." So the boy could understand Sam's going. But he couldn't understand why now, in March, six months before the moon for hunting.

"If Jobaker's dead like they say," he said, "and Sam hasn't got anybody but us at all kin to him, why does he want to go to the Big Bottom now, when it will be six months before we get there?"

"Maybe that's what he wants," McCaslin said. "Maybe he wants to get away from you a little while."

But that was all right. McCaslin and other grown people often said things like that and he paid no attention to them, just as he paid no attention to Sam saying he wanted to go to the Big Bottom to live. After all, he would have to live there for six months, because there would be no use in going at all if he was going to turn right around and come back. And, as Sam himself had told him, he already knew all about hunting in this settled country that Sam or anybody else could teach him. So it would be all right. Summer, then the bright days after the first frost, then the cold and himself on the wagon with McCaslin this time and the moment would come and he would draw the blood, the big blood which would make him a man, a hunter, and Sam would come back home with them and he too would have outgrown the child's pursuit of rabbits and possums. Then he too would make one before the winter fire, talking of the old hunts and the hunts to come as hunters talked.

So Sam departed. He owned so little that he could carry it. He walked. He would neither let McCaslin send him in the wagon, nor take a mule to ride. No one saw him go even. He was just gone one morning, the cabin which had never had very much in it, vacant and empty, the shop in which there never had been very much done, standing idle. Then November came at last, and now the boy made one—himself and his cousin McCaslin and Tennie's Jim, and Major de Spain and General Compson and Walter Ewell and Boon and old Uncle Ash to do the cooking, waiting for them in Jefferson with the other wagon, and the surrey in which he and McCaslin and General Compson and Major de Spain would ride.

Sam was waiting at the camp to meet them. If he was glad to seem them, he did not show it. And if, when they broke camp two weeks later to return home, he was sorry to see them go, he did not show that either. Because he did not come back with them. It was only the boy who returned, returning solitary and alone to the settled familiar land, to follow for eleven months the childish business of rabbits and such while he waited to go back, having brought with him, even from his brief first sojourn, an unforgettable sense of the big woods—not a quality dangerous or particularly inimical, but profound, sentient, gigantic and brooding, amid which he had been permitted to go to and fro at will, unscathed, why he knew not, but dwarfed and, until he had drawn honorably blood worthy of being drawn, alien.

Then November, and they would come back. Each morning Sam would take the boy out to the stand allotted him. It would be one of the poorer stands of course, since he was only ten and eleven and twelve and he had never even seen a deer running yet. But they would stand there, Sam a little behind him and without a gun himself, as he had been standing when the boy shot the running rabbit when he was eight years old. They would stand there in the November dawns, and after a while they would hear the dogs. Sometimes the chase would sweep up and past quite close, belling and invisible; once they heard the two heavy reports of Boon Hogganbeck's old gun with which he had never killed anything larger than a squirrel and that sitting, and twice they heard the flat unreverberant clap of Walter Ewell's rifle, following which you did not even wait to hear his horn.

"I'll never get a shot," the boy said. "I'll never kill one."

"Yes you will," Sam said. "You wait. You'll be a hunter. You'll be a man."

But Sam wouldn't come out. They would leave him there. He would come as far as the road where the surrey waited, to take the riding horses back, and that was all. The men would ride the horses and Uncle Ash and Tennie's Jim and the boy would follow in the wagon with Sam, with the camp equipment and the trophies, the meat, the heads, the antlers, the good ones, the wagon winding on among the tremendous gums and cypresses and oaks where no axe save that of the hunter had ever sounded, between the impenetrable walls of cane and brier—the two changing yet constant walls just beyond which the wilderness whose mark he had brought away forever on his spirit even from that first two weeks seemed to lean, stooping a little, watching them and listening, not quite inimical because they were too small, even those such as Walter and Major de Spain and old General Compson who had killed many deer and bear, their sojourn too brief and too harmless to excite to that, but just brooding, secret, tremendous, almost inattentive.

Then they would emerge, they would be out of it, the line as sharp as the demarcation of a doored wall. Suddenly skeleton cotton- and corn-fields would flow away on either hand, gaunt and motionless beneath the gray rain; there would be a house, barns, fences, where the hand of man had clawed for an instant, holding, the wall of the wilderness behind them now, tremendous and still and seemingly impenetrable in the gray and fading light, the very tiny orifice through which they had emerged apparently swallowed up. The surrey would be waiting, his cousin McCaslin and Major de Spain and General Compson and Walter and Boon dismounted beside it. Then

Sam would get down from the wagon and mount one of the horses and, with the others on a rope behind him, he would turn back. The boy would watch him for a while against that tall and secret wall, growing smaller and smaller against it, never looking back. Then he would enter it, returning to what the boy believed, and thought that his cousin McCaslin believed, was his loneliness and solitude.

2.

So the instant came. He pulled trigger and Sam Fathers marked his face with the hot blood which he had spilled and he ceased to be a child and became a hunter and a man. It was the last day. They broke camp that afternoon and went out, his cousin and Major de Spain and General Compson and Boon on the horses, Walter Ewell and the negroes in the wagon with him and Sam and his hide and antlers. There could have been (and were) other trophies in the wagon. But for him they did not exist, just as for all practical purposes he and Sam Fathers were still alone together as they had been that morning. The wagon wound and jolted between the slow and shifting yet constant walls from beyond and above which the wilderness watched them pass, less than inimical now and never to be inimical again since the buck still and forever leaped, the shaking gun-barrels coming constantly and forever steady at last, crashing, and still out of his instant of immortality the buck sprang, forever immortal;—the wagon jolting and bouncing on, the moment of the buck, the shot, Sam Fathers and himself and the blood with which Sam had marked him forever one with the wilderness which had accepted him since Sam said that he had done all right, when suddenly Sam reined back and stopped the wagon and they all heard the unmistakable and unforgettable sound of a deer breaking cover.

Then Boon shouted from beyond the bend of the trail and while they sat motionless in the halted wagon, Walter and the boy already reaching for their guns, Boon came galloping back, flogging his mule with his hat, his face wild and amazed as he shouted down at them. Then the other riders came around the bend, also spurring.

"Get the dogs!" Boon cried. "Get the dogs! If he had a nub on his head, he had fourteen points! Laying right there by the road in that pawpaw thicket! If I'd a knowed he was there, I could have cut his throat with my pocket knife!"

"Maybe that's why he run," Walter said. "He saw you never had your gun." He was already out of the wagon with his rifle. Then the boy was out too with his gun, and the other riders came up and Boon got off his mule somehow and was scrabbling and clawing among the duffel in the wagon, still shouting, "Get the dogs! Get the dogs!" And it seemed to the boy too that it would take them forever to decide what to do—the old men in whom the blood ran cold and slow, in whom during the intervening years between them and himself the blood had become a different and colder substance from that which ran in him and even in Boon and Walter.

"What about it, Sam?" Major de Spain said. "Could the dogs bring him back?"

"We wont need the dogs," Sam said. "If he dont hear the dogs behind him, he will circle back in here about sundown to bed."

"All right," Major de Spain said. "You boys take the horses. We'll go on out to the road in the wagon and wait there." He and General Compson and McCaslin got into the wagon and Boon and Walter and Sam and the boy mounted the horses and turned back and out of the trail. Sam led them for an hour through the gray and unmarked afternoon whose light was little different from what it had been at dawn and which would become darkness without any graduation between. Then Sam stopped them.

"This is far enough," he said. "He'll be coming upwind, and he dont want to smell the mules." They tied the mounts in a thicket. Sam led them on foot now, unpathed through the markless afternoon, the boy pressing close behind him, the two others, or so it seemed to the boy, on his heels. But they were not. Twice Sam turned his head slightly and spoke back to him across his shoulder, still walking: "You got time. We'll get there fore he does."

So he tried to go slower. He tried deliberately to decelerate the dizzy rushing of time in which the buck which he had not even seen was moving, which it seemed to him must be carrying the buck farther and farther and more and more irretrievably away from them even though there were no dogs behind him now to make him run, even though, according to Sam, he must have completed his circle now and was heading back toward them. They went on; it could have been another hour or twice that or less than half, the boy could not have said. Then they were on a ridge. He had never been in here before and he could not see that it was a ridge. He just knew that the earth had risen slightly because the underbrush had thinned a little, the ground sloping invisibly away toward a dense wall of cane. Sam stopped. "This is it," he said. He spoke to Walter and Boon: "Follow this ridge and you will come to two crossings. You will see the tracks. If he crosses, it will be at one of these three."

Walter looked about for a moment. "I know it," he said. "I've even seen your deer. I was in here last Monday. He aint nothing but a yearling."

"A yearling?" Boon said. He was panting from the walking. His face still looked a little wild. "If the one I saw was any yearling, I'm still in kindergarden."

"Then I must have seen a rabbit," Walter said. "I always heard you quit school altogether two years before the first grade."

Boon glared at Walter. "If you dont want to shoot him, get out of the way," he said. "Set down somewhere. By God, I——"

"Aint nobody going to shoot him standing here," Sam said quietly.

"Sam's right," Walter said. He moved, slanting the worn, silver-colored barrel of his rifle downward to walk with it again. "A little more moving and a little more quiet too. Five miles is still Hogganbeck range, even if we wasn't downwind." They went on. The boy could still hear Boon talking, though presently that ceased too. Then once more he and Sam stood motionless together against a tremendous pin oak in a little thicket, and again there was nothing. There was only the soaring and sombre solitude in the dim light, there was the thin murmur of the faint cold rain which had not ceased all day. Then, as if it had waited for them to find their positions and become still, the wilderness breathed again. It seemed to lean inward above them, above himself and Sam and Walter and Boon in their separate lurking-places, tremendous, attentive, impartial and omniscient, the buck moving in it somewhere, not running yet since he had not been pursued, not frightened yet and never fearsome but just alert also as they were alert, perhaps already circling back, perhaps quite near, perhaps conscious also of the eye of the ancient immortal Umpire. Because he was just twelve then, and that morning something had happened to him: in less than a second he had ceased forever to be the child he was yesterday. Or perhaps that made no difference, perhaps even a city-bred man, let alone a child, could not have understood it; perhaps only a country-bred one could comprehend loving the life he spills. He began to shake again.

"I'm glad it's started now," he whispered. He did not move to speak; only his lips shaped the expiring words: "Then it will be gone when I raise the gun——"

Nor did Sam. "Hush," he said.

"Is he that near?" the boy whispered. "Do you think——"

"Hush," Sam said. So he hushed. But he could not stop the shaking. He did not try, because he knew it would go away when he needed the steadiness; had not Sam Fathers already consecrated and absolved him from weakness and regret too? not from love and pity for all which lived and ran and then ceased to live in a second in the very midst of splendor and speed, but from weakness and regret. So they stood motionless, breathing deep and quiet and steady. If there had been any sun, it would be near to setting now; there was a condensing, a densifying, of what he had thought was the gray and unchanging light until he realised suddenly that it was his own breathing, his heart, his blood—something, all things, and that Sam Fathers had marked him indeed, not as a mere hunter, but with something Sam had had in his turn of his vanished and forgotten people. He stopped breathing then; there was only his heart, his blood, and in the following silence the wilderness ceased to breathe also, leaning, stooping overhead with its breath held, tremendous and impartial and waiting. Then the shaking stopped too, as he had known it would, and he drew back the two heavy hammers of the gun.

Then it had passed. It was over. The solitude did not

breathe again yet; it had merely stopped watching him and was looking somewhere else, even turning its back on him, looking on away up the ridge at another point, and the boy knew as well as if he had seen him that the buck had come to the edge of the cane and had either seen or scented them and faded back into it. But the solitude did not breathe again. It should have suspired again then but it did not. It was still facing, watching, what it had been watching and it was not here, not where he and Sam stood; rigid, not breathing himself, he thought, cried *No! No!*, knowing already that it was too late, thinking with the old despair of two and three years ago: *I'll never get a shot*. Then he heard it—the flat single clap of Walter Ewell's rifle which never missed. Then the mellow sound of the horn came down the ridge and something went out of him and he knew then he had never expected to get the shot at all.

"I reckon that's it," he said. "Walter got him." He had raised the gun slightly without knowing it. He lowered it again and had lowered one of the hammers and was already moving out of the thicket when Sam spoke.

"Wait."

"Wait?" the boy cried. And he would remember that—how he turned upon Sam in the truculence of a boy's grief over the missed opportunity, the missed luck. "What for? Dont you hear that horn?"

And he would remember how Sam was standing. Sam had not moved. He was not tall, squat rather and broad, and the boy had been growing fast for the past year or so and there was not much difference between them in height, yet Sam was looking over the boy's head and up the ridge toward the sound of the horn and the boy knew that Sam did not even see him; that Sam knew he was still there beside him but he did not see the boy. Then the boy saw the buck. It was coming down the ridge, as if it were walking out of the very sound of the horn which related its death. It was not running, it was walking, tremendous, unhurried, slanting and tilting its head to pass the antlers through the undergrowth, and the boy standing with Sam beside him now instead of behind him as Sam always stood, and the gun still partly aimed and one of the hammers still cocked.

Then it saw them. And still it did not begin to run. It just stopped for an instant, taller than any man, looking at them; then its muscles suppled, gathered. It did not even alter its course, not fleeing, not even running, just moving with that winged and effortless ease with which deer move, passing within twenty feet of them, its head high and the eye not proud and not haughty but just full and wild and unafraid, and Sam standing beside the boy now, his right arm raised at full length, palm-outward, speaking in that tongue which the boy had learned from listening to him and Joe Baker in the blacksmith shop, while up the ridge Walter Ewell's horn was still blowing them in to a dead buck.

"Oleh, Chief," Sam said. "Grandfather."

When they reached Walter, he was standing with his back toward them, quite still, bemused almost, looking down at his feet. He didn't look up at all.

"Come here, Sam," he said quietly. When they reached him he still did not look up, standing above a little spike buck which had still been a fawn last spring. "He was so little I pretty near let him go," Walter said. "But just look at the track he was making. It's pretty near big as a cow's. If there were any more tracks here besides the ones he is laying in, I would swear there was another buck here that I never even saw."

3.

It was dark when they reached the road where the surrey waited. It was turning cold, the rain had stopped, and the sky was beginning to blow clear. His cousin and Major de Spain and General Compson had a fire going. "Did you get him?" Major de Spain said.

"Got a good-sized swamp-rabbit with spike horns," Walter said. He slid the little buck down from his mule. The boy's cousin McCaslin looked at it.

"Nobody saw the big one?" he said.

"I dont even believe Boon saw it," Walter said. "He probably jumped somebody's stray cow in that thicket." Boon started cursing, swearing at Walter and at Sam for not getting the dogs in the first place and at the buck and all.

"Never mind," Major de Spain said. "He'll be here for us next fall. Let's get started home."

It was after midnight when they let Walter out at his gate two miles from Jefferson and later still when they took General Compson to his house and then returned to Major de Spain's, where he and McCaslin would spend the rest of the night since it was still seventeen miles home. It was cold, the sky was clear now; there would be a heavy frost by sunup and the ground was already frozen beneath the horses' feet and the wheels and beneath their own feet as they crossed Major de Spain's yard and entered the house, the warm dark house, feeling their way up the dark stairs until Major de Spain found a candle and lit it, and into the strange room and the big deep bed, the still cold sheets until they began to warm to their bodies and at last the shaking stopped and suddenly he was telling McCaslin about it while McCaslin listened, quietly until he had finished. "You dont believe it," the boy said. "I know you dont——"

"Why not?" McCaslin said. "Think of all that has happened here, on this earth. All the blood hot and strong for living, pleasuring, that has soaked back into it. For grieving and suffering too, of course, but still getting something out of it for all that, getting a lot out of it, because after all you dont have to continue to bear what you believe is suffering; you can always choose to stop that, put an end to that. And even suffering and grieving is better than nothing; there is only one thing worse than not being alive, and that's shame. But you cant be alive forever, and you always wear out life long before you have exhausted the possibilities of living. And all that must be somewhere; all that could not have been invented and created just to be thrown away. And the earth is shallow; there is not a great deal of it before you come to the rock. And the earth dont want to just keep things, hoard them; it wants to use them again. Look at the seed, the acorns, at what happens even to carrion when you try to bury it: it refuses too, seethes and struggles too until it reaches light and air again, hunting the sun still. And they—" the boy saw his hand in silhouette for a moment against the window beyond which, accustomed to the darkness now, he could see sky where the scoured and icy stars glittered "—they dont want it, need it. Besides, what would it want, itself, knocking around out there, when it never had enough time about the earth as it was, when there is plenty of room about the earth, plenty of places still unchanged from what they were when the blood used and pleasured in them while it was still blood?"

"But we want them," the boy said. "We want them too. There is plenty of room for us and them too."

"That's right," McCaslin said. "Suppose they dont have substance, cant cast a shadow——"

"But I saw it!" the boy cried. "I saw him!"

"Steady," McCaslin said. For an instant his hand touched the boy's flank beneath the covers. "Steady. I know you did. So did I. Sam took me in there once after I killed my first deer."

The Bear

I.

THERE was a man and a dog too this time. Two beasts, counting Old Ben, the bear, and two men, counting Boon Hogganbeck, in whom some of the same blood ran which ran in Sam Fathers, even though Boon's was a plebeian strain of it and only Sam and Old Ben and the mongrel Lion were taintless and incorruptible.

He was sixteen. For six years now he had been a man's hunter. For six years now he had heard the best of all talking. It was of the wilderness, the big woods, bigger and older than any recorded document:—of white man fatuous enough to believe he had bought any fragment of it, of Indian ruthless enough to pretend that any fragment of it had been his to convey; bigger than Major de Spain and the scrap he pretended to, knowing better; older than old Thomas Sutpen of whom Major de Spain had had it and who knew better; older even than old Ikkemotubbe, the Chickasaw chief, of whom old Sutpen had had it and who knew better in his turn. It was of the men, not white nor black nor red but men, hunters, with the will and hardihood to endure and the humility and skill to survive, and the dogs and the bear and deer juxtaposed and reliefed against it, ordered and compelled by and within the wilderness in the ancient and unremitting contest according to the ancient and immitigable rules which voided all regrets and brooked no quarter;—the best game of all, the best of all breathing and forever the best of all listening, the voices quiet and weighty and deliberate for retrospection and recollection and exactitude among the concrete trophies—the racked guns and the heads and skins—in the libraries of town houses or the offices of plantation houses or (and best of all) in the camps themselves where the intact and still-warm meat yet hung, the men who had slain it sitting before the burning logs on hearths when there were houses and hearths or about the smoky blazing of piled wood in front of stretched tarpaulins when there were not. There was always a bottle present, so that it would seem to him that those fine fierce instants of heart and brain and courage and wiliness and speed were concentrated and distilled into that brown liquor which not women, not boys and children, but only hunters drank, drinking not of the blood they spilled but some condensation of the wild immortal spirit, drinking it moderately, humbly even, not with the pagan's base and baseless hope of acquiring thereby the virtues of cunning and strength and speed but in salute to them. Thus it seemed to him on this December morning not only natural but actually fitting that this should have begun with whisky.

He realised later that it had begun long before that. It had already begun on that day when he first wrote his age in two ciphers and his cousin McCaslin brought him for the first time to the camp, the big woods, to earn for himself from the wilderness the name and state of hunter provided he in his turn were humble and enduring enough. He had already inherited then, without ever having seen it, the big old bear with one trap-ruined foot that in an area almost a hundred miles square had earned for himself a name, a definite designation like a living man:—the long legend of corn-cribs broken down and rifled, of shoats and grown pigs and even calves carried bodily into the woods and devoured and traps and deadfalls overthrown and dogs mangled and slain and shotgun and even rifle shots delivered at point-blank range yet with no more effect than so many peas blown through a tube by a child—a corridor of wreckage and destruction beginning back before the boy was born, through which sped, not fast but rather with the ruthless and irresistible deliberation of a locomotive, the shaggy tremendous shape. It ran in his knowledge before he ever saw it. It loomed and towered in his dreams before he even saw the unaxed woods where it left its crooked print, shaggy, tremendous, red-eyed, not malevolent but just big, too big for the dogs which tried to bay it, for the horses which tried to ride it down, for the men and the bullets they fired into it; too big for the very country which was its constricting scope. It was as if the boy had already divined what his senses and intellect had not encompassed yet: that doomed wilderness whose edges were being constantly and punily gnawed at by men with plows and axes who feared it because it was wilderness, men myriad and nameless even to one another in the land where the old bear had earned a name, and through which ran not even a mortal beast but an anachronism indomitable and invincible out of an old dead time, a phantom, epitome and apotheosis of the old wild life which the little puny humans swarmed and hacked at in a fury of abhorrence and fear like pygmies about the ankles of a drowsing elephant;—the old bear, solitary, indomitable, and alone; widowered childless and absolved of mortality—old Priam reft of his old wife and outlived all his sons.

Still a child, with three years then two years then one year yet before he too could make one of them, each November he would watch the wagon containing the dogs and the bedding and food and guns and his cousin McCaslin and Tennie's Jim and Sam Fathers too until Sam moved to the camp to live, depart for the Big Bottom, the big woods. To him, they were going not to hunt bear and deer but to keep yearly rendezvous with the bear which they did not even intend to kill. Two weeks later they would return, with no trophy, no skin. He had not expected it. He had not even feared that it might be in the wagon this time with the other skins and heads. He did not even tell himself that in three years or two years or one year more he would be present and that it might even be his gun. He believed that only after he had served his apprenticeship in the woods which would prove him worthy to be a hunter, would he even be permitted to distinguish the crooked print, and that even then for two November weeks he would merely make another minor one, along with his cousin and Major de Spain and General Compson and Walter Ewell and Boon and the dogs which feared to bay it and the shotguns and rifles which failed even to bleed it, in the yearly pageant-rite of the old bear's furious immortality.

His day came at last. In the surrey with his cousin and Major de Spain and General Compson he saw the wilderness through a slow drizzle of November rain just above the ice point as it seemed to him later he always saw it or at least always remembered it—the tall and endless wall of dense November woods under the dissolving afternoon and the year's death, sombre, impenetrable (he could not even discern yet how, at what point they could possibly hope to enter it even though he knew that Sam Fathers was waiting there with the wagon), the surrey moving through the skeleton stalks of cotton and corn in the last of open country, the last trace of man's puny gnawing at the immemorial flank, until, dwarfed by that perspective into an almost ridiculous diminishment, the surrey itself seemed to have ceased to move (this too to be completed later, years later, after he had grown to a man and had seen the sea) as a solitary small boat hangs in lonely immobility, merely tossing up and down, in the infinite waste of the ocean while the water and then the apparently impenetrable land which it nears without appreciable progress, swings slowly and opens the widening inlet which is the anchorage. He entered it. Sam was waiting, wrapped in a quilt on the wagon seat behind the patient and steaming mules. He entered his novitiate to the true wilderness with Sam beside him as he had begun his apprenticeship in miniature to manhood after the rabbits and such with Sam beside him, the two of them wrapped in the damp, warm, negro-rank quilt while the wilderness closed behind his entrance as it had opened momentarily to accept him, opening before his advancement as it closed behind his progress, no fixed path the wagon followed but a channel nonexistent ten yards ahead of it and ceasing to exist ten yards after it had passed, the wagon progressing not by its own volition but by attrition of their intact yet fluid circumambience, drowsing, earless, almost lightless.

It seemed to him that at the age of ten he was witnessing his own birth. It was not even strange to him. He had experienced it all before, and not merely in dreams. He saw the camp—a paintless six-room bungalow set on piles above the spring high-water—and he knew already how it was going to look. He helped in the rapid orderly disorder of their establishment in it and even his motions were familiar to him, foreknown. Then for two weeks he ate the coarse, rapid food—the shapeless sour bread, the wild strange meat, venison and bear and turkey and coon which he had never tasted before—which men ate, cooked by men who were hunters first and cooks afterward; he slept in harsh sheetless blankets as hunters slept. Each morning the gray of dawn found him and Sam Fathers on the stand, the crossing, which had been allotted him. It was the poorest one, the most barren. He had expected that; he had not dared yet to hope even to himself that he would even hear the running dogs this first time. But he did hear them. It was on the third morning—a murmur, sourceless, almost indistinguishable, yet he knew what it was although he had never before heard that many dogs running at once, the murmur swelling into separate and distinct voices until he could call the five dogs which his cousin owned from among the others. "Now," Sam said, "slant your gun up a little and draw back the hammers and then stand still."

But it was not for him, not yet. The humility was there; he had learned that. And he could learn the patience. He was only ten, only one week. The instant had passed. It seemed to him that he could actually see the deer, the buck, smoke-colored, elongated with speed, vanished, the woods, the gray solitude still ringing even when the voices of the dogs had died away; from far away across the sombre woods and the gray half-liquid morning there came two shots. "Now let your hammers down," Sam said.

He did so. "You knew it too," he said.

"Yes," Sam said. "I want you to learn how to do when you didn't shoot. It's after the chance for the bear or the deer has done already come and gone that men and dogs get killed."

"Anyway, it wasn't him," the boy said. "It wasn't even a bear. It was just a deer."

"Yes," Sam said, "it was just a deer."

Then one morning, it was in the second week, he heard the dogs again. This time before Sam even spoke he readied the too-long, too-heavy, man-size gun as Sam had taught him, even though this time he knew the dogs and the deer were coming less close than ever, hardly within hearing even. They didn't sound like any running dogs he had ever heard before even. Then he found that Sam, who had taught him first of all to cock the gun and take position where he could see best in all directions and then never to move again, had himself moved and up beside him. "There," he said. "Listen." The boy listened, to no ringing chorus strong and fast on a free scent but a moiling yapping an octave too high and with something more than indecision and even abjectness in it which he could not yet recognise, reluctant, not even moving very fast, taking a long time to pass out of hearing, leaving even then in the air that echo of thin and almost human hysteria, abject, almost humanly grieving, with this time nothing ahead of it, no sense of a fleeing unseen smoke-colored shape. He could hear Sam breathing at his shoulder. He saw the arched curve of the old man's inhaling nostrils.

"It's Old Ben!" he cried, whispering.

Sam didn't move save for the slow gradual turning of his head as the voices faded on and the faint steady rapid arch and collapse of his nostrils. "Hah," he said. "Not even running. Walking."

"But up here!" the boy cried. "Way up here!"

"He do it every year," Sam said. "Once. Ash and Boon say he comes up here to run the other little bears away. Tell them to get to hell out of here and stay out until the hunters are gone. Maybe." The boy no longer heard anything at all, yet still Sam's head continued to turn gradually and steadily until the back of it was toward him. Then it turned back and looked down at him—the same face, grave, familiar, expressionless until it smiled, the same old man's eyes from which as he watched there faded slowly a quality darkly and fiercely lambent, passionate and proud. "He dont care no more for bears than he does for dogs or men neither. He come to see who's here, who's new in camp this year, whether he can shoot or not, can stay or not. Whether we got the dog yet that can bay and hold him until a man gets there with a gun. Because he's the head bear. He's the man." It faded, was gone; again they were the eyes as he had known them all his life. "He'll let them follow him to the river. Then he'll send them home. We might as well go too; see how they look when they get back to camp."

The dogs were there first, ten of them huddled back under the kitchen, himself and Sam squatting to peer back into the obscurity where they crouched, quiet, the eyes rolling and luminous, vanishing, and no sound, only that effluvium which the boy could not quite place yet, of something more than dog, stronger than dog and not just animal, just beast even. Because there had been nothing in front of the abject and painful yapping except the solitude, the wilderness, so that when the eleventh hound got back about mid-afternoon and he and Tennie's Jim held the passive and still trembling bitch while Sam daubed her tattered ear and raked shoulder with turpentine and axle-grease, it was still no living creature but only the wilderness which, leaning for a moment, had patted lightly once her temerity. "Just like a man," Sam said. "Just like folks. Put off as long as she could having to be brave, knowing all the time that sooner or later she would have to be brave once so she could keep on calling herself a dog, and knowing before hand what was going to happen when she done it."

He did not know just when Sam left. He only knew that he was gone. For the next three mornings he rose and ate breakfast and Sam was not waiting for him. He went to his stand alone; he found it without help now and stood on it as Sam had taught him. On the third morning he heard the dogs again, running strong and free on a true scent again, and he readied the gun as he had learned to do and heard the hunt sweep past and on since he was not ready yet, had not deserved other yet in just one short period of two weeks as compared to all the long life which he had already dedicated to the wilderness with patience and humility; he heard the shot again, one shot, the single clapping report of Walter Ewell's rifle. By now he could not only find his stand and then return to camp without guidance, by using the compass his cousin had given him he reached Walter waiting beside the buck and the moiling of dogs over the cast entrails before any of the others except Major de Spain and Tennie's Jim on the horses, even before Uncle Ash arrived with the one-eyed wagon-mule which did not mind the smell of blood or even, so they said, of bear.

It was not Uncle Ash on the mule. It was Sam, returned. And Sam was waiting when he finished his dinner and, himself on the one-eyed mule and Sam on the other one of the wagon team, they rode for more than three hours through the rapid shortening sunless afternoon, following no path, no trail even that he could discern, into a section of country he had never seen before. Then he understood why Sam had made him ride the one-eyed mule which would not spook at the smell of blood, of wild animals. The other one, the sound one, stopped short and tried to whirl and bolt even as Sam got down, jerking and wrenching at the rein while Sam held it, coaxing it forward with his voice since he did not dare risk hitching it, drawing it forward while the boy dismounted from the marred one which would stand. Then, standing beside Sam in the thick great gloom of ancient woods and the winter's dying afternoon, he looked quietly down at the rotted log scored and gutted with claw-marks and, in the wet earth beside it, the print of the enormous warped two-toed foot. Now he knew what he had heard in the hounds' voices in the woods that morning and what he had smelled when he peered under the kitchen where they huddled. It was in him too, a little different because they were brute beasts and he was not, but only a little different—an eagerness, passive; an abjectness, a sense of his own fragility and impotence against the timeless woods, yet without doubt or dread; a flavor like brass in the sudden run of saliva in his mouth, a hard sharp constriction either in his brain or his stomach, he could not tell which and it did not matter; he knew only that for the first time he realised that the bear which had run in his listening and loomed in his dreams since before he could remember and which therefore must have existed in the listening and the dreams of his cousin and Major de Spain and even old General Compson before they began to remember in their turn, was a mortal animal and that they had departed for the camp each November with no actual intention of slaying it, not because it could not be slain but because so far they had no actual hope of being able to. "It will be tomorrow," he said.

"You mean we will try tomorrow," Sam said. "We aint got the dog yet."

"We've got eleven," he said. "They ran him Monday."

"And you heard them," Sam said. "Saw them too. We aint got the dog yet. It wont take but one. But he aint there. Maybe he aint nowhere. The only other way will be for him to run by accident over somebody that had a gun and knowed how to shoot it."

"That wouldn't be me," the boy said. "It would be Walter or Major or——"

"It might," Sam said. "You watch close tomorrow. Because he's smart. That's how come he has lived this long. If he gets hemmed up and has got to pick out somebody to run over, he will pick out you."

"How?" he said. "How will he know. . . ." He ceased.

"You mean he already knows me, that I aint never been to the Big Bottom before, aint had time to find out yet whether I . . . . . ." He ceased again, staring at Sam; he said humbly, not even amazed: "It was me he was watching. I dont reckon he did need to come but once."

"You watch tomorrow," Sam said. "I reckon we better start back. It'll be long after dark now before we get to camp."

The next morning they started three hours earlier than they had ever done. Even Uncle Ash went, the cook, who called himself by profession a camp cook and who did little else save cook for Major de Spain's hunting and camping parties, yet who had been marked by the wilderness from simple juxtaposition to it until he responded as they all did, even the boy who until two weeks ago had never even seen the wilderness, to a hound's ripped ear and shoulder and the print of a crooked foot in a patch of wet earth. They rode. It was too far to walk: the boy and Sam and Uncle Ash in the wagon with the dogs, his cousin and Major de Spain and General Compson and Boon and Walter and Tennie's Jim riding double on the horses; again the first gray light found him, as on that first morning two weeks ago, on the stand where Sam had placed and left him. With the gun which was too big for him, the breech-loader which did not even belong to him but to Major de Spain and which he had fired only once, at a stump on the first day to learn the recoil and how to reload it with the paper shells, he stood against a big gum tree beside a little bayou whose black still water crept without motion out of a cane-brake, across a small clearing and into the cane again, where, invisible, a bird, the big woodpecker called Lord-to-God by negroes, clattered at a dead trunk. It was a stand like any other stand, dissimilar only in incidentals to the one where he had stood each morning for two weeks; a territory new to him yet no less familiar than that other one which after two weeks he had come to believe he knew a little—the same solitude, the same loneliness through which frail and timorous man had merely passed without altering it, leaving no mark nor scar, which looked exactly as it must have looked when the first ancestor of Sam Fathers' Chickasaw predecessors crept into it and looked about him, club or stone axe or bone arrow drawn and ready, different only because, squatting at the edge of the kitchen, he had smelled the dogs huddled and cringing beneath it and saw the raked ear and side of the bitch that, as Sam had said, had to be brave once in order to keep on calling herself a dog, and saw yesterday in the earth beside the gutted log, the print of the living foot. He heard no dogs at all. He never did certainly hear them. He only heard the drumming of the woodpecker stop short off, and knew that the bear was looking at him. He never saw it. He did not know whether it was facing him from the cane or behind him. He did not move, holding the useless gun which he knew now he would never fire at it, now or ever, tasting in his saliva that taint of brass which he had smelled in the huddled dogs when he peered under the kitchen.

Then it was gone. As abruptly as it had stopped, the woodpecker's dry hammering set up again, and after a while he believed he even heard the dogs—a murmur, scarce a sound even, which he had probably been hearing for a time, perhaps a minute or two, before he remarked it, drifting into hearing and then out again, dying away. They came nowhere near him. If it was dogs he heard, he could not have sworn to it; if it was a bear they ran, it was another bear. It was Sam himself who emerged from the cane and crossed the bayou, the injured bitch following at heel as a bird dog is taught to walk. She came and crouched against his leg, trembling. "I didn't see him," he said. "I didn't, Sam."

"I know it," Sam said. "He done the looking. You didn't hear him neither, did you?"

"No," the boy said. "I——"

"He's smart," Sam said. "Too smart." Again the boy saw in his eyes that quality of dark and brooding lambence as Sam looked down at the bitch trembling faintly and steadily against the boy's leg. From her raked shoulder a few drops of fresh blood clung like bright berries. "Too big. We aint got the dog yet. But maybe some day."

Because there would be a next time, after and after. He was only ten. It seemed to him that he could see them, the two of them, shadowy in the limbo from which time emerged and became time: the old bear absolved of mortality and himself who shared a little of it. Because he recognised now what he had smelled in the huddled dogs and tasted in his own saliva, recognised fear as a boy, a youth, recognises the existence of love and passion and experience which is his heritage but not yet his patrimony, from entering by chance the presence or perhaps even merely the bedroom of a woman who has loved and been loved by many men. *So I will have to see him*, he thought, without dread or even hope. *I will have to look at him*. So it was in June of the next summer. They were at the camp again, celebrating Major de Spain's and General Compson's birthdays. Although the one had been born in September and the other in the depth of winter and almost thirty years earlier, each June the two of them and McCaslin and Boon and Walter Ewell (and the boy too from now on) spent two weeks at the camp, fishing and shooting squirrels and turkey and running coons and wildcats with the dogs at night. That is, Boon and the negroes (and the boy too now) fished and shot squirrels and ran the coons and cats, because the proven hunters, not only Major de Spain and old General Compson (who spent those two weeks sitting in a rocking chair before a tremendous iron pot of Brunswick stew, stirring and tasting, with Uncle Ash to quarrel with about how he was making it and Tennie's Jim to pour whisky into the tin dipper from which he drank it) but even McCaslin and Walter Ewell who were still young enough, scorned such other than shooting the wild gobblers with pistols for wagers or to test their marksmanship.

That is, his cousin McCaslin and the others thought he was hunting squirrels. Until the third evening he believed that Sam Fathers thought so too. Each morning he would leave the camp right after breakfast. He had his own gun now, a new breech-loader, a Christmas gift; he would own and shoot it for almost seventy years, through two new pairs of barrels and locks and one new stock, until all that remained of the original gun was the silver-inlaid trigger-guard with his and McCaslin's engraved names and the date in 1878. He found the tree beside the little bayou where he had stood that morning. Using the compass, he ranged from that point; he was teaching himself to be better than a fair woodsman without even knowing he was doing it. On the third day he even found the gutted log where he had first seen the print. It was almost completely crumbled now, healing with unbelievable speed, a passionate and almost visible relinquishment, back into the earth from which the tree had grown. He ranged the summer woods now, green with gloom, if anything actually dimmer than they had been in November's gray dissolution, where even at noon the sun fell only in windless dappling upon the earth which never completely dried and which crawled with snakes—moccasins and watersnakes and rattlers, themselves the color of the dappled gloom so that he would not always see them until they moved; returning to camp later and later, first day, second day, passing in the twilight of the third evening the little log pen enclosing the log barn where Sam was putting up the stock for the night. "You aint looked right yet," Sam said.

He stopped. For a moment he didn't answer. Then he said peacefully, in a peaceful rushing burst, as when a boy's miniature dam in a little brook gives way: "All right. Yes. But how? I went to the bayou. I even found that log again. I——"

"I reckon that was all right. Likely he's been watching you. You never saw his foot?"

"I . . . . ." the boy said. "I didn't——I never thought——"

"It's the gun," Sam said. He stood beside the fence, motionless, the old man, son of a negro slave and a Chickasaw chief, in the battered and faded overalls and the frayed five-cent straw hat which had been the badge of the negro's slavery and was now the regalia of his freedom. The camp—the clearing, the house, the barn and its tiny lot with which Major de Spain in his turn had scratched punily and evanescently at the wilderness—faded in the dusk, back into the immemorial darkness of the woods. *The gun*, the boy thought. *The gun*. "You will have to choose," Sam said.

He left the next morning before light, without breakfast, long before Uncle Ash would wake in his quilts on the kitchen floor and start the fire. He had only the compass and a stick for the snakes. He could go almost a mile before he would need to see the compass. He sat on a log, the invisible compass in his hand, while the secret night-sounds which had ceased at his movements, scurried again and then fell still for good and the owls ceased and gave over to the waking day birds and there was light in the gray wet woods and he could see the compass. He went fast yet still quietly, becoming steadily better and better as a woodsman without yet having time to realise it; he jumped a doe and a fawn, walked them out of the bed, close enough to see them—the crash of undergrowth, the white scut, the fawn scudding along behind her, faster than he had known it could have run. He was hunting right, upwind, as Sam had taught him, but that didn't matter now. He had left the gun; by his own will and relinquishment he had accepted not a gambit, not a choice, but a condition in which not only the bear's heretofore inviolable anonymity but all the ancient rules and balances of hunter and hunted had been abrogated. He would not even be afraid, not even in the moment when the fear would take him completely: blood, skin, bowels, bones, memory from the long time before it even became his memory:—all save that thin clear quenchless lucidity which alone differed him from this bear and from all the other bears and bucks he would follow during almost seventy years, to which Sam had said: "Be scared. You cant help that. But dont be afraid. Aint nothing in the woods going to hurt you if you dont corner it or it dont smell that you are afraid. A bear or a deer has got to be scared of a coward the same as a brave man has got to be."

By noon he was far beyond the crossing on the little bayou, farther into the new and alien country than he had ever been, travelling now not only by the compass but by the old, heavy, biscuit-thick silver watch which had been his father's. He had left the camp nine hours ago; nine hours from now, dark would already have been an hour old. He stopped, for the first time since he had risen from the log when he could see the compass face at last, and looked about, mopping his sweating face on his sleeve. He had already relinquished, of his will, because of his need, in humility and peace and without regret, yet apparently that had not been enough, the leaving of the gun was not enough. He stood for a moment—a child, alien and lost in the green and soaring gloom of the markless wilderness. Then he relinquished completely to it. It was the watch and the compass. He was still tainted. He removed the linked chain of the one and the looped thong of the other from his overalls and hung them on a bush and leaned the stick beside them and entered it.

When he realised he was lost, he did as Sam had coached and drilled him: made a cast to cross his backtrack. He had not been going very fast for the last two or three hours, and he had gone even less fast since he left the compass and watch on the bush. So he went slower still now, since the tree could not be very far; in fact, he found it before he really expected to and turned and went to it. But there was no bush beneath it, no compass nor watch, so he did next as Sam had coached and drilled him: made this next circle in the opposite direction and much larger, so that the pattern of the two of them would bisect his track somewhere, but crossing no trace nor mark anywhere of his feet or any feet, and now he was going faster though still not panicked, his heart beating a little more rapidly but strong and steady enough, and this time it was not even the tree because there was a down log beside it which he had never seen before and beyond the log a little swamp, a seepage of moisture somewhere between earth and water, and he did what Sam had coached and drilled him as the next and the last, seeing as he sat down on the log the crooked print, the warped indentation in the wet ground which while he looked at it continued to fill with water until it was level full and the water began to overflow and the sides of the print began to dissolve away. Even as he looked up he saw the next one, and, moving, the one beyond it; moving, not hurrying, running, but merely keeping pace with them as they appeared before him as though they were being shaped out of thin air just one constant pace short of where he would lose them forever and be lost forever himself, tireless, eager, without doubt or dread, panting a little above the strong rapid little hammer of his heart, emerging suddenly into a little glade and the wilderness coalesced. It rushed, soundless, and solidified—the tree, the bush, the compass and the watch glinting where a ray of sunlight touched them. Then he saw the bear. It did not emerge, appear: it was just there, immobile, fixed in the green and windless noon's hot dappling, not as big as he had dreamed it but as big as he had expected, bigger, dimensionless against the dappled obscurity, looking at him. Then it moved. It crossed the glade without haste, walking for an instant into the sun's full glare and out of it, and stopped again and looked back at him across one shoulder.

Then it was gone. It didn't walk into the woods. It faded, sank back into the wilderness without motion as he had watched a fish, a huge old bass, sink back into the dark depths of its pool and vanish without even any movement of its fins.

2.

So he should have hated and feared Lion. He was thirteen then. He had killed his buck and Sam Fathers had marked his face with the hot blood, and in the next November he killed a bear. But before that accolade he had become as competent in the woods as many grown men with the same experience. By now he was a better woodsman than most grown men with more. There was no territory within twenty-five miles of the camp that he did not know—bayou, ridge, landmark trees and path; he could have led anyone direct to any spot in it and brought them back. He knew game trails that even Sam Fathers had never seen; in the third fall he found a buck's bedding-place by himself and unbeknown to his cousin he borrowed Walter Ewell's rifle and lay in wait for the buck at dawn and killed it when it walked back to the bed as Sam had told him how the old Chickasaw fathers did.

By now he knew the old bear's footprint better than he did his own, and not only the crooked one. He could see any one of the three sound prints and distinguish it at once from any other, and not only because of its size. There were other bears within that fifty miles which left tracks almost as large, or at least so near that the one would have appeared larger only by juxtaposition. It was more than that. If Sam Fathers had been his mentor and the backyard rabbits and squirrels his kindergarten, then the wilderness the old bear ran was his college and the old male bear itself, so long unwifed and childless as to have become its own ungendered progenitor, was his alma mater.

He could find the crooked print now whenever he wished, ten miles or five miles or sometimes closer than that, to the camp. Twice while on stand during the next three years he heard the dogs strike its trail and once even jump it by chance, the voices high, abject, almost human in their hysteria. Once, still-hunting with Walter Ewell's rifle, he saw it cross a long corridor of down timber where a tornado had passed. It rushed through rather than across the tangle of trunks and branches as a locomotive would, faster than he had ever believed it could have moved, almost as fast as a deer even because the deer would have spent most of that distance in the air; he realised then why it would take a dog not only of abnormal courage but size and speed too ever to bring it to bay. He had a little dog at home, a mongrel, of the sort called fyce by Negroes, a ratter, itself not much bigger than a rat and possessing that sort of courage which had long since stopped being bravery and had become foolhardiness. He brought it with him one June and, timing them as if they were meeting an appointment with another human being, himself carrying the fyce with a sack over its head and Sam Fathers with a brace of the hounds on a rope leash, they lay downwind of the trail and actually ambushed the bear. They were so close that it turned at bay although he realised later this might have been from surprise and amazement at the shrill and frantic uproar of the fyce. It turned at bay against the trunk of a big cypress, on its hind feet; it seemed to the boy that it would never stop rising, taller and taller, and even the two hounds seemed to have taken a kind of desperate and despairing courage from the fyce. Then he realised that the fyce was actually not going to stop. He flung the gun down and ran. When he overtook and grasped the shrill, frantically pinwheeling little dog, it seemed to him that he was directly under the bear. He could smell it, strong and hot and rank. Sprawling, he looked up where it loomed and towered over him like a thunderclap. It was quite familiar, until he remembered: this was the way he had used to dream about it.

Then it was gone. He didn't see it go. He knelt, holding the frantic fyce with both hands, hearing the abased wailing of the two hounds drawing further and further away, until Sam came up, carrying the gun. He laid it quietly down beside the boy and stood looking down at him. "You've done seed him twice now, with a gun in your hands," he said. "This time you couldn't have missed him."

The boy rose. He still held the fyce. Even in his arms it continued to yap frantically, surging and straining toward the fading sound of the hounds like a collection of live wire springs. The boy was panting a little. "Neither could you," he said. "You had the gun. Why didn't you shoot him?"

Sam didn't seem to have heard. He put out his hand and touched the little dog in the boy's arms which still yapped and strained even though the two hounds were out of hearing now. "He's done gone," Sam said. "You can slack off and rest now, until next time." He stroked the little dog until it began to grow quiet under his hand. "You's almost the one we wants," he said. "You just aint big enough. We aint got that one yet. He will need to be just a little bigger than smart, and a little braver than either." He withdrew his hand from the fyce's head and stood looking into the woods where the bear and the hounds had vanished. "Somebody is going to, someday."

"I know it," the boy said. "That's why it must be one of us. So it wont be until the last day. When even he dont want it to last any longer."

So he should have hated and feared Lion. It was in the fourth summer, the fourth time he had made one in the celebration of Major de Spain's and General Compson's birthday. In the early spring Major de Spain's mare had foaled a horse colt. One evening when Sam brought the horses and mules up to stable them for the night, the colt was missing and it was all he could do to get the frantic mare into the lot. He had thought at first to let the mare lead him back to where she had become separated from the foal. But she would not do it. She would not even feint toward any particular part of the woods or even in any particular direction. She merely ran, as if she couldn't see, still frantic with terror. She whirled and ran at Sam once, as if to attack him in some ultimate desperation, as if she could not for the moment realise that he was a man and a long-familiar one. He got her into the lot at last. It was too dark by that time to back-track her, to unravel the erratic course she had doubtless pursued.

He came to the house and told Major de Spain. It was an animal, of course, a big one, and the colt was dead now, wherever it was. They all knew that. "It's a panther," General Compson said at once. "The same one. That doe and fawn last March." Sam had sent Major de Spain word of it when Boon Hogganbeck came to the camp on a routine visit to see how the stock had wintered—the doe's throat torn out, and the beast had run down the helpless fawn and killed it too.

"Sam never did say that was a panther," Major de Spain

said. Sam said nothing now, standing behind Major de Spain where they sat at supper, inscrutable, as if he were just waiting for them to stop talking so he could go home. He didn't even seem to be looking at anything. "A panther might jump a doe, and he wouldn't have much trouble catching the fawn afterward. But no panther would have jumped that colt with the dam right there with it. It was Old Ben," Major de Spain said. "I'm disappointed in him. He has broken the rules. I didn't think he would have done that. He has killed mine and McCaslin's dogs, but that was all right. We gambled the dogs against him; we gave each other warning. But now he has come into my house and destroyed my property, out of season too. He broke the rules. It was Old Ben, Sam." Still Sam said nothing, standing there until Major de Spain should stop talking. "We'll back-track her tomorrow and see," Major de Spain said.

Sam departed. He would not live in the camp; he had built himself a little hut something like Joe Baker's, only stouter, tighter, on the bayou a quarter-mile away, and a stout log crib where he stored a little corn for the shoat he raised each year. The next morning he was waiting when they waked. He had already found the colt. They did not even wait for breakfast. It was not far, not five hundred yards from the stable—the three-months' colt lying on its side, its throat torn out and the entrails and one ham partly eaten. It lay not as if it had been dropped but as if it had been struck and hurled, and no cat-mark, no claw-mark where a panther would have gripped it while finding its throat. They read the tracks where the frantic mare had circled and at last rushed in with that same ultimate desperation with which she had whirled on Sam Fathers yesterday evening, and the long tracks of dead and terrified running and those of the beast which had not even rushed at her when she advanced but had merely walked three or four paces toward her until she broke, and General Compson said, "Good God, what a wolf!"

Still Sam said nothing. The boy watched him while the men knelt, measuring the tracks. There was something in Sam's face now. It was neither exultation nor joy nor hope. Later, a man, the boy realised what it had been, and that Sam had known all the time what had made the tracks and what had torn the throat out of the doe in the spring and killed the fawn. It had been foreknowledge in Sam's face that morning. *And he was glad*, he told himself. *He was old. He had no children, no people, none of his blood anywhere above earth that he would ever meet again. And even if he were to, he could not have touched it, spoken to it, because for seventy years now he had had to be a negro. It was almost over now and he was glad.*

They returned to camp and had breakfast and came back with guns and the hounds. Afterward the boy realised that they also should have known then what killed the colt as well as Sam Fathers did. But that was neither the first nor the last time he had seen men rationalise from and even act upon their misconceptions. After Boon, standing astride the colt, had whipped the dogs away from it with his belt, they snuffed at the tracks. One of them, a young dog hound without judgment yet, bayed once, and they ran for a few feet on what seemed to be a trail. Then they stopped, looking back at the men, eager enough, not baffled, merely questioning, as if they were asking "Now what?" Then they rushed back to the colt, where Boon, still astride it, slashed at them with the belt.

"I never knew a trail to get cold that quick," General Compson said.

"Maybe a single wolf big enough to kill a colt with the dam right there beside it dont leave scent," Major de Spain said.

"Maybe it was a hant," Walter Ewell said. He looked at Tennie's Jim. "Hah, Jim?"

Because the hounds would not run it, Major de Spain had Sam hunt out and find the tracks a hundred yards further on and they put the dogs on it again and again the young one bayed and not one of them realised then that the hound was not baying like a dog striking game but was merely bellowing like a country dog whose yard has been invaded. General Compson spoke to the boy and Boon and Tennie's Jim: to the squirrel hunters. "You boys keep the dogs with you this morning. He's probably hanging around somewhere, waiting to get his breakfast off the colt. You might strike him."

But they did not. The boy remembered how Sam stood watching them as they went into the woods with the leashed hounds—the Indian face in which he had never seen anything until it smiled, except that faint arching of the nostrils on that first morning when the hounds had found Old Ben. They took the hounds with them on the next day, though when they reached the place where they hoped to strike a fresh trail, the carcass of the colt was gone. Then on the third morning Sam was waiting again, this time until they had finished breakfast. He said, "Come." He led them to his house, his little hut, to the corn-crib beyond it. He had removed the corn and had made a deadfall of the door, baiting it with the colt's carcass; peering between the logs, they saw an animal almost the color of a gun or pistol barrel, what little time they had to examine its color or shape. It was not crouched nor even standing. It was in motion, in the air, coming toward them—a heavy body crashing with tremendous force against the door so that the thick door jumped and clattered in its frame, the animal, whatever it was, hurling itself against the door again seemingly before it could have touched the floor and got a new purchase to spring from. "Come away," Sam said, "fore he break his neck." Even when they retreated the heavy and measured crashes continued, the stout door jumping and clattering each time, and still no sound from the beast itself—no snarl, no cry.

"What in hell's name is it?" Major de Spain said.

"It's a dog," Sam said, his nostrils arching and collapsing faintly and steadily and that faint, fierce milkiness in his eyes again as on that first morning when the hounds had struck the old bear. "It's the dog."

"*The* dog?" Major de Spain said.

"That's gonter hold Old Ben."

"Dog the devil," Major de Spain said. "I'd rather have Old Ben himself in my pack than that brute. Shoot him."

"No," Sam said.

"You'll never tame him. How do you ever expect to make an animal like that afraid of you?"

"I dont want him tame," Sam said; again the boy watched his nostrils and the fierce milky light in his eyes. "But I almost rather he be tame than scared, of me or any man or any thing. But he wont be neither, of nothing."

"Then what are you going to do with it?"

"You can watch," Sam said.

Each morning through the second week they would go to

Sam's crib. He had removed a few shingles from the roof and had put a rope on the colt's carcass and had drawn it out when the trap fell. Each morning they would watch him lower a pail of water into the crib while the dog hurled itself tirelessly against the door and dropped back and leaped again. It never made any sound and there was nothing frenzied in the act but only a cold and grim indomitable determination. Toward the end of the week it stopped jumping at the door. Yet it had not weakened appreciably and it was not as if it had rationalised the fact that the door was not going to give. It was as if for that time it simply disdained to jump any longer. It was not down. None of them had ever seen it down. It stood, and they could see it now—part mastiff, something of Airedale and something of a dozen other strains probably, better than thirty inches at the shoulders and weighing as they guessed almost ninety pounds, with cold yellow eyes and a tremendous chest and over all that strange color like a blued gun-barrel.

Then the two weeks were up. They prepared to break camp. The boy begged to remain and his cousin let him. He moved into the little hut with Sam Fathers. Each morning he watched Sam lower the pail of water into the crib. By the end of that week the dog was down. It would rise and half stagger, half crawl to the water and drink and collapse again. One morning it could not even reach the water, could not raise its forequarters even from the floor. Sam took a short stick and prepared to enter the crib. "Wait," the boy said. "Let me get the gun——"

"No," Sam said. "He cant move now." Nor could it. It lay on its side while Sam touched it, its head and the gaunted body, the dog lying motionless, the yellow eyes open. They were not fierce and there was nothing of petty malevolence in them, but a cold and almost impersonal malignance like some natural force. It was not even looking at Sam nor at the boy peering at it between the logs.

Sam began to feed it again. The first time he had to raise its head so it could lap the broth. That night he left a bowl of broth containing lumps of meat where the dog could reach it. The next morning the bowl was empty and the dog was lying on its belly, its head up, the cold yellow eyes watching the door as Sam entered, no change whatever in the cold yellow eyes and still no sound from it even when it sprang, its aim and co-ordination still bad from weakness so that Sam had time to strike it down with the stick and leap from the crib and slam the door as the dog, still without having had time to get its feet under it to jump again seemingly, hurled itself against the door as if the two weeks of starving had never been.

At noon that day someone came whooping through the woods from the direction of the camp. It was Boon. He came and looked for a while between the logs, at the tremendous dog lying again on its belly, its head up, the yellow eyes blinking sleepily at nothing: the indomitable and unbroken spirit. "What we better do," Boon said, "is to let that son of a bitch go and catch Old Ben and run him on the dog." He turned to the boy his weather-reddened and beetling face. "Get your traps together. Cass says for you to come on home. You been in here fooling with that horse-eating varmint long enough."

Boon had a borrowed mule at the camp; the buggy was waiting at the edge of the bottom. He was at home that night. He told McCaslin about it. "Sam's going to starve him again until he can go in and touch him. Then he will feed him again. Then he will starve him again, if he has to."

"But why?" McCaslin said. "What for? Even Sam will never tame that brute."

"We dont want him tame. We want him like he is. We just want him to find out at last that the only way he can get out of that crib and stay out of it is to do what Sam or somebody tells him to do. He's the dog that's going to stop Old Ben and hold him. We've already named him. His name is Lion."

Then November came at last. They returned to the camp. With General Compson and Major de Spain and his cousin and Walter and Boon he stood in the yard among the guns and bedding and boxes of food and watched Sam Fathers and Lion come up the lane from the lot—the Indian, the old man in battered overalls and rubber boots and a worn sheepskin coat and a hat which had belonged to the boy's father; the tremendous dog pacing gravely beside him. The hounds rushed out to meet them and stopped, except the young one which still had but little of judgment. It ran up to Lion, fawning. Lion didn't snap at it. He didn't even pause. He struck it rolling and yelping for five or six feet with a blow of one paw as a bear would have done and came on into the yard and stood, blinking sleepily at nothing, looking at no one, while Boon said, "Jesus. Jesus.—Will he let me touch him?"

"You can touch him," Sam said. "He dont care. He dont care about nothing or nobody."

The boy watched that too. He watched it for the next two years from that moment when Boon touched Lion's head and then knelt beside him, feeling the bones and muscles, the power. It was as if Lion were a woman—or perhaps Boon was the woman. That was more like it—the big, grave, sleepy-seeming dog which, as Sam Fathers said, cared about no man and no thing; and the violent, insensitive, hard-faced man with his touch of remote Indian blood and the mind almost of a child. He watched Boon take over Lion's feeding from Sam and Uncle Ash both. He would see Boon squatting in the cold rain beside the kitchen while Lion ate. Because Lion neither slept nor ate with the other dogs though none of them knew where he did sleep until in the second November, thinking until then that Lion slept in his kennel beside Sam Fathers' hut, when the boy's cousin McCaslin said something about it to Sam by sheer chance and Sam told him. And that night the boy and Major de Spain and McCaslin with a lamp entered the back room where Boon slept—the little, tight, airless room rank with the smell of Boon's unwashed body and his wet hunting-clothes—where Boon, snoring on his back, choked and waked and Lion raised his head beside him and looked back at them from his cold, slumbrous yellow eyes.

"Damn it, Boon," McCaslin said. "Get that dog out of here. He's got to run Old Ben tomorrow morning. How in hell do you expect him to smell anything fainter than a skunk after breathing you all night?"

"The way I smell aint hurt my nose none that I ever noticed," Boon said.

"It wouldn't matter if it had," Major de Spain said. "We're not depending on you to trail a bear. Put him outside. Put him under the house with the other dogs."

Boon began to get up. "He'll kill the first one that happens to yawn or sneeze in his face or touches him."

"I reckon not," Major de Spain said. "None of them are going to risk yawning in his face or touching him either, even asleep. Put him outside. I want his nose right tomorrow. Old Ben fooled him last year. I dont think he will do it again."

Boon put on his shoes without lacing them; in his long soiled underwear, his hair still tousled from sleep, he and Lion went out. The others returned to the front room and the poker game where McCaslin's and Major de Spain's hands waited for them on the table. After a while McCaslin said, "Do you want me to go back and look again?"

"No," Major de Spain said. "I call," he said to Walter Ewell. He spoke to McCaslin again. "If you do, dont tell me. I am beginning to see the first sign of my increasing age: I dont like to know that my orders have been disobeyed, even when I knew when I gave them that they would be.—A small pair," he said to Walter Ewell.

"How small?" Walter said.

"Very small," Major de Spain said.

And the boy, lying beneath his piled quilts and blankets waiting for sleep, knew likewise that Lion was already back in Boon's bed, for the rest of that night and the next one and during all the nights of the next November and the next one. He thought then: *I wonder what Sam thinks. He could have Lion with him, even if Boon is a white man. He could ask Major or McCaslin either. And more than that. It was Sam's hand that touched Lion first and Lion knows it.* Then he became a man and he knew that too. It had been all right. That was the way it should have been. Sam was the chief, the prince; Boon, the plebeian, was his huntsman. Boon should have nursed the dogs.

On the first morning that Lion led the pack after Old Ben, seven strangers appeared in the camp. They were swampers: gaunt, malaria-ridden men appearing from nowhere, who ran trap-lines for coons or perhaps farmed little patches of cotton and corn along the edge of the bottom, in clothes but little better than Sam Fathers' and nowhere near as good as Tennie's Jim's, with worn shotguns and rifles, already squatting patiently in the cold drizzle in the side yard when day broke. They had a spokesman; afterward Sam Fathers told Major de Spain how all during the past summer and fall they had drifted into the camp singly or in pairs and threes, to look quietly at Lion for a while and then go away: "Mawnin, Major. We heerd you was aimin to put that ere blue dawg on that old two-toed bear this mawnin. We figgered we'd come up and watch, if you dont mind. We wont do no shooting, lessen he runs over us."

"You are welcome," Major de Spain said. "You are welcome to shoot. He's more your bear than ours."

"I reckon that aint no lie. I done fed him enough cawn to have a sheer in him. Not to mention a shoat three years ago."

"I reckon I got a sheer too," another said. "Only it aint in the bear." Major de Spain looked at him. He was chewing tobacco. He spat. "Hit was a heifer calf. Nice un too. Last year. When I finally found her, I reckon she looked about like that colt of yourn looked last June."

"Oh," Major de Spain said. "Be welcome. If you see game in front of my dogs, shoot it."

Nobody shot Old Ben that day. No man saw him. The dogs jumped him within a hundred yards of the glade where the boy had seen him that day in the summer of his eleventh year. The boy was less than a quarter-mile away. He heard the jump but he could distinguish no voice among the dogs that he did not know and therefore would be Lion's, and he thought, believed, that Lion was not among them. Even the fact that they were going much faster than he had ever heard them run behind Old Ben before and that the high thin note of hysteria was missing now from their voices was not enough to disabuse him. He didn't comprehend until that night, when Sam told him that Lion would never cry on a trail. "He gonter growl when he catches Old Ben's throat," Sam said. "But he aint gonter never holler, no more than he ever done when he was jumping at that two-inch door. It's that blue dog in him. What you call it?"

"Airedale," the boy said.

Lion was there; the jump was just too close to the river. When Boon returned with Lion about eleven that night, he swore that Lion had stopped Old Ben once but that the hounds would not go in and Old Ben broke away and took to the river and swam for miles down it and he and Lion went down one bank for about ten miles and crossed and came up the other but it had begun to get dark before they struck any trail where Old Ben had come up out of the water, unless he was still in the water when he passed the ford where they crossed. Then he fell to cursing the hounds and ate the supper Uncle Ash had saved for him and went off to bed and after a while the boy opened the door of the little stale room thunderous with snoring and the great grave dog raised its head from Boon's pillow and blinked at him for a moment and lowered its head again.

When the next November came and the last day, the day which it was now becoming traditional to save for Old Ben, there were more than a dozen strangers waiting. They were not all swampers this time. Some of them were townsmen, from other county seats like Jefferson, who had heard about Lion and Old Ben and had come to watch the great blue dog keep his yearly rendezvous with the old two-toed bear. Some of them didn't even have guns and the hunting-clothes and boots they wore had been on a store shelf yesterday.

This time Lion jumped Old Ben more than five miles from the river and bayed and held him and this time the hounds went in, in a sort of desperate emulation. The boy heard them; he was that near. He heard Boon whooping; he heard the two shots when General Compson delivered both barrels, one containing five buckshot, the other a single ball, into the bear from as close as he could force his almost unmanageable horse. He heard the dogs when the bear broke free again. He was running now; panting, stumbling, his lungs bursting, he reached the place where General Compson had fired and where Old Ben had killed two of the hounds. He saw the blood from General Compson's shots, but he could go no further. He stopped, leaning against a tree for his breathing to ease and his heart to slow, hearing the sound of the dogs as it faded on and died away.

In camp that night—they had as guests five of the still terrified strangers in new hunting coats and boots who had been lost all day until Sam Fathers went out and got them—he heard the rest of it: how Lion had stopped and held the bear again but only the one-eyed mule which did not mind the smell of wild blood would approach and Boon was riding the mule and Boon had never been known to hit anything. He shot at the bear five times with his pump gun, touching nothing, and Old Ben killed another hound and broke free once more and reached the river and was gone. Again Boon and Lion hunted as far down one bank as they dared. Too far; they crossed in the first of dusk and dark overtook them within a mile. And this time Lion found the broken trail, the blood perhaps, in the darkness where Old Ben had come up out of the water, but Boon had him on a rope, luckily, and he got down from the mule and fought Lion hand-to-hand until he got him back to camp. This time Boon didn't even curse. He stood in the door, muddy, spent, his huge gargoyle's face tragic and still amazed. "I missed him," he said. "I was in twenty-five feet of him and I missed him five times."

"But we have drawn blood," Major de Spain said. "General Compson drew blood. We have never done that before."

"But I missed him," Boon said. "I missed him five times. With Lion looking right at me."

"Never mind," Major de Spain said. "It was a damned fine race. And we drew blood. Next year we'll let General Compson or Walter ride Katie, and we'll get him."

Then McCaslin said, "Where is Lion, Boon?"

"I left him at Sam's," Boon said. He was already turning away. "I aint fit to sleep with him."

So he should have hated and feared Lion. Yet he did not. It seemed to him that there was a fatality in it. It seemed to him that something, he didn't know what, was beginning; had already begun. It was like the last act on a set stage. It was the beginning of the end of something, he didn't know what except that he would not grieve. He would be humble and proud that he had been found worthy to be a part of it too or even just to see it too.

3.

It was December. It was the coldest December he had ever remembered. They had been in camp four days over two weeks, waiting for the weather to soften so that Lion and Old Ben could run their yearly race. Then they would break camp and go home. Because of these unforeseen additional days which they had had to pass waiting on the weather, with nothing to do but play poker, the whisky had given out and he and Boon were being sent to Memphis with a suitcase and a note from Major de Spain to Mr Semmes, the distiller, to get more. That is, Major de Spain and McCaslin were sending Boon to get the whisky and sending him to see that Boon got back with it or most of it or at least some of it.

Tennie's Jim waked him at three. He dressed rapidly, shivering, not so much from the cold because a fresh fire already boomed and roared on the hearth, but in that dead winter hour when the blood and the heart are slow and sleep is incomplete. He crossed the gap between house and kitchen, the gap of iron earth beneath the brilliant and rigid night where dawn would not begin for three hours yet, tasting, tongue palate and to the very bottom of his lungs the searing dark, and entered the kitchen, the lamplit warmth where the stove glowed, fogging the windows, and where Boon already sat at the table at breakfast, hunched over his plate, almost in his plate, his working jaws blue with stubble and his face innocent of water and his coarse, horse-mane hair innocent of comb—the quarter Indian, grandson of a Chickasaw squaw, who on occasion resented with his hard and furious fists the intimation of one single drop of alien blood and on others, usually after whisky, affirmed with the same fists and the same fury that his father had been the full-blood Chickasaw and even a chief and that even his mother had been only half white. He was four inches over six feet; he had the mind of a child, the heart of a horse, and little hard shoe-button eyes without depth or meanness or generosity or viciousness or gentleness or anything else, in the ugliest face the boy had ever seen. It looked like somebody had found a walnut a little larger than a football and with a machinist's hammer had shaped features into it and then painted it, mostly red; not Indian red but a fine bright ruddy color which whisky might have had something to do with but which was mostly just happy and violent out-of-doors, the wrinkles in it not the residue of the forty years it had survived but from squinting into the sun or into the gloom of cane-brakes where game had run, baked into it by the camp fires before which he had lain trying to sleep on the cold November or December ground while waiting for daylight so he could rise and hunt again, as though time were merely something he walked through as he did through air, aging him no more than air did. He was brave, faithful, improvident and unreliable; he had neither profession job nor trade and owned one vice and one virtue: whisky, and that absolute and unquestioning fidelity to Major de Spain and the boy's cousin McCaslin. "Sometimes I'd call them both virtues," Major de Spain said once. "Or both vices," McCaslin said.

He ate his breakfast, hearing the dogs under the kitchen, wakened by the smell of frying meat or perhaps by the feet overhead. He heard Lion once, short and peremptory, as the best hunter in any camp has only to speak once to all save the fools, and none other of Major de Spain's and McCaslin's dogs were Lion's equal in size and strength and perhaps even in courage, but they were not fools; Old Ben had killed the last fool among them last year.

Tennie's Jim came in as they finished. The wagon was outside. Ash decided he would drive them over to the log-line where they would flag the outbound log-train and let Tennie's Jim wash the dishes. The boy knew why. It would not be the first time he had listened to old Ash badgering Boon.

It was cold. The wagon wheels banged and clattered on the frozen ground; the sky was fixed and brilliant. He was not shivering, he was shaking, slow and steady and hard, the food he had just eaten still warm and solid inside him while his outside shook slow and steady around it as though his stomach floated loose. "They wont run this morning," he said. "No dog will have any nose today."

"Cep Lion," Ash said. "Lion dont need no nose. All he need is a bear." He had wrapped his feet in towsacks and he had a quilt from his pallet bed on the kitchen floor drawn over his head and wrapped around him until in the thin brilliant starlight he looked like nothing at all that the boy had ever seen before. "He run a bear through a thousand-acre icehouse. Catch him too. Them other dogs dont matter because they aint going to keep up with Lion nohow, long as he got a bear in front of him."

"What's wrong with the other dogs?" Boon said. "What the hell do you know about it anyway? This is the first time you've had your tail out of that kitchen since we got here except to chop a little wood."

"Aint nothing wrong with them," Ash said. "And long as it's left up to them, aint nothing going to be. I just wish I had knowed all my life how to take care of my health good as them hounds knows."

"Well, they aint going to run this morning," Boon said. His voice was harsh and positive. "Major promised they wouldn't until me and Ike get back."

"Weather gonter break today. Gonter soft up. Rain by night." Then Ash laughed, chuckled, somewhere inside the quilt which concealed even his face. "Hum up here, mules!" he said, jerking the reins so that the mules leaped forward and snatched the lurching and banging wagon for several feet before they slowed again into their quick, short-paced, rapid plodding. "Sides, I like to know why Major need to wait on you. It's Lion he aiming to use. I aint never heard tell of you bringing no bear nor no other kind of meat into this camp."

Now Boon's going to curse Ash or maybe even hit him, the boy thought. But Boon never did, never had; the boy knew he never would even though four years ago Boon had shot five times with a borrowed pistol at a negro on the street in Jefferson, with the same result as when he had shot five times at Old Ben last fall. "By God," Boon said, "he aint going to put Lion or no other dog on nothing until I get back tonight. Because he promised me. Whip up them mules and keep them whipped up. Do you want me to freeze to death?"

They reached the log-line and built a fire. After a while the log-train came up out of the woods under the paling east and Boon flagged it. Then in the warm caboose the boy slept again while Boon and the conductor and brakeman talked about Lion and Old Ben as people later would talk about Sullivan and Kilrain and, later still, about Dempsey and Tunney. Dozing, swaying as the springless caboose lurched and clattered, he would hear them still talking, about the shoats and calves Old Ben had killed and the cribs he had rifled and the traps and deadfalls he had wrecked and the lead he probably carried under his hide—Old Ben, the two-toed bear in a land where bears with trap-ruined feet had been called Two-Toe or Three-Toe or Cripple-Foot for fifty years, only Old

Ben was an extra bear (the head bear, General Compson called him) and so had earned a name such as a human man could have worn and not been sorry.

They reached Hoke's at sunup. They emerged from the warm caboose in their hunting clothes, the muddy boots and stained khaki and Boon's blue unshaven jowls. But that was all right. Hoke's was a sawmill and commissary and two stores and a loading-chute on a sidetrack from the main line, and all the men in it wore boots and khaki too. Presently the Memphis train came. Boon bought three packages of popcorn-and-molasses and a bottle of beer from the news butch and the boy went to sleep again to the sound of his chewing.

But in Memphis it was not all right. It was as if the high buildings and the hard pavements, the fine carriages and the horse cars and the men in starched collars and neckties made their boots and khaki look a little rougher and a little muddier and made Boon's beard look worse and more unshaven and his face look more and more like he should never have brought it out of the woods at all or at least out of reach of Major de Spain or McCaslin or someone who knew it and could have said, "Dont be afraid. He wont hurt you." He walked through the station, on the slick floor, his face moving as he worked the popcorn out of his teeth with his tongue, his legs spraddled and stiff in the hips as if he were walking on buttered glass, and that blue stubble on his face like the filings from a new gun-barrel. They passed the first saloon. Even through the closed doors the boy could seem to smell the sawdust and the reek of old drink. Boon began to cough. He coughed for something less than a minute. "Damn this cold," he said. "I'd sure like to know where I got it."

"Back there in the station," the boy said.

Boon had started to cough again. He stopped. He looked at the boy. "What?" he said.

"You never had it when we left camp nor on the train either." Boon looked at him, blinking. Then he stopped blinking. He didn't cough again. He said quietly:

"Lend me a dollar. Come on. You've got it. If you ever had one, you've still got it. I dont mean you are tight with your money because you aint. You just dont never seem to ever think of nothing you want. When I was sixteen a dollar bill melted off of me before I even had time to read the name of the bank that issued it." He said quietly: "Let me have a dollar, Ike."

"You promised Major. You promised McCaslin. Not till we get back to camp."

"All right," Boon said in that quiet and patient voice. "What can I do on just one dollar? You aint going to lend me another."

"You're damn right I aint," the boy said, his voice quiet too, cold with rage which was not at Boon, remembering: Boon snoring in a hard chair in the kitchen so he could watch the clock and wake him and McCaslin and drive them the seventeen miles in to Jefferson to catch the train to Memphis; the wild, never-bridled Texas paint pony which he had persuaded McCaslin to let him buy and which he and Boon had bought at auction for four dollars and seventy-five cents and fetched home wired between two gentle old mares with pieces of barbed wire and which had never even seen shelled corn before and didn't even know what it was unless the grains were bugs maybe and at last (he was ten and Boon had been ten all his life) Boon said the pony was gentled and with a towsack over its head and four negroes to hold it they backed it into an old two-wheeled cart and hooked up the gear and he and Boon got up and Boon said, "All right, boys. Let him go" and one of the negroes—it was Tennie's Jim—snatched the towsack off and leaped for his life and they lost the first wheel against a post of the open gate only at that moment Boon caught him by the scruff of the neck and flung him into the roadside ditch so he only saw the rest of it in fragments: the other wheel as it slammed through the side gate and crossed the back yard and leaped up onto the gallery and scraps of the cart here and there along the road and Boon vanishing rapidly on his stomach in the leaping and spurting dust and still holding the reins until they broke too and two days later they finally caught the pony seven miles away still wearing the hames and the headstall of the bridle around its neck like a duchess with two necklaces at one time. He gave Boon the dollar.

"All right," Boon said. "Come on in out of the cold."

"I aint cold," he said.

"You can have some lemonade."

"I dont want any lemonade."

The door closed behind him. The sun was well up now. It was a brilliant day, though Ash had said it would rain before night. Already it was warmer; they could run tomorrow. He felt the old lift of the heart, as pristine as ever, as on the first day; he would never lose it, no matter how old in hunting and pursuit: the best, the best of all breathing, the humility and the pride. He must stop thinking about it. Already it seemed to him that he was running, back to the station, to the tracks themselves: the first train going south; he must stop thinking about it. The street was busy. He watched the big Norman draft horses, the Percherons; the trim carriages from which the men in the fine overcoats and the ladies rosy in furs descended and entered the station. (They were still next door to it but one.) Twenty years ago his father had ridden into Memphis as a member of Colonel Sartoris' horse in Forrest's command, up Main street and (the tale told) into the lobby of the Gayoso hotel where the Yankee officers sat in the leather chairs spitting into the tall bright cuspidors and then out again, scot-free——

The door opened behind him. Boon was wiping his mouth on the back of his hand. "All right," he said. "Let's go tend to it and get the hell out of here."

They went and had the suitcase packed. He never knew where or when Boon got the other bottle. Doubtless Mr Semmes gave it to him. When they reached Hoke's again at sundown, it was empty. They could get a return train to Hoke's in two hours; they went straight back to the station as Major de Spain and then McCaslin had told Boon to do and then ordered him to do and had sent the boy along to see that he did. Boon took the first drink from his bottle in the wash-room. A man in a uniform cap came to tell him he couldn't drink there and looked at Boon's face once and said nothing. The next time he was pouring into his water glass beneath the edge of a table in the restaurant when the manager (she was a woman) did tell him he couldn't drink there and he went back to the wash-room. He had been telling the negro waiter and all the other people in the restaurant who couldn't help but hear him and who had never heard of Lion and didn't want to, about Lion and Old Ben. Then he happened to think of the zoo. He had found out that there was another train to Hoke's at three oclock and so they would spend the time at the zoo and take the three oclock train until he came back from the wash-room for the third time. Then they would take the first train back to camp, get Lion and come back to the zoo where, he said, the bears were fed on ice cream and lady fingers and he would match Lion against them all.

So they missed the first train, the one they were supposed to take, but he got Boon onto the three oclock train and they were all right again, with Boon not even going to the wash-room now but drinking in the aisle and talking about Lion and the men he buttonholed no more daring to tell Boon he couldn't drink there than the man in the station had dared.

When they reached Hoke's at sundown, Boon was asleep. The boy waked him at last and got him and the suitcase off the train and he even persuaded him to eat some supper at the saw-mill commissary. So he was all right when they got in the caboose of the log-train to go back into the woods, with the sun going down red and the sky already overcast and the ground would not freeze tonight. It was the boy who slept now, sitting behind the ruby stove while the springless caboose jumped and clattered and Boon and the brakeman and the conductor talked about Lion and Old Ben because they knew what Boon was talking about because this was home. "Overcast and already thawing," Boon said. "Lion will get him tomorrow."

It would have to be Lion, or somebody. It would not be Boon. He had never hit anything bigger than a squirrel that anybody ever knew, except the negro woman that day when he was shooting at the negro man. He was a big negro and not ten feet away but Boon shot five times with the pistol he had borrowed from Major de Spain's negro coachman and the negro he was shooting at outed with a dollar-and-a-half mail-order pistol and would have burned Boon down with it only it never went off, it just went snicksnicksnicksnicksnick five times and Boon still blasting away and he broke a plate glass window that cost McCaslin forty-five dollars and hit a negro woman who happened to be passing in the leg only Major de Spain paid for that; he and McCaslin cut cards, the plate glass window against the negro woman's leg. And the first day on stand this year, the first morning in camp, the buck ran right over Boon; he heard Boon's old pump gun go whow. whow. whow. whow. whow. and then his voice: "God damn, here he comes! Head him! Head him!" and when he got there the buck's tracks and the five exploded shells were not twenty paces apart.

There were five guests in camp that night, from Jefferson: Mr Bayard Sartoris and his son and General Compson's son and two others. And the next morning he looked out the window, into the gray thin drizzle of daybreak which Ash had predicted, and there they were, standing and squatting beneath the thin rain, almost two dozen of them who had fed Old Ben corn and shoats and even calves for ten years, in their worn hats and hunting coats and overalls which any town negro would have thrown away or burned and only the rubber boots strong and sound, and the worn and blueless guns and some even without guns. While they ate breakfast a dozen more arrived, mounted and on foot: loggers from the camp thirteen miles below and sawmill men from Hoke's and the only gun among them that one which the log-train conductor carried: so that when they went into the woods this morning Major de Spain led a party almost as strong, excepting that some of them were not armed, as some he had led in the last darkening days of '64 and '65. The little yard would not hold them. They overflowed it, into the lane where Major de Spain sat his mare while Ash in his dirty apron thrust the greasy cartridges into his carbine and passed it up to him and the great grave blue dog stood at his stirrup not as a dog stands but as a horse stands, blinking his sleepy topaz eyes at nothing, deaf even to the yelling of the hounds which Boon and Tennie's Jim held on leash.

"We'll put General Compson on Katie this morning," Major de Spain said. "He drew blood last year; if he'd had a mule then that would have stood, he would have——"

"No," General Compson said. "I'm too old to go helling through the woods on a mule or a horse or anything else anymore. Besides, I had my chance last year and missed it. I'm going on a stand this morning. I'm going to let that boy ride Katie."

"No; wait," McCaslin said. "Ike's got the rest of his life to hunt bears in. Let somebody else——"

"No," General Compson said. "I want Ike to ride Katie. He's already a better woodsman than you or me either and in another ten years he'll be as good as Walter."

At first he couldn't believe it, not until Major de Spain spoke to him. Then he was up, on the one-eyed mule which would not spook at wild blood, looking down at the dog motionless at Major de Spain's stirrup, looking in the gray streaming light bigger than a calf, bigger than he knew it actually was—the big head, the chest almost as big as his own, the blue hide beneath which the muscles flinched or quivered to no touch since the heart which drove blood to them loved no man and no thing, standing as a horse stands yet different from a horse which infers only weight and speed while Lion inferred not only courage and all else that went to make up the will and desire to pursue and kill, but endurance, the will and desire to endure beyond all imaginable limits of flesh in order to overtake and slay. Then the dog looked at him. It moved its head and looked at him across the trivial uproar of the hounds, out of the yellow eyes as depthless as Boon's, as free as Boon's of meanness or generosity or gentleness or viciousness. They were just cold and sleepy. Then it blinked, and he knew it was not looking at him and never had been, without even bothering to turn its head away.

That morning he heard the first cry. Lion had already vanished while Sam and Tennie's Jim were putting saddles on the mule and horse which had drawn the wagon and he watched the hounds as they crossed and cast, snuffing and whimpering, until they too disappeared. Then he and Major de Spain and Sam and Tennie's Jim rode after them and heard the first cry out of the wet and thawing woods not two hundred yards ahead, high, with that abject, almost human quality he had come to know, and the other hounds joining in until the gloomed woods rang and clamored. They rode then. It seemed to him that he could actually see the big blue dog boring on, silent, and the bear too: the thick, locomotive-like shape which he had seen that day four years ago crossing the blow-down, crashing on ahead of the dogs faster than he had believed it could have moved, drawing away even from the running mules. He heard a shotgun, once. The woods had opened, they were going fast, the clamor faint and fading on ahead; they passed the man who had fired—a swamper, a pointing arm, a gaunt face, the small black orifice of his yelling studded with rotten teeth.

He heard the changed note in the hounds' uproar and two hundred yards ahead he saw them. The bear had turned. He saw Lion drive in without pausing and saw the bear strike him aside and lunge into the yelling hounds and kill one of them almost in its tracks and whirl and run again. Then they were in a streaming tide of dogs. He heard Major de Spain and Tennie's Jim shouting and the pistol sound of Tennie's Jim's leather thong as he tried to turn them. Then he and Sam Fathers were riding alone. One of the hounds had kept on with Lion though. He recognised its voice. It was the young hound which even a year ago had had no judgment and which, by the lights of the other hounds anyway, still had none. *Maybe that's what courage is*, he thought. "Right," Sam said behind him. "Right. We got to turn him from the river if we can."

Now they were in cane: a brake. He knew the path through it as well as Sam did. They came out of the undergrowth and struck the entrance almost exactly. It would traverse the brake and come out onto a high open ridge above the river. He heard the flat clap of Walter Ewell's rifle, then two more. "No," Sam said. "I can hear the hound. Go on."

They emerged from the narrow roofless tunnel of snapping and hissing cane, still galloping, onto the open ridge below which the thick yellow river, reflectionless in the gray and streaming light, seemed not to move. Now he could hear the hound too. It was not running. The cry was a high frantic yapping and Boon was running along the edge of the bluff, his old gun leaping and jouncing against his back on its sling made of a piece of cotton plowline. He whirled and ran up to them, wild-faced, and flung himself onto the mule behind the boy. "That damn boat!" he cried. "It's on the other side! He went straight across! Lion was too close to him! That little hound too! Lion was so close I couldn't shoot! Go on!" he cried, beating his heels into the mule's flanks. "Go on!"

They plunged down the bank, slipping and sliding in the thawed earth, crashing through the willows and into the water. He felt no shock, no cold, he on one side of the swimming mule, grasping the pommel with one hand and holding his gun above the water with the other, Boon opposite him. Sam was behind them somewhere, and then the river, the water about them, was full of dogs. They swam faster than the mules; they were scrabbling up the bank before the mules touched bottom. Major de Spain was whooping from the bank they had just left and, looking back, he saw Tennie's Jim and the horse as they went into the water.

Now the woods ahead of them and the rain-heavy air were one uproar. It rang and clamored; it echoed and broke against the bank behind them and reformed and clamored and rang until it seemed to the boy that all the hounds which had ever bayed game in this land were yelling down at him. He got his leg over the mule as it came up out of the water. Boon didn't try to mount again. He grasped one stirrup as they went up the bank and crashed through the undergrowth which fringed the bluff and saw the bear, on its hind feet, its back against a tree while the bellowing hounds swirled around it and once more Lion drove in, leaping clear of the ground.

This time the bear didn't strike him down. It caught the dog in both arms, almost loverlike, and they both went down. He was off the mule now. He drew back both hammers of the gun but he could see nothing but moiling spotted hound-bodies until the bear surged up again. Boon was yelling something, he could not tell what; he could see Lion still clinging to the bear's throat and he saw the bear, half erect, strike one of the hounds with one paw and hurl it five or six feet and then, rising and rising as though it would never stop, stand erect again and begin to rake at Lion's belly with its forepaws. Then Boon was running. The boy saw the gleam of the blade in his hand and watched him leap among the hounds, hurdling them, kicking them aside as he ran, and fling himself astride the bear as he had hurled himself onto the mule, his legs locked around the bear's belly, his left arm under the bear's throat where Lion clung, and the glint of the knife as it rose and fell.

It fell just once. For an instant they almost resembled a piece of statuary: the clinging dog, the bear, the man astride its back, working and probing the buried blade. Then they went down, pulled over backward by Boon's weight, Boon underneath. It was the bear's back which reappeared first but at once Boon was astride it again. He had never released the knife and again the boy saw the almost infinitesimal movement of his arm and shoulder as he probed and sought; then the bear surged erect, raising with it the man and the dog too, and turned and still carrying the man and the dog it took two or three steps toward the woods on its hind feet as a man would have walked and crashed down. It didn't collapse, crumple. It fell all of a piece, as a tree falls, so that all three of them, man dog and bear, seemed to bounce once.

He and Tennie's Jim ran forward. Boon was kneeling at the bear's head. His left ear was shredded, his left coat sleeve was completely gone, his right boot had been ripped from knee to instep; the bright blood thinned in the thin rain down his leg and hand and arm and down the side of his face which was no longer wild but was quite calm. Together they prized Lion's jaws from the bear's throat. "Easy, goddamn it," Boon said. "Cant you see his guts are all out of him?" He began to remove his coat. He spoke to Tennie's Jim in that calm voice: "Bring the boat up. It's about a hundred yards down the bank there. I saw it." Tennie's Jim rose and went away. Then, and he could not remember if it had been a call or an exclamation from Tennie's Jim or if he had glanced up by chance, he saw Tennie's Jim stooping and saw Sam Fathers lying motionless on his face in the trampled mud.

The mule had not thrown him. He remembered that Sam was down too even before Boon began to run. There was no mark on him whatever and when he and Boon turned him over, his eyes were open and he said something in that tongue which he and Joe Baker had used to speak together. But he couldn't move. Tennie's Jim brought the skiff up; they could hear him shouting to Major de Spain across the river. Boon wrapped Lion in his hunting coat and carried him down to the skiff and they carried Sam down and returned and hitched the bear to the one-eyed mule's saddle-bow with Tennie's Jim's leash-thong and dragged him down to the skiff and got him into it and left Tennie's Jim to swim the horse and the two mules back across. Major de Spain caught the bow of the skiff as Boon jumped out and past him before it touched the bank. He looked at Old Ben and said quietly: "Well." Then he walked into the water and leaned down and touched Sam and Sam looked up at him and said something in that old tongue he and Joe Baker spoke. "You dont know what happened?" Major de Spain said.

"No, sir," the boy said. "It wasn't the mule. It wasn't anything. He was off the mule when Boon ran in on the bear. Then we looked up and he was lying on the ground." Boon was shouting at Tennie's Jim, still in the middle of the river.

"Come on, goddamn it!" he said. "Bring me that mule!"

"What do you want with a mule?" Major de Spain said.

Boon didn't even look at him. "I'm going to Hoke's to get the doctor," he said in that calm voice, his face quite calm beneath the steady thinning of the bright blood.

"You need a doctor yourself," Major de Spain said. "Tennie's Jim——"

"Damn that," Boon said. He turned on Major de Spain. His face was still calm, only his voice was a pitch higher. "Cant you see his goddamn guts are all out of him?"

"Boon!" Major de Spain said. They looked at one another. Boon was a good head taller than Major de Spain; even the boy was taller now than Major de Spain.

"I've got to get the doctor," Boon said. "His goddamn guts——"

"All right," Major de Spain said. Tennie's Jim came up out of the water. The horse and the sound mule had already scented Old Ben; they surged and plunged all the way up to the top of the bluff, dragging Tennie's Jim with them, before he could stop them and tie them and come back. Major de Spain unlooped the leather thong of his compass from his buttonhole and gave it to Tennie's Jim. "Go straight to Hoke's," he said. "Bring Doctor Crawford back with you. Tell him there are two men to be looked at. Take my mare. Can you find the road from here?"

"Yes, sir," Tennie's Jim said.

"All right," Major de Spain said. "Go on." He turned to the boy. "Take the mules and the horse and go back and get the wagon. We'll go on down the river in the boat to Coon bridge. Meet us there. Can you find it again?"

"Yes, sir," the boy said.

"All right. Get started."

He went back to the wagon. He realised then how far they had run. It was already afternoon when he put the mules into the traces and tied the horse's lead-rope to the tail-gate. He reached Coon bridge at dusk. The skiff was already there. Before he could see it and almost before he could see the water he had to leap from the tilting wagon, still holding the reins, and work around to where he could grasp the bit and then the ear of the plunging sound mule and dig his heels and hold it until Boon came up the bank. The rope of the led horse had already snapped and it had already disappeared up the road toward camp. They turned the wagon around and took the mules out and he led the sound mule a hundred yards up the road and tied it. Boon had already brought Lion up to the wagon and Sam was sitting up in the skiff now and when they raised him he tried to walk, up the bank and to the wagon and he tried to climb into the wagon but Boon did not wait; he picked Sam up bodily and set him on the seat. Then they hitched Old Ben to the one-eyed mule's saddle again and dragged him up the bank and set two skid-poles into the open tail-gate and got him into the wagon and he went and got the sound mule and Boon fought it into the traces, striking it across its hard hollow-sounding face until it came into position and stood trembling. Then the rain came down, as though it had held off all day waiting on them.

They returned to camp through it, through the streaming and sightless dark, hearing long before they saw any light the horn and the spaced shots to guide them. When they came to Sam's dark little hut he tried to stand up. He spoke again in the tongue of the old fathers; then he said clearly: "Let me out. Let me out."

"He hasn't got any fire," Major said. "Go on!" he said sharply.

But Sam was struggling now, trying to stand up. "Let me out, master," he said. "Let me go home."

So he stopped the wagon and Boon got down and lifted Sam out. He did not wait to let Sam try to walk this time. He carried him into the hut and Major de Spain got light on a paper spill from the buried embers on the hearth and lit the lamp and Boon put Sam on his bunk and drew off his boots and Major de Spain covered him and the boy was not there, he was holding the mules, the sound one which was trying again to bolt since when the wagon stopped Old Ben's scent drifted forward again along the streaming blackness of air, but Sam's eyes were probably open again on that profound look which saw further than them or the hut, further than the death of a bear and the dying of a dog. Then they went on, toward the long wailing of the horn and the shots which seemed each to linger intact somewhere in the thick streaming air until the next spaced report joined and blended with it, to the lighted house, the bright streaming windows, the quiet faces as Boon entered, bloody and quite calm, carrying the bundled coat. He laid Lion, blood coat and all, on his stale sheetless pallet bed which not even Ash, as deft in the house as a woman, could ever make smooth.

The sawmill doctor from Hoke's was already there. Boon would not let the doctor touch him until he had seen to Lion. He wouldn't risk giving Lion chloroform. He put the entrails back and sewed him up without it while Major de Spain held his head and Boon his feet. But he never tried to move. He lay there, the yellow eyes open upon nothing while the quiet men in the new hunting clothes and in the old ones crowded into the little airless room rank with the smell of Boon's body and garments, and watched. Then the doctor cleaned and disinfected Boon's face and arm and leg and bandaged them and, the boy in front with a lantern and the doctor and McCaslin and Major de Spain and General Compson following, they went to Sam Fathers' hut. Tennie's Jim had built up the fire; he squatted before it, dozing. Sam had not moved since Boon had put him in the bunk and Major de Spain had covered him with the blankets, yet he opened his eyes and looked from one to another of the faces and when McCaslin touched his shoulder and said, "Sam. The doctor wants to look at you," he even drew his hands out of the blanket and began to fumble at his shirt buttons until McCaslin said, "Wait. We'll do it." They undressed him. He lay there—the copper-brown, almost hairless body, the old man's body, the old man, the wild man not even one generation from the woods, childless, kinless, peopleless—motionless, his eyes open but no longer looking at any of them, while the doctor examined him and drew the blankets up and put the stethoscope back into his bag and snapped the bag and only the boy knew that Sam too was going to die.

"Exhaustion," the doctor said. "Shock maybe. A man his age swimming rivers in December. He'll be all right. Just make him stay in bed for a day or two. Will there be somebody here with him?"

"There will be somebody here," Major de Spain said.

They went back to the house, to the rank little room where Boon still sat on the pallet bed with Lion's head under his hand while the men, the ones who had hunted behind Lion and the ones who had never seen him before today, came quietly in to look at him and went away. Then it was dawn and they all went out into the yard to look at Old Ben, with his eyes open too and his lips snarled back from his worn teeth and his mutilated foot and the little hard lumps under his skin which were the old bullets (there were fifty-two of them, buckshot rifle and ball) and the single almost invisible slit under his left shoulder where Boon's blade had finally found his life. Then Ash began to beat on the bottom of the dishpan with a heavy spoon to call them to breakfast and it was the first time he could remember hearing no sound from the dogs under the kitchen while they were eating. It was as if the old bear, even dead there in the yard, was a more potent terror still than they could face without Lion between them.

The rain had stopped during the night. By midmorning the thin sun appeared, rapidly burning away mist and cloud, warming the air and the earth; it would be one of those windless Mississippi December days which are a sort of Indian summer's Indian summer. They moved Lion out to the front gallery, into the sun. It was Boon's idea. "Goddamn it," he said, "he never did want to stay in the house until I made him. You know that." He took a crowbar and loosened the floor boards under his pallet bed so it could be raised, mattress and all, without disturbing Lion's position, and they carried him out to the gallery and put him down facing the woods.

Then he and the doctor and McCaslin and Major de Spain went to Sam's hut. This time Sam didn't open his eyes and his breathing was so quiet, so peaceful that they could hardly see that he breathed. The doctor didn't even take out his stethoscope nor even touch him. "He's all right," the doctor said. "He didn't even catch cold. He just quit."

"Quit?" McCaslin said.

"Yes. Old people do that sometimes. Then they get a good night's sleep or maybe it's just a drink of whisky, and they change their minds."

They returned to the house. And then they began to arrive—the swamp-dwellers, the gaunt men who ran trap-lines and lived on quinine and coons and river water, the farmers of little corn- and cotton-patches along the bottom's edge whose fields and cribs and pig-pens the old bear had rifled, the loggers from the camp and the sawmill men from Hoke's and the town men from further away than that, whose hounds the old bear had slain and traps and deadfalls he had wrecked and whose lead he carried. They came up mounted and on foot and in wagons, to enter the yard and look at him and then go on to the front where Lion lay, filling the little yard and overflowing it until there was almost a hundred of them squatting and standing in the warm and drowsing sunlight, talking quietly of hunting, of the game and the dogs which ran it, of hounds and bear and deer and men of yesterday vanished from the earth, while from time to time the great blue dog would open his eyes, not as if he were listening to them but as though to look at the woods for a moment before closing his eyes again, to remember the woods or to see that they were still there. He died at sundown.

Major de Spain broke camp that night. They carried Lion into the woods, or Boon carried him that is, wrapped in a quilt from his bed, just as he had refused to let anyone else touch Lion yesterday until the doctor got there; Boon carrying Lion, and the boy and General Compson and Walter and still almost fifty of them following with lanterns and lighted pine-knots—men from Hoke's and even further, who would have to ride out of the bottom in the dark, and swampers and trappers who would have to walk even, scattering toward the little hidden huts where they lived. And Boon would let nobody else dig the grave either and lay Lion in it and cover him and then General Compson stood at the head of it while the blaze and smoke of the pine-knots streamed away among the winter branches and spoke as he would have spoken over a man. Then they returned to camp. Major de Spain and McCaslin and Ash had rolled and tied all the bedding. The mules were hitched to the wagon and pointed out of the bottom and the wagon was already loaded and the stove in the kitchen was cold and the table was set with scraps of cold food and bread and only the coffee was hot when the boy ran into the kitchen where Major de Spain and McCaslin had already eaten. "What?" he cried. "What? I'm not going."

"Yes," McCaslin said, "we're going out tonight. Major wants to get on back home."

"No!" he said. "I'm going to stay."

"You've got to be back in school Monday. You've already missed a week more than I intended. It will take you from now until Monday to catch up. Sam's all right. You heard Doctor Crawford. I'm going to leave Boon and Tennie's Jim both to stay with him until he feels like getting up."

He was panting. The others had come in. He looked rapidly and almost frantically around at the other faces. Boon had a fresh bottle. He upended it and started the cork by striking the bottom of the bottle with the heel of his hand and drew the cork with his teeth and spat it out and drank. "You're damn right you're going back to school," Boon said. "Or I'll burn the tail off of you myself if Cass dont, whether you are sixteen or sixty. Where in hell do you expect to get without education? Where would Cass be? Where in hell would I be if I hadn't never went to school?"

He looked at McCaslin again. He could feel his breath coming shorter and shorter and shallower and shallower, as if there were not enough air in the kitchen for that many to breathe. "This is just Thursday. I'll come home Sunday night on one of the horses. I'll come home Sunday, then. I'll make up the time I lost studying Sunday night. McCaslin," he said, without even despair.

"No, I tell you," McCaslin said. "Sit down here and eat your supper. We're going out to——"

"Hold up, Cass," General Compson said. The boy did not know General Compson had moved until he put his hand on his shoulder. "What is it, bud?" he said.

"I've got to stay," he said. "I've got to."

"All right," General Compson said. "You can stay. If missing an extra week of school is going to throw you so far behind you'll have to sweat to find out what some hired pedagogue put between the covers of a book, you better quit altogether.—And you shut up, Cass," he said, though McCaslin had not spoken. "You've got one foot straddled into a farm and the other foot straddled into a bank; you aint even got a good hand-hold where this boy was already an old man long before you damned Sartorises and Edmondses invented farms and banks to keep yourselves from having to find out what this boy was born knowing and fearing too maybe but without being afraid, that could go ten miles on a compass because he wanted to look at a bear none of us had ever got near enough to put a bullet in and looked at the bear and came the ten miles back on the compass in the dark; maybe by God that's the why and the wherefore of farms and banks.—I reckon you still aint going to tell what it is?"

But still he could not. "I've got to stay," he said.

"All right," General Compson said. "There's plenty of grub left. And you'll come home Sunday, like you promised McCaslin? Not Sunday night: Sunday."

"Yes, sir," he said.

"All right," General Compson said. "Sit down and eat, boys," he said. "Let's get started. It's going to be cold before we get home."

They ate. The wagon was already loaded and ready to depart; all they had to do was to get into it. Boon would drive them out to the road, to the farmer's stable where the surrey had been left. He stood beside the wagon, in silhouette on the sky, turbaned like a Paythan and taller than any there, the bottle tilted. Then he flung the bottle from his lips without even lowering it, spinning and glinting in the faint starlight, empty. "Them that's going," he said, "get in the goddamn wagon. Them that aint, get out of the goddamn way." The others got in. Boon mounted to the seat beside General Compson and the wagon moved, on into the obscurity until the boy could no longer see it, even the moving density of it amid the greater night. But he could still hear it, for a long while: the slow, deliberate banging of the wooden frame as it lurched from rut to rut. And he could hear Boon even when he could no longer hear the wagon. He was singing, harsh, tuneless, loud.

That was Thursday. On Saturday morning Tennie's Jim left on McCaslin's woods-horse which had not been out of the bottom one time now in six years, and late that afternoon rode through the gate on the spent horse and on to the commissary where McCaslin was rationing the tenants and the wage-hands for the coming week, and this time McCaslin forestalled any necessity or risk of having to wait while Major de Spain's surrey was being horsed and harnessed. He took their own, and with Tennie's Jim already asleep in the back seat he drove in to Jefferson and waited while Major de Spain changed to boots and put on his overcoat, and they drove the thirty miles in the dark of that night and at daybreak on Sunday morning they swapped to the waiting mare and mule and as the sun rose they rode out of the jungle and onto the low ridge where they had buried Lion: the low mound of unannealed earth where Boon's spade-marks still showed and beyond the grave the platform of freshly cut saplings bound between four posts and the blanket-wrapped bundle upon the platform and Boon and the boy squatting between the platform and the grave until Boon, the bandage removed, ripped, from his head so that the long scoriations of Old Ben's claws resembled crusted tar in the sunlight, sprang up and threw down upon them with the old gun with which he had never been known to hit anything although McCaslin was already off the mule, kicked both feet free of the irons and vaulted down before the mule had stopped, walking toward Boon.

"Stand back," Boon said. "By God, you wont touch him. Stand back, McCaslin." Still McCaslin came on, fast yet without haste.

"Cass!" Major de Spain said. Then he said "Boon! You, Boon!" and he was down too and the boy rose too, quickly, and still McCaslin came on not fast but steady and walked up to the grave and reached his hand steadily out, quickly yet still not fast, and took hold of the gun by the middle so that he and Boon faced one another across Lion's grave, both holding the gun, Boon's spent indomitable amazed and frantic face almost a head higher than McCaslin's beneath the black scoriations of beast's claws and then Boon's chest began to heave as though there were not enough air in all the woods, in all the wilderness, for all of them, for him and anyone else, even for him alone.

"Turn it loose, Boon," McCaslin said.

"You damn little spindling——" Boon said. "Dont you know I can take it away from you? Dont you know I can tie it around your neck like a damn cravat?"

"Yes," McCaslin said. "Turn it loose, Boon."

"This is the way he wanted it. He told us. He told us exactly how to do it. And by God you aint going to move him. So we did it like he said, and I been sitting here ever since to keep the damn wildcats and varmints away from him and by God——" Then McCaslin had the gun, downslanted while he pumped the slide, the five shells snicking out of it so fast that the last one was almost out before the first one touched the ground and McCaslin dropped the gun behind him without once having taken his eyes from Boon's.

"Did you kill him, Boon?" he said. Then Boon moved. He turned, he moved like he was still drunk and then for a moment blind too, one hand out as he blundered toward the big tree and seemed to stop walking before he reached the tree so that he plunged, fell toward it, flinging up both hands and catching himself against the tree and turning until his back was against it, backing with the tree's trunk his wild spent scoriated face and the tremendous heave and collapse of his chest, McCaslin following, facing him again, never once having moved his eyes from Boon's eyes. "Did you kill him, Boon?"

"No!" Boon said. "No!"

"Tell the truth," McCaslin said. "I would have done it if he had asked me to." Then the boy moved. He was between them, facing McCaslin; the water felt as if it had burst and sprung not from his eyes alone but from his whole face, like sweat.

"Leave him alone!" he cried. "Goddamn it! Leave him alone!"

4.

then he was twenty-one. He could say it, himself and his cousin juxtaposed not against the wilderness but against the tamed land which was to have been his heritage, the land which old Carothers McCaslin his grandfather had bought with white man's money from the wild men whose grandfathers without guns hunted it, and tamed and ordered or believed he had tamed and ordered it for the reason that the human beings he held in bondage and in the power of life and death had removed the forest from it and in their sweat scratched the surface of it to a depth of perhaps fourteen inches in order to grow something out of it which had not been there before and which could be translated back into the money he who believed he had bought it had had to pay to get it and hold it and a reasonable profit too: and for which reason old Carothers McCaslin, knowing better, could raise his children, his descendants and heirs, to believe the land was his to hold and bequeath since the strong and ruthless man has a cynical foreknowledge of his own vanity and pride and strength and a contempt for all his get: just as, knowing better, Major de Spain and his fragment of that wilderness which was bigger and older than any recorded deed: just as, knowing better, old Thomas Sutpen, from whom Major de Spain had had his fragment for money: just as Ikkemotubbe, the Chickasaw chief from whom Thomas Sutpen had had the fragment for money or rum or whatever it was, knew in his turn that not even a fragment of it had been his to relinquish or sell

not against the wilderness but against the land, not in pursuit and lust but in relinquishment, and in the commissary as it should have been, not the heart perhaps but certainly the solar-plexus of the repudiated and relinquished: the square, galleried, wooden building squatting like a portent above the fields whose laborers it still held in thrall '65 or no and placarded over with advertisements for snuff and cures for chills and salves and potions manufactured and sold by white men to bleach the pigment and straighten the hair of negroes that they might resemble the very race which for two hundred years had held them in bondage and from which for another hundred years not even a bloody civil war would have set them completely free

himself and his cousin amid the old smells of cheese and salt meat and kerosene and harness, the ranked shelves of tobacco and overalls and bottled medicine and thread and plow-bolts, the barrels and kegs of flour and meal and molasses and nails, the wall pegs dependant with plowlines and plow-collars and hames and trace-chains, and the desk and the shelf above it on which rested the ledgers in which McCaslin recorded the slow outward trickle of food and supplies and equipment which returned each fall as cotton made and ginned and sold (two threads frail as truth and impalpable as equators yet cable-strong to bind for life them who made the cotton to the land their sweat fell on), and the older ledgers clumsy and archaic in size and shape, on the yellowed pages of which were recorded in the faded hand of his father Theophilus and his uncle Amodeus during the two decades before the Civil War, the manumission in title at least of Carothers McCaslin's slaves:

'Relinquish,' McCaslin said. 'Relinquish. You, the direct male descendant of him who saw the opportunity and took it, bought the land, took the land, got the land no matter how, held it to bequeath, no matter how, out of the old grant, the first patent, when it was a wilderness of wild beasts and wilder men, and cleared it, translated it into something to bequeath to his children, worthy of bequeathment for his descendants' ease and security and pride and to perpetuate his name and accomplishments. Not only the male descendant but the only and last descendant in the male line and in the third generation, while I am not only four generations from old Carothers, I derived through a woman and the very McCaslin in my name is mine only by sufferance and courtesy and my grandmother's pride in what that man accomplished whose legacy and monument you think you can repudiate.' and he

'I cant repudiate it. It was never mine to repudiate. It was never Father's and Uncle Buddy's to bequeath me to repudiate because it was never Grandfather's to bequeath them to bequeath me to repudiate because it was never old Ikkemotubbe's to sell to Grandfather for bequeathment and repudiation. Because it was never Ikkemotubbe's fathers' fathers' to bequeath Ikkemotubbe to sell to Grandfather or any man because on the instant when Ikkemotubbe discovered, realised, that he could sell it for money, on that instant it ceased ever to have been his forever, father to father to father, and the man who bought it bought nothing.'

'Bought nothing?' and he

'Bought nothing. Because He told in the Book how He created the earth, made it and looked at it and said it was all right, and then He made man. He made the earth first and peopled it with dumb creatures, and then He created man to be His overseer on the earth and to hold suzerainty over the earth and the animals on it in His name, not to hold for himself and his descendants inviolable title forever, generation after generation, to the oblongs and squares of the earth, but to hold the earth mutual and intact in the communal anonymity of brotherhood, and all the fee He asked was pity and humility and sufferance and endurance and the sweat of his face for bread. And I know what you are going to say,' he said: 'That nevertheless Grandfather——' and McCaslin

'——did own it. And not the first. Not alone and not the first since, as your Authority states, man was dispossessed of Eden. Nor yet the second and still not alone, on down through the tedious and shabby chronicle of His chosen sprung from Abraham, and of the sons of them who dispossessed Abraham, and of the five hundred years during which half the known world and all it contained was chattel to one city as this plantation and all the life it contained was chattel and revokeless thrall to this commissary store and those ledgers yonder during your grandfather's life, and the next thousand years while men fought over the fragments of that collapse until at last even the fragments were exhausted and men snarled over the gnawed bones of the old world's worthless evening until an accidental egg discovered to them a new hemisphere. So let me say it: That nevertheless and notwithstanding old Carothers did own it. Bought it, got it, no matter; kept it, held it, no matter; bequeathed it: else why do you stand here relinquishing and repudiating? Held it, kept it for fifty years until you could repudiate it, while He—this Arbiter, this Architect, this Umpire—condoned——or did He? looked down and saw——or did He? Or at least did nothing: saw, and could not, or did not see; saw, and would not, or perhaps He would not see——perverse, impotent, or blind: which?' and he

'Dispossessed.' and McCaslin

'What?' and he

'Dispossessed. Not impotent: He didn't condone; not blind, because He watched it. And let me say it. Dispossessed of Eden. Dispossessed of Canaan, and those who dispossessed Him dispossessed Him dispossessed, and the five hundred years of absentee landlords in the Roman bagnios, and the thousand years of wild men from the northern woods who dispossessed them and devoured their ravished substance ravished in turn again and then snarled in what you call the old world's worthless twilight over the old world's gnawed bones, blasphemous in His name until He used a simple egg to discover to them a new world where a nation of people could be founded in humility and pity and sufferance and pride of one to another. And Grandfather did own the land nevertheless and notwithstanding because He permitted it, not impotent and not condoning and not blind because He ordered and watched it. He saw the land already accursed even as Ikkemotubbe and Ikkemotubbe's father old Issetibbeha and old Issetibbeha's fathers too held it, already tainted even before any white man owned it by what Grandfather and his kind, his fathers, had brought into the new land which He had vouchsafed them out of pity and sufferance, on condition of pity and humility and sufferance and endurance, from that old world's corrupt and worthless twilight as though in the sailfuls of the old world's tainted wind which drove the ships——' and McCaslin

'Ah.'

'——and no hope for the land anywhere so long as Ikkemotubbe and Ikkemotubbe's descendants held it in unbroken succession. Maybe He saw that only by voiding the land for a time of Ikkemotubbe's blood and substituting for it another blood, could He accomplish His purpose. Maybe He knew already what that other blood would be, maybe it was more than justice that only the white man's blood was available and capable to raise the white man's curse, more than vengeance when——' and McCaslin

'Ah.'

'——when He used the blood which had brought in the evil to destroy the evil as doctors use fever to burn up fever, poison to slay poison. Maybe He chose Grandfather out of all of them He might have picked. Maybe He knew that Grandfather himself would not serve His purpose because Grandfather was born too soon too, but that Grandfather would have descendants, the right descendants; maybe He had foreseen already the descendants Grandfather would have, maybe He saw already in Grandfather the seed progenitive of the three generations He saw it would take to set at least some of His lowly people free——' and McCaslin

'The sons of Ham. You who quote the Book: the sons of Ham.' and he

'There are some things He said in the Book, and some things reported of Him that He did not say. And I know what you will say now: That if truth is one thing to me and another thing to you, how will we choose which is truth? You dont need to choose. The heart already knows. He didn't have His Book written to be read by what must elect and choose, but by the heart, not by the wise of the earth because maybe they dont need it or maybe the wise no longer have any heart, but by the doomed and lowly of the earth who have nothing else to read with but the heart. Because the men who wrote His Book for Him were writing about truth and there is only one truth and it covers all things that touch the heart.' and McCaslin

'So these men who transcribed His Book for Him were sometime liars.' and he

'Yes. Because they were human men. They were trying to write down the heart's truth out of the heart's driving complexity, for all the complex and troubled hearts which would beat after them. What they were trying to tell, what He wanted said, was too simple. Those for whom they transcribed His words could not have believed them. It had to be expounded in the everyday terms which they were familiar with and could comprehend, not only those who listened but those who told it too, because if they who were that near to Him as to have been elected from among all who breathed and spoke language to transcribe and relay His words, could comprehend truth only through the complexity of passion and lust and hate and fear which drives the heart, what distance back to truth must they traverse whom truth could only reach by word-of-mouth?' and McCaslin

'I might answer that, since you have taken to proving your

points and disproving mine by the same text, I dont know. But I dont say that, because you have answered yourself: No time at all if, as you say, the heart knows truth, the infallible and unerring heart. And perhaps you are right, since although you admitted three generations from old Carothers to you, there were not three. There were not even completely two. Uncle Buck and Uncle Buddy. And they not the first and not alone. A thousand other Bucks and Buddies in less than two generations and sometimes less than one in this land which so you claim God created and man himself cursed and tainted. Not to mention 1865.' and he

'Yes. More men than Father and Uncle Buddy,' not even glancing toward the shelf above the desk, nor did McCaslin. They did not need to. To him it was as though the ledgers in their scarred cracked leather bindings were being lifted down one by one in their fading sequence and spread open on the desk or perhaps upon some apocryphal Bench or even Altar or perhaps before the Throne Itself for a last perusal and contemplation and refreshment of the Allknowledgeable before the yellowed pages and the brown thin ink in which was recorded the injustice and a little at least of its amelioration and restitution faded back forever into the anonymous communal original dust

the yellowed pages scrawled in fading ink by the hand first of his grandfather and then of his father and uncle, bachelors up to and past fifty and then sixty, the one who ran the plantation and the farming of it and the other who did the housework and the cooking and continued to do it even after his twin married and the boy himself was born

the two brothers who as soon as their father was buried moved out of the tremendously-conceived, the almost barnlike edifice which he had not even completed, into a one-room log cabin which the two of them built themselves and added other rooms to while they lived in it, refusing to allow any slave to touch any timber of it other than the actual raising into place the logs which two men alone could not handle, and domiciled all the slaves in the big house some of the windows of which were still merely boarded up with odds and ends of plank or with the skins of bear and deer nailed over the empty frames: each sundown the brother who superintended the farming would parade the negroes as a first sergeant dismisses a company, and herd them willynilly, man woman and child, without question protest or recourse, into the tremendous abortive edifice scarcely yet out of embryo, as if even old Carothers McCaslin had paused aghast at the concrete indication of his own vanity's boundless conceiving: he would call his mental roll and herd them in and with a hand-wrought nail as long as a flenching-knife and suspended from a short deer-hide thong attached to the door-jamb for that purpose, he would nail to the door of that house which lacked half its windows and had no hinged back door at all, so that presently and for fifty years afterward, when the boy himself was big enough to hear and remember it, there was in the land a sort of folk-tale: of the countryside all night long full of skulking McCaslin slaves dodging the moonlit roads and the Patrol-riders to visit other plantations, and of the unspoken gentlemen's agreement between the two white men and the two dozen black ones that, after the white man had counted them and driven the home-made nail into the front door at sundown, neither of the white men would go around behind the house and look at the back door, provided that all the negroes were behind the front one when the brother who drove it drew out the nail again at daybreak

the twins who were identical even in their handwriting, unless you had specimens side by side to compare, and even when both hands appeared on the same page (as often happened, as if, long since past any oral intercourse, they had used the diurnally advancing pages to conduct the unavoidable business of the compulsion which had traversed all the waste wilderness of North Mississippi in 1830 and '40 and singled them out to drive) they both looked as though they had been written by the same perfectly normal ten-year-old boy, even to the spelling, except that the spelling did not improve as one by one the slaves which Carothers McCaslin had inherited and purchased—Roscius and Phoebe and Thucydides and Eunice and their descendants, and Sam Fathers and his mother for both of whom he had swapped an underbred trotting gelding to old Ikkemotubbe, the Chickasaw chief from whom he had likewise bought the land, and Tennie Beauchamp whom the twin Amodeus had won from a neighbor in a poker-game, and the anomaly calling itself Percival Brownlee which the twin Theophilus had purchased, neither he nor his brother ever knew why apparently, from Bedford Forrest while he was still only a slave-dealer and not yet a general (It was a single page, not long and covering less than a year, not seven months in fact, begun in the hand which the boy had learned to distinguish as that of his father:

> *Percavil Brownly 26yr Old. cleark @ Bookepper. bought from N.B.Forest at Cold Water 3 Mar 1856 $265. dolars*

and beneath that, in the same hand:

> *5 mar 1856 No bookepper any way Cant read. Can write his Name but I already put that down My self Says he can Plough but dont look like it to Me. sent to Feild to day Mar 5 1856*

and the same hand:

> *6 Mar 1856 Cant plough either Says he aims to be a Precher so may be he can lead live stock to Crick to Drink*

and this time it was the other, the hand which he now recognised as his uncle's when he could see them both on the same page:

> *Mar 23th 1856 Cant do that either Except one at a Time Get shut of him*

then the first again:

> *24 Mar 1856 Who in hell would buy him*

then the second:

> *19th of Apr 1856 Nobody You put yourself out of Market at Cold Water two months ago I never said sell him Free him*

the first:

> *22 Apr 1856 Ill get it out of him*

the second:

> *Jun 13th 1856 How $1 per yr 265$ 265 yrs Wholl sign his Free paper*

then the first again:

1 Oct 1856 Mule josephine Broke Leg @ shot Wrong stall wrong niger wrong everything $100. dolars

and the same:

2 Oct 1856 Freed Debit McCaslin @ McCaslin $265. dolars

then the second again:

Oct 3th Debit Theophilus McCaslin Niger 265$ Mule 100$ 365$ He hasnt gone yet Father should be here

then the first:

3 Oct 1856 Son of a bitch wont leave What would father done

the second:

29th of Oct 1856 Renamed him

the first:

31 Oct 1856 Renamed him what

the second:

Chrstms 1856 Spintrius

) took substance and even a sort of shadowy life with their passions and complexities too as page followed page and year year; all there, not only the general and condoned injustice and its slow amortization but the specific tragedy which had not been condoned and could never be amortized, the new page and the new ledger, the hand which he could now recognise at first glance as his father's:

Father dide Lucuis Quintus Carothers McCaslin. Callina 1772 Missippy 1837. Dide and burid 27 June 1837

Roskus. rased by Granfather in Callina Dont know how old. Freed 27 June 1837 Dont want to leave. Dide and Burid 12 Jan 1841

Fibby Roskus Wife. bought by granfather in Callina says Fifty Freed 27 June 1837 Dont want to leave. Dide and burd 1 Aug 1849

Thucydus Roskus @ Fibby Son born in Callina 1779. Refused 10acre peace fathers Will 28 Jun 1837 Refused Cash offer $200. dolars from A. @ T. McCaslin 28 Jun 1837 Wants to stay and work it out

and beneath this and covering the next five pages and almost that many years, the slow, day-by-day accrument of the wages allowed him and the food and clothing—the molasses and meat and meal, the cheap durable shirts and jeans and shoes and now and then a coat against rain and cold—charged against the slowly yet steadily mounting sum of balance (and it would seem to the boy that he could actually see the black man, the slave whom his white owner had forever manumitted by the very act from which the black man could never be free so long as memory lasted, entering the commissary, asking permission perhaps of the white man's son to see the ledger-page which he could not even read, not even asking for the white man's word, which he would have had to accept for the reason that there was absolutely no way under the sun for him to test it, as to how the account stood, how much longer before he could go and never return, even if only as far as Jefferson seventeen miles away) on to the double pen-stroke closing the final entry:

3 Nov 1841 By Cash to Thucydus McCaslin $200. dolars Set Up blaksmith in J. Dec 1841 Dide and burid in J. 17 feb 1854

Eunice Bought by Father in New Orleans 1807 $650. dolars. Marrid to Thucydus 1809 Drownd in Crick Cristmas Day 1832

and then the other hand appeared, the first time he had seen it in the ledger to distinguish it as his uncle's, the cook and housekeeper whom even McCaslin, who had known him and the boy's father for sixteen years before the boy was born, remembered as sitting all day long in the rocking chair from which he cooked the food, before the kitchen fire on which he cooked it:

June 21th 1833 Drownd herself

and the first:

23 Jun 1833 Who in hell ever heard of a niger drownding him self and the second, unhurried, with a complete finality; the two identical entries might have been made with a rubber stamp save for the date:

Aug 13th 1833 Drownd herself

and he thought *But why? But why?* He was sixteen then. It was neither the first time he had been alone in the commissary nor the first time he had taken down the old ledgers familiar on their shelf above the desk ever since he could remember. As a child and even after nine and ten and eleven, when he had learned to read, he would look up at the scarred and cracked backs and ends but with no particular desire to open them, and though he intended to examine them someday because he realised that they probably contained a chronological and much more comprehensive though doubtless tedious record than he would ever get from any other source, not alone of his own flesh and blood but of all his people, not only the whites but the black ones too, who were as much a part of his ancestry as his white progenitors, and of the land which they had all held and used in common and fed from and on and would continue to use in common without regard to color or titular ownership, it would only be on some idle day when he was old and perhaps even bored a little since what the old books contained would be after all these years fixed immutably, finished, unalterable, harmless. Then he was sixteen. He knew what he was going to find before he found it. He got the commissary key from McCaslin's room after midnight while McCaslin was asleep and with the commissary door shut and locked behind him and the forgotten lantern stinking anew the rank dead icy air, he leaned above the yellowed page and thought not Why drowned herself, but thinking what he believed his father had thought when he found his brother's first comment: Why did Uncle Buddy think she had drowned herself? finding, beginning to find on the next succeeding page what he knew he would find, only this was still not it because he already knew this:

Tomasina called Tomy Daughter of Thucydus @ Eunice Born 1810 dide in Child bed June 1833 and Burd. Yr stars fell

nor the next:

Turl Son of Thucydus @ Eunice Tomy born Jun 1833 yr stars fell Fathers will

and nothing more, no tedious recording filling this page of wages day by day and food and clothing charged against them, no entry of his death and burial because he had outlived his white half-brothers and the books which McCaslin kept did not include obituaries: just *Fathers will* and he had seen that too: old Carothers' bold cramped hand far less legible than his sons' even and not much better in spelling, who while capitalising almost every noun and verb, made no effort to punctuate or construct whatever, just as he made no effort either to explain or obfuscate the thousand-dollar legacy to the son of an unmarried slave-girl, to be paid only at the child's coming-of-age, bearing the consequence of the act of which there was still no definite incontrovertible proof that he acknowledged, not out of his own substance but penalising his sons with it, charging them a cash forfeit on the accident of their own paternity; not even a bribe for silence toward his own fame since his fame would suffer only after he was no longer present to defend it, flinging almost contemptuously, as he might a cast-off hat or pair of shoes, the thousand dollars which could have had no more reality to him under those conditions than it would have to the negro, the slave who would not even see it until he came of age, twenty-one years too late to begin to learn what money was. *So I reckon that was cheaper than saying My son to a nigger* he thought. *Even if My son wasn't but just two words. But there must have been love* he thought. *Some sort of love. Even what he would have called love: not just an afternoon's or a night's spittoon* There was the old man, old, within five years of his life's end, long a widower and, since his sons were not only bachelors but were approaching middleage, lonely in the house and doubtless even bored since his plantation was established now and functioning and there was enough money now, too much of it probably for a man whose vices even apparently remained below his means; there was the girl, husbandless and young, only twenty-three when the child was born: perhaps he had sent for her at first out of loneliness, to have a young voice and movement in the house, summoned her, bade her mother send her each morning to sweep the floors and make the beds and the mother acquiescing since that was probably already understood, already planned: the only child of a couple who were not field hands and who held themselves something above the other slaves not alone for that reason but because the husband and his father and mother too had been inherited by the white man from his father, and the white man himself had travelled three hundred miles and better to New Orleans in a day when men travelled by horseback or steamboat, and bought the girl's mother as a wife for

and that was all. The old frail pages seemed to turn of their own accord even while he thought *His own daughter. His own daughter. No No Not even him* back to that one where the white man (not even a widower then) who never went anywhere any more than his sons in their time ever did and who did not need another slave, had gone all the way to New Orleans and bought one. And Tomey's Terrel was still alive when the boy was ten years old and he knew from his own observation and memory that there had already been some white in Tomey's Terrel's blood before his father gave him the rest of it; and looking down at the yellowed page spread beneath the yellow glow of the lantern smoking and stinking in that rank chill midnight room fifty years later, he seemed to see her actually walking into the icy creek on that Christmas day six months before her daughter's and her lover's (*Her first lover's* he thought. *Her first*) child was born, solitary, inflexible, griefless, ceremonial, in formal and succinct repudiation of grief and despair who had already had to repudiate belief and hope

that was all. He would never need look at the ledgers again nor did he; the yellowed pages in their fading and implacable succession were as much a part of his consciousness and would remain so forever, as the fact of his own nativity:

> *Tennie Beauchamp 21yrs Won by Amodeus McCaslin from Hubert Beauchamp Esqre Possible Strait against three Treys in sigt Not called 1859 Marrid to Tomys Turl 1859*

and no date of freedom because her freedom, as well as that of her first surviving child, derived not from Buck and Buddy McCaslin in the commissary but from a stranger in Washington and no date of death and burial, not only because McCaslin kept no obituaries in his books, but because in this year 1883 she was still alive and would remain so to see a grandson by her last surviving child:

Amodeus McCaslin Beauchamp Son of tomys Turl @ Tennie Beauchamp 1859 dide 1859

then his uncle's hand entire, because his father was now a member of the cavalry command of that man whose name as a slave-dealer he could not even spell: and not even a page and not even a full line:

Dauter Tomes Turl and tenny 1862

and not even a line and not even a sex and no cause given though the boy could guess it because McCaslin was thirteen then and he remembered how there was not always enough to eat in more places than Vicksburg:

Child of tomes Turl and Tenny 1863

and the same hand again and this one lived, as though Tennie's perseverance and the fading and diluted ghost of old Carothers' ruthlessness had at last conquered even starvation: and clearer, fuller, more carefully written and spelled than the boy had yet seen it, as if the old man, who should have been a woman to begin with, trying to run what was left of the plantation in his brother's absence in the intervals of cooking and caring for himself and the fourteen-year-old orphan, had taken as an omen for renewed hope the fact that this nameless inheritor of slaves was at least remaining alive long enough to receive a name:

James Thucydus Beauchamp Son of Tomes Turl and Tenny Beauchamp Born 29th december 1864 and both Well Wanted to call him Theophilus but Tride Amodeus McCaslin and Callina McCaslin and both dide so Disswaded Them Born at Two clock A,m,both Well

but no more, nothing; it would be another two years yet before the boy, almost a man now, would return from the abortive trip into Tennessee with the still-intact third of old Carothers' legacy to his negro son and his descendants, which as the three surviving children established at last one by one their apparent intention of surviving, their white half-uncles had increased to a thousand dollars each, conditions permitting, as they came of age, and completed the page himself as far as it would ever be completed when that day was long passed beyond which a man born in 1864 (or 1867 either, when he himself saw light) could have expected or himself hoped or even wanted to be still alive; his own hand now, queerly enough resembling neither his father's nor his uncle's nor even McCaslin's, but like that of his grandfather's save for the spelling:

Vanished sometime on night of his twenty-first birthday Dec 29 1885. Traced by Isaac McCaslin to Jackson Tenn. and there lost. His third of legacy $1000.00 returned to McCaslin Edmonds Trustee this day Jan 12 1886

but not yet: that would be two years yet, and now his father's again, whose old commander was now quit of soldiering and slave-trading both; once more in the ledger and then not again and more illegible than ever, almost indecipherable at all from the rheumatism which now crippled him and almost completely innocent now even of any sort of spelling as well as punctuation, as if the four years during which he had followed the sword of the only man ever breathing who ever sold him a negro, let alone beat him in a trade, had convinced him not only of the vanity of faith and hope but of orthography too:

Miss sophonsiba b dtr t t @ t 1869

but not of belief and will because it was there, written, as McCaslin had told him, with the left hand, but there in the ledger one time more and then not again, for the boy himself was a year old, and when Lucas was born six years later, his father and uncle had been dead inside the same twelvemonths almost five years; his own hand again, who was there and saw it, 1886, she was just seventeen, two years younger than himself, and he was in the commissary when McCaslin entered out of the first of dusk and said, 'He wants to marry Fonsiba,' like that: and he looked past McCaslin and saw the man, the stranger, taller than McCaslin and wearing better clothes than McCaslin and most of the other white men the boy knew habitually wore, who entered the room like a white man and stood in it like a white man, as though he had let McCaslin precede him into it not because McCaslin's skin was white but simply because McCaslin lived there and knew the way, and who talked like a white man too, looking at him past McCaslin's shoulder rapidly and keenly once and then no more, without further interest, as a mature and contained white man not impatient but just pressed for time might have looked. 'Marry Fonsiba?' he cried. 'Marry Fonsiba?' and then no more either, just watching and listening while McCaslin and the Negro talked:

'To live in Arkansas, I believe you said.'

'Yes. I have property there. A farm.'

'Property? A farm? You own it?'

'Yes.'

'You dont say Sir, do you?'

'To my elders, yes.'

'I see. You are from the North.'

'Yes. Since a child.'

'Then your father was a slave.'

'Yes. Once.'

'Then how do you own a farm in Arkansas?'

'I have a grant. It was my father's. From the United States. For military service.'

'I see,' McCaslin said. 'The Yankee army.'

'The United States army,' the stranger said; and then himself again, crying it at McCaslin's back:

'Call Aunt Tennie! I'll go get her! I'll——' But McCaslin was not even including him; the stranger did not even glance back toward his voice, the two of them speaking to one another again as if he were not even there:

'Since you seem to have it all settled,' McCaslin said, 'why have you bothered to consult my authority at all?'

'I dont,' the stranger said. 'I acknowledge your authority only so far as you admit your responsibility toward her as a female member of the family of which you are the head. I dont ask your permission. I——'

'That will do!' McCaslin said. But the stranger did not falter. It was neither as if he were ignoring McCaslin nor as if he had failed to hear him. It was as though he were making, not at all an excuse and not exactly a justification, but simply a statement which the situation absolutely required and demanded should be made in McCaslin's hearing whether McCaslin listened to it or not. It was as if he were talking to himself, for himself to hear the words spoken aloud. They faced one another, not close yet at slightly less than foils' distance, erect, their voices not raised, not impactive, just succinct:

'——I inform you, notify you in advance as chief of her family. No man of honor could do less. Besides, you have, in your way, according to your lights and upbringing——'

'That's enough, I said,' McCaslin said. 'Be off this place by full dark. Go.' But for another moment the other did not move, contemplating McCaslin with that detached and heatless look, as if he were watching reflected in McCaslin's pupils the tiny image of the figure he was sustaining.

'Yes,' he said. 'After all, this is your house. And in your fashion you have. . . . . But no matter. You are right. This is enough.' He turned back toward the door; he paused again but only for a second, already moving while he spoke: 'Be easy. I will be good to her.' Then he was gone.

'But how did she ever know him?' the boy cried. 'I never even heard of him before! And Fonsiba, that's never been off this place except to go to church since she was born——'

'Ha,' McCaslin said. 'Even their parents dont know until too late how seventeen-year-old girls ever met the men who marry them too, if they are lucky.' And the next morning they were both gone, Fonsiba too. McCaslin never saw her again, nor did he, because the woman he found at last five months later was no one he had ever known. He carried a third of the three-thousand-dollar fund in gold in a money-belt, as when he had vainly traced Tennie's Jim into Tennessee a year ago. They—the man—had left an address of some sort with Tennie, and three months later a letter came, written by the man although McCaslin's wife Alice had taught Fonsiba to read and write too a little. But it bore a different postmark from the address the man had left with Tennie, and he travelled by rail as far as he could and then by contracted stage and then by a hired livery rig and then by rail again for a distance: an experienced traveller by now and an experienced bloodhound too and a successful one this time because he would have to be; as the slow interminable empty muddy December miles crawled and crawled and night followed night in hotels, in roadside taverns of rough logs and containing little else but a bar, and in the cabins of strangers and the hay of lonely barns, in none of which he dared undress because of his secret golden girdle like that of a disguised one of the Magi travelling incognito and not even hope to draw him but only determination and desperation, he would tell himself: *I will have to find her. I will have to. We have already lost one of them. I will have to find her this time.* He did. Hunched in the slow and icy rain, on a spent hired horse splashed to the chest and higher, he saw it—a single log edifice with a clay chimney which seemed in process of being flattened by the rain to a nameless and valueless rubble of dissolution in that roadless and even pathless waste of unfenced fallow and wilderness jungle—no barn, no stable, not so much as a hen-coop: just a log cabin built by hand and no clever hand either, a meagre pile of clumsily-cut firewood sufficient for about one day and not even a gaunt hound to come bellowing out from under the house when he rode up—a farm only in embryo, perhaps a good farm, maybe even a plantation someday, but not now, not for years yet and only then with labor, hard and enduring and unflagging work and sacrifice; he shoved open the crazy kitchen door in its awry frame and entered an icy gloom where not even a fire for cooking burned and after another moment saw, crouched into the wall's angle behind a crude table, the coffee-colored face which he had known all his life but knew no more, the body which had been born within a hundred yards of the room that he was born in and in which some of his own blood ran but which was now completely inheritor of generation after generation to whom an unannounced white man on a horse was a white man's hired Patroller wearing a pistol sometimes and a blacksnake whip always; he entered the next room, the only other room the cabin owned, and found, sitting in a rocking chair before the hearth, the man himself, reading—sitting there in the only chair in the house, before that miserable fire for which there was not wood sufficient to last twenty-four hours, in the same ministerial clothing in which he had entered the commissary five months ago and a pair of gold-framed spectacles which, when he looked up and then rose to his feet, the boy saw did not even contain lenses, reading a book in the midst of that desolation, that muddy waste fenceless and even pathless and without even a walled shed for stock to stand beneath: and over all, permeant, clinging to the man's very clothing and exuding from his skin itself, that rank stink of baseless and imbecile delusion, that boundless rapacity and folly, of the carpet-bagger followers of victorious armies.

'Dont you see?' he cried. 'Dont you see? This whole land, the whole South, is cursed, and all of us who derive from it, whom it ever suckled, white and black both, lie under the curse? Granted that my people brought the curse onto the land: maybe for that reason their descendants alone can—not resist it, not combat it—maybe just endure and outlast it until the curse is lifted. Then your people's turn will come because we have forfeited ours. But not now. Not yet. Dont you see?'

The other stood now, the unfrayed garments still ministerial even if not quite so fine, the book closed upon one finger to keep the place, the lenseless spectacles held like a music master's wand in the other workless hand while the owner of it spoke his measured and sonorous imbecility of the boundless folly and the baseless hope: 'You're wrong. The curse you whites brought into this land has been lifted. It has been voided and discharged. We are seeing a new era, an era dedicated, as our founders intended it, to freedom, liberty and equality for all, to which this country will be the new Canaan——'

'Freedom from what? From work? Canaan?' He jerked his arm, comprehensive, almost violent: whereupon it all seemed to stand there about them, intact and complete and visible in the drafty, damp, heatless, negro-stale negro-rank sorry room—the empty fields without plow or seed to work them, fenceless against the stock which did not exist within or without the walled stable which likewise was not there. 'What corner of Canaan is this?'

'You are seeing it at a bad time. This is winter. No man farms this time of year.'

'I see. And of course her need for food and clothing will stand still while the land lies fallow.'

'I have a pension,' the other said. He said it as a man might say *I have grace* or *I own a gold mine*. 'I have my father's pension too. It will arrive on the first of the month. What day is this?'

'The eleventh,' he said. 'Twenty days more. And until then?'

'I have a few groceries in the house from my credit account with the merchant in Midnight who banks my pension check for me. I have executed to him a power of attorney to handle it for me as a matter of mutual——'

'I see. And if the groceries dont last the twenty days?'

'I still have one more hog.'

'Where?'

'Outside,' the other said. 'It is customary in this country to allow stock to range free during the winter for food. It comes up from time to time. But no matter if it doesn't; I can probably trace its footprints when the need——'

'Yes!' he cried. 'Because no matter: you still have the pension check. And the man in Midnight will cash it and pay himself out of it for what you have already eaten and if there is any left over, it is yours. And the hog will be eaten by then or you still cant catch it, and then what will you do?'

'It will be almost spring then,' the other said. 'I am planning in the spring——'

'It will be January,' he said. 'And then February. And then more than half of March——' and when he stopped again in the kitchen she had not moved, she did not even seem to breathe or to be alive except her eyes watching him; when he took a step toward her it was still not movement because she could have retreated no further: only the tremendous fathomless ink-colored eyes in the narrow, thin, too thin coffee-colored face watching him without alarm, without recognition, without hope. 'Fonsiba,' he said. 'Fonsiba. Are you all right?'

'I'm free,' she said. Midnight was a tavern, a livery stable, a big store (that would be where the pension check banked itself as a matter of mutual elimination of bother and fret, he thought) and a little one, a saloon and a blacksmith shop. But there was a bank there too. The president (the owner, for all practical purposes) of it was a translated Mississippian who had been one of Forrest's men too: and his body lightened of the golden belt for the first time since he left home eight days ago, with pencil and paper he multiplied three dollars by twelve months and divided it into one thousand dollars; it would stretch that way over almost twenty-eight years and for twenty-eight years at least she would not starve, the banker promising to send the three dollars himself by a trusty messenger on the fifteenth of each month and put it into her actual hand, and he returned home and that was all because in 1874 his father and his uncle were both dead and the old ledgers never again came down from the shelf above the desk to which his father had returned them for the last time that day in 1869. But he could have completed it:

Lucas Quintus Carothers McCaslin Beauchamp. Last surviving son and child of Tomey's Terrel and Tennie Beauchamp. March 17, 1874

except that there was no need: not *Lucius Quintus* @c @c @c, but *Lucas Quintus*, not refusing to be called Lucius, because he simply eliminated that word from the name; not denying, declining the name itself, because he used three quarters of it; but simply taking the name and changing, altering it, making it no longer the white man's but his own, by himself composed, himself selfprogenitive and nominate, by himself ancestored, as, for all the old ledgers recorded to the contrary, old Carothers himself was

and that was all: 1874 the boy; 1888 the man, repudiated denied and free; 1895 and husband but no father, unwidowered but without a wife, and found long since that no man is ever free and probably could not bear it if he were; married then and living in Jefferson in the little new jerrybuilt bungalow which his wife's father had given them: and one morning Lucas stood suddenly in the doorway of the room where he was reading the Memphis paper and he looked at the paper's dateline and thought *It's his birthday. He's twenty-one today* and Lucas said: 'Whar's the rest of that money old Carothers left? I wants it. All of it.'

that was all: and McCaslin

'More men than that one Buck and Buddy to fumble-heed that truth so mazed for them that spoke it and so confused for them that heard yet still there was 1865:' and he

'But not enough. Not enough of even Father and Uncle

Buddy to fumble-heed in even three generations not even three generations fathered by Grandfather not even if there had been nowhere beneath His sight any but Grandfather and so He would not even have needed to elect and choose. But He tried and I know what you will say. That having Himself created them He could have known no more of hope than He could have pride and grief but He didn't hope He just waited because He had made them: not just because He had set them alive and in motion but because He had already worried with them so long: worried with them so long because He had seen how in individual cases they were capable of anything any height or depth remembered in mazed incomprehension out of heaven where hell was created too and so He must admit them or else admit His equal somewhere and so be no longer God and therefore must accept responsibility for what He Himself had done in order to live with Himself in His lonely and paramount heaven. And He probably knew it was vain but He had created them and knew them capable of all things because He had shaped them out of the primal Absolute which contained all and had watched them since in their individual exaltation and baseness and they themselves not knowing why nor how nor even when: until at last He saw that they were all Grandfather all of them and that even from them the elected and chosen the best the very best He could expect (not hope mind: not hope) would be Bucks and Buddies and not even enough of them and in the third generation not even Bucks and Buddies but——' and McCaslin

'Ah:' and he

'Yes. If He could see Father and Uncle Buddy in Grandfather He must have seen me too. —an Isaac born into a later life than Abraham's and repudiating immolation: fatherless and therefore safe declining the altar because maybe this time the exasperated Hand might not supply the kid——' and McCaslin

'Escape:' and he

'All right. Escape.—Until one day He said what you told Fonsiba's husband that afternoon here in this room: *This will do. This is enough*: not in exasperation or rage or even just sick to death as you were sick that day: just *This is enough* and looked about for one last time, for one time more since He had created them, upon this land this South for which He had done so much with woods for game and streams for fish and deep rich soil for seed and lush springs to sprout it and long summers to mature it and serene falls to harvest it and short mild winters for men and animals and saw no hope anywhere and looked beyond it where hope should have been, where to East North and West lay illimitable that whole hopeful continent dedicated as a refuge and sanctuary of liberty and freedom from what you called the old world's worthless evening and saw the rich descendants of slavers, females of both sexes, to whom the black they shrieked of was another specimen another example like the Brazilian macaw brought home in a cage by a traveller, passing resolutions about horror and outrage in warm and air-proof halls: and the thundering cannonade of politicians earning votes and the medicine-shows of pulpiteers earning Chautauqua fees, to whom the outrage and the injustice were as much abstractions as Tariff or Silver or Immortality and who employed the very shackles of its servitude and the sorry rags of its regalia as they did the other beer and banners and mottoes redfire and brimstone and sleight-of-hand and musical handsaws: and the whirling wheels which manufactured for a profit the pristine replacements of the shackles and shoddy garments as they wore out and spun the cotton and made the gins which ginned it and the cars and ships which hauled it, and the men who ran the wheels for that profit and established and collected the taxes it was taxed with and the rates for hauling it and the commissions for selling it: and He could have repudiated them since they were His creation now and forever more throughout all their generations until not only that old world from which He had rescued them but this new one too which He had revealed and led them to as a sanctuary and refuge were become the same worthless tideless rock cooling in the last crimson evening except that out of all that empty sound and bootless fury one silence, among that loud and moiling all of them just one simple enough to believe that horror and outrage were first and last simply horror and outrage and was crude enough to act upon that, illiterate and had no words for talking or perhaps was just busy and had no time to, one out of them all who did not bother Him with cajolery and adjuration then pleading then threat and had not even bothered to inform Him in advance what he was about so that a lesser than He might have even missed the simple act of lifting the long ancestral musket down from the deer-horns above the door, whereupon He said *My name is Brown too* and the other *So is mine* and He *Then mine or yours cant be because I am against it* and the other *So am I* and He triumphantly *Then where are you going with that gun?* and the other told him in one sentence one word and He: amazed: Who knew neither hope nor pride nor grief *But your Association, your Committee, your Officers. Where are your Minutes, your Motions, your Parliamentary Procedures?* and the other *I aint against them. They are all right I reckon for them that have the time. I am just against the weak because they are niggers being held in bondage by the strong just because they are white.* So He turned once more to this land which He still intended to save because He had done so much for it——' and McCaslin

'What?' and he

'—to these people He was still committed to because they were His creations——' and McCaslin

'Turned back to us? His face to us?' and he

'—whose wives and daughters at least made soups and jellies for them when they were sick and carried the trays through the mud and the winter too into the stinking cabins and sat in the stinking cabins and kept fires going until crises came and passed but that was not enough: and when they were very sick had them carried into the big house itself into the company room itself maybe and nursed them there which the white man would have done too for any other of his cattle that was sick but at least the man who hired one from a livery wouldn't have and still that was not enough: so that He said and not in grief either Who had made them and so could know no more of grief than He could of pride or hope: *Apparently they can learn nothing save through suffering, remember nothing save when underlined in blood*——' and McCaslin

'Ashby on an afternoon's ride, to call on some remote maiden cousins of his mother or maybe just acquaintances of hers, comes by chance upon a minor engagement of outposts and dismounts and with his crimson-lined cloak for target leads a handful of troops he never saw before against an entrenched position of backwoods-trained riflemen. Lee's battle-order, wrapped maybe about a handful of cigars and doubtless thrown away when the last cigar was smoked, found by a Yankee Intelligence officer on the floor of a saloon behind the Yankee lines after Lee had already divided his forces before Sharpsburg. Jackson on the Plank Road, already rolled up the flank which Hooker believed could not be turned and, waiting only for night to pass to continue the brutal and incessant slogging which would fling that whole wing back into Hooker's lap where he sat on a front gallery in Chancellorsville drinking rum toddies and telegraphing Lincoln that he had defeated Lee, is shot from among a whole covey of minor officers and in the blind night by one of his own patrols, leaving as next by seniority Stuart that gallant man born apparently already horsed and sabred and already knowing all there was to know about war except the slogging and brutal stupidity of it: and that same Stuart off raiding Pennsylvania hen-roosts when Lee should have known of all of Meade just where Hancock was on Cemetery Ridge: and Longstreet too at Gettysburg and that same Longstreet shot out of saddle by his own men in the dark by mistake just as Jackson was. His face to us? His face to us?' and he

'How else have made them fight? Who else but Jacksons and Stuarts and Ashbys and Morgans and Forrests?—the farmers of the central and middle-west, holding land by the acre instead of the tens or maybe even the hundreds, farming it themselves and to no single crop of cotton or tobacco or cane, owning no slaves and needing and wanting none and already looking toward the Pacific coast, not always as long as two generations there and having stopped where they did stop only through the fortuitous mischance that an ox died or a wagon-axle broke. And the New England mechanics who didn't even own land and measured all things by the weight of water and the cost of turning wheels and the narrow fringe of traders and ship-owners still looking backward across the Atlantic and attached to the continent only by their counting-houses. And those who should have had the alertness to see: the wildcat manipulators of mythical wilderness townsites; and the astuteness to rationalise: the bankers who held the mortgages on the land which the first were only waiting to abandon and on the railroads and steamboats to carry them still further west, and on the factories and the wheels and the rented tenements those who ran them lived in; and the leisure and scope to comprehend and fear in time and even anticipate: the Boston-bred (even when not born in Boston) spinster descendants of long lines of similarly-bred and likewise spinster aunts and uncles whose hands knew no callus except that of the indicting pen, to whom the wilderness itself began at the top of tide and who looked, if at anything other than Beacon Hill, only toward heaven—not to mention all the loud rabble of the camp-followers of pioneers: the bellowing of politicians, the mellifluous choiring of self-styled men of God, the——' and McCaslin

'Here, here. Wait a minute:' and he

'Let me talk now. I'm trying to explain to the head of my family something which I have got to do which I dont quite understand myself, not in justification of it but to explain it if I can. I could say I dont know why I must do it but that I do know I have got to because I have got myself to have to live with for the rest of my life and all I want is peace to do it in. But you are the head of my family. More. I knew a long time ago that I would never have to miss my father, even if you are just finding out that you have missed your son.—the drawers of bills and the shavers of notes and the schoolmasters and the self-ordained to teach and lead and all that horde of the semi-literate with a white shirt but no change for it, with one eye on themselves and watching each other with the other one. Who else could have made them fight: could have struck them so aghast with fear and dread as to turn shoulder to shoulder and face one way and even stop talking for a while and even after two years of it keep them still so wrung with terror that some among them would seriously propose moving their very capital into a foreign country lest it be ravaged and pillaged by a people whose entire white male population would have little more than filled any one of their larger cities: except Jackson in the Valley and three separate armies trying to catch him and none of them ever knowing whether they were just retreating from a battle or just running into one and Stuart riding his whole command entirely around the biggest single armed force this continent ever saw in order to see what it looked like from behind and Morgan leading a cavalry charge against a stranded man-of-war. Who else could have declared a war against a power with ten times the area and a hundred times the men and a thousand times the resources, except men who could believe that all necessary to conduct a successful war was not acumen nor shrewdness nor politics nor diplomacy nor money nor even integrity and simple arithmetic but just love of land and courage——'

'And an unblemished and gallant ancestry and the ability to ride a horse,' McCaslin said. 'Dont leave that out.' It was evening now, the tranquil sunset of October mazy with windless woodsmoke. The cotton was long since picked and ginned, and all day now the wagons loaded with gathered corn moved between field and crib, processional across the enduring land. 'Well, maybe that's what He wanted. At least, that's what He got.' This time there was no yellowed procession of fading and harmless ledger-pages. This was chronicled in a harsher book and McCaslin, fourteen and fifteen and sixteen, had seen it and the boy himself had inherited it as Noah's grandchildren had inherited the Flood although they had not been there to see the deluge: that dark corrupt and bloody time while three separate peoples had tried to adjust not only to one another but to the new land which they had created and inherited too and must live in for the reason that those who had lost it were no less free to quit it than those who had gained it were:—those upon whom freedom and equality had been dumped overnight and without warning or preparation or any training in how to employ it or even just endure it and who misused it not as children would nor yet because they had been so long in bondage and then so suddenly freed, but misused it as human beings always misuse freedom, so that he thought *Apparently there is a wisdom beyond even that learned through suffering necessary for a man to distinguish between liberty and license*; those who had fought for four years and lost to preserve a condition under which that franchisement was anomaly and paradox, not because they were opposed to freedom as freedom but for the old reasons for which man (not the generals and politicians but man) has always fought and died in wars: to preserve a status quo or to establish a better future one to endure for his children; and lastly, as if that were not enough for bitterness and hatred and fear, that third race even more alien to the people whom they resembled in pigment and in whom even the same blood ran, than to the people whom they did not,—that race threefold in one and alien even among themselves save for a single fierce will for rapine and pillage, composed of the sons of middleaged Quartermaster lieutenants and Army sutlers and contractors in military blankets and shoes and transport mules, who followed the battles they themselves had not fought and inherited the conquest they themselves had not helped to gain, sanctioned and protected even if not blessed, and left their bones and in another generation would be engaged in a fierce economic competition of small sloven farms with the black men they were supposed to have freed and the white descendants of fathers who had owned no slaves anyway whom they were supposed to have disinherited and in the third generation would be back once more in the little lost county seats as barbers and garage mechanics and deputy sheriffs and mill- and gin-hands and power-plant firemen, leading, first in mufti then later in an actual formalised regalia of hooded sheets and passwords and fiery christian symbols, lynching mobs against the race their ancestors had come to save: and of all that other nameless horde of speculators in human misery, manipulators of money and politics and land, who follow catastrophe and are their own protection as grasshoppers are and need no blessing and sweat no plow or axehelve and batten and vanish and leave no bones, just as they derived apparently from no ancestry, no mortal flesh, no act even of passion or even of lust: and the Jew who came without protection too since after two thousand years he had got out of the habit of being or needing it, and solitary, without even the solidarity of the locusts and in this a sort of courage since he had come thinking not in terms of simple pillage but in terms of his great-grandchildren, seeking yet some place to establish them to endure even though forever alien: and unblessed: a pariah about the face of the Western earth which twenty centuries later was still taking revenge on him for the fairy tale with which he had conquered it. McCaslin had actually seen it, and the boy even at almost eighty would never be able to distinguish certainly between what he had seen and what had been told him: a lightless and gutted and empty land where women crouched with the huddled children behind locked doors and men armed in sheets and masks rode the silent roads and the bodies of white and black both, victims not so much of hate as of desperation and despair, swung from lonely limbs: and men shot dead in polling-booths with the still wet pen in one hand and the unblotted ballot in the other: and a United States marshal in Jefferson who signed his official papers with a crude cross, an ex-slave called Sickymo, not at all because his ex-owner was a doctor and apothecary but because, still a slave, he would steal his master's grain alcohol and dilute it with water and peddle it in pint bottles from a cache beneath the roots of a big sycamore tree behind the drug store, who had attained his high office because his half-white sister was the concubine of the Federal A.P.M.: and this time McCaslin did not even say Look but merely lifted one hand, not even pointing, not even specifically toward the shelf of ledgers but toward the desk, toward the corner where it sat beside the scuffed patch on the floor where two decades of heavy shoes had stood while the white man at the desk added and multiplied and subtracted. And again he did not need to look because he had seen this himself and, twenty-three years after the Surrender and twenty-four after the Proclamation, was still watching it: the ledgers, new ones now and filled rapidly, succeeding one another rapidly and containing more names than old Carothers or even his father and Uncle Buddy had ever dreamed of; new names and new faces to go with them, among which the old names and faces that even his father and uncle would have recognised, were lost, vanished—Tomey's Terrel dead, and even the tragic and miscast Percival Brownlee, who couldn't keep books and couldn't farm either, found his true niche at last, reappeared in 1862 during the boy's father's absence and had apparently been living on the plantation for at least a month before his uncle found out about it, conducting impromptu revival meetings among negroes, preaching and leading the singing also in his high sweet true soprano voice and disappeared again on foot and at top speed, not behind but ahead of a body of raiding Federal horse and reappeared for the third and last time in the entourage of a travelling

Army paymaster, the two of them passing through Jefferson in a surrey at the exact moment when the boy's father (it was 1866) also happened to be crossing the Square, the surrey and its occupants traversing rapidly that quiet and bucolic scene and even in that fleeting moment and to others beside the boy's father giving an illusion of flight and illicit holiday like a man on an excursion during his wife's absence with his wife's personal maid, until Brownlee glanced up and saw his late co-master and gave him one defiant female glance and then broke again, leaped from the surrey and disappeared this time for good and it was only by chance that McCaslin, twenty years later, heard of him again, an old man now and quite fat, as the well-to-do proprietor of a select New Orleans brothel; and Tennie's Jim gone, nobody knew where, and Fonsiba in Arkansas with her three dollars each month and the scholar-husband with his lenseless spectacles and frock coat and his plans for the spring; and only Lucas was left, the baby, the last save himself of old Carothers' doomed and fatal blood which in the male derivation seemed to destroy all it touched, and even he was repudiating and at least hoping to escape it;—Lucas, the boy of fourteen whose name would not even appear for six years yet among those rapid pages in the bindings new and dustless too since McCaslin lifted them down daily now to write into them the continuation of that record which two hundred years had not been enough to complete and another hundred would not be enough to discharge; that chronicle which was a whole land in miniature, which multiplied and compounded was the entire South, twenty-three years after surrender and twenty-four from emancipation—that slow trickle of molasses and meal and meat, of shoes and straw hats and overalls, of plowlines and collars and heel-bolts and buckheads and clevises, which returned each fall as cotton—the two threads frail as truth and impalpable as equators yet cable-strong to bind for life them who made the cotton to the land their sweat fell on: and he

'Yes. Binding them for a while yet, a little while yet. Through and beyond that life and maybe through and beyond the life of that life's sons and maybe even through and beyond that of the sons of those sons. But not always, because they will endure. They will outlast us because they are——' it was not a pause, barely a falter even, possibly appreciable only to himself, as if he couldn't speak even to McCaslin, even to explain his repudiation, that which to him too, even in the act of escaping (and maybe this was the reality and the truth of his need to escape) was heresy: so that even in escaping he was taking with him more of that evil and unregenerate old man who could summon, because she was his property, a human being because she was old enough and female, to his widower's house and get a child on her and then dismiss her because she was of an inferior race, and then bequeath a thousand dollars to the infant because he would be dead then and wouldn't have to pay it, than even he had feared. 'Yes. He didn't want to. He had to. Because they will endure. They are better than we are. Stronger than we are. Their vices are vices aped from white men or that white men and bondage have taught them: improvidence and intemperance and evasion—not laziness: evasion: of what white men had set them to, not for their aggrandisement or even comfort but his own——' and McCaslin

'All right. Go on: Promiscuity. Violence. Instability and lack of control. Inability to distinguish between mine and thine——' and he

'How distinguish, when for two hundred years mine did not even exist for them?' and McCaslin

'All right. Go on. And their virtues——' and he

'Yes. Their own. Endurance——' and McCaslin

'So have mules:' and he

'—and pity and tolerance and forbearance and fidelity and love of children——' and McCaslin

'So have dogs:' and he

'—whether their own or not or black or not. And more: what they got not only not from white people but not even despite white people because they had it already from the old free fathers a longer time free than us because we have never been free——' and it was in McCaslin's eyes too, he had only to look at McCaslin's eyes and it was there, that summer twilight seven years ago, almost a week after they had returned from the camp before he discovered that Sam Fathers had told McCaslin: an old bear, fierce and ruthless not just to stay alive but ruthless with the fierce pride of liberty and freedom, jealous and proud enough of liberty and freedom to see it threatened not with fear nor even alarm but almost with joy, seeming deliberately to put it into jeopardy in order to savor it and keep his old strong bones and flesh supple and quick to defend and preserve it; an old man, son of a Negro slave and an Indian king, inheritor on the one hand of the long chronicle of a people who had learned humility through suffering and learned pride through the endurance which survived the suffering, and on the other side the chronicle of a people even longer in the land than the first, yet who now existed there only in the solitary brotherhood of an old and childless Negro's alien blood and the wild and invincible spirit of an old bear; a boy who wished to learn humility and pride in order to become skillful and worthy in the woods but found himself becoming so skillful so fast that he feared he would never become worthy because he had not learned humility and pride though he had tried, until one day an old man who could not have defined either led him as though by the hand to where an old bear and a little mongrel dog showed him that, by possessing one thing other, he would possess them both; and a little dog, nameless and mongrel and many-fathered, grown yet weighing less than six pounds, who couldn't be dangerous because there was nothing anywhere much smaller, not fierce because that would have been called just noise, not humble because it was already too near the ground to genuflect, and not proud because it would not have been close enough for anyone to discern what was casting that shadow and which didn't even know it was not going to heaven since they had already decided it had no immortal soul, so that all it could be was brave even though they would probably call that too just noise. *'And you didn't shoot,' McCaslin said. 'How close were you?'*

'I dont know,' he said. 'There was a big wood tick just inside his off hind leg. I saw that. But I didn't have the gun then.'

'But you didn't shoot when you had the gun,' McCaslin said. 'Why?' But McCaslin didn't wait, rising and crossing the room, across the pelt of the bear he had killed two years ago and the bigger one McCaslin had killed before he was born, to the bookcase beneath the mounted head of his first buck, and returned with the book and sat down again and opened it. 'Listen,' he said. He read

the five stanzas aloud and closed the book on his finger and looked up. 'All right,' he said. 'Listen,' and read again, but only one stanza this time and closed the book and laid it on the table. 'She cannot fade, though thou hast not thy bliss,' McCaslin said: 'Forever wilt thou love, and she be fair.'

'He's talking about a girl,' he said.

'He had to talk about something,' McCaslin said. Then he said, 'He was talking about truth. Truth is one. It doesn't change. It covers all things which touch the heart—honor and pride and pity and justice and courage and love. Do you see now?' He didn't know. Somehow it had seemed simpler than that, simpler than somebody talking in a book about a young man and a girl he would never need to grieve over because he could never approach any nearer and would never have to get any further away. He had heard about an old bear and finally got big enough to hunt it and he hunted it four years and at last met it with a gun in his hands and he didn't shoot. Because a little dog——But he could have shot long before the fyce covered the twenty yards to where the bear waited, and Sam Fathers could have shot at any time during the interminable minute while Old Ben stood on his hind legs over them. . . . . He ceased. McCaslin watched him, still speaking, the voice, the words as quiet as the twilight itself was: 'Courage and honor and pride, and pity and love of justice and of liberty. They all touch the heart, and what the heart holds to becomes truth, as far as we know truth. Do you see now?' and he could still hear them, intact in this twilight as in that one seven years ago, no louder still because they did not need to be because they would endure: and he had only to look at McCaslin's eyes beyond the thin and bitter smiling, the faint lip-lift which would have had to be called smiling;—his kinsman, his father almost, who had been born too late into the old time and too soon for the new, the two of them juxtaposed and alien now to each other against their ravaged patrimony, the dark and ravaged fatherland still prone and panting from its etherless operation:

'Habet then.—So this land is, indubitably, of and by itself cursed:' and he

'Cursed:' and again McCaslin merely lifted one hand, not even speaking and not even toward the ledgers: so that, as the stereopticon condenses into one instantaneous field the myriad minutiae of its scope, so did that slight and rapid gesture establish in the small cramped and cluttered twilit room not only the ledgers but the whole plantation in its mazed and intricate entirety—the land, the fields and what they represented in terms of cotton ginned and sold, the men and women whom they fed and clothed and even paid a little cash money at Christmas-time in return for the labor which planted and raised and picked and ginned the cotton, the machinery and mules and gear with which they raised it and their cost and upkeep and replacement—that whole edifice intricate and complex and founded upon injustice and erected by ruthless rapacity and carried on even yet with at times downright savagery not only to the human beings but the valuable animals too, yet solvent and efficient and, more than that: not only still intact but enlarged, increased; brought still intact by McCaslin, himself little more than a child then, through and out of the debacle and chaos of twenty years ago where hardly one in ten survived, and enlarged and increased and would continue so, solvent and efficient and intact and still increasing so long as McCaslin and his McCaslin successors lasted, even though their surnames might not even be Edmonds then: and he: 'Habet too. Because that's it: not the land, but us. Not only the blood, but the name too; not only its color but its designation: Edmonds, white, but, a female line, could have no other but the name his father bore; Beauchamp, the elder line and the male one, but, black, could have had any name he liked and no man would have cared, except the name his father bore who had no name——' and McCaslin

'And since I know too what you know I will say now, once more let me say it: And one other, and in the third generation too, and the male, the eldest, the direct and sole and white and still McCaslin even, father to son to son——' and he

'I am free:' and this time McCaslin did not even gesture, no inference of fading pages, no postulation of the stereoptic whole, but the frail and iron thread strong as truth and impervious as evil and longer than life itself and reaching beyond record and patrimony both to join him with the lusts and passions, the hopes and dreams and griefs, of bones whose names while still fleshed and capable even old

Carothers' grandfather had never heard: and he: 'And of that too:' and McCaslin

'Chosen, I suppose (I will concede it) out of all your time by Him as you say Buck and Buddy were from theirs. And it took Him a bear and an old man and four years just for you. And it took you fourteen years to reach that point and about that many, maybe more, for Old Ben, and more than seventy for Sam Fathers. And you are just one. How long then? How long?' and he

'It will be long. I have never said otherwise. But it will be all right because they will endure——' and McCaslin

'And anyway, you will be free.——No, not now nor ever, we from them nor they from us. So I repudiate too. I would deny even if I knew it were true. I would have to. Even you can see that I could do no else. I am what I am; I will be always what I was born and have always been. And more than me. More than me, just as there were more than Buck and Buddy in what you called His first plan which failed:' and he

'And more than me:' and McCaslin

'No. Not even you. Because mark. You said how on that instant when Ikkemotubbe realised that he could sell the land to Grandfather, it ceased forever to have been his. All right; go on: Then it belonged to Sam Fathers, old Ikkemotubbe's son. And who inherited from Sam Fathers, if not you? co-heir perhaps with Boon, if not of his life maybe, at least of his quitting it?' and he

'Yes. Sam Fathers set me free.' And Isaac McCaslin, not yet Uncle Ike, a long time yet before he would be uncle to half a county and still father to none, living in one small cramped fireless rented room in a Jefferson boarding-house where petit juries were domiciled during court terms and itinerant horse- and mule-traders stayed, with his kit of brand-new carpenter's tools and the shotgun McCaslin had given him with his name engraved in silver and old General Compson's compass (and, when the General died, his silver-mounted horn too) and the iron cot and mattress and the blankets which he would take each fall into the woods for more than sixty years and the bright tin coffee-pot

there had been a legacy, from his Uncle Hubert Beauchamp, his godfather, that bluff burly roaring childlike man from whom Uncle Buddy had won Tomey's Terrel's wife Tennie in the poker-game in 1859—'posible strait against three Treys in sigt Not called'—; no pale sentence or paragraph scrawled in cringing fear of death by a weak and trembling hand as a last desperate sop flung backward at retribution, but a Legacy, a Thing, possessing weight to the hand and bulk to the eye and even audible: a silver cup filled with gold pieces and wrapped in burlap and sealed with his godfather's ring in the hot wax, which (intact still) even before his Uncle Hubert's death and long before his own majority, when it would be his, had become not only a legend but one of the family lares. After his father's and his Uncle Hubert's sister's marriage they moved back into the big house, the tremendous cavern which old Carothers had started and never finished, cleared the remaining negroes out of it and with his mother's dowry completed it, at least the rest of the windows and doors and moved into it, all of them save Uncle Buddy who declined to leave the cabin he and his twin had built, the move being the bride's notion and more than just a notion and none ever to know if she really wanted to live in the big house or if she knew before hand that Uncle Buddy would refuse to move: and two weeks after his birth in 1867, the first time he and his mother came down stairs, one night and the silver cup sitting on the cleared dining-room table beneath the bright lamp and while his mother and his father and McCaslin and Tennie (his nurse: carrying him)—all of them again but Uncle Buddy—watched, his Uncle Hubert rang one by one into the cup the bright and glinting mintage and wrapped it into the burlap envelope and heated the wax and sealed it and carried it back home with him where he lived alone now without even his sister either to hold him down as McCaslin said or to try to raise him up as Uncle Buddy said, and (dark times then in Mississippi) Uncle Buddy said most of the niggers gone and the ones that didn't go even Hub Beauchamp could not have wanted: but the dogs remained and Uncle Buddy said Beauchamp fiddled while Nero foxhunted

they would go and see it there; at last his mother would prevail and they would depart in the surrey, once more all save Uncle Buddy and McCaslin to keep Uncle Buddy company until one winter Uncle Buddy began to fail and from then on it was himself, beginning to remember now, and his mother and Tennie and Tomey's Terrel to drive: the twenty-two miles into the next county, the twin gate-posts on one of which McCaslin could remember the half-grown boy blowing a fox-horn at breakfast dinner and supper-time and jumping down to open to any passer who happened to hear it but where there were no gates at all now, the shabby and over-grown entrance to what his mother still insisted that people call Warwick because her brother was if truth but triumphed and justice but prevailed the rightful earl of it, the paintless house which outwardly did not change but which on the inside seemed each time larger because he was too little to realise then that there was less and less in it of the fine furnishings, the rosewood and mahogany and walnut which for him had never existed anywhere anyway save in his mother's tearful lamentations and the occasional piece small enough to be roped somehow onto the rear or the top of the carriage on their return (And he remembered this, he had seen it: an instant, a flash, his mother's soprano 'Even my dress! Even my dress!' loud and outraged in the barren unswept hall; a face young and female and even lighter in color than Tomey's Terrel's for an instant in a closing door; a swirl, a glimpse of the silk gown and the flick and glint of an ear-ring: an apparition rapid and tawdry and illicit yet somehow even to the child, the infant still almost, breathless and exciting and evocative: as though, like two limpid and pellucid streams meeting, the child which he still was had made serene and absolute and perfect rapport and contact through that glimpsed nameless illicit hybrid female flesh with the boy which had existed at that stage of inviolable and immortal adolescence in his uncle for almost sixty years; the dress, the face, the ear-rings gone in that same aghast flash and his uncle's voice: 'She's my cook! She's my new cook! I had to have a cook, didn't I?' then the uncle himself, the face alarmed and aghast too yet still innocently and somehow even indomitably of a boy, they retreating in their turn now, back to the front gallery, and his uncle again, pained and still amazed, in a sort of desperate resurgence if not of courage at least of self-assertion: 'They're free now! They're folks too just like we are!' and his mother: 'That's why! That's why! My mother's house! Defiled! Defiled!' and his uncle: 'Damn it, Sibbey, at least give her time to pack her grip:' then over, finished, the loud uproar and all, himself and Tennie and he remembered Tennie's inscrutable face at the broken shutterless window of the bare room which had once been the parlor while they watched, hurrying down the lane at a stumbling trot, the routed compounder of his uncle's uxory: the back, the nameless face which he had seen only for a moment, the once-hooped dress ballooning and flapping below a man's overcoat, the worn heavy carpet-bag jouncing and banging against her knee, routed and in retreat true enough and in the empty lane solitary young-looking and forlorn yet withal still exciting and evocative and wearing still the silken banner captured inside the very citadel of respectability, and unforgettable.)

the cup, the sealed inscrutable burlap, sitting on the shelf in the locked closet, Uncle Hubert unlocking the door and lifting it down and passing it from hand to hand: his mother, his father, McCaslin and even Tennie, insisting that each take it in turn and heft it for weight and shake it again to prove the sound, Uncle Hubert himself standing spraddled before the cold unswept hearth in which the very bricks themselves were crumbling into a litter of soot and dust and mortar and the droppings of chimney-sweeps, still roaring and still innocent and still indomitable: and for a long time he believed nobody but himself had noticed that his uncle now put the cup only into his hands, unlocked the door and lifted it down and put it into his hands and stood over him until he had shaken it obediently until it sounded then took it from him and locked it back into the closet before anyone else could have offered to touch it, and even later, when competent not only to remember but to rationalise, he could not say what it was or even if it had been anything because the parcel was still heavy and still rattled, not even when, Uncle Buddy dead and his father, at last and after almost seventy-five years in bed after the sun rose, said: 'Go get that damn cup. Bring that damn Hub Beauchamp too if you have to:' because it still rattled though his uncle no longer put it even into his hands now but carried it himself from one to the other, his mother, Mc-

Caslin, Tennie, shaking it before each in turn, saying: 'Hear it? Hear it?' his face still innocent, not quite baffled but only amazed and not very amazed and still indomitable: and, his father and Uncle Buddy both gone now, one day without reason or any warning the almost completely empty house in which his uncle and Tennie's ancient and quarrelsome great-grandfather (who claimed to have seen La Fayette and McCaslin said in another ten years would be remembering God) lived, cooked and slept in one single room, burst into peaceful conflagration, a tranquil instantaneous sourceless unanimity of combustion, walls floors and roof: at sunup it stood where his uncle's father had built it sixty years ago, at sundown the four blackened and smokeless chimneys rose from a light white powder of ashes and a few charred ends of planks which did not even appear to have been very hot: and out of the last of evening, the last one of the twenty-two miles, on the old white mare which was the last of that stable which McCaslin remembered, the two old men riding double up to the sister's door, the one wearing his fox-horn on its braided deerhide thong and the other carrying the burlap parcel wrapped in a shirt, the tawny wax-daubed shapeless lump sitting again and on an almost identical shelf and his uncle holding the half-opened door now, his hand not only on the knob but one foot against it and the key waiting in the other hand, the face urgent and still not baffled but still and even indomitably not very amazed and himself standing in the half-opened door looking quietly up at the burlap shape become almost three times its original height and a good half less than its original thickness and turning away and he would remember not his mother's look this time nor yet Tennie's inscrutable expression but McCaslin's dark and aquiline face grave insufferable and bemused: then one night they waked him and fetched him still half-asleep into the lamp light, the smell of medicine which was familiar by now in that room and the smell of something else which he had not smelled before and knew at once and would never forget, the pillow, the worn and ravaged face from which looked out still the boy innocent and immortal and amazed and urgent, looking at him and trying to tell him until McCaslin moved and leaned over the bed and drew from the top of the nightshirt the big iron key on the greasy cord which suspended it, the eyes saying Yes Yes Yes now, and cut the cord and unlocked the closet and brought the parcel to the bed, the eyes still trying to tell him even when he took the parcel so that was still not it, the hands still clinging to the parcel even while relinquishing it, the eyes more urgent than ever trying to tell him but they never did; and he was ten and his mother was dead too and McCaslin said, 'You are almost halfway now. You might as well open it:' and he: 'No. He said twenty-one:' and he was twenty-one and McCaslin shifted the bright lamp to the center of the cleared dining-room table and set the parcel beside it and laid his open knife beside the parcel and stood back with that expression of old grave intolerant and repudiating and he lifted it, the burlap lump which fifteen years ago had changed its shape completely overnight, which shaken gave forth a thin weightless not-quite-musical curiously muffled clatter, the bright knife-blade hunting amid the mazed intricacy of string, the knobby gouts of wax bearing his uncle's Beauchamp seal rattling onto the table's polished top and, standing amid the collapse of burlap folds, the unstained tin coffee-pot still brand new, the handful of copper coins and now he knew what had given them the muffled sound: a collection of minutely-folded scraps of paper sufficient almost for a rat's nest, of good linen bond, of the crude ruled paper such as negroes use, of raggedly-torn ledger-pages and the margins of newspapers and once the paper label from a new pair of overalls, all dated and all signed, beginning with the first one not six months after they had watched him seal the silver cup into the burlap on this same table in this same room by the light even of this same lamp almost twenty-one years ago:

I owe my Nephew Isaac Beauchamp McCaslin five (5) pieces Gold which I,O.U constitues My note of hand with Interest at 5 percent.

Hubert Fitz-Hubert Beauchamp

at Warwick 27 Nov 1867

and he: 'Anyway he called it Warwick:' once at least, even if no more. But there was more:

Isaac 24 Dec 1867 I.O.U. 2 pieces Gold H.Fh.B.

I.O.U. Isaac 1 piece Gold 1 Jan 1868 H.Fb.B.

then five again then three then one then one then a long time and what dream, what dreamed splendid recoup, not of any injury or betrayal of trust because it had been merely a loan; nay, a partnership:

I.O.U. Beauchamp McCaslin or his heirs twenty-five (25) pieces Gold This & All preceeding constituting My notes of hand at twenty (20) percentum compounded annually. This date of 19th January 1873

Beauchamp

no location save that in time and signed by the single not name but word as the old proud earl himself might have scrawled Neville: and that made forty-three and he could not remember himself of course but the legend had it at fifty, which balanced: one: then one: then one: then one and then the last three and then the last chit, dated after he came to live in the house with them and written in the shaky hand not of a beaten old man because he had never been beaten to know it but of a tired old man maybe and even at that tired only on the outside and still indomitable, the simplicity of the last one the simplicity not of resignation but merely of amazement, like a simple comment or remark, and not very much of that:

One silver cup. Hubert Beauchamp

and McCaslin: 'So you have plenty of coppers anyway. But they are still not old enough yet to be either rarities or heirlooms. So you will have to take the money:' except that he didn't hear McCaslin, standing quietly beside the table and looking peacefully at the coffee-pot and the pot sitting one night later on the mantel above what was not even a fireplace in the little cramped icelike room in Jefferson as McCaslin tossed the folded banknotes onto the bed and, still standing (there was nowhere to sit save on the bed) did not even remove his hat and overcoat: and he

'As a loan. From you. This one:' and McCaslin

'You cant. I have no money that I can lend to you. And you will have to go to the bank and get it next month because I wont bring it to you:' and he could not hear McCaslin now either, looking peacefully at McCaslin, his kinsman, his father almost yet no kin now as, at the last, even fathers and sons are no kin: and he

'It's seventeen miles, horseback and in the cold. We could both sleep here:' and McCaslin

'Why should I sleep here in my house when you wont sleep yonder in yours?' and gone, and he looking at the bright rustless unstained tin and thinking and not for the first time how much it takes to compound a man (Isaac McCaslin for instance) and of the devious intricate choosing yet unerring path that man's (Isaac McCaslin's for instance) spirit takes among all that mass to make him at last what he is to be, not only to the astonishment of them (the ones who sired the McCaslin who sired his father and Uncle Buddy and their sister, and the ones who sired the Beauchamp who sired his Uncle Hubert and his Uncle Hubert's sister) who believed they had shaped him, but to Isaac McCaslin too

as a loan and used it though he would not have had to: Major de Spain offered him a room in his house as long as he wanted it and asked nor would ever ask any question, and old General Compson more than that, to take him into his own room, to sleep in half of his own bed and more than Major de Spain because he told him baldly why: 'You sleep with me and before this winter is out, I'll know the reason. You'll tell me. Because I dont believe you just quit. It looks like you just quit but I have watched you in the woods too much and I dont believe you just quit even if it does look damn like it:' using it as a loan, paid his board and rent for a month and bought the tools, not simply because he was good with his hands because he had intended to use his hands and it could have been with horses, and not in mere static and hopeful emulation of the Nazarene as the young gambler buys a spotted shirt because the old gambler won in one yesterday, but (without the arrogance of false humility and without the false humbleness of pride, who intended to earn his bread, didn't especially want to earn it but had to earn it and for more than just bread) because if the Nazarene had found carpentering good for the life and ends He had assumed and elected to serve, it would be all right too for Isaac McCaslin even though Isaac McCaslin's ends, although simple enough in their apparent motivation, were and would be always incomprehensible to him, and his life, invincible enough in its needs, if he could have helped himself, not being the Nazarene, he would not have chosen it: and paid it back. He had forgotten the thirty dollars which McCaslin would put into the bank in his name each month, fetched it in to him and flung it onto the bed that first one time but no more; he had a partner now or rather he was the partner: a blasphemous profane clever old dipsomaniac who had built blockade-runners in Charleston in '62 and '3 and had been a ship's carpenter since and appeared in Jefferson two years ago nobody knew from where nor why and spent a good part of his time since recovering from delirium tremens in the jail; they had put a new roof on the stable of the bank's president and (the old man in jail again still celebrating that job) he went to the bank to collect for it and the president said, 'I should borrow from you instead of paying you:' and it had been seven months now and he remembered for the first time, two-hundred-and-ten dollars, and this was the first job of any size and when he left the bank the account stood at two-twenty, two-forty to balance, only twenty dollars more to go, then it did balance though by then the total had increased to three hundred and thirty and he said, 'I will transfer it now:' and the president said, 'I cant do that. McCaslin told me not to. Haven't you got another initial you could use and open another account?' but that was all right, the coins the silver and the bills as they accumulated knotted into a handkerchief and the coffee-pot wrapped in an old shirt as when Tennie's great-grandfather had fetched it from Warwick eighteen years ago, in the bottom of the iron-bound trunk which old Carothers had brought from Carolina and his landlady said, 'Not even a lock! And you dont even lock your door, not even when you leave!' and himself looking at her as peacefully as he had looked at McCaslin that first night in this same room, no kin to him at all yet more than kin as those who serve you even for pay are your kin and those who injure you are more than brother or wife

and had the wife now, got the old man out of jail and fetched him to the rented room and sobered him by superior strength, did not even remove his own shoes for twenty-four hours, got him up and got food into him and they built the barn this time from the ground up and he married her: an only child, a small girl yet curiously bigger than she seemed at first, solider perhaps, with dark eyes and a passionate heart-shaped face, who had time even on that farm to watch most of the day while he sawed timbers to the old man's measurements: and she: 'Papa told me about you. That farm is really yours, isn't it?' and he

'And McCaslin's:' and she

'Was there a will leaving half of it to him?' and he

'There didn't need to be a will. His grandmother was my father's sister. We were the same as brothers:' and she

'You are the same as second cousins and that's all you ever will be. But I dont suppose it matters:' and they were married, they were married and it was the new country, his heritage too as it was the heritage of all, out of the earth, beyond the earth yet of the earth because his too was of the earth's long chronicle, his too because each must share with another in order to come into it and in the sharing they become one: for that while, one: for that little while at least, one: indivisible, that while at least irrevocable and unrecoverable, living in a rented room still but for just a little while and that room wall-less and topless and floorless in glory for him to leave each morning and return to at night; her father already owned the lot in town and furnished the material and he and his partner would build it, her dowry from one: her wedding-present from three, she not to know it until the bungalow was finished and ready to be moved into and he never knew who told her, not her father and not his partner and not even in drink though for a while he believed that, himself coming home from work and just time to wash and rest a moment before going down to supper, entering no rented cubicle since it would still partake of glory even after they would have grown old and lost it: and he saw her face then, just before she spoke: 'Sit down:' the two of them sitting on the bed's edge, not even touching yet, her face strained and terrible, her voice a passionate and expiring whisper of immeasurable promise: 'I love you. You know I love you. When are we going to move?' and he

'I didn't—I didn't know——Who told you——' the hot fierce palm clapped over his mouth, crushing his lips into his teeth, the fierce curve of fingers digging into his cheek and only the palm slacked off enough for him to answer:

'The farm. Our farm. Your farm:' and he

'I——' then the hand again, finger and palm, the whole enveloping weight of her although she still was not touching him save the hand, the voice: 'No! No!' and the fingers themselves seeming to follow through the cheek the impulse to speech as it died in his mouth, then the whisper, the breath again, of love and of incredible promise, the palm slackening again to let him answer:

'When?' and he

'I——' then she was gone, the hand too, standing, her back to him and her head bent, the voice so calm now that for an instant it seemed no voice of hers that he ever remembered: 'Stand up and turn your back and shut your eyes:' and repeated before he understood and stood himself with his eyes shut and heard the bell ring for supper below stairs and the calm voice again: 'Lock the door:' and he did so and leaned his forehead against the cold wood, his eyes closed, hearing his heart and the sound he had begun to hear before he moved until it ceased and the bell rang again below stairs and he knew it was for them this time and he heard the bed and turned and he had never seen her naked before, he had asked her to once, and why: that he wanted to see her naked because he loved her and he wanted to see her looking at him naked because he loved her but after that he never mentioned it again, even turning his face when she put the nightgown on over her dress to undress at night and putting the dress on over the gown to remove it in the morning and she would not let him get into bed beside her until the lamp was out and even in the heat of summer she would draw the sheet up over them both before she would let him turn to her: and the landlady came up the stairs up the hall and rapped on the door and then called their names but she didn't move, lying still on the bed outside the covers, her face turned away on the pillow, listening to nothing, thinking of nothing, not of him anyway he thought then the landlady went away and she said, 'Take off your clothes:' her head still turned away, looking at nothing, thinking of nothing, waiting for nothing, not even him, her hand moving as though with volition and vision of its own, catching his wrist at the exact moment when he paused beside the bed so that he never paused but merely changed the direction of moving, downward now, the hand drawing him and she moved at last, shifted, a movement one single complete inherent not practiced and one time older than man, looking at him now, drawing him still downward with the one hand down and down and he neither saw nor felt it shift, palm flat against his chest now and holding him away with the same apparent lack of any effort or any need for strength, and not looking at him now, she didn't need to, the chaste woman, the wife, already looked upon all the men who ever rutted and now her whole body had changed, altered, he had never seen it but once and now it was not even the one he had seen but composite of all woman-flesh since man that ever of its own will reclined on its back and opened, and out of it somewhere, without any movement of lips even, the dying and invincible whisper: 'Promise:' and he 'Promise?'

'The farm.' He moved. He had moved, the hand shifting from his chest once more to his wrist, grasping it, the arm still lax and only the light increasing pressure of the fingers as though arm and hand were a piece of wire cable with one looped end, only the hand tightening as he pulled against it. 'No,' he said. 'No:' and she was not looking at him still but not like the other but still the hand: 'No, I tell you. I wont. I cant. Never:' and still the hand and he said, for the last time, he tried to speak clearly and he knew it was still gently and he thought, *She already knows more than I with all the man-listening in camps where there was nothing to read ever even heard of. They are born already bored with what a boy approaches only at fourteen and fifteen with blundering and aghast trembling*: 'I cant. Not ever. Remember:' and still the steady and invincible hand and he said Yes and he thought, *She is lost. She was born lost. We were all born lost* then he stopped thinking and even saying Yes, it was like nothing he had ever dreamed, let alone heard in mere man-talking until after a no-time he returned and lay spent on the insatiate immemorial beach and again with a movement one time more older than man she turned and freed herself and on their wedding night she had cried and he thought she was crying now at first, into the tossed and wadded pillow, the voice coming from somewhere between the pillow and the cachinnation: 'And that's all. That's all from me. If this dont get you that son you talk about, it wont be mine:' lying on her side, her back to the empty rented room, laughing and laughing

5.

He went back to the camp one more time before the lumber company moved in and began to cut the timber. Major de Spain himself never saw it again. But he made them welcome to use the house and hunt the land whenever they liked, and in the winter following the last hunt when Sam Fathers and Lion died, General Compson and Walter Ewell invented a plan to corporate themselves, the old group, into a club and lease the camp and the hunting privileges of the woods—an invention doubtless of the somewhat childish old General but actually worthy of Boon Hogganbeck himself. Even the boy, listening, recognised it for the subterfuge it was: to change the leopard's spots when they could not alter the leopard, a baseless and illusory hope to which even McCaslin seemed to subscribe for a while, that once they had persuaded Major de Spain to return to the camp he might revoke himself, which even the boy knew he would not do. And he did not. The boy never knew what occurred when Major de Spain declined. He was not present when the subject was broached and McCaslin never told him. But when June came and the time for the double birthday celebration there was no mention of it and when November came no one spoke of using Major de Spain's house and he never knew whether or not Major de Spain knew they were going on the hunt though without doubt old Ash probably told him: he and McCaslin and General Compson (and that one was the General's last hunt too) and Walter and Boon and Tennie's Jim and old Ash loaded two wagons and drove two days and almost forty miles beyond any country the boy had ever seen before and lived in tents for the two weeks. And the next spring they heard (not from Major de Spain) that he had sold the timber-rights to a Memphis lumber company and in June the boy came to town with McCaslin one Saturday and went to Major de Spain's office—the big, airy, book-lined second-storey room with windows at one end opening upon the shabby hinder purlieus of stores and at the other a door giving onto the railed balcony above the Square, with its curtained alcove where sat a cedar water-bucket and a sugar-bowl and spoon and tumbler and a wicker-covered demijohn of whiskey, and the bamboo-and-paper punkah swinging back and forth above the desk while old Ash in a tilted chair beside the entrance pulled the cord.

"Of course," Major de Spain said. "Ash will probably like to get off in the woods himself for a while, where he wont have to eat Daisy's cooking. Complain about it, anyway. Are you going to take anybody with you?"

"No sir," he said. "I thought that maybe Boon——" For six months now Boon had been town-marshal at Hoke's; Major de Spain had compounded with the lumber company—or perhaps compromised was closer, since it was the lumber company who had decided that Boon might be better as a town-marshal than head of a logging gang.

"Yes," Major de Spain said. "I'll wire him today. He can meet you at Hoke's. I'll send Ash on by the train and they can take some food in and all you will have to do will be to mount your horse and ride over."

"Yes sir," he said. "Thank you." And he heard his voice again. He didn't know he was going to say it yet he did know, he had known it all the time: "Maybe if you. . . . . ." His voice died. It was stopped, he never knew how because Major de Spain did not speak and it was not until his voice ceased that Major de Spain moved, turned back to the desk and the papers spread on it and even that without moving because he was sitting at the desk with a paper in his hand when the boy entered, the boy standing there looking down at the short plumpish gray-haired man in sober fine broadcloth and an immaculate glazed shirt whom he was used to seeing in boots and muddy corduroy, unshaven, sitting the shaggy powerful long-hocked mare with the worn Winchester carbine across the saddlebow and the great blue dog standing motionless as bronze at the stirrup, the two of them in that last year and to the boy anyway coming to resemble one another somehow as two people competent for love or for business who have been in love or in business together for a long time sometimes do. Major de Spain did not look up again.

"No. I will be too busy. But good luck to you. If you have it, you might bring me a young squirrel."

"Yes sir," he said. "I will."

He rode his mare, the three-year-old filly he had bred and raised and broken himself. He left home a little after midnight and six hours later, without even having sweated her, he rode into Hoke's, the tiny log-line junction which he had always thought of as Major de Spain's property too although Major de Spain had merely sold the company (and that many years ago) the land on which the sidetracks and loading-platforms and the commissary store stood, and looked about in shocked and grieved amazement even though he had had forewarning and had believed himself prepared: a new planing-mill already half completed which would cover two or three acres and what looked like miles and miles of stacked steel rails red with the light bright rust of newness and of piled crossties sharp with creosote, and wire corrals and feeding-troughs for two hundred mules at least and the tents for the men who drove them; so that he arranged for the care and stabling of his mare as rapidly as he could and did not look any more, mounted into the log-train caboose with his gun and climbed into the cupola and looked no more save toward the wall of wilderness ahead within which he would be able to hide himself from it once more anyway.

Then the little locomotive shrieked and began to move: a rapid churning of exhaust, a lethargic deliberate clashing of slack couplings travelling backward along the train, the exhaust changing to the deep slow clapping bites of power as the caboose too began to move and from the cupola he watched the train's head complete the first and only curve in the entire line's length and vanish into the wilderness, dragging its length of train behind it so that it resembled a small dingy harmless snake vanishing into weeds, drawing him with it too until soon it ran once more at its maximum clattering speed between the twin walls of unaxed wilderness as of old. It had been harmless once. Not five years ago Walter Ewell had shot a six-point buck from this same moving caboose, and there was the story of the half-grown bear: the train's first trip in to the cutting thirty miles away, the bear between the rails, its rear end elevated like that of a playing puppy while it dug to see what sort of ants or bugs they might contain or perhaps just to examine the curious symmetrical squared barkless logs which had appeared apparently from nowhere in one endless mathematical line overnight, still digging until the driver on the braked engine not fifty feet away blew the whistle at it, whereupon it broke frantically and took the first tree it came to: an ash sapling not much bigger than a man's thigh and climbed as high as it could and clung there, its head ducked between its arms as a man (a woman perhaps) might have done while the brakeman threw chunks of ballast at it, and when the engine returned three hours later with the first load of outbound logs the bear was halfway down the tree and once more scrambled back up as high as it could and clung again while the train passed and was still there when the engine went in again in the afternoon and still there when it came back out at dusk; and Boon had been in Hoke's with the wagon after a barrel of flour that noon when the train-crew told about it and Boon and Ash, both twenty years younger then, sat under the tree all that night to keep anybody from shooting it and the next morning Major de Spain had the log-train held at Hoke's and just before sundown on the second day, with not only Boon and Ash but Major de Spain and General Compson and Walter and McCaslin, twelve then, watching, it came down the tree after almost thirty-six hours without even water and McCaslin told him how for a minute they thought it was going to stop right there at the barrow-pit where they were standing and drink, how it looked at the water and paused and looked at them and at the water again, but did not, gone, running, as bears run, the two sets of feet, front and back, tracking two separate though parallel courses.

It had been harmless then. They would hear the passing log-train sometimes from the camp; sometimes, because nobody bothered to listen for it or not. They would hear it going in, running light and fast, the light clatter of the trucks, the exhaust of the diminutive locomotive and its shrill peanut-parcher whistle flung for one petty moment and absorbed by the brooding and inattentive wilderness without even an echo. They would hear it going out, loaded, not quite so fast now yet giving its frantic and toylike illusion of crawling speed, not whistling now to conserve steam, flinging its bitten laboring miniature puffing into the immemorial woodsface with frantic and bootless vainglory, empty and noisy and puerile, carrying to no destination or purpose sticks which left nowhere any scar or stump as the child's toy loads and transports and unloads its dead sand and rushes back for more, tireless and unceasing and rapid yet never quite so fast as the Hand which plays with it moves the toy burden back to load the toy again. But it was different now. It was the same train, engine cars and caboose, even the same enginemen brakeman and conductor to whom Boon, drunk then sober then drunk again then fairly sober once more all in the space of fourteen hours, had bragged that day two years ago about what they were going to do to Old Ben tomorrow, running with its same illusion of frantic rapidity between the same twin walls of impenetrable and impervious woods, passing the old landmarks, the old game crossings over which he had trailed bucks wounded and not wounded and more than once seen them, anything but wounded, bolt out of the woods and up and across the embankment which bore the rails and ties then down and into the woods again as the earth-bound supposedly move but crossing as arrows travel, groundless, elongated, three times its actual length and even paler, different in color, as if there were a point between immobility and absolute motion where even mass chemically altered, changing without pain or agony not only in bulk and shape but in color too, approaching the color of wind, yet this time it was as though the train (and not only the train but himself, not only his vision which had seen it and his memory which remembered it but his clothes too, as garments carry back into the clean edgeless blowing of air the lingering effluvium of a sick-room or of death) had brought with it into the doomed wilderness even before the actual axe the shadow and portent of the new mill not even finished yet and the rails and ties which were not even laid; and he knew now what he had known as soon as he saw Hoke's this morning but had not yet thought into words: why Major de Spain had not come back, and that after this time he himself, who had had to see it one time other, would return no more.

Now they were near. He knew it before the engine-driver whistled to warn him. Then he saw Ash and the wagon, the reins without doubt wrapped once more about the brake-lever as within the boy's own memory Major de Spain had been forbidding him for eight years to do, the train slowing, the slackened couplings jolting and clashing again from car to car, the caboose slowing past the wagon as he swung down with his gun, the conductor leaning out above him to signal the engine, the caboose still slowing, creeping, although the engine's exhaust was already slatting in mounting tempo against the unechoing wilderness, the crashing of draw-bars once more travelling backward along the train, the caboose picking up speed at last. Then it was gone. It had not been. He could no longer hear it. The wilderness soared, musing, inattentive, myriad, eternal, green; older than any mill-shed, longer than any spur-line. "Mr Boon here yet?" he said.

"He beat me in," Ash said. "Had the wagon loaded and ready for me at Hoke's yistiddy when I got there and setting on the front steps at camp last night when I got in. He already been in the woods since fo daylight this morning. Said he gwine up to the Gum Tree and for you to hunt up that way and meet him." He knew where that was: a single big sweet-gum just outside the woods, in an old clearing; if you crept up to it very quietly this time of year and then ran suddenly into the clearing, sometimes you caught as many as a dozen squirrels in it, trapped, since there was no other tree near they could jump to. So he didn't get into the wagon at all.

"I will," he said.

"I figured you would," Ash said. "I fotch you a box of shells." He passed the shells down and began to unwrap the lines from the brake-pole.

"How many times up to now do you reckon Major has told you not to do that?" the boy said.

"Do which?" Ash said. Then he said: "And tell Boon Hoganbeck dinner gonter be on the table in a hour and if yawl want any to come on and eat it."

"In an hour?" he said. "It aint nine oclock yet." He drew

out his watch and extended it face-toward Ash. "Look." Ash didn't even look at the watch.

"That's town time. You aint in town now. You in the woods."

"Look at the sun then."

"Nemmine the sun too," Ash said. "If you and Boon Hogganbeck want any dinner, you better come on in and get it when I tole you. I aim to get done in that kitchen because I got my wood to chop. And watch your feet. They're crawling."

"I will," he said.

Then he was in the woods, not alone but solitary; the solitude closed about him, green with summer. They did not change, and, timeless, would not, anymore than would the green of summer and the fire and rain of fall and the iron cold and sometimes even snow

the day, the morning when he killed the buck and Sam marked his face with its hot blood, they returned to camp and he remembered old Ash's blinking and disgruntled and even outraged disbelief until at last McCaslin had had to affirm the fact that he had really killed it: and that night Ash sat snarling and unapproachable behind the stove so that Tennie's Jim had to serve the supper and waked them with breakfast already on the table the next morning and it was only half-past one oclock and at last out of Major de Spain's angry cursing and Ash's snarling and sullen rejoinders the fact emerged that Ash not only wanted to go into the woods and shoot a deer also but he intended to and Major de Spain said, 'By God, if we dont let him we will probably have to do the cooking from now on:' and Walter Ewell said, 'Or get up at midnight to eat what Ash cooks:' and since he had already killed his buck for this hunt and was not to shoot again unless they needed meat, he offered his gun to Ash until Major de Spain took command and allotted that gun to Boon for the day and gave Boon's unpredictable pump gun to Ash, with two buckshot shells but Ash said, 'I got shells:' and showed them, four: one buck, one of number three shot for rabbits, two of bird-shot and told one by one their history and their origin and he remembered not Ash's face alone but Major de Spain's and Walter's and General Compson's too, and Ash's voice: 'Shoot? In course they'll shoot! Genl Cawmpson guv me this un'——the buckshot——'right outen the same gun he kilt that big buck with eight years ago. And this un'——it was the rabbit shell: triumphantly——'is oldern thisyer boy!' And that morning he loaded the gun himself, reversing the order: the bird-shot, the rabbit, then the buck so that the buckshot would feed first into the chamber, and himself without a gun, he and Ash walked beside Major de Spain's and Tennie's Jim's horses and the dogs (that was the snow) until they cast and struck, the sweet strong cries ringing away into the muffled falling air and gone almost immediately, as if the constant and unmurmuring flakes had already buried even the unformed echoes beneath their myriad and weightless falling, Major de Spain and Tennie's Jim gone too, whooping on into the woods; and then it was all right, he knew as plainly as if Ash had told him that Ash had now hunted his deer and that even his tender years had been forgiven for having killed one, and they turned back toward home through the falling snow—that is, Ash said, 'Now whut?' and he said, 'This way'——himself in front because, although they were less than a mile from camp, he knew that Ash, who had spent two weeks of his life in the camp each year for the last twenty, had no idea whatever where they were, until quite soon the manner in which Ash carried Boon's gun was making him a good deal more than just nervous and he made Ash walk in front, striding on, talking now, an old man's garrulous monologue beginning with where he was at the moment then of the woods and of camping in the woods and of eating in camps then of eating then of cooking it and of his wife's cooking then briefly of his old wife and almost at once and at length of a new light-colored woman who nursed next door to Major de Spain's and if she didn't watch out who she was switching her tail at he would show her how old was an old man or not if his wife just didn't watch him all the time, the two of them in a game trail through a dense brake of cane and brier which would bring them out within a quarter-mile of camp, approaching a big fallen tree-trunk lying athwart the path and just as Ash, still talking, was about to step over it the bear, the yearling, rose suddenly beyond the log, sitting up, its forearms against its chest and its wrists limply arrested as if it had been surprised in the act of covering its face to pray: and after a certain time Ash's gun yawed jerkily up and he said, 'You haven't got a shell in the barrel yet. Pump it:' but the gun already snicked and he said, 'Pump it. You haven't got a shell in the barrel yet:' and Ash pumped the action and in a certain time the gun steadied again and snicked and he said, 'Pump it:' and watched the buckshot shell jerk, spinning heavily, into the cane. This is the rabbit shot: he thought and the gun snicked and he thought: The next is bird-shot: and he didn't have to say Pump it; he cried, 'Dont shoot! Dont shoot!' but that was already too late too, the light dry vicious snick! before he could speak and the bear turned and dropped to all-fours and then was gone and there was only the log, the cane, the velvet and constant snow and Ash said, 'Now whut?' and he said, 'This way. Come on:' and began to back away down the path and Ash said, 'I got to find my shells:' and he said, 'Goddamn it, goddamn it, come on:' but Ash leaned the gun against the log and returned and stooped and fumbled among the cane roots until he came back and stooped and found the shells and they rose and at that moment the gun, untouched, leaning against the log six feet away and for that while even forgotten by both of them, roared, bellowed and flamed, and ceased: and he carried it now, pumped out the last mummified shell and gave that one also to Ash and, the action still open, himself carried the gun until he stood it in the corner behind Boon's bed at the camp

——; summer, and fall, and snow, and wet and saprife spring in their ordered immortal sequence, the deathless and immemorial phases of the mother who had shaped him if any had toward the man he almost was, mother and father both to the old man born of a Negro slave and a Chickasaw chief who had been his spirit's father if any had, whom he had revered and harkened to and loved and lost and grieved: and he would marry someday and they too would own for their brief while that brief unsubstanced glory which inherently of itself cannot last and hence why glory: and they would, might, carry even the remembrance of it into the time when flesh no longer talks to flesh because memory at least does last: but still the woods would be his mistress and his wife.

He was not going toward the Gum Tree. Actually he was getting farther from it. Time was and not so long ago either when he would not have been allowed here without someone with him, and a little later, when he had begun to learn how much he did not know, he would not have dared be here without someone with him, and later still, beginning to ascertain, even if only dimly, the limits of what he did not know, he could have attempted and carried it through with a compass, not because of any increased belief in himself but because McCaslin and Major de Spain and Walter and General Compson too had taught him at last to believe the compass regardless of what it seemed to state. Now he did not even use the compass but merely the sun and that only subconsciously, yet he could have taken a scaled map and plotted at any time to within a hundred feet of where he actually was; and sure enough, at almost the exact moment when he expected it, the earth began to rise faintly, he passed one of the four concrete markers set down by the lumber company's surveyor to establish the four corners of the plot which Major de Spain had reserved out of the sale, then he stood on the crest of the knoll itself, the four corner-markers all visible now, blanched still even beneath the winter's weathering, lifeless and shockingly alien in that place where dissolution itself was a seething turmoil of ejaculation tumescence conception and birth, and death did not even exist. After two winters' blanketings of leaves and the flood-waters of two springs, there was no trace of the two graves anymore at all. But those who would have come this far to find them would not need headstones but would have found them as Sam Fathers himself had taught him to find such: by bearings on trees: and did, almost the first thrust of the hunting knife finding (but only to see if it was still there) the round tin box manufactured for axle-grease and containing now Old Ben's dried mutilated paw, resting above Lion's bones.

He didn't disturb it. He didn't even look for the other grave where he and McCaslin and Major de Spain and Boon had laid Sam's body, along with his hunting horn and his knife and his tobacco-pipe, that Sunday morning two years ago; he didn't have to. He had stepped over it, perhaps on it. But that was all right. *He probably knew I was in the woods this morning long before I got here*, he thought, going on to the tree which had supported one end of the platform where Sam lay when McCaslin and Major de Spain found them—the tree, the other axle-grease tin nailed to the trunk, but weathered, rusted, alien too yet healed already into the wilderness' concordant generality, raising no tuneless note, and empty, long since empty of the food and tobacco he had put into it that day, as empty of that as it would presently be of this which he drew from his pocket—the twist of tobacco, the new bandanna handkerchief, the small paper sack of the peppermint candy which Sam had used to love; that gone too, almost before he had turned his back, not vanished but merely translated into the myriad life which printed the dark mold of these secret and sunless places with delicate fairy tracks, which, breathing and biding and immobile, watched him from beyond every twig and leaf until he moved, moving again, walking on; he had not stopped, he had only paused, quitting the knoll which was no abode of the dead because there was no death, not Lion and not Sam: not held fast in earth but free in earth and not in earth but of earth, myriad yet undiffused of every myriad part, leaf and twig and particle, air and sun and rain and dew and night, acorn oak and leaf and acorn again, dark and dawn and dark and dawn again in their immutable progression and, being myriad, one: and Old Ben too, Old Ben too; they would give him his paw back even, certainly they would give him his paw back: then the long challenge and the long chase, no heart to be driven and outraged, no flesh to be mauled and bled—— Even as he froze himself, he seemed to hear Ash's parting admonition. He could even hear the voice as he froze, immobile, one foot just taking his weight, the toe of the other just lifted behind him, not breathing, feeling again and as always the sharp shocking inrush from when Isaac McCaslin long yet was not, and so it was fear all right but not fright as he looked down at it. It had not coiled yet and the buzzer had not sounded either, only one thick rapid contraction, one loop cast sideways as though merely for purchase from which the raised head might start slightly backward, not in fright either, not in threat quite yet, more than six feet of it, the head raised higher than his knee and less than his knee's length away, and old, the once-bright markings of its youth dulled now to a monotone concordant too with the wilderness it crawled and lurked: the old one, the ancient and accursed about the earth, fatal and solitary and he could smell it now: the thin sick smell of rotting cucumbers and something else which had no name, evocative of all knowledge and an old weariness and of pariah-hood and of death. At last it moved. Not the head.

The elevation of the head did not change as it began to glide away from him, moving erect yet off the perpendicular as if the head and that elevated third were complete and all: an entity walking on two feet and free of all laws of mass and balance and should have been because even now he could not quite believe that all that shift and flow of shadow behind that walking head could have been one snake: going and then gone; he put the other foot down at last and didn't know it, standing with one hand raised as Sam had stood that afternoon six years ago when Sam led him into the wilderness and showed him and he ceased to be a child, speaking the old tongue which Sam had spoken that day without premeditation either: "Chief," he said: "Grandfather."

He couldn't tell when he first began to hear the sound, because when he became aware of it, it seemed to him that he had been already hearing it for several seconds—a sound as though someone were hammering a gun-barrel against a piece of railroad iron, a sound loud and heavy and not rapid yet with something frenzied about it, as though the hammerer were not only a strong man and an earnest one but a little hysterical too. Yet it couldn't be on the log-line because, although the track lay in that direction, it was at least two miles from him and this sound was not three hundred yards away. But even as he thought that, he realised where the sound must be coming from: whoever the man was and whatever he was doing, he was somewhere near the edge of the clearing where the Gum Tree was and where he was to meet Boon. So far, he had been hunting as he advanced, moving slowly and quietly and watching the ground and the trees both. Now he went on, his gun unloaded and the barrel slanted up and back to facilitate its passage through brier and undergrowth, approaching as it grew louder and louder that steady savage somehow queerly hysterical beating of metal on metal, emerging from the woods, into the old clearing, with the solitary gum tree directly before him. At first glance the tree seemed to be alive with frantic squirrels. There appeared to be forty or fifty of them leaping and darting from branch to branch until the whole tree had become one green maelstrom of mad leaves, while from time to time, singly or in twos and threes, squirrels would dart down the trunk then whirl without stopping and rush back up again as though sucked violently back by the vacuum of their fellows' frenzied vortex. Then he saw Boon, sitting, his back against the trunk, his head bent, hammering furiously at something on his lap. What he hammered with was the barrel of his dismembered gun, what he hammered at was the breech of it. The rest of the gun lay scattered about him in a half-dozen pieces while he bent over the piece on his lap his scarlet and streaming walnut face, hammering the disjointed barrel against the gun-breech with the frantic abandon of a madman. He didn't even look up to see who it was. Still hammering, he merely shouted back at the boy in a hoarse strangled voice:

"Get out of here! Dont touch them! Dont touch a one of them! They're mine!"

Delta Autumn

SOON NOW they would enter the Delta. The sensation was familiar to him. It had been renewed like this each last week in November for more than fifty years—the last hill, at the foot of which the rich unbroken alluvial flatness began as the sea began at the base of its cliffs, dissolving away beneath the unhurried November rain as the sea itself would dissolve away.

At first they had come in wagons: the guns, the bedding, the dogs, the food, the whisky, the keen heart-lifting anticipation of hunting; the young men who could drive all night and all the following day in the cold rain and pitch a camp in the rain and sleep in the wet blankets and rise at daylight the next morning and hunt. There had been bear then. A man shot a doe or a fawn as quickly as he did a buck, and in the afternoons they shot wild turkey with pistols to test their stalking skill and marksmanship, feeding all but the breast to the dogs. But that time was gone now. Now they went in cars, driving faster and faster each year because the roads were better and they had farther and farther to drive, the territory in which game still existed drawing yearly inward as his life was drawing inward, until now he was the last of those who had once made the journey in wagons without feeling it and now those who accompanied him were the sons and even grandsons of the men who had ridden for twenty-four hours in the rain or sleet behind the steaming mules. They called him 'Uncle Ike' now, and he no longer told anyone how near eighty he actually was because he knew as well as they did that he no longer had any business making such expeditions, even by car.

In fact, each time now, on that first night in camp, lying aching and sleepless in the harsh blankets, his blood only faintly warmed by the single thin whisky-and-water which he allowed himself, he would tell himself that this would be his last. But he would stand that trip—he still shot almost as well as he ever had, still killed almost as much of the game he saw as he ever killed; he no longer even knew how many deer had fallen before his gun—and the fierce long heat of the next summer would renew him. Then November would come again, and again in the car with two of the sons of his old companions, whom he had taught not only how to distinguish between the prints left by a buck or a doe but between the sound they made in moving, he would look ahead past the jerking arc of the windshield wiper and see the land flatten suddenly and swoop, dissolving away beneath the rain as the sea itself would dissolve, and he would say, "Well, boys, there it is again."

This time though, he didn't have time to speak. The driver of the car stopped it, slamming it to a skidding halt on the greasy pavement without warning, actually flinging the two passengers forward until they caught themselves with their braced hands against the dash. "What the hell, Roth!" the man in the middle said. "Cant you whistle first when you do that? Hurt you, Uncle Ike?"

"No," the old man said. "What's the matter?" The driver didn't answer. Still leaning forward, the old man looked sharply past the face of the man between them, at the face of his kinsman. It was the youngest face of them all, aquiline, saturnine, a little ruthless, the face of his ancestor too, tempered a little, altered a little, staring sombrely through the streaming windshield across which the twin wipers flicked and flicked.

"I didn't intend to come back in here this time," he said suddenly and harshly.

"You said that back in Jefferson last week," the old man said. "Then you changed your mind. Have you changed it again? This aint a very good time to——"

"Oh, Roth's coming," the man in the middle said. His name was Legate. He seemed to be speaking to no one, as he was looking at neither of them. "If it was just a buck he was coming all this distance for, now. But he's got a doe in here. Of course a old man like Uncle Ike cant be interested in no doe, not one that walks on two legs—when she's standing up, that is. Pretty light-colored, too. The one he was after them nights last fall when he said he was coon-hunting, Uncle Ike. The one I figured maybe he was still running when he was gone all that month last January. But of course a old man like Uncle Ike aint got no interest in nothing like that." He chortled, still looking at no one, not completely jeering.

"What?" the old man said. "What's that?" But he had not even so much as glanced at Legate. He was still watching his kinsman's face. The eyes behind the spectacles were the blurred eyes of an old man, but they were quite sharp too; eyes which could still see a gun-barrel and what ran beyond it as well as any of them could. He was remembering himself now: how last year, during the final stage by motor boat in to where they camped, a box of food had been lost overboard and how on the next day his kinsman had gone back to the nearest town for supplies and had been gone overnight. And when he did return, something had happened to him. He would go into the woods with his rifle each dawn when the others went, but the old man, watching him, knew that he was not hunting. "All right," he said. "Take me and Will on to shelter where we can wait for the truck, and you can go on back."

"I'm going in," the other said harshly. "Dont worry. Because this will be the last of it."

"The last of deer hunting, or of doe hunting?" Legate said. This time the old man paid no attention to him even by speech. He still watched the young man's savage and brooding face.

"Why?" he said.

"After Hitler gets through with it? Or Smith or Jones or Roosevelt or Willkie or whatever he will call himself in this country?"

"We'll stop him in this country," Legate said. "Even if he calls himself George Washington."

"How?" Edmonds said. "By singing God bless America in bars at midnight and wearing dime-store flags in our lapels?"

"So that's what's worrying you," the old man said. "I aint noticed this country being short of defenders yet, when it needed them. You did some of it yourself twenty-odd years ago, before you were a grown man even. This country is a little mite stronger than any one man or group of men, outside of it or even inside of it either. I reckon, when the time comes and some of you have done got tired of hollering we are whipped if we dont go to war and some more are hollering we are whipped if we do, it will cope with one Austrian paper-hanger, no matter what he will be calling himself. My pappy and some other better men than any of them you named tried once to tear it in two with a war, and they failed."

"And what have you got left?" the other said. "Half the people without jobs and half the factories closed by strikes. Half the people on public dole that wont work and half that couldn't work even if they would. Too much cotton and corn and hogs, and not enough for people to eat and wear. The country full of people to tell a man how he cant raise his own cotton whether he will or wont, and Sally Rand with a sergeant's stripes and not even the fan couldn't fill the army rolls. Too much not-butter and not even the guns——"

"We got a deer camp—if we ever get to it," Legate said. "Not to mention does."

"It's a good time to mention does," the old man said. "Does and fawns both. The only fighting anywhere that ever had anything of God's blessing on it has been when men fought to protect does and fawns. If it's going to come to fighting, that's a good thing to mention and remember too."

"Haven't you discovered in—how many years more than seventy is it?—that women and children are one thing there's never any scarcity of?" Edmonds said.

"Maybe that's why all I am worrying about right now is that ten miles of river we still have got to run before we can make camp," the old man said. "So let's get on."

They went on. Soon they were going fast again, as Edmonds always drove, consulting neither of them about the speed just as he had given neither of them any warning when he slammed the car to stop. The old man relaxed again. He watched, as he did each recurrent November while more than sixty of them passed, the land which he had seen change. At first there had been only the old towns along the River and the old towns along the hills, from each of which the planters with their gangs of slaves and then of hired laborers had wrested from the impenetrable jungle of water-standing cane and cypress, gum and holly and oak and ash, cotton patches which as the years passed became fields and then plantations. The paths made by deer and bear became roads and then highways, with towns in turn springing up along them and along the rivers Tallahatchie and Sunflower which joined and became the Yazoo, the River of the Dead of the Choctaws—the thick, slow, black, unsunned streams almost without current, which once each year ceased to flow at all and then reversed, spreading, drowning the rich land and subsiding again, leaving it still richer.

Most of that was gone now. Now a man drove two hundred miles from Jefferson before he found wilderness to hunt in. Now the land lay open from the cradling hills on the East to the rampart of levee on the West, standing horseman-tall with cotton for the world's looms—the rich black land, imponderable and vast, fecund up to the very doorsteps of the negroes who worked it and of the white men who owned it; which exhausted the hunting life of a dog in one year, the working life of a mule in five and of a man in twenty—the land in which neon flashed past them from the little countless towns and countless shining this-year's automobiles sped past them on the broad plumb-ruled highways, yet in which the only permanent mark of man's occupation seemed to be the tremendous gins, constructed in sections of sheet iron and in a week's time though they were, since no man, millionaire though he be, would build more than a roof and walls to shelter the camping equipment he lived from when he knew that once each ten years or so his house would be flooded to the second storey and all within it ruined;—the land across which there came now no scream of panther but instead the long hooting of locomotives: trains of incredible length and drawn by a single engine, since there was no gradient anywhere and no elevation save those raised by forgotten aboriginal hands as refuges from the yearly water and used by their Indian successors to sepulchre their fathers' bones, and all that remained of that old time were the Indian names on the little towns and usually pertaining to water—Aluschaskuna, Tillatoba, Homochitto, Yazoo.

By early afternoon, they were on water. At the last little Indian-named town at the end of pavement they waited until the other car and the two trucks—the one carrying the bedding and tents and food, the other the horses—overtook them. They left the concrete and, after another mile or so, the gravel too. In caravan they ground on through the ceaselessly dissolving afternoon, with skid-chains on the wheels now, lurching and splashing and sliding among the ruts, until presently it seemed to him that the retrograde of his remembering had gained an inverse velocity from their own slow progress, that the land had retreated not in minutes from the last spread of gravel but in years, decades, back toward what it had been when he first knew it: the road they now followed once more the ancient pathway of bear and deer, the diminishing fields they now passed once more scooped punily and terrifically by axe and saw and mule-drawn plow from the wilderness' flank, out of the brooding and immemorial tangle, in place of ruthless mile-wide parallelograms wrought by ditching and dyking machinery.

They reached the river landing and unloaded, the horses to go overland down stream to a point opposite the camp and swim the river, themselves and the bedding and food and dogs and guns in the motor launch. It was himself, though no horseman, no farmer, not even a countryman save by his distant birth and boyhood, who coaxed and soothed the two horses, drawing them by his own single frail hand until, backing, filling, trembling a little, they surged, halted, then sprang scrambling down from the truck, possessing no affinity for them as creatures, beasts, but being merely insulated by his years and time from the corruption of steel and oiled moving parts which tainted the others.

Then, his old hammer double gun which was only twelve years younger than he standing between his knees, he watched even the last puny marks of man—cabin, clearing, the small and irregular fields which a year ago were jungle and in which the skeleton stalks of this year's cotton stood almost as tall and rank as the old cane had stood, as if man had had to marry his planting to the wilderness in order to conquer it—fall away and vanish. The twin banks marched with wilderness as he remembered it—the tangle of brier and cane impenetrable even to sight twenty feet away, the tall tremendous soaring of oak and gum and ash and hickory which had rung to no axe save the hunter's, had echoed to no machinery save the beat of old-time steam boats traversing it or to the snarling of launches like their own of people going into it to dwell for a week or two weeks because it was still wilderness.

There was some of it left, although now it was two hundred miles from Jefferson when once it had been thirty. He had watched it, not being conquered, destroyed, so much as retreating since its purpose was served now and its time an outmoded time, retreating southward through this inverted-apex, this ∇-shaped section of earth between hills and River until what was left of it seemed now to be gathered and for the time arrested in one tremendous density of brooding and inscrutable impenetrability at the ultimate funnelling tip.

They reached the site of their last-year's camp with still two hours left of light. "You go on over under that driest tree and set down," Legate told him. "—if you can find it. Me and these other young boys will do this." He did neither. He was not tired yet. That would come later. *Maybe it wont come at all this time*, he thought, as he had thought at this point each November for the last five or six of them. *Maybe I will go out on stand in the morning too*; knowing that he would not, not even if he took the advice and sat down under the driest shelter and did nothing until camp was made and supper cooked. Because it would not be the fatigue. It would be because he would not sleep tonight but would lie instead wakeful and peaceful on the cot amid the tent-filling snoring and the rain's whisper as he always did on the first night in camp; peaceful, without regret or fretting, telling himself that was all right too, who didn't have so many of them left as to waste one sleeping.

In his slicker he directed the unloading of the boat—the tents, the stove, the bedding, the food for themselves and the dogs until there should be meat in camp. He sent two of the negroes to cut firewood; he had the cook-tent raised and the stove up and a fire going and supper cooking while the big tent was still being staked down. Then in the beginning of dusk he crossed in the boat to where the horses waited, backing and snorting at the water. He took the lead-ropes and with no more weight than that and his voice, he drew them down into the water and held them beside the boat with only their heads above the surface, as though they actually were suspended from his frail and strengthless old man's hands, while the boat recrossed and each horse in turn lay prone in the shallows, panting and trembling, its eyes rolling in the dusk, until the same weightless hand and unraised voice gathered it surging upward, splashing and thrashing up the bank.

Then the meal was ready. The last of light was gone now save the thin stain of it snared somewhere between the river's surface and the rain. He had the single glass of thin whisky-and-water, then, standing in the churned mud beneath the stretched tarpaulin, he said grace over the fried slabs of pork, the hot soft shapeless bread, the canned beans and molasses and coffee in iron plates and cups—the town food, brought along with them—then covered himself again, the others following. "Eat," he said. "Eat it all up. I dont want a piece of town meat in camp after breakfast tomorrow. Then you boys will hunt. You'll have to. When I first started hunting in this bottom sixty years ago with old General Compson and Major de Spain and Roth's grandfather and Will Legate's too, Major de Spain wouldn't allow but two pieces of foreign grub in his camp. That was one side of pork and one ham of beef. And not to eat for the first supper and breakfast neither. It was to save until along toward the end of camp when everybody was so sick of bear meat and coon and venison that we couldn't even look at it."

"I thought Uncle Ike was going to say the pork and beef was for the dogs," Legate said, chewing. "But that's right; I remember. You just shot the dogs a mess of wild turkey every evening when they got tired of deer guts."

"Times are different now," another said. "There was game here then."

"Yes," the old man said quietly. "There was game here then."

"Besides, they shot does then too," Legate said. "As it is now, we aint got but one doe-hunter in ——"

"And better men hunted it," Edmonds said. He stood at the end of the rough plank table, eating rapidly and steadily as the others ate. But again the old man looked sharply across at the sullen, handsome, brooding face which appeared now darker and more sullen still in the light of the smoky lantern. "Go on. Say it."

"I didn't say that," the old man said. "There are good men everywhere, at all times. Most men are. Some are just unlucky, because most men are a little better than their circumstances give them a chance to be. And I've known some that even the circumstances couldn't stop."

"Well, I wouldn't say——" Legate said.

"So you've lived almost eighty years," Edmonds said. "And that's what you finally learned about the other animals you lived among. I suppose the question to ask you is, where have you been all the time you were dead?"

There was a silence; for the instant even Legate's jaw stopped chewing while he gaped at Edmonds. "Well, by God, Roth——" the third speaker said. But it was the old man who spoke, his voice still peaceful and untroubled and merely grave:

"Maybe so," he said. "But if being what you call alive would have learned me any different, I reckon I'm satisfied, wherever it was I've been."

"Well, I wouldn't say that Roth——" Legate said.

The third speaker was still leaning forward a little over the table, looking at Edmonds. "Meaning that it's only because folks happen to be watching him that a man behaves at all," he said. "Is that it?"

"Yes," Edmonds said. "A man in a blue coat, with a badge on it watching him. Maybe just the badge."

"I deny that," the old man said. "I dont——"

The other two paid no attention to him. Even Legate was listening to them for the moment, his mouth still full of food and still open a little, his knife with another lump of something balanced on the tip of the blade arrested halfway to his mouth. "I'm glad I dont have your opinion of folks," the third speaker said. "I take it you include yourself."

"I see," Edmonds said. "You prefer Uncle Ike's opinion of circumstances. All right. Who makes the circumstances?"

"Luck," the third said. "Chance. Happen-so. I see what you are getting at. But that's just what Uncle Ike said: that now and then, maybe most of the time, man is a little better than the net result of his and his neighbors' doings, when he gets the chance to be."

This time Legate swallowed first. He was not to be stopped this time. "Well, I wouldn't say that Roth Edmonds was a poor hunter or a unlucky one neither. A man that can hunt one doe every day and night for two weeks and still have the same doe left to hunt on again next year——"

"Have some meat," the man next to him said.

"——aint no unlucky—— What?" Legate said.

"Have some meat." The other offered the dish.

"I got some," Legate said.

"Have some more," the third speaker said. "You and Roth Edmonds both. Have a heap of it. Clapping your jaws together that way with nothing to break the shock." Someone chortled. Then they all laughed, with relief, the tension broken. But the old man was speaking, even into the laughter, in that peaceful and still untroubled voice:

"I still believe. I see proof everywhere. I grant that man made a heap of his circumstances, him and his living neighbors between them. He even inherited some of them already made, already almost ruined even. A while ago Henry Wyatt there said how there used to be more game here. There was. So much that we even killed does. I seem to remember Will Legate mentioning that too——" Someone laughed, a single guffaw, stillborn. It ceased and they all listened, gravely, looking down at their plates. Edmonds was drinking his coffee, sullen, brooding, inattentive.

"Some folks still kill does," Wyatt said. "There wont be just one buck hanging in this bottom tomorrow night without any head to fit it."

"I didn't say all men," the old man said. "I said most men. And not just because there is a man with a badge to watch us. We probably wont even see him unless maybe he will stop here about noon tomorrow and eat dinner with us and check our licenses——"

"We dont kill does because if we did kill does in a few years there wouldn't even be any bucks left to kill, Uncle Ike," Wyatt said.

"According to Roth yonder, that's one thing we wont never have to worry about," the old man said. "He said on the way here this morning that does and fawns—I believe he said women and children—are two things this world aint ever lacked. But that aint all of it," he said. "That's just the mind's reason a man has to give himself because the heart dont always have time to bother with thinking up words that fit together. God created man and He created the world for him to live in and I reckon He created the kind of world He would have wanted to live in if He had been a man—the ground to walk on, the big woods, the trees and the water, and the game to live in it. And maybe He didn't put the desire to hunt and kill game in man but I reckon He knew it was going to be there, that man was going to teach it to himself, since he wasn't quite God himself yet——"

"When will he be?" Wyatt said.

"I think that every man and woman, at the instant when it dont even matter whether they marry or not, I think that whether they marry then or afterward or dont never, at that instant the two of them together were God."

"Then there are some Gods in this world I wouldn't want to touch, and with a damn long stick," Edmonds said. He set his coffee cup down and looked at Wyatt. "And that includes myself, if that's what you want to know. I'm going to bed." He was gone. There was a general movement among the others. But it ceased and they stood again about the table, not looking at the old man, apparently held there yet by his quiet and peaceful voice as the heads of the swimming horses had been held above the water by his weightless hand. The three negroes—the cook and his helper and old Isham—were sitting quietly in the entrance of the kitchen tent, listening too, the three faces dark and motionless and musing.

"He put them both here: man, and the game he would follow and kill, foreknowing it. I believe He said, 'So be it.' I reckon He even foreknew the end. But He said, 'I will give him his chance. I will give him warning and foreknowledge too, along with the desire to follow and the power to slay. The woods and fields he ravages and the game he devastates will be the consequence and signature of his crime and guilt, and his punishment.'—Bed time," he said. His voice and inflection did not change at all. "Breakfast at four oclock, Isham. We want meat on the ground by sunup time."

There was a good fire in the sheet-iron heater; the tent was warm and was beginning to dry out, except for the mud underfoot. Edmonds was already rolled into his blankets, motionless, his face to the wall. Isham had made up his bed too—the strong, battered iron cot, the stained mattress which was not quite soft enough, the worn, often-washed blankets which as the years passed were less and less warm enough. But the tent was warm; presently, when the kitchen was cleaned up and readied for breakfast, the young negro would come in to lie down before the heater, where he could be roused to put fresh wood into it from time to time. And then, he knew now he would not sleep tonight anyway; he no longer needed to tell himself that perhaps he would. But it was all right now. The day was ended now and night faced him, but alarmless, empty of fret. *Maybe I came for this*, he thought: *Not to hunt, but for this. I would come anyway, even if only to go back home tomorrow*. Wearing only his bagging woolen underwear, his spectacles folded away in the worn case beneath the pillow where he could reach them readily and his lean body fitted easily into the old worn groove of mattress and blankets, he lay on his back, his hands crossed on his breast and his eyes closed while the others undressed and went to bed and the last of the sporadic talking died into snoring. Then he opened his eyes and lay peaceful and quiet as a child, looking up at the motionless belly of rain-murmured canvas upon which the glow of the heater was dying slowly away and would fade still further until the young negro, lying on two planks before it, would sit up and stoke it and lie back down again.

They had a house once. That was sixty years ago, when the Big Bottom was only thirty miles from Jefferson and old Major de Spain, who had been his father's cavalry commander in '61 and -2 and -3 and -4, and his cousin (his older brother; his father too) had taken him into the woods for the first time. Old Sam Fathers was alive then, born in slavery, son of a Negro slave and a Chickasaw chief, who had taught him how to shoot, not only when to shoot but when not to; such a November dawn as tomorrow would be and the old man led him straight to the great cypress and he had known the buck would pass exactly there because there was something running in Sam Fathers' veins which ran in the veins of the buck too, and they stood there against the tremendous trunk, the old man of seventy and the boy of twelve, and there was nothing save the dawn until suddenly the buck was there, smoke-colored out of nothing, magnificent with speed:

and Sam Fathers said, 'Now. Shoot quick and shoot slow:' and the gun levelled rapidly without haste and crashed and he walked to the buck lying still intact and still in the shape of that magnificent speed and bled it with Sam's knife and Sam dipped his hands into the hot blood and marked his face forever while he stood trying not to tremble, humbly and with pride too though the boy of twelve had been unable to phrase it then: *I slew you; my bearing must not shame your quitting life. My conduct forever onward must become your death*; marking him for that and for more than that: that day and himself and McCaslin juxtaposed not against the wilderness but against the tamed land, the old wrong and shame itself, in repudiation and denial at least of the land and the wrong and shame even if he couldn't cure the wrong and eradicate the shame, who at fourteen when he learned of it had believed he could do both when he became competent and when at twenty-one he became competent he knew that he could do neither but at least he could repudiate the wrong and shame, at least in principle, and at least the land itself in fact, for his son at least: and did, thought he had: then (married then) in a rented cubicle in a back-street stock-traders' boarding-house, the first and last time he ever saw her naked body, himself and his wife juxtaposed in their turn against that same land, that same wrong and shame from whose regret and grief he would at least save and free his son and, saving and freeing his son, lost him. They had the house then. That roof, the two weeks of each November which they spent under it, had become his home. Although since that time they had lived during the two fall weeks in tents and not always in the same place two years in succession and now his companions were the sons and even the grandsons of them with whom he had lived in the house and for almost fifty years now the house itself had not even existed, the conviction, the sense and feeling of home, had been merely transferred into the canvas. He owned a house in Jefferson, a good house though small, where he had had a wife and lived with her and lost her, ay, lost her even though he had lost her in the rented cubicle before he and his old clever dipsomaniac partner had finished the house for them to move into it: but lost her, because she loved him. But women hope for so much. They never live too long to still believe that anything within the scope of their passionate wanting is likewise within the range of their passionate hope: and it was still kept for him by his dead wife's widowed niece and her children and he was comfortable in it, his wants and needs and even the small trying harmless crochets of an old man looked after by blood at least related to the blood which he had elected out of all the earth to cherish. But he spent the time within those walls waiting for November, because even this tent with its muddy floor and the bed which was not wide enough nor soft enough nor even warm enough, was his home and these men, some of whom he only saw during these two November weeks and not one of whom even bore any name he used to know—De Spain and Compson and Ewell and Hogganbeck—were more his kin than any. Because this was his land——

The shadow of the youngest negro loomed. It soared, blotting the heater's dying glow from the ceiling, the wood billets thumping into the iron maw until the glow, the flame, leaped high and bright across the canvas. But the negro's shadow still remained, by its length and breadth, standing, since it covered most of the ceiling, until after a moment he raised himself on one elbow to look. It was not the negro, it was his kinsman; when he spoke the other turned sharp against the red firelight the sullen and ruthless profile.

"Nothing," Edmonds said. "Go on back to sleep."

"Since Will Legate mentioned it," McCaslin said, "I remember you had some trouble sleeping in here last fall too. Only you called it coon-hunting then. Or was it Will Legate called it that?" The other didn't answer. Then he turned and went back to his bed. McCaslin, still propped on his elbow, watched until the other's shadow sank down the wall and vanished, became one with the mass of sleeping shadows. "That's right," he said. "Try to get some sleep. We must have meat in camp tomorrow. You can do all the setting up you want to after that." He lay down again, his hands crossed again on his breast, watching the glow of the heater on the canvas ceiling. It was steady again now, the fresh wood accepted, being assimilated; soon it would begin to fade again, taking with it the last echo of that sudden upflare of a young man's passion and unrest. Let him lie awake for a little while, he thought; He will lie still some day for a long time without even dissatisfaction to disturb him. And lying awake here, in these surroundings, would soothe him if anything could, if anything could soothe a man just forty years old. Yes, he thought; Forty years old or thirty, or even the trembling and sleepless ardor of a boy; already the tent, the rain-murmured canvas globe, was once more filled with it. He lay on his back, his eyes closed, his breathing quiet and peaceful as a child's, listening to it—that silence which was never silence but was myriad. He could almost see it, tremendous, primeval, looming, musing downward upon this puny evanescent clutter of human sojourn which after a single brief week would vanish and in another week would be completely healed, traceless in the unmarked solitude. Because it was his land, although he had never owned a foot of it. He had never wanted to, not even after he saw plain its ultimate doom, watching it retreat year by year before the onslaught of axe and saw and log-lines and then dynamite and tractor plows, because it belonged to no man. It belonged to all; they had only to use it well, humbly and with pride. Then suddenly he knew why he had never wanted to own any of it, arrest at least that much of what people called progress, measure his longevity at least against that much of its ultimate fate. It was because there was just exactly enough of it. He seemed to see the two of them—himself and the wilderness—as coevals, his own span as a hunter, a woodsman, not contemporary with his first breath but transmitted to him, assumed by him gladly, humbly, with joy and pride, from that old Major de Spain and that old Sam Fathers who had taught him to hunt, the two spans running out together, not toward oblivion, nothingness, but into a dimension free of both time and space where once more the untreed land warped and wrung to mathematical squares of rank cotton for the frantic old-world people to turn into shells to shoot at one another, would find ample room for both—the names, the faces of the old men he had known and loved and for a little while outlived, moving again among the shades of tall unaxed trees and sightless brakes where the wild strong immortal game ran forever before the tireless belling immortal hounds, falling and rising phoenix-like to the soundless guns.

He had been asleep. The lantern was lighted now. Outside in the darkness the oldest negro, Isham, was beating a spoon against the bottom of a tin pan and crying, "Raise up and get yo foa clock coffy. Raise up and get yo foa clock coffy," and the tent was full of low talk and of men dressing, and Legate's voice, repeating: "Get out of here now and let Uncle Ike sleep. If you wake him up, he'll go out with us. And he aint got any business in the woods this morning."

So he didn't move. He lay with his eyes closed, his breathing gentle and peaceful, and heard them one by one leave the tent. He listened to the breakfast sounds from the table beneath the tarpaulin and heard them depart—the horses, the dogs, the last voice until it died away and there was only the sound of the negroes clearing breakfast away. After a while he might possibly even hear the first faint clear cry of the first hound ring through the wet woods from where the buck had bedded, then he would go back to sleep again——The tent-flap swung in and fell. Something jarred sharply against the end of the cot and a hand grasped his knee through the blanket before he could open his eyes. It was Edmonds, carrying a shotgun in place of his rifle. He spoke in a harsh, rapid voice:

"Sorry to wake you. There will be a——"

"I was awake," McCaslin said. "Are you going to shoot that shotgun today?"

"You just told me last night you want meat," Edmonds said. "There will be a——"

"Since when did you start having trouble getting meat with your rifle?"

"All right," the other said, with that harsh, restrained, furious impatience. Then McCaslin saw in his hand a thick oblong: an envelope. "There will be a message here some time this morning, looking for me. Maybe it wont come. If it does, give the messenger this and tell h— say I said No."

"A what?" McCaslin said. "Tell who?" He half rose onto his elbow as Edmonds jerked the envelope onto the blanket, already turning toward the entrance, the envelope striking solid and heavy and without noise and already sliding from the bed until McCaslin caught it, divining by feel through the paper as instantaneously and conclusively as if he had opened the envelope and looked, the thick sheaf of banknotes. "Wait," he said. "Wait:"—more than the blood kinsman, more even than the senior in years, so that the other paused, the canvas lifted, looking back, and McCaslin saw that outside it was already day. "Tell her No," he said. "Tell her." They stared at one another—the old face, wan, sleep-raddled above the tumbled bed, the dark and sullen younger one at once furious and cold. "Will Legate was right. This is what you called coon-hunting. And now this." He didn't raise the envelope. He made no motion, no gesture to indicate it. "What did you promise her that you haven't the courage to face her and retract?"

"Nothing!" the other said. "Nothing! This is all of it. Tell her I said No." He was gone. The tent flap lifted on an in-waft of faint light and the constant murmur of rain, and fell again, leaving the old man still half-raised onto one elbow, the envelope clutched in the other shaking hand. Afterward it seemed to him that he had begun to hear the approaching boat almost immediately, before the other could have got out of sight even. It seemed to him that there had been no interval whatever: the tent flap falling on the same out-waft of faint and rain-filled light like the suspiration and expiration of the same breath and then in the next second lifted again—the mounting snarl of the outboard engine, increasing, nearer and nearer and louder and louder then cut short off, ceasing with the absolute instantaneity of a blown-out candle, into the lap and plop of water under the bows as the skiff slid in to the bank, the youngest negro, the youth, raising the tent flap beyond which for that instant he saw the boat—a small skiff with a negro man sitting in the stern beside the up-slanted motor—then the woman entering, in a man's hat and a man's slicker and rubber boots, carrying the blanket-swaddled bundle on one arm and holding the edge of the unbuttoned raincoat over it with the other hand: and bringing something else, something intangible, an effluvium which he knew he would recognise in a moment because Isham had already told him, warned him, by sending the young negro to the tent to announce the visitor instead of coming himself, the flap falling at last on the young negro and they were alone—the face indistinct and as yet only young and with dark eyes, queerly colorless but not ill and not that of a country woman despite the garments she wore, looking down at him where he sat upright on the cot now, clutching the envelope, the soiled undergarment bagging about him and the twisted blankets huddled about his hips.

"Is that his?" he cried. "Dont lie to me!"

"Yes," she said. "He's gone."

"Yes. He's gone. You wont jump him here. Not this time. I dont reckon even you expected that. He left you this. Here." He fumbled at the envelope. It was not to pick it up, because it was still in his hand; he had never put it down. It was as if he had to fumble somehow to co-ordinate physically his heretofore obedient hand with what his brain was commanding of it, as if he had never performed such an action before, extending the envelope at last, saying again, "Here. Take it. Take it:" until he became aware of her eyes, or not the eyes so much as the look, the regard fixed now on his face with that immersed contemplation, that bottomless and intent candor, of a child. If she had ever seen either the envelope or his movement to extend it, she did not show it.

"You're Uncle Isaac," she said.

"Yes," he said. "But never mind that. Here. Take it. He said to tell you No." She looked at the envelope, then she took it. It was sealed and bore no superscription. Nevertheless, even after she glanced at the front of it, he watched her hold it in the one free hand and tear the corner off with her teeth and manage to rip it open and tilt the neat sheaf of bound notes onto the blanket without even glancing at them and look into the empty envelope and take the edge between her teeth and tear it completely open before she crumpled and dropped it.

"That's just money," she said.

"What did you expect? What else did you expect? You have known him long enough or at least often enough to have got that child, and you dont know him any better than that?"

"Not very often. Not very long. Just that week here last fall, and in January he sent for me and we went West, to New Mexico. We were there six weeks, where I could at least sleep in the same apartment where I cooked for him and looked after his clothes——"

"But not marriage," he said. "Not marriage. He didn't promise you that. Dont lie to me. He didn't have to."

"No. He didn't have to. I didn't ask him to. I knew what I was doing. I knew that to begin with, long before honor I imagine he called it told him the time had come to tell me in so many words what his code I suppose he would call it would forbid him forever to do. And we agreed. Then we agreed again before he left New Mexico, to make sure. That that would be all of it. I believed him. No, I dont mean that; I mean I believed myself. I wasn't even listening to him any-more by then because by that time it had been a long time since he had had anything else to tell me for me to have to hear. By then I wasn't even listening enough to ask him to please stop talking. I was listening to myself. And I believed it. I must have believed it. I dont see how I could have helped but believe it, because he was gone then as we had agreed and he didn't write as we had agreed, just the money came to the bank in Vicksburg in my name but coming from nobody as we had agreed. So I must have believed it. I even wrote him last month to make sure again and the letter came back un-opened and I was sure. So I left the hospital and rented my-self a room to live in until the deer season opened so I could make sure myself and I was waiting beside the road yesterday when your car passed and he saw me and so I was sure."

"Then what do you want?" he said. "What do you want? What do you expect?"

"Yes," she said. And while he glared at her, his white hair awry from the pillow and his eyes, lacking the spectacles to focus them, blurred and irisless and apparently pupilless, he saw again that grave, intent, speculative and detached fixity like a child watching him. "His great great—— Wait a minute.—great great *great* grandfather was your grandfather. McCaslin. Only it got to be Edmonds. Only it got to be more than that. Your cousin McCaslin was there that day when your father and Uncle Buddy won Tennie from Mr Beauchamp for the one that had no name but Terrel so you called him Tomey's Terrel, to marry. But after that it got to be Edmonds." She regarded him, almost peacefully, with that unwinking and heatless fixity—the dark wide bottomless eyes in the face's dead and toneless pallor which to the old man looked anything but dead, but young and incredibly and even ineradicably alive—as though she were not only not looking at anything, she was not even speaking to anyone but herself. "I would have made a man of him. He's not a man yet. You spoiled him. You, and Uncle Lucas and Aunt Mollie. But mostly you."

"Me?" he said. "Me?"

"Yes. When you gave to his grandfather that land which didn't belong to him, not even half of it by will or even law."

"And never mind that too," he said. "Never mind that too. You," he said. "You sound like you have been to college even. You sound almost like a Northerner even, not like the draggle-tailed women of these Delta peckerwoods. Yet you meet a man on the street one afternoon just because a box of groceries happened to fall out of a boat. And a month later you go off with him and live with him until he got a child on you: and then, by your own statement, you sat there while he took his hat and said goodbye and walked out. Even a Delta peckerwood would look after even a draggle-tail better than that. Haven't you got any folks at all?"

"Yes," she said. "I was living with one of them. My aunt, in Vicksburg. I came to live with her two years ago when my father died; we lived in Indianapolis then. But I got a job, teaching school here in Aluschaskuna, because my aunt was a widow, with a big family, taking in washing to sup——"

"Took in what?" he said. "Took in washing?" He sprang, still seated even, flinging himself backward onto one arm, awry-haired, glaring. Now he understood what it was she had brought into the tent with her, what old Isham had already told him by sending the youth to bring her in to him—the pale lips, the skin pallid and dead-looking yet not ill, the dark and tragic and foreknowing eyes. *Maybe in a thousand or two thousand years in America*, he thought. *But not now! Not now!* He cried, not loud, in a voice of amazement, pity, and outrage: "You're a nigger!"

"Yes," she said. "James Beauchamp—you called him Tennie's Jim though he had a name—was my grandfather. I said you were Uncle Isaac."

"And he knows?"

"No," she said. "What good would that have done?"

"But you did," he cried. "But you did. Then what do you expect here?"

"Nothing."

"Then why did you come here? You said you were waiting in Aluschaskuna yesterday and he saw you. Why did you come this morning?"

"I'm going back North. Back home. My cousin brought me up the day before yesterday in his boat. He's going to take me on to Leland to get the train."

"Then go," he said. Then he cried again in that thin not loud and grieving voice: "Get out of here! I can do nothing for you! Cant nobody do nothing for you!" She moved; she was not looking at him again, toward the entrance. "Wait," he said. She paused again, obediently still, turning. He took up the sheaf of banknotes and laid it on the blanket at the foot of the cot and drew his hand back beneath the blanket. "There," he said.

Now she looked at the money, for the first time, one brief blank glance, then away again. "I dont need it. He gave me money last winter. Besides the money he sent to Vicksburg. Provided. Honor and code too. That was all arranged."

"Take it," he said. His voice began to rise again, but he stopped it. "Take it out of my tent." She came back to the cot and took up the money; whereupon once more he said, "Wait:" although she had not turned, still stooping, and he put out his hand. But, sitting, he could not complete the reach until she moved her hand, the single hand which held the money, until he touched it. He didn't grasp it, he merely touched it—the gnarled, bloodless, bone-light bone-dry old man's fingers touching for a second the smooth young flesh where the strong old blood ran after its long lost journey back to home. "Tennie's Jim," he said. "Tennie's Jim." He drew the hand back beneath the blanket again; he said harshly now: "It's a boy, I reckon. They usually are, except that one that was its own mother too."

"Yes," she said. "It's a boy." She stood for a moment longer, looking at him. Just for an instant her free hand moved as though she were about to lift the edge of the raincoat away from the child's face. But she did not. She turned again when once more he said Wait and moved beneath the blanket.

"Turn your back," he said. "I am going to get up. I aint got my pants on." Then he could not get up. He sat in the huddled blanket, shaking, while again she turned and looked down at him in dark interrogation. "There," he said harshly, in the thin and shaking old man's voice. "On the nail there. The tent-pole."

"What?" she said.

"The horn!" he said harshly. "The horn." She went and got it, thrust the money into the slicker's side pocket as if it were a rag, a soiled handkerchief, and lifted down the horn, the one which General Compson had left him in his will, covered with the unbroken skin from a buck's shank and bound with silver.

"What?" she said.

"It's his. Take it."

"Oh," she said. "Yes. Thank you."

"Yes," he said, harshly, rapidly, but not so harsh now and soon not harsh at all but just rapid, urgent, until he knew that his voice was running away with him and he had neither intended it nor could stop it: "That's right. Go back North. Marry: a man in your own race. That's the only salvation for you—for a while yet, maybe a long while yet. We will have to wait. Marry a black man. You are young, handsome, almost white; you could find a black man who would see in you what it was you saw in him, who would ask nothing of you and expect less and get even still less than that, if it's revenge you want. Then you will forget all this, forget it ever happened, that he ever existed——" until he could stop it at last and did, sitting there in his huddle of blankets during the instant when, without moving at all, she blazed silently down at him. Then that was gone too. She stood in the gleaming and still dripping slicker, looking quietly down at him from under the sodden hat.

"Old man," she said, "have you lived so long and forgotten so much that you dont remember anything you ever knew or felt or even heard about love?"

Then she was gone too. The waft of light and the murmur of the constant rain flowed into the tent and then out again as the flap fell. Lying back once more, trembling, panting, the blanket huddled to his chin and his hands crossed on his breast, he listened to the pop and snarl, the mounting then fading whine of the motor until it died away and once again the tent held only silence and the sound of rain. And cold too: he lay shaking faintly and steadily in it, rigid save for the shaking. This Delta, he thought: This Delta. *This land which man has deswamped and denuded and derivered in two generations so that white men can own plantations and commute every night to Memphis and black men own plantations and ride in jim crow cars to Chicago to live in millionaires' mansions on Lakeshore Drive, where white men rent farms and live like niggers and niggers crop on shares and live like animals, where cotton is planted and grows man-tall in the very cracks of the sidewalks, and usury and mortgage and bankruptcy and measureless wealth, Chinese and African and Aryan and Jew, all breed and spawn together until no man has time to say which one is which nor cares.* . . . . . No wonder the ruined woods I used to know dont cry for retribution! he thought: The people who have destroyed it will accomplish its revenge.

The tent flap jerked rapidly in and fell. He did not move save to turn his head and open his eyes. It was Legate. He went quickly to Edmonds' bed and stooped, rummaging hurriedly among the still-tumbled blankets.

"What is it?" he said.

"Looking for Roth's knife," Legate said. "I come back to get a horse. We got a deer on the ground." He rose, the knife in his hand, and hurried toward the entrance.

"Who killed it?" McCaslin said. "Was it Roth?"

"Yes," Legate said, raising the flap.

"Wait," McCaslin said. He moved, suddenly, onto his elbow. "What was it?" Legate paused for an instant beneath the lifted flap. He did not look back.

"Just a deer, Uncle Ike," he said impatiently. "Nothing extra." He was gone; again the flap fell behind him, wafting out of the tent again the faint light and the constant and grieving rain. McCaslin lay back down, the blanket once more drawn to his chin, his crossed hands once more weightless on his breast in the empty tent.

"It was a doe," he said.

Go Down, Moses

1.

THE FACE was black, smooth, impenetrable; the eyes had seen too much. The negroid hair had been treated so that it covered the skull like a cap, in a single neat-ridged sweep, with the appearance of having been lacquered, the part trimmed out with a razor, so that the head resembled a bronze head, imperishable and enduring. He wore one of those sports costumes called ensembles in the men's shop advertisements, shirt and trousers matching and cut from the same fawn-colored flannel, and they had cost too much and were draped too much, with too many pleats; and he half lay on the steel cot in the steel cubicle just outside which an armed guard had stood for twenty hours now, smoking cigarettes and answering in a voice which was anything under the sun but a southern voice or even a negro voice, the questions of the spectacled young white man sitting with a broad census-taker's portfolio on the steel stool opposite:

"Samuel Worsham Beauchamp. Twenty-six. Born in the country near Jefferson, Mississippi. No family. No——"

"Wait." The census-taker wrote rapidly. "That's not the name you were sen—lived under in Chicago."

The other snapped the ash from the cigarette. "No. It was another guy killed the cop."

"All right. Occupation——"

"Getting rich too fast."

"—none." The census-taker wrote rapidly. "Parents."

"Sure. Two. I dont remember them. My grandmother raised me."

"What's her name? Is she still living?"

"I dont know. Mollie Worsham Beauchamp. If she is, she's on Carothers Edmonds' farm seventeen miles from Jefferson, Mississippi. That all?"

The census-taker closed the portfolio and stood up. He was a year or two younger than the other. "If they dont know who you are here, how will they know—how do you expect to get home?"

The other snapped the ash from the cigarette, lying on the

steel cot in the fine Hollywood clothes and a pair of shoes better than the census-taker would ever own. "What will that matter to me?" he said.

So the census-taker departed; the guard locked the steel door again. And the other lay on the steel cot smoking until after a while they came and slit the expensive trousers and shaved the expensive coiffure and led him out of the cell.

2.

On that same hot, bright July morning the same hot bright wind which shook the mulberry leaves just outside Gavin Stevens' window blew into the office too, contriving a semblance of coolness from what was merely motion. It fluttered among the county-attorney business on the desk and blew in the wild shock of prematurely white hair of the man who sat behind it—a thin, intelligent, unstable face, a rumpled linen suit from whose lapel a Phi Beta Kappa key dangled on a watch chain—Gavin Stevens, Phi Beta Kappa, Harvard, Ph.D., Heidelberg, whose office was his hobby, although it made his living for him, and whose serious vocation was a twenty-two-year-old unfinished translation of the Old Testament back into classic Greek. Only his caller seemed impervious to it, though by appearance she should have owned in that breeze no more of weight and solidity than the intact ash of a scrap of burned paper—a little old negro woman with a shrunken, incredibly old face beneath a white headcloth and a black straw hat which would have fitted a child.

"Beauchamp?" Stevens said. "You live on Mr Carothers Edmonds' place."

"I done left," she said. "I come to find my boy." Then, sitting on the hard chair opposite him and without moving, she began to chant. "Roth Edmonds sold my Benjamin. Sold him in Egypt. Pharaoh got him——"

"Wait," Stevens said. "Wait, Aunty." Because memory, recollection, was about to mesh and click. "If you dont know where your grandson is, how do you know he's in trouble? Do you mean that Mr Edmonds has refused to help you find him?"

"It was Roth Edmonds sold him," she said. "Sold him in

Egypt. I dont know whar he is. I just knows Pharaoh got him. And you the Law. I wants to find my boy."

"All right," Stevens said. "I'll try to find him. If you're not going back home, where will you stay in town? It may take some time, if you dont know where he went and you haven't heard from him in five years."

"I be staying with Hamp Worsham. He my brother."

"All right," Stevens said. He was not surprised. He had known Hamp Worsham all his life, though he had never seen the old Negress before. But even if he had, he still would not have been surprised. They were like that. You could know two of them for years; they might even have worked for you for years, bearing different names. Then suddenly you learn by pure chance that they are brothers or sisters.

He sat in the hot motion which was not breeze and listened to her toiling slowly down the steep outside stairs, remembering the grandson. The papers of that business had passed across his desk before going to the District Attorney five or six years ago—Butch Beauchamp, as the youth had been known during the single year he had spent in and out of the city jail: the old Negress' daughter's child, orphaned of his mother at birth and deserted by his father, whom the grandmother had taken and raised, or tried to. Because at nineteen he had quit the country and come to town and spent a year in and out of jail for gambling and fighting, to come at last under serious indictment for breaking and entering a store.

Caught red-handed, whereupon he had struck with a piece of iron pipe at the officer who surprised him and then lay on the ground where the officer had felled him with a pistol-butt, cursing through his broken mouth, his teeth fixed into something like furious laughter through the blood. Then two nights later he broke out of jail and was seen no more—a youth not yet twenty-one, with something in him from the father who begot and deserted him and who was now in the State Penitentiary for manslaughter—some seed not only violent but dangerous and bad.

And that's who I am to find, save, Stevens thought. Because he did not for one moment doubt the old Negress' instinct. If she had also been able to divine where the boy was and what his trouble was, he would not have been surprised, and it was only later that he thought to be surprised at how quickly he did find where the boy was and what was wrong.

His first thought was to telephone Carothers Edmonds, on whose farm the old Negress' husband had been a tenant for years. But then, according to her, Edmonds had already refused to have anything to do with it. Then he sat perfectly still while the hot wind blew in his wild white mane. Now he comprehended what the old Negress had meant. He remembered now that it was Edmonds who had actually sent the boy in to Jefferson in the first place: he had caught the boy breaking into his commissary store and had ordered him off the place and had forbidden him ever to return. *And not the sheriff, the police*, he thought. *Something broader, quicker in scope*. . . . . He rose and took his old fine worn panama and descended the outside stairs and crossed the empty square in the hot suspension of noon's beginning, to the office of the county newspaper. The editor was in—an older man but with hair less white than Stevens', in a black string tie and an old-fashioned boiled shirt and tremendously fat.

"An old nigger woman named Mollie Beauchamp," Stevens said. "She and her husband live on the Edmonds place. It's her grandson. You remember him—Butch Beauchamp, about five or six years ago, who spent a year in town, mostly in jail, until they finally caught him breaking into Rouncewell's store one night? Well, he's in worse trouble than that now. I dont doubt her at all. I just hope, for her sake as well as that of the great public whom I represent, that his present trouble is very bad and maybe final too——"

"Wait," the editor said. He didn't even need to leave his desk. He took the press association flimsy from its spike and handed it to Stevens. It was datelined from Joliet, Illinois, this morning:

Mississippi negro, on eve of execution for murder of Chicago policeman, exposes alias by completing census questionnaire. Samuel Worsham Beauchamp——

Five minutes later Stevens was crossing again the empty square in which noon's hot suspension was that much nearer. He had thought that he was going home to his boarding house for the noon meal, but he found that he was not. *Besides, I didn't lock my office door*, he thought. Only, how under the sun she could have got to town from those seventeen miles. She may even have walked. "So it seems I didn't mean what I said I hoped," he said aloud, mounting the outside stairs again, out of the hazy and now windless sunglare, and entered his office. He stopped. Then he said,

"Good morning, Miss Worsham."

She was quite old too—thin, erect, with a neat, old-time piling of white hair beneath a faded hat of thirty years ago, in rusty black, with a frayed umbrella faded now until it was green instead of black. He had known her too all his life. She lived alone in the decaying house her father had left her, where she gave lessons in china-painting and, with the help of Hamp Worsham, descendant of one of her father's slaves, and his wife, raised chickens and vegetables for market.

"I came about Mollie," she said. "Mollie Beauchamp. She said that you——"

He told her while she watched him, erect on the hard chair where the old Negress had sat, the rusty umbrella leaning against her knee. On her lap, beneath her folded hands, lay an old-fashioned beaded reticule almost as big as a suitcase. "He is to be executed tonight."

"Can nothing be done? Mollie's and Hamp's parents belonged to my grandfather. Mollie and I were born in the same month. We grew up together as sisters would."

"I telephoned," Stevens said. "I talked to the Warden at Joliet, and to the District Attorney in Chicago. He had a fair trial, a good lawyer—of that sort. He had money. He was in a business called numbers, that people like him make money in." She watched him, erect and motionless. "He is a murderer, Miss Worsham. He shot that policeman in the back. A bad son of a bad father. He admitted, confessed it afterward."

"I know," she said. Then he realised that she was not looking at him, not seeing him at least. "It's terrible."

"So is murder terrible," Stevens said. "It's better this way." Then she was looking at him again.

"I wasn't thinking of him. I was thinking of Mollie. She mustn't know."

"Yes," Stevens said. "I have already talked with Mr Wilmoth at the paper. He has agreed not to print anything. I will telephone the Memphis paper, but it's probably too late for that. . . . . If we could just persuade her to go on back home this afternoon, before the Memphis paper. . . . . Out there, where the only white person she ever sees is Mr Edmonds, and I will telephone him; and even if the other darkies should hear about it, I'm sure they wouldn't. And then maybe in about two or three months I could go out there and tell her he is dead and buried somewhere in the North. . . . ." This time she was watching him with such an expression that he ceased talking; she sat there, erect on the hard chair, watching him until he had ceased.

"She will want to take him back home with her," she said.

"Him?" Stevens said. "The body?" She watched him. The expression was neither shocked nor disapproving. It merely embodied some old, timeless, female affinity for blood and grief. Stevens thought: *She has walked to town in this heat. Unless Hamp brought her in the buggy he peddles eggs and vegetables from.*

"He is the only child of her oldest daughter, her own dead first child. He must come home."

"He must come home," Stevens said as quietly. "I'll attend to it at once. I'll telephone at once."

"You are kind." For the first time she stirred, moved. He watched her hands draw the reticule toward her, clasping it. "I will defray the expenses. Can you give me some idea——?"

He looked her straight in the face. He told the lie without batting an eye, quickly and easily. "Ten or twelve dollars will cover it. They will furnish a box and there will be only the transportation."

"A box?" Again she was looking at him with that expression curious and detached, as though he were a child. "He is her grandson, Mr Stevens. When she took him to raise, she gave him my father's name—Samuel Worsham. Not just a box, Mr Stevens. I understand that can be done by paying so much a month."

"Not just a box," Stevens said. He said it in exactly the same tone in which he had said He must come home. "Mr Edmonds will want to help, I know. And I understand that old Luke Beauchamp has some money in the bank. And if you will permit me——"

"That will not be necessary," she said. He watched her open the reticule; he watched her count onto the desk twenty-five dollars in frayed bills and coins ranging down to nickels and dimes and pennies. "That will take care of the immediate expenses. I will tell her— You are sure there is no hope?"

"I am sure. He will die tonight."

"I will tell her this afternoon that he is dead then."

"Would you like for me to tell her?"

"I will tell her," she said.

"Would you like for me to come out and see her, then, talk to her?"

"It would be kind of you." Then she was gone, erect, her feet crisp and light, almost brisk, on the stairs, ceasing. He telephoned again, to the Illinois warden, then to an undertaker in Joliet. Then once more he crossed the hot, empty square. He had only to wait a short while for the editor to return from dinner.

"We're bringing him home," he said. "Miss Worsham and you and me and some others. It will cost——"

"Wait," the editor said. "What others?"

"I dont know yet. It will cost about two hundred. I'm not counting the telephones; I'll take care of them myself. I'll get something out of Carothers Edmonds the first time I catch him; I dont know how much, but something. And maybe fifty around the square. But the rest of it is you and me, because she insisted on leaving twenty-five with me, which is just twice what I tried to persuade her it would cost and just exactly four times what she can afford to pay——"

"Wait," the editor said. "Wait."

"And he will come in on Number Four the day after tomorrow and we will meet it, Miss Worsham and his grandmother, the old nigger, in my car and you and me in yours. Miss Worsham and the old woman will take him back home, back where he was born. Or where the old woman raised him. Or where she tried to. And the hearse out there will be fifteen more, not counting the flowers——"

"Flowers?" the editor cried.

"Flowers," Stevens said. "Call the whole thing two hundred and twenty-five. And it will probably be mostly you and me. All right?"

"No it aint all right," the editor said. "But it dont look like I can help myself. By Jupiter," he said, "even if I could help myself, the novelty will be almost worth it. It will be the first time in my life I ever paid money for copy I had already promised before hand I wont print."

"Have already promised before hand you will not print," Stevens said. And during the remainder of that hot and now windless afternoon, while officials from the city hall, and justices of the peace and bailiffs come fifteen and twenty miles from the ends of the county, mounted the stairs to the empty office and called his name and cooled their heels a while and then went away and returned and sat again, fuming, Stevens passed from store to store and office to office about the square—merchant and clerk, proprietor and employee, doctor dentist lawyer and barber—with his set and rapid speech: "It's to bring a dead nigger home. It's for Miss Worsham. Never mind about a paper to sign: just give me a dollar. Or a half a dollar then. Or a quarter then."

And that night after supper he walked through the breathless and star-filled darkness to Miss Worsham's house on the edge of town and knocked on the paintless front door. Hamp Worsham admitted him—an old man, belly-bloated from the vegetables on which he and his wife and Miss Worsham all three mostly lived, with blurred old eyes and a fringe of white hair about the head and face of a Roman general.

"She expecting you," he said. "She say to kindly step up to the chamber."

"Is that where Aunt Mollie is?" Stevens said.

"We all dar," Worsham said.

So Stevens crossed the lamplit hall (he knew that the entire house was still lighted with oil lamps and there was no running water in it) and preceded the Negro up the clean, paintless stairs beside the faded wallpaper, and followed the old Negro along the hall and into the clean, spare bedroom with its unmistakable faint odor of old maidens. They were all there, as Worsham had said—his wife, a tremendous light-colored woman in a bright turban leaning in the door, Miss

Worsham erect again on a hard straight chair, the old Negress sitting in the only rocking chair beside the hearth on which even tonight a few ashes smoldered faintly.

She held a reed-stemmed clay pipe but she was not smoking it, the ash dead and white in the stained bowl; and actually looking at her for the first time, Stevens thought: *Good Lord, she's not as big as a ten-year-old child.* Then he sat too, so that the four of them—himself, Miss Worsham, the old Negress and her brother—made a circle about the brick hearth on which the ancient symbol of human coherence and solidarity smoldered.

"He'll be home the day after tomorrow, Aunt Mollie," he said. The old Negress didn't even look at him; she never had looked at him.

"He dead," she said. "Pharaoh got him."

"Oh yes, Lord," Worsham said. "Pharaoh got him."

"Done sold my Benjamin," the old Negress said. "Sold him in Egypt." She began to sway faintly back and forth in the chair.

"Oh yes, Lord," Worsham said.

"Hush," Miss Worsham said. "Hush, Hamp."

"I telephoned Mr Edmonds," Stevens said. "He will have everything ready when you get there."

"Roth Edmonds sold him," the old Negress said. She swayed back and forth in the chair. "Sold my Benjamin."

"Hush," Miss Worsham said. "Hush, Mollie. Hush now."

"No," Stevens said. "No he didn't, Aunt Mollie. It wasn't Mr Edmonds. Mr Edmonds didn't——" *But she cant hear me*, he thought. She was not even looking at him. She never had looked at him.

"Sold my Benjamin," she said. "Sold him in Egypt."

"Sold him in Egypt," Worsham said.

"Roth Edmonds sold my Benjamin."

"Sold him to Pharaoh."

"Sold him to Pharaoh and now he dead."

"I'd better go," Stevens said. He rose quickly. Miss Worsham rose too, but he did not wait for her to precede him. He went down the hall fast, almost running; he did not even know whether she was following him or not. *Soon I will be outside*, he thought. *Then there will be air, space, breath.* Then he could hear her behind him—the crisp, light, brisk yet unhurried feet as he had heard them descending the stairs from his office, and beyond them the voices:

"Sold my Benjamin. Sold him in Egypt."

"Sold him in Egypt. Oh yes, Lord."

He descended the stairs, almost running. It was not far now; now he could smell and feel it: the breathing and simple dark, and now he could manner himself to pause and wait, turning at the door, watching Miss Worsham as she followed him to the door—the high, white, erect, old-time head approaching through the old-time lamplight. Now he could hear the third voice, which would be that of Hamp's wife—a true constant soprano which ran without words beneath the strophe and antistrophe of the brother and sister:

"Sold him in Egypt and now he dead."

"Oh yes, Lord. Sold him in Egypt."

"Sold him in Egypt."

"And now he dead."

"Sold him to Pharaoh."

"And now he dead."

"I'm sorry," Stevens said. "I ask you to forgive me. I should have known. I shouldn't have come."

"It's all right," Miss Worsham said. "It's our grief."

And on the next bright hot day but one the hearse and the two cars were waiting when the southbound train came in. There were more than a dozen cars, but it was not until the train came in that Stevens and the editor began to notice the number of people, Negroes and whites both. Then, with the idle white men and youths and small boys and probably half a hundred Negroes, men and women too, watching quietly, the Negro undertaker's men lifted the gray-and-silver casket from the train and carried it to the hearse and snatched the wreaths and floral symbols of man's ultimate and inevitable end briskly out and slid the casket in and flung the flowers back and clapped-to the door.

Then, with Miss Worsham and the old Negress in Stevens' car with the driver he had hired and himself and the editor in the editor's, they followed the hearse as it swung into the long hill up from the station, going fast in a whining lower gear until it reached the crest, going pretty fast still but with an unctuous, an almost bishoplike purr until it slowed into the square, crossing it, circling the Confederate monument and the courthouse while the merchants and clerks and barbers and professional men who had given Stevens the dollars and half-dollars and quarters and the ones who had not, watched quietly from doors and upstairs windows, swinging then into the street which at the edge of town would become the country road leading to the destination seventeen miles away, already picking up speed again and followed still by the two cars containing the four people—the high-headed erect white woman, the old Negress, the designated paladin of justice and truth and right, the Heidelberg Ph.D.—in formal component complement to the Negro murderer's catafalque: the slain wolf.

When they reached the edge of town the hearse was going quite fast. Now they flashed past the metal sign which said Jefferson. Corporate Limit. and the pavement vanished, slanting away into another long hill, becoming gravel. Stevens reached over and cut the switch, so that the editor's car coasted, slowing as he began to brake it, the hearse and the other car drawing rapidly away now as though in flight, the light and unrained summer dust spurting from beneath the fleeing wheels; soon they were gone. The editor turned his car clumsily, grinding the gears, sawing and filling until it was back in the road facing town again. Then he sat for a moment, his foot on the clutch.

"Do you know what she asked me this morning, back there at the station?" he said.

"Probably not," Stevens said.

"She said, 'Is you gonter put hit in de paper?' "

"What?"

"That's what I said," the editor said. "And she said it again: 'Is you gonter put hit in de paper? I wants hit all in de paper. All of hit.' And I wanted to say, 'If I should happen to know how he really died, do you want that in too?' And by Jupiter, if I had and if she had known what we know even, I believe she would have said yes. But I didn't say it. I just said, 'Why, you couldn't read it, Aunty.' And she said, 'Miss Belle will show me whar to look and I can look at hit. You put hit in de paper. All of hit.' "

"Oh," Stevens said. *Yes*, he thought. *It doesn't matter to her now. Since it had to be and she couldn't stop it, and now that it's all over and done and finished, she doesn't care how he died. She just wanted him home, but she wanted him to come home right. She wanted that casket and those flowers and the hearse and she wanted to ride through town behind it in a car.* "Come on," he said. "Let's get back to town. I haven't seen my desk in two days."

INTRUDER IN THE DUST

I.

IT WAS just noon that Sunday morning when the sheriff reached the jail with Lucas Beauchamp though the whole town (the whole county too for that matter) had known since the night before that Lucas had killed a white man.

He was there, waiting. He was the first one, standing lounging trying to look occupied or at least innocent, under the shed in front of the closed blacksmith's shop across the street from the jail where his uncle would be less likely to see him if or rather when he crossed the Square toward the post-office for the eleven oclock mail.

Because he knew Lucas Beauchamp too—as well that is as any white person knew him. Better than any maybe unless it was Carothers Edmonds on whose place Lucas lived seventeen miles from town, because he had eaten a meal in Lucas' house. It was in the early winter four years ago; he had been only twelve then and it had happened this way: Edmonds was a friend of his uncle; they had been in school at the same time at the State University, where his uncle had gone after he came back from Harvard and Heidelberg to learn enough law to get himself chosen County Attorney, and the day before Edmonds had come in to town to see his uncle on some county business and had stayed the night with them and at supper that evening Edmonds had said to him:

'Come out home with me tomorrow and go rabbit hunting:' and then to his mother: 'I'll send him back in tomorrow afternoon. I'll send a boy along with him while he's out with his gun:' and then to him again: 'He's got a good dog.'

'He's got a boy,' his uncle said and Edmonds said:

'Does his boy run rabbits too?' and his uncle said:

'We'll promise he wont interfere with yours.'

So the next morning he and Aleck Sander went home with Edmonds. It was cold that morning, the first winter cold-snap; the hedgerows were rimed and stiff with frost and the standing water in the roadside drainage ditches was skimmed with ice and even the edges of the running water in the Nine Mile branch glinted fragile and scintillant like fairy glass and from the first farmyard they passed and then again and again and again came the windless tang of woodsmoke and they could see in the back yards the black iron pots already steaming while women in the sunbonnets still of summer or men's old felt hats and long men's overcoats stoked wood under them and the men with crokersack aprons tied with wire over their overalls whetted knives or already moved about the pens where hogs grunted and squealed, not quite startled, not alarmed but just alerted as though sensing already even though only dimly their rich and immanent destiny; by nightfall the whole land would be hung with their spectral intact tallowcolored empty carcasses immobilised by the heels in attitudes of frantic running as though full tilt at the center of the earth.

And he didn't know how it happened. The boy, one of Edmonds' tenant's sons, older and larger than Aleck Sander who in his turn was larger than he although they were the same age, was waiting at the house with the dog—a true rabbit dog, some hound, a good deal of hound, maybe mostly hound, redbone and black-and-tan with maybe a little pointer somewhere once, a potlicker, a nigger dog which it took but one glance to see had an affinity a rapport with rabbits such as people said Negroes had with mules—and Aleck Sander already had his tapstick—one of the heavy nuts which bolt railroad rails together, driven onto a short length of broomhandle—which Aleck Sander could throw whirling end over end at a running rabbit pretty near as accurately as he could shoot the shotgun—and Aleck Sander and Edmonds' boy with tapsticks and he with the gun they went down through the park and across a pasture to the creek where Edmonds' boy knew the footlog was and he didn't know how it happened, something a girl might have been expected and even excused for doing but nobody else, halfway over the footlog and not even thinking about it who had walked the top rail of a fence many a time twice that far when all of a sudden the known familiar sunny winter earth was upside down and flat on his face and still holding the gun he was rushing not away from the earth but away from the bright sky and he could remember still the thin bright tinkle of the breaking ice and how he didn't even feel the shock of the water but only of the air when he came up again. He had dropped the gun too so he had to dive, submerge again to find it, back out of the icy air into the water which as yet felt neither, neither cold or not and where even his sodden garments—boots and thick pants and sweater and hunting coat—didn't even feel heavy but just slow, and found the gun and tried again for bottom then thrashed one-handed to the bank and treading water and clinging to a willow-branch he reached the gun up until someone took it; Edmonds' boy obviously since at that moment Aleck Sander rammed down at him the end of a long pole, almost a log whose first pass struck his feet out from under him and sent his head under again and almost broke his hold on the willow until a voice said:

'Get the pole out of his way so he can get out'—just a voice, not because it couldn't be anybody else but either Aleck Sander or Edmonds' boy but because it didn't matter whose: climbing out now with both hands among the willows, the skim ice crinkling and tinkling against his chest, his clothes like soft cold lead which he didn't move in but seemed rather to mount into like a poncho or a tarpaulin: up the bank until he saw two feet in gum boots which were neither Edmonds' boy's nor Aleck Sander's and then the legs, the overalls rising out of them and he climbed on and stood up and saw a Negro man with an axe on his shoulder, in a heavy sheeplined coat and a broad pale felt hat such as his grandfather had used to wear, looking at him and that was when he saw Lucas Beauchamp for the first time that he remembered or rather for the first time because you didn't forget Lucas Beauchamp; gasping, shaking and only now feeling the shock of the cold water, he looked up at the face which was just watching him without pity commiseration or anything else, not even surprise: just watching him, whose owner had made no effort whatever to help him up out of the creek, had in fact ordered Aleck Sander to desist with the pole which had been the one token toward help that anybody had made—a face which in his estimation might have been under fifty or even forty except for the hat and the eyes, and inside a Negro's skin but that was all even to a boy of twelve shaking with cold and still panting from shock and exertion because what looked out of it had no pigment at all, not even the white man's lack of it, not arrogant, not even scornful: just intractable and composed. Then Edmonds' boy said something to the man, speaking a name: something Mister Lucas: and then he knew who the man was, remembering the rest of the story which was a piece, a fragment of the county's chronicle which few if any knew better than his uncle: how the man was son of one of old Carothers McCaslin's, Edmonds' great grandfather's, slaves who had been not just old Carothers' slave but his son too: standing and shaking steadily now for what seemed to him another whole minute while the man stood looking at him with nothing whatever in his face. Then the man turned, speaking not even back over his shoulder, already walking, not even waiting to see if they heard, let alone were going to obey:

'Come on to my house.'

'I'll go back to Mr Edmonds',' he said. The man didn't look back. He didn't even answer.

'Tote his gun, Joe,' he said.

So he followed, with Edmonds' boy and Aleck Sander following him, in single file along the creek toward the bridge and the road. Soon he had stopped shaking; he was just cold and wet now and most of that would go if he just kept moving. They crossed the bridge. Ahead now was the gate where the drive went up through the park to Edmonds' house. It was almost a mile; he would probably be dry and warm both by the time he got there and he still believed he was going to turn in at the gate and even after he knew that he wasn't or anyway hadn't, already beyond it now, he was still telling himself the reason was that, although Edmonds was a bachelor and there were no women in the house, Edmonds himself might refuse to let him out of the house again until he could be returned to his mother, still telling himself this even after he knew that the true reason was that he could no more imagine himself contradicting the man striding on ahead of him than he could his grandfather, not from any fear of nor even the threat of reprisal but because like his grandfather the man striding ahead of him was simply incapable of conceiving himself by a child contradicted and defied.

So he didn't even check when they passed the gate, he didn't even look at it and now they were in no well-used tended lane leading to tenant or servant quarters and marked by walking feet but a savage gash half gully and half road mounting a hill with an air solitary independent and intractable too and then he saw the house, the cabin and remembered the rest of the story, the legend: how Edmonds' father had deeded to his Negro first cousin and his heirs in perpetuity the house and the ten acres of land it sat in—an oblong of earth set forever in the middle of the two thousand acre plantation like a postage stamp in the center of an envelope—the paintless wooden house, the paintless picket fence whose paintless latchless gate the man kneed open still without stopping or once looking back and, he following and Aleck Sander and Edmonds' boy following him, strode on into the yard. It would have been grassless even in summer; he could imagine it, completely bare, no weed no sprig of anything, the dust each morning swept by some of Lucas' womenfolks with a broom made of willow switches bound together, into an intricate series of whorls and overlapping loops which as the day advanced would be gradually and slowly defaced by the droppings and the cryptic three-toed prints of chickens like (remembering it now at sixteen) a terrain in miniature out of the age of the great lizards, the four of them walking in what was less than walk because its surface was dirt too yet more than path, the footpacked strip running plumbline straight between two borders of tin cans and empty bottles and shards of china and earthenware set into the ground, up to the paintless steps and the paintless gallery along whose edge sat more cans but larger—empty gallon buckets which had once contained molasses or perhaps paint and wornout water or milk pails and one five-gallon can for kerosene with its top cut off and half of what had once been somebody's (Edmonds' without doubt) kitchen hot water tank sliced longways like a banana—out of which flowers had grown last summer and from which the dead stalks and the dried and brittle tendrils still leaned and drooped, and beyond this the house itself, gray and weathered and not so much paintless as independent of and intractable to paint so that the house was not only the one possible continuation of the stern untended road but was its crown too as the carven ailanthus leaves are the Greek column's capital.

Nor did the man pause yet, up the steps and across the gallery and opened the door and entered and he and then Edmonds' boy and Aleck Sander followed: a hall dim even almost dark after the bright outdoors and already he could smell that smell which he had accepted without question all his life as being the smell always of the places where people with any trace of Negro blood live as he had that all people named Mallison are Methodists, then a bedroom: a bare worn quite clean paintless rugless floor, in one corner and spread with a bright patchwork quilt a vast shadowy tester bed which had probably come out of old Carothers McCaslin's house, and a battered cheap Grand Rapids dresser and then for the moment no more or at least little more; only later would he notice—or remember that he had seen—the cluttered mantel on which sat a kerosene lamp hand-painted with flowers and a vase filled with spills of twisted newspaper and above the mantel the colored lithograph of a three-year-old calendar in which Pocahontas in the quilled fringed buckskins of a Sioux or Chippewa chief stood against a balustrade of Italian marble above a garden of formal cypresses and shadowy in the corner opposite the bed a chromo portrait of two people framed heavily in gold-painted wood on a gold-painted easel. But he hadn't seen that at all yet because that was behind him and all he now saw was the fire—the clay-daubed fieldstone chimney in which a halfburned backlog glowed and smoldered in the gray ashes and beside it in a rocking chair something which he thought was a child until he saw the face, and then he did pause long enough to look at her because he was about to remember something else his uncle had told him about or at least in regard to Lucas Beauchamp, and looking at her he realised for the first time how old the man actually was, must be—a tiny old almost doll-sized woman much darker than the man, in a shawl and an apron, her head bound in an immaculate white cloth on top of which sat a painted straw hat bearing some kind of ornament. But he couldn't think what it was his uncle had said or told him and then he forgot that he had remembered even the having been told, sitting in the chair himself now squarely before the hearth where Edmonds' boy was building up the fire with split logs and pine slivers and Aleck Sander squatting tugged off the wet boots and then his trousers and standing he got out of the coat and sweater and his shirt, both of them having to dodge around and past and under the man who stood straddled on the hearth, his back to the fire in the gum boots and the hat and only the sheepskin coat removed and then the old woman was beside him again less tall than he and Aleck Sander even at twelve, with another of the bright patchwork quilts on her arm.

'Strip off,' the man said.

'No I——' he said.

'Strip off,' the man said. So he stripped off the wet unionsuit too and then he was in the chair again in front of the now bright and swirling fire, enveloped in the quilt like a cocoon, enclosed completely now in that unmistakable odor of Negroes—that smell which if it were not for something that was going to happen to him within a space of time measurable now in minutes he would have gone to his grave never once pondering speculating if perhaps that smell were really not the odor of a race nor even actually of poverty but perhaps of a condition: an idea: a belief: an acceptance, a passive acceptance by them themselves of the idea that being Negroes they were not supposed to have facilities to wash properly or often or even to wash bathe often even without the facilities to do it with; that in fact it was a little to be preferred that they did not. But the smell meant nothing now or yet; it was still an hour yet before the thing would happen and it would be four years more before he would realise the extent of its ramifications and what it had done to him and he would be a man grown before he would realise, admit that he had accepted it. So he just smelled it and then dismissed it because he was used to it, he had smelled it off and on all his life and would continue to: who had spent a good part of that life in Paralee's, Aleck Sander's mother's cabin in their back yard where he and Aleck Sander played in the bad weather when they were little and Paralee would cook whole meals for them halfway between two meals at the house and he and Aleck Sander would eat them together, the food tasting the same to each; he could not even imagine an existence from which the odor would be missing to return no more. He had smelled it forever, he would smell it always; it was a part of his inescapable past, it was a rich part of his heritage as a Southerner; he didn't even have to dismiss it, he just no longer smelled it at all as the pipe smoker long since never did smell at all the cold pipereek which is as much a part of his clothing as their buttons and buttonholes, sitting drowsing a little even in the warm huddled rankness of the quilt, rousing a little when he heard Edmonds' boy and Aleck Sander get up from where they had been squatting against the wall and leave the room, but not much, sinking again into the quilt's warm reek while there stood over him still, back to the fire and hands clasped behind him and except for the clasped hands and the missing axe and the sheeplined coat exactly as when he had looked up out of the creek and seen him first, the man in the gum boots and the faded overalls of a Negro but with a heavy gold watch-chain looping across the bib of the overalls and shortly after they entered the room he had been conscious of the man turning and taking something from the cluttered mantel and putting it into his mouth and later he had seen what it was: a gold toothpick such as his own grandfather had used: and the hat was a worn handmade beaver such as his grandfather had paid thirty and forty dollars apiece for, not set but raked slightly above the face pigmented like a Negro's but with a nose high in the bridge and even hooked a little and what looked out through it or from behind it not black nor white either, not arrogant at all and not even scornful: just intolerant inflexible and composed.

Then Aleck Sander came back with his clothes, dried now and still almost hot from the stove and he dressed, stamping into his stiffened boots; Edmonds' boy squatting again against the wall was still eating something from his hand and he said: 'I'll have my dinner at Mr Edmonds'.'

The man neither protested nor acquiesced. He didn't stir; he was not even looking at him. He just said, inflexible and calm: 'She done already dished it up now:' and he went on past the old woman who stood aside from the door to let him pass, into the kitchen: an oilcloth-covered table set in the bright sunny square of a southern window where—he didn't know how he knew it since there were no signs, traces, soiled plates to show it—Edmonds' boy and Aleck Sander had already eaten, and sat down and ate in his turn of what obviously was to be Lucas' dinner—collard greens, a slice of sidemeat fried in flour, big flat pale heavy half-cooked biscuits, a glass of buttermilk: nigger food too, accepted and then dismissed also because it was exactly what he had expected, it was what Negroes ate, obviously because it was what they liked, what they chose; not (at twelve: he would be a man grown before he experienced his first amazed dubiety at this) that out of their long chronicle this was all they had had a chance to learn to like except the ones who ate out of white folks' kitchens but that they had elected this out of all eating because this was their palates and their metabolism; afterward, ten minutes later and then for the next four years he would be trying to tell himself that it was the food which had thrown him off. But he would know better; his initial error, misjudgment had been there all the time, not even needing to be abetted by the smell of the house and the quilt in order to survive what had looked out (and not even at him: just looked out) from the man's face; rising at last and with the coin, the half-dollar already in his hand going back into the other room: when he saw for the first time because he happened to be facing it now the gold-framed portrait-group on its gold easel and he went to it, stooping to peer at it in its shadowy corner where only the gold leaf gleamed, before he knew he was going to do it. It had been retouched obviously; from behind the round faintly prismatic glass dome as out of a seer's crystal ball there looked back at him again the calm intolerant face beneath the swaggering rake of the hat, a tieless starched collar clipped to a white starched shirt with a collarbutton shaped like a snake's head and almost as large, the watch-chain looped now across a broadcloth vest inside a broadcloth coat and only the toothpick missing, and beside him the tiny doll-like woman in another painted straw hat and a shawl; that is it must have been the woman though it looked like nobody he had ever seen before and then he realised it was more than that: there was something ghastly, almost intolerably wrong about it or her: when she spoke and he looked up, the man still standing straddled before the fire and the woman sitting again in the rocking chair in its old place almost in the corner and she was not looking at him now and he knew she had never looked at him since he re-entered yet she said:

'That's some more of Lucas' doings:' and he said,

'What?' and the man said,

'Molly dont like it because the man that made it took her headrag off:' and that was it, she had hair; it was like looking at an embalmed corpse through the hermetic glass lid of a coffin and he thought *Molly. Of course* because he remembered now what it was his uncle had told him about Lucas or about them. He said:

'Why did he take it off?'

'I told him to,' the man said. 'I didn't want no field nigger picture in the house:' and he walked toward them now, putting the fist holding the half-dollar back into his pocket and scooping the dime and the two nickels—all he had—into the palm with it, saying,

'You came from town. My uncle knows you—Lawyer Gavin Stevens.'

'I remember your mamma too,' she said. 'She use to be Miss Maggie Dandridge.'

'That was my grandmother,' he said. 'My mother's name was Stevens too:' and extended the coins: and in the same second in which he knew she would have taken them he knew that only by that one irrevocable second was he forever now too late, forever beyond recall, standing with the slow hot blood as slow as minutes themselves up his neck and face, forever with his dumb hand open and on it the four shameful fragments of milled and minted dross, until at last the man had something that at least did the office of pity.

'What's that for?' the man said, not even moving, not even tilting his face downward to look at what was on his palm: for another eternity and only the hot dead moveless blood until at last it ran to rage so that at least he could bear the shame: and watched his palm turn over not flinging the coins but spurning them downward ringing onto the bare floor, bouncing and one of the nickels even rolling away in a long swooping curve with a dry minute sound like the scurry of a small mouse: and then his voice:

'Pick it up!'

And still nothing, the man didn't move, hands clasped behind him, looking at nothing; only the rush of the hot dead heavy blood out of which the voice spoke, addressing nobody: 'Pick up his money:' and he heard and saw Aleck Sander and Edmonds' boy reach and scurry among the shadows near the floor. 'Give it to him,' the voice said: and saw Edmonds' boy drop his into Aleck Sander's palm and felt Aleck Sander's hand fumble the coins at his own dropped hand and then into it. 'Now go on and shoot your rabbit,' the voice said. 'And stay out of that creek.'

II.

AND THEY WALKED again in the bright cold (even though it was noon now and about as warm as it would ever get today probably), back across the creek bridge and (suddenly: looking around, they had gone almost a half-mile along the creek and he didn't even remember it) the dog put a rabbit into a brier patch beside a cottonfield and yapping hysterically hoicked it out again, the small frantic tawny-colored blob looking one instant spherical and close-coupled as a croquet ball and the next one long as a snake, bursting out of the thicket ahead of the dog, the small white flare of its scut zigzagging across the skeletoned cottonrows like the sail of a toy boat on a windy pond while across the thicket Aleck Sander yelled:

'Shoot him! Shoot him!' then 'Whyn't you shoot him?' and then he turned without haste and walked steadily to the creek and drew the four coins from his pocket and threw them out into the water: and sleepless in bed that night he knew that the food had been not just the best Lucas had to offer but all he had to offer; he had gone out there this morning as the guest not of Edmonds but of old Carothers McCaslin's plantation and Lucas knew it when he didn't and so Lucas had beat him, stood straddled in front of the hearth and without even moving his clasped hands from behind his back had taken his own seventy cents and beat him with them, and writhing with impotent fury he was already thinking of the man whom he had never seen but once and that only twelve hours ago, as within the next year he was to learn every white man in that whole section of the county had been thinking about him for years: *We got to make him be a nigger first. He's got to admit he's a nigger. Then maybe we will accept him as he seems to intend to be accepted.* Because he began at once to learn a good deal more about Lucas. He didn't hear it: he learned it, all that anyone who knew that part of the county could tell him about the Negro who said 'ma'am' to women just as any white man did and who said 'sir' and 'mister' to you if you were white but who you knew was thinking neither and he knew you knew it but who was not even waiting, daring you to make the next move, because he didn't even care. For instance, this.

It was a Saturday afternoon three years ago at the crossroads store four miles from Edmonds' place where at some time during Saturday afternoon every tenant and renter and freeholder white or black in the neighborhood would at least pass and usually stop, quite often even to buy something, the saddled trace-galled mules and horses tied among the willows and birches and sycamores in the trampled mud below the spring and their riders overflowing the store itself out onto the dusty banquette in front, standing or squatting on their heels drinking bottled sodapop and spitting tobacco and rolling without hurry cigarettes and striking deliberate matches to smoked-out pipes; this day there were three youngish white men from the crew of a nearby sawmill, all a little drunk, one of whom had a reputation for brawling and violence, and Lucas came in in the worn black broadcloth suit which he wore to town and on Sundays and the worn fine hat and the heavy watch-chain and the toothpick and something happened, the story didn't say or perhaps didn't even know what, perhaps the way Lucas walked, entered speaking to no one and went to the counter and made his purchase (it was a five cent carton of gingersnaps) and turned and tore the end from the carton and removed the toothpick and put it into his breast pocket and shook one of the gingersnaps into his palm and put it into his mouth, or perhaps just nothing was enough, the white man on his feet suddenly saying something to Lucas, saying 'You goddamn biggity stiffnecked stinking burrheaded Edmonds sonofabitch:' and Lucas chewed the gingersnap and swallowed and the carton already tilted again over his other hand, turned his head quite slowly and looked at the white man a moment and then said:

'I aint a Edmonds. I dont belong to these new folks. I belongs to the old lot. I'm a McCaslin.'

'Keep on walking around here with that look on your face and what you'll be is crowbait,' the white man said. For another moment or at least a half one Lucas looked at the white man with a calm speculative detachment; slowly the carton in one of his hands tilted further until another gingersnap dropped into his other palm, then lifting the corner of his lip he sucked an upper tooth, quite loud in the abrupt silence but with no implication whatever of either derision or rebuttal or even disagreement, with no implication of anything at all but almost abstractedly, as a man eating gingersnaps in the middle of a hundred-mile solitude would—if he did—suck a tooth, and said:

'Yes, I heard that idea before. And I notices that the folks that brings it up aint even Edmondses:' whereupon the white man even as he sprang up reached blindly back where on the counter behind him lay a half-dozen plow singletrees and snatched one of them up and had already started the downswing when the son of the store's proprietor, himself a youngish active man, came either around or over the counter and grasped the other so that the singletree merely flew harmlessly across the aisle and crashed against the cold stove; then another man was holding the man too.

'Get out of here, Lucas!' the proprietor's son said over his shoulder. But still Lucas didn't move, quite calm, not even scornful, not even contemptuous, not even very alert, the gaudy carton still poised in his left hand and the small cake in the right, just watching while the proprietor's son and his companion held the foaming and cursing white man. 'Get to hell out of here, you damn fool!' the proprietor's son shouted: and only then did Lucas move, without haste, turning without haste and going on toward the door, raising his right hand to his mouth so that as he went out the door they could see the steady thrust of his chewing.

Because there was the half-dollar. The actual sum was seventy cents of course and in four coins but he had long since during that first few fractions of a second transposed translated them into the one coin one integer in mass and weight out of all proportion to its mere convertible value; there were times in fact when, the capacity of his spirit for regret or perhaps just simple writhing or whatever it was at last spent for a moment and even quiescent, he would tell himself *At least I have the half-dollar, at least I have something* because now not only his mistake and its shame but its protagonist too—the man, the Negro, the room, the moment, the day itself—had annealed vanished into the round hard symbol of the coin and he would seem to see himself lying watching regretless and even peaceful as day by day the coin swelled to its gigantic maximum, to hang fixed at last forever in the black vault of his anguish like the last dead and waneless moon and himself, his own puny shadow gesticulant and tiny against it in frantic and vain eclipse: frantic and vain yet indefatigable too because he would never stop, he could never give up now who had debased not merely his manhood but his whole race too; each afternoon after school and all day Saturday, unless there was a ballgame or he went hunting or there was something else he wanted or needed to do, he would go to his uncle's office where he would answer the telephone or run errands, all with some similitude of responsibility even if not actually of necessity; at least it was an intimation of his willingness to carry some of his own weight. He had begun it when he was a child, when he could scarcely remember, out of that blind and absolute attachment to his mother's only brother which he had never tried to reason about, and he had done it ever since; later, at fifteen and sixteen and seventeen he would think of the story of the boy and his pet calf which he lifted over the pasture fence each day; years passed and they were a grown man and a bull still being lifted over the pasture fence each day.

He deserted his calf. It was less than three weeks to Christmas; every afternoon after school and all day Saturday he was either in the Square or where he could see it, watch it. It was cold for another day or two, then it got warm, the wind softened then the bright sun hazed over and it rained yet he still walked or stood about the street where the store windows were already filling with toys and Christmas goods and fireworks and colored lights and evergreen and tinsel or behind the steamy window of the drugstore or barbershop watched the country faces, the two packages—the four two-for-a-quarter cigars for Lucas and the tumbler of snuff for his wife—in their bright Christmas paper in his pocket, until at last he saw Edmonds and gave them to him to deliver Christmas morning. But that merely discharged (with doubled interest) the seventy cents; there still remained the dead monstrous heatless disc which hung nightly in the black abyss of the rage and impotence: *If he would just be a nigger first, just for one second, one little infinitesimal second:* so in February he began to save his money—the twenty-five cents his father gave him each week as allowance and the twenty-five cents his uncle paid him as office salary—until in May he had enough and with his mother helping him chose the flowered imitation silk dress and sent it by mail to Molly Beauchamp, care of Carothers Edmonds R.F.D. and at last he had something like ease because the rage was gone and all he could not forget was the grief and the shame; the disc still hung in the black vault but it was almost a year old now and so the vault itself was not so black with the disc paling and he could even sleep under it as even the insomniac dozes at last under his waning and glareless moon. Then it was September; school would begin in another week. He came home one afternoon and his mother was waiting for him.

'Here's something for you,' she said. It was a gallon bucket of fresh homemade sorghum molasses and he knew the answer at once long before she finished speaking: 'Somebody from Mr Edmonds' place sent it to you.'

'Lucas Beauchamp,' he said, cried almost. 'How long has he been gone? Why didn't he wait for me?'

'No,' his mother said. 'He didn't bring it himself. He sent it in. A white boy brought it on a mule.'

And that was all. They were right back where they had started; it was all to do over again; it was even worse this time because this time Lucas had commanded a white hand to pick up his money and give it back to him. Then he realised that he couldn't even start over again because to take the can of molasses back and fling it into Lucas' front door would only be the coins again for Lucas again to command somebody to pick up and return, not to mention the fact that he would have to ride a Shetland pony which he had outgrown and was ashamed of except that his mother wouldn't agree yet to let him have a fullsized horse or at least the kind of fullsized horse he wanted and that his uncle had promised him, seventeen miles in order to reach the door to fling it through. This would have to be all; whatever would or could set him free was beyond not merely his reach but even his ken; he could only wait for it if it came and do without it if it didn't.

And four years later he had been free almost eighteen months and he thought it was all: old Molly dead and her and Lucas' married daughter moved with her husband to Detroit and he heard now at last by chance remote and belated hearsay that Lucas was living alone in the house, solitary kinless and intractable, apparently not only without friends even in his own race but proud of it. He had seen him three times more, on the Square in town and not always on Saturday—in fact it would be a year from the last time before he would realise that he had never seen him in town on Saturday when all the other Negroes and most of the whites too from the country came in, nor even that the occasions when he did see him were almost exactly a year apart and that the reason he saw him then was not that Lucas' presence had happened to coincide with his own chance passage through the Square but that he had coincided with Lucas' annual and necessary visits—but on weekdays like the white men who were not farmers but planters, who wore neckties and vests like the merchants and doctors and lawyers themselves, as if he refused, declined to accept even that little of the pattern not only of Negro but of country Negro behavior, and always in the worn brushed obviously once-expensive black broadcloth suit of the portrait-photograph on the gold easel and the raked fine hat and the boiled white shirt of his own grandfather's time and the tieless collar and the heavy watch-chain and the gold toothpick like the one his own grandfather had carried in his upper vest pocket: the first time in the second winter; he had spoken first though Lucas had remembered him at once; he thanked him for the molasses and Lucas had answered exactly as his grandfather himself might, only the words, the grammar any different:

'They turned out good this year. When I was making um I remembered how a boy's always got a sweet tooth for good molasses:' and went on, saying over his shoulder: 'Dont fall in no more creeks this winter:' and saw him twice more after that—the black suit, the hat, the watch-chain but the next time he didn't have the toothpick and this time Lucas looked straight at him, straight into his eyes from five feet away and passed him and he thought *He has forgotten me. He doesn't even remember me anymore* until almost the next year when his uncle told him that Molly, the old wife, had died a year ago. Nor did he bother, take time to wonder then how his uncle (obviously Edmonds had told him) happened to know about it because he was already counting rapidly backward; he said thought with a sense of vindication, easement, triumph almost: *She had just died then. That was why he didn't see me. That was why he didn't have the toothpick:* thinking with a kind of amazement: *He was grieving. You dont have to not be a nigger in order to grieve* and then he found that he was waiting, haunting the Square almost as he had done two years ago when he was watching for Edmonds to give him the two Christmas presents to deliver, through the next two then three then four months before it occurred to him that when he had seen Lucas in town it had always been only once each year in January or February and then for the first time he realised why: he had come in to pay the yearly taxes on his land. So it was late January, a bright cold afternoon. He stood on the bank corner in the thin sun and saw Lucas come out of the courthouse and cross the Square directly toward him, in the black suit and the tieless shirt and the fine old hat at its swaggering rake, walking so erect that the coat touched him only across the shoulders from which it hung and he could already see the cocked slanted glint of the gold toothpick and he could feel the muscles of his face, waiting and then Lucas looked up and once more looked straight into his eyes for perhaps a quarter of a minute and then away and came straight on and then even side-stepped a little in order to pass him and passed him and went on; nor did he look back either, standing at the curb-edge in the thin cold sun thinking *He didn't even fail to remember me this time. He didn't even know me. He hasn't even bothered to forget me:* thinking in a sort of peace even: *It's over. That was all* because he was free, the man who for three years had obsessed his life waking and sleeping too had walked out of it. He would see him again of course; without doubt they would pass on the street in town like this once each year for the rest of Lucas' life but that would be all: the one no longer the man but only the ghost of him who had ordered the two Negro boys to pick up his money and give it back to him; the other only the memory of the child who had offered it and then flung it down, carrying into manhood only the fading tagend of that old once-frantic shame and anguish and need not for revenge, vengeance but simply for re-equalization, reaffirmation of his masculinity and his white blood. And someday the one would not even be any longer the ghost of the man who had ordered the coins picked up and to the other the shame and anguish would no longer be a thing remembered and recallable but merely a breath a whisper like the bitter-sweet-sour taste of the sheep sorrel eaten by the boy in his dead childhood, remembered only in the instant of tasting and forgotten before it could be placed and remembered; he could imagine them as old men meeting, quite old, at some point in that agony of naked inesthetisable nerve-ends which for lack of a better word men call being alive at which not only their elapsed years but the half-century of discrepancy between them would be as indistinguishable and uncountable as that many sand grains in a coal pile and he saying to Lucas: *I was the boy who when you gave me half of your dinner tried to pay you with some things which people in those days called seventy cents worth of money and so all I could think of to save my face was to fling it on the floor? Dont you remember?* and Lucas: *Was that me?* or vice versa, turned around and it was Lucas saying *I was the man when you throwed your money on the floor and wouldn't pick it up I had to have two niggers pick it up and hand it back to you? Dont you remember?* and he this time: *Was that me?* Because it was over now. He had turned the other cheek and it had been accepted. He was free.

Then he came back through the Square late that Saturday afternoon (there had been a ball game on the High School field) and he heard that Lucas had killed Vinson Gowrie out at Fraser's store; word had come for the sheriff about three oclock and had been relayed on by another party-line telephone down into the opposite corner of the county where the sheriff had gone this morning on business and where a messenger might quite possibly find him some time between now and tomorrow's sunup: which would make little difference since even if the sheriff had been in his office he would probably be too late since Fraser's store was in Beat Four and if Yoknapatawpha County was the wrong place for a nigger to shoot a white man in the back then Beat Four was the last place even in Yoknapatawpha County a nigger with any judgment—or any other stranger of any color—would have chosen to shoot anybody least of all one named Gowrie before or behind either; already the last car full of the young men and some not so young whose business addresses not only on Saturday afternoons but all week too were the poolhall and the barbershop and some of whom even had some vague connection with cotton or automobiles or land- and stock-sales, who bet on prizefights and punchboards and national ballgames, had long since left the Square to hurry the fifteen miles to park along the highway in front of the constable's house where the constable had taken Lucas and the story said had handcuffed him to a bedpost and was now sitting over him with a shotgun (and Edmonds too of course by now; even a fool country constable would have had sense enough to send for Edmonds only four miles away even before hollering for the sheriff) in case the Gowries and their connections decided not to wait until they had buried Vinson first; of course Edmonds would be there; if Edmonds had been in town today he would certainly have seen him at some time during the morning and before he went to the ballpark and since he had not obviously Edmonds had been at home, only four miles away; a messenger could have reached him and Edmonds himself could have been at the constable's house almost before the other messenger had memorised the sheriff's telephone and the message to give him and then rode to the nearest telephone where he could use either: which—Edmonds (again something nagged for a second's flash at his attention) and the constable—would be two while the Lord Himself would have to stop to count the Gowries and Ingrums and Workitts and if Edmonds was busy eating supper or reading the paper or counting his money or something the constable would be just one even with the shotgun: but then he was free, hardly even pausing really, walking on to the corner where he would turn for home and not until he saw how much of sun, how much was left of afternoon still in the street then turned back retracing his steps for several yards before he remembered why in the world he didn't cut straight across the now almost empty Square to the outside stairs leading up to the office.

Though of course there was really no reason to expect his uncle to be in the office this late on Saturday afternoon but once on the stairs he could at least throw that away, happening to be wearing rubber soles today though even then the wooden stairs creaked and rumbled unless you trod the inside edge close to the wall: thinking how he had never really appreciated rubber soles before, how nothing could match them for giving you time to make up your mind what you really wanted to do and then he could see the office door closed now although it was still too early for his uncle to have had the lights on but besides the door itself had that look which only locked doors have so even hard soles wouldn't have mattered, unlocking the door with his key then locking it with the thumb-latch behind him and crossed to the heavy swivel roller chair which had been his grandfather's before his uncle's and sat down behind the littered table which his uncle used in place of the rolltop desk of his grandfather's old time and across which the county's legal business had passed longer than he could remember, since in fact his memory was memory or anyway his, and so battered table and dogeared faded papers and the needs and passions they represented and the measured and bounded county too were all coeval and one, the last of the sun coming through the mulberry tree then the window behind him onto the table the stacked untidy papers the inkwell the tray of paperclips and fouled rusted penpoints and pipecleaners and the overturned corncob pipe in its spill of ash beside the stained unwashed coffeecup and saucer and the colored mug from the Heidelberg *stube* filled with twisted spills of newspaper to light the pipes with like the vase sitting on Lucas' mantel that day and before he even knew he had thought of it he rose taking up the cup and saucer and crossed the room picking up the coffeepot and the kettle too in passing and in the lavatory emptied the grounds and rinsed the pot and cup and filled the kettle and set it and the pot the cup and saucer back on the shelf and returned to the chair and sat down again after really no absence at all, still in plenty of time to watch the table and all its familiar untidy clutter all fading toward one anonymity of night as the sunlight died: thinking remembering how his uncle had said that all man had was time, all that stood between him and the death he feared and abhorred was time yet he spent half of it inventing ways of getting the other half past: and suddenly he remembered from nowhere what it was that had been nagging at his attention: Edmonds was not at home nor even in Mississippi; he was in a hospital in New Orleans being operated on for gallstones, the heavy chair making a rumbling clatter on the wooden floor almost as loud as a wagon on a wooden bridge as he rose and then stood beside the table until the echo died away and there was only the sound of his breathing: because he was free: and then he moved: because his mother would know what time baseball games finished even if she couldn't have heard the yelling from across the edge of town and she would know that even he could use up only so much of twilight getting home, locking the door behind him then down the stairs again, the Square filled with dusk now and the first lights coming on in the drugstore (they had never been off in the barbershop and the poolhall since the bootblack and the porter unlocked the doors and swept out the hair and cigarette stubs at six oclock this morning) and the mercantile ones too so that the rest of the county except Beat Four would have somewhere to wait until word could come in from Fraser's store that all was okeydoke again and they could unpark the trucks and cars and wagons and mules from the back streets and alleys and go home and go to bed: turning the corner this time and now the jail, looming, lightless except for the one crossbarred rectangle in the upper front wall where on ordinary nights the nigger crapshooters and whiskey-peddlers and razor-throwers would be yelling down to their girls and women on the street below and where Lucas would have been these three hours now (very likely banging on the steel door for somebody to bring him his supper or perhaps having already had it and now merely to complain about its quality since without doubt he would consider that his right too along with the rest of his lodging and keep) except that people seemed to hold that the one sole end of the entire establishment of public office was to elect one man like Sheriff Hampton big enough or at least with sense and character enough to run the county and then fill the rest of the jobs with cousins and inlaws who had failed to make a living at everything else they ever tried. But then he was free and besides it was probably all over by now and even if it wasn't he knew what he was going to do and there was plenty of time yet for that, tomorrow would be time enough for that; all he would need to do tonight was to give Highboy about two extra cups of oats against tomorrow and at first he believed he was or at least in a moment was going to be ravenously hungry himself, sitting down at the familiar table in the familiar room among the bright linen and silver and the water glasses and the bowl of narcissus and gladioli and a few roses in it too and his uncle said,

'Your friend Beauchamp seems to have done it this time.'

'Yes,' he said. 'They're going to make a nigger out of him once in his life anyway.'

'Charles!' his mother said.—eating rapidly, eating quite a lot and talking rapidly and quite a lot too about the ballgame and waiting to get hungry any minute any second now until suddenly he knew that even the last bite had been too much, still chewing at it to get it down to where it would swallow, already getting up.

'I'm going to the picture show,' he said.

'You haven't finished,' his mother said: then she said, 'The show doesn't begin for almost an hour yet:' and then not even just to his father and uncle but to all time all A.D. of Our Lord one thousand and nine hundred and thirty and forty and fifty: 'I dont want him to go to town tonight. I dont want——' and then at last one wail one cry to the supreme: his father himself: out of that nightraddled dragonregion of fears and terrors in which women—mothers anyway—seemed from choice almost to dwell: 'Charlie——' until his uncle put his napkin down and rose too and said:

'Then here's your chance to wean him. I want him to do an errand for me anyway:' and out: on the front gallery in the dark cool and after a while his uncle said: 'Well? Go on.'

'Aint you coming?' he said. Then he said, 'But why? Why?'

'Does that matter?' his uncle said, and then said what he had already heard when he passed the barbershop going on two hours ago now: 'Not now. Not to Lucas nor anybody else of his color out there.' But he had already thought of that himself not just before his uncle said it but even before whoever it had been in front of the barbershop two hours ago did, and for that matter the rest of it too: 'In fact the true why is not what crisis he faced beyond which life would be no longer bearable until he shot a white man in the back but why of all white men he must pick a Gowrie to shoot and out of all possible places Beat Four to do it in. —Go on. But dont be late. After all a man ought to be kind even to his parents now and then.'

And sure enough one of the cars and for all he knew maybe all of them had got back to the barbershop and the poolhall so apparently Lucas was still chained and peaceful to the bedpost and the constable sitting over him (it was probably a rocking chair) with the cold shotgun and probably the constable's wife had served their supper there and Lucas with a good appetite, sharp set for his since he not only wouldn't have to pay for it but you dont shoot somebody every day in the week: and at last it seemed to be more or less authentic that the sheriff had finally got the word and sent word back that he would return to town late tonight and would fetch Lucas in early tomorrow morning and he would have to do something, pass the time somehow until the picture show was out so he might as well go to it and he crossed the Square to the courthouse yard and sat down on a bench in the dark cool empty solitude among the bitten shadows the restless unwindy vernal leaves against the starry smore of heaven where he could watch the lighted marquee in front of the picture show and perhaps the sheriff was right; he seemed able to establish enough contact with Gowries and Ingrums and Workitts and McCallums to persuade them to vote for him every eight years so maybe he knew approximately what they would do under given situations or perhaps the people in the barbershop were right and the Ingrums and Gowries and Workitts were waiting not until they had buried Vinson tomorrow but simply because it would be Sunday in three hours now and they didn't want to have to hurry, bolt through the business in order to finish it by midnight and not violate the Sabbath: then the first of the crowd dribbled then flowed beneath the marquee blinking into the light and even fumbling a little for a second or even a minute or two yet, bringing back into the shabby earth a fading remnant of the heart's celluloid and derring dream so he could go home now, in fact he would have to: who knew by simple instinct when picture shows were over just as she did when ballgames were and though she would never really forgive him for being able to button his own buttons and wash behind his ears at least she accepted it and would not come after him herself but merely send his father and by starting now ahead of the picture show's dispersal he would have the empty street until he got home, until he reached the corner of the yard in fact and his uncle stepped out from beside the hedge, hatless, smoking one of the cob pipes.

'Listen,' his uncle said. 'I talked to Hampton down at Peddlers Field Old Town and he had already telephoned Squire Fraser and Fraser himself went to Skipworth's house and saw Lucas handcuffed to the bedpost and it's all right, everything's quiet out there tonight and tomorrow morning Hampton will have Lucas locked up in the jail——'

'I know,' he said. 'They wont lynch him until after midnight tomorrow night, after they have buried Vinson and got rid of Sunday:' walking on: 'It's all right with me. Lucas didn't have to work this hard not to be a nigger just on my account.' Because he was free: in bed: in the cool familiar room in the cool familiar dark because he knew what he was going to do and he had forgotten after all to tell Aleck Sander to give Highboy the extra feed against tomorrow but in the morning would do just as well because he was going to sleep tonight because he had something about ten thousand times quicker than just sheep to count; in fact he was going to go to sleep so fast he probably wouldn't have time to count more than about ten of them: with rage, an almost unbearable excruciation of outrage and fury: any white man to shoot in the back but this one of all white men at all: youngest of a family of six brothers one of whom had already served a year in federal penitentiary for armed resistance as an army deserter and another term at the state penal farm for making whiskey, and a ramification of cousins and inlaws covering a whole corner of the county and whose total number probably even the old grandmothers and maiden aunts couldn't have stated offhand—a connection of brawlers and farmers and foxhunters and stock- and timber-traders who would not even be the last anywhere to let one of its number be killed by anyone but only among the last since it in its turn was integrated and interlocked and intermarried with other brawlers and foxhunters and whiskeymakers not even into a simple clan or tribe but a race a species which before now had made their hill stronghold good against the county and the federal government too, which did not even simply inhabit nor had merely corrupted but had translated and transmogrified that whole region of lonely pine hills dotted meagrely with small tilted farms and peripatetic sawmills and contraband whiskey-kettles where peace officers from town didn't even go unless they were sent for and strange white men didn't wander far from the highway after dark and no Negro at any time—where as a local wit said once the only stranger ever to enter in with impunity was God and He only by daylight and on Sunday—into a synonym for independence and violence: an idea with physical boundaries like a quarantine for plague so that solitary unique and alone out of all the county it was known to the rest of the county by the number of its survey co-ordinate—Beat Four—as in the middle twenties people knew where Cicero Illinois was and who lived there and what they did who neither knew nor cared what state Chicago was in: and since this was not enough choosing the one moment when the one man white or black—Edmonds—out of all Yoknapatawpha County or Mississippi or America or the world too for that matter who would have had any inclination let alone power and ability (and here he had to laugh even though he was just about to go to sleep, remembering how he had even thought at first that if Edmonds had been at home it would have made any difference anywhere, remembering the face the angle of the hat the figure straddled baronial as a duke or a squire or a congressman before the fire hands clasped behind it and not even looking down at them but just commanding two nigger boys to pick up the coins and give them back to him, not even needing to remember his uncle reminding him ever since he had got big enough to understand the words that no man could come between another man and his destiny because even his uncle for all Harvard and Heidelberg couldn't have pointed out the man with enough temerity and delusion just to come between Lucas and merely what he wanted to do) to try to stand between Lucas and the violent fate he had courted was lying flat on his back in a New Orleans operating room: yet that was what Lucas had had to pick, that time that victim and that place: another Saturday afternoon and the same store where he had already had trouble with a white man at least once before: chose the first suitable convenient Saturday afternoon and with an old single action Colt pistol of a calibre and type not even made anymore which was exactly the sort of pistol Lucas would own exactly as no other still alive man in the county owned a gold toothpick lay in wait at the store—the one sure place where sooner or later on Saturday afternoon that whole end of the county would pass—until the victim appeared and shot him and nobody knew why yet and as far as he had discovered that afternoon or even when he finally left the Square that night nobody had even wondered yet since why didn't matter least of all to Lucas since apparently he had been working for twenty or twentyfive years with indefatigable and unflagging concentration toward this one crowning moment; followed him into the woods about one good spit from the store and shot him in the back within hearing distance of the crowd around it and was still standing over the body the fired pistol put neatly away into his hip pocket again when the first ones reached the scene where he would without doubt have been lynched immediately out of hand except for the same Doyle Fraser who had saved him from the singletree seven years ago and old Skipworth, the constable—a little driedup wizened stonedeaf old man not much larger than a half-grown boy with a big nickelplated pistol loose in one coat pocket and in the other a guttapercha eartrumpet on a rawhide thong around his neck like a foxhorn, who on this occasion anyway revealed an almost gratuitous hardihood and courage, getting Lucas (who made no resistance whatever, merely watching this too with that same calm detached not even scornful interest) out of the crowd and took him to his home and chained him to the bedpost until the sheriff could come and get him and bring him in to town and keep him while the Gowries and Workitts and Ingrums and the rest of their guests and connections could get Vinson buried and Sunday passed and so be fresh and untrammelled for the new week and its duties and believe it or not even the night passed, the tentative roosters at false dawn then the interval then the loud fairy clangor of the birds and through the east window he could see the trees against gray light and then the sun itself high and furious above the trees glaring at him and it was already late, this of course must happen to him too: but then he was free and he would feel better after breakfast and he could always say he was going to Sunday school but then he wouldn't have to say anything by going out the back, strolling: across the back yard and into the lot and across it and through the woods to the railroad to the depot and then back to the Square then he thought of a simpler way than that and then quit thinking about it at all, through the front hall and across the front gallery and down the walk to the street and it was here he would remember later having first noticed that he had seen no Negro except Paralee when she brought his breakfast; by ordinary at this hour on Sunday morning he would have seen on almost every gallery housemaids or cooks in their fresh Sunday aprons with brooms or perhaps talking from gallery to gallery across the contiguous yardspaces and the children too fresh and scrubbed for Sunday school with clutched palm-sweaty nickels though perhaps it was a little too early for that or perhaps by mutual consent or even interdiction there would be no Sunday school today, only church and so at some mutual concorded moment say about halfpast eleven all the air over Yoknapatawpha County would reverberate soundlessly like heatshimmer with one concerted adjuration calm the hearts of these bereaved and angry men vengeance is mine saith the lord thou shalt not kill except that this was a little late too, they should have mentioned this to Lucas yesterday, past the jail the barred second storey window whose interstices on an ordinary Sunday would have been thick with dark hands and beyond them even a glint now and then of eye-whites in the shadows and the mellow voices calling and laughing down to the Negro girls and women passing or stopping along the street and this was when he realised that except for Paralee he had seen no Negro since yesterday afternoon though it would be tomorrow before he would learn that the ones who lived in the Hollow and Freedmantown hadn't come to work at all since Saturday night: nor on the

Square either, not even in the barbershop where Sunday morning was the bootblack's best day shining shoes and brushing clothes and running errands and drawing baths for the bachelor truckdrivers and garage hands who lived in rented rooms and the young men and the ones not so young who worked hard all week in the poolhall and the sheriff really had finally got back to town and had even torn himself away from his Sunday to go for Lucas: listening: hearing the talk: a dozen of them who had hurried out to Fraser's store yesterday afternoon and returned empty-handed (and he gathered one car full had even gone back last night, yawning and lounging now and complaining of lack of sleep: and that to be added to Lucas' account too) and he had heard all this before too and had even thought of it himself before that:

'I wonder if Hampton took a shovel with him. That's all he's going to need.'

'They'll lend him a shovel out there.'

'Yes—if there's anything to bury. They have gasoline even in Beat Four.'

'I thought old Skipworth was going to take care of that.'

'Sure. But that's Beat Four. They'll do what Skipworth tells them as long as he's got the nigger. But he's going to turn him over to Hampton. That's when it'll happen. Hope Hampton might be sheriff in Yoknapatawpha County but he's just another man in Beat Four.'

'No. They wont do nothing today. They're burying Vinson this afternoon and to burn a nigger right while the funeral's going on wouldn't be respectful to Vinson.'

'That's so. It'll probably be tonight.'

'On Sunday night?'

'Is that the Gowries' fault? Lucas ought to thought of that before he picked out Saturday to kill Vinson on.'

'I dont know about that. Hope Hampton's going to be a hard man to take a prisoner away from too.'

'A nigger murderer? Who in this county or state either is going to help him protect a nigger that shoots white men in the back?'

'Or the South either.'

'Yes. Or the South either.' He had heard it all before: outside again now: only his uncle might decide to come to town before time to go for the noon mail at the post office and if his uncle didn't see him then he really could tell his mother he didn't know where he was and of course he thought first of the empty office but if he went there that's exactly where his uncle would come too: because—and he remembered again that he had forgot to give Highboy the extra feed this morning too but it was too late now and besides he was going to carry feed with him anyway—he knew exactly what he was going to do: the sheriff had left town about nine oclock; the constable's house was fifteen miles away on a gravel road not too good but the sheriff should certainly go there and be back with Lucas by noon even if he stopped to make a few votes while there; long before that time he would go home and saddle Highboy and tie a sack of feed behind the saddle and turn him in a straight line in the opposite direction from Fraser's store and ride in that one undeviable direction for twelve hours which would be about midnight tonight and feed Highboy and rest him until daylight or even longer if he decided to and then ride the twelve hours back which would be eighteen actually or maybe even twenty-four or even thirty-six but at least all over finished done, no more fury and outrage to have to lie in bed with like trying to put yourself to sleep counting sheep and he turned the corner and went along the opposite side of the street and under the shed in front of the closed blacksmith shop, the heavy double wooden doors not locked with a hasp or latch but with a padlocked chain passed through an augerhole in each one so that the slack of the chain created an insag almost like an alcove; standing in it nobody could have seen him from either up the street or down it nor even passing along it (which would not be his mother anyway today) unless they stopped to look and now the bells began ringing in mellow unhurried discordant strophe and antistrophe from steeple to pigeonswirled steeple across the town, streets and Square one sudden decorous flow of men in their dark suits and women in silks and parasols and girls and young men two and two, flowing and decorous beneath that mellow uproar into that musical clamor: gone, Square and street empty again though still the bells rang on for a while yet, skydwellers, groundless denizens of the topless air too high too far insentient to the crawling earth then ceasing stroke by hasteless stroke from the subterrene shudder of organs and the cool frantic monotone of the settled pigeons. Two years ago his uncle had told him that there was nothing wrong with cursing; on the contrary it was not only useful but substituteless but like everything else valuable it was precious only because the supply was limited and if you wasted it on nothing on its urgent need you might find yourself bankrupt so he said *What the hell am I doing here* then answered himself the obvious answer: not to see Lucas, he had seen Lucas but so that Lucas could see him again if he so wished, to look back at him not just from the edge of mere uniqueless death but from the gasoline-roar of apotheosis. Because he was free. Lucas was no longer his responsibility, he was no longer Lucas' keeper; Lucas himself had discharged him.

Then suddenly the empty street was full of men. Yet there were not many of them, not two dozen, some suddenly and quietly from nowhere. Yet they seemed to fill it, block it, render it suddenly interdict as though not that nobody could pass them, pass through it, use it as a street but that nobody would dare, would even approach near enough to essay the gambit as people stay well away from a sign saying High Voltage or Explosive. He knew, recognised them all; some of them he had even seen and listened to in the barbershop two hours ago—the young men or men under forty, bachelors, the homeless who had the Saturday and Sunday baths in the barbershop—truckdrivers and garagehands, the oiler from the cotton gin, a sodajerker from the drugstore and the ones who could be seen all week long in or around the poolhall who did nothing at all that anyone knew, who owned automobiles and spent money nobody really knew exactly how they earned on weekends in Memphis or New Orleans brothels—the men who his uncle said were in every little Southern town, who never really led mobs nor even instigated them but were always the nucleus of them because of their mass availability. Then he saw the car; he recognised it too even in the distance without knowing or for that matter stopping to wonder how, himself moving out of his concealing doorway into the street and then across it to the edge of the crowd which made no sound but just stood there blocking the sidewalk beside the jail fence and overflowing into the street while the car came up not fast but quite deliberately, almost decorously as a car should move on Sunday morning, and drew in to the curb in front of the jail and stopped. A deputy was driving it. He made no move to get out. Then the rear door opened and the sheriff emerged—a big, a tremendous man with no fat and little hard pale eyes in a cold almost bland pleasant face who without even glancing at them turned and held the door open. Then Lucas got out, slowly and stiffly, exactly like a man who has spent the night chained to a bedpost, fumbling a little and bumping or at least raking his head against the top of the door so that as he emerged his crushed hat tumbled from his head onto the pavement almost under his feet. And that was the first time he had ever seen Lucas without the hat on and in the same second he realised that with the possible exception of Edmonds they there in the street watching him were probably the only white people in the county who had ever seen him uncovered: watching as, still bent over as he had emerged from the car, Lucas began to reach stiffly for the hat. But already in one vast yet astonishingly supple stoop the sheriff had picked it up and handed it back to Lucas who still bent over seemed to fumble at the hat too. Yet almost at once the hat was creased back into its old shape and now Lucas was standing up, erect except for his head, his face as he brushed the hat back and forth against the sleeve of his forearm rapid and light and deft as you stroke a razor. Then his head, his face went back and up too and in a motion not quite sweeping he set the hat back on his head at the old angle which the hat itself seemed to assume as if he had flung it up, and erect now in the black suit crumpled too from whatever night he had spent (there was a long grimed smear down one entire side from shoulder to ankle as if he had been lying on an unswept floor a long time in one position without being able to change it) Lucas looked at them for the first time and he thought *Now. He will see me now* and then he thought *He saw me. And that's all* and then he thought *He hasn't seen anybody* because the face was not even looking at them but just toward them, arrogant and calm and with no more defiance in it than fear: detached, impersonal, almost musing, intractable and composed, the eyes blinking a little in the sunlight even after the sound, an indraw of breath went up from somewhere in the crowd and a single voice said:

'Knock it off again, Hope. Take his head too this time.'

'You boys get out of here,' the sheriff said. 'Go back to the barbershop:' turning, saying to Lucas: 'All right. Come on.' And that was all, the face for another moment looking not at them but just toward them, the sheriff already walking toward the jail door when Lucas turned at last to follow him and by hurrying a little he could even get Highboy saddled and be out of the lot before his mother began to send Aleck Sander to look for him to come and eat dinner. Then he saw Lucas stop and turn and he was wrong because Lucas even knew where he was in the crowd before he turned, looking straight at him before he got turned around even, speaking to him:

'You, young man,' Lucas said. 'Tell your uncle I wants to see him:' then turned again and walked on after the sheriff, still a little stiffly in the smeared black suit, the hat arrogant and pale in the sunlight, the voice in the crowd saying:

'Lawyer hell. He wont even need an undertaker when them Gowries get through with him tonight:' walking on past the sheriff who himself had stopped now and was looking back at them, saying in his mild cold bland heatless voice:

'I told you folks once to get out of here. I aint going to tell you again.'

III.

So if he had gone straight home from the barbershop this morning and saddled Highboy when he first thought of it he would be ten hours away by now, probably fifty miles.

There were no bells now. What people on the street now would have been going to the less formal more intimate evening prayer-meeting, walking decorously across the shadow-bitten darkness from streetlamp to streetlamp; so in keeping with the Sabbath's still suspension that he and his uncle would have been passing them steadily, recognising them yards ahead without knowing or even pausing to speculate on when or how or why they had done so—not by silhouette nor even the voice needed: the presence, the aura perhaps; perhaps merely the juxtaposition: this living entity at this point at this moment on this day, as is all you need to recognise the people with, among whom you have lived all your life—stepping off the concrete onto the bordering grass to pass them, speaking (his uncle) to them by name, perhaps exchanging a phrase, a sentence then on, onto the concrete again.

But tonight the street was empty. The very houses themselves looked close and watchful and tense as though the people who lived in them, who on this soft May night (those who had not gone to church) would have been sitting on the dark galleries for a little while after supper in rocking chairs or porchswings, talking quietly among themselves or perhaps talking from gallery to gallery when the houses were close enough. But tonight they passed only one man and he was not walking but standing just inside the front gate to a small neat shoebox of a house built last year between two other houses already close enough together to hear one anothers' toilets flush (his uncle had explained that: 'When you were born and raised and lived all your life where you cant hear anything but owls at night and roosters at dawn and on damp days when sound carries your nearest neighbor chopping wood two miles away, you like to live where you can hear and smell people on either side of you every time they flush a drain or open a can of salmon or of soup.'), himself darker than shadow and certainly stiller—a countryman who had moved to town a year ago and now owned a small shabby side street grocery whose customers were mostly Negroes, whom they had not even seen until they were almost on him though he had already recognised them or at least his uncle some distance away and was waiting for them, already speaking to his uncle before they came abreast of him:

'Little early, aint you, Lawyer? Them Beat Four folks have got to milk and then chop wood to cook breakfast tomorrow with before they can eat supper and get in to town.'

'Maybe they'll decide to stay at home on a Sunday night,' his uncle said pleasantly, passing on: whereupon the man said almost exactly what the man in the barbershop had said this morning (and he remembered his uncle saying once how little of vocabulary man really needed to get comfortably and even efficiently through his life, how not only in the individual but within his whole type and race and kind a few simple clichés served his few simple passions and needs and lusts):

'Sho now. It aint their fault it's Sunday. That sonofabitch ought to thought of that before he taken to killing white men on a Saturday afternoon.' Then he called after them as they went on, raising his voice: 'My wife aint feeling good tonight, and besides I dont want to stand around up there just looking at the front of that jail. But tell um to holler if they need help.'

'I expect they know already they can depend on you, Mr Lilley,' his uncle said. They went on. 'You see?' his uncle said. 'He has nothing against what he calls niggers. If you ask him, he will probably tell you he likes them even better than some white folks he knows and he will believe it. They are probably constantly beating him out of a few cents here and there in his store and probably even picking up things—packages of chewing gum or bluing or a banana or a can of sardines or a pair of shoelaces or a bottle of hair-straightener—under their coats and aprons and he knows it; he probably even gives them things free of charge—the bones and spoiled meat out of his butcher's icebox and spoiled candy and lard. All he requires is that they act like niggers. Which is exactly what Lucas is doing: blew his top and murdered a white man—

which Mr Lilley is probably convinced all Negroes want to do—and now the white people will take him out and burn him, all regular and in order and themselves acting exactly as he is convinced Lucas would wish them to act: like white folks; both of them observing implicitly the rules: the nigger acting like a nigger and the white folks acting like whitefolks and no real hard feelings on either side (since Mr Lilley is not a Gowrie) once the fury is over; in fact Mr Lilley would probably be one of the first to contribute cash money toward Lucas' funeral and the support of his widow and children if he had them. Which proves again how no man can cause more grief than that one clinging blindly to the vices of his ancestors.'

Now they could see the Square, empty too—the amphitheatric lightless stores, the slender white pencil of the Confederate monument against the mass of the courthouse looming in columned upsoar to the dim quadruple face of the clock lighted each by a single faint bulb with a quality as intransigeant against those four fixed mechanical shouts of adjuration and warning as the glow of a firefly. Then the jail and at that moment, with a flash and glare and wheel of lights and a roar of engine at once puny against the vast night and the empty town yet insolent too, a car rushed from nowhere and circled the Square; a voice, a young man's voice squalled from it—no words, not even a shout: a squall significant and meaningless—and the car rushed on around the Square, completing the circle back to nowhere and died away. They turned in at the jail.

It was of brick, square, proportioned, with four brick columns in shallow basrelief across the front and even a brick cornice under the eaves because it was old, built in a time when people took time to build even jails with grace and care and he remembered how his uncle had said once that not courthouses nor even churches but jails were the true records of a county's, a community's history, since not only the cryptic forgotten initials and words and even phrases cries of defiance and indictment scratched into the walls but the very bricks and stones themselves held, not in solution but in suspension, intact and biding and potent and indestructible, the agonies and shames and griefs with which hearts long since unmarked and unremembered dust had strained and perhaps burst. Which was certainly true of this one because it and one of the churches were the oldest buildings in the town, the courthouse and everything else on or in the Square having been burned to rubble by Federal occupation forces after a battle in 1864. Because scratched into one of the panes of the fanlight beside the door was a young girl's single name, written by her own hand into the glass with a diamond in that same year and sometimes two or three times a year he would go up onto the gallery to look at it, it cryptic now in reverse, not for a sense of the past but to realise again the eternality, the deathlessness and changelessness of youth—the name of one of the daughters of the jailer of that time (and his uncle who had for everything an explanation not in facts but long since beyond dry statistics into something far more moving because it was truth: which moved the heart and had nothing whatever to do with what mere provable information said, had told him this too: how this part of Mississippi was new then, as a town a settlement a community less than fifty years old, and all the men who had come into it less long ago almost than even the oldest's lifetime were working together to secure it, doing the base jobs along with the splendid ones not for pay or politics but to shape a land for their posterity, so that a man could be the jailer then or the innkeeper or farrier or vegetable peddler yet still be what the lawyer and planter and doctor and parson called a gentleman) who stood at that window that afternoon and watched the battered remnant of a Confederate brigade retreat through the town, meeting suddenly across that space the eyes of the ragged unshaven lieutenant who led one of the broken companies, scratching into the glass not his name also, not only because a young girl of that time would never have done that but because she didn't know his name then, let alone that six months later he would be her husband.

In fact it still looked like a residence with its balustraded wooden gallery stretching across the front of the lower floor. But above that the brick wall was windowless except for the single tall crossbarred rectangle and he thought again of the Sunday nights which seemed now to belong to a time as dead as Nineveh when from suppertime until the jailer turned the lights out and yelled up the stairs for them to shut up, the dark limber hands would lie in the grimed interstices while the mellow untroubled repentless voices would shout down to the women in the aprons of cooks or nurses and the girls in their flash cheap clothes from the mail order houses or the other young men who had not been caught yet or had been caught and freed yesterday, gathered along the street. But not tonight and even the room behind it was dark though it was not yet eight oclock and he could see, imagine them not huddled perhaps but certainly all together, within elbow's touch whether they were actually touching or not and certainly quiet, not laughing tonight nor talking either, sitting in the dark and watching the top of the stairs because this would not be the first time when to mobs of white men not only all black cats were gray but they didn't always bother to count them either.

And the front door was open, standing wide to the street which he had never seen before even in summer although the ground floor was the jailer's living quarters, and tilted in a chair against the back wall so that he faced the door in full sight of the street, was a man who was not the jailer nor even one of the sheriff's deputies either. Because he had recognised him too: Will Legate, who lived on a small farm two miles from town and was one of the best woodsmen, the finest shot and the best deer-hunter in the county, sitting in the tilted chair holding the colored comic section of today's Memphis paper, with leaning against the wall beside him not the handworn rifle with which he had killed more deer (and even running rabbits with it) than even he remembered but a double barrelled shotgun, who apparently without even lowering or moving the paper had already seen and recognised them even before they turned in at the gate and was now watching them steadily as they came up the walk and mounted the steps and crossed the gallery and entered: at which moment the jailer himself emerged from a door to the right—a snuffy untidy potbellied man with a harried concerned outraged face, wearing a heavy pistol holstered onto a cartridge belt around his waist which looked as uncomfortable and out of place as a silk hat or a fifth century iron slavecollar, who shut the door behind him, already crying at his uncle:

'He wont even shut and lock the front door! Just setting there with that durn funny paper waiting for anybody that wants to to walk right in!'

'I'm doing what Mr Hampton told me to,' Legate said in his pleasant equable voice.

'Does Hampton think that funny paper's going to stop them folks from Beat Four?' the jailer cried.

'I dont think he's worrying about Beat Four yet,' Legate said still pleasantly and equably. 'This here's just for local consumption now.'

His uncle glanced at Legate. 'It seems to have worked. We saw the car—or one of them—make one trip around the Square as we came up. I suppose it's been by here too.'

'Oh, once or twice,' Legate said. 'Maybe three times. I really aint paid much mind.'

'And I hope to hell it keeps on working,' the jailer said. 'Because you sure aint going to stop anybody with just that one britch-loader.'

'Sure,' Legate said. 'I dont expect to stop them. If enough folks get their minds made up and keep them made up, aint anything likely to stop them from what they think they want to do. But then, I got you and that pistol to help me.'

'Me?' the jailer cried. 'Me get in the way of them Gowries and Ingrums for seventy-five dollars a month? Just for one nigger? And if you aint a fool, you wont neither.'

'Oh I got to,' Legate said in his easy pleasant voice. 'I got to resist. Mr Hampton's paying me five dollars for it.' Then to his uncle: 'I reckon you want to see him.'

'Yes,' his uncle said. 'If it's all right with Mr Tubbs.'

The jailer stared at his uncle, irate and harried. 'So you got to get mixed up in it too. You cant let well enough alone neither.' He turned abruptly. 'Come on:' and led the way through the door beside which Legate's chair was tilted, into the back hall where the stairway rose to the upper floor, snapping on the light switch at the foot of the stairs and began to mount them, his uncle then he following while he watched the hunch and sag of the holster at the jailer's hip. Suddenly the jailer seemed about to stop; even his uncle thought so, stopping too but the jailer went on, speaking over his shoulder: 'Dont mind me. I'm going to do the best I can; I taken an oath of office too.' His voice rose a little, still calm, just louder: 'But dont think nobody's going to make me admit I like it. I got a wife and two children; what good am I going to be to them if I get myself killed protecting a goddamn stinking nigger?' His voice rose again; it was not calm now: 'And how am I going to live with myself if I let a passel of nogood sonabitches take a prisoner away from me?' Now he stopped and turned on the step above them, higher than both, his face once more harried and frantic, his voice frantic and outraged: 'Better for everybody if them folks had took him as soon as they laid hands on him yesterday——'

'But they didn't,' his uncle said. 'I dont think they will. And if they do, it wont really matter. They either will or they wont and if they dont it will be all right and if they do we will do the best we can, you and Mr Hampton and Legate and the rest of us, what we have to do, what we can do. So we dont need to worry about it. You see?'

'Yes,' the jailer said. Then he turned and went on, unsnapping his keyring from his belt under the pistol belt, to the heavy oak door which closed off the top of the stairs (It was one solid handhewn piece over two inches thick, locked with a heavy modern padlock in a handwrought iron bar through two iron slots which like the heavy rosette-shaped hinges were handwrought too, hammered out over a hundred years ago in the blacksmith shop across the street where he had stood yesterday; one day last summer a stranger, a city man, an architect who reminded him somehow of his uncle, hatless and tieless, in tennis shoes and a pair of worn flannel trousers and what was left of a case of champagne in a convertible-top car which must have cost three thousand dollars, driving not through town but into it, not hurting anyone but just driving the car up onto the pavement and across it through a plate glass window, quite drunk, quite cheerful, with less than fifty cents in cash in his pocket but all sorts of identification cards and a check folder whose stubs showed a balance in a New York bank of over six thousand dollars, who insisted on being put in jail even though the marshal and the owner of the window both were just trying to persuade him to go to the hotel and sleep it off so he could write a check for the window and the wall: until the marshal finally put him in jail where he went to sleep at once like a baby and the garage sent for the car and the next morning the jailer telephoned the marshal at five oclock to come and get the man out because he had waked the whole household up talking from his cell across to the niggers in the bullpen. So the marshal came and made him leave and then he wanted to go out with the street gang to work and they wouldn't let him do that and his car was ready too but he still wouldn't leave, at the hotel that night and two nights later his uncle even brought him to supper, where he and his uncle talked for three hours about Europe and Paris and Vienna and he and his mother listening too though his father had excused himself: and still there two days after that, still trying from his uncle and the mayor and the board of aldermen and at last the board of supervisors themselves to buy the whole door or if they wouldn't sell that, at least the bar and slots and the hinges.) and unlocked it and swung it back.

But already they had passed out of the world of man, men: people who worked and had homes and raised families and tried to make a little more money than they perhaps deserved by fair means of course or at least by legal, to spend a little on fun and still save something against old age. Because even as the oak door swung back there seemed to rush out and down at him the stale breath of all human degradation and shame—a smell of creosote and excrement and stale vomit and incorrigibility and defiance and repudiation like something palpable against the thrust and lift of their bodies as they mounted the last steps and into a passage which was actually a part of the main room, the bullpen, cut off from the rest of the room by a wall of wire mesh like a chicken run or a dog-kennel, inside which in tiered bunks against the farther wall lay five Negroes, motionless, their eyes closed but no sound of snoring, no sound of any sort, lying there immobile orderly and composed under the dusty glare of the single shadeless bulb as if they had been embalmed, the jailer stopping again, his own hands gripped into the mesh while he glared at the motionless shapes. 'Look at them,' the jailer said in that voice too loud, too thin, just under hysteria: 'Peaceful as lambs but aint a damned one of them asleep. And I dont blame them, with a mob of white men boiling in here at midnight with pistols and cans of gasoline.—Come on,' he said and turned and went on. Just beyond there was a door in the mesh, not padlocked but just hooked with a hasp and staple such as you might see on a dog-kennel or a corncrib but the jailer passed it.

'You put him in the cell, did you?' his uncle said.

'Hampton's orders,' the jailer said over his shoulder. 'I dont know what the next white man that figgers he cant rest good until he kills somebody is going to think about it. I taken all the blankets off the cot though.'

'Maybe because he wont be here long enough to have to go to sleep?' his uncle said.

'Ha ha,' the jailer said in that strained high harsh voice without mirth: 'Ha ha ha ha:' and following behind his uncle he thought how of all human pursuits murder has the most deadly need of privacy; how man will go to almost any lengths to preserve the solitude in which he evacuates or makes love but he will go to any length for that in which he takes life, even to homicide, yet by no act can he more completely and irrevocably destroy it: a modern steel barred door this time with a built-in lock as large as a woman's handbag which the jailer unlocked with another key on the ring and then turned, the sound of his feet almost as rapid as running back down the corridor until the sound of the oak door at the head of the stairs cut them off, and beyond it the cell lighted by another single dim dusty flyspecked bulb behind a wire screen cupped to the ceiling, not much larger than a broom closet and in fact just wide enough for the double bunk against the wall, from both beds of which not just the blankets but the mattresses too had been stripped, he and his uncle entering and still all he saw yet was the first thing he had seen: the hat and the black coat hanging neatly from a nail in the wall: and he would remember afterward how he thought in a gasp, a surge of relief: *They've already got him. He's gone. It's too late. It's already over now*. Because he didn't know what he had expected, except that it was not this: a careful spread of newspaper covering neatly the naked springs of the lower cot and another section as carefully placed on the upper one so it would shield his eyes from the light and Lucas himself lying on the spread papers, asleep, on his back, his head pillowed on one of his shoes and his hands folded on his breast, quite peacefully or as peacefully as old people sleep, his mouth open and breathing in faint shallow jerky gasps; and he stood in an almost unbearable surge not merely of outrage but of rage, looking down at the face which for the first time, defenceless at last for a moment, revealed its age, and the lax gnarled old man's hands which only yesterday had sent a bullet into the back of another human being, lying still and peaceful on the bosom of the old-fashioned collarless boiled white shirt closed at the neck with the oxidising brass button shaped like an arrow and almost as large as the head of a small snake, thinking: *He's just a nigger after all for all his high nose and his stiff neck and his gold watch-chain and refusing to mean mister to anybody even when he says it. Only a nigger could kill a man, let alone shoot him in the back, and then sleep like a baby as soon as he found something flat enough to lie down on;* still looking at him when without moving otherwise Lucas closed his mouth and his eyelids opened, the eyes staring up for another second, then still without the head moving at all the eyeballs turned until Lucas was looking straight at his uncle but still not moving: just lying there looking at him.

'Well, old man,' his uncle said. 'You played hell at last.' Then Lucas moved. He sat up stiffly and swung his legs stiffly over the edge of the cot, picking one of them up by the knee between his hands and swinging it around as you open or close a sagging gate, groaning, grunting not just frankly and unabashed and aloud but comfortably, as the old grunt and groan with some long familiar minor stiffness so used and accustomed as to be no longer even an ache and which if they were ever actually cured of it, they would be bereft and lost; he listening and watching still in that rage and now amazement too at the murderer not merely in the shadow of the gallows but of a lynch-mob, not only taking time to groan over a stiffness in his back but doing it as if he had all the long rest of a natural life in which to be checked each time he moved by the old familiar catch.

'Looks like it,' Lucas said. 'That's why I sent for you. What you going to do with me?'

'Me?' his uncle said. 'Nothing. My name aint Gowrie. It aint even Beat Four.'

Moving stiffly again Lucas bent and peered about his feet, then he reached under the cot and drew out the other shoe and sat up again and began to turn creakily and stiffly to look behind him when his uncle reached and took the first shoe from the cot and dropped it beside the other. But Lucas didn't put them on. Instead he sat again, immobile, his hands on his knees, blinking. Then with one hand he made a gesture which completely dismissed Gowries, mob, vengeance, holocaust and all. 'I'll worry about that when they walks in here,' he said. 'I mean the law. Aint you the county lawyer?'

'Oh,' his uncle said. 'It's the District Attorney that'll hang you or send you to Parchman—not me.'

Lucas was still blinking, not rapidly: just steadily. He watched him. And suddenly he realised that Lucas was not looking at his uncle at all and apparently had not been for three or four seconds.

'I see,' Lucas said. 'Then you can take my case.'

'Take your case? Defend you before the judge?'

'I'm gonter pay you,' Lucas said. 'You dont need to worry.'

'I dont defend murderers who shoot people in the back,' his uncle said.

Again Lucas made the gesture with one of the dark gnarled hands. 'Let's forgit the trial. We aint come to it yet.' And now he saw that Lucas was watching his uncle, his head lowered so that he was watching his uncle upward from beneath through the grizzled tufts of his eyebrows—a look shrewd secret and intent. Then Lucas said: 'I wants to hire somebody——' and stopped. And watching him, he thought, remembered an old lady, dead now, a spinster, a neighbor who wore a dyed transformation and had always on a pantry shelf a big bowl of homemade teacakes for all the children on the street, who one summer (he couldn't have been over seven or eight then) taught all of them to play Five Hundred: sitting at the card table on her screened side gallery on hot summer mornings and she would wet her fingers and take a card from her hand and lay it on the table, her hand not still poised over it of course but just lying nearby until the next player revealed exposed by some movement or gesture of triumph or exultation or maybe by just simple increased hard breathing his intention to trump or overplay it, whereupon she would say quickly: 'Wait. I picked up the wrong one' and take up the card and put it back into her hand and play another one. That was exactly what Lucas had done. He had sat still before but now he was absolutely immobile. He didn't even seem to be breathing.

'Hire somebody?' his uncle said. 'You've got a lawyer. I had already taken your case before I came in here. I'm going to tell you what to do as soon as you have told me what happened.'

'No,' Lucas said. 'I wants to hire somebody. It dont have to be a lawyer.'

Now it was his uncle who stared at Lucas. 'To do what?'

He watched them. Now it was no childhood's game of stakeless Five Hundred. It was more like the poker games he had overlooked. 'Are you or aint you going to take the job?' Lucas said.

'So you aint going to tell me what you want me to do until after I have agreed to do it,' his uncle said. 'All right,' his uncle said. 'Now I'm going to tell you what to do. Just exactly what happened out there yesterday?'

'So you dont want the job,' Lucas said. 'You aint said yes or no yet.'

'No!' his uncle said, harsh, too loud, catching himself but already speaking again before he had brought his voice back down to a sort of furious explicit calm: 'Because you aint got any job to offer anybody. You're in jail, depending on the grace of God to keep those damned Gowries from dragging you out of here and hanging you to the first lamp post they come to. Why they ever let you get to town in the first place I still dont understand——'

'Nemmine that now,' Lucas said. 'What I needs is——'

'Nemmine that!' his uncle said. 'Tell the Gowries to never mind it when they bust in here tonight. Tell Beat Four to just forget it——' He stopped; again with an effort you could almost see he brought his voice back to that furious patience. He drew a deep breath and expelled it. 'Now. Tell me exactly what happened yesterday.'

For another moment Lucas didn't answer, sitting on the bunk, his hands on his knees, intractable and composed, no longer looking at his uncle, working his mouth faintly as if he were tasting something. He said: 'They was two folks, partners in a sawmill. Leastways they was buying the lumber as the sawmill cut it——'

'Who were they?' his uncle said.

'Vinson Gowrie was one of um.'

His uncle stared at Lucas for a long moment. But his voice was quite calm now. 'Lucas,' he said, 'has it ever occurred to you that if you just said mister to white people and said it like you meant it, you might not be sitting here now?'

'So I'm to commence now,' Lucas said. 'I can start off by saying mister to the folks that drags me out of here and builds a fire under me.'

'Nothing's going to happen to you—until you go before the judge,' his uncle said. 'Dont you know that even Beat Four dont take liberties with Mr Hampton—at least not here in town?'

'Shurf Hampton's home in bed now.'

'But Mr Will Legate's sitting down stairs with a shotgun.'

'I aint 'quainted with no Will Legate.'

'The deer hunter? The man that can hit a running rabbit with a thirty-thirty rifle?'

'Hah,' Lucas said. 'Them Gowries aint deer. They might be cattymounts and panthers but they aint deer.'

'All right,' his uncle said. 'Then I'll stay here if you'll feel better. Now. Go on. Vinson Gowrie and another man were buying lumber together. What other man?'

'Vinson Gowrie's the only one that's public yet.'

'And he got public by being shot in broad daylight in the back,' his uncle said. 'Well, that's one way to do it.—All right,' his uncle said. 'Who was the other man?'

Lucas didn't answer. He didn't move; he might not even have heard, sitting peaceful and inattentive, not even really waiting: just sitting there while his uncle watched him. Then his uncle said:

'All right. What were they doing with it?'

'They was yarding it up as the mill cut it, gonter sell it all at once when the sawing was finished. Only the other man was hauling it away at night, coming in late after dark with a truck and picking up a load and hauling it over to Glasgow or Hollymount and selling it and putting the money in his pocket.'

'How do you know?'

'I seen um. Watched um.' Nor did he doubt this for a moment because he remembered Ephriam, Paralee's father before he died, an old man, a widower who would pass most of the day dozing and waking in a rocking chair on Paralee's gallery in summer and in front of the fire in winter and at night would walk the roads, not going anywhere, just moving, at times five and six miles from town before he would return at dawn to doze and wake all day in the chair again.

'All right,' his uncle said. 'Then what?'

'That's all,' Lucas said. 'He was just stealing a load of lumber every night or so.'

His uncle stared at Lucas for perhaps ten seconds. He said in a voice of calm, almost hushed amazement: 'So you took your pistol and went to straighten it out. You, a nigger, took a pistol and went to rectify a wrong between two white men. What did you expect? What else did you expect?'

'Nemmine expecting,' Lucas said. 'I wants——'

'You went to the store,' his uncle said, 'only you happened to find Vinson Gowrie first and followed him into the woods and told him his partner was robbing him and naturally he cursed you and called you a liar whether it was true or not, naturally he would have to do that; maybe he even knocked you down and walked on and you shot him in the back——'

'Never nobody knocked me down,' Lucas said.

'So much the worse,' his uncle said. 'So much the worse for you. It's not even self defense. You just shot him in the back. And then you stood there over him with the fired pistol in your pocket and let the white folks come up and grab you. And if it hadn't been for that little shrunk-up rheumatic constable who had no business being there in the first place and in the second place had no business whatever, at the rate of a dollar a prisoner every time he delivered a subpoena or served a warrant, having guts enough to hold off that whole damn Beat Four for eighteen hours until Hope Hampton saw fit or remembered or got around to bringing you in to jail——holding off that whole countryside that you nor all the friends you could drum up in a hundred years——'

'I aint got friends,' Lucas said with stern and inflexible

pride, and then something else though his uncle was already talking:

'You're damned right you haven't. And if you ever had that pistol shot would have blown them to kingdom come too—— What?' his uncle said. 'What did you say?'

'I said I pays my own way,' Lucas said.

'I see,' his uncle said. 'You dont use friends; you pay cash. Yes. I see. Now you listen to me. You'll go before the grand jury tomorrow. They'll indict you. Then if you like I'll have Mr Hampton move you to Mottstown or even further away than that, until court convenes next month. Then you'll plead guilty; I'll persuade the District Attorney to let you do that because you're an old man and you never were in trouble before; I mean as far as the judge and the District Attorney will know since they dont live within fifty miles of Yoknapatawpha County. Then they wont hang you; they'll send you to the penitentiary; you probably wont live long enough to be paroled but at least the Gowries cant get to you there. Do you want me to stay in here with you tonight?'

'I reckon not,' Lucas said. 'They kept me up all last night and I'm gonter try to get some sleep. If you stay here you'll talk till morning.'

'Right,' his uncle said harshly, then to him: 'Come on:' already moving toward the door. Then his uncle stopped. 'Is there anything you want?'

'You might send me some tobacco,' Lucas said. 'If them Gowries leaves me time to smoke it.'

'Tomorrow,' his uncle said. 'I dont want to keep you awake tonight:' and went on, he following, his uncle letting him pass first through the door so that he stepped aside in his turn and stood looking back into the cell while his uncle came through the door and drew it after him, the heavy steel plunger crashing into its steel groove with a thick oily sound of irrefutable finality like that ultimate cosmolined doom itself when as his uncle said man's machines had at last effaced and obliterated him from the earth and, purposeless now to themselves with nothing left to destroy, closed the last carborundum-grooved door upon their own progenitorless apotheosis behind one clockless lock responsive only to the last stroke of eternity, his uncle going on, his feet ringing and echoing down the corridor and then the sharp rattle of his knuckles on the oak door while he and Lucas still looked at one another through the steel bars, Lucas standing too now in the middle of the floor beneath the light and looking at him with whatever it was in his face so that he thought for a second that Lucas had spoken aloud. But he hadn't, he was making no sound: just looking at him with that mute patient urgency until the jailer's feet thumped nearer and nearer on the stairs and the slotted bar on the door rasped back.

And the jailer locked the bar again and they passed Legate still with his funny paper in the tilted chair beside the shotgun facing the open door, then outside, down the walk to the gate and the street, following through the gate where his uncle had already turned toward home: stopping, thinking *a nigger a murderer who shoots white people in the back and aint even sorry.*

He said: 'I imagine I'll find Skeets McGowan loafing somewhere on the Square. He's got a key to the drugstore. I'll take Lucas some tobacco tonight.' His uncle stopped.

'It can wait till morning,' his uncle said.

'Yes,' he said, feeling his uncle watching him, not even wondering what he would do if his uncle said no, not even waiting really, just standing there.

'All right,' his uncle said. 'Dont be too long.' So he could have moved then. But still he didn't.

'I thought you said nothing would happen tonight.'

'I still dont think it will,' his uncle said. 'But you cant tell. People like the Gowries dont attach a great deal of importance to death or dying. But they do put a lot of stock in the dead and how they died—particularly their own. If you get the tobacco, let Tubbs carry it up to him and you come on home.'

So he didn't have to say even yes this time, his uncle turning first then he turned and walked toward the Square, walking on until the sound of his uncle's feet had ceased, then standing until his uncle's black silhouette had changed to the white gleam of his linen suit and then that faded beyond the last arclight and if he had gone on home and got Highboy as soon as he recognised the sheriff's car this morning that would be eight hours and almost forty miles, turning then and walking back toward the gate with Legate's eyes watching him, already recognising him across the top of the funny paper even before he reached the gate and if he just went straight on now he could follow the lane behind the hedge and across into the lot and saddle Highboy and go out by the pasture gate and turn his back on Jefferson and nigger murderers and all and let Highboy go as fast as he wanted to go and as far as he wanted to go even when he had blown himself at last and agreed to walk, just so his tail was still turned to Jefferson and nigger murderers: through the gate and up the walk and across the gallery and again the jailer came quickly through the door at the right, his expression already giving way to the one of harried outrage.

'Again,' the jailer said. 'Dont you never get enough?'

'I forgot something,' he said.

'Let it wait till morning,' the jailer said.

'Let him get it now,' Legate said in his equable drawl. 'If he leaves it there till morning it might get trompled on.' So the jailer turned; again they mounted the stairs, again the jailer unlocked the bar across the oak door.

'Never mind the other one,' he said. 'I can attend to it through the bars:' and didn't wait, the door closed behind him, he heard the bar slide back into the slot but still all he had to do was just to rap on it, hearing the jailer's feet going away back down the stairs but even then all he had to do was just to yell loud and bang on the floor and Legate anyway would hear him, thinking *Maybe he will remind me of that goddamn plate of collards and sidemeat or maybe he'll even tell me I'm all he's got, all that's left and that will be enough*——walking fast, then the steel door and Lucas had not moved, still standing in the middle of the cell beneath the light, watching the door when he came up to it and stopped and said in a voice as harsh as his uncle's had ever been:

'All right. What do you want me to do?'

'Go out there and look at him,' Lucas said.

'Go out where and look at who?' he said. But he understood all right. It seemed to him that he had known all the time what it would be; he thought with a kind of relief *So that's all it is* even while his automatic voice was screeching with outraged disbelief: 'Me? *Me?*' It was like something you have dreaded and feared and dodged for years until it seemed like all your life, then despite everything it happened to you and all it was was just pain, all it did was hurt and so it was all over, all finished, all right.

'I'll pay you,' Lucas said.

So he wasn't listening, not even to his own voice in amazed incredulous outrage: 'Me go out there and dig up that grave?' He wasn't even thinking anymore *So this is what that plate of meat and greens is going to cost me*. Because he had already passed that long ago when that something—whatever it was—had held him here five minutes ago looking back across the vast, the almost insuperable chasm between him and the old Negro murderer and saw, heard Lucas saying something to him not because he was himself, Charles Mallison junior, nor because he had eaten the plate of greens and warmed himself at the fire, but because he alone of all the white people Lucas would have a chance to speak to between now and the moment when he might be dragged out of the cell and down the steps at the end of a rope, would hear the mute unhoping urgency of the eyes. He said:

'Come here.' Lucas did so, approaching, taking hold of two of the bars as a child stands inside a fence. Nor did he remember doing so but looking down he saw his own hands holding to two of the bars, the two pairs of hands, the black ones and the white ones, grasping the bars while they faced one another above them. 'All right,' he said. 'Why?'

'Go and look at him,' Lucas said. 'If it's too late when you get back, I'll sign you a paper now saying I owes you whatever you think it's worth.'

But still he wasn't listening; he knew it: only to himself: 'I'm to go seventeen miles out there in the dark——'

'Nine,' Lucas said. 'The Gowries buries at Caledonia Chapel. You takes the first right hand up into the hills just beyond the Nine-Mile branch bridge. You can be there in a half hour in your uncle's automobile.'

'——I'm to risk having the Gowries catch me digging up that grave. I aim to know why. I dont even know what I'll be looking for. Why?'

'My pistol is a fawty-one Colt,' Lucas said. Which it would be; the only thing he hadn't actually known was the calibre—that weapon workable and efficient and well cared for yet as archaic peculiar and unique as the gold toothpick, which had probably (without doubt) been old Carothers McCaslin's pride a half century ago.

'All right,' he said. 'Then what?'

'He wasn't shot with no fawty-one Colt.'

'What was he shot with?'

But Lucas didn't answer that, standing there on his side of the steel door, his hands light-clasped and motionless around the two bars, immobile save for the faint movement of his breathing. Nor had he expected Lucas to and he knew that Lucas would never answer that, say any more, any further to any white man, and he knew why, as he knew why Lucas had waited to tell him, a child, about the pistol when he would have told neither his uncle nor the sheriff who would have been the one to open the grave and look at the body; he was surprised that Lucas had come as near as he had to telling his uncle about it and he realised, appreciated again that quality in his uncle which brought people to tell him things they would tell nobody else, even tempting Negroes to tell him what their nature forbade them telling white men: remembering old Ephriam and his mother's ring that summer five years ago—a cheap thing with an imitation stone; two of them in fact, identical, which his mother and her room-mate at Sweetbriar Virginia had saved their allowances and bought and exchanged to wear until death as young girls will, and the room-mate grown and living in California with a daughter of her own at Sweetbriar now and she and his mother had not seen one another in years and possibly never would again yet his mother still kept the ring: then one day it disappeared; he remembered how he would wake late at night and see lights burning downstairs and he would know she was still searching for it: and all this time old Ephriam was sitting in his home-made rocking chair on Paralee's front gallery until one day Ephriam told him that for half a dollar he would find the ring and he gave Ephriam the half dollar and that afternoon he left for a week at a Scout camp and returned and found his mother in the kitchen where she had spread newspapers on the table and emptied the stone crock she and Paralee kept the cornmeal in onto it and she and Paralee were combing through the meal with forks and for the first time in a week he remembered the ring and went back to Paralee's house and there was Ephriam sitting in the chair on the gallery and Ephriam said, 'Hit's under the hawg-trough at your pa's farm:' nor did Ephriam need to tell him how then because he had already remembered by then: Mrs Downs: an old white woman who lived alone in a small filthy shoebox of a house that smelled like a foxden on the edge of town in a settlement of Negro houses, in and out of which Negroes came and went steadily all day long and without doubt most of the night: who (this not from Paralee who seemed always to not know or at least to have no time at the moment to talk about it, but from Aleck Sander) didn't merely tell fortunes and cure hexes but found things: which was where the half dollar had gone and he believed at once and so implicitly that the ring was now found that he dismissed that phase at once and forever and it was only the thing's secondary and corollary which moved his interest, saying to Ephriam: 'You've known all this week where it was and you didn't even tell them?' and Ephriam looked at him a while, rocking steadily and placidly and sucking at his cold ashfilled pipe with each rock like the sound of a small asthmatic cylinder: 'I mought have told your maw. But she would need help. So I waited for you. Young folks and womens, they aint cluttered. They can listen. But a middle-year man like your paw and your uncle, they cant listen. They aint got time. They're too busy with facks. In fact, you mought bear this in yo mind; someday you mought need it. If you ever needs to get anything done outside the common run, dont waste yo time on the menfolks; get the womens and children to working at it.' And he remembered his father's not rage so much as outrage, his almost furious repudiation, his transference of the whole thing into a realm of assailed embattled moral principle, and even his uncle who until now had had no more trouble than he believing things that all other grown people doubted for the sole reason that they were unreasonable, while his mother went serenely and stubbornly about her preparations to go out to the farm which she hadn't visited in over a year and even his father hadn't seen it since months before the ring was missing and even his uncle refused to drive the car so his father hired a man from the garage and he and his mother went out to the farm and with the help of the overseer found under the trough where the hogs were fed, the ring. Only this was no obscure valueless little ring exchanged twenty years ago between two young girls but the death by shameful violence of a man who would die not because he was a murderer but because his skin was black. Yet this was all Lucas was going to tell him and he knew it was all; he thought in a kind of raging fury: *Believe? Believe what?* because Lucas was not even asking him to believe anything; he was not even asking a favor, making no last desperate plea to his humanity and pity but was even going to pay him provided the price was not too high, to go alone seventeen miles (no, nine: he remembered at least that he had heard that now) in the dark and risk being caught violating the grave of a member of a clan of men already at the pitch to commit the absolute of furious and bloody outrage, without even telling him why. Yet he tried it again, as he knew Lucas not only knew he was going to but knew that he knew what answer he would get:

'What gun was he shot with, Lucas?' and got exactly what even Lucas knew he had expected:

'I'm gonter pay you,' Lucas said. 'Name yo price at anything in reason and I will pay it.'

He drew a long breath and expelled it while they faced each other through the bars, the bleared old man's eyes watching him, inscrutable and secret. They were not even urgent now and he thought peacefully *He's not only beat me, he never for one second had any doubt of it*. He said: 'All right. Just for me to look at him wouldn't do any good, even if I could tell about the bullet. So you see what that means. I've got to dig him up, get him out of that hole before the Gowries catch me, and in to town where Mr Hampton can send to Memphis for an expert that can tell about bullets.' He looked at Lucas, at the old man holding gently to the bars inside the cell and not even looking at him anymore. He drew a long breath again. 'But the main thing is to get him up out of the ground where somebody can look at him before the . . . . .' He looked at Lucas. 'I'll have to get out there and dig him up and get back to town before midnight or one oclock and maybe even midnight will be too late. I dont see how I can do it. I cant do it.'

'I'll try to wait,' Lucas said.

IV.

THERE WAS a weathered battered second-hand-looking pickup truck parked at the curb in front of the house when he reached home. It was now well past eight oclock; it was a good deal more than a possibility that there remained less than four hours for his uncle to go to the sheriff's house and convince him and then find a J.P. or whoever they would have to find and wake and then convince too to open the grave (in lieu of permission from the Gowries, which for any reason whatever, worst of all to save a nigger from being burned over a bonfire, the President of the United States himself let alone a country sheriff would never get) and then go out to Caledonia church and dig up the body and get back to town with it in time. Yet this of all nights would be one when a farmer whose stray cow or mule or hog had been impounded by a neighbor who insisted on collecting a dollar pound fee before he would release it, must come in to see his uncle, to sit for an hour in his uncle's study saying yes or no or I reckon not while his uncle talked about crops or politics, one of which his uncle knew nothing about and the other the farmer didn't, until the man would get around to telling what he came for.

But he couldn't stand on ceremony now. He had been walking pretty fast since he left the jail but he was trotting now, catacorner across the lawn, onto the gallery and across it into the hall past the library where his father would still be sitting under one reading lamp with the Memphis paper's Sunday crossword puzzle page and his mother under the other one with the new Book-of-the-Month book, and on back to what his mother used to try to call Gavin's study but which Paralee and Aleck Sander had long since renamed the office so that everyone now called it that. The door was closed; he could hear the murmur of the man's voice beyond it during the second in which without even stopping he rapped twice and at the same time opened the door and entered, already saying:

'Good evening, sir. Excuse me. Uncle Gavin——'

Because the voice was his uncle's; seated opposite his uncle beyond the desk, instead of a man with a shaved sunburned neck in neat tieless Sunday shirt and pants, was a woman in a plain cotton print dress and one of the round faintly dusty-looking black hats set squarely on the top of her head such as his grandmother had used to wear and then he recognised her even before he saw the watch—small gold in a hunting case suspended by a gold brooch on her flat bosom almost like and in almost exactly the same position as the heart sewn on the breast of the canvas fencing vest—because since his grandmother's death no other woman in his acquaintance wore or even owned one and in fact he should have recognised the pickup truck: Miss Habersham, whose name was now the oldest which remained in the county. There had been three once: Doctor Habersham and a tavern keeper named Holston and a Huguenot younger son named Grenier who had ridden horseback into the county before its boundaries had ever been surveyed and located and named, when Jefferson was a Chickasaw trading post with a Chickasaw word to designate it out of the trackless wilderness of canebrake and forest of that time but all gone now, vanished except the one even from the county's spoken recollection: Holston merely the name of the hotel on the Square and few in the county to know or care where the word came from, and the last of the blood of Louis Grenier the *élégante*, the *dilettante*, the Paris-educated architect who had practised a little of law but had spent most of his time as a planter and painter (and more amateur as a raiser of food and cotton than with canvas and brush) now warmed the bones of an equable cheerful middleaged man with the mind and face of a child who lived in a half-shed half-den he built himself of discarded boards and pieces of flattened stovepipe and tin cans on the bank of the river twenty miles away, who didn't know his age and couldn't write even the Lonnie Grinnup which he now called himself and didn't even know that the land he squatted on was the last lost scrap of the thousands of acres which his ancestor had been master of and only Miss Habersham remained: a kinless spinster of seventy living in the columned colonial house on the edge of town which had not been painted since her father died and had neither water nor electricity in it, with two Negro servants (and here again something nagged for an instant at his mind his attention but already in the same second gone, not even dismissed: just gone) in a cabin in the back yard, who (the wife) did the cooking while Miss Habersham and the man raised chickens and vegetables and peddled them about town from the pickup truck. Until two years ago they had used a plump aged white horse (it was said to be twenty years old when he first remembered it, with a skin beneath the burnished white hairs as clean and pink as a baby's) and a buggy. Then they had a good season or something and Miss Habersham bought the pickup truck second hand and every morning winter and summer they would be seen about the streets from house to house, Miss Habersham at the wheel in cotton stockings and the round black hat which she had been wearing for at least forty years and the clean print dresses which you could see in the Sears Roebuck catalogues for two dollars and ninety-eight cents with the neat small gold watch pinned to the flat unmammary front and the shoes and the gloves which his mother said were made to her measure in a New York shop and cost thirty and forty dollars a pair for the one and fifteen and twenty for the other, while the Negro man trotted his vast belly in and out of the houses with a basket of bright greens or eggs in one hand and the plucked naked carcass of a chicken in the other;—recognised, remembered, even (his attention) nagged at and already dismissed because there wasn't time, saying rapidly:

'Good evening, Miss Habersham. Excuse me. I've got to speak to Uncle Gavin:' then again to his uncle: 'Uncle Gavin——'

'So is Miss Habersham,' his uncle said quick and immediate, in a tone a voice which in ordinary times he would have recognised at once; at an ordinary time he might even have comprehended the implication of what his uncle had said. But not now. He didn't actually hear it. He wasn't listening. In fact he really didn't have time to talk himself, saying rapid yet calm too, merely urgent and even that only to his uncle because he had already forgotten Miss Habersham, even her presence:

'I've got to speak to you:' and only then stopped not because he had finished, he hadn't even begun yet, but because for the first time he was hearing his uncle who hadn't even paused, sitting half sideways in the chair, one arm thrown over the back and the other hand holding the burning cob pipe on the table in front of him, still speaking in that voice like the idle flicking of a small limber switch:

'So you took it up to him yourself. Or maybe you didn't even bother with tobacco. And he told you a tale. I hope it was a good one.'

And that was all. He could go now, in fact should. For that matter he should never have stopped on his way through the hall or even come into the house at all but on around it where he could have called Aleck Sander on his way to the stable; Lucas had told him that thirty minutes ago in the jail when even he had come almost to the point and even under the very shadow of the Gowries had in the end known better than to try to tell his uncle or any other white man. Yet still he didn't move. He had forgotten Miss Habersham. He had dismissed her; he had said 'Excuse me' and so evanished her not only from the room but the moment too as the magician with one word or gesture disappears the palm tree or the rabbit or the bowl of roses and only they remained, the three of them: he at the door and still holding it, half in the room which he had never actually entered and shouldn't have come even that far and half already back out of it in the hall where he should never have wasted time passing to begin with, and his uncle half sprawled behind the table littered with papers too and another of the German beermugs filled with paper spills and probably a dozen of the corncob pipes in various stages of char, and half a mile away the old kinless friendless opinionated arrogant hardheaded intractable independent (insolent too) Negro man alone in the cell where the first familiar voice he would hear would probably be old one-armed Nub Gowrie's in the hall below saying, 'Git out of the way, Will Legate. We've come for that nigger', while outside the quiet lamplit room the vast millrace of time roared not toward midnight but dragging midnight with it, not to hurl midnight into wreckage but to hurl the wreckage of midnight down upon them in one poised skyblotting yawn: and he knew now that the irrevocable moment was not when he said 'All right' to Lucas through the steel door of the cell but when he would step back into the hall and close this one behind him. So he tried again, still calm, not even rapid now, not even urgent: just specious explicit and reasonable:

'Suppose it wasn't his pistol that killed him.'

'Of course,' his uncle said. 'That's exactly what I would claim myself if I were Lucas—or any other Negro murderer for that matter or any ignorant white murderer either for the matter of that. He probably even told you what he fired his pistol at. What was it? a rabbit, or maybe a tin can or a mark on a tree just to see if it really was loaded, really would go off. But let that pass. Grant it for the moment: then what? What do you suggest? No; what did Lucas tell you to do?'

And he even answered that: 'Couldn't Mr Hampton dig him up and see?'

'On what grounds? Lucas was caught within two minutes after the shot, standing over the body with a recently-fired pistol in his pocket. He never denied having fired it; in fact he refused to make any statement at all, even to me, his lawyer—the lawyer he himself sent for. And how risk it? I'd just as soon go out there and shoot another one of his sons as to tell Nub Gowrie I wanted to dig his boy's body up out of the ground it had been consecrated and prayed into. And if I went that far, I'd heap rather tell him I just wanted to exhume it up to dig the gold out of its teeth than to tell him the reason was to save a nigger from being lynched.'

'But suppose——' he said.

'Listen to me,' his uncle said with a sort of weary yet indomitable patience: 'Try to listen. Lucas is locked behind a proof steel door. He's got the best protection Hampton or anybody else in this county can possibly give him. As Will Legate said, there are enough people in this county to pass him and Tubbs and even that door if they really want to. But I dont believe there are that many people in this county who really want to hang Lucas to a telephone pole and set fire to him with gasoline.'

And now too. But he still tried. 'But just suppose——' he said again and now he heard for the third time almost exactly what he had heard twice in twelve hours, and he marvelled again at the paucity, the really almost standardised meagreness not of individual vocabularies but of Vocabulary itself, by means of which even man can live in vast droves and herds even in concrete warrens in comparative amity: even his uncle too:

'Suppose it then. Lucas should have thought of that before he shot a white man in the back.' And it was only later that he would realise his uncle was speaking to Miss Habersham too now; at the moment he was neither rediscovering her presence in the room nor even discovering it; he did not even remember that she had already long since ceased to exist, turning, closing the door upon the significantless speciosity of his uncle's voice: 'I've told him what to do. If anything was going to happen, they would have done it out there, at home, in their own back yard; they would never have let Mr Hampton get to town with him. In fact, I still dont understand why they did. But whether it was luck or mismanagement or old Mr Gowrie is failing with age, the result is good; he's all right now and I'm going to persuade him to plead guilty to manslaughter; he's old and I think the District Attorney will accept it. He'll go to the penitentiary and perhaps in a few years if he lives———' and closed the door, who had heard it all before and would no more, out of the room which he had never completely entered anyway and shouldn't have stopped at at all, releasing the knob for the first time since he had put his hand on it and thinking with the frantic niggling patience of a man in a burning house trying to gather up a broken string of beads: *Now I'll have to walk all the way back to the jail to ask Lucas where it is:* realising how Lucas probability doubts and everything else to the contrary he actually had expected his uncle and the sheriff would take charge and make the expedition, not because he thought they would believe him but simply because he simply could not conceive of himself and Aleck Sander being left with it: until he remembered that Lucas had already taken care of that too, foreseen that too; remembering not with relief but rather with a new burst of rage and fury beyond even his own concept of his capacity how Lucas had not only told him what he wanted but exactly where it was and even how to get there and only then as afterthought asked him if he would:—hearing the crackle of the paper on his father's lap beyond the library door and smelling the cigar burning in the ashtray at his hand and then he saw the blue wisp of its smoke float slowly out the open door as his father must have picked it up in some synonymous hiatus or throe and puffed it once: and (remembering) even by what means to get out there and back and he thought of himself opening the door again and saying to his uncle: *Forget Lucas. Just lend me your car* and then walking into the library and saying to his father who would have their car keys in his pocket until he would remember when he undressed to leave them where his mother could find them tomorrow: *Let me have the keys, Pop. I want to run out to the country and dig up a grave;* he even remembered Miss Habersham's pickup truck in front of the house (not Miss Habersham; he never thought of her again. He just remembered a motor vehicle sitting empty and apparently unwatched on the street not fifty yards away); the key might be, probably was, still in the switch and the Gowrie who caught him robbing his son's or brother's or cousin's grave might as well catch a car-thief too.

Because (quitting abandoning emerging from scattering with one sweep that confetti-swirl of raging facetiae) he realised that he had never doubted getting out there and even getting the body up. He could see himself reaching the church, the graveyard without effort nor even any great elapse of time; he could see himself singlehanded even having the body up and out still with no effort, no pant and strain of muscles and lungs nor laceration of the shrinking sensibilities. It was only then that the whole wrecked and tumbling midnight which peer and pant though he would he couldn't see past and beyond, would come crashing down on him. So (moving: he had not stopped since the first second's fraction while he closed the office door) he flung himself bodily with one heave into a kind of deadly reasonableness of enraged calculation, a calm sagacious and desperate rationality not of pros and cons because there were no pros: the reason he was going out there was that somebody had to and nobody else would and the reason somebody had to was that not even Sheriff Hampton (vide Will Legate and the shotgun stationed in the lower hall of the jail like on a lighted stage where anybody approaching would have to see him or them before they even reached the gate) were completely convinced that the

Gowries and their kin and friends would not try to take Lucas out of the jail tonight and so if they were all in town tonight trying to lynch Lucas there wouldn't be anybody hanging around out there to catch him digging up the grave and if that was a concrete fact then its obverse would be concrete too: if they were not in town after Lucas tonight then any one of the fifty or a hundred men and boys in the immediate connection by blood or just foxhunting and whiskeymaking and pine lumbertrading might stumble on him and Aleck Sander: and that too, that again: he must go on a horse for the same reason: that nobody else would except a sixteen-year-old boy who owned nothing to go on but a horse and he must even choose here: either to go alone on the horse in half the time and spend three times the time getting the body up alone because alone he would not only have to do all the digging but the watching and listening too, or take Aleck Sander with him (he and Aleck Sander had travelled that way before on Highboy for even more than ten miles—a big rawboned gelding who had taken five bars even under a hundred and seventy-five pounds and a good slow canter even with two up and a long jolting driving trot as fast as the canter except that not even Aleck Sander could stand it very long behind the saddle and then a shuffling nameless halfrun halfwalk which he could hold for miles under both of them, Aleck Sander behind him for the first mile at the canter then trotting beside the horse holding to the off stirrup for the next one) and so get the body up in a third of the time at the risk of having Aleck Sander keeping Lucas company when the Gowries came with the gasoline: and suddenly he found himself escaped back into the confetti exactly as you put off having to step finally into the cold water, thinking seeing hearing himself trying to explain that to Lucas too:

We have to use the horse. We cant help it: and Lucas:

You could have axed him for the car: and he:

He would have refused. Dont you understand? He wouldn't only have refused, he would have locked me up where I couldn't even have walked out there, let alone had a horse: and Lucas:

All right, all right. I aint criticising you. After all, it aint you them Gowries is fixing to set afire:—moving down the hall to the back door: and he was wrong; not when he had said All right to Lucas through the steel bars nor when he had stepped back into the hall and closed the office door behind him, but here was the irrevocable moment after which there would be no return; he could stop here and never pass it, let the wreckage of midnight crash harmless and impotent against these walls because they were strong, they would endure; they were home, taller than wreckage, stronger than fear;—not even stopping, not even curious to ask himself if perhaps he dared not stop, letting the screen door quietly to behind him and down the steps into the vast furious vortex of the soft May night and walking fast now across the yard toward the dark cabin where Paralee and Aleck Sander were no more asleep than all the other Negroes within a mile of town would sleep tonight, not even in bed but sitting quietly in the dark behind the closed doors and shuttered windows waiting for what sound what murmur of fury and death to breathe the spring dark: and stopped and whistled the signal he and Aleck Sander had been using to one another ever since they learned to whistle, counting off the seconds until the moment should come to repeat it, thinking how if he were Aleck Sander he wouldn't come out of the house to anybody's whistle tonight either when suddenly with no sound and certainly no light behind to reveal him by Aleck Sander stood out from the shadows, walking, already quite near in the moonless dark, a little taller than he though there was only a few months' difference between them: and came up, not even looking at him but past, over his head, toward the Square as if looking could make a lofting trajectory like a baseball, over the trees and the streets and the houses, to drop seeing into the Square—not the homes in the shady yards and the peaceful meals and the resting and the sleep which were the end and the reward, but the Square: the edifices created and ordained for trade and government and judgment and incarceration where strove and battled the passions of men for which the rest and the little death of sleep were the end and the escape and the reward.

'So they aint come for old Lucas yet,' Aleck Sander said.

'Is that what your people think about it too?' he said.

'And so would you,' Aleck Sander said. 'It's the ones like Lucas makes trouble for everybody.'

'Then maybe you better go to the office and sit with Uncle Gavin instead of coming with me.'

'Going where with you?' Aleck Sander said. And he told him, harsh and bald, in four words:

'Dig up Vinson Gowrie.' Aleck Sander didn't move, still looking past and over his head toward the Square. 'Lucas said it wasn't his gun that killed him.'

Still not moving Aleck Sander began to laugh, not loud and with no mirth: just laughing; he said exactly what his uncle had said hardly a minute ago: 'So would I,' Aleck Sander said. He said: 'Me? Go out there and dig that dead white man up? Is Mr Gavin already in the office or do I just sit there until he comes?'

'Lucas is going to pay you,' he said. 'He told me that even before he told me what it was.'

Aleck Sander laughed, without mirth or scorn or anything else: with no more in the sound of it than there is anything in the sound of breathing but just breathing. 'I aint rich,' he said. 'I dont need money.'

'At least you'll saddle Highboy while I hunt for a flashlight, wont you?' he said. 'You're not too proud about Lucas to do that, are you?'

'Certainly,' Aleck Sander said, turning.

'And get the pick and shovel. And the long tie-rope. I'll need that too.'

'Certainly,' Aleck Sander said. He paused, half turned. 'How you going to tote a pick and shovel both on Highboy when he dont even like to see a riding switch in your hand?'

'I dont know,' he said and Aleck Sander went on and he turned back toward the house and at first he thought it was his uncle coming rapidly around the house from the front, not because he believed that his uncle might have suspected and anticipated what he was about because he did not, his uncle had dismissed that too immediately and thoroughly not only from conception but from possibility too, but because he no longer remembered anyone else available for it to have been and even after he saw it was a woman he assumed it was his mother, even after he should have recognised the hat, right up to the instant when Miss Habersham called his name and his first impulse was to step quickly and quietly around the corner of the garage, from where he could reach the lot fence still unseen and climb it and go on to the stable and so go out the pasture gate without passing the house again at all, flashlight or not but it was already too late: calling his name: 'Charles:' in that tense urgent whisper then came rapidly up and stopped facing him, speaking in that tense rapid murmur:

'What did he tell you?' and now he knew what it was that had nudged at his attention back in his uncle's office when he had recognised her and then in the next second flashed away: old Molly, Lucas' wife, who had been the daughter of one of old Doctor Habersham's, Miss Habersham's grandfather's, slaves, she and Miss Habersham the same age, born in the same week and both suckled at Molly's mother's breast and grown up together almost inextricably like sisters, like twins, sleeping in the same room, the white girl in the bed, the Negro girl on a cot at the foot of it almost until Molly and Lucas married, and Miss Habersham had stood up in the Negro church as godmother to Molly's first child.

'He said it wasn't his pistol,' he said.

'So he didn't do it,' she said, rapid still and with something even more than urgency in her voice now.

'I dont know,' he said.

'Nonsense,' she said. 'If it wasn't his pistol——'

'I dont know,' he said.

'You must know. You saw him—talked to him——'

'I dont know,' he said. He said it calmly, quietly, with a kind of incredulous astonishment as though he had only now realised what he had promised, intended: 'I just dont know. I still dont know. I'm just going out there . . . . . .' He stopped, his voice died. There was an instant a second in which he even remembered he should have been wishing he could recall it, the last unfinished sentence. Though it was probably already too late and she had already done herself what little finishing the sentence needed and at any moment now she would cry, protest, ejaculate and bring the whole house down on him. Then in the same second he stopped remembering it. She said:

'Of course:' immediate murmurous and calm; he thought for another half of a second that she hadn't understood at all and then in the other half forgot that too, the two of them facing each other indistinguishable in the darkness across the tense and rapid murmur: and then he heard his own voice speaking in the same tone and pitch, the two of them not conspiratorial exactly but rather like two people who have irrevocably accepted a gambit they are not at all certain they can cope with: only that they will resist it: 'We dont even know it wasn't his pistol. He just said it wasn't.'

'Yes.'

'He didn't say whose it was nor whether or not he fired it. He didn't even tell you he didn't fire it. He just said it wasn't his pistol.'

'Yes.'

'And your uncle told you there in his study that that's just exactly what he would say, all he could say.' He didn't answer that. It wasn't a question. Nor did she give him time. 'All right,' she said. 'Now what? To find out if it wasn't his pistol—find out whatever it was he meant? Go out there and what?'

He told her, as baldly as he had told Aleck Sander, explicit and succinct: 'Look at him:' not even pausing to think how here he should certainly have anticipated at least a gasp. 'Go out there and dig him up and bring him to town where somebody that knows bullet holes can look at the bullet hole in him——'

'Yes,' Miss Habersham said. 'Of course. Naturally he wouldn't tell your uncle. He's a Negro and your uncle's a man:' and now Miss Habersham in her turn repeating and paraphrasing and he thought how it was not really a paucity a meagreness of vocabulary, it was in the first place because the deliberate violent blotting out obliteration of a human life was itself so simple and so final that the verbiage which surrounded it enclosed it insulated it intact into the chronicle of man had of necessity to be simple and uncomplex too, repetitive, almost monotonous even; and in the second place, vaster than that, adumbrating that, because what Miss Habersham paraphrased was simple truth, not even fact and so there was not needed a great deal of diversification and originality to express it because truth was universal, it had to be universal to be truth and so there didn't need to be a great deal of it just to keep running something no bigger than one earth and so anybody could know truth; all they had to do was just to pause, just to stop, just to wait: 'Lucas knew it would take a child—or an old woman like me: someone not concerned with probability, with evidence. Men like your uncle and Mr Hampton have had to be men too long, busy too long.—Yes?' she said. 'Bring him in to town where someone who knows can look at the bullet hole. And suppose they look at it and find out it was Lucas's pistol?' And he didn't answer that at all, nor had she waited again, saying, already turning: 'We'll need a pick and shovel. I've got a flashlight in the truck——'

'We?' he said.

She stopped; she said almost patiently: 'It's fifteen miles out there——'

'Ten,' he said.

'—a grave is six feet deep. It's after eight now and you may have only until midnight to get back to town in time——' and something else but he didn't even hear it. He wasn't even listening. He had said this himself to Lucas only fifteen minutes ago but it was only now that he understood what he himself had said. It was only after hearing someone else say it that he comprehended not the enormity of his intention but the simple inert unwieldy impossible physical vastness of what he faced; he said quietly, with hopeless indomitable amazement:

'We cant possibly do it.'

'No,' Miss Habersham said. 'Well?'

'Ma'am?' he said. 'What did you say?'

'I said you haven't even got a car.'

'We were going on the horse.'

Now she said, 'We?'

'Me and Aleck Sander.'

'Then we'll have three,' she said. 'Get your pick and shovel. They'll begin to wonder in the house why they haven't heard my truck start.' She moved again.

'Yessum,' he said. 'Drive on down the lane to the pasture gate. We'll meet you there.'

He didn't wait either. He heard the truck start as he climbed the lot fence; presently he could see Highboy's blaze in the black yawn of the stable hallway; Aleck Sander jerked the buckled girth-strap home through the keeper as he came up. He unsnapped the tie-rope from the bit-ring before he remembered and remembered and snapped it back and rove the other end through its knot around the wall-ring and looped it and the reins up over Highboy's head and led him out of the hallway and got up.

'Here,' Aleck Sander said reaching up the pick and shovel but Highboy had already begun to dance even before he could have seen them as he always did even at a hedge switch and he set him back hard and steadied him as Aleck Sander said 'Stand still!' and gave Highboy a loud slap on the rump, passing up the pick and shovel and he steadied them across the saddle-bow and managed to hold Highboy back on his heels for another second, long enough to free his foot from the near stirrup for Aleck Sander to get his foot into it, Highboy moving then in a long almost buck-jump as Aleck Sander swung up behind and still trying to run until he steadied him again with one hand, the pick and shovel jouncing on the saddle, and turned him across the pasture toward the gate. 'Hand me them damn shovels and picks,' Aleck Sander said. 'Did you get the flashlight?'

'What do you care?' he said. Aleck Sander reached his spare hand around him and took the pick and shovel; again for a second Highboy could actually see them but this time he had both hands free for the snaffle and the curb too. 'You aint going anywhere to need a flashlight. You just said so.'

They had almost reached the gate. He could see the dark blob of the halted truck against the pale road beyond it; that is, he could believe he saw it because he knew it was there. But Aleck Sander actually saw it: who seemed able to see in the dark almost like an animal. Carrying the pick and shovel, Aleck Sander had no free hand, nevertheless he had one with which he reached suddenly again and caught the reins outside his own hands and jerked Highboy almost back to a squat and said in a hissing whisper: 'What's that?'

'It's Miss Eunice Habersham's truck,' he said. 'She's going with us. Turn him loose, confound it!' wrenching the reins from Aleck Sander, who released them quickly enough now, saying,

'She's gonter take the truck:' and not even dropping the pick and shovel but flinging them clattering and clanging against the gate and slipping down himself and just in time because now Highboy stood erect on his hind feet until he struck him hard between the ears with the looped tie-rope.

'Open the gate,' he said.

'We wont need the horse,' Aleck Sander said. 'Unsaddle and bridle him here. We'll put um up when we get back.'

Which was what Miss Habersham said; through the gate now and Highboy still sidling and beating his hooves while Aleck Sander put the pick and shovel into the back of the truck as though he expected Aleck Sander to throw them at him this time, and Miss Habersham's voice from the dark cab of the truck:

'He sounds like a good horse. Has he got a four-footed gait too?'

'Yessum,' he said. 'Nome,' he said. 'I'll take the horse too. The nearest house is a mile from the church but somebody might still hear a car. We'll leave the truck at the bottom of the hill when we cross the branch.' Then he answered that too before she had time to say it: 'We'll need the horse to bring him back down to the truck.'

'Heh,' Aleck Sander said. It wasn't laughing. But then nobody thought it was. 'How do you reckon that horse is going to tote what you dug up when he dont even want to tote what you going to do the digging with?' But he had already thought of that too, remembering his grandfather telling of the old days when deer and bear and wild turkey could be hunted in Yoknapatawpha County within twelve miles of Jefferson, of the hunters: Major de Spain who had been his grandfather's cousin and old General Compson and Uncle Ike McCaslin, Carothers Edmonds' great-uncle, still alive at ninety, and Boon Hogganbeck whose mother's mother had been a Chickasaw woman and the Negro Sam Fathers whose father had been a Chickasaw chief, and Major de Spain's one-eyed hunting mule Alice who wasn't afraid even of the smell of bear and he thought how if you really were the sum of your ancestry it was too bad the ancestors who had evoluted him into a secret resurrector of country graveyards hadn't thought to equip him with a descendant of that unspookable one-eyed mule to transport his subjects on.

'I dont know,' he said.

'Maybe he'll learn by the time we get back to the truck,' Miss Habersham said. 'Can Aleck Sander drive?'

'Yessum,' Aleck Sander said.

Highboy was still edgy; held down he would merely have lathered himself to no end so since it was cool tonight for the first mile he actually kept in sight of the truck's tail-light. Then he slowed, the light fled diminishing on and vanished beyond a curve and he settled Highboy into the shambling halfrun halfwalk which no show judge would ever pass but which covered ground; nine miles of it to be covered and he thought with a kind of ghastly amusement that at last he would have time to think, thinking how it was too late to think now, not one of the three of them dared think now, if they had done but one thing tonight it was at least to put all thought ratiocination contemplation forever behind them; five miles from town and he would cross (probably Miss Habersham and Aleck Sander in the truck already had) the invisible surveyor's line which was the boundary of Beat Four: the notorious, the fabulous almost and certainly least of all did any of them dare think now, thinking how it was never difficult for an outlander to do two things at once which Beat Four wouldn't like since Beat Four already in advance didn't like most of the things which people from town (and from most of the rest of the county too for that matter) did: but that it remained for them, a white youth of sixteen and a Negro one of the same and an old white spinster of seventy to elect and do at the same time the two things out of all man's vast reservoir of invention and capability that Beat Four would repudiate and retaliate on most violently: to violate the grave of one of its progeny in order to save a nigger murderer from its vengeance.

But at least they would have some warning (not speculating on who the warning could help since they who would be warned were already six and seven miles from the jail and still moving away from it as fast as he dared push the horse) because if Beat Four were coming in tonight he should begin to pass them soon (or they pass him)—the battered mudstained cars, the empty trucks for hauling cattle and lumber, and the saddled horses and mules. Yet so far he had passed nothing whatever since he left town; the road lay pale and empty before and behind him too; the lightless houses and cabins squatted or loomed beside it, the dark land stretched away into the darkness strong with the smell of plowed earth and now and then the heavy scent of flowering orchards lying across the road for him to ride through like stagnant skeins of smoke so maybe they were making better time than even he had hoped and before he could stop it he had thought *Maybe we can, maybe we will after all;*—before he could leap and spring and smother and blot it from thinking not because he couldn't really believe they possibly could and not because you dont dare think whole even to yourself the entirety of a dear hope or wish let alone a desperate one else you yourself have doomed it but because thinking it into words even only to himself was like the struck match which doesn't dispel the dark but only exposes its terror—one weak flash and glare revealing for a second the empty road's the dark and empty land's irrevocable immitigable negation.

Because—almost there now; Aleck Sander and Miss Habersham had already arrived probably a good thirty minutes ago and he took a second to hope Aleck Sander had had forethought enough to drive the truck off the road where anybody passing would not see it, then in the same second he knew that of course Aleck Sander had done that and it was not Aleck Sander he had ever doubted but himself for even for one second doubting Aleck Sander—he had not seen one Negro since leaving town, with whom at this hour on Sunday night in May the road should have been constant as beads almost—the men and young women and girls and even a few old men and women and even children before it got too late, but mostly the men the young bachelors who since last Monday at daylight had braced into the shearing earth the lurch and heave of plows behind straining and surging mules then at noon Saturday had washed and shaved and put on the clean Sunday shirts and pants and all Saturday night had walked the dusty roads and all day Sunday and all Sunday night would still walk them until barely time to reach home and change back into the overalls and the brogans and catch and gear up the mules and forty-eight hours even bedless save for the brief time there was a woman in it be back in the field again the plow's point set into the new furrow when Monday's sun rose: but not now, not tonight: where in town except for Paralee and Aleck Sander he had seen none either for twenty-four hours but he had expected that, they were acting exactly as Negroes and whites both would have expected Negroes to act at such a time; they were still there, they had not fled, you just didn't see them—a sense a feeling of their constant presence and nearness: black men and women and children breathing and waiting inside their barred and shuttered houses, not crouching cringing shrinking, not in anger and not quite in fear: just waiting, biding since theirs was an armament which the white man could not match nor—if he but knew it—even cope with: patience; just keeping out of sight and out of the way,—but not here, no sense feeling here of a massed adjacence, a dark human presence biding and unseen; this land was a desert and a witness, this empty road its postulate (it would be some time yet before he would realise how far he had come: a provincial Mississippian, a child who when the sun set this same day had appeared to be—and even himself believed, provided he had thought about it at all—still a swaddled unwitting infant in the long tradition of his native land—or for that matter a witless foetus itself struggling—if he was aware that there had been any throes—blind and insentient and not even yet awaked in the simple painless convulsion of emergence) of the deliberate turning as with one back of the whole dark people on which the very economy of the land itself was founded, not in heat or anger nor even regret but in one irremediable invincible inflexible repudiation, upon not a racial outrage but a human shame.

Now he was there; Highboy tightened and even began to drive a little, even after nine miles, smelling water and now he could see distinguish the bridge or at least the gap of lighter darkness where the road spanned the impenetrable blackness of the willows banding the branch and then Aleck Sander stood out from the bridge rail; Highboy snorted at him then he recognised him too, without surprise, not even remembering how he had wondered once if Aleck Sander would have forethought to hide the truck, not even remembering that he had expected no less, not stopping, checking Highboy back to a walk across the bridge then giving him his head to turn from the road beyond the bridge and drop in stiff fore-legged jolts down toward the water invisible for a moment longer then he too could see the reflected wimpling where it caught the sky: until Highboy stopped and snorted again then heaved suddenly up and back, almost unseating him.

'He smell quicksand,' Aleck Sander said. 'Let him wait till he gets home, anyway. I'd rather be doing something else than what I am too.'

But he took Highboy a little further down the bank where he might get down to the water but again he only feinted at it so he pulled away and back onto the road and freed the stirrup for Aleck Sander, Highboy again already in motion when Aleck Sander swung up. 'Here,' Aleck Sander said but he had already swung Highboy off the gravel and into the narrow dirt road turning sharp toward the black loom of the ridge and beginning almost at once its long slant up into the hills though even before it began to rise the strong constant smell of pines was coming down on them with no wind behind it yet firm and hard as a hand almost, palpable against the moving body as water would have been. The slant steepened under the horse and even carrying double he essayed to run at it as was his habit at any slope, gathering and surging out until he checked him sharply back and even then he had to hold him hard-wristed in a strong lurching uneven walk until the first level of the plateau flattened and even as Aleck Sander said 'Here' again Miss Habersham stood out of the obscurity at the roadside carrying the pick and shovel. Aleck Sander slid down as Highboy stopped. He followed.

'Stay on,' Miss Habersham said. 'I've got the tools and the flashlight.'

'It's a half mile yet,' he said. 'Up hill. This aint a sidesaddle but maybe you could sit sideways. Where's the truck?' he said to Aleck Sander.

'Behind them bushes,' Aleck Sander said. 'We aint holding a parade. Leastways I aint.'

'No no,' Miss Habersham said. 'I can walk.'

'We'll save time,' he said. 'It must be after ten now. He's gentle. That was just when Aleck Sander threw the pick and shovel——'

'Of course,' Miss Habersham said. She handed the tools to Aleck Sander and approached the horse.

'I'm sorry it aint——' he said.

'Pah,' she said and took the reins from him and before he could even brace his hand for her foot she put it in the stirrup and went up as light and fast as either he or Aleck Sander could have done, onto the horse astride so that he had just time to avert his face, feeling her looking down in the darkness at his turned head. 'Pah,' she said again. 'I'm seventy years old. Besides, we'll worry about my skirt after we are done with this:'—moving Highboy herself before he had hardly time to take hold of the bit, back into the road when Aleck Sander said:

'Hush.' They stopped, immobile in the long constant invisible flow of pine. 'Mule coming down the hill,' Aleck Sander said.

He began to turn the horse at once. 'I dont hear anything,' Miss Habersham said. 'Are you sure?'

'Yessum,' he said, turning Highboy back off the road: 'Aleck Sander's sure.' And standing at Highboy's head among the trees and undergrowth, his other hand lying on the horse's nostrils in case he decided to nicker at the other animal, he heard it too—the horse or mule coming steadily down the road from the crest. It was unshod probably; actually the only sound he really heard was the creak of leather and he wondered (without doubting for one second that he had) how Aleck Sander had heard it at all the two minutes and more it had taken the animal to reach them. Then he could see it or that is where it was passing them—a blob, a movement, a darker shadow than shadow against the pale dirt of the road, going on down the hill, the soft steady shuffle and screak of leather dying away, then gone. But they waited a moment more.

'What was that he was toting on the saddle in front of him?' Aleck Sander said.

'I couldn't even see whether it was a man on it or not,' he said.

'I couldn't see anything,' Miss Habersham said. He led the horse back into the road. 'Suppose——' she said.

'Aleck Sander will hear it in time,' he said. So once more Highboy surged strong and steady at the steepening pitch, he carrying the shovel and clutching the leather under Miss Habersham's thin hard calf on one side and Aleck Sander with the pick on the other, mounting, really moving quite fast through the strong heady vivid living smell of the pines which did something to the lungs, the breathing as (he imagined: he had never tasted it. He could have—the sip from the communion cup didn't count because it was not only a sip but sour consecrated and sharp: the deathless blood of our Lord not to be tasted, moving not downward toward the stomach but upward and outward into the Allknowledge between good and evil and the choice and the repudiation and the acceptance forever—at the table at Thanksgiving and Christmas but he had never wanted to.) wine did to the stomach. They were quite high now, the ridged land opening and tumbling away invisible in the dark yet with the sense, the sensation of height and space; by day he could have seen them, ridge on pine-dense ridge rolling away to the east and the north in similitude of the actual mountains in Carolina and before that in Scotland where his ancestors had come from but he hadn't seen yet, his breath coming a little short now and he could not only hear but feel too the hard short blasts from Highboy's lungs as he was actually trying to run at this slope too even carrying a rider and dragging two, Miss Habersham steadying him, holding him down until they came out onto the true crest and Aleck Sander said once more 'Here' and Miss Habersham turned the horse out of the road because he could still see nothing until they were off the road and only then he distinguished the clearing not because it was a clearing but because in a thin distillation of starlight there stood, canted a little where the earth had sunk, the narrow slab of a marble headstone. And he could hardly see the church (weathered, unpainted, of wood and not much larger than a single room) at all even when he led Highboy around behind it and tied the reins to a sapling and unsnapped the tie-rope from the bit and went back to where Miss Habersham and Aleck Sander were waiting.

'It'll be the only fresh one,' he said. 'Lucas said there hasn't been a burying here since last winter.'

'Yes,' Miss Habersham said. 'The flowers too. Aleck Sander's already found it.' But to make sure (he thought quietly, he didn't know to whom: *I'm going to make a heap more mis-*

takes but dont let this be one of them.) he hooded the flashlight in his wadded handkerchief so that one thin rapid pencil touched for a second the raw mound with its meagre scattering of wreaths and bouquets and even single blooms and then for another second the headstone adjacent to it, long enough to read the engraved name:

AMANDA WORKITT
wife of
N.B. Forrest Gowrie
1878 1926
birth death

then snapped it off and again the darkness came in and the strong scent of the pines and they stood for a moment beside the raw mound, doing nothing at all. 'I hate this,' Miss Habersham said.

'You aint the one,' Aleck Sander said. 'It's just a half a mile back to the truck. Down hill too.'

She moved; she was first. 'Move the flowers,' she said. 'Carefully. Can you see?'

'Yessum,' Aleck Sander said. 'Aint many. Looks like they throwed them at it too.'

'But we wont,' Miss Habersham said. 'Move them carefully.' And it must be nearing eleven now; they would not possibly have time; Aleck Sander was right: the thing to do was to go back to the truck and drive away, back to town and through town and on, not to stop, not even to have time to think for having to keep on driving, steering, keeping the truck going in order to keep on moving, never to come back; but then they had never had time, they had known that before they ever left Jefferson and he thought for an instant how if Aleck Sander really had meant it when he said he would not come and if he would have come alone in that case and then (quickly) he wouldn't think about that at all, Aleck Sander using the shovel for the first shift while he used the pick though the dirt was still so loose they didn't really need the pick (and if it hadn't been still loose they couldn't have done it at all even by daylight); two shovels would have done and faster too but it was too late for that now until suddenly Aleck Sander handed him the shovel and climbed out of the hole and vanished and (not even using the flashlight) with that same sense beyond sight and hearing both which had realised that what Highboy smelled at the branch was quicksand and which had discovered the horse or the mule coming down the hill a good minute before either he or Miss Habersham could begin to hear it, returned with a short light board so that both of them had shovels now and he could hear the *chuck!* and then the faint swish as Aleck Sander thrust the board into the dirt and then flung the load up and outward, expelling his breath, saying 'Hah!' each time—a sound furious raging and restrained, going faster and faster until the ejaculation was almost as rapid as the beat of someone running: 'Hah! . . . Hah! . . . Hah!' so that he said over his shoulder:

'Take it easy. We're doing all right:' straightened his own back for a moment to mop his sweating face and seeing as always Miss Habersham in motionless silhouette on the sky above him in the straight cotton dress and the round hat on the exact top of her head such as few people had seen in fifty years and probably no one at any time looking up out of a halfway rifled grave: more than halfway because spading again he heard the sudden thud of wood on wood, then Aleck Sander said sharply:

'Go on. Get out of here and gimme room:' and flung the board up and out and took, jerked the shovel from his hands and he climbed out of the pit and even as he stooped groping Miss Habersham handed him the coiled tie-rope.

'The flashlight too,' he said and she handed him that and he stood too while the strong hard immobile flow of the pines bleached the sweat from his body until his wet shirt felt cold on his flesh and invisible below him in the pit the shovel rasped and scraped on wood, and stooping and hooding the light again he flashed it downward upon the unpainted lid of the pine box and switched it off.

'All right,' he said. 'That's enough. Get out:' and Aleck Sander with the last shovel of dirt released the shovel too, flinging the whole thing arcing out of the pit like a javelin and followed it in one motion, and carrying the rope and the light he dropped into the pit and only then remembered he would need a hammer, crowbar—something to open the lid with and the only thing of that nature would be what Miss Habersham might happen to have in the truck a half-mile away and the walk back uphill, stooping to feel, examine the catch or whatever it was to be forced when he discovered that the lid was not fastened at all: so that straddling it, balancing himself on one foot he managed to open the lid up and back and prop it with one elbow while he shook the rope out and found the end and snapped on the flashlight and pointed it down and then said, 'Wait.' He said, 'Wait.' He was still saying 'Wait' when he finally heard Miss Habersham speaking in a hissing whisper:

'Charles. . . . . Charles.'

'This aint Vinson Gowrie,' he said. 'This man's name is Montgomery. He's some kind of a shoestring timber-buyer from over in Crossman County.'

V.

THEY HAD to fill the hole back up of course and besides he had the horse. But even then it was a good while until daylight when he left Highboy with Aleck Sander at the pasture gate and tried remembered to tiptoe into the house but at once his mother her hair loose and in her nightdress wailed from right beside the front door: 'Where have you been?' then followed him to his uncle's door and then while his uncle was putting some clothes on: 'You? Digging up a grave?' and he with a sort of weary indefatigable patience, just about worn out himself now from riding and digging then turning around and undigging and then riding again, somehow managing to stay that one jump ahead of what he had really never hoped to beat anyway:

'Aleck Sander and Miss Habersham helped:' which if anything seemed to be worse though she was still not loud: just amazed and inexpugnable until his uncle came out fully dressed even to his necktie but not shaved and said,

'Now Maggie, do you want to wake Charley?' then following them back to the front door and this time she said—and he thought again how you could never really beat them because of their fluidity which was not just a capacity for mobility but a willingness to abandon with the substanceless promptitude of wind or air itself not only position but principle too; you didn't have to marshal your forces because you already had them: superior artillery, weight, right justice and precedent and usage and everything else and made your attack and cleared the field, swept all before you—or so you thought until you discovered that the enemy had not retreated at all but had already abandoned the field and had not merely abandoned the field but had usurped your very battlecry in the process; you believed you had captured a citadel and instead found you had merely entered an untenable position and then found the unimpaired and even unmarked battle set up again in your unprotected and unsuspecting rear—she said:

'But he's got to sleep! He hasn't even been to bed!' so that he actually stopped until his uncle said, hissed at him:

'Come on. What's the matter with you? Dont you know she's tougher than you and me both just as old Habersham was tougher than you and Aleck Sander put together; you might have gone out there without her to drag you by the hand but Aleck Sander wouldn't and I'm still not so sure you would when you came right down to it.' So he moved on too beside his uncle toward where Miss Habersham sat in the truck behind his uncle's parked car (it had been in the garage at nine oclock last night; later when he had time he would remember to ask his uncle just where his mother had sent him to look for him). 'I take that back,' his uncle said. 'Forget it. Out of the mouths of babes and sucklings and old ladies——' he paraphrased. 'Quite true, as a lot of truth often is, only a man just dont like to have it flung in his teeth at three oclock in the morning. And dont even forget your mother, which of course you cant; she has already long since seen to that. Just remember that they can stand anything, accept any fact (it's only men who burk at facts) provided they dont have to face it; can assimilate it with their heads turned away and one hand extended behind them as the politician accepts the bribe. Look at her: who will spend a long contented happy life never abating one jot of her refusal to forgive you for being able to button your own pants.'

And still a good while until daylight when his uncle stopped the car at the sheriff's gate and led the way up the short walk and onto the rented gallery. (Since he couldn't succeed himself, although now in his third term the elapsed time covering Sheriff Hampton's tenure was actually almost twice as long as the twelve years of his service. He was a countryman, a farmer and son of farmers when he was first elected and now owned himself the farm and house where he had been born, living in the rented one in town during his term of office then returning to the farm which was his actual home at each expiration, to live there until he could run for—and be elected—sheriff again.)

'I hope he's not a heavy sleeper,' Miss Habersham said.

'He aint asleep,' his uncle said. 'He's cooking breakfast.'

'Cooking breakfast?' Miss Habersham said: and then he knew that, for all her flat back and the hat which had never shifted from the exact top of her head as though she kept it balanced there not by any pins but simply by the rigid unflagging poise of her neck as Negro women carry a whole family wash, she was about worn out with strain and lack of sleep too.

'He's a country man,' his uncle said. 'Any food he eats after daylight in the morning is dinner. Mrs Hampton's in Memphis with their daughter waiting for the baby and the only woman who'll cook a man's breakfast at half past three a. m. is his wife. No hired town cook's going to do it. She comes at a decent hour about eight oclock and washes the dishes.' His uncle didn't knock. He started to open the door then stopped and looked back past both of them to where Aleck Sander stood at the bottom of the front steps. 'And dont you think you're going to get out of it just because your mama dont vote,' he told Aleck Sander. 'You come on too.'

Then his uncle opened the door and at once they smelled the coffee and the frying hogmeat, walking on linoleum toward a faint light at the rear of the hall then across a linoleum-floored diningroom in rented Grand Rapids mission into the kitchen, into the hard cheerful blast of a woodstove where the sheriff stood over a sputtering skillet in his undershirt and pants and socks, his braces dangling and his hair mussed and tousled with sleep like that of a ten-year-old boy, a battercake turner in one hand and a cuptowel in the other. The sheriff had already turned his vast face toward the door before they entered it and he watched the little hard pale eyes flick from his uncle to Miss Habersham to himself and then to Aleck Sander and even then it was not the eyes which widened so much for that second but rather the little hard black pupils which had tightened in that one flick to pinpoints. But the sheriff said nothing yet, just looking at his uncle now and now even the little hard pupils seemed to expand again as when an expulsion of breath untightens the chest and while the three of them stood quietly and steadily watching the sheriff his uncle told it, rapid and condensed and succinct, from the moment in the jail last night when his uncle had realised that Lucas had started to tell—or rather ask—him something, to the one when he had entered his uncle's room ten minutes ago and waked him up, and stopped and again they watched the little hard eyes go flick. flick. flick. across their three faces then back to his uncle again, staring at his uncle for almost a quarter of a minute without even blinking. Then the sheriff said:

'You wouldn't come here at four oclock in the morning with a tale like that if it wasn't so.'

'You aint listening just to two sixteen-year-old children,' his uncle said. 'I remind you that Miss Habersham was there.'

'You dont have to,' the sheriff said. 'I haven't forgot it. I dont think I ever will.' Then the sheriff turned. A gigantic man and in the fifties too, you wouldn't think he could move fast and he didn't really seem to yet he had taken another skillet from a nail in the wall behind the stove and was already turning toward the table (where for the first time he noticed, saw the side of smoked meat) before he seemed to have moved at all, picking up a butcher knife from beside the meat before his uncle could even begin to speak:

'Have we got time for that? You've got to drive sixty miles to Harrisburg to the District Attorney; you'll have to take Miss Habersham and these boys with you for witnesses to try and persuade him to originate a petition for the exhumation of Vinson Gowrie's body——'

The sheriff wiped the handle of the knife rapidly with the cuptowel. 'I thought you told me Vinson Gowrie aint in that grave.'

'Officially he is,' his uncle said. 'By the county records he is. And if you, living right here and knowing Miss Habersham and me all your political life, had to ask me twice, what do you think Jim Halladay is going to do?—Then you've got to drive sixty miles back here with your witnesses and the petition and get Judge Maycox to issue an order——'

The sheriff dropped the cuptowel onto the table. 'Have I?' he said mildly, almost inattentively: so that his uncle stopped perfectly still watching him as the sheriff turned from the table, the knife in his hand.

'Oh,' his uncle said.

'I've thought of something else too,' the sheriff said. 'I'm surprised you aint. Or maybe you have.'

His uncle stared at the sheriff. Then Aleck Sander—he was behind them all, not yet quite through the diningroom door into the kitchen—said in a voice as mild and impersonal as though he were reading off a slogan catch-phrase advertising some object he didn't own and never expected to want:

'It mought not a been a mule. It mought have been a horse.'

'Maybe you've thought of it now,' the sheriff said.

'Oh,' his uncle said. He said: 'Yes.' But Miss Habersham was already talking. She had given Aleck Sander one quick hard look but now she was looking at the sheriff again as quick and as hard.

'So do I,' she said. 'And I think we deserve better than secrecy.'

'I do too, Miss Eunice,' the sheriff said. 'Except that the one that needs considering right now aint in this room.'

'Oh,' Miss Habersham said. She said 'Yes' too. She said, 'Of course:' already moving, meeting the sheriff halfway between the table and the door and taking the knife from him and going on to the table when he passed her and came on toward the door, his uncle then he then Aleck Sander moving out of the way as the sheriff went on into the diningroom and across it into the dark hall, shutting the door behind him: and then he was wondering why the sheriff hadn't finished dressing when he got up; a man who didn't mind or had to or anyway did get up at half-past three in the morning to cook himself some breakfast would hardly mind getting up five minutes earlier and have time to put his shirt and shoes on too then Miss Habersham spoke and he remembered her; a lady's presence of course was why he had gone to put on the shirt and shoes without even waiting to eat the breakfast and Miss Habersham spoke and he jerked, without moving heaved up out of sleep, having been asleep for seconds maybe even minutes on his feet as a horse sleeps but Miss Habersham was still only turning the side of meat onto its edge to cut the first slice. She said: 'Cant he telephone to Harrisburg and have the District Attorney telephone back to Judge Maycox?'

'That's what he doing now,' Aleck Sander said. 'Telephoning.'

'Maybe you'd better go to the hall where you can overhear good what he's saying,' his uncle told Aleck Sander. Then his uncle looked at Miss Habersham again; he too watched her slicing rapid slice after slice of the bacon as fast and even almost as a machine could have done it. 'Mr Hampton says we wont need any papers. We can attend to it ourselves without bothering Judge Maycox——'

Miss Habersham released the knife. She didn't lay it down, she just opened her hand and in the same motion picked up the cuptowel and was wiping her hands as she turned from the table, crossing the kitchen toward them faster, a good deal faster than even the sheriff had moved. 'Then what are we wasting time here for?' she said. 'For him to put on his necktie and coat?'

His uncle stepped quickly in front of her. 'We cant do anything in the dark,' he said. 'We must wait for daylight.'

'We didn't,' Miss Habersham said. Then she stopped; it was either that or walk over his uncle though his uncle didn't touch her, just standing between her and the door until she had to stop at least for the second for his uncle to get out of the way: and he looked at her too, straight, thin, almost shapeless in the straight cotton dress beneath the round exactitude of the hat and he thought *She's too old for this* and then corrected it: *No a woman a lady shouldn't have to do this* and then remembered last night when he had left the office and walked across the back yard and whistled for Aleck Sander and he knew he had believed—and he still believed it—that he would have gone alone even if Aleck Sander had stuck to his refusal but it was only after Miss Habersham came around the house and spoke to him that he knew he was going to go through with it and he remembered again what old Ephriam had told him after they found the ring under the hog trough: *If you got something outside the common run that's got to be done and cant wait, dont waste your time on the menfolks; they works on what your uncle calls the rules and the cases. Get the womens and the children at it; they works on the circumstances.* Then the hall door opened. He heard the sheriff cross the diningroom to the kitchen door. But the sheriff didn't enter the kitchen, stopping in the door, standing in it even after Miss Habersham said in a harsh, almost savage voice:

'Well?' and he hadn't put on his shoes nor even picked up the dangling galluses and he didn't seem to have heard Miss Habersham at all: just standing looming bulging in the door looking at Miss Habersham—not at the hat, not at her eyes nor even her face: just at her—as you might look at a string of letters in Russian or Chinese which someone you believed had just told you spelled your name, saying at last in a musing baffled voice:

'No:' then turning his head to look at him and saying, 'It aint you neither:' then turning his head further until he was looking at Aleck Sander while Aleck Sander slid his eyes up at the sheriff then slid them away again then slid them up again. 'You,' the sheriff said. 'You're the one. You went out there in the dark and helped dig up a dead man. Not only that, a dead white man that the rest of the white folks claimed another nigger had murdered. Why? Was it because Miss Habersham made you?'

'Never nobody made me,' Aleck Sander said. 'I didn't even know I was going. I had done already told Chick I didn't aim to. Only when we got to the truck everybody seemed to just take it for granted I wasn't going to do nothing else but go and before I knowed it I wasn't.'

'Mr Hampton,' Miss Habersham said. Now the sheriff looked at her. He even heard her now.

'Haven't you finished slicing that meat yet?' he said. 'Give me the knife then.' He took her by the arm, turning her back to the table. 'Aint you done enough rushing and stewing around tonight to last you a while? It'll be daylight in fifteen minutes and folks dont start lynchings in daylight. They might finish one by daylight if they had a little trouble or bad luck and got behind with it. But they dont start them by daylight because then they would have to see one anothers' faces. How many can eat more than two eggs?'

They left Aleck Sander with his breakfast at the kitchen table and carried theirs into the diningroom, he and his uncle and Miss Habersham carrying the platter of fried eggs and meat and the pan of biscuits baked last night and warmed again in the oven until they were almost like toast and the coffeepot in which the unstrained grounds and the water had been boiling together until the sheriff had thought to remove the pot from the hot part of the stove; four of them although the sheriff had set five places and they had barely sat down when the sheriff raised his head listening though he himself heard nothing, then rose and went into the dark hall and toward the rear of the house and then he heard the sound of the back door and presently the sheriff came back with Will Legate though minus the shotgun, and he turned his head enough to look out the window behind him and sure enough it was daylight.

The sheriff served the plates while his uncle and Legate passed theirs and the sheriff's cup to Miss Habersham at the coffeepot. Then at once he seemed to have been hearing for a long time the sheriff from a great distance saying '. . . boy . . . boy . . .' then 'Wake him up, Gavin. Let him eat his breakfast before he goes to sleep:' and he jerked, it was still only daylight, Miss Habersham was still pouring coffee into the same cup and he began to eat, chewing and even swallowing, rising and falling as though to the motion of the chewing along the deep soft bottomless mire of sleep, into then out of the voices buzzing of old finished things no longer concern of his: the sheriff's:

'Do you know Jake Montgomery, from over in Crossman County? Been in and out of town here for the last six months or so?' then Legate's:

'Sure. A kind of jackleg timber buyer now. Used to run a place he called a restaurant just across the Tennessee line out of Memphis, though I never heard of nobody trying to buy nothing that had to be chewed in it, until a man went and got killed in it one night two-three years ago. They never did know just how much Jake did or didn't have to do with it but the Tennessee police run him back across the Mississippi line just on principle. Since then I reckon he's been laying around his pa's farm over beyond Glasgow. Maybe he's waiting until he figgers folks have forgot about that other business and he can set up again in another place on a highway with a hole under the floor big enough to hide a case of whiskey in.'

'What was he doing around here?' the sheriff said: then Legate:

'Buying timber, aint he? Aint him and Vinson Gowrie . . . . .' Then Legate said with the barest inflection, '*Was?*' and then with no inflection at all: 'What is he doing?' and he this time, his own voice indifferent along the soft deep edge of sleep, too indifferent to bother if it were aloud or not:

'He aint doing anything now.'

But it was better afterward, out of the stale warm house again into the air, the morning, the sun in one soft high level golden wash in the highest tips of the trees, gilding the motionless obese uprush of the town water tank in spiderlegged elongate against the blue, the four of them in his uncle's car once more while the sheriff stood leaned above the driver's window, dressed now even to a bright orange-and-yellow necktie, saying to his uncle:

'You run Miss Eunice home so she can get some sleep. I'll pick you up at your house in say an hour——'

Miss Habersham in the front seat with his uncle said 'Pah.' That was all. She didn't curse. She didn't need to. It was far more definite and final than just cursing. She leaned forward to look past his uncle at the sheriff. 'Get in your car and go to the jail or wherever you'll go to get somebody to do the digging this time. We had to fill it up again because we knew you wouldn't believe it even yet unless you saw it there yourself. Go on,' she said. 'We'll meet you out there. Go on,' she said.

But the sheriff didn't move. He could hear him breathing, vast subterrene and deliberate, like sighing almost. 'Of course I dont know about you,' the sheriff said. 'A lady without nothing but a couple thousand chickens to feed and nurse and water and a vegetable farm hardly five acres big to run, might not have nothing to do all day. But these boys anyway have got to go to school. Leastways I never heard about any rule in the School Board to give holidays for digging up corpses.'

And that even stopped her. But she didn't sit back yet. She still leaned forward where she could look past his uncle at the sheriff and he thought again *She's too old for this, to have to do this:* only if she hadn't then he and Aleck Sander, what she and his uncle and the sheriff all three and his mother and father and Paralee too would have called children, would have had to do it;—not would have done it but would have had to do it to preserve not even justice and decency but innocence: and he thought of man who apparently had to kill man not for motive or reason but simply for the sake the need the compulsion of having to kill man, inventing creating his motive and reason afterward so that he could still stand up among man as a rational creature: whoever had had to kill

Vinson Gowrie had then to dig him up dead and slay another to put in his vacated grave so that whoever had to kill him could rest; and Vinson Gowrie's kin and neighbors who would have to kill Lucas or someone or anyone, it would not really matter who, so that they could lie down and breathe quiet and even grieve quiet and so rest. The sheriff's voice was mild, almost gentle even: 'You go home. You and these boys have done fine. Likely you saved a life. Now you go home and let us attend to the rest of it. That wont be any place for a lady out there.'

But Miss Habersham was just stopped, nor even that for long: 'It wasn't for a man either last night.'

'Wait, Hope,' his uncle said. Then his uncle turned to Miss Habersham. 'Your job's in town here,' he said. 'Dont you know that?' Now Miss Habersham watched his uncle. But she still hadn't sat back in the seat, giving no ground to anyone yet; watching, it was as though she had not at all exchanged one opponent for another but without pause or falter had accepted them both, asking no quarter, crying no odds. 'Will Legate's a farmer,' his uncle said. 'Besides being up all night. He's got to go home and see to his own business for a little while.'

'Hasn't Mr Hampton got other deputies?' Miss Habersham said. 'What are they for?'

'They're just men with guns,' his uncle said. 'Legate himself told Chick and me last night that if enough men made up their minds and kept them made up, they would pass him and Mr Tubbs both in time. But if a woman, a lady, a white lady . . . . .' His uncle stopped, ceased; they stared at each other; watching them he thought again of his uncle and Lucas in the cell last night (it was last night, of course; it seemed like years now); again except for the fact that his uncle and Miss Habersham were actually looking into each other's physical eyes instead of bending each upon the other that absolute concentration of all the senses in the sum of which mere clumsy fallible perception weighed little more than the ability to read Sanskrit would, he might have been watching the last two stayers in a poker-pot. '. . . . just to sit there, in sight, where the first one that passes can have the word spread long before Beat Four can even get the truck cranked up to start to town . . . . . while we go out there and finish it for good, for ever——'

Miss Habersham leaned slowly back until her back came against the seat. She said: 'So I'm to sit there on that staircase with my skirts spread or maybe better with my back against the balustrade and one foot propped against the wall of Mrs Tubbs' kitchen while you men who never had time yesterday to ask that old nigger a few questions and so all he had last night was a boy, a child——' His uncle said nothing. The sheriff leaned above the window breathing vast subterranean sighs, not breathing hard but just as a big man seems to have to breathe. Miss Habersham said: 'Drive me home first. I've got some mending to do. I aint going to sit there all morning doing nothing so that Mrs Tubbs will think she has to talk to me. Drive me home first. I realised an hour ago what a rush and hurry you and Mr Hampton are in but you can spare the time for that. Aleck Sander can bring my truck to the jail on his way to school and leave it in front of the gate.'

'Yessum,' his uncle said.

VI.

SO THEY DROVE Miss Habersham home, out to the edge of town and through the shaggy untended cedar grove to the paintless columned portico where she got out and went into the house and apparently on through it without even stopping because at once they could hear her somewhere in the back yelling at someone—the old Negro man probably who was Molly's brother and Lucas' brother-in-law—in her strong voice strained and a little high from sleeplessness and fatigue, then she came out again carrying a big cardboard box full of what looked like unironed laundry and long limp webs and ropes of stockings and got back into the car and they drove back to the Square through the fresh quiet morning streets: the old big decaying wooden houses of Jefferson's long-ago foundation set like Miss Habersham's deep in shaggy untended lawns of old trees and rootbound scented and flowering shrubs whose very names most people under fifty no longer knew and which even when children lived in them seemed still to be spellbound by the shades of women, old women still spinsters and widows waiting even seventy-five years later for the slow telegraph to bring them news of Tennessee and Virginia and Pennsylvania battles, which no longer even faced the street but peered at it over the day-after-tomorrow shoulders of the neat small new one-storey houses designed in Florida and California set with matching garages in their neat plots of clipped grass and tedious flowerbeds, three and four of them now, a subdivision now in what twenty-five years ago had been considered a little small for one decent front lawn, where the prosperous young married couples lived with two children each and (as soon as they could afford it) an automobile each and the memberships in the country club and the bridge clubs and the junior rotary and chamber of commerce and the patented electric gadgets for cooking and freezing and cleaning and the neat trim colored maids in frilled caps to run them and talk to one another over the telephone from house to house while the wives in sandals and pants and painted toenails puffed lipstick-stained cigarettes over shopping bags in the chain groceries and drug stores.

Or would have been and should have been; Sunday and they might have passed, accepted a day with no one to plug and unplug the humming sweepers and turn the buttons on the stoves as a day off a vacation or maybe an occasion like a baptising or a picnic or a big funeral but this was Monday, a new day and a new week, rest and the need to fill time and conquer boredom was over, children fresh for school and husband and father for store or office or to stand around the Western Union desk where the hourly cotton reports came in; breakfast must be forward and the pandemoniac bustle of exodus yet still no Negro had they seen—the young ones with straightened hair and makeup in the bright trig tomorrow's clothes from the mailorder houses who would not even put on the Harper's Bazaar caps and aprons until they were inside the white kitchens and the older ones in the ankle-length homemade calico and gingham who wore the long plain homemade aprons all the time so that they were no longer a symbol but a garment, not even the men who should have been mowing the lawns and clipping the hedges; not even (crossing the Square now) the street department crews who should have been flushing the pavement with hoses and sweeping up the discarded Sunday papers and empty cigarette packs; across the Square and on to the jail where his uncle got out too and went up the walk with Miss Habersham and up the steps and through the still-open door where he could still see Legate's empty chair still propped against the wall and he heaved himself bodily again out of the long soft timeless rushing black of sleep to find as usual that no time had passed, his uncle still putting his hat back on and turning to come back down the walk to the car. Then they stopped at home, Aleck Sander already out of the car and gone around the side of the house and vanished and he said,

'No.'

'Yes,' his uncle said. 'You've got to go to school. Or better still, to bed and to sleep.—Yes,' his uncle said suddenly: 'and Aleck Sander too. He must stay at home today too. Because this mustn't be talked about, not one word about it until we have finished it. You understand that.'

But he wasn't listening, he and his uncle were not even talking about the same thing, not even when he said 'No' again and his uncle out of the car and already turning toward the house stopped and looked back at him and then stood looking at him for a good long moment and then said,

'We are going at this a little hindpart-before, aint we? I'm the one who should be asking you if I can go.' Because he was thinking about his mother, not just remembered about her because he had done that as soon as they crossed the Square five minutes ago and the simplest thing would have been to get out of his uncle's car there and go and get in the sheriff's car and simply stay in it until they were ready to go back out to the church and he had probably thought about it at the time and would even have done it probably if he hadn't been so wornout and anticlimaxed and dull for sleep and he knew he couldn't cope with her this time even if he had been completely fresh; the very fact that he had already done it twice in eleven hours, once by secrecy and once by sheer surprise and rapidity of movement and of mass, but doomed him completer now to defeat and rout: musing on his uncle's naive and childlike rationalising about school and bed when faced with that fluid and implacable attack, when once more his uncle read his mind, standing beside the car and looking down at him for another moment with compassion and no hope even though he was a bachelor of fifty thirty-five years free of woman's dominion, his uncle too knowing remembering how she would use the excuses of his education and his physical exhaustion only less quicker than she would have discarded them; who would listen no more to rational reasons for his staying at home than for—civic duty or simple justice or humanity or to save a life or even the peace of his own immortal soul—his going. His uncle said:

'All right. Come on. I'll talk to her.'

He moved, getting out; he said suddenly and quietly, in amazement not at despair of hope but at how much hopelessness you could really stand: 'You're just my uncle.'

'I'm worse than that,' his uncle said. 'I'm just a man.' Then his uncle read his mind again: 'All right. I'll try to talk to Paralee too. The same condition obtains there; motherhood doesn't seem to have any pigment in its skin.'

And his uncle too was probably thinking how you not only couldn't beat them, you couldn't even find the battlefield in time to admit defeat before they had moved it again; he remembered, it was two years ago now, he had finally made the high school football team or that is he had won or been chosen for one of the positions to make an out-of-town trip because the regular player had been injured in practice or fallen behind in his grades or maybe his mother either wouldn't let him go, something, he had forgotten exactly what because he had been too busy all that Thursday and Friday racking his brains in vain to think how to tell his mother he was going to Mottstown to play on the regular team, right up to the last minute when he had to tell her something and so did: baldly: and weathered it since his father happened to be present (though he really hadn't calculated it that way—not that he wouldn't have if he hadn't been too worried and perplexed with a blending of anger and shame and shame at being angry and ashamed ((crying at her at one point: 'Is it the team's fault that I'm the only child you've got?')) to think of it) and left that Friday afternoon with the team feeling as he imagined a soldier might feel wrenching out of his mother's restraining arms to go fight a battle for some shameful cause; she would grieve for him of course if he fell and she would even look on his face again if he didn't but there would be always ineradicable between them the ancient green and perennial adumbration: so that all that Friday night trying to go to sleep in a strange bed and all the next forenoon too waiting for the game to start he thought better for the team if he had not come since he probably had too much on his mind to be worth anything to it: until the first whistle blew and on and afterward until bottom-most beneath the piled mass of both teams, the ball clutched to his chest and his mouth and nostrils both full of the splashed dried whitewash marking the goal line he heard and recognised above all the others that one voice shrill triumphant and bloodthirsty and picked up at last and the wind thumped back into him he saw her foremost in the crowd not sitting in the grandstand but among the ones trotting and even running up and down the sideline following each play, then in the car that evening on the way back to Jefferson, himself in the front seat beside the hired driver and his mother and three of the other players in the back and her voice as proud and serene and pitiless as his own could have been: 'Does your arm still hurt?'——entering the hall and only then discovering that he had expected to find her still just inside the front door still in the loose hair and the nightdress and himself walking back even after three hours into the unbroken uninterrupted wail. But instead it was his father already roaring who came out of the diningroom and still at it even with his uncle yelling back almost into his face:

'Charley. Charley. Dammit, will you wait?' and only then his mother fully dressed, brisk busy and composed, coming up the hall from the back, the kitchen, saying to his father without even raising her voice:

'Charley. Go back and finish your breakfast. Paralee isn't feeling well this morning and she doesn't want to be all day getting dinner ready:' then to him—the fond constant familiar face which he had known all his life and therefore could neither have described it so that a stranger could recognise it nor recognise it himself from anyone's description but only brisk calm and even a little inattentive now, the wail a wail only because of the ancient used habit of its verbiage: 'You haven't washed your face:' nor even pausing to see if he followed, on up the stairs and into the bathroom, even turning on the tap and putting the soap into his hands and standing with the towel open and waiting, the familiar face wearing the familiar expression of amazement and protest and anxiety and invincible repudiation which it had worn all his life each time he had done anything removing him one more step from infancy, from childhood: when his uncle had given him the Shetland pony someone had taught to take eighteen- and twentyfour-inch jumps and when his father had given him the first actual powder-shooting gun and the afternoon when the groom delivered Highboy in the truck and he got up for the first time and Highboy stood on his hind legs and her scream and the groom's calm voice saying, 'Hit him hard over the head when he does that. You dont want him falling over backward on you' but the muscles merely falling into the old expression through inattention and long usage as her voice had merely chosen by inattention and usage the long-worn verbiage of wailing because there was something else in it now—the same thing which had been there in the car that afternoon when she said, 'Your arm doesn't hurt at all now does it?' and on the other afternoon when his father came home and found him jumping Highboy over the concrete watertrough in the lot, his mother leaning on the fence watching and his father's fury of relief and anger and his mother's calm voice this time: 'Why not? The trough isn't near as tall as that flimsy fence-thing you bought him that isn't even nailed together:' so that even dull for sleep he recognised it and turned his face and hands dripping and cried at her in amazed and incredulous outrage: 'You aint going too! You cant go!' then even dull for sleep realising the fatuous naivete of anyone using cant to her on any subject and so playing his last desperate card: 'If you go, then I wont! You hear me? I wont go!'

'Dry your face and comb your hair,' she said. 'Then come on down and drink your coffee.'

That too. Paralee was all right too apparently because his uncle was at the telephone in the hall when he entered the diningroom, his father already roaring again before he had even sat down:

'Dammit, why didn't you tell me last night? Dont you ever again——'

'Because you wouldn't have believed him either,' his uncle said coming in from the hall. 'You wouldn't have listened either. It took an old woman and two children for that, to believe truth for no other reason than that it was truth, told by an old man in a fix deserving of pity and belief, to someone capable of the pity even when none of them really believed him. Which you didn't at first,' his uncle said to him. 'When did you really begin to believe him? When you opened the coffin, wasn't it? I want to know, you see. Maybe I'm not too old to learn either. When was it?'

'I dont know,' he said. Because he didn't know. It seemed to him that he had known all the time. Then it seemed to him that he had never really believed Lucas. Then it seemed to him that it had never happened at all, heaving himself once more with no movement up out of the long deep slough of sleep but at least to some elapse of time now, he had gained that much anyway, maybe enough to be safe on for a while like the tablets night truck drivers took not as big hardly as a shirt button yet in which was concentrated enough wakefulness to reach the next town because his mother was in the room now brisk and calm, setting the cup of coffee down in front of him in a way that if Paralee had done it she would have said that Paralee had slopped it at him: which, the coffee, was why neither his father nor his uncle had even looked at her, his father on the contrary exclaiming,

'Coffee? What the devil is this? I thought the agreement was when you finally consented for Gavin to buy that horse that he would neither ask for nor even accept a spoonful of coffee until he was eighteen years old:' and his mother not even listening, with the same hand and in the same manner half shoving and half popping the cream pitcher then the sugar bowl into his reach and already turning back toward the kitchen, her voice not really hurried and impatient: just brisk:

'Drink it now. We're already late:' and now they looked at her for the first time: dressed, even to her hat, with in the crook of her other arm the straw basket out of which she had darned his and his father's and his uncle's socks and stockings ever since he could remember, though his uncle at first saw only the hat and for a moment seemed to join him in the same horrified surprise he had felt in the bathroom.

'Maggie!' his uncle said. 'You cant! Charley——'

'I dont intend to,' his mother said, not even stopping. 'This time you men will have to do the digging. I'm going to the jail:' already in the kitchen now and only her voice coming back: 'I'm not going to let Miss Habersham sit there by herself with the whole county gawking at her. As soon as I help Paralee plan dinner we'll——' but not dying fading: ceasing, quitting: since she had dismissed them though his father still tried once more:

'He's got to go to school.'

But even his uncle didn't listen. 'You can drive Miss Eunice's truck, cant you?' his uncle said. 'There wont be a Negro school today for Aleck Sander to be going to so he can leave it at the jail. And even if there was I doubt if Paralee's going to let him cross the front yard inside the next week.' Then his uncle seemed even to have heard his father or at least decided to answer him: 'Nor any white school either for that matter if this boy hadn't listened to Lucas, which I wouldn't, and to Miss Habersham, which I didn't. Well?' his uncle said. 'Can you stay awake that long? You can get a nap once we are on the road.'

'Yes sir,' he said. So he drank the coffee which the soap and water and hard toweling had unfogged him enough to know he didn't like and didn't want but not enough for him to choose what simple thing to do about it: that is not drink it: tasting sipping then adding more sugar to it until each—coffee and sugar—ceased to be either and became a sickish quinine sweet amalgam of the worst of both until his uncle said,

'Dammit, stop that,' and got up and went to the kitchen and returned with a saucepan of heated milk and a soup bowl and dumped the coffee into the bowl and poured the hot milk into it and said, 'Go on. Forget about it. Just drink it.' So he did, from the bowl in both hands like water from a gourd, hardly tasting it and still his father flung a little back in his chair looking at him and talking, asking him just how scared Aleck Sander was and if he wasn't even scareder than Aleck Sander only his vanity wouldn't allow him to show it before a darky and to tell the truth now, neither of them would have touched the grave in the dark even enough to lift the flowers off of it if Miss Habersham hadn't driven them at it: his uncle interrupting:

'Aleck Sander even told you then that the grave had already been disturbed by someone in a hurry, didn't he?'

'Yes sir,' he said and his uncle said:

'Do you know what I'm thinking now?'

'No sir,' he said.

'I'm being glad Aleck Sander couldn't completely penetrate darkness and call out the name of the man who came down the hill carrying something in front of him on the mule.' And he remembered that: the three of them all thinking it but not one of them saying it: just standing invisible to one another above the pit's invisible inky yawn.

'Fill it up,' Miss Habersham said. They did, the (five times now) loosened dirt going down much faster than it came up though it seemed forever in the thin starlight filled with the constant sound of the windless pines like one vast abateless hum not of amazement but of attention, watching, curiosity; amoral, detached, not involved and missing nothing. 'Put the flowers back,' Miss Habersham said.

'It'll take time,' he said.

'Put them back,' Miss Habersham said. So they did.

'I'll get the horse,' he said. 'You and Aleck Sander——'

'We'll all go,' Miss Habersham said. So they gathered up the tools and the rope (nor did they use the flashlight again) and Aleck Sander said 'Wait' and found by touch the board he had used for a shovel and carried that until he could push it back under the church and he untied Highboy and held the stirrup but Miss Habersham said, 'No. We'll lead him. Aleck Sander can walk exactly behind me and you walk exactly behind Aleck Sander and lead the horse.'

'We could go faster——' he said again and they couldn't see her face: only the thin straight shape, the shadow, the hat which on anyone else wouldn't even have looked like a hat but on her as on his grandmother looked exactly right, like exactly nothing else, her voice not loud, not much louder than breathing, as if she were not even moving her lips, not to anyone, just murmuring:

'It's the best I know to do. I dont know anything else to do.'

'Maybe we all ought to walk in the middle,' he said, loud, too loud, twice louder than he had intended or even thought; it should carry for miles especially over a whole countryside already hopelessly waked and alerted by the sleepless sibilant what Paralee probably and old Ephriam certainly and Lucas too would call 'miration' of the pines. She was looking at him now. He could feel it.

'I'll never be able to explain to your mother but Aleck Sander hasn't got any business here at all,' she said. 'Youall walk exactly behind me and let the horse come last:' and turned and went on though what good that would do he didn't know because in his understanding the very word 'ambush' meant 'from the flank, the side': back in single file that way down the hill to where Aleck Sander had driven the truck into the bushes: and he thought *If I were him this is where it would be* and so did she; she said, 'Wait.'

'How can you keep on standing in front of us if we dont

stay together?' he said. And this time she didn't even say This is all I can think of to do but just stood there so that Aleck Sander walked past her and on into the bushes and started the truck and backed it out and swung it to point down the hill, the engine running but no lights yet and she said, 'Tie the reins up and let him go. Wont he come home?'

'I hope so,' he said. He got up.

'Then tie him to a tree,' she said. 'We will come back and get him as soon as we have seen your uncle and Mr Hampton——'

'Then we can all watch him ride down the road with maybe a horse or the mule in front of him too,' Aleck Sander said. He raced the engine then let it idle again. 'Come on, get in. He's either here watching us or he aint and if he aint we're all right and if he is he's done waited too late now when he let us get back to the truck.'

'Then you ride right behind the truck,' she said. 'We'll go slow——'

'Nome,' Aleck Sander said; he leaned out. 'Get started; we're going to have to wait for you anyway when we get to town.'

So—he needed no urging—he let Highboy down the hill, only holding his head up; the truck's lights came on and it moved and once on the flat even in the short space to the highroad Highboy was already trying to run but he checked him back and up onto the highroad, the lights of the truck fanning up and out as it came down onto the flat then he slacked the curb, Highboy beginning to run, clashing the snaffle as always, thinking as always that one more champing regurge would get it forward enough to get his teeth on it, running now when the truck lights swung up onto the highroad too, his feet in eight hollow beats on the bridge and he leaned into the dark hard wind and let him go, the truck lights not even in sight during the full half-mile until he slowed him into the long reaching hard road-gait and almost a mile then before the truck overtook and then passed and the ruby tail-lamp drew on and away and then was gone but at least he was out of the pines, free of that looming downwatching sibilance uncaring and missing nothing saying to the whole circumambience: Look. Look: but then they were still saying it somewhere and they had certainly been saying it long enough for all Beat Four, Gowries and Ingrums and Workitts and Frasers and all to have heard it by this time so he wouldn't think about that and so he stopped thinking about it now, all in the same flash in which he had remembered it, swallowing the last swallow from the bowl and setting it down as his father more or less plunged up from the table, clattering his chairlegs back across the floor, saying:

'Maybe I better go to work. Somebody'll have to earn a little bread around here while the rest of you are playing cops and robbers:' and went out and apparently the coffee had done something to what he called his thinking processes or anyway the processes of what people called thinking because now he knew the why for his father too—the rage which was relief after the event which had to express itself some way and chose anger not because he would have forbidden him to go but because he had had no chance to, the pseudo-scornful humorous impugnment of his and Aleck Sander's courage which blinked not even as much at a rifled grave in the dark as it did at Miss Habersham's will,—in fact the whole heavy-handed aspersion of the whole thing by reducing it to the terms of a kind of kindergarten witch-hunt: which was probably merely the masculine form of refusing also to believe that he was what his uncle called big enough to button his pants and so he dismissed his father, hearing his mother about to emerge from the kitchen and pushing his chair back and getting up himself when suddenly he was thinking how coffee was already a good deal more than he had known but nobody had warned him that it produced illusions like cocaine or opium: seeing watching his father's noise and uproar flick and vanish away like blown smoke or mist, not merely revealing but exposing the man who had begot him looking back at him from beyond the bridgeless abyss of that begetting not with just pride but with envy too; it was his uncle's abnegant and rhetorical self-lacerating which was the phony one and his father was gnawing the true bitter irremediable bone of all which was dismatchment with time, being born too soon or late to have been himself sixteen and gallop a horse ten miles in the dark to save an old nigger's insolent and friendless neck.

But at least he was awake. The coffee had accomplished

that anyway. He still needed to doze only now he couldn't; the desire to sleep was there but it was wakefulness now he would have to combat and abate. It was after eight now; one of the county schoolbusses passed as he prepared to drive Miss Habersham's truck away from the curb and the street would be full of children too fresh for Monday morning with books and paper bags of recess-time lunches and behind the schoolbus was a string of cars and trucks stained with country mud and dust so constant and unbroken that his uncle and his mother would already have reached the jail before he ever managed to cut into it because Monday was stock-auction day at the sales barns behind the Square and he could see them, the empty cars and trucks rank on dense rank along the courthouse curb like shoats at a feed-trough and the men with their stock-trader walkingsticks not even stopping but gone straight across the Square and along the alley to the sales barns to chew tobacco and unlighted cigars from pen to pen amid the ammonia-reek of manure and liniment and the bawling of calves and the stamp and sneeze of horses and mules and the secondhand wagons and plow gear and guns and harness and watches and only the women (what few of them that is since stock-sale day unlike Saturday was a man's time) remained about the Square and the stores so that the Square itself would be empty except for the parked cars and trucks until the men would come back for an hour at noon to meet them at the cafes and restaurants.

Whereupon this time he jerked himself, no reflex now, not even out of sleep but illusion, who had carried hypnosis right out of the house with him even into the bright strong sun of day, even driving the pickup truck which before last night he would not even have recognised yet which since last night had become as inexpugnable a part of his memory and experience and breathing as hiss of shovelled dirt or the scrape of a metal blade on a pine box would ever be, through a mirage-vacuum in which not simply last night had not happened but there had been no Saturday either, remembering now as if he had only this moment seen it that there had been no children in the schoolbus but only grown people and in the stream of cars and trucks following it and now following him where he had finally cut in, a few of which even on stock-auction Monday (on Saturday half of the flat open beds would have been jammed and packed with them, men women and children in the cheap meagre finery in which they came to town) should have carried Negroes, there had not been one dark face.

Nor one school-bound child on the street although he had heard without listening enough of his uncle at the telephone to know that the superintendent had called whether to have school today or not and his uncle had told him yes, and in sight of the Square now he could see already three more of the yellow busses supposed and intended to bring the county children in to school but which their owner-contractor-operators translated on Saturdays and holidays into pay-passenger transport and then the Square itself, the parked cars and trucks as always as should be but the Square itself anything but empty: no exodus of men toward the stock pens nor women into the stores so that as he drove the pickup into the curb behind his uncle's car he could see already where visible and sense where not a moil and mass of movement, one dense pulse and hum filling the Square as when the crowd overflows the carnival midway or the football field, flowing into the street and already massed along the side opposite to the jail until the head of it had already passed the blacksmith's where he had stood yesterday trying to be invisible as if they were waiting for a parade to pass (and almost in the middle of the street so that the still unbroken stream of cars and trucks had to detour around them a clump of a dozen or so more like the group in a reviewing stand in whose center in its turn he recognised the badged official cap of the town marshal who at this hour on this day would have been in front of the schoolhouse holding up traffic for children to cross the street and he did not have to remember that the marshal's name was Ingrum, a Beat Four Ingrum come to town as the apostate sons of Beat Four occasionally did to marry a town girl and become barbers and bailiffs and night-watchmen as petty Germanic princelings would come down out of their Brandenburg hills to marry the heiresses to European thrones)—the men and the women and not one child, the weathered country faces and sunburned necks and backs of hands, the clean faded tieless earthcolored shirts and pants and print cotton dresses thronging the Square and the street as though the stores themselves were closed and locked, not even staring yet at the blank front of the jail and the single barred window which had been empty and silent too for going on forty-eight hours now but just gathering, condensing, not expectant nor in anticipation nor even attentive yet but merely in that preliminary settling down like the before-curtain in a theatre: and he thought that was it: holiday: which meant a day for children yet here turned upside down: and suddenly he realised that he had been completely wrong; it was not Saturday which had never happened but only last night which to them had not happened yet, that not only they didn't know about last night but there was nobody, not even Hampton, who could have told them because they would have refused to believe him; whereupon something like a skim or a veil like that which crosses a chicken's eye and which he had not even known was there went flick! from his own and he saw them for the first time—the same weathered still almost inattentive faces and the same faded clean cotton shirts and pants and dresses but no crowd now waiting for the curtain to rise on a stage's illusion but rather the one in the courtroom waiting for the sheriff's officer to cry Oyez Oyez Oyez This honorable court; not even impatient because the moment had not even come yet to sit in judgment not on Lucas Beauchamp, they had already condemned him, but on Beat Four, come not to see what they called justice done nor even retribution exacted but to see that Beat Four should not fail its white man's high estate.

So that he had stopped the truck was out and had already started to run when he stopped himself: something of dignity something of pride remembering last night when he had instigated and in a way led and anyway accompanied the stroke which not one of the responsible elders but had failed even to recognise its value, let alone its need, and something of caution too remembering how his uncle had said almost nothing was enough to put a mob in motion so perhaps even a child running toward the jail would have been enough: then he remembered again the faces myriad yet curiously identical in their lack of individual identity, their complete relinquishment of individual identity into one We not even impatient, not even hurryable, almost gala in its complete obliviousness of its own menace, not to be stampeded by a hundred running children: and then in the same flash the obverse: not to be halted or deflected by a hundred times a hundred of them, and having realised its sheer hopelessness when it was still only an intention and then its physical imponderability when it entered accomplishment he now recognised the enormity of what he had blindly meddled with and that his first instinctive impulse—to run home and fling saddle and bridle on the horse and ride as the crow flies into the last stagger of exhaustion and then sleep and then return after it was all over—had been the right one (who now simply because he happened not to be an orphan had not even that escape) because it seemed to him now that he was responsible for having brought into the light and glare of day something shocking and shameful out of the whole white foundation of the county which he himself must partake of too since he too was bred of it, which otherwise might have flared and blazed merely out of Beat Four and then vanished back into its darkness or at least invisibility with the fading embers of Lucas' crucifixion.

But it was too late now, he couldn't even repudiate, relinquish, run: the jail door still open and opposite it now he could see Miss Habersham sitting in the chair Legate had sat in, the cardboard box on the floor at her feet and a garment of some sort across her lap; she was still wearing the hat and he could see the steady motion of her hand and elbow and it seemed to him he could even see the flash and flick of the needle in her hand though he knew he could not at this distance; but his uncle was in the way so he had to move further along the walk but at that moment his uncle turned and came out the door and recrossed the veranda and then he could see her too in the second chair beside Miss Habersham; a car drew up to the curb behind him and stopped and now without haste she chose a sock from the basket and slipped the darningegg into it; she even had the needle already threaded stuck in the front of her dress and now he could distinguish the flash and glint of it and maybe that was because he knew so well the motion, the narrow familiar suppleness of the hand which he had watched all his life but at least no man could have disputed him that it was his sock.

'Who's that?' the sheriff said behind him. He turned. The sheriff sat behind the wheel of his car, his neck and shoulders bowed and hunched so he could peer out below the top of the window-frame. The engine was still running and he saw in the back of the car the handles of two shovels and the pick too which they would not need and on the back seat quiet and motionless save for the steady glint and blink of their eyewhites, two Negroes in blue jumpers and the soiled black-ringed convict pants which the street gangs wore.

'Who would it be?' his uncle said behind him too but he didn't turn this time nor did he even listen further because three men came suddenly out of the street and stopped beside the car and as he watched five or six more came up and in another moment the whole crowd would begin to flow across the street; already a passing car had braked suddenly (and then the following one behind it) at first to keep from running over them and then for its occupants to lean out looking at the sheriff's car where the first man to reach it had already stooped to peer into it, his brown farmer's hands grasping the edge of the open window, his brown weathered face thrust into the car curious divinant and abashless while behind him his massed duplicates in their felt hats and sweat-stained panamas listened.

'What you up to, Hope?' the man said. 'Dont you know the Grand Jury'll get you, wasting county money this way? Aint you heard about that new lynch law the Yankees passed? the folks that lynches the nigger is supposed to dig the grave?'

'Maybe he's taking them shovels out there for Nub Gowrie and them boys of his to practice with,' the second said.

'Then it's a good thing Hope's taking shovel hands too,' the third said. 'If he's depending on anybody named Gowrie to dig a hole or do anything else that might bring up a sweat, he'll sure need them.'

'Or maybe they aint shovel hands,' the fourth said. 'Maybe it's them the Gowries are going to practice on.' Yet even though one guffawed they were not laughing, more than a dozen now crowded around the car to take one quick all-comprehensive glance into the back of it where the two Negroes sat immobile as carved wood staring straight ahead at nothing and no movement even of breathing other than an infinitesimal widening and closing of the whites around their eyeballs, then looking at the sheriff again with almost exactly the expression he had seen on the faces waiting for the spinning tapes behind a slotmachine's glass to stop.

'I reckon that'll do,' the sheriff said. He thrust his head and one vast arm out the window and with the arm pushed the nearest ones back and away from the car as effortlessly as he would have opened a curtain, raising his voice but not much: 'Willy.' The marshal came up; he could already hear him:

'Gangway, boys. Lemme see what the high sheriff's got on his mind this morning.'

'Why dont you get these folks out of the street so them cars can get to town?' the sheriff said. 'Maybe they want to stand around and look at the jail too.'

'You bet,' the marshal said. He turned, shoving his hands at the nearest ones, not touching them, as if he were putting into motion a herd of cattle. 'Now boys,' he said.

They didn't move, looking past the marshal still at the sheriff, not at all defiant, not really daring anyone: just tolerant, goodhumored, debonair almost.

'Why, Sheriff,' a voice said, then another:

'It's a free street, aint it, Sheriff? You town folks wont mind us just standing on it long as we spend our money with you, will you?'

'But not to block off the other folks trying to get to town to spend a little,' the sheriff said. 'Move on now. Get them out of the street, Willy.'

'Come on, boys,' the marshal said. 'There's other folks besides you wants to get up where they can watch them bricks.' They moved then but still without haste, the marshal herding them back across the street like a woman driving a flock of hens across a pen, she to control merely the direction not the speed and not too much of that, the fowls moving ahead of her flapping apron not recalcitrant, just unpredictable, fearless of her and not yet even alarmed; the halted car and the ones behind it moved too, slowly, dragging at creeping pace their loads of craned faces; he could hear the marshal shouting at the drivers: 'Get on. Get on. There's cars behind you——'

The sheriff was looking at his uncle again. 'Where's the other one?'

'The other what?' his uncle said.

'The other detective. The one that can see in the dark.'

'Aleck Sander,' his uncle said. 'You want him too?'

'No,' the sheriff said. 'I just missed him. I was just surprised to find one human in this county with taste and judgment enough to stay at home today. You ready? Let's get started.'

'Right,' his uncle said. The sheriff was notorious as a driver who used up a car a year as a heavy handed sweeper wears out brooms: not by speed but by simple friction; now the car actually shot away from the curb and almost before he could watch it, was gone. His uncle went to theirs and opened the door. 'Jump in,' his uncle said.

Then he said it; at least this much was simple: 'I'm not going.'

His uncle paused and now he saw watching him the quizzical saturnine face, the quizzical eyes which given a little time didn't miss much; had in fact as long as he had known them never missed anything until last night.

'Ah,' his uncle said. 'Miss Habersham is of course a lady but this other female is yours.'

'Look at them,' he said, not moving, barely moving his lips even. 'Across the street. On the Square too and nobody but Willy Ingrum and that damn cap——'

'Didn't you hear them talking to Hampton?' his uncle said.

'I heard them,' he said. 'They were not even laughing at their own jokes. They were laughing at him.'

'They were not even taunting him,' his uncle said. 'They were not even jeering at him. They were just watching him. Watching him and Beat Four, to see what would happen. These people just came to town to see what either or both of them are going to do.'

'No,' he said. 'More than that.'

'All right,' his uncle said, quite soberly too now.

'Granted. Then what?'

'Suppose——' But his uncle interrupted:

'Suppose Beat Four comes in and picks up your mother's and Miss Habersham's chairs and carries them out into the yard where they'll be out of the way? Lucas aint in that cell. He's in Mr Hampton's house, probably sitting in the kitchen right now eating his breakfast. What did you think Will

Legate was doing coming in by the back door within fifteen minutes of when we got there and told Mr Hampton? Aleck Sander even heard him telephoning.'

'Then what's Mr Hampton in such a hurry for?' he said: and his uncle's voice was quite sober now: but just sober, that was all:

'Because the best way to stop having to suppose or deny either is for us to get out there and do what we have to do and get back here. Jump in the car.'

VII.

THEY NEVER SAW the sheriff's car again until they reached the church. Nor for him was the reason sleep who in spite of the coffee might have expected that and in fact had. Up to the moment when at the wheel of the pickup he had got near enough to see the Square and then the mass of people lining the opposite side of the street in front of the jail he had expected that as soon as he and his uncle were on the road back to the church, coffee or no coffee he would not even be once more fighting sleep but on the contrary would relinquish and accept it and so in the nine miles of gravel and the one of climbing dirt regain at least a half-hour of the eight he had lost last night and—it seemed to him now—the three or four times that many he had spent trying to quit thinking about Lucas Beauchamp the night before.

And when they reached town a little before three this morning nobody could have persuaded him that by this time, almost nine oclock, he would not have made back at least five and a half hours of sleep even if not the full six, remembering how he—and without doubt Miss Habersham and Aleck Sander too—had believed that as soon as they and his uncle entered the sheriff's house that would be all of it; they would enter the front door and lay into the sheriff's broad competent ordained palm as you drop your hat on the hall table in passing, the whole night's nightmare of doubt and indecision and sleeplessness and strain and fatigue and shock and amazement and (he admitted it) some of fear too. But it hadn't happened and he knew now that he had never really expected it to; the idea had ever entered their heads only because they had been worn out, spent not so much from sleeplessness and fatigue and strain as exhausted by shock and amazement and anticlimax; he had not even needed the massed faces watching the blank brick front of the jail nor the ones which had crossed the street and even blocked it while they crowded around the sheriff's car, to read and then dismiss its interior with that one mutual concordant glance comprehensive abashless trustless and undeniable as the busy parent pauses for an instant to check over and anticipate the intentions of a loved though not too reliable child. If he needed anything he certainly had that—the faces the voices not even taunting and not even jeering: just perspicuant jocular and without pity—poised under the first relaxation of succumbence like a pin in the mattress so he was as wide awake as his uncle even who had slept all night or at least most of it, free of town now and going fast now, passing within the first mile the last of the cars and trucks and then no more of them because all who would come to town today would by this time be inside that last rapidly contracting mile—the whole white part of the county taking advantage of the good weather and the good allweather roads which were their roads because their taxes and votes and the votes of their kin and connections who could bring pressure on the congressmen who had the giving away of the funds had built them, to get quickly into the town which was theirs too since it existed only by their sufferance and support to contain their jail and their courthouse, to crowd and jam and block its streets too if they saw fit: patient biding and unpitying, neither to be hurried nor checked nor dispersed nor denied since theirs was the murdered and the murderer too; theirs the affronter and the principle affronted: the white man and the bereavement of his vacancy, theirs the right not just to mere justice but vengeance too to allot or withhold.

They were going quite fast now, faster than he could ever remember his uncle driving, out the long road where he had ridden last night on the horse but in daylight now, morning's bland ineffable May; now he could see the white bursts of dogwood in the hedgerows marking the old section-line surveys or standing like nuns in the cloistral patches and bands of greening woods and the pink and white of peach and pear and the pinkwhite of the first apple trees in the orchards which last night he had only smelled: and always beyond and around them the enduring land—the fields geometric with furrows where corn had been planted when the first doves began to call in late March and April, and cotton when the first whippoorwills cried at night around the beginning of May a week ago: but empty, vacant of any movement and any life—the farmhouses from which no smoke rose because breakfast was long over by now and no dinner to be cooked where none would be home to eat it, the paintless Negro cabins where on Monday morning in the dust of the grassless treeless yards halfnaked children should have been crawling and scrabbling after broken cultivator wheels and wornout automobile tires and empty snuff-bottles and tin cans and in the back yards smoke-blackened iron pots should have been bubbling over wood fires beside the sagging fences of vegetable patches and chickenruns which by nightfall would be gaudy with drying overalls and aprons and towels and unionsuits: but not this morning, not now; the wheels and the giant-doughnuts of chewed rubber and the bottles and cans lying scattered and deserted in the dust since that moment Saturday afternoon when the first voice shouted from inside the house, and in the back yards the pots sitting empty and cold among last Monday's ashes among the empty clotheslines and as the car flashed past the blank and vacant doors he would catch one faint gleam of fire on hearth and no more see but only sense among the shadows the still white roll of eyes; but most of all, the empty fields themselves in each of which on this day at this hour on the second Monday in May there should have been fixed in monotonous repetition the land's living symbol—a formal group of ritual almost mystic significance identical and monotonous as milestones tying the county-seat to the county's ultimate rim as milestones would: the beast the plow and the man integrated in one foundationed into the frozen wave of their furrow tremendous with effort yet at the same time vacant of progress, ponderable immovable and immobile like groups of wrestling statuary set against the land's immensity—until suddenly (they were eight miles from town; already the blue-green lift of the hills was in sight) he said with an incredulous an almost shocked amazement who except for Paralee and Aleck Sander and Lucas had not seen one in going on forty-eight hours:

'There's a nigger.'

'Yes,' his uncle said. 'Today is the ninth of May. This county's got half of a hundred and forty-two thousand acres to plant yet. Somebody's got to stay home and work:' —the car rushing boring up so that across the field's edge and the perhaps fifty yards separating them he and the Negro behind the plow looked eye to eye into each other's face before the Negro looked away—the face black and gleamed with sweat and passionate with effort, tense concentrated and composed, the car flashing past and on while he leaned first out the open window to look back then turned in the seat to see back through the rear window, watching them still in their rapid unblurred diminishment—the man and the mule and the wooden plow which coupled them furious and solitary, fixed and without progress in the earth, leaning terrifically against nothing.

They could see the hills now; they were almost there—the long lift of the first pine ridge standing across half the horizon and beyond it a sense a feel of others, the mass of them seeming not so much to stand rush abruptly up out of the plateau as to hang suspended over it as his uncle had told him the Scottish highlands did except for this sharpness and color; that was two years ago, maybe three and his uncle had said, 'Which is why the people who chose by preference to live on them on little patches which wouldn't make eight bushels of corn or fifty pounds of lint cotton an acre even if they were not too steep for a mule to pull a plow across (but then they dont want to make the cotton anyway, only the corn and not too much of that because it really doesn't take a great deal of corn to run a still as big as one man and his sons want to fool with) are people named Gowrie and McCallum and Fraser and Ingrum that used to be Ingraham and Workitt that used to be Urquhart only the one that brought it to America and then Mississippi couldn't spell it either, who love brawling and fear God and believe in Hell——' and it was as though his uncle had read his mind, holding the speedometer needle at fifty-five into the last mile of gravel (already the road was beginning to slant down toward the willow-and-cypress bottom of the Nine-Mile branch) speaking, that is volunteering to speak for the first time since they left town:

'Gowrie and Fraser and Workitt and Ingrum. And in the valleys along the rivers, the broad rich easy land where a man can raise something he can sell openly in daylight, the people named Littlejohn and Greenleaf and Armstead and Millingham and Bookwright——' and stopped, the car dropping on down the slope, increasing speed by its own weight; now he could see the bridge where Aleck Sander had waited for him in the dark and below which Highboy had smelled quicksand.

'We turn off just beyond it,' he said.

'I know,' his uncle said. '—And the ones named Sambo, they live in both, they elect both because they can stand either because they can stand anything.' The bridge was quite near now, the white railing of the entrance yawned rushing at them. 'Not all white people can endure slavery and apparently no man can stand freedom (Which incidentally—the premise that man really wants peace and freedom—is the trouble with our relations with Europe right now, whose people not only dont know what peace is but—except for Anglo Saxons—actively fear and distrust personal liberty; we are hoping without really any hope that our atom bomb will be enough to defend an idea as obsolete as Noah's Ark.); with one mutual instantaneous accord he forces his liberty into the hands of the first demagogue who rises into view: lacking that he himself destroys and obliterates it from his sight and ken and even remembrance with the frantic unanimity of a neighborhood stamping out a grass-fire. But the people named Sambo survived the one and who knows? they may even endure the other.—And who knows——'

Then a gleam of sand, a flash and glint of water; the white rail streamed past in one roar and rush and rattle of planking and they were across. *He'll have to slow down now* he thought but his uncle didn't, merely declutching, the car rolling on its own momentum which carried it still too fast through a slewing skidding turn into the dirt road and on for fifty yards bouncing among the ruts until the last of flat land died headlong into the first gentle slant, its momentum still carrying the car in high speed gear yet up the incline until then after he saw the tracks where Aleck Sander had driven the pickup off the road into the bushes and where he had stood ready with his hand poised over Highboy's nostrils while the horse or the mule, whichever it was, had come down the hill with the burden in front of the rider which even Aleck Sander with his eyes like an owl or mink or whatever else hunts at night, had failed to descry (and he remembered again not just his uncle at the table this morning but himself standing in the yard last night during that moment after Aleck Sander walked away and before he recognised Miss Habersham when he actually believed he was coming out alone to do what must be done and he told himself now as he had at the table: *I wont think about that.*); almost there now, practically were there in fact: what remained of space intervened not even to be measured in miles.

Though that little at a crawl, the car whining in second gear now against the motionless uprush of the main ridge and the strong constant resinous downflow of the pines where the dogwood looked indeed like nuns now in the long green corridors, up and onto the last crest, the plateau and now he seemed to see his whole native land, his home—the dirt, the earth which had bred his bones and those of his fathers for six generations and was still shaping him into not just a man but a specific man, not with just a man's passions and aspirations and beliefs but the specific passions and hopes and convictions and ways of thinking and acting of a specific kind and even race: and even more: even among a kind and race specific and unique (according to the lights of most, certainly of all of them who had thronged into town this morning to stand across the street from the jail and crowd up around the sheriff's car, damned unique) since it had also integrated into him whatever it was that had compelled him to stop and listen to a damned highnosed impudent Negro who even if he wasn't a murderer had been about to get if not about what he deserved at least exactly what he had spent the sixty-odd years of his life asking for—unfolding beneath him like a map in one slow soundless explosion: to the east ridge on green ridge tumbling away toward Alabama and to the west and south the checkered fields and the woods flowing on into the blue and gauzed horizon beyond which lay at last like a cloud the long wall of the levee and the great River itself flowing not merely from the north but out of the North circumscribing and outland—the umbilicus of America joining the soil which was his home to the parent which three generations ago it had failed in blood to repudiate; by turning his head he could see the faint stain of smoke which was town ten miles away and merely by looking ahead he could see the long reach of rich bottom land marked off into the big holdings, the plantations (one of which was Edmonds where the present

Edmonds and Lucas both had been born, stemming from the same grandfather) along their own little river (though even in his grandfather's memory steamboats had navigated it) and then the dense line of river jungle itself: and beyond that stretching away east and north and west not merely to where the ultimate headlands frowned back to back upon the waste of the two oceans and the long barrier of Canada but to the uttermost rim of earth itself, the North: not north but North, outland and circumscribing and not even a geographical place but an emotional idea, a condition of which he had fed from his mother's milk to be ever and constant on the alert not at all to fear and not actually anymore to hate but just—a little wearily sometimes and sometimes even with tongue in cheek—to defy: who had brought from infancy with him a childhood's picture which on the threshold of manhood had found no reason or means to alter and which he had no reason to believe in his old age would alter either: a curving semicircular wall not high (anyone who really wanted to could have climbed it; he believed that any boy already would) from the top of which with the whole vast scope of their own rich teeming never-ravaged land of glittering undefiled cities and unburned towns and unwasted farms so long-secured and opulent you would think there was no room left for curiosity, there looked down upon him and his countless row on row of faces which resembled his face and spoke the same language he spoke and at times even answered to the same names he bore yet between whom and him and his there was no longer any real kinship and soon there would not even be any contact since the very mutual words they used would no longer have the same significance and soon after that even this would be gone because they would be too far asunder even to hear one another: only the massed uncountable faces looking down at him and his in fading amazement and outrage and frustration and most curious of all, gullibility: a volitionless, almost helpless capacity and eagerness to believe anything about the South not even provided it be derogatory but merely bizarre enough and strange enough: whereupon once more his uncle spoke at complete one with him and again without surprise he saw his thinking not be interrupted but merely swap one saddle for another:

'It's because we alone in the United States (I'm not speaking of Sambo right now; I'll get to him in a minute) are a homogeneous people. I mean the only one of any size. The New Englander is too of course back inland from the coastal spew of Europe which this country quarantined unrootable into the rootless ephemeral cities with factory and foundry and municipal paychecks as tight and close as any police could have done it, but there are no longer enough of him just as there are not of the Swiss who are not a people so much as a neat clean small quite solvent business. So we are not really resisting what the outland calls (and we too) progress and enlightenment. We are defending not actually our politics or beliefs or even our way of life, but simply our homogeneity from a federal government to which in simple desperation the rest of this country has had to surrender voluntarily more and more of its personal and private liberty in order to continue to afford the United States. And of course we will continue to defend it. We (I mean all of us: Beat Four will be unable to sleep at night until it has cancelled Lucas Beauchamp ((or someone else)) against Vinson Gowrie in the same color of ink, and Beat One and Two and Three and Five who on heatless principle intend to see that Beat Four makes that cancellation) dont know why it is valuable. We dont need to know. Only a few of us know that only from homogeneity comes anything of a people or for a people of durable and lasting value—the literature, the art, the science, that minimum of government and police which is the meaning of freedom and liberty, and perhaps most valuable of all a national character worth anything in a crisis—that crisis we shall face someday when we meet an enemy with as many men as we have and as much material as we have and—who knows?—who can even brag and boast as we brag and boast.

'That's why we must resist the North: not just to preserve ourselves nor even the two of us as one to remain one nation because that will be the inescapable by-product of what we will preserve: which is the very thing that three generations ago we lost a bloody war in our own back yards so that it remain intact: the postulate that Sambo is a human being living in a free country and hence must be free. That's what we are really defending: the privilege of setting him free ourselves: which we will have to do for the reason that nobody else can since going on a century ago now the North tried it and have been admitting for seventy-five years now that they failed. So it will have to be us. Soon now this sort of thing wont even threaten anymore. It shouldn't now. It should never have. Yet it did last Saturday and it probably will again, perhaps once more, perhaps twice more. But then no more, it will be finished; the shame will still be there of course but then the whole chronicle of man's immortality is in the suffering he has endured, his struggle toward the stars in the stepping-stones of his expiations. Someday Lucas Beauchamp can shoot a white man in the back with the same impunity to lynch-rope or gasoline of another white man; in time he will vote anywhen and anywhere a white man can and send his children to the same school anywhere the white man's children go and travel anywhere the white man travels as the white man does it. But it wont be next Tuesday. Yet people in the North believe it can be compelled even into next Monday by the simple ratification by votes of a printed paragraph: who have forgotten that although a long quarter-century ago Lucas Beauchamp's freedom was made an article in our constitution and Lucas Beauchamp's master was not merely beaten to his knees but trampled for ten years on his face in the dust to make him swallow it, yet only three short generations later they are faced once more with the necessity of passing legislation to set Lucas Beauchamp free.

'And as for Lucas Beauchamp, Sambo, he's a homogeneous man too, except that part of him which is trying to escape not even into the best of the white race but into the second best—the cheap shoddy dishonest music, the cheap flash baseless overvalued money, the glittering edifice of publicity foundationed on nothing like a card-house over an abyss and all the noisy muddle of political activity which used to be our minor national industry and is now our national amateur pastime—all the spurious uproar produced by men deliberately fostering and then getting rich on our national passion for the mediocre: who will even accept the best provided it is debased and befouled before being fed to us: who are the only people on earth who brag publicly of being second-rate, i.e., lowbrows. I dont mean that Sambo. I mean the rest of him who has a better homogeneity than we have and proved it by finding himself roots into the land where he had actually to displace white men to put them down: because he had patience even when he didn't have hope, the long view even when there was nothing to see at the end of it, not even just the will but the desire to endure because he loved the old few simple things which no one wanted to take from him: not an automobile nor flash clothes nor his picture in the paper but a little of music (his own), a hearth, not his child but any child, a God a heaven which a man may avail himself a little of at any time without having to wait to die, a little earth for his own sweat to fall on among his own green shoots and plants. We—he and us—should confederate: swap him the rest of the economic and political and cultural privileges which are his right, for the reversion of his capacity to wait and endure and survive. Then we would prevail; together we would dominate the United States; we would present a front not only impregnable but not even to be threatened by a mass of people who no longer have anything in common save a frantic greed for money and a basic fear of a failure of national character which they hide from one another behind a loud lip-service to a flag.'

Now they were there and not too long behind the sheriff. For though the car was already drawn off the road into the grove in front of the church, the sheriff was still standing beside it and one of the Negroes was just passing the pick backward out of the car to the other prisoner who stood holding both the shovels. His uncle drew in beside it and stopped and now in daylight he could see the church, for the first time actually who had lived within ten miles of it all his life and must have passed it, seen it at least half that many times. Yet he could not remember ever having actually looked at it before—a plank steepleless box no larger than some of the one-room cabins hill people lived in, paintless too yet (curiously) not shabby and not even in neglect or disrepair because he could see where sections of raw new lumber and scraps and fragments of synthetic roofing had been patched and carpentered into the old walls and shingles with a savage almost insolent promptitude, not squatting nor crouching nor even sitting but standing among the trunks of the high strong constant shaggy pines, solitary but not forlorn, intractable and independent, asking nothing of any, making compromise with none and he remembered the tall slender spires which said Peace and the squatter utilitarian belfries which said Repent and he remembered one which even said Beware but this one said simply: Burn: and he and his uncle got out; the sheriff and the two Negroes carrying the tools were already inside the fence and he and his uncle followed, through the sagging gate in the low wire enclosure massed with honeysuckle and small odorless pink and white climbing roses and he saw the graveyard too for the first time, who had not only violated a grave in it but exploded one crime by exposing another—a fenced square of earth less large than garden plots he had seen and which by September would probably be choked and almost impenetrable and wellnigh invisible with sagegrass and ragweed and beggarlice, out of which stood without symmetry or order like bookmarks thrust at random into a ledger or toothpicks in a loaf and canted always slightly as if they had taken their own frozen perpendicular from the limber unresting never-quite-vertical pines, shingle-thin slabs of cheap gray granite of the same weathered color as the paintless church as if they had been hacked out of its flank with axes (and carved mottoless with simple names and dates as though there had been nothing even their mourners remembered of them than that they had lived and they had died) and it had been neither decay nor time which had compelled back into the violated walls the raw new patching of unplaned paintless lumber but the simple exigencies of mortality and the doom of flesh.

He and his uncle threaded on among them to where the sheriff and the two Negroes already stood above the fresh raw mound which likewise he who had violated it now actually saw for the first time. But they hadn't begun to dig yet. Instead the sheriff had even turned, looking back at him until he and his uncle came up and stopped too.

'Now what?' his uncle said.

But the sheriff was speaking to him in the mild heavy voice: 'I reckon you and Miss Eunice and your secretary were mighty careful not to let anybody catch you at this business last night, weren't you?'

His uncle answered: 'This is hardly the thing you'd want an audience at, is it?'

But the sheriff was still looking at him. 'Then why didn't they put the flowers back?'

Then he saw them too—the artificial wreath, the tedious intricate contrivance of wire and thread and varnished leaves and embalmed blooms which someone had brought or sent out from the florist in town, and the three bunches of wilted garden and field flowers tied with cotton string, all of which Aleck Sander had said last night looked as if they had been thrown at or onto the grave and which he remembered Aleck Sander and himself moving aside out of the way and which he knew they had put back after they filled the hole back up; he could remember Miss Habersham telling them twice to put them back even after he himself had protested about the un-need or at least the waste of time; perhaps he could even remember Miss Habersham herself helping to put them back: or then perhaps he didn't remember them being put back at all but merely thought he did because they obviously hadn't been, lying now tossed and inextricable to one side and apparently either he or Aleck Sander had trodden on the wreath though it didn't really matter now, which was what his uncle was just saying:

'Never mind now. Let's get started. Even when we finish here and are on the way back to town we will still be only started.'

'All right, boys,' the sheriff said to the Negroes. 'Jump to it. Let's get out of here——' and there was no sound, he heard nothing to warn him, he just looked up and around as his uncle and the sheriff did and saw, coming not down the road but around from behind the church as though from among the high windy pines themselves, a man in a wide pale hat and a clean faded blue shirt whose empty left sleeve was folded neatly back and pinned cuff to shoulder with a safety-pin, on a small trim claybank mare showing too much eye-white and followed by two younger men riding double on a big saddleless black mule with a rope-burn on its neck and followed in their turn (and keeping carefully clear of the mule's heels) by two gaunt Trigg foxhounds, coming at a rapid trot across the grove to the gate where the man stopped the mare and swung himself lightly and rapidly down with his one hand and dropped the reins across the mare's neck and came with that light wiry almost springy rapidity through the gate and up to them—a short lean old man with eyes as pale as the sheriff's and a red weathered face out of which jutted a nose like the hooked beak of an eagle, already speaking in a high thin strong uncracked voice:

'What's going on around here, Shurf?'

'I'm going to open this grave, Mr Gowrie,' the sheriff said.

'No Shurf,' the other said, immediate, with no change whatever in the voice: not disputative, nothing: just a statement: 'Not that grave.'

'Yes, Mr Gowrie,' the sheriff said. 'I'm going to open it.'

Without haste or fumbling, almost deliberate in fact, the old man with his one hand unbuttoned two buttons on the front of his shirt and thrust the hand inside, hunching his hip slightly around to meet the hand and drew from inside the shirt a heavy nickel-plated pistol and still with no haste but no pause either thrust the pistol into his left armpit, clamping it butt-forward against his body by the stub of the arm while his one hand buttoned the shirt, then took the pistol once more into the single hand not pointing it at anything, just holding it.

But long before this he had seen the sheriff already moving, moving with really incredible speed not toward the old man but around the end of the grave, already in motion even before the two Negroes turned to run, so that when they whirled they seemed to run full tilt into the sheriff as into a cliff, even seeming to bounce back a little before the sheriff grasped them one in each hand as if they were children and then in the next instant seemed to be holding them both in one hand like two rag dolls, turning his body so that he was between them and the little wiry old man with the pistol, saying in that mild even lethargic voice:

'Stop it. Dont you know the worst thing that could happen to a nigger would be dodging loose in a pair of convict pants around out here today?'

'That's right, boys,' the old man said in his high inflectionless voice. 'I aint going to hurt you. I'm talking to the Shurf here. Not my boy's grave, Shurf.'

'Send them back to the car,' his uncle murmured rapidly. But the sheriff didn't answer, still looking at the old man.

'Your boy aint in that grave, Mr Gowrie,' the sheriff said. And watching he thought of all the things the old man might have said—the surprise, the disbelief, the outrage perhaps, even the thinking aloud: *How do you come to know my boy aint there?*—the rationalising by reflective in which he might have paraphrased the sheriff speaking to his uncle six hours ago: *You wouldn't be telling me this if you didn't know it was so;* watching, even following the old man as he cut straight across all this and he thought suddenly with amazement: *Why, he's grieving:* thinking how he had seen grief twice now in two years where he had not expected it or anyway anticipated it, where in a sense a heart capable of breaking had no business being: once in an old nigger who had just happened to outlive his old nigger wife and now in a violent foulmouthed godless old man who had happened to lose one of the six lazy idle violent more or less lawless a good deal more than just more or less worthless sons, only one of whom had ever benefitted his community and kind and that only by the last desperate resort of getting murdered out of it: hearing the high flat voice again immediate and strong and without interval, inflectionless, almost conversational:

'Why, I just hope you dont tell me the name of the fellow that proved my boy aint there, Shurf. I just hope you wont mention that:'—little hard pale eyes staring at little hard pale eyes, the sheriff's voice mild still, inscrutable now:

'No, Mr Gowrie. It aint empty:' and later, afterward, he realised that this was when he believed he knew not perhaps why Lucas had ever reached town alive because the reason for that was obvious: there happened to be no Gowrie present at the moment but the dead one: but at least how the old man and two of his sons happened to ride out of the woods behind the church almost as soon as he and the sheriff and his uncle reached the grave, and certainly why almost forty-eight hours afterward Lucas was still breathing. 'It's Jake Montgomery down there,' the sheriff said.

The old man turned, immediate, not hurriedly and even quickly but just easily as if his spare small fleshless frame offered neither resistance to the air nor weight to the motive muscles, and shouted toward the fence where the two younger men still sat the mule identical as two clothing store dummies and as immobile, not even having begun yet to descend until the old man shouted: 'Here, boys.'

'Never mind,' the sheriff said. 'We'll do it.' He turned to the two Negroes. 'All right. Get your shovels——'

'I told you,' his uncle murmured rapidly again. 'Send them back to the car.'

'That's right, Lawyer—Lawyer Stevens, aint it?' the old man said. 'Get 'em away from here. This here's our business. We'll attend to it.'

'It's my business now, Mr Gowrie,' the sheriff said.

The old man raised the pistol, steadily and without haste, bending his elbow until it came level, his thumb curling up and over the hammer cocking it so that it came already cocked level or not quite, not quite pointing at anything somewhere about the height of the empty belt-loops on the sheriff's trousers. 'Get them out of here, Shurf,' the old man said.

'All right,' the sheriff said without moving. 'You boys go back to the car.'

'Further than that,' the old man said. 'Send 'em back to town.'

'They're prisoners, Mr Gowrie,' the sheriff said. 'I cant do that.' He didn't move. 'Go back and get in the car,' he told them. They moved then, walking not back toward the gate but directly away across the enclosure, walking quite fast, lifting their feet and knees in the filthy barred trousers quite high, walking quite fast by the time they reached the opposite fence and half stepping half hopping over it and only then changing direction back toward the two cars so that until they reached the sheriff's car they would never be any nearer the two white men on the mule than when they had left the grave: and he looked at them now sitting the mule identical as two clothes pins on a line, the identical faces even weathered exactly alike, surly quick-tempered and calm, until the old man shouted again:

'All right, boys:' and they got down as one, at the same time even like a trained vaudeville team and again as one stepped with the same left leg over the fence, completely ignoring the gate: the Gowrie twins, identical even to the clothing and shoes except that one wore a khaki shirt and the other a sleeveless jersey; about thirty, a head taller than their father and with their father's pale eyes and the nose too except that it was not the beak of an eagle but rather that of a hawk, coming up with no word, no glance even for any of them from the bleak composed humorless faces until the old man pointed with the pistol (he saw that the hammer was down now anyway) at the two shovels and said in his high voice which sounded almost cheerful even:

'Grab 'em, boys. They belong to the county; if we bust one it aint anybody's business but the Grand Jury's:'—the twins, facing each other now at opposite ends of the mound and working again in that complete almost choreographic unison: the next two youngest before the dead one, Vinson; fourth and fifth of the six sons:—Forrest, the oldest who had not only wrenched himself free of his fiery tyrant of a father but had even got married and for twenty years now had been manager of a delta cotton plantation above Vicksburg; then Crawford, the second one who had been drafted on the second day of November 1918 and on the night of the tenth (with a bad luck in guessing which, his uncle said, should not happen to any man—a point of view in which in fact his federal captors themselves seemed to concur since his term in the Leavenworth prison had been only one year) had deserted and lived for almost eighteen months in a series of caves and tunnels in the hills within fifteen miles of the federal courthouse in Jefferson until he was captured at last after something very like a pitched battle (though luckily for him nobody was seriously hurt) during which he made good his cave for thirty-odd hours armed with (and, his uncle said, a certain consistency and fitness here: a deserter from the United States army defending his freedom from the United States government with a piece of armament captured from the enemy whom he had refused to fight) an automatic pistol which one of the McCallum boys had taken from a captured German officer and traded shortly after he got home for a brace of Gowrie foxhounds, and served his year and came home and the town next heard of him in Memphis where it was said he was (1) running liquor up from New Orleans,

(2) acting as a special employer-bonded company officer during a strike, but anyway coming back to his father's home suddenly where nobody saw much of him until a few years back when the town began to hear of him as having more or less settled down, dealing in a little timber and cattle and even working a little land; and Bryan, the third one who was the actual force, power, cohering element, whatever you might call it, in or behind the family farm which fed them all; then the twins, Vardaman and Bilbo who spent their nights squatting in front of smoldering logs and stumps while the hounds ran foxes and their days sleeping flat on the naked planks of the front gallery until dark came and time to cast the hounds again; and the last one, Vinson, who even as a child had shown an aptitude for trading and for money so that now, though dead at only twenty-eight, he was not only said to own several small parcels of farmland about the county but was the first Gowrie who could sign his name to a check and have any bank honor it;—the twins, kneedeep then waistdeep, working with a grim and sullen speed, robotlike and in absolute unison so that the two shovels even seemed to ring at the same instant on the plank box and even then seeming to communicate by no physical means as birds or animals do: no sound no gesture: simply one of them released his shovel in a continuation of the same stroke which flung the dirt and then himself flowed effortless up out of the pit and stood among the rest of them while his brother cleaned off what remained of dirt from the top of the coffin, then tossed his shovel up and out without even looking and—as he himself had done last night—kicked the last of the earth away from the edge of the lid and stood on one leg and grasped the lid and heaved it up and over and away until all of them standing along the rim of the grave could look down past him into the box.

It was empty. There was nothing in it at all until a thin trickle of dirt flowed down into it with a whispering pattering sound.

VIII.

AND HE would remember it: the five of them standing at the edge of the pit above the empty coffin, then with another limber flowing motion like his twin's the second Gowrie came up out of the grave and stooped and with an air of rapt displeased even faintly outraged concern began to brush and thump the clay particles from the lower legs of his trousers, the first twin moving as the second stooped, going straight to him with a blind unhurried undeviable homing quality about him like the other of a piece of machinery, the other spindle say of a lathe, travelling on the same ineluctable shaft to its socket, and stooped too and began to brush and strike the dirt from the back of his brother's trousers; and this time almost a spadeful of dirt slid down across the outslanted lid and rattled down into the empty box, almost loud enough or with mass and weight enough to produce a small hollow echo.

'Now he's got two of them,' his uncle said.

'Yes,' the sheriff said. 'Where?'

'Durn two of them,' old Gowrie said. 'Where's my boy, Shurf?'

'We're going to find him now, Mr Gowrie,' the sheriff said. 'And you were smart to bring them hounds. Put your pistol up and let your boys catch them dogs and hold them till we get straightened out here.'

'Never you mind the pistol nor the dogs neither,' old Gowrie said. 'They'll trail and they'll ketch anything that ever run or walked either. But my boy and that Jake Montgomery—if it was Jake Montgomery whoever it was found laying in my son's coffin—never walked away from here to leave no trail.'

The sheriff said, 'Hush now, Mr Gowrie.' The old man glared back up at the sheriff. He was not trembling, not eager, baffled, amazed, not anything. Watching him he thought of one of the cold lightblue tearshaped apparently heatless flames which balance themselves on even less than tiptoe over gasjets.

'All right,' the old man said. 'I'm hushed. And now you get

started. You're the one that seems to know all about this, that sent me word out to my breakfast table at six oclock this morning to meet you here. Now you get started.'

'That's what we're going to do,' the sheriff said. 'We're going to find out right now where to start.' He turned to his uncle, saying in the mild rational almost diffident voice: 'It's say around eleven oclock at night. You got a mule or maybe it's a horse, anyway something that can walk and tote a double load, and a dead man across your saddle. And you aint got much time; that is, you aint got all of time. Of course it's around eleven oclock, when most folks is in bed, and a Sunday night too when folks have got to get up early tomorrow to start a new week in the middle of cotton-planting time, and there aint any moon and even if folks might still be moving around you're in a lonely part of the country where the chances all are you wont meet nobody. But you still got a dead man with a bullet hole in his back and even at eleven oclock day's going to come sooner or later. All right. What would you do?'

They looked, stared at one another, or that is his uncle stared—the too-thin bony eager face, the bright intent rapid eyes, and opposite the sheriff's vast sleepy face, the eyes not staring, apparently not even looking, blinking almost drowsily, the two of them cutting without speech across all that too: 'Of course,' his uncle said. 'Into the earth again. And not far, since as you said daylight comes sooner or later even when it's still just eleven oclock. Especially when he still had time to come back and do it all over again, alone, by himself, no hand but his on the shovel.—And think of that too: the need, the terrible need, not just to have it all to do again but to have to do it again for the reason he had; to think that he had done all he possibly could, all anyone could have asked or expected him to do or even dreamed that he would have to do; was as safe as he could hope to be—and then to be drawn back by a sound, a noise or perhaps he blundered by sheer chance on the parked truck or perhaps it was just his luck, his good fortune, whatever god or djinn or genie looks after murderers for a little while, keeps him secure and safe until the other fates have had time to spin and knot the rope,—anyway to have to crawl, tie the mule or horse or whatever it was to a tree and crawl on his belly back up here to lie (who knows? perhaps just behind the fence yonder) and watch a meddling old woman and two children who should have been two hours ago in bed ten miles away, wreck the whole careful edifice of his furious labor, undo the work not merely of his life but of his death too. . . . . .' His uncle stopped, and now he saw the bright almost luminous eyes glaring down at him: 'And you. You couldn't have had any idea Miss Habersham was coming with you until you got home. And without her, you could have had no hope whatever that Aleck Sander would come with you alone at all. So if you ever really had any idea of coming out here alone to dig this grave up, dont even tell me——'

'Let that be now,' the sheriff said. 'All right. Somewhere in the ground. And what sort of ground? What dirt digs easiest and fastest for a man in a hurry and by himself even if he has a shovel? What sort of dirt could you hope to hide a body in quick even if you never had nothing but a pocket knife?'

'In sand,' his uncle said immediately, rapidly, almost indifferently, almost inattentively. 'In the bed of the branch. Didn't they tell you at three oclock this morning that they saw him going there with it? What are we waiting for?'

'All right,' the sheriff said. 'Let's go then.' Then to him: 'Show us exactly where——'

'Except that Aleck Sander said it might not have been a mule,' he said.

'All right,' the sheriff said. 'Horse then. Show us exactly where . . . .'

He would remember it: watching the old man clap the pistol again butt-forward into his armpit and clamp it there with the stump of the arm while the one hand unbuttoned the shirt then took the pistol from the armpit and thrust it back inside the shirt then buttoned the shirt again then turned even faster quicker than the two sons half his age, already in front of everybody when he hopped back over the fence and went to the mare and caught reins and pommel all in one hand, already swinging up: then the two cars dropping in second speed against gravity back down the steep pitch until he said 'Here' where the pickup's tracks slewed off the road into the bushes then back into the road again and his uncle stopped:

and he watched the fierce old stump-armed man jump the buckskin mare up out of the road into the woods on the opposite side already falling away down toward the branch, then the two hounds flowing up the bank behind him and then the mule with the two identical wooden-faced sons on it: then he and his uncle were out of the car, the sheriff's car bumper to bumper behind them, hearing the mare crashing on down toward the branch and then the old man's high flat voice shouting at the hounds:

'Hi! Hi! Hum on boy! At him, Ring!' and then his uncle:

'Handcuff them through the steering wheel:' and then the sheriff:

'No. We'll need the shovels:' and he had climbed the bank too, listening off and downward toward the crashing and the shouts, then his uncle and the sheriff and the two Negroes carrying the shovels were beside him. Although the branch crossed almost at right angles the highway just beyond where the dirt road forked away, it was almost a quarter-mile from where they now stood or walked rather and although they could all hear old Gowrie still whooping at the dogs and the crashing of the mare and the mule too in the dense thicket below, the sheriff didn't go that way, bearing instead off along the hill almost parallel with the road for several minutes and only beginning to slant away from it when they came out into the sawgrass and laurel and willow-choked flat between the hill and the branch: and on across that, the sheriff in front until he stopped still looking down then turned his head and looked back at him, watching him as he and his uncle came up.

'Your secretary was right the first time,' the sheriff said. 'It was a mule.'

'Not a black one with a rope-burn,' his uncle said. 'Surely not that. Not even a murderer is that crassly and arrogantly extrovert.'

'Yes,' the sheriff said. 'That's why they're dangerous, why we must destroy them or lock them up:' and looking down he saw them too: the narrow delicate almost finicking muleprints out of all proportion to the animal's actual size, mashed pressed deep, too deep for any one mule no matter how heavy carrying just one man, into the damp muck, the tracks filled with water and even as he watched a minute aquatic beast of some sort shot across one of them leaving a tiny threadlike spurt of dissolving mud; and standing in the trail, now that they had found it they could see the actual path itself through the crushed shoulder-high growth in suspension held like a furrow across a field or the frozen wake of a boat, crossing the marsh arrow-straight until it vanished into the jungle which bordered the branch. They followed it, walking in it, treading the two sets of prints not going and returning but both going in the same direction, now and then the print of the same hoof superposed on its previous one, the sheriff still in the lead talking again, speaking aloud but without looking back as though—he thought at first—to no one:

'He wouldn't come back this way. The first time he didn't have time. He went back straight up the hill that time, woods or not and dark or not. That was when he heard whatever it was he heard.' Then he knew who the sheriff was talking to: 'Maybe your secretary was whistling up there or something. Being in a graveyard that time of night.'

Then they stood on the bank of the branch itself—a broad ditch a channel through which during the winter and spring rains a torrent rushed but where now there flowed a thin current scarcely an inch deep and never much over a yard wide from pool to pool along the blanched sand—and even as his uncle said, 'Surely the fool——' the sheriff ten yards or so further along the bank said:

'Here it is:' and they went to him and then he saw where the mule had stood tied to a sapling and then the prints where the man himself had thrashed on along the bank, his prints also deeper than any man no matter how heavy should have made and he thought of that too: the anguish, the desperation, the urgency in the black dark and the briers and the dizzy irrevocable fleeing on seconds, carrying a burden man was not intended to carry: then he was hearing a snapping and thrashing of underbrush still further along the bank and then the mare and then old Gowrie shouted and then another crash which would be the mule coming up and then simple pandemonium: the old man shouting and cursing and the yelping of the hounds and the thudding sound a man's shoe makes against a dog's ribs: but they couldn't hurry anymore, thrashing and crashing their own way through the tearing clinging briers and vines until they could look down into the ditch and the low mound of fresh shaled earth into which the two hounds had been digging and old Gowrie still kicking at them and cursing, and then they were all down in the ditch except the two Negroes.

'Hold up, Mr Gowrie,' the sheriff said. 'That aint Vinson.' But the old man didn't seem to hear him. He didn't even seem aware that anyone else was there; he seemed even to have forgot why he was kicking the dogs: that he had merely set out to drive them back from the mound, still hobbling and hopping after them on one leg and the other poised and cocked to kick even after they had retreated from the mound and were merely trying to dodge past him and get out of the ditch into safety, still kicking at them and cursing after the sheriff caught him by his one arm and held him.

'Look at the dirt,' the sheriff said. 'Cant you see? He hardly took time to bury it. This was the second one, when he was in the hurry, when it was almost daylight and he had to get it hidden?' and they could all see now—the low hummock of fresh dirt lying close under the bank and in the bank above it the savage ragged marks of the shovel as if he had hacked at the bank with the edge of the blade like swinging an axe (and again: thinking: the desperation the urgency the frantic hand-to-hand combat with the massy intolerable inertia of the earth itself) until enough of it shaled off and down to hide what he had to hide.

This time they didn't need even the shovels. The body was barely covered; the dogs had already exposed it and he realised now the true magnitude of the urgency and desperation: the frantic and desperate bankrupt in time who had not even enough of it left to hide the evidence of his desperation and the reason for his urgency; it had been after two oclock when he and Aleck Sander, even two of them working with furious speed, had got the grave filled back up again: so that by the time the murderer, not only alone but who had already moved six feet of dirt and then put it back once since the sun set yesterday, had the second body out and the grave filled for the second time it must have been daylight, later than daylight perhaps, the sun itself watching him while he rode for the second time down the hill and across to the branch; morning itself watching him while he tumbled the body beneath the bank's overhang then hacked furiously from it just enough dirt to hide the body temporarily from sight with something of that frantic desperation of the wife flinging her peignoir over the lover's forgotten glove:—lying (the body) face down and only the back of the crushed skull visible until the old man stooped and with his one hand jerked it stiffly over onto its back.

'Yep,' old Gowrie said in the high brisk carrying voice: 'It's that Montgomery, damned if it aint:' and rose lean and fast as a tripped watch-spring yelling shouting at the hounds again: 'Hi boys! Find Vinson!' and then his uncle shouting too to make himself heard:

'Wait, Mr Gowrie. Wait:' then to the sheriff: 'He was a fool then just because he didn't have time, not because he is a fool. I just dont believe it twice——' looking around, his eyes darting. Then he stopped them on the twins. He said sharply: 'Where's the quicksand?'

'What?' one of the twins said.

'The quicksand,' his uncle said. 'The quicksand bed in the branch here. Where is it?'

'Quicksand?' old Gowrie said. 'Sonabitch, Lawyer. Put a man in quicksand? my boy in quicksand?'

'Shut up, Mr Gowrie,' the sheriff said. Then to the twin: 'Well? Where?'

But he answered first. He had been intending to for a second or so. Now he did: 'It's by the bridge:' then—he didn't know why: and then that didn't matter either—'It wasn't Aleck Sander that time. It was Highboy.'

'*Under* the highway bridge,' the twin corrected. 'Where it's been all the time.'

'Oh,' the sheriff said. 'Which one was Highboy?' And he was about to answer that: then suddenly the old man seemed to have forgot about his mare too, whirling, already running before any of them moved and even before he himself moved, running for several strides against the purchaseless sand while they watched him, before he turned and with that same cat-like agility he mounted the mare with, clawed himself one-handed up the steep bank and was thrashing and crashing on out of sight before anybody else except the two Negroes who had never quitted it were even up the bank.

'Jump,' the sheriff said to the twins: 'Catch him.' But they didn't. They thrashed and crashed on after him, one of the twins in front then the rest of them and the two Negroes pell mell through the briers and brush, on back along the branch and out of the jungle into the cleared right-of-way below the road at the bridge; he saw the sliding hoofmarks where Highboy had come almost down to the water and then refused, the stream the water crowded over against the opposite concrete revetment flowing in a narrow band whose nearer edge faded without demarcation into an expanse of wet sand as smooth and innocent and markless of surface as so much milk; he stepped sprang over a long willow pole lying above the bank-edge and coated for three or four feet up its length with a thin patina of dried sand like when you thrust a stick into a bucket or vat of paint and even as the sheriff shouted to the twin in front 'Grab him, you!' he saw the old man jump feet first off the bank and with no splash no disturbance of any sort continue right on not through the bland surface but past it as if he had jumped not into anything but past the edge of a cliff or a window-sill and then stopping half-disappeared as suddenly with no shock or jolt: just fixed and immobile as if his legs had been cut off at the loins by one swing of a scythe, leaving his trunk sitting upright on the bland depthless milk-like sand.

'All right, boys!' old Gowrie cried, brisk and carrying: 'Here he is. I'm standing on him.'

And one twin got the rope bridle from the mule and the leather one and the saddle girth from the mare and using the shovels like axes the Negroes hacked willow branches while the rest of them dragged up other brush and poles and whatever else they could reach or find or free and now both twins and the two Negroes, their empty shoes sitting on the bank, were down in the sand too and steadily there came down from the hills the ceaseless strong murmur of the pines but no other sound yet although he strained his ears listening in both directions along the road, not for the dignity of death because death has no dignity but at least for the decorum of it: some little at least of that decorum which should be every man's helpless right until the carrion he leaves can be hidden from the ridicule and the shame, the body coming out now feet first, gallowsed up and out of the inscrutable suck to the heave of the crude tackle then free of the sand with a faint smacking plop like the sound of lips perhaps in sleep and in the bland surface nothing: a faint wimple wrinkle already fading then gone like the end of a faint secret fading smile, and then on the bank now while they stood about and over it and he was listening harder than ever now with something of the murderer's own frantic urgency both ways along the road though there was still nothing: only hearing recognising his own voice apparently long after everyone else had, watching the old man coated to the waist with the same thin patina of sand like the pole, looking down at the body, his face wrenched and his upper lip wrenched upward from the lifeless porcelain glare and the pink bloodless gums of his false teeth:

'Oh gee, Uncle Gavin, oh gee, Uncle Gavin, let's get him away from the road, at least let's get him back into the woods——'

'Steady,' his uncle said. 'They've all passed now. They're all in town now:' and still watching as the old man stooped and began to brush clumsily with his one hand at the sand clogged into the eyes and nostrils and mouth, the hand looking curious and stiff at this which had been shaped so supple and quick to violence: to the buttons on the shirt and the butt and hammer of the pistol: then the hand went back and began to fumble at the hip pocket but already his uncle had produced a handkerchief and extended it but that was too late too as kneeling now the old man jerked out the tail of his shirt and bending to bring it close, wiped the or at the dead face with it then bending tried to blow the wet sand from it as though he had forgotten the sand was still damp. Then the old man stood up again and said in the high flat carrying voice in which there was still no real inflection at all:

'Well, Shurf?'

'It wasn't Lucas Beauchamp, Mr Gowrie,' the sheriff said. 'Jake Montgomery was at Vinson's funeral yesterday. And while Vinson was being buried Lucas Beauchamp was locked up in my jail in town.'

'I aint talking about Jake Montgomery, Shurf,' old Gowrie said.

'Neither am I, Mr Gowrie,' the sheriff said. 'Because it wasn't Lucas Beauchamp's old forty-one Colt that killed Vinson either.'

And watching he thought *No! No! Dont say it! Dont ask!* and for a while he believed the old man would not as he stood facing the sheriff but not looking at him now because his wrinkled eyelids had come down hiding his eyes but only in the way they do when somebody looks down at something at his feet so you couldn't really say whether the old man had closed them or was just looking down at what lay on the ground between him and the sheriff. But he was wrong; the eyelids went up again and again the old man's hard pale eyes were looking at the sheriff; again his voice to nine hundred men out of nine hundred and one would have sounded just cheerful:

'What was it killed Vinson, Shurf?'

'A German Luger automatic, Mr Gowrie,' the sheriff said. 'Like the one Buddy McCallum brought home from France in 1919 and traded that summer for a pair of foxhounds.'

And he thought how this was where the eyelids might even should have closed again but again he was wrong: only until the old man himself turned, quick and wiry, already in motion, already speaking peremptory and loud, not brookless of opposition or argument, simply incapable of conceiving either:

'All right, sons. Let's load our boy on the mule and take him home.'

IX.

AND TWO OCLOCK that afternoon in his uncle's car just behind the truck (it was another pickup; they—the sheriff—had commandeered it, with a slatted cattle frame on the bed which one of the Gowrie twins had known would be standing in the deserted yard of the house two miles away which had the telephone too—and he remembered how he wondered what the truck was doing there, how they had got to town themselves who had left it—and the Gowrie had turned the switch on with a table fork which by the Gowrie's direction he had found in the unlocked kitchen when his uncle went in to telephone the coroner and the Gowrie was driving it) blinking rapidly and steadily not against glare so much as something hot and gritty inside his eyelids like a dust of ground glass (which certainly could and even should have been dust after twenty-odd miles of sand and gravel roads in one morning except that no simple dust refused as this did to moisten at all with blinking) it seemed to him that he saw crowding the opposite side of the street facing the jail not just the county, not just Beat One and Two and Three and Five in their faded tieless khaki and denim and print cotton but the town too—not only the faces he had seen getting out of the Beat Four-dusty cars in front of the barbershop and the poolhall Saturday afternoon and then in the barbershop Sunday morning and again here in the street Sunday noon when the sheriff drove up with Lucas, but the others who except for the doctors and lawyers and ministers were not just the town but the Town: merchants and cotton-buyers and automobile dealers and the younger men who were the clerks in the stores and cotton offices and salesrooms and mechanics in the garages and filling stations on the way back to work from lunch—who without even waiting for the sheriff's car to get close enough to be recognised had already turned and begun to flow back toward the Square like the turn of a tide, already in motion when the sheriff's car reached the jail, already pouring back into the Square and converging in that one direction across it when first the sheriff then the truck then his uncle turned into the alley beyond the jail leading to the loading ramp at the undertaker's back door where the coroner was waiting for them: so that moving not only parallel with them beyond the intervening block but already in advance, it would even reach the undertaker's first; and then suddenly and before he could even turn in the seat to look back he knew that it had even boiled into the alley behind them and in a moment a second now it would roar down on them, overtake and snatch them up in order: his uncle's car then the truck then the sheriff's like three hencoops and sweep them on and fling them at last in one inextricable aborted nowworthless jumble onto the ramp at the coroner's feet; still not moving yet it seemed to him that he was already leaning out the window or maybe actually clinging to the fleeing runningboard yelling back at them in a kind of unbearable unbelieving outrage:

'You fools, dont you see you are too late, that you'll have to start all over again now to find a new reason?' then turning in the seat and looking back through the rear window for a second or maybe two he actually saw it not faces but a face, not a mass nor even a mosaic of them but a Face: not even ravening nor uninsatiate but just in motion, insensate, vacant of thought or even passion: an Expression significantless and without past like the one which materialises suddenly after seconds or even minutes of painful even frantic staring from the innocent juxtaposition of trees and clouds and landscape in the soap-advertisement puzzle-picture or on the severed head in the news photo of the Balkan or Chinese atrocity: without dignity and not even evocative of horror: just neckless slack-muscled and asleep, hanging suspended face to face with him just beyond the glass of the back window yet in the same instant rushing and monstrous down at him so that he actually started back and had even begun to think *In a second more it will* when flick! it was gone, not only the Face but the faces, the alley itself empty behind them: nobody and nothing in it at all and in the street beyond the vacant mouth less than a dozen people now standing looking up the alley after them who even as he looked turned also and began to move back toward the Square.

He hesitated only an instant. *They've all gone around to the front* he thought rapid and quite calm, having a little trouble (he noticed that the car was stopped now) getting his hand onto the door handle, remarking the sheriff's car and the truck both stopped too at the loading ramp where four or five men were lifting a stretcher up to the truck's open endgate and he even heard his uncle's voice behind him:

'Now we're going home and put you to bed before your mother has a doctor in to give us both a squirt with a needle:' then finding the handle and out of the car, stumbling a little but only once, then his heels although he was not running at all pounding too hard on the concrete, his leg-muscles cramped from the car or perhaps even charley-horsed from thrashing up and down branch bottoms not to mention a night spent digging and undigging graves but at least the jarring was clearing his head somewhat or maybe it was the wind of motion doing it; anyway if he was going to have delusions at least he would have a clear brain to look at them with: up the walkway between the undertaker's and the building next to it though already too late of course, the Face in one last rush and surge long since by now already across the Square and the pavement, in one last crash against then right on through the plate glass window trampling to flinders the little bronze-and-ebony membership plaque in the national funeraleers association and the single shabby stunted palm in its maroon earthenware pot and exploding to tatters the sunfaded purple curtain which was the last frail barrier shielding what was left of what Jake Montgomery had of what was left of his share of human dignity.

Then out of the walkway onto the sidewalk, the Square, and stopped dead still for what seemed to him the first time since he and his uncle left the supper table and walked out of the house a week or a month or a year ago or whenever it had been that last Sunday night was. Because this time he didn't even need the flick. They were there of course nose-pressed to the glass but there were not even enough of them to block the pavement let alone compound a Face; less than a dozen here too and some most of them were even boys who should have been in school at this hour—not one country face nor even one true man because even the other four or five were the man-sized neither men nor boys who were always there when old epileptic Uncle Hogeye Mosby from the poorhouse fell foaming into the gutter or when Willy Ingrum finally managed to shoot through the leg or loins what some woman had telephoned him was a mad-dog: and standing at the entrance to the walkway while his uncle came pounding up it behind him, blinking painfully his painful moistureless eyelids he watched why: the Square not empty yet because there were too many of them but getting empty, the khaki and denim and the printed cotton streaming into it and across it toward the parked cars and trucks, clotting and crowding at the doors while one by one they crawled and climbed into the seats and beds and cabs; already starters were whining and engines catching and racing and idling and gears scraping and grinding while the passengers still hurried toward them and now not one but five or six at once backed away from the curb and turned and straightened out with people still running toward them and scrambling aboard and then he could no longer have kept count of them even if he had ever tried, standing beside his uncle watching them condense into four streams into the four main streets leading out of town in the four directions, already going fast even before they were out of the Square, the faces for one last moment more looking not back but out, not at anything, just out just once and that not for long and then no more, vanishing rapidly in profile and seeming already to be travelling much faster than the vehicle which bore them, already by their faces out of town long before they had passed from view: and twice more even from the car; his mother standing suddenly not touching him, come obviously through the walkway too from the jail right past where they were probably still hoicking Montgomery out of the truck but then his uncle had told him they could stand anything provided they still retained always the right to refuse to admit it was visible, saying to his uncle:

'Where's the car?' then not even waiting to be answered, turning back into the walkway ahead of them, walking slender and erect and rigid with her back looking and her heels clicking and popping on the concrete as they did at home when he and Aleck Sander and his father and uncle all four had better walk pretty light for a while, back past the ramp where only the sheriff's empty car and the empty truck stood now and on to the alley where she was already holding open the door of the car when he and his uncle got there and saw them again crossing the mouth of the alley like across a stage—the cars and trucks, the faces in invincible profile not amazed not aghast but in a sort of irrevocable repudiation, shooting across the alley-mouth so constant and unbroken and so many of them it was like the high school senior class or maybe an itinerant one-night travelling troupe giving the Battle of San Juan Hill and you not only didn't hear you didn't even need to not listen to the muted confused backstage undersounds to the same as see the marching or charging troops as soon as they reached the wings break into a frantic stumbling run swapping coats and caps and fake bandages as they doubled back behind the rippling cheesecloth painted with battle and courage and death to fall in on their own rear and at heroic attention cross the footlights again.

'We'll take Miss Habersham home first,' he said.

'Get in,' his mother said and one turn to the left into the street behind the jail and he could still hear them and another turn to the left into the next cross street and there they were again fleeing across that proscenium too unbroken and breakless, the faces rigid in profile above the long tearing sound of cement and rubber and it had taken him two or three minutes in the pickup this morning to find a chance just to get into it and go the same way it was going; it would take his uncle five or ten to find a hole to get through it and go back to the jail.

'Go on,' his mother said. 'Make them let you in:' and he knew they were not going by the jail at all; he said:

'Miss Habersham——'

'How do I do it?' his uncle said. 'Just shut both eyes and mash hard with my right foot?' and perhaps did; they were in the stream too now turning with it toward home which was all right, he had never worried about getting into it but getting out of it again before that frantic pellmell not of flight then if any liked that better so just call it evacuation swept them on into nightfall to spew them at last hours and miles away high and dry and battered and with the wind knocked out of them somewhere along the county's ultimate scarcemapped perimeter to walk back in the dark: saying again:

'Miss Habersham——'

'She has her truck,' his uncle said. 'Dont you remember?' —who had been doing nothing else steadily for five minutes now, even trying three times to say it: Miss Habersham in the truck and her house not half a mile away and all holding her back was she couldn't possibly get to it, the house on one side and the truck on the other of that unpierceable barrier of rushing bumper-locked cars and trucks and so almost as interdict to an old maiden lady in a second-hand vegetable-peddler's pickup as if it were in Mongolia or the moon: sitting in the truck with the engine running and the gears meshed and her foot on the accelerator independent solitary and forlorn erect and slight beneath the exact archaic even moribund hat waiting and watching and wanting only but nothing but to get through it so she could put the darned clothes away and feed the chickens and eat supper and get some rest too after going on thirty-six hours which to seventy must have been worse than a hundred to sixteen, watching and waiting that dizzying profiled blur for a while even a good while but not forever not too long because she was a practical woman who hadn't taken long last night to decide that the way to get a dead body up out of a grave was to go out to the grave and dig it up and not long now to decide that the way to get around an obstruction especially with the sun already tumbling down the west was to go around it, the truck in motion now running along parallel with the obstruction and in its direction, forlorn and solitary still yet independent still too and only a little nervous, perhaps just realising that she was already driving a little faster than she was used and liked to, faster in fact than she had ever driven before and even then not keeping abreast of it but only beside it because it was going quite fast now: one endless profiled whizz: and now she would know that when the gap came perhaps she would not have the skill or strength or speed or quickness of eye or maybe even the simple nerve: herself going faster and faster and so intent trying to not miss the gap with one eye and watch where she was going with the other that she wouldn't realise until afterward that she had made the turn going not south but east now and not just her house diminishing rapidly and squarely behind her but Jefferson too because they or it was not moving in just one direction out of town but in all of them on all the main roads leading away from the jail and the undertaker's and Lucas Beauchamp and what was left of Vinson Gowrie and Montgomery like the frantic scattering of waterbugs on a stagnant pond when you drop a rock into it: so she would be more desperate than ever now with all distance fleeing between her and home and another night coming on, nerving herself for any gap or crevice now, the battered pickup barely skimming the ground beside that impenetrable profiled blur drawing creeping closer and closer beside it when the inevitable happened: some failure of eye or tremor of hand or an involuntary flick of the eyelid on alertness's straining glare or maybe simple topography: a stone or clod in the path as inaccessible to indictment as God but anyway too close and then too late, the truck snatched up and into the torrent of ballbearing rubber and refinanced pressed steel and hurled pell mell on still gripping the useless steering wheel and pressing the gelded accelerator solitary and forlorn across the long peaceful creep of late afternoon, into the mauve windless dome of dusk, faster and faster now toward one last crescendo just this side of the county line where they would burst scattering into every crossroad and lane like rabbits or rats nearing at last their individual burrows, the truck slowing and then stopping a little crossways in the road perhaps where momentum had spewed it because she was safe now, in Crossman County and she could turn south again now along the edge of Yoknapatawpha turning on the lights now going as fast as she dared along the fringing unmarked country roads; full night now and in Mott County now she could even turn west at last watching her chance to turn north and make her dash, nine and ten oclock along the markless roads fringing the imaginary line beyond which the distant frantic headlights flashed and darted plunging into their burrows and dens; Okatoba County soon and midnight and surely she could turn north then back into Yoknapatawpha, wan and spent solitary and indomitable among the crickets and treefrogs and lightningbugs and owls and whippoorwills and the hounds rushing bellowing out from under the sleeping houses and even at last a man in his nightshirt and unlaced shoes, carrying a lantern:

Where you trying to go, lady?

I'm trying to get to Jefferson.

Jefferson's behind you, lady.

I know. I had to detour around an arrogant insufferable old nigger who got the whole county upset trying to pretend he murdered a white man: when suddenly he discovered that he was going to laugh, discovering it almost in time, not quite in time to prevent it but in time to begin to stop it pretty quick, really more surprised than anything else, until his mother said harshly:

'Blow the horn. Blow them out of the way' and he discovered that it was not laughing at all or anyway not just laughing, that is the sound it was making was about the same as laughing but there was more of it and it felt harder, seemed to be having more trouble getting out and the harder it felt and sounded the less and less he could seem to remember what he must have been laughing at and his face was suddenly wet not with a flow but a kind of burst and spring of water; anyway there he was, a hulking lump the second largest of the three of them, more bigger than his mother than his uncle was than he, going on seventeen years old and almost a man yet because three in the car were so crowded he couldn't help but feel a woman's shoulder against his and her narrow hand on his knee sitting there like a spanked child before he had even had warning enough to begin to stop it.

'They ran,' he said.

'Pull out, damn you,' his mother said. 'Go around them:' which his uncle did, on the wrong side of the street and going almost as fast as he had driven this morning on the way to the church trying to keep in sight of the sheriff and it wasn't because his mother had rationalised that since all of them were already in town trying their best to get out of it there wouldn't be anybody to be coming toward the Square on that side of the street so it was simply just having one in the car with you even if she wasn't driving it, that's all you needed to do: remembering them once before in a car and his uncle driving and his uncle said then,

'All right, how do I do it, just shut both eyes and mash the accelerator?' and his mother said,

'How many collisions did you ever see with women driving both of them?' and his uncle said,

'All right, touché, maybe it's because one of them's car is still in the shop where a man ran into it yesterday:' then he could no longer see them but only hear the long tearing without beginning or end and leaving no scar of tires and pavement in friction like the sound of raw silk and luckily the house was on the same wrong side of the street too and carrying the sound into the yard with him too and now he could do something about the laughing by taking a moment to put his hand on whatever it was that seemed to have got him started and bringing it out into the light where even he could see it wasn't that funny; about ten thousand miles of being funny enough to set his mother swearing; he said:

'They ran' and at once knew that was wrong, almost too late even while he was standing right there looking at himself, walking fast across the yard until he stopped and not jerked just pulled his arm away and said, 'Look, I'm not crippled. I'm just tired. I'm going up to my room and lie down a while:' and then to his uncle: 'I'll be all right then. Come up and call me in about fifteen minutes:' then stopped and turned again to his uncle: 'I'll be ready in fifteen minutes:' and went on this time carrying it into the house with him and even in his room too he could still hear it even through the drawn shades and the red jumping behind his eyelids until he started up onto one elbow under his mother's hand too again to his uncle just beyond the footboard:

'Fifteen minutes. You wont go without me? You promise?'

'Sure,' his uncle said. 'I wont go without you. I'll just——'

'Will you please get to hell out of here, Gavin?' his mother said and then to him, 'Lie down' and he did and there it still was even through even against the hand, the narrow slim cool palm but too dry too rough and maybe even too cool, the dry hot gritty feel of his skull better than the feel of the hand on it because at least he was used to it by now, he had had it long enough, even rolling his head but about as much chance to escape that one frail narrow inevictible palm as to roll your forehead out from under a birthmark and it was not even a face now because their backs were toward him but the back of a head, the composite one back of one Head one fragile mushfilled bulb indefensible as an egg yet terrible in its concorded unanimity rushing not at him but away.

'They ran,' he said. 'They saved their consciences a good ten cents by not having to buy him a package of tobacco to show they had forgiven him.'

'Yes,' his mother said. 'Just let go:' which was like telling a man dangling with one hand over a cliff to just hold on: who wanted nothing right now but a chance to let go and relinquish into the nothing of sleep what little of nothing he still had who last night had wanted to go to sleep and could have but didn't have time and now wanted more than ever to go to sleep and had all the time in the world for the next fifteen minutes (or the next fifteen days or fifteen years as far as anybody knew because there was nothing anybody could do but hope Crawford Gowrie would decide to come in and hunt up the sheriff and say All right I did it because all they had was Lucas who said that Vinson Gowrie wasn't shot with a forty-one Colt or anyway his, Lucas's forty-one Colt and Buddy McCallum to say or not say Yes I swapped Crawford Gowrie a German pistol twenty-five years ago; not even Vinson Gowrie for somebody from the Memphis police to come and look at and say what bullet killed him because the sheriff had already let old Gowrie take him back home and wash the quicksand off and bury him again tomorrow: where this time Hampton and his uncle could go out there tomorrow night and dig him up) only he had forgotten how: or maybe that was it and he didn't dare relinquish into nothing what little he had left: which was nothing: no grief to be remembered nor pity nor even awareness of shame, no vindication of the deathless aspiration of man by man to man through the katharsis of pity and shame but instead only an old man for whom grief was not even a component of his own but merely a temporary phenomenon of his slain son jerking a strange corpse over onto its back not in appeasement to its one mute indicting cry not for pity not for vengeance but for justice but just to be sure he had the wrong one, crying cheery abashless and loud: 'Yep it's that damned Montgomery damned if it aint', and a Face; who had no more expected Lucas to be swept out of his cell shoulder high on a tide of expiation and set for his moment of vindication and triumph on the base say of the Confederate monument (or maybe better on the balcony of the postoffice building beneath the pole where the national flag flew) than he had expected such for himself and Aleck Sander and Miss Habersham: who (himself) not only had not wanted that but could not have accepted it since it would have abrogated and made void the whole sum of what part he had done which had to be anonymous else it was valueless: who had wanted of course to leave his mark too on his time in man but only that, no more than that, some mark on his part in earth but humbly, waiting wanting humbly even, not really hoping even, nothing (which of course was everything) except his own one anonymous chance too to perform something passionate and brave and austere not just in but into man's enduring chronicle worthy of a place in it (who knew? perhaps adding even one anonymous jot to the austerity of the chronicle's brave passion) in gratitude for the gift of his time in it, wanting only that and not even with hope really, willing to accept the fact that he had missed it because he wasn't worthy, but certainly he hadn't expected this:—not a life saved from death nor even a death saved from shame and indignity nor even the suspension of a sentence but merely the grudging pretermission of a date; not indignity shamed with its own shameful cancellation, not sublimation and humility with humility and pride remembered nor the pride of courage and passion nor of pity nor the pride and austerity and grief, but austerity itself debased by what it had gained, courage and passion befouled by what they had had to cope with;—a Face, the composite Face of his native kind his native land, his people his blood his own with whom it had been his joy and pride and hope to be found worthy to present one united unbreakable front to the dark the abyss the night—a Face monstrous unravening omniverous and not even uninsatiate, not frustrated nor even thwarted, not biding nor waiting and not even needing to be patient since yesterday today and tomorrow are Is: Indivisible: One (his uncle for this too, anticipating this too two or three or four years ago as his uncle had everything else which as he himself became more and more a man he had found to be true: 'It's all *now* you see. Yesterday wont be over until tomorrow and tomorrow began ten thousand years ago. For every Southern boy fourteen years old, not once but whenever he wants it, there is the instant when it's still not yet two oclock on that

July afternoon in 1863, the brigades are in position behind the rail fence, the guns are laid and ready in the woods and the furled flags are already loosened to break out and Pickett himself with his long oiled ringlets and his hat in one hand probably and his sword in the other looking up the hill waiting for Longstreet to give the word and it's all in the balance, it hasn't happened yet, it hasn't even begun yet, it not only hasn't begun yet but there is still time for it not to begin against that position and those circumstances which made more men than Garnett and Kemper and Armstead and Wilcox look grave yet it's going to begin, we all know that, we have come too far with too much at stake and that moment doesn't need even a fourteen year old boy to think *This time. Maybe this time* with all this much to lose and all this much to gain: Pennsylvania, Maryland, the world, the golden dome of Washington itself to crown with desperate and unbelievable victory the desperate gamble, the cast made two years ago; or to anyone who ever sailed even a skiff under a quilt sail, the moment in 1492 when somebody thought *This is it:* the absolute edge of no return, to turn back now and make home or sail irrevocably on and either find land or plunge over the world's roaring rim. A small voice, a sound sensitive lady poet of the time of my youth said *the scattered tea goes with the leaves and every day a sunset dies:* a poet's extravagance which as quite often mirrors truth but upside down and backward since the mirror's unwitting manipulator busy in his preoccupation has forgotten that the back of it is glass too: because if they only did, instead of which yesterday's sunset and yesterday's tea both are inextricable from the scattered indestructible uninfusable grounds blown through the endless corridors of tomorrow, into the shoes we will have to walk in and even the sheets we will have ((or try)) to sleep between: because you escape nothing, you flee nothing; the pursuer is what is doing the running and tomorrow night is nothing but one long sleepless wrestle with yesterday's omissions and regrets.'): who had pretermitted not even a death nor even a death to Lucas but merely Lucas, Lucas in ten thousand Sambo-avatars to scurry unheeding and not even aware through that orifice like mice through the slot of a guillotine until at the One unheeding moment the unheeding unwitting uncaring chopper falls; tomorrow or at least tomorrow or at most tomorrow and perhaps this time to intervene where angels fear no white and black children sixteen and an old white spinster long on the way to eighty; who ran, fled not even to deny Lucas but just to keep from having to send up to him by the drugstore porter a can of tobacco not at all to say they were sorry but so they wouldn't have to say out loud that they were wrong: and spurned the cliff away in one long plunge up and up slowing into it already hearing it, only the most faintly oscillant now hearing it listening to it, not moving yet nor even opening his eyes as he lay for a moment longer listening to it, then opened them and then his uncle too stood silhouetted against the light beyond the footboard in that utter that complete that absolute silence now with nothing in it now but the breathing of darkness and the treefrogs and bugs: no fleeing nor repudiation nor for this moment more even urgency anywhere in the room or outside it either above or below or before or behind the tiny myriad beast-sounds and the vast systole and diastole of summer night.

'It's gone,' he said.

'Yes,' his uncle said. 'They're probably all in bed asleep by now. They got home to milk and even have time before dark to chop wood for tomorrow's breakfast too.'

Which made once though still he didn't move. 'They ran,' he said.

'No,' his uncle said. 'It was more than that.'

'They ran,' he said. 'They reached the point where there was nothing left for them to do but admit that they were wrong. So they ran home.'

'At least they were moving,' his uncle said: which made twice: who hadn't even needed the first cue since not only the urgency the need the necessity to move again or rather not really to have stopped moving at all at that moment four or five or six hours or whatever it had been ago when he really believed he was going to lie down for only fifteen minutes (and which incidentally knew fifteen minutes whether he apparently did or not) hadn't come back, it had never been anywhere to come back from because it was still there, had been there all the time, never for one second even vacated even from behind the bizarre phantasmagoriae whose ragtag and bobends still befogged him, with or among which he had wasted nearer fifteen hours than fifteen minutes; it was still there or at least his unfinished part in it which was not even a minuscule but rather a minutecule of his uncle's and the sheriff's in the unfinishability of Lucas Beauchamp and Crawford Gowrie since as far as they knew before he lost track this morning neither of them knew what they were going to do next even before Hampton had disposed of what little of evidence they had by giving it back to old one-armed pistol Gowrie where even two children and an old woman couldn't get it back this time; the need not to finish anything but just to keep moving not even to remain where they were but just desperately to keep up with it like having to run on a treadmill not because you wanted to be where the treadmill was but simply not to be flung pellmell still running frantically backward off the whole stage out of sight, and not waiting static for the moment to flow back into him again and explode him up into motion but rather already in endless motion like the treadmill's endless band less than an inch's fraction above the ultimate point of his nose and chest where the first full breath would bring him into its snatching orbit, himself lying beneath it like a hobo trapped between the rails under a speeding train, safe only so long as he did not move.

So he moved; he said 'Time:' swinging his legs over: 'What time is it? I said fifteen minutes. You promised——'

'It's only nine-thirty,' his uncle said. 'Plenty of time for a shower and your supper too. They wont leave before we get there.'

'They?' he said: up onto his bare feet (he had not undressed except his shoes and sox) already reaching for his slippers. 'You've been back to town. Before we get there? We're not going with them?'

'No,' his uncle said. 'It'll take both of us to hold Miss Habersham back. She's going to meet us at the office. So move along now; she's probably already waiting for us.'

'Yes,' he said. But he was already unfastening his shirt and his belt and trousers too with the other hand, all ready to step in one motion out of both. And this time it was laughing. It was all right. You couldn't even hear it. 'So that was why,' he said. 'So their women wouldn't have to chop wood in the dark with half-awake children holding lanterns.'

'No,' his uncle said. 'They were not running from Lucas. They had forgotten about him——'

'That's exactly what I'm saying,' he said. 'They didn't even wait to send him a can of tobacco and say It's all right, old man, everybody makes mistakes and we wont hold this one against you.'

'Was that what you wanted?' his uncle said. 'The can of tobacco? That would have been enough?—Of course it wouldn't. Which is one reason why Lucas will ultimately get his can of tobacco; they will insist on it, they will have to. He will receive installments on it for the rest of his life in this county whether he wants them or not and not just Lucas but *Lucas: Sambo* since what sets man writhing sleepless in bed at night is not having injured his fellow so much as having been wrong; the mere injury (if he cannot justify it with what he calls logic) he can efface by destroying the victim and the witnesses but the mistake is his and that is one of his cats which he always prefers to choke to death with butter. So Lucas will get his tobacco. He wont want it of course and he'll try to resist it. But he'll get it and so we shall watch right here in Yoknapatawpha County the ancient oriental relationship between the savior and the life he saved turned upside down: Lucas Beauchamp once the slave of any white man within range of whose notice he happened to come, now tyrant over the whole county's white conscience. And they—Beat One and Two and Three and Five—knew that too so why take time now to send him a ten-cent can of tobacco when they have got to spend the balance of their lives doing it? So they had dismissed him for the time. They were not running from him, they were running from Crawford Gowrie; they simply repudiated not even in horror but in absolute unanimity a shall-not and should not which without any warning whatever turned into a *must*-not. *Thou shalt not kill* you see—no accusative, heatless: a simple moral precept; we have accepted it in the distant anonymity of our forefathers, had it so long, cherished it, fed it, kept the sound of it alive and the very words themselves unchanged, handled it so long that all the corners are now worn smoothly off; we can sleep right in the bed with it; we have even distilled our own antidotes for it as the foresighted housewife keeps a solution of mustard or handy eggwhites on the same shelf with the ratpoison; as familiar as grandpa's face, as unrecognisable as grandpa's face beneath the turban of an Indian prince, as abstract as grandpa's flatulence at the family supper-table; even when it breaks down and the spilled blood stands sharp and glaring in our faces we still have the precept, still intact, still true: *we shall not kill* and maybe next time we even wont. But *thou shalt not kill thy mother's other child.* It came right down into the street that time to walk in broad daylight at your elbow, didn't it?'

'So for a lot of Gowries and Workitts to burn Lucas Beauchamp to death with gasoline for something he didn't even do is one thing but for a Gowrie to murder his brother is another.'

'Yes,' his uncle said.

'You cant say that,' he said.

'Yes,' his uncle said. '*Thou shalt not kill* in precept and even when you do, precept still remains unblemished and scarless: *Thou shalt not kill* and who knows, perhaps next time maybe you wont. But *Gowrie must not kill Gowrie's brother:* no maybe about it, no next time to maybe not Gowrie kill Gowrie because there must be no first time. And not just for Gowrie but for all: Stevens and Mallison and Edmonds and McCaslin too; if we are not to hold to the belief that that point not just shall not but must not and *can*not come at which Gowrie or Ingrum or Stevens or Mallison may shed Gowrie or Ingrum or Stevens or Mallison blood, how hope ever to reach that one where *Thou shalt not kill at all*, where Lucas Beauchamp's life will be secure not despite the fact that he is Lucas Beauchamp but because he is?'

'So they ran to keep from having to lynch Crawford Gowrie,' he said.

'They wouldn't have lynched Crawford Gowrie,' his uncle said. 'There were too many of them. Dont you remember, they packed the street in front of the jail and the Square too all morning while they still believed Lucas had shot Vinson Gowrie in the back without bothering him at all?'

'They were waiting for Beat Four to come in and do it.'

'Which is exactly what I am saying—granted for the moment that that's true. That part of Beat Four composed of Gowries and Workitts and the four or five others who wouldn't have given a Gowrie or Workitt either a chew of tobacco and who would have come along just to see the blood, is small enough to produce a mob. But not all of them together because there is a simple numerical point at which a mob cancels and abolishes itself, maybe because it has finally got too big for darkness, the cave it was spawned in is no longer big enough to conceal it from light and so at last whether it will or no it has to look at itself, or maybe because the amount of blood in one human body is no longer enough, as one peanut might titillate one elephant but not two or ten. Or maybe it's because man having passed into mob passes then into mass which abolishes mob by absorption, metabolism, then having got too large even for mass becomes man again conceptible of pity and justice and conscience even if only in the recollection of his long painful aspiration toward them, toward that something anyway of one serene universal light.'

'So man is always right,' he said.

'No,' his uncle said. 'He tries to be if they who use him for their own power and aggrandisement let him alone. Pity and justice and conscience too—that belief in more than the divinity of individual man (which we in America have debased into a national religion of the entrails in which man owes no duty to his soul because he has been absolved of soul to owe duty to and instead is static heir at birth to an inevictible quit-claim on a wife a car a radio and an old-age pension) but in the divinity of his continuity as Man; think how easy it would have been for them to attend to Crawford Gowrie: no mob moving fast in darkness watching constantly over its shoulder but one indivisible public opinion: that peanut vanishing beneath a whole concerted trampling herd with hardly one elephant to really know the peanut had even actually been there since the main reason for a mob is that the individual red hand which actually snapped the thread may vanish forever into one inviolable confraternity of namelessness: where in this case that one would have had no more reason to lie awake at night afterward than a paid hangman. They didn't want to destroy Crawford Gowrie. They repudiated him. If they had lynched him they would have taken only his life. What they really did was worse: they deprived him to the full extent of their capacity of his citizenship in man.'

He didn't move yet. 'You're a lawyer.' Then he said, 'They were not running from Crawford Gowrie or Lucas Beauchamp either. They were running from themselves. They ran home to hide their heads under the bedclothes from their own shame.'

'Exactly correct,' his uncle said. 'Haven't I been saying that all the time? There were too many of them. This time there were enough of them to be able to run from shame, to have found unbearable the only alternative which would have been the mob's: which (the mob) because of its smallness and what it believed was its secretness and tightness and what it knew to be its absolute lack of trust in one another, would have chosen the quick and simple alternative of abolishing knowledge of the shame by destroying the witness to it. So as you like to put it they ran.'

'Leaving you and Mr Hampton to clean up the vomit, which even dogs dont do. Though of course Mr Hampton is a paid dog and I reckon you might be called one too.—Because dont forget Jefferson either,' he said. 'They were clearing off out of sight pretty fast too. Of course some of them couldn't because it was still only the middle of the afternoon so they couldn't shut up the stores and run home too yet; there still might be a chance to sell each other a nickel's worth of something.'

'I said Stevens and Mallison too,' his uncle said.

'Not Stevens,' he said. 'And not Hampton either. Because somebody had to finish it, somebody with a strong enough stomach to mop a floor. The sheriff to catch (or try to or hope to or whatever it is you are going to do) the murderer and a lawyer to defend the lynchers.'

'Nobody lynched anybody to be defended from it,' his uncle said.

'All right,' he said. 'Excuse them then.'

'Nor that either,' his uncle said. 'I'm defending Lucas Beauchamp. I'm defending Sambo from the North and East and West—the outlanders who will fling him decades back not merely into injustice but into grief and agony and violence too by forcing on us laws based on the idea that man's injustice to man can be abolished overnight by police. Sambo will suffer it of course; there are not enough of him yet to do anything else. And he will endure it, absorb it and survive because he is Sambo and has that capacity; he will even beat us there because he has the capacity to endure and survive but he will be thrown back decades and what he survives to may not be worth having because by that time divided we may have lost America.'

'But you're still excusing it.'

'No,' his uncle said. 'I only say that the injustice is ours, the South's. We must expiate and abolish it ourselves, alone and without help nor even (with thanks) advice. We owe that to Lucas whether he wants it or not (and this Lucas anyway wont) not because of his past since a man or a race either if he's any good can survive his past without even needing to escape from it and not because of the high quite often only too rhetorical rhetoric of humanity but for the simple indubitable practical reason of his future: that capacity to survive and absorb and endure and still be steadfast.'

'All right,' he said again. 'You're still a lawyer and they still ran. Maybe they intended for Lucas to clean it up since he came from a race of floor-moppers. Lucas and Hampton and you since Hampton ought to do something now and then for his money and they even elected you to a salary too. Did they think to tell you how to do it? what to use for bait to get Crawford Gowrie to come in and say All right, boys, I pass. Deal them again. Or were they too busy being ——being . . . .'

His uncle said quietly: 'Righteous?'

Now he completely stopped. But only for a second. He said, 'They ran,' calm and completely final, not even contemptuous, flicking the shirt floating away behind him and at the same moment dropping the trousers and stepping barefoot out of them in nothing now but shorts. 'Besides, it's all right. I dreamed through all that; I dreamed through them too, dreamed them away too; let them stay in bed or milking their cows before dark or chopping wood before dark or after or by lanterns or not lanterns either. Because they were not the dream; I just passed them to get to the dream——' talking quite fast now, a good deal faster than he realised until it would be too late: 'It was something . . . somebody . . . something about how maybe this was too much to expect of us, too much for people just sixteen or going on eighty or ninety or whatever she is to have to bear, and then right off I was answering what you told me, you remember, about the English boys not much older than me leading troops and flying scout aeroplanes in France in 1918? how you said that by 1918 all British officers seemed to be either subalterns of seventeen or one-eyed or one-armed or one-legged colonels of twenty-three?'—checking then or trying to because he had got the warning at last quite sharp not as if he had heard suddenly in advance the words he was going to say but as if he had discovered suddenly not what he had already said but where it was going, what the ones he had already spoken were going to compel him to say in order to bring them to a stop: but too late of course like mashing suddenly on the brake pedal going downhill then discovering to your horror that the brake rod had snapped: '—only there was something else too——I was trying . . . . . ' and stopped them at last feeling the hot hard blood burn all the way up his neck into his face and nowhere even to look not because he was standing there almost naked to begin with but because no clothes nor expression nor talking either smoke-screened anything from his uncle's bright grave eyes.

'Yes?' his uncle said. Then his uncle said, 'Yes. Some things you must always be unable to bear. Some things you must never stop refusing to bear. Injustice and outrage and dishonor and shame. No matter how young you are or how old you have got. Not for kudos and not for cash: your picture in the paper nor money in the bank either. Just to refuse to bear them. That it?'

'Who, me,' he said, moving now already crossing the room, not even waiting for the slippers. 'I haven't been a Tenderfoot scout since I was twelve years old.'

'Of course not,' his uncle said. 'But just regret it; dont be ashamed.'

X.

PERHAPS EATING had something to do with it, not even pausing while he tried with no particular interest nor curiosity to compute how many days since he had sat down to a table to eat and then in the same chew as it were remembering that it had not been one yet since even though already half asleep he had eaten a good breakfast at the sheriff's at four this morning: remembering how his uncle (sitting across the table drinking coffee) had said that man didn't necessarily eat his way through the world but by the act of eating and maybe only by that did he actually enter the world, get himself into the world: not through it but into it, burrowing into the world's teeming solidarity like a moth into wool by the physical act of chewing and swallowing the substance of its warp and woof and so making, translating into a part of himself and his memory, the whole history of man or maybe even relinquishing by mastication, abandoning, eating into it to be annealed, the proud vainglorious minuscule which he called his memory and his self and his I-Am into that vast teeming anonymous solidarity of the world from beneath which the ephemeral rock would cool and spin away to dust not even remarked and remembered since there was no yesterday and tomorrow didn't even exist so maybe only an ascetic living in a cave on acorns and spring water was really capable of vainglory and pride; maybe you had to live in a cave on acorns and spring water in rapt impregnable contemplation of your vainglory and righteousness and pride in order to keep up to that high intolerant pitch of its worship which brooked no compromise: eating steadily and quite a lot too and at what even he knew by this time was too fast since he had been hearing it for sixteen years and put his napkin down and rose and one last wail from his mother (and he thought how women couldn't really stand anything except tragedy and poverty and physical pain; how this morning when he was where at sixteen he had no business being and doing what even at twice sixteen he had no business doing: chasing over the country with the sheriff digging up murdered corpses out of a ditch: she had been a hundred times less noisy than his father and a thousand times more valuable, yet now when all he intended was to walk to town with his uncle and sit for an hour or so in the same office in which he had already spent a probably elapsed quarter of his life, she had completely abolished Lucas Beauchamp and Crawford Gowrie both and had gone back indefatigable to the day fifteen years ago when she had first set out to persuade him he couldn't button his pants):

'But why cant Miss Habersham come here to wait?'

'She can,' his uncle said. 'I'm sure she can find the house again.'

'You know what I mean,' she said. 'Why dont you make her? Sitting around a lawyer's office until twelve oclock at night is no place for a lady.'

'Neither was digging up Jake Montgomery last night,' his uncle said. 'But maybe this time we will break Lucas Beauchamp of making this constant drain on her gentility. Come along, Chick:' and so out of the house at last, not walking out of the house into it because he had brought it out of the house with him, having at some point between his room and the front door not acquired it nor even simply entered it nor even actually regained it but rather expiated his aberration from it, become once more worthy to be received into it since it was his own or rather he was its and so it must have been the eating, he and his uncle once more walking the same street almost exactly as they had walked it not twenty-two hours ago which had been empty then with a sort of aghast recoiled consternation: because it was not empty at all now, deserted and empty of movement certainly running as vacant of life from streetlamp to streetlamp as a dead street through an abandoned city but not really abandoned not really withdrawn but only making way for them who could do it better, only making way for them who could do it right, not to interfere or get in the way or even offer suggestion or even permit (with thanks) advice to them who would do it right and in their own homely way since it was their own grief and their own shame and their own expiation, laughing again now but it was all right, thinking: *Because they always have me and Aleck Sander and Miss Habersham, not to mention Uncle Gavin and a sworn badge-wearing sheriff:* when suddenly he realised that that was a part of it too—that fierce desire that they should be perfect because they were his and he was theirs, that furious intolerance of any one single jot or tittle less than absolute perfection—that furious almost instinctive leap and spring to defend them from anyone anywhere so that he might excoriate them himself without mercy since they were his own and he wanted no more save to stand with them unalterable and impregnable: one shame if shame must be, one expiation since expiation must surely be but above all one unalterable durable impregnable one: one people one heart one land: so that suddenly he said,

'Look——' and stopped but as always no more was needed:

'Yes?' his uncle said, then when he said no more: 'Ah, I see. It's not that they were right but that you were wrong.'

'I was worse,' he said. 'I was righteous.'

'It's all right to be righteous,' his uncle said. 'Maybe you were right and they were wrong. Just dont stop.'

'Dont stop what?' he said.

'Even bragging and boasting is all right too,' his uncle said. 'Just dont stop.'

'Dont stop what?' he said again. But he knew what now; he said,

'Aint it about time you stopped being a Tenderfoot scout too?'

'This is not Tenderfoot,' his uncle said. 'This is the third degree. What do you call it?——'

'Eagle scout,' he said.

'Eagle scout,' his uncle said. 'Tenderfoot is, Dont accept. Eagle scout is, Dont stop. You see? No, that's wrong. Dont bother to see. Dont even bother to not forget it. Just dont stop.'

'No,' he said. 'We dont need to worry about stopping now. It seems to me what we have to worry about now is where we're going and how.'

'Yes you do,' his uncle said. 'You told me yourself about fifteen minutes ago, dont you remember? About what Mr Hampton and Lucas were going to use for bait to fetch Crawford Gowrie in to where they could put Mr Hampton's hand on him? They're going to use Lucas——'

And he would remember: himself and his uncle standing beside the sheriff's car in the alley beside the jail watching Lucas and the sheriff emerge from the jail's side door and cross the dark yard toward them. It was quite dark in fact since the street light at the corner didn't reach this far nor any sound either; only a little after ten oclock and on Monday night too yet the sky's dark bowl cupped as though in a vacuum like the old bride's bouquet under its glass bell the town, the Square which was more than dead: abandoned: because he had gone on to look at it, without stopping leaving his uncle standing at the corner of the alley who said after him:

'Where are you going?' but not even answering, walking the last silent and empty block, ringing his footfalls deliberate and unsecret into the hollow silence, unhurried and solitary but nothing at all of forlorn, instead with a sense a feeling not possessive but proprietary, vicegeral, with humility still, himself not potent but at least the vessel of a potency like the actor looking from wings or perhaps empty balcony down upon the waiting stage vacant yet garnished and empty yet, nevertheless where in a moment now he will walk and posture in the last act's absolute cynosure, himself in himself nothing and maybe no world-beater of a play either but at least his to finish it, round it and put it away intact and unassailable, complete: and so onto into the dark and empty Square stopping as soon as he could perceive at effortless once that whole dark lifeless rectangle with but one light anywhere and that in the cafe which stayed open all night on account of the long-haul trucks whose (the cafe's) real purpose some said, the real reason for the grant of its license by the town was to keep Willy Ingrum's nocturnal counterpart awake who although the town had walled him off a little cubbyhole of an office in an alley with a stove and a telephone he wouldn't stay there but used instead the cafe where there was somebody to talk to and he could be telephoned there of course but some people old ladies especially didn't like to page the policeman in an allnight jukejoint coffee stall so the office telephone had been connected to a big burglar alarm bell on the outside wall loud enough for the counterman or a truck driver in the cafe to hear it and tell him it was ringing, and the two lighted second-storey windows (and he thought that Miss Habersham really had persuaded his uncle to give her the key to the office and then he thought that that was wrong, his uncle had persuaded her to take the key since she would just as soon have sat in the parked truck until they came—and then added If she had waited because that was certainly wrong and what had really happened was that his uncle had locked her up in the office to give the sheriff and Lucas time to get out of town) but since the lights in a lawyer's office were liable to burn any time the lawyer or the janitor forgot to turn them off when they left and the cafe like the power plant was a public institution they didn't count and even the cafe was just lighted (he couldn't see into it from here but he could have heard and he thought how that, formally shutting off the jukebox for twelve hours had probably been the night marshal's first official act besides punching every hour the time clock on the wall at the bank's back door since the mad-dog scare last August) and he remembered the other the normal Monday nights when no loud fury of blood and revenge and racial and family solidarity had come roaring in from Beat Four (or Beat One or Two or Three or Five for that matter or for the matter of that from the purlieus of the urban Georgian porticoes themselves) to rattle and clash among the old bricks and the old trees and the Doric capitals and leave them for one night anyway stricken: ten oclock on Monday night and although the first run of the film at the picture show would be forty or fifty minutes over now a few of the patrons who had come in late would still be passing homeward and all the young men sitting since that time drinking coca cola and playing nickels into the drugstore jukebox would certainly be, strolling timeless and in no haste since they were going nowhere since the May night itself was their destination and they carried that with them walking in it and (stock-auction day) even a few belated cars and trucks whose occupants had stayed in for the picture show too or to visit and take supper with kin or friends and now at last dispersing nightward sleepward tomorrow-ward about the dark mile-compassing land, remembering no longer ago than last night when he had thought it was empty too until he had had time to listen to it a moment and realised that it was not empty at all: a Sunday night but with more than Sunday night's quiet, the sort of quiet in fact that no night had any business with and of all nights Sunday night never, which had been Sunday night only because they had already named the calendar when the sheriff brought Lucas in to jail: an emptiness you could call emptiness provided you called vacant and empty the silent and lifeless terrain in front of a mobilised army or peaceful the vestibule to a powder magazine or quiet the spillway under the locks of a dam—a sense not of waiting but of incrementation, not of people—women and old folks and children—but of men not so much grim as grave and not so much tense as quiet, sitting quietly and not even talking much in back rooms and not just the bath-cabinets and johns behind the barbershop and the shed behind the poolhall stacked with soft drink cases and littered with empty whiskey bottles but the stock-rooms of stores and garages and behind the drawn shades of the offices themselves whose owners even the proprietors of the stores and garages conceded to belong not to a trade but a profession, not waiting for an event a moment in time to come to them but for a moment in time when in almost volitionless concord they themselves would create the event, preside at and even serve an instant which was not even six or twelve or fifteen hours belated but was instead simply the continuation of the one when the bullet struck Vinson Gowrie and there had been no time between and so for all purposes Lucas was already dead since he had died then on the same instant when he had forfeited his life and theirs was merely to preside at his suttee, and now tonight to remember because tomorrow it would be over, tomorrow of course the Square would wake and stir, another day and it would fling off hangover, another and it would even fling off shame so that on Saturday the whole county with one pierceless unanimity of click and pulse and hum would even deny that the moment had ever existed when they could have been mistaken: so that he didn't even need to remind himself in the absolute the utter the complete silence that the town was not dead nor even abandoned but only withdrawn giving room to do what homely thing must be done in its own homely way without help or interference or even (thank you) advice: three amateurs, an old white spinster and a white child and a black one to expose Lucas's wouldbe murderer, Lucas himself and the county sheriff to catch him and so one last time: remembering: his uncle while he still stood barefoot on the rug with both edges of the unbuttoned shirt arrested in his hands thirty minutes ago and when they were mounting the last pitch of hill toward the church eleven hours ago and on what must have been a thousand other times since he had got big enough to listen and to understand and to remember:—*to defend not Lucas nor even the union of the United States but the United States from the outlanders North East and West who with the highest of motives and intentions (let us say) are essaying to divide it at a time when no people dare risk division by using federal laws and federal police to abolish Lucas's shameful condition, there may not be in any random one thousand Southerners one who really grieves or even is really concerned over that condition nevertheless neither is there always one who would himself lynch Lucas no matter what the occasion yet not one of that nine hundred ninety-nine plus that other first one making the thousand whole again would hesitate to repulse with force (and one would still be that lyncher) the outlander who came down here with force to intervene or punish him, you say (with sneer) You must know Sambo well to arrogate to yourself such calm assumption of his passivity and I reply I dont know him at all and in my opinion no white man does but I do know the Southern white man not only the nine hundred and ninety-nine but that one other too because he is our own too and more than that, that one other does not exist only in the South, you will see allied not North and East and West and Sambo against a handful of white men in the South but a paper alliance of theorists and fanatics and private and personal avengers plus a number of others under the assumption of enough physical miles to afford a principle against and possibly even outnumbered a concorded South which has drawn recruits whether it would or no from your own back-areas, not just your hinterland but the fine cities of your cultural pride your Chicagoes and Detroits and Los Angeleses and wherever else live ignorant people who fear the color of any skin or shape of nose save their own and who will grasp this opportunity to vent on Sambo the whole sum of their ancestral horror and scorn and fear of Indian and Chinese and Mexican and Carib and Jew, you will force us the one out of that first random thousand and the nine hundred and ninety-nine out of the second who do begrieve Lucas's shameful condition and would improve it and have and are and will until (not tomorrow perhaps) that condition will be abolished to be not forgotten maybe but at least remembered with less of pain and bitterness since justice was relinquished to him by us rather than torn from us and forced on him both with bayonets, willynilly into alliance with them with whom we have no kinship whatever in defence of a principle which we ourselves begrieve and abhor, we are in the position of the German after 1933 who had no other alternative between being either a Nazi or a Jew or the present Russian (European too for that matter) who hasn't even that but must be either a Communist or dead, only we must do it and we alone without help or interference or even (thank you) advice since only we can if Lucas's equality is to be anything more than its own prisoner inside an impregnable barricade of the direct heirs of the victory of 1861–1865 which probably did more than even John Brown to stalemate Lucas's freedom which still seems to be in check going on a hundred years after Lee surrendered and when you say Lucas must not wait for that tomorrow because that tomorrow will never come because you not only cant you wont then we can only repeat Then you shall not and say to you Come down here and look at us before you make up your mind and you reply No thanks the smell is bad enough from here and we say Surely you will at least look at the dog you plan to housebreak, a people divided at a time when history is still showing us that the anteroom to dissolution is division and you say At least we perish in the name of humanity and we reply When all is stricken but that nominative pronoun and that verb what price Lucas's humanity then* and turned and ran the short dead empty block back to the corner where his uncle had gone on without waiting and then up the alley too to where the sheriff's car stood, the two of them watching the sheriff and Lucas cross the dark yard toward them the sheriff in front and Lucas about five feet behind walking not fast but just intently, neither furtive nor covert but exactly like two men simply busy not exactly late but with no time to dawdle, through the gate and across to the car where the sheriff opened the back door and said,

'Jump in,' and Lucas got in and the sheriff closed the door and opened the front one and crawled grunting into it, the whole car squatting onto its springs and rims when he let himself down into the seat and turned the switch and started the engine, his uncle standing at the window now holding the rim of it in both hands as though he thought or hoped suddenly on some second thought to hold the car motionless before it could begin to move, saying what he himself had been thinking off and on for thirty or forty minutes:

'Take somebody with you.'

'I am,' the sheriff said. 'Besides I thought we settled all this three times this afternoon.'

'That's still just one no matter how many times you count Lucas,' his uncle said.

'You let me have my pistol,' Lucas said, 'and wont nobody have to do no counting. I'll do it:' and he thought how many times the sheriff had probably told Lucas by now to shut up, which may have been why the sheriff didn't say it now: except that (suddenly) he did, turning slowly and heavily and grunting in the seat to look back at Lucas, saying in the plaintive heavily-sighing voice:

'After all the trouble you got into Saturday standing with that pistol in your pocket in the same ten feet of air a Gowrie was standing in, you want to take it in your hand and walk around another one. Now I want you to hush and stay hushed. And when we begin to get close to Whiteleaf bridge I want you to be laying on the floor close up against the seat behind me and still hushed. You hear me?'

'I hear you,' Lucas said. 'But if I just had my pistol——' but the sheriff had already turned to his uncle:

'No matter how many times you count Crawford Gowrie he's still just one too:' and then went on in the mild sighing reluctant voice which nevertheless was already answering his uncle's thought before even his uncle could speak it: 'Who would he get?' and he thought of that too remembering the long tearing rubber-from-cement sound of the frantic cars and trucks scattering pellmell hurling themselves in aghast irrevocable repudiation in all directions toward the county's outmost unmapped fastnesses except that little island in Beat Four known as Caledonia Church, into sanctuary: the old the used the familiar, home where the women and older girls and children could milk and chop wood for tomorrow's breakfast while the little ones held lanterns and the men and older sons after they had fed the mules against tomorrow's plowing would sit on the front gallery waiting for supper into the twilight: the whippoorwills: night: sleep: and this he could even see (provided that even a murderer's infatuation could bring Crawford Gowrie ever again into the range and radius of that nub arm which—since Crawford was a Gowrie too—in agreement here with the sheriff he didn't believe—and he knew now why Lucas had ever left Fraser's store alive Saturday afternoon, let alone ever got alive out of the sheriff's car at the jail: that the Gowries themselves had known he hadn't done it so they were just marking time waiting for somebody else, maybe Jefferson to drag him out into the street until he remembered—a flash, something almost like shame—the blue shirt squatting and the stiff awkward single hand trying to brush the wet sand from the dead face and he knew that whatever the furious old man might begin to think tomorrow he held nothing against Lucas then because there was no room for anything but his son)—night, the diningroom perhaps and again seven Gowrie men in the twenty-year womanless house because Forrest had come up from Vicksburg for the funeral yesterday and was probably still there this morning when the sheriff sent word out for old Gowrie to meet him at the church, a lamp burning in the center of the table among the crusted sugarbowls and molasses jugs and ketchup and salt and pepper in the same labeled containers they had come off the store shelf in and the old man sitting at the head of it his one arm lying on the table in front of him and the big pistol under his hand pronouncing judgment sentence doom and execution too on the Gowrie who had cancelled his own Gowriehood with his brother's blood, then the dark road the truck (not commandeered this time because Vinson had owned one new and big and powerful convertible for either logs or cattle) the same twin driving it probably and the body boomed down onto the runninggear like a log itself with the heavy logchains, fast out of Caledonia out of Beat Four into the dark silent waiting town fast still up the quiet street across the Square to the sheriff's house and the body tumbled and flung onto the sheriff's front gallery and perhaps the truck even waiting while the other Gowrie twin rang the doorbell. 'Stop worrying about Crawford,' the sheriff said. 'He aint got anything against me. He votes for me. His trouble right now is having to kill extra folks like Jake Montgomery when all he ever wanted was just to keep Vinson from finding out he had been stealing lumber from him and Uncle Sudley Workitt. Even if he jumps onto the runningboard before I have time to keep up with what's going on he'll still have to waste a minute or two trying to get the door open so he can see exactly where Lucas is—provided by that time Lucas is doing good and hard what I told him to do, which I sure hope for his sake he is.'

'I'm going to,' Lucas said. 'But if I just had my——'

'Yes,' his uncle said in the harsh voice: 'Provided he's there.'

The sheriff sighed. 'You sent the message.'

'What message I could,' his uncle said. 'However I could. A message making an assignation between a murderer and a policeman, that whoever finally delivers it to the murderer wont even know was intended for the murderer, that the murderer himself will not only believe he wasn't intended to get it but that it's true.'

'Well,' the sheriff said, 'he'll either get it or he wont get it and he'll either believe it or he wont believe it and he'll either be waiting for us in Whiteleaf bottom or he wont and if he aint me and Lucas will go on to the highway and come back to town.' He raced the engine let it idle again; now he turned on the lights. 'But he may be there. I sent a message too.'

'All right,' his uncle said. 'Why is that, Mr Bones?'

'I got the mayor to excuse Willy Ingrum so he could go out and set up with Vinson again tonight and before Willy left I told him in confidence I was going to run Lucas over to Hollymount tonight through the old Whiteleaf cutoff so Lucas can testify tomorrow at Jake Montgomery's inquest and reminded Willy that they aint finished the Whiteleaf fill yet and cars have to cross it in low gear and told him to be sure not to mention it to anybody.'

'Oh,' his uncle said, not quite turning the door loose yet. 'No matter who might have claimed Jake Montgomery alive he belongs to Yoknapatawpha County now.—But then,' he said briskly, turning the door loose now, 'we're after just a murderer, not a lawyer.—All right,' he said. 'Why dont you get started?'

'Yes,' the sheriff said. 'You go on to your office and watch out for Miss Eunice. Willy may have passed her on the street too and if he did she might still beat us to Whiteleaf bridge in that pickup.'

Then into the Square this time to cross it catacornered to where the pickup stood nosedin empty to the otherwise empty curb and up the long muted groan and rumble of the stairway to the open office door and passing through it he thought without surprise how she was probably the only woman he knew who would have withdrawn the borrowed key from the lock as soon as she opened the strange door not to leave the key on the first flat surface she passed but to put it back into the reticule or pocket or whatever she had put it in when it was lent to her and she wouldn't be sitting in the chair behind the table either and wasn't, sitting instead bolt upright in the hat but another dress which looked exactly like the one she had worn last night and the same handbag on her lap with the eighteen dollar gloves clasped on top of it and the flat-heeled thirty dollar shoes planted side by side on the floor in front of the hardest straightest chair in the room, the one beside the door which nobody ever really sat in no matter how crowded the office and only moving to the easy chair behind the table after his uncle had spent a good two minutes insisting and finally explained it might be two or three hours yet because she had the gold brooch watch on her bosom open when they came in and seemed to think that by this time the sheriff should not only have been back with Crawford Gowrie but probably on the way to the penitentiary with him: then he in his usual chair beside the water cooler and finally his uncle even struck the match to the cob pipe still talking not just through the smoke but into it with it:

'——what happened because some of it we even know let alone what Lucas finally told us by watching himself like a hawk or an international spy to keep from telling us anything that would even explain him let alone save him, Vinson and Crawford were partners buying the timber from old man Sudley Workitt who was Mrs Gowrie's second or fourth cousin or uncle or something, that is they had agreed with old Sudley on a price by the board foot but to be paid him when the lumber was sold which was not to be until the last tree was cut and Crawford and Vinson had delivered it and got their money and then they would pay old Sudley his, hiring a mill and crew to fell and saw and stack it right there within a mile of old Sudley's house and not one stick to be moved until it was all cut. Only—except this part we dont really know yet until Hampton gets his hands on Crawford except it's got to be this way or what in the world were you all doing digging Jake Montgomery out of Vinson's grave?—and every time I think about this part of it and remember you three coming back down that hill to the exact spot where two of you heard him and one of you even saw riding past the man who already with one murdered corpse on the mule in front of him experienced such a sudden and urgent alteration of plan that when Hampton and I got there hardly six hours later there was nobody in the grave at all——'

'But he didn't,' Miss Habersham said.

'—What?' his uncle said. '. . . Where was I? Oh yes.—only Lucas Beauchamp taking his walk one night heard something and went and looked or maybe he was actually passing and saw or maybe he already had the idea which was why he took the walk or that walk that night and saw a truck whether he recognised it or not being loaded in the dark with that lumber which the whole neighborhood knew was not to be moved until the mill itself closed up and moved away which would be some time yet and Lucas watched and listened and maybe he even went over into Crossman County to Glasgow and Hollymount until he knew for sure not only who was moving some of that lumber every night or so, not much at a time, just exactly not quite enough for anyone who was not there every day to notice its absence (and the only people there every day or even interested even to that extent were Crawford who represented himself and his brother and uncle who owned the trees and the resulting lumber and so could do what they liked with it—the one of which was running about the country all day long attending to his other hot irons and the other an old rheumatic man to begin with and half blind on top of that who couldn't have seen anything even if he could have got that far from his house—and the mill crew who were hired by the day and so wouldn't have cared even if they had known what was going on at night as long as they got their pay every Saturday) but what he was doing with it, maybe learning even as far as Jake Montgomery though Lucas's knowing about Jake made no difference except that by getting himself murdered and into Vinson's grave Jake probably saved Lucas's life. But even when Hope told me how he had finally got that much out of Lucas in his kitchen this morning when Will Legate brought him from the jail and we were driving you home it explained only part of it because I was still saying what I had been saying ever since you all woke me this morning and Chick told me what Lucas had told him about the pistol: But why Vinson? Why did Crawford have to kill Vinson in order to obliterate the witness to his thieving? not that it shouldn't have worked of course since Lucas really should have died as soon as the first white man came in sight of him standing over Vinson's body with the handle of that pistol hunching the back of his coat, but why do it this way, by the bizarre detour of fratricide? so now that we had something really heavy enough to talk to Lucas with I went straight to Hampton's house this afternoon into the kitchen and there was Hampton's cook sitting on one side of the table and Lucas on the other eating greens and cornbread not from a plate but out of the two-gallon pot itself and I said,

'"And you let him catch you—and I dont mean Crawford——' and he said,

'"No. I means Vinson too. Only it was too late then, the truck was done already loaded and pulling out fast without no lights burning or nothing and he said Whose truck is that? and I never said nothing."

'"All right," I said. "Then what?"

'"That's all," Lucas said. "Nothing."

'"Didn't he have a gun?"

'"I dont know," Lucas said. "He had a stick:" and I said,

'"All right. Go on:" and he said,

'"Nothing. He just stood there a minute with the stick drawed back and said Tell me whose truck that was and I never said nothing and he lowered the stick back down and turned and then I never saw him no more."

'"So you took your pistol," I said, "and went——" and he said,

'"I never had to. He come to me, I mean Crawford this time, at my house the next night and was going to pay me to tell him whose truck that was, a heap of money, fifty dollars, he showed it to me and I said I hadn't decided yet whose truck it was and he said he would leave me the money anyhow while I decided and I said I had already decided what I was going to do, I would wait until tomorrow—that was Friday night—for some kind of a evidence that Mr Workitt and Vinson had got their share of that missing timber money."

'"Yes?" I said. "Then what?"

'"Then I would go and tell Mr Workitt he better——"

'"Say that again," I said. "Slow."

'"Tell Mr Workitt he better count his boards."

'"And you, a Negro, were going up to a white man and tell him his niece's sons were stealing from him—and a Beat Four white man on top of that. Dont you know what would have happened to you?"

'"It never had no chance," he said. "Because it was the next day—Sat-dy—I got the message—" and I should have known then about the pistol because obviously Gowrie knew about it; his message couldn't have been *have replaced stolen money, would like your personal approval, bring your pistol and be sociable*—something like that so I said,

'"But why the pistol?" and he said,

'"It was Sat-dy," and I said,

'"Yes, the ninth. But why the pistol?" and then I understood; I said: "I see. You wear the pistol when you dress up on Saturday just like old Carothers did before he gave it to you:" and he said,

'"Sold it to me," and I said,

'"All right, go on," and he said,

'"—got the message to meet him at the store only——"' and now his uncle struck the match again and puffed the pipe still talking, talking through the pipe stem with the smoke as though you were watching the words themselves: 'Only he never got to the store, Crawford met him in the woods sitting on a stump beside the path waiting for him almost before Lucas had left home good and now it was Crawford about the pistol, right off before Lucas could say good afternoon or were Vinson and Mr Workitt glad to get the money or anything, saying "Even if it will still shoot you probably couldn't hit anything with it" and so you can probably finish it yourself; Lucas said how Crawford finally put up a half dollar that Lucas couldn't hit the stump from fifteen feet away and Lucas hit it and Crawford gave him the half dollar and they walked on the other two miles toward the store until Crawford told Lucas to wait there, that Mr Workitt was sending a signed receipt for his share of the missing lumber to the store and Crawford would go and fetch it back so Lucas could see it with his own eyes and I said,

'"And you didn't suspicion anything even then?" and he said,

'"No. He cussed me so natural." And at least you can finish that, no need to prove any quarrel between Vinson and Crawford nor rack your brains very deep to imagine what Crawford said and did to have Vinson waiting at the store and then send him in front along the path since no more than this will do it: "All right. I've got him. If he still wont tell whose truck that was we'll beat it out of him:" because that doesn't really matter either, enough that the next Lucas saw was Vinson coming down the path from the store in a good deal of a hurry Lucas said but probably what he meant was impatient, puzzled and annoyed both but probably mostly annoyed, probably doing exactly what Lucas was doing: waiting for the other to speak and explain except that Vinson quit waiting first according to Lucas, still walking saying getting as far as "So you changed your mind——" when Lucas said he tripped over something and kind of bucked down onto his face and presently Lucas remembered that he had heard the shot and realised that what Vinson had tripped over was his brother Crawford, then the rest of them were there Lucas said before he even had time to hear them running through the woods and I said,

'"I reckon it looked to you right then that you were getting ready to trip pretty bad over Vinson, old Skipworth and Adam Fraser or not" but at least I didn't say But why didn't you explain then and so at least Lucas didn't have to say Explain what to who: and so he was all right— I dont mean Lucas of course, I mean Crawford, no mere child of misfortune he——' and there it was again and this time he knew what it was, Miss Habersham had done something he didn't know what, no sound and she hadn't moved and it wasn't even that she had got any stiller but something had occurred, not something happened to her from the outside in but something from the inside outward as though she not only hadn't been surprised by it but had decreed authorised it but she hadn't moved at all not even to take an extra breath and his uncle hadn't even noticed that much '—but rather chosen and elected peculiar and unique out of man by the gods themselves to prove not to themselves because they had never doubted it but to man by this his lowest common denominator that he has a soul, driven at last to murder his brother——'

'He put him in quicksand,' Miss Habersham said.

'Yes,' his uncle said. 'Ghastly wasn't it.—by the simple mischance of an old Negro man's insomnambulism and then having got away with that by means of a plan a scheme so simple and water-tight in its biological and geographical psychology as to be what Chick here would call a natural, then to be foiled here by the fact that four years ago a child whose presence in the world he was not even aware of fell into a creek in the presence of that same Negro insomnambulist because this part we dont really know either and with Jake Montgomery in his present condition we probably never will though that doesn't really matter either since the fact still remains, why else was he in Vinson's grave except that in buying the lumber from Crawford (we found that out by a telephone call to the lumber's ultimate consignee in Memphis this afternoon) Jake Montgomery knew where it came from too since knowing that would have been Jake's nature and character too and indeed a factor in his middleman's profit and so when Vinson Crawford's partner tripped suddenly on death in the woods behind Fraser's store Jake didn't need a crystal ball to read that either and so if this be surmise then make the most of it or give Mr Hampton and me a better and we'll swap, Jake knew about Buddy McCallum's old war trophy too and I like to think for Crawford's sake——' and there it was again and still no outward sign but this time his uncle saw or felt or sensed (or however it was) it too and stopped and even for a second seemed about to speak then in the next one forgot it apparently, talking again: '—that maybe Jake named the price of his silence and even collected it or an installment on it perhaps intending all the time to convict Crawford of the murder, perhaps with his contacts all established to get still more money or perhaps he didn't like Crawford and wanted revenge or perhaps a purist he drew the line at murder and simply dug Vinson up to load him on the mule and take him in to the sheriff but anyway on the night after the funeral somebody with a conceivable reason for digging Vinson up dug him up, which must have been Jake, and somebody who not only didn't want Vinson dug up but had a conceivable reason to be watching the someone who would have had a conceivable reason for digging him up, knew that he had been dug up within in—you said it was about ten when you and Aleck Sander parked the truck and it got dark enough for digging up graves about seven that night so that leaves three hours—and that's what I mean about Crawford,' his uncle said and this time he noticed that his uncle had even stopped, expecting it and it came but still no sound no movement, the hat immobile and exact the neat precision of the clasped gloves and the handbag on her lap the shoes planted and motionless side by side as if she had placed them into a chalked diagram on the floor: '—watching there in the weeds behind the fence seeing himself not merely betrayed out of the blackmail but all the agony and suspense to go through again not to mention the physical labor who since one man already knew that the body couldn't bear examination by trained policemen, could never know how many others might know or suspect so the body would have to come out of the grave now though at least he had help here whether the help knew it or not so he probably waited until Jake had the body out and was all ready to load it onto the mule (and we found that out too, it was the Gowrie's plow mule, the same one the twins were riding this morning; Jake borrowed it himself late that Sunday afternoon and when you guess which Gowrie he borrowed it from you'll be right: it was Crawford) and he wouldn't have risked the pistol now anyway anymore than he would have used it if he could, who would rather have paid Jake over again the amount of the blackmail for the privilege of using whatever it was he crushed Jake's skull with and put him into the coffin and filled the grave back up—and here it is again, the desperate the dreadful urgency, the loneliness the pariah-hood having not only the horror and repudiation of all man against him but having to struggle with the sheer inertia of earth and the terrible heedless rush of time but even beating all that coalition at last, the grave decent again even to the displaced flowers and the evidence of his original crime at last disposed and secure—' and it would have been again but this time his uncle didn't pause '— then to straighten up at last and for the first time draw a full breath since the moment when Jake had approached him rubbing his thumb against the tips of the same fingers—and then to hear whatever it was that sent him plunging back up the hill then crawling creeping to lie once more panting but this time not merely in rage and terror but in almost incredulous disbelief that one single man could be subject to this much bad luck, watching you three not only undo his work for the second time but double it now since you not only exposed Jake Montgomery but you refilled the grave and even put the flowers back: who couldn't afford to let his brother Vinson be found in that grave but durst not let Jake Montgomery be found in it when (as he must have known) Hope Hampton got there tomorrow:' and stopped this time waiting for her to say it and she did:

'He put his brother in quicksand.'

'Ah,' his uncle said. 'That moment may come to anyone when simply nothing remains to be done with your brother or husband or uncle or cousin or mother-in-law except destroy them. But you dont put them in quicksand. Is that it?'

'He put him in quicksand,' she said with calm and implacable finality, not moving nor stirring except her lips to speak until then she raised her hand and opened the watch pinned to her bosom and looked at it.

'They haven't reached Whiteleaf bottom yet,' his uncle said. 'But dont worry, he'll be there, my message might have reached him but no man in this county can possibly escape hearing anything ever told Willy Ingrum under the pledge of secrecy, because there's nothing else he can do you see because murderers are gamblers and like the amateur gambler the amateur murderer believes first not in his luck but in long shots, that the long shot will win simply because it's a long shot but besides that, say he already knew he was lost and nothing Lucas could testify about Jake Montgomery or anyone else could harm him further and that his one last slim chance was to get out of the country, or say he knew even that was vain, knew for sure that he was running through the last few pence and pennies of what he could still call freedom, suppose he even knew for certain that tomorrow's sun would not even rise for him,—what would you want to do first, one last act and statement of your deathless principles before you left your native land for good and maybe even the world for good if your name was Gowrie and your blood and thinking and acting had been Gowrie all your life and you knew or even only believed or even only hoped that at a certain moment in an automobile creeping in low gear through a lonely midnight creek bottom would be the cause and reason for all your agony and frustration and outrage and grief and shame and irreparable loss and that not even a white man but a nigger and you still had the pistol with at least one of the old original ten German bullets in it.—But dont worry,' he said quickly: 'Dont worry about Mr Hampton. He probably wont even draw his pistol, I aint certain in fact that he has one because he has a way of carrying right along with him into all situations maybe not peace, maybe not abatement of the base emotions but at least a temporary stalemate of crude and violent behavior just by moving slow and breathing hard, this happened two or three terms ago back in the twenties, a Frenchman's Bend lady naming no names at feud with another lady over something which began (we understood) over the matter of a prize cake at a church supper bazaar, whose—the second lady's—husband owned the still which had been supplying Frenchman's Bend with whiskey for years bothering nobody until the first lady made official demand on Mr Hampton to go out there and destroy the still and arrest the operator and then in about a week or ten days came in to town herself and told him that if he didn't she was going to report him to the governor of the state and the president in Washington so Hope went that time, she had not only given him explicit directions but he said there was a path to it knee-deep in places where it had been trodden for years beneath the weight of stopper-full gallon jugs so that you could have followed it even without the flashlight which he had and sure enough there was the still in as nice a location as you could want, cozy and sheltered yet accessible too with a fire burning under the kettle and a Negro tending it who of course didn't know who owned it nor ran it nor anything about it even before he recognised Hampton's size and finally even saw his badge: who Hope said offered him a drink first and then did fetch him a gourd of branch water and then made him comfortable sitting against a tree, even chunking the fire up to dry his wet feet while he waited for the owner to come back, quite comfortable Hope said, the two of them there by the fire in the darkness talking about one thing and another and the Negro asking him from time to time if he wouldn't like another gourd of water until Hampton said the mockingbird was making so confounded much racket that finally he opened his eyes blinking for a while in the sunlight until he got them focussed and there the mockingbird was on a limb not three feet above his head and before they loaded up the still to move it away somebody had gone to the nearest house and fetched back a quilt to spread over him and a pillow to put under his head and Hope said he noticed the pillow even had a fresh slip on it when he took it and the quilt to Varner's store to be returned with thanks to whoever owned them and came on back to town. And another time——'

'I'm not worrying,' Miss Habersham said.

'Of course not,' his uncle said. 'Because I know Hope Hampton——'

'Yes,' Miss Habersham said. 'I know Lucas Beauchamp.'

'Oh,' his uncle said. Then he said, 'Yes.' Then he said, 'Of course.' Then he said, 'Let's ask Chick to plug in the kettle and we'll have coffee while we wait, what do you think?'

'That will be nice,' Miss Habersham said.

XI.

FINALLY he even got up and went to one of the front windows looking down into the Square because if Monday was stock-auction and trade day then Saturday was certainly radio and automobile day; on Monday they were mostly men and they drove in and parked the cars and trucks around the Square and went straight to the sales barns and stayed there until time to come back to the Square and eat dinner and then went back to the sales barns and stayed there until time to come and get in the cars and trucks and drive home before full dark. But not Saturday; they were men and women and children too then and the old people and the babies and the young couples to buy the licenses for the weddings in the country churches tomorrow, come in to do a week's shopping for staples and delicacies like bananas and twenty-five cent sardines and machine-made cakes and pies and clothes and stockings and feed and fertilizer and plow-gear: which didn't take long for any of them and no time at all for some of them so that some of the cars never really became permanently stationary at all and within an hour or so many of the others had joined them moving steadily processional and quite often in second gear because of their own density round and round the Square then out to the end of the tree-dense residential streets to turn and come back and circle round and round the Square again as if they had come all the way in from the distant circumambient settlements and crossroads stores and isolate farms for that one purpose of enjoying the populous coming and going and motion and recognising one another and the zephyr-like smoothness of the paved streets and alleys themselves as well as looking at the neat new painted small houses among their minute neat yards and flowerbeds and garden ornaments which in the last few years had come to line them as dense as sardines or bananas; as a result of which the radios had to play louder than ever through their supercharged amplifiers to be heard above the mutter of exhausts and swish of tires and the grind of gears and the constant horns, so that long before you even reached the Square you not only couldn't tell where one began and another left off but you didn't even have to try to distinguish what any of them were playing or trying to sell you.

But this one seemed to be even a Saturday among Saturdays so that presently his uncle had got up from behind the table and come to the other window too, which was why they happened to see Lucas before he reached the office though that was not yet; he was still standing (so he thought) alone at the window looking down into the Square thronged and jammed as he couldn't remember it before—the bright sunny almost hot air heavy with the smell of blooming locust from the courthouse yard, the sidewalks dense and massed and slow with people black and white come in to town today as if by concert to collect at compound and so discharge not merely from balance but from remembering too that other Saturday only seven days ago of which they had been despoiled by an old Negro man who had got himself into the position where they had had to believe he had murdered a white man—that Saturday and Sunday and Monday only a week past yet which might never have been since nothing of them remained: Vinson and his brother Crawford (in his suicide's grave and strangers would be asking for weeks yet what sort of jail and sheriff Yoknapatawpha County had where a man locked in it for murder could still get hold of a Luger pistol even if it didn't have but one bullet in it and for that many weeks nobody in Yoknapatawpha County would still be able to tell him) side by side near their mother's headstone in Caledonia churchyard and Jake Montgomery over in Crossman County where somebody probably claimed him too for the same reason somebody did Crawford and Miss Habersham sitting in her own hall now mending the stockings until time to feed the chickens and Aleck Sander down there on the Square in a flash Saturday shirt and a pair of zoot pants and a handful of peanuts or bananas too and he standing at the window watching the dense unhurried unhurryable throng and the busy almost ubiquitous flash and gleam on Willy Ingrum's cap-badge but mostly and above all the motion and the noise, the radios and the automobiles—the jukeboxes in the drugstore and the poolhall and the cafe and the bellowing amplifiers on the outside walls not only of the record-andsheetmusic store but the army-and-navy supply store and both feed stores and (that they might falter) somebody standing on a bench in the courthouse yard making a speech into another one with a muzzle like a siege gun bolted to the top of an automobile, not to mention the ones which would be running in the apartments and the homes where the housewives and the maids made up the beds and swept and prepared to cook dinner so that nowhere inside the town's uttermost ultimate corporate rim should man woman or child citizen or guest or stranger be threatened with one second of silence; and the automobiles because explicitly speaking he couldn't see the Square at all: only the dense impenetrable mass of tops and hoods moving in double line at a snail's crawl around the Square in a sharp invisible aura of carbon monoxide and blatting horns and a light intermittent clashing of bumpers, creeping slowly one by one into the streets leading away from the Square while the other opposite line crept as slowly one by one into it; so dense and slow dowelled into one interlocked mosaic so infinitesimal of motion as to be scarcely worthy of the word that you could have crossed the Square walking on them—or even out to the edge of town for that matter or even on a horse for that matter, Highboy for instance to whom the five or six foot jump from one top across the intervening hood to the next top would have been nothing or say the more or less motionless tops were laid with one smooth continuous surface of planks like a bridge and not Highboy but a gaited horse or a horse with one gait: a hard driving rack seven feet in the air like a bird and travelling fast as a hawk or an eagle: with a feeling in the pit of his stomach as if a whole bottle of hot sodapop had exploded in it thinking of the gallant the splendid the really magnificent noise a horse would make racking in any direction on a loose plank bridge two miles long when suddenly his uncle at the other window said,

'The American really loves nothing but his automobile: not his wife his child nor his country nor even his bank-account first (in fact he doesn't really love that bank-account nearly as much as foreigners like to think because he will spend almost any or all of it for almost anything provided it is valueless enough) but his motorcar. Because the automobile has become our national sex symbol. We cannot really enjoy anything unless we can go up an alley for it. Yet our whole background and raising and training forbids the subrose and surreptitious. So we have to divorce our wife today in order to remove from our mistress the odium of mistress in order to divorce our wife tomorrow in order to remove from our mistress and so on. As a result of which the American woman has become cold and undersexed; she has projected her libido onto the automobile not only because its glitter and gadgets and mobility pander to her vanity and incapacity (because of the dress decreed upon her by the national retailers association) to walk but because it will not maul her and tousle her, get her all sweaty and disarranged. So in order to capture and master anything at all of her anymore the American man has got to make that car his own. Which is why let him live in a rented rathole though he must he will not only own one but renew it each year in pristine virginity, lending it to no one, letting no other hand ever know the last secret forever chaste forever wanton intimacy of its pedals and levers, having nowhere to go in it himself and even if he did he would not go where scratch or blemish might deface it, spending all Sunday morning washing and polishing and waxing it because in doing that he is caressing the body of the woman who has long since now denied him her bed.'

'That's not true,' he said.

'I am fifty-plus years old,' his uncle said. 'I spent the middle fifteen of them fumbling beneath skirts. My experience was that few of them were interested in love or sex either. They wanted to be married.'

'I still dont believe it,' he said.

'That's right,' his uncle said. 'Dont. And even when you are fifty and plus, still refuse to believe it.' And that was when they saw Lucas crossing the Square, probably at the same time—the cocked hat and the thin fierce glint of the tilted gold toothpick and he said,

'Where do you suppose it was all the time? I never did see it. Surely he had it with him that afternoon, a Saturday when he was not only wearing that black suit but he even had the pistol? Surely he never left home without the toothpick too.'

'Didn't I tell you?' his uncle said. 'That was the first thing he did when Mr Hampton walked into Skipworth's house where Skipworth had Lucas handcuffed to the bedpost—gave Hampton the toothpick and told him to keep it until he called for it.'

'Oh,' he said. 'He's coming up here.'

'Yes,' his uncle said. 'To gloat. Oh,' he said quickly, 'he's a gentleman; he wont remind me to my face that I was wrong; he's just going to ask me how much he owes me as his lawyer.'

Then in his chair beside the water cooler and his uncle once more behind the table they heard the long airy rumble and creek of the stairs then Lucas' feet steadily though with no haste and Lucas came tieless and even collarless this time except for the button but with an old-time white waistcoat not soiled so much as stained under the black coat and the worn gold loop of the watch-chain—the same face which he had seen for the first time when he climbed dripping up out of the icy creek that morning four years ago, unchanged, to which nothing had happened since not even age—in the act of putting the toothpick into one of the upper waistcoat pockets as he came through the door, saying generally,

'Gentle-men,' then to him: 'Young man——' courteous and intractable, more than bland: downright cheerful almost, removing the raked swagger of the hat: 'You aint fell in no more creeks lately, have you?'

'That's right,' he said. 'I'm saving that until you get some more ice on yours.'

'You'll be welcome without waiting for a freeze,' Lucas said.

'Have a seat, Lucas,' his uncle said but he had already begun to, taking the same hard chair beside the door which nobody else but Miss Habersham had ever chosen, a little akimbo as though he were posing for a camera, the hat laid crownup back across his forearm, looking at both of them still and saying again,

'Gentle-men.'

'You didn't come here for me to tell you what to do so I'm going to tell you anyway,' his uncle said.

Lucas blinked rapidly once. He looked at his uncle. 'I cant

say I did.' Then he said cheerily: 'But I'm always ready to listen to good advice.'

'Go and see Miss Habersham,' his uncle said.

Lucas looked at his uncle. He blinked twice this time. 'I aint much of a visiting man,' he said.

'You were not much of a hanging man either,' his uncle said. 'But you dont need me to tell you how close you came.'

'No,' Lucas said. 'I dont reckon I do. What do you want me to tell her?'

'You cant,' his uncle said. 'You dont know how to say thank you. I've got that fixed too. Take her some flowers.'

'Flowers?' Lucas said. 'I aint had no flowers to speak of since Molly died.'

'And that too,' his uncle said. 'I'll telephone home. My sister'll have a bunch ready. Chick'll drive you up in my car to get them and then take you out to Miss Habersham's gate.'

'Nemmine that,' Lucas said. 'Once I got the flowers I can walk.'

'And you can throw the flowers away too,' his uncle said. 'But I know you wont do one and I dont think you'll do the other in the car with Chick.'

'Well,' Lucas said. 'If wont nothing else satisfy you——' (And when he got back to town and finally found a place three blocks away to park the car and mounted the stairs again his uncle was striking the match, holding it to the pipe and speaking through with into the smoke: 'You and Booker T. Washington, no that's wrong, you and Miss Habersham and Aleck Sander and Sheriff Hampton, and Booker T. Washington because he did only what everybody expected of him so there was no real reason why he should have while you all did not only what nobody expected you to but all Jefferson and Yoknapatawpha County would have risen in active concord for once to prevent you if they had known in time and even a year from now some ((when and if they do at all)) will remember with disapproval and distaste not that you were ghouls nor that you defied your color because they would have passed either singly but that you violated a white grave to save a nigger so you had every reason why you should have. Just dont stop:' and he:

'You dont think that just because it's Saturday afternoon

again somebody is hiding behind Miss Habersham's jasmine bush with a pistol aimed at her waiting for Lucas to walk up to the front steps. Besides Lucas didn't have his pistol today and besides that Crawford Gowrie——' and his uncle:

'Why not, what's out yonder in the ground at Caledonia Church was Crawford Gowrie for only a second or two last Saturday and Lucas Beauchamp will be carrying his pigment into ten thousand situations a wiser man would have avoided and a lighter escaped ten thousand times after what was Lucas Beauchamp for a second or so last Saturday is in the ground at his Caledonia Church too, because that Yoknapatawpha County which would have stopped you and Aleck Sander and Miss Habersham last Sunday night are right actually, Lucas's life the breathing and eating and sleeping is of no importance just as yours and mine are not but his unchallengeable right to it in peace and security and in fact this earth would be much more comfortable with a good deal fewer Beauchamps and Stevenses and Mallisons of all colors in it if there were only some painless way to efface not the clumsy room-devouring carcasses which can be done but the memory which cannot—that inevictible immortal memory awareness of having once been alive which exists forever still ten thousand years afterward in ten thousand recollections of injustice and suffering, too many of us not because of the room we take up but because we are willing to sell liberty short at any tawdry price for the sake of what we call our own which is a constitutional statutory license to pursue each his private postulate of happiness and contentment regardless of grief and cost even to the crucifixion of someone whose nose or pigment we dont like and even these can be coped with provided that few of others who believe that a human life is valuable simply because it has a right to keep on breathing no matter what pigment its lungs distend or nose inhales the air and are willing to defend that right at any price, it doesn't take many three were enough last Sunday night even one can be enough and with enough ones willing to be more than grieved and shamed Lucas will no longer run the risk of needing without warning to be saved:' and he:

'Maybe not three the other night. One and two halves would be nearer right:' and his uncle:

'I said it's all right to be proud. It's all right even to boast. Just dont stop.')——and came to the table and laid the hat on it and took from the inside coat pocket a leather snap-purse patina-ed like old silver and almost as big as Miss Habersham's handbag and said,

'I believe you got a little bill against me.'

'What for?' his uncle said.

'For representing my case,' Lucas said. 'Name whatever your fee is within reason. I want to pay it.'

'Not me,' his uncle said. 'I didn't do anything.'

'I sent for you,' Lucas said. 'I authorised you. How much do I owe you?'

'Nothing,' his uncle said. 'Because I didn't believe you. That boy there is the reason you're walking around today.'

Now Lucas looked at him, holding the purse in one hand and the other hand poised to unsnap it—the same face to which it was not that nothing had happened but which had simply refused to accept it; now he opened the purse. 'All right. I'll pay him.'

'And I'll have you both arrested,' his uncle said, 'you for corrupting a minor and him for practising law without a license.'

Lucas looked back to his uncle; he watched them staring at one another. Then once more Lucas blinked twice. 'All right,' he said. 'I'll pay the expenses then. Name your expenses at anything within reason and let's get this thing settled.'

'Expenses?' his uncle said. 'Yes, I had an expense sitting here last Tuesday trying to write down all the different things you finally told me in such a way that Mr Hampton could get enough sense out of it to discharge you from the jail and so the more I tried it the worse it got and the worse it got the worse I got until when I came to again my fountain pen was sticking up on its point in the floor down here like an arrow. Of course the paper belongs to the county but the fountain pen was mine and it cost me two dollars to have a new point put in it. You owe me two dollars.'

'Two dollars?' Lucas said. He blinked twice again. Then he blinked twice again. 'Just two dollars?' Now he just blinked once, then he did something with his breath: not a sigh, simply a discharge of it, putting his first two fingers into the purse: 'That dont sound like much to me but then I'm a farming man and you're a lawing man and whether you know your business or not I reckon it aint none of my red wagon as the music box says to try to learn you different:' and drew from the purse a worn bill crumpled into a ball not much larger than a shriveled olive and opened it enough to read it then opened it out and laid it on the desk and from the purse took a half dollar and laid it on the desk then counted onto the desk from the purse one by one four dimes and two nickels and then counted them again with his forefinger, moving them one by one about half an inch, his lips moving under the moustache, the purse still open in the other hand, then he picked up two of the dimes and a nickel and put them into the hand holding the open purse and took from the purse a quarter and put it on the desk and looked down at the coins for a rapid second then put the two dimes and the nickel back on the desk and took up the half dollar and put it back into the purse.

'That aint but six bits,' his uncle said.

'Nemmine that,' Lucas said and took up the quarter and dropped it back into the purse and closed it and watching Lucas he realised that the purse had at least two different compartments and maybe more, a second almost elbow-deep section opening beneath Lucas' fingers and for a time Lucas stood looking down into it exactly as you would look down at your reflection in a well then took from that compartment a knotted soiled cloth tobacco sack bulging and solid looking which struck on the desk top with a dull thick chink.

'That makes it out,' he said. 'Four bits in pennies. I was aiming to take them to the bank but you can save me the trip. You want to count um?'

'Yes,' his uncle said. 'But you're the one paying the money. You're the one to count them.'

'It's fifty of them,' Lucas said.

'This is business,' his uncle said. So Lucas unknotted the sack and dumped the pennies out on the desk and counted them one by one moving each one with his forefinger into the first small mass of dimes and nickels, counting aloud, then snapped the purse shut and put it back inside his coat and with the other hand shoved the whole mass of coins and the crumpled bill across the table until the desk blotter stopped them and took a bandana handkerchief from the side pocket of the coat and wiped his hands and put the handkerchief back and stood again intractable and calm and not looking at either of them now while the fixed blaring of the radios and the blatting creep of the automobile horns and all the rest of the whole County's Saturday uproar came up on the bright afternoon.

'Now what?' his uncle said. 'What are you waiting for now?'

'My receipt,' Lucas said.

REQUIEM FOR A NUN

Contents

ACT I

The Courthouse
(A Name for the City)

THE COURTHOUSE is less old than the town, which began somewhere under the turn of the century as a Chickasaw Agency trading-post and so continued for almost thirty years before it discovered, not that it lacked a depository for its records and certainly not that it needed one, but that only by creating or anyway decreeing one, could it cope with a situation which otherwise was going to cost somebody money;

The settlement had the records; even the simple dispossession of Indians begot in time a minuscule of archive, let alone the normal litter of man's ramshackle confederation against environment—that time and that wilderness;—in this case, a meagre, fading, dogeared, uncorrelated, at times illiterate sheaf of land grants and patents and transfers and deeds, and tax- and militia-rolls, and bills of sale for slaves, and counting-house lists of spurious currency and exchange rates, and liens and mortgages, and listed rewards for escaped or stolen Negroes and other livestock, and diary-like annotations of births and marriages and deaths and public hangings and land-auctions, accumulating slowly for those three decades in a sort of iron pirate's chest in the back room of the postoffice-tradingpost-store, until that day thirty years later when, because of a jailbreak compounded by an ancient monster iron padlock transported a thousand miles by horseback from Carolina, the box was removed to a small new leanto room like a wood- or tool-shed built two days ago against one outside wall of the morticed-log mud-chinked shake-down jail; and thus was born the Yoknapatawpha County courthouse: by simple fortuity, not only less old than even the jail, but come into existence at all by chance and accident: the box containing the documents not moved from any place, but simply to one; removed from the trading-post back room not for any reason inherent in either the back room or the box, but on the contrary: which—the box—was not only in nobody's way in the back room, it was even missed when gone since it had served as another seat or stool among the powder- and whiskey-kegs and firkins of salt and lard about the stove on winter nights; and was moved at all for the simple reason that suddenly the settlement (overnight it would become a town without having been a village; one day in about a hundred years it would wake frantically from its communal slumber into a rash of Rotary and Lion Clubs and Chambers of Commerce and City Beautifuls: a furious beating of hollow drums toward nowhere, but merely to sound louder than the next little human clotting to its north or south or east or west, dubbing itself city as Napoleon dubbed himself emperor and defending the expedient by padding its census rolls—a fever, a delirium in which it would confound forever seething with motion and motion with progress. But that was a hundred years away yet; now it was frontier, the men and women pioneers, tough, simple, and durable, seeking money or adventure or freedom or simple escape, and not too particular how they did it.) discovered itself faced not so much with a problem which had to be solved, as a Damocles sword of dilemma from which it had to save itself;

Even the jailbreak was fortuity: a gang—three or four—of Natchez Trace bandits (twenty-five years later legend would begin to affirm, and a hundred years later would still be at it, that two of the bandits were the Harpes themselves, Big Harpe anyway, since the circumstances, the method of the breakout left behind like a smell, an odor, a kind of gargantuan and bizarre playfulness at once humorous and terrifying, as if the settlement had fallen, blundered, into the notice or range of an idle and whimsical giant. Which—that they were the Harpes—was impossible, since the Harpes and even the last of Mason's ruffians were dead or scattered by this time, and the robbers would have had to belong to John Murrel's organization—if they needed to belong to any at all other than the simple fraternity of rapine.) captured by chance by an incidental band of civilian more-or-less militia and brought in to the Jefferson jail because it was the nearest one, the militia band being part of a general muster at Jefferson two days before for a Fourth of July barbecue, which by the second day had been refined by hardy elimination into one drunken brawling which rendered even the hardiest survivors vulnerable enough to be ejected from the settlement by the civilian residents, the band which was to make the capture having been carried, still comatose, in one of the evicting wagons to a swamp four miles from Jefferson known as Hurricane Bottoms, where they made camp to regain their strength or at least their legs, and where that night the four—or three—bandits, on their way across country to their hideout from their last exploit on the Trace, stumbled onto the campfire. And here report divided; some said that the sergeant in command of the militia recognised one of the bandits as a deserter from his corps, others said that one of the bandits recognised in the sergeant a former follower of his, the bandit's, trade. Anyway, on the fourth morning all of them, captors and prisoners, returned to Jefferson in a group, some said in confederation now seeking more drink, others said that the captors brought their prizes back to the settlement in revenge for having been evicted from it. Because these were frontier, pioneer, times, when personal liberty and freedom were almost a physical condition like fire or flood, and no community was going to interfere with anyone's morals as long as the amoralist practised somewhere else, and so Jefferson, being neither on the Trace nor the River but lying about midway between, naturally wanted no part of the underworld of either;

But they had some of it now, taken as it were by surprise, unawares, without warning to prepare and fend off. They put the bandits into the log-and-mudchinking jail, which until now had had no lock at all since its clients so far had been amateurs—local brawlers and drunkards and runaway slaves—for whom a single heavy wooden beam in slots across the outside of the door like on a corncrib, had sufficed. But they had now what might be four—three—Dillingers or Jesse Jameses of the time, with rewards on their heads. So they locked the jail; they bored an auger hole through the door and another through the jamb and passed a length of heavy chain through the holes and sent a messenger on the run across to the postoffice-store to fetch the ancient Carolina lock from the last Nashville mail-pouch—the iron monster weighing almost fifteen pounds, with a key almost as long as a bayonet, not just the only lock in that part of the country, but the oldest lock in that cranny of the United States, brought there by one of the three men who were what was to be Yoknapatawpha County's coeval pioneers and settlers, leaving in it the three oldest names—Alexander Holston, who came as half groom and half bodyguard to Doctor Samuel Habersham, and half nurse and half tutor to the doctor's eight-year-old motherless son, the three of them riding horeseback across Tennessee from the Cumberland Gap along with Louis Grenier, the Huguenot younger son who brought the first slaves into the country and was granted the first big land patent and so became the first cotton planter; while Doctor Habersham, with his worn black bag of pills and knives and his brawny taciturn bodyguard and his half orphan child, became the settlement itself (for a time, before it was named, the settlement was known as Doctor Habersham's, then Habersham's, then simply Habersham; a hundred years later, during a schism between two ladies' clubs over the naming of the streets in order to get free mail delivery, a movement was started, first, to change the name back to Habersham; then, failing that, to divide the town in two and call one half of it Habersham after the old pioneer doctor and founder)—friend of old Issetibbeha, the Chickasaw chief (the motherless Habersham boy, now a man of twenty-five, married one of Issetibbeha's grand-daughters and in the thirties emigrated to Oklahoma with his wife's dispossessed people), first unofficial, then official Chickasaw agent until he resigned in a letter of furious denunciation addressed to the President of the United States himself; and—his charge and pupil a man now—Alexander Holston became the settlement's first publican, establishing the tavern still known as the Holston House, the original log walls and puncheon floors and hand-morticed joints of which are still buried somewhere beneath the modern pressed glass and brick veneer and neon tubes. The lock was his:

Fifteen pounds of useless iron lugged a thousand miles through a desert of precipice and swamp, of flood and drouth and wild beasts and wild Indians and wilder white men, displacing that fifteen pounds better given to food or seed to plant food or even powder to defend with, to become a fixture, a kind of landmark, in the bar of a wilderness ordinary, locking and securing nothing, because there was nothing behind the heavy bars and shutters needing further locking and securing; not even a paper weight because the only papers in the Holston House were the twisted spills in an old powder horn above the mantel for lighting tobacco; always a little in the way, since it had constantly to be moved: from bar to shelf to mantel then back to bar again until they finally thought about putting it on the bi-monthly mail-pouch; familiar, known, presently the oldest unchanged thing in the settlement, older than the people since Issetibbeha and Doctor Habersham were dead, and Alexander Holston was an old man crippled with arthritis, and Louis Grenier had a settlement of his own on his vast plantation, half of which was not even in Yoknapatawpha County, and the settlement rarely saw him; older than the town, since there were new names in it now even when the old blood ran in them—Sartoris and Stevens, Compson and McCaslin and Sutpen and Coldfield—and you no longer shot a bear or deer or wild turkey simply by standing for a while in your kitchen door, not to mention the pouch of mail—letters and even newspapers—which came from Nashville every two weeks by a special rider who did nothing else and was paid a salary for it by the Federal government; and that was the second phase of the monster Carolina lock's transubstantiation into the Yoknapatawpha County courthouse;

The pouch didn't always reach the settlement every two weeks, nor even always every month. But sooner or later it did, and everybody knew it would, because it—the cowhide saddlebag not even large enough to hold a full change of clothing, containing three or four letters and half that many badly-printed one- and two-sheet newspapers already three or four months out of date and usually half and sometimes wholly misinformed or incorrect to begin with—was the

United States, the power and the will to liberty, owning liegence to no man, bringing even into that still almost pathless wilderness the thin peremptory voice of the nation which had wrenched its freedom from one of the most powerful peoples on earth and then again within the same lifespan successfully defended it; so peremptory and audible that the man who carried the pouch on the galloping horse didn't even carry any arms except a tin horn, traversing month after month, blatantly, flagrantly, almost contemptuously, a region where for no more than the boots on his feet, men would murder a traveller and gut him like a bear or deer or fish and fill the cavity with rocks and sink the evidence in the nearest water; not even deigning to pass quietly where other men, even though armed and in parties, tried to move secretly or at least without uproar, but instead announcing his solitary advent as far ahead of himself as the ring of the horn would carry. So it was not long before Alexander Holston's lock had moved to the mail-pouch. Not that the pouch needed one, having come already the three hundred miles from Nashville without a lock. (It had been projected at first that the lock remain on the pouch constantly. That is, not just while the pouch was in the settlement, but while it was on the horse between Nashville and the settlement too. The rider refused, succinctly, in three words, one of which was printable. His reason was the lock's weight. They pointed out to him that this would not hold water, since not only—the rider was a frail irascible little man weighing less than a hundred pounds—would the fifteen pounds of lock even then fail to bring his weight up to that of a normal adult male, the added weight of the lock would merely match that of the pistols which his employer, the United States government, believed he carried and even paid him for having done so, the rider's reply to this being succinct too though not so glib: that the lock weighed fifteen pounds either at the back door of the store in the settlement, or at that of the postoffice in Nashville. But since Nashville and the settlement were three hundred miles apart, by the time the horse had carried it from one to the other, the lock weighed fifteen pounds to the mile times three hundred miles, or forty-five hundred pounds. Which was manifest nonsense, a physical impossibility either in lock or horse. Yet indubitably fifteen pounds times three hundred miles was forty-five hundred something, either pounds or miles,—especially as while they were still trying to unravel it, the rider repeated his first three succinct—two unprintable—words.) So less than ever would the pouch need a lock in the back room of the trading-post, surrounded and enclosed once more by civilization, where its very intactness, its presence to receive a lock, proved its lack of that need during the three hundred miles of rapine-haunted Trace; needing a lock as little as it was equipped to receive one, since it had been necessary to slit the leather with a knife just under each jaw of the opening and insert the lock's iron mandible through the two slits and clash it home, so that any other hand with a similar knife could have cut the whole lock from the pouch as easily as it had been clasped onto it. So the old lock was not even a symbol of security: it was a gesture of salutation, of free men to free men, of civilization to civilization across not just the three hundred miles of wilderness to Nashville, but the fifteen hundred to Washington: of respect without servility, allegiance without abasement to the government which they had helped to found and had accepted with pride but still as free men, still free to withdraw from it at any moment when the two of them found themselves no longer compatible, the old lock meeting the pouch each time on its arrival, to clasp it in iron and inviolable symbolism, while old Alec Holston, childless bachelor, grew a little older and grayer, a little more arthritic in flesh and temper too, a little stiffer and more rigid in bone and pride too, since the lock was still his, he had merely lent it, and so in a sense he was the grandfather in the settlement of the inviolability not just of government mail, but of a free government of free men too, so long as the government remembered to let men live free, not under it but beside it;

That was the lock; they put it on the jail. They did it quickly, not even waiting until a messenger could have got back from the Holston House with old Alec's permission to remove it from the mail-pouch or use it for the new purpose. Not that he would have objected on principle nor refused his permission except by simple instinct; that is, he would probably have been the first to suggest the lock if he had known in time or thought of it first, but he would have refused at once if he thought the thing was contemplated without consulting him. Which everybody in the settlement knew, though this was not at all why they didn't wait for the messenger. In fact, no messenger had ever been sent to old Alec; they didn't have time to send one, let alone wait until he got back; they didn't want the lock to keep the bandits in, since (as was later proved) the old lock would have been no more obstacle for the bandits to pass than the customary wooden bar; they didn't need the lock to protect the settlement from the bandits, but to protect the bandits from the settlement. Because the prisoners had barely reached the settlement when it developed that there was a faction bent on lynching them at once, out of hand, without preliminary—a small but determined gang which tried to wrest the prisoners from their captors while the militia was still trying to find someone to surrender them to, and would have succeeded except for a man named Compson, who came to the settlement a few years ago with a race-horse, which he swapped to Ikkemotubbe, Issetibbeha's successor in the chiefship, for a square mile of what was to be the most valuable land in the future town of Jefferson, who, legend said, drew a pistol and held the ravishers at bay until the bandits could be got into the jail and the auger holes bored and someone sent to fetch old Alec Holston's lock. Because there were indeed new names and faces too in the settlement now—faces so new as to have (to the older residents) no discernible antecedents other than mammalinity, nor past other than the simple years which had scored them; and names so new as to have no discernible (nor discoverable either) antecedents or past at all, as though they had been invented yesterday, report dividing again: to the effect that there were more people in the settlement that day than the militia sergeant whom one or all of the bandits might recognise;

So Compson locked the jail, and a courier with the two best horses in the settlement—one to ride and one to lead—cut through the woods to the Trace to ride the hundred-odd miles to Natchez with news of the capture and authority to dicker for the reward; and that evening in the Holston House kitchen was held the settlement's first municipal meeting, prototype not only of the town council after the settlement would be a town, but of the chamber of commerce when it would begin to proclaim itself a city, with Compson presiding, not old Alec, who was quite old now, grim, taciturn, sitting even on a hot July night before a smoldering log in his vast chimney, his back even turned to the table (he was not interested in the deliberation; the prisoners were his already since his lock held them; whatever the conference decided would have to be submitted to him for ratification anyway before anyone could touch his lock to open it) around which the progenitors of the Jefferson city fathers sat in what was almost a council of war, not only discussing the collecting of the reward, but the keeping and defending it. Because there were two factions of opposition now: not only the lynching party, but the militia band too, who now claimed that as prizes the prisoners still belonged to their original captors; that they   the militia   had merely surrendered the prisoners' custody but had relinquished nothing of any reward: on the prospect of which, the militia band had got more whiskey from the trading-post store and had built a tremendous bonfire in front of the jail, around which they and the lynching party had now confederated in a wassail or conference of their own. Or so they thought. Because the truth was, that Compson, in the name of a crisis in the public peace and welfare, had made a formal demand on the professional bag of Doctor Peabody, old Doctor Habersham's successor, and the three of them—Compson, Peabody, and the post trader (his name was Ratcliffe; a hundred years later it would still exist in the county, but by that time it had passed through two inheritors who had dispensed with the eye in the transmission of words, using only the ear, so that by the time the fourth one had been compelled by simple necessity to learn to write it again, it had lost the 'c' and the final 'fe' too) added the laudanum to the keg of whiskey and sent it as a gift from the settlement to the astonished militia sergeant, and returned to the Holston House kitchen to wait until the last of the uproar died; then the law-and-order party made a rapid sortie and gathered up all the comatose opposition, lynchers and captors too, and dumped them all into the jail with the prisoners and locked the door again and went home to bed—until the next morning, when the first arrivals were met by a scene resembling an outdoor stage setting: which was how the legend of the mad Harpes started: a thing not just fantastical but incomprehensible, not just whimsical but a little terrifying (though at least it was bloodless, which would have contented neither Harpe): not just the lock gone from the door nor even just the door gone from the jail, but the entire wall gone, the mud-chinked axe-morticed logs unjointed neatly and quietly in the darkness and stacked as neatly to one side, leaving the jail open to the world like a stage on which the late insurgents still lay sprawled and various in deathlike slumber, the whole settlement gathered now to watch Compson trying to kick at least one of them awake, until one of the Holston slaves—the cook's husband, the waiter-groom-hostler—ran into the crowd shouting, 'Whar de lock, whar de lock, ole Boss say whar de lock.'

It was gone (as were three horses belonging to three of the lynching faction). They couldn't even find the heavy door and the chain, and at first they were almost betrayed into believing that the bandits had had to take the door in order to steal the chain and lock, catching themselves back from the very brink of this wanton accusation of rationality. But the lock was gone; nor did it take the settlement long to realise that it was not the escaped bandits and the aborted reward, but the lock, and not a simple situation which faced them, but a problem which threatened, the slave departing back to the Holston House at a dead run and then reappearing at the dead run almost before the door, the walls, had had time to hide him, engulf and then eject him again, darting through the crowd and up to Compson himself now, saying, 'Ole Boss say fetch de lock'——not send the lock, but bring the lock. So Compson and his lieutenants (and this was where the mail rider began to appear, or rather, to emerge—the fragile wisp of a man ageless hairless and toothless, who looked too frail even to approach a horse, let alone ride one six hundred miles every two weeks, yet who did so, and not only that but had wind enough left not only to announce and precede but even follow his passing with the jeering musical triumph of the horn:—a contempt for possible—probable—despoilers matched only by that for the official dross of which he might be despoiled, and which agreed to remain in civilised bounds only so long as the despoilers had the taste to refrain)—repaired to the kitchen where old Alec still sat before his smoldering log, his back still to the room, and still not turning it this time either. And that was all. He ordered the immediate return of his lock. It was not even an ultimatum, it was a simple instruction, a decree, impersonal, the mail rider now well into the fringe of the group, saying nothing and missing nothing, like a weightless desiccated or fossil bird, not a vulture of course nor even quite a hawk, but say a pterodactyl chick arrested just out of the egg ten glaciers ago and so old in simple infancy as to be worn and weary ancestor of all subsequent life. They pointed out to old Alec that the only reason the lock could be missing was that the bandits had not had time or been able to cut it out of the door, and that even three fleeing madmen on stolen horses would not carry a six-foot oak door very far, and that a party of Ikkemotubbe's young men were even now trailing the horses westward toward the River and that without doubt the lock would be found at any moment, probably under the first bush at the edge of the settlement: knowing better, knowing that there was no limit to the fantastic and the terrifying and the bizarre, of which the men were capable who already, just to escape from a log jail, had quietly removed one entire wall and stacked it in neat piecemeal at the roadside, and that they nor old Alec neither would ever see his lock again;

Nor did they; the rest of that afternoon and all the next day too, while old Alec still smoked his pipe in front of his smoldering log, the settlement's sheepish and raging elders hunted for it, with (by now: the next afternoon) Ikkemotubbe's Chickasaws helping too, or anyway present, watching: the wild men, the wilderness's tameless evictant children looking only the more wild and homeless for the white man's denim and butternut and felt and straw which they wore, standing or squatting or following, grave attentive and interested, while the white men sweated and cursed among the bordering thickets of their punily-clawed foothold; and always the rider, Pettigrew, ubiquitous, everywhere, not helping search himself and never in anyone's way, but always present, inscrutable, saturnine, missing nothing: until at last toward sundown Compson crashed savagely out of the last bramble-brake and flung the sweat from his face with a full-armed sweep sufficient to repudiate a throne, and said,

'All right, god damn it, we'll pay him for it.' Because they had already considered that last gambit; they had already realised its seriousness from the very fact that Peabody had tried to make a joke about it which everyone knew that even Peabody did not think humorous:

'Yes——and quick too, before he has time to advise with Pettigrew and price it by the pound.'

'By the pound?' Compson said.

'Pettigrew just weighed it by the three hundred miles from Nashville. Old Alec might start from Carolina. That's fifteen thousand pounds.'

'Oh,' Compson said. So he blew in his men by means of a foxhorn which one of the Indians wore on a thong around his neck, though even then they paused for one last quick conference; again it was Peabody who stopped them.

'Who'll pay for it?' he said. 'It would be just like him to want a dollar a pound for it, even if by Pettigrew's scale he had found it in the ashes of his fireplace.' They—Compson anyway—had probably already thought of that; that, as much as Pettigrew's presence, was probably why he was trying to rush them into old Alec's presence with the offer so quickly that none would have the face to renege on a pro rata share. But Peabody had torn it now. Compson looked about at them, sweating, grimly enraged.

'That means Peabody will probably pay one dollar,' he said. 'Who pays the other fourteen? Me?' Then Ratcliffe, the trader, the store's proprietor, solved it—a solution so simple, so limitless in retroact, that they didn't even wonder why nobody had thought of it before; which not only solved the problem but abolished it; and not just that one, but all problem, from now on into perpetuity, opening to their vision like the rending of a veil, like a glorious prophecy, the vast splendid limitless panorama of America: that land of boundless opportunity, that bourne, created not by nor of the people, but for the people, as was the heavenly manna of old, with no return demand on man save the chewing and swallowing since out of its own matchless Allgood it would create produce train support and perpetuate a race of laborers dedicated to the single purpose of picking the manna up and putting it into his lax hand or even between his jaws,—illimitable, vast, without beginning or end, not even a trade or a craft but a beneficence as are sunlight and rain and air, inalienable and immutable.

'Put it on the Book,' Ratcliffe said—the Book: not a ledger, but *the* ledger, since it was probably the only thing of its kind between Nashville and Natchez, unless there might happen to be a similar one a few miles south at the first Chocktaw agency at Yalo Busha,—a ruled, paper-backed copybook such as might have come out of a schoolroom, in which accrued, with the United States as debtor, in Mohataha's name (the Chickasaw matriarch, Ikkemotubbe's mother and old Issetibbeha's sister, who—she could write her name, or anyway make something with a pen or pencil which was agreed to be, or at least accepted to be, a valid signature—signed all the conveyances as her son's kingdom passed to the white people, regularising it in law anyway) the crawling tedious list of calico and gunpowder, whiskey and salt and snuff and denim pants and osseous candy drawn from Ratcliffe's shelves by her descendants and subjects and Negro slaves. That was all the settlement had to do: add the lock to the list, the account. It wouldn't even matter at what price they entered it. They could have priced it on Pettigrew's scale of fifteen pounds times the distance not just to Carolina but to Washington itself, and nobody would ever notice it probably; they could have charged the United States with seventeen thousand five hundred dollars worth of the fossilised and indestructible candy, and none would ever read the entry. So it was solved, done, finished, ended. They didn't even have to discuss it. They didn't even think about it anymore, unless perhaps here and there to marvel (a little speculatively probably) at their own moderation, since they wanted nothing—least of all, to escape any just blame—but a fair and decent adjustment of the lock. They went back to where old Alec still sat with his pipe in front of his dim hearth. Only they had overestimated him; he didn't want any money at all, he wanted his lock. Whereupon what little remained of Compson's patience went too.

'Your lock's gone,' he told old Alec harshly. 'You'll take fifteen dollars for it,' he said, his voice already fading, because even that rage could recognise impasse when it saw it. Nevertheless, the rage, the impotence, the sweating, the *too much*—whatever it was—forced the voice on for one word more: 'Or——' before it stopped for good and allowed Peabody to fill the gap:

'Or else?' Peabody said, and not to old Alec, but to Compson. 'Or else what?' Then Ratcliffe saved that too.

'Wait,' he said. 'Uncle Alec's going to take fifty dollars for his lock. A guarantee of fifty dollars. He'll give us the name of the blacksmith back in Cal'lina that made it for him, and we'll send back there and have a new one made. Going and coming and all'll cost about fifty dollars. We'll give Uncle Alec the fifty dollars to hold as a guarantee. Then when the new lock comes, he'll give us back the money. All right, Uncle Alec?' And that could have been all of it. It probably would have been, except for Pettigrew. It was not that they had forgotten him, nor even assimilated him. They had simply sealed—healed him off (so they thought)—him into their civic crisis as the desperate and defenseless oyster immobilises its atom of inevictable grit. Nobody had seen him move yet he now stood in the center of them where Compson and Ratcliffe and Peabody faced old Alec in the chair. You might have said that he had oozed there, except for that adamantine quality which might (in emergency) become invisible but never insubstantial and never in this world fluid; he spoke in a voice bland, reasonable and impersonal, then stood there being looked at, frail and childsized, impermeable as diamond and manifest with portent, bringing into that backwoods room a thousand miles deep in pathless wilderness, the whole vast incalculable weight of federality, not just representing the government nor even himself just the government; for that moment at least, he was the United States.

'Uncle Alec hasn't lost any lock,' he said. 'That was Uncle Sam.'

After a moment someone said, 'What?'

'That's right,' Pettigrew said. 'Whoever put that lock of Holston's on that mail bag either made a voluntary gift to the United States, and the same law covers the United States government that covers minor children: you can give something to them, but you cant take it back, or he or they done something else.'

They looked at him. Again after a while somebody said something; it was Ratcliffe. 'What else?' Ratcliffe said. Pettigrew answered, still bland, impersonal, heatless and glib:

'Committed a violation of act of Congress as especially made and provided for the defacement of government property, penalty of five thousand dollars or not less than one year in a Federal jail or both. For whoever cut them two slits in the bag to put the lock in, act of Congress as especially made and provided for the injury or destruction of government property, penalty of ten thousand dollars or not less than five years in a Federal jail or both.' He did not move even yet; he simply spoke directly to old Alec: 'I reckon you're going to have supper here same as usual sooner or later or more or less.'

'Wait,' Ratcliffe said. He turned to Compson. 'Is that true?'

'What the hell difference does it make whether it's true or not?' Compson said. 'What do you think he's going to do as soon as he gets to Nashville?' He said violently to Pettigrew: 'You were supposed to leave for Nashville yesterday. What were you hanging around here for?'

'Nothing to go to Nashville for,' Pettigrew said. 'You dont want any mail. You aint got anything to lock it up with.'

'So we aint,' Ratcliffe said. 'So we'll let the United States find the United States' lock.' This time Pettigrew looked at no one. He wasn't even speaking to anyone, anymore than old Alec had been when he decreed the return of his lock:

'Act of Congress as made and provided for the unauthorised removal and or use or willful or felonious use or misuse or loss of government property, penalty the value of the article plus five hundred to ten thousand dollars or thirty days to twenty years in a Federal jail or both. They may even make a new one when they read where you have charged a postoffice department lock to the bureau of Indian affairs.' He moved; now he was speaking to old Alec again: 'I'm going out to my horse. When this meeting is over and you get back to cooking, you can send your nigger for me.'

Then he was gone. After a while Ratcliffe said, 'What do you reckon he aims to get out of this? A reward?' But that was wrong; they all knew better than that.

'He's already getting what he wants,' Compson said, and cursed again. 'Confusion. Just damned confusion.' But that was wrong too; they all knew that too, though it was Peabody who said it:

'No. Not confusion. A man who will ride six hundred miles through this country every two weeks, with nothing for protection but a foxhorn, aint really interested in confusion any more than he is in money.' So they didn't know yet what was in Pettigrew's mind. But they knew what he would do. That is, they knew that they did not know at all, either what he would do, or how, or when, and that there was nothing whatever that they could do about it until they discovered why. And they saw now that they had no possible means to discover that; they realised now that they had known him for three years now, during which, fragile and inviolable and undeviable and preceded for a mile or more by the strong sweet ringing of the horn, on his strong and tireless horse he would complete the bi-monthly trip from Nashville to the settlement and for the next three or four days would live among them, yet that they knew nothing whatever about him, and even now knew only that they dared not, simply dared not, take any chance, sitting for a while longer in the darkening room while old Alec still smoked, his back still squarely turned to them and their quandary too; then dispersing to their own cabins for the evening meal—with what appetite they could bring to it, since presently they had drifted back through the summer darkness when by ordinary they would have been already in bed, to the back room of Ratcliffe's store now, to sit again while Ratcliffe recapitulated in his mixture of bewilderment and alarm (and something else which they recognised was respect as they realised that he—Ratcliffe—was unshakably convinced that Pettigrew's aim was money; that Pettigrew had invented or evolved a scheme so richly rewarding that he—Ratcliffe—had not only been unable to forestall him and do it first, he—

Ratcliffe—couldn't even guess what it was after he had been given a hint) until Compson interrupted him.

'Hell,' Compson said. 'Everybody knows what's wrong with him. It's ethics. He's a damned moralist.'

'Ethics?' Peabody said. He sounded almost startled. He said quickly: 'That's bad. How can we corrupt an ethical man?'

'Who wants to corrupt him?' Compson said. 'All we want him to do is stay on that damned horse and blow whatever extra wind he's got into that damned horn.'

But Peabody was not even listening. He said, 'Ethics,' almost dreamily. He said, 'Wait.' They watched him. He said suddenly to Ratcliffe: 'I've heard it somewhere. If anybody here knows it, it'll be you. What's his name?'

'His name?' Ratcliffe said. 'Pettigrew's? Oh. His christian name.' Ratcliffe told him. 'Why?'

'Nothing,' Peabody said. 'I'm going home. Anybody else coming?' He spoke directly to nobody and said and would say no more, but that was enough: a straw perhaps, but at least a straw; enough anyway for the others to watch and say nothing either as Compson got up to and said to Ratcliffe,

'You coming?' and the three of them walked away together, beyond earshot then beyond sight too. Then Compson said, 'All right. What?'

'It may not work,' Peabody said. 'But you two will have to back me up. When I speak for the whole settlement, you and Ratcliffe will have to make it stick. Will you?'

Compson cursed. 'But at least tell us a little of what we're going to guarantee.' So Peabody told them, some of it, and the next morning entered the stall in the Holston House stable where Pettigrew was grooming his ugly hammerheaded ironmuscled horse.

'We decided not to charge that lock to old Mohataha, after all,' Peabody said.

'That so?' Pettigrew said. 'Nobody in Washington would ever catch it. Certainly not the ones that can read.'

'We're going to pay for it ourselves,' Peabody said. 'In fact, we're going to do a little more. We've got to repair that jail wall anyhow; we've got to build one wall anyway. So by building three more, we will have another room. We got to build one anyway, so that dont count. So by building an extra three-wall room, we will have another four-wall house. That will be the courthouse.' Pettigrew had been hissing gently between his teeth at each stroke of the brush, like a professional Irish groom. Now he stopped, the brush and his hand arrested in midstroke, and turned his head a little.

'Courthouse?'

'We're going to have a town,' Peabody said. 'We already got a church—that's Whitfield's cabin. And we're going to build a school too soon as we get around to it. But we're going to build the courthouse today; we've already got something to put in it to make it a courthouse: that iron box that's been in Ratcliffe's way in the store for the last ten years. Then we'll have a town. We've already even named her.'

Now Pettigrew stood up, very slowly. They looked at one another. After a moment Pettigrew said, 'So?'

'Ratcliffe says your name's Jefferson,' Peabody said.

'That's right,' Pettigrew said. 'Thomas Jefferson Pettigrew. I'm from old Ferginny.'

'Any kin?' Peabody said.

'No,' Pettigrew said. 'My ma named me for him, so I would have some of his luck.'

'Luck?' Peabody said.

Pettigrew didn't smile. 'That's right. She didn't mean luck. She never had any schooling. She didn't know the word she wanted to say.'

'Have you had it?' Peabody said. Nor did Pettigrew smile now. 'I'm sorry,' Peabody said. 'Try to forget it.' He said: 'We decided to name her Jefferson.' Now Pettigrew didn't seem to breathe even. He just stood there, small, frail, less than boysize, childless and bachelor, incorrigibly kinless and tieless, looking at Peabody. Then he breathed, and raising the brush, he turned back to the horse and for an instant Peabody thought he was going back to the grooming. But instead of making the stroke, he laid the hand and the brush against the horse's flank and stood for a moment, his face turned away and his head bent a little. Then he raised his head and turned his face back toward Peabody.

'You could call that lock "axle grease" on that Indian account,' he said.

'Fifty dollars worth of axle grease?' Peabody said.

'To grease the wagons for Oklahoma,' Pettigrew said.

'So we could,' Peabody said. 'Only her name's Jefferson now. We cant ever forget that anymore now.' And that was the courthouse—the courthouse which it had taken them almost thirty years not only to realise they didn't have, but to discover that they hadn't even needed, missed, lacked; and which, before they had owned it six months, they discovered was nowhere near enough. Because somewhere between the dark of that first day and the dawn of the next, something happened to them. They began that same day; they restored the jail wall and cut new logs and split out shakes and raised the little floorless lean-to against it and moved the iron chest from Ratcliffe's back room; it took only the two days and cost nothing but the labor and not much of that per capita since the whole settlement was involved to a man, not to mention the settlement's two slaves—Holston's man and the one belonging to the German blacksmith—; Ratcliffe too, all he had to do was put up the bar across the inside of his back door, since his entire patronage was countable in one glance sweating and cursing among the logs and shakes of the half dismantled jail across the way opposite—including Ikkemotubbe's Chickasaws, though these were neither sweating nor cursing: the grave dark men dressed in their Sunday clothes except for the trousers, pants, which they carried rolled neatly under their arms or perhaps tied by the two legs around their necks like capes or rather hussars' dolmans where they had forded the creek, squatting or lounging along the shade, courteous, interested, and reposed (even old Mohataha herself, the matriarch, barefoot in a purple silk gown and a plumed hat, sitting in a gilt brocade empire chair in a wagon behind two mules, under a silver-handled Paris parasol held by a female slave child)—because they (the other white men, his confreres, or—during this first day—his co-victims) had not yet remarked the thing—quality—something—esoteric, eccentric, in Ratcliffe's manner, attitude,—not an obstruction nor even an impediment, not even when on the second day they discovered what it was, because he was among them, busy too, sweating and cursing too, but rather like a single chip, infinitesimal, on an otherwise unbroken flood or tide, a single body or substance alien and unreconciled, a single thin almost unheard voice crying thinly out of the roar of a mob: 'Wait, look here, listen——'

Because they were too busy raging and sweating among the dismantled logs and felling the new ones in the adjacent woods and trimming and notching and dragging them out and mixing the tenuous clay mud to chink them together with; it was not until the second day that they learned what was troubling Ratcliffe, because now they had time, the work going no slower, no lessening of sweat but on the contrary, if anything the work going even a little faster because now there was a lightness in the speed and all that was abated was the rage and the outrage, because somewhere between the dark and the dawn of the first and the second day, something had happened to them—the men who had spent that first long hot endless July day sweating and raging about the wrecked jail, flinging indiscriminately and savagely aside the dismantled logs and the log-like laudanum-smitten inmates in order to rebuild the one, cursing old Holston and the lock and the four—three—bandits and the eleven militiamen who had arrested them, and Compson and Pettigrew and Peabody and the United States of America,—the same men met at the project before sunrise on the next day which was already promising to be hot and endless too, but with the rage and the fury absent now, quiet, not grave so much as sobered, a little amazed, diffident, blinking a little perhaps, looking a little aside from one another, a little unfamiliar even to one another in the new jonquil-colored light, looking about them at the meagre huddle of crude cabins set without order and every one a little awry to every other and all dwarfed to dollhouses by the vast loom of the woods which enclosed them—the tiny clearing clawed punily not even into the flank of pathless wilderness but into the loin, the groin, the secret parts, which was the irrevocable cast die of their lives, fates, pasts and futures—not even speaking for a while yet since each one probably believed (a little shamefaced too) that the thought was solitarily his, until at last one spoke for all and then it was all right since it had taken one conjoined breath to shape that sound, the speaker speaking not loud, diffidently, tentatively, as you insert the first light tentative push of wind into the mouthpiece of a strange untried foxhorn: 'By God. Jefferson.'

'Jefferson, Mississippi,' a second added.

'Jefferson, Yoknapatawpha County, Mississippi,' a third corrected; who, which one, didn't matter this time either since it was still one conjoined breathing, one compound dreamstate, mused and static, well capable of lasting on past sunrise too, though they probably knew better too since Compson was still there: the gnat, the thorn, the catalyst:

'It aint until we finish the goddamned thing,' Compson said. 'Come on. Let's get at it.' So they finished it that day, working rapidly now, with speed and lightness too, concentrated yet inattentive, to get it done and that quickly, not to finish it but to get it out of the way, behind them; not to finish it quickly in order to own, possess it sooner, but to be able to obliterate, efface, it the sooner, as if they had also known in that first yellow light that it would not be near enough, would not even be the beginning; that the little lean-to room they were building would not even be a pattern and could not even be called practice, working on until noon, the hour to stop and eat, by which time Louis Grenier had arrived from Frenchman's Bend (his plantation: his manor, his kitchens and stables and kennels and slave quarters and gardens and promenades and fields which a hundred years later will have vanished, his name and his blood too, leaving nothing but the name of his plantation and his own fading corrupted legend like a thin layer of the native ephemeral yet inevictable dust on a section of country surrounding a little lost paintless crossroads store) twenty miles away behind a slave coachman and footman in his imported English carriage and what was said to be the finest matched team outside of Natchez or Nashville, and Compson said, 'I reckon that'll do,'—all knowing what he meant: not abandonment: to complete it, of course, but so little remained now that the two slaves could finish it. The four in fact, since, although as soon as it was assumed that the two Grenier Negroes would lend the two local ones a hand, Compson demurred on the grounds that who would dare violate the rigid protocol of bondage by ordering a stable-servant, let alone a house-servant, to do manual labor, not to mention having the temerity to approach old Louis Grenier with the suggestion. Peabody nipped that at once.

'One of them can use my shadow,' he said. 'It never blenched out there with a white doctor standing in it,' and even offered to be emissary to old Grenier, except that Grenier himself forestalled them. So they ate Holston's noon ordinary, while the Chickasaws, squatting unmoving still where the creep of shade had left them in the full fierce glare of July noon about the wagon where old Mohataha still sat under her slave-borne Paris parasol, ate their lunches too which (Mohataha's and her personal retinue's came out of a woven white-oak withe fishbasket in the wagonbed) they appeared to have carried in from what, patterning the white people, they called their plantation too, under their arms inside the rolled-up trousers. Then they moved back to the front gallery and—not the settlement anymore now: the town; it had been a town for thirty-one hours now—watched the four slaves put up the final log and pin down the final shake on the roof and hang the door and then, Ratcliffe leading something like the court chamberlain across a castle courtyard, cross back to the store and enter and emerge carrying the iron chest, the grave Chickasaws watching too the white man's slaves sweating the white man's ponderable dense inscrutable medicine into its new shrine. And now they had time to find out what was bothering Ratcliffe.

'That lock,' Ratcliffe said.

'What?' somebody said.

'That Indian axle grease,' Ratcliffe said.

'What?' they said again. But they knew, understood, now. It was neither lock nor axle grease; it was the fifteen dollars which could have been charged to the Indian Department on Ratcliffe's books and nobody would have ever found it, noticed it, missed it. It was not greed on Ratcliffe's part, and least of all was he advocating corruption. The idea was not even new to him; it did not need any casual man on a horse riding in to the settlement once every two or three weeks, to reveal to him that possibility; he had thought of that the first time he had charged the first sack of peppermint candy to the first one of old Mohataha's forty-year-old grandchildren and had refrained from adding two zeroes to the ten or fifteen cents for ten years now, wondering each time why he did refrain, amazed at his own virtue or at least his strength of will. It was a matter of principle. It was he—they: the settlement (town now)—who had thought of charging the lock to the United States as a provable lock, a communal risk, a concrete ineradicable object, win lose or draw, let the chips fall where they may on that dim day when some federal inspector might, just barely might, audit the Chickasaw affairs; it was the United States itself which had voluntarily offered to show them how to transmute the inevictable lock into proofless and ephemeral axle grease—the little scrawny childsized man, solitary unarmed impregnable and unalarmed, not even defying them, not even advocate and representative of the United States, but *the* United States, as though the United States had said, 'Please accept a gift of fifteen dollars,' (the town had actually paid old Alec fifteen dollars for the lock; he would accept no more) and they had not even declined it but simply abolished it since, as soon as Petttigrew breathed it into sound, the United States had already forever lost it; as though Pettigrew had put the actual ponderable fifteen gold coins into—say, Compson's or Peabody's—hands and they had dropped them down a rathole or a well, doing no man any good, neither restoration to the ravaged nor emolument to the ravager, leaving in fact the whole race of man, as long as it endured, forever and irrevocably fifteen dollars deficit, fifteen dollars in the red;

That was Ratcliffe's trouble. But they didn't even listen. They heard him out of course, but they didn't even listen. Or perhaps they didn't even hear him either, sitting along the shade on Holston's gallery, looking, seeing, already a year away; it was barely the tenth of July; there was the long summer, the bright soft dry fall until the November rains, but they would require not two days this time but two years and maybe more, with a winter of planning and preparation before hand. They even had an instrument available and waiting, like providence almost: a man named Sutpen who had come into the settlement that same spring—a big gaunt friendless passionworn untalkative man who walked in a fading aura of anonymity and violence like a man just entered a warm room or at least a shelter, out of a blizzard, bringing with him thirty-odd men slaves even wilder and more equivocal than the native wild men, the Chickasaws, to whom the settlement had become accustomed, who (the new Negroes) spoke no English but instead what Compson, who had visited New Orleans, said was the Carib-Spanish-French of the Sugar Islands, and who (Sutpen) had bought or proved on or anyway acquired a tract of land in the opposite direction and was apparently bent on establishing a place on an ever more ambitious and grandiose scale than Grenier's; he had even brought with him a tame Parisian architect—or captive rather, since it was said in Ratcliffe's back room that the man slept at night in a kind of pit at the site of the chateau he was planning, tied wrist to wrist with one of his captor's Carib slaves; indeed, the settlement had only to see him once to know that he was no dociler than his captor, any more than the weasel or rattlesnake is no less untame than the wolf or bear before which it gives way until completely and hopelessly cornered:—a man no larger than Pettigrew, with humorous sardonic undefeated eyes which had seen everything and believed none of it, in the broad expensive hat and brocaded waistcoat and ruffled wrists of a half-artist half-boulevardier; and they—Compson perhaps, Peabody certainly—could imagine him in his mudstained brier-slashed brocade and lace standing in a trackless wilderness dreaming colonnades and porticoes and fountains and promenades in the style of David, with just behind each elbow an identical giant half-naked Negro not even watching him, only breathing, moving each time he took a step or shifted like his shadow repeated in two and blown to gigantic size;

So they even had an architect. He listened to them for perhaps a minute in Ratcliffe's back room. Then he made an indescribable gesture and said, 'Bah. You do not need advice. You are too poor. You have only your hands, and clay to make good brick. You dont have any money. You dont even have anything to copy: how can you go wrong?' But he taught them how to mold the brick; he designed and built the kiln to bake the brick in, plenty of them since they had probably known from that first yellow morning too that one edifice was not going to be enough. But although both were conceived in the same instant and planned simultaneously during the same winter and built in continuation during the next three years, the courthouse of course came first, and in March, with stakes and hanks of fishline, the architect laid out in a grove of oaks opposite the tavern and the store, the square and simple foundations, the irrevocable design not only of the courthouse but of the town too, telling them as much: 'In fifty years you will be trying to change it in the name of what you will call progress. But you will fail; but you will never be able to get away from it.' But they had already seen that, standing thigh-deep in wilderness also but with more than a vision to look at since they had at least the fishline and the stakes, perhaps less than fifty years, perhaps—who knew?—less than twenty-five even: a Square, the courthouse in its grove the center; quadrangular around it, the stores, two storey, the offices of the lawyers and doctors and dentists, the lodge-rooms and auditoriums, above them; school and church and tavern and bank and jail each in its ordered place; the four broad diverging avenues straight as plumb-lines in the four directions, becoming the network of roads and by-roads until the whole county would be covered with it: the hands, the prehensile fingers clawing dragging lightward out of the disappearing wilderness year by year as up from the bottom of the receding sea, the broad rich fecund burgeoning fields, pushing thrusting each year further and further back the wilderness and its denizens—the wild bear and deer and turkey, and the wild men (or not so wild anymore, familiar now, harmless now, just obsolete: anachronism out of an old dead time and a dead age; regrettable of course, even actually regretted by the old men, fiercely as old Doctor Habersham did, and with less fire but still as irreconciliable and stubborn as old Alec Holston and a few others were still doing, until in a few more years the last of them would have passed and vanished in their turn too, obsolescent too: because this was a white man's land; that was its fate, or not even fate but destiny, its high destiny in the roster of the earth);—the veins, arteries, life- and pulse-stream along which would flow the aggrandisement of harvest: the gold: the cotton and the grain;

But above all, the courthouse: the center, the focus, the hub; sitting looming in the center of the county's circumference like a single cloud in its ring of horizon, laying its vast shadow to the uttermost rim of horizon; musing, brooding, symbolic and ponderable, tall as cloud, solid as rock, dominating all: protector of the weak, judiciate and curb of the passions and lusts, repository and guardian of the aspirations and the hopes; rising course by brick course during that first summer, simply square, simplest Georgian colonial (this, by the Paris architect who was creating at Sutpen's Hundred something like a wing of Versailles glimpsed in a Lilliput's gothic nightmare—in revenge, Gavin Stevens would say a hundred years later, when Sutpen's own legend in the county would include the anecdote of the time the architect broke somehow out of his dungeon and tried to flee and Sutpen and his Negro headman and hunter ran him down with dogs in the swamp and brought him back) since, as the architect had told them, they had no money to buy bad taste with nor even anything from which to copy what bad taste might still have been within their compass; this one too still costing nothing but the labor and—the second year now—most of that was slave since there were still more slave owners in the settlement which had been a town and named for going on two years now, already a town and already named when the first ones waked up on that yellow morning two years back:—men other than Holston and the blacksmith (Compson was one now) who owned one or two or three Negroes, besides Grenier and Sutpen who had set up camps beside the creek in Compson's pasture for the two gangs of their Negroes to live in until the two buildings—the courthouse and the jail—should be completed. But not altogether slave, the boundmen, the unfree, because there were still the white men too, the same ones who on that hot July morning two and now three years ago had gathered in a kind of outraged unbelief to fling, hurl up in raging sweating impotent fury the little three-walled lean-to,—the same men (with affairs of their own they might have been attending to or work of their own or for which they were being hired, paid, that they should have been doing) standing or lounging about the scaffolding and the stacks of brick and puddles of clay mortar for an hour or two hours or half a day, then putting aside one of the Negroes and taking his place with trowel or saw or adze, unbidden or unreproved either since there was none present with the right to order or deny; a stranger might have said probably for that reason, simply because now they didn't have to, except that it was more than that, working peacefully now that there was no outrage and fury, and twice as fast because there was no urgency since this was no more to be hurried by man or men than the burgeoning of a crop, working (this paradox too to anyone except men like Grenier and Compson and Peabody who had grown from infancy among slaves, breathed the same air and even suckled the same breast with the sons of Ham: black and white, free and unfree, shoulder to shoulder in the same tireless lift and rhythm as if they had the same aim and hope, which they did have as far as the Negro was capable, as even Ratcliffe, son of a long pure line of Anglo-Saxon mountain people and—destined—father of an equally long and pure line of white trash tenant farmers who never owned a slave and never would since each had and would imbibe with his mother's milk a personal violent antipathy not at all to slavery but to black skins, could have explained: the slave's simple child's mind had fired at once with the thought that he was helping to build not only the biggest edifice in the country, but probably the biggest he had ever seen; this was all but this was enough) as one because it was theirs, bigger than any because it was the sum of all and, being the sum of all, it must raise all of their hopes and aspirations level with its own aspirant and soaring cupola, so that, sweating and tireless and unflagging, they would look about at one another a little shyly, a little amazed, with something like humility too, as if they were realising, or were for a moment at least capable of believing, that men, all men, including themselves, were a little better, purer maybe even, than they had thought, expected, or even needed to be. Though they were still having a little trouble with Ratcliffe: the money, the Holston lock-Chickasaw axle grease fifteen dollars; not trouble really because it had never been an obstruction even three years ago when it was new, and now after three years even the light impedeless chip was worn by familiarity and custom to less than a toothpick: merely present, merely visible, or that is, audible: and no trouble *with* Ratcliffe because he made one too contraposed the toothpick;

more: he was its chief victim, sufferer, since where with the others was mostly inattention, a little humor, now and then a little fading annoyance and impatience, with him was shame, bafflement, a little of anguish and despair like a man struggling with a congenital vice, hopeless, indomitable, already defeated. It was not even the money anymore now, the fifteen dollars. It was the fact that they had refused it and, refusing it, had maybe committed a fatal and irremediable error. He would try to explain it: 'It's like Old Moster and the rest of them up there that run the luck, would look down at us and say, Well well, looks like them durn peckerwoods down there dont want them fifteen dollars we was going to give them free-gratis-for-nothing. So maybe they dont want nothing from us. So maybe we better do like they seem to want, and let them sweat and swivet and scrabble through the best they can by themselves.'

Which they—the town—did, though even then the courthouse was not finished for another six years. Not but that they thought it was: complete: simple and square, floored and roofed and windowed, with a central hallway and the four offices—sheriff and tax assessor and circuit- and chancery-clerk (which—the chancery-clerk's office—would contain the ballot boxes and booths for voting)—below, and the courtroom and jury-room and the judge's chambers above,—even to the pigeons and English sparrows, migrants too but not pioneers, inevictably urban in fact, come all the way from the Atlantic coast as soon as the town became a town with a name, taking possession of the gutters and eave-boxes almost before the final hammer was withdrawn, uxorious and interminable the one, garrulous and myriad the other. Then in the sixth year old Alec Holston died and bequeathed back to the town the fifteen dollars it had paid him for the lock; two years before, Louis Grenier had died and his heirs still held in trust on demand the fifteen hundred dollars his will had devised it, and now there was another newcomer in the county, a man named John Sartoris, with slaves and gear and money too like Grenier and Sutpen, but who was an even better stalemate to Sutpen than Grenier had been because it was apparent at once that he, Sartoris, was the sort of man who could even cope with Sutpen in the sense that a man with a sabre or even a small sword and heart enough for it, could cope with one with an axe; and that summer (Sutpen's Paris architect had long since gone back to whatever place he came from and to which he had made his one abortive midnight try to return, but his trickle, flow of bricks had never even faltered: his molds and kilns had finished the jail and were now raising the walls of two churches and by the half-century would have completed what would be known through all north Mississippi and east Tennessee as *the* Academy, *the* Female Institute) there was a committee: Compson and Sartoris and Peabody (and *in absentia* Sutpen: nor would the town ever know exactly how much of the additional cost Sutpen and Sartoris made up): and the next year the eight disjointed marble columns were landed from an Italian ship at New Orleans, into a steamboat up the Mississippi to Vicksburg, and into a smaller steamboat up the Yazoo and Sunflower and Tallahatchie, to Ikkemotubbe's old landing which Sutpen now owned, and thence the twelve miles by oxen into Jefferson: the two identical four-column porticoes, one on the north and one on the south, each with its balcony of wrought-iron New Orleans grillwork, on one of which—the south one—in 1861 Sartoris would stand in the first Confederate uniform the town had ever seen, while in the Square below the Richmond mustering officer enrolled and swore in the regiment which Sartoris as its colonel would take to Virginia as a part of Bee, to be Jackson's extreme left in front of the Henry house at First Manassas, and from both of which each May and November for a hundred years, bailiffs in their orderly appointive almost hereditary succession would cry without inflection or punctuation either 'oyes oyes honorable circuit court of yoknapatawpha county come all and ye shall be heard' and beneath which for that same length of time too except for the seven years between '63 and '70 which didn't really count a century afterward except to a few irreconciliable old ladies, the white male citizens of the county would pass to vote for county and state offices, because when in '63 a United States military force burned the Square and the business district, the courthouse survived. It didn't escape: it simply survived: harder than axes, tougher than fire, more fixed than dynamite;

encircled by the tumbled and blackened ruins of lesser walls, it still stood, even the topless smoke-stained columns, gutted of course and roofless, but immune, not one hair even out of the Paris architect's almost forgotten plumb, so that all they had to do (it took nine years to build; they needed twenty-five to restore it) was put in new floors for the two storeys and a new roof, and this time with a cupola with a four-faced clock and a bell to strike the hours and ring alarms; by this time the Square, the banks and the stores and the lawyers' and doctors' and dentists' offices, had been restored, and the English sparrows were back too which had never really deserted—the garrulous noisy independent swarms which, as though concomitant with, inextricable from regularised and roted human quarreling, had appeared in possession of cornices and gutter-boxes almost before the last nail was driven—and now the pigeons also, interminably murmurous, nesting in, already usurping, the belfry even though they couldn't seem to get used to the bell, bursting out of the cupola at each stroke of the hour in frantic clouds, to sink and burst and whirl again at each succeeding stroke, until the last one: then vanishing back through the slatted louvers until nothing remained but the frantic and murmurous cooing like the fading echoes of the bell itself, the source of the alarm never recognised and even the alarm itself unremembered, as the actual stroke of the bell is no longer remembered by the vibration-fading air. Because they—the sparrows and the pigeons—endured, durable, a hundred years, the oldest things there except the courthouse centennial and serene above the town most of whose people now no longer even knew who Doctor Habersham and old Alec Holston and Louis Grenier were, had been; centennial and serene above the change: the electricity and gasoline, the neon and the crowded cacophonous air; even Negroes passing in beneath the balconies and into the chancery clerk's office to cast ballots too, voting for the same white-skinned rascals and demagogues and white supremacy champions that the white ones did,—durable: every few years the county fathers, dreaming of bakhshish, would instigate a movement to tear it down and erect a new modern one, but someone would at the last moment defeat them; they will try it again of course and be defeated perhaps once again or even maybe twice again, but no more than that. Because its fate is to stand in the hinterland of America: its doom is its longevity; like a man, its simple age is its own reproach, and after the hundred years, will become unbearable. But not for a little while yet; for a little while yet the sparrows and the pigeons: garrulous myriad and independent the one, the other uxorious and interminable, at once frantic and tranquil—until the clock strikes again which even after a hundred years, they still seem unable to get used to, bursting in one swirling explosion out of the belfry as though the hour, instead of merely adding one puny infinitesimal more to the long weary increment since Genesis, had shattered the virgin pristine air with the first loud dingdong of time and doom.

Scene I

Courtroom. 5:30 P.M. November thirteenth.

The Curtain is down. As the lights begin to go up:

MAN'S VOICE (behind the curtain)
Let the prisoner stand.

The curtain rises, symbolising the rising of the prisoner in the dock, and revealing a section of the courtroom. It does not occupy the whole stage, but only the upper left half, leaving the other half and the bottom of the stage in darkness, so that the visible scene is not only spotlighted but elevated slightly too, a further symbolism which will be clearer when Act II opens—the symbolism of the elevated tribunal of justice of which this, a County court, is only the intermediate, not the highest, stage.

This is a section of the court—the bar, the judge, officers, the opposing lawyers, the jury. The defense lawyer is Gavin Stevens, about fifty. He looks more like a poet than a lawyer and actually is: a bachelor, descendant of one of the pioneer Yoknapatawpha County families, Harvard and Heidelberg educated, and returned to his native soil to be a sort of bucolic Cincinnatus, champion not so much of truth as of justice, or of justice as he sees it, constantly involving himself, often for no pay, in affairs of equity and passion and even crime too among his people, white and Negro both, sometimes directly contrary to his office of County Attorney which he has held for years, as is the present business.

The prisoner is standing. She is the only one standing in the room—a Negress, quite black, about thirty—that is, she could be almost anything between twenty and forty—with a calm impenetrable almost bemused face, the tallest, highest there with all eyes on her but she herself not looking at any of them, but looking out and up as though at some distant corner of the room, as though she were alone in it. She is—or until recently, two months ago to be exact—a domestic servant, nurse to two white children, the second of whom, an infant, she smothered in its cradle two months ago, for which act she is now on trial for her life. But she has probably done many things else—chopped cotton, cooked for working gangs—any sort of manual labor within her capacities, or rather, limitations in time and availability, since her principal reputation in the little Mississippi town where she was born is that of a tramp—a drunkard, a casual prostitute, being beaten by some man or cutting or being cut by his wife or his other sweetheart. She has probably been married, at least once. Her name—or so she calls it and would probably spell it if she could spell—is Nancy Mannigoe.

There is a dead silence in the room while everybody watches her.

JUDGE

Have you anything to say before the sentence of the court is pronounced upon you?

Nancy neither answers nor moves; she doesn't even seem to be listening.

JUDGE

That you, Nancy Mannigoe, did on the thirteenth day of September, wilfully and with malice aforethought kill and murder the infant child of Mr and

Mrs Gowan Stevens in the town of Jefferson and the County of Yoknapatawpha . . . . . .

It is the sentence of this court that you be taken from hence back to the county jail of Yoknapatawpha County and there on the thirteenth day of March be hanged by the neck until you are dead. And may God have mercy on your soul.

NANCY (quite loud in the silence, to no one, quite calm, not moving)

Yes, Lord.

There is a gasp, a sound, from the invisible spectators in the room, of shock at this unheard-of violation of procedure: the beginning of something which might be consternation and even uproar, in the midst of, or rather above which, Nancy herself does not move. The judge bangs his gavel, the bailiff springs up, the curtain starts hurriedly and jerkily down as if the judge, the officers, the court itself were jerking frantically at it to hide this disgraceful business; from somewhere among the unseen spectators there comes the sound of a woman's voice—a moan, wail, sob perhaps.

BAILIFF (loudly)

Order! Order in the court! Order!

The curtain descends rapidly, hiding the scene, the lights fade rapidly into darkness: a moment of darkness: then the curtain rises smoothly and normally on:

SCENE II

Stevens living-room. 6:00 P.M. November thirteenth.

Living-room, a center table with a lamp, chairs, a sofa left rear, floor-lamp, wall-bracket lamps, a door L enters from hall, double doors rear stand open on a dining-room, a fire-place R with gas logs. The atmosphere of the room is smart, modern, up-to-date, yet the room itself has the air of another time—the high ceiling, the cornices, some of the furniture; it has the air of being in an old house, an ante-bellum house descended at last to a spinster survivor who has modernised it (vide the gas fire and the two overstuffed chairs) into apartments rented to young couples or families who can afford to pay that much rent in order to live on the right street among other young couples who belong to the right church and the country club.

Sound of feet, then the lights come on as if someone about to enter had pressed a wall switch, then the door L opens and Temple enters, followed by Gowan, her husband, and the lawyer, Gavin Stevens. She is in the middle twenties, very smart, soignée, in an open fur coat, wearing a hat and gloves and carrying a handbag. Her air is brittle and tense, yet controlled. Her face shows nothing as she crosses to the center table and stops.

Gowan is three or four years older. He is almost a type; there were many of him in America, the South, between the two great wars: only children of financially secure parents living in city apartment hotels, alumni of the best colleges, South or East, where they belonged to the right clubs; married now and raising families yet still alumni of their schools, performing acceptably jobs they themselves did not ask for, usually concerned with money: cotton futures, or stocks, or bonds. But this face is a little different, a little more than that. Something has happened to it—tragedy—something, against which it had had no warning, and to cope with which (as it discovered) no equipment, yet which it has accepted and is trying, really and sincerely and selflessly (perhaps for the first time in its life) to do its best with according to its code. He and Stevens wear their overcoats, carrying their hats. Stevens stops just inside the room. Gowan drops his hat onto the sofa in passing and goes on to where Temple stands at the table, stripping off one of her gloves.

TEMPLE (takes cigarette from box on the table: mimics the prisoner; her voice, harsh, reveals for the first time repressed, controlled, hysteria)

Yes, God. Guilty, God. Thank you, God. If that's your attitude toward being hung, what else can you expect from a judge and jury except to accommodate you?

GOWAN

Stop it, Boots. Hush now. Soon as I light the fire, I'll buy a drink.

(to Stevens)

Or maybe Gavin will do the fire while I do the butler.

TEMPLE (takes up lighter)

I'll do the fire. You get the drinks. Then Uncle Gavin wont have to stay. After all, all he wants to do is say, Goodbye and send me a postcard. He can almost do that in two words, if he tries hard. Then he can go home.

She crosses to the hearth and kneels and turns the gas valve, the lighter ready in her other hand.

GOWAN (anxiously)

Now, Boots.

TEMPLE (snaps lighter, holds flame to the jet)

Will you for God's sake please get me a drink?

GOWAN

Sure, honey.

(he turns: to Stevens)

Drop your coat anywhere.

He exits into the dining-room. Stevens does not move, watching Temple as the log takes fire.

TEMPLE (still kneeling, her back to Stevens)

If you're going to stay, why dont you sit down? Or vice versa. Backward. Only, it's the first one that's backward: if you're not sitting down, why dont you go? Let me be bereaved and vindicated, but at least let me do it in privacy, since God knows if any one of the excretions should take place in privacy, triumph should be the one——

Stevens watches her. Then he crosses to her, taking the handkerchief from his breast pocket, stops behind her and extends the handkerchief down where she can see it. She looks at it, then up at him. Her face is quite calm.

TEMPLE

What's that for?

STEVENS

It's all right. It's dry too.

(still extending the handkerchief)

For tomorrow, then.

TEMPLE (rises quickly)

Oh, for cinders. On the train. We're going by air; hadn't Gowan told you? We leave from the Memphis airport at midnight; we're driving up after supper. Then California tomorrow morning; maybe we'll even go on to Hawaii in the spring. No; wrong season: Canada, maybe. Lake Louise in May and June——

(she stops, listens a moment toward the dining-room doors)

So why the handkerchief? Not a threat, because you dont have anything to threaten me with, do you? And if you dont have anything to threaten me with, I must not have anything you want, so it cant be a bribe either, can it?

(they both hear the sound from beyond the dining-room doors which indicates that Gowan is approaching. Temple lowers her voice again, rapidly)

Put it this way then. I dont know what you want, because I dont care. Because whatever it is, you wont get it from me.

(the sound is near now—footsteps, clink of glass)

Now he'll offer you a drink, and then he'll ask you too what you want, why you followed us home. I've already answered you. No. If what you came for is to see me weep, I doubt if you'll even get that. But you certainly wont get anything else. Not from me. Do you understand that?

STEVENS

I hear you.

TEMPLE

Meaning, you dont believe it. All right, *touché* then.

(quicker, tenser)

I refused to answer your question; now I'll ask you one: How much do you—

(as Gowan enters, she changes what she was saying so smoothly in mid-sentence that anyone entering would not even realise that the pitch of her voice had altered)

—are her lawyer, she must have talked to you; even a dope fiend that murders a little baby must have what she calls some excuse for it, even a nigger dope-fiend and a white baby——or maybe even more, a nigger dope-fiend and a white baby——

GOWAN

I said, stop it, Boots.

He carries a tray containing a pitcher of water, a bowl of ice, three empty tumblers and three whiskey glasses already filled. The bottle itself protrudes from his topcoat pocket. He approaches Temple and offers the tray.

GOWAN

That's right. I'm going to have one myself. For a change. After eight years. Why not?

TEMPLE

Why not?

(looks at the tray)

Not highballs?

GOWAN

Not this one.

She takes one of the filled glasses. He offers the tray to Stevens, who takes the second one. Then he sets the tray on the table and takes up the third glass.

GOWAN

Nary a drink in eight years; count 'em. So maybe this will be a good time to start again. At least, it wont be too soon.

(to Stevens)

Drink up. A little water behind it?

As though not aware that he had done so, he sets his untasted glass back on the tray, splashes water from the pitcher into a tumbler and hands the tumbler to Stevens as Stevens empties his glass and lowers it, taking the tumbler. Temple has not touched hers either.

GOWAN

Now maybe Defense Attorney Stevens will tell us what he wants here.

STEVENS

Your wife has already told you. To say goodbye.

GOWAN

Then say it. One more for the road, and where's your hat, huh?

He takes the tumbler from Stevens and turns back to the table.

TEMPLE (sets her untasted glass back on the tray)

And put ice in it this time, and maybe even a little water. But first, take Uncle Gavin's coat.

GOWAN (takes bottle from his pocket and makes a highball for Stevens in the tumbler)

That wont be necessary. If he could raise his arm in a white courtroom to defend a murdering nigger, he can certainly bend it in nothing but a wool overcoat—at least to take a drink with the victim's mother.

(quickly: to Temple)

Sorry. Maybe you were right all the time, and I was wrong. Maybe we've both got to keep on saying things like that until we can get rid of them, some of them, a little of them——

TEMPLE

All right, why not. Here goes then.

(she is watching, not Gowan but Stevens, who watches her in return, grave and soberly)

Dont forget the father too, dear.

GOWAN (mixing the drink)

Why should I, dear? How could I, dear? Except that the child's father is unfortunately just a man. In the eyes of the law, men are not supposed to suffer: they are merely appellants or appellees. The law is tender only of women and children—particularly of women, particularly particular of nigger dope-fiend whores who murder white children.

(hands the highball to Stevens, who takes it)

So why should we expect Defense Attorney Stevens to be tender of a man or a woman who just happen to be the parents of the child that got murdered?

TEMPLE (harshly)

Will you for God's sake please get through? Then will you for God's sake please hush?

GOWAN (quickly: turns)

Sorry.

(he turns toward her, sees her hand empty, then sees her full glass beside his own on the tray)

No drink?

TEMPLE

I dont want it. I want some milk.

GOWAN

Right. Hot, of course.

TEMPLE

Please.

GOWAN (turning)

Right. I thought of that too. I put a pan on to heat while I was getting the drinks.

(crossing toward dining-room exit)

Dont let Uncle Gavin get away until I get back. Lock the door, if you have to. Or maybe just telephone that nigger freedom agent—what's his name?——

He exits. They dont move until the slap of the pantry door sounds.

TEMPLE (rapid and hard)

How much do you know?

(rapidly)

Dont lie to me; dont you see there's not time?

STEVENS

Not time for what? Before your plane leaves tonight? She has a little time yet—four months, until March, the thirteenth of March——

TEMPLE

You know what I mean—her lawyer—seeing her every day—just a nigger, and you a white man—even if you needed anything to frighten her with—you could just buy it from her with a dose of cocaine or a pint of . . . .

(she stops, stares at him, in a sort of amazement, despair; her voice is almost quiet)

Oh, God, oh, God, she hasn't told you anything. It's me; I'm the one that's—— Dont you see? It's that I cannot believe—will not believe —— impossible——

STEVENS

Impossible to believe that all human beings really dont—as you would put it—stink? Even—as you put it—dope-fiend nigger whores? No, she told me nothing more.

TEMPLE (prompts)

Even if there was anything more.

STEVENS

Even if there was.

TEMPLE

Then what is it you think you know? Never mind where you got it; just tell me what you think it is.

STEVENS

There was a man there that night.

TEMPLE (quick, glib, almost before he has finished)

Gowan.

STEVENS

That night? When Gowan had left with Bucky at six that morning to drive to New Orleans in a car?

TEMPLE (quick, harsh)

So I was right. Did you frighten her, or just buy it?

(interrupts herself)

I'm trying. I'm really trying. Maybe it wouldn't be so hard if I could just understand why they dont stink—what reason they would have for not stinking . . . . . .

(she stops; it is as if she had heard a sound presaging Gowan's return, or perhaps simply knew by instinct or from knowledge of her own house, that he had had time to heat a cup of milk. Then continues, rapid and quiet)

There was no man there. You see? I told you, warned you, that you would get nothing from me. Oh, I know; you could have put me on the stand at any time, under oath; of course, your jury wouldn't have liked it—that wanton crucifixion of a bereaved mamma, but what's that in the balance with justice? I dont know why you didn't. Or maybe you still intend to—provided you can catch us before we cross the Tennessee line tonight.

(quick, tense, hard)

All right. I'm sorry. I know better. So maybe it's just my own stinking after all that I find impossible to doubt.

(the pantry door slaps again; they both hear it)

Because I'm not even going to take Gowan with me when I say goodbye and go up stairs.—And who knows——

She stops. Gowan enters, carrying a small tray bearing a glass of milk, a salt-shaker and a napkin, and comes to the table.

GOWAN

What are you talking about now?

TEMPLE

Nothing. I was telling Uncle Gavin that he had something of Virginia or some sort of gentleman in him too that he must have inherited from you through your grandfather, and that I'm going up to give Bucky his bath and supper.

(she touches the glass for heat, then takes it up: to Gowan)

Thank you, dear.

GOWAN

Right, dear.

(to Stevens)

You see? Not just a napkin: the right napkin. That's how I'm trained.

(he stops suddenly, noticing Temple, who has done nothing apparently: just standing there holding the milk. But he seems to know what is going on: to her)

What's this for?

TEMPLE

I dont know.

He moves; they kiss, not long but not a peck either; definitely a kiss between a man and a woman. Then, carrying the milk, Temple crosses toward the hall door.

TEMPLE (to Stevens)

Goodbye then until next June. Bucky will send you and Maggie a postcard.

(she goes on to the door, pauses and looks back at Stevens)

I may even be wrong about Temple Drake's odor too; if you should happen to hear something you haven't heard yet and it's true, I may even ratify it. Maybe you can even believe that—if you can believe you are going to hear anything that you haven't heard yet.

STEVENS

Do you?

TEMPLE (after a moment)

Not from me, Uncle Gavin. If someone wants to go to heaven, who am I to stop them? Goodnight. Goodbye.

She exits, closes the door. Stevens, very grave, turns back and sets his highball down on the tray.

GOWAN

Drink up. After all, I've got to eat supper and do some packing too. How about it?

STEVENS

About what? the packing, or the drink? What about you? I thought you were going to have one.

GOWAN

Oh, sure, sure.

(takes up the small filled glass)

Maybe you had better go on and leave us to our revenge.

STEVENS

I wish it could comfort you.

GOWAN

I wish to God it could. I wish to God that what I wanted was only revenge. An eye for an eye—were ever words emptier? Only, you have got to have lost the eye to know it.

STEVENS

Yet she still has to die.

GOWAN

Why not? Even if she would be any loss—a nigger whore, a drunkard, a dope-fiend——

STEVENS

—a vagabond, a tramp, hopeless until one day Mr

and Mrs Gowan Stevens out of simple pity and humanity picked her up out of the gutter to give her one more chance——

(Gowan stands motionless, his hand tightening slowly about the glass. Stevens watches him)

And then in return for it——

GOWAN

Look, Uncle Gavin. Why dont you go for God's sake home? Or to hell, or anywhere out of here?

STEVENS

I am, in a minute. Is that why you think—why you would still say she has to die?

GOWAN

I dont. I had nothing to do with it. I wasn't even the plaintiff. I didn't even instigate—that's the word, isn't it?—the suit. My only connection with it was, I happened by chance to be the father of the child she—— Who in hell ever called that a drink?

He dashes the whiskey, glass and all, into the ice bowl, quickly catches up one of the empty tumblers in one hand and at the same time, tilts the whiskey bottle over it, pouring. At first he makes no sound, but at once it is obvious that he is laughing: laughter which begins normally enough, but almost immediately it is out of hand, just on hysteria, while he still pours whiskey into the glass, which in a moment now will overflow, except that Stevens reaches his hand and grasps the bottle and stops it.

STEVENS

Stop it. Stop it, now. Here.

He takes the bottle from Gowan, sets it down, takes the tumbler and tilts part of its contents into the other empty one, leaving at least a reasonable, a believable, drink, and hands it to Gowan. Gowan takes it, stopping the crazy laughter, gets hold of himself again.

GOWAN (holding the glass untasted)

Eight years. Eight years on the wagon—and this is what I got for it: my child murdered by a dope-fiend nigger whore that wouldn't even run so that a cop or somebody could have shot her down like the mad-dog—— You see? Eight years without the drink, and so I got whatever it was I was buying by not drinking, and now I've got whatever it was I was paying for and it's paid for and so I can drink again. And now I dont want the drink. You see? Like whatever it was I was buying I not only didn't want, but what I was paying for it wasn't worth anything, wasn't even any loss. So I have a laugh coming. That's triumph. Because I got a bargain even in what I didn't want. I got a cut rate. I had two children. I had to pay only one of them to find out it wasn't really costing me anything—— Half price: a child, and a dope-fiend nigger whore on a public gallows: that's all I had to pay for immunity.

STEVENS

There's no such thing.

GOWAN

From the past. From my folly. My drunkenness. My cowardice, if you like——

STEVENS

There's no such thing as past either.

GOWAN

That is a laugh, that one. Only, not so loud, huh? to disturb the ladies—disturb Miss Drake—Miss Temple Drake.—Sure, why not cowardice. Only, for euphony, call it simple over-training. You know? Gowan Stevens, trained at Virginia to drink like a gentleman, gets drunk as ten gentlemen, takes a country college girl, a maiden: who knows? maybe even a virgin, cross country by car to another country college ball game, gets drunker than twenty gentlemen, gets lost, gets still drunker than forty gentlemen, wrecks the car, passes eighty gentlemen now, passes completely out while the maiden the virgin is being kidnapped into a Memphis whorehouse——

(he mumbles an indistinguishable word)

STEVENS

What?

GOWAN

Sure; cowardice. Call it cowardice; what's a little euphony between old married people?

STEVENS

Not the marrying her afterward, at least. What——

GOWAN

Sure. Marrying her was purest Old Virginia. That was indeed the hundred and sixty gentlemen.

STEVENS

The intent was, by any other standards too. The prisoner in the whorehouse; I didn't quite hear——

GOWAN (quickly: reaching for it)

Where's your glass? Dump that slop——Here——

STEVENS (holds glass)

This will do. What was that you said about held prisoner in the whorehouse?

GOWAN (harshly)

That's all. You heard it.

STEVENS

You said 'and loved it'.

(they stare at each other)

Is that what you can never forgive her for?—not for having been the instrument creating that moment in your life which you can never recall nor forget nor explain nor condone nor even stop thinking about, but because she herself didn't even suffer, but on the contrary, even liked it—that month or whatever it was like the episode in the old movie of the white girl held prisoner in the cave by the bedouin prince?—That you had to lose not only your bachelor freedom, but your man's self-respect in the chastity of his wife and your child too, to pay for something your wife hadn't even lost, didn't even regret, didn't even miss? Is that why this poor lost doomed crazy Negro woman must die?

GOWAN (tensely)

Get out of here. Go on.

STEVENS

In a minute.—Or else, blow your own brains out: stop having to remember, stop having to be forever unable to forget: nothing; to plunge into nothing and sink and drown forever and forever, never again to have to remember, never again to wake in the night writhing and sweating because you cannot, can never not, stop remembering? What else happened during that month, that time while that madman held her prisoner there in that Memphis house, that nobody but you and she know about, maybe not even you know about?

Still staring at Stevens, slowly and deliberately Gowan sets the glass of whiskey back on the tray and takes up the bottle and swings it bottom up back over his head. The stopper is out, and at once the whiskey begins to pour out of it, down his arm and sleeve and onto the floor. He does not seem to be aware of it even. His voice is tense, barely articulate.

GOWAN

So help me, Christ. . . . . . So help me, Christ.

A moment, then Stevens moves, without haste, sets his own glass back on the tray and turns, taking his hat as he passes the sofa, and goes on to the door and exits. Gowan stands a moment longer with the poised bottle, now empty. Then he draws a long shuddering breath, seems to rouse, wake, sets the empty bottle back on the tray, notices his untasted whiskey glass, takes it up, a moment: then turns and throws the glass crashing into the fireplace, against the burning gas logs, and stands, his back to the audience, and draws another long shuddering breath and then draws both hands hard down his face, then turns, looking at his wet sleeve, takes out his handkerchief and dabs at his sleeve as he comes back to the table, puts the handkerchief back in his pocket and takes the folded napkin from the small tray beside the salt cellar and wipes his sleeve with it, sees he is doing no good, tosses the crumpled napkin back onto the whiskey tray; and now, outwardly quite calm again, as though nothing had happened, he gathers the glasses back onto the big tray, puts the small tray and the napkin onto it too and takes up the tray and walks quietly toward the dining-room door as the lights begin to go down.

The lights go completely down. The stage is dark.

The lights go up.

Scene III

Stevens living-room. 10:00 P.M. March eleventh.

The room is exactly as it was four months ago, except that the only light burning is the lamp on the table, and the sofa has been moved so that it partly faces the audience, with a small motionless blanket-wrapped object lying on it, and one of the chairs placed between the lamp and the sofa so that the shadow of its back falls across the object on the sofa, making it more or less indistinguishable, and the dining-room doors are now closed. The telephone sits on the small stand in the corner R as in scene 2.

The hall door opens. Temple enters, followed by Stevens. She now wears a long housecoat; her hair is tied back with a ribbon as though prepared for bed. This time Stevens carries the topcoat and the hat too; his suit is different. Apparently she has already warned Stevens to be quiet; his air anyway shows it. She enters, stops, lets him pass her. He pauses, looks about the room, sees the sofa, stands looking at it.

STEVENS

This is what they call a plant.

He crosses to the sofa, Temple watching him, and stops, looking down at the shadowed object. He quietly draws aside the shadowing chair and reveals a little boy, about four, wrapped in the blanket, asleep.

TEMPLE

Why not? Dont the philosophers and other gynecologists tell us that women will strike back with any weapon, even their children?

STEVENS (watching the child)

Including the sleeping pill you told me you gave Gowan?

TEMPLE

All right.

(approaches table)

If I would just stop struggling: how much time we could save. I came all the way back from California, but I still cant seem to quit. Do you believe in coincidence?

STEVENS (turns)

Not unless I have to.

TEMPLE (at table, takes up a folded yellow telegraph form, opens it, reads)

Dated Jefferson, March sixth. 'You have a week yet

until the thirteenth. But where will you go then?' signed Gavin.

She folds the paper back into its old creases, folds it still again. Stevens watches her.

STEVENS

Well? This is the eleventh. Is that the coincidence?

TEMPLE

No. This is.

(she drops, tosses the folded paper onto the table, turns)

It was that afternoon—the sixth. We were on the beach, Bucky and I. I was reading, and he was—oh, talking mostly, you know—'Is California far from Jefferson, mamma?' and I say 'Yes, darling'—you know: still reading or trying to, and he says, 'How long will we stay in California, mamma?' and I say, 'Until we get tired of it' and he says, 'Will we stay here until they hang Nancy, mamma?' and it's already too late then; I should have seen it coming but it's too late now; I say, 'Yes, darling' and then he drops it right in my lap, right out of the mouths of—how is it?—babes and sucklings? 'Where will we go then, mamma?' And then we come back to the hotel, and there you are too. Well?

STEVENS

Well what?

TEMPLE

All right. Let's for God's sake stop.

(goes to a chair)

Now that I'm here, no matter whose fault it was, what do you want? A drink? Will you drink? At least, put your coat and hat down.

STEVENS

I dont even know yet. That's why you came back——

TEMPLE (interrupts)

I came back? It wasn't I who——

STEVENS (interrupts)

—who said, let's for God's sake stop.

They stare at each other: a moment.

TEMPLE

All right. Put down your coat and hat.

Stevens lays his hat and coat on a chair. Temple sits down. Stevens takes a chair opposite, so that the sleeping child on the sofa is between them in background.

TEMPLE

So Nancy must be saved. So you send for me, or you and Bucky between you, or anyway here you are and here I am. Because apparently I know something I haven't told yet, or maybe you know something I haven't told yet. What do you think you know?

(quickly; he says nothing)

All right. What do you know?

STEVENS

Nothing. I dont want to know it. All I——

TEMPLE

Say that again.

STEVENS

Say what again?

TEMPLE

What is it you think you know?

STEVENS

Nothing. I——

TEMPLE

All right. Why do you think there is something I haven't told yet?

STEVENS

You came back. All the way from California——

TEMPLE

Not enough. Try again.

STEVENS

You were there.

(with her face averted, Temple reaches her hand to the table, fumbles until she finds the cigarette box, takes a cigarette and with the same hand fumbles until she finds the lighter, draws them back to her lap)

At the trial. Every day. All day, from the time court opened——

TEMPLE (still not looking at him, supremely casual, puts the cigarette into her mouth, talking around it, the cigarette bobbing)

The bereaved mother——

STEVENS

Yes, the bereaved mother——

TEMPLE (the cigarette bobbing: still not looking at him)

——herself watching the accomplishment of her revenge; the tigress over the body of her slain cub——

STEVENS

—who should have been too immersed in grief to have thought of revenge—to have borne the very sight of her child's murderer . . . .

TEMPLE (not looking at him)

Methinks she doth protest too much?

Stevens doesn't answer. She snaps the lighter on, lights the cigarette, puts the lighter back on the table. Leaning, Stevens pushes the ashtray along the table until she can reach it. Now she looks at him.

TEMPLE

Thanks. Now let grandmamma teach you how to suck an egg. It doesn't matter what I know, what you think I know, what might have happened. Because we wont even need it. All we need is an affidavit. That she is crazy. Has been for years.

STEVENS

I thought of that too. Only it's too late. That should have been done about five months ago. The trial is over now. She has been convicted and sentenced. In the eyes of the law, she is already dead. In the eyes of the law, Nancy Mannigoe doesn't even exist. Even if there wasn't a better reason than that. The best reason of all.

TEMPLE (smoking)

Yes?

STEVENS

We haven't got one.

TEMPLE (smoking)

Yes?

(she sits back in the chair, smoking rapidly, looking at Stevens. Her voice is gentle, patient, only a little too rapid, like the smoking)

That's right. Try to listen. Really try. I am the affidavit; what else are we doing here at ten oclock at night barely a day from her execution? What else did I—as you put it—come all the way back from California for, not to mention a—as you have probably put that too—faked coincidence to save—as I would put it I suppose—my face? All we need now is to decide just how much of what to put in the affidavit. Do try; maybe you had better have a drink after all.

STEVENS

Later, maybe. I'm dizzy enough right now with just perjury and contempt of court.

TEMPLE

What perjury?

STEVENS

Not venal then, worse: inept. After my client is not only convicted but sentenced, I turn up with the prosecution's chief witness offering evidence to set the whole trial aside——

TEMPLE

Tell them I forgot this. Or tell them I changed my mind. Tell them the district attorney bribed me to keep my mouth shut——

STEVENS (peremptory yet quiet)

Temple.

She puffs rapidly at the cigarette, removes it from her mouth.

TEMPLE

Or better still; wont it be obvious? a woman whose child was smothered in its crib, wanting vengeance, capable of anything to get the vengeance; then when she has it, realising she cant go through with it, cant sacrifice a human life for it, even a nigger whore's?

STEVENS

Stop it. One at a time. At least, let's talk about the same thing.

TEMPLE

What else are we talking about except saving a condemned client whose trained lawyer has already admitted that he has failed?

STEVENS

Then you really dont want her to die. You did invent the coincidence.

TEMPLE

Didn't I just say so? At least, let's for God's sake stop that, cant we?

STEVENS

Done. So Temple Drake will have to save her.

TEMPLE

Mrs Gowan Stevens will.

STEVENS

Temple Drake.

She stares at him, smoking, deliberately now. Deliberately she removes the cigarette and, still watching him, reaches and snubs it out in the ashtray.

STEVENS

All right. Tell me again. Maybe I'll even understand this time, let alone listen. We produce—turn up with—a sworn affidavit that this murdress was crazy when she committed the crime.

TEMPLE

You did listen, didn't you? Who knows——

STEVENS

Based on what?

TEMPLE

——What?

STEVENS

The affidavit. Based on what?

(she stares at him)

On what proof?

TEMPLE

Proof?

STEVENS

Proof. What will be in the affidavit? What are we going to affirm now that for some reason, any reason, we—you—we didn't see fit to bring up or anyway didn't bring up until after she——

TEMPLE

How do I know? You're the lawyer. What do you want in it? What do such affidavits have in them, need to have in them, to make them work, make them sure to work? Dont you have samples in your law books—reports, whatever you call them—that you can copy and have me swear to? Good ones, certain ones? At least, while we're committing whatever this is, pick out a good one, such a good one that nobody, not even an untrained lawyer, can punch holes in it . . . . .

Her voice ceases. She stares at him, while he continues to look steadily back at her, saying nothing, just looking at her, until at last she draws a loud harsh breath; her voice is harsh too.

TEMPLE

What do you want then? What more do you want?

STEVENS

Temple Drake.

TEMPLE (quick, harsh, immediate)

No. Mrs Gowan Stevens.

STEVENS (implacable and calm)

Temple Drake. The truth.

TEMPLE

Truth? We're trying to save a condemned murdress whose lawyer has already admitted that he has failed. What has truth got to do with that?

(rapid, harsh)

We? I, *I*, the mother of the baby she murdered; not you, Gavin Stevens, the lawyer, but I, Mrs Gowan Stevens, the mother. Cant you get it through your head that I will do anything, *any*thing?

STEVENS

Except one. Which is all. We're not concerned with death. That's nothing: any handful of petty facts and sworn documents can cope with that. That's all finished now; we can forget it. What we are trying to deal with now is injustice. Only truth can cope with that. Or love.

TEMPLE (harshly)

Love. Oh, God. Love.

STEVENS

Call it pity then. Or courage. Or simple honor, honesty, or a simple desire for the right to sleep at night.

TEMPLE

You prate of sleep, to me, who learned six years ago how not even to realise anymore that I didn't mind not sleeping at night?

STEVENS

Yet you invented the coincidence.

TEMPLE

Will you for Christ's sake stop? Will you . . . . . All right. Then if her dying is nothing, what do you want? What in God's name do you want?

STEVENS

I told you. Truth.

TEMPLE

And I told you that what you keep on harping at as truth, has nothing to do with this. When you go before the—What do you call this next collection of trained lawyers? supreme court?—what you will need will be facts, papers, documents, sworn to, incontrovertible, that no other lawyer trained or untrained either can punch holes in, find any flaw in.

STEVENS

We're not going to the supreme court.

(she stares at him)

That's all finished. If that could have been done, would have sufficed, I would have thought of that, attended to that, four months ago. We're going to the governor. Tonight

TEMPLE

The governor?

STEVENS

Perhaps he wont save her either. He probably wont.

TEMPLE

Then why ask him? Why?

STEVENS

I've told you. Truth.

TEMPLE (in quiet amazement)

For no more than that. For no better reason than that. Just to get it told, breathed aloud, into words, sound. Just to be heard by, told to, someone, anyone, any stranger none of whose business it is, can possibly be, simply because he is capable of hearing, comprehending it. Why blink your own rhetoric? Why dont you go on and tell me it's for the good of my soul—if I have one?

STEVENS

I did. I said, so you can sleep at night.

TEMPLE

And I told you I forgot six years ago even what it was to miss the sleep.

She stares at him. He doesn't answer, looking at her. Still watching him, she reaches her hand to the table, toward the cigarette box, then stops, is motionless, her hand suspended, staring at him.

TEMPLE

There is something else, then. We're even going to get the true one this time. All right. Shoot.

He doesn't answer, makes no sign, watching her. A moment: then she turns her head and looks toward the sofa and the sleeping child. Still looking at the child, she rises and crosses to the sofa and stands looking down at the child; her voice is quiet.

TEMPLE

So it was a plant, after all; I just didn't seem to know for who.

(she looks down at the child)

I threw my remaining child at you. Now you threw him back.

STEVENS

But I didn't wake him.

TEMPLE

Then I've got you, lawyer. What would be better for his peace and sleep than to hang his sister's murderer?

STEVENS

No matter by what means, in what lie?

TEMPLE

Nor whose.

STEVENS

Yet you invented the coincidence.

TEMPLE

Mrs Gowan Stevens did.

STEVENS

Temple Drake did. Mrs Gowan Stevens is not even fighting in this class. This is Temple Drake's.

TEMPLE

Temple Drake is dead.

STEVENS

The past is never dead. It's not even past.

She comes back to the table, takes a cigarette from the box, puts it in her mouth and reaches for the lighter. He leans as though to hand it to her, but she has already found it, snaps it on and lights the cigarette, talking through the smoke.

TEMPLE

Listen. How much do you know?

STEVENS

Nothing.

TEMPLE

Swear.

STEVENS

Would you believe me?

TEMPLE

No. But swear anyway.

STEVENS

All right. I swear.

TEMPLE (crushes cigarette into tray)

Then listen. Listen carefully.

(she stands, tense, rigid, facing him, staring at him)

Temple Drake is dead. Temple Drake will have been dead six years longer than Nancy Mannigoe will ever be. If all Nancy Mannigoe has to save her is Temple Drake, then God help Nancy Mannigoe. Now get out of here.

She stares at him; another moment. Then he rises, still watching her; she stares steadily and implacably back. Then he moves.

TEMPLE

Goodnight.

STEVENS

Goodnight.

He goes back to the chair, takes up his coat and hat, then goes on to the hall door, has put his hand on the knob.

TEMPLE

Gavin.

(he pauses, his hand on the knob, and looks back at her)

Maybe I'll have the handkerchief, after all.

(he looks at her a moment longer, then releases the knob, takes the handkerchief from his breast pocket as he crosses back toward her, extends it. She doesn't take it)

All right. What will I have to do? What do you suggest, then?

STEVENS

Everything.

TEMPLE

Which of course I wont. I will not. You can understand that, cant you? At least you can hear it. So let's start over, shall we? How much will I have to tell?

STEVENS

Everything.

TEMPLE

Then I wont need the handkerchief, after all. Goodnight. Close the front door when you go out, please. It's getting cold again.

He turns, crosses again to the door without stopping nor looking back, exits, closes the door behind him. She is not watching him either now. For a moment after the door has closed, she doesn't move. Then she makes a gesture something like Gowan's in scene 2, except that she merely presses her palms for a moment hard against her face, her face calm, expressionless, cold, drops her hands, turns, picks up the crushed cigarette from beside the tray and puts it into the tray and takes up the tray and crosses to the fireplace, glancing down at the sleeping child as she passes the sofa, empties the tray into the fireplace and returns to the table and puts the tray on it and this time pauses at the sofa and stoops and tucks the blanket closer about the sleeping child and then goes on to the telephone and lifts the receiver.

TEMPLE (into the phone)

Two three nine, please.

(while she stands waiting for the answer, there is a slight movement in the darkness beyond the open door at rear, just enough silent movement to show that something or someone is there or has moved there. Temple is unaware of it since her back is turned. Then she speaks into the phone)

Maggie? Temple. . . . Yes, suddenly . . . Oh, I dont know; perhaps we got bored with sunshine . . . . Of course, I may drop in tomorrow. I wanted to leave a message for Gavin . . . I know; he just left here. Something I forgot . . . If you'll ask him to call me when he comes in . . . . Yes . . . . Wasn't it. . . . . Yes . . . . If you will . . . Thank you.

(she puts the receiver down and starts to turn back into the room when the telephone rings. She turns back, takes up the receiver, speaks into it)

Hello . . . Yes. Coincidence again; I had my hand on it; I had just called Maggie . . . . Oh, the filling station. I didn't think you had had time. I can be ready in thirty minutes. Your car, or ours? . . . All right. Listen . . . Yes, I'm here. Gavin . . . How much will I have to tell?

(hurriedly)

Oh, I know: you've already told me eight or ten times. But maybe I didn't hear it right. How much will I have to tell?

(she listens a moment, quiet, frozen-faced, then slowly begins to lower the receiver toward the stand; she speaks quietly, without inflection)

Oh, God. Oh, God.

(she puts the receiver down, crosses to the sofa, snaps off the table lamp and takes up the child and crosses to the door to the hall, snaps off the remaining room lights as she goes out, so that the only light in the room now enters from the hall. As soon as she has disappeared from sight, Gowan enters from the door at rear, dressed except for his coat, vest and tie. He has obviously taken no sleeping pill. He goes to the phone and stands quietly beside it, facing the hall door and obviously listening until Temple is safely away. Now the hall light snaps off, and the stage is in complete darkness)

GOWAN'S VOICE (quietly)

Two three nine, please . . . Good evening, Aunt Maggie. Gowan . . . All right, thank you . . .

Sure, sometime tomorrow. As soon as Uncle Gavin comes in, will you have him call me? I'll be right here. Thank you.

(sound of the receiver as he puts it back)

(Curtain)

ACT II

The Golden Dome
(Beginning Was τὸ ἕν*)*

JACKSON. Alt. 294 ft. Pop. (A.D.1950) 201,092.
Located by an expedition of three Commissioners selected appointed and dispatched for that single purpose, on a high bluff above Pearl River at the approximate geographical center of the State, to be not a market nor industrial town, nor even as a place for men to live, but to be a capital, the Capital of a Commonwealth;

In the beginning was already decreed this rounded knob, this gilded pustule, already before and beyond the steamy chiaroscuro, untimed unseasoned winterless miasma not any one of water or earth or life yet all of each, inextricable and indivisible; that one seethe one spawn one mother-womb, one furious tumescence, father-mother-one, one vast incubant ejaculation already fissionating in one boiling moil of litter from the celestial experimental Work Bench; that one spawning crawl and creep printing with three-toed mastodonic tracks the steamy-green swaddling clothes of the coal and the oil, above which the pea-brained reptilian heads curved the heavy leather-flapped air;

Then the ice, but still this knob, this pimple-dome, this buried half-ball hemisphere; the earth lurched, heaving darkward the long continental flank, dragging upward beneath the polar cap that furious equatorial womb, the shutter-lid of cold severing off into blank and heedless void one last sound, one cry, one puny myriad indictment already fading and then no more, the blind and tongueless earth spinning on, looping the long recordless astral orbit, frozen, tideless, yet still was there this tiny gleam, this spark, this gilded crumb of man's eternal aspiration, this golden dome preordained and impregnable, this minuscule foetus-glint tougher than ice and harder than freeze; the earth lurched again, sloughing; the ice with infinitesimal speed, scouring out the valleys, scoring the hills, and vanished; the earth tilted further to recede the sea rim by necklace-rim of crustacean husks in recessional contour lines like the concentric whorls within the sawn stump telling the tree's age, baring south by recessional south toward that mute and beckoning gleam the confluent continental swale, baring to light and air the broad blank mid-continental page for the first scratch of orderly recording—a laboratory-factory covering what would be twenty states, established and ordained for the purpose of manufacturing one: the ordered unhurried whirl of seasons, of rain and snow and freeze and thaw and sun and drouth to aereate and slack the soil, the conflux of a hundred rivers into one vast father of rivers carrying the rich dirt, the rich garnering, south and south, carving the bluffs to bear the long march of the river towns, flooding the Mississippi lowlands, spawning the rich alluvial dirt layer by vernal layer, raising inch by foot by year by century the surface of the earth which in time (not distant now, measured against that long signatureless chronicle) would tremble to the passing of trains like when the cat crosses the suspension bridge;

The rich deep black alluvial soil which would grow cotton taller than the head of a man on a horse, already one jungle one brake one impassable density of brier and cane and vine interlocking the soar of gum and cypress and hickory and pinoak and ash, printed now by the tracks of unalien shapes—bear and deer and panthers and bison and wolves and alligators and the myriad smaller beasts, and unalien men to name them too perhaps—the (themselves) nameless though recorded predecessors who built the mounds to escape the spring floods and left their meagre artifacts: the obsolete and the dispossessed, dispossessed by those who were dispossessed in turn because they too were obsolete: the wild Algonquian, Chickasaw and Choctaw and Natchez and Pascagoula, peering in virgin astonishment down from the tall bluffs at a Chippeway canoe bearing three Frenchmen—and had barely time to whirl and look behind him at ten and then a hundred and then a thousand Spaniards come overland from the Atlantic Ocean: a tide, a wash, a thrice flux-and-ebb of motion so rapid and quick across the land's slow alluvial chronicle as to resemble the limber flicking of the magician's one hand before the other holding the deck of inconstant cards: the Frenchman for a moment, then the Spaniard for perhaps two, then the Frenchman for another two and then the Spaniard again for another and then the Frenchman for that one last second, half-breath; because then came the Anglo-Saxon, the pioneer, the tall man, roaring with Protestant scripture and boiled whiskey, Bible and jug in one hand and (like as not) a native tomahawk in the other, brawling, turbulent not through viciousness but simply because of his over-revved glands; uxorious and polygamous: a married invincible bachelor, dragging his gravid wife and most of the rest of his mother-in-law's family behind him into the trackless infested forest, spawning that child as like as not behind the barricade of a rifle-crotched log mapless leagues from nowhere and then getting her with another one before reaching his final itch-footed destination, and at the same time scattering his ebullient seed in a hundred dusky bellies through a thousand miles of wilderness; innocent and gullible, without bowels for avarice or compassion or forethought either, changing the face of the earth: felling a tree which took two hundred years to grow, in order to extract from it a bear or a capful of wild honey;

Obsolete too: still felling the two-hundred-year-old tree when the bear and the wild honey were gone and there was nothing in it anymore but a raccoon or a possum whose hide was worth at the most two dollars, turning the earth into a howling waste from which he would be the first to vanish, not even on the heels but synchronous with the slightly darker wild men whom he had dispossessed, because, like them, only the wilderness could feed and nourish him; and so disappeared, strutted his roaring eupeptic hour, and was no more, leaving his ghost, pariah and proscribed, scriptureless now and armed only with the highwayman's, the murderer's, pistol, haunting the fringes of the wilderness which he himself had helped to destroy, because the river towns marched now recessional south by south along the processional bluffs: St Louis, Paducah, Memphis, Helena, Vicksburg, Natchez,

Baton Rouge, peopled by men with mouths full of law, in broadcloth and flowered waistcoats, who owned Negro slaves and Empire beds and buhl cabinets and ormolu clocks, who strolled and smoked their cigars along the bluffs beneath which in the shanty and flatboat purlieus he rioted out the last of his doomed evening, losing his worthless life again and again to the fierce knives of his drunken and worthless kind;—this in the intervals of being pursued and harried in his vanishing avatars of Harpe and Hare and Mason and Murrel, either shot on sight or hoicked, dragged out of what remained of his secret wilderness haunts along the overland Natchez Trace (one day someone brought a curious seed into the land and inserted it into the earth, and now vast fields of white not only covered the waste places which with his wanton and heedless axe he had made, but were effacing, thrusting back the wilderness even faster than he had been able to, so that he barely had a screen for his back when, crouched in his thicket, he glared at his dispossessor in impotent and incredulous and uncomprehending rage) into the towns to his formal apotheosis in a courtroom and then a gallows or the limb of a tree;

Because those days were gone, the old brave innocent tumultuous eupeptic tomorrowless days; the last broadhorn and keelboat (Mike Fink was a legend; soon even the grandfathers would no longer claim to remember him, and the river hero was now the steamboat gambler wading ashore in his draggled finery from the towhead where the captain had marooned him) had been sold piecemeal for firewood in Chartres and Toulouse and Dauphine street, and Choctaw and Chickasaw braves, in short hair and overalls and armed with mule-whips in place of war-clubs and already packed up to move west to Oklahoma, watched steamboats furrowing even the shallowest and remotest wilderness streams where tumbled gently to the motion of the paddle-wheels, the gutted rock-weighted bones of Hare's and Mason's murderees; a new time, a new age, millennium's beginning; one vast single net of commerce webbed and veined the mid-continent's fluvial embracement; New Orleans, Pittsburgh, and Fort Bridger, Wyoming, were suburbs one to the other, inextricable in destiny; men's mouths were full of law and order, all men's mouths were round with the sound of money; one unanimous golden affirmation ululated the nation's boundless immeasurable forenoon: profit plus regimen equals security: a nation of commonwealths; that crumb, that dome, that gilded pustule, that Idea risen now, suspended like a balloon or a portent or a thundercloud above what used to be wilderness, drawing, holding the eyes of all: Mississippi: a state, a commonwealth; triumvirate in legislative, judiciary, executive, but without a capital, functioning as though from a field headquarters, operating as though still en route toward that high inevitable place in the galaxy of commonwealths, so in 1820 from its field p.c. at Columbia the legislature selected appointed and dispatched the three Commissioners Hinds Lattimore and Patton, not three politicians and less than any three political timeservers but soldiers engineers and patriots—soldier to cope with the reality, engineer to cope with the aspiration, patriot to hold fast to the dream—three white men in a Choctaw pirogue moving slowly up the empty reaches of a wilderness river as two centuries ago the three Frenchmen had drifted in their Northern birchbark down that vaster and emptier one;

But not drifting, these: paddling: because this was upstream, bearing not volitionless into the unknown mystery and authority, but establishing in the wilderness a point for men to rally to in conscience and free will, scanning, watching the dense inscrutable banks in their turn too, conscious of the alien incorrigible eyes too perhaps but already rejectant of them, not that the wilderness's dark denizens, already dispossessed at Doak's Stand, were less inveterate now, but because this canoe bore not the meek and bloody cross of Christ and Saint Louis, but the scales the blindfold and the sword,—up the river to Le Fleur's Bluff, the trading-post store on the high mild promontory established by the Canadian *voyageur*, whose name, called and spelled 'Leflore' now, would be borne by the half-French half-Choctaw hereditary first chief of the Choctaw nation who, siding with the white men at the Council of Dancing Rabbit, would remain in Mississippi after his people departed for the west, to become in time among the first of the great slave-holding cotton planters and leave behind him a county and its seat named for himself and a plantation named in honor of a French king's mistress,—stopping at last though still paddling slowly to hold the pirogue against the current, looking not up at the dark dispossessed faces watching them from the top of the bluff, but looking staring rather from one to another among themselves in the transfixed boat, saying, 'This is the city. This is the State';

1821, General Hinds and his co-commissioners, with Abraham DeFrance, superintendent of public buildings at Washington, to advise them, laid out the city according to Thomas Jefferson's plan to Territorial Governor Claiborne seventeen years ago, and built the statehouse, thirty by forty feet of brick and clay and native limestone yet large enough to contain the dream; the first legislature convened in it in the new year 1822;

And named the city after the other old hero, hero Hinds' brother-in-arms on beaten British and Seminole fields and presently to be President—the old duellist, the brawling lean fierce mangy durable old lion who set the well-being of the Nation above the White House, and the health of his new political party above either, and above them all set, not his wife's honor, but the principle that honor must be defended whether it was or not since, defended, it was, whether or not;—Jackson, that the new city created not for a city but a central point for the governance of men, might partake of the successful soldier's courage and endurance and luck, and named the area surrounding it 'Hinds County' after the lesser hero, as the hero's quarters, even empty, not only partake of his dignity but even guard and increase its stature;

And needed them, the luck at least: in 1829 the Senate passed a bill authorising the removal of the capital to Clinton, the House defeated it; in 1830 the House itself voted to move to Port Gibson on the Mississippi, but with the next breath reconsidered, reneged, the following day they voted to move to Vicksburg but nothing came of that either, no records (Sherman burned them in 1863 and notified his superior, General Grant, by note of hand with comfortable and encouraging brevity.) to show just what happened this time: a trial, a dry run perhaps or perhaps still enchannelled by a week's or a month's rut of habit or perhaps innocent in juvenility, absent or anyway missing the unanimous voice or presence of the three patriot-dreamers who forced the current and bore the dream, like a child with dynamite: innocent of its own power for alteration: until in 1832, perhaps in simple self-defense or perhaps in simple weariness, a constitution was written designating Jackson as the capital if not in perpetuity at least in escrow until 1850, when (hoped perhaps) a maturer legislature would be composed of maturer men outgrown or anyway become used to the novelty of manipulation;

Which by that time was enough; Jackson was secure, impregnable to simple toyment; fixed and founded strong, it would endure always; men had come there to live and the railroads had followed them, crossing off with steel cancellations the age of the steamboat: in '36 to Vicksburg, in '37 to Natchez, then last of all the junction of two giving a route from New Orleans to Tennessee and the Southern railroad to New York and the Atlantic ocean; secure and fixed: in 1836 Old Hickory himself addressed the legislature in its own halls, five years later Henry Clay was entertained under that roof; it knew the convention called to consider Clay's last compromise, it saw that Convention in 1861 which declared Mississippi to be the third star in that new galaxy of commonwealths dedicated to the principle that voluntary communities of men shall be not just safe but even secured from Federal meddling, and knew General Pemberton while defending that principle and right, and Joseph Johnston: and Sherman: and fire: and nothing remained, a City of Chimneys (once pigs rooted in the streets; now rats did) ruled over by a general of the United States army while the new blood poured in: men who had followed, pressed close the Federal field armies with spoiled grain and tainted meat and spavined mules, now pressing close the Federal provost-marshals with carpet bags stuffed with blank ballot-forms on which freed slaves could mark their formal X's;

* * *

But endured; the government, which fled before Sherman in 1863, returned in '65, and even grew too despite the fact that a city government of carpet-baggers held on long after the State as a whole had dispossessed them; in 1869 Tougaloo College for Negroes was founded, in 1884 Jackson College for Negroes was brought from Natchez, in 1898 Campbell College for Negroes removed from Vicksburg; Negro leaders developed by these schools intervened when in 1868 one 'Buzzard' Egglestone instigated the use of troops to drive Governor Humphries from the executive offices and mansion; in 1887 Jackson women sponsored the Kermis Ball lasting three days to raise money for a monument to the Confederate dead; in 1884 Jefferson Davis spoke for his last time in public at the old Capitol; in 1890 the state's greatest convention drew up the present constitution;

And still the people and the railroads: the New Orleans and Great Northern down the Pearl River valley, the Gulf Mobile and Northern northeast; Alabama and the eastern black prairies were almost a commuter's leap and a line to Yazoo City and the upper river towns made of the Great Lakes five suburban ponds; the Gulf and Ship Island opened the south Mississippi lumber boom and Chicago voices spoke among the magnolias and the odor of jasmine and oleander; population doubled and trebled in a decade, in 1892 Millsaps College opened its doors to assume its place among the first establishments for higher learning; then the natural gas and the oil, Texas and Oklahoma license plates flitted like a migration of birds about the land and the tall flames from the vent-pipes stood like incandescent plumes above the century-cold ashes of Choctaw camp-fires and the vanished imprints of deer; and in 1903 the new Capitol was completed—the golden dome, the knob, the gleamy crumb, the gilded pustule longer than the miasma and the gigantic ephemeral saurians, more durable than the ice and the pre-night cold, soaring, hanging as one blinding spheroid above the center of the Commonwealth, incapable of being either looked full or evaded, peremptory, irrefragible, and reassuring;

* * *

In the roster of Mississippi names:
Claiborne. Humphries. Dickson. McLaurin. Barksdale. Lamar. Prentiss. Davis. Sartoris. Compson;

In the roster of cities:
JACKSON. Alt. 294 ft. Pop. (A.D. 1950) 201,092.
Railroads: Illinois Central, Yazoo & Mississippi Valley, Alabama & Vicksburg, Gulf & Ship Island.
Bus: Tri-State Transit, Varnado, Thomas, Greyhound, Dixie-Greyhound, Teche-Greyhound, Oliver.
Air: Delta, Chicago & Southern.
Transport: Street busses, Taxis.
Accommodations: Hotels, Tourist camps, Rooming houses.
Radio: WJDX, WTJS.
Diversions: chronic: S.I.A.A. Basketball Tournament, Music Festival, Junior Auxiliary Follies, May Day Festival, State Tennis Tournament, Red Cross Water Pageant, State Fair, Junior Auxiliary Style Show, Girl Scouts Horseshow, Feast of Carols.
Diversions: acute: Religion, Politics.

Scene I

Office of the Governor of the State. 2:00 A.M. March twelfth.

The whole bottom of the stage is in darkness, as in Scene 1, Act I, so that the visible scene has the effect of being held in the beam of a spotlight. Suspended too, since it is upper L and even higher above the shadow of the stage proper than the same in Scene 1, Act I, carrying still further the symbolism of the still higher, the last, the ultimate seat of judgment.

It is a corner or section of the office of the Governor of the Commonwealth, late at night, about two a.m.—a clock on the wall says two minutes past two—, a massive flat-topped desk bare except for an ashtray and a telephone, behind it a high-backed heavy chair like a throne; on the wall behind and above the chair, is the emblem, official badge, of the State, sovereignty (a mythical one, since this is rather the State of which Yoknapatawpha County is a unit)—an eagle, the blind scales of justice, a device in Latin perhaps, against a flag. There are two other chairs in front of the desk, turned slightly to face each other, the length of the desk between them.

The Governor stands in front of the high chair, between it and the desk, beneath the emblem on the wall. He is symbolic too: no known person, neither old nor young; he might be someone's idea not of God but of Gabriel perhaps, the Gabriel not before the Crucifixion but after it. He has obviously just been routed out of bed or at least out of his study or dressing-room; he wears a dressing gown, though there is a collar and tie beneath it, and his hair is neatly combed.

Temple and Stevens have just entered. Temple wears the same fur coat, hat, bag, gloves etc. as in Act I, Scene 2, Stevens is dressed exactly as he was in Scene 3, Act I, is carrying his hat. They are moving toward the two chairs at either end of the desk.

STEVENS

Good morning, Henry. Here we are.

GOVERNOR

Yes. Sit down.

(as Temple sits down)

Does Mrs Stevens smoke?

STEVENS

Yes. Thank you.

He takes a pack of cigarettes from his topcoat pocket, as though he had come prepared for the need, emergency. He works one of them free and extends the pack to Temple. The Governor puts one hand into his dressing gown pocket and withdraws it, holding something in his closed fist.

TEMPLE (takes the cigarette)

What, no blindfold?

(the Governor extends his hand across the desk. It contains a lighter.

Temple puts the cigarette into her mouth. The Governor snaps on the lighter)

But of course, the only one waiting execution is back there in Jefferson. So all we need to do here is, fire away, and hope that at least the volley rids us of the metaphor.

GOVERNOR

Metaphor?

TEMPLE

The blindfold. The firing squad. Or is metaphor wrong? Or maybe it's the joke. But dont apologise; a joke that has to be diagrammed is like trying to excuse an egg, isn't it? The only thing you can do is, bury them both, quick.

(the Governor approaches the flame to Temple's cigarette. She leans and accepts the light, then sits back)

Thanks.

The Governor closes the lighter, sits down in the tall chair behind the desk, still holding the lighter in his hand, his hands resting on the desk before him. Stevens sits down in the other chair across from Temple, laying the pack of cigarettes on the desk beside him.

GOVERNOR

What has Mrs Gowan Stevens to tell me?

TEMPLE

Not tell you: ask you. No, that's wrong. I could have asked you to revoke or commute or whatever you do to a sentence to hang when we—Uncle Gavin telephoned you last night.

(to Stevens)

Go on. Tell him. Aren't you the mouthpiece?—isn't that how you say it? Dont lawyers always tell their patients—I mean clients—never to say anything at all: to let them do all the talking?

GOVERNOR

That's only before the client enters the witness stand.

TEMPLE

So this is the witness stand.

GOVERNOR

You have come all the way here from Jefferson at two oclock in the morning. What would you call it?

TEMPLE

All right. Touché then. But not Mrs Gowan Stevens: Temple Drake. You remember Temple: the all-Mississippi debutante whose finishing school was the Memphis sporting house? About eight years ago, remember? Not that anyone, certainly not the sovereign state of Mississippi's first paid servant, need be reminded of that, provided they could read newspapers eight years ago or were kin to somebody who could read eight years ago or even had a friend who could or even just hear or even just remember or just believe the worst or even just hope for it.

GOVERNOR

I think I remember. What has Temple Drake to tell me then?

TEMPLE

That's not first. The first thing is, how much will I have to tell? I mean, how much of it that you dont already know, so that I wont be wasting all of our times telling it over? It's two oclock in the morning; you want to—maybe even need to—sleep some, even if you are our first paid servant; maybe even because of that—— You see? I'm already lying. What does it matter to me how much sleep the state's first paid servant loses, anymore than it matters to the first paid servant, a part of whose job is being paid to lose sleep over Nancy Mannigoes and Temple Drakes?

STEVENS

Not lying.

TEMPLE

All right. Stalling, then. So maybe if his excellency or his honor or whatever they call him, will answer the question, we can get on.

STEVENS

Why not let the question go, and just get on?

GOVERNOR (to Temple)

Ask me your question. How much of what do I already know?

TEMPLE (after a moment: she doesn't answer at first, staring at the Governor: then:)

Uncle Gavin's right. Maybe you are the one to ask the questions. Only, make it as painless as possible. Because it's going to be a little . . . . painful, to put it euphoniously—at least 'euphonious' is right, isn't it?—no matter who bragged about blindfolds.

GOVERNOR

Tell me about Nancy—Mannihoe, Mannikoe—how does she spell it?

TEMPLE

She doesn't. She cant. She cant read or write either. You are hanging her under Mannigoe, which may be wrong too, though after tomorrow morning it wont matter.

GOVERNOR

Oh yes, Manigault. The old Charleston name.

STEVENS

Older than that. Maingault. Nancy's heritage—or anyway her patronym—runs Norman blood.

GOVERNOR

Why not start by telling me about her.

TEMPLE

You are so wise. She was a dope-fiend whore that my husband and I took out of the gutter to nurse our children. She murdered one of them and is to be hung tomorrow morning. We—her lawyer and I—have come to ask you to save her.

GOVERNOR

Yes. I know all that. Why?

TEMPLE

Why am I, the mother whose child she murdered, asking you to save her? Because I have forgiven her.

(the Governor watches her, he and Stevens both do, waiting. She stares back at the Governor, steadily, not defiant: just alert)

Because she was crazy.

(the Governor watches her: she stares back, puffing rapidly at the cigarette)

All right. You dont mean why I am asking you to save her, but why I—we hired a whore and a tramp and a dope-fiend to nurse our children.

(she puffs rapidly, talking through the smoke)

To give her another chance—a human being too, even a nigger dope-fiend whore——

STEVENS

Nor that, either.

TEMPLE (rapidly, with a sort of despair)

Oh yes, not even stalling now. Why cant you stop lying? You know: just stop for a while or a time like you can stop playing tennis or running or dancing or drinking or eating sweets during Lent. You know: not to reform: just to quit for a while, clear your system, rest up for a new tune or set or lie? All right. It was to have someone to talk to. And now you see? I'll have to tell the rest of it in order to tell you why I had to have a dope-fiend whore to talk to, why Temple Drake, the white woman, the all-Mississippi debutante, descendant of long lines of statesmen and soldiers high and proud in the high proud annals of our sovereign state, couldn't find anybody except a nigger dope-fiend whore that could speak her language——

GOVERNOR

Yes. This far, this late at night. Tell it.

TEMPLE (she puffs rapidly at the cigarette, leans and crushes it out in the ashtray and sits erect again. She speaks in a hard rapid brittle emotionless voice)

Whore, dope-fiend; hopeless, already damned before she was ever born, whose only reason for living was to get the chance to die a murdress on the gallows.—Who not only entered the home of the socialite Gowan Stevenses out of the gutter, but made her debut into the public life of her native city while lying in the gutter with a white man trying to kick her teeth or at least her voice back down her throat.—You remember, Gavin: what was his name? it was before my time in Jefferson, but you remember: the cashier in the bank, the pillar of the church or anyway in the name of his childless wife; and this Monday morning and still drunk, Nancy comes up while he is unlocking the front door of the bank and fifty people standing at his back to get in, and Nancy comes into the crowd and right up to him and says, 'Where's my two dollars, white man?' and he turned and struck her, knocked her across the pavement into the gutter and then ran after her, stomping and kicking at her face or anyway her voice which was still saying 'Where's my two dollars, white man?' until the crowd caught and held him still kicking at the face lying in the gutter, spitting blood and teeth and still saying, 'It was two dollars more than two weeks ago and you done been back twice since'——

She stops speaking, presses both hands to her face for an instant, then removes them.

TEMPLE

No, no handkerchief; Lawyer Stevens and I made a dry run on handkerchiefs before we left home tonight. Where was I?

GOVERNOR (quotes her)

'It was already two dollars'——

TEMPLE

So now I've got to tell all of it. Because that was just Nancy Mannigoe. Temple Drake was in more than just a two-dollar Saturday night house. But then, I said touché, didn't I?

She leans forward and starts to take up the crushed cigarette from the ashtray. Stevens picks up the pack from the desk and prepares to offer it to her. She withdraws her hand from the crushed cigarette and sits back.

TEMPLE (to the proffered cigarette in Stevens' hand)

No thanks; I wont need it, after all. From here out, it's merely anticlimax. *Coup de grace*. The victim never feels that, does he?—Where was I?

(quickly)

Never mind. I said that before too, didn't I?

(she sits for a moment, her hands gripped in her lap, motionless)

There seems to be some of this, quite a lot of this, which even our first paid servant is not up on; maybe because he has been our first paid servant for less than two years yet. Though that's wrong too; he could read eight years ago, couldn't he? In fact, he couldn't have been elected governor of even Mississippi if he hadn't been able to read at least three years in advance, could he?

STEVENS

Temple.

TEMPLE (to Stevens)

Why not? It's just stalling, isn't it?

GOVERNOR (watching Temple)

Hush, Gavin.

(to Temple)

Coup de grace not only means mercy, but is. Deliver it. Give her the cigarette, Gavin.

TEMPLE (sits forward again)

No thanks. Really.

(after a second)

Sorry.

(quickly)

You'll notice, I always remember to say that, always remember my manners,—'raising' as we put it. Showing that I really sprang from gentlefolks, not Norman knights like Nancy did, but at least people who dont insult the host in his own house, especially at two oclock in the morning. Only, I just sprang too far, where Nancy merely stumbled modestly: a lady again, you see.

(after a moment)

There again. I'm not even lying now: I'm faulting—what do they call it? burking. You know: here we are at the fence again; we've got to jump it this time, or crash. You know: slack the snaffle, let her mouth it a little, take hold, a light hold, just enough to have something to jump against; then touch her. So here we are, right back where we started, and so we can start over. So how much will I have to tell, say, speak out loud so that anybody with ears can hear it, about Temple Drake that I never thought that anything on earth, least of all the murder of my child and the execution of a nigger dope-fiend whore, would ever make me tell? That I came here at two oclock in the morning to wake you up to listen to, after eight years of being safe or at least quiet? You know: how much will I have to tell, to make it good and painful of course, but quick too, so that you can revoke or commute the sentence or whatever you do to it, and we can all go back home to sleep or at least to bed? Painful of course, but just painful enough—— I think you said 'euphoniously' was right, didn't you?

GOVERNOR

Death is painful. A shameful one, even more so—which is not too euphonious, even at best.

TEMPLE

Oh, death. We're not talking about death now. We're talking about shame. Nancy Mannigoe has no shame; all she has is, to die. But touché for me too; haven't I brought Temple Drake all the way here at two oclock in the morning for the reason that all Nancy Mannigoe has, is to die?

STEVENS

Tell him, then.

TEMPLE

He hasn't answered my question yet.

(to Governor)

Try to answer it. How much will I have to tell? Dont just say 'everything'. I've already heard that.

GOVERNOR

I know who Temple Drake was: the young woman student at the University eight years ago who left the school one morning on a special train of students to attend a baseball game at another college, and disappeared from the train somewhere during its run, and vanished, nobody knew where, until she reappeared six weeks later as a witness in a murder trial in Jefferson, produced by the lawyer of the man who, it was then learned, had abducted her and held her prisoner——

TEMPLE

—in the Memphis sporting house: dont forget that.

GOVERNOR

—in order to produce her to prove his alibi in the murder——

TEMPLE

—that Temple Drake knew had done the murder for the very good reason that——

STEVENS

Wait. Let me play too. She got off the train at the instigation of a young man who met the train at an intermediate stop with an automobile, the plan being to drive on to the ball game in the car, except that the young man was drunk at the time and got drunker, and wrecked the car and stranded both of them at the moonshiner's house where the murder happened, and from which the murderer kidnapped her and carried her to Memphis, to hold her until he would need his alibi. Afterward he—the young man with the automobile, her escort and protector at the moment of the abduction—married her. He is her husband now. He is my nephew.

TEMPLE (to Stevens, bitterly)

You too. So wise too. Why cant you believe in truth? At least that I'm trying to tell it. At least trying now to tell it.

(to Governor)

Where was I?

GOVERNOR (quotes)

That Temple Drake knew had done the murder for the very good reason that——

TEMPLE

Oh yes. —for the very good reason that she saw him do it, or at least his shadow: and so produced by his lawyer in the Jefferson courtroom so that she could swear away the life of the man who was accused of it. Oh yes, that's the one. And now I've already told you something you nor nobody else but the Memphis lawyer knew, and I haven't even started. You see? I cant even bargain with you. You haven't even said yes or no yet, whether you can save her or not, whether you want to save her or not, will consider saving her or not; which, if either of us, Temple Drake or Mrs Gowan Stevens either, had any sense, would have demanded first of you.

GOVERNOR

Do you want to ask me that first?

TEMPLE

I cant. I dont dare. You might say no.

GOVERNOR

Then you wouldn't have to tell me about Temple Drake.

TEMPLE

I've got to do that. I've got to say it all, or I wouldn't be here. But unless I can still believe that you might say yes, I dont see how I can. Which is another touché for somebody: God, maybe—if there is one. You see? That's what's so terrible. We dont even need Him. Simple evil is enough. Even after eight years, it's still enough. It was eight years ago that

Uncle Gavin said—oh yes, he was there too; didn't you just hear him? He could have told you all of this or anyway most of it over the telephone and you could be in bed asleep right this minute—said how there is a corruption even in just looking at evil, even by accident; that you cant haggle, traffic, with putrefaction—you cant, you dont dare——

(she stops, tense, motionless)

GOVERNOR

Take the cigarette now.

(to Stevens)

Gavin——

(Stevens takes up the pack and prepares to offer the cigarette)

TEMPLE

No thanks. It's too late now. Because here we go. If we cant jump the fence, we can at least break through it——

STEVENS (interrupts)

Which means that anyway one of us will get over standing up.

(as Temple reacts)

Oh yes, I'm still playing; I'm going to ride this one too. Go ahead.

(prompting)

Temple Drake——

TEMPLE

—Temple Drake, the foolish virgin; that is, a virgin as far as anybody went on record to disprove, but a fool certainly by anybody's standards and computation; seventeen, and more of a fool than simply being a virgin or even being seventeen could excuse or account for; indeed, showing herself capable of a height of folly which even seven or three, let alone mere virginity, could scarcely have matched——

STEVENS

Give the brute a chance. Try at least to ride him at the fence and not just through it.

TEMPLE

You mean the Virginia gentleman.

(to Governor)

That's my husband. He went to the University of Virginia, trained, Uncle Gavin would say, at Virginia not only in drinking but in gentility too——

STEVENS

—and ran out of both at the same instant that day eight years ago when he took her off the train and wrecked the car at the moonshiner's house.

TEMPLE

But relapsed into one of them at least because at least he married me as soon as he could.

(to Stevens)

You dont mind my telling his excellency that, do you?

STEVENS

A relapse into both of them. He hasn't had a drink since that day either. His excellency might bear that in mind too.

GOVERNOR

I will. I have.

(he makes just enough of a pause to cause them both to stop and look at him)

I almost wish——

(they are both watching him; this is the first intimation we have that something is going on here, an undercurrent: that the Governor and Stevens know something which Temple doesn't: to Temple)

He didn't come with you.

STEVENS (mildly yet quickly)

Wont there be time for that later, Henry?

TEMPLE (quick, defiant, suspicious, hard)

Who didn't?

GOVERNOR

Your husband.

TEMPLE (quick and hard)

Why?

GOVERNOR

You have come here to plead for the life of the murdress of your child. Your husband was its parent too.

TEMPLE

You're wrong. We didn't come here at two oclock in the morning to save Nancy Mannigoe. Nancy Mannigoe is not even concerned in this because Nancy Mannigoe's lawyer told me before we ever left Jefferson that you were not going to save Nancy Mannigoe. What we came here and waked you up at two oclock in the morning for is just to give Temple Drake a good fair honest chance to suffer—you know: just anguish for the sake of anguish, like that Russian or somebody who wrote a whole book about suffering, not suffering for or about anything, just suffering, like somebody unconscious not really breathing for anything but just breathing. Or maybe that's wrong too and nobody really cares, suffers, anymore about suffering than they do about truth or justice or Temple Drake's shame or Nancy Mannigoe's worthless nigger life——

She stops speaking, sitting quite still, erect in the chair, her face raised slightly, not looking at either of them while they watch her.

GOVERNOR

Give her the handkerchief now.

Stevens takes a fresh handkerchief from his pocket, shakes it out and extends it toward Temple. She does not move, her hands still clasped in her lap. Stevens rises, crosses, drops the handkerchief into her lap, returns to his chair.

TEMPLE

Thanks really. But it doesn't matter now; we're too near the end; you could almost go on down to the car and start it and have the engine warming up while I finish.

(to Governor)

You see? All you'll have to do now is just be still and listen. Or not even listen if you dont want to: but just be still, just wait. And not long either now, and then we can all go to bed and turn off the light. And then, night: dark: sleep even maybe, when with the same arm you turn off the light and pull the covers up with, you can put away forever Temple Drake and whatever it is you have done about her, and Nancy Mannigoe and whatever it is you have done about her, if you're going to do anything, if it even matters anyhow whether you do anything or not, and none of it will ever have to bother us anymore. Because Uncle Gavin was only partly right. It's not that you must never even look on evil and corruption; sometimes you cant help that, you are not always warned. It's not even that you must resist it always. Because you've got to start much sooner than that. You've got to be already prepared to resist it, say no to it, long before you see it; you must have already said no to it long before you even know what it is. I'll have the cigarette now, please.

Stevens takes up the pack, rising and working the end of a cigarette free, and extends the pack. She takes the cigarette, already speaking again while Stevens puts the pack on the desk and takes up the lighter which the Governor, watching Temple, shoves across the desk where Stevens can reach it. Stevens snaps the lighter on and holds it out. Temple makes no effort to light the cigarette, holding the cigarette in her hand and talking. Then she lays the cigarette unlighted on the ashtray and Stevens closes the lighter and sits down again, putting the lighter down beside the pack of cigarettes.

TEMPLE

Because Temple Drake liked evil. She only went to the ball game because she would have to get on a train to do it, so that she could slip off the train the first time it stopped, and get into the car to drive a hundred miles with a man——

STEVENS

—who couldn't hold his drink.

TEMPLE (to Stevens)

All right. Aren't I just saying that?

(to Governor)

An optimist. Not the young man; he was just doing the best he knew, could. It wasn't him that suggested the trip: it was Temple——

STEVENS

It was his car though. Or his mother's.

TEMPLE (to Stevens)

All right. All right.

(to Governor)

No, Temple was the optimist: not that she had foreseen, planned ahead either: she just had unbounded faith that her father and brothers would know evil when they saw it, so all she had to do was, do the one thing which she knew they would forbid her to do if they had the chance. And they were right about the evil, and so of course she was right too, though even then it was not easy: she even had to drive the car for a while after we began to realise that the young man was wrong, had graduated too soon in the drinking part of his Virginia training——

STEVENS
It was Gowan who knew the moonshiner and insisted on going there.

TEMPLE
—and even then——

STEVENS
He was driving when you wrecked.

TEMPLE (to Stevens: quick and harsh)
And married me for it. Does he have to pay for it twice? It wasn't really worth paying for once, was it?
(to Governor)
And even then——

GOVERNOR
How much was it worth?

TEMPLE
Was what worth?

GOVERNOR
His marrying you.

TEMPLE
You mean to him, of course. Less than he paid for it.

GOVERNOR
Is that what he thinks too?
(they stare at one another, Temple alert, quite watchful, though rather impatient than anything else)

You're going to tell me something that he doesn't know, else you would have brought him with you. Is that right?

TEMPLE

Yes.

GOVERNOR

Would you tell it if he were here?

(Temple is staring at the Governor. Unnoticed by her, Stevens makes a faint movement. The Governor stops him with a slight motion of one hand which also Temple does not notice)

Now that you have come this far, now that, as you said, you have got to tell it, say it aloud, not to save Nan—this woman, but because you decided before you left home tonight that there is nothing else to do but tell it.

TEMPLE

How do I know whether I would or not?

GOVERNOR

Suppose he was here—sitting in that chair where Gav—your uncle is——

TEMPLE

—or behind the door or in one of your desk drawers, maybe? He's not. He's at home. I gave him a sleeping pill.

GOVERNOR

But suppose he was, now that you have got to say it. Would you still say it?

TEMPLE

All right. Yes. Now will you please shut up too and let me tell it? How can I, if you and Gavin wont hush and let me? I cant even remember where I was.—Oh yes. So I saw the murder, or anyway the shadow of it, and the man took me to Memphis, and I know that too, I had two legs and I could see, and I could have simply screamed up the main street of any of the little towns we passed, just as I could have walked away from the car after Gow—we ran it into the tree, and stopped a wagon or a car which would have carried me to the nearest town or railroad station or even back to school or for that matter, right on back home into my father's or brothers' hands. But not me, not Temple. I choose the murderer——

STEVENS (to Governor)

He was a psychopath, though that didn't come out in the trial, and when it did come out, or could have come out, it was too late. I was there; I saw that too: a little black thing with an Italian name, like a neat and only slightly deformed cockroach: a hybrid, sexually incapable. But then, she will tell you that too.

TEMPLE (with bitter sarcasm)

Dear Uncle Gavin.

(to Governor)

Oh yes, that too, her bad luck too: to plump for a thing which didn't even have sex for his weakness, but just murder——

(she stops, sitting motionless, erect, her hands clenched on her lap, her eyes closed)

If you both would just hush, just let me. I seem to be like trying to drive a hen into a barrel. Maybe if you would just try to act like you wanted to keep her out of it, from going into it——

GOVERNOR

Dont call it a barrel. Call it a tunnel. That's a thoroughfare, because the other end is open too. Go through it. There was no—sex.

TEMPLE

Not from him. He was worse than a father or uncle. It was worse than being the wealthy ward of the most indulgent trust or insurance company: carried to Memphis and shut up in that Manuel Street sporting house like a ten-year-old bride in a Spanish convent, with the madam herself more eagle-eyed than any mamma—and the Negro maid to guard the door while the madam would be out, to wherever she would go, wherever the madams of cat houses go on their afternoons out, to pay police court fines or protection or to the bank or maybe just visiting, which would not be so bad because the maid would unlock the door and come inside and we could——

(she falters, pauses for less than a second; then quickly)

Yes, that's why—talk. A prisoner of course, and maybe not in a very gilded cage, but at least the prisoner was. I had perfume by the quart; some salesgirl chose it of course, and it was the wrong kind, but at least I had it, and he bought me a fur coat—with nowhere to wear it of course because he wouldn't let me out, but I had the coat—and snazzy underwear and negligees, selected also by salesgirls but at least the best or anyway the most expensive—the taste at least of the big end of an underworld big shot's wallet. Because he wanted me to be contented, you see; and not only contented, he didn't even mind if I was happy too: just so I was there when or in case the police finally connected him with that Mississippi murder; not only didn't mind if I was happy, he even made the effort himself to see that I was. And so at last we have come to it, because now I have got to tell you this too to give you a valid reason why I waked you up at two in the morning to ask you to save a murdress.

She stops speaking, reaches and takes the unlighted cigarette from the tray, then realises it is unlit. Stevens takes up the lighter from the desk and starts to get up. Still watching Temple, the Governor makes to Stevens a slight arresting signal with his hand. Stevens pauses, then pushes the lighter along the desk to where Temple can reach it, and sits back down. Temple takes the lighter, snaps it on, lights the cigarette, closes the lighter and puts it back on the desk. But after only one puff at the cigarette, she lays it back on the tray and sits again as before, speaking again.

TEMPLE

Because I still had the two arms and legs and eyes; I could have climbed down the rainspout at any time, the only difference being that I didn't. I would never leave the room except late at night, when he would come in a closed car the size of an undertaker's wagon, and he and the chauffeur on the front seat, and me and the madam in the back, rushing at forty and fifty and sixty miles an hour up and down the back alleys of the redlight district. Which—the back alleys—was all I ever saw of them too. I was not even permitted to meet or visit with or even see the other girls in my own house, not even to sit with them after work and listen to the shop talk while they counted their chips or blisters or whatever they would do sitting on one another's beds in the elected dormitory. . . .

(she pauses again, continues in a sort of surprise, amazement)

Yes, it was like the dormitory at school: the smell: of women, young women all busy thinking not about men but just man: only a little stronger, a little calmer, less excited,—sitting on the temporarily idle beds discussing the exigencies—that's surely the right one, isn't it?—of their trade. But not me, not Temple: shut up in that room twenty-four hours a day, with nothing to do but hold fashion shows in the fur coat and the flash pants and negligees, with nothing to see it but a two-foot mirror and a Negro maid; hanging bone dry and safe in the middle of sin and pleasure like being suspended twenty fathoms deep in an ocean diving bell. Because he wanted her to be contented, you see. He even made the last effort himself. But Temple didn't want to be just contented. So she had to do what us sporting girls call fall in love.

GOVERNOR

Ah.

STEVENS

That's right.

TEMPLE (quickly: to Stevens)

Hush.

STEVENS (to Temple)

Hush yourself.

(to Governor)

He—Vitelli—they called him Popeye—brought the man there himself. He—the young man——

TEMPLE

Gavin! No, I tell you!

STEVENS (to Temple)

You are drowning in an orgasm of abjectness and moderation when all you need is truth.

(to Governor)

—was known in his own circles as Red, Alabama Red; not to the police, or not officially, since he was not a criminal, or anyway not yet, but just a thug, probably cursed more by simple eupepsia than by anything else. He was a houseman—the bouncer—at the nightclub, joint, on the outskirts of town, which Popeye owned and which was Popeye's headquarters. He died shortly afterward in the alley behind Temple's prison, of a bullet from the same pistol which had done the Mississippi murder, though Popeye too was dead, hanged in Alabama for a murder he did not commit, before the pistol was ever found and connected with him.

GOVERNOR

I see. This—Popeye——

STEVENS

—discovered himself betrayed by one of his own servants, and took a princely vengeance on his honor's smircher? You will be wrong. You underrate this *precieux*, this flower, this jewel. Vitelli. What a name for him. A hybrid, impotent. He was hanged the next year, to be sure. But even that was wrong: his very effacement debasing, flouting, even what dignity man has been able to lend to necessary human abolishment. He should have been crushed somehow under a vast and mindless boot, like a spider. He didn't sell her; you violate and outrage his very memory with that crass and material impugnment. He was a purist, an amateur always; he did not even murder for base profit. It was not even for simple lust. He was a gourmet, a sybarite, centuries, perhaps hemispheres before his time; in spirit and glands he was of that age of princely despots to whom the ability even to read was vulgar and plebeian and, reclining on silk amid silken airs and scents, had eunuch slaves for that office, commanding death to the slave at the end of each reading, each evening, that none else alive, even a eunuch slave, shall have shared in, partaken of, remembered, the poem's evocation.

GOVERNOR

I dont think I understand.

STEVENS

Try to. Uncheck your capacity for rage and revulsion—the sort of rage and revulsion it takes to step on a worm. If Vitelli cannot evoke that in you, his life will have been indeed a desert.

TEMPLE

Or dont try to. Just let it go. Just for God's sake let it go. I met the man, how doesn't matter, and I fell what I called in love with him and what it was or what I called it doesn't matter either because all that matters is that I wrote the letters——

GOVERNOR

I see. This is the part that her husband didn't know.

TEMPLE (to Governor)

And what does that matter either? Whether he knows or not? What can another face or two or name or two matter, since he knows that I lived for six weeks in a Manuel Street brothel? Or another body or two in the bed? Or three or four? I'm trying to tell it, enough of it. Cant you see that? But cant you make him let me alone so I can. Make him, for God's sake, let me alone.

GOVERNOR (to Stevens: watching Temple)

No more, Gavin.

(to Temple)

So you fell in love.

TEMPLE

Thank you for that. I mean, the 'love.' Except that I didn't even fall, I was already there: the bad, the lost: who could have climbed down the gutter or lightning rod any time and got away, or even simpler than that: disguised myself as the nigger maid with a stack of towels and a bottle opener and change for ten dollars, and walked right out the front door. So I wrote the letters. I would write one each time . . . afterward, after they—he left, and sometimes I would write two or three when it would be two or three days between, when they—he wouldn't——

GOVERNOR

What? What's that?

TEMPLE

—you know: something to do, be doing, filling the time, better than the fashion parades in front of the two-foot glass with nobody to be disturbed even by the . . . pants, or even no pants. Good letters——

GOVERNOR

Wait. What did you say?

TEMPLE

I said they were good letters, even for——

GOVERNOR

You said, after *they* left.

(they look at one another. Temple doesn't answer: to Stevens, though still watching Temple)

Am I being told that this . . . Vitelli would be there in the room too?

STEVENS

Yes. That was why he brought him. You can see now what I meant by connoisseur and gourmet.

GOVERNOR:

And what you meant by the boot too. But he's dead. You know that.

STEVENS

Oh yes. He's dead. And I said 'purist' too. To the last: hanged the next summer in Alabama for a murder he didn't even commit and which nobody involved in the matter really believed he had committed, only not even his lawyer could persuade him to admit that he couldn't have done it if he had wanted to, or wouldn't have done it if the notion had struck him. Oh yes, he's dead too; we haven't come here for vengeance.

GOVERNOR (to Temple)

Yes. Go on. The letters.

TEMPLE

The letters. They were good letters. I mean——good ones.

(staring steadily at the Governor)

What I'm trying to say is, they were the kind of letters that if you had written them to a man, even eight years ago, you wouldn't—would—rather your husband didn't see them, no matter what he thought about your—past.

(still staring at the Governor as she makes her painful confession)

Better than you would expect from a seventeen-year-old amateur. I mean, you would have wondered how anybody just seventeen and not even through freshman in college, could have learned the—right words. Though all you would have needed probably would be an old dictionary from back in Shakespeare's time when, so they say, people hadn't learned how to blush at words. That is, anybody except Temple Drake, who didn't need a dictionary, who was a fast learner and so even just one lesson would have been enough for her, let alone three or four or a dozen or two or three dozen.

(staring at the Governor)

No, not even one lesson because the bad was already there waiting, who hadn't even heard yet that you must be already resisting the corruption not only before you look at it but before you even know what it is, what you are resisting. So I wrote the letters, I dont know how many, enough, more than enough because just one would have been enough. And that's all.

GOVERNOR

All?

TEMPLE

Yes. You've certainly heard of blackmail. The letters turned up again of course. And of course, being Temple Drake, the first way to buy them back that Temple Drake thought of, was to produce the material for another set of them.

STEVENS (to Temple)

Yes, that's all. But you've got to tell him why it's all.

TEMPLE

I thought I had. I wrote some letters that you would have thought that even Temple Drake might have been ashamed to put on paper, and then the man I wrote them to died, and I married another man and reformed, or thought I had, and bore two children and hired another reformed whore so that I would have somebody to talk to, and I even thought I had forgotten about the letters until they turned up again and then I found out that I not only hadn't forgot about the letters, I hadn't even reformed——

STEVENS

All right. Do you want me to tell it, then?

TEMPLE

And you were the one preaching moderation.

STEVENS

I was preaching against orgasms of it.

TEMPLE (bitterly)

Oh, I know. Just suffering. Not for anything: just suffering. Just because it's good for you, like calomel or ipecac.

(to Governor)

All right. What?

GOVERNOR

The young man died——

TEMPLE

Oh yes.—Died, shot from a car while he was slipping up the alley behind the house, to climb up the same drainpipe I could have climbed down at any time and got away, to see me—the one time, the first time, the only time when we thought we had dodged, fooled him, could be alone together, just the two of us, after all the . . . other ones.—If love can be, mean anything, except the newness, the learning, the peace, the privacy: no shame: not even conscious that you are naked because you are just using the nakedness because that's a part of it; then he was dead, killed, shot down right in the middle of thinking about me, when in just one more minute maybe he would have been in the room with me, when all of him except just his body was already in the room with me and the door locked at last for just the two of us alone, and then it was all over and as though it had never been, happened, it had to be as though it had never happened, except that that was even worse——

(rapidly)

Then the courtroom in Jefferson and I didn't care, not about anything anymore, and my father and brothers waiting and then the year in Europe, Paris, and I still didn't care, and then after a while it really did get easier. You know. People are lucky. They are wonderful. At first you think that you can bear only so much and then you will be free. Then you find out that you can bear anything, you really can and then it wont even matter. Because suddenly it could be as if it had never been, never happened. You know: somebody—Hemingway, wasn't it?—wrote a book about how it had never actually happened to a g—woman, if she just refused to accept it, no matter who remembered, bragged. And besides, the ones who could—remember were both dead. Then Gowan came to Paris that winter and we were married—at the Embassy, with a reception afterward at the Crillon, and if that couldn't fumigate an American past, what else this side of heaven could you hope for to remove stink? Not to mention a new automobile and a honeymoon in a rented hideaway built for his European mistress by a Mohammedan prince at Cap Ferrat. Only——

(she pauses, falters, for just an instant, then goes on)

—we—I thought we—I didn't want to efface the stink really——

(rapidly now, tense, erect, her hands gripped again into fists on her lap)

You know: just the marriage would be enough: not the Embassy and the Crillon and Cap Ferrat but just to kneel down, the two of us, and say 'We have sinned, forgive us'. And then maybe there would be the love this time—the peace, the quiet, the no shame that I . . . . didn't——missed that other time——

(falters again, then rapidly again, glib and succinct)

Love, but more than love too: not depending on just love to hold two people together, make them better than either one would have been alone, but tragedy, suffering, having suffered and caused grief; having something to have to live with even when, because, you knew both of you could never forget it. And then I began to believe something even more than that: that there was something even better, stronger, than tragedy to hold two people together: forgiveness. Only, that seemed to be wrong. Only maybe it wasn't the forgiveness that was wrong, but the gratitude; and maybe the only thing worse than having to give gratitude constantly all the time, is having to accept it——

STEVENS

Which is exactly backward. What was wrong wasn't——

GOVERNOR

Gavin.

STEVENS

Shut up yourself, Henry. What was wrong wasn't Temple's good name. It wasn't even her husband's conscience. It was his vanity: the Virginia-trained aristocrat caught with his gentility around his knees like the guest in the trick Hollywood bathroom. So the forgiving wasn't enough for him, or perhaps he hadn't read Hemingway's book. Because after about a year, his restiveness under the onus of accepting the gratitude began to take the form of doubting the paternity of their child.

TEMPLE

Oh God. Oh God.

GOVERNOR

Gavin.

(Stevens stops)

No more, I said. Call that an order.

(to Temple)

Yes. Tell me.

TEMPLE

I'm trying to. I expected our main obstacle in this would be the bereaved plaintiff. Apparently though it's the defendant's lawyer. I mean, I'm trying to tell you about one Temple Drake, and our Uncle Gavin is showing you another one. So already you've got two different people begging for the same clemency; if everybody concerned keeps on splitting up into two people, you wont even know who to pardon, will you? And now that I mention it, here we are, already back to Nancy Mannigoe, and now surely it shouldn't take long. Let's see, we'd got back to Jefferson too, hadn't we? Anyway, we are now. I mean, back in Jefferson, back home. You know: face it: the disgrace: the shame, face it down, good and down forever, never to haunt us more; together, a common front to stink because we love each other and have forgiven all, strong in our love and mutual forgiveness. Besides having everything else: the Gowan Stevenses, young, popular: a new bungalow on the right street to start the Saturday night hangovers in, a country club with a country club younger set of rallying friends to make it a Saturday night hangover worthy the name of Saturday night country club hangover, a pew in the right church to recover from it in provided of course they were not too hungover even to get to church. Then the son and heir came; and now we have Nancy: nurse: guide: mentor, catalyst, glue, whatever you want to call it, holding the whole lot of them together—not just a magnetic center for the heir apparent and the other little princes or princesses in their orderly succession, to circle around, but for the two bigger hunks too of mass or matter or dirt or whatever it is shaped in the image of God, in a semblance at least of order and respectability and peace; not ole cradle-rocking black mammy at all, because the Gowan Stevenses are young and modern, so young and modern that all the other young country club set applauded when they took an ex-dope-fiend nigger whore out of the gutter to nurse their children, because the rest of the young country club set didn't know that it wasn't the Gowan Stevenses but Temple Drake who had chosen the ex-dope-fiend nigger whore for the reason that an ex-dope-fiend nigger whore was the only animal in Jefferson that spoke Temple Drake's language——

(quickly takes up the burning cigarette from the tray and puffs at it, talking through the puffs)

Oh yes, I'm going to tell this too. A confidante. You know: the big-time ball player, the idol on the pedestal, the worshipped; and the worshipper, the acolyte, the one that never had and never would, no matter how willing or how hard she tried, get out of the sand-lots, the bush league. You know: the long afternoons, with the last electric button pressed on the last cooking or washing or sweeping gadget and the baby safely asleep for a while, and the two sisters in sin swapping trade or anyway avocational secrets over coca colas in the quiet kitchen. Somebody to talk to, as we all seem to need, want, have to have, not to converse with you nor even agree with you, but just keep quiet and listen. Which is all that people really want, really need; I mean, to behave themselves, keep out of one another's hair; the maladjustments which they tell us breed the arsonists and rapists and murderers and thieves and the rest of the anti-social enemies, are not really maladjustments but simply because the embryonic murderers and thieves didn't have anybody to listen to them: which is an idea the catholic church discovered two thousand years ago only it just didn't carry it far enough or maybe it was too busy being the church to have time to bother with man, or maybe it wasn't the church's fault at all but simply because it had to deal with human beings and maybe if the world was just populated with a kind of creature half of which were dumb, couldn't do anything but listen, couldn't even escape from having to listen to the other half, there wouldn't even be any war. Which was what Temple had: somebody paid by the week just to listen, which you would have thought would have been enough; and then the other baby came, the infant, the doomed sacrifice (though of course we dont know that yet) and you would have thought that this was surely enough, that now even Temple Drake would consider herself safe, could be depended on, having two—what do sailors call them? oh yes, sheet-anchors—now. Only it wasn't enough. Because Hemingway was right. I mean, the g—woman in his book. All you have got to do is, refuse to accept. Only, you have got to . . . . refuse——

STEVENS

Now, the letters——

GOVERNOR (watching Temple)

Be quiet, Gavin.

STEVENS

No, I'm going to talk a while now. We'll even stick to the sports metaphor and call it a relay race, with the senior member of the team carrying the . . . baton, twig, switch, sapling, tree—whatever you want to call the symbolical wood, up what remains of the symbolical hill.

(the lights flicker, grow slightly dimmer, then flare back up and steady again, as though in a signal, a warning)

The letters. The blackmail. The blackmailer was Red's younger brother—a criminal of course, but at least a man——

TEMPLE

No! No!

STEVENS (to Temple)

Be quiet too. It only goes up a hill, not over a precipice. Besides, it's only a stick. The letters were not first. The first thing was the gratitude. And now we have even come to the husband, my nephew. And when I say 'past,' I mean that part of it which the husband knows so far, which apparently was enough in his estimation. Because it was not long before she discovered, realised, that she was going to spend a good part of the rest of her days (nights too) being forgiven for it; in being not only constantly reminded—well, maybe not specifically reminded, but say made—kept—aware of it in order to be forgiven for it so that she might be grateful to the forgiver, but in having to employ more and more of what tact she had—and the patience which she probably didn't know she had, since until now she had never occasion to need patience—to make the gratitude—in which she had probably had as little experience as she had had with patience—acceptable to meet with, match, the high standards of the forgiver. But she was not too concerned. Her husband—my nephew—had made what he probably considered the supreme sacrifice to expiate his part in her past; she had no doubts of her capacity to continue to supply whatever increasing degree of gratitude the increasing appetite—or capacity—of its addict would demand, in return for the sacrifice which, so she believed, she had accepted for the same reason of gratitude. Besides, she still had the legs and the eyes; she could walk away, escape, from it at any moment she wished, even though her past might have shown her that she probably would not use the ability to locomote to escape from threat and danger. Do you accept that?

GOVERNOR

All right. Go on.

STEVENS

Then she discovered that the child—the first one—was on the way. For that first instant, she must have known something almost like frenzy. Now she couldn't escape, she had waited too long. But it was worse than that. It was as though she realised for the first time that you—everyone—must, or anyway may have to, pay for your past; that past is something like a promissory note with a trick clause in it which, as long as nothing goes wrong, can be manumitted in an orderly manner, but which fate or luck or chance, can foreclose on you without warning. That is, she had known, accepted, this all the time and dismissed it because she knew that she could cope, was invulnerable through simple integration, own-woman-ness. But now there would be a child, tender and defenseless. But you never really give up hope, you know, not even after you finally realise that people not only can bear anything, but probably will have to, so probably even before the frenzy had had time to fade, she found a hope: which was the child's own tender and defenseless innocence: that God—if there was one—would protect the child—not her: she asked no quarter and wanted none; she could cope, either cope or bear it, but the child from the sight draft of her past—because it was innocent, even though she knew better, all her observation having shown her that God either would not or could not—anyway, did not—save innocence just because it was innocent; that when He said 'Suffer little children to come unto Me' He meant exactly that: He meant suffer; that the adults, the fathers, the old in and capable of sin, must be ready and willing—nay, eager—to suffer at any time, that the little children shall come unto Him unanguished, unterrified, undefiled. Do you accept that?

GOVERNOR

Go on.

STEVENS

So at least she had ease. Not hope: ease. It was precarious of course, a balance, but she could walk a tightrope too. It was as though she had struck, not a bargain, but an armistice with God—if there was one. She had not tried to cheat; she had not tried to evade the promissory note of her past by intervening the blank check of a child's innocence—it was born now, a little boy, a son, her husband's son and heir—between. She had not tried to prevent the child; she had simply never thought about pregnancy in this connection, since it took the physical fact of the pregnancy to reveal to her the existence of that promissory note bearing her post-dated signature. And since God—if there was one—must be aware of that, then she too would bear her side of the bargain by not demanding on Him a second time since He—if there was one—would at least play fair, would be at least a gentleman. And that?

GOVERNOR

Go on.

STEVENS

So you can take your choice about the second child. Perhaps she was too busy between the three of them to be careful enough: between the three of them: the doom, the fate, the past; the bargain with God; the forgiveness and the gratitude. Like the Juggler says, not with three insentient replaceable Indian clubs or balls, but three glass bulbs filled with nitroglycerin and not enough hands for one even: one hand to offer the atonement with and another to receive the forgiveness with and a third needed to offer the gratitude, and still a fourth hand more and more imperative as time passed to sprinkle in steadily and constantly increasing doses a little more and a little more of the sugar and seasoning on the gratitude to keep it palatable to its swallower—that perhaps: she just didn't have time to be careful enough, or perhaps it was desperation, or perhaps this was when her husband first refuted or implied or anyway impugned—whichever it was—his son's paternity. Anyway, she was pregnant again; she had broken her word, destroyed her talisman, and she probably knew fifteen months before the letters that this was the end, and when the man appeared with the old letters she probably was not even surprised: she had merely been wondering for fifteen months what form the doom would take. And accept this too——

The lights flicker and dim further, then steady at that point.

STEVENS

And relief too. Because at last it was over; the roof had fallen, avalanche had roared; even the helplessness and the impotence were finished now, because now even the old fragility of bone and meat was no longer a factor;—and, who knows? because of that fragility, a kind of pride, triumph: you have waited for destruction: you endured; it was inevitable, inescapable, you had no hope. Nevertheless, you did not merely cringe, crouching, your head, vision, buried in your arms; you were not watching that poised arrestment all the time, true enough, but that was not because you feared it but because you were too busy putting one foot before the other, never for one instant really flagging, faltering, even though you knew it was in vain;—triumph in the very fragility which no longer need concern you now, for the reason that the all, the very worst, which catastrophe can do to you, is crush and obliterate the fragility; you were the better man, you outfaced even catastrophe, outlasted it, compelled it to move first; you did not even defy it, not even contemptuous: with no other tool or implement but that worthless fragility, you held disaster off as with one hand you might support the weightless silken canopy of a bed, for six long years while it, with all its weight and power, could not possibly prolong the obliteration of your fragility over five or six seconds; and even during that five or six seconds you would still be the better man, since all that it—the catastrophe—could deprive you of, you yourself had already written off six years ago as being, inherently of and because of its own fragile self, worthless.

GOVERNOR

And now, the man.

STEVENS

I thought you would see it too. Even the first one stuck out like a sore thumb. Yes, he——

GOVERNOR

The first what?

STEVENS (pauses, looks at the Governor)

The first man, Red. Dont you know anything at all about women? I never saw Red or this next one, his brother, either, but all three of them, the other two and her husband, probably all look enough alike or act enough alike—maybe by simply making enough impossible unfulfillable demands on her or by being drawn to her enough to accept, risk, almost incredible conditions—to be at least first cousins. Where have you been all your life?

GOVERNOR

All right. The man.

STEVENS

At first, all he thought of, planned on, was interested in, intended, was the money—to collect for the letters, and beat it, get the hell out. Of course, even at the end, all he was really after was still the money, not only after he found out that he would have to take her and the child too to get it, but even when it looked like all he was going to get, at least for a while, was just a runaway wife and a six-months-old infant. In fact, Nancy's error, her really fatal action on that fatal and tragic night, was in not giving the money and the jewels both to him when she found where Temple had hidden them, and getting the letters and getting rid of him forever, instead of hiding the money and jewels from Temple in her turn—which was what Temple herself thought too apparently, since she—Temple—told him a lie about how much the money was, telling him it was only two hundred dollars when it was actually almost two thousand. So you would have said that he wanted the money indeed, and just how much, how badly, to have been willing to pay that price for it. Or maybe he was being wise—'smart', he would have called it—beyond his years and time, and without having actually planned it that way, was really inventing a new and safe method of kidnapping: that is, pick an adult victim capable of signing her own checks—also with an infant in arms for added persuasion—and not forcing but actually persuading her to come along under her own power and then—still peaceably—extracting the money later at your leisure, using the tender welfare of the infant as a fulcrum for your lever. Or maybe we're both wrong and both should give credit—what little of it—where credit—what little of it—is due, since it was just the money with her too at first, though he was probably still thinking it was just the money at the very time when, having got her own jewelry together and found where her husband kept the key to the strongbox (and I imagine, even opened it one night after her husband was in bed asleep and counted the money in it or at least made sure there was money in it or anyway that the key would actually open it), she found herself still trying to rationalise why she had not paid over the money and got the letters and destroyed them and so rid herself forever of her Damocles' roof. Which was what she did not do. Because Hemingway—his girl—was quite right: all you have got to do is, refuse to accept it. Only, you have got to be told truthfully beforehand what you must refuse; the gods owe you that—at least a clear picture and a clear choice. Not to be fooled by . . . who knows? probably even gentleness, after a fashion, back there on those afternoons or whenever they were in the Memphis . . . . all right: honeymoon, even with a witness; in this case certainly anything much better lacked, and indeed, who knows? (I am Red now) even a little of awe, incredulous hope, incredulous amazement, even a little of trembling at this much fortune, this much luck dropping out of the very sky itself, into his embrace; at least (Temple now) no gang: even rape become tender: only one, an individual, still refusable, giving her at least (this time) the similitude of being wooed, of an opportunity to say Yes first, letting her even believe she could say either one of yes or no. I imagine that he (the new one, the blackmailer) even looked like his brother—a younger Red, the Red of a few years even before she knew him, and—if you will permit it—less stained, so that in a way it may have seemed to her that here at last even she might slough away the six years' soilure of struggle and repentance and terror to no avail. And if this is what you meant, then you are right too: a man, at least a man, after six years of that sort of forgiving which debased not only the forgiven but the forgiven's gratitude too,—a bad man of course, a criminal by intent regardless of how cramped his opportunities may have been up to this moment; and, capable of blackmail, vicious and not merely competent to, but destined to, bring nothing but evil and disaster and ruin to anyone foolish enough to enter his orbit, cast her lot with his. But—by comparison, that six years of comparison—at least a man—a man so single, so hard and ruthless, so impeccable in amorality, as to have a kind of integrity, purity, who would not only never need nor intend to forgive anyone anything, he would never even realise that anyone expected him to forgive anyone anything; who wouldn't even bother to forgive her if it ever dawned on him that he had the opportunity, but instead would simply black her eyes and knock a few teeth out and fling her into the gutter: so that she could rest secure forever in the knowledge that, until she found herself with a black eye and or spitting teeth in the gutter, he would never even know he had anything to forgive her for.

This time, the lights do not flicker. They begin to dim steadily toward and then into complete darkness as Stevens continues.

STEVENS

Nancy was the confidante, at first, while she—Nancy—still believed probably that the only problem, factor, was how to raise the money the blackmailer demanded, without letting the boss, the master, the husband find out about it; finding, discovering—this is still Nancy—realising probably that she had not really been a confidante for a good while, a long while before she discovered that what she actually was, was a spy: on her employer: not realising until after she had discovered that, although Temple had taken the money and the jewels too from her husband's strongbox, she—Temple—still hadn't paid them over to the blackmailer and got the letters, that the payment of the money and jewels was less than half of Temple's plan.

The lights go completely out. The stage is in complete darkness. Stevens' voice continues.

STEVENS

That was when Nancy in her turn found where Temple had hidden the money and jewels, and—Nancy—took them in her turn and hid them from Temple; this was the night of the day Gowan left for a week's fishing at Aransas Pass, taking the older child, the boy, with him, to leave the child for a week's visit with its grandparents in New Orleans until Gowan would pick him up on his way home from Texas.

(to Temple: in the darkness)

Now. Tell him.

The stage is in complete darkness.

Scene II

Interior, Temple's private sitting- or dressing-room. 9:30 P.M. September thirteenth *ante*.

The lights go up, lower R, as in Act I in the transition from the courtroom to the Stevens living room, though instead of the living room, the scene is now Temple's private apartment. A door L, enters from the house proper. A door R, leads into the nursery where the child is asleep in its crib. At rear, french windows open onto a terrace; this is a private entrance to the house itself from outdoors. At L, a closet door stands open. Garments are scattered over the floor about it, indicating that the closet has been searched, not hurriedly so much as savagely and ruthlessly and thoroughly. At R, is a fireplace of gas logs. A desk against the rear wall is open and shows traces of the same savage and ruthless search. A table center, bears Temple's hat, gloves and bag, also a bag such as is associated with infants; two bags, obviously Temple's, are packed and closed and sit on the floor beside the table. The whole room indicates Temple's imminent departure, and that something has been vainly yet savagely and completely, perhaps even frantically, searched for.

When the lights go up, Pete is standing in the open closet door, holding a final garment, a negligee, in his hands. He is about 25. He does not look like a criminal. That is, he is not a standardised recognisable criminal or gangster type, quite. He looks almost like the general conception of a college man, or a successful young automobile or appliance salesman. His clothes are ordinary, neither flashy nor sharp, simply what everybody wears. But there is a definite 'untamed' air to him. He is handsome, attractive to women, not at all unpredictable because you—or they—know exactly what he will do, you just hope he wont do it this time. He has a hard, ruthless quality, not immoral but unmoral.

He wears a light weight summer suit, his hat is shoved onto the back of his head so that, engaged as he is at present, he looks exactly like a youthful city detective in a tough moving picture. He is searching the flimsy negligee, quickly and without gentleness, drops it and turns, finds his feet entangled in the other garments on the floor and without pausing, kicks himself free and crosses to the desk and stands looking down at the litter on it which he has already searched thoroughly and savagely once, with a sort of bleak and contemptuous disgust.

Temple enters, L. She wears a dark suit for travelling beneath a light weight open coat, is hatless, carries the fur coat which we have seen, and a child's robe or blanket over the same arm, and a filled milk bottle in the other hand. She pauses long enough to glance at the littered room. Then she comes on in and approaches the table. Pete turns his head; except for that, he doesn't move.

PETE

Well?

TEMPLE

No. The people where she lives say they haven't seen her since she left to come to work this morning.

PETE

I could have told you that.

(he glances at his wrist watch)

We've still got time. Where does she live?

TEMPLE (at the table)

And then what? hold a lighted cigarette against the sole of her foot?

PETE

It's fifty dollars, even if you are accustomed yourself to thinking in hundreds. Besides the jewelry. What do you suggest then? call the cops?

TEMPLE

No. You wont have to run. I'm giving you an out.

PETE

An out?

TEMPLE

No dough, no snatch. Isn't that how you would say it?

PETE

Maybe I dont get you.

TEMPLE

You can quit now. Clear out. Leave. Get out from under. Save yourself. Then all you'll have to do is, wait till my husband gets back, and start over.

PETE

Maybe I still dont get you.

TEMPLE

You've still got the letters, haven't you?

PETE

Oh, the letters.

He reaches inside his coat, takes out the packet of letters and tosses it onto the table.

There you are.

TEMPLE

I told you two days ago I didn't want them.

PETE

Sure. That was two days ago.

They watch one another a moment. Then Temple dumps the fur coat and the robe from her arm, onto the table, sets the bottle carefully on the table, takes up the packet of letters and extends her other hand to Pete.

TEMPLE

Give me your lighter.

Pete produces the lighter from his pocket and hands it to her. That is, he extends it, not moving otherwise, so that she has to take a step or two toward him to reach and take it. Then she turns and crosses to the hearth, snaps the lighter on. It misses fire two or three times, then lights. Pete has not moved, watching her. She stands motionless a moment, the packet of letters in one hand, the burning lighter in the other. Then she turns her head and looks back at him. For another moment they watch one another.

PETE

Go ahead. Burn them. The other time I gave them to you, you turned them down so you could always change your mind and back out. Burn them.

They watch one another for another moment. Then she turns her head and stands now, her face averted, the lighter still burning. Pete watches her for another moment.

PETE

Then put that junk down and come here.

She snaps out the lighter, turns, crosses to the table, putting the packet of letters and the lighter on the table as she passes it, and goes on to where Pete has not moved. At this moment, Nancy appears in the door L. Neither of them see her. Pete puts his arms around Temple.

PETE

I offered you an out too.

(he draws her closer)

Baby.

TEMPLE

Dont call me that.

PETE (tightens his arms, caressing and savage too)

Red did. I'm as good a man as he was. Aint I?

They kiss. Nancy moves quietly through the door and stops just inside the room, watching them. She now wears the standardised department store maidservant's uniform, but without cap and apron, beneath a light weight open topcoat; on her head is a battered almost shapeless felt hat which must have once belonged to a man. Pete breaks the kiss.

PETE

Come on. Let's get out of here. I've even got moral or something. I dont even want to put my hands on you in his house——

He sees Nancy across Temple's shoulder, and reacts. Temple reacts to him, turns quickly and sees Nancy too. Nancy comes on into the room.

TEMPLE (to Nancy)
What are you doing here?

NANCY
I brought my foot. So he can hold that cigarette against it.

TEMPLE
So you're not just a thief: you're a spy too.

PETE
Maybe she's not a thief either. Maybe she brought it back.

(they watch Nancy, who doesn't answer)

Or maybe she didn't. Maybe we had better use that cigarette.

(to Nancy)

How about it? Is that what you came back for, sure enough?

TEMPLE (to Pete)
Hush. Take the bags and go on to the car.

PETE (to Temple but watching Nancy)
I'll wait for you. There may be a little something I can do here, after all.

TEMPLE
Go on, I tell you! Let's for God's sake get away from here. Go on.

Pete watches Nancy for a moment longer, who stands facing them but not looking at anything, motionless, almost bemused, her face sad, brooding and inscrutable. Then Pete turns, goes to the table, picks up the lighter, seems about to pass on, then pauses again and with almost infinitesimal hesitation, takes up the packet of letters, puts it back inside his coat, takes up the two packed bags and crosses to the french window, passing Nancy, who is still looking at nothing and no one.

PETE (to Nancy)

Not that I wouldn't like to, you know. For less than fifty bucks even. For old lang zyne.

He transfers the bags to one hand, opens the french window, starts to exit, pauses half way out and looks back at Temple.

I'll be listening, in case you change your mind about the cigarette.

He goes on out, draws the door to after him. Just before it closes, Nancy speaks.

NANCY

Wait.

Pete stops, begins to open the door again.

TEMPLE (quickly: to Pete)

Go on! Go on! For God's sake go on!

Pete exits, shuts the door after him. Nancy and Temple face each other.

NANCY

Maybe I was wrong to think that just hiding that money and diamonds was going to stop you. Maybe I ought to have give it to him yesterday as soon as I found where you had hid it. Then wouldn't nobody between here and Chicago or Texas seen anything of him but his dust.

TEMPLE

So you did steal it. And you saw what good that did, didn't you?

NANCY

If you can call it stealing, then so can I. Because wasn't but part of it yours to begin with. Just the diamonds was yours. Not to mention that money is almost two thousand dollars, that you told me was just two hundred and that you told him was even less than that, just fifty. No wonder he wasn't worried—about just fifty dollars. He wouldn't even be worried if he knowed it was even the almost two thousand it is, let alone the two hundred you told me it was. He aint even worried about whether or not you'll have any money at all when you get out to the car. He knows that all he's got to do is, just wait and keep his hand on you and maybe just mash hard enough with it, and you'll get another passel of money and diamonds too out of your husband or your pa. Only, this time he'll have his hand on you and you'll have a little trouble telling him it's just fifty dollars instead of almost two thousand——

Temple steps quickly forward and slaps Nancy across the face. Nancy steps back. As she does so, the packet of money and the jewel box fall to the floor from inside her topcoat. Temple stops, looking down at the money and jewels. Nancy recovers.

NANCY

Yes, there it is, that caused all the grief and ruin. If you hadn't been somebody that would have a box of diamonds and a husband that you could find almost two thousand dollars in his britches pocket while he was asleep, that man wouldn't have tried to sell you them letters. Maybe if I hadn't taken and hid it, you would have give it to him before you come to this. Or maybe if I had just give it to him yesterday and got the letters, or maybe if I was to take it out to where he's waiting in that car right now, and say, Here, man, take your money——

TEMPLE

Try it. Pick it up and take it out to him, and see. If you'll wait until I finish packing, you can even carry the bag.

NANCY

I know. It aint even the letters anymore. Maybe it never was. It was already there in whoever could write the kind of letters that even eight years afterward could still make grief and ruin. The letters never did matter. You could have got them back at any time; he even tried to give them to you twice——

TEMPLE

How much spying have you been doing?

NANCY

All of it.—You wouldn't even needed money and diamonds to get them back. A woman dont need it. All she needs is womanishness to get anything she wants from men. You could have done that right here in the house, without even tricking your husband into going off fishing.

TEMPLE

A perfect example of whore morality. But then, if I can say whore, so can you, cant you? Maybe the difference is, I decline to be one in my husband's house.

NANCY

I aint talking about your husband. I aint even talking about you. I'm talking about two little children.

TEMPLE

So am I. Why else do you think I sent Bucky on to his grandmother, except to get him out of a house where the man he has been taught to call his father, may at any moment decide to tell him he has none? As clever a spy as you must surely have heard my husband——

NANCY (interrupts)

I've heard him. And I heard you too. You fought back—that time. Not for yourself, but for that little child. But now you have quit.

TEMPLE

Quit?

NANCY

Yes. You gave up. You gave up the child too. Willing to risk never seeing him again maybe.

(Temple doesn't answer)

That's right. You dont need to make no excuses to me. Just tell me what you must have already strengthened your mind up to telling all the rest of the folks that are going to ask you that. You are willing to risk it. Is that right?

(Temple doesn't answer)

All right. We'll say you have answered it. So that settles Bucky. Now answer me this one. Who are you going to leave the other one with?

TEMPLE

Leave her with? A six-months-old baby?

NANCY

That's right. Of course you cant leave her. Not with nobody. You cant no more leave a six-months-old baby with nobody while you run away from your husband with another man, than you can take a six-months-old baby with you on that trip. That's what I'm talking about. So maybe you'll just leave it in there in that cradle; it'll cry for a while, but it's too little to cry very loud and so maybe wont nobody hear it and come meddling, especially with the house shut up and locked until Mr Gowan gets back next week, and probably by that time it will have hushed——

TEMPLE

Are you really trying to make me hit you again?

NANCY

Or maybe taking her with you will be just as easy, at least until the first time you write Mr Gowan or your pa for money and they dont send it as quick as your new man thinks they ought to, and he throws you and the baby both out. Then you can just drop it into a garbage can and no more trouble to you or anybody, because then you will be rid of both of them——

(Temple makes a convulsive movement, then catches herself)

Hit me. Light you a cigarette too. I told you and him both I brought my foot. Here it is.

(she raises her foot slightly)

I've tried everything else; I reckon I can try that too.

TEMPLE (repressed, furious)

Hush. I tell you for the last time. Hush.

NANCY

I've hushed.

She doesn't move. She is not looking at Temple. There is a slight change in her voice or manner, though we only realise later that she is not addressing Temple.

I've tried. I've tried everything I know. You can see that.

TEMPLE

Which nobody will dispute. You threatened me with my children, and even with my husband—if you can call my husband a threat. You even stole my elopement money. Oh yes, nobody will dispute that you tried. Though at least you brought the money back. Pick it up.

NANCY

You said you dont need it.

TEMPLE

I dont. Pick it up.

NANCY

No more do I need it.

TEMPLE

Pick it up, anyway. You can keep your next week's pay out of it when you give it back to Mr Gowan.

Nancy stoops and gathers up the money, and gathers the jewelry back into its box, and puts them on the table.

TEMPLE (quieter)

Nancy.

(Nancy looks at her)

I'm sorry. Why do you force me to this—hitting and screaming at you, when you have always been so good to my children and me—my husband too—all of us—trying to hold us together in a household, a family, that anybody should have known all the time couldn't possibly hold together? even in decency, let alone happiness?

NANCY

I reckon I'm ignorant. I dont know that yet. Besides, I aint talking about any household or happiness neither——

TEMPLE (with sharp command)

Nancy!

NANCY

—I'm talking about two little children——

TEMPLE

I said, hush.

NANCY

I cant hush. I'm going to ask you one more time. Are you going to do it?

TEMPLE

Yes!

NANCY

Maybe I am ignorant. You got to say it out in words yourself, so I can hear them. Say, I'm going to do it.

TEMPLE

You heard me. I'm going to do it.

NANCY

Money or no money.

TEMPLE

Money or no money.

NANCY

Children or no children.

(Temple doesn't answer)

To leave one with a man that's willing to believe the child aint got no father, willing to take the other one to a man that dont even want no children——

(they stare at one another)

If you can do it, you can say it.

TEMPLE

Yes! Children or no children! Now get out of here. Take your part of that money, and get out. Here——

Temple goes quickly to the table, removes two or three bills from the mass of banknotes, and hands them to Nancy, who takes them. Temple takes up the rest of the money, takes up her bag from the table and opens it. Nancy crosses quietly toward the nursery, picking up the milk bottle from the table as she passes, and goes on. With the open bag in one hand and the money in the other, Temple notices Nancy's movement.

TEMPLE

What are you doing?

NANCY (still moving)

This bottle has got cold. I'm going to warm it in the bathroom.

Then Nancy stops and looks back at Temple, with something so strange in her look that Temple, about to resume putting the money into the bag, pauses too, watching Nancy. When

Nancy speaks, it is like the former speech: we dont realise until afterward what it signifies.

NANCY

I tried everything I knowed. You can see that.

TEMPLE (peremptory, commanding)

Nancy.

NANCY (quietly, turning on)

I've hushed.

She exits through the door into the nursery. Temple finishes putting the money into the bag, and closes it and puts it back on the table. Then she turns to the baby's bag. She tidies it, checks rapidly over its contents, takes up the jewel box and stows it in the bag and closes the bag. All this takes about two minutes; she has just closed the bag when Nancy emerges quietly from the nursery, without the milk bottle, and crosses, pausing at the table only long enough to put back on it the money Temple gave her, then starts on toward the opposite door through which she first entered the room.

TEMPLE

Now what?

Nancy goes on toward the other door. Temple watches her.

Nancy.

(Nancy pauses, still not looking back)

Dont think too hard of me.

(Nancy waits, immobile, looking at nothing. When Temple doesn't continue, she moves again toward the door)

If I—it ever comes up, I'll tell everybody you did your best. You tried. But you were right. It wasn't even the letters. It was me.

(Nancy moves on)

Goodbye, Nancy.

(Nancy reaches the door)

You've got your key. I'll leave your money here on the table. You can get it——

(Nancy exits)

Nancy!

There is no answer. Temple looks a moment longer at the empty door, shrugs, moves, takes up the money Nancy left, glances about, crosses to the littered desk and takes up a paper-weight and returns to the table and puts the money beneath the weight; now moving rapidly and with determination, she takes up the blanket from the table and crosses to the nursery door and exits through it. A second or two, then she screams. The lights flicker and begin to dim, fade swiftly into complete darkness, over the scream.

The stage is in complete darkness.

Scene III

Same as Scene I. Governor's Office. 3:09 A.M. March twelfth.

The lights go on upper L. The scene is the same as before, Scene I, except that Gowan Stevens now sits in the chair behind the desk where the Governor had been sitting, and the Governor is no longer in the room. Temple now kneels before the desk, facing it, her arms on the desk and her face buried in her arms. Stevens now stands beside and over her. The hands of the clock show nine minutes past three.

Temple does not know that the Governor has gone and that her husband is now in the room.

TEMPLE (her face still hidden)

And that's all. The police came, and the murdress still sitting in a chair in the kitchen in the dark, saying 'Yes, Lord, I done it', and then in the cell at the jail still saying it——

(Stevens leans and touches her arm, as if to help her up. She resists, though still not raising her head)

Not yet. It's my cue to stay down here until his honor or excellency grants our plea, isn't it? Or have I already missed my cue forever even if the sovereign state should offer me a handkerchief right out of its own elected public suffrage dressing-gown pocket? Because see?

(she raises her face, quite blindly, tearless, still not looking toward the chair where she could see Gowan instead of the Governor, into the full glare of the light)

Still no tears.

STEVENS

Get up, Temple.

(he starts to lift her again, but before he can do so, she rises herself, standing, her face still turned away from the desk, still blind; she puts her arm up almost in the gesture of a little girl about to cry, but instead she merely shields her eyes from the light while her pupils readjust)

TEMPLE

Nor cigarette either; this time it certainly wont take long, since all you have to say is, No.

(still not turning her face to look, even though she is now speaking directly to the Governor whom she still thinks is sitting behind the desk)

Because you aren't going to save her, are you? Because all this was not for the sake of her soul because her soul doesn't need it, but for mine.

STEVENS (gently)

Why not finish first? Tell the rest of it. You had started to say something about the jail.

TEMPLE

The jail. They had the funeral the next day—Gowan had barely reached New Orleans, so he chartered an airplane back that morning—and in Jefferson, everything going to the graveyard passes the jail, or going anywhere else for that matter, passing right under the upstairs barred windows—the bullpen and the cells where the Negro prisoners—the crapshooters and whiskey-peddlers and vagrants and the murderers and murdresses too—can look down and enjoy it, enjoy the funerals too. Like this. Some white person you know is in a jail or a hospital, and right off you say, How ghastly: not at the shame or the pain, but the walls, the locks, and before you even know it, you have sent them books to read, cards, puzzles to play with. But not Negroes. You dont even think about the cards and puzzles and books. And so all of a sudden you find out with a kind of terror, that they have not only escaped having to read, they have escaped having to escape. So whenever you pass the jail, you can see them—no, not them, you dont see them at all, you just see the hands among the bars of the windows, not tapping or fidgeting or even holding, gripping the bars like white hands would be, but just lying there among the interstices, not just at rest, but even restful, already shaped and easy and unanguished to the handles of the plows and axes and hoes, and the mops and brooms and the rockers of white folks' cradles, until even the steel bars fitted them too without alarm or anguish. You see? not gnarled and twisted with work at all, but even limbered and suppled by it, smoothed and even softened, as though with only the penny-change of simple sweat they had already got the same thing the white ones have to pay dollars by the ounce jar for. Not immune to work, and in compromise with work is not the right word either, but in confederacy with work and so free from it; in armistice, peace;—the same long supple hands serene and immune to anguish, so that all the owners of them need to look out with, to see with—to look out at the outdoors—the funerals, the passing, the people, the freedom, the sunlight, the free air—are just the hands: not the eyes: just the hands lying there among the bars and looking out, that can see the shape of the plow or hoe or axe before daylight comes; and even in the dark, without even having to turn on the light, can not only find the child, the baby—not her child but yours, the white one—but the trouble and discomfort too—the hunger, the wet didy, the unfastened safety-pin—and see to remedy it. You see. If I could just cry. There was another one, a man this time, before my time in Jefferson but Uncle Gavin will remember this too. His wife had just died—they had been married only two weeks—and he buried her and so at first he tried just walking the country roads at night for exhaustion and sleep, only that failed and then he tried getting drunk so he could sleep, and that failed and then he tried fighting and then he cut a white man's throat with a razor in a dice game and so at last he could sleep for a little while; which was where the sheriff found him, asleep on the wooden floor of the gallery of the house he had rented for his wife, his marriage, his life, his old age. Only that waked him up, and so in the jail that afternoon, all of a sudden it took the jailer and a deputy and five other Negro prisoners just to throw him down and hold him while they locked the chains on him;—lying there on the floor with more than a half dozen men panting to hold him down, and what do you think he said? 'Look like I just cant quit thinking. Look like I just cant quit.'

(she ceases, blinking, rubs her eyes and then extends one hand blindly toward Stevens, who has already shaken out his handkerchief and hands it to her. There are still no tears on her face; she merely takes the handkerchief and dabs, pats at her eyes with it as if it were a powder-puff, talking again)

But we have passed the jail, haven't we? We're in the courtroom now. It was the same there; Uncle Gavin had rehearsed her, of course, which was easy, since all you can say when they ask you to answer to a murder charge is, Not Guilty. Otherwise, they cant even have a trial; they would have to hurry out and find another murderer before they could take the next official step. So they asked her, all correct and formal among the judges and lawyers and bailiffs and jury and the Scales and the Sword and the flag and the ghosts of Coke upon Littleton upon Bonaparte and Julius Caesar and all the rest of it, not to mention the eyes and the faces which were getting a moving picture show for free since they had already paid for it in the taxes, and nobody really listening since there was only one thing she could say. Except that she didn't say it: just raising her head enough to be heard plain—not loud: just plain—and said, 'Guilty, Lord'——like that, disrupting and confounding and dispersing and flinging back two thousand years, the whole edifice of corpus juris and rules of evidence we have been working to make stand up by itself ever since Caesar, like when without even watching yourself or even knowing you were doing it, you would reach out your hand and turn over a chip and expose to air and light and vision the frantic and aghast turmoil of an antbed. And moved the chip again, when even the ants must have thought there couldn't be another one within her reach: when they finally explained to her that to say she was not guilty, had nothing to do with truth but only with law, and this time she said it right, Not Guilty, and so then the jury could tell her she lied and everything was all correct again and, as everybody thought, even safe, since now she wouldn't be asked to say anything at all anymore. Only, they were wrong; the jury said Guilty and the judge said Hang and now everybody was already picking up his hat to go home, when she picked up that chip too: the judge said, 'And may God have mercy on your soul' and Nancy answered: 'Yes, Lord.'

(she turns suddenly, almost briskly, speaking so briskly that her momentum carries on past the instant when she sees and recognises Gowan sitting where she had thought all the time that the Governor was sitting and listening to her)

And that is all, this time. And so now you can tell us. I know you're not going to save her, but now you can say so. It wont be difficult. Just one word——

(she stops, arrested, utterly motionless, but even then she is first to recover)

Oh God.

(Gowan rises quickly. Temple whirls to Stevens)

Why is it you must always believe in plants? Do you have to? Is it because you have to? Because you are a lawyer? No, I'm wrong. I'm sorry; I was the one that started us hiding gimmicks on each other, wasn't it?

(quickly: turning to Gowan)

Of course; you didn't take the sleeping pill at all. Which means you didn't even need to come here for the Governor to hide you behind the door or under the desk or wherever it was he was trying to tell me you were hiding and listening, because after all the governor of a southern state has got to try to act like he regrets having to aberrate from being a gentleman——

STEVENS (to Temple)

Stop it.

GOWAN

Maybe we both didn't start hiding soon enough—by about eight years—not in desk drawers either, but in two abandoned mine shafts, one in Siberia and the other at the South Pole, maybe.

TEMPLE

All right. I didn't mean hiding. I'm sorry.

GOWAN

Dont be. Just draw on your eight years' interest for that.

(to Stevens)

All right, all right; tell me to shut up too.

(to no one directly)

In fact, this may be the time for me to start saying sorry for the next eight-year term. Just give me a little time. Eight years of gratitude might be a habit a little hard to break. So here goes.

(to Temple)

I'm sorry. Forget it.

TEMPLE

I would have told you.

GOWAN

You did. Forget it. You see how easy it is? You could have been doing that yourself for eight years: every time I would say 'Say sorry, please', all you would need would be to answer: 'I did. Forget it.'

(to Stevens)

I guess that's all, isn't it? We can go home now.

(he starts to come around the desk)

TEMPLE

Wait.

(Gowan stops; they look at each other)

Where are you going?

GOWAN

I said home, didn't I? To pick up Bucky and carry him back to his own bed again.

(they look at one another)

You're not even going to ask me where he is now?

(answers himself)

Where we always leave our children when the clutch——

STEVENS (to Gowan)
Maybe I will say shut up this time.

GOWAN
Only let me finish first. I was going to say, 'with our handiest kinfolks.'
(to Temple)
I carried him to Maggie's.

STEVENS (moving)
I think we can all go now. Come on.

GOWAN
So do I.
(he comes on around the desk, and stops again; to Temple)
Make up your mind. Do you want to ride with me, or Gavin?

STEVENS (to Gowan)
Go on. You can pick up Bucky.

GOWAN
Right.
(he turns, starts toward the steps front, where Temple and Stevens entered, then stops)
That's right. I'm probably still supposed to use the spy's entrance.
(he turns back, starts around the desk again, toward the door at rear, sees Temple's gloves and bag on the desk, and takes them up and holds them out to her: roughly almost)
Here. This is what they call evidence; dont forget these.
(Temple takes the bag and gloves. Gowan goes on toward the door at rear)

TEMPLE (after him)

Did you have a hat and coat?

(he doesn't answer. He goes on, exits)

Oh God. Again.

STEVENS (touches her arm)

Come on.

TEMPLE (not moving yet)

Tomorrow and tomorrow and tomorrow——

STEVENS (speaking her thought, finishing the sentence)

—he will wreck the car again against the wrong tree, in the wrong place, and you will have to forgive him again, for the next eight years until he can wreck the car again in the wrong place, against the wrong tree——

TEMPLE

I was driving it too. I was driving some of the time too.

STEVENS (gently)

Then let that comfort you.

(he takes her arm again, turns her toward the stairs)

Come on. It's late.

TEMPLE (holds back)

Wait. He said, No.

STEVENS

Yes.

TEMPLE

Did he say why?

STEVENS

Yes. He cant.

TEMPLE

Cant? The Governor of a state, with all the legal power to pardon or at least reprieve, cant?

STEVENS

That's just law. If it was only law, I could have plead insanity for her at any time, without bringing you here at two oclock in the morning——

TEMPLE

And the other parent too; dont forget that. I dont know yet how you did it . . . . Yes, Gowan was here first; he was just pretending to be asleep when I carried Bucky in and put him in his bed; yes, that was what you called that leaking valve, when we stopped at the filling station to change the wheel: to let him get ahead of us——

STEVENS

All right. He wasn't even talking about justice. He was talking about a child, a little boy——

TEMPLE

That's right. Make it good: the same little boy to hold whose normal and natural home together, the murdress, the nigger, the dope-fiend whore, didn't hesitate to cast the last gambit—and maybe that's the wrong word too, isn't it?—she knew and had: her own debased and worthless life. Oh yes, I know that answer too; that was brought out here tonight too: that a little child shall not suffer in order to come unto Me. So good can come out of evil.

STEVENS

It not only can, it must.

TEMPLE

So touché, then. Because what kind of natural and normal home can that little boy have where his father may at any time tell him he has no father?

STEVENS

Haven't you been answering that question every day for eight years? Didn't Nancy answer it for you when she told you how you had fought back, not for yourself, but for that little boy? Not to show the father that he was wrong, nor even to prove to the little boy that the father was wrong, but to let the little boy learn with his own eyes that nothing, not even that, which could possibly enter that house, could ever harm him?

TEMPLE

But I quit. Nancy told you that too.

STEVENS

She doesn't think so now. Isn't that what she's going to prove Friday morning?

TEMPLE

Friday. The black day. The day you never start on a journey. Except that Nancy's journey didn't start at daylight or sunup or whenever it is polite and tactful to hang people, day after tomorrow. Her journey started that morning eight years ago when I got on the train at the University——

(she stops: a moment; then quietly)

Oh God, that was Friday too; that baseball game was Friday——

(rapidly)

You see? Dont you see? It's nowhere near enough yet. Of course he wouldn't save her. If he did that, it would be over: Gowan could just throw me out, which he may do yet, or I could throw Gowan out, which I could have done until it got too late now, too late forever now, or the judge could have thrown us both out and given Bucky to an orphanage, and it would be all over. But now it can go on, tomorrow and tomorrow and tomorrow, forever and forever and forever——

STEVENS (gently tries to start her)
Come on.

TEMPLE (holding back)
Tell me exactly what he did say. Not tonight: it couldn't have been tonight—or did he say it over the telephone, and we didn't even need——

STEVENS
He said it a week ago——

TEMPLE
Yes, about the same time when you sent the wire. What did he say?

STEVENS (quotes)
'Who am I, to have the brazen temerity and hardihood to set the puny appanage of my office in the balance against that simple undeviable aim? Who am I, to render null and abrogate the purchase she made with that poor crazed lost and worthless life?'

TEMPLE (wildly)
And good too—good and mellow too. So it was not even in hopes of saving her life, that I came here at two oclock in the morning. It wasn't even to be told that he had already decided not to save her. It was not even to confess to my husband, but to do it in the hearing of two strangers, something which I had spent eight years trying to expiate so that my husband wouldn't have to know about it. Dont you see? That's just suffering. Not for anything: just suffering.

STEVENS

You came here to affirm the very thing which Nancy is going to die tomorrow morning to postulate: that little children, as long as they are little children, shall be intact, unanguished, untorn, unterrified.

TEMPLE (quietly)

All right. I have done that. Can we go home now?

STEVENS

Yes.

(she turns, moves toward the steps, Stevens beside her. As she reaches the first step, she falters, seems to stumble slightly, like a sleepwalker. Stevens steadies her, but at once she frees her arm, and begins to descend)

TEMPLE (on the first step: to no one, still with that sleepwalker air)

To save my soul—if I have a soul. If there is a God to save it—a God who wants it——

(Curtain)

ACT III

The Jail

(Nor Even Yet Quite Relinquish——)

SO, ALTHOUGH in a sense the jail was both older and less old than the courthouse, in actuality, in time, in observation and memory, it was older even than the town itself. Because there was no town until there was a courthouse, and no courthouse until (like some unsentient unweaned creature torn violently from the dug of its dam) the floorless lean-to rabbit-hutch housing the iron chest was reft from the log flank of the jail and transmogrified into a by-neo-Greek-out-of-Georgian-England edifice set in the center of what in time would be the town Square (as a result of which, the town itself had moved one block south—or rather, no town then and yet, the courthouse itself the catalyst: a mere dusty widening of the trace, trail, pathway in a forest of oak and ash and hickory and sycamore and flowering catalpa and dogwood and judas tree and persimmon and wild plum, with on one side old Alec Holston's tavern and coaching-yard, and a little further along, Ratcliffe's trading-post-store and the blacksmith's, and diagonal to all of them, en face and solitary beyond the dust, the log jail; moved—the town—complete and intact, one block southward, so that now, a century and a quarter later, the coaching-yard and Ratcliffe's store were gone and old Alec's tavern and the blacksmith's were a hotel and a garage, on a main thoroughfare true enough but still a business side-street, and the jail across from them, though transformed also now into two storeys of Georgian brick by the hand ((or anyway pocketbooks)) of Sartoris and Sutpen and Louis Grenier, faced not even on a side-street but on an alley);

And so, being older than all, it had seen all: the mutation and the change: and, in that sense, had recorded them (indeed, as Gavin Stevens, the town lawyer and the county amateur Cincinnatus, was wont to say, if you would peruse in unbroken—ay, overlapping—continuity the history of a community, look not in the church registers and the courthouse records, but beneath the successive layers of calsomine and creosote and whitewash on the walls of the jail, since only in that forcible carceration does man find the idleness in which to compose, in the gross and simple terms of his gross and simple lusts and yearnings, the gross and simple recapitulations of his gross and simple heart); invisible and impacted, not only beneath the annual inside creosote-and-whitewash of bullpen and cell, but on the blind outside walls too, first the simple mud-chinked log ones and then the symmetric brick, not only the scrawled illiterate repetitive unimaginative doggerel and the perspectiveless almost prehistoric sexual picture-writing, but the images, the panorama not only of the town but of its days and years until a century and better had been accomplished, filled not only with its mutation and change from a halting-place: to a community: to a settlement: to a village: to a town, but with the shapes and motions, the gestures of passion and hope and travail and endurance, of the men and women and children in their successive overlapping generations long after the subjects which had reflected the images were vanished and replaced and again replaced, as when you stand say alone in a dim and empty room and believe, hypnotised beneath the vast weight of man's incredible and enduring *Was*, that perhaps by turning your head aside you will see from the corner of your eye the turn of a moving limb—a gleam of crinoline, a laced wrist, perhaps even a Cavalier plume—who knows? provided there is will enough, perhaps even the face itself three hundred years after it was dust—the eyes, two jellied tears filled with arrogance and pride and satiety and knowledge of anguish and foreknowledge of death, saying no to death across twelve generations, asking still the old same unanswerable question three centuries after that which reflected them had learned that the answer didn't matter, or—better still—had forgotten the asking of it—in the shadowy fathomless dreamlike depths of an old mirror which has looked at too much too long;

But not in shadow, not this one, this mirror, these logs: squatting in the full glare of the stump-pocked clearing during those first summers, solitary on its side of the dusty widening marked with an occasional wheel but mostly by the prints of horses and men: Pettigrew's private pony express until he and it were replaced by a monthly stagecoach from Memphis, the race horse which Jason Compson traded to Ikkemotubbe, old Mohataha's son and the last ruling Chickasaw chief in that section, for a square of land so large that, as the first formal survey revealed, the new courthouse would have been only another of Compson's outbuildings had not the town Corporation bought enough of it (at Compson's price) to forefend themselves being trespassers, and the saddlemare which bore Doctor Habersham's worn black bag (and which drew the buggy after Doctor Habersham got too old and stiff to mount the saddle), and the mules which drew the wagon in which, seated in a rocking chair beneath a French parasol held by a Negro slave girl, old Mohataha would come to town on Saturdays (and came that last time to set her capital X on the paper which ratified the dispossession of her people forever, coming in the wagon that time too, barefoot as always but in the purple silk dress which her son, Ikkemotubbe, had brought her back from France, and a hat crowned with the royal-colored plume of a queen, beneath the slave-held parasol still and with another female slave child squatting on her other side holding the crusted slippers which she had never been able to get her feet into, and in the back of the wagon the petty rest of the unmarked Empire flotsam her son had brought to her which was small enough to be moved; driving for the last time out of the woods into the dusty widening before Ratcliffe's store where the Federal land agent and his marshal waited for her with the paper, and stopped the mules and sat for a little time, the young men of her body guard squatting quietly about the halted wagon after the eight-mile walk, while from the gallery of the store and of Holston's tavern the settlement—the Ratcliffes and Compsons and Peabodys and Pettigrews ((not Grenier and Holston and Habersham, because Louis Grenier declined to come in to see it, and for the same reason old Alec Holston sat alone on that hot afternoon before the smoldering log in the fireplace of his taproom, and Doctor Habersham was dead and his son had already departed for the West with his bride, who was Mohataha's grand-daughter, and his father-in-law, Mohataha's son, Ikkemotubbe))—looked on, watched: the inscrutable ageless wrinkled face, the fat shapeless body dressed in the cast-off garments of a French queen, which on her looked like the Sunday costume of the madam of a rich Natchez or New Orleans brothel, sitting in a battered wagon inside a squatting ring of her household troops, her young men dressed in their Sunday clothes for travelling too: then she said, 'Where is this Indian territory?' And they told her: West. 'Turn the mules west,' she said, and someone did so, and she took the pen from the agent and made her X on the paper and handed the pen back and the wagon moved, the young men rising too, and she vanished so across that summer afternoon to that terrific and infinitesimal creak and creep of ungreased wheels, herself immobile beneath the rigid parasol, grotesque and regal, bizarre and moribund, like obsolescence's self riding off the stage on its own obsolete catafalque, looking not once back, not once back toward home);

But most of all, the prints of men—the fitted shoes which Doctor Habersham and Louis Grenier had brought from the Atlantic seaboard, the cavalry boots in which Alec Holston had ridden behind Francis Marion, and—more myriad almost than leaves, outnumbering all the others lumped together—the moccasins, the deerhide sandals of the forest, worn not by the Indians but by white men, the pioneers, the long hunters, as though they had not only vanquished the wilderness but had even stepped into the very footgear of them they dispossessed (and mete and fitting so, since it was by means of his feet and legs that the white man conquered America; the closed and split U's of his horses and cattle overlay his own prints always, merely consolidating his victory);—(the jail) watched them all, red men and white and black—the pioneers, the hunters, the forest men with rifles, who made the same light rapid soundless toed-in almost heelless prints as the red men they dispossessed and who in fact dispossessed the red men for that reason: not because of the grooved barrel but because they could enter the red man's milieu and make the same footprints that he made; the husbandman printing deep the hard heels of his brogans because of the weight he bore on his shoulders: axe and saw and plow-stock, who dispossessed the forest man for the obverse reason: because with his saw and axe he simply removed, obliterated, the milieu in which alone the forest man could exist; then the land speculators and the traders in slaves and whiskey who followed the husbandmen, and the politicians who followed the land speculators, printing deeper and deeper the dust of that dusty widening, until at last there was no mark of Chickasaw left in it anymore; watching (the jail) them all, from the first innocent days when Doctor Habersham and his son and Alec Holston and Louis Grenier were first guests and then friends of Ikkemotubbe's Chicksaw clan; then an Indian agent and a land-office and a trading-post, and suddenly Ikkemotubbe and his Chickasaws were themselves the guests without being friends of the federal government; then Ratcliffe, and the trading-post was no longer simply an Indian trading-post, though Indians were still welcome, of course (since, after all, they owned the land or anyway were on it first and claimed it), then Compson with his race horse and presently Compson began to own the Indian accounts for tobacco and calico and jeans pants and cooking-pots on Ratcliffe's books (in time he would own Ratcliffe's books too) and one day Ikkemotubbe owned the race horse and Compson owned the land itself, some of which the city fathers would have to buy from him at his price in order to establish a town; and Pettigrew with his tri-weekly mail, and then a monthly stage and the new faces coming in faster than old Alec Holston, arthritic and irascible, hunkered like an old surly bear over his smoldering hearth even in the heat of summer (he alone now of that original three, since old Grenier no longer came in to the settlement, and old Doctor Habersham was dead, and the old Doctor's son, in the opinion of the settlement, had already turned Indian and renegade even at the age of twelve or fourteen) any longer made any effort, wanted, to associate names with; and now indeed the last moccasin print vanished from that dusty widening, the last toed-in heel-less light soft quick long-striding print pointing west for an instant, then trodden from the sight and memory of man by a heavy leather heel engaged not in the traffic of endurance and hardihood and survival, but in money,—taking with it (the print) not only the moccasins but the deer-hide leggins and jerkin too, because Ikkemotubbe's Chickasaws now wore eastern factory-made jeans and shoes sold them on credit out of Ratcliffe's and Compson's general store, walking in to the settlement on the white man's Saturday, carrying the alien shoes rolled neatly in the alien pants under their arms, to stop at the bridge over Compson's creek long enough to bathe their legs and feet before donning the pants and shoes, then coming on to squat all day on the store gallery eating cheese and crackers and peppermint candy (bought on credit too out of Compson's and Ratcliffe's showcase) and now not only they but Habersham and Holston and Grenier too were there on sufferance, anachronistic and alien, not really an annoyance yet but simply a discomfort;

Then they were gone; the jail watched that: the halted ungreased unpainted wagon, the span of underfed mules attached to it by fragments of eastern harness supplemented by raw deer-hide thongs, the nine young men—the wild men, tameless and proud, who even in their own generation's memory had been free and, in that of their fathers, the heirs of kings—squatting about it, waiting, quiet and composed, not even dressed in the ancient forest-softened deerskins of their freedom but in the formal regalia of the white man's inexplicable ritualistic sabbaticals: broadcloth trousers and white shirts with boiled-starch bosoms (because they were travelling now; they would be visible to outworld, to strangers:—and carrying the New England-made shoes under their arms too since the distance would be long and walking was better barefoot), the shirts collarless and cravatless true enough and with the tails worn outside, but still board-rigid, gleaming, pristine, and in the rocking chair in the wagon, beneath the slave-borne parasol, the fat shapeless old matriarch in the regal sweat-stained purple silk and the plumed hat, barefoot too of course but, being a queen, with another slave to carry her slippers, putting her cross to the paper and then driving on, vanishing slowly and terrifically to the slow and terrific creak and squeak of the ungreased wagon—apparently and apparently only, since in reality it was as though, instead of putting an inked cross at the foot of a sheet of paper, she had lighted the train of a mine set beneath a dam, a dyke, a barrier already straining, bulging, bellying, not only towering over the land but leaning, looming, imminent with collapse, so that it only required the single light touch of the pen in that brown illiterate hand, and the wagon did not vanish slowly and terrifically from the scene to the terrific sound of its ungreased wheels, but was swept, hurled, flung not only out of Yoknapatawpha County and Mississippi but the United States too, immobile and intact—the wagon, the mules, the rigid shapeless old Indian woman and the nine heads which surrounded her—like a float or a piece of stage property dragged rapidly into the wings across the very backdrop and amid the very bustle of the property-men setting up for the next scene and act before the curtain had even had time to fall;

There was no time; the next act and scene itself clearing its own stage without waiting for property-men; or rather, not even bothering to clear the stage but commencing the new act and scene right in the midst of the phantoms, the fading wraiths of that old time which had been exhausted, used up, to be no more and never return: as though the mere and simple orderly ordinary succession of days was not big enough, comprised not scope enough, and so weeks and months and years had to be condensed and compounded into one burst, one surge, one soundless roar filled with one word: town: city: with a name: Jefferson; men's mouths and their incredulous faces (faces to which old Alec Holston had long since ceased trying to give names or, for that matter, even to recognise) were filled with it; that was only yesterday, and by tomorrow the vast bright rush and roar had swept the very town one block south, leaving in the tideless backwater of an alley on a sidestreet the old jail which, like the old mirror, had already looked at too much too long, or like the patriarch who, whether or not he decreed the conversion of the mud-chinked cabin into a mansion, had at least foreseen it, is now not only content but even prefers the old chair on the back gallery, free of the rustle of blue prints and the uproar of bickering architects in the already dismantled living-room;

* * *

It (the old jail) didn't care, tideless in that backwash, insulated by that city block of space from the turmoil of the town's birthing, the mud-chinked log walls even carcerant of the flotsam of an older time already on its rapid way out too: an occasional runaway slave or drunken Indian or shoddy would-be heir of the old tradition of Mason or Hare or Harpe (biding its time until, the courthouse finished, the jail too would be translated into brick, but, unlike the courthouse, merely a veneer of brick, the old mud-chinked logs of the ground floor still intact behind the patterned and symmetric sheath); no longer even watching now, merely cognizant, remembering: only yesterday was a wilderness ordinary, a store, a smithy, and already today was not a town, a city, but *the* town and city: named; not a courthouse but *the* courthouse, rising surging like the fixed blast of a rocket, not even finished yet but already looming, beacon focus and lodestar, already taller than anything else, out of the rapid and fading wilderness,—not the wilderness receding from the rich and arable fields as tide recedes, but rather the fields themselves, rich and inexhaustible to the plow, rising sunward and airward out of swamp and morass, themselves thrusting back and down brake and thicket, bayou and bottom and forest, along with the copeless denizens—the wild men and animals—which once haunted them, wanting, dreaming, imagining, no other;—lodestar and pole, drawing the people—the men and women and children, the maidens, the marriageable girls and the young men, flowing, pouring in with their tools and goods and cattle and slaves and gold money, behind ox- or mule-teams, by steamboat up Ikkemotubbe's old river from the Mississippi; only yesterday Pettigrew's pony express had been displaced by a stage-coach, yet already there was talk of a railroad less than a hundred miles to the north, to run all the way from Memphis to the Atlantic Ocean;

Going fast now: only seven years, and not only was the courthouse finished, but the jail too: not a new jail of course but the old one veneered over with brick, into two storeys, with white trim and iron-barred windows: only its face lifted, because behind the veneer were still the old ineradicable bones, the old ineradicable remembering: the old logs immured intact and lightless between the tiered symmetric bricks and the whitewashed plaster, immune now even to having to look, see, watch that new time which in a few years more would not even remember that the old logs were there behind the brick or had ever been, an age from which the drunken Indian had vanished, leaving only the highwayman, who had wagered his liberty on his luck, and the runaway nigger who, having no freedom to stake, had wagered merely his milieu; that rapid, that fast: Sutpen's untameable Paris architect long since departed, vanished (one hoped) back to wherever it was he had made that aborted midnight try to regain and had been overtaken and caught in the swamp, not (as the town knew now) by Sutpen and Sutpen's wild West Indian headman and Sutpen's bear hounds, nor even by Sutpen's destiny nor even by his (the architect's) own, but by that of the town: the long invincible arm of Progress itself reaching into that midnight swamp to pluck him out of that bayed circle of dogs and naked Negroes and pine torches, and stamped the town with him like a rubber signature and then released him, not flung him away like a squeezed-out tube of paint, but rather (inattentive too) merely opening its fingers, its hand; stamping his (the architect's) imprint not on just the courthouse and the jail, but on the whole town, the flow and trickle of his bricks never even faltering, his molds and kilns building the two churches and then that Female Academy a certificate from which, to a young woman of North Mississippi or West Tennessee, would presently have the same mystic significance as an invitation dated from Windsor castle and signed by Queen Victoria would for a young female from Long Island or Philadelphia;

That fast now: tomorrow, and the railroad did run unbroken from Memphis to Carolina, the light-wheeled bulb-stacked wood-burning engines shrieking among the swamps and cane-brakes where bear and panther still lurked, and through the open woods where browsing deer still drifted in pale bands like unwinded smoke: because they—the wild animals, the beasts—remained, they coped, they would endure; a day, and they would flee, lumber, scuttle across the clearings already overtaken and relinquished by the hawk-shaped shadows of mail planes; they would endure, only the wild men were gone; indeed, tomorrow, and there would be grown men in Jefferson who could not even remember a drunken Indian in the jail; another tomorrow—so quick, so rapid, so fast—and not even a highwayman anymore of the old true sanguinary girt and tradition of Hare and Mason and the mad Harpes; even Murrell, their thrice-compounded heir and apotheosis, who had taken his heritage of simple rapacity and bloodlust and converted it into a bloody dream of outlaw-empire, was gone, finished, as obsolete as Alexander, checkmated and stripped not even by man but by Progress, by a pierceless front of middleclass morality, which refused him even the dignity of execution as a felon, but instead merely branded him on the hand like an Elizabethan pickpocket—until all that remained of the old days for the jail to incarcerate was the runaway slave, for his little hour more, his little minute yet while the time, the land, the nation, the American earth, whirled faster and faster toward the plunging precipice of its destiny;

That fast, that rapid: a commodity in the land now which until now had dealt first in Indians: then in acres and sections and boundaries:—an economy: Cotton: a king: omnipotent and omnipresent: a destiny of which (obvious now) the plow and the axe had been merely the tools; not plow and axe which had effaced the wilderness, but Cotton: petty globules of Motion weightless and myriad even in the hand of a child, incapable even of wadding a rifle, let alone of charging it, yet potent enough to sever the very taproots of oak and hickory and gum, leaving the acre-shading tops to wither and vanish in one single season beneath that fierce minted glare; not the rifle nor the plow which drove at last the bear and deer and panther into the last jungle fastnesses of the river bottoms, but Cotton; not the soaring cupola of the courthouse drawing people into the country, but that same white tide sweeping them in: that tender skim covering the winter's brown earth, burgeoning through spring and summer into September's white surf crashing against the flanks of gin and warehouse and ringing like bells on the marble counters of the banks: altering not just the face of the land, but the complexion of the town too, creating its own parasitic aristocracy not only behind the columned porticoes of the plantation houses, but in the counting-rooms of merchants and bankers and the sanctums of lawyers, and not only these last, but finally nadir complete: the county offices too: of sheriff and tax-collector and bailiff and turnkey and clerk; doing overnight to the old jail what Sutpen's architect with all his brick and iron smithwork, had not been able to accomplish,—the old jail which had been unavoidable, a necessity, like a public comfort-station, and which, like the public comfort-station, was not ignored but simply by mutual concord, not seen, not looked at, not named by its purpose and aim, yet which to the older people of the town, in spite of Sutpen's architect's face-lifting, was still the old jail—now translated into an integer, a moveable pawn on the county's political board like the sheriff's star or the clerk's bond or the bailiff's wand of office; converted indeed now, elevated (an apotheosis) ten feet above the level of the town, so that the old buried log walls now contained the living-quarters for the turnkey's family and the kitchen from which his wife catered, at so much a meal, to the city's and the county's prisoners—perquisite not for work or capability for work, but for political fidelity and the numerality of votable kin by blood or marriage;—a jailor or turnkey, himself someone's cousin and with enough other cousins and inlaws of his own to have assured the election of sheriff or chancery- or circuit-clerk,—a failed farmer who was not at all the victim of his time but on the contrary, was its master, since his inherited and inescapable incapacity to support his family by his own efforts, had matched him with an era and a land where government was founded on the working premise of being primarily an asylum for ineptitude and indigence, for the private business failures among your or your wife's kin whom otherwise you yourself would have to support,—so much his destiny's master that, in a land and time where a man's survival depended not only on his ability to drive a straight furrow and to fell a tree without maiming or destroying himself, that fate had supplied to him one child: a frail anemic girl with narrow workless hands lacking even the strength to milk a cow, and then capped its own vanquishment and eternal subjugation by the paradox of giving him for his patronymic the designation of the vocation at which he was to fail: Farmer; this was the incumbent, the turnkey, the jailor; the old tough logs which had known Ikkemotubbe's drunken Chickasaws and brawling teamsters and trappers and flatboatmen (and—for that one short summer night—the four highwaymen, one of whom might have been the murderer, Wiley Harpe), were now the bower framing a window in which mused hour after hour and day and month and year, the frail blonde girl not only incapable of (or at least excused from) helping her mother cook, but even of drying the dishes after her mother (or father perhaps) washed them,—musing, not even waiting for anyone or anything, as far as the town knew, not even pensive, as far as the town knew: just musing amid her blonde hair in the window facing the country town street, day after day and month after month and—as the town remembered it—year after year for what must have been three or four of them, inscribing at some moment the fragile and indelible signature of her meditation in one of the panes of it (the window): her frail and workless name, scratched by a diamond ring in her frail and workless hand, and the date: *Cecilia Farmer April 16th 1861*;

At which moment the destiny of the land, the nation, the South, the State, the County, was already whirling into the plunge of its precipice, not that the State and the South knew it, because the first seconds of fall always seem like soar: a weightless deliberation preliminary to a rush not downward but upward, the falling body reversed during that second by transubstantiation into the upward rush of earth; a soar, an apex, the South's own apotheosis of its destiny and its pride, Mississippi and Yoknapatawpha County not last in this, Mississippi among the first of the eleven to ratify secession, the regiment of infantry which John Sartoris raised and organised with Jefferson for its headquarters, going to Virginia numbered Two in the roster of Mississippi regiments, the jail watching that too but just by cognizance from a block away: that noon, the regiment not even a regiment yet but merely a voluntary association of untried men who knew they were ignorant and hoped they were brave, the four sides of the

Square lined with their fathers or grandfathers and their mothers and wives and sisters and sweethearts, the only uniform present yet that one in which Sartoris stood with his virgin sabre and his pristine colonel's braid on the courthouse balcony, bareheaded too while the Baptist minister prayed and the Richmond mustering officer swore the regiment in; and then (the regiment) gone; and now not only the jail but the town too hung without motion in a tideless backwash: the plunging body advanced far enough now into space as to have lost all sense of motion, weightless and immobile upon the light pressure of invisible air, gone now all diminishment of the precipice's lip, all increment of the vast increaseless earth: a town of old men and women and children and an occasional wounded soldier (John Sartoris himself, deposed from his colonelcy by a regimental election after Second Manassas, came home and oversaw the making and harvesting of a crop on his plantation before he got bored and gathered up a small gang of irregular cavalry and carried it up into Tennessee to join Forrest), static in quo, rumored, murmured of war only as from a great and incredible dreamy distance, like far summer thunder: until the spring of '64, the once-vast fixed impalpable increaseless and threatless earth now one omnivorous roar of rock (a roar so vast and so spewing, flinging ahead of itself, like the spray above the maelstrom, the preliminary anesthetic of shock so that the agony of bone and flesh will not even be felt, as to contain and sweep along with it the beginning, the first ephemeral phase, of this story, permitting it to boil for an instant to the surface like a chip or a twig—a match-stick or a bubble say, too weightless to give resistance for destruction to function against: in this case, a bubble, a minute globule which was its own impunity, since what it—the bubble—contained, having no part in rationality and being contemptuous of fact, was immune even to the rationality of rock)—a sudden battle centering around Colonel Sartoris's plantation house four miles to the north, the line of a creek held long enough for the main Confederate body to pass through Jefferson to a stronger line on the river heights south of the town, a rear-guard action of cavalry in the streets of the town itself (and this was the story, the beginning of it; all of it too, the town might have been justified in thinking, presuming they had had time to see, notice, remark and then remember, even that little)—the rattle and burst of pistols, the hooves, the dust, the rush and scurry of a handful of horsemen led by a lieutenant, up the street past the jail, and the two of them—the frail and useless girl musing in the blonde mist of her hair beside the window-pane where three or four (or whatever it was) years ago she had inscribed with her grandmother's diamond ring her paradoxical and significantless name (and where, so it seemed to the town, she had been standing ever since), and the soldier gaunt and tattered, battle-grimed and fleeing and undefeated, looking at one another for that moment across the fury and pell mell of battle;

Then gone; that night the town was occupied by Federal troops; two nights later, it was on fire (the Square, the stores and shops and the professional offices), gutted (the courthouse too), the blackened jagged topless jumbles of brick wall enclosing like a ruined jaw the blackened shell of the courthouse between its two rows of topless columns, which (the columns) were only blackened and stained, being tougher than fire: but not the jail, it escaped, untouched, insulated by its windless backwater from fire; and now the town was as though insulated by fire or perhaps cauterised by fire from fury and turmoil, the long roar of the rushing omnivorous rock fading on to the east with the fading uproar of the battle: and so in effect it was a whole year in advance of Appomattox (only the undefeated undefeatable women, vulnerable only to death, resisted, endured, irreconciliable); already, before there was a name for them (already their prototype before they even existed as a species), there were carpetbaggers in Jefferson—a Missourian named Redmond, a cotton- and quartermaster-supplies-speculator, who had followed the Northern army to Memphis in '61 and (nobody knew exactly how or why) had been with (or at least on the fringe of) the military household of the brigadier commanding the force which occupied Jefferson, himself—Redmond—going no further, stopping, staying, none knew the why for that either, why he elected Jefferson, chose that alien fire-gutted site (himself one, or at least the associate, of them who had set the match) to be his future home; and a German private, a blacksmith, a deserter from a Pennsylvania regiment, who appeared in the summer of '64, riding a mule, with (so the tale told later, when his family of daughters had become matriarchs and grandmothers of the town's new aristocracy) for saddle-blanket sheaf on sheaf of virgin and uncut United States banknotes, so Jefferson and Yoknapatawpha County had mounted Golgotha and passed beyond Appomattox a full year in advance, with returned soldiers in the town, not only the wounded from the battle of Jefferson, but whole men: not only the furloughed from Forrest in Alabama and Johnston in Georgia and Lee in Virginia, but the stragglers, the unmaimed flotsam and refuse of that single battle now drawing its final constricting loop from the Atlantic Ocean at Old Point Comfort, to Richmond: to Chattanooga: to Atlanta: to the Atlantic Ocean again at Charleston, who were not deserters but who could not rejoin any still-intact Confederate unit for the reason that there were enemy armies between, so that in the almost faded twilight of that land, the knell of Appomattox made no sound; when in the spring and early summer of '65 the formally and officially paroled and disbanded soldiers began to trickle back into the county, there was anticlimax; they returned to a land which not only had passed through Appomattox over a year ago, it had had that year in which to assimilate it, that whole year in which not only to ingest surrender but (begging the metaphor, the figure) to convert, metabolise it, and then defecate it as fertilizer for the four-years' fallow land they were already in train to rehabilitate a year before the Virginia knell rang the formal change, the men of '65 returning to find themselves alien in the very land they had been bred and born in and had fought for four years to defend, to find a working and already solvent economy based on the premise that it could get along without them; (and now the rest of this story, since it occurs, happens, here: not yet June in '65; this one had indeed wasted no time getting back: a stranger, alone; the town did not even know it had ever seen him before, because the other time was a year ago and had lasted only while he galloped through it firing a pistol backward at a Yankee army, and he had been riding a horse—a fine though a little too small and too delicate blooded mare—where now he rode a big mule, which for that reason—its size—was a better mule than the horse was a horse, but it was still a mule, and of course the town could not know that he had swapped the mare for the mule on the same day that he traded his lieutenant's sabre—he still had the pistol—for the stocking full of seed corn he had seen growing in a Pennsylvania field and had not let even the mule have one mouthful of it during the long journey across the ruined land between the Atlantic seaboard and the Jefferson jail, riding up to the jail at last, still gaunt and tattered and dirty and still undefeated and not fleeing now but instead making or at least planning a single-handed assault against what any rational man would have considered insurmountable odds ((but then, that bubble had ever been immune to the ephemerae of facts)); perhaps, probably—without doubt: apparently she had been standing leaning musing in it for three or four years in 1864; nothing had happened since, not in a land which had even anticipated Appomattox, capable of shaking a meditation that rooted, that durable, that veteran—the girl watched him get down and tie the mule to the fence, and perhaps while he walked from the fence to the door he even looked for a moment at her, though possibly, perhaps even probably, not, since she was not his immediate object now, he was not really concerned with her at the moment, because he had so little time, he had none, really: still to reach Alabama and the small hill farm which had been his father's and would now be his, if—no, when—he could get there, and it had not been ruined by four years of war and neglect, and even if the land was still plantable, even if he could start planting the stocking of corn tomorrow, he would be weeks and even months late; during that walk to the door and as he lifted his hand to knock on it, he must have thought with a kind of weary and indomitable outrage of how, already months late, he must still waste a day or maybe even two or three of them before he could load the girl onto the mule behind him and head at last for Alabama,—this, at a time when of all things he would require patience and a clear head, trying for them ((courtesy too, which would be demanded now)), patient and urgent and polite, undefeated, trying to explain, in terms which they could understand or at least accept, his simple need and the urgency of it, to the mother and father whom he had never seen before and whom he never intended, or anyway anticipated, to see again, not that he had anything for or against them either: he simply intended to be too busy for the rest of his life, once they could get on the mule and start for home; not seeing the girl then, during the interview, not even asking to see her for a moment when the interview was over, because he had to get the license now and then find the preacher: so that the first word he ever spoke to her was a promise delivered through a stranger; it was probably not until they were on the mule—the frail useless hands whose only strength seemed to be that sufficient to fold the wedding license into the bosom of her dress and then cling to the belt around his waist—that he looked at her again or ((both of them)) had time to learn one another's middle name);

That was the story, the incident, ephemeral of an afternoon in late May, unrecorded by the town and the county because they had little time too: which (the county and the town) had anticipated Appomattox and kept that lead, so that in effect Appomattox itself never overhauled them; it was the long pull of course, but they had—as they would realise later—that priceless, that unmatchable year; on New Year's Day, 1865, while the rest of the South sat staring at the northeast horizon beyond which Richmond lay, like a family staring at the closed door to a sick-room, Yoknapatawpha County was already nine months gone in reconstruction; by New Year's of '66, the gutted walls (the rain of two winters had washed them clean of the smoke and soot) of the Square had been temporarily roofed and were stores and shops and offices again, and they had begun to restore the courthouse: not temporary, this, but restored, exactly as it had been, between the two columned porticoes, one north and one south, which had been tougher than dynamite and fire, because it was the symbol: the County and the City: and they knew how, who had done it before; Colonel Sartoris was home now, and General Compson, the first Jason's son, and though a tragedy had happened to Sutpen and his pride—a failure not of his pride nor even of his own bones and flesh, but of the lesser bones and flesh which he had believed capable of supporting the edifice of his dream—they still had the old plans of his architect and even the architect's molds, and even more: money, (strangely, curiously) Redmond, the town's domesticated carpet-bagger, symbol of a blind rapacity almost like a biological instinct, destined to cover the South like a migration of locusts; in the case of this man, arriving a full year before its time and now devoting no small portion of the fruit of his rapacity to restoring the very building the destruction of which had rung up the curtain for his appearance on the stage, had been the formal visa on his passport to pillage; and by New Year's of '76, this same Redmond with his money and Colonel Sartoris and General Compson had built a railroad from Jefferson north into Tennessee to connect with the one from Memphis to the Atlantic ocean; nor content there either, north or south: another ten years (Sartoris and Redmond and Compson quarrelled, and Sartoris and Redmond bought—probably with Redmond's money—Compson's interest in the railroad, and the next year Sartoris and Redmond had quarrelled and the year after that, because of simple physical fear, Redmond killed Sartoris from ambush on the Jefferson Square and fled, and at last even Sartoris's supporters—he had no friends: only enemies and frantic admirers—began to understand the result of that regimental election in the fall of '62) and the railroad was a part of that system covering the whole South and East like the veins in an oak leaf and itself mutually adjunctive to the other intricate systems covering the rest of the United States, so that you could get on a train in Jefferson now and, by changing and waiting a few times, go anywhere in North America;

No more into the United States, but into the *rest* of the United States, because the long pull was over now; only the aging unvanquished women were unreconciled, irreconcilable, reversed and irrevocably reverted against the whole moving unanimity of panorama until, old unordered vacant pilings above a tide's flood, they themselves had an illusion of motion, facing irreconciliably backward toward the old lost battles, the old aborted cause, the old four ruined years whose very physical scars ten and twenty and twenty-five changes of season had annealed back into the earth; twenty-five and then thirty-five years; not only a century and an age, but a way of thinking died; the town itself wrote the epilogue and epitaph: 1900, on Confederate Decoration Day, Mrs Virginia DuPre, Colonel Sartoris's sister, twitched a lanyard and the spring-restive bunting collapsed and flowed, leaving the marble effigy—the stone infantryman on his stone pedestal on the exact spot where forty years ago the Richmond officer and the local Baptist minister had mustered in the Colonel's regiment, and the old men in the gray and braided coats (all officers now, none less in rank than captain) tottered into the sunlight and fired shotguns at the bland sky and raised their cracked quavering voices in the shrill hackle-lifting yelling which Lee and Jackson and Longstreet and the two Johnstons (and Grant and Sherman and Hooker and Pope and McClellan and Burnside too for the matter of that) had listened to amid the smoke and the din; epilogue and epitaph, because apparently neither the U.D.C. ladies who instigated and bought the monument, nor the architect who designed it nor the masons who erected it, had noticed that the marble eyes under the shading marble palm stared not toward the north and the enemy, but toward the south, toward (if anything) his own rear,—looking perhaps, the wits said (could say now, with the old war thirty-five years past and you could even joke about it—except the women, the ladies, the unsurrendered, the irreconciliable, who even after another thirty-five years would still get up and stalk out of picture houses showing *Gone With The Wind*), for reinforcements; or perhaps not a combat soldier at all, but a provost marshal's man looking for deserters, or perhaps himself for a safe place to run to: because that old war was dead; the sons of those tottering old men in gray had already died in blue coats in Cuba, the macabre mementos and testimonials and shrines of the new war already usurping the earth before the blasts of blank shotgun shells and the weightless collapsing of bunting had unveiled the final ones to the old;

Not only a new century and a new way of thinking, but of acting and behaving too: now you could go to bed in a train in Jefferson and wake up tomorrow morning in New Orleans or Chicago; there were electric lights and running water in almost every house in town except the cabins of Negroes; and now the town bought and brought from a great distance a kind of gray crushed ballast-stone called macadam, and paved the entire street between the depot and the hotel, so that no more would the train-meeting hacks filled with drummers and lawyers and court-witnesses need to lurch and heave and strain through the winter mud-holes; every morning a wagon came to your very door with artificial ice and put it in your icebox on the back gallery for you, the children in rotational neighborhood gangs following it (the wagon), eating the fragments of ice which the Negro driver chipped off for them; and that summer a specially-built sprinkling-cart began to make the round of the streets each day; a new time, a new age: there were screens in windows now; people (white people) could actually sleep in summer night air, finding it harmless, uninimical: as though there had waked suddenly in man (or anyway in his womenfolks) a belief in his inalienable civil right to be free of dust and bugs;

Moving faster and faster: from the speed of two horses on either side of a polished tongue, to that of thirty then fifty then a hundred under a tin bonnet no bigger than a washtub: which from almost the first explosion, would have to be controlled by police; already in a back yard on the edge of town, an ex blacksmith's-apprentice, a grease-covered man with the eyes of a visionary monk, was building a gasoline buggy, casting and boring his own cylinders and rods and cams, inventing his own coils and plugs and valves as he found he needed them, which would run, and did: crept popping and stinking out of the alley at the exact moment when the banker Bayard Sartoris, the Colonel's son, passed in his carriage: as a result of which, there is on the books of Jefferson today a law prohibiting the operation of any mechanically-propelled vehicle on the streets of the corporate town: who (the same banker Sartoris) died in one (such was progress, that fast, that rapid) lost from control on an icy road by his (the banker's) grandson, who had just returned from (such was progress) two years of service as a combat airman on the Western Front and now the camouflage paint is weathering slowly from a French point-seventy-five field piece squatting on one flank of the base of the Confederate monument, but even before it faded there was neon in the town and A.A.A. and C.C.C. in the county, and W.P.A. ("and XYZ and etc.," as "Uncle Pete" Gombault, a lean clean tobacco-chewing old man, incumbent of a political sinecure under the designation of United States marshal—an office held back in reconstruction times, when the State of Mississippi was a United States military district, by a Negro man who was still living in 1925—fire-maker, sweeper, janitor and furnace-attendant to five or six lawyers and doctors and one of the banks—and still known as "Mulberry" from the avocation which he had followed before and during and after his incumbency as marshal: peddling illicit whiskey in pint and half-pint bottles from a cache beneath the roots of a big mulberry tree behind the drugstore of his pre-1865 owner—put it) in both; W.P.A. and XYZ marking the town and the county as war itself had not: gone now were the last of the forest trees which had followed the shape of the Square, shading the unbroken second-storey balcony onto which the lawyers' and doctors' offices had opened, which shaded in its turn the fronts of the stores and the walkway beneath; and now was gone even the balcony itself with its wrought-iron balustrade on which in the long summer afternoons the lawyers would prop their feet to talk; and the continuous iron chain looping from wooden post to post along the circumference of the courthouse yard, for the farmers to hitch their teams to; and the public watering trough where they could water them, because gone was the last wagon to stand on the Square during the spring and summer and fall Saturdays and trading-days, and not only the Square but the streets leading into it were paved now, with fixed signs of interdiction and admonition applicable only to something capable of moving faster than thirty miles an hour; and now the last forest tree was gone from the courthouse yard too, replaced by formal synthetic shrubs contrived and schooled in Wisconsin greenhouses, and in the courthouse (the city hall too) a courthouse and city hall gang, in miniature of course (but that was not its fault but the fault of the city's and the county's size and population and wealth) but based on the pattern of Chicago and Kansas City and Boston and Philadelphia (and which, except for its minuscularity, neither Philadelphia nor Boston nor Kansas City nor Chicago need have blushed at) which every three or four years would try again to raze the old courthouse in order to build a new one, not that they did not like the old one nor wanted the new, but because the new one would bring into the town and county that much more increment of unearned federal money;

And now the paint is preparing to weather from an anti-tank howitzer squatting on rubber tires on the opposite flank of the Confederate monument; and gone now from the fronts of the stores are the old brick made of native clay in Sutpen's architect's old molds, replaced now by sheets of glass taller than a man and longer than a wagon and team, pressed intact in Pittsburgh factories and framing interiors bathed now in one shadowless corpse-glare of fluorescent light; and, now and at last, the last of silence too: the county's hollow inverted air one resonant boom and ululance of radio: and thus no more Yoknapatawpha's air nor even Mason and Dixon's air, but America's: the patter of comedians, the baritone screams of female vocalists, the babbling pressure to buy and buy and still buy arriving more instantaneous than light, two thousand miles from New York and Los Angeles; one air, one nation: the shadowless fluorescent corpse glare bathing the sons and daughters of men and women, Negro and white both, who were born to and who passed all their lives in denim overalls and calico, haggling by cash or the installment-plan for garments copied last week out of *Harper's Bazaar* or *Esquire* in East Side sweat-shops: because an entire generation of farmers has vanished, not just from Yoknapatawpha's but from Mason and Dixon's earth: the self-consumer: the machine which displaced the man because the exodus of the man left no one to drive the mule, now that the machine was threatening to extinguish the mule; time was when the mule stood in droves at daylight in the plantation mule-lots across the plantation road from the serried identical ranks of two-room shotgun shacks in which lived in droves with his family the Negro tenant- or share- or furnish-hand who bridled him (the mule) in the lot at sunup and followed him through the plumb-straight monotony of identical furrows and back to the lot at sundown, with (the man) one eye on where the mule was going and the other eye on his (the mule's) heels; both gone now: the one, to the last of the forty- and fifty- and sixty-acre hill farms inaccessible from unmarked dirt roads, the other to New York and Detroit and Chicago and Los Angeles ghettos, or nine out of ten of him that is, the tenth one mounting from the handles of a plow to the springless bucket seat of a tractor, dispossessing and displacing the other nine just as the tractor had dispossessed and displaced the other eighteen mules to whom that nine would have been complement; then Warsaw and Dunquerque displaced that tenth in his turn, and now the planter's not-yet-drafted son drove the tractor: and then Pearl Harbor and Tobruk and Utah Beach displaced that son, leaving the planter himself on the seat of the tractor, for a little while that is—or so he thought, forgetting that victory or defeat both are bought at the same exorbitant price of change and alteration; one nation, one world: young men who had never been further from Yoknapatawpha County than Memphis or New Orleans (and that not often), now talked glibly of street intersections in Asiatic and European capitals, returning no more to inherit the long monotonous endless unendable furrows of Mississippi cotton fields, living now (with now a wife and next year a wife and child and the year after that a wife and children) in automobile trailers or G.I. barracks on the outskirts of liberal arts colleges, and the father and now grandfather himself still driving the tractor across the gradually diminishing fields between the long looping skeins of electric lines bringing electric power from the Appalachian mountains, and the subterrene steel veins bringing the natural gas from the western plains, to the little lost lonely farmhouses glittering and gleaming with automatic stoves and washing machines and television antennae;

One nation: no longer anywhere, not even in Yoknapatawpha County, one last irreconciliable fastness of stronghold from which to enter the United States, because at last even the last old sapless indomitable unvanquished widow or maiden aunt had died and the old deathless Lost Cause had become a faded (though still select) social club or caste, or form of behavior when you remembered to observe it on the occasions when young men from Brooklyn, exchange students at Mississippi or Arkansas or Texas universities, vended tiny confederate battle flags among the thronged Saturday afternoon ramps of football stadia; one world: the tank gun: captured from a regiment of Germans in an African desert by a regiment of Japanese in American uniforms, whose mothers and fathers at the time were in a California detention camp for enemy aliens, and carried (the gun) seven thousand miles back to be set halfway between, as a sort of secondary flying buttress to a memento of Shiloh and The Wilderness; one universe, one cosmos: contained in one America: one towering frantic edifice poised like a card-house over the abyss of the mortgaged generations; one boom, one peace: one swirling rocket-roar filling the glittering zenith as with golden feathers, until the vast hollow sphere of his air, the vast and terrible burden beneath which he tries to stand erect and lift his battered and indomitable head—the very substance in which he lives and, lacking which, he would vanish in a matter of seconds—is murmurous with his fears and terrors and disclaimers and repudiations and his aspirations and dreams and his baseless hopes, bouncing back at him in radar waves from the constellations;

And still—the old jail—endured, sitting in its rumorless cul-de-sac, its almost seasonless backwater in the middle of that rush and roar of civic progress and social alteration and change like a collarless (and reasonably clean: merely dingy: with a day's stubble and no garters to his socks) old man sitting in his suspenders and stocking feet, on the back kitchen steps inside a walled courtyard; actually not isolated by location so much as insulated by obsolescence: on the way out of course (to disappear from the surface of the earth along with the rest of the town on the day when all America, after cutting down all the trees and levelling the hills and mountains with bulldozers, would have to move underground to make room for, get out of the way of, the motor cars) but like the track-walker in the tunnel, the thunder of the express mounting behind him, who finds himself opposite a niche or crack exactly his size in the wall's living and impregnable rock, and steps into it, inviolable and secure while destruction roars past and on and away, grooved ineluctably to the spidery rails of its destiny and destination; not even—the jail—worth selling to the United States for some matching allocation out of the federal treasury; not even (so fast, so far, was Progress) anymore a real pawn, let alone knight or rook, on the County's political board, not even plum in true worth of the word: simply a modest sinecure for the husband of someone's cousin, who had failed not as a father but merely as a fourth-rate farmer or day-laborer;

It survived, endured; it had its inevictable place in the town and the county; it was even still adding modestly not just to its but to the town's and the county's history too: somewhere behind that dingy brick facade, between the old durable hand-molded brick and the cracked creosote-impregnated plaster of the inside walls (though few in the town or county any longer knew that they were there) were the old notched and morticed logs which (this, the town and county did remember; it was part of its legend) had held someone who might have been Wiley Harpe; during that summer of 1864, the federal brigadier who had fired the Square and the courthouse had used the jail as his provost-marshal's guard-house; and even children in high school remembered how the jail had been host to the Governor of the State while he discharged a thirty-day sentence for contempt of court for refusing to testify in a paternity suit brought against one of his lieutenants: but isolate, even its legend and record and history, indisputable in authenticity yet a little oblique, elliptic or perhaps just ellipsoid, washed thinly over with a faint quiet cast of apocrypha: because there were new people in the town now, strangers, outlanders, living in new minute glass-walled houses set as neat and orderly and antiseptic as cribs in a nursery ward, in new subdivisions named Fairfield or Longwood or Halcyon Acres which had once been the lawn or back yard or kitchen garden of the old residences (the old obsolete columned houses still standing among them like old horses surged suddenly out of slumber in the middle of a flock of sheep), who had never seen the jail; that is, they had looked at it in passing, they knew where it was, when their kin or friends or acquaintances from the East or North or California visited them or passed through Jefferson on the way to New Orleans or Florida, they could even repeat some of its legend or history to them: but they had had no contact with it, it was not a part of their lives; they had the automatic stoves and furnaces and milk deliveries and lawns the size of installment-plan rugs; they had never had to go to the jail on the morning after Juneteenth or July Fourth or Thanksgiving or Christmas or New Year's (or for that matter, on almost any Monday morning) to pay the fine of houseman or gardener or handyman so that he could hurry on home (still wearing his hangover or his barely-stanched razor-slashes) and milk the cow or clean the furnace or mow the lawn;

So only the old citizens knew the jail anymore, not old people but old citizens: men and women old not in years but in the constancy of the town, or against that constancy, concordant (not coeval of course, the town's date was a century and a quarter ago now, but in accord against that continuation) with that thin durable continuity born a hundred and twenty-five years ago out of a handful of bandits captured by a drunken militia squad, and a bitter ironical incorruptible wilderness mail-rider, and a monster wrought-iron padlock,—that steadfast and durable and unhurryable continuity against or across which the vain and glittering ephemerae of progress and alteration washed in substanceless repetitive evanescent scarless waves, like the wash and glare of the neon sign on what was still known as the Holston House diagonally opposite, which would fade with each dawn from the old brick walls of the jail and leave no trace; only the old citizens still knew it: the intractable and obsolescent of the town who still insisted on wood-burning ranges and cows and vegetable gardens and handymen who had to be taken out of hock on the mornings after Saturday nights and holidays; or the ones who actually spent the Saturday- and holiday-nights inside the barred doors and windows of the cells or bullpen for drunkenness or fighting or gambling—the servants, housemen and gardeners and handymen, who would be extracted the next morning by their white folks, and the others (what the town knew as the New Negro, independent of that commodity) who would sleep there every night beneath the thin ruby checker-barred wash and fade of the hotel sign, while they worked their fines out on the street; and the County, since its cattle-thieves and moonshiners went to trial from there, and its murderers—by electricity now (so fast, that fast, was Progress)—to eternity from there; in fact it was still, not a factor perhaps, but at least an integer, a cipher, in the county's political establishment; at least still used by the Board of Supervisors, if not as a lever, at least as something like Punch's stuffed club, not intended to break bones, not aimed to leave any permanent scars;

So only the old knew it, the irreconciliable Jeffersonians and Yoknapatawphians who had (and without doubt firmly intended to continue to have) actual personal dealings with it on the blue Monday mornings after holidays, or during the semi-yearly terms of Circuit or Federal Court:—until suddenly you, a stranger, an outlander say from the East or the North or the Far West, passing through the little town by simple accident, or perhaps relation or acquaintance or friend of one of the outland families which had moved into one of the pristine and recent subdivisions, yourself turning out of your way to fumble among road signs and filling stations out of frank curiosity, to try to learn, comprehend, understand what had brought your cousin or friend or acquaintance to elect to live here—not specifically here, of course, not specifically Jefferson, but such as here, such as Jefferson—, suddenly you would realise that something curious was happening or had happened here: that instead of dying off as they should as time passed, it was as though these old irreconciliables were actually increasing in number; as though with each interment of one, two more shared that vacancy: where in 1900, only thirty-five years afterward, there could not have been more than two or three capable of it, either by knowledge or memory of leisure, or even simple willingness and inclination, now, in 1951, eighty-six years afterward, they could be counted in dozens (and in 1965, a hundred years afterward, in hundreds because—by now you had already begun to understand why your kin or friend or acquaintance had elected to come to such as this with his family and call it his life—by then the children of that second outland invasion following a war, would also have become not just Mississippians but Jeffersonians and Yoknapatawphians: by which time—who knows?—not merely the pane, but the whole window, perhaps the entire wall, may have been removed and embalmed intact into a museum by an historical, or anyway a cultural, club of ladies,—why, by that time, they may not even know, or even need to know: only that the windowpane bearing the girl's name and the date is that old, which is enough; has lasted that long: one small rectangle of wavy, crudely-pressed, almost opaque glass, bearing a few faint scratches apparently no more durable than the thin dried slime left by the passage of a snail, yet which has endured a hundred years) who are capable and willing too to quit whatever they happen to be doing—sitting on the last of the wooden benches beneath the last of the locust and chinaberry trees among the potted conifers of the new age dotting the courthouse yard, or in the chairs along the shady sidewalk before the Holston House, where a breeze always blows—to lead you across the street and into the jail and (with courteous neighborly apologies to the jailor's wife stirring or turning on the stove the peas and grits and side-meat—purchased in bargain-lot quantities by shrewd and indefatigable peditation from store to store—which she will serve to the prisoners for dinner or supper at so much a head—plate—payable by the County, which is no mean factor in the sinecure of her husband's incumbency) into the kitchen and so to the cloudy pane bearing the faint scratches which, after a moment, you will descry to be a name and a date;

Not at first, of course, but after a moment, a second, because at first you would be a little puzzled, a little impatient because of your illness-at-ease from having been dragged without warning or preparation into the private kitchen of a strange woman cooking a meal; you would think merely *What? So what?* annoyed and even a little outraged, until suddenly, even while you were thinking it, something has already happened: the faint frail meaningless even inference-less scratching on the ancient poor-quality glass you stare at, has moved, under your eyes, even while you stared at it, coalesced, seeming actually to have entered into another sense than vision: a scent, a whisper, filling that hot cramped strange room already fierce with the sound and reek of frying pork-fat: the two of them in conjunction—the old milky obsolete glass, and the scratches on it: that tender ownerless obsolete girl's name and the old dead date in April almost a century ago—speaking, murmuring, back from, out of, across from, a time as old as lavender, older than album or stereopticon, as old as daguerrotype itself;

And being a stranger and a guest would have been enough, since, a stranger and a guest, you would have shown the simple courtesy and politeness of asking the questions naturally expected of you by the host or anyway volunteer guide, who had dropped whatever he was doing (even if that had been no more than sitting with others of his like on a bench in a courthouse yard or on the sidewalk before a hotel) in order to bring you here; not to mention your own perfectly natural desire for, not revenge perhaps, but at least compensation, restitution, vindication, for the shock and annoyance of having been brought here without warning or preparation, into the private quarters of a strange woman engaged in something as intimate as cooking a meal; but by now you had not only already begun to understand why your kin or friend or acquaintance had elected, not Jefferson but such as Jefferson, for his life, but you had heard that voice, that whisper, murmur, frailer than the scent of lavender, yet (for that second anyway) louder than all the seethe and fury of frying fat; so you ask the questions, not only which are expected of you, but whose answers you yourself must have if you are to get back into your car and fumble with any attention and concentration among the road signs and filling stations, to get on to wherever it is you had started when you stopped by chance or accident in Jefferson for an hour or a day or a night, and the host—guide—answers them, to the best of his ability out of the town's composite heritage of remembering that long back, told, repeated, inherited to him by his father; or rather, his mother: from her mother: or better still, to him when he himself was a child, direct from his great-aunt: the spinsters, maiden and childless out of a time when there were too many women because too many of the young men were maimed or dead: the indomitable and undefeated, maiden progenitresses of spinster and childless descendants still capable of rising up and stalking out in the middle of *Gone With The Wind*;

And again one sense assumes the office of two or three: not only hearing, listening, and seeing too, but you are even standing on the same spot, the same boards she did that day she wrote her name into the window and on the other one three years later watching and hearing through and beyond that faint fragile defacement the sudden rush and thunder: the dust: the crackle and splatter of pistols: then the face, gaunt, battle-dirty, stubbled-over; urgent of course, but merely harried, harassed; not defeated, turned for a fleeing instant across the turmoil and the fury, then gone: and still the girl in the window (the guide—host—has never said one or the other; without doubt in the town's remembering after a hundred years it has changed that many times from blonde to dark and back to blonde again: which doesn't matter, since in your own remembering that tender mist and vail will be forever blonde) not even waiting: musing; a year, and still not even waiting: meditant, not even unimpatient: just patienceless, in the sense that blindness and zenith are colorless; until at last the mule, not out of the long northeastern panorama of defeat and dust and fading smoke, but drawn out of it by that impregnable, that invincible, that incredible, that terrifying passivity, coming at that one fatigueless unflagging jog all the way from Virginia,—the mule which was a better mule in 1865 than the blood mare had been a horse in '-2 and '-3 and '-4, for the reason that this was now 1865, and the man, still gaunt and undefeated: merely harried and urgent and short of time to get on to Alabama and see the condition of his farm—or (for that matter) if he still had a farm, and now the girl, the fragile and workless girl not only incapable of milking a cow but of whom it was never even demanded, required, suggested, that she substitute for her father in drying the dishes, mounting pillion on a mule behind a paroled cavalry subaltern out of a surrendered army who had swapped his charger for a mule and the sabre of his rank and his defeatless pride for a stocking full of seed corn, whom she had not known or even spoken to long enough to have learned his middle name or his preference in food, or told him hers, and no time for that even now: riding, hurrying toward a country she had never seen, to begin a life which was not even simple frontier, engaged only with wilderness and shoeless savages and the tender hand of God, but one which had been rendered into a desert (assuming that it was still there at all to be returned to) by the iron and fire of civilization;

Which was all your host (guide) could tell you, since that was all he knew, inherited, inheritable from the town: which was enough, more than enough in fact, since all you needed was the face framed in its blonde and delicate vail behind the scratched glass; yourself, the stranger, the outlander from New England or the prairies or the Pacific Coast, no longer come by the chance or accident of kin or friend or acquaintance or roadmap, but drawn too from ninety years away by that incredible and terrifying passivity, watching in your turn through and beyond that old milk-dim disfigured glass that shape, that delicate frail and useless bone and flesh departing pillion on a mule without one backward look, to the reclaiming of an abandoned and doubtless even ravaged (perhaps even usurped) Alabama hill farm,—being lifted onto the mule (the first time he touched her probably, except to put the ring on: not to prove nor even to feel, touch, if there actually was a girl under the calico and the shawls; there was no time for that yet; but simply to get her up so they could start), to ride a hundred miles to become the farmless mother of farmers (she would bear a dozen, all boys, herself no older, still fragile, still workless among the churns and stoves and brooms and stacks of wood which even a woman could split into kindlings; unchanged), bequeathing to them in their matronymic the heritage of that invincible inviolable ineptitude;

Then suddenly, you realise that that was nowhere near enough, not for that face;—bridehood, motherhood, grandmotherhood, then widowhood and at last the grave,—the long peaceful connubial progress toward matriarchy in a rocking chair nobody else was allowed to sit in, then a headstone in a country churchyard;—not for that passivity, that stasis, that invincible captaincy of soul which didn't even need to wait but simply to be, breathe tranquilly, and take food,—infinite not only in capacity but in scope too: that face, one maiden muse which had drawn a man out of the running pell mell of a cavalry battle, a whole year around the long iron perimeter of duty and oath, from Yoknapatawpha County, Mississippi, across Tennessee into Virginia and up to the fringe of Pennsylvania before it curved back into its closing fade along the headwaters of the Appomattox river and at last removed from him its iron hand: where, a safe distance at last into the rainy woods from the picket lines and the furled flags and the stacked muskets, a handful of men leading spent horses, the still-warm pistols still loose and quick for the hand in the unstrapped scabbards, gathered in the failing twilight—privates and captains, sergeants and corporals and subalterns—talking a little of one last desperate cast southward where (by last report) Johnston was still intact, knowing that they would not, that they were done not only with vain resistance but with indominability too; already departed this morning in fact for Texas, the West, New Mexico: a new land even if not yet (spent too—like the horses—from the long harassment and anguish of remaining indomitable and undefeated) a new hope, putting behind them for good and all the loss of both: the young dead bride;—drawing him (that face) even back from this too, from no longer having to remain undefeated too: who swapped the charger for the mule and the sabre for the stocking of seed corn: back across the whole ruined land and the whole disastrous year by that virgin inevictable passivity more inescapable than lodestar;

Not that face; that was nowhere near enough: no symbol there of connubial matriarchy, but fatal instead with all insatiate and deathless sterility; spouseless, barren, and undescended; not even demanding more than that: simply requiring it, requiring all,—Lilith's lost and insatiable face drawing the substance—the will and hope and dream and imagination—of all men (you too: yourself and the host too) into that one bright fragile net and snare; not even to be caught, over-flung, by one single unerring cast of it, but drawn to watch in patient and thronging turn the very weaving of the strangling golden strands;—drawing the two of you from almost a hundred years away in your turn—yourself the stranger, the outlander from B.A. or (perhaps even) M.A. at Harvard or Northwestern or Stanford, passing through Jefferson by chance or accident on the way to somewhere else, and the host who in three generations has never been out of Yoknapatawpha further than a few prolonged Saturday nights in Memphis or New Orleans, who has heard of Jenny Lind, not because he has heard of Mark Twain and Mark Twain spoke well of her, but for the same reason that Mark Twain spoke well of her: not that she sang songs, but that she sang them in the old West in the old days, and the man sanctioned by public affirmation to wear a pistol openly in his belt is an inevictable part of the Missouri and the Yoknapatawpha dream too, but never of Duse or Bernhardt or Maximilian of Mexico, let alone whether the Emperor of Mexico even ever had a wife or not (saying—the host—: 'You mean, she was one of them? maybe even that emperor's wife?' and you: 'Why not? Wasn't she a Jefferson girl?')—to stand, in this hot strange little room furious with frying fat, among the roster and chronicle, the deathless murmur of the sublime and deathless names and the deathless faces, the faces omnivorous and insatiable and forever incontent: demon-nun and angel-witch; empress, siren, Erinys: Mistinguette too, invincibly possessed of a half-century more of years than the mere three score or so she bragged and boasted, for you to choose among, which one she was,—not *might* have been, nor even *could* have been, but *was*: so vast, so limitless in capacity is man's imagination to disperse and burn away the rubble-dross of fact and probability, leaving only truth and dream,—then gone, you are outside again, in the hot noon sun: late; you have already wasted too much time: to unfumble among the road signs and filling stations to get back onto a highway you know, back into the United States; not that it matters since you know again now that there is no time: no space: no distance: a fragile and workless scratching almost depthless in a sheet of old barely transparent glass, and (all you had to do was look at it a while; all you have to do now is remember it) there is the clear undistanced voice as though out of the delicate antenna-skeins of radio, further than empress's throne, than splendid insatiation, even than matriarch's peaceful rocking chair, across the vast instantaneous intervention, from the long long time ago: *'Listen, stranger; this was myself: this was I'.*

SCENE I

Interior, the Jail. 10:30 A.M. March twelfth.

The common room, or 'bull-pen'. It is on the second floor. A heavy barred door at L is the entrance to it, to the entire cell-block, which—the cells—are indicated by a row of steel doors, each with its own individual small barred window, lining the right wall. A narrow passage at the far end of the right wall leads to more cells. A single big heavily-barred window in the rear wall looks down into the street. It is mid-morning of a sunny day.

The door, L, opens with a heavy clashing of the steel lock, and swings back and outward. Temple enters, followed by Stevens and the Jailor. Temple has changed her dress, but wears the fur coat and the same hat. Stevens is dressed exactly as he was in Act II. The Jailor is a typical small-town turnkey, in shirt-sleeves and no necktie, carrying the heavy keys on a big iron ring against his leg as a farmer carries a lantern, say. He is drawing the door to behind him as he enters.

Temple stops just inside the room. Stevens perforce stops also. The Jailor closes the door and locks it on the inside with another clash and clang of steel, and turns.

JAILOR

Well, Lawyer, singing school will be over after tonight, huh?

(to Temple)

You been away, you see. You dont know about this, you aint kept up with what's——

(he stops himself quickly; he is about to commit what he would call a very bad impoliteness, what in the tenets of his class and kind would be the most grave of gaucherie and bad taste: referring directly to a recent bereavement in the presence of the bereaved, particularly one of this nature, even though by this time tomorrow the State itself will have made restitution with the perpetrator's life. He tries to rectify it)

Not that I wouldn't too, if I'd a been the ma of the very——

(stopping himself again; this is getting worse than ever; now he not only is looking at Stevens, but actually addressing him)

Every Sunday night, and every night since last Sunday except last night—come to think of it, Lawyer, where was you last night? We missed you—Lawyer here and Na—the prisoner have been singing hymns in her cell. The first time, he just stood out there on the sidewalk while she stood in that window yonder. Which was all right, not doing no harm, just singing church hymns. Because all of us home folks here in Jefferson and Yoknapatawpha County both know Lawyer Stevens, even if some of us might have thought he got a little out of line——

(again it is getting out of hand; he realises it, but there is nothing he can do now; he is like someone walking a foot-log: all he can do is move as fast as he dares until he can reach solid ground or at least pass another log to leap to)

defending a nigger murderer, let alone when it was his own niece was mur——

(and reaches another log and leaps to it without stopping: at least one running at right angles for a little distance into simple generality)

—maybe suppose some stranger say, some durn Yankee tourist, happened to be passing through in a car, when we get enough durn criticism from Yankees like it is,—besides, a white man standing out there in the cold, while a durned nigger murderer is up here all warm and comfortable; so it happened that me and Mrs Tubbs hadn't went to prayer meeting that night, so we invited him to come in; and to tell the truth, we come to enjoy it too. Because as soon as they found out there wasn't going to be no objection to it, the other nigger prisoners (I got five more right now, but I taken them out back and locked them up in the coal house so you could have some privacy) joined in too, and by the second or third Sunday night, folks was stopping along the street to listen to them instead of going to regular church. Of course, the other niggers would just be in and out over Saturday and Sunday night for fighting or gambling or vagrance or drunk, so just about the time they would begin to get in tune, the whole choir would be a complete turn-over. In fact, I had a idea at one time to have the Marshal comb the nigger dives and joints not for drunks and gamblers, but basses and baritones.

(he starts to laugh, guffaws once, then catches himself; he looks at Temple with something almost gentle, almost articulate, in his face, taking ((as though)) by the horns, facing frankly and openly the dilemma of his own inescapable vice)

Excuse me, Mrs Stevens. I talk too much. All I want to say is, this whole county, not a man or woman, wife or mother either in the whole state of Mississippi, that dont— dont feel——

(stopping again, looking at Temple)

There I am, still at it, still talking too much. Wouldn't you like for Mrs Tubbs to bring you up a cup of coffee or maybe a coca cola? She's usually got a bottle or two of sody pop in the icebox.

TEMPLE

No thank you, Mr Tubbs. If we could just see Nancy——

JAILOR (turning)

Sure, sure.

He crosses toward the rear, R, and disappears into the passage.

TEMPLE

The blindfold again. Out of a coca cola bottle this time or a cup of county-owned coffee.

Stevens takes the same pack of cigarettes from his overcoat pocket, though Temple has declined before he can even offer them.

TEMPLE

No thanks. My hide's toughened now. I hardly feel it. People. They're really innately, inherently gentle and compassionate and kind. That's what wrings, wrenches . . . . something. Your entrails, maybe. The member of the mob who holds up the whole ceremony for seconds or even minutes while he dislodges a family of bugs or lizards from the log he is about to put on the fire——

(there is the clash of another steel door off-stage as the Jailor unlocks Nancy's cell. Temple pauses, turns and listens, then continues rapidly)

And now I've got to say 'I forgive you, sister' to the nigger who murdered my baby. No: it's worse: I've even got to transpose it, turn it around. I've got to start off my new life being forgiven again. How can I say that? Tell me. How can I?

She stops again and turns further as Nancy enters from the rear alcove, followed by the Jailor, who passes Nancy and comes on, carrying the ring of keys once more like a farmer's lantern.

JAILOR (to Stevens)

Okay, Lawyer. How much time you want? Thirty minutes? an hour?

STEVENS

Thirty minutes should be enough.

JAILOR (still moving toward the exit L)

Okay.

(to Temple)

You sure you dont want that coffee or a coca cola? I could bring you up a rocking chair——

TEMPLE

Thank you just the same, Mr Tubbs.

JAILOR

Okay.

(at the exit door, unlocking it)

Thirty minutes, then.

He unlocks the door, opens it, exits, closes and locks it behind him; the lock clashes, his footsteps die away. Nancy has slowed and stopped where the Jailor passed her; she now stands about six feet to the rear of Temple and Stevens. Her face is calm, unchanged. She is dressed exactly as before, except for the apron; she still wears the hat.

NANCY (to Temple)

You been to California, they tell me. I used to think maybe I would get there too, some day. But I waited too late to get around to it.

TEMPLE

So did I. Too late and too long. Too late when I went to California, and too late when I came back. That's it: too late and too long, not only for you, but for me too; already too late when both of us should have got around to running, like from death itself, from the very air anybody breathed named Drake or Mannigoe.

NANCY

Only, we didn't. And you come back, yesterday evening. I heard that too. And I know where you were last night, you and him both.

(indicating Stevens)

You went to see the Mayor.

TEMPLE

Oh God, the mayor. No: the Governor, the Big Man himself, in Jackson. Of course; you knew that as soon as you realised that Mr Gavin wouldn't be here last night to help you sing, didn't you? In fact, the only thing you cant know about it, is what the Governor told us. You cant know that yet, no matter how clairvoyant you are, because we—the Governor and Mr Gavin and I—were not even talking about you; the reason I—we had to go and see him was not to beg or plead or bind or loose, but because it would be my right, my duty, my privilege—— Dont look at me, Nancy.

NANCY

I'm not looking at you. Besides, it's all right. I know what the Governor told you. Maybe I could have told you last night what he would say, and saved you the trip. Maybe I ought to have:—sent you the word as soon as I heard you were back home, and knowed what you and him——

(again she indicates Stevens with that barely discernible movement of her head, her hands still folded across her middle as though she still wore the absent apron)

—both would probably be up to. Only, I didn't. But it's all right——

TEMPLE

Why didn't you? Yes, look at me. This is worse, but the other is terrible.

NANCY

What?

TEMPLE

Why didn't you send me the word?

NANCY

Because that would have been hoping: the hardest thing of all to break, get rid of, let go of, the last thing of all poor sinning man will turn aloose. Maybe it's because that's all he's got. Leastways, he hold onto it, hangs onto it. Even with salvation laying right in his hand, and all he's got to do is, choose between it; even with salvation already in his hand and all he needs is just to shut his fingers, old sin is still too strong for him, and sometimes before he even knows it, he has throwed salvation away just grabbling back at hoping. But it's all right——

STEVENS

You mean, when you have salvation, you dont have hope?

NANCY

You dont even need it. All you need, all you have to do, is just believe. So maybe——

STEVENS

Believe what?

NANCY

Just believe.—So maybe it's just as well that all I did last night, was just to guess where you all went. But I know now, and I know what the Big Man told you. And it's all right. I finished all that a long time back, that same day in the judge's court. No: before that even: in the nursery that night, before I even lifted my hand——

TEMPLE (convulsively)

Hush. Hush.

NANCY

All right. I've hushed. Because it's all right. I can get low for Jesus too. I can get low for Him too.

TEMPLE

Hush! Hush! At least, dont blaspheme. But who am I, to challenge the language you talk about Him in, when He Himself certainly cant challenge it, since that's the only language He arranged for you to learn?

NANCY

What's wrong with what I said? Jesus is a man too. He's got to be. Menfolks listens to somebody because of what he says. Women dont. They dont care what he said. They listens because of what he is.

TEMPLE

Then let Him talk to me. I can get low for Him too, if that's all He wants, demands, asks. I'll do anything He wants if He'll just tell me what to do. No: how to do it. I know what to do, what I must do, what I've got to do. But how? We—I thought that all I would have to do would be to come back and go to the Big Man and tell him that it wasn't you who killed my baby, but I did it eight years ago that day when I slipped out the back door of that train, and that would be all. But we were wrong. Then I—we thought that all it would be was, for me just to come back here and tell you you had to die; to come all the way two thousand miles from California, to sit up all night driving to Jackson and talking for an hour or two and then driving back, to tell you you had to die; not just to bring you the news that you had to die, because any messenger could do that, but just so it could be me that would have to sit up all night and talk for the hour or two hours and then bring you the news back. You know: not to save you, that wasn't really concerned in it: but just for me, just for the suffering and the paying: a little more suffering simply because there was a little more time left for a little more of it, and we might as well use it since we were already paying for it; and that would be all, it would be finished then. But we were wrong again. That was all, only for you. You wouldn't be any worse off if I had never come back from California. You wouldn't even be any worse off. And this time tomorrow, you wont be anything at all. But not me. Because there's tomorrow, and tomorrow, and tomorrow. All you've got to do is, just to die. But let Him tell me what to do. No: that's wrong; I know what to do, what I'm going to do; I found that out that same night in the nursery too. But let Him tell me how. How? Tomorrow, and tomorrow, and still tomorrow. How?

NANCY

Trust in Him.

TEMPLE

Trust in Him. Look what He has already done to me. Which is all right; maybe I deserved it; at least I'm not the one to criticise or dictate to Him. But look what He did to you. Yet you can still say that. Why? Why? Is it because there isn't anything else?

NANCY

I dont know. But you got to trust Him. Maybe that's your pay for the suffering.

STEVENS

Whose suffering, and whose pay? Just each one's for his own?

NANCY

Everybody's. All suffering. All poor sinning man's.

STEVENS

The salvation of the world is in man's suffering. Is that it?

NANCY

Yes sir.

STEVENS

How?

NANCY

I dont know. Maybe when folks are suffering, they will be too busy to get into devilment, wont have time to worry and meddle one another.

TEMPLE

But why must it be suffering? He's omnipotent, or so they tell us. Why couldn't He have invented something else? Or, if it's got to be suffering, why cant it be just your own? why cant you buy back your own sins with your own agony? Why do you and my little baby both have to suffer just because I decided to go to a baseball game eight years ago? Do you have to suffer everybody else's anguish just to believe in God? What kind of God is it that has to blackmail His customers with the whole world's grief and ruin?

NANCY

He dont want you to suffer. He dont like suffering neither. But He cant help Himself. He's like a man that's got too many mules. All of a sudden one morning, he looks around and sees more mules than he can count at one time even, let alone find work for, and all he knows is that they are his, because at least dont nobody else want to claim them, and that the pasture fence was still holding them last night where they cant harm themselves nor nobody else the least possible. And that when Monday morning comes, he can walk in there and hem some of them up and even catch them if he's careful about not never turning his back on the ones he aint hemmed up. And that, once the gear is on them, they will do his work and do it good, only he's still got to be careful about getting too close to them, or forgetting that another one of them is behind him, even when he is feeding them. Even when it's Saturday noon again, and he is turning them back into the pasture, where even a mule can know it's got until Monday morning anyway to run free in mule sin and mule pleasure.

STEVENS

You have got to sin, too?

NANCY

You aint *got* to. You cant help it. And He knows that. But you can suffer. And He knows that too. He dont tell you not to sin, He just asks you not to. And He dont tell you to suffer. But He gives you the chance. He gives you the best He can think of, that you are capable of doing. And He will save you.

STEVENS

You too? a murdress? In heaven?

NANCY

I can work.

STEVENS

The harp, the raiment, the singing, may not be for Nancy Mannigoe—not now. But there's still the work to be done—the washing and sweeping, maybe even the children to be tended and fed and kept from hurt and harm and out from under the grown folks' feet?

(he pauses a moment. Nancy says nothing, immobile, looking at no one)

Maybe even that baby?

(Nancy doesn't move, stir, not looking at anything apparently, her face still, bemused, expressionless)

That one too, Nancy? Because you loved that baby, even at the very moment when you raised your hand against it, knew that there was nothing left but to raise your hand?

(Nancy doesn't answer nor stir)

A heaven where that little child will remember nothing of your hands but gentleness because now this earth will have been nothing but a dream that didn't matter? Is that it?

TEMPLE

Or maybe not that baby, not mine, because, since I destroyed mine myself when I slipped out the back end of that train that day eight years ago, I will need about all the forgiving and forgetting that one six-months-old baby is capable of. But the other one: yours: that you told me about, that you were carrying six months gone, and you went to the picnic or dance or frolic or fight or whatever it was, and the man kicked you in the stomach and you lost it? That one too?

STEVENS (to Nancy)

What? Its father kicked you in the stomach while you were pregnant?

NANCY

I dont know.

STEVENS

You dont know who kicked you?

NANCY

I know that. I thought you meant its pa.

STEVENS

You mean, the man who kicked you wasn't even its father?

NANCY

I dont know. Any of them might have been.

STEVENS

Any of them? You dont have any idea who its father was?

NANCY (looks at Stevens impatiently)

If you backed your behind into a buzz-saw, could you tell which tooth hit you first?

(to Temple)

What about that one?

TEMPLE

Will that one be there too, that never had a father and never was even born, to forgive you? Is there a heaven for it to go to so it can forgive you? Is there a heaven, Nancy?

NANCY

I dont know. I believes.

TEMPLE

Believe what?

NANCY

I dont know. But I believes.

They all pause at the sound of feet approaching beyond the exit door, all are looking at the door as the key clashes again in the lock and the door swings out and the Jailor enters, drawing the door to behind him.

JAILOR (locking the door)

Thirty minutes, Lawyer. You named it, you know: not me.

STEVENS

I'll come back later.

JAILOR (turns and crosses toward them)

Provided you dont put it off too late. What I mean, if you wait until tonight to come back, you might have some company; and if you put it off until tomorrow, you wont have no client.

(to Nancy)

I found that preacher you want. He'll be here about sundown, he said. He sounds like he might even be another good baritone. And you cant have too many, especially as after tonight you wont need none, huh? No hard feelings, Nancy. You committed about as horrible a crime as this county ever seen, but you're fixing to pay the law for it, and if the child's own mother——

(he falters, almost pauses, catches himself and continues briskly, moving again)

There, talking too much again. Come on, if Lawyer's through with you. You can start taking your time at daylight tomorrow morning, because you might have a long hard trip.

He passes her and goes briskly on toward the alcove at rear. Nancy turns to follow.

TEMPLE (quickly)

Nancy.

(Nancy doesn't pause. Temple continues, rapidly)

What about me? Even if there is one and somebody waiting in it to forgive me, there's still tomorrow and tomorrow. And suppose tomorrow and tomorrow, and then nobody there, nobody waiting to forgive me——

NANCY (moving on after the Jailor)

Believe.

TEMPLE

Believe what, Nancy? Tell me.

NANCY

Believe.

She exits into the alcove behind the Jailor. The steel door offstage clangs, the key clashes. Then the Jailor reappears, approaches, and crosses toward the exit. He unlocks the door and opens it out again, pauses.

JAILOR

Yes sir. A long hard way. If I was ever fool enough to commit a killing that would get my neck into a noose, the last thing I would want to see would be a preacher. I'd a heap rather believe there wasn't nothing after death, than to risk the station where I was probably going to get off.

(he waits, holding the door, looking back at them. Temple stands motionless until Stevens touches her arm slightly. Then she moves, stumbles slightly and infinitesimally, so infinitesimally and so quickly recovered that the Jailor has barely time to react to it, though he does so: with quick concern, with that quality about him almost gentle, almost articulate, turning from the door, even leaving it open as he starts quickly toward her)

Here; you set down on the bench; I'll get you a glass of water.

(to Stevens)

Durn it, Lawyer, why did you have to bring her——

TEMPLE (recovered)

I'm all right.

She walks steadily toward the door. The Jailor watches her.

JAILOR

You sure?

TEMPLE (walking steadily and rapidly toward him and the door now)

Yes. Sure.

JAILOR (turning back toward the door)

Okay. I sure dont blame you. Durned if I see how even a murdering nigger can stand this smell.

He passes on out the door and exits, invisible though still holding the door and waiting to lock it. Temple, followed by Stevens, approaches the door.

JAILOR'S VOICE (off-stage: surprised)

Howdy. Gowan, here's your wife now.

TEMPLE (walking)

Anyone to save it. Anyone who wants it. If there is none, I'm sunk. We all are. Doomed. Damned.

STEVENS (walking)

Of course we are. Hasn't He been telling us that for going on two thousand years?

GOWAN'S VOICE (off-stage)

Temple.

TEMPLE

Coming.

They exit. The door closes in, clashes, the clash and clang of the key as the Jailor locks it again; the three pairs of footsteps sound and begin to fade in the outer corridor.

(Curtain)

A FABLE

To my daughter,
JILL

To William Bacher and Henry Hathaway of Beverly Hills, California, who had the basic idea from which this book grew into its present form; to James Street in whose volume, *Look Away*, I read the story of the hanged man and the bird; and to Hodding Carter and Ben Wasson of the Levee Press, who published in a limited edition the original version of the story of the stolen racehorse, I wish to make grateful acknowledgment.

W.F.

Wednesday

Long before the first bugles sounded from the barracks within the city and the cantonments surrounding it, most of the city was already awake. These did not need to rise from the straw mattresses and thin pallet beds of their hive-dense tenements, because few of them save the children had ever lain down. Instead, they had huddled all night in one vast tongueless brotherhood of dread and anxiety, about the thin fires of braziers and meagre hearths, until the night wore at last away and a new day of anxiety and dread had begun.

Because the original regiment had been raised in this district, raised in person, in fact, by one of the glorious blackguards who later became Napoleon's marshals, who delivered the regiment into the Emperor's own hand, and along with it became one of the fiercest stars in that constellation which filled half the sky with its portent and blasted half the earth with its lightning. And most of its subsequent replacements had been drawn from this same district, so that most of these old men were not only veterans of it in their time, and these male children already dedicated to it when their time should come, but all these people were parents and kin, not only the actual old parents and kin of the doomed men, but fathers and mothers and sisters and wives and sweethearts whose sons and brothers and husbands and fathers and lovers might have been among the doomed men except for sheer blind chance and luck.

Even before the bugles' echoes died away, the warrened purlieus were already disgorging them. A French or British or American aviator (or a German either for that matter, if he had had the temerity and the luck) could have watched it best: hovel and tenement voiding into lane and alley and nameless *cul-de-sac*, and lane and alley and *cul-de-sac* compounding into streets as the trickles became streams and the streams became rivers, until the whole city seemed to be pouring down the broad boulevards converging like wheel-spokes into the *Place de Ville*, filling the *Place* and then, pressed on by the weight of its own converging mass, flowing like an unrecoiling wave up to the blank gates of the *Hôtel* where the three sentries of the three co-embattled nations flanked the three empty flagstaffs awaiting the three concordant flags.

They met the first troops here. It was a body of garrison cavalry, drawn up across the mouth of the wide main boulevard leading from the *Place* to the old gate in what had once been the city's ancient eastern wall, already in position and waiting as though the murmur of the flood's beginning had preceded it, right into the bedroom of the town-major himself. But the crowd paid no attention to the cavalry. It just continued to press on into the *Place*, slowing and stopping now because of its own massy congested weight, merely stirring and shifting constantly and faintly within its own mass while it stared, mazed and patient in the rising light, at the *Hôtel* door.

Then the sunrise gun crashed from the old citadel above the city; the three flags broke simultaneously from nowhere and climbed the three staffs. What they broke and climbed and peaked in was still dawn, hanging motionless for a moment. But when they streamed on the first morning breeze, they streamed into sunlight, flinging into sunlight the three mutual colors—the red for courage and pride, the white for purity and constancy, the blue for honor and truth. Then the empty boulevard behind the cavalry filled suddenly with sunlight which flung suddenly the tall shadows of the men and the horses outward upon the crowd as though the cavalry were charging it.

Only it was the people advancing on the cavalry. The mass made no sound. It was almost orderly, merely irresistible in the concord of its frail components like a wave in its drops. For an instant the cavalry—there was an officer present, though a sergeant-major seemed to be in charge—did nothing. Then the sergeant-major shouted. It was not a command, because the troop did not stir. It sounded like nothing whatever, in fact: unintelligible: a thin forlorn cry hanging for a fading instant in the air like one of the faint, sourceless, musical cries of the high invisible larks now filling the sky above the city. His next shout though was a command. But it was already too late; the crowd had already underswept the military, irresistible in that passive and invincible humility, carrying its fragile bones and flesh into the iron orbit of the hooves and sabres with an almost inattentive, a humbly and passively contemptuous disregard, like martyrs entering an arena of lions.

For another instant, the cavalry held. And even then, it did not break. It just began to move in retrograde while still facing forward, as though it had been picked up bodily—the white-rolled eyes of the short-held horses, the high, small faces of the riders gaped with puny shouting beneath the raised sabres, all moving backward like the martial effigies out of a gutted palace or mansion or museum being swept along on the flood which had obliterated to instantaneous rubble the stone crypts of their glorious privacy. Then the mounted officer freed himself. For a moment, he alone seemed to be moving, because he alone was stationary above the crowd which was now parting and flowing on either side of him. Then he actually was moving, forward, breasting the still short-bitted horse, iron-held, into and through the moving crowd; a voice cried once somewhere beneath the horse—a child, a woman, possibly a man's voice eunuch-keened by fear or pain—as he forced the horse on, feinting and dodging the animal through the human river which made no effort to avoid him, which accepted the horse as water accepts a thrusting prow. Then he was gone. Accelerating now, the crowd poured into the boulevard. It flung the cavalry aside and poured on, blotting the intersecting streets as it passed them as a river in flood blots up its tributary creeks, until at last that boulevard too was one dense seething voiceless lake.

But before that, the infantry had already arrived, debouching from the *Place de Ville* on the crowd's rear long before the cavalry officer could have reported to the officer of the day, who would have dispatched the orderly, who would have summonsed the batman, who would have interrupted at his ablutions and shaving the adjutant, who would have waked the town-major in his nightcap, who would have telephoned or sent a runner to the infantry commander in the citadel. It was a whole battalion, armed except for packs, emerging from the *Place de Ville* in close route column, led by a light tank with its visor closed for action, which as it advanced, parted the crowd like a snow-plow, thrusting the divided parting back from either curb like the snow-plow's jumbled masses, the infantry deploying into two parallel files behind the advancing tank, until at last the whole boulevard from the *Place* to the old gate was clear and empty again between the two thin lines of interlocked bayonetted rifles. A slight commotion rose at one point behind the dyke of bayonets, but its area was not ten feet and it did not spread, and only those near it knew that anything was happening or had happened. And when a platoon sergeant stooped under the interlocked rifles and shouldered his way in, there was not much to see either: only a young woman, a girl, thin and poorly dressed, who had fainted. She lay as she had fallen: a thin huddle of shabby, travel-stained garments, as if she had come a long distance and mostly on foot or in farm carts, lying in the narrow grave-shaped space they had made for her to fall in, and, if such had been her intention, die in, while those who apparently had made no room for her to stand erect and breathe in, stood looking quietly down at her as people will, until someone makes the first move. The sergeant made it.

'At least pick her up,' he said savagely. 'Get her up out of the street where she wont be trampled.' A man moved then, but as he and the sergeant stooped, the woman opened her eyes; she even tried to help as the sergeant hauled her to her feet, not roughly, just impatient at the stupidly complicating ineptitude of civilians at all times, particularly at this one now which kept him from his abandoned post. 'Who does she belong to?' he said. There was no answer: only the quiet attentive faces. Apparently he had expected none. He was already glancing about, though he had probably already seen that it would be impossible to get her out of the crowd, even if anyone had offered to take charge of her. He looked at her again;

he started to speak again, to her this time, but stopped himself, furious and contained—a thick man of forty, moustached like a Sicilian brigand and wearing the service and campaign ribbons of three continents and two hemispheres on his tunic, whose racial stature Napoleon had shortened two or three inches a hundred years ago as Caesar had shortened that of the Italians and Hannibal that of the nameless pediment-pieces of his glory,—a husband and father who should (perhaps even could and would) have been a custodian of wine-casks in the Paris Halles if he and the Paris Halles had been cast on some other stage than this. He glanced again at the patient faces. 'Doesn't anybody——'

'She's hungry,' a voice said.

'All right,' the sergeant said. 'Has anybody——' But the hand had already extended the bread. It was the heel of a loaf, soiled and even a little warm from the pocket it had been carried in. The sergeant took it. But when he offered it to her, she refused it, quickly, glancing quickly about with something like fright in her face, her eyes, as if she were looking for an avenue of escape. The sergeant thrust the bread into her hands. 'Here,' he said harshly, with that roughness which was not unkindness but just impatience, 'eat it. You'll have to stay and look at him too, whether you want to or not.'

But she refused again, repudiating the bread, not the gift of it but the bread itself, and not to whoever had offered it, but to herself. It was as if she were trying to keep her eyes from looking at the bread, and knew that she could not. Even while they watched her, she surrendered. Her eyes, her whole body, denied her mouth's refusal, her eyes already devouring the bread before her hand reached to take it, snatching it from the sergeant and holding it to her face between both hands as though to hide either the bread from a ravisher, or her voracity from those who watched her, gnawing at the bread like a species of rodent, her eyes darting constantly above the concealing hands, not quite furtive, not quite secret: just anxious, watchful, and terrified,—a quality which glowed and faded and then glowed again like a coal she breathed on. But she was all right now, and the sergeant had begun to turn away, when the same voice spoke again. Without doubt, it belonged to the hand which had tendered the bread, though if the sergeant remarked it now, he gave no sign. But without doubt he did remark now that the face did not belong here at all, not now, at this time, this place—not just in France, but in forty kilometres of the Western Front, on this or any Wednesday in late May in 1918—; a man not so young actually, but rather simply youthful-looking, and this not merely in contrast to the other men among (or above rather; he was that tall, that unblemished) whom he stood, sound and erect and standing easily in a faded smock and rough trousers and stained shoes like a road-mender or perhaps a plasterer, who, to be here on this day on this place on the earth, must have been a soldier invalided safely and securely and forever out since the fifth day of August almost four years ago now, yet who, if this was so, didn't show it, and if the sergeant remarked it or thought it, there was only the flicker of his glance to reveal that he had. The first time the man spoke, he had addressed the sergeant; this time, the sergeant had no doubt of it.

'But now she has eaten bread,' the man said. 'With that morsel, she should have bought immunity from her anguish, not?'

In fact, the sergeant had turned away, already in motion, when the voice, the murmur, stopped him—the murmur not so much gentle as just quiet, not so much tentative as bland, and possessing, for last of all the qualities, innocence: so that in the second, the instant of pause before he even began to turn back, he could see, feel all the quiet attentive faces watching, not him nor the speaker either, but as though looking at something intangible which the man's voice had created in the very air between them. Then the sergeant saw it too. It was the cloth he wore. Turning and looking back, not only at the man who had spoken but at all the faces surrounding him, it seemed to him that he was looking, out of a sort of weary, prolonged, omniscient grief and sorrow so long borne and accustomed that, now when he happened to remember it, it was no longer even regret, at the whole human race across the insuperable barrier of the vocation and livelihood to which twenty years ago he had not merely dedicated but relinquished too, not just his life but his bones and flesh; it seemed to him that the whole ring of quiet attentive faces was stained with a faint, ineradicable, reflected horizon-blue. It had always been so; only the tint had changed—the drab and white of the desert and the tropics, the sharp full red-and-blue of the old uniform, and now the chameleon-azure of this present one since three years ago. He had expected that, not only expected, but accepted, relinquishing volition and the fear of hunger and decision to the extent of even being paid a few sure sous a day for the privilege and right, at no other cost than obedience and the exposure and risk of his tender and brittle bones and flesh, of immunity forever for his natural appetites. So for twenty years now he had looked at the anonymous denizens of the civilian world from the isolation, insulation, of that unchallengeable immunity, with a sort of contempt as alien intruders, rightless, on simple sufferance, himself and his interknit and interlocked kind in the impregnable fraternity of valor and endurance breasting through it behind the sharp and cleaving prow of their stripe and bars and stars and ribbons, like an armored ship (or, since a year ago now, a tank) through a shoal of fish. But now something had happened. Looking about at the waiting faces (all except the young woman's; she alone was not watching him, the end of the heel of bread still cupped against her chewing face between her slender dirt-stained hands, so that it was not he alone, but the two of them, himself and the kinless and nameless girl, who seemed to stand in a narrow well of unbreathing), it seemed to him with a kind of terror that it was himself who was the alien, and not just alien but obsolete; that on that day twenty years ago, in return for the right and the chance to wear on the battle-soiled breast of his coat the battle-grimed symbolical candy-stripes of valor and endurance and fidelity and physical anguish and sacrifice, he had sold his birthright in the race of man. But he did not show it. The candy-stripes themselves were the reason that he could not, and his wearing of them the proof that he would not.

'And so?' he said.

'It was the whole regiment,' the tall man said dreamily, in his murmurous, masculine, gentle, almost musing baritone. 'All of it. At zero, nobody left the trench except the officers and a few N.C.O.'s. That's right, not?'

'And so?' the sergeant said again.

'Why didn't the boche attack?' the tall man said. 'When they saw that we were not coming over? that something had happened to the attack? The drum-fire was all right, and the rolling barrage too, only when it lifted and the moment came, only the section leaders had climbed out of the trench, but that the men themselves were not coming? They must have seen that, not? When you have been facing another front only a thousand metres away for four years, you can see an attack fail to start, and probably why. And you cant say it was because of the barrage; that's why you get out of the trench in the first place and charge: to get out from under somebody's shelling—sometimes your own, not?'

The sergeant looked only at the tall man; he needed to do no more since he could feel the others—the quiet, attentive, quietly-breathing faces, listening, missing nothing. 'A field marshal,' the sergeant said in a bitter contemptuous voice. 'Maybe it's time somebody looked into that uniform you are wearing.' He held out his hand. 'Let's have a look at them.'

The tall man looked calmly and peacefully down at him a moment longer. Then his hand went somewhere under the smock and reappeared and extended the papers, folded once, stained and soiled and dog-eared at the crease. The sergeant took and opened them. Yet even then, he did not seem to be looking at the papers, his glance instead now flicking rapidly again about the other motionless intent faces, while the tall man still looked down at him, serene and waiting, and then speaking again, remote, calm, almost absently, conversational:

'And at noon yesterday, our whole front stopped except for token artillery, one gun to a battery each ten thousand metres, and at fifteen hours the British and the Americans stopped too, and when it got quiet you could hear the boche doing the same thing, so that by sundown yesterday there was no more gunfire in France except the token ones since they had to leave them for a little longer yet since all that silence, falling suddenly out of the sky on the human race after going on four years, might have destroyed it——' Rapidly and in one motion, the sergeant refolded the papers and extended them back toward the man, or apparently so, since before the man could raise his hand to take them, the sergeant's hand had grasped the front of his smock, gripping as one the crumple of the papers and the wadded mass of the rough cloth, jerking, though actually it was not the tall man but the sergeant who moved, the sergeant's brigand's face nose to nose with the other's, his rotting discolored teeth gaped for speech, though still empty of it because the other man was still talking in that calm unhurried murmur: 'And now General of Division Gragnon is bringing the whole lot of them back here to ask the Generalissimo to let him shoot them, since that much peace and silence, falling without warning on the human race——'

'Not even a field marshal,' the sergeant said in his furious, seething voice: 'an advocate.' He said, in that harsh furious murmur no louder than the other man's had been, to which the static attentive faces ringing them about seemed not to listen or even hear anymore than they had listened to or heard the other man while he spoke, anymore than the young woman herself did or was, still gnawing and tearing steadily at the bread behind her huddled hands, but only watching them, intent and incurious as deaf people. 'Ask the bastards you have come here to look at if they think anybody has quit.'

'I know that too,' the other said. 'I just said so. You saw my papers.'

'So will the provost-marshal's adjutant,' the sergeant said, and flung, not the other man, but himself away and turned again, still clutching the crumpled papers and using his elbows and hands both this time to open his path back to the boulevard; then he stopped again suddenly and jerked his head up, and as they watched, he seemed to raise his whole body in order to look past and above the crowded heads and faces, in the direction of the old city gate. Then they all heard it, not only the sergeant already ducking back under the interlocked rifles, but even the young woman, who even stopped chewing behind her cupped hands to listen too, when as one the heads and the packed bodies turned away from her and toward the boulevard, not because so light on them had been the impact of her trouble and the spectacle of its alleviation, but because of the sound now coming up the boulevard from the old city gate like a wind beginning. Except for the shouts of the section leaders of the deployed infantry aligning each curb, the sound was not voices yet so much as a sigh, an exhalation, travelling from breast to breast up the boulevard. It was as if the night's anxiety, quiescent for a time beneath the simple weight of waiting, now that the new day was about to reveal the actuality which in darkness had only been a dread, was gathering itself to flow over them like the new day itself in one great blinding wave, as the first car entered the city.

It contained the three generals. It came fast, so fast that the shouts of the section leaders and the clash of rifles as each section presented arms and then clashed back to 'at ease', were not only continuous but overlapping, so that the car seemed to progress on one prolonged crash of iron as on invisible wings with steel feathers,—a long, dusty open car painted like a destroyer and flying the pennon of the supreme commander of all the allied armies, the three generals sitting side by side in the tonneau amid a rigid glitter of aides,—the three old men who held individual command over each of the three individual armies, and the one of that three who, by mutual consent and accord, held supreme command over all (and, by that token and right, over everything beneath and on and above the distracted half-continent)—the Briton, the American, and between them the Generalissimo: the slight gray man with a face wise, intelligent, and unbelieving, who no longer believed in anything but his disillusion and his intelligence and his limitless power—flashing across that terrified and aghast amazement and then gone, as the section leaders shouted again and the boots and the rifles crashed back to simple alert.

The lorries were right behind it. They were coming fast too, in close order and seemingly without end, since this was the whole regiment. But still there was no concerted, no definite, human sound yet, not even the crashing ejaculation of salute this time, but only the stir, the shift of movement in the crowd itself, pacing the first lorry in that silence which was still aghast and not quite believing, in which the anguish and terror seemed to rise to each lorry as it approached, and enclose it as it passed, and follow it as it sped on, broken only now and then when someone—a woman—cried out at one of the passing faces—a face which, because of the lorry's speed, had already passed and vanished before recognition became a fact, and the roar of the next lorry had already drowned it before the recognition became a cry, so that the lorries seemed to be travelling even faster than the car, as though the car, with half a continent supine before its bonnet, possessed the gift of leisure, where the lorries, whose destination could be computed in seconds now, had only the spur of shame.

They were open, with high, slatted sides as though for the transportation of cattle, packed like cattle with standing men, bareheaded, disarmed, stained from the front lines, with something desperate and defiant in the unshaven and sleepless faces which glared down at the crowd as if they had never seen human beings before, or could not see these now, or at least could not recognise them as human beings. They were like the faces of sleepwalkers looking backward across nightmares, recognising no one and no familiar things, glaring down across the fleeing irrevocable instant as if they were being hurried to execution itself, flashing on, rapid and successive and curiously identical, not despite the fact that each had an individuality and a name, but because of it; identical not because of an identical doom, but because each carried into that mutual doom a name and an individuality, and that most complete privacy of all: the capacity for that solitude in which every man has to die,—flashing on as if they had no part nor interest in, and were not even aware of, the violence and speed with which or in which they rigidly moved, like phantoms or apparitions or perhaps figures cut without depth from tin or cardboard and snatched in violent repetition across a stage set for a pantomime of anguish and fatality.

And now there was a concerted sound: a faint yelling beginning somewhere in the *Place de Ville*, which the first lorry would be reaching about now. It was high, thin with distance, prolonged, not vindictive but defiant, with at the same time a curiously impersonal quality, as if the men it came from were not making, producing it, but merely passing through it as through a sudden noisy though harmless burst of spring rain. It came in fact from the *Hôtel de Ville*, which the first lorries were now passing, where the three sentries now stood at attention beneath the three flags hanging windless now in the following stillness of the dawn breeze, and where on the stone steps before the door the old generalissimo, the other two generals having followed him out of the halted car, had now stopped and turned, the two lesser generals stopping and turning with him, both on a step higher than his and so taller than he, both as gray as he, both slightly behind him though not behind each other, while the first lorry passed, and the hatless, dishevelled, somnambulistic men in it, waked perhaps at sight of the three flags or perhaps by the simple isolation of the three old men after the crowded boulevard, but waking anyway, and in that same instant divining, identifying the three gaudy panoplied old men, not merely by their juxtaposition to the three flags but by their isolation, like that of three plague carriers in the empty center of an aghast and fleeing city, or perhaps the three survivors of a city swept by plague, immune and impervious, gaudy and panoplied and seemingly as harmless in time as a photograph posed and fading since these fifty or sixty years,—but—the men in the lorries—anyway waking, as one man, and as one man yelling, shaking their clenched hands down at the three impassive figures, the yelling passing from lorry to lorry as each entered the yelling and sped on, until the last one seemed to trail behind it a cloud of doomed and forlorn repudiation filled with gaped faces and threatening fists like the fading cloud of its own dust.

It was like dust, still hanging in the air long after the object—the motion, the friction, the body, the momentum, speed—which had produced it was gone and vanished. Because the whole boulevard was filled with yelling now, not defiant now but just amazed and incredulous, the two backflung parallel banks of massed bodies and wan faces now gaped and frantic with adjuration. Because there was still one more lorry. It came fast too; although there were two hundred yards between it and the last one preceding it, this one seemed to be travelling twice as fast as the others, just as the others had seemed to be travelling twice as fast as the pennoned car containing the three generals. Yet it seemed to move in complete silence. There was something almost furtive about it. Where the others had seemed to pass noisily, violently almost, in a kind of defiant valedictory of shame and despair, this one came and was gone with a sort of noiseless, celeritous effacement, as if the men who drove it abhorred, not its destination at all, but rather its contents.

It was open, like the others, indistinguishable from the others, except by its cargo. Because, where the others had been packed with standing men, this one carried only thirteen. They were hatless and dirty and battle-stained too, but they were manacled, chained to one another and to the lorry itself like wild beasts, so that at first glance they looked not merely like foreigners but like creatures of another race, another species; alien, bizarre, and strange, even though they wore on their collar-tabs the same regimental numerals, to the rest of the regiment which had not only preceded them by that reduceless gap but which had even seemed to be fleeing from them, not only by their chains and isolation, but by their very expressions and attitudes too: where the faces in the other fleeing lorries had been dazed and spent, like those of men too long under ether, the faces of these thirteen were merely grave, attentive, watchful. Then you saw that four of the thirteen were really foreigners, alien not only by their gyves and isolation to the rest of the regiment but against the whole panorama of city and soil across which the lorry was rushing them,—the faces of four mountain men in a country which had no mountains, of peasants in a land which no longer had a peasantry; alien even among the other nine among whom they were chained and shackled, since where the other nine were grave and watchful and a little—not too much—concerned, three of the four who were not Frenchmen were merely a little puzzled, alert too, almost decorous, curious and interested: the mountain peasants whom they resembled, entering for the first time a strange valley market-town, say; men overtaken suddenly by an uproar in a tongue which they had no hope of comprehending and, indeed, not much interest in, and therefore no concern in its significance;—three of the four who were not Frenchmen, that is, because now the crowd itself had discerned that the fourth one was alien still somehow even to the other three, if only in being the sole object of its vituperation and terror and fury. Because it was to—against—this one man that the crowd was raising its voices and its clenched hands, having barely glanced at the other twelve. He stood near the front, his hands resting quietly on the top rail, so that the loop of chain between his wrists and the corporal's stripes on his sleeve were both visible, with an alien face like all the other twelve, a mountain peasant's face like the last three, a little younger than several of them, looking down at the fleeing sea of eyes and gaped mouths and fists with the same watchfulness as the other twelve, but with neither the bafflement nor the concern:—a face merely interested, attentive, and calm, with something else in it which none of the others had: a comprehension, understanding, utterly free of compassion, as if he had already anticipated without censure or pity the uproar which rose and paced and followed the lorry as it sped on.

It crossed in its turn the *Place de Ville*, where the three generals still stood like a posed camera group on the steps of the *Hôtel*. Perhaps this time it was the simple juxtaposition of the three flags which were just beginning to stir in the reversed day wind, since certainly none of the other three who were not Frenchmen, and possibly none of the whole twelve, seemed to remark the significance of the three dissimilar banners, nor even to see the three starred and braided old men standing beneath them. It was only the thirteenth man who seemed to notice, see, remark; only the gaze of the corporal in passing as he and the old supreme general, whom no man in any of the other lorries could say had ever looked definitely at any one of them, stared full at one another across the moment which could not last because of the vehicle's speed,—the peasant's face above the corporal's chevrons and the shackled wrists in the speeding lorry, and the gray inscrutable face above the stars of supreme rank and the bright ribbons of honor and glory on the *Hôtel* steps, looking at one another across the fleeing instant. Then the lorry was gone. The old generalissimo turned, his two confreres turning with him, flanking him in rigid protocol; the three sentries clashed and stamped to present arms as the limber and glittering young aide sprang and opened the door.

This time, the commotion went almost unnoticed, not only because of the yelling and uproar, but because the crowd itself was moving now. It was the young woman again, the one who had fainted. She was still gnawing at the bread when the last lorry came up. Then she ceased, and those nearest remembered later that she moved, cried out, and tried to run, to break through the crowd and into the street as if to intercept or overtake the lorry. But by that time, they were all moving toward the street, even those at whose backs she was clawing and scrabbling and at whose faces she was trying to cry, say something through the mass of chewed bread in her mouth. So they stopped remembering her at all, and there remained only the man who had given her the bread, upon whose chest she was still hammering with the hand which still clutched the fragment of the morsel, while she tried to cry something at him through the wet mass in her mouth.

Then she began to spit the chewed bread at him, not deliberately, intentionally, but because there was not time to turn her head aside and void her mouth for speech, already screaming something at him through the spew and spray of mastication. But the man was already running too, wiping his face on his sleeve, vanishing into the crowd as it burst at last through the interlocked rifles and poured into the street. Still clutching what remained of the bread, she ran too. For a while, she even kept up with them, running and darting between and among them with an urgency apparently even greater than theirs, as the whole mass of them poured up the boulevard after the fleeing lorries. But presently the ones she had passed began to overtake her in turn and pass her; soon she was running in a fading remnant of dispersal, panting and stumbling, seeming to run now in spent and frantic retrograde to the whole city's motion, the whole world's, so that when she reached the *Place de Ville* at last, and stopped, all mankind seemed to have drained away and vanished, bequeathing, relicting to her the broad, once-more empty boulevard and the *Place* and even, for that moment, the city and the earth itself;—a slight woman, not much more than a girl, who had been pretty once, and could be again, with sleep and something to eat and a little warm water and soap and a comb, and whatever it was out of her eyes, standing in the empty *Place*, wringing her hands.

Monday
Monday Night

When the attack was first offered him, the general commanding the division which contained the regiment said immediately: 'Of course. Thanks. What is it?' Because it seemed to him that here at last was the chance which he had needed and wanted for more years than he cared to remember, so many years in fact that he had, as he realised now, given up hope of ever getting. Because at some moment in his past which even he could not specifically postulate, something had happened to him, or at least to his career.

It seemed to him that he had been intended by fate itself to be the perfect soldier: pastless, unhampered, and complete. His first recollection had been a Pyrenean orphanage run by a Catholic sisterhood, where there was no record of his parentage whatever, even to be concealed. At seventeen, he was an enlisted private; at twenty-four, he had been three years a sergeant and of such destined promise that his regimental commander (himself a self-made man who had risen from the ranks) gave no one any rest until the protégé also had his chance for officers' school; by 1914 he had established a splendid record as a desert colonel of Spahis, and, immediately in France itself, the beginning of an unimpeachable one as a brigadier, so that to those who believed in him and watched his career (he had no influence either, and no friends too save those, like the obscure colonel of his sergeantcy, whom he had made, earned himself by his own efforts and record) there seemed no limit to his destiny save the premature end of the war itself.

Then something happened. Not to him: he had not changed, he was still competent, still unhampered and complete. He seemed merely to have lost or mislaid somewhere, at some point, the old habit or mantle or aura (or affinity for) of almost monotonous success in which he had seemed to move as in his garments, as if not he but his destiny had slowed down, not changed: just slowed down for the time being: which idea his superiors themselves seemed to hold, since he got in due time (in fact, a little sooner than some) the next star for his hat and not only the division which went with it but the opportunities too, indicating that his superiors still believed that at any moment now he might recover, or rediscover, the secret of the old successfulness.

But that was two years ago now, and for a year now even the opportunities had ceased, as though at last even the superiors had come around to his own belief that the high tide of his hopes and aspirations had fluxed three years ago, three years before the last backwash of his destiny finally ebbed from beneath him, leaving him stranded a mere general of division still in a war already three years defunctive. It—the war—would hang on a while yet, of course; it would take the Americans, the innocent newcomers, another year probably to discover that you cannot really whip Germans: you can only exhaust them. It might even last another ten years or even another twenty, by which time France and Britain would have vanished as military and even political integers and the war would have become a matter of a handful of Americans who didn't even have ships to go back home in, battling with limbs from shattered trees and the rafters from ruined houses and the stones from fences of weed-choked fields and the broken bayonets and stocks of rotted guns and rusted fragments wrenched from crashed aeroplanes and burned tanks, against the skeletons of German companies stiffened by a few Frenchmen and Britons tough enough like himself to endure still, to endure as he would always, immune to nationality, to exhaustion, even to victory—by which time he hoped he himself would be dead.

Because by ordinary he believed himself incapable of hoping: only of daring, without fear or qualm or regret within the iron and simple framework of the destiny which he believed would never betray him so long as he continued to dare without question or qualm or regret, but which apparently had abandoned him, leaving him only the capacity to dare, until two days ago when his corps commander sent for him. The corps commander was his only friend in France, or anywhere else above earth, for that matter. They had been subalterns together in the same regiment into which he had been commissioned. But Lallemont, though a poor man too, had along with ability just enough of the sort of connections which not only made the difference between division and corps command at the same length of service, but placed Lallemont quite favorably for the next vacant army command. Though when Lallemont said, 'I've something for you, if you want it,' he realised that what he had thought was the capacity to dare was still soiled just a little with the baseless hoping which is the diet of weaklings. But that was all right too: who, even though apparently abandoned by destiny, still had not been wrong in dedicating his life as he had: even though abandoned, he had never let his chosen vocation down; and sure enough in his need, the vocation had remembered him.

So he said, 'Thanks. What?' Lallemont told him. Whereupon for a moment he believed that he had not understood. But this passed, because in the next one he saw the whole picture. The attack was already doomed in its embryo, and whoever commanded it, delivered it, along with it. It was not that his trained professional judgment told him that the affair, as the corps commander presented it, would be touch-and-go and hence more than doubtful. That would not have stopped him. On the contrary, that would have been a challenge, as if the old destiny had not abandoned him at all. It was because that same trained judgment saw at once that this particular attack was intended to fail: a sacrifice already planned and doomed in some vaster scheme, in which it would not matter either way, whether the attack failed or not: only that the attack must be made: and more than that, since here the whole long twenty-odd years of training and dedication paid him off in clairvoyance; he saw the thing not only from its front and public view, but from behind it too: the cheapest attack would be one which must fail, harmlessly to all if delivered by a man who had neither friends nor influence to make people with five stars on the General Staff, or civilians with red rosettes in the Quai d'Orsay, squirm. He didn't for even one second think of the old gray man in the *Hôtel de Ville* at Chaulnesmont. He thought for even less time than that: *Lallemont is saving his own neck.* He thought—and now he knew that he was indeed lost—*It's Mama Bidet.* But he only said:

'I cant afford a failure.'

'There will be a ribbon,' the corps commander said.

'I dont have enough rank to get the one they give for failures.'

'Yes,' the corps commander said. 'This time.'

'So it's that bad,' the division commander said. 'That serious. That urgent. All between Bidet and his baton, is one infantry division. And that one, mine.' They stared at one another. Then the corps commander started to speak. The division commander didn't permit him to. 'Stow it,' the division commander said. That is, that's what he conveyed. What he spoke was a phrase pithy succinct and obscene out of his life as an N.C.O. in the African regiment recruited from the prison- and gutter-sweepings of Europe before he and the corps commander had ever seen one another. He said: 'So I have no choice.'

'You have no choice,' the corps commander said.

The division commander always watched his attacks from the nearest forward observer's post; it had been his habit always; that was a part of his record too. This time, he had one especially prepared, on an elevation, revetted and sandbagged behind a steel plate, with one telephone line direct to corps headquarters and another to the artillery commander; here, synchronised watch in hand while the preliminary barrage wailed and screeched overhead onto the German wire, he looked down upon his own front line and on the opposite one which even those who had assigned him the attack didn't intend to breach, as from a balcony seat at the opera. Or box seat, and not just any box, but the royal one: the victim by regal dispensation watching in solitary splendor the preparations for his execution, watching not the opera's final scene, but his own before he moved, irrevocable and forever, into some back-area job in that region whose function was to arm and equip the combat divisions who reaped the glorious death and the immortal renown; from now on, his to reap every hope save glory, and every right save the chance to die for it. He could desert, of course, but where? to whom? The only people who would accept a failed French general would be people so far free of the war: the Dutch, who were off the normal course of German invasions, and the Spanish, who were too poor even to make a two-day excursion to it, like the Portuguese did, for excitement and change of scene—in which case—the Spanish one—he would not even be paid for risking his life and what remained of his reputation, until he corrected that: thinking how war and drink are the two things man is never too poor to buy. His wife and children may be shoeless; someone will always buy him drink or weapons, thinking *More than that. The last person a man planning to set up in the wine trade would approach for a loan, would be a rival wine-dealer. A nation preparing for war can borrow from the very nation it aims to destroy.*

Then he didn't even have a failure. He had a mutiny. When the barrage lifted, he was not even watching the scene beneath him, but was already looking at his watch-face. He didn't need to watch. After watching them from beneath his stars for three years now, he had become an expert, not merely in forecasting failure, but in predicting almost exactly when, where, at what point in time and terrain, they would become void and harmless;—this, even when he was not familiar with the troops making the attack, which in the present case he was, having selected this particular regiment the day before because he knew, on the one hand, not only the condition of the regiment but its colonel's belief in it and the record of his success with it; and on the other, its value as measured against each of the other three in the division; he knew it would deliver the attack near enough to the maximum demanded of him, yet if the foreordained failure meant its temporary wreckage or even permanent ruin, this would weigh less in the strength and morale of the division than that of any of the other three; he could never, breathing, have been convinced or even told that he had chosen the regiment out of his division exactly as the group commander had chosen the division out of his armies.

So he simply followed the jerking watch-hand, waiting for it to establish the point when all the men who were to get through the wire, would be beyond it. Then he looked up and saw nothing, nothing at all in the space beyond the wire which by now should have been filled with running and falling men; he saw only a few figures crouching along his own parapet, not advancing at all but apparently yelling, screaming and gesticulating, downward into the trench—the officers and N.C.O.'s, the company and section leaders who obviously had been betrayed as he had been. Because he knew at once what had happened. He was quite calm; he thought without passion or even astonishment: *So this was reserved for me too* as he dropped the binocular back into its case on his chest and snapped the cover down and spoke to the aide beside him, indicating the line to Corps Headquarters: 'Say that the attack failed to leave the trench. Tell them to ratify me to Artillery. Say I'm on my way out now', and took the other telephone himself and spoke down it: 'Gragnon. I want two barrages. Re-range one on the enemy wire. Range the other on the communication trenches behind the —th Regiment and continue until you have a remand from Corps', and put the telephone down and turned toward the exit.

'Sir!' the aide at the other telephone cried. 'Here's General Lallemont himself!' But the division commander didn't even pause, not until the tunnel broached at last into light, and then only long enough to listen for a moment to the screeching crescendo of shells overhead, listening with a sort of impersonal detached attentiveness, as if he were a messenger, a runner, sent there to ascertain whether or not the guns were still firing, and to return and report. It had been twenty years now, the first scrap of braid not even tarnished on his sleeve, since he had accepted, established as the first stone in the edifice of his career: *A commander must be so hated, or at least feared by his troops that, immunised by that fury, they will attempt any odds, any time, anywhere.* He stood, not stopped, just paused, his face lifted too, like the runner taking that simple precaution against the possibility that those to whom he would report might demand the authority of his eyes too, or order him to walk the whole distance back again to rectify the oversight, thinking: *Except that I didn't intend that they should hate me so much they would refuse to attack at all because I didn't think then that a commander could be hated that much, apparently didn't know even this morning that soldiers could hate that much, being soldiers;* thinking quietly: *Of course. Countermand the barrage, stop it, let them come over; the whole thing will be obliterated then, effaced, and I need only say that they were ready for me before my attack ever started, with none to refute me since those who could will no longer be alive;* thinking with what he considered not even sardonicism nor even wittiness, but just humor: *With a regiment which has already mutinied holding the line, they will overrun and destroy the whole division in ten or fifteen minutes. Then even those who are giving him the baton will appreciate the value of their gift;*—already walking again, on for another thousand metres, almost to the end of the communication trench where his car would be waiting; and this time he did stop, utterly; he didn't know how long it had been going on nor even how long he had been hearing it: no puny concentration now of guns behind one single regimental front; it seemed to him that he could hear the fury spreading battery to battery in both directions along the whole front until every piece in the entire sector must be in frantic action. *They did come over,* he thought. *They did. The whole line has collapsed; not just one mutinied regiment, but the whole line of us;* already turned to run back up the trench before he could catch himself, telling himself, *It's too late; you cant get back in time now,*—catching himself back into sanity, or at least into trained military logic and reason, even if he did have to use what he thought was humor (and this time called wittiness too, the wit perhaps of despair) in order to do it: *Nonsense. What reason could they have had for an assault at this moment? How could the boche have known even before I did, that one of my regiments was going to mutiny? And even if they did know it, how could they afford to give Bidet his German marshalcy at the rate of just one regiment at a time?*—walking on again, saying quietly aloud this time: 'That's the clatter a falling general makes.'

Two field howitzers were firing almost over his waiting car. They had not been there at dawn when he left it, and his driver could not have heard him if he had spoken, which he did not: one peremptory gesture as he got in, sitting rigid and calm and parallel now for a while to the pandemonium of guns stretching further than hearing did; still quite calm when he got out of the car at Corps Headquarters, not even seeing at first that the corps commander was already waiting for him at the door, then reversing in midstride and returning to the car, still striding rigidly on when the corps commander overtook him and put one hand on his arm and began to draw him aside toward where the corps car waited. The corps commander spoke the army commander's name. 'He's waiting for us,' he said.

'And then, Bidet,' the division commander said. 'I want authority from Bidet's own lips to shoot them.'

'In with you,' the corps commander said, touching him again, almost shoving him into the car, then following, closing the door himself, the car already in motion, so that the orderly had to leap for the running board; soon they were running fast too beside, beneath the horizon's loud parallel, the division commander rigid, erect, immobile, staring ahead, while the corps commander, leaning back, watched him, or what was visible of the calm and invincible face. 'And suppose he refuses,' the corps commander said.

'I hope he does,' the division commander said. 'All I ask is to be sent under arrest to Chaulnesmont.'

'Listen to me,' the corps commander said. 'Cant you see that it will not matter to Bidet whether it failed or not or how it failed or even whether it was made or not? that he will get his baton just the same, anyway?'

'Even if the boche destroys us?'

'Destroys us?' the corps commander said. 'Listen.' He jerked his hand toward the east where, fast though they were moving, the division commander might have realised now that the uproar still reached further and faster than hearing moved. 'The boche doesn't want to destroy us, any more than we would want, could afford, to destroy him. Cant you understand? either of us, without the other, couldn't exist? that even if nobody was left in France to confer Bidet's baton, some boche would be selected, even if there remained only one private, and elevated high enough in French rank to do it? That Bidet didn't choose you for this because you were Charles Gragnon, but because you were General of Division Gragnon at this time, this day, this hour?'

'Us?' the division commander repeated.

'Us!' the corps commander said.

'So I failed, not in a front line at six this morning, but the day before yesterday in your headquarters—or maybe ten years ago, or maybe forty-seven years ago.'

'You did not fail at all,' the corps commander said.

'I lost a whole regiment. And not even by an attack: by a provost marshal's machinegun squad.'

'Does it matter how they will die?'

'It does to me. How it dies is the reason it died. That's my record.'

'Bah,' the corps commander said.

'Since what I lost was merely Charles Gragnon. While what I saved was France——'

'You saved us,' the corps commander said.

'Us?' the division commander repeated again.

'Us,' the corps commander said in that voice harsh and strong with pride: 'the lieutenants, the captains, the majors and colonels and sergeants all with the same privilege: the opportunity to lie someday in the casket of a general or a marshal among the flags of our nation's glory in the palace of the Invalides——'

'Except that the Americans and British and Germans dont call theirs "Invalides".'

'All right, all right,' the corps commander said. '—merely in return for fidelity and devotion and accepting a little risk, gambling a petty stake which, lacking glory, was no better than any vegetable's to begin with, and deserved no less of obscurity for its fate. Failed,' he said. 'Failed. Charles Gragnon, from sergeant to general of division before he was forty-five years old—that is, forty-seven——'

'And then lost.'

'So did the British lieutenant general who commanded that army in Picardy two months ago.'

'And whatever boche it was who lost contact or mislaid his maps and compass in Belgium three years ago,' the division commander said. 'And the one who thought they could come through at Verdun. And the one who thought the Chemin des Dames would be vulnerable, having a female name.' He said: 'So it's not we who conquer each other, because we are not even fighting each other. It's simple nameless war which decimates our ranks. All of us: captains and colonels, British and American and German and us, shoulder to shoulder, our backs to the long invincible wall of our glorious tradition, giving and asking . . . . . Asking? not even accepting quarter——'

'Bah,' the corps commander said again. 'It is man who is our enemy: the vast seething moiling spiritless mass of him. Once to each period of his inglorious history, one of us appears with the stature of a giant, suddenly and without warning in the middle of a nation as a dairymaid enters a buttery, and with his sword for paddle he heaps and pounds and stiffens the malleable mass and even holds it cohered and purposeful for a time. But never for always, nor even for very long: sometimes before he can even turn his back, it has relinquished, dis-cohered, faster and faster flowing and seeking back to its own base anonymity. Like that out there this morning——' again the corps commander made the brief indicative gesture.

'Like what out there?' the division commander said; whereupon the corps commander said almost exactly what the group commander would say within the next hour:

'It cannot be that you dont even know what happened.'

'I lost Charles Gragnon.'

'Bah,' the corps commander said. 'We have lost nothing. We were merely faced without warning by an occupational hazard. We hauled them up out of their ignominious mud by their bootstraps; in one more little instant they might have changed the world's face. But they never do. They collapse, as yours did this morning. They always will. But not us. We will even drag them willy-nilly up again, in time, and they will collapse again. But not us. It wont be us.'

The army commander was waiting too; the car had barely to stop for him. As soon as it was in motion again, the division commander made for the second time his request in the flat, calm, almost dispassionate voice: 'I shall shoot them, of course.' The army commander didn't answer. The division commander had not expected him to. He would not have heard any answer because he was not even listening to the other two voices murmuring to one another in brief, rapid, half-finished phrases as the corps commander briefed, reviewed to the army commander by number and designation, the regiments in the other divisions on either flank of his own, until the two voices had locked block into regimental block the long mosaic of the whole army front.

And—not only no sound of guns here, but never at any time—they were challenged at the chateau gates and entered the park, a guide on the running board now so that they didn't even pause at the carved rococo entrance but went on around to the side, across a courtyard bustling with orderlies and couriers and popping motorcycles, passing—and the division commander neither noticed nor cared here either—two cars flying the pennons of two other army commanders, and a third car which was British, and a fourth one which had not even been manufactured on this side of the Atlantic, and on to a *porte cochere* at the back of the chateau and so directly into the shabby cluttered cubicle not much larger than a clothes press, notched into the chateau's Italianate *bijou* like a rusted spur in a bride's cake, from which the group commander conducted the affairs of his armies.

They were all there: the commanders of the two other armies which composed the group of armies, their heavy moustaches, already shaped to noon's spoon, richly luxuriant from the daily ritual of soup; the English chief of staff who could have looked no more indomitably and rigidly youthful if the corset had been laced in full view on the outside of his tunic, with his bright ribbons and wisps of brass and scarlet tabs and his white hair and moustache and his blue eyes the color of icy war; and the American colonel with the face of a Boston shipping magnate (which indeed he was, or at least the entailed scion of one)—or rather, an eighteenth century face: the face of that predecessor or forefather who at twenty-five had retired rich from the quarter deck of a Middle Passage slaver, and at thirty had his name illuminated in colored glass above his Beacon Hill pew. He was the guest, the privileged, since for three years it had not even been his nation's war, who had brought already into the conclave the privileged guest's air of prim, faintly spinsterish disapproval—an air, quality, appearance too, almost Victorian in fact, from his comfortable old man's shoes and the simple leather putties of a Northumberland drover (both—shoes and putties—beautifully polished but obviously purchased at different times and places and so never to match in color, and neither matching the ordnance belt which obviously had been acquired in two places also, making four different tones of leather) and the simple flareless breeches cut from the same bolt as the short-tailed jacket rising unblemished by any brass to the high-boned throat with its prim piping of linen collar backside foremost like the dog-collar of a priest. (There was an anecdote about that uniform, or rather about its wearer, the colonel, going the rounds of messes six months ago, about how, shortly after the American headquarters had been set up, a junior officer—no Bostonian, this: a New Yorker—had appeared before the colonel one morning in the Bedford cords of a British officer and a long skirted tunic cut by a London tailor, though it did have the high closed throat; the colonel would meet many duplicates of it later, but not then because that was 1917; the youth appearing a little sheepishly, probably a little fearfully, wishing perhaps, as many another pioneer has done, that he had let someone else be first, before the cold banker's eyes of his superior, saying presently: 'You think I shouldn't have done it? It's bad form, taste, aping——'; then the colonel, pleasant, immediate: 'Why not? They taught us the art of war in 1783 by losing one to us; they should not object to lending us the clothes in 1917 to win one for them.')

And, cynosure of all, the Mama Bidet, the General Cabinet, the Marshal d'Aisance of the division commander's calm and icelike implacability not for justice for himself but for vindication of his military record, who—the group commander—had brought twenty-five years ago into the African sunglare not a bent for war (that would reveal later) and not even a simple normal thirst for glory and rank, but a cold, pitiless preoccupation with the mucous membrane buttoned inside his army breeches, which accompanied (even preceded) him from troop to squadron to regiment to brigade, division and corps and army and army group as he advanced and rose, more immune to harm as his stars increased in number and his gift for war found field and scope, but no more pitiless—the short, healthy, pot-bellied little man who looked like a green grocer retired happy and cheerful at fifty, and then ten years later dressed not too willingly for a masquerade in the ill-fitting private's tunic without a single ribbon on it nor even any insigne of rank, whose real name had been an authority for fifteen years among textbook soldiers on how to keep troops fit, and a byword for four years among field commanders on how to fight them.

He didn't ask the division commander to sit down when the army- and corps-commanders did; as far as the division commander could have affirmed, the group commander had not even remarked his presence, leaving him to stand while that unbidden and uncaring part of his attention recorded the tedious recapitulation of regiments and divisions, not merely by their positions in the front but by their past records and the districts of their derivation and their officers' names and records, the army commander talking, rapid and succinct, nothing still of alarm in the voice and not very much of concern: just alertness, precision, care. Nor did it seem to the division commander watching—or not specifically watching the group commander because he was not really watching anything: just looking steadily at or toward the group commander as he had been doing ever since he entered, aware suddenly that he not only could not remember when he had blinked his eyes last, but that he felt no need to blink them—that the group commander was listening either, though he must have been, quietly and courteously and inattentively; until suddenly the division commander realised that the group commander had been looking at him for several seconds. Then the others seemed to become aware of it too; the army commander stopped talking, then said:

'This is Gragnon. It was his division.'

'Ah yes,' the group commander said. He spoke directly to the division commander in the same tone, pleasant and inflectionless: 'Many thanks. You may return to your troops,' and turned again to the army commander. 'Yes?' Then for another half minute, the army commander's voice; and now the division commander, rigid and unblinking, was looking at nothing at all, rigid and unblinking still until the army commander's voice stopped again, the division commander not even bothering to bring vision back behind his eyes even after the group commander spoke to him again: 'Yes?'

Standing not quite at attention, looking not at anything but merely staring at rigid eyelevel above the group commander's head, the division commander made his formal request for permission to have the whole regiment executed. The group commander heard him through. There was nothing whatever in the group commander's face.

'Endorsed as received,' he said. 'Return to your troops.' The division commander did not move. He might not have heard even. The group commander sat back in his chair and spoke to the army commander without even turning his head: 'Henri. Will you conduct these gentlemen to the little drawing room and have them bring wine, whisky, tea, whatever they fancy?' He said to the American colonel in quite passable English: 'I have heard of your United States coca cola. My regrets and apologies that I do not have that for you yet. But soon we hope, eh?'

'Thank you, General,' the colonel said in better than passable French: 'The only European terms we decline to accept are German ones.'

Then they were gone; the door closed behind them. The division commander had not moved. The group commander looked at him. His voice was still merely pleasant, not even quizzical: 'A general of division. You have come a long way from Africa, Sergeant Gragnon.'

'So have you,' the division commander said, '—Mama Bidet.'—speaking in his cold, flat voice, with no inflection nor emphasis either, the name given not secretly so much as merely when he was out of earshot, or perhaps not even that but simply from the inviolable security of their rankless state, by the men in ranks to the group commander soon after he came out as a subaltern into the African regiment in which the division commander was already a sergeant: 'A long way, Monsieur the General Cabinet, Monsieur soon-to-be the Marshal d'Aisance.' And still nothing in the group commander's face; his voice was still calm, yet there now crept into it a shadow of something else, something speculative and even a little astonished, though the division commander would prove that he at least had not remarked it. Then the group commander said:

'I seem to have been more right than even I knew or

hoped. When you came in, I felt that perhaps I owed you an apology. Now I am sure of it.'

'You demean yourself,' the division commander said. 'How could a man doubting his own infallibility get that many stars? And how could a man with that many stars retain any doubts about anything?'

The group commander looked at the division commander for another moment. Then he said: 'It cant be possible that you dont even see that it has already ceased to matter whether these three thousand men or these four men die or not. That there is already more to this than the execution of twice three thousand men could remedy or even change.'

'Speak for yourself,' the division commander said. 'I have seen ten times three thousand dead Frenchmen.' He said, 'You will say, Slain by other Frenchmen?' He said, repeated, rote-like, cold, unemphasised, almost telegraphic: '*Comité des Forges. De Ferrovie. S.P.A.D.* The people at Billancourt. Not to mention the English and Americans, since they are not French, at least not until they have conquered us. What will it matter to the three thousand or the ten times three thousand, when they are dead? Nor matter to us who killed them, if we are successful?'

'By "successful" you mean "victorious",' the group commander said. 'And by "we" of course, you mean France.'

In his flat, cold voice the division commander repeated the simple, explicit, soldierly expletive of the Cambronne legend.

'A fact, but not a rejoinder,' the group commander said.

The division commander said the word again. 'For me, a ribbon tomorrow; for you, a baton before you die. Since mine is worth only a regiment, yours will certainly be cheap at that.'

Presently the group commander said: 'What you are really asking me for, is to endorse you for a court-martial. You're offering me the choice between sending you to the commander-in-chief, and compelling you to go yourself.' The division commander did not move. He was not going to. They both knew it. 'Return to your headquarters,' the group commander said. 'You will be notified there when the Marshal will see you at Chaulnesmont.'

He returned to Corps Headquarters with the corps commander, and got his own car; he would probably not even remember that the corps commander did not ask him to lunch. He would not have cared. He would have declined anyway. The group commander had told him to return to his own headquarters: an order. He was probably not even aware that he was disobeying it, getting into his car and saying briefly to the driver: 'The line.' Though it would be too late. It was nearing two oclock; the regiment would long since have been evacuated and disarmed and replaced; it would be too late to watch it pass now and so see for himself that it was done, just as he had paused in the communication trench to make sure that the artillery was still firing. He was going back as a chef might return two or three hours afterward to the kitchen where a dish he had been preparing had burned or perhaps exploded, not to help nor even advise in tidying up, but merely to see what might remain with some of the litter removed; not to regret it, because that would be a waste of regret, but just to see, to check; not even thinking about it, not thinking about anything, immobile and calm in the moving car, carrying inside him like a liquid sealed in a vacuum bottle that cold, inflexible undeviable determination for justice to his rank at any cost, vindication of his record at all.

So at first he did not realise what had startled, shocked him. He said sharply: 'Stop.' and sat in the halted car in the ringing silence which he hadn't even heard yet because he had never heard anything here before but guns: no longer a starred, solitary man in a staff car behind a French battle-front, but a solitary boy lying on his stomach on a stone wall outside the Pyrenean village where, for all any records stated or knowledge remembered, he had been born an orphan; listening now to the same cicada chirring and buzzing in a tangle of cordite-blasted weeds beyond the escarpment landmarked since last winter by the skeleton tail of a crashed German aeroplane. Then he heard the lark too, high and invisible, almost liquid but not quite, like four small gold coins dropped without haste into a cup of soft silver, he and the driver staring at one another until he said, loud and harsh: 'Drive on!'—moving on again; and sure enough, there was the lark again, incredible and serene, and then again the unbearable golden silence, so that he wanted to clap his hands to his ears, bury his head, until at last the lark once more relieved it.

Though the two batteries at the camouflaged corner were not firing now, they were not only still there, but a section of heavy howitzers was flanked on them, the gunners watching him quietly as he approached, chop-striding, bull-chested, virile, in appearance impervious and indestructible, starred and exalted and, within this particular eye-range of earth, supreme and omnipotent still, yet who, because of those very stars, didn't dare ask whoever was senior here when he had ceased to fire, let alone where his orders to do so had come from, thinking how he had heard all his military life about the ineradicable mark which war left on a man's face, without ever having seen it himself, but at least he had seen now what peace did to men's faces. Because he knew now that the silence extended much further than one divisional front or even than the two flanking ones; knowing now what the corps commander and the group commander both had meant when they had said in almost the same words: 'It cannot be that you dont even know what is happening', thinking *I am not even to have a court-martial for incompetence. Now that the war is over, they wont have to allow me a court because nobody will care any longer, nobody compelled by simple military regulations to see that my record receives justice.*

'Who commands here?' he said. But before the captain could answer, a major appeared from beyond the guns. 'Gragnon here,' the division commander said. 'You're standing to, of course.'

'Yes, General,' the major said. 'That was the order which came up with the remand. What is it, General? What's happening?'—saying the last of it to the division commander's back, because he had already turned, striding on, rigidly erect and only a little blind; then a battery did fire, two kilometres and perhaps more to the south: a salvo, a ragged thud; and, chop-striding, unhurried, burly and virile and indestructible, there occurred inside him a burst, a giving-away, a flow of something which if he had still been the unfathered unmothered boy secure in the privacy of his abandoned Pyrenean wall, would have been tears, no more visible then than now, no more then than now of grief, but of inflexibility. Then another battery fired, one salvo, less than a kilometre away this time, the division commander not faltering, merely altering direction in midstride and instead of entering the communication trench he rapidly climbed the escarpment, into the pocked field beyond it, not running still but walking so fast that he was a considerable distance away when the next battery fired, this time one of those he had just left, firing its salvo in its turn as if whoever had created the silence were underlining it, calling men's attention to it with the measured meaningless slams, saying with each burst of puny uproar, 'Hear it? Hear it?'

His first brigade's headquarters was the cellar of a ruined farm. There were several people there, but he was not inside long enough to have recognised any of them, even if he had wanted to or tried. Almost immediately, he was outside again, wrenching his arm from the hand of the aide who had been with him in the observation post when the attack failed. But he did take the flask, the brandy insentient as stale water in his throat, slightly warm from the aide's body-heat, tasteless. Because here at last was one of the rare moments in the solitude and pride of command when he could be General Gragnon without being General of Division Gragnon too. 'What——' he said.

'Come,' the aide said rapidly. But the division commander jerked his arm from the aide's hand again, not following but preceding the aide for a short distance into the farmyard, then stopping and turning.

'Now,' he said.

'They didn't even tell you?' the aide said. He didn't answer, immobile, bull-like and indestructible; and, bull-like and indestructible, quite calm. The aide told him. 'They are stopping it. Our whole front—I dont mean just our division and corps, but the whole French front—remanded at noon except for air patrols and artillery like that yonder at the corner. And the air people are not crossing: just patrolling up and down our front, and the orders to the artillery were to range, not on the boche, but between us and them, on what the Americans call no-man's land. And the boche is doing the same thing with his artillery and air; and the order is out for the British and Americans to remand at fifteen hours, to see if the boche will do the same thing in front of them.' The division commander stared at him. 'It's not just our division: it's all of them: us and the boche too.' Then the aide saw that even now the division commander did not understand. 'It's the men,' the aide said. 'The ranks. Not just that regiment, nor even our division, but all the private soldiers in our whole front, the boche too, since he remanded too as soon as our barrage lifted, which would have been his chance to attack since he must have seen that our regiment had refused, mutinied; he went further than we have, because he is not even using artillery: only his air people, not crossing either, just patrolling up and down his front. Though of course they wont know for sure about the British and the Americans and the boche in front of them until fifteen hours. It's the men; not even the sergeants knew, suspected anything, had any warning. And nobody knows if they just happened to set a date in advance which coincided with our attack, or if they had a prearranged signal which our regiment put up when it knew for certain that it was going over this morning——'

'You lie,' the division commander said. 'The men?'

'Yes. Everybody in the line below sergeant——'

'You lie,' the division commander said. He said with a vast, a spent, an indomitable patience: 'Cant you understand? Cant you see the difference between a single regiment getting the wind up—a thing which can and might happen to any regiment, at any time; to the same regiment which took a trench yesterday and which tomorrow, simply because it turned tail today, will take a village or even a walled town? And you try to tell me this (using again the succinct soldierly noun). The men,' he said. 'Officers—marshals and generals—decreed that business this morning and decreed it as a preordained failure; staff officers and experts made the plans for it within the specifications of failure; I supplied the failure with a mutinying regiment, and still more officers and generals and marshals will collect the cost of it out of my reputation. But the men. I have led them in battle all my life. I was always under the same fire they were under. I got them killed: yes; but I was there too, leading them, right up to the day when they gave me so many stars that they could forbid me to anymore. But not the men. They understand even if you cannot. Even that regiment would have understood; they knew the risk they took when they refused to leave the trench. Risk? Certainty. Because I could have done nothing else. Not for my reputation, not even for my own record or the record of the division I command, but for the future safety of the men, the rank and file of all the other regiments and divisions whose lives might be thrown away tomorrow or next year by another regiment shirking, revolting, refusing, that I was going to have them executed——' thinking, *Was. I'm already saying was; not is: was,* while the aide stared at him in incredulous amazement.

'Is it possible?' the aide said. 'Do you really contend that they are stopping the war just to deprive you of your right, as commander of the division, to execute that regiment?'

'Not my reputation,' the division commander said quickly, 'not even my own record. But the division's record and good name. What else could it be? What other reason could they have——' blinking rapidly and painfully while the aide took the flask from his pocket and uncapped it and nudged it against the division commander's hand. 'The men,' the division commander said.

'Here,' the aide said. The division commander took the flask.

'Thanks,' he said; he even started to raise the flask to his lips. 'The men,' he said. 'The troops. All of them. Defying, revolting, not against the enemy, but against us, the officers, who not only went where they went, but led them, went first, in front, who desired for them nothing but glory, demanded of them nothing but courage. . . . .'

'Drink, General,' the aide said. 'Come now.'

'Ah yes,' the division commander said. He drank and returned the flask; he said, 'Thanks,' and made a motion, but before he could complete it the aide, who had been in his military family since he got his first brigadier's star, had already produced a handkerchief, immaculate and laundered, still folded as the iron pressed it. 'Thanks,' the division commander said again, taking the handkerchief and wiping his moustache, and then stood again, the handerchief open now in his hand, blinking rapidly and painfully. Then he said, simply and distinctly: 'Enough of this.'

'General?' the aide said.

'Eh? What?' the division commander said. Then he was blinking again, steadily though not painfully now, not really fast. 'Well——' he said. He turned.

'Shall I come too?' the aide said.

'No no,' the division commander said, already walking on. 'You stay here. They may need you. There might be something else. . . . .' his voice not fading but simply ceasing, already chop-striding again, virile and impregnable, the gunners now standing along the crest of the opposite escarpment as he approached, carrying the loose handkerchief in his hand as though bearing under orders a flag of truce of which he himself was inflexibly ashamed and grieved. The major saluted him. He returned it and got into the car. It moved at once; the driver had already turned it around. The boche crash was not far; soon they reached it. 'Stop here,' he said. He got out. 'Drive on. I'll overtake you in a moment;' not even waiting for the car to move but already climbing the bank into the cordite-blasted weeds, still carrying the handkerchief. This was the place; he had marked it, though naturally his sudden advent would have alarmed the tiny beast. But it would still be here; by squatting and hunting patiently enough, parting the weed-stems gently enough, he could probably see it in the Pyrenean grass, crouching and unterrified, merely waiting for him to become still, resume the solitude which was his origin and his ancestry and his birthright, the Sisters—the Father himself when he would arrive with his inconsolable dedicated eyes and his hands gentle enough but sonless, which had never caressed nor struck in anger and love and fear and hope and pride, boy's flesh sprung from his flesh and bearing his immortality in the same intolerant love and hope and pride, wiser perhaps than the Sisters were, less tender than they were tender, but no less compassionate, knowing nothing as the Sisters knew nothing too—saying: 'The Mother of Christ, the Mother of all, is your mother;' not enough, because he didn't want the mother of all nor the mother of Christ either: he wanted the mother of One; only necessary to become still and wait until the tiny creature was accustomed to his sudden advent, then the first sound would come, tentative, brief: a rising, almost an interrogative inflection, almost a test as if to learn if he were really there and ready; then he would whisper the one word against the noon-fierce stone under his face: and he had been right: not the Pyrenean cicada of course, but certainly its northern sister, the miniature sound insistent and impersonal and constant and unobtrusive, steadfast somewhere among the jumble of rusted engine and guns and blackened wires and charred sticks—a purring sound such as he imagined might be made by the sleeping untoothed mouth itself around the sleeping nipple.

His divisional headquarters was what its owner called his country house, built by a man who had made several millions on the Paris Bourse and returned to the district of his birth to install an Argentine mistress, establishing not only the symbol and monument, but bringing the proof of his success back to the scene of his childhood and youth, his *I*-told-you-so to the elders, mayor and doctor and advocate and judge, who had said he would never amount to anything; and who was well served not only in his patriotism but in his devotion too when the military demanded the use of it, since the Argentine had quitted Paris only under pressure in the first place.

The message from Corps Headquarters was waiting for him: *Chaulnesmont. Tomorrow 15 hours. You are expected. You will confine yourself to quarters until the motor car calls for you,* crumpling the message and the aide's handkerchief into his tunic pocket; and, home again (what home he had ever had since when, at eighteen, he had first donned the uniform which from then on would be his home as the turtle's shell is its domicile), there opened before him an attenuation, an emptiness, of the next five or six or seven hours until it would be dark. He thought of drink. He was not a drinking man; he not only never thought of it until he saw it, it was as though he had forgot it existed until someone actually put it into his hand, as the aide had done the flask. But he dismissed the idea as immediately and completely and for exactly the same reason as if he had been a drinking man: although he had officially ceased to be General of Division Gragnon the moment he received the corps commander's order for him to put himself under arrest, General of Division Gragnon would have to continue to exist for another five or six or seven hours, perhaps even for another day or two yet.

Then suddenly he knew what he would do, quitting the official quarters for his private ones, passing his own bedroom—a small, panelled closet called by the millionaire the gunroom and containing a shotgun which had never been fired and a mounted stag's head (not a very good one) and a stuffed trout, both bought in the same shop with the gun—and went on to the room in which three of his aides slept—the lovenest itself, which seemed to retain even yet something of the Argentine, though none could have said what it was, since nothing remained of her, unless it was some inconsolable ghost perhaps of what northerners conceived, believed, to be antipodal libidinous frenzy—and found the volume in the battered chest in which it was the duty of one of the aides to transport about with them the unofficial effects of the headquarters entourage. And now the book's dead owner was present again too: a former member of his staff, a thin, over-tall, delicately- and even languidly-made man regarding whose sexual proclivities the division commander had had his doubts (very likely wrong) without really caring one way or the other, who had entered the (then) brigadier's military family shortly before he received his division, who, the general discovered, was the nameless product of an orphanage too—which fact, not the book, the reading itself, the division commander would admit to himself with a sort of savage self-contempt in his secret moments, was what caused him to be so constantly aware of the other not quite sipping and not quite snatching and certainly not buried in the book because he was a satisfactory aide, until at last it seemed to the division commander that the battered and dogeared volume was the aide and the man himself merely that aide's orderly: until one evening while they were waiting for a runner from the front lines with a return concerning some prisoners which a brigadier had neglected to sign (the aide was his divisional JAG), he asked and then listened in cold, inattentive amazement to the answer he got:

'I was a couturier. In Paris——'

'A what?' the division commander said.

'I made women's clothes. I was good at it. I was going to be better some day. But that wasn't what I wanted. I wanted to be brave.'

'Be what?' the division commander said.

'You know: a hero. Instead, I made women's clothes. So I thought of becoming an actor—Henry V—Tartuffe better than nothing—even Cyrano. But that would be just acting, pretence—somebody else, not me. Then I knew what to do. Write it.'

'Write it?'

'Yes. The plays. Myself write the plays, rather than just act out somebody else's idea of what is brave. Invent myself the glorious deeds and situations, create myself the people brave enough to perform and face and endure them.'

'And that wouldn't have been make-believe too?' the general said.

'It would have been me that wrote them, invented them, created them.' Nor did the general discern humility either: a quality humble yet dogged too, even if it was sheep-like. 'I would at least have done that.'

'Oh,' the general said. 'And this is the book.'

'No no,' the aide said. 'Another man wrote this one. I haven't written mine yet.'

'Haven't written it yet? You have had time here'; not even knowing that he had expressed the contempt nor even that he had tried to conceal it, or that perhaps he might have tried. And now the aide was not humble, not even dogged; certainly the general would not have recognised despair, though he might indomitability:

'I dont know enough yet. I had to wait to stop the books to find out——'

'In books? What in books?'

'About being brave. About glory, and how men got it, and how they bore it after they got it, and how other people managed to live with them after they got it; and honor and sacrifice, and the pity and compassion you have to have to be worthy of honor and sacrifice, and the courage it takes to pity, and the pride it takes to deserve the courage——'

'Courage, to pity?' the general said.

'Yes. Courage. When you stop to pity, the world runs over you. It takes pride to be that brave.'

'Pride in what?' the general said.

'I dont know yet. That's what I'm trying to find out.' Nor did the general recognise serenity then, since he probably called it something else. 'And I will find it. It's in the books.'

'In this book?' the general said.

'Yes,' the aide said, and he died, or that is, the general found him missing one morning, or rather failed to find him at all one morning. It was two hours before he found where the aide was, and another three or four hours before he learned exactly what the aide had done, and he never did learn why and how the aide had come to be there, inside the lines, where a general of division's Assistant Judge Advocate General had no right nor business whatever, sitting—this was how the runner told it—beside a regimental runner behind a wall near a corner much used by staff cars, on which, so the runner claimed he had told the aide, the enemy had registered a gun only that morning. And everybody had been warned of it, yet the car came on anyway, still coming on even after the aide sprang to his feet and began to wave his arms to stop the car. But it refused to stop, still coming on even after the aide ran out into the open road, still trying to wave the car off even after the runner said that he could hear the shell coming, and that the aide himself must have heard it also; and how the aide could not possibly have known that the car contained not only a wealthy American expatriate, a widow whose only son was in a French air squadron a few kilometres away and who was supporting near Paris an asylum for war-orphaned children, but a well-connected Paris staff-major too. And there had been nothing to pin the medal on when it came through, and nothing to identify to bury it with either, so that the medal also was still in the battered chest which the aide's successors in their succession superintended from post to post; and the division commander took the book out and read the title and then read it again in mounting exasperation, reading it aloud, saying aloud almost, *All right. Blas wrote it. But what's the name of the book?* until he realised that the word he was looking at was the name of the book and therefore the book would have to be about a man, thinking *Yes,* remembering scraps, fragments, echoes from that night two years ago, saying the name aloud this time: 'Gil Blas,' listening, concentrated, if perhaps there might come out of the closed pages, through the cover itself and into the simple name, something, some echo of the thunder, the clanging crash, the ringing bugles and the horns, the—— *What was it?* he thought. *The glory, the honor and the courage and the pride*——

He returned to his bedroom, carrying the book. Save for his field cot and chest and desk, the furniture still belonged to the owner of the house and of the Argentine. It had the look of having been bought all in one shop too, probably over the telephone. He drew the single chair into the light from the window beside the stuffed fish and sat down and began to read, slowly, rigidly, not moving his lips even, inflexible in fortitude and suffering as if he were sitting fifty years ago for his portrait. After a while it was dusk. The door opened, hesitated, opened more and quietly and a batman entered and came to the table and prepared to light the lamp on it, the division commander not even looking up to say 'Yes', even when the soft gout of light plopped and burst soundless and brilliant on the open page in his hands, still reading when the batman went out, still reading until the tray was on the table beside the lamp and the batman had gone again. Then he put the book carefully down and turned to the tray, immobile again for a second, facing, somewhat as he had faced the book before opening it, the tray bearing the covered dish and the loaf and plate and cutlery and glass, and the bottle of wine and one of rum and one of *cassis* which he had been looking at on this tray for three years now—the same bottles which he had never touched, the same corks started each day and then driven home again and even dusted freshly over, the same liquid level in each as when vintner and distiller had bottled them. Nor did he use the knife and fork when he ate alone from the tray like this, eating not with voracity, nothing at all really gross about the feeding: simply putting the food rapidly and efficiently into himself with his fingers and sops of the bread. Then with only the slightest pause, not of indecision but simply to remember which pocket, he drew out the aide's handkerchief and carefully wiped his moustache and fingers and tossed the handkerchief onto the tray and thrust the chair away from the table and took up the book and paused again, immobile, the book half raised, though none could have said whether he was looking at the open page or out the open window which he now faced, looking at or listening to the spring-filled darkness, the myriad peaceful silence, which it framed. Then he raised the book further and entered, strode into it as a patient enters a dentist's office for the last petty adjustment before paying the bill, and read again, rigid and inflexible above the pages' slow increment in which he missed, skipped, elided, no single word, with a cold, incredulous, respectful amazement, not at the shadows of men and women, because they were inventions and naturally he didn't believe them—besides being in another country and long ago and therefore even if they had been real, they could never impinge, affect, the course of his life and its destruction—but at the capacity and industry and (he admitted it) the competence of the man who could remember all this and write it down.

He waked immediately, completely prescient. He even picked up the fallen book before looking at his watch; no start of concern nor dismay, as though he knew beforehand that he would be able to reach the chateau in plenty of time before dawn. Not that it would make any difference; he had simply planned to see the group commander tonight, and slept without intending to sleep and waked without needing to be waked, in plenty of time to see the group commander while technically at least it was still tonight.

So it was not dawn yet when the sentry at the lodge passed him (he was alone in the car, driving himself) through the gates and into the drive running straight and over-arched now through the spring darkness loud with predawn nightingales, up to the chateau. A successful highwayman had established its site and the park it sat in, a distant connection of a French queen had restored it in the Italian style of his native land; his marquis descendants had owned it: then the Republic: then a marshal of Napoleon: then a Levantine millionaire; for the last four years now, for all practical purposes, it had been the property of the general commanding the circumambient group of French armies. And the division commander had not noticed the nightingales until he was inside the park and it may have been at this moment that he realised that he himself would never own either: army command or chateau, or nightingales for doomed division commanders, coming to resign their pasts and their futures both, to listen to. And still not dawn when he slammed the car to a stop before the dark pile less of Louis than Florentine and more of baroque than either, jerking it up exactly as he would the over-ridden horse and getting out and flinging the door backward behind him against the night's silence as he would have flung the reins to a groom without even pausing to see if the animal's head were secure or not, then mounting the broad shallow steps to the stone terrace with its carved balustrade and urns garlanded in carven stone. Nor was even all the old gothic quite absent either: a pile of horse-droppings two or three days old on the terrace beside the door, as if the old princely highwayman himself had returned, or perhaps had only left day before yesterday, which the division commander glanced at in passing, thinking how forage grown from this northern chalk-loam soil merely gave a horse windy size, distending the animal simply by its worthless passing bulk: nothing of speed and bottom like the hard, lean, light desert-bred ones bone- and flesh-bred to endure on almost nothing, contemptuous even of that. And not just horses: man too, thinking *Able was I ere I saw France again,* thinking how always a man's simple longevity outlives his life and we are all our own paupers, derelict; thinking, as men had thought and said before him, that no soldier should be permitted to survive his first engagement under fire and then not thinking at all, chop-striding to the door and rapping on it, deliberate, peremptory, and loud.

He saw the candle, heard the feet. The door opened: no dishevelled Faubourg Saint Germain aide, this, but a private soldier: a middle-aged man in unlaced infantry boots and dangling braces, holding his trousers up with the other candleless hand over a soiled lavender civilian shirt whose collarless neckband was clasped by a tarnished brass button the size and shape of a wolf's fang. Even the man appeared no different; certainly the shirt was not: he (the division commander) might have been looking at both that day fifteen years ago when Bidet got his captaincy at last and an instructorship at the *École Militaire*, and he and the wife, who had followed him a subaltern to Africa even though she herself got no further than a loft in the Oran native town, could sleep every night under the same roof again at last, the same soldier but with a baize apron over the soiled violet shirt, scrubbing the stoop or the staircase while the wife stood over him like a sergeant herself, with a vast bunch of keys at her waist to jangle at each of his convulsive starts when she would murmur at him, and in the same baize apron waiting on table at meals; and apparently the same soldier (or at least one as large) but certainly the same shirt eight years later when Bidet was a colonel with enough pay to keep a horse too, waiting on table with a white apron now over the collarless shirt and the vast bunch of keys jangling against authentic satin now or even the true funereal silk at each of his convulsive starts, the same heavy boots under the apron bringing amid the viands the smell of stable manure now, the same giant thumb in the bowls of soup.

He followed the candle into the same bedroom at which the knightly highwayman, along with the shade of the imperial marshal, would have looked in contemptuous unbelief, in which the marquis descendants of the Florentine might or might not have slept, but in which the Levantine without doubt did, and saw something else which, he realised now, he had not expected to find changed either, though the man who wore them had. Standing at the foot of the bed, he faced across the fretted garlanded painted footboard the group commander sitting against the piled pillows in the same flannel nightcap and nightshirt which he too had brought to Africa that day twenty-five years ago when he had had to leave his wife under the broiling eaves of the Oran native house because they had no money then (he the only child of the widow living—or trying to—on the pension of her husband, a Savoyard schoolmaster, she one of the six daughters of a retired sergeant-major of marines) while the husband was absent for almost two years on his first subaltern's tour of outpost duty;—facing the man who even now did not look like even a French soldier and who on that first day twenty-five years ago seemed to have been completely and even criminally miscast, looking then himself like a consumptive school teacher, condemned not just to simple failure but to destitution and suicide too, who weighed then less than a hundred pounds (he was stouter now, almost plump in fact, and somewhere in his career like that of a delayed rocket, the glasses had vanished too) and wearing spectacles of such fierce magnification that he was almost blind without them, and even with them too since for a third of the time the lenses were sweated to opaqueness and he spent another third wiping them dry with the end of his burnous in order to see at all before sweating them blind again, and who had brought into the field life of that regiment of desert cavalry something of the monastery, something of the cold fierce blinkless intolerant glare which burns at midnight in the dedicated asepsis of clinical or research laboratories: that pitiless preoccupation with man, not as an imperial implement, least of all as that gallant and puny creature bearing undismayed on his frail bones and flesh the vast burden of his long inexplicable incomprehensible tradition and journey, not even in fact as a functioning animal but as a functioning machine in the same sense that the earthworm is: alive purely and simply for the purpose of transporting, without itself actually moving, for the distance of its corporeal length, the medium in which it lives, which, given time, would shift the whole earth that infinitesimal inch, leaving at last its own blind insatiate jaws chewing nothing above the spinning abyss: that cold, scathing, contemptuous preoccupation with body vents and orifices and mucous membrane as though he himself owned neither, who declared that no army was better than its anus, since even without feet it could still crawl forward and fight, and so earned his nickname because of his inflexible belief in his doctrine—a nickname spoken at first in contempt and derision, then in alarm and anger and then rage and then concerned and impotent fury since his inflexible efforts to prove his doctrine soon extended beyond his own platoon, into troops and squadrons where, still a simple junior lieutenant of cavalry and not even a medical officer, he had no right nor business at all; and then spoken no longer in ridicule nor even contumely and anger anywhere, because presently the whole African establishment knew how, sitting in a tent, he had told his regimental commander how to recover two scouts captured one night by a band of mounted tribesmen who vanished afterward like antelope; and it worked, and later, still sitting in a tent, told the general himself how to avail to a hitherto dry outpost a constant supply of drinking water, and that worked too; and moved from the classroom colonelcy to the command of a field division in 1914 and three years later was the competent and successful commander of an army group and already unofficially next but one to a marshal's baton while still less than fifty-five years old, sitting in his flannel nightshirt and cap in the gaudy bed in the rococo room lighted by the cheap candle in its tin candlestick which the batman had set on the bedside table, like an ex-grocer alderman surprised, but neither alarmed nor even concerned, in a sumptuous bordello.

'You were right,' the division commander said. 'I wont go to Chaulnesmont.'

'You have wrestled all night,' the group commander said. 'With what angel?'

'What?' the division commander said. He blinked for only a second. Then he said, firmly and calmly, like a man stepping firmly forward into complete darkness, drawing a folded paper from his tunic as he did so and dropping it onto the group commander's covered knees: 'It didn't take that long.'

The group commander didn't touch the paper. He merely looked at it. He said pleasantly: 'Yes?'

'It's my resignation,' the division commander said.

'You think it's over, then?'

'What?' the division commander said. 'Oh. The war. No, it's not over. They'll have something I can do as a civilian. I was even a fair veterinary in the old days, Farrier, too. Or maybe I could even run a production line (that's what they call it, isn't it?) in a munitions plant.'

'And then?' the group commander said.

The division commander looked at him, though only for a second. 'Oh. When it is over, you mean. I'm leaving France then. Maybe to the south Pacific. An island. . . . . .'

'Like Gauguin,' the group commander said gently.

'Who?'

'Another man who one day discovered that he had had enough of France too and went to the south Pacific and became a painter.'

'This is another place,' the division commander said immediately. 'There wont be enough people on this one to need their houses painted.'

The group commander reached his hand and took up the folded paper and turned and, the paper still folded, held the corner of it to the candle-flame until it took fire and then burst blazing, the group commander holding it for a second longer before he dropped it hissing into the chamber-pot beside the bed and in the same motion slid himself down the pillows until he was reclining again, already drawing the covers up. 'Chaulnesmont,' he said. 'At three tomorrow—— Bah, it's already tomorrow.' And then the division commander was aware of it too: the alteration, day, the invincible oblivious tomorrow which follows always, undeviable by man and to man immune; no longer ago than yesterday saw him and his fury, the first tomorrow will have forgotten both. It was even a second or so before he realised that the group commander was still talking to him: '—if the world thinks it wishes to stop fighting for twenty-five or thirty years, let it. But not this way. Not like a group of peasants in a half-mown field suddenly shouldering their scythes and lunch-pails and walking off. Chaulnesmont this afternoon.'

'Because there are rules,' the division commander said harshly. 'Our rules. We shall enforce them, or we shall die—the captains and the colonels—no matter what the cost——'

'It wasn't we who invented war,' the group commander said. 'It was war which created us. From the loins of man's furious ineradicable greed sprang the captains and the colonels to his necessity. We are his responsibilty; he shall not shirk it.'

'But not me,' the division commander said.

'You,' the group commander said. 'We can permit even our own rank and file to let us down on occasion; that's one of the prerequisites of their doom and fate as rank and file forever. They may even stop the wars, as they have done before and will again; ours merely to guard them from the knowledge that it was actually they who accomplished that act. Let the whole vast moil and seethe of man confederate in stopping wars if they wish, so long as we can prevent them learning that they have done so. A moment ago you said that we must enforce our rules, or die. It's no abrogation of a rule that will destroy us. It's less. The simple effacement from man's memory of a single word will be enough. But we are safe. Do you know what that word is?'

The division commander looked at him for a moment. He said: 'Yes?'

'Fatherland,' the group commander said. Now he raised the top of the covers, preparatory to drawing them back over his head and face. 'Yes, let them believe they can stop it, so long as they dont suspect that they have.' The covers were already moving; now only the group commander's nose and eyes and the nightcap remained in sight. 'Let them believe that tomorrow they will end it; then they wont begin to ponder if perhaps today they can. Tomorrow. And still tomorrow. And again tomorrow. That's the hope you will vest them in. The three stars that Sergeant Gragnon won by his own strength, with help from man nor God neither, have damned you, General. Call yours martyrdom for the world; you will have saved it. Chaulnesmont this afternoon.'

And now the division commander was no longer a general, still less the sergeant of twenty-five years ago whose inflexible pride it had been to accept odds from no man. 'But to me,' he said. 'What will happen to me?'

And now even the nightcap had vanished and only the muffled voice came from beneath the covers. 'I dont know,' it said. 'It will be glorious.'

Tuesday Night

Some time after midnight that Tuesday (it was Wednesday now) two British privates were resting on the firestep of a front-line trench below the Bethune slag-heap. Two months ago they were looking at it not only from another angle but from another direction; until then, the line's relation to it seemed fixed to a longer life than memory's. But since the break-through there had been no fixed line at all. The old corridor had still remained of course, roofed over with the shriek and stink of cordite, but attached to the earth only at the two ends: the one somewhere on the Channel and the other somewhere up the roof of France, so that it seemed to belly before the Teutonic gale like a clothesline about to carry away in a wind. And since three oclock yesterday afternoon (yesterday morning rather, noon when the French quit) it had merely hung in its spent bulge against the arrested weight of the Germanic air, even roofless now since with dark the last patrolling aircraft had gone to roost and there remained only the flares arching up from behind the flickerless wire with a faint hiss, a prolonged whispered sniff, to bloom and parachute and hang against the dark with the cold thick texture and color of the working lights in a police morgue, then sliding silently down the black air like drops of grease on a window-pane, and far away to the North the spaced blink and thump of a single gun, a big one, with no following burst at all, as though it were firing at the Channel, the North Sea itself fifty miles away, or perhaps at some target even vaster and more immune than that: at Cosmos, space, infinity, lifting its voice against the Absolute, the ultimate I-Am, harmless: the iron maw of Dis, toothless, unwearyable, incapable, bellowing.

One of the privates was a sentry. He stood on the firestep, leaning slightly against the wall beside the sand-bagged aperture in which his rifle lay loaded and cocked and with the safety off. In civil life he had indubitably been a horse-groom, because even in khaki and even after four years of infantryman's war he still moved, stood in an aura, effluvium of stalls and tack-rooms—a hard-faced jockey-sized man who seemed to have brought on his warped legs even into the French and Flemish mud something of hard, light, razor-edge horses and betting-rings, who even wore the steel helmet at the same vicious rake of the filthy heavy-checked cap which would have been the badge of his old dead calling and dedication. But this was only inference, from his appearance and general air, not from anything he ever told anyone; even his mates in the battalion who had stayed alive long enough to have known him four years knew nothing about his past, as if he did not have one, had not even been born until the fourth of August 1914—a paradox who had no business in an infantry battalion at all, and an enigma to the extent that six months after he entered the battalion (this was about Christmas, 1914) the colonel commanding it had been summoned to Whitehall to make a specific report on him. Because the authorities had discovered that eleven privates in the battalion had made the man beneficiary of their soldiers' life assurance policies; by the time the colonel reached the war ministry, the number had increased to twenty, and although the colonel had made an intensive two-days' investigation of his own before leaving the battalion, he knew little more than they in London did. Because the company officers knew nothing about it, and from the N.C.O.'s he got only rumor and hearsay, and from the men themselves, only a blank and respectful surprised innocence as to the man's very existence, the sum of which was, that the (eleven when the war office got its first report, and twenty by the time the colonel reached London, and—the colonel had been absent from the battalion twelve hours now—nobody knew how many more by this time) men had approached the battalion sergeant-major all decorously and regularly and apparently of their own free will and desire, and made the request which, since none of them had legal heirs, was their right to make, and the Empire's duty to acquiesce to. As for the man himself——

'Yes,' the staff-major who was doing the informal questioning, said. 'What did he say about it?' and then, after a moment: 'You didn't even question him?'

This time, the colonel did shrug. 'Why?' he said.

'Quite,' the major said. 'Though I should have been tempted—if only to learn what he can be selling them.'

'I should rather know what the ones who have legal heirs and cant make over the insurance, are paying him instead,' the colonel said.

'Their souls, obviously,' the major said. 'Since their deaths are already pledged.' And that was all. In the whole King's Regulations, through which had been winnowed and tested and proved every conceivable khaki or blue activity and posture and intention, with a rule provided for it and a penalty provided for the rule, there was nothing to cover it: who (the man) had infringed no discipline, trafficked with no enemy, failed to shine no brass nor wrap properly any puttie nor salute any officer. Yet still the colonel sat there, until the major, a little more than curious now, said, 'What? Say it.'

'I cant,' the colonel said. 'Because the only word I can think of is love,'—explaining that: the stupid, surly, dirty, unsocial, really unpleasant man, who apparently neither gambled nor drank (during the last two months, the battalion sergeant-major and the colonel's orderly sergeant had sacrificed—unofficially, of course—no little of their own free time and slumber too, walking suddenly into dugouts and rest billets and estaminets, ascertaining that), who, in the light of day, seemed to have no friends at all, yet each time the sergeant-major or the orderly sergeant entered one of the dugouts or billets, they would find it jammed with men. And not the same men either, but each time there would be a new set of faces, so that in each period between two pay-days, the entire battalion roll could have been called by anyone detailed to sit beside the man's bunk; indeed, on pay-day itself, or for a day or two days after it, the line, queue, had been known to extend into the street, as when people wait to enter a cinema, while the dugout, the room, itself would be jammed to the door with men standing or sitting or squatting about the bunk or corner in which the man himself lay quite often asleep, morose and resigned and not even talking, like people waiting in a dentist's anteroom;—waiting, that was it, as both the sergeant-major and the sergeant realised, if for nothing else except for them—the sergeant-major and the sergeant—to leave.

'Why dont you give him a stripe?' the major said. 'If it's devotion, why not employ it for the greater glory of English arms?'

'How?' the colonel said. 'Try to buy with one file, the man who already owns the battalion?'

'Perhaps you should assign your own insurance and pay-book over to him.'

'Yes,' the colonel said. 'If he gives me time to.' And that was all. The colonel spent fourteen hours with his wife. At noon the next day, he was in Boulogne again; at six that afternoon, his car entered the village where the battalion was in rest billets. 'Stop here,' the colonel said, and sat for a moment in the car, looking at the queue of men which was moving infinitesimally toward and through the gate into one of those sweating stone courtyards which for a thousand years the French have been dotting about the Picard and Artois and Flanders countryside, apparently for the purpose of housing between battles the troops of the allied nations come to assist in preserving them. *No,* the colonel thought, *not a cinema; the anticipation is not great enough, although the urgency is twice as strong. They are like the parade outside a latrine.* 'Drive on,' he said.

The other private was a battalion runner. He was sitting on the firestep, his unslung rifle propped beside him, himself half-propped, half-reclining against the trench-wall, his boots and putties not caked with the drying mud of trenches but dusted with the recent powdery dust of roads; even his attitude showed not so much indolence, but fatigue, physical exhaustion. Except that it was not spent exhaustion, but the contrary: with something tense behind it, so that the exhaustion did not seem to possess him, but rather he seemed to wear it as he did the dust, sitting there for five or six minutes now, all of which he had spent talking, and with nothing of exhaustion in his voice either. Back in the old spanking time called peace, he had been not only a successful architect, but a good one, even if (in private life) an aesthete and even a little precious; at this hour of those old dead days, he would have been sitting in a Soho restaurant or studio (or, his luck good, even in a Mayfair drawing room or even—at least once or twice or perhaps three times—boudoir), doing a little more than his share of the talking about art or politics or life or both or all three. He had been among the first London volunteers, a private at Loos; without even a lance corporal's stripe on his sleeve, he had extricated his platoon and got it back alive across the Canal; he commanded the platoon for five days at Passchendaele and was confirmed in it, posted from the battlefield to officers' school and had carried his single pip for five months into 1916 on the night when he came off duty and entered the dugout where his company commander was shaving out of a Maconochie tin.

'I want to resign,' he said.

Without stopping the razor nor even moving enough to see the other's reflection in the mirror, the company commander said, 'Dont we all.' Then he stopped the razor. 'You must be serious. All right. Go up the trench and shoot yourself through the foot. Of course, they never really get away with it. But——'

'I see,' the other said. 'No, I dont want to get out.' He touched the pip on his left shoulder rapidly with his right finger tips and dropped the hand. 'I just dont want this anymore.'

'You want to go back to ranks,' the company commander said. 'You love man so well you must sleep in the same mud he sleeps in.'

'That's it,' the other said. 'It's just backward. I hate man so. Hear him?' Again the hand moved, an outward motion, gesture, and dropped again. 'Smell him, too.' That was already in the dugout also, sixty steps down though it was: not just the rumble and mutter, but the stench too, the smell, the soilure, the stink of simple usage: not the dead bones and flesh rotting in the mud, but because the live bones and flesh had used the same mud so long to sleep and eat in. 'When I, knowing what I have been, and am now, and will continue to be—assuming of course that I shall continue among the chosen beneath the boon of breathing, which I probably shall, some of us apparently will have to, dont ask me why of that either—, can, by the simple coincidence of wearing this little badge on my coat, have not only the power, with a whole militarised government to back me up, to tell vast herds of man what to do, but the impunitive right to shoot him with my own hand when he doesn't do it, then I realise how worthy of any fear and abhorrence and hatred he is.'

'Not just your hatred and fear and abhorrence,' the company commander said.

'Right,' he said. 'I'm merely the one who cant face it.'

'Wont face it,' the company commander said.

'Cant face it,' he said.

'Wont face it,' the company commander said.

'All right,' he said. 'So I must get back into the muck with him. Then maybe I'll be free.'

'Free of what?' the company commander said.

'All right,' he said. 'I dont know either. Maybe of having to perform forever at inescapable intervals that sort of masturbation about the human race people call hoping. That would be enough. I had thought of going straight to Brigade. That would save time. But then, the colonel might get his back up for being overslaughed. I'm looking for what K.R. and O. would call channels, I suppose. Only I dont seem to know anybody who ever read that book.'

It was not that easy. The battalion commander refused to endorse him; he found himself in the presence of a brigadier twenty-seven years old, less than four years out of Sandhurst today, in a Mons Star, M.C. and bar, D.S.O. and a French *Croix de Guerre* and a thing from the Belgian monarch and three wound stripes, who could not—not would not, could not—even believe what he was hearing, let alone understand what his importuner was talking about, who said, 'I daresay you've already thought of shooting yourself in the foot. Raise the pistol about sixty inches first. You might as well get out front of the parapet too, what? Better still, get past the wire while you're about it.'

But it was quite simple, when he finally thought of the method. He waited until his leave came up. He would have to do that; desertion was exactly what he did not want. In London he found a girl, a young woman, not a professional, not really a good-standing amateur yet, two or three months pregnant from any one of three men, two of whom had been killed inside the same fortnight and mile by Nieppe Forest, and the other now in Mesopotamia, who didn't understand either and therefore (so he thought at the time) was willing to help him for a price—a price twice what she suggested and which represented his whole balance at Cox's—in a plot whose meretricity and shabbiness only American moving pictures were to match: the two of them taken in *delicto* so outrageously *flagrante* and public, so completely unequivocal and incapable of other than one interpretation, that anyone, even the field-rank moralists in charge of the conduct of Anglo-Saxon-derived junior officers, should have refused point blank to accept or even believe it.

It worked though. The next morning, in a Knightsbridge barracks anteroom, a staff officer spokesman offered, as an alternative to preserve the regiment's honor, the privilege which he had requested of his company commander and then the battalion commander, and finally of the brigadier himself in France three months ago; and three nights later, passing through Victoria station to file into a coach full of private soldiers in the same returning train which had brought him by officers' first class up from Dover ten days ago, he found he had been wrong about the girl, whom at first he didn't even remember after she spoke to him. 'It didn't work,' she said.

'Yes,' he said. 'It worked.'

'But you're going back. I thought you wanted to lose the commission so you wouldn't have to go back.' Then she was clinging to him, cursing him and crying too. 'You were lying all the time, then. You wanted to go back. You just wanted to be a poor bloody private again.' She was pulling at his arm. 'Come on. The gates are still open.'

'No,' he said, holding back. 'It's all right.'

'Come on,' she said, jerking at him. 'I know these things. There's a train you can take in the morning; you wont be reported absent until tomorrow night in Boulogne.' The line began to move. He tried to move with it. But she clung only the harder. 'Cant you see?' she cried. 'I cant get the money to give back to you until tomorrow morning.'

'Let go,' he said. 'I must get aboard and find a corner to sleep in.'

'The train wont go for two hours yet. How many of them do you think I've seen leave? Come on. My room isn't ten minutes from here.'

'Let go now,' he said, moving on. 'Goodbye.'

'Just two hours.' A sergeant shouted at him. It had been so long since an N.C.O. had spoken to him this way, that he did not realise at once himself was meant. But he had already freed himself with a sudden sharp hard movement; a carriage door was open behind him, then he was in the compartment, dropping his pack and rifle onto a jumble of others, stumbling among a jumble of legs, pulling the door behind him as she cried through the closing gap: 'You haven't told me where to send the money.'

'Goodbye,' he said, closing the door, leaving her on the step, clinging on somehow even after the train was moving, her gaped urgent face moving parallel beyond the voiceless glass until an M.P. on the platform jerked her off, her face, not the train, seeming to flee suddenly with motion, in another instant gone.

He had gone out in 1914 with the Londoners. His commission was in them. This time, he was going out to a battalion of Northumberland Borderers. His record had preceded him; a corporal was waiting on the Boulogne quai to take him to the R.T.O. anteroom. The lieutenant had been with him at officers' school.

'So you put up a job on them,' the lieutenant said. 'Dont tell me: I dont want to know why. You're going out to the —th. I know James (the lieutenant colonel commanding it). Cut my teeth with him in the Salient last year. You dont want to go in a platoon. What about a telephonist—a sergeant-major's man?'

'Let me be a runner,' he said. So a runner he was. The word from the R.T.O. lieutenant had been too good; not just his record but his past had preceded him to the battalion also, up to the lieutenant colonel himself before he had been a week in the battalion, possibly because he, the runner, was entitled to wear (he did not wear it since it was the officer's branch of the decoration and, among the men he would now mess and sleep with, that ribbon up on his private's tunic would have required too much breath) one of the same candy-stripes which the colonel (he was not a professional soldier either) did; that, and one other matter, though he would never believe that the two were more than incidentally connected.

'Look here,' the colonel said. 'You haven't come here to stir up anything. You ought to know that the only possible thing is to get on with it, finish it and bloody well have done. We already have one man who could be a trouble-maker—unless he oversteps in time for us to learn what he is up to.' He named the man. 'He's in your company.'

'I couldn't,' the runner said. 'They wont talk to me yet. I probably couldn't persuade them to anything even if they would talk to me and I wanted to.'

'Not even (the colonel named the private again)? You dont know what he's up to either?'

'I dont think I'm an agitator,' the runner said. 'I know I'm not a spy. This is gone now, remember,' he said, touching his shoulder lightly with the opposite hand.

'Though I doubt if you can stop remembering that you once had it,' the colonel said. 'It's your own leg you're pulling, you know. If you really hate man, all you need do is take your pistol back to the latrines and rid yourself of him.'

'Yes sir,' the runner said, completely wooden.

'Hate Germans, if you must hate someone.'

'Yes sir,' the runner said.

'Well? Cant you answer?'

'All the Germans with all their kith and kin are not enough to make up man.'

'They are for me—now,' the colonel said. 'And they had better be for you too now. Dont force me to compel you to remember that pip. Oh, I know it too: the men who, in hopes of being recorded as victorious prime- or cabinet-ministers, furnish men for this. The men who, in order to become millionaires, supply the guns and shells. The men who, hoping to be addressed someday as Field Marshal or Viscount Plugstreet or Earl of Loos, invent the gambles they call plans.

The men who, to win a war, will go out and dig up if possible, invent if necessary, an enemy to fight against. Is that a promise?'

'Yes,' the runner said.

'Right,' the colonel said. 'Carry on. Just remember.' Which he did, sometimes when on duty but mostly during the periods when the battalion was in rest billets, carrying the unloaded rifle slung across his back which was his cognizance, his badge of office, with somewhere in his pocket some—any—scrap of paper bearing the colonel's or the adjutant's signature in case of emergency. At times he managed lifts from passing transport—lorries, empty ambulances, an unoccupied sidecar. At times while in rest areas he even wangled the use of a motorbike himself, as if he actually were a dispatch rider; he could be seen sitting on empty petrol tins in scout- or fighter- or bomber-squadron hangars, in the material sheds of artillery or transport parks, at the back doors of field stations and hospitals and divisional chateaux, in kitchens and canteens and at the toy-sized zinc bars of village estaminets, as he had told the colonel, not talking but listening.

So he learned about the thirteen French soldiers almost at once—or rather, the thirteen men in French uniforms—who had been known for a year now among all combat troops below the grade of sergeant in the British forces and obviously in the French too, realising at the same moment that not only had he been the last man below sergeant in the whole Allied front to hear about them, but why: who five months ago had been an officer too, by the badges on his tunic also forever barred and interdict from the right and freedom to the simple passions and hopes and fears—sickness for home, worry about wives and allotment pay, the weak beer and the shilling a day which wont even buy enough of that; even the right to be afraid of death,—all that confederation of fellowship which enables man to support the weight of war; in fact, the surprise was that, having been an officer once, he had been permitted to learn about the thirteen men at all.

His informant was an A.S.C. private more than sixty years old, member of and lay preacher to a small nonconformist congregation in Southwark; he had been half porter and half confidential servant with an unblemished record to an Inns of

Court law firm, as his father had been before him and his son was to be after, except that at the Old Bailey assizes in the spring of 1914 the son would have been sent up for breaking and burglary, except that the presiding judge was not only a humanitarian but a member of the same philatelist society to which the head of the law firm belonged; whereupon the son was permitted to enlist instead the next day and in August went to Belgium and was reported missing at Mons all in the same three weeks and was accepted so by all save his father, who received leave of absence to enlist from the law firm for the single reason that his employers did not believe he could pass the doctors; eight months later the father was in France too; a year after that he was still trying to get, first, leave of absence; then, failing that, transfer to some unit near enough to Mons to look for his son although it had been a long time now since he had mentioned the son, as if he had forgot the reason and remembered only the destination, still a lay preacher, still half nightwatchman and half nurse, unimpeachable of record, to the succession of (to him) children who ran a vast ammunition dump behind St Omer, where one afternoon he told the runner about the thirteen French soldiers.

'Go and listen to them,' the old porter said. 'You can speak foreign; you can understand them.'

'I thought you said that the nine who should have spoken French, didn't, and that the other four couldn't speak anything at all.'

'They dont need to talk,' the old porter said. 'You dont need to understand. Just go and look at him.'

'Him?' the runner said. 'So it's just one now?'

'Wasn't it just one before?' the old porter said. 'Wasn't one enough then to tell us the same thing all them two thousand years ago: that all we ever needed to do was just to say, Enough of this;—us, not even the sergeants and corporals, but just us, all of us, Germans and Colonials and Frenchmen and all the other foreigners in the mud here, saying together: Enough. Let them that's already dead and maimed and missing be enough of this;—a thing so easy and simple that even human man, as full of evil and sin and folly as he is, can understand and believe it this time. Go and look at him.'

But he didn't see them, not yet. Not that he couldn't have

found them; at any time they would be in the British zone, against that khaki monotone that clump of thirteen men in horizon blue, even battle-stained, would have stood out like a cluster of hyacinths in a Scottish moat. He didn't even try yet. He didn't dare; he had been an officer himself, even though for only eight months, and even though he had repudiated it something ineradicable of it still remained, as the unfrocked priest or repentant murderer, even though unfrocked at heart and reformed at heart, carries forever about him like a catalyst the indelible effluvium of the old condition; it seemed to him that he durst not be present even on the fringe of whatever surrounding crowd, even to walk, pass through, let alone stop, within the same air of that small blue clump of hope; this, even while telling himself that he did not believe it, that it couldn't be true, possible, since if it were possible, it would not need to be hidden from Authority; that it would not matter whether Authority knew about it or not, since even ruthless and all-powerful and unchallengeable Authority would be impotent before that massed unresisting undemanding passivity. He thought: *They could execute only so many of us before they will have worn out the last rifle and pistol and expended the last live shell,* visualising it: first, the anonymous fringe of subalterns and junior clerks to which he had once belonged, relegated to the lathes and wheels to keep them in motion rifling barrels and filling shell-cases; then, the frenzy and the terror mounting, the next layer: the captains and majors and secretaries and attachés with their martial harness and ribbons and striped trousers and brief-cases among the oilcans and the flying shafts; then the field officers: colonels and senators and Members; then, last and ultimate, the ambassadors and ministers and lesser generals themselves frantic and inept among the slowing wheels and melting bearings, while the old men, the last handful of kings and presidents and field marshals and spoiled-beef and shoe-peg barons, their backs to the last crumbling rampart of their real, their credible, their believable world, wearied, spent, not with blood-glut at all but with the eye-strain of aiming and the muscle-tension of pointing and the finger-cramp of squeezing, fired the last puny scattered and markless fusillade as into the face of the sea itself. It's not that I dont believe it, he said. It's because it cant be true. We cant be saved now; even He doesn't want us anymore now.

So he believed that he was not even waiting: just watching. It was winter again now, the long unbroken line from Alps to sea lying almost quiescent in mud's foul menopause; this would be the time for them, with even front-line troops free for a little while to remember when they were warm and dry and clean; for him and the other twelve—(thinking, almost impatiently, *All right, all right, they are thirteen too*),—a soil not only unfallow now but already tumescent even, having a little space to think now, to remember and to dread, thinking (the runner) how it was not the dying but the indignity of the method: even the condemned murderer is better off, with an hour set and fixed far enough in the future to allow time to summon fortitude to face it well, and privacy to hide the lack in case the fortitude failed; not to receive both the sentence and its execution all in one unprepared flash, not even at rest but running, stumbling, laden with jangling iron like a pack-mule in the midst of death which can take him from any angle, front rear or above, panting, vermin-covered, stinking with his own reek, without even privacy in which to drop the dung and water he carried. He even knew what he was watching for: for the moment in the stagnancy when Authority would finally become aware of the clump of alien incongruous blue in its moat. Which would be at any time now; what he was watching was a race. Winter was almost over; they—the thirteen—had had time, but it was running out. It would be spring soon: the jocund bright time beginning to be mobile and dry underfoot; and even before that they in the Whitehalls and Quai d'Orsays and Unter den Somethings and Gargleplatzes would have thought of something anew, even if it had to be something which had already failed before. And suddenly he knew why it would not matter to Authority whether they knew about the thirteen men or not. They didn't need to, having not only authority but time too on their side; no need for them to hunt down and hoick out and execute a mere thirteen men: their very avocation was its own defender and emollient.

And it had run out. It was already spring; the Americans (1918 now) were in it now, rushing frantically across the

Atlantic ocean before it was too late and the scraps were all gone, and the break-through had come: the old stale Germanic tide washing again over the Somme and Picard towns which you might have thought had served their apprenticeship, washing along the Aisne a month later so that clerks in Paris bureaus were once more snapping the locks on the worn and homeless attaché-cases; May and even the Marne again, American troops counter-attacking this time among the ruined towns which you would think might have had absolution too. Except that he was not thinking now, he was too busy; for two weeks now he and his heretofore unfired rifle had been in an actual platoon, part of a rearguard, too busy remembering how to walk backward to think, using in place of the harassing ordeal of thought, a fragment out of the old time before he had become incapable of believing, out of Oxford probably (he could even see the page) though now it seemed much younger than that, too young to have endured this far at all:

lo, I have committed
fornication. But that was in another country; and
besides, the wench is dead

So when it finally happened, he had no warning. The wave had stopped, and he was a runner again; he had got back from Division Headquarters at dawn and two hours later he was asleep in the bunk of a man on a fatigue party, when an orderly summoned him to the office. 'You can drive a motorbike,' the colonel said.

He thought *You should know*. He said: 'Yes sir.'

'You're going to Corps Headquarters. They want couriers. A lorry will pick up you and the others at Division.'

He didn't even think *Other what?* He just thought *They have killed the serpent, and now they have got to get rid of the fragments,* and returned to Division Headquarters, where eight more runners from the other battalions and a lorry waited, the nine of them by that special transport to serve as special couriers out of Corps Headquarters which by ordinary bristled with couriers, not warned still, knowing no more yet, not even wondering, not even caring; fixed behind a faint wry grimace which was almost smiling in the midst of what was not ruin at all because he had known it of old too long, too long of old: *Yes* he thought *a bigger snake than even they had anticipated having to destroy and efface*. Nor did he learn anymore at Corps Headquarters, nor during the next two hours while at top speed now he delivered and exchanged and received dispatches from and to people whom even his travels had never touched before—not to orderly room N.C.O.'s but in person to majors and colonels and sometimes even generals, at transport and artillery parks, with columns of transport and artillery camouflaged beside roads and waiting for darkness to move, at batteries in position and Flying Corps wing offices and forward aerodromes—no longer even wondering now behind that fixed thin grimace which might have been smiling: who had not for nothing been a soldier in France for twenty-one months and an officer for five of them, and so knew what he was looking at when he saw it: the vast cumbrous machinery of war grinding to its clumsy halt in order to reverse itself to grind and rumble in a new direction,—the proprietorless wave of victory exhausted by its own ebb and returned by its own concomitant flux, spent not by its own faded momentum but as though bogged down in the refuse of its own success; afterward, it seemed to him that he had been speeding along those back-area roads for days before he realised what he had been travelling through; he would not even recall afterward at what moment, where, what anonymous voice from a passing lorry or another motorbike or perhaps in some orderly room where he lay one dispatch down in the act of taking up another, which said: 'The French quit this morning——' merely riding on, speeding on into the full burst of sun before he realised what he had heard.

It was an hour after noon before he finally found a face: that of a corporal standing before a cafe in a village street—a face which had been in the anteroom of the old battalion when he was an officer in it: and slowed the machine in and stopped, still straddling it; it was the first time.

'Nah,' the corporal said. 'It was just one regiment. Fact is, they're putting one of the biggest shoots yet in jerry's support and communications along the whole front right this minute. Been at it ever since dawn——'

'But one regiment quit,' the runner said. 'One did.' Now the corporal was not looking at him at all.

'Have a wet,' the corporal said.

'Besides,' the runner said gently, 'you're wrong. The whole French front quit at noon.'

'But not ours,' the corporal said.

'Not yet,' the runner said. 'That may take a little time.' The corporal was not looking at him. Now the corporal said nothing whatever. With a light, rapid gesture the runner touched one shoulder with the opposite hand. 'There's nothing up here now,' he said.

'Have a wet,' the corporal said, not looking at him.

And an hour later he was close enough to the lines to see the smoke-and-dust pall as well as hear the frantic uproar of the concentrated guns along the horizon; at three oclock, though twelve miles away at another point, he heard the barrage ravel away into the spaced orderly harmless-seeming poppings as of salutes or signals, and it seemed to him that he could see the whole long line from the sea-beaches up the long slant of France to old tired Europe's rooftree, squatted and crouched with filthy and noisome men who had forgot four years ago how to stand erect anymore, amazed and bewildered and unable to believe it either, forewarned and filled with hope though (he knew it now) they must have been; he thought, said aloud almost: *Yes, that's it. It's not that we didn't believe: it's that we couldn't, didn't know how anymore. That's the most terrible thing they have done to us. That's the most terrible.*

That was all, then. For almost twenty-four hours in fact, though he didn't know it then. A sergeant-major was waiting for them as they returned, gathered again at Corps Headquarters that night—the nine from his Division and perhaps two dozen others from other units in the Corps. 'Who's senior here?' the sergeant-major said. But he didn't even wait on himself: he glanced rapidly about at them again and with the unerring instinct of his vocation chose a man in the middle thirties who looked exactly like what he probably was—a demoted lance corporal out of a 1912 Northwest Frontier garrison. 'You're acting sergeant,' the sergeant-major said. 'You will indent for suppers and bedding here.' He looked at them again. 'I suppose it's no use to tell you not to talk.'

'Talk about what?' one said. 'What do we know to talk about.'

'Talk about that then,' the sergeant-major said. 'You are relieved until reveille. Carry on.' And that was all then. They slept on a stone floor in a corridor; they were given breakfast (a good one; this was a Corps Headquarters) before reveille went even; what bugles they—he, the runner—heard were at other Division and Corps Headquarters and parks and depots where the motorcycle took him during another day like yesterday in his minuscule walking-on (riding-on) part in bringing war to a pause, a halt, a stop; morning noon and afternoon up and down back areas not beneath a pall of peace but a thrall of dreamlike bustling for a holiday. The night again, the same sergeant-major was waiting for them—the nine from his Division and the two dozen others. 'That's all,' the sergeant-major said. 'Lorries are waiting to take you back in.' *That's all,* he thought. *All you have to do, all you need to do, all He ever asked and died for eighteen hundred and eighty-five years ago,* in the lorry now with his group of the thirty-odd others, the afterglow of sunset fading out of the sky like the tideless shoreless sea of despair itself ebbing away, leaving only the peaceful grief and the hope; when the lorry stopped and presently he leaned out to see what was wrong—a road which it was unable to cross because of transport on it, a road which he remembered as running southeast from up near Boulogne somewhere, now so dense with hooded and lightless lorries moving nose to tail like a line of elephants that their own lorry had to put them down here, to find their ways home as best they might, his companions dispersing, leaving him standing there in the last of afterglow while the vans crawled endless past him, until a head, a voice called his name from one of them, saying, 'Hurry, get up quick . . . . something to show you,' so that he had to run to overtake it and had already begun to swing himself up before he recognised it: the old watchman from the St Omer ammunition dump, who had come to France four years ago to search for his son and who had been the first to tell him about the thirteen French soldiers.

Three hours after midnight he was sitting on the firestep where the sentry leaned at the aperture while the spaced star-shells sniffed and plopped and whispered down the greasy dark and the remote gun winked and thudded and after a while winked and thudded again. He was talking in a voice which, whatever else it contained, it was not exhaustion—a voice dreamy and glib, apparently not only inattentive to itself but seemingly incapable of compelling attention anywhere. Yet each time he spoke, the sentry without even removing his face from the aperture would give a start, a motion convulsive and intolerable, like someone goaded almost beyond endurance.

'One regiment,' the runner said. 'One French regiment. Only a fool would look on war as a condition; it's too expensive. War is an episode, a crisis, a fever the purpose of which is to rid the body of fever. So the purpose of a war is to end the war. We've known that for six thousand years. The trouble was, it took us six thousand years to learn how to do it. For six thousand years we labored under the delusion that the only way to stop a war was to get together more regiments and battalions than the enemy could, or vice versa, and hurl them upon each other until one lot was destroyed and, the one having nothing left to fight with, the other could stop fighting. We were wrong, because yesterday morning, by simply declining to make an attack, one single French regiment stopped us all.'

This time the sentry didn't move, leaning—braced rather—against the trench-wall beneath the vicious rake of his motionless helmet, peering apparently almost idly through the aperture save for that rigidity about his back and shoulders—a kind of immobility on top of immobility—as though he were braced not against the dirt wall but rather against the quiet and empty air behind him. Nor had the runner moved either, though from his speech it was almost as if he had turned his face to look directly at the back of the sentry's head. 'What do you see?' he said. 'No novelty, you think?—the same stinking strip of ownerless valueless frantic dirt between our wire and theirs, which you have been peering at through a hole in a sandbag for four years now? the same war which we had come to believe did not know how to end itself, like the amateur orator searching desperately for a definitive preposition? You're wrong. You can go out there now, at least during the next fifteen minutes say, and not die probably. Yes, that may be the novelty: you can go out there now and stand erect and look about you—granted of course that any of us really ever can stand erect again. But we will learn how. Who knows? in four or five years we may even have got our neck-muscles supple enough simply to duck our heads again in place of merely bowing them to await the stroke, as we have been doing for four years now; in ten years, certainly.' The sentry didn't move, like a blind man suddenly within range of a threat, the first warning of which he must translate through some remaining secondary sense, already too late to fend with. 'Come,' the runner said. 'You're a man of the world. Indeed, you have been a man of this world since noon yesterday, even if they didn't bother to tell you so until fifteen oclock. In fact, we are all men of this world now, all of us who died on the fourth day of August four years ago——'

The sentry moved again with that convulsive start; he said in a harsh thick furious murmur: 'For the last time. I warned you.'

'—all the fear and the doubt, the agony and the grief and the lice Because it's over. Isn't it over?'

'Yes!' the sentry said.

'Of course it's over. You came out in . . . fifteen, wasn't it? You've seen a lot of war too. Of course you know when one is over.'

'It is over!' the sentry said. 'Didn't you hear the . . . .ing guns stop right out there in front of you?'

'Then why dont we go home?'

'Can they draw the whole . . . .ing line out at once? Leave the whole . . . .ing front empty at one time?'

'Why not?' the runner said. 'Isn't it over?' It was as if he had fixed the sentry as the matador does the bull, leaving the animal capable only of watching him. 'Over. Finished. Done. No more parades. Tomorrow we shall go home; by this time tomorrow night we shall have hoicked from the beds of our wives and sweethearts the manufacturers of walking-out shoe-pegs and Enfield primers——' He thought rapidly *He's going to kick me*. He said, 'All right. Sorry. I didn't know you had a wife.'

'No more I have,' the sentry said in his shaking whisper. 'So will you stow it now? Will you for bleeding Christ?'

'Of course you haven't. How wise you are. A girl in a High Street pub, of course. Or perhaps a city girl—a Greater City girl, Houndsditch or Bermondsey, towarding forty but not looking within five years of it, and's had her troubles too—who hasn't?—but suppose she does, who wouldn't choose her and lucky, who can appreciate a man, to one of these young tarts swapping cove for cove with each leave train——'

The sentry began to curse, in the same harsh spent furious monotone, cursing the runner with obscene and dull unimagination out of the stalls and tack-rooms and all the other hinder purlieus of what must have been his old vocation, until at the same moment the runner sat quickly and lightly up and the sentry began to turn back to the aperture in a series of jerks like a mechanical toy running down, murmuring again in his shaking furious voice: 'Remember. I told you' as two men came around the traverse and up the trench in single file, indistinguishable in their privates' uniforms save for the officer's stick and the sergeant's chevrons.

'Post?' the officer said.

'Two-nine,' the sentry said. The officer had lifted his foot to the firestep when he saw, seemed to see, the runner.

'Who's that?' he said. The runner began to stand up, promptly enough but without haste. The sergeant pronounced his name.

'He was in that special draft of runners Corps drew out yesterday morning. They were dismissed to dugouts as soon as they reported back tonight, and told to stop there. This man was, anyway.'

'Oh,' the officer said. That was when the sergeant pronounced the name. 'Why aren't you there?'

'Yes sir,' the runner said, picking up the rifle and turning quite smartly, moving back down the trench until he had vanished beyond the traverse. The officer completed his stride onto the firestep; now both the helmets slanted motionless and twinlike between the sandbags while the two of them peered through the aperture. Then the sentry said, murmured so quietly that it seemed impossible that the sergeant six feet away could have heard him:

'Nothing more's come up I suppose, sir?' For another half minute the officer peered through the aperture. Then he turned and stepped down to the duckboards, the sentry turning with him, the sergeant moving again into file behind him, the officer himself already beginning to move when he spoke:

'When you are relieved, go down your dugout and stay there.' Then they were gone. The sentry began to turn back toward the aperture. Then he stopped. The runner was now standing on the duckboards below him; while they looked at one another the star-shell sniffed and traced its sneering arc and plopped into parachute, the faint glare washing over the runner's lifted face and then, even after the light itself had died, seeming to linger still on it as if the glow had not been refraction at all but water or perhaps grease; he spoke in a tense furious murmur not much louder than a whisper:

'Do you see now? Not for us to ask what nor why but just go down a hole in the ground and stay there until they decide what to do. No: just how to do it because they already know what. Of course they wont tell us. They wouldn't have told us anything at all if they hadn't had to, hadn't had to tell us something, tell the rest of you something before the ones of us who were drawn out yesterday for special couriers out of Corps would get back in tonight and tell you what we had heard. And even then, they told you just enough to keep you in the proper frame of mind so that, when they said Go down the dugouts and stay there you would do it. And even I wouldn't have known any more in time if on the way back in tonight I hadn't blundered onto that lorry train.

'No: that's wrong too; just known in time that they are already up to something. Because all of us know by now that something is wrong. Dont you see? something happened down there yesterday morning in the French front, a regiment failed—burked—mutinied, we dont know what and are not going to know what because they aren't going to tell us. Besides, it doesn't matter what happened. What matters is, what happened afterward. At dawn yesterday a French regiment did something—did or failed to do something which a regiment in a front line is not supposed to do or fail to do, and as a result of it, the entire war in western Europe took a recess at three oclock yesterday afternoon. Dont you see? When you are in battle and one of your units fails, the last thing you do, dare do, is quit. Instead, you snatch up everything else you've got and fling it in as quick and hard as you can, because you know that that's exactly what the enemy is going to do as soon as he discovers or even suspects you have trouble on your side. Of course you're going to be one unit short of him when you meet; your hope, your only hope, is that if you can only start first and be going the fastest, momentum and surprise might make up a little of it.

'But they didn't. Instead, they took a recess, remanded, the French at noon, us and the Americans three hours later. And not only us, but jerry too. Dont you see? How can you remand in war, unless your enemy agrees too? And why should jerry have agreed, after squatting under the sort of barrage which four years had trained him to know meant that an attack was coming, then no attack came or failed or whatever it was it did, and four years had certainly trained him to the right assumption for that; when the message, signal, request—whatever it was—came over suggesting a remand, why should he have agreed to it, unless he had a reason as good as the one we had, maybe the same reason we had? The same reason; those thirteen French soldiers apparently had no difficulty whatever going anywhere they liked in our back-areas for three years, why weren't they across yonder in jerry's too, since we all know that, unless you've got the right properly signed paper in your hand, it's a good deal more difficult to go to Paris from here than to Berlin; any time you want to go east from here, all you need is a British or French or American uniform. Or perhaps they didn't even need to go themselves, perhaps just wind, moving air, carried it. Or perhaps not even moving air but just air, spreading by attrition from invisible and weightless molecule to molecule as disease, smallpox spreads, or fear, or hope—just enough of us, all of us in the mud here saying together, Enough of this, let's have done with this.

'Because dont you see? they cant have this. They cant permit this, to stop it at all yet, let alone allow it to stop itself this way—the two shells in the river and the race already underway and both crews without warning simply unshipping the oars from the locks and saying in unison: We're not going to pull anymore. They cant yet. It's not finished yet, like an unfinished cricket or rugger match which started according to a set of mutually accepted rules formally and peaceably agreed on, and must finish by them, else the whole theory of arbitration, the whole tried and proven step-by-step edifice of politics and economy on which the civilised concord of nations is based, becomes so much wind. More than that: that thin and tensioned girder of steel and human blood which carries its national edifice soaring glorious and threatful among the stars, in dedication to which young men are transported free of charge and even with pay, to die violently in places that even the map-makers and -dividers never saw, that a pilgrim stumbling on it a hundred or a thousand years afterward may still be able to say Here is a spot that is (anyway was once) forever England or France or America. And not only cant, dare not: they wont. They have already started not to. Because listen. On the way back up tonight, I got a lift in a lorry. It was carrying AA shells. It was in a column almost three miles long, all chock full of AA shells. Think of it: three miles of AA shells; think of having enough shells to measure it in miles, which apparently they did not have in front of Amiens two months ago. But then, naturally it takes more ammunition to recess a war for ten minutes than to stop a mere offensive. The lorry was in charge of an old man I knew who had been waiting for three years at an ammo dump at St Omer for his application to go through for leave and permission to go to Mons and search for his son who hadn't or didn't or couldn't or didn't want to—anyway, failed to—come back that afternoon four years ago. He showed me one of the shells. It was blank. Not dud: blank, complete and intact except that there was no shrapnel in it; it would fire and even burst, harmless. It looked all right on the outside; I doubt if its father in his West End club (or Birmingham or Leeds or Manchester or wherever people live who make shells) would have known the difference, and only a dyed-in-the-wool archie bloke could. It was amazing, really; they must have worked like beaver all last night and today too there at the dump, altering, gelding three miles of shells—or maybe they had them all ready beforehand, in advance; maybe after four years, even Anglo-Saxons can learn to calculate ahead in war——' talking, the voice not dreamy now: just glib and rapid, he (the runner) in the moving lorry now, the three of them, himself, the old man and the driver, crowded into the close and lightless cab so that he could feel the whole frail length of the old man's body tense and exultant against him, remembering how at first his voice had sounded as cracked and amazed as the old man's, but soon no more: the two voices running along side by side as logical in unreason, rational and inconsequent as those of two children:

'Perhaps you'd better tell me again. Maybe I have forgot.'

'For the signal!' the old man cried. 'The announcement! To let the whole world know that He has risen!'

'A signal of AA shells? Three miles of AA shells? Wouldn't one gun be enough to herald Him? And if one gun, why hold His resurrection up long enough to run three miles of shells through it? Or if one shell to each gun, why only three miles of guns? Why not enough for every gun between Switzerland and the Channel? Aren't the rest of us to be notified too? To welcome Him too? Why not just bugles, horns? He would recognise horns; they wouldn't frighten Him.'

'Dont the Book itself say he will return in thunder and lightning?'

'But not gunpowder,' the runner said.

'Then let man make the noise!' the cracked voice cried. 'Let man shout hallelujah and jubilee with the very things he has been killing with!'—rational and fantastic, like children, and as cruel too:

'And fetch your son along with Him?' the runner said.

'My son?' the old man said. 'My son is dead.'

'Yes,' the runner said. 'That's what I meant. Isn't that what you mean too?'

'Pah,' the old man said; it sounded almost like spitting. 'What does it matter, whether or not He brings my son back with Him? my son, or yours, or any other man's? *My* son? Even the whole million of them we have lost since that day four years ago, the billion since that day eighteen hundred and eighty-five years ago. The ones He will restore to life are the ones that would have died since eight oclock this morning

My son? *My* son?'—then (the runner) out of the lorry again (The column had stopped. It was near the lines, just under them in fact, or what had been the front line until three oclock this afternoon; the runner knew that at once, although he had never been here before. But he had not only been an infantryman going in and out of them for twenty-odd months, for seven months he had been a runner going in and out of them every night, so he had no more doubt of where he was than would the old wolf or lynx when he was near a trap-line.), walking up the column toward the halted head of it, and stopped in shadow and watched M.P.'s and armed sentries splitting the column into sections with a guide for each leading lorry, each section as it was detached turning from the road into the fields and woods beyond which lay the front; and not long to watch this either, because almost at once a corporal with his bayonet fixed came quickly around the lorry in whose shadow he stood.

'Get back to your lorry,' the corporal ordered.

He identified himself, naming his battalion and its vector.

'What the bleeding . . . . are you doing down here?' the corporal said.

'Trying to get a lift.'

'Not here,' the corporal said. 'Hop it. Sharp, now'—and (the corporal) still watching him until darkness hid him again; then he too left the road, into a wood, walking toward the lines now; and (telling it, sprawled on the firestep beneath the rigid and furious sentry almost as though he drowsed, his eyes half-closed, talking in the glib, dreamy, inconsequent voice) how from the shadows again he watched the crew of an anti-aircraft battery, with hooded torches, unload the blank shells from one of the lorries, and tumble their own live ammunition back into it, and went on until he saw the hooded lights again and watched the next lorry make its exchange; and at midnight was in another wood—or what had been a wood, since all that remained now was a nightingale somewhere behind him—, not walking now but standing with his back against the blasted corpse of a tree, hearing still above the bird's idiot reiteration the lorries creeping secretly and steadily through the darkness, not listening to them, just hearing them, because he was searching for something which he had lost, mislaid, for the moment, though when he thought that he had put the digit of his recollection on it at last, it was wrong, flowing rapid and smooth through his mind, but wrong: *In Christ is death at end in Adam that began:*—true, but the wrong one: not the wrong truth but the wrong moment for it, the wrong one needed and desired; clearing his mind again and making the attempt again, yet there it was again: *In Christ is death at end in Adam that*—— still true, still wrong, still comfortless; and then, before he had thought his mind was clear again, the right one was there, smooth and intact and instantaneous, seeming to have been there for a whole minute while he was still fretting its loss:

> —but that was in another country;—and besides
> the wench is dead

And this time the flare went up from their own trench, not twenty yards away beyond the up traverse, so near this time that after the green corpse-glare died the sentry could have discerned that what washed over the runner's face was neither the refraction assumed nor the grease it resembled, but the water it was: 'A solid corridor of harmless archie batteries, beginning at our parapet and exactly the width of the range at which a battery in either wall would decide there wasn't any use in even firing at an aeroplane flying straight down the middle of it, running back to the aerodrome at Villeneuve Blanche, so that to anyone not a general it would look all right—and if there was just enough hurry and surprise about it, maybe even to the men themselves carrying the shells running to the guns ramming them home and slamming the blocks and pulling the lanyards and blistering their hands snatching the hot cases out fast enough to get out of the way of the next one, let alone the ones in front lines trying to cringe back out of man's sight in case the aeroplane flying down the corridor to Villeneuve wasn't carrying ammunition loaded last night at whatever the Hun calls his Saint Omer, it would still look and sound all right, even if the Hun continued not falling all the way back to Villeneuve because Flying Corps people say archie never hits anything anyway——

'So you see what we must do, before that German emissary

or whatever he will be, can reach Paris or Chaulnesmont or wherever he is to go, and he and whoever he is to agree with, have agreed, not on what to do because that is no problem: only on how, and goes back home to report it. We dont even need to start it; the French, that one French regiment, has already taken up the load. All we need is, not to let it drop, falter, pause for even a second. We must do it now, tomorrow—tomorrow? it's already tomorrow; it's already today now—do as that French regiment did, the whole battalion of us: climb over this parapet tomorrow morning and get through the wire, with no rifles, nothing, and walk toward jerry's wire until he can see us, enough of him can see us—a regiment of him or a battalion or maybe just a company or maybe even just one because even just one will be enough. You can do it. You own the whole battalion, every man in it under corporal, beneficiary of every man's insurance in it who hasn't got a wife and I.O.U.'s for their next month's pay of all the rest of them in that belt around your waist. All you'll need is just to tell them to when you say Follow me; I'll go along to the first ones as soon as you are relieved, so they can see you vouch for me. Then others will see you vouch for me when I vouch for them, so that by daylight or by sunup anyway, when jerry can see us, all the rest of Europe can see us, will have to see us, cant help but see us——' He thought: *He's really going to kick me this time, and in the face.* Then the sentry's boot struck the side of his jaw, snapping his head back even before his body toppled, the thin flow of water which sheathed his face flying at the blow like a thin spray of spittle or perhaps of dew or rain from a snapped leaf, the sentry kicking at him again as he went over backward onto the firestep, and was still stamping his boot at the unconscious face when the officer and the sergeant ran back around the traverse, still stamping at the prone face and panting at it:

'Will you for Christ's sake now? Will you? Will you?' when the sergeant jerked him bodily down to the duck-boards. The sentry didn't even pause, whirling while the sergeant held him, and slashing his reversed rifle blindly across the nearest face. It was the officer's, but the sentry didn't even wait to see, whirling again back toward the firestep though the sergeant still gripped him in one arm around his middle, still—the sentry—striking with the rifle-butt at the runner's bleeding head when the sergeant fumbled his pistol out with his free hand and thumbed the safety off.

'As you were,' the officer said, jerking the blood from his mouth, onto his wrist and flinging it away. 'Hold him.' He spoke without turning his head, toward the corner of the down traverse, raising his voice a little: 'Two-eight. Pass the word for corporal.'

The sentry was actually foaming now, apparently not even conscious that the sergeant was holding him, still jabbing the rifle-butt at or at least toward the runner's peaceful and bloody head, until the sergeant spoke almost against his ear.

'Two-seven . . . . for corporal,' a voice beyond the down traverse said; then fainter, beyond that, another:

'Two-six . . . . . corporal.'

'Use yer boot,' the sergeant muttered. 'Kick his . . . .ing teeth in.'

Monday
Tuesday
Wednesday

He had already turned back toward the aerodrome when he saw the Harry Tate. At first he just watched it, merely alerting himself to overshoot it safely; they looked so big and were travelling so slowly that you always made the mistake of overestimating them if you were not careful. Then he saw that the thing obviously not only hoped but actually believed that it could cut him off—a Harry Tate, which usually had two Australians in it or one general-and-pilot, this one indubitably a general since only by some esoteric factor like extreme and even overwhelming rank could an R.E.8 even hope to catch an S.E. and send it to earth.

Which was obviously what this one intended to do, he throttling back now until the S.E. was hanging on its airscrew just above stalling. And it was a general: the two aeroplanes broadside on for a second or so, a hand in a neat walking-out glove from the observer's seat gesturing him peremptorily downward until he waggled his wings in acknowledgment and put his nose down for home, thinking, *Why me? What've I done now? Besides, how did they know where I was?*——having suddenly a sort of vision of the whole sky full of lumbering R.E.8's, each containing a general with a list compiled by frantic telephone of every absent unaccounted-for scout on the whole front, hunting them down one by one out of back-areas and harrying them to earth.

Then he reached the aerodrome and saw the ground signal-strip laid out on it; he hadn't seen one since ground school and for a goodish while he didn't even know what it was; not until he saw the other aeroplanes on the ground or landing or coming in to land, did he recognise it to be the peremptory emergency signal to all aircraft to come down, landing in his turn faster and harder than people liked to land S.E.'s because of their unhappy ground habits, taxi-ing in to the tarmac where, even before he could switch off, the mechanic was shouting at him: 'The mess, sir! Right away! The major wants you at the mess right away!'

'What?' he said. 'Me?'

'Everyone, sir,' the mechanic said. 'The whole squadron, sir. Best hurry.'

He jumped down to the tarmac, already running, so young in breathing that he wouldn't be nineteen for another year yet and so young in war that, although the Royal Air Force was only six weeks old, his was not the universal tunic with RFC badges superposed on the remnants of old regimental insigne which veteran transfers wore, and he didn't even own the old official Flying Corps tunic at all: his was the new RAF thing not only unmartial but even a little epicene, with its cloth belt and no shoulder-straps like the coat of the adult leader of a neo-Christian boys' club and the narrow pale blue ring around each cuff and the hat-badge like a field marshal's until you saw, remarked, noticed the little modest dull gold pin on either side of it like lingerie-clips or say the christening's gift-choice by god-fathers whose good taste had had to match their pocketbooks.

A year ago he was still in school, waiting not for his eighteenth birthday and legal age for joining up, but for his seventeenth one and the expiration, discharge, of a promise to his widowed mother (he was the only child) to stick it out until then. Which he did, even making good marks, even while his mind, his whole being, was sleepless and athirst with the ringing heroic catalogue: Ball: McCudden: Mannock: Bishop: Barker: Rhys Davies: and above all, simply: England. Three weeks ago he was still in England, waiting in Pilot's Pool for posting to the front—a certificated stationary engine scout pilot to whom the King had inscribed *We*

Reposing Trust and Confidence in Our Trusty and Well-Beloved Gerald David . . . but already too late, gazetted not into the RFC but into the RAF. Because the RFC had ceased to exist on April Fool's day, two days before his commission came through: whereupon that March midnight had seemed to him a knell. A door had closed on glory; immortality itself had died in unprimered anti-climax: not his to be the old commission in the old glorious corps, the brotherhood of heroes to which he had dedicated himself even at the cost of that wrench to his mother's heart; not his the old commission which Albert Ball had carried with him into immortality and which Bishop and Mannock and McCudden still bore in their matchless records; his only the new thing not flesh nor fowl nor good red herring: who had waited one whole year acquiescent to his mother's unrational frantic heart fiercely and irrevocably immune to glory, and then another year in training, working like a beaver, like the very proverbial Trojan, to compensate for his own inability to say no to a woman's tears.

It was too late; those who had invented for him the lingerie pins and the official slacks in place of pink Bedfords and long boots and ordnance belt, had closed the door even to the anteroom of heroes. In Valhalla's un-national halls the un-national shades, Frenchman and German and Briton, conqueror and conquered alike—Immelman and Guynemer, Boelcke and Ball—identical not in the vast freemasonry of death but in the closed select one of flying, would clash their bottomless mugs, but not for him. Their inheritors—Bishop and Mannock and Voss and McCudden and Fonck and Barker and Richthofen and Nungesser—would still cleave the earth-foundationed air, pacing their fleeing shadows on the scudding canyon-walls of cumulae, furloughed and immune, secure in immortality even while they still breathed, but it would not be his. Glory and valor would still exist of course as long as men lived to reap them. It would even be the same valor in fact, but the glory would be another glory. And that would be his: some second form of Elysium, a cut above dead infantry perhaps, but little more: who was not the first to think *What had I done for motherland's glory had motherland but matched me with her need.*

And now apparently even what remained was to be denied him: three weeks spent in practice, mostly gunnery (he was quite good at it, astonishing even himself), at the aerodrome; one carefully chaperoned trip—the major, Bridesman, his flight commander, himself and one other new and unblooded tyro—up to the lines to show them what they looked like and how to find the way back; and yesterday he was in his hut after lunch trying to compose a letter to his mother when Bridesman thrust his head in and gave him the official notice which he had been waiting for now ever since his seventeenth birthday: 'Levine. Jobs tomorrow. Eleven oclock. Before we take off, I'll try again to remind you to try to remember what we have been trying to tell you to remember.' Then this morning he had gone up for what would be the last of his unchallenged airy privacy, the farewell to his apprenticeship, what might be called the valedictory of his maidenhood, when the general in the Harry Tate sent him back to earth, to spring down almost before the aeroplane stopped rolling and, spurred again by the mechanic, run to the mess, already the last one since everyone else was there except the flight which was still out, finding the major already talking, one knee crooked easily across the corner of the table; he (the major) had just got back from Wing Headquarters, where he had met the general commanding, who had come straight from Poperinghe: the French had asked for an armistice; it would go into effect at noon—twelve hours. But it meant nothing: they (the squadron) were to remember that; the British hadn't asked for any armistice, nor the Americans either; and having known the French, fought beside them for almost four years now, he (the major) didn't yet believe it meant anything with them. However, there would be a truce, a remand, for an hour or two hours or perhaps a whole day. But it was a French truce; it wasn't ours—looking about at them, nonchalant and calm and even negligent, speaking in that same casual negligent voice and manner with which he could carry the whole squadron through a binge night, through exuberance and pandemonium and then, with none realising it until afterward, back into sufficient sobriety to cope with the morrow's work, which was not the least of the reasons why, even though no hun-getter, he was one of the most popular and capable squadron commanders in France, though he (the child) had not been there long enough to know that. But he did know that here was the true authentic voice of that invincible island which, with not merely the eighteen years he had but the rest of his promised span which he might very likely lose doing it, he would in joy and pride defend and in gratitude preserve: 'Because we aren't quitting. Not us nor the Americans either. It's not over. Nobody declared it for us; nobody but us shall make our peace. Flights will stand by as usual. Carry on.'

He didn't think *Why* yet. He just thought *What*. He had never heard of a recess in war. But then, he knew so little about war; he realised now that he knew nothing about war. He would ask Bridesman, glancing about the room where they were already beginning to disperse, and in the first moment realising that Bridesman was not there, and in the next one that none of the flight commanders were there: not only Bridesman, but Witt and Sibleigh too, which in Witt's case obviously meant that he still had C Flight out on the mid-morning job, and which—the fact that C Flight was still carrying on with the war—ratified the major's words; C Flight hadn't quit, and if he knew Bridesman (and after three weeks he certainly should) B hadn't either, glancing at his watch now: half after ten, thirty minutes yet before B would go up; he would have time to finish the letter to his mother which Bridesman had interrupted yesterday; he could even—since the war would officially begin for him in thirty minutes—write the other one, the succinct and restrained and modestly heroic one to be found among his gear afterward by whoever went through it and decided what should be sent back to his mother: thinking how the patrol went up at eleven and the remand would begin at twelve, which would leave him an hour—no, it would take them ten minutes to get to the lines, which would leave fifty minutes; if fifty minutes was long enough for him to at least make a start after Bishop's and McCudden's and Mannock's records, it would be long enough for him to get shot down in too: already moving toward the door when he heard engines: a flight: taking off: then running up to the hangars, where he learned that it was not even B Flight, shouting at the sergeant, incredulous and amazed:

'Do you mean that all three flight commanders and all the deputies have gone out in one patrol?' and then heard the guns begin, not like any heavy firing he had ever heard before, but furious and simultaneous and vast in extent—a sound already in existence to the south-east before audibility began and still in existence to the north-west when audibility ceased. 'They're coming over!' he shouted. 'The French have betrayed us! They just got out of the way and let them through!'

'Yes sir,' the flight sergeant said. 'Hadn't you better get along to the office? They may be wanting you.'

'Right,' he said, already running, back up the vacant aerodrome beneath the sky furious with the distant guns, into the office which was worse than empty: the corporal not only sitting as always behind the telephone, but looking at him across the dogeared copy of *Punch* which he had been looking at when he first saw him three weeks ago. 'Where's the major?' he cried.

'Down at Wing, sir,' the corporal said.

'Down at Wing?' he cried, incredulous, already running again: through the opposite door, into the mess, and saw everyone of the squadron's new replacements like himself except himself, all sitting quietly about as though the adjutant had not merely arrested them but was sitting guard over them, and the adjutant himself sitting at the end of the mess table with his pipe and wound stripe and observer's O and single wing above the Mons Star ribbon, and the squadron chessboard and the folded sheet of last Sunday's *Times* chess problem laid out before him; and he (the child) shouting, 'Cant you hear them? Cant you?' so that he couldn't hear the adjutant at all for his own noise, until the adjutant began to shout too:

'Where have you been?'

'Hangars,' he said. 'I was to go on the patrol.'

'Didn't anyone tell you to report to me here?'

'Report?' he said. 'Flight Sergeant Conventicle—— No,' he said.

'You're——'

'Levine.'

'Levine. You've been here three weeks. Not long enough to have learned that this squadron is run by people especially appointed and even qualified for it. In fact, when they gave you those badges, they gave you a book of rules to go with them, to prevent you needing ever to rack your brains like this. Perhaps you haven't yet had time to glance through it.'

'Yes,' he said. 'What do you want with me?'

'To sit down somewhere and be quiet. As far as this squadron is concerned, the war stopped at noon. There'll be no more flying here until further notice. As for those guns, they began at twelve hours. The major knew that beforehand. They will stop at fifteen hours. Now you know that in advance too——'

'Stop?' he said. 'Dont you see——'

'Sit down!' the adjutant said.

'—if we stop now, we are beat, have lost——'

'Sit down!'

He stopped then. Then he said: 'Am I under arrest?'

'Do you want to be?'

'Right,' he said. He sat down. It was twenty-two minutes past twelve hours; now it was not the Nissen walls which trembled, but the air they contained. Presently, or in time that is, it was thirteen hours, then fourteen, all that distant outside fury reduced now to a moiling diastole of motes where the sun slanted into the western windows; getting on for fifteen hours now and the squadron itself reduced to a handful of tyros who barely knew in which direction the front lay, under command of a man who had never been anything but a poor bloody observer to begin with and had even given that up now for a chessboard: they still sat there: he, and the other new men who had—must have—brought out from England with them the same gratitude and pride and thirst and hope—— Then he was on his feet, hearing the silence still falling like a millstone into a well; then they were all moving as one, through the door and outside into that topless gape from which the walls and roof of distant gunfire had been ripped, snatched, as a cyclone rips the walls and roof from the rectangle of vacancy which a moment ago had been a hangar, leaving audibility with nothing now to lean against, outbursting into vacuum as the eardrums crack with altitude, until at last even that shocking crash died away.

'That seems to be it,' a voice said behind him.

'Seems to be what?' he said. 'It's not over! Didn't you hear what the major said? The Americans aren't quitting either! Do you think Monaghan' (Monaghan was an American, in B Flight too; although he had been out only ten weeks, he already had a score of three and a fraction) 'is quitting? And even if they do——' and stopped, finding them all watching him, soberly and quietly, as if he were a flight commander himself; one said:

'What do you think, Levine?'

'Me?' he said. 'About what?' *Ask Collyer,* he thought. *He's running the nursery now;* bitterly too now: *Ask Collyer*——the pipe, the balding head, the plump bland face which at this moment was England's sole regent over this whole square half-mile of French dirt, custodian of her honor and pride, who three years ago had probably brought out to France (he, Collyer, according to squadron folklore, had been ridden down by a Uhlan with a lance inside the war's first weeks and turned flying observer and came out again and within a week of that managed somehow to live through a F.E. crash after his pilot was dead and since then, carrying the same single pip and—the legend said—the same cold pipe, had been a squadron adjutant) the same feeling, belief, hunger—whatever you want to call it—as intolerant and unappeasable as his own, and then lost it or put it aside as he had put the war itself forever away, secure and immune in his ground job where no thirst for victory nor tumescence of valor could trouble him more; thinking, *Oh yes, ask Collyer,* finishing the thought which the cessation of the guns had interrupted inside the mess: *He has quit too. He gave up so long ago that he doesn't even remember now that he hasn't even lost anything.—I heard the death of England* he said quietly to himself, then aloud: 'Think about what? That noise? Nothing. That's what it sounds like, doesn't it?'

At five oclock the major was delivered almost onto the office stoop by the general commanding the brigade's Harry Tate. Just before sunset two lorries drove onto the aerodrome; watching from his hut he saw infantry with rifles and tin hats get down and parade for a moment on the dusty grass behind the office and then disperse in squads and at sunset the patrol of flight commanders and deputies which had gone out at noon in the similitude of B Flight had not returned, three times longer than any patrol ever stayed out or than any S.E. could stay up on its petrol. And he dined with a mess (the major was not present though a few of the older men—including the infantry officer—were; he didn't know where they had been nor when returned) half of whom he knew knew nothing either and the other half he didn't know how much they knew or cared;—a meal which was not long before the adjutant got up and stopped just long enough to say, not speaking to the older people at all: 'You aren't confined to quarters. Just put it that almost any place you can think of is out of bounds.'

'Even the village?' someone said.

'Even Villeneuve Blanche, sink of iniquity though it be not. You might all go home with Levine and curl up with his book. That's where he should be.' Then he stopped again. 'That means the hangars too.'

'Why should we go to the hangars this time of night?' one said.

'I dont know,' the adjutant said. 'Dont.' Then the others dispersed but not he, he was still sitting there after the orderlies had cleared the mess for the night and still there when the motor car came up, not stopping at the mess but going on around to the office and through the thin partition he heard people enter the office and then the voices: the major and Bridesman and the other two flight commanders and no S.E. had landed on this aerodrome after dark even if he hadn't heard the car but then that was all right, aeroplanes were not even new replacements, they were not only insentient and so couldn't ask questions and talk back, you could even jettison them where they wouldn't even need to be watched by infantry and he couldn't have heard what the voices were saying even if he had tried, just sitting there when the voices stopped short and a second later the door opened and the adjutant paused an instant then came on, pulling the door after him, saying: 'Get along to your hut.'

'Right,' he said, rising. But the adjutant came on into the

mess, shutting the door behind him; his voice was really kind now:

'Why dont you let it alone?'

'I am,' he said. 'I dont know how to do anything else because I dont know how it can be over if it's not over nor how it can be not over if it's over——'

'Go to your hut,' the adjutant said. He went out into the darkness, the silence, walking on in the direction of the huts as long as anyone from the mess might still see him, then giving himself another twenty steps for good measure before he turned away toward the hangars, thinking how his trouble was probably very simple, really: he simply had never heard silence before; he had been thirteen, almost fourteen, when the guns began, but perhaps even at fourteen you still could not bear silence: you denied it at once and immediately began to try to do something about it as children of six or ten do: as a last resort, when even noise failed, fleeing into closets, cupboards, corners under beds or pianos, lacking any other closeness and darkness in which to escape it; walking around the corner of the hangar as the challenge came, and saw the crack of light under the hangar doors which were not only closed but padlocked—a thing never before seen by him or anyone else in this or any squadron, himself standing quite still now with the point of the bayonet about six inches from his stomach.

'All right,' he said. 'What do I do now?'

But the man didn't even answer. 'Corporal of the guard!' he shouted. 'Post Number Four!' Then the corporal appeared.

'Second Lieutenant Levine,' he said. 'My aeroplane's in this hangar——'

'Not if you're General Haig and your sword's in there,' the corporal said.

'Right,' he said, and turned. And for a moment he even thought of Conventicle, the Flight Sergeant; he had been a soldier long enough by now to have learned that there were few, if any, military situations which the simple cry of 'Sergeant!' would not resolve. It was mainly this of course, yet there was a little of something else too: the rapport, not between himself and Conventicle perhaps, but between their two races—the middle-aged bog-complected man out of that race, all of whom he had ever known were named Evans or Morgan except the two or three named Deuteronomy or Tabernacle or Conventicle out of the Old Testament—that morose and musical people who knew dark things by simply breathing, who seemed to be born without dread or concern into knowledge of and rapport with man's sunless and subterrene origins which had better never have seen light at all, whose own misty and music-ed names no other men could pronounce even, so that when they emerged from their fens and fastnesses into the rational world where men still tried to forget their sombre beginnings, they permitted themselves to be designated by the jealous and awesome nouns out of the old fierce Hebraic annals in which they as no other people seemed at home, as Napoleon in Austria had had his (the child's) people with their unpronounceable names fetched before him and said 'Your name is Wolf' or 'Hoff' or 'Fox' or 'Berg' or 'Schneider', according to what they looked like or where they lived or what they did. But he considered this only a moment. There was only one sure source, knowing now that even this one would not be too certain. But nothing else remained: Bridesman's and Cowrie's hut (That was one of the dangled prerequisites for being brave enough to get to be a captain: half a hut to yourself. The major had a whole one.), Cowrie looking at him from the pillow as Bridesman sat up in the other cot and lit the candle and told him.

'Certainly it's not over. It's so far from over that you're going on jobs tomorrow. Does that satisfy you?'

'All right,' he said. 'But what happened? What is it? An armed sentry stopped me at the hangars thirty minutes ago and turned out the guard and the hangar doors were locked and a light inside and I could hear people doing something, only I couldn't pass the bayonet and when they drove me away I heard a lorry and saw a torch moving about down at that archie battery this side the village and of course that's fresh ammo being hurried up since archie quit at noon today too and naturally they'll need a lot of ammo to quit with too——'

'If I tell you, will you let be and go to your hut and go to bed?'

'Right,' he said. 'That's all I ever wanted: just to know. If they've beat us, I want to stand my share too——'

'Beat us be blowed. There's nobody in this war any longer capable of beating anyone, unless the Americans might in time——'

'And welcome,' Cowrie said. But Bridesman was still talking:

'A French regiment mutinied this morning—refused to go over. When they—the French—began to poke about to learn why, it seems that—— But it's all right.'

'How all right?'

'It was only their infantry disaffected. Only troops holding the line. But the other regiments didn't do anything. The others all seemed to know in advance that the one was going to refuse, but all the others did seem to be just waiting about to see what was going to happen to it. But they—the French—took no chances. They pulled the regiment out and replaced it and moved up guns and put down a heavy barrage all along their front, just like we did this afternoon. To give ourselves time to see what was what. That's all.'

'How that's all?' he said. Cowrie had put a cigarette into his mouth and, raised onto one elbow, was reaching for the candle when the hand stopped, less than a fraction of a second before it moved on. 'What was the hun doing all this time?' He said quietly: 'So it's over.'

'It's not over,' Bridesman said harshly. 'Didn't you just hear what the major said at noon today?'

'Oh yes,' he said serenely. 'It's over. All the poor bloody stinking infantry everywhere, Frenchmen, Americans, Germans, us . . . So that's what they're hiding.'

'Hiding?' Bridesman said. 'Hiding what? There's nothing to hide. It's not over, I tell you. Didn't you just hear me say we have a job tomorrow?'

'All right,' he said. 'It's not over. How can it be not over then?'

'Because it isn't. What do you think we put down that barrage for today—we and the French and the Americans too—the whole front from the Channel in—blasting away a half year's supply of ammo for except to keep the hun off until we can know what to do?'

'Know to do what? What are they doing in our hangar tonight?'

'Nothing!' Bridesman said.

'What are they doing in B Flight's hangar, Bridesman?' he said. The cigarette pack lay on the packing case which served for a table between the two cots. Bridesman half turned and reached his hand but before he had touched the pack Cowrie, lying back on one arm beneath his head, without looking around extended the cigarette already burning in his own hand. Bridesman took it.

'Thanks,' he said. He said: 'I dont know.' He said harsh and strong: 'I dont want to know. All I know is, we have a job tomorrow and you're on it. If you've a good reason for not going, say it and I'll take someone else.'

'No,' he said. 'Goodnight.'

'Goodnight,' someone said.

But it wasn't tomorrow. There was nothing tomorrow: only dawn and then daylight and then morning. No dawn patrol went out because he would have heard it, being already and long since awake. Nor were there any aeroplanes on the tarmac when he crossed to the mess for breakfast, and nothing on the blackboard where Collyer occasionally saw fit to scrawl things in chalk which no one really ever read, himself sitting long at the cleared table where Bridesman would more or less have to see him sooner or later, provided he wanted to. From here he could see across the aerodrome to the blank and lifeless hangars and watch the two-hourly relief of the pacing guards through the long coma-ed forenoon, the morning reft of all progress beneath the bland sky and the silence.

Then it was noon; he watched the Harry Tate land and taxi up to the office and switch off, and the trench coat get down from the observer's seat and remove the helmet and goggles and toss them into the cockpit and draw out the stick and the red and brazen hat. Then all of them at lunch: the general and his pilot and the infantry officer and the whole squadron, the first lunch he could remember from which at least one flight and sometimes two were not absent, the general saying it not quite as well as the major because it took him longer, but saying the same thing:

'It's not over. Not that we needed the French. We should

simply have drawn back to the Channel ports and let the hun have Paris. It wouldn't be the first time. 'Change would have got windy, but it wouldn't have been their first time either. But that's all past now. We have not only kept the hun fooled, the French have got their backs into it again. Call this a holiday, since like all holidays it will be over soon. And there are some of you I think wont be sorry either'—naming them off because he did keep up with records, knew them all '—Thorpe, Osgood, De Marchi, Monaghan—who are doing damned well and will do better because the French have had their lesson now and so next time it will be the long vac. proper because when the guns stop next, it will be on the other side of the Rhine. Plenty of revs, and carry on.' And no sound, though maybe no one expected any, everyone following outside to where the Harry Tate's engine was already ticking over and the major helped put the stick and the red hat back into the cockpit and get the helmet out and get it on the general and the general back into the Harry Tate and the major said 'Shun!' saluting and the general jerked his thumbed fist upward and the Harry Tate trundled away.

Then afternoon, and nothing either. He still sat in the mess where Bridesman could see or find him if he liked, not waiting now any less than he had been waiting during the forenoon, because he knew now that he had not been waiting then, had not believed it then, not to mention that Bridesman had had to look at him at lunch because he had sat right across the table from him. The whole squadron did in fact: sat or idled about the mess—that is, the new ones, the tyros, the huns like himself—Villeneuve Blanche, even Villeneuve which Collyer called that sink, still out of bounds (which fact—the out of bounds—was probably the first time in all its history that anyone not born there had specifically wanted to go there). He could have gone to his hut too; there was a letter to his mother in it that he had not finished yet, except that now he could not finish it because the cessation of the guns yesterday had not only deleted all meaning from the words but effaced the very foundation of their purpose and aim.

But he went to the hut and got a book out and lay down on his cot with it. Perhaps it was simply to show, prove to, the old flesh, the bones and the meat, that he was not waiting for anything. Or perhaps to teach them to relinquish, abnegate. Or perhaps it was not the bones and meat so much as the nerves, muscles, which had been trained by a government in a serious even though temporary crisis to follow one highly specialised trade, then the government passed the crisis, solved the dilemma needing it, before he had had the chance to repay the cost of the training. Not glory: just to repay the cost. The laurel of glory, provided it was even moderately leafed, had human blood on; that was permissible only when motherland itself was at stake. Peace abolished it, and that man who would choose between glory and peace had best let his voice be small indeed——

But this was not reading; *Gaston de la Tour* at least deserved to be read by whoever held it open looking at it, even lying down. So he read, peaceful, resigned, no longer thirsting now. Now he even had a future, it would last forever now; all he needed was to find something to do with it, now that the only trade he had been taught—flying armed aircraft in order to shoot down (or try to) other armed aircraft—was now obsolete. It would be dinner time soon, and eating would exhaust, get rid of, a little of it, four, perhaps, counting tea, even five hours out of each twenty-four, if one only remembered to eat slowly enough, then eight off for sleeping or even nine if you remembered to go slowly enough about that too, would leave less than half to have to cope with. Except that he would not go to tea or dinner either today; he had yet almost a quarter-pound of the chocolate his mother had sent last week and whether he preferred chocolate to tea and dinner would not matter. Because they—the new ones, the tyros, the huns—would probably be sent back home tomorrow, and he would return to London if he must without ribbons on his coat, but at least he would not go back with a quarter-pound of chocolate melting in his hand like a boy returning half asleep from a market fair. And anyone capable of spreading eating and sleeping over fourteen hours out of twenty-four, should be able to stretch *Gaston de la Tour* over what remained of this coma-ed and widowed day, until it met the night: the dark: and the sleep.

Then tomorrow, it had just gone three Pip Emma, he was

not only not waiting for anything, it had been twenty-four hours now since he had had to remind himself that he was not waiting for anything, when the orderly room corporal stood suddenly in the door of the hut.

'What?' he said. 'What?'

'Yes sir,' the corporal said. 'A patrol sir. Going up in thirty minutes.'

'The whole squadron?'

'Captain Bridesman just said you, sir.'

'In only thirty minutes?' he said. 'Damn it, why couldn't t—— Right,' he said. 'Thirty minutes. Thanks.' Because he would have to finish the letter now, and it was not that thirty minutes was not long enough to finish it in, but that they were not long enough to get back into the mood, belief in which the letter had been necessary. Except for signing it and folding it into the envelope, he would not even have needed to get the letter out. Because he remembered it:

> *. . . not dangerous at all, really. I knew I could fly before I came out, and I have got to be pretty good on the range and even Captain Bridesman admits now that I'm not a complete menace to life in formation, so maybe when I settle down I might be of some value in the squadron after all*

and what else could one add? what else say to a woman who was not only a mother, but an only and half-orphan mother too? which was backward, of course, but anybody would know what he meant; who knew? perhaps one of the anybody could even suggest a postscript: like this say:

> *P.S. A delightful joke on you: they declared a recess at noon two days ago and if you had only known it, you would not have needed to worry at all from then until three oclock this afternoon; you could have gone out to tea two afternoons with a clear conscience, which I hope you did, and even stayed for dinner too though I do hope you remembered what sherry always does to your complexion*

Except that there was not even time for that. He heard engines; looking out, he saw three busses outside now in front of the hangar, the engines running and mechanics about them and the sentry standing again in front of the closed hangar doors. Then he saw a strange staff-car on the grass plot beside the office and he wrote 'love, David' at the foot of the letter and folded and licked it into the envelope and in the mess again now he saw the major's batman cross toward the office carrying an armful of flying kit; apparently Bridesman hadn't left the office at all, except that a moment later he saw Bridesman coming up from the hangars already dressed for the patrol, so the gear was not his. Then the office door opened and Bridesman came out, saying, 'All right, get your——' and stopped, because he already had it: maps, gloves, helmet, scarf, his pistol inside the knee pocket of the sidcott. Then they were outside, walking toward the three aeroplanes in front of B hangar.

'Just three,' he said. 'Who else is going?'

'The major,' Bridesman said.

'Oh,' he said. 'Why did he pick me?'

'I dont know. Out of a hat, I think. I can wash you out if you dont like it. It wont matter. I think he really picked you out of a hat.'

'Why should I not like it?' he said. Then he said, 'I just thought——' and then stopped.

'Thought what?' Bridesman said.

'Nothing,' he said. Then he was telling it, he didn't know why: 'I thought that maybe the major found out about it somehow, and when he wanted one of the new blokes on this job, he remembered about me—' telling it: that morning when he had been supposed simply to be out practicing, contour chasing probably, and instead had spent that forty or fifty seconds right down on the carpet with the unarmed aeroplane over the hun trenches or at least what he thought was the hun front line: 'You dont get frightened then; it's not until later, afterward. And then—— It's like the dentist's drill, already buzzing before you have even opened your mouth. You've got to open your mouth and you know you're going to all right, only you know at the same time that neither knowing you are going to nor opening it either, is going to help because even after you have closed it again, the thing will buzz at you again and you'll have to open it again the next moment or tomorrow or maybe it wont be until six months from now, but it will buzz again and you will have to open again because there's nowhere else you can go . . . .' He said: 'Maybe that's all of it. Maybe when it's too late and you cant help yourself anymore, you dont really mind getting killed——'

'I dont know,' Bridesman said. 'You didn't get even one bullet hole?'

'No,' he said. 'Maybe I shall this time.' And this time Bridesman did stop.

'Listen,' Bridesman said. 'This is a job. You know what jobs in this squadron are for.'

'Yes. To find huns.'

'And then bust them.'

'You sound like Monaghan: "Oh, I just ran up behind and busted the ass off the son of a bitch." '

'You do that too,' Bridesman said. 'Come on.' They went on. But he had needed only one glance at the three aeroplanes.

'Your bus is not back yet,' he said.

'No,' Bridesman said. 'I'm taking Monaghan's.' Then the major came and they took off. As he passed the office, he saw a smallish closed van turn in from the road but he didn't have time to look then, not until he was off and up and from the turn could really look down. It was the sort of van provost marshals' people used; and climbing for formation, he saw not one car but two behind the mess—not ordinary muddy staff cars but the sort which detached Life and Horse Guards officers on the staffs of corps- and army-commanders were chauffeured about in. Now he drew in opposite Bridesman across the major's tail-plane, still climbing but to the southward, so that they would approach the lines squarely, and did so, still climbing; Bridesman waggled his wings and turned away and he did likewise long enough to clear the Vickers, into Germany or anyway toward Germans, and traversed the Lewis on its quadrant and fired it off too and closed in again. Now the major turned back north-west parallel above the front, still climbing and nothing below now to reveal, expose it as front lines although he hadn't seen it but twice to have learned to know it again—only two kite balloons about a mile apart above the British trenches and two others almost exactly opposite them above the German ones, no dust no murk no gout and drift of smoke purposeless and unorigined and convoluted with no sound out of nothing and already fading and already replaced, no wink of guns as he had seen them once though perhaps at this height you didn't see flashes anyway: nothing now but the correlative to a map, looking now as it would look on that day when as the general said the last gun would cease beyond the Rhine—for that little space before the earth with one convulsive surge would rush to cover and hide it from the light of day and the sight of man——

He broke off to turn when the major did. They were crossing now, still climbing, right over the upper British balloon, heading straight for the German one. Then he saw it too—a white salvo bursting well below them and in front and then four single bursts pointing away eastward like four asterisks. But he never had time to look where it was pointing because at the same instant German archie burst all around them—or would have, because the major was diving slightly now, going east. But still he could see nothing yet except the black hun archie. It seemed to be everywhere; he flew right through a burst of it, cringing, shrinking convulsively into himself while he waited for the clang and whine which he had heard before. But maybe they were going too fast now, he and the major really diving now, and he noticed for the first time that Bridesman was gone, he didn't know what had become of him nor when, and then he saw it: a two-seater: he didn't know what kind because he had never seen a German two-seater in the air before nor any other German for that matter. Then Bridesman came vertically down in front of him and putting his nose down after Bridesman, he discovered that the major had vanished and forgot that too, he and Bridesman going almost straight down, the German right under them now, going west; he could see Bridesman's tracer going right into it until Bridesman pulled out and away, then his own tracer though he never could seem to get right on the two-seater before he had to pull out and away too, the archie already waiting for him before he was clear even, as though the hun batteries were simply shooting it up here without caring whom it hit or even watching to see. One actually seemed to burst between his upper and lower right-hand planes; he thought, *Maybe the reason I dont hear any clang is because this one is going to shoot me down before I have time to.* Then he found the two-seater again. That is, not the aeroplane but the white bursts of British archie telling him or them where it was, and an S.E. (it would have to be the major; Bridesman couldn't possibly have got that far by now) diving toward the bursts. Then Bridesman was just off his wing-tip again, the two of them going full out now in the pocking cloud of black archie like two sparrows through a swirl of dead leaves; and then he saw the balloons and noticed or remembered or perhaps simply saw the sun.

He saw them all—the two-seater apparently emerged neatly and exactly from between the two German balloons and, in its aureole of white archie, flying perfectly straight and perfectly level on a line which would carry it across No-man's Land and exactly between the two British ones, the major behind and above the two-seater and Bridesman and himself perhaps a mile back in their cloud of black archie, the four of them like four beads sliding on a string and two of them not even going very fast because he and Bridesman were up with the major almost at once. And perhaps it was the look on his face, the major glancing quickly at him then motioning him and Bridesman back into formation. But he didn't even throttle back and then Bridesman was following him, the two of them passing the major and he thought, *Maybe I was wrong, maybe hun archie doesn't clang and it was ours I heard that day,* still thinking that when, slightly ahead of Bridesman, they closed that gap too and flew into the white archie enclosing the two-seater before someone could tell the gunners they could stop now too, the last white wisp of it vanishing in the last fading drift about him and Bridesman now and there was the two-seater flying straight and level and sedate toward the afternoon sun and he pressed the button and nudged and ruddered the tracer right onto it, walking the tracer the whole length of it and return—the engine, the back of the pilot's head then the observer sitting as motionless as though in a saloon car on the way to the opera, the unfired machine gun slanting back and down from its quadrant behind the observer like a rolled umbrella hanging from a rail, then the observer turned without haste and looked right into the tracer, right at him, and with one hand deliberately raised the goggles—a Prussian face, a Prussian general's face; he had seen too many caricatures of the Hohenzollern Crown Prince in the last three years not to know a Prussian general when he saw one—and with the other hand put up a monocle at him and looked at him through it, then removed the monocle and faced front again.

Then he pulled away and went past; there was the aerodrome right under them now, until he remembered the archie battery just outside the village where he had seen the torch last night and heard the lorry; from the tight vertical turn he could look straight down at the gunners, shaking his hand at them and yelling: 'Come on! Come on! This is your last chance!' and slanted away and came back diving, walking the tracer right through the gun and the pale still up-turned discs of the faces watching him about it; as he pulled up he saw another man whom he had not seen before standing just on the edge of the wood behind the battery; the gentlest nudge on stick and rudder brought this one squarely into the Aldis itself this time and, pulling up at last to get over the trees, he knew that he should have got something very close to a possible ten somewhere about that one's navel. Then the aerodrome again; he saw the two-seater squaring away to land, the two S.E.'s above and behind it, herding it down; he himself was too high even if he had not been much too fast; even after the vicious sideslip he might still wipe off the S.E.'s frail undercarriage, which was easy enough to do even with sedate landings. But it held, stood up; he was down first, rolling now and for a moment he couldn't remember where he had seen it then he did remember, beginning to turn as soon as he dared (Someday they would put brakes on them; those who flew them now and lived would probably see it.) and turning: a glimpse of brass and scarlet somewhere near the office, and the infantry in column coming around the corner of the office; he was taxi-ing fast now back along the tarmac past the hangars where three mechanics began to run toward him until he waved them off, taxi-ing on toward the corner of the field and there it was where he had seen it last week and he switched off and got down, the two-seater on the ground too now and Bridesman and the major landing while he watched, the three of them taxi-ing on in a clump like three waddling geese toward the office where the scarlet and brass gleamed beautiful and refulgent in the sun in front of the halted infantry. But he was running a little heavily now in his flying boots and so the ritual had already begun when he arrived—the major and Bridesman on foot now with the adjutant and Thorpe and Monaghan and the rest of B Flight, in the center of them the three Poperinghe a.d.c.'s splendid in scarlet and brass and glittering Guards badges, behind them the infantry officer with his halted platoon deployed into two open files, all facing the German aeroplane.

'Bridesman,' he said but at that moment the major said ' 'Shun!' and the infantry officer shouted 'Present—— *harms*!' and at salute now he watched the German pilot jump down and jerk to attention beside the wing while the man in the observer's seat removed the helmet and goggles and dropped them somewhere and from somewhere inside the cockpit drew out a cap and put it on and did something rapidly with his empty hand like a magician producing a card and set the monocle into his eye and got down from the aeroplane and faced the pilot and said something rapid in German and the pilot stood himself back at ease and then snapped something else at the pilot and the pilot jerked back to attention and then with no more haste than when he had removed the helmet but still a little quicker than anyone could have stopped it drew a pistol from somewhere and even aimed it for a second while the rigid pilot (he looked about eighteen himself) stared not even at the pistol's muzzle but at the monocle and shot the pilot through the center of the face and turned almost before the body jerked and began to fall and swapped the pistol to the other gloved hand and had started to return the salute when Monaghan jumped across the pilot's body and flung the other German back into the aeroplane before Bridesman and Thorpe caught and held him.

'Fool,' Bridesman said. 'Dont you know hun generals dont fight strangers?'

'Strangers?' Monaghan said. 'I'm no stranger. I'm trying to kill the son of a bitch. That's why I came two thousand miles over here: to kill them all so I can get to hell back home!'

'Bridesman,' he said again but again the major said ''Shun there! Shun!' and at salute again he watched the German straighten up (he hadn't even lost the monocle) and flip the pistol over until he held it by the barrel and extend it butt first to the major who took it, and then draw a handkerchief from his cuff and brush off the breast and sleeve of his tunic where Monaghan had touched him and look at Monaghan for just a second with nothing behind the monocle at all as he put the handkerchief back into the cuff and clicked and jerked as he returned the salute and walked forward straight at the group as though it were not there and he didn't even need to see it part and even scramble a little to get out of the way for him to stride through, the three Guards officers falling in behind, between the two open infantry files, toward the mess; the major said to Collyer:

'Move this. I dont know whether they want it or not, but neither do we, here.'

'Bridesman,' he said again.

'Pah,' Bridesman said, spitting, hard. 'We shant need to go to the mess. I've a bottle in the hut.' Then Bridesman overtook him. 'Where are you going?'

'It will only take a moment,' he said. Then apparently Bridesman saw, noticed the aeroplane too.

'What's wrong with your bus? You got down all right.'

'Nothing,' he said. 'I left it there because there's an empty petrol tin in the weeds we can set the tail up on.' The tin was there: a faint and rusting gleam in the dying end of day. 'Because it's over, isn't it? That's what they want with that hun general of course. Though why they had to do it this way, when all somebody needed was just to hold out a white sheet or tablecloth; they must have a tablecloth at Pop and surely jerry's got one at his headquarters that he took away from a Frenchwoman; and somebody owes something for that poor bloodstained taxi-driver he—— Which was not like the book either: he did it backward; first he should have unpinned the iron cross from his own coat and hung it on the other one and then shot him——'

'You fool,' Bridesman said. 'You bloody fool.'

'All right. This will only take a moment.'

'Let it be,' Bridesman said. 'Just let it be.'

'I just want to see,' he said. 'Then I shall. It wont take but a moment.'

'Will you let it be then? Will you promise?'

'Of course. What else can I do? I just want to see'—and set the empty petrol tin in position and lifted the S.E.'s tail and swung it around onto the tin and it was just right: in a little better than flying angle: almost in a flat shallow glide, the nose coming down just right; and Bridesman really saying No now.

'I'll be damned if I will.'

'Then I'll have to get . . .' he hesitated: a second: then rapidly, cunningly: '. . . Monaghan. He'll do it. Especially if I can overtake the van or the staff-car or whichever it is, and borrow the jerry general's hat. Or maybe just the monocle will be enough——no: just the pistol to hold in my hand.'

'Take your own word for it,' Bridesman said. 'You were there. You saw what they shot at us, and what we were shooting at that two-seater. You were right on him for five or six seconds once. I watched your tracer rake him from the engine right on back through the monocle.'

'So were you,' he said. 'Get in.'

'Why dont you just let it be?'

'I have. Long ago. Get in.'

'Do you call this letting be?'

'It's like a cracked record on the gramophone, isn't it?'

'Chock the wheels,' Bridesman said. He found two chocks for the wheels and steadied the fuselage while Bridesman got into the cockpit. Then he went around to face the nose and it was all right; he could see the slant of the cowl and the Aldis slanting a little since he was taller than most, a little high still. But then he could raise himself on his toes and he intended to put his arms over his face anyway in case there was something left of whatever it was they had loaded the cartridges with last night by the time it had travelled twenty feet, though he never had actually seen any of them strike, bounce off the two-seater, and he had been right on top of it for the five or six seconds Bridesman had talked about. And the airscrew was already in open position so the constantinesco would be working or not working or whatever it was doing when it let bullets pass. So all he had to do was line up the tube of the Aldis on Bridesman's head behind the wind screen, except that Bridesman was leaning out around the screen, talking again: 'You promised.'

'That's right,' he said. 'It will be all right then.'

'You're too close,' Bridesman said. 'It's still tracer. It can still burn you.'

'Yes,' he said, backing away, still facing the little black port out of which the gun shot, 'I wondered how they did that. I thought tracer was the bullet itself burning up. However did they make tracer without a bullet in it? do you know? I mean, what are they? bread pellets maybe? No, bread would have burned up in the breech. Maybe they are wood pellets dipped in phosphorus. Which is a little amusing, isn't it? our hangar last night locked tight as . . . . with an armed guard walking back and forth in the dark and the cold outside and inside somebody, maybe Collyer; a chess player ought to be good with a knife, whittling sounds philosophical too and they say chess is a philosopher's game, or maybe it was a mechanic who will be a corporal tomorrow or a corporal who will be a sergeant tomorrow even if it is over because they can give a corporal another stripe even on the way home or at least before he is demobbed. Or maybe they'll even still keep the Air Force since a lot of people came into it out of the cradle before they had time to learn to do anything else but fly, and even in peace these ones will still have to eat at least now and then——' still backing away because Bridesman was still waving him back, still keeping the Aldis aligned; '—out here three years, and nothing, then one night he sits in a locked hangar with a pen knife and a lap-full of wooden blocks and does what Ball nor McCudden nor Mannock nor Bishop nor none of them ever did: brought down a whole German general: and get the barnacle at Buckingham palace his next leave—except that there wont be any, there's nothing now to be on leave from, and even if there was, what decoration will they give for that, Bridesman?—All right,' he said, 'all right, I'll cover my face too——'

Except that he wouldn't really need to now; the line of fire was already slanting into the ground, and this much further away it would cross well down his chest. And so he took one last sight on the Aldis for alignment and bowed his head a little and crossed both arms before his face and said, 'All right.' Then the chattering rattle, the dusky rose winking in miniature in the watch-crystal on his lifted wrist and the hard light stinging (They were pellets of some sort; if he had been three feet from the muzzle instead of about thirty, they would have killed him as quickly as actual bullets would have. And even as it was, he had leaned into the burst, not to keep from being beaten back but to keep from being knocked down: during which—the falling backward—the angle, pattern, would have walked up his chest and he would probably have taken the last of the burst in his face before Bridesman could have stopped it.) bitter *thock-thock-thock-thock* on his chest and the slow virulent smell of burning cloth before he felt the heat.

'Get it off!' Bridesman was shouting. 'You cant put it out! Get the sidcott off, damn it!' Then Bridesman was wrenching at the overall too, ripping it down as he kicked out of the flying boots and then out of the overall and the slow invisible smoldering stink. 'Are you satisfied now?' Bridesman said. 'Are you?'

'Yes, thanks,' he said. 'It's all right now.—Why did he have to shoot his pilot?'

'Here,' Bridesman said, 'get it away from the bus——' catching up the overall by one leg as though to fling it away until he caught hold of it.

'Wait,' he said. 'I've got to get my pistol out. If I dont, they'll charge me with it!' He took the pistol from the sidcott's knee pocket and dropped it into his tunic pocket.

'Now then,' Bridesman said. But he held on.

'Incinerator,' he said. 'We cant leave it lying about here.'

'All right,' Bridesman said. 'Come along.'

'I'll put it in the incinerator and meet you at the hut.'

'Bring it on to the hut and let the batman put it in the incinerator.'

'It's like the cracked record again isn't it?' he said. Then Bridesman released his leg of the sidcott though he didn't move yet.

'Then you'll come along to the hut.'

'Of course,' he said. 'Besides, I'll have to stop at the hangars and tell them to roll me in.—But why did he have to shoot his pilot, Bridesman?'

'Because he is a German,' Bridesman said with a sort of calm and raging patience. 'Germans fight wars by the rule-books. By the book, a German pilot who lands an undamaged German aeroplane containing a German lieutenant general on an enemy aerodrome, is either a traitor or a coward, and he must die for it. That poor bloody bugger probably knew while he was eating his breakfast sausage and beer this morning what was going to happen to him. If the general hadn't done it here, they would probably shoot the general himself as soon as they got their hands on him again. Now get rid of that thing and come on to the hut.'

'Right,' he said. Then Bridesman went on and at first he didn't dare roll up the overall to carry it. Then he thought what difference could it possibly make now. So he rolled up the overall and picked up his flying boots and went back to the hangars. B's was open now and they were just rolling in the major's and Bridesman's busses; the rule-book wouldn't let them put the German two-seater under a British shed probably, but on the contrary it would doubtless compel at least six Britons (who, since the infantry were probably all gone now, would be air mechanics unaccustomed both to rifles and having to stop up all night) to pass the night in relays walking with guns around it. 'I had a stoppage,' he told the first mechanic. 'There was a live shell in. Captain Bridesman helped me clear it. You can roll me in now.'

'Yes sir,' the mechanic said. He went on, carrying the rolled overall gingerly, around the hangars and on in the dusk toward the incinerator behind the men's mess, then suddenly he turned sharply again and went to the latrines; it would be pitch dark inside, unless someone was already there with a torch (Collyer had a tin candle-stick; passed going or coming from the latrines, cloistral indeed he would look, tonsured and with his braces knotted about his waist under his open warm). It was dark and the smell of the sidcott was stronger than ever inside. He put the flying boots down and unrolled it but even in the pitch dark there was nothing to see: only the slow thick invisible burning; and he had heard that too: a man in B Flight last year who had got a tracer between the bones of his lower leg and they were still whittling the bone away as the phosphorus rotted it; Thorpe told him that next time they were going to take off the whole leg at the knee to see if that would stop it. Of course the bloke's mistake was in not putting off until day after tomorrow say, going on that patrol (Or tomorrow, for that matter. Or today, except that Collyer wouldn't have let him.) only how could he have known that a year ago, when he himself knew one in the squadron who hadn't discovered it until people shot blank archie at him and couldn't seem to believe it even then? rolling up the sidcott again and fumbling for a moment in the pitch dark (It wasn't quite dark after you got used to it. The canvas walls had gathered a little luminousness, as if delayed day would even begin inside them after it was done outdoors.) until he found the boots. Outside, it was not at all night yet; night wouldn't even begin for two or three hours yet and this time he went straight to Bridesman's hut, pausing only long enough to lay the rolled sidcott against the wall beside the door. Bridesman was in his shirt sleeves, washing; on the box between his and Cowrie's beds a bottle of whisky sat between his and Cowrie's toothmugs. Bridesman dried his hands and without stopping to roll down his sleeves, dumped the two toothbrushes from the mugs and poured whisky into them and passed Cowrie's mug to him.

'Down with it,' Bridesman said. 'If the whisky's any good at all, it will burn up whatever germs Cowrie put in it or that you'll leave.' They drank. 'More?' Bridesman said.

'No thanks. What will they do with the aeroplanes?'

'What will what?' Bridesman said.

'The aeroplanes. Our busses. I didn't have time to do anything with mine. But I might have, if I had had time. You know: wash it out. Taxi it into something—another aeroplane standing on the tarmac, yours maybe. Finish it, do for two of them at once, before they can sell them to South America or the Levantine. So nobody in a comic opera general's suit can lead the squadron's aeroplanes in some air force that wasn't even in this at all. Maybe Collyer'll let me fly mine once more. Then I shall crash it——'

Bridesman was walking steadily toward him with the bottle. 'Up the mug,' Bridesman said.

'No thanks. I suppose you dont know just when we'll go home.'

'Will you drink, or wont you?' Bridesman said.

'No thanks.'

'All right,' Bridesman said. 'I'll give you a choice: drink, or shut up—let be—napoo. Which will you have?'

'Why do you keep on saying let be? Let be what? Of course I know the infantry must go home first—the p.b.i. in the mud for four years, out after two weeks and no reason to be glad or even amazed that you are still alive, because all you came out for is to get your rifle clean and count your iron rations so you can go back in for two weeks, and so no reason to be amazed until it's over. Of course they must go home first, throw the bloody rifle away forever and maybe after two weeks even get rid of the lice. Then nothing to do forever more but work all day and sit in pubs in the evenings and then go home and sleep in a clean bed with your wife——'

Bridesman held the bottle almost like he was going to strike him with it. 'Your word's worth damn all. Up the mug.'

'Thanks,' he said. He put the mug back on the box.—'All right,' he said. 'I've let be.'

'Then cut along and wash and come to the mess. We'll get one or two others and go to Madame Milhaud's to eat.'

'Collyer told us again this morning none of us were to leave the aerodrome. He probably knows. It's probably as hard to stop a war as it is to start one. Thanks for the whisky.' He went out. He could already smell it even before he was outside the hut and he stooped and took up the overall and went to his hut. It was empty of course; there would probably be a celebration, perhaps even a binge in the mess tonight. Nor did he light the lamp: dropping the flying boots and shoving them under his bed with his foot, then he put the rolled sidcott carefully on the floor beside the bed and lay down on it, lying quietly on his back in that spurious semblance of darkness and the time for sleeping which walls held, smelling the slow burning, and still there when he heard Burk cursing something or someone and the door banged back and Burk said,

'Holy Christ, what's that stink?'

'It's my sidcott,' he said from the bed while someone lit the lamp. 'It's on fire.'

'What the bloody hell did you bring it in here for?' Burk said. 'Do you want to burn down the hut?'

'All right,' he said, swinging his legs over and getting up and then taking up the overall while the others watched him curiously for a moment more, De Marchi at the lamp still holding the burning match in one hand. 'What's the matter? No binge tonight?' Then Burk was cursing Collyer again even before De Marchi said,

'Collyer closed the bar.' He went outside; it was not even night yet, he could still read his watch: twenty-two hours (no, simple ten oclock p.m. now because now time was back in mufti too) and he went around the corner of the hut and put the overall on the ground beside the wall, not too close to it, the whole northwest one vast fading church window while he listened to the silence crowded and myriad with tiny sounds which he had never heard before in France and didn't know even existed there because they were England. Then he couldn't remember whether he had actually heard them in English nights either or whether someone had told him about them, because four years ago when such peaceful night-sounds were legal or at least *de rigeur*, he had been a child looking forward to no other uniform save that of the Boy Scouts. Then he turned; he could still smell it right up to the door and even inside too though inside of course he couldn't really have sworn whether he actually smelled it or not. They were all in bed now and he got into pyjamas and put out the lamp and got into bed properly, rigid and quiet on his back. The snoring had already begun—Burk always snored and always cursed anyone who told him he did—so he could hear nothing but night passing, time passing, the grains of it whispering in a faint rustling whisper from or into whatever it was it ran from or into, and he swung his legs quietly over again and reached under the bed and found the flying boots and put them on and stood up and found his warm quietly and put it on and went out, already smelling it before he reached the door and on around the corner and sat down with his back against the wall beside the overall, not any darker now than it had been at twenty-two (no, ten p.m. now), the vast church window merely wheeling slowly eastward until almost before you knew it now it would fill, renew with light and then the sun, and then tomorrow.

But they would not wait for that. Already the long lines of infantry would be creeping in the darkness up out of the savage bitter fatal stinking ditches and scars and caves where they had lived for four years now, blinking with amazement and unbelief, looking about them with dawning incredulous surmise, and he tried listening, quite hard, because surely he should be able to hear it since it would be much louder, noisier than any mere dawning surmise and unbelief: the single voice of all the women in the western world, from what used to be the Russian front to the Atlantic ocean and beyond it too, Germans and French and English and Italians and Canadians and Americans and Australians—not just the ones who had already lost sons and husbands and brothers and sweethearts, because that sound had been in the air from the moment the first one fell, troops had been living with that sound for four years now; but the one which had begun only yesterday or this morning or whenever the actual instant had been, from the women who would have lost a son or brother or husband or sweetheart today or tomorrow if it hadn't stopped and now wouldn't have to since it had (not his women, his mother of course because she had lost nothing and had really risked nothing; there hadn't been that much time)—a sound much noisier than mere surmise, so much noisier that men couldn't believe it quite yet even, where women could and did believe anything they wanted to, making (didn't want to nor even need to make) no distinction between the sound of relief and the sound of anguish.

Not his mother in the house on the River beyond Lambeth where he had been born and lived ever since and from which, until he died ten years ago, his father would go in to the City each day to manage the London office of a vast American cotton establishment; they—his father and mother—had begun too late if he were the man on whom she was to bestow her woman's capacity for fond anguish, she the woman for whom (as history insisted—and from the talk he had had to listen to in messes he was inclined to admit that at least history believed it knew what it was talking about—men always had) he was to seek garlands or anyway sprigs of laurel at the cannon's mouth. He remembered, it was the only time, he and two others were celebrating their commissions, pooled their resources and went to the Savoy and McCudden came in, either just finished getting some more ribbons or some more huns, very likely both, in fact indubitably both, and it was an ovation, not of men but of women, the three of them watching while women who seemed to them more beautiful and almost as myriad as angels, flung themselves upward like living bouquets about that hero's feet; and how, watching, they thought it whether they said it aloud or not: 'Wait.'

But there hadn't been time; there was only his mother still, and he thought with despair how women were not moved one jot by glory and when they were mothers too, they were even irascible about uniforms. And suddenly he knew that his mother would be the noisiest of any anywhere, the noisiest of all, who had never for one instant had any intention of losing anything in the war and now had been proved in the sight of the whole world to have been right. Because women didn't care who won or lost wars, they didn't even care whether anybody did. And then he knew that it really didn't matter, not to England: Ludendorff could come on over Amiens and turn for the coast and get into his boats and cross the Channel and storm whatever he thought fit between Goodwin Sands and Land's End and Bishop's Rock and take London too and it wouldn't matter. Because London signified England like the foam signifies the beer, but the foam is not the beer and nobody would waste much time or breath grieving, nor would Ludendorff have time to breathe either or spend gloating, because he would still have to envelop and reduce every tree in every wood and every stone in every wall in all England, not to mention three men in every pub that he would have to tear down brick by brick to get to them. And it would not matter when he did, because there would be another pub at the next crossroads with three more men in it and there were simply just not that many Germans nor anybody else in Europe or anywhere else, and he unrolled the sidcott; at first there had been a series of little smoldering overlapping rings across the front of it, but now it had become one single sprawling ragged loop spreading, creeping up toward the collar and down toward the belt and across toward each armpit, until by morning the whole front would be gone probably. Because it was constant, steadfast, invincible and undeviable; you could depend on it as Ball had, and McCudden and Bishop and Rhys Davies and Barker, and Boelcke and Richthofen and Immelman and Guynemer and Nungesser and the Americans like Monaghan who had been willing to die even before their country was even in it to give them a roster of names to brag about; and the troops on the ground, in the mud, the poor bloody infantry—all of them who hadn't asked to be safe nor even to not be let down again tomorrow always by the brass hats who had done the best they could too probably, but asked only that the need for the unsafeness and the fact that all of them had dared it and a lot of them had accepted it and in consequence were now no more, be held by the nations at Paris and Berlin and Washington and London and Rome immune and unchallengeable above all save brave victory itself and as brave defeat, to the one of which it would give glory and from the other efface the shame.

Tuesday
Wednesday

The next time anyone might have seen or noticed her to remember, would have been at the old eastern city gate. And they would have noticed her then only because she had been there so long, standing beside the arch and staring at each face as it entered, then looking quickly on to the next one even before the first one had passed her.

But nobody noticed her to remember. Nobody except her lingered about the gate to notice anything. Even the ones who were still crowding steadily up to pass through the gate, had already entered the city in mind and spirit long before their bodies reached it, their anxiety and dread already one with the city's vast and growing reservoir of it, while their bodies still choked the slow converging roads.

They had begun to arrive yesterday, Tuesday, when news of the regiment's mutiny and arrest first reached the district and before the regiment itself had even been brought back to Chaulnesmont for the old supreme generalissimo himself to decide its fate. They continued to pour into the city all that night, and this morning they still came, on the heels of the regiment, in the very dust of the lorries which had rushed it back to the city and into it and through it without stopping, coming on foot and in clumsy farm carts, to crowd through the gate where the young woman stood scanning each face with strained and indefatigable rapidity,—villagers and farmers, laborers and artisans and publicans and clerks and smiths: other men who in their turn had served in the regiment, other men and women who were parents and kin of the men who belonged to it now and, because of that fact, were now under close guard beneath the threat of execution in the prisoners' compound on the other side of the town;—other men and women who, but for sheer blind chance and luck, might have been the parents and kin this time, and—some of them—would certainly be the next.

It was little they knew on that first day when they left their homes, and they would learn but little more from the others on the same mutual errand of desperation and terror whom they met or overtook or were overtaken by, before they reached the city: only that at dawn yesterday morning, the regiment had mutinied, refused to make an attack. It had not failed in an attack: it had simply refused to make one, to leave the trench, not before nor even as the attack started, but afterward;—had, with no prewarning, no intimation even to the most minor lance-corporal among the officers designated to lead it, declined to perform that ritual act which, after four years, had become as much and as inescapable a part of the formal ritual of war as the Grand March which opens the formal ball each evening during a season of festival or carnival;—the regiment had been moved up into the lines the night before, after two weeks of rest and refitting which could have disabused even the rawest replacement of what was in store for it, let alone the sudden moil and seethe of activity through which it fumbled in the darkness on the way up: the dense loom and squat of guns, the lightless lurch and crawl of caissons and lorries which could only be ammunition; then the gunfire itself, concentrated on the enemy-held hill sufficient to have notified both lines for kilometres in either direction that something was about to happen at this point, the wire-cutting parties out and back, and at dawn the whole regiment standing under arms, quiet and docile while the barrage lifted from the enemy's wire to hurdle his front and isolate him from reinforcement; and still no warning, no intimation; the company- and section-leaders, officers and N.C.O.'s, had already climbed out of the trench when they looked back and saw that not one man had moved to follow: no sign nor signal from man to man, but the entire three thousand spread one-man deep across a whole regimental front, acting without intercommunication as one man, as—reversed, of course—a line of birds on a telephone wire all leave the wire at the same instant like one bird, and that the general commanding the division of which the regiment was a unit, had drawn it out and put it under arrest, and at noon on that same day, Monday, all activity on the whole French front and the German one opposite it from the Alps to the Aisne, except air patrols and spaced token artillery salvos almost like signal guns, had ceased, and by three oclock that afternoon, the American and British fronts and the enemy one facing them from the Aisne to the sea, had done likewise, and now the general commanding the division of which the regiment was a unit, was sending the regiment back to Grand Headquarters at Chaulnesmont, where he himself would appear at three oclock on Wednesday afternoon (nor did they pause to wonder, let alone doubt, how an entire civilian countryside managed to know two days in advance, not only the purpose and intent but the hour too, of a high military staff conference) and, with the support or at least acquiescence of his own immediate superiors—the commander of the corps to which the division belonged, and of the army to which the corps belonged—demand in person of the old generalissimo permission to execute every man in it.

That was all they knew now as they hurried toward the city—old people and women and children, parents and wives and children and kin and mistresses of the three thousand men whom the old generalissimo at Chaulnesmont could destroy tomorrow by merely lifting his finger,—a whole converging countryside flowing toward the city, panting and stumbling, aghast and frantic, torn not even between terror and hope, but only by anguish and terror; destinationless even, since they had no hope: not quitting their homes and fields and shops to hurry to the city, but hoicked by anguish and terror, out of their huts and hovels and ditches, and drawn to the city whether they would or not: out of the villages and farms and into the city by simple grief to grief, since grief and anxiety, like poverty, take care of their own; to crowd into the already crowded city with no other will and desire except to relinquish their grief and anxiety into the city's vast conglomerate of all the passions and forces—fear, and grief, and despair, and impotence, and unchallengeable power and terror and invincible will; to partake of and share in all by breathing the same air breathed by all, and therefore both: by the grieving and the begrieved on one hand, and on the other the lone gray man supreme, omnipotent and inaccessible behind the carved stone door and the sentries and the three symbolical flags of the *Hôtel de Ville*, who dealt wholesale in death and who could condemn the whole regiment and miss its three thousand men no more from the myriads he dealt in, than he would miss the nod of his head or the reverse of the lifted hand which would save them. Because they did not believe that the war was over. It had gone on too long to cease, finish, overnight, at a moment's notice, like this. It had merely arrested itself; not the men engaged in it, but the war itself, War, impervious and even inattentive to the anguish, the torn flesh, the whole petty surge and resurge of victories and defeats like the ephemeral repetitive swarm and swirl of insects on a dung-heap, saying, 'Hush. Be quiet a moment' to the guns and the cries of the wounded too,—that whole ruined band of irredeemable earth from the Alps to the sea, studded with faces watching in lipless and lidless detachment, for a moment, a day or two days, for the old gray man at Chaulnesmont to lift that hand. Besides, it did not matter. They had got used to the war now, after four years. In four years, they had even learned how to live with it, beside it; or rather, beneath it as beneath a fact or condition of nature, of physical laws—the privations and deprivations, the terror and the threat like the loom of an arrested tornado or a tidal wave beyond a single frail dyke; the maiming and dying too of husbands and fathers and sweethearts and sons, as though bereavement by war were a simple occupational hazard of marriage and parenthood and childbearing and love. And not only just while the war lasted, but after it was officially over too, as if the only broom War knew or had to redd up its vacated room with, was Death; as though every man touched by even one second's flick of its mud and filth and physical fear, had been discharged only under condition of a capital sentence like a fatal disease;—so does War ignore its own recessment until it has ground also to dust the last cold and worthless cinder of its satiety and the tag-ends of its unfinished business; whether the war had ceased or not, the men of the regiment would still have had to die individually before their time, but since the regiment as a unit had been responsible for its cessation, the regiment would surely have to die, as a unit, by the old obsolete methods of war, if for no other reason than to enable its executioners to check their rifles back into the quartermasters' stores in order to be disbanded and demobilised. In fact, the only thing that could save the regiment would be the resumption of the war: which was their paradox, their bereavement: that, by mutinying, the regiment had stopped the war; it had saved France (France? England too; the whole West, since nothing else apparently had been able to stop the Germans since the March breakthrough in front of Amiens) and this was to be its reward; the three thousand men who had saved France and the world, would lose their lives, not in the act of it, but only after the fact, so that, to the men who had saved the world, the world they saved would not be worth the price they paid for it,—not to them, of course, the three thousand men in the regiment; they would be dead: the world, the West, France, all, would not matter to them; but to the wives and parents and children and brothers and sisters and sweethearts who would have lost all in order to save France and the world; they saw themselves no longer as one unit integrated into one resistance, one nation, mutual in suffering and dread and deprivation, against the German threat, but solitary, one small district, one clan, one family almost, embattled against all that Western Europe whom *their* sons and fathers and husbands and lovers were having to save. Because, no matter how much longer the threat of the war might have continued, some at least of the lovers and sons and fathers and husbands might have escaped with no more than an injury, while, now that the terror and the threat were past, all of their fathers and lovers and husbands and sons would have to die.

But when they reached the city, they found no placid lake of grieving resignation. Rather, it was a cauldron of rage and consternation, because now they learned that the regiment had not mutinied by mutual concord and design, either planned or spontaneous, but instead had been led, cajoled, betrayed into revolt by a single squad of twelve soldiers and their corporal; that the entire three thousand men had been corrupted into capital crime and through it, right up into the shadow of the rifles which would be its punishment, by thirteen men, four of whom, including the corporal-leader, were not only not Frenchmen by birth, but not even naturalised Frenchmen. In fact, only one of them—the corporal—could even speak French. Even the army records did not seem to know what their nationality was; their very presence in a French regiment or the French army in France was contradictory and obfuscated, though indubitably they had, must have, got there through or by means of some carelessly reported or recorded Foreign Legion draft, since armies never really lost anything for good, once it was described and numbered and dated and countersigned onto a scrap of paper; the boot, bayonet, camel or even regiment, might vanish and leave no physical trace, but not the record of it and the name and rank and designation of whoever had it last, or anyway signed for it last. The other nine of the squad were Frenchmen, but only three of them were less than thirty years old, and two of them were over fifty. But all nine of them had unimpeachable service records extending back not only to August, 1914, but on to the day when the oldest of them turned eighteen and was drafted thirty-five years ago.

And by the next morning, Wednesday, they knew the rest of it. By then, this part of it was not even waiting for them to reach the city. It was running out to meet them on the thronged converging roads like wind or fire through dry grass: how, not only warned and alerted by the barrage that an attack was coming, the German observation posts must have actually seen the men refuse to leave the trench after their officers, yet no counter-attack came; and how, even during their best, their priceless opportunity, which was during the confusion and turmoil while the revolted and no longer to-be-trusted regiment was having to be relieved in broad daylight, still the enemy made no counter-move, not even a barrage on the communication lines where the relieved and the relieving regiments would have to pass each other, so that, an hour after the regiment had been relieved and put under arrest, all infantry activity in the sector had stopped, and two hours after that, the general commanding the regiment's division and his corps commander and their army commander, and an American staff-colonel and the British commander-in-chief's chief of staff, were behind locked doors with the general commanding the entire Group of Armies, where, as report and rumor thickened, it emerged that not only the private soldiers in the division's other three regiments, but those in both the divisions flanking it, knew in advance that the attack was to be made and that the selected regiment was going to refuse. And that (staff- and provost-officers with their sergeants and corporals were moving fast now, spurred by amazement and alarm and incredulity too, while the telephones shrilled and the telegraphs chattered and the dispatch-riders' motorcycles roared in and out of the courtyard) not only were the foreign corporal and his strange conglomerate squad known personally to every private in those three divisions, but for over two years now the thirteen men—the obscure corporal whose name few knew and even they could not pronounce it, whose very presence in the regiment, along with that of the other three apparently of the same middle-European nationality, was an enigma, since none of them seemed to have any history at all beyond the day when they had appeared, materialised seemingly out of nowhere and nothingness in the quartermaster's store-room where they had been issued uniforms and equipment, and the nine others who were authentic and, until this morning, unimpeachable French men and French soldiers, had been spending their leaves and furloughs for two years now among the combat-troop rest-billets not only throughout the entire French Army zone, but the American and the British ones too, sometimes individually, but usually as the intact squad, —the entire thirteen, three of whom couldn't even speak French, and their corporal-leader only enough of it to hold his rating, visiting for days and sometimes weeks at a time, not only among French troops, but American and British too;—which was the moment when the inspectors and inquisitors in their belts and tabs and pips and bars and eagles and wreaths and stars, realised the . . . not enormity, but monstrosity, incredibility; the monstrous incredibility, the incredible monstrosity, with which they were confronted: the moment when they learned that during three of these two-week leave-periods, two last year and the third last month, less than three weeks ago, the entire squad had vanished from France itself, vanished one night with their passes and transport and ration warrants from their rest-billets, and reappeared one morning two weeks later in ranks again, with the passes and warrants still unstamped and intact;—monstrous and incredible, since there was but one place on earth since almost four years now where thirteen men in uniform could have gone without having their papers stamped, needing no papers at all in fact, only darkness and a pair of wire-cutters; they—the inquisitors and examiners, the inspectors-general and the provost-marshals flanked now by platoons of N.C.O.'s and M.P.'s with pistols riding light to the hand in the unstrapped holsters—were moving rapidly indeed now, with a sort of furious calm, along, among that unbroken line of soiled, stained, unchevroned and braidless men designated only by serial numbers, stretching from Alsace to the Channel, who for almost four years now had been standing in sleepless rotation behind their cocked and loaded rifles in the apertures of that one continuous firestep, but who now were not watching the opposite German line at all but, as though they had turned their backs on war, were watching them, the inquisitors, the inspectors, the alarmed and outraged and amazed; until a heliograph in a French observation post began to blink, and one behind the German line facing it answered; and at noon that Monday, the whole French front and the German one opposite it fell silent, and at three oclock the American and the British fronts and the German one facing them followed suit, so that when night fell, both the dense subterrene warrens lay as dead as Pompeii or Carthage beneath the constant watchful arch and plop of rockets and the slow wink and thud of back-area guns.

So now they had a protagonist for anguishment, an object for execration, stumbling and panting on that Wednesday morning through the kilometres' final converging, above which the city soared into the sunlight the spires and crenellations of its golden diadem, pouring, crowding through the old city gates, becoming one with that vast subterrene of warrened shadow out of which, until yesterday, the city's iron and martial splendor had serenely stood, but which now had become one seethe and turmoil which had overflowed the boulevard at dawn and was still pouring across the city after the fleeing lorries.

As the lorries sped across the city, they soon outdistanced the crowd, though when its vanguard emerged also onto the sunny plain beyond, the lorries were in sight again, fleeing in a sucking swirl of primrose-colored dust toward the camouflage-painted huddle of the prison-compound a kilometre and a half away.

But for a moment, the crowd seemed unable to discern or distinguish the lorries. It stopped, bunching onto itself like a blind worm thrust suddenly into sunlight, recoiling into arrestment, so that motion itself seemed to repudiate it in one fleeing ripple like a line of invisible wind running down a windrow of wheat. Then they distinguished or located the speeding dust, and broke, surged, not running now, because—old men and women and children—they had run themselves out crossing the city, and no longer shouting now either because they had spent themselves voiceless too, but hurrying, panting, stumbling, beginning—now that they were clear of the city—to spread out fanwise across the plain, so that already they no longer resembled a worm, but rather again that wave of water which had swept at dawn across the *Place de Ville*.

They had no plan: only motion, like a wave; fanned out now across the plain, they—or it—seemed to have more breadth than depth, like a wave, seeming, as they approached the compound, to increase in speed as a wave does nearing the sand, on, until it suddenly crashed against the wire barrier, and hung for an instant and then burst, split into two lesser waves which flowed in each direction along the fence until each spent itself. And that was all. Instinct, anguish, had started them; motion had carried all of them for an hour, and some of them for twenty-four, and brought them here and flung them like a cast of refuse along the fence (It—the compound—had been a factory once, back in the dead vanished days of what the nations called peace: a rectangle of brick walls covered with peaceful ivy then, converted last year into a training- and replacement-depot by the addition of half a hundred geometric plank-and-paper barracks composed of material bought with American money and sawn into numbered sections by American machines in America, and shipped overseas and clapped up by American engineers and artisans, into an eyesore, monument, and portent of a nation's shocking efficiency and speed, and converted again yesterday into a man-proof pen for the mutinied regiment, by the addition of barricades of electrified wire and searchlight towers and machine-gun platforms and pits and an elevated catwalk for guards; French sappers and service troops were still weaving more barricades and stringing more of the lethal wire to crown them.) and then abandoned them, leaving them lying along the barrier in an inextricable mass like victims being resurrected after a holocaust, staring through the taut, vicious, unclimbable strands beyond which the regiment had vanished as completely as though it had never existed, while all circumambience—the sunny spring, the jocund morning, the lark-loud sky, the glinting pristine wire (which, even when close enough to be touched, still had an appearance gossamer and ephemeral like Christmas tinsel, giving to the working parties immersed in its coils the inconsequential air of villagers decorating for a parish festival), the empty parade and the blank lifeless barracks and the Senegalese guarding them, lounging haughtily overhead along the catwalks and lending a gaudy, theatrical insouciance to the raffish shabbiness of their uniforms like that of an American blackface minstrel troupe dressed hurriedly out of pawnshops—seemed to muse down at them, contemplative, inattentive, inscrutable, and not even interested.

And that was all. Here they had wanted to come for twenty-four hours now, and here at last they were, lying like the cast of spent flotsam along the fence, not even seeing the wire against which they lay, let alone anything beyond it, for the half-minute perhaps which it took them to realise, not that they had had no plan when they came here, nor even that the motion which had served in lieu of plan, had been motion only so long as it had had room to move in, but that motion itself had betrayed them by bringing them here at all, not only in the measure of the time it had taken them to cover the kilometre and a half between the city and the compound, but in that of the time it would take them to retrace back to the city and the *Place de Ville*, which they comprehended now they should never have quitted in the first place, so that, no matter what speed they might make getting back to it, they would be too late. Nevertheless, for still another half minute they lay immobile against the fence beyond which the fatigue parties, wrestling slowly among their interminable tinsel coils, paused to look quietly and incuriously back at them, and the gaudy Senegalese, lounging in lethargic disdain among their machine guns above both the white people engaged in labor inside the fence and the ones engaged in anguish outside it, smoked cigarettes and stroked idly the edges of bayonets with broad dark spatulate thumbs and didn't bother to look at them at all.

Nor could even the aviator stationed and motionless in the hard blue wind, have said exactly where among them the facing-about began as, like the blind headless earth-brute which, apparently without any organ either to perceive alarm or select a course to evade it, can move at instantaneous notice and instantaneous speed in either direction, the crowd began to flow back to the city, turning and beginning to move all at one instant as birds do, hurrying again, weary and indefatigable, indomitable in their capacity not alone for endurance but for frenzy as well, streaming immediately once more between two files of troops stretching the whole distance back to the city—(apparently a whole brigade of cavalry this time, drawn up and facing, across the cleared path, a like number of infantry, without packs again but with bayonets still fixed and with grenades too now, with at one point, the nozzle and looped hose of a flame thrower, and at the far, the city, end of the cleared path, the tank again, half-seen beyond the arch of the gate like a surly, not-too-courageous dog peering from its kennel) without seeming to have remarked either the arrival of the troops nor to notice, let alone have any curiosity about, their presence now. Nor did the troops pay any attention to the people, alerted of course, but actually almost lounging on the horses and the grounded rifles while the crowd poured between them, as though to the troops themselves and to those who had ordered them here, the crowd was like the herd of western cattle which, once got into motion about its own vortex, is its own warrant both of its own security and of the public's peace.

They recrossed the city, back into the *Place de Ville*, filling it again, right up to the spear-tipped iron fence beyond which the three sentries flanked the blank door beneath the three morning-windy flags. They still crowded into the *Place* long after there was no more room, still convinced that, no matter how fast they had come back from the compound, they would be too late, knowing that no courier carrying the order for the execution could possibly have passed them on the road, yet convinced that one must indubitably have done so. Yet they still crowded in, as if the last belated ones could not accept the back-passed word, but must see, or try to see, for themselves that they had missed the courier and were too late; until even if they had wished to stream, stumble, pant back to the compound and at least be where they could hear the volley which would bereave them, there would have been no room to turn around in and begin to run; immobilised and fixed by their own density in that stone sink whose walls were older than Clovis and Charlemagne—until suddenly it occurred to them that they could not be late, it was impossible for them to be late; that, no matter what errors and mistakes of time or direction or geography they might make, they could no more be late for the execution than they could prevent it, since the only reason for the whole vast frantic and anguished influx to the city was, to be there when the regiment's division commander arrived to ask the old gray general behind the closed stone door facing them, to allow him to have the regiment shot, and the division general was not even due there until three oclock this afternoon.

So all they needed to do now, was just to wait. It was a little after nine oclock now. At ten, three corporals, an American, a Briton, and a Frenchman, flanked each by an armed soldier of his nation, came out of the archway from the rear of the *Hôtel*, and exchanged each the sentry of his nation and marched the relieved man back through the archway. Then it was noon. Their shadows crept in from the west and centered; the same three corporals came with three fresh sentries and relieved the three posts and went away; it was the hour when, in the old dead time called peace, men went home to eat and rest a little perhaps, but none stirred; their shadows crept eastward, lengthening again; at two oclock, the three corporals came for the third time; the three sets of three paced and stamped for the third time through the two-hourly ritual, and departed.

This time, the car came so fast up the boulevard that it outstripped its own heralding. The crowd had only time to press frantically back and let it enter the *Place* and then anneal behind it as it shot across the *Place* and stopped before the *Hôtel* in a bursting puff of dust from its clapped-to brakes. It was a staff car also, but stained with dust and caked with dried mud too, since it had come not only from the army zone, but out of the lines themselves, even if its pennon did bear the five stars of an army commander. Though, after these four years, even the children read that much, and if it had flown no pennon at all, even the children would have recognised two of the men in it—the squat, bull-chested man who commanded the regiment's division, who was already beginning to stand up before the car stopped, and the tall, scholarly-looking man who would be the division commander's army-group commander's chief-of-staff, the division commander springing out of the car before the orderly beside the driver in the front seat had time to get down and open the tonneau door, and already chop-striding his short stiff cavalry legs toward the blank, sentry-flanked entrance to the *Hôtel* before the staff officer had even begun to move.

Then the staff officer rose too, taking up a longish object from the seat beside him, and in the next second they—the crowd—had recognised it, swaying forward out of their immobilised recoil and making a sound now, not of execration, because it was not even directed at the division commander; even before they learned about the foreign corporal, they had never really blamed him, and even with the corporal, although they could still dread the division commander as the postulate of their fear and the instrument of their anguish, they had not blamed him: not only a French soldier, but a brave and faithful one, he could have done nothing else but what he was doing, believed nothing else except what he believed, since it was because of such as he that France had endured this long, surrounded and embattled by jealousy and envy—a soldier: that not only his own honor and that of his division, but the honor of the entire profession of command, from files and squads to armies and groups of them, had been compromised; a Frenchman: that the security of the motherland itself had been jeopardised or at least threatened. Later, afterward, it would seem to them, some of them, that, during the four or five seconds before they recognised the significance of what the staff officer had taken up from the seat of the car, there had been a moment when they had felt for him something almost like pity: not only a Frenchman and a soldier, but a Frenchman and a soldier who had to be a man first, to have been a Frenchman and become a soldier, yet who, to gain the high privilege of being a brave and faithful Frenchman and soldier, had had to forfeit and abdicate his right in the estate of man,—where theirs would be only to suffer and grieve, his would be to decree it; he could share only in the bereaving, never in the grief; victim, like they, of his own rank and high estate.

Then they saw what the staff officer had in his hand. It was a sabre. He—the staff officer—had two: wearing one buckled to his ordnance belt, and carrying one, its harness furled about the hilt and sheath, which he was tucking under his arm as he too descended from the car. And even the children knew what that meant: that the division commander too was under arrest, and now they made the sound; it was as though only now, for the first time, had they actually realised that the regiment was going to die,—a sound not even of simple agony, but of relinquishment, acceptance almost, so that the division commander himself paused and turned and they seemed to look at, see him too for the first time—victim not even of his rank and high estate, but like them, of that same instant in geography and in time which had destroyed the regiment, but with no rights in its fate; solitary, kinless, alone, pariah and orphan both from them whose decree of orphanage he would carry out, and from them whom he would orphan; repudiated in advance by them from whom he had bought the high privilege of endurance and fidelity and abnegation with the forfeiture of his birthright in humanity, in compassion and pity and even in the right to die;—

standing for a moment yet, looking back at them, then turned, already chop-striding again toward the stone steps and the blank door, the staff officer with the furled sabre under his arm following, the three sentries clashing to present arms as the division commander strode up the steps and past them and himself jerked open the door's black yawn before anyone else could have moved to do it, and entered—the squat, short figure kinless, indomitable, and doomed, vanishing rigidly and without a backward look, across that black threshold as though (to the massed faces and eyes watching) into Abyss or into Hell.

And now it was too late. If they could have moved, they might at least have reached the compound wire in time to hear the knell; now, because of their own immobilisation, they would have only the privilege of watching the executioner prepare the empty rope. In a moment now, the armed couriers and outriders would appear and kick into life the motorcycles waiting in the areaway; the cars would draw up to the door, and the officers themselves would emerge—not the old supreme general, not the two lesser ones, not even the division commander, compelled to that last full measure of expiation by watching the doom whose mouthpiece he had been,—not any of these, but the provost-marshals, the specialists: they who by avocation and affinity had been called and as by bishops selected and trained and dedicated into the immutable hierarchy of War to be major-domos to such as this, to preside with all the impunity and authority of civilised usage over the formal orderly shooting of one set of men by another wearing the same uniform, lest there be flaw or violation in the right; trained for this moment and this end as race-horses are brought delicately, with all man's skill and knowledge and care, up to the instant of the springing barrier and the grandstands' roar, of St Leger or Derby; the pennoned staff cars would roar away, rapid and distancing, feeding them fading dust once more back to the compound which they knew now they should never have left; even if they could have moved, only by the most frantic speed could they more than reach the compound fence in time merely to hear and see the clapping away of echoes and the wisping away of smoke which made them orphaned and childless and relict, but now they could not even move enough to face about: the whole *Place* one aspic of gaped faces from which rose that sound not yelling but half murmuring and half wailing, while they stared at the gray, tomblike pile into which the two generals in their panoply and regalia and tools of glory, had vanished as into a tomb for heroes, and from which, when something did emerge, it would now be Death,—glaring at it, anguished and aghast, unable to move anywhere, unless the ones in front might perhaps fling themselves upon and beneath the cavalcade before it could start, and so destroy it, and, dying themselves with it, bequeath to the doomed regiment at least that further span of breathing comprised in the time necessary to form a new one.

But nothing happened. A courier did appear after a while from the archway, but he was only an ordinary dispatch-rider, and alone; his whole manner declared that he had no concern whatever in anything regarding them or their trouble. He didn't even look at them, so that the sound, never too loud, ceased while he straddled one of the waiting motorcycles and kicked it to life and moved away, not even in the direction of the compound but toward the boulevard, pushing the popping mechanism along between his straddled legs since, in the crowd, there was no chance whatever of running it fast enough to establish its balance, the crowd parting just enough to let him through and then closing behind him again, his urgent, constant adjurations for passage marking his progress, lonely, urgent and irritable, like the crying of a lost wildfowl; after a while two more came out, identical, even to the air of private and leisurely independence, and departed on two more of the machines, their cries too marking their infinitesimal and invisible progress: 'Give way, you bastards . . . . offspring of sheep and camels . . .'

And that was all. Then it was sunset. As they stood in the turning flood of night, the ebb of day rang abruptly with an orderly discordant diapason of bugles, orderly because they all sounded at once, discordant because they sounded not one call, but three: the *Battre aux Champs* of the French, the *Last Post* of the English, the *Retreat* of the Americans, beginning inside the city and spreading from cantonment and depot to cantonment and depot, rising and falling within its own measured bruit as the bronze throat of orderly and regulated War proclaimed and affirmed the end of day, clarion and sombre above the parade rite of *Mount* and *Stand Down* as the old guards, custodians of today, relinquished to tomorrow's, the six sergeants themselves appearing this time, each with his old guard or his new, the six files in ordered tramp and wheel facing each its rigid counterpart juxtaposed, the barked commands in the three different tongues ringing in the same discordant unison as the bugles, in staccato *poste* and *riposte* as the guards exchanged and the three sentries of the new ones assumed the posts. Then the sunset gun went from the old citadel, deliberate and profound, as if a single muffled drumstick had been dropped once against the inverted bowl of hollow and resonant air, the sound fading slowly and deliberately, until at last, with no suture to mark its annealment, it was lost in the murmur of bunting with which the flags, bright blooms of glory myriad across the embattled continent, sank, windless again, down.

They were able to move now. The fading whisper of the gun and the descending flags might have been the draining away of what had been holding them gelid; there would even be time to hasten home and eat, and then return. So they were almost running, walking only when they had to and running again when they could, wan, indomitable and indefatigable, as the morning's ebb flowed back through the twilight, the darkling, the night-annealing city, toward the warrens and tenements where it had risen. They were like the recessed shift out of a factory furiously abridging the ordered retinue of day and dark producing shells say, for a retreating yet unconquered army, their eyes bloodshot from the fumes, their hair and garments stinking with the reek, hurrying to eat and then return, already eating the waiting food while they still ran toward it, and already back at the clanking flashing unstopping machines while still chewing and swallowing the food they would not taste.

Tuesday
Wednesday
Wednesday Night

It was late spring of 1916 when the runner joined the battalion. The whole brigade had been moved from Flanders down into Picardy, in billets near Amiens, resting and refitting and receiving replacements to be an integer in what would be known afterward as the First Battle of the Somme—an affair which would give even those who had survived to remember Loos and the Canal, not only something to blench for but the discovery that something even remained to blench with.

He had debarked that same dawn from the Dover leave packet. A lorry had given him a lift from Boulogne; he got directions from the first man he met and in time entered the brigade office with his posting order already in his hand, expecting to find a corporal or a sergeant or at most the brigade adjutant, but found instead the brigadier himself sitting at the desk with an open letter, who said:

'Afternoon. As you were a moment, will you?' The runner did so and watched enter a captain whom he was to know as commander of one of the companies in the battalion to which he would be assigned, followed by a thin wiry surly-looking private who, even to the runner's first glance, seemed to have between his bowed legs and his hands the shape of a horse, the brigadier saying pettishly, 'Stand at ease; stand at ease,' then opened the folded letter and glanced at it, then looked at the private and said: 'This came by special courier this morning. From Paris. Someone from America is trying to find you. Someone important enough for the French government to have located you through channels and then send a special courier up from Paris. Someone named—' and glanced at the letter again: '—Reverend Tobe Sutterfield.'

And now the runner was watching the private too, already looking at him in time not only to hear but to see him say, quick and harsh and immediately final: 'No.'

'Sir,' the captain prompted.

'No what?' the brigadier said. 'An American. A blackamoor minister. You dont know who it is?'

'No,' the private said.

'He seemed to think you might say that. He said to remind you of Missouri.'

'No,' the private said, rigid and harsh and final. 'I was never in Missouri. I dont know anything about him.'

'Say sir,' the captain said.

'That's your last word?' the brigadier said.

'Yes sir,' the private said.

'All right,' the brigadier said. 'Carry on.' Then they were gone and, rigid at attention, he (the runner) felt rather than saw the brigadier open the brigade order and begin to read it and then look up at him—no movement of the head at all: merely an upward flick of the eyes, steady for a moment, then down to the order again: thinking (the runner) quietly: *Not this time. There's too much rank:* thinking: *It wont even be the colonel, but the adjutant.* Which by ordinary could have been as much as two weeks later since, a runner formally assigned to a combat battalion, his status was the same as any other member of it and he too would be officially 'resting' until they went back up the lines; and, except for coincidence, probably would have been: reporting (the runner) not to the battalion sergeant-major but to Coincidence, entering his assigned billet two hours later, and in the act of stowing his kit into a vacant corner, saw again the man he had seen two hours ago in the brigadier's office—the surly, almost insubordinate stable-aura-ed private who by his appearance would have pined and died one day after he was removed further from Whitechapel than a Newmarket paddock perhaps, yet who was not only important enough to be approached through official channels by some American individual or agent or agency himself or itself important enough to use the French government for messenger, but important enough to repudiate the approach—seated this time on a bunk with a thick leather money-belt open on one knee and a small dirty dogeared notebook on the other, and three or four other privates facing him in turn, to each of which he counted out a few French notes from the money-belt and then made a notation with the stub of a pencil in the notebook.

And the next day, the same scene; and the day after that, and the one after that, directly after the morning parade for roll-call and inspection; the faces different faces and varying in number: two, or three, sometimes only one: but always one, the worn money-belt getting a little thinner but apparently inexhaustible, anyway bottomless, the pencil stub making the tedious entries in the grimed notebook; then the fifth day, after noon mess; it was payday and, approaching the billet, for a moment the runner thought wildly that part of the pay parade was taking place there: a line, a queue of men extending out into the street, waiting to creep one by one inside, so that the runner had trouble entering his own domicile, to stand now and watch the whole affair in reverse: the customers, clients, patients—whatever they were—now paying the grimed frayed wads of French notes back into the money belt, the tedious pencil stub still making the tedious entries; and still standing there watching when the orderly whom he had seen that first morning in the brigade anteroom, entered and broke through the line, saying to the man on the bunk: 'Come on. You're for it this time. It's a bleeding f. . .ing motorcar from Paris with a bleeding f. . .ing prime minister in it,'—watching (the runner) the man on the bunk without haste stow the notebook and the pencil-stub into the money-belt and strap it up and turn and roll the belt into the blanket behind him and rise and follow the orderly, the runner speaking to the nearest of the now broken and dispersing line:

'What is it? What's the money for? He's gone now; why dont you just help yourselves while he's not here to put it down against you?' and still getting only the watchful, secretive, already dispersing stares, and not waiting even for that: himself outside too now, in the cobbled street, and saw that too: one of the long black funereal French motorcars such as high government officials use, with a uniformed driver and a French staff-captain in the front seat and a British one and a thin Negro youth on the two small jump seats and behind them in the rear seat, a middle-aged woman in rich furs who could be nothing but a rich American (the runner did not recognise her though almost any Frenchman would since her money partially supported a French air squadron in which her only son was a pilot) and a Frenchman who was not the prime minister but (the runner did recognise this) was at least a high Cabinet secretary for something, and sitting between them, an old Negro in a worn brushed tophat, with the serene and noble face of an idealised Roman consul; the owner of the money-belt rigid and wooden, staring but at nothing, saluting but saluting no one, just saluting, then rigid and wooden again and ten feet away while the old Negro man leaned, speaking to him, then the old Negro himself descended from the car, the runner watching that too, and not only the runner but the entire circumambience: the six people still in the car, the orderly who had fetched the man from the bunk, the thirty-odd men who had been in the creeping line when the orderly broke through it, having followed into the street to stand before the billet door, watching too, perhaps waiting: the two of them drawn aside now, the owner of the money-belt still rigid, wooden, invincibly repudiant while the serene and noble head, the calm imperial chocolate-colored face, still talked to him, murmured: barely a minute, then the Negro turned and went back to the car and got into it, the runner not waiting to watch that either, already following the white man back toward the billet, the waiting group before the door parting to let him through, then crowding in after him until the runner stopped the last one by touching, grasping his sleeve.

'The money,' the runner said. 'What is it?'

'It's the Association,' the man said.

'All right, all right,' the runner said, almost testily. 'How do you get it? Can anybody. . . . .'

'Right,' the man said. 'You take ten bob. Then on the next payday you begin paying him sixpence a day for thirty days.'

'If you're still alive,' the runner said.

'Right,' the other said. 'When you have paid up you can start over again.'

'But suppose you're not,' the runner said. But this time the man merely looked at him, so that he said, almost pettishly again:

'All right, all right, I'm not really that stupid; to still be alive a year from now is worth six hundred percent. of anything.' But still the man looked at him, with something so curious in his face, behind his eyes, that the runner said quickly, 'Yes. What?'

'You're new,' the other said.

'Yes,' the runner said. 'I was in London last week. Why?'

'The rate aint so high, if you're a . . . .' the voice stopping, ceasing, the eyes still watching him so curiously, so intently, that it seemed to the runner that his own gaze was drawn, as though by some physical force, down the man's side to where his hand hung against his flank: at which instant the hand flicked out in a gesture, a signal, so brief, so rapid before it became again immobile against its owner's khaki leg, that the runner could hardly believe he had seen it.

'What?' the runner said. 'What?' But now the face was closed, inscrutable; the man was already turning away.

'Why dont you ask him what you want to know?' he said. 'He wont bite yer. He wont even make you take the ten bob, if you dont want.'

The runner watched the long car back and fill in the narrow street, to return wherever it came from: nor had he even seen the battalion adjutant yet, who at worst could be no more than captain and very likely not even as old as he: so the preliminaries would not take long, probably no more than this: what Hollywood in a few more years would coin a word for: double-take: then the adjutant: *Oh, you're that one. Why haven't you got up your M.C.? Or did they take that back too, along with the pip?*

Then he: *I dont know. Could I wear an M.C. on this?*

Then the adjutant: *I dont know either. What else did you want? You're not due here until Orderly Room Monday.*

Then he would ask: who by now had divined who the rich American woman would be, since for two years now Europe—France anyway—had been full of them—the wealthy

Philadelphia and Wall Street and Long Island names whose money supported ambulance units and air squadrons in the French front—the committees, organizations, of officially nonbelligerent amateurs by means of which America fended off not Germans but war itself; he could ask then, saying, *But why here? Granted that they have one with at the head of it an old blackamoor who looks like a nonconformist preacher, why did the French government send him up here in a State motor-car for a two-minute visit with a private soldier in a British infantry battalion?*—oh yes, he could ask, getting nothing probably except the old Negro's name, which he already knew and hence was not what he lacked, needed, must have if there were peace: which took another three days from that Monday when, reporting at Orderly Room, he became officially a member of the battalion family and could cultivate the orderly corporal in charge of the battalion correspondence and so hold at last in his own hands the official document signed by the chief-of-staff at Poperinghe, containing not only the blackamoor's name but the rich and organ-rolling one of the organization, committee, which he headed: *Les Amis Myriades et Anonymes à la France de Tout le Monde*—a title, a designation, so embracing, so richly sonorous with grandeur and faith, as to have freed itself completely from man and his agonies, majestic in empyrean, as weightless and palpless upon the anguished earth as the adumbration of a cloud. And if he had hoped to get anything at all, even that much, let alone anything more, from the owner of the money-belt, he would have been wrong indeed there: which (the failure) cost him five shillings in francs: hunting the man down and stopping him by simply getting in front of him and standing there, saying baldly and bluntly:

'Who is Reverend Tobe Sutterfield?' then still standing there for better than another minute beneath the harsh spent vituperation, until he could say at last: 'Are you finished now? Then I apologise. All I really want is ten bob:' and watched his name go down into the little dogeared book and took the francs which he would not even spend, so that the thirty sixpences would go back to their source in the original notes. But at least he had established a working, a speaking relationship; because of his orderly-room contact, he was able to use it, not needing to block the way this time to speak:

'Best keep this a staff matter, though I think you should know. We're going back in tonight.' The man looked at him. 'Something is going to happen. They have brought too many troops down here. It's a battle. The ones who thought up Loos cant rest on their laurels forever, you know.' Still the man only looked at him. 'It's your money. So you can protect yourself. Who knows? you may be one of the ones to stay alive. Instead of letting us bring you only sixpence a day, demand it all at once and bury it somewhere.' Still the man just looked at him, not even with contempt; suddenly the runner thought, with humility, abasement almost: *He has ethics, like a banker, not to his clients because they are people, but because they are clients. Not pity: he would bankrupt any—all—of them without turning a hair, once they had accepted the gambit; it's ethics toward his vocation, his trade, his profession. It's purity. No: it's even more than that: it's chastity, like Caesar's wife,*—watching it; the battalion went in that night, and he was right: when it came out again—the sixty-odd percent. which was left of it—it bore forever across its memory like the sear of a heated poker, the name of the little stream not much wider in places than a good downwind spit, and the other Somme names—Arras and Albert, Bapaume and St Quentin and Beaumont Hamel—ineradicable, to last as long as the capacity for breathing would, the capacity for tears,—saying (the runner) this time:

'You mean that all that out there is just a perfectly healthy and normal panic, like a market-crash: necessary to keep the body itself strong and hale? that the ones who died and will still die in it, were allotted to do so, like the little brokers and traders without wit or intelligence or perhaps just enough money backing, whose high destiny it is to commit suicide in order to keep the edifice of finance solvent?' And still the other only looked at him, not even contemptuous, not even with pity: just waiting until the runner had finished this time. Then he said:

'Well? Do you want the tanner, or dont you?'

The runner took the money, the francs. He spent them, this time, seeing for the first time, thinking, how finance was like poetry, demanding, requiring a giver and a taker too in order to endure; singer and listener, banker and borrower, buyer and seller, both ethical, unimpugnable, immaculate in devotion and faith; thinking *I was the one who failed; I was the debaser, the betrayer*, spending the money this time, usually at one blow, in modest orgies of food and drink for whoever would share it with him, fulfilling his sixpence-by-sixpence contract, then borrowing the ten shillings again, with the single-mindedness of a Roman Catholic at his devotions or expiating a penance: through that fall, that winter; it would be spring soon and now his leave would be coming up again and he thought, quietly, without grief, without regret: *Of course I could go back home, back to London. Because what else can you do to a cashiered subaltern in this year of Our Lord One Nine One Seven but give him a rifle and a bayonet and I already have those;* when, suddenly and peacefully, he knew what he would do with that freedom, that liberty which he no longer had any use for because there was no more any place for it on the earth; and this time he would ask not for shillings but pounds, setting its valuation not in shillings but in pounds, not only on his pilgrimage back to when and where the lost free spirit of man once existed, but on that which made the pilgrimage possible, asking for ten of them and himself setting the rate and interest at ten shillings a day for thirty days.

'Going to Paris to celebrate your f. . .ing D.C.M. are you?' the other said.

'Why not?' he said: and took the ten pounds in francs and with the ghost of his lost youth dead fifteen years now, he retraced the perimeter of his dead life when he had not only hoped but believed, concentric about the once-sylvan vale where squatted the gray and simple stone of Saint Sulpice, saving for the last the narrow crooked passageway in which he had lived for three years, passing the Sorbonne but only slowing, not turning in, and the other familiar Left Bank places—quai and bridge, gallery and garden cafe—where he had spent his rich leisure and his frugal money; it was not until the second solitary and sentimental morning, after coffee (and *Figaro*: today was April eighth, an English liner, this time practically full of Americans, had been torpedoed yesterday off Ireland; he thought peacefully, tearless: *They'll have to come in now; we can destroy both hemispheres now*) at the Deux Magots, taking the long way, through the Luxembourg Gardens again among the nursemaids and maimed soldiers (another spring, perhaps by this autumn even, there would be American uniforms too) and the stained effigies of gods and queens, into the rue Vaugirard, already looking ahead to discern the narrow crevice which would be the rue Servandoni and the garret which he had called home (perhaps Monsieur and Madame Gargne, *patron* and *patronne*, would still be there to greet him), when he saw it—the banner, the lettered cloth strip fastened above the archway where the ducal and princely carriages had used to pass, affirming its grandiose and humble declaration out of the old faubourg of aristocrats: *Les Amis Myriades et Anonymes à la France de Tout le Monde*, and, already one in a thin steady trickle of people—soldiers and civilians, men and women, old and young—entered something which seemed to him afterward like a dream: a vestibule, an anteroom, where a strong hale plain woman of no age, in a white coif like a nun, sat knitting, who said:

'Monsieur?'

'Monsieur le président, Madame, s'il vous plaît. Monsieur le Révérend Sutterfield:' and who (the woman) said again, with no pause in the click and flick of the needles:

'Monsieur?'

'Le chef de bureau, Madame. Le directeur. Monsieur Le Réverénd Sutterfield.'

'Ah,' the woman said. 'Monsieur Tooleyman:' and, still knitting, rose to precede, guide, conduct him: a vast marble-floored hall with gilded cornices and hung with chandeliers and furnished, crowded, heterogeneous and without order, with wooden benches and the sort of battered chairs you rent for a few sous at band concerts in parks, murmurous not with the voices but as though with the simple breathing, the inspiration and suspiration of the people—the soldiers maimed and unmaimed, the old men and women in black veils and armbands and the young women here and there carrying a child against or even beneath the complete weeds of bereavement and grieving—singly or in small groups like family groups about the vast room murmurous also still of dukes and princes and millionaires, facing the end of the room across which was suspended another of the cloth banners, the lettered strip like that one above the gateway and lettered like it: *Les Amis Myriades et Anonymes à la France de Tout le Monde:* not looking at the banner, not watching it; not like people in church: it was not subdued enough for that, but perhaps like people in a railway station where a train has been indefinitely delayed; then the rich curve of a stairway, the woman stopping and standing aside, still knitting and not even looking up to speak:

'Prière de monter, monsieur:' and he did so: who had traversed a cloud, now mounting to the uttermost airy nepenthelene pinnacle: a small chamber like a duchess's boudoir in heaven converted temporarily to represent a business office in a charade: a new innocent and barren desk and three hard and innocent chairs and behind the desk the serene and noble face in its narrow clasp of white wool rising now from the horizon-blue of an infantry corporal's uniform which by its look had lain only yesterday still on a supply sergeant's shelves, and slightly behind him the pole-thin Negro youth in the uniform and badges of a French sub-lieutenant which looked almost as new, himself facing them across it, the voices also serenely congruous and inconsequential, like dream:

'Yes, it used to be Sutterfield. But I changed it. To make it easier for the folks. From the Association.'

'Oh. Tout le Monde.'

'Yes. Tooleyman.'

'So you came up that day to see . . . . I was about to say friend——'

'Yes, he aint quite ready yet. It was to see if he needed money.'

'Money? He?'

'The horse,' the old Negro said. 'That they claimed we stole. Except that we couldn't have stole it, even if we had wanted to. Because it never belonged to no man to be stole from. It was the world's horse. The champion. No, that's wrong too. Things belonged to it, not it to things. Things and people both. He did. I did. All three of us did before it was over.'

'He?' the runner said.

'Mistairy.'

'Mist what?' the runner said.

'Harry,' the youth said. 'That's how he pronounced it.'

'Oh,' the runner said, with a sort of shame. 'Of course. Mistairy——'

'That's right,' the old Negro said. 'He kept on trying to get me to say just Airy, but I reckon I was too old.' So he told it: what he had seen, watched at first hand, and what he had divined from what he had seen, watched: which was not all; the runner knew that, thinking, *A protagonist. If I'm to run with the hare and be the hounds too, I must have a protagonist,* even while the youth, speaking for the first time, answered that:

'It was the deputy marshal that sent the New Orleans lawyer.'

'The who?' the runner said.

'The Federal deputy marshal,' the youth said. 'The head man of the folks chasing us.'

'All right,' the runner said. 'Tell me.'

† † †

It was 1912, two years before the war; the horse was a three-year-old running horse, but such a horse that even the price which the Argentine hide-and-wheat prince paid for it at the Newmarket sale, although an exceptional one, was not an outrageous one. Its groom was the sentry, the man with the ledger and the money-belt. He went out to America with it, whereupon within the next twenty-four months three things happened to him which changed completely not only his life but his character too, so that when late in 1914 he returned to England to enlist, it was as though somewhere behind the Mississippi Valley hinterland where within the first three months he had vanished, a new man had been born, without past, without griefs, without recollections.

He was not merely included in the sale of the horse, he was compelled into it. And not by the buyer nor even the seller, but by the sold: the chattel: the horse itself, with an imperiousness not even to be temporised with, let alone denied. It was not because he was the exceptional groom, which he might have been, nor even the first rate one which he actually was. It was because there had developed apparently on sight between the man and the animal something which was no mere rapport but an affinity, not from understanding to understanding but from heart to heart and glands to glands, so that unless the man was present or at least nearby, the horse was not even less than a horse: it was no longer a horse at all: not at all intractable and anything but unpredictable, because it was quite predictable in fact; not only dangerous, but in effect, for all its dedicated and consecrated end and purpose—the long careful breeding and selecting which finally produced it to be sold for the price it brought to perform the one rite for which it had been shaped—worthless, letting none save the one man enter the same walls or fence with it to groom or feed it, no jockey or exercise boy to approach and mount it until the man bade it; and even then, with the rider actually up, not even running until—whatever the communication was: voice, touch, whatever—the man had set it free.

So the Argentine bought the groom too, for a sum left in escrow in a London bank, to become the groom's on his return to England after being formally discharged. By the horse of course, since nothing else could, which (the horse) in the end discharged and absolved them all, the old Negro telling this part of it since this was where he—they—himself and his grandson—came into it:—the horse which before the groom came into its life, merely won races, but which after his advent, began to break records; three weeks after it first felt his hand and heard his voice, it set a mark ('The race was named the Sillinger,' the old Negro said. 'It was like our Derby at home.') which seven years later was still standing; and in its first South American race, although only two weeks out of the ship after a month and a half at sea, it set one not likely to be touched at any time. ('Not nowhere. At no time. By no horse,' the old Negro said.) And the next day it was bought by a United States oil baron for a price which even the Argentine millionaire could not refuse, and two weeks later landed in New Orleans, where the old Negro, a preacher on Sunday and the rest of the week a groom and hostler in the new owner's Kentucky breeding and training stables, met it; and two nights later the train drawing the van containing the horse and the two grooms, the white one and the black one, plunged through a flood-weakened trestle: out of which confusion and mischance were born the twenty-two months from which the English groom emerged at last a practicing Baptist: a Mason: and one of his time's most skillful manipulators of or players at dice.

Sixteen of the twenty-two were the months during which the five separately organised though now grimly unified groups—the Federal government, the successive state police forces and the railway's and the insurance company's and the oil baron's private detectives—pursued the four of them—the crippled horse and the English groom and the old Negro and the twelve-year-old child who rode it—up and down and back and forth through the section of the Mississippi watershed between Illinois and the Gulf of Mexico and Kansas and Alabama, where on three legs the horse had been running in remote back-country quarter-races and winning most of them, the old Negro telling it, grave and tranquil, serenely and peacefully inconsequential, like listening to a dream, until presently the runner five years afterward was seeing what the Federal deputy marshal had five years ago while in the middle of it: not a theft, but a passion, an immolation, an apotheosis—no gang of opportunists fleeing with a crippled horse whose value, even whole, had ceased weeks back to equal the sum spent on its pursuit, but the immortal pageant-piece of the tender legend which was the crowning glory of man's own legend beginning when his first paired children lost well the world and from which paired prototypes they still challenged paradise, still paired and still immortal against the chronicle's grimed and bloodstained pages: Adam and Lilith and Paris and Helen and Pyramus and Thisbe and all the other recordless Romeos and their Juliets, the world's oldest and most shining tale limning in his brief turn the warp-legged foul-mouthed English horse-groom as ever Paris or Lochinvar or any else of earth's splendid rapers: the doomed glorious frenzy of a love-story, pursued not by an unclosed office file nor even the raging frustration of the millionaire owner, but by its own inherent doom since, being immortal, the story, the legend, was not to be owned by any one of the pairs who added to its shining and tragic increment, but only to be used, passed through, by each in their doomed and homeless turn.

He didn't tell how they did it: only that they did it: as if, once it was done, how no longer mattered; that if something must be done, it is done, and then hardship or anguish or even impossibility no longer signify:—got the frantic and injured horse out of the demolished car and into the bayou where it could swim while they held its head above water—('He found a boat,' the old Negro said. 'If you could call it a boat. Whittled out of a log and done already turned over before you even put your foot in it. They called them pirogues. They talked gobble talk there, like they do here.')—then out of the bayou too, into such complete invisibility that when the railroad detectives reached the scene the next morning, it was as if the flood itself had washed the three of them away. It was a hummock, a small island in the swamp not a mile from the collapsed trestle, where a work-train and crew had arrived the next morning to rebuild the bridge and the track, and from which (They got the horse as far up out of the water as they could the first night, and the old Negro was left to attend it. 'I just give it water, and kept a mud pack on the hip and tried to keep the gnats and flies and mosquitoes away,' the old Negro said.) the groom returned at dawn on the third day, with a block-and-tackle bearing the railroad company's stencil in the pirogue, and food for themselves and the horse and canvas for the sling and cradle and plaster of Paris for the case—('I know what you're going to ask now,' the old Negro said. 'Where we got the money for all that. He got it like he done the boat,' telling that too: the cockney horse-groom who had never been further from London than Epsom or Doncaster yet who in two years of America had become a Mason and a Baptist, who in only two weeks in the forecastle of the American freighter up from Buenos Aires had discovered or anyway revealed to himself that rapport with and affinity for dice, who on the first return to the scene of the wreck had picked up the block-and-tackle simply because he happened to pass it, since his true destination had been the bunk-car where the Negro work-gang slept, waking them, the white man in his swamp-fouled alien jodhpurs and the black ones in undershirts or dungaree pants or in nothing at all, squatting around a spread blanket beneath the smoking lantern and the bank notes and the coins and the clicking and scuttering dice.)—and in the pitch dark—he had brought back no lantern, no light; it would not only have been dangerous to show one, he didn't even need one: scornfully, even contemptuously, who from his tenth year had known the bodies of horses as the blind man knows the room he durst not leave: any more than he would have brought back a veterinary, not only not needing one but he would not have let any hand save his or the old Negro's touch the horse, even if the horse had permitted it—they suspended the horse and set the hip and built the immobilising cast.

Then the weeks while the ruined hip knitted and the search-parties, with every exit to the swamp watched and guarded, continued to drag the bayou beneath the trestle, and to splash and curse among the moccasins and rattlesnakes and alligators of the swamp itself, long after they (the pursuers) had come to believe that the horse was dead for the simple reason that it must be dead, since that particular horse could not be anything else but dead and still be invisible, and that the owner would in the end gain only the privilege of venting his vengeance on the thieves. And once each week, as soon as it was dark enough and the search-parties had withdrawn for the night, the groom would depart in the pirogue, to return before dawn two or three days later with another supply of food and forage; two and three days now because the trestle was repaired now; once more trains roared hollowly across it in the night and the work-gang and that source of revenue or income was gone, back to New Orleans where it had come from and now the white man was going to New Orleans himself, bucking the professional games on baize-covered tables beneath electric lights and now not even the old Negro—(a horseman, a groom, merely by accident, but by avocation and dedication a minister of God, sworn dedicated enemy of sin yet who apparently without qualm or hesitation had long since drawn and then forgot it the line of his rectitude to include the magnificent ruined horse and all who were willing to serve it)—would know how far he sometimes had to go before he found another spread blanket beneath a smoked lantern or, as a last resort, the electric-lit baize table, where, although in their leathern cup the dice were as beyond impugnment as Caesar's wife, the counters—chips, money—

still accrued, whether or not to the benison of his gift or to the simple compulsion of his need.

Then months, not only within daily earshot of the trains once more thundering across the repaired trestle but of the search parties themselves (to whom at times either of them could have spoken without even raising his voice), the search continuing long after the ones who did the cursing and splashing and the frantic recoiling from the sluggish thrash or vicious buzz of startled moccasins and rattlesnakes all believed that the horse was long since dead and vanished forever into the sleepless insatiable appetites of eels and gars and turtles and the thief himself fled, out of the country and out of the nation and perhaps even out of the continent and the hemisphere, but continuing nevertheless because the railroad company had for stake an expensive set of triple blocks and over two hundred feet of two-inch cable, and the insurance company owned banks and barge lines and chain stores from Portland, Maine to Oregon and so could afford not to lose even a one-dollar horse, let alone a fifty thousand dollar one, and the horse's owner that bottomless purse which would not miss the value of the sixty race horses he still owned, in order to revenge himself on the thief of the sixty-first, and the Federal police had more at stake than even the state ones who could only share in the glory and the reward: they had a file to be closed out—until one day a United Press flash came, relayed last night from Washington to the Federal deputy, of how a horse, a valuable Thoroughbred and running on three legs, in charge of or at least accompanied by a small bandy-legged foreigner who could barely speak English, and a middle-aged Negro preacher, and ridden by a twelve-year-old Negro boy, had run away from the whole field in a three-furlong race at Weatherford, Texas—('We walked it,' the old Negro said, before the runner could ask him. 'At night. It needed that much to get used to itself again. To stop remembering that trustle and get limbered up again and start being a horse. When daylight come, we would hide in the woods again.' And afterwards too, telling that too: how they didn't dare else: run one race and then leave directly afterward without even stopping almost, because as soon as that three-legged horse won a race the whole world would hear about it and they had to stay at least one day ahead of them.)—and got there one day too late, to learn that the Negro preacher and the snarling contemptuous foreigner had appeared suddenly from nowhere exactly in time to enter the three-legged Thoroughbred in a race on which the foreigner had betted sums ranging (by this time) all the way from ten to a thousand dollars, at odds ranging all the way from one to ten to one to a hundred, the three-legged horse breaking so fast from the post that the barrier seemed actually to have sprung behind it, and running so fast that the trailing field appeared, if anything, to be running in another and later race, and so far ahead at the finish that the jockey seemed to have no control over it at all—if anyone, let alone a child of twelve or at most thirteen who rode the race without saddle at all but simply a bellyband and a surcingle to hold on to (this informant had seen the race), could have held it after the barrier dropped, the horse crossing the finish line at full speed and apparently bent on making another circuit of the track had not the white foreigner, leaning on the rail beyond the finish line, spoken a single word to it in a voice you could not have heard fifteen feet away.

And the next place where they were within even three days of the horse was at Willow Springs, Iowa, and next to that, Bucyrus, Ohio, and the next time they were almost two weeks behind—an inaccessible valley in the east Tennessee mountains three months later, so remote not only from railroads but even telegraphs and telephones too, that the horse had been running and winning races for ten days before the pursuit ever heard of it; this was indubitably where he joined, was received into, the order of Masons: since this was the first time they had stopped for longer than one afternoon, the horse able now to run for ten undisturbed days before the pursuit even heard about it, so that, when the pursuers left the valley, they were twice ten days behind the horse, since after two weeks of patient asking and listening up and down that thirty-mile-long mountain-cradled saucer, again, as at the scene of the original disappearance, they had not found one human being who had ever heard of the three-legged horse and the two men and the child, let alone seen them.

So when they heard of the horse next in central Alabama, it was already gone from there, moving west again, the pursuers still a month behind across Mississippi: across the Mississippi River into Arkansas, pausing only as a bird pauses: not alighting, though the last thing the pause could have been called was hovering since the horse would be running, once more at that incredible, that unbelievable, speed (and at the incredible and unbelievable odds too; by report and rumor the two men—the aged Negro man of God, and the foul-mouthed white one to whom to grant the status of man was merely to accept Darkness' emissary in the stead of its actual prince and master—had won tens of thousands of dollars) as if their mundane progress across America were too slow to register on the eye, and only during those incredible moments against a white rail did the horse and the three adjunctive human beings become visible.

Whereupon the Federal deputy, the titular-by-protocol leader of the pursuit, found that, suddenly and with no warning, something had happened to him which was to happen five years later in Paris to a British soldier even whose name he would never hear. He—the deputy—was a poet, not the writing kind, or anyway not yet, but rather still one of Homer's mere mute orphan godchildren sired by blind chance into a wealthy and political New Orleans family and who, by that family's standards, had failed at Harvard and then wasted two years at Oxford before the family found out about it and fetched him home where, after some months under the threat of the full marshalate, he compromised with his father on the simple deputyship. And so that night—it was in Arkansas, in a new paint-rank hotel room in a little booming logging town, itself less old than last year—he realised what it was about the whole business that he refused to accept ever since Weatherford, Texas, and then in the next second dismissed it forever because what remained had not only to be the answer but the truth too; or not even *the* truth, but *truth*, because truth was truth: it didn't have to be anything; it didn't even care whether it was so or not even, looking (the deputy) at it not even in triumph but in humility, because an old Negro minister had already seen it with one glance going on two years ago now—a minister, a man of God, sworn and dedicated enemy of man's lusts and follies, yet who from that first moment had not only abetted theft and gambling, but had given to the same cause the tender virgin years of his own child as ever of old had Samuel's father or Abraham his Isaac; and not even with pride because at last he had finally seen the truth even if it did take him a year, but at least pride in the fact that from the very first, as he knew now, he had performed his part in the pursuit with passion and regret. So ten minutes later he waked his second-in-command, and two days later in the New York office he said, 'Give it up. You'll never catch him.'

'Meaning you wont,' the owner of the horse said.

'If you like it that way,' the deputy said. 'I've resigned.'

'You should have done that eight months ago when you quit.'

'Touché then,' the deputy said. 'If that makes you feel better too. Maybe what I'm trying to do now is apologise because I didn't know it eight months ago too.' He said: 'I know about what you have spent so far. You know what the horse is now. I'll give you my check for that amount. I'll buy your ruined horse from you. Call it off.' The owner told him what he had actually paid for the horse. It was almost as much as the public believed. 'All right,' the deputy said. 'I cant give you a check for that much, but I'll sign a note for it. Even my father wont live forever.' The owner pressed a button. A secretary entered. The owner spoke briefly to the secretary, who went out and returned and laid a check on the desk before the owner, who signed the check and pushed it across to the deputy. It was for a sum still larger than the difference between the horse's cost and that of the pursuit to date. It was made out to the deputy.

'That's your fee for catching my horse and deporting that Englishman and bringing my nigger back in handcuffs,' the owner said. The deputy folded the check twice and tore it across twice, the owner's thumb already on the buzzer as the deputy dropped the fragments carefully into an ashtray and was already standing to leave when the secretary opened the door again. 'Another check,' the owner said without even turning his head. 'Add to it the reward for the capture of the men who stole my horse.'

But he didn't even wait for that one, and it was Oklahoma before he (ex now) overtook the pursuit, joining it now as the private young man with money in his pocket—or who had had it once and lost or spent it—had used to join Marlborough's Continental Tours (and indeed meeting among them who a week ago had been his companions in endeavor the same cold-fronted unanimity of half-contempt which the private young men would meet among Marlborough's professionals). Then the little bleak railway stations between a cattle-chute and a water-tank, the men in broad hats and heeled boots already clumped about the placard offering for a stolen horse a reward such as even Americans had never seen before—the reproduction of a newspaper photograph made in Buenos Aires of the man and the horse together, with a printed description of both—a face as familiar and recognisable now to the central part of the United States (Canada and Mexico too) as that of a president or a female murderer, but above all, the sum, the amount of the reward—the black, succinct evocation of that golden dream, that shining and incredible heap of dollars to be had by any man for the simple turn of a tongue, always ahead of them (of the pursuit certainly, and, the deputy now believed, of the pursued too), disseminating the poison faster than they advanced, faster even than the meteor-course of love and sacrifice, until already the whole Mississippi-Missouri-Ohio watershed must be corrupt and befouled and at last the deputy knew that the end was in sight: thinking how it was no wonder that man had never been able to solve the problems of his span upon earth, since he has taken no steps whatever to educate himself, not in how to manage his lusts and follies; they harm him only in sporadic, almost individual instances; but in how to cope with his own blind mass and weight: seeing them—the man and the horse and the two Negroes whom they had snatched as it were willy nilly into that fierce and radiant orbit—doomed not at all because passion is ephemeral (which was why they had never found any better name for it, which was why Eve and the Snake and Mary and the Lamb and Ahab and the Whale and Androcles and Balzac's African deserter, and all the celestial zoology of horse and goat and swan and bull, were the firmament of man's history instead of the mere rubble of his past), nor even because the rape was theft and theft is wrong and wrong shall not prevail, but simply because, due to the sheer repetition of zeros behind a dollar-mark on a printed placard, everyone within eyerange or tonguespread (which was every human capable of seeing and hearing between Canada and Mexico and the Rockies and the Appalachians) would be almost frantically attuned to the merest whisper regarding the horse's whereabouts.

No, it would not be much longer now, and for an instant he thought, toyed with the idea, of confounding corruption with corruption: using the equivalent of the check which in New York he had offered to write, to combat the reward, and put that away because that would fail too: not that corrupting corruption would merely spread corruption that much further, but because the idea merely created an image which even a poet must regard as only a poet's fantastic whimsy: Mammon's David ringing for a moment anyway Mammon's Goliath's brazen invincible unregenerate skull. It was not long now, the end was actually in sight when the course, the run (as if it too knew that this was near the end) turned sharply back south and east across Missouri and into the closing V where the St Francis river entered the Mississippi, haunted still by the ghosts of the old bank-and-railroad bandits who had refuged there; then over, finished, done: an afternoon, a little lost branch-line county seat with a fairgrounds and a rail-less half-mile track, the pursuers crossing the infield in the van of a growing crowd of local people, town and swamp and farm, all men, silent, watching, not crowding them at all yet: just watching; and now for the first time they laid eyes on the thief whom they had pursued now for almost fifteen months: the foreigner, the Englishman leaning in the doorless frame of the fallen stable, the butt of the still-warm pistol protruding from the waistband of his filthy jodhpurs, and behind him the body of the horse shot neatly once through the star on its forehead and beyond the horse the Roman senator's head and the brushed worn frock coat of the old Negro preacher, and beyond him in turn, in deeper shadow still, the still white eyeballs of the child; and that night in the jail cell the ex-deputy (still a lawyer even though the prisoner violently and obscenely repudiated him) said:

'I would have done it too of course. But tell me why—— No, I know why. I know the reason. I know it's true: I just want to hear you say it, hear both of us say it so I'll know it's real'——already—or still—speaking even through the other's single vicious obscene contemptuous epithet: 'You could have surrendered the horse at any time and it could have stayed alive, but that was not it: not just to keep it alive, anymore than for the few thousands or the few hundred thousands that people will always be convinced you won on it'——stopping then and even waiting, or anyway watching, exultant and calm while the prisoner cursed, not toward him nor even just at him, but him, the ex-deputy, steadily and for perhaps a full minute, with harsh and obscene unimagination, then the ex-deputy speaking again, rapid and peaceful and soothing: 'All right, all right. The reason was so that it could run, keep on running, keep on losing races at least, finish races at least even if it did have to run them on three legs, did run them on three legs because it was a giant and didn't need even three legs to run them on but only one with a hoof at the end to qualify as a horse. While they would have taken it back to the Kentucky farm and shut it up in a whorehouse where it wouldn't need any legs at all, not even a sling suspended from a travelling crane geared by machinery to the rhythm of ejaculation, since a skillful pander with a tin cup and a rubber glove'——exultant and quite calm, murmuring: 'Fathering colts forever more; they would have used its ballocks to geld its heart with for the rest of its life, except that you saved it because any man can be a father, but only the best, the brave——' and left in the middle of the spent dull repetitive cursing and from New Orleans the next morning sent back the best lawyer which even he, with all the vast scope of his family's political affiliations and his own semiprofessional and social ones, could find—a lawyer whose like the little lost Missouri town had probably never seen before, nor anyone else for that matter, as having come four hundred miles to defend a nameless foreign horsethief—telling the lawyer what he had seen there: the curious, watching attitude of the town——

'A mob,' the lawyer said, with a sort of unction almost. 'It's a long time since I have coped with a mob.'

'No no,' the client said quickly. 'They are just watching, waiting for something, I didn't have time to find out what.'

And the lawyer saw that too. He found more than that: arriving on the second morning after an all-night drive in his private chauffeured limousine, and within thirty minutes was on the telephone back to his client in New Orleans, because the man he had come to defend was gone, vanished, not escaped from the jail but freed from it, the lawyer sitting at the telephone where he could look out into the quiet square almost empty of movement, from which nobody watched him now nor for that matter had ever actually looked at him, but where he was conscious of them—not so much the dour, slow-speaking, half-western half-southern faces, but of the waiting, the attention.

And not only the white man, the two Negroes were gone too, the lawyer on the New Orleans telephone again that evening, not because it had taken him this long to learn these meagre details, but simply because he realised now that this was all he was going to find out here, by inquiry or purchase or just by simple listening, no matter how much longer he stayed: how the two Negroes had never reached the jail at all but had vanished apparently into thin air somewhere between it and the courthouse, where the ex-deputy's Federal successor had formally relinquished the three prisoners to the local sheriff; only the white man ever to reach the jail, because the ex-deputy had seen him there, and he gone too now, not even freed so much as just vanished, the lawyer discovering five minutes after his arrival that there was no prisoner, and at the end of thirty no felon, and by mid-afternoon no crime even, the body of the horse having vanished too sometime during that first night, and nobody had moved it nor seen anyone moving it nor heard of anyone who might have moved it or in fact even knew that it was missing.

But the pursuit had long ago learned about all there was to know about those two weeks in the eastern Tennessee valley last fall, and the ex-deputy had briefed the lawyer, and so to the lawyer there was no mystery about it; he had already divined the solution: there would be Masons in Missouri too—an opinion which the client in New Orleans didn't even bother to ignore, let alone acknowledge, not the ex-deputy's but the poet's voice actually babbling at his end of the wire while the lawyer was still talking:

'About the money,' the lawyer said. 'They searched him, of course——'

'All right, all right,' the ex-deputy said. —right perhaps, justice certainly, might not have prevailed, but something more important had——

'He had only ninety-four dollars and a few cents,' the lawyer said.

'The old Negro has got the rest of it in the tail of that frock-coat,' the ex-deputy said.——truth, love, sacrifice, and something else even more important than they: some bond between or from man to his brother man stronger than even the golden shackles which coopered precariously his ramshackle earth——

'I'll be damned,' the lawyer said. 'Of course that's where the money is. Why the hell I didn't—— Hush, and listen to me a minute. There's nothing more I can do here, so I'm coming back to town as soon as they unlock the garage in the morning and I can get my car. But you are already on the scene, you can do it quicker than I can by telephone from here. Get in touch with your people and get notices spread up and down the valley as quick as you can—placards, descriptions of all three of them——'

'No,' the ex-deputy said. 'You must stay there. If anything further comes out of the charge, it will have to originate there. You must be there to protect him.'

'The only one who will need protection here is the first man who tries to lay a hand on the man who earned as much money as they believe he did, with nothing but his bare hands and a three-legged horse,' the lawyer said. 'He's a fool. If he had stayed here, he could have had the sheriff's badge without even running for it. But I can do everything necessary by telephone from my office until we catch them.'

'I said from the first that you didn't understand,' the ex-deputy said. 'No: that you still did not believe me, even after I tried to tell you. I dont want to find him—them. I had my turn at bat, and struck out. You stay there. That's what you are for,' the ex-deputy said, and hung up. Though still the lawyer didn't move, his end of the connection still open, the smoke from his cigar standing like a balanced pencil on a carven hand until the other New Orleans number answered and he spoke to his confidential clerk, describing the two Negroes, rapid and explicit and succinct:

'Cover all the river towns from St Louis to Basin Street. Watch the cabin or stable or whatever it is in Lexington, of course; if he doesn't go back home himself, he might try to send the child back.'

'You're in the middle of a pretty good place to look for him now,' the clerk said. 'If the sheriff there wont——'

'Listen to me,' the lawyer said. 'Listen carefully. He must not reappear here under any condition. He must not be found at all until he can be picked up for something like vagrancy in some city big enough for nobody to know who he is, or care. Under no condition must he come into the clutches of any local officers in any town or hamlet small enough even to have heard of that three-legged horse, let alone seen it. Do you understand?'

A moment: then the clerk: 'So they really did win that much money.'

'Do as I tell you,' the lawyer said.

'Of course,' the clerk said. 'Only you're too late. The owner of the horse has already beat you. The police here have had that notice ever since yesterday, and I imagine the police everywhere have it by now—description, reward and all. They even know where the money is: in the tail-pocket of that preacher's coat the nigger wears. It's too bad every house he passes dont have a wireless, like ships do. Then he would know how valuable he is, and he would have something to trade with you on.'

'Do as I tell you,' the lawyer said; that was the second day; then the third day and the lawyer had established his headquarters or post of command in the judge's chambers next the courtroom in the courthouse, not by the consent or even acquiescence of the judge who was a circuit judge and merely followed the itinerary of his court and did not live in the town and was not even consulted, nor by the acquiescence of the town either but by its will, so that it did not even matter whether the judge was a Mason too or not; and in the barbershop that day the lawyer saw last night's St Louis paper bearing something which even purported to be a photograph of the old Negro, with the usual description and even a guess at the amount of money in the tail of the frock-coat, the barber, busy with another client, having apparently glanced at least once at the lawyer where he stood looking at the paper, because the barber said, 'That many folks hunting for him ought to find him,' then silence and then a voice from the other end of the shop, speaking to nothing and no one and with no inflection: 'Several thousand dollars.'

Then the fourth day, when the Department of Justice investigator and the one from the sheriff's bonding company arrived (the first St Louis reporter had reached the scene one train ahead of the U.P. man from Little Rock) and from his high small quiet borrowed window the lawyer watched the two strangers and the sheriff and the two men who would be the sheriff's local bondsmen, cross the square not to the front door of the bank but around to the discreet side one which led directly to the president's office; five minutes there, then out again, the two strangers stopping while the sheriff and the two local men scattered briskly and vanished, the two strangers looking after them until the Federal man removed his hat and seemed to be studying the inside of it for a moment, a second. Then he turned briskly, leaving the bonding company's man still looking out across the square, and crossed to the hotel and entered it, moving briskly now, and reappeared with his strapped bag and sat down on the bench opposite the bus stop; and then the bonding company's man moved too and crossed to the hotel and reappeared with his bag.

Then the fifth day and the sixth and even the two reporters had returned to where they came from and there remained in the town no stranger save the lawyer; nor was he a stranger anymore now, though he was never to know by what means the town had learned or divined that he was there not to prosecute but to shield; and at times during that idleness and waiting, he would imagine, envision himself actually in court with the man whom he had not only no expectation but even intention, of ever seeing at all—a picture of himself not engaged in just one more monotonous legal victory, but as a—perhaps *the*—figure in a pageant which in reality would be an historical commemoration, in fact, even more than that: the affirmation of a creed, a belief, the declaration of an undying faith, the postulation of an invincible way of life: the loud strong voice of America itself out of the westward roar of the tremendous and battered yet indomitably virgin continent, where nothing save the vast unmoral sky limited what a man could try to do, nor even the sky limit his success and the adulation of his fellow man; even the defence he would employ would be in the old fine strong American tradition of rapine, its working precedent having been already established in this very—or anyway approximate—land by an older and more successful thief than any English groom or Negro preacher: John Murrell himself, himself his own attorney: the rape was not a theft but merely a misdemeanor, since the placard offering the reward before the horse's demise had constituted a legal power of attorney authorising any man's hand to the body of the horse, and its violation had been a simple breach of trust, the burden of the proof of which lay with the pursuers since they would have to prove that the man had not been trying simply to find the owner and restore him his property all the time.

This, out of daydream's idle unexpectation, because the lawyer did not really expect ever to see either of them since the owner or the Federal Government would indubitably catch them first, right up to the morning of the seventh day when there was a knock at the jail's kitchen door—a knock not much louder than audibility, yet quite firm; and, firm, yet not at all peremptory: just polite, courteous and firm: a knock not often heard at the back door of a small Missouri jail, nor even quite at the back door of an Arkansas or Louisiana or Mississippi plantation house, where it might sooner have been at home, the turnkey's wife wiping her hands on her apron as she turned from the sink and opened the door on a middleageless Negro man in a worn brushed frock-coat and carrying a napless tophat, whom she did not recognise because she had not expected to see him there, possibly because he was alone, the boy, the child still standing five minutes later just inside the mouth of the alley beside the jail, where neither he nor the old one gave any sign of recognition whatever, although his grandfather—handcuffed now to the turnkey—actually brushed him in passing. But her husband recognised him at once, not by the face, he scarcely glanced at that, but by the coat: the worn dusty broadcloth garment which—not the man but the coat, and not even the whole coat but the elbow-deep, suitcase-roomy tails of it—the county and state police of five contiguous commonwealths had been blocking roads and searching farm wagons and automobiles and freight trains and the Jim Crow cars of passenger ones, and depot lavatories, charging in pairs and threes with shotguns and drawn pistols through the pool halls and burial associations and the kitchens and bedrooms of Negro tenements for sixty-five hours now, trying to find. As did the town too: the turnkey and his shackled prize had scarcely left the jail before they began to gather behind them a growing tail of men and youths and small boys like that of a rising kite, which in the street leading to the square the turnkey could still tell himself that he was leading, and which while crossing the square toward the courthouse he even still looked like he was, walking faster and faster, almost dragging the prisoner at the other end of the chain joining them, until at last he broke and even took one step actually running before he stopped and turned to face the pressing crowd, drawing the pistol from its holster all in one blind motion like the hopeless and furious repudiation of the boy turning, once more whole, stainless and absolved, to hurl his toy pistol into the very face of the charging elephant, victim no more of terror but of pride, and cried in a thin forlorn voice which itself was like the manless voice of a boy:

'Stop, men! This hyer's the Law!'—who, without doubt if they had run at him, would have stood his ground, still holding the pistol which he had not and would not even cock, dying without a struggle beneath the trampling feet in that one last high second of his badge and warrant:—a small, mild, ordinary man whom you have seen in his ten thousands walking the streets of little American towns, and some not so little either, not just in the vast central Valley but on the eastern and western watersheds and the high mountain plateaus too, who had received his job and office out of that inexhaustible reservoir of nepotism from which, during the hundred-odd years since the republic's founding, almost that many millions of its children had received not just their daily bread but a little something over for Saturday and Christmas too, since, coeval with the republic, it was one of the prime foundations,—in this case, from the current sheriff, whose remote kinswoman, to his unending surprise and unbelief even ten years afterward, the turnkey had somehow managed to marry;—a man so quiet so mild and so ordinary that none remarked the manner in which he accepted and affirmed the oath when sworn into his office: merely somebody else's nameless and unknown cousin by blood or maybe just marriage, promising to be as brave and honest and loyal as anyone could or should expect for the pay he would receive during the next four years in a position he would lose the day the sheriff went out of office, turning to meet his one high moment as the male mayfly concentrates his whole one day of life in the one evening act of procreation and then relinquishes it. But the crowd was not running at him: only walking, and that only because he was between them and the courthouse, checking for an instant at sight of the drawn pistol, until a voice said: 'Take that thing away from him before he hurts somebody:' and they did: a hand, not ungently nor even unkindly, wrenching the pistol firmly from him, the crowd moving again, converging on him, the same voice, not impatient so much as irascible, speaking to him by name this time:

'Gwan, Irey. Get out of the sun': so that, turning again, the turnkey faced merely another gambit, he must choose all over again: either to acquiesce forever more to man or sever himself forever more from the human race by the act—getting either himself or the prisoner free from one end or the other of the steel chain joining them—which would enable him to flee. Or not flee, not flight; who to dispute the moment's heroic image even in that last second: no puny fumbling with a blind mechanical insentient key, but instead one single lightning-stroke of sword or scimitar across the betraying wrist, and then running, the scarlet-spurting stump inevictably aloft like an unbowed pennon's staff or the undefeated lance's headless shank, not even in adjuration but in abdication of all man and his corruption.

But there was not even time for that; his only choice was against being trampled as, shoulder to shoulder now with his captive and, if anything, slightly behind him, they moved on in the center of the crowd, across the square and into the courthouse, a firm hand now grasping him above the elbow and thrusting him firmly on exactly as he had nightlily dreamed ever since he assumed his office of himself in the act of doing, as soon as he found a felon either small enough or mild enough to permit him, through the corridor and up the stairs to the judge's chambers, where the New Orleans lawyer gave one start of outrage then of astonishment and then the infinitesimal flicker which never reached his face at all nor even his eyes, until the same calm merely irascible voice said, 'This aint big enough. We'll use the courtroom' and he (the lawyer) was moving too, the three of them now—himself, the turnkey and the prisoner like three hencoops on a flood—filling the little room with a sibilant sound as though all the ghosts of Coke upon Littleton upon Blackstone upon Napoleon upon Julius Caesar had started up and back in one inextricable rustle, one aghast and dusty cry, and through the opposite door into the courtroom itself, where suddenly the lawyer was not only himself free of the crowd, he had managed (quite skilfully for all his bulk: a man not only tall but big, in rich dark broadcloth and an immaculate pique waistcoat and a black cravat bearing a single pearl like the egg of a celestial humming bird) to extricate the turnkey and the prisoner too, in the same motion kneeing the swing gate in the low railing enclosing Bench and witness stand and jury box and counsels' tables, and thrust the other two through it and followed and let the gate swing back while the crowd itself poured on into the auditorium.

People were entering now not only through the judge's chambers but through the main doors at the back too, not just men and boys now but women also—young girls who already at eight and nine in the morning had been drinking coca cola in the drugstores, and housewives testing meat and cabbages in the groceries and markets, or matching scraps of lace and buttons over drygoods counters—until not just the town but the county itself, all of which had probably seen the three-legged horse run, and most of which had contributed at least one or two each of the dollars (by now the total had reached the thirty thousands) which the two men had won and which the old Negro preacher had escaped with and indubitably concealed—seemed to be converging steadily into the courthouse, ringing with unhurried thunder the corridor and stairs and the cavernous courtroom itself, filling row by row the hard pew-like wooden benches until the last reverberation faded behind the cool frantic pulsing of pigeons in the clock tower on the roof and the brittle chitter and rattle of sparrows in the sycamores and locusts in the yard, and the calm merely irascible voice said—and not from behind any face but as though no one man spoke but rather the room itself: 'All right, Mister. Commence.'

And, standing with his prize behind the railing's flimsy sanctuary, bayed, trapped in fact, between the little wooden barrier which a child could step over in one stride like a degree of latitude or of honesty, and the sacred dais to which, even before he saw it, he had already lost his appeal, not alone except for his two companions nor even despite them, but in fact because of them, for a moment yet the lawyer watched Man pouring steadily into the tabernacle, the shrine itself, of his last tribal mysteries, entering it without temerity or challenge, because why not? it was his, he had decreed it, built it, sweated it up: not out of any particular need nor any long agony of hope, because he was not aware of any lack or long history of agony or that he participated in any long chronicle of frustrated yearning, but because he wanted it, could afford it, or anyway was going to have it whether he could afford it or not: to be no symbol nor cradle nor any mammalian apex, harbor where the incredible cockleshell of his invincible dream made soundings at last from the chartless latitudes of his lost beginnings and where, like that of the enduring sea, the voice of his affirmation roared murmuring home to the atoll-dais of his unanimity where no mere petty right, but blind justice itself, reigned ruthless and inattentive amid the deathless invincible smells of his victories: his stale tobacco spit and his sweat. Because to begin with, he was not *he* but *they*, and *they* only by electing to be, because what he actually was, was *I* and in the first place he was not a mammal and as for his chartless latitudes, he not only knew exactly where he came from six thousand years ago, but that in three score and ten or thereabouts he was going back there; and as for affirmation, the mark of a free man was his right to say *no* for no other reason except *no*, which answered for the unanimity too; and the floor was his because he had built it, paid for it, and who could spit on it if not he. And perhaps the lawyer had even read Dickens and Hugo once long ago when he was a young man, looking now across the flimsy barrier into no brick-and-plaster barn built yesterday by the God-fearing grandfathers of other orderly and decorous and God-fearing Missouri farmers, but back a hundred years into the stone hall older than Orleans or Capet or Charlemagne, filled with the wooden sabots until yesterday reeking with plowed land and manure, which had stained and fouled the trampled silks and lilies which had lasted a thousand years and were to have endured ten thousand more; and the caps of Mediterranean fishermen, and the smocks of cobblers and porters and road-menders stiffening with the crimson smears of the hands which had rent and cast down the silks and the lilies, looking out at them not even with mere awe and respect, not alone alarm, but with triumph and pride: pride in the triumph of man, and that out of all his kind, time and geography had matched him with this hour:—America, the United States in this April of Our Lord one thousand nine hundred and fourteen, where man had had a hundred and forty years in which to become so used to liberty that the simple unchallenged right to attend its ordered and regimented charades sufficed to keep him quiet and content; looking out at them a moment longer, then he turned and struck the handcuffs a sharp and almost musical blow and thundered down at the turnkey: 'What does this mean? Dont you know that no man shall be put twice in the same jeopardy?' then turned again and spoke into the room in that same voice like the rich snore of an organ: 'This man has been illegally arrested. The law compels his right to consult a lawyer. We will recess for ten minutes,' and turned again and opened the gate in the railing this time by thrusting the other two through it and on ahead of him toward the door to the judge's chambers, not even looking back as five men rose at the back of the room and went out through the main doors, and thrust the Negro and the turnkey into the judge's chambers and followed and shut the door and—the turnkey told this afterward—without even stopping, went on to the opposite door and opened it and was already standing in it when the five men from the courtroom came around the corner.

'Five minutes, gentlemen,' the lawyer said. 'Then we will resume in the courtroom,' and closed the door and came back to where the turnkey and the Negro stood. But he didn't even look at the Negro; and the turnkey, spent, exhausted, almost comatose from courage and excitement, discovered, realised with a kind of outraged unbelief that the lawyer, who had voluntarily given himself only ten minutes to do whatever he intended to do, was apparently going to use up some of them smoking, watching the lawyer produce the cigar from an upper pocket of the white vest which looked as if it had come right out from under the washerwoman's smoothing-iron five minutes ago—a pocket which contained three more just like it. Then the turnkey recognised its brand and therefore its cost—one dollar—because he had owned one once (and on the following Sunday morning smoked it) through the mistake of a stranger under the impression that it was the sheriff who had married his, the turnkey's, sister instead of he who had married the sheriff's brother's wife's niece, recognised it with grief and outrage too, the same thing happening again but this time a thousand times worse: the man who gave him the other cigar had asked nothing of him, whereas he knew now and at last what the lawyer wanted, was after, had been after all the while, setting the price of his, the turnkey's, corruption at that of one one-dollar cigar: this was the forty thousand dollars which the nigger had escaped with and hidden so good that even the Federal Government couldn't find it. Then the grief and outrage was not even outrage, let alone grief; it was triumph and pride and even joy too, since not only had the lawyer already lost even before he laid eyes on the nigger, he (the lawyer) wasn't even going to find it out until he (the turnkey) got good and ready to tell him, waiting for the lawyer to speak first, with no organ in the voice either now, which instead was as hard and calm and cold and vacant of trash as that of his wife's uncle-by-marriage:

'You've got to get him out of town. It's your only chance.' And maybe his (the turnkey's) voice wasn't too calm and maybe to a big city lawyer it didn't sound too hard either. But even one as big as this one could have heard the finality in it and, if he listened, the scorn and the contempt and the pleasure too:

'I can think of another. In fact, I'm fixing right now to take it.' Then to the nigger: 'Come on:' already moving toward the corridor door, drawing the nigger after him, and already reaching from the snap on his belt the ring containing the handcuff key. 'You're thinking of that money. I aint. Because it aint mine to think about. It's his, half of it is that is; whether or not a nigger aint got any business with half of forty thousand dollars aint none of my business nor yours neither. And soon as I unlock these handcuffs, he can go and get it,' and turned the knob and had opened the door when the voice stopped him—the hard calm not even loud voice behind him sounding like somebody dropping pebbles into a churn:

'Neither am I. Because there's not any money. I'm not even thinking about you. I'm thinking about your bondsmen:' and (the turnkey) heard the match and turned in time to watch the flame's hunchy squat at the drawing cigar's tip and the first pale gout of smoke hiding for an instant the lawyer's face.

'That's all right too,' the turnkey said. 'I been living in the jail two years already. So I wont even have to move. I expect I can even stand chain-gang work too.'

'Pah,' the lawyer said, not through smoke but in smoke, by means of smoke, the puff, the gout, the pale rich costly balloon bursting, vanishing, leaving the hard calm not loud word as durable and single as a piece of gravel or a buckshot: 'When you arrested this man the second time, you broke the law. As soon as you turn him loose, he wont have to hunt for a lawyer because there are probably a dozen of them from Memphis and Saint Louis and Little Rock waiting down there in the yard now, just hoping you will have no more sense than to turn him loose. They're not going to put you in jail. They're not even going to sue you. Because you haven't got any money or know where any is, anymore than this nigger does. They're going to sue your bondsmen—whoever they were and whatever it was they thought you could do for them—and your—what is it? brother-in-law?—the sheriff.'

'They were my——' he started to say kinsmen, but they

were not, they were his wife's kinsmen; he had plenty of his own, but none of them—or all of them together, for that matter—had enough money in a bank anywhere to guarantee a bond. Then he started to say friends, but they were his wife's family's friends too. But then it didn't matter what he said, because the voice had already read his mind:

'—which makes it harder; you might leave your own kinfolks holding the sack, but these are the sheriff's friends and you've got to sleep in the same bed with his niece every night.' Which was wrong too, since three years and two months and thirteen nights ago now, but that didn't matter either, the cigar smoking in the judge's ashtray now, and the voice: 'Come back here': and he returned, drawing the Negro with him, until they stood facing the white vest with its loop of watch-chain like a section of gold plow-trace, and the voice: 'You've got to get him into a jail somewhere where they can hold him long enough for you to put a charge on him that the law will accept. They can turn him loose the next day or the next minute if they want to; all you want is to have him on record as having been charged with a legal crime or misdemeanor by a legally qualified officer of a legally constituted court, then when his lawyers sue your bondsmen for false arrest, they can tell them to go chase themselves.'

'What charge?' the turnkey said.

'What's the next big jail from here? Not a county seat: a town with at least five thousand people in it?' The turnkey told him. 'All right. Take him there. Take my car; it's in the hotel garage; I'll telephone my driver from here. Only, you'll——but surely I dont need to tell you how to spirit a prisoner out of the clutches of a mob.' Which was true too, that was a part of the turnkey's dream too; he had planned it all, run it through his mind, out to the last splendid and victorious gesture, time and again since that moment two years ago when he had laid his hand on the Book and sworn the oath, not that he really expected it to happen but to be prepared against that moment when he should be called upon to prove not merely his fitness for his office but his honor and courage as a man, by preserving and defending the integrity of his oath in the very face of them by whose sufferance he held his office.

'Yes,' he said. 'Only——'

'All right,' the lawyer said. 'Unlock that damn thing. Here, give me the key:' and took it from his hand and unlocked the handcuffs and flung them onto the table, where they made again that faint musical note.

'Only——' the turnkey said again.

'Now go around by the corridor and shut the big door to the courtroom and lock it on the outside.'

'That wont stop them—hold them——'

'Dont worry about them. I'll attend to that. Go on.'

'Yes,' he said, and turned, then stopped again. 'Wait. What about them fellows outside the door there?' For perhaps two or three seconds the lawyer didn't say anything at all, and when he did speak, it was as though there was nobody else in the room, or in fact as though he was not even speaking aloud:

'Five men. And you a sworn officer of the law, armed. You might even draw your pistol. They're not dangerous, if you're careful.'

'Yes,' he said, and turned again and stopped again, not looking back: just stopping as he had turned. 'That charge.'

'Vagrancy,' the lawyer said.

'Vagrancy?' he said. 'A man owning half of forty-five thousand dollars?'

'Pah,' the lawyer said. 'He doesn't own half of anything, even one dollar. Go on.' But now it was he who didn't move; maybe he didn't look back, but he didn't move either, talking himself this time, and calm enough too:

'Because this thing is all wrong. It's backwards. The law spirits a nigger prisoner out of jail and out of town, to protect him from a mob that wants to take him out and burn him. All these folks want to do is to set this one free.'

'Dont you think the law should cut both ways?' the lawyer said. 'Dont you think it should protect people who didn't steal forty-five thousand dollars too?'

'Yes,' the turnkey said; and now he looked at the lawyer, his hand on the doorknob again but not turning it yet. 'Only that aint the question I want to ask anyway. And I reckon you got an answer to this one too and I hope it's a good one—' speaking calm and slow and clear himself too: 'This is all to it.

I just take him to Blankton long enough to get a legal charge on the books. Then he can go.'

'Look at his face,' the lawyer said. 'He hasn't got any money. He doesn't even know where any is. Neither of them do, because there never was any and what little there might have been, that cockney swipe threw away long ago on whores and whisky.'

'You still aint answered,' the turnkey said. 'As soon as the charge is on the books, he can go.'

'Yes,' the lawyer said. 'Lock the courtroom doors first. Then come back for the nigger.' Then the turnkey opened the door; the five men stood there but he didn't even falter: on through and past them; then suddenly, instead of following the corridor to the courtroom's rear door as the lawyer had ordered him, he turned toward the stairs, moving fast now, not running: just moving fast, down the stairs and along the hall to the office of his wife's uncle-in-law, deserted now, and into the office, around the partition and straight to the drawer and opened it and without even faltering, took from beneath the mass of old discharged warrants and incomplete subpoenas and paper clips and rubber stamps and corroded pen points, the spare office pistol and slipped it into the empty holster and returned to the hall and mounted the opposite stairway which brought him to the main courtroom doors and drew them quietly to even as a face, then three, then a dozen, turned to look at him, and turned the key in the lock and withdrew it and put it into his pocket, already hurrying again, even running now, back to the judge's chambers where the lawyer had put the receiver back on its hook and pushed the telephone away and reached for the cigar in the ashtray and actually looked for the first time at the Negro, drawing the cigar to life in one slow inhale-exhale and through the smoke for the first time examined the calm no-aged Roman senator's face framed in a narrow unclosed circlet of grizzled hair clasping the skull like a caesar's laurels above the aged worn carefully brushed carefully mended frock coat, and then spoke, the two of them in succinct flat *poste-riposte* that was almost monotone:

'You haven't got any money, have you?'

'No.'

'You dont even know where any is, do you?'

'No.'

'Because there's not any. There never was. And even that little, your white bully boy threw away before you even saw it——'

'You're wrong. And you believe you're wrong too. Because I know——'

'All right. Maybe it was even a whole hundred dollars.'

'More than that.'

'More than thirty thousand dollars?' and only the faintest hesitation here; no faulting: only an interval: the voice still strong, still invincibly unshaken and unshakable:

'Yes.'

'How much more than thirty thousand dollars? . . . . All right. How much more than a hundred dollars? . . . Did you ever have a hundred dollars? Ever see a hundred dollars? . . . All right. You know it's more than a hundred dollars, but you dont know how much more. Is that it?'

'Yes. But you dont need to worry——'

'And you came back to get your half of the hundred dollars anyway.'

'I came back to tell him goodbye before he goes back home.'

'Back home?' the lawyer said quickly. 'You mean, England? Did he tell you that?' and the other, insuperably calm, insuperably intractable:

'How could he told me? Because he wouldn't need to. When a man comes to the place where he aint got anything left worth spending or losing, he always goes back home. But you dont need to worry, because I know what you're fixing to do: lock me up in the jail until he hears about it in the newspapers and comes back. And you're right, because that's what he'll do, because he needs me too. And you dont need to worry about how much money it is; it'll be enough for all the lawyers too.'

'Like the loaves and the fishes?' the lawyer said. But this time it was not an interval; there was no answer at all, serenely nothing, and the interval was the lawyer's to put an end to: 'So he's the one who needs you. Yet he's the one who has the forty thousand dollars. How can anyone with forty thousand dollars need you?' and again the interval, intractable and serene, again the lawyer's to break: 'Are you an ordained minister?'

'I dont know. I bears witness.'

'To what? God?'

'To man. God dont need me. I bears witness to Him of course, but my main witness is to man.'

'The most damning thing man could suffer would be a valid witness before God.'

'You're wrong there,' the Negro said. 'Man is full of sin and nature, and all he does dont bear looking at, and a heap of what he says is a shame and a mawkery. But cant no witness hurt him. Someday something might beat him, but it wont be Satan,' and turned, both of them, at the sound of the door and saw the turnkey inside the room, trying to hold the corridor door, braced against its slow remorseless movement until the yawn's full inswing dismissed him completely into the wall and the five men from the corridor entered, the lawyer already moving before they had got inside the room, crossing to the opposite courtroom door, saying over his shoulder: 'This way, gentlemen,' and opened the door and stood aside holding it: no gesture or motion commanding nor even peremptory as, docile and simultaneous as five sheep, they filed across the room after him like five of the identical targets ducks or clay pipes or stars—traversing on their endless chain the lilliputian range of a shooting-gallery, and on through the door, the lawyer following on the last one's heels and saying over his shoulder to the turnkey or the Negro or perhaps both or perhaps neither: 'Five minutes,' and followed, on and then through the five men who had stopped, huddled, blocking the narrow passage as if they had walked full tilt, as into an invisible wall, into the room's massed and waiting cynosure; and on through the swing gate into the enclosure, to stop facing the massed room in almost the same prints he had stood in ten minutes ago, solitary this time but anything but alone amid, against, as a frieze or tapestry, that titanic congeries, invincible and judgmatical, of the long heroic roster who were the milestones of the rise of man—the giants who coerced compelled directed and, on occasion, actually led his myriad moil: Caesar and Christ, Bonaparte and Peter and

Mazarin, Marlborough and Alexander, Genghis and Talleyrand and Warwick, Marlborough and Bryan, Bill Sunday, General Booth and Prester John, prince and bishop, Norman, dervish, plotter and khan, not for the power and glory nor even the aggrandisement; these were merely secondarily concomitant and even accidental; but for man: by putting some of him in one motion in one direction, by him of him and for him, to disjam the earth, get him for a little while at least out of his own way;—standing there a moment, then two, then three, not accepting but compelling the entire blast of the cynosure as in the twilit room the mirror concentrates to itself all of light and all else owns visibility only at second hand; four then five then six, while breathed no sound no sigh no sound of breathing even save the watch-chain's golden sough and the thin insistent music of the pearl, still holding as in his palm like putty, the massed anonymity and the waiting as the sculptor holds for another moment yet the malleable obedient unimpatient clay, or the conductor across his balanced untensile hands the wand containing within its weightless pencil-gleam all the loud fury and love and anguish.

Then he moved his hand, feeling as he did so the whole vast weight of the watching and the attention concentrate in one beam upon it as the magician's hand compels, and took out the watch and snapped it open, seeing even as he calculated the elapsed creep of the hands, within the lid's mellow concavity as in the seer's crystal ball, the shadowy miniatures of the turnkey and the prisoner who should be well into the square by now and even perhaps already in the alley leading to the hotel garage; even at the moment there came into the room the rising roar of an automobile engine, then the sound of the car itself rushing fast into the square and across and out of it, rushing on at that contemptuous and reckless gait at which his insolent Negro driver always drove when, under his master's orders, the car contained passengers whom the driver considered beneath him or beneath the car's splendor—a swaggering demi-d'Artagnan of a mulatto murderer whom the lawyer had let remain in the penitentiary at hard labor for exactly one year and one day, as the handler wires the dead game bird to the neck of the intractable hunting dog, then getting him out on parole, not that he (the lawyer) held any brief even for the murder of this particular woman, but because of the way it had been done; apparently with the razor already naked in his hand, the man had not driven the woman out of the cabin, but had simply harried and chivvied her through a scene which, as the lawyer imagined it, must have had the quality of ballet, until the woman broke and ran out of the house screaming into the moonlit lane, running without doubt toward the sanctuary of the white kitchen where she worked, until the man without haste overtook her, not to catch, grasp at her, but simply ran past her with one single neat surgeon-like back-handed slash of the razor, running into then out of the instant's immobility into which all motion flowed in one gesture of formulated epicene, almost finicking, even niggardly fatal violence like the bullfighter's, the two of them running on side by side for two or three paces in the moonlight until the woman fell, the man not even spotted and the blade itself barely befouled, as if he had severed not a jugular but a scream and restored merely to the midnight, silence.

So the lawyer could have stopped now, with one word leaving them once more fixed, as with one twitch of his cape the espada does the bull, and walk again through the door to the judge's chambers and on to the hotel and pack and strap his bag. But he did not: who owed this little more, as the old pagan, before he quaffed it empty, tilted always from the goblet's brimming rim one splash at least upon the hearth, not to placate but simply in recognition of them who had matched him with his hour upon the earth; in one of the houses on one of the best streets in one of the most unassailable sections of New Orleans, he owned a picture, a painting, no copy but proved genuine and coveted, for which he had paid more than he liked to remember even though it had been validated by experts before he bought it and revalidated twice since and for which he had been twice offered half again what he had paid for it, and which he had not liked then and still didn't and was not even certain he knew what it meant, but which was his own now and so he didn't even have to pretend that he liked it, which—so he believed then, with more truth than any save himself knew—he affirmed to have bought for the sole purpose of not having to pretend that he liked it; one evening, alone in his study (wifeless and childless, in the house too save for the white-jacketed soft-footed not tamed but merely tractable mulatto murderer) suddenly he found himself looking at no static rectangle of disturbing Mediterranean blues and saffrons and ochres, nor even at the signboard affirming like a trumpet-blast the inevictable establishment in coeval space of the sum of his past—the house in its unimpeachable street, the membership in clubs some of whose doors were older than the state and behind which his father's name would, could, never have disturbed the air, and the cryptic numbers which opened his lock boxes and monotonous incrementation of his securities-lists—but instead was looking at the cognizance of his destiny like the wind-hard banner of the old Norman earl beneath whose vast shadow not just bankers and politicians clicked and sprang nor governors and lieutenants blenched and trembled but at the groaning tables in whose kitchens and sculleries or even open courtyards and kennels daily sixty thousand who wore no swords and spurs and owned no surnames made the one last supreme sacrifice: the free gift of their pauperism, and (the lawyer) thought: *I didn't really earn this. I didn't have time. I didn't even need to earn to earn it; man out of his boundless and incalculable folly foisted it on me before I even had time to resist him;* and closed the watch and put it back into the waistcoat pocket and then the voice, not even raised, murmurous, ventriloquial, sourceless, as though it were not even he but circumambience, the room, the high unsubstanced air itself somewhere about or among the soaring and shadowy cornices, not speaking to the faces but rather descending, not as sound but as benison, as light itself upon the docile, the enduring, the triumphing heads:

'Ladies, gentlemen—' then not louder: merely sharp peremptory and succinct, like the report of a small whip or a toy pistol: 'Democrats: On the fourth of November two years ago there rose from the ballot boxes of America the sun of a thousand years of peace and prosperity such as the world has never seen; on the fourth day of November two years from now, we will see it set again, if the octopus of Wall Street and the millionaire owners of New England factories have their way, waiting and watching their chance to erect once more the barricade of a Yankee tariff between the Southern farmer and the hungry factories and cheap labor of the old world in Europe already entered into its own millennium of peace and reason, freed at last after two thousand years of war and the fear of war, panting only to exchange at a price you can afford to accept, your wheat and corn and cotton for the manufactured goods necessary to your life and happiness and that of your children at a price you can afford to pay, affirming again that inalienable right decreed by our forefathers a hundred and twenty-six years ago of liberty and free trade: the right of man to sell the produce of his own sweat and labor wherever and whenever he wants to, without fear or favor of New York capitalists or New England factory owners already spending like water the money ground out of the child labor of their sweat-shops, to divert to the farthest corners of the earth the just profits of your sweat and labor, so that not your wives and children, but those of African savages and heathen Chinese will have the good roads and the schools and the cream separators and the automobiles——' then already in motion before he stopped speaking, crossing rapidly to the gate in the railing as with one concerted unhaste the entire room stood up, not flowing so much as swaying toward the main doors at the back, since almost at once a voice said from the doors:

'Hit's locked,' the sway not even pausing, only reversing and becoming a flow: one murmurous hollow roaring of feet, not running: merely shuffling yet as the crowd flowed back toward and into the narrow passage leading to the judge's chambers, where the lawyer, passing rapidly through the swing gate, now stood between them and the door; and even as he thought, *My first mistake was moving* he made another.

'Stand back, men,' he said and even raised his hand, palm out, seeing, marking for the first time, faces, individual faces and eyes which least of all were those of individuals now, but rather one single face bearing steadily down on him and overwhelming him until suddenly he was moving backward: no shock, no concussion, but simply enclosed, accepted into one moving envelopement; he stumbled once but immediately what felt like a dozen quick firm impersonal hands steadied and even turned him and then checked him while others reached past him and opened the door to the judge's chambers, not flinging nor even sweeping him aside, but evacuating, voiding him back into the wall as the crowd flowed on across the little room to the opposite corridor door, already emptying the room before they had had time to fill it, so that he knew that the first ones out had gone around to the main courtroom doors and unlocked them, so that not only the corridor but the whole building was murmuring again with the hollow unhurried thunder of feet while he stood for a moment more against the wall with in the center of the once immaculate waistcoat the print, not smeared: just blurred, not hurried, just firm and plain and light, of a hand.

And suddenly, in outrage and prescience, he started, actually sprang almost, already knowing what he would see before he reached the window, looking through it down into the square where they had already halted, the turnkey already facing back toward the courthouse as he fumbled inside his coat; except there were three of them now and the lawyer thought, rapid, inattentive and with no surprise: *Oh yes, the child who rode the horse* and looked no more at the turnkey scrabbling clumsily beneath his coat-tail but watched instead the deliberate pour of the crowd from the courthouse portal, already spreading as it converged toward the three waiting figures like the remorseless unhurried flow of spilled ink across a table cloth, thinking (the lawyer) how only when he is mounted on something—anything, from a footstool through a horse or rostrum to a flagpole or a flying machine—is man vulnerable and familiar; that on his own feet and in motion, he is terrible; thinking with amazement and humility and pride too, how no mere immobile mass of him, no matter how large nor apparently doing or about to do no matter what, nor even the mass of him in motion mounted on something which, not he but it, was locomotive, but the mass of him moving of itself in one direction, toward one objective by means of his own frail clumsily-jointed legs and feet;—not Ghengis' bone horns nor Murat's bugles, let alone the golden voice of Demosthenes or Cicero, or the trumpet-blast of Paul or John Brown or Pitt or Calhoun or Daniel Webster, but the children dying of thirst amid Mesopotamian mirages and the wild men out of the northern woods who walked into Rome carrying even their houses on their backs and Moses' forty-year scavengers and the tall men carrying a rifle or an axe and a bag of beads who changed the color of the American race (and in the lawyer's own memory the last individual: cowboy who marked the whole of western America with the ranging dung of his horse and the oxidising hulls of his sardine and tomato cans, exterminated from the earth by a tide of men with wire-stretchers and pockets full of staples); thinking with pride and awe too, how threatful only in locomotion and dangerous only in silence; neither in lust nor appetite nor greed lay wombed the potency of his threat, but in silence and meditation: his ability to move *en masse* at his own impulse, and silence in which to fall into thought and then action as into an open manhole; with exultation too, since none knew this better than the lords proprietors of his massed breathing, the hero-giant precentors of his seething moil, who used his spendthrift potency in the very act of curbing and directing it, and ever had and ever would: in Detroit today an old-time bicycle-racer destined to be one of the world's giants, his very surname an adjectival noun in the world's mouth, who had already put half a continent on wheels by families, and in twenty-five more would have half a hemisphere on wheels individually, and in a thousand would have already effaced the legs from a species just as that long-ago and doubtless at the time not-even-noticed twitch of Cosmos drained the seas into continents and effaced the gills from their fish. But that was not yet; that would be peace, and to attain that, the silence must be conquered too: the silence in which man had space to think and in consequence act on what he believed he thought or thought he believed: the silence in which the crowd walked, flowed steadily across the square toward the three waiting figures and out of which the turnkey cried in his thin high manless voice, dragging the new pistol in its turn from beneath his coat skirts:

'Stop, men! I'm going to count three!' and began to count: 'One — Two ——' staring, even glaring at the faces which were not rushing at him nor did they even seem to walk at him, but rather towered down and over him, feeling again the pistol neither wrenched nor snatched but just wrung firmly from him and then other hands had him too. 'You durn fools!' he cried, struggling. But how say it? how tell them? You had to be honorable about money, no matter who had it; if you were not honorable about money, pitying the weak did them no good because about all they got from you then was just pity. Besides, it was already too late to try to tell them, even if there had been no other reason, the firm, quite kind, almost gentle hands not only holding him up but even lifting, raising him, and then they were even carrying him as two kinless bachelors might carry a child between them, his feet remembering earth but no longer touching it; then raising him still further until he could see, between and past the heads and shoulders, the ringed circumference of faces not grim and never angry: just unanimous and attentive, and in the center of it the old Negro in the worn frock coat and the thin chocolate-colored adolescent boy with eyeballs of that pure incredible white which Flemish painters knew how to grind; then the owner of the calm irascible voice spoke again and now for the first time the turnkey could see and recognise him: no lawyer or merchant or banker or any other civic leader, but himself a gambler who bucked from choice the toughest game of all: ownership of a small peripatetic sawmill where he had gone to work at the age of fifteen as the sole support of a widowed mother and three unmarried sisters, and now at forty owned the mill and a wife and two daughters and one grand-daughter of his own, speaking at last into a silence in which there was not even the sound of breathing:

'How much did you and that fellow really win on that horse? A hundred dollars?'

'More,' the old Negro said.

'A thousand?'

'More than that': and now indeed there was no stir, no breath: only one vast suspension as if the whole bright April morning leaned:

'Was it forty thousand? . . . . All right. Was it half of forty thousand? How much did you see? How much did you count? Can you count to a thousand dollars?'

'It was a heap,' the old Negro said: and now they breathed: one stir, one exhalation, one movement; the day, the morning once more relinquished, the voice its valedictory:

'There'll be a train at the depot in twenty-five minutes. You be on it when it leaves and dont come back. We dont like rich niggers here.'

† † †

'So we got on the train,' the old Negro said, 'and rode to the next station. Then we got out and walked. It was a far piece, but we knowed where he would be now, if they would just let him alone—' the blue haze-cradled valley where the corners of Georgia and Tennessee and Carolina meet, where he had appeared suddenly from nowhere that day last summer with a three-legged racehorse and an old Negro preacher and the Negro child who rode the horse, and stayed two weeks during which the horse outran every other one within fifty miles, and finally one brought all the way from Knoxville to try to cope with it, then (the four of them) vanished again overnight six hours ahead of a horde of Federal agents and sheriffs and special officers like the converging packs of a state- or nation-wide foxhunt.

'And we was right; he must a come straight back there from the Missouri jail because it was still June. They told us about it: a Sunday morning in the church and likely it was the preacher that seen him first because he was already facing that way, before the rest of them turned their heads and recognised him too standing against the back wall just inside the door like he hadn't never left—' the runner seeing it too, seeing almost as much as the Federal ex-deputy would have seen if he had been there:—the morose, savage, foul-mouthed, almost inarticulate (only the more so for the fact that occasionally a fragment of what he spoke sounded a little like what the valley knew as English) foreigner who moved, breathed, not merely in an aura of bastardy and bachelordom but of homelessness too, like a half-wild pedigreeless pariah dog: fatherless, wifeless, sterile and perhaps even impotent too, mis-shapen, savage and foul: the world's portionless and intractable and inconsolable orphan, who brought without warning into that drowsing vacuum an aggregation bizarre, mobile and amazing as a hippodrome built around a comet: two Negroes and the ruined remnant of the magnificent and incredible horse whose like even on four legs the valley or the section either had never seen before, into a country where a horse was any milkless animal capable of pulling a plow or a cart on weekdays and carrying sacks of corn to the mill on Saturdays and bearing as many of the family as could cling to its gaunt ridgepole to the church on Sundays, and where there not only were none, but there never had been any Negroes; whose people, man and boy from sixty-odd down to fourteen and thirteen, had fifty years ago quitted their misty unmapped eyries to go for miles and even weeks on foot to engage in a war in which they had no stake and, if they had only stayed at home, no contact, in order to defend their land from Negroes; not content merely to oppose and repudiate their own geopolitical kind and their common economic derivation, they must confederate with its embattled enemies, stealing, creeping (once at a crossroads tavern a party of them fought something resembling a pitched battle with a Confederate recruiting party) by night through the Confederate lines to find and join a Federal army, to fight not against slavery but against Negroes, to abolish the Negro by freeing him from them who might bring Negroes among them exactly as they would have taken their rifles down from the pegs or deer antlers above hearth and doorway to repel, say, a commercial company talking about bringing the Indians back.

Hearing it too: 'Except it wasn't two weeks we was there that first time. It was fifteen days. The first two they spent just looking at us. They would come from all up and down the valley, walking or on horses and mules or the whole family in the wagon, to set in the road in front of the store where we would be squatting on the gallery eating cheese and crackers and sardines, looking at us. Then the men and boys would go around behind the store where we had built a pen out of rails and scraps of boards and pieces of rope, to stand and look at the horse. Then we begun to run and by the fifth day we had outrun every horse in the whole valley and had done won even one mortgage on a ten-acre corn-patch up on the mountain, and by the seventh day we was running against horses brought all the way in from the next counties across what they called the Gap. Then six days more, with the folks in the valley betting on our horse now, until the fifteenth day when they brought that horse from Knoxville that had run at Churchill Downs back home once, and this time it was not just the valley folks but folks from all that part of Tennessee watching that three-legged horse without even no saddle (we never used no bridle neither: just a one-rein hackamore and a belly-band for this boy to hold on to) outrun that Knoxville horse the first time at five furlongs and the next time at a full mile for double stakes, with not just the folks in the valley but the folks from the other counties too betting on it now, so that everybody or anyway every family in that part of Tennessee had a share in what it won—'

'That's when he was taken into the Masons,' the runner said. 'During that two weeks.'

'Fifteen days,' the old Negro said. 'Yes, there was a lodge there.—then just before daylight the next morning a man on a mule rid down from the Gap, just about a hour ahead of them—' the runner hearing this too as the old Negro himself had heard it a year afterward: when the sun rose the automobile itself stood in front of the store—the first automobile which the soil of the valley had ever emprinted and which some of the old people and children had ever seen, driven part of the way over the gap trail but indubitably hauled and pushed and probably even carried here and there for the rest of the distance, and inside the store the sheriff of the county and the city strangers in their city hats and neckties and shoes smelling, stinking of excise officers, revenuers, while already the horses and mules and wagons of yesterday flowed back down from the coves and hills, the riders and occupants dismounting at once now, to pause for a moment to look quietly and curiously at the automobile as though at a medium-sized rattlesnake, then crowding into the store until it would hold no more of them, facing not the city strangers standing in a tight wary clump in front of the cold spit-marked stove in its spit-marked sandbox, they had looked at them once and then no more, but rather the sheriff, so that, since the sheriff was one of them, bore one of the names which half the valley bore and the valley had all voted for him and in fact, except for his dime-store cravat and their overalls, even looked like them, it was as though the valley merely faced itself.

'They stole the horse,' the sheriff said. 'All the man wants is just to get it back.' But no reply: only the quiet, grave, courteous, not really listening but just waiting faces, until one of the city strangers said in a bitter city voice:

'Wait——' already stepping quickly past the sheriff, his hand already inside the buttoned front of his city coat when the sheriff said in his flat hill voice:

'You wait,' his hand inside the other's buttoned coat too, already covering the other smaller one, plucking it out of the coat and holding easily in the one grasp both the small city hand and the flat city pistol so that they looked like toys in it, not wrenching but merely squeezing the pistol out of the hand and dropping it into his own coat pocket, and said, 'Well boys, let's get on,' moving, walking, his companions in their white shirts and coat sleeves and pants legs and shoes creased and polished two days ago in Chattanooga hotels, heeling him, compact and close, while the faces, the lane opened: through the store, the lane, the faces closing behind: across the gallery and down the steps, the silent lane still opening and closing behind them until they reached the automobile; 1914 then, and young mountain men had not yet learned how to decommission an automobile simply by removing the distributor or jamming the carburetor. So they had used what they did know: a ten-pound hammer from the blacksmith's shop, not knowing even then the secret of the thing's life beneath the hood and so over-finding it: the fine porcelain dust of shattered plugs and wrenched and battered wires and dented pipes and even the mute half-horse-shoe prints of the hammer punctuating the spew of oil and gasoline and even the hammer itself immobile against an overalled leg in plain view; and now the city man, cursing in his furious bitter voice, was scrabbling with both hands at the sheriff's coat until the sheriff grasped both of them in his one and held the man so; and, facing them now across the ruined engine, again it was merely the valley facing itself. 'The automobile dont belong to the government,' the sheriff said. 'It belongs to him. He will have to pay to have it fixed.'

Nor anything yet for a moment. Then a voice: 'How much?'

'How much?' the sheriff said over his shoulder.

'How much?' the city man said. 'A thousand dollars, for all I know. Maybe two thousand——'

'We'll call it fifty,' the sheriff said, releasing the hands and removing the trim pearl-colored city hat from the city head and with his other hand took from his trousers pocket a small crumple of banknotes and separated one and dropped it into the hat, holding the hat upside down and as though baited with the single bill, toward the nearest of the crowd: 'Next,' he said.

'Except that they had to look quick, because before the preacher could say the benediction so they could get up and even tell him howdy, he was done gone from there too. But quick as he left, it wasn't before the word could begin to spread:' telling that too: thirty-seven in the church that morning so in effect the whole valley was and by midafternoon or sundown anyway every cove and hill and run knew he was back: alone: without the horse: and broke, and hungry; not gone again: just disappeared, out of sight: for the time: so that they knew they had only to wait, to bide until the moment, which was that night in the loft above the postoffice-store—'It was the lodge-room. They used it for they politic too, and for the court, but mostly for the poker- and crap-games that they claimed had been running there ever since the valley was first settled and the store was built. There was a regular outside staircase going up to it that the lawyers and judges and politicians and Masons and Eastern Stars used, but mainly it was a ladder nailed flat to the back wall outside, leading up to a back window, that everybody in the valley knowed about but not one of them would ever claim he even seen, let alone climbed. And inside there was a jug always full of white mountain whisky setting on the shelf with the water-bucket and the gourd, that everybody in the valley knowed was there just like they done the ladder but that nobody could see while the court or the lodge or a meeting was going on:' telling it:

An hour after dark when the six or seven men (including the store's clerk) squatting around the spread blanket on the floor beneath the lantern ('It was Sunday night. They just shot craps on Sunday night. They wouldn't allow no poker.') heard his feet on the ladder and watched him crawl through the window and then didn't look at him anymore while he went to the jug and poured himself a drink into the gourd dipper, not watching him exactly as not one of them would have offered him as a gift the actual food or as a loan the money to buy it with, not even when he turned and saw the coin, the half-dollar, on the floor beside his foot where ten seconds ago no coin had been, nor when he picked it up and interrupted the game for two or three minutes while he compelled them one by one to disclaim the coin's ownership, then knelt into the circle and bet the coin and cast the dice and drew down the original half-dollar and pyramided for two more casts, then passed the dice and, rising, left the original coin on the floor where he had found it and went to the trap door and the ladder which led down into the store's dark interior and with no light descended and returned with a wedge of cheese and a handful of crackers and interrupted the game again to hand the clerk one of the coins he had won and took his change and, squatting against the wall and with no sound save the steady one of his chewing, ate what the valley knew was his first food since he returned to it, reappeared in the church ten hours ago; and—suddenly—the first since he had vanished with the horse and the two Negroes ten months ago.

'They just took him back, like he hadn't never even been away. It was more than that. It was like there never had been no more than what they seen now: no horse to win races on three legs and never had been because they probably never even asked him what had become of it, never no two niggers like me and this boy, never no money to ask him how much of it he won like all them folks back there in Missouri done, not even no time between that one a year ago last summer and this one—' no interval of fall and winter and spring, no flame of oak and hickory nor drive of sleet nor foam and rush of laurel and rhododendron down the mountainsides into summer again; the man himself (the runner seeing this too out of the listening, the hearing) unchanged and not even any dirtier: just alone this time (though not as well as the Federal ex-deputy could have seen it)—the same savage and bandy misanthrope in the foul raked checked cap and the cheap imitation tweed jacket and the bagging Bedford cords ('He called them jodhpurs. They would have held three of him. He said they was made in a place called Savile Row for what he called the second largest duke in the Irish peerage.') squatting on the store's front gallery beneath the patent medicine and tobacco and baking powder placards and the announcements and adjurations of candidates for sheriff and representative and district attorney (this was 1914, an even year; they had already been defeated and forgotten and there remained only their fading photographs joblotted from the lowest bidder and not looking like them anyway, which no one had expected, but merely like any candidate, which was all that any hoped, dotting the countryside on telephone poles and fences and the wooden rails of bridges and the flanks of barns and already fading beneath the incrementation of time and weather, like ejaculations: a warning: a plea: a cry):

'Just squatting there at first, not doing nothing and not nobody bothering him, even to try to talk to him, until Sunday when he would be in the church again, setting in the last pew at the back where he could get out first after the benediction. He was sleeping on a straw tick in the lodge room over the store and eating out of the store too because he had won that much that first night. He could have had a job; they told me about that too: him squatting on the gallery one morning when some fellow brought a horse in to the blacksmith that he had tried to shoe himself and quicked it in the nigh hind, the horse plunging and kicking and squealing every time they tried to touch it until at last they was trying to cross-tie it up and maybe even have to throw it to pull the quick shoe, until he got up and went in and laid his hand on its neck a minute and talked to it and then just tied the halter rein in the ring and picked up the foot and pulled the shoe and reset it. The blacksmith offered him a steady job right there but he never even answered, just back on the gallery squatting again, then Sunday in the back pew in the church again where he could get out first, before anybody could try to talk to him. Because they couldn't see his heart.'

'His heart?' the runner said.

'Yes,' the old Negro said. 'Then he did vanish, because the next time they seed him they wouldn't have knowed him except for the cap, the coat and them Irish britches gone now and wearing over-halls and a hickory shirt. Except that they would have had to gone out there to seen that, because he was a farmer now, a wage-hand, likely not getting much more than his board and lodging and washing because the place he was working on hadn't hardly supported the two folks that was already trying to live on it—' the runner seeing that now almost as well as the Federal ex-deputy could have seen it:—a childless couple of arthritic middleage: two heirs of misfortune drawn as though by some mutual last resort into the confederation of matrimony as inversely two heirs of great wealth or of royalty might have been,—a one-room-and-leanto cabin, a hovel almost, clinging paintless to a sheer pitch of mountainside in a straggling patch of corn standing in niggard monument to the incredible, the not just back- but heart-breaking labor which each meagre stalk represented: moloch-effigy of self-sustenance which did not reward man's sweat but merely consumed his flesh;—the man who ten months ago had walked in the company of giants and heroes and who even yesterday, even without the horse and solitary and alone, had still walked in its magnificent gigantic shadow, now in faded overalls milking a gaunt hill cow and splitting firewood and (the three of them, distinguishable at any distance from one another only because one wore the checked cap and another a skirt) hoeing the lean and tilted corn, coming down the mountain to squat, not talking yet not actually mute either, among them on the gallery of the store on Saturday afternoon; and on the next morning, Sunday, again in his back pew in the church, always in that clean fresh rotation of faded blue which was not the regalia of his metamorphosis and the badge of all plodding enduring husbandry, but which hid and concealed even the horse-warped curvature of his legs, obliterating, effacing at last the last breath or recollection of the old swaggering aura bachelor, footfree and cavalier, so that (it was July now) there remained (not the heart) only the foul raked heavily-checked cap talking (not the heart talking of passion and bereavement) among the empty Tennessee hills of the teeming metropolitan outland:

'Then he was gone. It was August; the mail rider had brought the Chattanooga and Knoxville papers back over the Gap that week and the next Sunday the preacher made the prayer for all the folks across the water swamped again in battle and murder and sudden death, and the next Saturday night they told me how he taken his last degree in Masonry and how that time they tried to talk to him because the Chattanooga and Knoxville papers was coming over the Gap every day now and they was reading them too: about that battle——'

'Mons,' the runner said.

'Mons,' the old Negro said.—'saying to him, "Them was your folks too, wasn't they?" and getting the sort of answer there wasn't no reply to except just to hit him. And when the next Sunday came, he was gone. Though at least this time they knowed where, so that when we finally got there that day——'

'What?' the runner said. 'It took you from June until August to travel from Missouri to Tennessee?'

'It wasn't August,' the old Negro said. 'It was October. We walked. We would have to stop now and then to find work to earn money to eat on. That taken a while, because this boy never had no size then, and I never knowed nothing but horses and preaching, and any time I stopped to do either one, somebody might have asked me who I was.'

'You mean you had to bring the money to him first before you could even draw travel expenses from it?'

'There wasn't no money,' the old Negro said. 'There never was none, except just what we needed, had to have. Never nobody but that New Orleans lawyer ever believed there was. We never had time to bother with winning a heap of money to have to take care of. We had the horse. To save that horse that never wanted nothing and never knowed nothing but just to run out in front of all the other horses in a race, from being sent back to Kentucky to be just another stud-horse for the rest of its life. We had to save it until it could die still not knowing nothing and not wanting nothing but just to run out in front of everything else. At first he thought different, aimed different. But not long. It was during that time when we was walking to Texas. We was hiding in the woods one day by a creek and I talked to him and that evening I baptised him in the creek into my church. And after that he knowed too that betting was a sin. We had to do a little of it, win a little money to live on, buy feed for it and grub for us. But that was all. God knowed that too. That was all right with Him.'

'Are you an ordained minister?' the runner said.

'I bears witness,' the old Negro said.

'But you're not an ordained priest. Then how could you confirm him into your church?'

'Hush, Pappy,' the youth said.

'Wait,' the runner said. 'I know. He made you a Mason too.'

'Suppose he did,' the old Negro said. 'You and this boy are alike. You think maybe I never had no right to make him a christian, but you know he never had no business making me a Mason. But which do you think is the lightest to undertake: to tell a man to act like the head Mason thinks he ought to act, that's just another man trying to know what's right to do, or to tell him how the head of Heaven *knows* he ought to act, that's God and *knows* what's right to ease his suffering and save him?'

'All right,' the runner said. 'It was October——'

'Only this time they knowed where he was. "France?" I says, with this boy already jerking at my sleeve and saying, "Come on, Grampaw. Come on, Grampaw." "Which way is that?" I says. "Is that in Tennessee too?"

' "Come on, Grampaw," this boy says. "I knows where it is." '

'Yes,' the runner said to the youth. 'I'll get to you in a moment too.' He said to the old Negro: 'So you came to France. I wont even ask how you did that with no money. Because that was God. Wasn't it?'

'It was the Society,' the youth said. Only he didn't say 'society': he said 'société'.

'Yes,' the runner said to the youth. He said in French, his best French: the glib smart febrile *argot* immolated into the international *salons* via the nightclubs from the Paris gutter: 'I wondered who did the talking for him. It was you, was it?'

'Someone had to,' the youth said, in still better French, the French of the Sorbonne, the Institute, the old Negro listening, peaceful and serene, until he said:

'His mamma was a New Orleans girl. She knowed gobble talk. That's where he learned it.'

'But not the accent,' the runner said. 'Where did you get that?'

'I dont know,' the youth said. 'I just got it.'

'Could you "just get" Greek or Latin or Spanish the same way?'

'I aint tried,' the youth said. 'I reckon I could, if they aint no harder than this one.'

'All right,' the runner said, to the old Negro now. 'Did you have the Society before you left America?' and heard that, insequent and without order or emphasis, like dream too: they were in New York, who a year ago had not known that the earth extended further than the distance between Lexington, Kentucky, and Louisville until they walked on it, trod with their actual feet the hard enduring ground bearing the names Louisiana and Missouri and Texas and Arkansas and Ohio and Tennessee and Alabama and Mississippi—words which until then had been as foundationless and homeless as the ones meaning Avalon or Astalot or Ultima Thule. Then immediately there was a woman in it, a 'lady', not young, richly in furs—

'I know,' the runner said. 'She was in the car with you that day last spring when you came up to Amiens. The one whose son is in the French air squadron that she is supporting.'

'Was,' the youth said. 'Her boy is dead. He was a volunteer, one of the first airmen killed in the French service. That's when she began to give money to support the squadron.'

'Because she was wrong,' the old Negro said.

'Wrong?' the runner said. 'Oh. Her dead son's monument is a machine to kill as many Germans as possible because one German killed him? Is that it? And when you told her so, it was just like that morning in the woods when you talked to the horse-thief and then baptised him in the creek and saved him? All right, tell me.'

'Yes,' the old Negro said, and told it: the three of them traversing a succession almost like avatars: from what must have been a Park Avenue apartment, to what must have been a Wall Street office, to another office, room: a youngish man with a black patch over one eye and a cork leg and a row of miniature medals on his coat, and an older man with a minute red thing like a toy rosebud in his buttonhole, talking gobble talk to the lady and then to the youth too—

'A French consulate?' the runner said. 'Looking for a British soldier?'

'It was Verdun,' the youth said.

'Verdun?' the runner said. 'That was just last year—1916. It took you until 1916——'

'We was walking and working. Then Pappy begun to hear them——'

'There was too many of them,' the old Negro said. 'Men and boys, marching for months down into one muddy ditch to kill one another. There was too many of them. There wasn't room to lay quiet and rest. All you can kill is man's meat. You cant kill his voice. And if there is enough of the meat, without even room to lay quiet and rest, you can hear it too.'

'Even if it's not saying anything but Why?' the runner said. 'What can trouble you more than having a human man saying to you, Tell me why. Tell me how. Show me the way?'

'And you can show him the way?'

'I can believe,' the old Negro said.

'So because you believed, the French government sent you to France.'

'It was the lady,' the youth said. 'She paid for it.'

'She believed too,' the old Negro said. 'All of them did. The money didn't count no more now because they all knowed by now that just money had done already failed.'

'All right,' the runner said. 'Anyway, you came to France—' hearing it: a ship; there was a committee of at least one or two at Brest, even if they were just military, staff officers to expedite, not a special train maybe but at least one with precedence over everything not military; the house, palace, sonorous and empty, was already waiting for them in Paris. Even if the banner to go above the ducal gates was not ready yet, thought of yet into the words. But that was not long and the house, the palace, was not empty long either: first the women in black, the old ones and the young ones carrying babies, then the maimed men in trench-stained horizon blue, coming in to sit for a while on the hard temporary benches, not always even to see him since he was still occupied in trying to trace down his companion, his Mistairy, telling that too: from the Paris war office to the Department of State, to Downing Street to Whitehall and then out to Poperinghe, until the man's whereabouts were ascertained at last: who (that Newmarket horse and its legend were known and remembered in Whitehall too) could have gone out as groom to the commander-in-chief himself's horse if he had chosen, but enlisted instead into the Londoners until, having barely learned how to wrap his spiral putties, he found himself in a posting which would have left him marooned for the duration as groom-farrier-hostler in a troop of Guards cavalry had he not taught the sergeant in charge of the draft to shoot dice in the American fashion and so won his escape from him, and for two years now had been a private in a combat battalion of Northumberland Borderers.

'Only when you finally found him, he barely spoke to you,' the runner said.

'He aint ready yet,' the old Negro said. 'We can wait. There's plenty of time yet.'

'We?' the runner said. 'You and God too?'

'Yes. Even if it will be over next year.'

'The war? This war? Did God tell you that?'

'It's all right. Laugh at Him. He can stand that too.'

'What else can I do but laugh?' the runner said. 'Hadn't He rather have that than the tears?'

'He's got room for both of them. They're all the same to Him; He can grieve for both of them.'

'Yes,' the runner said. 'Too much of it. Too many of them. Too often. There was another one last year, called the Somme; they give ribbons now not for being brave because all men are brave if you just frighten them enough. You must have heard of that one; you must have heard them too.'

'I heard them too,' the old Negro said.

'Les Amis à la France de Tout le Monde,' the runner said. 'Just to believe, to hope. That little. So little. Just to sit together in the anguished room and believe and hope. And that's enough? like the doctor when you're ill: you know he cant cure you just by laying his hands on you and you dont expect him to: all you need is someone to say "Believe and hope. Be

of good cheer". But suppose it's already too late for a doctor now; all that will serve now is a surgeon, someone already used to blood, up there where the blood already is.'

'Then He would have thought of that too.'

'Then why hasn't He sent you up there, instead of here to live on hot food in clean bugless clothes in a palace?'

'Maybe because He knows I aint brave enough,' the old Negro said.

'Would you go if He sent you?'

'I would try,' the old Negro said. 'If I could do the work, it wouldn't matter to Him or me neither whether I was brave.'

'To believe and to hope,' the runner said. 'Oh yes, I walked through that room downstairs; I saw them; I was walking along the street and happened by simple chance to see that placard over the gate. I was going somewhere else, yet here I am too. But not to believe and hope. Because man can bear anything, provided he has something left, a little something left: his integrity as a creature tough and enduring enough not only not to hope but not even to believe in it and not even to miss its lack; to be tough and to endure until the flash, crash, whatever it will be, when he will no longer be anything and none of it will matter anymore, even the fact that he was tough and, until then, did endure.'

'That's right,' the old Negro said, peaceful and serene, 'maybe it is tomorrow you got to go back. So go on now and have your Paris while you got a little time.'

'Aha,' the runner said. 'Ave Bacchus and Venus, morituri te salutant, eh? Wouldn't you have to call that sin?'

'Evil is a part of man, evil and sin and cowardice, the same as repentance and being brave. You got to believe in all of them, or believe in none of them. Believe that man is capable of all of them, or he aint capable of none. You can go out this way if you want to, without having to meet nobody.'

'Thanks,' the runner said. 'Maybe what I need is to have to meet somebody. To believe. Not in anything: just to believe. To enter that room down there, not to escape from anything but to escape into something, to flee mankind for a little while. Not even to look at that banner because some of them probably cant even read it, but just to sit in the same room for a while with that affirmation, that promise, that hope. If I only could. You only could. Anybody only could. Do you know what the loneliest experience of all is? But of course you do: you just said so. It's breathing.'

'Send for me,' the old Negro said.

'Oh yes—if I only could.'

'I know,' the old Negro said. 'You aint ready yet neither. But when you are, send for me.'

'Are what?' the runner said.

'When you needs me.'

'What can I need you for, when it will be over next year? All I've got to do is just stay alive.'

'Send for me,' the old Negro said.

'Goodbye,' the runner said.

† † †

Descending, retracing his steps, they were still there in the vast cathedral-like room, not only the original ones but the steady trickle of new arrivals, entering, not even to look at the lettered banner but just to sit for awhile inside the same walls with that innocent and invincible affirmation. And he had been right: it was August now and there were American uniforms in France, not as combat units yet but singly, still learning: they had a captain and two subalterns posted to the battalion, to blood themselves on the old Somme names, preparatory to, qualifying themselves to, lead their own kind into the ancient familiar abbatoir; he thought: *Oh yes, three more years and we will have exhausted Europe. Then we—hun and allies together—will transfer the whole business intact to the fresh trans-Atlantic pastures, the virgin American stage, like a travelling minstrel troupe.*

Then it was winter; later, remembering it, it would seem to him that it might actually have been the anniversary of the Son of Man, a gray day and cold, the gray cobbles of that village *Place de Ville* gleaming and wimpled like the pebbles beneath the surface of a brook when he saw the small augmenting crowd and joined it too, from curiosity then, seeing across the damp khaki shoulders the small clump of battle-stained horizon blue whose obvious or at least apparent leader bore a French corporal's insigne, the faces alien and strange and bearing an identical lostness, like—some of them at least—those of men who have reached a certain point or place or situation by simple temerity and who no longer have any confidence even in the temerity, and three or four of which were actually foreign faces reminding him of the ones the French Foreign Legion was generally believed to have recruited out of European jails. And if they had been talking once, they stopped as soon as he came up and was recognised, the faces, the heads above the damp khaki shoulders turning to recognise him and assume at once that expression tentative, reserved and alert with which he had become familiar ever since the word seeped down (probably through a corporal-clerk) from the orderly room that he had been an officer once.

So he came away. He learned in the orderly room that they were correctly within military protocol: they had passes, to visit the homes of one or two or three of them in villages inside the British zone. Then from the battalion padre he even began to divine why. Not learn why: divine it. 'It's a staff problem,' the padre said. 'It's been going on for a year or two. Even the Americans are probably familiar with them by now. They just appear, with their passes all regularly issued and visa-ed, in troop rest-billets. They are known, and of course watched. The trouble is, they have done no——' and stopped, the runner watching him.

'You were about to say, "done no harm yet",' the runner said. 'Harm?' he said gently. 'Problem? Is it a problem and harmful for men in front-line trenches to think of peace, that after all, we can stop fighting if enough of us want to?'

'To think it; not to talk it. That's mutiny. There are ways to do things, and ways not to do them.'

'Render under Caesar?' the runner said.

'I cannot discuss this subject while I bear this,' the padre said, his hand flicking for an instant toward the crown on his cuff.

'But you wear this too,' the runner said, his hand in its turn indicating the collar and the black V inside the tunic's lapels.

'God help us,' the padre said.

'Or we, God,' the runner said. 'Maybe the time has now come for that': and went away from there too, the winter following its course too toward the spring and the next final battle which would end the war, during which he would hear of them again, rumored from the back areas of the (now three) army zones, watched still by the (now) three intelligence sections but still at stalemate because still they had caused no real harm, at least not yet; in fact, the runner had now begun to think of them as a formally accepted and even dispatched compromise with the soldier's natural and inevictable belief that he at least would not be killed, as orderly batches of whores were sent up back areas to compromise with man's natural and normal sex, thinking (the runner) bitterly and quietly, as he had thought before: *His prototype had only man's natural propensity for evil to contend with; this one faces all the scarlet-and-brazen impregnability of general staffs.*

And this time (it was May again, the fourth one he had seen from beneath the brim of a steel helmet, the battalion had gone in again two days ago and he had just emerged from Corps Headquarters at Villeneuve Blanche) when he saw the vast black motor car again there was such a shrilling of N.C.O.s' whistles and a clashing of presented arms that he thought at first it was full of French and British and American generals until he saw that only one was a general: the French one: then recognised them all: in the rear seat beside the general the pristine blue helmet as unstained and innocent of exposure and travail as an uncut sapphire above the Roman face and the unstained horizon-blue coat with its corporal's markings, and the youth in the uniform now of an American captain, on the second jump seat beside the British staff-major, the runner half-wheeling without even breaking stride, to the car and halted one pace short then took that pace and clapped his heels and saluted and said to the staff-major in a ringing voice: 'Sir!' then in French to the French general—an old man with enough stars on his hat to have been at least an army commander: 'Monsieur the general.'

'Good morning, my child,' the general said.

'With permission to address monsieur the director your companion?'

'Certainly, my child,' the general said.

'Thank you, my general,' the runner said, then to the old Negro: 'You missed him again.'

'Yes,' the old Negro said. 'He aint quite ready yet. And dont forget what I told you last year. Send for me.'

'And dont you forget what I told you last year too,' the runner said, and took that pace backward then halted again. 'But good luck to you, anyway; he doesn't need it,' he said and clapped his heels again and saluted and said again to the staff-major or perhaps to no one at all in the ringing and empty voice: 'Sir!'

And that was all, he thought; he would never see either of them again—that grave and noble face, the grave and fantastic child. But he was wrong. It was not three days until he stood in the ditch beside the dark road and watched the lorries moving up toward the lines laden with what the old St Omer watchman told him were blank anti-aircraft shells, and not four when he waked, groaning and choking on his own blood until he could turn his head and spit (his lip was cut and he was going to lose two teeth—spitting again, he had already lost them—and now he even remembered the rifle-butt in his face), hearing already (that was what had waked, roused him) the terror of that silence.

He knew at once where he was: where he always was asleep or on duty either: lying (someone had even spread his blanket over him) on the dirt ledge hacked out of the wall of the tiny cave which was the ante-room to the battalion dugout. And he was alone: no armed guard sitting across from him as he realised now he had expected, nor was he even manacled: nothing save himself lying apparently free on his familiar ledge in that silence which was not only above ground but down here too: no telephonist at the switchboard opposite, none of the sounds—voices, movement, the coming and going of orderlies and company commanders and N.C.O.'s—all the orderly disorder of a battalion p.c. functioning normally in a cramped space dug forty feet down into the earth—which should have been coming from the dugout itself;—only the soundless roar of the massed weight of shored and poised dirt with which all subterrene animals—badgers and miners and moles—are deafened until they no longer hear it. His watch (curiously it was not broken) said 10:19, whether Ack Emma or Pip Emma he could not tell down here, except that it could not be, it must not be Pip Emma; he could not, he must not have been here going on twenty hours; the seven which Ack Emma would signify would already be too many. So he knew at least where they would be, the whole p.c. of them—colonel, adjutant, sergeant-major and the telephonist with his temporarily spliced and extended line—topside too, crouching behind the parapet, staring through periscopes across that ruined and silent emptiness at the opposite line, where their opposite German numbers would be crouching also behind a parapet, gazing too through periscopes across that vernal desolation, that silence, expectant too, alerted and amazed.

But he did not move yet. It was not that it might already be too late; he had already refused to believe that and so dismissed it. It was because the armed man might be in the dugout itself, guarding the only exit there. He even thought of making a sound, a groan, something to draw the man in; he even thought of what he would say to him: *Dont you see? We dont know what they are up to, and only I seem to have any fears or alarms. If I am wrong, we will all die sooner or later anyway. If I am right and you shoot me here, we will all surely die.* Or better still: *Shoot me. I shall be the one man out of this whole four years who died calmly and peacefully and reposed in dry clothing instead of panting, gasping, befouled with mud to the waist or drenched completely in the sweat of exertion and anguish.* But he didn't do it. He didn't need to. The dugout was empty also. The armed man might be at the top of the stairs instead of the foot of them but then there or thereabouts would be where the colonel and his orderly room and periscope were too; besides, he would have to face, risk the rifle somewhere and it wouldn't matter where since it contained only (for him) one bullet while what he was armed with was capable of containing all of time, all of man.

He found his helmet at once. He would have no rifle, of course, but even as he dismissed this he had one: leaning against the wall behind the sergeant-major's desk (oh yes, what he was armed with even equipped him at need with that which his own armament was even superior to) and yes, there it still was in the sergeant-major's desk: the pass issued to him Monday to pass him out to Corps Headquarters and then back, so that he didn't even expect to find a guard at the top of the fifty-two steps leading up and debouching into the trench: only the transubstantiated orderly room as he had foreknown—colonel, adjutant, sergeant-major, telephone periscopes and all, his speech all ready on his tongue when the sergeant-major turned and looked back at him.

'Latrine,' he said.

'Right,' the sergeant-major said. 'Be smart about it. Then report back here.'

'Yessir,' he said and two hours later he was again among the trees from which he had watched the torches moving about the archie battery two nights ago; three hours after that he saw the three aeroplanes—they were S.E.5's—in the sky which had been empty of aircraft for forty-eight hours now, and saw and heard the frantic uproar of shells above where the enemy front would be. Then he saw the German aeroplane too, watched it fly arrow-straight and apparently not very fast, enclosed by the pocking of white British archie which paced it, back across No-man's Land, the three S.E.'s in their pocking of black hun archie zooming and climbing and diving at the German; he watched one of them hang on the German's tail for what must have been a minute or two, the two aircraft apparently fastened rigidly together by the thin threads of tracer. And still the German flew steadily and sedately on, descending, descending now even as it passed over him and the battery behind—near—which he lurked opened on it in that frenzy of frantic hysterical frustration common to archie batteries; descending, vanishing just above the trees, and suddenly he knew where: the aerodrome just outside Villeneuve Blanche, vanishing sedately and without haste downward, enclosed to the last in that empty similitude of fury, the three S.E.5's pulling up and away in one final zoom; and, as if that were not enough to tell him what he had to do, he saw one of them roll over at the top of its loop and, frozen and immobile, watched it in its plan as it dove, rushed straight down at the battery itself, its nose flicking and winking with the tracer which was now going straight into the battery and the group of gunners standing quietly about it, down and down past what he would have thought was the instant already too late to save itself from crashing in one last inextricable jumble into the battery, then levelling, himself watching the rapid pattering walk of the tracer across the intervening ground toward him until now he was looking directly into the flicking wink and the airman's helmeted and goggled face behind and above it, so near that they would probably recognise one another if they ever saw each other again—the two of them locked in their turn for a moment, an instant by the thin fiery thread of a similitude of death (afterward he would even remember the light rapid blow against his leg as if he had been tapped rapidly and lightly once by a finger), the aeroplane pulling level and with a single hard snarling downward blast of air, zooming, climbing on until the roaring whine died away, he not moving yet, immobile and still frozen in the ravelling fading snarl and the faint thin sulphur-stink of burning wool from the skirt of his tunic.

It was enough. He didn't even expect to get nearer the Villeneuve aerodrome than the first road-block, himself speaking to the corporal not even across a rifle but across a machine gun: 'I'm a runner from the —th Battalion.'

'I cant help that,' the corporal said. 'You dont pass here.' Nor did he really want to. He knew enough now. Ten hours later in the Villeneuve Blanche gendarme's uniform, he was in Paris, traversing again the dark and silent streets of the aghast and suspended city dense not only with French civil police but the military ones of the three nations patrolling the streets in armed motorcars, until he passed again beneath the lettered banner above the arched gateway.

Wednesday Night

To the young woman waiting just inside the old eastern city gate, that dispersal in the *Place de Ville* made a long faint hollow faraway rushing sound as remote and impersonal as a pouring of water or the wings of a tremendous migratory flock. With her head turned and arrested and one thin hand clutching the crossing of the shabby shawl on her breast, she seemed to listen to it almost inattentively while it filled the saffron sunset between the violet city and the cobalt-green firmament, and died away.

Then she turned back to where the road entered the city beneath the old arch. It was almost empty now, only a trickle approached and entered, the last of them, the dregs; when she turned back to it her face, though still wan and strained, was almost peaceful now, as if even the morning's anguish had been exhausted and even at last obliterated by the day of watching and waiting.

Then she was not even watching the road as her hand, releasing the shawl, brushed past the front of her dress and stopped, her whole body motionless while her hand fumbled at something through the cloth, fumbling at whatever it was as if even the hand didn't know yet what it was about to find. Then she thrust her hand inside the dress and brought the object out—the crust of the bread which the man had given her in the boulevard almost twelve hours ago, warm from her body and which by her expression she had completely forgotten, even the putting it there. Then she even forgot the bread again, clutching it to her mouth in one thin voracious fist, tearing at it with quick darting birdlike snatches as she once more watched the gate which those entering now approached with creeping and painful slowness. Because these were the dregs, the residue—the very old and the very young, belated not because they had had further to come but because some of them had been so long in life as long ago to have outlived the kin and friends who would have owned carts to lend or share with them, and the others had been too brief in it yet to have friends capable of owning carts and who had already been orphaned of kin by the regiment at Bethune and Souchez and the *Chemin des Dames* three years ago—all creeping cityward now at the pace of the smallest and weakest.

When she began suddenly to run, she was still chewing the bread, still chewing when she darted under the old twilit arch, running around an old woman and a child who were entering it without breaking stride but merely changing feet like a running horse at a jump, flinging the crust behind her, spurning it with her palm against the hollow purchaseless air as she ran toward a group of people coming up the now almost empty road—an old man and three women, one of them carrying a child. The woman carrying the child saw her and stopped. The second woman stopped too, though the others—an old man on a single crutch and carrying a small cloth-knotted bundle and leaning on the arm of an old woman who appeared to be blind—were still walking on when the young woman ran past them and up to the woman carrying the child and stopped facing her, her wan face urgent and frantic again.

'Marthe!' she said. 'Marthe!'

The woman answered, something rapid and immediate, not in French but in a staccato tongue full of harsh rapid consonants, which went with her face—a dark high calm ugly direct competent peasant's face out of the ancient mountainous central-European cradle, which, though a moment later she spoke in French and with no accent, was no kin whatever to the face of the child she carried, with its blue eyes and florid coloring filtered westward from Flanders. She spoke French at once, as if, having looked at the girl, she realised that, whether or not the girl had ever once understood the other tongue, she was past comprehending or remembering it now. Now the blind woman leading the crippled old man had stopped and turned and was coming back; and now you would have noticed for the first time the face of the second woman, the one who had stopped when the one carrying the child did. It was almost identical with the other's; they were indubitably sisters. At first glance, the second face was the older of the two. Then you saw that it was much younger. Then you realised that it had no age at all, it had all ages or none; it was the peaceful face of the witless.

'Hush now,' the woman carrying the child said. 'They wont shoot him without the others.' Then the blind woman dragged the old man up. She faced them all, but none in particular, motionless while she listened for the sound of the girl's breathing until she located it and turned quickly toward the girl her fierce cataracted stare.

'Have they got him?' she said.

'As we all know,' the woman with the child said quickly. She started to move again. 'Let's get on.'

But the blind woman didn't move, square and sightless in the road, blocking it, still facing the girl. 'You,' she said. 'I dont mean the fools who listened to him and who deserve to die for it. I mean that foreigner, that anarchist who murdered them. Have they got him? Answer me.'

'He's there too,' the woman carrying the child said, moving again. 'Come on.'

But still the blind woman didn't move, except to turn her face toward the woman with the child when she spoke. 'That's not what I asked,' she said.

'You heard me say they will shoot him too,' the woman carrying the child said. She moved again, as though to touch the blind woman with her hand and turn her. But before the hand touched her, the woman who could not even see had jerked her own up and struck it down.

'Let her answer me,' she said. She faced the girl again. 'They haven't shot him yet? Where's your tongue? You were full enough of something to say when you came up.' But the girl just stared at her.

'Answer her,' the woman carrying the child said.

'No,' the girl whispered.

'So,' the blind woman said. She had nothing to blink for or from, yet there was nothing else to call it but blinking. Then her face began to turn rapidly between the girl's and the woman's carrying the child. Even before she spoke, the girl seemed to shrink, staring at the blind woman in terrified anticipation. Now the blind woman's voice was silken, smooth. 'You too have kin in the regiment, eh? Husband—brother—a sweetheart?'

'Yes,' the woman carrying the child said.

'Which one of you?' the blind woman said.

'All three of us,' the woman carrying the child said. 'A brother.'

'A sweetheart too, maybe?' the blind woman said. 'Come, now.'

'Yes,' the woman carrying the child said.

'So, then,' the blind woman said. She jerked her face back to the girl. 'You,' she said. 'You may pretend you're from this district, but you dont fool me. You talk wrong. And you—' she jerked back to face the woman carrying the child again '—you're not even French. I knew that the minute the two of you came up from nowhere back yonder, talking about having given your cart to a pregnant woman. Maybe you can fool them that dont have anything but eyes, and nothing to do but believe everything they look at. But not me.'

'Angélique,' the old man said in a thin quavering disused voice. The blind woman paid no attention to him. She faced the two women. Or the three women, the third one too: the older sister who had not spoken yet, whom anyone looking at her would never know whether she was going to speak or not, and even when she did speak it would be in no language of the used and familiar passions: suspicion or scorn or fear or rage; who had not even greeted the girl who had called the sister by a christian name, who had stopped simply because the sister had stopped and apparently was simply waiting with peaceful and infinite patience for the sister to move again, watching each speaker in turn with serene inattention.

'So the anarchist who is murdering Frenchmen is your brother,' the blind woman said. Still facing the woman carrying the child, she jerked her head sideways toward the girl. 'What does she claim him as? a brother too, or maybe an uncle?'

'She is his wife,' the woman carrying the child said.

'His whore, maybe you mean,' the blind woman said.

'Maybe I'm looking at two more of them, even if both of you are old enough to be his grandmothers. Give me the child.' Again she moved as unerring as light toward the faint sound of the child's breathing and before the other could move snatched the child down from her shoulder and swung it onto her own. 'Murderers,' she said.

'Angélique,' the old man said.

'Pick it up,' the blind woman snapped at him. It was the cloth-knotted bundle; only the blind woman, who was still facing the three other women, not even the old man himself, knew that he had dropped it. He stooped for it, letting himself carefully and with excruciating slowness hand under hand down the crutch and picked it up and climbed the crutch hand over hand again. As soon as he was up her hand went out with that sightless unerring aim and grasped his arm, jerking him after her as she moved, the child riding high on her other shoulder and staring silently back at the woman who had been carrying it; she was not only holding the old man up, she was actually leading the way. They went on to the old arch and passed beneath it. The last of sunset was gone even from the plain now.

'Marthe,' the girl said to the woman who had carried the child. Now the other sister spoke, for the first time. She was carrying a bundle too—a small basket neatly covered with an immaculate cloth tucked neatly down.

'That's because he's different,' she said with peaceful triumph. 'Even people in the towns can see it.'

'Marthe!' the girl said again. This time she grasped the other's arm and began to jerk at it. 'That's what they're all saying! They're going to kill him!'

'That's why,' the second sister said with that serene and happy triumph.

'Come on,' Marthe said, moving. But the girl still clung to her arm.

'I'm afraid,' she said. 'I'm afraid.'

'We cant do anything just standing here and being afraid,' Marthe said. 'We're all one now. It is the same death, no matter who calls the tune or plays it or pays the fiddler. Come, now. We're still in time, if we just go on.' They went on toward the old dusk-filling archway, and entered it. The sound of the crowd had ceased now. It would begin again presently though, when, having eaten, the city would hurry once more back to the *Place de Ville*. But now what sound it was making was earthy, homely, inturned and appeased, no longer the sound of thinking and hope and dread, but of the peaceful diurnal sublimation of viscera; the very air was colored not so much by twilight as by the smoke of cooking drifting from windows and doorways and chimneys and from braziers and naked fires burning on the cobbles themselves where even the warrens had overflowed, gleaming rosily on the spitted hunks of horses and the pots and on the faces of the men and children squatting about them and the women bending over them with spoons or forks.

That is, until a moment ago. Because when the two women and the girl entered the gate, the street as far as they could see it lay arrested and immobilised under a deathlike silence, rumor having moved almost as fast as anguish did, though they never saw the blind woman and the old man again. They saw only the back-turned squatting faces about the nearest fire and the face of the woman turned too in the act of stooping or rising, one hand holding the fork or spoon suspended over the pot, and beyond them faces at the next fire turning to look, and beyond them people around the third fire beginning to stand up to see, so that even Marthe had already stopped for a second when the girl grasped her arm again.

'No, Marthe!' she said. 'No!'

'Nonsense,' Marthe said. 'Haven't I told you we are all one now?' She freed her arm, not roughly, and went on. She walked steadily into the firelight, into the thin hot reek of the meat, the squatting expressionless faces turning like the heads of owls to follow her, and stopped facing across the closed circle the woman with the spoon. 'God be with all here this night and tomorrow,' she said.

'So here you are,' the woman said. 'The murderer's whores.'

'His sisters,' Marthe said. 'This girl is his wife.'

'We heard that too,' the woman said. The group at the next fire had left it now, and the one beyond it. But of the three strangers only the girl seemed aware that the whole street was crowding quietly up, growing denser and denser, not staring at them yet, the faces even lowered or turned a little aside and only the gaunt children staring, not at the three strangers but at the covered basket which the sister carried. Marthe had not once even glanced at any of them.

'We have food,' she said. 'We'll share with you for a share in your fire.' Without turning her head she said something in the mountain tongue, reaching her hand back as the sister put the handle of the basket into it. She extended the basket toward the woman with the spoon. 'Here,' she said.

'Hand me the basket,' the woman said. A man in the squatting circle took the basket from Marthe and passed it to her. Without haste the woman put the spoon back into the pot, pausing to give the contents a single circular stir, turning her head to sniff at the rising steam, then in one motion she released the spoon and turned and took the basket from the man and swung her arm back and flung the basket at Marthe's head. It spun once, the cloth still neatly tucked. It struck Marthe high on the shoulder and caromed on, revolving again and emptying itself (it was food) just before it struck the other sister in the chest. She caught it. That is, although none had seen her move, she now held the empty basket easily against her breast with one hand while she watched the woman who threw it, interested and serene.

'You're not hungry,' she said.

'Did that look like we want your food?' the woman said.

'That's what I said,' the sister said. 'Now you dont have to grieve.' Then the woman snatched the spoon from the pot and threw it at the sister. But it missed. That is, as the woman stooped and scrabbled for the next missile (it was a wine bottle half full of vinegar) she realised that the spoon had struck nothing, that none of the three strangers had even ducked, as though the spoon had vanished into thin air as it left her hand. And when she threw the bottle she couldn't see the three women at all. It struck a man in the back and caromed vanishing as the whole crowd surged, baying the three strangers in a little ring of space like hounds holding fixed but still immune some animal not feared but which had completely confounded them by violating all the rules of chase and flight, so that, as hounds fall still and for a moment even cease to whimper, the crowd even stopped yelling and merely held the three women in a ring of gaped suspended uproar until the woman who threw the spoon broke through, carrying a tin mug and two *briquettes* and flung them without aim, the crowd baying and surging again as Marthe turned, half carrying the girl in one arm and pushing the sister on ahead with the other hand, walking steadily, the crowd falling away in front and closing behind so that the flexing intact ring itself seemed to advance as they did like a miniature whirlpool in a current, then the woman, screaming now, darted and stooped to a scatter of horse droppings among the cobbles and began to hurl the dried globules which might have been *briquettes* too but for hue and durability. Marthe stopped and turned, the girl half hanging from the crook of her arm, the sister's ageless interested face watching from behind her shoulder, while refuse of all sorts—scraps of food, rubbish, sticks, cobbles from the street itself—rained about them. A thread of blood appeared suddenly at the corner of her mouth but she didn't move, until after a time her immobility seemed to stay the missiles too and the gaped crowding faces merely bayed at them again, the sound filling the alley and roaring from wall to wall until the reverberations had a quality not only frantic but cachinnant, recoiling and compounding as it gathered strength, rolling on alley by alley and street to street until it must have been beating along the boulevards' respectable fringes too.

Because the patrol—it was a mounted provost marshal's party—met them at the first corner. The crowd broke, burst, because this was a charge. The yelling rose a whole octave without transition like flipping over a playing card, as motionless again the three women watched the crowd stream back upon them; they stood in a rushing vacuum while the mass divided and swept past on either hand, in front of and beneath and behind the running horses, the cobble-clashing fire-ringing hooves and the screams dying away into the single vast murmur of the whole city's tumult, leaving the alley empty save for the three women when the N.C.O. leader of the patrol reined his horse and held it, short-bitted, ammoniac and reek-spreading and bouncing a little against the snaffle, while he glared down at them. 'Where do you live?' he said. They didn't answer, staring up at him—the wan girl, the tall calm woman, the quicking and serene approval of the sister. The N.C.O. listened for an instant to the distant tumult. Then he looked at them again. 'All right,' he said harshly. 'Get out of town while you can. Come on now. Get started.'

'We belong here too,' Marthe said. For a second he glared down at them, he and the horse in high sharp fading silhouette against the sky itself filled with anguish and fury.

'Is the whole damned world crowding here to crucify a bastard the army's going to fix anyway?' he said in thin furious exasperation.

'Yes,' Marthe said. Then he was gone. He slacked the horse; its iron feet clashed and sparked on the cobbles; the hot reek sucked after it, pungent for a fading instant, then even the galloping had faded into the sound of the city. 'Come,' Marthe said. They went on. At first she seemed to be leading them away from the sound. But presently she seemed to be leading them straight back to it. She turned into an alley, then into another not smaller but emptier, deserted, with an air about it of back premises. But she seemed to know where she was going or at least what she was looking for. She was almost carrying the girl now until the sister moved up unbidden and exchanged the empty basket to the other arm and took half the girl's weight and then they went quite rapidly, on to the end of the alley and turned the wall and there was what Marthe had gone as directly to as if she had not only known it was there but had been to it before—an empty stone stall, a byre or stable niched into the city's night-fading flank. There was even a thin litter of dry straw on the stone floor and once inside although the sound was still audible it was as though they had established armistice with the tumult and the fury, not that it should evacuate the city in their favor but at least it should approach no nearer. Marthe didn't speak, she just stood supporting the girl while the sister set down the empty basket and knelt and with quick deft darting motions like a little girl readying a doll's house she spread the straw evenly and then removed her shawl and spread it over the straw and still kneeling helped Marthe lower the girl onto the shawl and took the other shawl which Marthe removed from her shoulders and spread it over the girl. Then they lowered themselves onto the straw on either side of the girl and as Marthe drew the girl to her for warmth the sister reached and got the basket and not even triumphant, with another of those clumsy darting childlike motions which at the same time were deft or least efficient or anyway successful, she took from the basket which everyone had seen empty itself when the woman at the fire threw it at her, a piece of broken bread a little larger than two fists. Again Marthe said nothing. She just took the bread from the sister and started to break it.

'In three,' the sister said and took the third fragment when Marthe broke it and put it back into the basket and they reclined again, the girl between them, eating. It was almost dark now. What little light remained seemed to have gathered about the door's worn lintel with a tender nebulous quality like a worn lost halo, the world outside but little lighter than the stone interior—the chill sweating stone which seemed not to conduct nor even contain but to exude like its own moisture the murmur of the unwearying city—a sound no longer auricularly but merely intellectually disturbing, like the breathing of a sick puppy or a sick child. But when the other sound began they stopped chewing. They stopped at the same instant; when they sat up it was together as though a spreader bar connected them, sitting each with a fragment of bread in one poised hand, listening. It was beneath the first sound, beyond it, human too but not the same sound at all because the old one had women in it—the mass voice of the ancient limitless mammalian capacity not for suffering but for grieving, wailing, to endure incredible anguish because it could become vocal without shame or self-consciousness, passing from gland to tongue without transition through thought—while the new one was made by men and though they didn't know where the prisoners' compound was nor even (nobody had taken time to tell them yet) that the regiment was in a compound anywhere, they knew at once what it was. 'Hear them?' the sister said, serene, in astonished and happy approval, so rapt that Marthe's movement caused her to look up only after the other had risen and was already stooping to rouse the girl; whereupon the sister reached again with that deft unthinking immediate clumsiness and took the fragment of bread from Marthe and put it and her own fragment back into the basket with the third one and rose to her knees and began to help raise the girl, speaking in a tone of happy anticipation. 'Where are we going now?' she said.

'To the Mayor,' Marthe said. 'Get the basket.' She did so; she had to gather up both the shawls too which delayed her a little, so that when she was on her feet Marthe, supporting the girl, had already reached the door. But even for a moment yet the sister didn't follow, standing clutching the shawls and the basket, her face lifted slightly in rapt and pleased astonishment in the murmurous last of light which seemed to have brought into the damp stone cubicle not merely the city's simple anguish and fury but the city itself in all its invincible and impervious splendor. Even inside the stone single-stalled stable it seemed to rise in glittering miniature, tower and spire tall enough and high enough to soar in sunlight still though dark had fallen, high enough and tall enough above earth's old miasmic mists for the glittering and splendid pinnacles never to be in darkness at all perhaps, invincible, everlasting, and vast.

'He will wear a fine sword here,' she said.

† † †

Shortly before sunset the last strand of wire enclosing the new compound had been run and joined and the electric current turned into it. Then the whole regiment, with the exception of the thirteen special prisoners who were in a separate cell to themselves, were turned out of the barracks. They were not released, they were evicted, not by simultaneous squads of guards nor even by one single roving detachment moving rapidly, alert compact and heavily armed, from barracks to barracks, but by individual Senegalese. Armed sometimes with a bayoneted rifle and sometimes merely with the naked bayonet carried like a brush knife or a swagger stick and sometimes with nothing at all, they appeared abruptly and without warning in each room and drove its occupants out, hustling them with scornful and contemptuous expedition toward the door, not even waiting to follow but going along with them, each one already well up into the middle of the group before it even reached the door and still pressing on toward the head of it, prodding each his own moving path with the reversed rifle or the bayonet's handle and, even within the ruck, moving faster than it moved, riding head and shoulders not merely above the moving mass but as though on it, gaudy ethiope and contemptuous, resembling harlequined trees uprooted say from the wild lands, the tameless antipodal fields, moving rigid and upright above the dull sluggish current of a city-soiled commercial canal. So the Senegalese would actually be leading each group when it emerged into its company street. Nor would they even stop then, not even waiting to pair off in couples, let alone in squads, but seeming to stride once or twice, still carrying the bayoneted rifles or the bayonets like the spears and knives of a lion or antelope hunt, and vanish as individual and abrupt as they had appeared.

So when the regiment, unarmed unshaven hatless and half-dressed, began to coalesce without command into the old sheeplike molds of platoons and companies, it found that nobody was paying any attention to it at all, that it had been deserted even by the bayonets which had evicted it out of doors. But for a while yet it continued to shuffle and grope for the old familiar alignments, blinking a little after the dark barracks, in the glare of sunset. Then it began to move. There were no commands from anywhere; the squads and sections simply fell in between the old file-markers and -closers and began to flow, drift as though by some gentle and even unheeded gravitation, into companies in the barracks streets, into battalions onto the parade ground, and stopped. It was not a regiment yet but rather a shapeless mass in which only the squads and platoons had any unity, as the coherence of an evicted city obtains only in the household groups which stick together not because the members are kin in blood but because they have eaten together and slept together and grieved and hoped and fought among themselves so long, huddling immobile and blinking beneath the high unclimbable wire and the searchlights and machine-gun platforms and the lounging scornful guards, all in silhouette on the sunset as if the lethal shock which charged the wire ten minutes ago had at the same instant electrocuted them all into inflexible arrestment against the end of time.

They were still huddled there when the new tumult began in the city. The sun had set, the bugles had rung and ceased, the gun had crashed from the old citadel and clapped and reverberated away, and the huddled regiment was already fading into one neutral mass in the middle of the parade ground when the first faint yelling came across the plain. But they did nothing at first, except to become more still, as dogs do at the rising note of a siren about to reach some unbearable pitch which the human ear will not hear at all. In fact, when they did begin to make the sound, it was not human at all but animal, not yelling but howling, huddling still in the dusk that fading and shapeless mass which might have been Protoplasm itself, eyeless and tongueless on the floor of the first dividing of the sea, palpant and vociferant with no motion nor sound of its own but instead to some gigantic uproar of the primal air-crashing tides' mighty copulation, while overhead on the catwalks and platforms the Senegalese lounged on their rifles or held to cigarettes the small windless flames of lighters contrived of spent cartridge cases, as if the glare of day had hidden until now that which the dusk exposed: that the electric shock which had fixed them in carbon immobility had left here and there one random not-yet-faded coal.

The dusk seemed to have revealed to them the lighted window too. It was in the old once-ivied wall of what had been the factory's main building; they might even have seen the man standing in it, though probably the window alone was enough. Not yelling but howling, they began to flow across the compound. But the night moved still faster; the mass of them had already faded completely into it before they had crossed the parade ground, so that it was the sound, the howling, which seemed to roll on and crash and recoil and roar again against the wall beneath the lighted window and the motionless silhouette of the man standing in it, and recoiled and roared again while a hurried bugle began to blat and whistles to shrill and a close body of white infantry came rapidly around the corner and began to push them away from the wall with short jabbing blows of rifle butts.

When the guard came for them, the corporal was still standing at the window, looking down at the uproar. The thirteen of them were in a small perfectly bare perfectly impregnable single-windowed cell which obviously had been a strong room of some sort back in the old dead time when the factory had been merely a factory. A single dingy electric bulb burned in the center of the ceiling behind a wire cage like the end of a rat-trap. It had been burning when they were herded into the room shortly after dawn this morning, and, since it was American electricity, or that is, was already being charged daily one day in advance to the Service of Supply of the American Expeditionary Force, it had been burning ever since. So as the day succumbed to evening, the faces of the thirteen men sitting quietly on the floor against one wall did not fade wanly back into the shadows but rather instead emerged, not even wan but, unshaven and therefore even more virile, gathering to themselves an even further ghastly and jaundiced strength.

When the first stir of movement went through the compound as the Senegalese began to evict the regiment from the barracks, the thirteen men sitting against the wall of the cell did not appear to respond to it, unless there might have been a further completer stillness and arrestment travelling as though from one to another among twelve of them—the half-turn of a face, the quick almost infinitesimal side-glancing of an eye toward the thirteenth one, the corporal, sitting in the center of them, who—the corporal—did not move at all until the first roar of yelling rolled across the parade ground and crashed like a wave against the wall beneath the window. Then the corporal rose to his feet, not quietly nor deliberately so much as easily, as mountain men move, and went to the window and, his hands lying as lightly and easily among the bars as they had lain on the lorry's top rail, stood looking down at the yelling. He didn't seem to be listening to it: just looking at it, watching it pour across the compound to break in one inaudible crash beneath the window, in the wan glow from which the men themselves were now visible—the clenched fists, the pale individual faces which, even gaped with yelling he may have recognised, having spent four years crouched with them behind bullet-snicked parapets or trying bitten-tongued to anneal into the stinking muck of shell craters beneath drum fire or rolling barrages or flattened immobile and unbreathing beneath the hiss and whisper of flares on night patrols. He seemed not to listen to it but to watch it, immobile and detached, while the frantic bugle yelped and the whistles shrilled and the infantry section burst on its collapsing flank and whirled it slowly away. He didn't move. He looked exactly like a stone-deaf man watching with interest but neither surprise nor alarm the pantomime of some cataclysm or even universal uproar which neither threatens nor even concerns him since to him it makes no sound at all.

Then heavy boots tramped and clashed in the corridor. The corporal turned from the window and this time the other twelve faces moved too, lifting as one and pacing along the wall the tramp of the invisible feet beyond it until the feet halted, so that they were all looking at the door when it opened and flung back and a sergeant (they were not Senegalese nor even white infantry this time, but provost marshal's people) stood in it and made a sweeping peremptory gesture with his arm. 'On your feet,' he said.

† † †

Still preceding the chief-of-staff, and pausing only long enough for the aide to open the door and get out of the way, the division commander entered the room. It was less large than a modern concert hall. In fact, it had been merely a boudoir back in the time of its dead duchess or marquise, and it still bore the imprint of that princely insensate (and, perhaps one of the duchesses or marquises had thought, impregnable) opulence in its valanced alcoves and pilastered medallioned ceiling and crystal chandeliers and sconces and mirrors and girandoles and buhl etageres and glazed cabinets of faience bibelots, and a white rug into which war-bleachened boots sank ankle-deep as into the muck of trenches say in the cold face of the moon, flooring bland and soft as cloud that majestic vista at the end of which the three old generals sat.

Backed by a hovering frieze of aides and staff, they sat behind a tremendous oblong table as bare and flat and richly austere as the top of a knight's or a bishop's sarcophagus, all three in the spectacles of old men and each with a thick identical sheaf of clipped papers before him, so that the whole group in their dust- or horizon-colored clothing and brass-and-scarlet-and-leather harness had a look paradoxical and bizarre, both scholarly and outlandish, like a pack of tameless forest beasts dressed in the regalia and set in the environment of civilised office and waiting in decorous and almost somnolent unhaste while the three old leaders sat for a specified time over the meaningless papers which were a part of the regalia too, until the moment came not to judge nor even condemn but just to fling away the impeding papers and garments and execute.

The windows were open, curtain and casement, so that there came into the room not only the afternoon light and air, but something of the city's tumult too—not sound, because the voices, even the sudden uproar of them which the division commander and the chief-of-staff had just left outside in the *Place de Ville*, didn't reach here. It was rather a sense, a quality as of the light itself, a reflection as of light itself from the massed faces below, refracted upward into the room through the open windows like light from disturbed water, pulsing and quivering faintly and constantly on the ceiling where nobody, not even the clerks and secretaries coming and going steadily on their endless minuscule errands, would notice it without they chanced to look up, unless like now, when something had caused the pulse to beat a little faster, so that when the division commander and the chief-of-staff entered, everyone in the room was looking at the door. Though almost as soon as they entered, that too died away and the refraction merely quivered again.

The division commander had never seen the room before. He did not look at it now. He just entered and paused for a rigid infinitesimal instant until the chief-of-staff came abreast on his right, the sabre between them now under the chief-of-staff's left arm. Then almost in step they trod the rug's blanched vista to the table and halted rigidly together while the chief-of-staff saluted and took from under his arm the dead sabre furled loosely in the dangling buckle-ends of its harness like a badly-rolled umbrella, and laid it on the table.

And staring rigidly at nothing while the chief-of-staff verbally performed the formal rite of his relinquishment, the division commander thought: *It's true. He knew me at once*, thinking, No: worse: that the old man had already known him long before anyone announced the two of them from an anteroom; that apparently he had come all the long way from that instant in the observation post two mornings back where his career died, merely to prove what all who knew the old marshal's name believed: that the old man remembered the name and face of every man in uniform whom he had ever seen—not only those out of the old regiment into which he had been commissioned from St Cyr, and the ranking commanders of his armies and corps whom he saw daily, but their staffs and secretaries and clerks, and the commanders of divisions and brigades and their staffs, and regimental and battalion and company officers and their orderlies and batmen and runners, and the privates whom he had decorated or reprimanded or condemned, and the N.C.O. leaders and degreeless file-closers of sections and platoons and squads whose inspection-opened ranks he had merely walked rapidly through once thirty and forty years ago, calling them all 'my child' just as he did his own handsome young personal aide and his ancient batman and his chauffeur: a six-and-a-half foot Basque with the face of a murderer of female children. He (the division commander) had seen no movement; his recollection on entering was that the old marshal had been holding the sheaf of papers open in his hand. Yet it was not only closed now, it was pushed slightly aside and the old marshal had removed the spectacles, holding them lightly in a mottled old man's hand almost completely hidden inside the round tremendous orifice of an immaculately laundered cuff detachable from an old-fashioned starched white civilian shirt, and looking for just a second into the spectacle-less eyes, the division commander remembered something Lallemont had said once: *If I were evil, I would hate and fear him. If I were a saint, I would weep. If I were wise, and both or either, I would despair.*

'Yes, General Gragnon?' the old general said.

Staring again not at anything but at simple eye-level above the old general's head, the division commander repeated orally the report which he had already recognised as soon as he entered the room—the verbatim typescripts signed by himself and endorsed by the corps commander, lying now in mimeographed triplicate before the three generals, and finished and stopped for a moment as the lecturer pauses to turn a page or sip from the glass of water, then repeated for the fourth time his official request for the regiment's execution; inflexible and composed before the table on which lay the triumvirate markers of his career's sepulture, the triplicate monument of what the group commander had called his glory, he discharged for the fourth time the regiment from the rolls of his division as though it had vanished two mornings ago in the face of a machine-gun battery or a single mine explosion. He hadn't changed it. It had been right thirty-six hours ago when his honor and integrity as its (or any regiment's) division commander compelled him to anticipate having to make it; it was still right the second after that when he discovered that that which had given him the chance to become commander of a division in exchange for the dedication of his honor and life, was compelling him to deliver it. So it was still right now for the very reason that it was the same honor and integrity which the beneficence had found worthy to be conferred with the three stars of his major general's rank, rather than the beneficence itself, which was making the demand, the compulsion.

Because the beneficence itself didn't need the gesture. As the group commander himself had practically told him this morning, what he was saying now had no connection at all beyond mere coincidence, with what lay on the table. The speech was much older than that moment two days ago in the observation post when he discovered that he was going to have to make it. Its conception was the moment he found he was to be posted to officers' school, its birth the day he received the commission, so that it had become, along with the pistol and sabre and the sublieutenant's badges, a part of the equipment with which he would follow and serve his destiny with his life as long as life lasted; its analogous coeval was that one of the live cartridges constant through the pistol's revolving cylinder, against the moment when he would discharge the voluntary lien he had given on his honor by expiating what a civilian would call bad luck and only a soldier disgrace, the—any—bad luck in it being merely this moment now, when the need compelled the speech yet at the same time denied the bullet. In fact, it seemed to him now that the two of them, speech and bullet, were analogous and coeval even in more than birth: analogous in the very incongruity of the origins from which they moved, not even shaped yet, toward their mutual end:—a lump of dross exhumed from the earth and become, under heat, brass, and under fierce and cunning pressure, a cartridge case; from a laboratory, a pinch, a spoonful, a dust, precipitate of earth's and air's primordial motion, the two condensed and combined behind a tiny locked grooved slug and all micrometered to a servant breech and bore not even within its cognizance yet, like a footman engaged from an employment agency over the telephone;—half Europe went to war with the other half and finally succeeded in dragging half the western hemisphere along: a plan, a design vast in scope, exalted in conception, in implication (and hope) terrifying, not even conceived here at Grand Headquarters by the three old generals and their trained experts and advisers in orderly conference, but conceived out of the mutual rage and fear of the three ocean-dividing nations themselves, simultaneously at Washington and London and Paris by some immaculate pollenization like earth's simultaneous leafage, and come to birth at a council not even held at Grand Headquarters but behind locked and guarded doors in the Quai d'Orsay—a council where trained military experts, dedicated as irrevocably to war as nuns are married to God, were outnumbered by those who were not only not trained for war, they were not even braided and panoplied for it—the Prime Ministers and Premiers and Secretaries, the cabinet members and senators and chancellors; and those who outnumbered even them: the board chairmen of the vast establishments which produced the munitions and shoes and tinned foods, and the modest unsung omnipotent ones who were the priests of simple money; and the others still who outnumbered even these: the politicians, the lobbyists, the owners and publishers of newspapers and the ordained ministers of churches, and all the other accredited travelling representatives of the vast solvent organizations and fraternities and movements which control by coercion or cajolery man's morals and actions and all his mass-value for affirmation or negation;—all that vast powerful terror-inspiring representation which, running all democracy's affairs in peace, come indeed into their own in war, finding their true apotheosis then, in iron conclave now decreeing for half the earth a design vast in its intention to demolish a frontier, and vaster still in its furious intent to obliterate a people; all in conclave so single that the old gray inscrutable supreme general with the face of one who long ago had won the right to believe in nothing whatever save man's deathless folly, didn't need to vote at all but simply to preside, and so presiding, contemplated the plan's birth and then watched it, not even needing to control it as it took its ordained undeviable course, descending from nations confederated to nations selected, to forces to army groups to armies to corps; all that gigantic long complex chronicle, at the end reduced to a simple regimental attack against a simple elevation of earth too small to show on a map, known only to its own neighborhood and even that by a number and a nickname dating back less than four years to the moment when someone had realised that you could see perhaps a quarter-mile further from its summit than its foot; an attack not allotted to a division but self-compelled to it by its own geography and logistics because the alternatives were either here or nowhere, this or nothing, and compelled to his particular division for the reason that the attack was doomed and intended as failure and his was the division among all with which failure could be bought cheapest, as another might be the division with which a river could be crossed or a village taken cheapest; he realised now that it had not been necessary for anyone to have foreseen the mutiny, because the mutiny itself didn't matter: the failure alone would have been enough, and how and why it failed, nobody cared, the mutiny flung in as lagniappe to that end whose sole aim had been to bring him to attention here before the table on which lay in its furled scabbard the corpse of his career, to repeat for the fourth time the speech, who had been denied the bullet, and finish it and stop.

'The whole regiment,' the old marshal said, repeating in his turn, in a voice inscrutable and pleasant and so void of anything as to seem almost warm, inattentive, almost impersonal.

'Not just this ring-leader and his twelve disciples. By all means, the nine of them who are Frenchmen yet still permitted themselves to be corrupted.'

'There was no ring-leader,' the division commander said, harsh and rigid. 'The regiment mutinied.'

'The regiment mutinied,' the old marshal repeated again. 'And suppose we do. What of the other regiments in your division, when they learn of it?'

'Shoot them,' the division commander said.

'And the other divisions in your corps, and the other corps on either side of you.'

'Shoot them,' the division commander said, and stood again inflexible and composed while the old marshal turned and translated quietly and rapidly to the British general and the American on either side of him, then turned back and said to the chief-of-staff:

'Thank you, General.' The chief-of-staff saluted. But the division commander did not wait for him, already about-facing, leaving the chief-of-staff once more the split of a second late since he had to perform his own manoeuver which even a crack drill-sergeant could not have done smoothly with no more warning than this, having in fact to take two long extra steps to get himself again on the division commander's right hand and failing—or almost—here too, so that it was the old marshal's personal aide who flanked the division commander, the chief-of-staff himself still half a pace behind, as they trod the white rug once more back to the now open door just outside which a provost marshal's officer correct with side-arms waited, though before they reached him, the division commander was even in front of the aide.

† † †

So the aide was flanking, not the division commander but the chief-of-staff, pacing him correctly on the left, back to the open door beyond which the provost officer waited while the division commander passed through it.

Whereupon the aide not only effaced from the room the entire significance of the surrendered sabre, he obliterated from it the whole gauche inference of war. As he stepped quickly and lightly and even a little swaggeringly toward the open door beyond which the division commander and the provost officer had vanished, it was as though, in declining in advance to hold the door for the division commander (even though the division commander had already declined the courtesy in advance by not waiting for it), he had not merely retaliated upon the junior general for the junior's affrontment to the senior general's precedence, he had used the junior as the instrument to postulate both himself and the chief-of-staff as being irrevocably alien and invincibly unconcerned with everything the room and those it contained represented—the very tall elegantly thin captain of twenty-eight or thirty with the face and body of a durable matinee idol, who might have been a creature from another planet, anachronistic and immune, inviolable, so invincibly homeless as to be completely and impregnably at home on this or any other planet where he might find himself: not even of tomorrow but of the day before it, projected by reverse avatar back into a world where what remained of lost and finished man struggled feebly for a moment yet among the jumbled ruins of his yesterdays—a creature who had survived intact the fact that he had no place, no business whatever, in war, who for all gain or loss to war's inexorable gambit or that of the frantic crumbling nations either, might as well have been floating gowned and capped (and with the golden tassel of a lordship too since he looked more like a scion than any duke's son) across an Oxford or Cambridge quadrangle, compelling those watching him and the chief-of-staff to condone the deodorization of war's effluvium even from the uniforms they wore, leaving them simply costumes, stepping rapidly and lightly and elegantly past the chief-of-staff to grasp the knob and shut the door until the latch caught, then turned the knob and opened the door and clicked not to attention but into a rigid brief inclination from the waist as the chief-of-staff passed through it.

Then he closed the door and turned and started back down the room, then in the same instant stopped again and now apparently essayed to efface from it even the rumor of war which had entered at second hand; motionless for that moment at the top of the splendid diminishing vista, there was about him like an aura a quality insouciant solitary and debonair like Harlequin *solus* on a second- or third-act stage as the curtain goes down or rises, while he stood with his head turned slightly aside, listening. Then he moved, rapid and boneless on his long boneless legs, toward the nearest window. But the old marshal spoke before he had taken the second step, saying quietly in English: 'Leave them open.'

The aide paid no attention whatever. He strode to the window and thrust his whole upper body out as he reached for the outswung casement and began to swing it in. Then he stopped. He said in French, not loud, in a sort of rapt amazement, dispassionate and momentary: 'It looks like a crowd at a race track waiting for the two-sou window to open—if they have such. No, they look like they are watching a burning pawnshop.'

'Leave it open,' the old general said in English. The aide paused again, the casement half closed. He turned his head and said in English too, perfectly, with no accent whatever, not even of Oxford, not even of Beacon Hill:

'Why not have them inside and be done with it? They cant hear what's going on out there.'

This time the old general spoke French. 'They dont want to know,' he said. 'They want only to suffer. Leave it open.'

'Yes sir,' the aide said in French. He flung the casement out again and turned. As he did so one leaf of the double doors in the opposite wall opened. It opened exactly six inches, by no visible means, and stopped. The aide didn't even glance toward it. He came on into the room, saying in that perfect accentless English, 'Dinner, gentlemen,' as both leaves of the door slid back.

The old general rose when the two other generals did but that was all. When the doors closed behind the last aide, he was already seated again. Then he pushed the closed folder further aside and folded the spectacles into their worn case and buttoned the case into one of his upper tunic pockets, and alone now in the vast splendid room from which even the city's tumult and anguish was fading as the afternoon light died from the ceiling, motionless in the chair whose high carven back topped him like the back of a throne, his hands hidden below the rich tremendous table which concealed most of the rest of him too and apparently not only immobile but immobilised beneath the mass and glitter of his braid and stars and buttons, he resembled a boy, a child, crouching amid the golden debris of the tomb not of a knight or bishop ravished in darkness but (perhaps the mummy itself) of a sultan or pharaoh violated by Christians in broad afternoon.

Then the same leaf of the double door opened again, exactly as before, for exactly six inches and no hand to show for it and making only the slightest of sounds, and even then giving the impression that if it had wanted to, it could have made none and that what it did make was only the absolute minimum to be audible at all, opening for that six inches and then moving no more until the old general said: 'Yes, my child.' Then it began to close, making no sound at all now that sound was no longer necessary, moving on half the distance back to closure with its fellow leaf when it stopped again and with no pause began to open again, still noiseless but quite fast now, so fast that it had opened a good eighteen inches and in another instant who or whatever moved it would of necessity reveal, expose him or itself, before the old general could or did speak. 'No,' he said. The door stopped. It didn't close, it just quit moving at all and seemed to hang like a wheel at balance with neither top nor bottom, hanging so until the old general spoke again: 'Leave them open.'

Then the door closed. It went all the way to this time, and the old general rose and came around the table and went to the nearest window, walking through the official end of day as across a threshold into night, because as he turned the end of the table the scattered bugles began to sound the three assemblies, and as he crossed the room the clash of boots and rifles came up from the courtyard, and when he reached the window the two guards were already facing one another for the first note of the three retreats and the formal exchange to begin. But the old general didn't seem to be watching it. He just stood in the window above the thronged motionless *Place* where the patient mass of people lay against the iron fence; nor did he turn his head when the door opened rapidly this time and the young aide entered, carrying a telephone whose extension flowed behind him across the white rug like the endless tail of a trophy, and went behind the table and with his foot drew up one of the chairs and sat down and set the telephone on the table and lifted the receiver and shot into view the watch on his other wrist and became motionless, the receiver to his ear and his eyes on the watch. Instead, he just stood there, a little back from the window and a little to one side, holding the curtain slightly aside, visible if anyone in the *Place* had thought to look up, while the scattered brazen adjurations died into the clash and stamp as the two guards came to *at ease* and the whole borderline, no longer afternoon yet not quite evening either, lay in unbreathing suspension until the bugles began again, the three this time in measured discordant unison, the three voices in the courtyard barking in unison too yet invincibly alien, the two groups of heavily armed men posturing rigidly at each other like a tribal ritual for religious immolation. He could not have heard the telephone, since the aide already had the receiver to his ear and merely spoke an acknowledging word into it, then listened a moment and spoke another word and lowered the receiver and sat waiting too while the bugles chanted and wailed like cocks in the raddled sunset, and died away.

'He has landed,' the aide said. 'He got down from the aeroplane and drew a pistol and called his pilot to attention and shot him through the face. They dont know why.'

'They are Englishmen,' the old general said. 'That will do.'

'Of course,' the aide said. 'I'm surprised they have as little trouble as they do in Continental wars. In any of their wars.' He said: 'Yes sir.' He rose to his feet. 'I had arranged to have this line open at five points between here and Villeneuve Blanche, so you could keep informed of his progress——'

'It is indistinguishable from his destination,' the old general said without moving. 'That will do.' The aide put the receiver back on its hook and took up the telephone and went back around the table, the limber endless line recoiling onto itself across the rug until he flicked the diminishing loop after him through the door, and closed it. At that moment the sunset gun thudded: no sound, but rather a postulation of vacuum, as though back into its blast-vacated womb the regurgitated martial day had poured in one reverberant clap; from just beyond the window came the screak and whisper of the three blocks and the three down-reeling lanyards and the same leaf of the door opened again for that exact six inches, paused, then without any sound opened steadily and unmotived on and still the old general stood while the thrice-alien voices barked, and beneath the three tenderly-borne mystical rags the feet of the three color guards rang the cobbled courtyard and, in measured iron diminution, the cobbled evening itself.

And now the mass beyond the fence itself began to move, flowing back across the *Place* toward the diverging boulevards, emptying the *Place*, already fading before it was out of the *Place*, as though with one long quiet inhalation evening was effacing the whole meek mist of man; now the old general stood above the city which, already immune to man's enduring, was now even free of his tumult. Or rather, the evening effaced not man from the *Place de Ville* so much as it effaced the *Place de Ville* back into man's enduring anguish and his invincible dust, the city itself not really free of either but simply taller than both. Because they endured, as only endurance can, firmer than rock, more invincible than folly, longer than grief, the darkling and silent city rising out of the darkling and empty twilight to lower like a tumescent thunderclap, since it was the effigy and the power, rising tier on inviolate tier out of that mazed chiaroscuro like a tremendous beehive whose crown challenged by day the sun and stemmed aside by night the celestial smore.

First and topmost were the three flags and the three supreme generals who served them: a triumvirate consecrated and anointed, a constellation remote as planets in their immutability, powerful as archbishops in their trinity, splendid as cardinals in their retinues and myriad as Brahmins in their blind followers; next were the three thousand lesser generals who were their deacons and priests and the hierarchate of their households, their acolytes and bearers of monstrance and host and censer: the colonels and majors who were in charge of the portfolios and maps and memoranda, the captains and subalterns who were in charge of the communications and errands which kept the portfolios and maps up to date, and the sergeants and corporals who actually carried the portfolios and mapcases and protected them with their lives and answered the telephone and ran the errands, and the privates who sat at the flickering switchboards at two and three and four oclock in the morning and rode the motorcycles in the rain and snow and drove the starred and pennoned cars and cooked the food for the generals and colonels and majors and captains and subalterns and made their beds and shaved them and cut their hair and polished their boots and brass; and inferior and nethermost even in that braided inviolate hierarchate: so crowded was the city with generals of high rank and their splendid and shining staffs that not only were subalterns and captains and even majors and colonels nothing, distinguishable from civilians only because they wore uniforms, there was even a nadir among these: men who had actually been in, come out of, the battle zone, as high in rank as majors and even colonels sometime, strayed into the glittering and gunless city through nobody knew what bizarre convulsion of that military metabolism which does everything to a man but lose him, which learns nothing and forgets nothing and loses nothing at all whatever and forever—no scrap of paper, no unfinished record or uncompleted memorandum no matter how inconsequential or trivial; a few of them were always there, not many but enough: platoon or section leaders and company commanders and battalion seconds stained with the filth of front lines who amid that thronged pomp and glitter of stars and crossed batons and braid and brass and scarlet tabs moved diffident and bewildered and ignored with the lost air of oafish peasants smelling of field and stable summoned to the castle, the Great House, for an accounting or a punishment: a wounded man armless legless or eyeless was stared at with the same aghast distasteful refusive pity and shock and outrage as a man in an epileptic seizure at high noon on a busy downtown corner; then the civilians: Antipas his friends and their friends, merchant and prince and bishop, administrator clacquer and absolver to ministrate the attempt and applaud the intention and absolve the failed result, and all the nephews and godsons of Tiberius in far Rome and their friends and the friends of the wives and the husbands of their friends come to dine with the generals and sell to the generals' governments the shells and guns and aircraft and beef and shoes for the generals to expend against the enemy, and their secretaries and couriers and chauffeurs who had got military deferment because the brief-cases had to be carried and the motorcars driven, and those who actually dwelled as *pater-familiae* among the city's boulevards and avenues and even less base streets already before the city entered its four-year apotheosis and while apotheosis obtained and would still (so they hoped) after apotheosis had ceased and been forgotten—mayor and burgher, doctor attorney director inspector and judge who held no particular letter from Tiberius in Rome yet whose contacts were still among generals and colonels and not captains and subalterns even if they were restricted to drawing rooms and dining tables, publican and smith and baker and grocer and wright whose contacts were not with captains nor subalterns nor with sergeants and corporals and privates neither since it was their wives who knitted behind the zinc bars and weighed and exchanged sous for the bread and greens and beat the underwear on the river's margin stones; and the women who were not the wives of directors or bakers, who traded not in war but because of war and who as in a sense two thousand nine hundred and ninety-seven of the generals were just one general were all one woman too whether staff colonels stood when they entered rooms or whether they lived on the same floor in modest *pensions* with Service Corps captains or boiled the soup of communications corporals or, troops themselves, received their partners in what is called love and perhaps even is from a sergeant's roll-call as a soldier receives his iron ration or boots and no need for that partner to put back on his tunic or greatcoat before going on into the lines because the sergeant who checked him into and out of that love which perhaps had never let him take either off, so that as often as not she carried into sleep with her that night a dead man's still warm and living seed; and then and last even anonymity's absolute whose nameless faceless mass cluttered old Jerusalem and old Rome too while from time to time governor and caesar flung them bread or a circus as in the old snowy pantomime the fleeing shepherd casts back to the pursuing wolves fragments of his lunch, a garment, and as a last resort the lamb itself—the laborers who owned today only the spending of what they earned yesterday, the beggars and thieves who did not always understand that what they did was beggary and theft, the lepers beneath city gate and temple door who did not even know they were not whole, who belonged neither to the military nor to the merchants and princes and bishops, who neither derived nor hoped for any benefit from army contracts nor battened by simply existing, breathing coeval with the prodigality and waste concomitant with a nation's mortal agony, that strange and constant few who each time are denied any opportunity whatever to share in the rich carnival of their country's wasting lifeblood, whose luck is out always with no kin nor friends who have kin or friends who have powerful kin or friends or patrons, who owned nothing in fact save a reversion in endurance without hope of betterment nor any spur of pride—a capacity for endurance which even after four years of existence as tolerated and rightless aliens on their own land and in their own city still enabled them without hope or pride even in the endurance to endure, asking or expecting no more than permission to exercise it, like a sort of immortality. Out of that enduring and anguished dust it rose, out of the dark Gothic dream, carrying the Gothic dream, arch- and buttress-winged, by knight and bishop, angels and saints and cherubim groined and pilastered upward into soaring spire and pinnacle where goblin and demon, gryphon and gargoyle and hermaphrodite yelped in icy soundless stone against the fading zenith. The old general dropped the curtain and began to turn from the window.

'You may close——' he said. Then he stopped. It was as though he didn't anticipate the sound so much as he simply foreknew it, already motionless when the sound came into the window—an uproar thin and distant across the city, not diffuse now but localised and still curiously localised by source even when it began to move as if it were directed at some small specific object no larger than a man and it was not the yelling which moved but the object of it retreating slowly before the yelling—not turning back to the window but simply arrested beside it. Hooves clattered suddenly in the *Place* and a body of cavalry crossed it at trot and entered the boulevard leading toward the old eastern gate, already at canter and went on. Then for a time the sound of the hooves seemed to have dissolved into, been smothered by the yelling, until suddenly the cavalry had ridden as though into the yelling as into a weightless mass of dead leaves, exploding them, flinging and hurling them, to reappear the next second like centaurs in furious soundless motion intact in an intact visible cloud of swirling frantic screams which continued to swirl and burst in that faint frenetic tossing even after the horses must indubitably have been gone, still swirling and tossing in scattered diminuendo when the other sound began. It came up beneath them, beginning not as sound at all but rather as light, diffused yet steady from across the plain beyond the city: the voices of men alone, choral almost, growing not in volume but in density as dawn itself increases, filling the low horizon beyond the city's black and soaring bulk with a band not of sound but light while above and into it the thin hysteric nearer screams and cries skittered and spun and were extinguished like sparks into water, still filling the horizon even after the voices themselves had ceased with a resonant humming like a fading sunset and heatless as aurora against which the black tremendous city seemed to rush skyward in one fixed iron roar out of the furious career of earth toward its furious dust, upreared and insensate as an iron ship's prow among the fixed insensate stars.

This time the old general turned from it. The single leaf of the door was now open about three feet and there stood beside it an old old man, not at all at attention but just standing there. He was hardly larger than a child, not stooped or humped and shrunken was not the word either. He was condensed, intact and unshriveled, the long ellipsoid of his life almost home again now, where rosy and blemishless, without memory or grieving flesh, mewling bald and toothless, he would once more possess but three things and would want no more: a stomach, a few surface nerves to seek warmth, a few cells capable of sleep. He was not a soldier. The very fact that he wore not only a heavy regulation infantryman's buttoned-back greatcoat but a steel helmet and a rifle slung across his back merely made him look less like one. He stood there in spectacles, in the faded coat which had been removed perhaps from its first (or last) owner's corpse—it still bore the darker vacancies where an N.C.O.'s chevrons and a regimental number had been removed, and neatly stitched together on the front of it, just above where the skirts folded back, was the suture where something (a bayonet obviously) had entered it, and within the last twenty-four hours it had been brushed carefully and ironed by hand by someone who could not see very well—and processed through a cleansing and delousing plant and then issued to him from a quartermaster's salvage depot, and the polished steel helmet and the clean polished rifle which looked as lovingly-tended and unused as a twelfth-century pike from a private museum, which he had never fired and did not know how to fire and would not have fired nor accepted a live cartridge for even if there was a single man in all the French armies who would have given him one. He had been the old general's batman for more than fifty years (except for the thirteen years beginning on the day more than forty years ago now when the old general, a captain with a brilliant and almost incredible future, had vanished not only from the army lists but from the ken of all the people who up to that time had thought they knew him also, to reappear thirteen years later in the army lists and the world too with the rank of brigadier and none to know whence nor why either although as regards the rank they did know how; his first official act had been to find his old batman, then a clerk in a commissary's office in Saigon, and have him assigned back to his old position and rating); he stood there healthily pink as an infant, ageless and serene in his aura of indomitable fidelity, invincibly hardheaded, incorrigibly opinionated and convinced, undeflectable in advice suggestion and comment and invincibly contemptuous of war and all its ramifications, constant durable faithful and insubordinate and almost invisible within the clutter and jumble of his martial parody so that he resembled an aged servant of some ancient ducal house dressed in ceremonial regalia for the annual commemoration of some old old event, some ancient defeat or glory of the House so long before his time that he had long ago forgotten the meaning and significance if he ever knew it, while the old general crossed the room and went back around the table and sat down again. Then the old batman turned and went back through the door and reappeared immediately with a tray bearing a single plain soup bowl such as might have come from an N.C.O.'s mess or perhaps from that of troops themselves, and a small stone jug and the end of a loaf and a battered pewter spoon and an immaculate folded damask napkin, and set the tray on the table before the old marshal and, the beautifully polished rifle gleaming and glinting as he bent and recovered and stood back, watched, fond and domineering and implacable, the old marshal's every move as the old marshal took up the bread and began to crumble it into the bowl.

When he entered St Cyr at seventeen, except for that fragment of his splendid fate which even here he could not escape, he seemed to have brought nothing of the glittering outside world he had left behind him but a locket—a small object of chased worn gold, obviously valuable or anyway venerable, resembling a hunting-case watch and obviously capable of containing two portraits; only capable of containing such since none of his classmates ever saw it open and in fact they only learned he possessed it through the circumstance that one or two of them happened to see it on a chain about his neck like a crucifix in the barracks bathroom one day. And even that scant knowledge was quickly adumbrated by the significance of that destiny which even these gates were incapable of severing him from—that of being not only the nephew of a Cabinet Minister, but the godson of the board chairman of that gigantic international federation producing munitions which, with a few alterations in the lettering stamped into the head of each cartridge- and shell-case, fitted almost every military rifle and pistol and light field-piece in all the western hemisphere and half the eastern too. Yet despite this, because of his secluded and guarded childhood, until he entered the Academy the world outside the Faubourg St Germain had scarcely ever seen him, and the world which began at the Paris *banlieu* had never even heard of him except as a male christian name. He was an orphan, an only child, the last male of his line, who had grown from infancy in the sombre insulate house of his mother's eldest sister in the rue Vaugirard—wife of a Cabinet Minister who was himself a nobody but a man of ruthless and boundless ambition, who had needed only opportunity and got it through his wife's money and connections, and—they were childless—had legally adopted her family by hyphenating its name onto his own, the child growing to the threshold of manhood not only that heir and heir to the power and wealth of his bachelor godfather, the *Comité de Ferrovie* chairman who had been his father's closest friend, but before any save his aunt's Faubourg St Germain *salons* and their servants and his tutors, could connect his face with his splendid background and his fabulous future.

So when he entered the Academy, none of the classmates with whom he was to spend the next four years (and probably the staff and the professors too) had ever seen him before. And he had been there probably twenty-four hours before any of them except one even connected his face with his great name. This one was not a youth too but instead already a man, twenty-two years old, who had entered the Academy two days before and was to stand Number Two to the other's One on the day of graduation, who on that first afternoon began to believe, and for the next fifteen years would continue, that he had seen at once in that seventeen-year-old face the promise of a destiny which would be the restored (this was 1873, two years after the capitulation and formal occupation of Paris) glory and destiny of France too. As for the rest of them, their first reaction was that of the world outside: surprise and amazement and for the moment downright unbelief, that he, this youth, was here at all. It was not because of his appearance of fragility and indurability; they simply read the face also into that fragility and indurability which, during that first instant when he seemed to be not entering the gates but rather framed immobilely by them, had fixed him as absolutely and irrevocably discrepant to that stone-bastioned iron maw of war's apprenticeship as a figure out of a stained glass cathedral window set by incomprehensible chance into the breached wall of a fort. It was because to them, his was the golden destiny of an hereditary crown prince of paradise. To them, he was not even a golden youth: he was *the* golden youth; to them inside the Academy and to all that world stretching from the Paris *banlieu* to the outermost rim where the word Paris faded, he was not even a Parisian but *the* Parisian: a millionaire and an aristocrat from birth, an orphan and an only child, not merely heir in his own right to more francs than anyone knew save the lawyers and bankers who guarded and nursed and incremented them, but to the incalculable weight and influence of the uncle who was the nation's first Cabinet member even though another did bear the title and the precedence, and of that godfather whose name opened doors which (a *Comité de Ferrovie* chairman's), because of their implications and commitments, or (a bachelor's) of their sex, gender, even that of a Cabinet Minister could not; who had only to reach majority in order to inherit that matchless of all catastrophes: the privilege of exhausting his life—or if necessary, shortening it—by that matchless means of all: being young, male, unmarried, an aristocrat, wealthy, secure by right of birth in Paris: that city which was the world too, since of all cities it was supreme, dreamed after and adored by all men, and not just when she was supreme in her pride but when—as now—she was abased from it. Indeed, never more dreamed after and adored than now, while in abasement; never more so than now because of what, in any other city, would have been abasement. Never more than now was she, not France's Paris but the world's, the defilement being not only a part of the adored immortality and the immaculateness and therefore necessary to them, but since it was the sort of splendid abasement of which only Paris was capable, being capable of it made her the world's Paris: conquered—or rather, not conquered, since, France's Paris, she was inviolate and immune to the very iron heel beneath which the rest of France (and, since she was the world's Paris too, the rest of the world also) lay supine and abased,—impregnable and immune: the desired, the civilised world's inviolate and forever unchaste, virgin barren and insatiable: the mistress who renewed her barren virginity in the very act of each barren recordless promiscuity, Eve and Lilith both to every man in his youth so fortunate and blessed as to be permitted within her omnivorous insatiable orbit; the victorious invading hun himself, bemazed not so much by his success as his sudden and incredible whereabouts, shuffling his hobbed boots in the perfumed anteroom, dreaming no less than one born to that priceless fate, on whom, herself immortal, she conferred brief immortality's godhead in exchange for no more than his young man's youth.

Yet here he was, just another anonymous one in a class of candidates for professional careers, not merely in the rigid hierarchy of an army but in an army which for the next fifty years would be struggling simply to survive, to emerge from the debacle and debasement of defeat in order not to be feared as a threat but merely respected as a monument. An Anglo-Saxon mind could, and almost any American would, have read into his presence here a young man's dream in which he would see himself, not by some irremediable sacrifice rescuing that adored city Andromeda-like from her brutal rock perhaps, but at least as one of Niobe's or Rachel's children clapping up sword and buckler. But not the Latin, the French mind; to it, that city had nothing to be saved from, who had strangled all man's heart in any one strand of her vagrant Lilith hair; who, barren, had no sons: they were her lovers, and when they went to war, it was for glory to lay before the altar of that unchaste unstale bed.

So only that single classmate ever believed other than that it was not the youth who repudiated paradise but paradise which repudiated its scion and heir; not he but his family which had put him where he was, not disinherited at all but disfranchised, segregated: the family which had compelled him into the army as—for them, their name and position—at best the isolation, quarantine, of whatever was the threat he had become or represented, and at worst the mausoleum of the shame which would be its result, and—for him—a refuge from the consequences. Because he was still who he was, male and solitary and heir; the family would still use the power and the influence, even though they had had to isolate and quarantine his failure to be what he might—should—have been. In fact, his family had not even merely bought absolution for him. On the contrary, they would gain a sort of blinding redundance on the great name's original splendor from the golden braid which his hat and sleeves would someday bear. Because even the single classmate believed that all that class (and presently the three ahead of it too) were eating and sleeping with one who would be a general at forty and—given any sort of opportunity for any kind of a military debacle worthy of the name inside the next thirty years—a marshal of France when the nation buried him.

Only he didn't use the influence, not in the next four years at least. He didn't even need it. He graduated not only at the top of the class but with the highest marks ever made at the Academy; such was his record that not even his classmates, who would not have been offered it no matter what grades they graduated with, were not even jealous of the Quartermaster captaincy which rumor said was waiting for him at the Academy's exit like a hat or a cloak on the arm of a footman at the exit from a theatre or a restaurant. Yet when he next came into their cognizance—which was immediately on the succeeding day, when the rest of the class had barely begun the regulation two weeks' leave before assuming duty—he didn't have the captaincy. He simply appeared at Toulon without it, still looking little different from what he had four years ago: not fragile so much as invincibly indurable, with his unblemished paybook for which he would have no more use than would the beggar for the king's farrier's nail or the king for the beggar's almsbox, and his untried spartan subaltern's kit and his virgin copy of the Manual of War (and the locket of course; his classmates had not forgot that; in fact they even knew now what the two portraits in it would be: the uncle and the godfather: his crucifix indeed, his talisman, his reliquary) but with no more captaincy than the guest or patron leaving the theatre or restaurant by a fire exit or rear alley would have hat or cloak when he reached the boulevard.

But—save that one—they believed they knew the answer to this. It was a gesture, not the youth's but the family's—one of those gestures of modesty and discretion of the potent and powerful who are powerful and potent enough to afford even discretion and modesty; they and he too were all waiting for the same thing: for the arrival of the great suave hearselike midnight-colored limousine bringing not the civilian secretary bearing the captaincy like a ducal coronet on a velvet cushion, but rather the uncle-Minister himself, who would walk the nephew back to the Quai d'Orsay and in that privacy fling away the meagre African subaltern's kit with the cold outrage of a cardinal plucking a copy of Martin Luther from the robe of a kneeling candidate for consecration. But that didn't happen either. The car would have come too late. Because, although the draft to which he would have been posted was not to leave for two weeks yet and its personnel had not even begun to arrive at the depot, he was gone after only one night, to Africa, to immediate field service, quietly, almost surreptitiously, with the same simple sublieutenant's rank and the same meagre equipment which the rest of them would have in their turn.

So now those who might have been jealous of him (not only his St Cyr coevals, junior and senior, who had no Minister-uncles and chairman-godfathers, but the career men who did have parents and guardians but not Cabinet members and *Comité de Ferrovie* chairmen, who hated him not because he had been offered the captaincy but because he had not accepted it) no longer had to be. Because they knew that they would never overtake him now: who would be removed forever more from envy and hence from hatred and fear both, the three of them, nephew godfather and uncle, going fast now, who had been ruthless even to the long tradition of nepotism, the youth hurried to whatever remote frontier where rampant indeed would be the uncle's and the godfather's power and will, with none save an occasional inspector-general to challenge it; no bounds to the family's ambition nor check to that which furthered it. They would be free, who had bought immunity from envy by simply outlasting it; when he reappeared, say two years from now as a colonel of twenty-three, he would be far beyond the range of any envy and jealousy, let alone theirs. Or perhaps it wouldn't even take two years, one might be enough, so great was their faith in, not just the uncle's and the godfather's power and will, but in rapacity itself: the compassionate, the omnipotent, the all-seeing and all-pervading; one day the Quai d'Orsay would gently out-breathe, and against that fierce African foreshore would officially beat a national unanimity loud and long enough not only to obfuscate the mere circumstances of fact, but to distract the mind from all curiosity regarding them; there would remain only the accomplishment and its protagonist juxtaposed without past on a stage without yesterday, like two masques for a pantomime furbished out of the bloodless lumber-room of literature, because by that time he would have escaped not merely from fear and hatred but from the long rigid mosaic of seniority itself, as irrevocably as does a girl from maidenhood; they would—could—even watch him now, heatless peaceful and immune to any remembered anguish—even see him again passing among the windy bunting and the paraded troops in the cheering Oran street in the Governor General's car, sitting on the right hand of the Governor General himself: the hero of twenty-two or -three who had not at all merely saved some whatever scrap or fragment of an empire, but had set again against the zenith the fierce similitude of a bird, be though as it was but one more lost feather of the eagles which seventy years ago had stooped at all Europe and Africa and Asia too, they watching without jealousy now nor even rancor, but rather with amazed admiration not merely for France but for invincible Man;—the hero still girlish-looking even after two years of African sun and solitude, still frail and fragile in the same way that adolescent girls appear incredibly delicate yet at the same time invincibly durable, like wisps of mist or vapor drifting checkless and insensate among the thunderous concrete-bedded mastodons inside a foundry; appearing now only the more durable because of the proven—no: reproven—fragility, at once frail yet at the same time intact and inviolable because of what in another had been not merely ruin but destruction too: like the saint in the old tale, the maiden who without hesitation or argument fee-ed in advance with her maidenhood the ferryman who set her across the stream and into heaven (an Anglo-Saxon fable too, since only an Anglo-Saxon could seriously believe that anything buyable at no more cost than that could really be worth a sainthood);—the hero, the sheeplike acclaiming mass with not one among them all to ask or even wonder what he had done or when or where, nor even against what or whom the victory, as he passed immune even to the uproar, across the cheering city to the quai and the destroyer (a cruiser maybe, a destroyer certainly) which would carry him to his Paris triumph and then return him, chief of a corps and commander of a department, or perhaps even Governor General himself.

But that didn't happen either. He crossed the Mediterranean and disappeared; when they followed in the order of their postings, they learned that he had gone on from the port base too, after even less than one night, to assigned duty somewhere in the interior, exactly where and on exactly what service, nobody at the port base knew either. But they had expected that. They believed they even knew where he would be: no place remote merely because it was far away and impossible to reach, like Brazzaville say, where the three pale faces—Commandant-governor, new subaltern, and halfbreed interpreter—would slumber hierarchate and superposed, benignant and inscrutable, irascible and hieroglyph like an American Indian totem pole in ebon Eden innocence; but a place really remote, not even passively isolate but actively and even aggressively private, like an oasis in the desert's heart itself, more blind than cave and circumferenced than safari—a silken tent odorous with burning pastille and murmurous with the dreamy *chock* of the woodcutter's axe and the pad of watercarriers' feet, where on a lion-robed divan he would await untimed destiny's hasteless accouchement. But they were wrong. He had left the port base the same day he arrived, for a station as famous in its circles as the Black Hole of Calcutta—a small outpost not only five hundred kilometres from anything resembling a civilised stronghold or even handhold, but sixty and more from its nearest support—a tiny lost compound manned by a sergeant's platoon out of a foreign legion battalion recruited from the gutter-sweepings of all Europe and South America and the Levant:—a well, a flagstaff, a single building of loop-holed clay set in a seared irreconciliable waste of sun and sand which few living men had ever seen, to which troops were sent as punishment or, incorrigibles, for segregation until heat and monotony on top of their natural and acquired vices divorced them permanently from mankind. He had gone straight there from the port base three years ago and (the only officer present and, for all practical purposes, the only white man too) had not only served out his own one-year tour of command, but that of his successor too, and was now ten months forward in that of what would have been his successor's successor; in the shock of that first second of knowledge it seemed to them—except that one—that earth itself had faltered, rapacity itself had failed, when regardless of whatever had been the nephew's old defalcation from his family's hope or dream seven or eight or ten years ago, even that uncle and that godfather had been incapable of saving him; this, until that single classmate picked up the whole picture and reversed it.

He was a Norman, son of a Caen doctor whose grandfather, while an art student in Paris, had become the friend and then the fanatic disciple of Camille Desmoulins until Robespierre executed them both, the great-grandson come to Paris to be a painter too but relinquished his dream to the Military Academy for the sake of France as the great-grandfather had done his to the guillotine for the sake of Man: who for all his vast peasant bones had looked at twenty-two even more indurable and brittly-keyed than ever had his obsession at seventeen,—a man with a vast sick flaccid moon of a face and hungry and passionate eyes, who had looked once at that one which to all the world else had been that of any seventeen-year-old youth and relinquished completely to it like a sixty-year-old longtime widower to that of a pubic unconscious girl, who picked up the three figures—uncle nephew and godfather—like so many paper dolls and turned them around and set them down again in the same positions and attitudes but obversed. Though this would be several years yet, almost ten in fact after that day when they had watched that sunstricken offing behind Oran accept that fragile stride and then close markless behind it like a painted backdrop, not only markless but impenetrable too; and not just a backdrop but Alice's looking-glass rather, through which he had stepped not into unreality but instead carrying unreality with him to establish it where before there had been none: four years from that day and he was still there at his little lost barren sunglared unfutured outpost: who, whether or not he had ever been an actual threat once, was now an enigma burying its ostrich-head from the staff commission which would drag him back to Paris and at least into vulnerable range of his old sybaritic renunciation; five years from that day and beginning the sixth voluntary tour of that duty which should have fallen to every officer in the Army List (every man everywhere) before it came to him, and (so grave the defalcation from which his family had had to bury him that not only was mere seniority confounded, but the immutable rotation of military leave too) not even the cafes of Casa Blanca or Oran or Algiers, let alone Paris, had ever seen him.

Then six years from that day and he had vanished from Africa too, none knew where except the Norman classmate's passionate and hungry hope, vanished not only from the knowledge of man but from the golden warp and woof of the legend too, leaving behind him only a name in the Army List, still with the old unchanged rank of sublieutenant but with nothing after it: not even dead, not even whereabouts unknown; and even this was another two years, by which time all of them who had feared him once, not only the old St Cyr class but its successors too, were scattered and diffused about the perimeter where the thrice-barred flag flew, until the afternoon when five of them, including the Norman classmate and a staff captain, met by chance in a Quai d'Orsay anteroom, were now sitting about a sidewalk table in front of the most adjacent cafe, the staff officer already four years a captain even though only five years out of St Cyr, descendant of a Napoleonic duchy whose founder or recipient had been a butcher then a republican then an imperialist then a duke, and his son a royalist then a republican again and—still alive and still a duke—then a royalist again: so that three of the four watching and listening to him thought how here was the true golden youth which that other one of eleven years ago whom he was talking about, had refused to be, realising, aware for the first time, not just what the other would have been by now, but—with that family and background and power—what matchless pinnacle he might have reached, since this one had behind him only simple proprietors of banks and manipulators of shares; the staff captain using the anteroom to serve his captaincy in, and three of the other four having reported to it that morning by mutual coincidence after three years on the Asiatic Station, and the fourth one, the junior, having been assigned to it right out of the gates themselves, the five of them coincidental about the cramped table on the crowded terrace while three of them—including the Norman giant who sat not among them so much as above them, immense and sick and apparently insensate as a boulder save for his flaccid and hungry face and the passionate and hungry eyes—listening while the staff captain, burly blunt brutal heavy-witted and assured and so loud that people at the other tables had begun to turn, talked about the almost-forgotten sublieutenant at his tiny lost post in the depths of Never-Never: who should have been the idol pattern and hope not merely for all career officers but for all golden youth everywhere, as was Bonaparte not merely for all soldiers but for every ancestorless

Frenchman qualified first in poverty, who was willing to hold life and conscience cheap enough: wondering (the staff captain) what could have been out there in that desert to hold for six years above a quartermaster captaincy, the sublieutenant-command of a stinking well enclosed by eight palm trees and inhabited by sixteen un-nationed cut-throats; what out there that Oran or Casa Blanca or even Paris couldn't match—what paradise within some camel-odored tent—what limbs old and weary and cunning with ancient pleasures that Montmartre bagnios (and even St Germain boudoirs) knew nothing of, yet so ephemeral, so incipient with satiation and at last actual revulsion, that after only six years the sultan-master must vacate it——

'Vacate it?' one of the three said. 'You mean he's gone? He actually left that place at last?'

'Not quite gone,' the staff captain said. 'Not until his relief arrives. After all, he accepted an oath to France, even he, even if he does hold from the *Comité de Ferrovie*. He failed. He lost a camel. There was a man too, even if he had spent most of his five enlistments in clink —' telling it: the soldier spawned by a Marseilles cesspool to be the ultimate and fatal nemesis of a woman a girl whom eighteen years ago he had corrupted and diseased and then betrayed into prostitution and at last murdered and had spent the eighteen years since as member of lost frontier garrisons such as this because this—the rim of oblivion—was the one place on earth where he could continue to walk and breathe and be fed and clothed: whose one fear now was that he might do something which would prompt someone to make him a corporal or a sergeant and so compel him back to some post within a day's walk of any community large enough to possess one civilian policeman, where not he would see a strange face but where some strange face would see him; he—the soldier, the trooper, had vanished along with the camel, obviously into the hands of an adjacent band or tribe of the Riffs who were the excuse for the garrison being where it was and the reason for its being armed. And though the man was a piece of government property too, even if not a very valuable one, that camel was a camel. Yet the commander of the post had apparently made no effort whatever to recover them; whereupon they—his listeners—might say that the commander's only failure in the matter had been that he had prevented a local war. Which was wrong. He had not stopped a war: he had simply failed to start one. Which was not his purpose there, not why he had been tested and found competent for that command: not to fail to start wars, but to preserve government property. So he had failed, and yesterday his official request to be relieved had forwarded to the Adjutant-General's desk——

The Norman was already on his feet while the staff captain was still talking; at least four of them knew how he heard of the command's vacancy but not even these knew how he managed to get the succession to it—a man without family or influence or money at all, with nothing in fact to front or fend for him in his profession save the dubious capacity of his vast ill body to endure, and the rating of Two in his St Cyr class; already, because of the rating, a sublieutenant of engineers and, because of the rating and his sick body both, in addition to the fact that he had just completed a tour of field service in Indo China, from now on secure for a Home Establishment post probably in Paris itself, until retirement age overtook him. Yet within an hour he was in the office of the Quartermaster General himself, using, having deliberately used the Number Two rating for the first (and probably the last) time in his life for the chance to stand facing the desk which he could not know or dream that someday he himself would sit behind, himself in his turn sole unchallengeable arbiter over the whereabouts and maintenance of every man wearing a French uniform.

'You? an Engineer?' the man facing him said.

'So was he:'—the voice eager, serene, not importunate so much as simply not to be denied: 'That's why, you see. Remember, I was Number Two to him in our class. When he leaves it, it belongs to me.'

'Then you remember this,' the other said, tapping the medical survey on the desk before him. 'This is why you are not going back to Saigon after your leave, why you are going on Home Establishment from now on. As for that, you wouldn't live a year out there in that——'

'You were about to say "hole",' he said. 'Isn't that its purpose: for the honorable disposal of that self-proven to have no place in the Establishment of Man?'

'Man?'

'France, then,' he said; and thirteen days later looked from the back of the camel across the glaring markless intervening miles, as a thousand years afterward the first pilgrim must have looked at the barely distinguishable midden which the native guide assured him had been, not Golgotha of course but Gethsemane, at the flagstaff and the sun-blanched walls in a nest of ragged and meagre palms; at sunset he stood inside them, rigid and immolant while the horn chanted and there descended on him in his turn that fringy raveling of empire's carapace; at first dark, the two camels rumbling and gurgling just beyond earshot above the waiting orderly, he stood at the gate beside the man who had been One to his Two in the old class six years ago, the two of them barely visible to one another, leaving only the voice serene and tender, passionate for suffering, sick with hope:

'I know. They thought you were hiding. They were afraid of you at first. Then they decided you were just a fool who insisted on becoming a marshal of France at fifty instead of forty-five, using the power and influence at twenty-one and -two and -three and -four and -five to evade at forty-five the baton you would have nothing left to fend off at fifty; the power and the influence to escape the power and influence, the world to escape the world; to free yourself of flesh without having to die, without having to lose the awareness that you were free of flesh: not to escape from it and you could not be immune to it nor did you want to be: only to be free of it, to be conscious always that you were merely at armistice with it at the price of constant and unflagging vigilance, because without that consciousness, flesh would not exist for you to be free of it and so there would be nothing anywhere for you to be free of. Oh yes, I knew: the English poet Byron's dream or wish or cry that all living women had but one single mouth for his kiss: the supreme golden youth who encompassed all flesh by putting, still virgin to it, all flesh away. But I knew better: who sought a desert not as Simeon did but as Anthony, using Mithridates and Heliogabalus not merely to acquire a roosting-place for contempt and scorn, but for fee to the cave where the lion itself lay down: who—the ones who feared you once—believed that they had seen ambition and greed themselves default before one seventeen-year-old child—had seen the whole vast hitherto invulnerable hegemony of ruthlessness and rapacity reveal itself unfearsome and hollow when even that uncle and that godfather could not cope with your crime or defalcation, as though so poor and thin was the ambition and greed to which even that uncle and that godfather were dedicant, that voracity itself had repudiated them who had been its primest pillars and its supremest crown and glory.

'Which could not be. That was not merely incredible, it was unbearable. Rapacity does not fail, else man must deny he breathes. Not rapacity: its whole vast glorious history repudiates that. It does not, cannot, must not fail. Not just one family in one nation privileged to soar cometlike into splendid zenith through and because of it, not just one nation among all the nations selected as heir to that vast splendid heritage; not just France, but all governments and nations which ever rose and endured long enough to leave their mark as such, had sprung from it and in and upon and by means of it became forever fixed in the amazement of man's present and the glory of his past; civilization itself is its password and Christianity its masterpiece, Chartres and the Sistine Chapel, the pyramids and the rock-wombed powder-magazines under the Gates of Hercules its altars and monuments, Michelangelo and Phidias and Newton and Ericsson and Archimedes and Krupp its priests and popes and bishops; the long deathless roster of its glory—Caesar and the Barcas and the two Macedonians, our own Bonaparte and the great Russian and the giants who strode nimbused in red hair like fire across the Aurora Borealis, and all the lesser nameless who were not heroes but, glorious in anonymity, at least served the destiny of heroes—the generals and admirals, the corporals and ratings of glory, the batmen and orderlies of renown, and the chairmen of boards and the presidents of federations, the doctors and lawyers and educators and churchmen who after nineteen centuries have rescued the son of heaven from oblivion and translated him from mere meek heir to earth to chairman of its board of trade; and those who did not even have names and designations to be anonymous from—the hands and the backs which carved and sweated aloft the stone blocks and painted the ceilings and invented the printing presses and grooved the barrels, down to the last indestructible voice which asked nothing but the right to speak of hope in Roman lion-pits and murmur the name of God from the Indian-anticked pyres in Canadian forests—stretching immutable and enduring further back than man's simple remembering recorded it. Not rapacity: it does not fail; suppose Mithridates' and Heliogabalus' heir had used his heritage in order to escape his inheritees: Mithridates and Heliogabalus were Heliogabalus and Mithridates still and that scurry from Oran was still only a mouse's, since one of Grimalkin's parents was patience too and that whole St Cyr-Toulon-Africa business merely flight, as when the maiden flees the ravisher not toward sanctuary but privacy, and just enough of it to make the victory memorable and its trophy a prize. Not rapacity, which like poverty, takes care of its own. Because it endures, not even because it is rapacity but because man is man, enduring and immortal; enduring not because he is immortal but immortal because he endures: and so with rapacity, which immortal man never fails since it is in and from rapacity that he gets, holds, his immortality—the vast, the all-being, the compassionate, which says to him only, Believe in Me; though ye doubt seventy times seven, ye need only believe again.

'But I know. I was there. I saw: that day eleven years ago: paused in that iron maw of war, not fragile actually: just fixed and immune in fragility like the figure in the stained window; not through any Alice's mirror into unreality, but just immune, moral opposed and invincibly apostate; if there still existed for you even in dream the splendid and glittering boulevards and faubourgs of your old cradle and your lost estate, it was merely as dream forever inextricable from your past and forever interdict from your destiny; inextricable the dream, yourself and the dream annealed, yourself interdict and free from that pain and that longing forever more; inextricable from that youth who is this man now, as is this little lost barren spot here inextricable forever from that destiny,—never that uncle's and that godfather's private donjon but rather the figment of that consecration's necessary tarryment for this time, this space, somewhere in time and space,—not the youth: the fragility; not to test the youth but to test the fragility: to measure and gauge and test; never an intractable and perverse child who fled, never an uncle and godfather coercing and compelling by attrition, starvation, but all of them, the trinity still intact because it had never been otherwise, testing as one the fragility's capacity for the destiny and the consecration, using the desert for yardstick as when in the old days the cadet would spend that last night of his maiden squiredom on his knees on the lonely chapel's stone floor before the cushion bearing the virgin spurs of his tomorrow's knighthood.

'That's what they think: not that man failed rapacity, but that man failed man; his own frail flesh and blood lets him down: the blood still runs but cooling now, into the second phase of his brief and furious span when the filling of his belly is better than glory or a throne, then on into the third and last one where anticipation of the latrine is more moving than even the spread of a girl's hair on the pillow. That's what they believe is to be your destiny and end. And ten years from now they will still know no better. Because your time, your moment, will not have come even in ten years. It will take longer than that. It will need a new time, a new age, a new century which doesn't even remember our old passions and failures; a new century from that one when man discovered God for a second and then lost Him, postulated by a new digit in the record of his hope and need; it will be more than twenty years even before the day, the moment when you will appear again, without past, as if you had never been. Because by that time you will no longer exist for them except in mutual remembering: a lay figure not only without life but integrated as myth only in mutual confederation: the property of no one of them because you will be the property of all, possessing unity and integration only when your custodians happen to meet from the ends of the earth (which is the French empire) and match fragments and make you whole for a moment; you will lie weightless across the face of France from Mozambique to Miquelon, and Devil's Island to the Treaty Ports like a barely remembered odor, a fading word, a habit, a legend—an effigy cut by a jigsaw for souvenirs, becoming whole only over a cafe or mess table in Brazzaville or Saigon or Cayenne or Tananarive, dovetailed for a moment or an hour as when boys match and exchange the pictures of the actresses and generals and presidents from the packs of cigarettes; not even the shadow of a breathing man but instead something synthetic and contrived like the composite one of the homely domestic objects contrived by the nurse's hand between the nursery lamp and the wall for the child to take into slumber with it: a balloon: a duck: Punchinello: *la gloire:* the head of a cat—a shadow cast backward on that arid curtain behind Oran beyond which you disappeared, not by the sun but by that quartermaster captain's commission the refusal of which first struck them with terror and rage, until after twenty years not you nor even your two powerful kinsmen will be real, but only that old fading parchment, and it real only because your refusal of it incorporated it onto your legend—the shopworn and now harmless vellum vainly dangling its fading seals and ribbons beside the rent beyond which you vanished in the oldest of comedies: the youth fleeing, the forsaken aging yet indomitable betrothed pursuing, abject, constant, undismayable, undeflectable, terrifying not in threat but in fidelity, until at last those who feared you once will have watched you pass out of enmity to amazement: to contempt: to unreality, and at last out of your race and kind altogether, into the dusty lumber room of literature.

'But not I,' he said, looming, visible only as a gaunt gigantic shape, sick, furious, murmuring: 'Because I know better. I knew that first moment eleven years ago when I looked and saw you standing there in that gate. I knew. I wont be here to see it of course (my last medical survey, you know: that marvelous and amazing thing, a human life, spanned and then—what's the Boer word?—outspanned by one dry and dusty page of doctor's jargon. They are wrong of course. I mean in the Quai d'Orsay. They didn't want to post me here at all, since in doing it they would in their opinion simply double the work of whatever clerk would not only have to relieve me but discharge me from the army list also and then post my successor before my tour here was even completed) and at first I grieved a little because once I thought that you might need me. I mean, need me other than for my simple seniority of hope in the condition of man. —That's right,' he said, though the other had made no sound: 'Laugh, at that dream, that vain hope too. Because you will not need anybody wherever it is you are going now in order to return from it. Mind you, I dont ask where. I was about to say "to find whom or what you will need to be your instrument" but I refrained from that in time too. So at least you dont need to laugh at that, since I know that you are going wherever it is you are going, in order to return from it when the time, the moment comes, in the shape of man's living hope. May I embrace you?'

'Must you?' the other said. Then: 'Should you?' Then quickly: 'Of course,' but before he moved the taller one had stooped, loomed downward from his vast and depthless height and took the smaller man's hand and kissed it and released it and, erect again, took the other's face between his two hands almost like a parent, a mother, and held it for a moment, then released it.

'With Christ in God,' he said. 'Go now.'

'So I'm to save France,' the other said.

'France,' he said, not even brusquely, not even contemptuously. 'You will save man. Farewell.'

And he was right for almost two years. That is, he was almost wrong. He did not remember the camel or litter—whatever it had been—at all; only a moment—probably, without doubt, in the base hospital in Oran—a face, a voice, probably a doctor's, marvelling not that he had failed to keep consciousness over that fierce and empty distance, but that he had kept life at all; then not much again, only motion: the Mediterranean: then he knew peacefully, not with joy or exultation: just peacefully, almost unattentively, unable yet (nor did that matter either) to raise his own head to look, that this was France, Europe, home. Then he could move his head and lift his hands too even if the vast peasant Norman frame did seem still to lie outside its transparent envelope; he said, weakly but aloud, with a sort of peaceful amazement, weakly, but at least aloud: 'I had forgot what winter looks like,' lying half-propped all day now on the glassed veranda above Zermatt watching the Matterhorn, watching not the ordered and nameless progression of days fade but rather the lesser earth, since always the great peak carried into the next one as in a gigantic hand, one clutch of light. But that was only the body and it was mending too; soon it would be as strong, not perhaps as it ever was nor even as it ever would but rather as it would ever need to be, since they were the same,—only the body: not the memory because it had forgotten nothing, not even for one second the face which had been the junior that afternoon two years ago around the table on the Quai d'Orsay terrace, come all the way from Paris just to see him——

'Not Paris,' the other said. 'Verdun. We're building fortifications there now which they will never pass again.'

'They?' he said peacefully. 'It's too late now.'

'Too late? Nonsense. The fever and the fury are still there, I grant you. It seems to be born in them; they probably cant help it. But it will be decades, perhaps a whole generation, before it reaches convulsion again.'

'Not for us,' he said. 'Too late for them.'

'Oh,' the other said, who did not see at all; he knew that. Then the other said: 'I brought this. It came out just after you left for Africa. You probably haven't seen it yet.' It was a page from the Gazette, yellowed, faded, almost three years old now, the other holding it spread while he looked at the rigid epitaph:

To Lieutenant-Colonel.
Sous-Lieutenant (and the name)
March 29, 1885

Relieved and Retired:
Lieutenant-Colonel (and the name)
March 29, 1885

'He never came back to Paris,' the other said. 'Not even to France——'

'No,' he said peacefully.

'So you were probably the last to see him.—You did see him, didn't you?'

'Yes,' he said.

'Then maybe you even know where he went. Where he is.'

'Yes,' he said peacefully.

'You mean he told you himself? I dont believe it.'

'Yes,' he said, 'it is nonsense, isn't it? Not for me to claim that he told me, but that he should have to have told anyone. He's in a Tibetan lamasery.'

'A what?'

'Yes. The east, the morning, which even the dead, even the pagan dead, lie facing, so that the first faint fall of shadow of the risen son of it can break their sleep.' Now he could feel the other watching him and there was something in the face but he would not bother about it yet, and when the other spoke there was something in the voice too but he would not bother about that yet either.

'They gave him a ribbon too,' the other said. 'It was the red one. He not only saved your post and garrison for you, he probably saved Africa. He prevented a war. Of course, they had to get rid of him afterward—ask for his resignation.'

'All right,' he said peacefully. Then he said, 'What?'

'The camel and the soldier he lost: the murderer—dont you remember? Surely, if he told you where he was going, he told you about that too.' Now the other was looking at him, watching him. 'There was a woman in it—not his, of course. You mean he didn't tell you?'

'Yes,' he said. 'He told me.'

'Then of course I wont have to.'

'Yes,' he said again. 'He told me.'

'She was a Riff, a native, belonging to the village, tribe, settlement, whatever it was, which was the reason for the post and the garrison being there; you must have seen that anyway while you were there,—a slave, valuable: nobody's wife or daughter or favorite it appeared, or anyway was reported: just simply merchantable. She died too, like the other one back in Marseilles eighteen years ago; the man's power over women was indeed a fatal one. Whereupon the next morning the camel—it was his—the commandant's—private mount: possibly a pet if you can—want to—pet a camel—and its groom, driver, mahout, whatever they are, had vanished and two dawns later the groom returned, on foot and thoroughly terrified, with the ultimatum from the chief, headman to the commandant, giving the commandant until the next dawn to send him the man (there were three involved but the chief would be content with the principal one) responsible for the woman's death and her spoliation as merchandise; else the chief and his men would invest the post and obliterate it and its garrison, which they could probably have done, if not immediately, certainly in the almost twelve months before the next inspector-general would turn up to look at it. So the commandant asked for a volunteer to slip away that night, before the ultimatum went into effect at dawn and the place was surrounded, and go to the next post and bring back a relieving force.—I beg your pardon?' But he had not spoken, rigid, himself the fragile one now, who was yet only barely erect from death.

'I thought you said "chose one",' the other said. 'He didn't need to choose. Because this was the man's one chance. He could have escaped at any time—hoarded food and water and stolen away on almost any night during the whole eighteen years, possibly reached the coast and perhaps even France. But where would he go then? who could have escaped only from Africa: never from himself, from the old sentence, from which all that saved him was his uniform, and that only while he wore it in the light of day. But now he could go. He was not even escaping, he was not even entering mere amnesty but absolution; from now on, the whole edifice of France would be his sponsor and his purifaction, even though he got back with the relief too late, because he not only had the commandant's word, but a signed paper also to avouch his deed and command all men by these presents to make good its reward.

'So the commandant didn't need to choose him: only accept him; and at sunset the garrison paraded and the man stepped out of ranks; and now the commandant should have taken the decoration from his own breast and pinned it on that of the sacrifice, except that the commandant had not got the ribbon yet (oh yes, I've thought of the locket too: to remove the chain from his own neck and cast it about the condemned's, but that is reserved for some finer, more durable instant in that rocket's course than the abolishment of a blackguard or the preservation of a flyspeck). So without doubt that would be the moment when he gave him the signed paper setting him free of his past, the man not knowing that that first step out of ranks had already set him free of whatever else breathing could do to him more; and the man saluted and about faced and marched out the gate into darkness. Into death. And I thought for a moment you had spoken again, were about to ask how, if the ultimatum would not take effect until dawn tomorrow, did the Riff chief discover that a scout would attempt to get out that night, and so have an ambush ready at the mouth of the wadi through which the scout would pass. Yes, how: the man himself probably asking that in the one last choked cry or scream remaining to him of indictment and repudiation, because he didn't know about the ribbon then either.

'Into darkness: night: the wadi. Into hell; even Hugo didn't think of that. Because from the looks of what remained of him, it took him most of that night to die; the sentry above the gate challenged at dawn the next morning, then the camel (not the plump missing one of course but an old mangy one, because the dead woman was valuable; and besides, one camel looks just like another in a Transport Office return) cantered in with the body tied on it, stripped of clothing and most of the flesh too. So the siege, the investment, was lifted; the enemy retired and that sunset the commandant buried its lone casualty (except for the better camel: and after all, the woman had been valuable) with a bugle and a firing-squad, and you relieved him and he departed, a lieutenant-colonel with the rosette in a Himalayan lamasery, leaving nothing behind him but that little corner of France which he saved, to be mausoleum and cenotaph of the man whom he tricked into saving it. A man,' the other said, watching him. 'A human being.'

'A murderer,' he said. 'A murderer twice——'

'Spawned into murder by a French cesspool.'

'But repudiated by all the world's cesspools: nationless twice, without fatherland twice since he had forfeited life, worldless twice since he was already forfeit to death, belonging to no man since he was not even his own——'

'But a man,' the other said.

'—speaking, thinking in French only because, nationless, he must of necessity use that tongue which of all is international; wearing that French uniform because inside a French uniform was the only place on earth where a murderer could be safe from his murder——'

'But bearing it, bearing at least without complaint his rewardless share of the vast glorious burden of empire where few other men dared or could; even behaving himself in his fashion: nothing in his record but a little drunkenness, a little thievery——'

'Until now,' he cried. '—only thievery, buggery, sodomy—until now.'

'—which were his sole defense against the corporal's or sergeant's warrant which would have been his death sentence. Asking nothing of none until his blind and valueless fate tangled with that of him who had already exhausted the *Comité de Ferrovie* and the French Army, and was now reduced to rooting about among the hogwallows and cesspools of the human race itself; who, already forfeit of life, owed nothing to France save the uniform he wore and the rifle he oiled and tended, who in return for filling on demand a man's width of space in a platoon front, asked and expected nothing save the right to hope to die in a barracks-bed still unregenerate, yet who had been tricked into giving his life, without even the chance to prepare himself, for that country which would guillotine him within fifteen minutes of putting its civilian hand on him.'

'He was a man,' the other said. 'Even dead, angels—justice itself—still fought for him. You were away at the time, so you have not heard this either. It was at the signing of the citation for that rosette. While bearing the parchment across to the desk for the Grand Commander's signature, the clerk (in private life an amateur Alpinist) stumbled and overturned a litre bottle of ink onto it, blotting out not merely the recipient's name but the entire record of the achievement. So they produced a new parchment. It reached the desk, but even as the Grand Commander reached his hand for the pen, a draft of air came from nowhere (if you know General Martel, you know that any room he stops in long enough to remove his hat, must be hermetically sealed)—came from nowhere and wafted the parchment twenty metres across the room and into the fire, where it vanished pouf! like celluloid. But to what avail, between them armed only with the flaming swords of clumsy mythology, and the *Comité de Ferrovie* snoring with revolving pistols and the rattling belch of Maxim guns? So now he has gone to a Tibetan lamasery. To repent.'

'To wait!' he cried. 'To prepare!'

'Yes,' the other said. 'That's what they call it too: *Der Tag*. So maybe I'd better hurry on back to Verdun and get on with our preparing and waiting too, since we are warned now that we shall need them both. Oh, I know. I was not there that day to see his face in that gate as you saw it. But at least I inherited it. We all did: not just that class, but all the others which came after yours and his. And at least we know now what we inherited: only fear, not anguish. A prophet discharged us of that by giving us a warning of it. So only the respect for the other need remain.'

'A murderer,' he said.

'But a man,' the other said, and was gone, leaving him not quite erect from death perhaps but at least with his back once more toward it; erect enough to be aware of the steadily diminishing numbers of his seniority: that diminishing reservoir on which the bark of his career floated, to be aground soon at this rate. In fact, that day would come when he would know that it was aground, revokable never more by any tide or wave or flood: who had believed all his life, if not in his durability, at least in the vast frame which the indurability clothed; whereupon in the next moment he would know that, aground or not, it—he—would never be abandoned; that that edifice which had accepted the gaunt frame's dedication would see always that there was at least one number between him and zero, even if it were only his own; so that the day came, *Der Tag*, the enemy poured, not through Verdun because his caller of that morning twenty-five years back had been right and they would not pass there, but through Flanders so fast and so far that a desperate rag-tag met them in Paris taxi-cabs and held them for the necessary desperate moment, and still behind his glassed veranda he heard how that Number One to his Two in the old St Cyr class was now Number One among all the desperate and allied peoples in Western Europe, and he said, *Even from here I will have seen the beginning of it,* then two months later he stood across a desk from the face which he had not seen in thirty years, which he had seen the first time in the St Cyr gate forty years ago and had been marked forever with it, looking not much older, still calm, composed, the body, the shoulders beneath it still frail and delicate yet doomed—no: not doomed: potent—to bear the fearful burden of man's anguish and terror and at last his hope, looking at him for a moment, then saying: 'The appointment of Quartermaster General is within my gift. Will you accept the office?' and he said to himself, with a sort of peaceful vindication not even of great and desperate hope now but of simple reason, logic: *I will even see the end, accomplishment of it too. I will even be present there.*

But that was a quarter of a century away yet, as the caller of ten minutes ago had prophesied; now he lay beneath his own peaceful tears while the nurse bent over him with a folded cloth, saying, weak but indomitable still, invincibly obdurate, incurable and doomed with hope, using the two 'he's' indiscriminately, as though the nurse too knew:

'Yes, he was a man. But he was young then, not much more than a child. These tears are not anguish: only grief.'

† † †

The room was now lighted candelabrum, sconce and girandole. The windows were closed now, curtain and casement; the room seemed now to hang insulate as a diving bell above the city's murmur where the people had already begun to gather again in the *Place* below. The jug and bowl were gone and the old general sat once more flanked by his two confreres behind the bare table, though among them now was a fourth figure as incongruous and paradoxical as a magpie in a bowl of goldfish—a bearded civilian sitting between the old generalissimo and the American in that black-and-white costume which to the Anglo-Saxon is the formal regalia for eating or seduction or other diversions of the dark, and to the Continental European and South American the rigid uniform for partitioning other governments or overthrowing his own. The young aide stood facing them. He said rapid and glib in French: 'The prisoners are here. The motorcar from Villeneuve Blanche will arrive at twenty-two hours. The woman about the spoon.'

'Spoon?' the old general said. 'Did we take her spoon? Return it.'

'No sir,' the aide said. 'Not this time. The three strange women. The foreigners. His Honor the Mayor's business.' For a moment the old general sat perfectly still. But there was nothing in his voice.

'They stole the spoon?'

Nor was there anything in the aide's either: rigid, inflectionless: 'She threw the spoon at them. It disappeared. She has witnesses.'

'Who saw one of them pick up the spoon and hide it,' the old general said.

The aide stood rigid, looking at nothing. 'She threw a basket too. It was full of food. The same one caught it in the air without spilling it.'

'I see,' the old general said. 'Does she come here to protest a miracle, or merely affirm one?'

'Yes sir,' the aide said. 'Do you want the witnesses too?'

'Let the strangers wait,' the old general said. 'Just the plaintiff.'

'Yes sir,' the aide said. He went out again by the smaller door at the end of the room. Though when in the next second almost he reappeared, he had not had time to get out of anyone's way. He returned not swept but tumbled, not in but rather on because he rose, loomed not half a head nor even a whole head but half a human being above a tight clump of shawled or kerchiefed women led by one of a short broad strong fifty-ish who stopped just at the edge of the white rug as if it were water and gave the room one rapid comprehensive look, then another rapid one at the three old men behind the table, then moved again unerringly toward the old generalissimo, leading her group, save the aide who had at last extricated himself beside the door, firmly out onto the blanched surface of the rug, saying in a strong immediate voice:

'That's right. Dont hope to conceal yourself—not behind a mayor anyway; there are too many of you for that. Once I would have said that the curse of this country is its forest of mayoral sashes and swords; I know better now. And after four years of this harassment, even the children can tell a general on sight—provided you can ever see one when you need him.'

'A third miracle then,' the old general said. 'Since your first postulate is proved by the confounding of your second.'

'Miracle?' the woman said. 'Bah. The miracle is that we have anything left after four years of being over-run by foreigners. And now, even Americans. Has France come to that sorry pass where you must not only rob us of our kitchen utensils but even import Americans in order to fight your battles? War, war, war. Dont you ever get tired of it?'

'Indubitably, Madame,' the old general said. 'Your spoon——'

'It vanished. Dont ask me where. Ask them. Or better: have some of your corporals and sergeants search them. It's true there are two of them beneath whose garments even a sergeant would not want to fumble. But none of them would object.'

'No,' the old general said. 'More should not be demanded of corporals and sergeants beyond the simple hazard of military life.' He spoke the aide's name.

'Sir,' the aide said.

'Go to the scene. Find the gentlewoman's spoon and return it to her.'

'I, sir?' the aide cried.

'Take a full company. On your way out, let the prisoners come in. —No: first, the three officers. They are here?'

'Yes sir,' the aide said.

'Good,' the old general said. He turned toward his two confreres, started to speak, paused, then spoke to the civilian; when he did so, the civilian began to rise from his seat with a sort of startled and diffuse alacrity. 'That should take care of the spoon,' the old general said. 'I believe the rest of your problem was the complaint of the three strange women that they have no place to sleep tonight.'

'That; and——' the mayor said.

'Yes,' the old general said. 'I will see them presently. Meanwhile, will you take care of finding quarters for them, or shall——'

'But certainly, General,' the mayor said.

'Thank you. Then, goodnight.' He turned to the woman. 'And to you also. And in peace; your spoon will be restored.' Now it was the mayor who was swept, carried—the magpie this time in a flock of pigeons or perhaps hens or maybe geese—back toward the door which the aide held open, and through it, the aide still looking back at the old general with his expression of shocked disbelief.

'A spoon,' the aide said. 'A company. I've never commanded one man, let alone a company of them. And even if I could, knew how, how can I find that spoon?'

'Of course you will find it,' the old general said. 'That will be the fourth miracle. Now, the three officers. But first take the three strange ladies to your office and ask them to wait there for me.'

'Yes sir,' the aide said. He went out and closed the door. It opened again; three men entered: a British colonel, a French major, an American captain, the two juniors flanking the colonel rigidly down the rug and to rigid attention facing the table while the colonel saluted.

'Gentlemen,' the old general said. 'This is not a parade. It is not even an inquiry: merely an identification.—Chairs, please,' he said without turning his head to the galaxy of staff behind him. 'Then the prisoners.' Three of the aides brought chairs around; now that end of the room resembled one end of an amphitheatre or a section of an American bleachers, the three generals and the three newcomers sitting in the beginning of a semi-circle against the bank of aides and staff as one of the aides who had fetched the chairs went on to the smaller door and opened it and stood aside. And now they could smell the men before they even entered—that thin strong ineradicable stink of front lines: of foul mud and burnt cordite and tobacco and ammonia and human filth. Then the thirteen men entered, led by the sergeant with his slung rifle and closed by another armed private, bare-headed, unshaven, alien, stained still with battle, bringing with them still another compounding of the smell—wariness, alertness, just a little of fear too but mostly just watchfulness, deploying a little clumsily as the sergeant spoke two rapid commands in French and halted them into line. The old general turned to the British colonel. 'Colonel?' he said.

'Yes sir,' the colonel said immediately. 'The corporal.' The old general turned to the American.

'Captain?' he said.

'Yes sir,' the American said. 'That's him. Colonel Beale's right—I mean, he cant be right——' But the old general was already speaking to the sergeant.

'Let the corporal remain,' he said. 'Take the others back to the ante-room and wait there.' The sergeant wheeled and barked, but the corporal had already paced once out of ranks, to stand not quite at attention but almost, while the other twelve wheeled into file, the armed private now leading and the sergeant last, up the room to the door, not through it yet but to it, because the head of the file faltered and fell back on itself for a moment and then gave way as the old general's personal aide entered and passed them and then himself gave way aside until the file had passed him, the sergeant following last and drawing the door after him, leaving the aide once more solus before it, boneless, tall, baffled still and incredulous still but not outraged now: merely disorganised. The British colonel said:

'Sir.' But the old general was looking at the aide at the door. He said in French:

'My child?'

'The three women,' the aide said. 'In my office now. While we have our hands on them, why dont——'

'Oh yes,' the old general said. 'Your authority for detached duty. Tell the Chief-of-Staff to let it be a reconnaissance, of—say—four hours. That should be enough.' He turned to the British colonel. 'Certainly, Colonel,' he said.

The colonel rose quickly, staring at the corporal—the high calm composed, not wary but merely watchful, mountain face looking, courteous and merely watchful, back at him. 'Boggan,' the colonel said. 'Dont you remember me? Lieutenant Beale?' But still the face only looked at him, courteous, interrogatory, not baffled: just blank, just waiting. 'We thought you were dead,' the colonel said. 'I——saw you——'

'I did more than that,' the American captain said. 'I buried him.' The old general raised one hand slightly at the captain. He said to the Briton:

'Yes, Colonel?'

'It was at Mons, four years ago. I was a subaltern. This man was in my platoon that afternoon when they . . . caught us. He went down before a lance. I . . . . saw the point come through his back before the shaft broke. The next two horses galloped over him. On him. I saw that too, afterward. I mean, just for a second or two, how his face looked after the last horse, before I—I mean, what had used to be his face——' He said, still staring at the corporal, his voice if anything even more urgent because of what its owner had now to cope with: 'Boggan!' But still the corporal only looked at him, courteous, attentive, quite blank. Then he turned and said to the old general in French:

'I'm sorry. I understand only French.'

'I know that,' the old general said also in French. He said in English to the Briton: 'Then this is not the man.'

'It cant be, sir,' the colonel said. 'I saw the head of that lance. I saw his face after the horses—— Besides, I—I saw——' He stopped and sat there, martial and glittering in his red tabs and badges of rank and the chain-wisps symbolising the mail in which the regiment had fought at Crecy and Agincourt seven and eight hundred years ago, with his face above them like death itself.

'Tell me,' the old general said gently. 'You saw what? You saw him again later, afterward? Perhaps I know already—the ghosts of your ancient English bowmen there at Mons?—in leather jerkins and hose and crossbows, and he among them in khaki and a steel helmet and an Enfield rifle? Was that what you saw?'

'Yes sir,' the colonel said. Then he sat erect; he said quite loudly: 'Yes sir.'

'But if this could be the same man,' the old general said.

'I'm sorry, sir,' the colonel said.

'You wont say either way: that he is or is not that man?'

'I'm sorry, sir,' the colonel said. 'I've got to believe in something.'

'Even if only death?'

'I'm sorry, sir,' the colonel said. The old general turned to the American.

'Captain?' he said.

'That puts us all in a fix, doesn't it?' the American captain said. 'All three of us; I dont know who's worst off. Because I didn't just see him dead: I buried him, in the middle of the Atlantic Ocean. His name is—was—no, it cant be because

I'm looking at him—wasn't Brzonyi. At least it wasn't last year. It was—damn it—I'm sorry sir—is Brzewski. He's from one of the coal towns back of Pittsburgh. I was the one that buried him. I mean, I commanded the burial party, read the service: you know. We were National Guard; you probably dont know what that means——'

'I know,' the old general said.

'Sir?' the captain said.

'I know what you mean,' the old general said. 'Continue.'

'Yes sir.—Civilians, organised our own company ourselves, to go out and die for dear old Rutgers—that sort of thing; elected our officers, notified the government who was to get what commission and then got hold of the Articles of War and tried to memorise as much of it as we could before the commission came back. So when the flu hit us, we were in the transport coming over last October, and when the first one died—it was Brzewski—we found out that none of us had got far enough in the manual to find out how to bury a dead soldier except me—I was a sha—second lieutenant then—and I just happened to have found out by accident the last night before we left because a girl had stood me up and I thought I knew why. I mean, who it was, who the guy was. And you know how it is: you think of all the things to do to get even, make her sorry; you lying dead right there where she's got to step over you to pass, and it's too late now and boy, wont that fix her——'

'Yes,' the old general said. 'I know.'

'Sir?' the captain said.

'I know that too,' the old general said.

'Of course you do—remember, anyway,' the captain said. 'Nobody's really that old, I dont care how——' going that far before he managed to stop himself. 'I'm sorry, sir,' he said.

'Dont be,' the old general said. 'Continue. So you buried him.'

'So that night just by chance or curiosity or maybe it was personal interest, I was reading up on what somebody would have to do to get rid of me afterward and make Uncle Sam's books balance, and so when Br——' he paused and glanced rapidly at the corporal, but only for a second, even less than that: barely a falter even: '—the first one died, I was elected, to certify personally with the M.O. that the body was a dead body and sign the certificate and drill the firing squad and then give the command to dump him overboard. Though by the time we got to Brest two weeks later, all the rest of them had had plenty of practice at it. So you see where that leaves us. I mean, him; he's the one in the fix: if I buried him in the middle of the Atlantic Ocean in October last year, then Colonel Beale couldn't have seen him killed at Mons in 1914. And if Colonel Beale saw him killed in 1914, he cant be standing here now waiting for you to shoot him tomor——' He stopped completely. He said quickly: 'I'm sorry, sir. I didn't——'

'Yes,' the old general said in his courteous and bland and inflectionless voice. 'Then Colonel Beale was wrong.'

'No sir,' the captain said.

'Then you wish to retract your statement that this is the man whose death you personally certified and whose body you saw sink into the Atlantic Ocean?'

'No sir,' the captain said.

'So you believe Colonel Beale.'

'If he says so, sir.'

'That's not quite an answer. Do you believe him?' He watched the captain. The captain looked as steadily back at him. Then the captain said:

'And that I certified him dead and buried him.' He said to the corporal, even in a sort of French: 'So you came back. I'm glad to see you and I hope you had a nice trip,' and looked back at the old general again, as steadily as he, as courteously and as firm, a good moment this time until the old general said in French:

'You speak my tongue also.'

'Thank you, sir,' the captain answered him. 'No other Frenchman ever called it that.'

'Do not demean yourself. You speak it well. What is your name?'

'Middleton, sir.'

'You have . . . twenty-five years, perhaps?'

'Twenty-four, sir.'

'Twenty-four. Some day you are going to be a very dangerous man, if you are not already so:' and said to the corporal: 'Thank you, my child. You may return to your squad,' and spoke a name over his shoulder without turning his head, though the aide had already come around the table as the corporal about-faced, the aide flanking him back to the door and through it and out, the American captain turning his head back in time to meet for another second yet the quiet and inscrutable eyes, the courteous, bland, almost gentle voice: 'Because his name is Brzonyi here too.' He sat back in the chair; again he looked like a masquerading child beneath the illusion of crushing and glittering weight of his blue-and-scarlet and gold and brass and leather, until even the five who were still sitting had the appearance of standing too, surrounding and enclosing him. He said in English: 'I must leave you presently, for a short time. But Major Blum speaks English. It is not as good as yours of course, nor as good as Captain Middleton's French, but it should do; one of our allies —Colonel Beale—saw him slain, and the other—Captain Middleton—buried him, so all that remains for us is to witness to his resurrection, and none more competent for that than Major Blum, who was graduated from the Academy into the regiment in 1913 and so was in it before and has been in it ever since the day when this ubiquitous corporal reached it. So the only question is—' he paused a second; it was as though he had even glanced about at them without even moving: the delicate and fragile body, the delicate face beautiful, serene, and terrifying '—who knew him first: Colonel Beale at Mons in August 1914, or Major Blum at Chalons in that same month—before of course Captain Middleton buried him at sea in 1917. But that is merely academic: identity—if there is such—has been established (indeed, it was never disputed): there remains only recapitulation, and Major Blum will do that.' He stood up; except for the two generals, the others rose quickly too and although he said rapidly: 'No no, sit down, sit down,' the three newcomers continued to stand. He turned to the French major. 'Colonel Beale has his ghostly bowmen in Belgium; at least we can match that with our archangels on the Aisne. Surely you can match that for us—the tremendous aerial shapes patrolling our front, and each time they are thickest, heaviest, densest, most archangelic, our corporal is there too perhaps, pacing with them—the usual night firing going on, just enough to make a sane man keep his head below the trench and be glad he has a trench to keep his head below, yet this corporal is outside the trench, between the parapet and the wire, pacing along as peacefully as a monk in his cloister while the great bright formless shapes pace the dark air beside and above him? or perhaps not even pacing but simply leaning on the wire contemplating that desolation like a farmer his turnip-field? Come, Major.'

'My imagination wears only a majority, sir,' the major said. 'It cannot compete with yours.'

'Nonsense,' the old general said. 'The crime—if any—is already established. If any? established? we did not even need to establish it; he did not even merely accept it in advance: he abrogated it. All that remains now is to find extenuation—pity, if we can persuade him to accept pity. Come, tell them.'

'There was the girl,' the major said.

'Yes,' the old general said. 'The wedding and the wine.'

'No sir,' the major said. 'Not quite now. You see, I can—how do you say?—*démentir*—*contredire*—say against——'

'Contradict,' the American captain said.

'Thank you,' the major said. '—contradict you here; my majority can cope with simple regimental gossip.'

'Tell them,' the old general said. So the major did, though that was after the old general had left the room—a little girl, a child going blind in one of the Aisne towns for lack of an operation which a certain famous Paris surgeon could perform, the corporal levying upon the troops of two nearby divisions, a franc here and two francs there until the surgeon's fee was raised and the child sent to him. And an old man; he had a wife, daughter and grandson and a little farm in 1914 but waited too long to evacuate it, unable until too late to tear himself away from what he possessed; his daughter and grandson vanished in the confusion which ended at the First Marne battle, his old wife died of exposure on the roadside, the old man returning alone to the village when it was freed again and he could, where, an idiot, name forgotten, grief and all forgotten, only moaning a little, drooling, grubbing for food in the refuse of army kitchens, sleeping in ditches and hedgerows on the spot of earth which he had owned once, until the corporal used one of his leaves to hunt out a remote kinsman of the old man's in a distant Midi village and levied again on the regiment for enough to send him there.

'And now,' the major said. He turned to the American captain. 'How to say, *touché*?'

'You're out,' the captain said. 'And I wish he was still present so I could hear you say it to him.'

'Bah,' the major said. 'He is a Frenchman. It is only a boche marshal that no man can speak to. And now, you're out, from him to me. Because now the wedding and the wine—' and told that—a village behind Montfaucon and only this past winter because they were American troops; they had just been paid, a dice game was going on, the floor littered with franc notes and half the American company crowded around them when the French corporal entered and without a word began to gather up the scattered money; for a time a true international incident was in the making until the corporal finally managed to communicate, explain, what it was about: a wedding: one of the young American soldiers, and a girl, an orphan refugee from somewhere beyond Rheims, who was now a sort of slavey in the local estaminet; she and the young American had—had——

'The rest of his company would say he had knocked her up,' the American captain said. 'But we know what you mean. Go on.' So the major did: the matter ending with the entire company not only attending the wedding but adopting it, taking charge of it, buying up all the wine in the village for the supper and inviting the whole countryside; adopting the marriage too: endowing the bride with a wedding gift sufficient to set up as a lady in her own right, to wait in her own single rented room until—if—her husband returned from his next tour in the lines. But that would be after the old general had left the room; now the three newcomers made way for him as he came around the table and paused and said:

'Tell them. Tell them how he got the medal too. What we seek now is not even extenuation, not even pity, but mercy—if there is such—if he will accept that either,' and turned and went on toward the small door: at which moment it opened and the aide who had taken the prisoner out stood at attention beside it for the old general to pass, then followed and closed the door behind them. 'Yes?' the old general said.

'They are in De Montigny's office,' the aide said. 'The youngest one, the girl, is a Frenchwoman. One of the older ones is the wife of a Frenchman, a farmer——'

'I know,' the old general said. 'Where is the farm?'

'Was, sir,' the aide said. 'It was near a village called Vienne-la-pucelle, north of St Mihiel. That country was all evacuated in 1914. On Monday morning Vienne-la-pucelle was under the enemy's front line.'

'Then she and her husband dont know whether they have a farm or not,' the old general said.

'No sir,' the aide said.

'Ah,' the old general said. Then he said again: 'Yes?'

'The motorcar from Villeneuve Blanche has just entered the courtyard.'

'Good,' the old general said. 'My compliments to our guest, and conduct him to my study. Serve his dinner there, and request his permission to receive us in one hour.'

The aide's office had been contrived three years ago by carpenters out of—or into—a corner of what had been a ballroom and then a courtroom. The aide saw it each twenty-four hours and obviously even entered it at least once during those periods because on a rack in the corner hung his hat and topcoat and a very fine beautifully-furled London umbrella, in juxtaposition to that hat and that coat as bizarre and paradox as a domino or a fan, until you realised that it could quite well have owed its presence there to the same thing which the only other two objects of any note in the room did: two bronzes which sat at either end of the otherwise completely bare desk—a delicate and furious horse poised weightless and epicene on one leg, and a savage and slumbrous head not cast, molded but cut by hand out of the amalgam by Gaudier-Brzeska. Otherwise the cubicle was empty save for a wooden bench against the wall facing the desk. When the old general entered, the three women were sitting on it, the two older ones on the outside and the younger one between them; as he crossed to the desk without yet looking at them, the younger one gave a quick, almost convulsive start, as though to get up, until one of the others stopped her with one hand. Then they sat again, immobile, watching him while he went around the desk and sat down behind the two bronzes and looked at them—the harsh high mountain face which might have been a twin of the corporal's except for the difference in age, the serene and peaceful one which showed no age at all or perhaps all ages, and between them the strained and anguished one of the girl. Then, as though on a signal, as if she had waited for him to complete the social amenity of sitting too, the peaceful one—she held on her lap a wicker basket neatly covered by an immaculate tucked-in cloth—spoke.

'I'm glad to see you, anyway,' she said. 'You look so exactly like what you are.'

'Marya,' the other older one said.

'Dont be ashamed,' the first one said. 'You cant help it. You should be pleased, because so many dont.' She was already rising. The other said again:

'Marya,' and even raised her hand again, but the first one came on to the desk, carrying the basket, beginning to raise her other hand as though to approach the basket with it as she reached the desk, then extending the hand until it lay on the desk. It now held a long handled iron spoon.

'That nice young man,' she said. 'At least you should be ashamed of that. Sending him out to tramp about the city at night with all those soldiers.'

'The fresh air will be good for him,' the old general said. 'He doesn't get much of it in here.'

'You could have told him.'

'I never said you had it. I only said I believed you could produce it when it was needed.'

'Here it is.' She released the spoon and laid that hand lightly on the one which held the tucked-in and undisturbed basket. Then immediately and peacefully but without haste she smiled at him, serene and uncritical. 'You really cant help it, can you? You really cant.'

'Marya,' the woman on the bench said. Again immediately but without haste, the smile went away. It was not replaced by anything: it just went away, leaving the face unchanged, uncritical, serene.

'Yes, Sister,' she said. She turned and went back to the bench where the other woman had risen now; again the girl had made that convulsive start to rise too; this time the tall woman's hard thin peasant hand was gripping her shoulder, holding her down.

'This is——' the old general said.

'His wife,' the tall woman said harshly. 'Who did you expect it to be?'

'Ah yes,' the old general said, looking at the girl; he said, in that gentle inflectionless voice: 'Marseilles? Toulon perhaps?' then named the street, the district, pronouncing the street name which was its by-word. The woman started to answer but the old general raised his hand at her. 'Let her answer,' he said, then to the girl: 'My child? A little louder.'

'Yes sir,' the girl said.

'Oh yes,' the woman said. 'A whore. How else do you think she got here—got the papers to come this far, to this place, except to serve France also?'

'But his wife too,' the old general said.

'His wife now,' the woman corrected. 'Accept that, whether you believe it or not.'

'I do both,' the old general said. 'Accept that from me too.' Then she moved, released the girl's shoulder and came toward the desk, almost to it in fact, then stopping as though at the exact spot from which her voice would be only a murmur to the two still on the bench when she spoke:

'Do you want to send them out first?'

'Why?' the old general said. 'So you are Magda.'

'Yes,' she said. 'Not Marthe: Magda. I wasn't Marthe until after I had a brother and had to cross half of Europe to face thirty years later the French general who would hold the refusal of his life. Not gift: refusal; and even that's wrong: the taking back of it.' She stood, tall, still, looking down at him. 'So you even knew us. I was about to say "Not remembered us, because you never saw us". But maybe that's wrong too and you did see us then. If you did, you would remember us even if I wasn't but nine then and Marya eleven, because as soon as I saw your face tonight I knew that it would never need to flee, hide from, fear or dread or grieve at having to remember anything it ever looked at. Marya might fail to see that maybe—Marya now too, since she also had to come all the way to France to watch the refusal of her half-brother's life, even if she doesn't need to fear or dread or grieve at having to remember either—but not I. Maybe Marya is why you remember us if you saw us then: because she was eleven then and in our country girls at eleven are not girls anymore, but women. But I wont say that, not because of the insult that would be even to our mother, let alone to you—our mother who had something in her—I dont mean her face—which did not belong in that village—that village? in all our mountains, all that country—while what you must have had—had? have—in you is something which all the earth had better beware and dread and be afraid of. The insult would have been to evil itself. I dont mean just that evil. I mean Evil, as if there was a purity in it, a severity, a jealousy like in God—a strictness of untruth incapable of compromise or second-best or substitute. A purpose, an aim in it, as though not just our mother but you neither could help yourselves; and not just you but our—mine and Marya's—father too: not two of you but three of you doing not what you would but what you must. That people, men and women, dont choose evil and accept it and enter it, but evil chooses the men and women by test and trial, proves and tests them and then accepts them forever until the time comes when they are consumed and empty and at last fail evil because they no longer have anything that evil can want or use; then it destroys them. So it wasn't just you, a stranger happened by accident into a country so far away and hard to get to that whole generations of us are born and live and die in it without even knowing or wondering or caring what might be on the other side of our mountains or even if the earth extends there. Not just a man come there by chance, having already whatever he would need to charm, trance, bewitch a weak and vulnerable woman, then finding a woman who was not only weak and vulnerable but beautiful too—oh yes, beautiful; if that was what you had had to plead, her beauty and your love, my face would have been the first to forgive you, since the jealousy would be not yours but hers—just to destroy her home, her husband's faith, her children's peace, and at last her life,—to drive her husband to repudiate her just to leave her children fatherless, then her to die in childbirth in a cow-byre behind a roadside inn just to leave them orphans, then at last have the right—privilege—duty, whatever you want to call it—to condemn that last and only male child to death just that the name which she betrayed shall be no more. Because that's not enough. It's nowhere near enough. It must be something much bigger than that, much more splendid, much more terrible: not our father gone all that long distance from our valley to seek a beautiful face to be the mother of his name's succession, then finding instead the fatal and calamitous one which would end it; not you blundered there by chance, but sent there to meet that beautiful and fatal face; not her so weak in pride and virtue, but rather doomed by that face from them;—not the three of you compelled there just to efface a name from man's history, because who on earth outside our valley ever heard that name, or cares? but instead to create a son for one of you to condemn to death as though to save the earth, save the world, save man's history, save mankind.'

She brought both hands up in front of her and let them rest there, the fist of one lying in the other palm. 'Of course you knew us. My folly was in even thinking I would need to bring you proof. So now I dont know just what to do with it, when to use it, like a knife capable of only one stroke or a pistol with just one bullet, which I cant afford to risk too soon and dare not wait too late. Maybe you even know the rest of it already too; I remember how wrong I was that you would not know who we are. Maybe your face is telling me now that you already know the rest of it, end of it, even if you weren't there, had served your destiny—or anyway hers—and gone away.'

'Tell me then,' the old general said.

'—if I must? Is that it? the ribbons and stars and braid that turned forty years of spears and bullets, yet not one of them to stop a woman's tongue?—Or try to tell you, that is, because I dont know; I was only nine then, I only saw and remembered; Marya too, even if she was eleven, because even then she already didn't need to dread or grieve for anything just because her face had looked at it. Not that we needed to look at this because it had been there all our lives, most of the valley's too. It was already ours, our—the valley's—pride (with a little awe in it) as another one might have a peak or glacier or waterfall—that speck, that blank white wall or dome or tower—whatever it was—which was first in all our valley that the sun touched and the last that lost it, still holding light long after the gulch we crouched in had lost what little it had ever snared. Yet it wasn't high either; high wasn't the right word either; you couldn't—we didn't—measure where it was that way. It was just higher than any of our men, even herdsmen and hunters, ever went. Not higher than they could but than they did, dared; no shrine or holy place because we knew them too and even the kind of men that lived in, haunted, served them; mountain men too before they were priests because we knew their fathers and our fathers had known their grandfathers, so they would be priests only afterward with what was left. Instead, it was an eyrie like where eagles nested, where people—men—came as if through the air itself (you), leaving no more trace of coming or arriving (yes, you) or departing (oh yes, you) than eagles would (oh yes, you too; if Marya and I ever saw you then, we did not remember it, nor when you saw us if you ever did except for our mother's telling; I almost said If our father himself ever saw you in the flesh because of course he did, you would have seen to that yourself: a gentleman honorable in gentleman fashion and brave too since it would have taken courage, our father having already lost too much for that little else to be dear spending), come there not to tremble on their knees on stone floors, but to think. To think: not that dreamy hoping and wishing and believing (but mainly just waiting) that we would think is thinking, but some fierce and rigid concentration that at any time—tomorrow, today, next moment, this one—will change the shape of the earth.

'Not high, just high enough to stand between us and the sky like a way-station to heaven, so no wonder when we died the rest of us believed the soul hadn't stopped there maybe but at least had paused to surrender half the coupon; no wonder when our mother was gone for that week in the spring, Marya and I knew where she had gone to; not dead: we had buried nothing, so she wouldn't have to pass it. But certainly there, since where else could she be—that face which had never belonged to, had no place in, our valley from the beginning, not to mention what we, even her children, had felt, sensed, behind that face which had no place in our mountains, among our kind of people anywhere; where else but there? not to think, to be accepted into that awesome and tremendous condition, because even her face and what was behind it could not match that, but at least to breathe, bathe in the lambence of that furious meditation. The wonder was that she came back. Not the valley's wonder but mine and Marya's too. Because we were children, we didn't know: we only watched and saw and knitted, knotted, tried to, what simple threads we had of implication; to us it was simply that the face, that something—whatever it was—in her that had never been ours and our father's anyway even if it had been wife to one and mother to the others, had at last simply done what from the beginning it had been doomed to do. Yet she came back. She didn't change forever that house, home, life and all, she had already done that by leaving as she did and coming back to it only compounded what she had already left there; she had been alien and a passing guest always anyhow, she couldn't possibly come back any more so. So Marya and I, even children, knew even more than the valley did that it couldn't last. The child, another child, a new brother or sister or whichever it would be next winter, meant nothing to us. Even if we were children, we knew about babies; who so young in our country as not to know, since in our country, our hard and unpiteous mountains, people used, had to use, needed, required, had nothing else to use, children as people in lands savage with dangerous animals used guns and bullets: to defend, preserve themselves, endure; we didn't see, as our father did, that child not the brand of sin but incontrovertible proof of something which otherwise he might have schooled himself to bear. He didn't turn her out of his house. Dont think that. It was us—she. He was just going to leave himself, put home, past, all the dreams and hopes that people call home; the rage, the impotence, the outraged masculinity—oh yes, heartbreak too: why not?—all behind him. It was she who cut that cord and left, swollen belly and all because it could not be long now, it was already winter and maybe we couldn't compute gestation but we had seen enough swelled female bellies to guess approximations.

'So we left. It was at night, after dark. He had left right after supper, we didn't know where, and now I would say, maybe just hunting dark and solitude and space and silence for what wasn't there or anywhere else for him either. And I know now why the direction we—she—took was west too, and where the money came from that we had for a while too until we couldn't pay for riding anymore and had to walk, because she—we—took nothing from that house except the clothes we wore and our shawls and a little food which Marya carried in that same basket yonder. And I could say here also: "But you were safe; it was not enough" except that I dont, not to you who have in you what all heaven too might do well to blench at. So we walked then, and still westward: who might not have learned to think in that place during that week but at least she had memorised something of geography. Then there was no more food except what we could beg, but it would not be long now even if we had had money left to ride with too. Then that night, it was already winter when we left home and now it was Christmas, the eve before; and now I dont remember if we were driven from the inn itself or just turned away or maybe perhaps it was our mother still who would cut even that cord too with man. I remember only the straw, the dark stable and the cold, nor whether it was Marya or I who ran back through the snow to beat on the closed kitchen door until someone came—only the light at last, the lantern, the strange and alien faces crowding downward above us, then the blood and lymph and wet: I, a child of nine and an eleven-year-old idiot sister trying to hide into what privacy we could that outraged betrayed abandon and forsaken nakedness while her closed hand fumbled at mine and she tried to speak, the hand still gripping, holding onto it even after I had given my word, my promise, my oath——'

She stood looking down at him, the closed fist of the one hand lying in the palm of the other. 'Not for you: for him. No, that's wrong; it was already for you, for this moment, that night thirty-five years ago when she first gripped it into my hand and tried to speak; I must have known even at nine that I would cross half of Europe to bring it to you some day, just as I must have known even at nine how vain the bringing it would be. A fate, a doom communicated, imposed on me by the mere touch of it against my flesh, before I even opened it to look inside and divine, surmise who the face belonged to, even before I—we—found the purse, the money which was to bring us here. Oh you were generous; nobody denied that. Because how could you have known that the money which was to have bought you immunity from the consequence of your youthful folly—a dowry if the child should be a girl, a tilted scrap of pasture and a flock to graze it if a boy, and a wife for him in time and so even the same grandchildren to immobilise your folly's partner forever beyond the geographic range of your vulnerability—would instead accomplish the exact opposite by paying our passage to Beirut and—with what was left over—becoming what was its original intent: a dowry?

'Because we could have stayed there, in our mountains, our country, among people whose kind we knew and whose kind knew us. We could have stayed right there at the inn, the village where we were because people are really kind, they really are capable of pity and compassion for the weak and orphaned and helpless because it is pity and compassion and they are weak and helpless and orphaned and people though of course you cannot, dare not believe that: who dare believe only that people are to be bought and used empty and then thrown away. In fact we did stay there for almost ten years. We worked of course, at the inn—in the kitchen, with the milk cows; in—for—the village too; being witless Marya had a way with simple unmartial creatures like cows and geese which were content to be simple cows and geese instead of lions and stags: but then so would we have worked back home, which was where for all their kindness, perhaps because of their kindness, they tried at first to persuade us to return.

'But not I. The doom might have been his, but the curse to hurry it, consummate it, at least was mine; I was the one now wearing the secret talisman, token, not to remember, cherish: no tender memento of devoted troth nor plighted desertion either: but lying instead against my flesh beneath my dress like a brand a fever a coal a goad driving me (I was his mother now; the doom that moved him would have to move me first; already at nine and ten and eleven I was the mother of two—the infant brother and the idiot sister two years my senior too—until at Beirut I found a father for them both) toward the day the hour the moment the instant when with his same blood he would discharge the one and expiate the other. Yes, the doom was his but at least I was its handmaiden: to bring you this, I must bring you the reason for its need too; to bring you this I must bring with me into your orbit the very object which would constitute and make imperative that need. Worse: by bringing it into your orbit I myself created the need which the token, the last desperate cast remaining to me, would be incapable of discharging.

'A curse and doom which in time was to corrupt the very kindly circumambience which harbored us because already you are trying to ask how in the world we managed to have to pass through Asia Minor in order to reach Western Europe, and I will tell you. It was not us. It was the village. No: it was all of us together: a confederation. France: a word a name a designation significant yet foundationless like the ones for grace or Tuesday or quarantine, esoteric and infrequent not just to us but to the ignorant and kindly people among whom we had found orphaned and homeless haven: who had barely heard of France either and did not care until our advent among them: whereupon it was as though they had established a living rapport with it through, by means of us who did not even know where it was except West and that we—I, dragging the other two with me—must go there: until presently we were known to the whole village—valley, district—as the little Franchini: the three who were going to—bound for—dedicated for—France as others might be for some distant and irrevocable state or condition like a nunnery or the top of Mount Everest—not heaven; everybody believes he will be on his way there just as soon as he finds time to really concentrate on it—but some peculiar and individual esoteric place to which no one really wants to go save in idle speculation yet which reflects a certain communal glory on the place which was host to the departure and witnessed the preparations.

'Because we had never heard of Beirut at all; it required older and more worldly than us to have known that Beirut even was, let alone that there was a French colony there, a garrison, official—in effect France, the nearest France to where we were. That is, the real France might have been nearer but that was overland and therefore expensive and we were poor; what we had to travel on was time and leisure. There was the purse of course which probably wouldn't have taken all three of us to France the quickest route anyway, even if there had not been a better reason than that to save the purse. So we spent what we had the most of, travelling as only the very poor or the very rich can; only they travel rapidly who are too rich to have time and too poor to have leisure: by sea, spending only enough of the purse to set the three of us in the nearest available official authentic fringe of France and still leave as much as possible over. Because I was nineteen now and in me we had now something even more mutually compoundable than the purse, of which we needed only enough to set me, not empty-handed, into the quickest marriage-range of the French husband who would be the passport of all three of us into the country where our brother's destiny waited for him.

'That was why Beirut. I had never heard of it but why should I have doubted when the village didn't? any more that in its or God's good time Beirut would appear at the end of the ship, the voyage than that the French husband would be waiting for me there. Which he was. I had never even heard his name before and I dont even recall all the circumstances of our meeting: only that it was not long and he was—is—a good man and has been a good husband to me and brother to Marya and father to him of whom I am apparently to have all the anguishes save the initial one of having borne him, and I have tried—will still try—to be a good wife to him. He was a soldier in the garrison. That is, doing his military service because he was bred a farmer and his time was just up; oh yes, it was that close; one more day and I would have missed him, which should have told me, warned me that what faced us was doom, not destiny, since only destiny is clumsy, inefficient, procrastinative, while doom never is. But I didn't know that then. I knew only that we must reach France, which we did: the farm—I wont even bother to tell you where it is——'

'I know where it is,' the old general said. She had been immobile all the while so she couldn't become stiller—a tall figure breathing so quietly that she didn't seem to be doing that either, clasping the closed fist into the other motionless palm, looking down at him.

'So we have already come to that,' she said. 'Of course you have learned where the farm is; how else could you know what spot to hesitate to give me permission to bury the flesh and bone of the flesh and bone you loved once—lusted after once at least—in? You even know already in advance the request I'll finally demand of you, since we both know now that this—' without uncrossing her hands she moved the closed one slightly then returned it to the other palm '—will be in vain.'

'Yes,' the old general said. 'I know that too.'

'And granted in advance too, since by that time he'll be no more a threat? No no, dont answer yet; let me believe a little longer that I could never have believed that anyone, not even you, could any more control the flux of the bowels of natural compassion than he could his physical ones. Where was I? oh yes, the farm. In that ship to Beirut I had heard them talk of landfall and harbor; by Beirut I even knew what haven meant and now at last in France I believed that we—he—had found them. Home: who had never known one before: four walls and a hearth to come back to at the end of day because they were mutually his walls and hearth; work to be done not for pay or the privilege of sleeping in a hay-loft or left-over food at a kitchen door but because the finished task was mutually his too to choose between its neglect and its completion. Because already he was not just a natural farmer: he was a good one, as though that half of his blood and background and heritage which was peasant had slept in untimed suspension until his destiny found and matched him with land, earth good and broad and rich and deep enough, so that by the end of the second year he was my husband's heir and would still be co-heir even if we had children of our own. And not just home but fatherland too; he was already a French subject; in ten more years he would be a French citizen too, a citizen of France, a Frenchman to all effect and purpose, and his very nameless origin would be as though it had never been.

'So now at last we—I, he—could forget you. No, not that: we couldn't forget you because you were why we were where we were, had at last found the harbor, haven where as they said in the ship, we could drop anchor and make fast and secure. Besides, he couldn't very well forget you because he had never heard of you yet. It was rather that I forgave you. Now at last I could stop seeking you, harrying, dragging two other people over the earth in order to find and face and reproach, compel, whatever it would be; remember, I was a child still even if I had been the mother of two since I was nine years old. It was as though it had been I in my ignorance who had misread you and owed you the apology and the shame where you in your wisdom had known all the time the one restitution for which he was fitted; that, because of that ineradicable peasant other half of his origin, any other relationship, juxtaposition, with you would have brought him only disaster, perhaps even to the point of destroying him. Oh yes, I believed now that you already knew this history, not only where we were but how and what we were doing there, hoped—yes, believed—there, that you had deliberately arranged and planned it to be even if you may not quite have anticipated that I should establish it intact on your own doorstep—haven and harbor and home not just for him but us too, Marya and me too: all four of us, not just yourself and the one you had begot but the other two whose origin you had had no part in, all branded forever more into one irremediable kinship by that one same passion which had created three of our lives and altered forever the course or anyway the pattern of your own; the four of us together even obliterating that passion's irremediable past in which you had not participated: in your own get you dispossessed your predecessor; in Marya and me you effaced even his seniority; and in Marya, her first child, you even affirmed to yourself the trophy of its virginity. More: in the two of us—not Marya this time because, unrational and witless, she was incapable of threatening you and, herself innocent of harm, was herself invulnerable even to you since the witless know only loss and absence: never bereavement—but he and I were not only your absolution but even your expiation too, as though in your design's first completion you had even foreseen this moment here now and had decreed already to me in proxy the last right and privilege of your dead abandoned paramour: to vaunt her virtue for constancy at the same time she heaped on you the reproach of her fall.

'So I didn't even need to forgive you either: we were all four one now in that workable mutual neither compassionate nor uncompassionate armistice and none of us neither needed or had the time to waste forgiving or reproaching one another because we would all be busy enough in supporting, balancing that condition of your expiation and our—his—reparations whose instrument you had been. Nor had I ever seen your face to remember either and now I began to believe that I never would, never would have to: that even when—if—the moment ever came when you would have, could no longer evade having, to face one another he alone would be enough and he would not require my ratification or support. No, it was the past itself which I had forgiven, could at last forgive now: swapped all that bitter and outraged impotence for the home—harbor—haven which was within the range of his capacities, which he was fitted and equipped for—more: would have chosen himself if he had had the choice—whose instrument you in your anonymity had been whether you actually intended for it to be in France or not, where, since he was free of you, the two others of us could be also. Then his military class was called. He went almost eagerly—not that he could have done else as I know, but then so do you know that there are ways and still ways of accepting what you have no choice of refusing. But he went almost eagerly and served his tour—I almost said time but didn't I just say he went almost eagerly?—and came back home and then I believed that he was free of you—that you and he also had struck a balance, an armistice in liability and threat; he was a French citizen and a Frenchman now not only legally but morally too since the date of his birth proved his right to the one and he had just doffed the uniform in which he himself had proved his right and worthiness to the other; not only was he free of you but each of you were free now of the other: you absolved of the liability since, having given him life, you had now created for him security and dignity in which to end it and so you owed him nothing; he absolved of threat since you no longer harmed him now and so you didn't need to fear him anymore.

'Yes, free of you at last, or so I thought. Or you were free of him that is, since he was the one who had better be afraid. If any minuscule of danger still remained for you in him, he himself would eradicate it now by the surest means of all: marriage, a wife and family; so many economic responsibilities to bear and discharge that he would have no time over to dream of his moral rights; a family, children: that strongest and most indissoluble bond of all to anneal him harmless forever more into his present and commit him irrevocable to his future and insulate him for good and always from the griefs and anguishes (he had none of course in the sense I mean because he still had never heard of you) of his past. But it seems that I was wrong. Wrong always in regard to you, wrong every time in what I thought you thought or felt or feared from him. Never more wrong than now, when apparently you had come to believe that bribing him with independence of you had merely scotched the snake, not killed it, and marriage would compound his threat in children any one of which might prove impervious to the bribe of a farm. Any marriage, even this one. And at first it looked like your own blood was trying to fend and shield you from this threat as though in a sort of instinctive filial loyalty. We had long ago designed marriage for him and, now that he was free, grown, a man, a citizen, heir to the farm because we—my husband and I—knew now that we would have no children, his military service forever (so we thought then) behind him, we began to plan one. Except that he refused twice, declined twice the candidates virtuous and solvent and suitable which we picked for him, and still in such a way that we could never tell if it was the girl he said no to or the institution. Perhaps both, being your son though as far as I know he still didn't know you even existed; perhaps both, having inherited both from you: the repudiation of the institution since his own origin had done without it; the choicy choosing of a partner since with him once passion had had to be enough because it was all and he in his turn felt, desired, believed that he deserved, no less to match his own inheritance with.

'Or was it even worse than that to you: your own son truly, demanding not even revenge on you but vengeance: refusing the two we picked who were not only solvent but virtuous too, for that one who had not even sold the one for the other but in bartering one had trafficked them both away? I didn't know, we didn't know: only that he had refused, declined, and still in that way I told you of less of refusal than negation, so that we just thought he wasn't ready yet, that he still wanted a little more of that young man's bachelor and tieless freedom which he had only regained—regained? found—yesterday when he doffed the uniform. So we could wait too and we did; more time passed but we still thought there was enough of it since marriage is long enough to have plenty of room for time behind it. Then—suddenly, with no warning to us who knew only work and bread, not politics and glory—it was 1914 and whether there had been time enough or not or he had been right to wait or not didn't matter. Because he didn't wait now either; he was gone that first week in the old uniform still stinking of the mothballs from the garret trunk but even that was no quicker nor faster than we were; you know where the farm is—was (no: still is since it will have to still be there in order to be a basis for what you will finally grant us) so I dont need to tell you how we left it either since a part of your trade is coping with the confused and anguished mass of the civilian homeless in order to make room for your victories.

'He didn't even wait to be called by his class. A stranger might have guessed it to be a young bachelor accepting even war as a last desperate cast to escape matrimony, but that stranger would be wrong of course, as he himself proved two years later. But we knew better. He was a Frenchman now. All France asked of him in return for that dignity and right and that security and independence was his willingness to defend it and them, and he had gone to do that. Then suddenly all France (all western Europe too for that matter) was loud with your name; every child even in France knew your face because you would save us—you, to be supreme of all, not to command our armies and the armies of our allies because they did not need to be commanded since the terror and the threat was their terror and threat too and all they needed was to be led, comforted, reassured and you were the one to do that because they had faith in you, believed in you. But I knew more. Not better: just more; I had only to match almost any newspaper with this—' again she moved slightly the closed hand lying in the other palm '—and now I knew not only who you were but what you were and where you were. No no, you didn't start this war just to further prove him as your son and a Frenchman, but rather since this war had to be, his own destiny, fate would use it to prove him to his father. You see? you and he together to be one in the saving of France, he in his humble place and you in your high and matchless one and victory itself would be that day when at last you would see one another face to face, he rankless still save for the proven bravery and constancy and devotion which the medal you would fasten to his breast would symbolise and affirm.

'It was the girl of course; his revenge and vengeance on you which you feared: a whore, a Marseilles whore to mother the grandchildren of your high and exalted blood. He told us of her on his leave in the second year. We—I—said no of course too, but then he had that of you also: the capacity to follow his will always. Oh yes, he told us of her: a good girl he said, leading through her own fate, necessity, compulsions (there is an old grandmother) a life which was not her life. And he was right. We saw that as soon as he brought her to us. She is a good girl, now anyway, since then anyway, maybe always a good girl as he believed or maybe only since she loved him. Anyway, who are we to challenge him and her, if what this proves is what love can do: save a woman as well as doom her. But no matter now. You will never believe, perhaps you dare not risk it, chance it, that he would never have made any claim on you: that this whore's children would bear not his father's name but my father's. You would never believe that they would never any more know whose blood they carried than he would have known except for this. But it's too late now. That's all over now; I had imagined you facing him for the first time on that last victorious field while you fastened a medal to his coat; instead you will see him for the first time—no, you wont even see him; you wont even be there—tied to a post, you to see him—if you were to see him, which you will not—over the shoulders and the aimed rifles of a firing-squad.'

The hand, the closed one, flicked, jerked, so fast that the eye almost failed to register it and the object seemed to gleam once in the air before it even appeared, already tumbling across the vacant top of the desk until it sprang open as though of its own accord and came to rest—a small locket of chased worn gold, opening like a hunting-case watch upon twin medallions, miniatures painted on ivory. 'So you actually had a mother. You really did. When I first saw the second face inside it that night, I thought it was your wife or sweetheart or mistress, and I hated you. But I know better now and I apologise for imputing to your character a capacity so weak as to have earned the human warmth of hatred.' She looked down at him. 'So I did wait too late to produce it, after all. No, that's wrong too. Any moment would have been too late; any moment I might have chosen to use it as a weapon the pistol would have misfired, the knife-blade shattered at the stroke. So of course you know what my next request will be.'

'I know it,' the old general said.

'And granted in advance of course, since then he can no longer threaten you. But at least it's not too late for him to receive the locket, even though it cannot save him. At least you can tell me that. Come. Say it: At least it's not too late for him to receive it.'

'It's not too late,' the old general said.

'So he must die.' They looked at one another. 'Your own son.'

'Then will he not merely inherit from me at thirty what I had already bequeathed to him at birth?'

By its size and location, the room which the old general called his study had probably been the chamber, cell of the old marquise's favorite lady-in-waiting or perhaps tiring-woman, though by its appearance now it might have been a library lifted bodily from an English country home and then reft of the books and furnishings. The shelves were empty now except for one wall, and those empty too save for a brief row of the text-books and manuals of the old general's trade, stacked neatly at one end of one shelf. Beneath this, against the wall, was a single narrow army cot pillowless beneath a neatly and immaculately drawn gray army blanket; at the foot of it sat the old general's battered field desk. Otherwise the room contained a heavyish, Victorian-looking, almost

American-looking table surrounded by four chairs in which the four generals were sitting. The table had been cleared of the remains of the German general's meal; an orderly was just going out with the final tray of soiled dishes. Before the old general sat a coffee service and its cups and a tray of decanters and glasses. The old general filled the cups and passed them. Then he took up one of the decanters.

'Schnaps, General, of course,' he said to the German general.

'Thanks,' the German general said. The old general filled and passed the glass. The old general didn't speak to the British general at all, he simply passed the port decanter and an empty glass to him, then a second empty glass.

'Since General (he called the American general's name) is already on your left.' He said to no one directly, calling the American general's name again: '—doesn't drink after dinner, as a rule. Though without doubt he will void it tonight.' Then to the American: 'Unless you will have brandy too?'

'Port, thank you, General,' the American said. 'Since we are only recessing an alliance: not abrogating it.'

'Bah,' the German general said. He sat rigid, bright with medals, the ground glass monocle (it had neither cord nor ribbon; it was not on his face, his head like an ear, but set as though inevictable into the socket of his right eye like an eyeball itself) fixed in a rigid opaque glare at the American general. 'Alliances. That is what is wrong each time. The mistake we—us, and you—and you—and you—' his hard and rigid stare jerking from face to face as he spoke '—have made always each time as though we will never learn. And this time, we are going to pay for it. Oh yes, we. Dont you realise that we know as well as you do what is happening, what is going to be the end of this by another twelve months? twelve months? bah. It wont last twelve months; another winter will see it. We know better than you do—' to the British general '—because you are on the run now and do not have time to do anything else. Even if you were not running, you probably would not realise it, because you are not a martial people. But we are. Our national destiny is for glory and war; they are not mysteries to us and so we know what we are looking at. So we will pay for that mistake. And since we will, you—and you—and you—' the cold and lifeless glare stopping again at the American '—who only think you came in late enough to gain at little risk—must pay also.' Then he was looking at none of them; it was almost as though he had drawn one rapid quiet and calming inhalation, still rigid though and still composed. 'But you will excuse me, please. It is too late for that now—this time. Our problem now is the immediate one. Also, first——' He rose, tossing his crumpled napkin onto the table and picking up the filled brandy glass, so rapidly that his chair scraped back across the floor and would have crashed over had not the American general put out a quick hand and saved it, the German general standing rigid, the brandy glass raised, his close uniform as unwrinkleable as mail against the easy coat of the Briton like the comfortable jacket of a game-keeper, and the American's like a tailor-made costume for a masquerade in which he would represent the soldier of fifty years ago, and the old general's which looked like a wife had got it out of a moth-balled attic trunk and cut some of it off and stitched some braid and ribbons and buttons on what remained. *'Hoch!'* the German general said and tossed the brandy down and with the same motion flung the empty glass over his shoulder to crash against the wall.

'Hoch,' the old general said courteously. He drank too but he set his empty glass back on the table. 'You must excuse us,' he said. 'We are not situated as you are; we cannot afford to break French glasses.' He took another brandy glass from the tray and began to fill it. 'Be seated, General,' he said. The German general didn't move.

'And whose fault is that?' he said, 'that we have been—ja, twice—compelled to destroy French property? Not yours and mine, not ours here, not the fault of any of us, all of us who have to spend the four years straining at each other from behind two wire fences. It's the politicians, the civilian imbeciles who compel us every generation to have to rectify the blunders of their damned international horse-trading——'

'Be seated, General,' the old general said.

'As you were!' the German general said. Then he caught himself. He made a rigid quarter-turn and clapped his heels to face the old general. 'I forgot myself for a moment. You will please to pardon it.' He reversed the quarter-turn, but without the heel-clap this time. His voice was milder now, quieter anyway. 'The same blunder because it is always the same alliance: only the pieces moved and swapped about. Perhaps they have to keep on doing, making the same mistake; being civilians and politicians, perhaps they cant help themselves. Or, being civilians and politicians, perhaps they dare not. Because they would be the first to vanish under that one which we would establish. Think of it, if you have not already: the alliance which would dominate all Europe. Europe? Bah. The world—Us, with you, France, and you, England—' he seemed to catch himself again for a second, turning to the American general. '—with you for—with your good wishes——'

'A minority stockholder,' the American said.

'Thank you,' the German general said. '—An alliance, the alliance which will conquer the whole earth—Europe, Asia, Africa, the islands;—to accomplish where Bonaparte failed, what Caesar dreamed of, what Hannibal didn't live long enough to do——'

'Who will be emperor?' the old general said. It was so courteous and mild that for a moment it didn't seem to register. The German general looked at him.

'Yes,' the British general said as mildly: 'Who?' The German general looked at him. There was no movement of the face at all: the monocle simply descended from the eye, down the face and then the tunic, glinting once or twice as it turned in the air, into the palm lifted to receive it, the hand shutting on it then opening again, the monocle already in position between the thumb and the first finger, to be inserted again; and in fact there had been no eyeball behind it: no scar nor healed suture even: only the lidless and empty socket glaring down at the British general.

'Perhaps now, General?' the old general said.

'Thanks,' the German general said. But still he didn't move. The old general set the filled brandy glass in front of his still-vacant place. 'Thanks,' the German general said. Still staring at the British general, he drew a handkerchief from his cuff and wiped the monocle and set it back into the socket; now the opaque oval stared down at the British general. 'You see why we have to hate you English,' he said. 'You are not soldiers.

Perhaps you cant be. Which is all right; if true, you cant help it; we dont hate you for that. We dont even hate you because you dont try to be. What we hate you for is because you wont even bother to try. You are in a war, you blunder through it somehow and even survive. Because of your little island you cant possibly get any bigger, and you know it. And because of that, you know that sooner or later you will be in another war, yet this time too you will not even prepare for it. Oh, you send a few of your young men to your military college, where they will be taught perfectly how to sit a horse and change a palace guard; they will even get some practical experience by transferring this ritual intact to little outposts beside rice-paddies or tea-plantations or Himalayan goat-paths. But that is all. You will wait until an enemy is actually beating at your front gate. Then you will turn out to repel him exactly like a village being turned out cursing and swearing on a winter night to salvage a burning hayrick—gather up your gutter-sweepings, the scum of your slums and stables and paddocks; they will not even be dressed to look like soldiers, but in the garments of ploughmen and ditchers and carters; your officers look like a country-house party going out to the butts for a pheasant drive. Do you see? getting out in front armed with nothing but walking sticks, saying, "Come along, lads. That seems to be enemy yonder and there appear to be a goodish number of them but I dare say not too many"—and then walking, strolling on, not even looking back to see if they are followed or not because they dont need to because they are followed, do follow, cursing and grumbling still and unprepared still, but they follow and die, still cursing and grumbling, still civilians. We have to hate you. There is an immorality, an outrageous immorality; you are not even contemptuous of glory: you are simply not interested in it: only in solvency.' He stood, rigid and composed, staring down at the British general; he said calmly, in a voice of composed and boundless despair: 'You are swine, you know.' Then he said, 'No,' and now in his voice there was a kind of invincibly incredulous outrage too. 'You are worse. You are unbelievable. When we are on the same side, we win—always; and the whole world gives you the credit for the victory: Waterloo. When we are against you, you lose—

always: Passchendaele, Mons, Cambrai and tomorrow Amiens —and you dont even know it——'

'If you please, General,' the old general said in his mild voice. The German general didn't even pause. He turned to the American.

'You also.'

'Swine?' the American said.

'Soldiers,' the German said. 'You are no better.'

'You mean, no worse, dont you?' the American said. 'I just got back from St Mihiel last night.'

'Then perhaps you can visit Amiens tomorrow,' the German said. 'I will conduct you.'

'General,' the old general said. This time the German general stopped and even looked at the old general. He said:

'Not yet. I am—how you say?—supplicant.' He said again: 'Supplicant.' Then he began to laugh, that is, up to the dead indomitable unregenerate eye, speaking not even to anyone, not even to himself: only to outraged and unregenerate incredulity: 'I, a German lieutenant general, come eighty-seven kilometres to request of—ja, insist on—an Englishman and a Frenchman the defeat of my nation. We—I—could have saved it by simply refusing to meet you here. I could save it now simply by walking out. I could have done it at your aerodrome this afternoon by using on myself the pistol which I employed to preserve even in defeat the integrity of what this—' he made a brief rapid gesture with one hand; with barely a motion of it he indicated his entire uniform—belts brass braid insigne and all '—represents, has won the right to stand for, preserves still that for which those of us who have died in it died for. Then this one, this blunder of the priests and politicians and civilian time-servers, would stop now, since in fact it already has, three days ago now. But I did not. I do not, as a result of which inside another year we—not us—' again without moving he indicated his uniform '—but they whose blunder we tried to rectify, will be done, finished; and with them, us too since now we are no longer extricable from them—oh yes, us too, let the Americans annoy our flank as much as they like: they will not pass Verdun either; by tomorrow we will have run you—' to the Briton '—out of Amiens and possibly even into what you call your ditch, and by next month your people—' to the old general now '—in Paris will be cramming your official sacred talismans into brief-cases on the way to Spain or Portugal. But it will be too late, it will be over, finished; twelve months from now and we—not they for this but we, us—will have to plead with you on your terms for their survival since already it is impossible to extricate theirs from ours. Because I am a soldier first, then a German, then—or hope to be—a victorious German. But that is not even second, but only third. Because this—' again he indicated the uniform '—is more important than any German or even any victory.' Now he was looking at all of them; his voice was quite calm, almost conversational now: 'That is our sacrifice: the whole German army against your one French regiment. But you are right. We waste time.' He looked at them, rapidly, erect still but not quite rigid. 'You are here. I am . . .' He looked at them again; he said again, 'Bah. For a little time anyway we dont need secrets. I am eighty-seven kilometres from here. I must return. As you say—' he faced the American general; his heels clapped again, a sound very loud in the quiet and insulate room '—this is only a recess: not an abrogation.' Still without moving, he looked rapidly from the American to the Briton then back again. 'You are admirable. But you are not soldiers—'

'All young men are brave,' the American said.

'Continue,' the German general said. 'Say it. Even Germans.'

'Even Frenchmen,' the old general said in his mild voice. 'Wouldn't we all be more comfortable if you would sit down?'

'A moment,' the German general said. He did not even look at the old general. 'We—' again without moving he looked rapidly from one to the other '—you two and I discussed this business thoroughly while your—what do I say? formal or mutual?—Commander-in-Chief was detained from us. We are agreed on what must be done; that was never any question. Now we need only to agree to do it in this little time we have out of the four years of holding one another off—we, Germans on one side, and you, English and French—' he turned to the American; again the heels clapped '—you Americans too; I have not forgot you.—on the other, engaging each the other with half a hand because the other hand and a half was required to defend our back areas from our own politicians and priests. During that discussion before your Commander-in-Chief joined us, something was said about decision.' He said again, 'Decision.' He didn't even say bah now. He looked rapidly again from the American to the Briton, to the American again. 'You,' he said.

'Yes,' the American general said. 'Decision implies choice.'

The German general looked at the Briton. 'You,' he said.

'Yes,' the British general said. 'God help us.'

The German general paused. 'Pardon?'

'Sorry,' the British general said. 'Let it be just yes then.'

'He said, God help us,' the American general said. 'Why?'

'Why?' the German general said. 'The why is to me?'

'We're both right this time,' the American general said. 'At least we dont have to cope with that.'

'So,' the German general said. 'That is both of you. Three of us.' He sat down, picked up the crumpled napkin and drew his chair up, and took up the filled brandy glass and sat back and erect again, into that same rigidity of formal attention as when he had been standing to toast his master, so that even sitting the rigidity had a sort of visible inaudibility like a soundless clap of heels, the filled glass at level with the fixed rigid glare of the opaque monocle; again without moving he seemed to glance rapidly at the other glasses. 'Be pleased to fill, gentlemen,' he said. But neither the Briton nor the American moved. They just sat there while across the table from them the German general sat with his lifted and rigid glass; he said, indomitable and composed, not even contemptuous: 'So then. All that remains is to acquaint your Commander-in-Chief with what part of our earlier discussion he might be inclined to hear. Then the formal ratification of our agreement.'

'Formal ratification of what agreement?' the old general said.

'Mutual ratification then,' the German general said.

'Of what?' the old general said.

'The agreement,' the German general said.

'What agreement?' the old general said. 'Do we need an agreement? Has anyone missed one?—The port is with you, General,' he said to the Briton. 'Fill, and pass.'

Thursday
Thursday Night

This time it was a bedroom. The grave and noble face was framed by a pillow, looking at him from beneath a flannel nightcap tied under the chin. The nightshirt was flannel too, open at the throat to reveal a small cloth bag, not new and not very clean and apparently containing something which smelled like asafoetida, on a soiled string like a necklace. The youth stood beside the bed in a brocade dressing gown.

'They were blank shells,' the runner said in his light dry voice. 'The aeroplane—all four of them—flew right through the bursts. The German one never even deviated, not even going fast, even when one of ours hung right on its tail from about fifty feet for more than a minute while I could actually see the tracer going into it. The same one—aeroplane—ours—dove at us, at me; I even felt one of whatever it was coming out of the gun hit me on the leg here. It was like when a child blows a garden pea at you through a tube except for the smell, the stink, the burning phosphorus. There was a German general in it, you see. I mean, in the German one. There had to be; either we had to send someone there or they had to send someone here. And since we—or the French—were the ones who started it, thought of it first, obviously it would be our right—privilege—duty to be host. Only it would have to look all right from beneath; they couldn't—couldn't dare anyway—issue a synchronised simultaneous order for every man on both sides to shut their eyes and count a hundred so they had to do the next best thing to make it look all regular, all orthodox to anyone they couldn't hide it from——'

'What?' the old Negro said.

'Dont you see yet? It's because they cant afford to let it stop like this. I mean, let us stop it. They dont dare. If they ever let us find out that we can stop a war as simply as men tired of digging a ditch decide calmly and quietly to stop digging the ditch——'

'I mean that suit,' the old Negro said. 'That policeman's suit. You just took it, didn't you?'

'I had to,' the runner said with that peaceful and terrible patience. 'I had to get out. To get back in too. At least back to where I hid my uniform. It used to be difficult enough to pass either way, in or out. But now it will be almost impossible to get back in. But dont worry about that; all I need——'

'Is he dead?' the old Negro said.

'What?' the runner said. 'Oh, the policeman. I dont know. Probably not.' He said with a sort of amazement: 'I hope not.' He said: 'I knew night before last—two nights ago, Tuesday night—what they were planning to do, though of course I had no proof then. I tried to tell him. But you know him, you've probably tried yourself to tell him something you couldn't prove or that he didn't want to believe. So I'll need something else. Not to prove it to him, make him believe it: there's not time enough left to waste that way. That's why I came here. I want you to make me a Mason too. Or maybe there's not even time for that either. So just show me the sign—like this——' he jerked, flicked his hand low against his flank, as near as he had been able to divine at the time or anyway remember now from the man two years ago on the day he joined the battalion. 'That will be enough. It will have to be; I'll bluff the rest of it through——'

'Wait,' the old Negro said. 'Tell me slow.'

'I'm trying to,' the runner said with that terrible patience. 'Every man in the battalion owes him his pay for weeks ahead, provided they live long enough to earn it and he lives long enough to collect it from them. He did it by making them all Masons or anyway making them believe they are Masons. He owns them, you see. They cant refuse him. All he will need to do is——'

'Wait,' the old Negro said. 'Wait.'

'Dont you see?' the runner said. 'If all of us, the whole battalion, at least one battalion, one unit out of the whole line to start it, to lead the way—leave the rifles and grenades and all behind us in the trench: simply climb barehanded out over the parapet and through the wire and then just walk on barehanded, not with our hands up for surrender but just open to show that we had nothing to hurt, harm anyone; not running, stumbling: just walking forward like free men,—just one of us, one man; suppose just one man, then multiply him by a battalion; suppose a whole battalion of us, who want nothing except just to go home and get themselves clean into clean clothes and work and drink a little beer in the evening and talk and then lie down and sleep and not be afraid. And maybe, just maybe that many Germans who dont want anything more too, or maybe just one German who doesn't want more than that, to put his or their rifles and grenades down and climb out too with their hands empty too not for surrender but just so every man could see there is nothing in them to hurt or harm either——'

'Suppose they dont,' the old Negro said. 'Suppose they shoot at us.' But the runner didn't even hear the us. He was still talking.

'Wont they shoot at us tomorrow anyway, as soon as they have recovered from the fright? as soon as the people at Chaulnesmont and Paris and Poperinghe and whoever it was in that German aeroplane this afternoon have had time to meet and compare notes and decide exactly where the threat, danger is, and eradicate it and then start the war again: tomorrow and tomorrow and tomorrow until the last formal rule of the game has been fulfilled and discharged and the last ruined player removed from sight and the victory immolated like a football trophy in a club-house show-case. That's all I want. That's all I'm trying to do. But you may be right. So you tell me.'

The old Negro groaned. He groaned peacefully. One hand came out from beneath the covers and turned them back and he swung his legs toward the edge of the bed and said to the youth in the dressing gown: 'Hand me my shoes and britches.'

'Listen to me,' the runner said. 'There's not time. It will be daylight in two hours and I've got to get back. Just show me how to make the sign, the signal.'

'You cant learn it right in that time,' the old Negro said. 'And even if you could, I'm going too. Maybe this is what I been hunting for too.'

'Didn't you just say the Germans might shoot at us?' the runner said. 'Dont you see? That's it, that's the risk: if some of the Germans do come out. Then they will shoot at us, both of them, their side and ours too—put a barrage down on all of us. They'll have to. There wont be anything else for them to do.'

'So your mind done changed about it,' the old Negro said.

'Just show me the sign, the signal,' the runner said. Again the old Negro groaned, peaceful, almost inattentive, swinging his legs on out of the bed. The innocent and unblemished corporal's uniform was hanging neatly on a chair, the shoes and the socks were placed neatly beneath it. The youth had picked them up and he now knelt beside the bed, holding one of the socks open for the old Negro's foot. 'Aren't you afraid?' the runner said.

'Aint we already got enough ahead of us without bringing that up?' the old Negro said pettishly. 'And I know what you're fixing to say next: How am I going to get up there? And I can answer that: I never had no trouble getting here to France; I reckon I can make them other just sixty miles. And I know what you are fixing to say after that one too: I cant wear this French suit up there neither, without no general with me. Only I dont need to answer that one because you done already answered it.'

'Kill a British soldier this time?' the runner said.

'You said he wasn't dead.'

'I said maybe he wasn't.'

'You said you hoped he wasn't. Dont never forget that.'

The runner was the last thing which the sentry would ever see. In fact, he was the first thing the sentry saw that morning except for the relief guard who had brought his breakfast and who now sat, his rifle leaning beside him against the dugout's opposite earthen shelf.

He had been under arrest for almost thirty hours now. That was all: just under arrest, as though the furious blows of the rifle-butt two nights ago had not simply hushed a voice which he could bear no longer but had somehow separated him from mankind; as if that aghast reversal, that cessation of four years of mud and blood and its accompanying convulsion of silence had cast him up on this buried dirt ledge with no other sign of man at all save the rotation of guards who brought him food and then sat opposite him until the time came for their relief. Yesterday and this morning too in ordained rote the orderly officer's sergeant satellite had appeared suddenly in the orifice, crying ''Shun!' and he had stood bareheaded while the guard saluted and the orderly officer himself entered and said, rapid and glib out of the glib and routine book: 'Any complaints?' and was gone again before he could have made any answer he did not intend to make. But that was all. Yesterday he had tried for a little while to talk to one of the rotated guards and since then some of them had tried to talk to him, but that was all of that too, so that in effect for over thirty hours now he had sat or sprawled and lay asleep on his dirt shelf, morose, sullen, incorrigible, foul-mouthed and snarling, not even waiting but just biding pending whatever it was they would finally decide to do with him or with the silence, both or either, if and when they did make up their minds.

Then he saw the runner. At the same moment he saw the pistol already in motion as the runner struck the guard between the ear and the rim of the helmet and caught him as he toppled and tumbled him onto the ledge and turned and the sentry saw the burlesque of a soldier entering behind him—the travesty of the wrapped putties, the tunic whose lower buttons would not even meet across the paunch not of sedentation but of age and above it, beneath the helmet, the chocolate face which four years ago he had tried to relegate and repudiate into the closed book of his past.

'That makes five,' the old Negro said.

'All right, all right,' the runner answered, rapidly and harshly. 'He's not dead either. Dont you think that by this time I have learned how to do it?' He said rapidly to the sentry: 'You dont need to worry either now. All we need from you now is inertia.' But the sentry was not even looking at him. He was looking at the old Negro.

'I told you to leave me alone,' he said. And it was the runner who answered him, in that same rapid and brittle voice:

'It's too late for that now. Because I am wrong; we dont want inertia from you: what we want is silence. Come along. Notice, I have the pistol. If I must, I shall use it. I've already used it six times, but only the flat of it. This time I'll use the trigger.' He said to the old Negro, in the rapid brittle and almost despairing voice: 'All right, this one will be dead. Then you suggest something.'

'You cant get away with this,' the sentry said.

'Who expects to?' the runner said. 'That's why we have no time to waste. Come along. You've got your investments to protect, you know; after a breathing spell like this and the fresh start it will give them, let alone the discovery of what can happen simply by letting the same men hang around in uniforms too long, the whole battalion will probably be wiped out as soon as they can get us up in gun-range again. Which may be this afternoon. They flew a German general over yesterday; without doubt he was at Chaulnesmont by late dinner last night, with our pooh-bahs and the American ones too already waiting for him and the whole affair settled and over with by the time the port passed (if German generals drink port, though why not, since we have had four years to prove to us even if all history had not already done it, that the biped successful enough to become a general had ceased to be a German or British or American or Italian or French one almost as soon as it never was a human one) and without doubt he is already on his way back and both sides are merely waiting until he is out of the way as you hold up a polo game while one of the visiting rajahs rides off the field——'

The sentry—in what time he had left—would remember it. He knew at once that the runner meant exactly what he said about the pistol; he had proof of that at once—of the flat side of it anyway—when he almost stumbled over the sprawled bodies of the orderly officer and his sergeant in the tunnel before he saw them. But it would seem to him that it was not the hard muzzle of the pistol in the small of his back, but the voice itself—the glib calm rapid desperate and despairing voice carrying, sweeping them into the next dugout where an entire platoon lay or sat along the earthen shelf, the faces turning as one to look at them as the runner thrust him in with the muzzle of the pistol and then thrust the old Negro forward too, saying:

'Make the sign. Go on. Make it.'—the tense calm desperate voice not even stopping then, as it seemed to the sentry that it never had: 'That's right, of course he doesn't need to make the sign. He has enough without. He has come from outside. So have I, for that matter but you wont even need to doubt me now, you need only look at him; some of you may even recognise Horn's D.C.M. on that tunic. But dont worry; Horn isn't dead any more than Mr Smith and Sergeant Bledsoe; I have learned to use the flat of this—' he raised the pistol for an instant into sight '—quite neatly now. Because here is our chance to have done with it, be finished with it, quit of it, not just the killing, the getting dead, because that's only a part of the nightmare, of the rot and the stinking and the waste——'

The sentry would remember it, incorrigible still, merely acquiescent, believing still that he was waiting, biding the moment when he or perhaps two or three of them at once would take the runner off guard and smother him, listening to the glib staccato voice, watching the turned faces listening to it too, believing still that he saw in them only astonishment, surprise, presently to fade into one incorrigible concert which he would match: 'And neither of us would have got back in if it had not been for his pass from the Ministry of War in Paris. So you dont even know yet what they have done to you. They've sealed you up in here—the whole front from the Channel to Switzerland. Though from what I saw in Paris last night—not only military police, the French and American and ours too, but the civilian police too—I wouldn't have thought they'd have enough left to seal anything with. But they have; the colonel himself could not have got back in this morning unless the pass bore the signature of that old man in the castle at Chaulnesmont. It's like another front, manned by all the troops in the three forces who cant speak the language belonging to the coat they came up from under the equator and half around the world to die in, in the cold and the wet—Senegalese and Moroccans and Kurds and Chinese and Malays and Indians—Polynesian Melanesian Mongol and

Negro who couldn't understand the password nor read the pass either: only to recognise perhaps by memorised rote that one cryptic hieroglyph. But not you. You cant even get out now, to try to come back in. No-man's Land is no longer in front of us. It's behind us now. Before, the faces behind the machine guns and the rifles at least thought Caucasian thoughts even if they didn't speak English or French or American; now they dont even think Caucasian thoughts. They're alien. They dont even have to care. They have tried for four years to get out of the white man's cold and mud and rain just by killing Germans, and failed. Who knows? by killing off the Frenchmen and Englishmen and Americans which they have bottled up here, they might all be on the way home tomorrow. So there is nowhere for us to go now but east——'

Now the sentry moved. That is, he did not move yet, he dared not yet: he simply made a single infinitesimal transition into a more convulsive rigidity, speaking now, harsh and obscene, cursing the rapt immobilised faces: 'Are you going to let them get away with this? Dont you know we're all going to be for it? They have already killed Lieutenant Smith and Sergeant Bledsoe——'

'Nonsense,' the runner said. 'They aren't dead. Didn't I just tell you I have learned how to use the flat of a pistol? It's his money. That's all. Everyone in the battalion owes him. He wants us to sit here and do nothing until he has earned his month's profit. Then he wants them to start it up again so we will be willing to bet him twenty shillings a month that we will be dead in thirty days. Which is what they are going to do—start it up again. You all saw those four aeroplanes yesterday, and all that archie. The archie were blank shells. There was a German general in the hun aeroplane. Last night he was at Chaulnesmont. He would have to have been; else, why did he come at all? why else wafted across on a cloud of blank archie shell, with three S.E.5's going through the motion of shooting him down with blank ammunition? Oh yes, I was there; I saw the lorries fetching up the shells night before last, and yesterday I stood behind one of the batteries firing them when one of the S.E.'s—that pilot would have been a child of course, too young for them to have dared inform him in advance, too young to be risked with the knowledge that fact and truth are not the same—dived and put a burst right into the battery and shot me in the skirt of my tunic with something—whatever it was—which actually stung a little for a moment. What else, except to allow a German general to visit the French and the British and the American ones in the Allied Commandery-in-Chief without alarming the rest of us bipeds who were not born generals but simply human beings? And since they—all four of them—would speak the same language, no matter what clumsy isolated national tongues they were compelled by circumstance to do it in, the matter probably took them no time at all and very likely the German one is already on his way back home at this moment, not even needing the blank shells now because the guns will be already loaded with live ones, merely waiting for him to get out of the way in order to resume, efface, obliterate forever this ghastly and incredible contretemps. So we have no time, you see. We may not even have an hour. But an hour will be enough, if only it is all of us, the whole battalion. Not to kill the officers; they themselves have abolished killing for a recess of three days. Besides, we wont need to, with all of us. If we had time, we could even draw lots: one man to each officer, to simply hold his hands while the rest of us go over. But the flat of a pistol is quicker and no more harmful really, as Mr Smith and Sergeant Bledsoe and Horn will tell you when they awake. Then never to touch pistol or rifle or grenade or machine gun again, to climb out of ditches forever and pass through the wire and then advance with nothing but our bare hands, to dare, defy the Germans not to come out too and meet us.' He said quickly, in the desperate and calmly despairing voice: 'All right: meet us with machine-gun fire, you will say. But the hun archie yesterday was blank too.' He said to the old Negro: 'Now, make them the sign. Have not you already proved that, if anything, it means brotherhood and peace?'

'You fools!' the sentry cried, except that he did not say fools: virulent and obscene out of his almost inarticulate paucity, struggling now, having defied the pistol in one outraged revulsion of repudiation before he realized that the hard little iron ring was gone from his spine and that the runner was merely holding him, he (the sentry) watching, glaring at the faces which he had thought were merely fixed in a surprise precursive to outrage too, looming, bearing down on him, identical and alien and concerted, until so many hard hands held him that he could not even struggle, the runner facing him now, the pistol poised flat on one raised palm, shouting at him:

'Stop it! Stop it! Make your choice, but hurry. You can come with us, or you can have the pistol. But decide.'

He would remember; they were topside now, in the trench, he could see a silent and moiling group within which or beneath which the major and two company commanders and three or four sergeants had vanished (they had taken the adjutant and the sergeant-major and the corporal signalman in the orderly dugout and the colonel still in bed) and in both directions along the trench he could see men coming up out of their holes and warrens, blinking in the light, dazed still yet already wearing on their faces that look of amazed incredulity fading with one amazed concert into dawning and incredulous hope. The hard hands still grasped him; as they lifted, flung him up onto the firestep and then over the lip of the parapet, he already saw the runner spring up and turn and reach down and pull the old Negro up beside him while other hands boosted from beneath, the two of them now standing on the parapet facing the trench, the runner's voice thin and high now with that desperate and indomitable despair:

'The sign! The sign! Give it us! Come on, men! If this is what they call staying alive, do you want that on these terms forever either?'

Then he was struggling again. He didn't even know he was about to, when he found himself jerking and thrashing, cursing, flinging, beating away the hands, not even realising then why, for what, until he found himself in the wire, striking, hitting backward at the crowding bodies at the entrance to the labyrinthine passageway which the night patrols used, hearing his own voice in one last invincible repudiation: 'F. . . them all! Bugger all of you!' crawling now, not the first one through because when he rose to his feet, running, the old Negro was panting beside him, while he shouted at the old Negro: 'Serve you f. . .ing well right! Didn't I warn you two years ago to stay away from me? Didn't I?'

Then the runner was beside him, grasping his arm and stopping him and turning him about, shouting: 'Look at them!' He did so and saw them, watched them, crawling on their hands and knees through the gaps in the wire as though up out of hell itself, faces clothes hands and all stained as though forever one single nameless and identical color from the mud in which they had lived like animals for four years, then rising to their feet as though in that four years they had not stood on earth, but had this moment returned to light and air from purgatory as ghosts stained forever to the nameless single color of purgatory. 'Over there too!' the runner cried, turning him again until he saw that also: the distant German wire one faint moil and pulse of motion, indistinguishable until it too broke into men rising erect; whereupon a dreadful haste came over him, along with something else which he had not yet time to assimilate, recognise, knowing, aware of only the haste; and not his haste but one haste, not only the battalion but the German one or regiment or what ever it was, the two of them running toward each other now, empty-handed, approaching until he could see, distinguish the individual faces but still all one face, one expression, and then he knew suddenly that his too looked like that, all of them did: tentative, amazed, defenseless, and then he heard the voices too and knew that his was one also—a thin murmuring sound rising into the incredible silence like a chirping of lost birds, forlorn and defenseless too; and then he knew what the other thing was even before the frantic uprush of the rockets from behind the two wires, German and British too.

'No!' he cried, 'no! Not to us!' not even realising that he had said 'we' and not 'I' for the first time in his life probably, certainly for the first time in four years, not even realising that in the next moment he had said 'I' again, shouting to the old Negro as he whirled about: 'What did I tell you? Didn't I tell you to let me alone?' Only it was not the old Negro, it was the runner, standing facing him as the first ranging burst of shells bracketed in. He never heard them, nor the wailing rumble of the two barrages either, nor saw nor heard little more of anything in that last second except the runner's voice crying out of the soundless rush of flame which enveloped half his body neatly from heel through navel through chin: 'They cant kill us! They cant! Not dare not: they cant!'

† † †

Except of course that he couldn't sit here save for a definitely physically limited length of time because after a while it would be daylight. Unless of course the sun really failed to rise tomorrow, which as they taught you in that subsection of philosophy they called dialectics which you were trying to swot through in order to try to swot through that section of being educated they called philosophy, was for the sake of argument possible. Only why shouldn't he be sitting here after daylight or for the rest of the day itself for that matter, since the only physical limitation to that would be when someone with the authority and compulsion to resist the condition of a young man in a second lieutenant's uniform sitting on the ground against the wall of a Nissen hut, had his attention called to it by a horn or whistle; and that greater condition which yesterday had sent three fairly expensive aeroplanes jinking up and down the sky with their Vickerses full of blank ammunition, might well abrogate that one too.

Then the first limitation had been discharged, because now it was day and none to know where the night had gone: not a dialectic this time, but he who didn't know where night had gone this soon, this quick. Or maybe it was a dialectic since as far as he knew only he had watched it out and since only he in waking had watched it out, to all the others still in slumber it still obtained, like the tree in darkness being no longer green, and since he who had watched it out still didn't know where it had gone, for him it was still night too. Then almost before he had had time to begin to bother to think that out and so have done with it, a bugle blowing *reveille* confounded him, the sound (that sound: who had never heard it before or even heard of it: a horn blowing at daybreak on a forward aerodrome where people did not even have guns but were armed only with maps and what Monaghan called monkey-wrenches) even getting him up onto his feet: that greater condition's abrogation which had now reabrogated. In fact, if he had been a cadet still, he would even know what crime whoever found him sitting there would charge him with: not shaving: and, standing now, he realised that he had even forgot his problem too, who had sat there all night thinking that he had none evermore, as though sitting so long within that peaceful stink had robbed olfactory of its single sense or perhaps the sidcott of its smell and only getting up restored them both. In fact, for a moment he toyed with the idea of unrolling the sidcott to see how far the burning had spread, except that if he did that and let the air in, the burning might spread faster, thinking, with a sort of peaceful amazement hearing himself: *Because it's got to last;* no more: not *last until*, just *last*.

At least he wouldn't take it inside with him so he left it against the wall and went around the hut and inside it—Burk and Hanley and De Marchi had not stirred so the tree was not green for some yet anyway—and got his shaving tackle and then picked up the sidcott again and went to the washroom; nor would the tree be quite green yet here either, and if not here, certainly not in the latrines. Though now it would because the sun was well up now and, once more smooth of face, the sidcott stinking peacefully under his arm, he could see movement about the mess, remembering suddenly that he had not eaten since lunch yesterday. But then there was the sidcott, when suddenly he realised that the sidcott would serve that too, turning and already walking. They—someone—had brought his bus back and rolled it in so he trod his long shadow toward only the petrol tin and put the sidcott into it and stood peaceful and empty while the day incremented, the infinitesimal ineluctable shortening of the shadows. It was going to rain probably, but then it always was anyway; that is, it always did on days-off from patrols, he didn't know why yet, he was too new. 'You will though,' Monaghan told him. 'Just wait till after the first time you've been good and scared'—pronouncing it 'skeered'.

So it would be all right now, the ones who were going to get up would have already had breakfast and the others would sleep on through till lunch; he could even take his shaving kit on to the mess without going to the hut at all: and stopped, he could not even remember when he had heard it last, that alien and divorced—that thick dense mute furious murmur to the north and east; he knew exactly where it would be because he had flown over the spot yesterday afternoon, thinking peacefully *I came home too soon. If I had only sat up there all night instead I could have seen it start again*—listening, motionless in midstride, hearing it murmur toward and into its crescendo and sustain a time, a while and then cut short off, murmuring in his ears for a little time still until he discovered that what he was actually listening to was a lark: and he had been right, the sidcott had served even better than it knew even or even perhaps intended, carrying him still intact across lunch too since it was after ten now. Provided he could eat enough of course, the food—the eggs and bacon and the marmalade—having no taste to speak of, so that only in that had he been wrong; then presently he was wrong there too, eating steadily on in the empty mess until at last the orderly told him there was simply no more toast.

Much better than the sidcott could have known to plan or even dream because during lunch the hut itself would be empty and for that while he could use his cot to do some of the reading he had imagined himself doing between patrols—the hero living by proxy the lives of heroes between the monotonous peaks of his own heroic derring: which he was doing for another moment or two while Bridesman stood in the door, until he looked up. 'Lunch?' Bridesman said.

'Late breakfast, thanks,' he said.

'Drink?' Bridesman said.

'Later, thanks,' he said: and moved in time, taking the book with him; there was a tree, he had discovered it in the first week—an old tree with two big roots like the arms of a chair on the bank above the cut through which the road ran past the aerodrome to Villeneuve Blanche so that you could sit like in a chair with the roots to prop the elbows which propped in turn the book, secure from war yet still of it, not that remote, in those days when they had called it war: who apparently were not decided yet what to call this now. And so now there would have been time enough, Bridesman would know by now what that had been this morning: thinking peacefully, the open book still propped before he began to move: *Yes, he will know by now. He will have to make the decision to tell me or not, but he will make it.*

Nor was there any reason to take the book to the hut because he might even read some more, entering and then leaving Bridesman's hut with the book still closed on one finger to mark his place, still strolling; he had never been walking fast anyway and finally stopping, empty and peaceful, only blinking a little, looking out across the empty field, the line of closed hangars, the mess and the office where a few people came and went. Not too many though; apparently Collyer had lifted the ban on Villeneuve Blanche; soon he would be looking at evening too and suddenly he thought of Conventicle but for an instant only and then no more because what could he say to Conventicle or they to each other? 'Well, Flight, Captain Bridesman tells me one of our battalions put their guns down this morning and climbed out of the trench and through the wire and met a similar unarmed German one until both sides could get a barrage down on them. So all we need now is just to stand by until time to take that jerry general home.' And then Conventicle: 'Yes sir. So I heard.'

And now he was looking at evening, the aftermath of sun, treading no shadow at all now to the petrol tin. Though almost at once he began to hurry a little, remembering not the sidcott but the burning; it had been more than twelve hours now since he left it in the tin and there might not be anything left of it. But he was in time: just the tin itself too hot to touch so that he kicked it over and tumbled the sidcott out, which would have to cool a little too. Which it did: not evening incrementing now but actual night itself, almost summer night this time at home in May; and in the latrine the tree once more was no longer green: only the stink of the sidcott which had lasted, he had wasted that concern, dropping it into the sink where it unfolded as of its own accord into visibility, into one last repudiation—the slow thick invincible smell of the burning itself visible now in creeping overlaps, almost gone now—only a beggar's crumb but perhaps there had been an instant in the beginning when only a crumb of fire lay on the face of darkness and the falling waters and he moved again, one of the cubicles had a wooden latch inside the door if you were there first and he was and latched the invisible door and drew the invisible pistol from his tunic pocket and thumbed the safety off.

† † †

Again the room was lighted, candelabrum sconce and girandole, curtain and casement once more closed against the swarm-dense city's unsleeping and anguished murmur; again the old general looked like a gaudy toy in his blanched and glittering solitude, just beginning to crumble the heel of bread into the waiting bowl as the smaller door opened and the youthful aide stood in it. 'He is here?' the old general said.

'Yes sir,' the aide said.

'Let him come in,' the old general said. 'Then let nobody else.'

'Yes sir,' the aide said and went out and closed the door and in a time opened it again; the old general had not moved except to put quietly down beside the bowl the uncrumbled bread, the aide entering and turning stiffly to attention beside the door as the Quartermaster General entered and came on a pace or two and then stopped, paused, the aide going back out the door and drawing it to behind him, the Quartermaster General standing for a moment longer—the gaunt gigantic peasant with his sick face and his hungry and stricken eyes, the two old men looking at one another for another moment, then the Quartermaster General partly raised one hand and dropped it and came on until he faced the table.

'Have you dined?' the old general said. The other didn't even answer.

'I know what happened,' he said. 'I authorised it, permitted it, otherwise it couldn't have. But I want you to tell me. Not admit, confess: affirm it, tell me to my face that we did this. Yesterday afternoon a German general was brought across the lines and here, to this house, into this house.'

'Yes,' the old general said. But the other still waited, inexorable. 'We did it then,' the old general said.

'Then this morning an unarmed British battalion met an unarmed German force between the lines until artillery from both sides was able to destroy them both.'

'We did it then,' the old general said.

'We did it,' the Quartermaster General said. 'We. Not British and American and French we against German them nor German they against American and British and French us, but We against all because we no longer belong to us. A subterfuge not of ours to confuse and mislead the enemy nor of the enemy to mislead and confuse us, but of We to betray all since all has had to repudiate us in simple defensive horror; no barrage by us or vice versa to prevent an enemy running over us with bayonets and hand grenades or vice versa, but a barrage by both of We to prevent naked and weaponless hand touching opposite naked and weaponless hand. We, you and I and our whole unregenerate and unregenerable kind; not only you and I and our tight close jealous unchallengeable hierarchy behind this wire and our opposite German one behind that one, but more, worse: our whole small repudiated and homeless species about the earth who not only no longer belong to man but even to earth itself since we have had to make this last base desperate cast in order to hold our last desperate and precarious place on it.'

'Sit down,' the old general said.

'No,' the other said. 'I was standing when I accepted this appointment. I can stand to divest myself of it.' He thrust one big fleshless hand rapidly inside his tunic then out again, though once more he stood just holding the folded paper in it, looking down at the old general. 'Because I didn't just believe in you. I loved you. I believed from that first moment when I saw you in that gate that day forty-seven years ago that you had been destined to save us. That you were chosen by destiny out of the paradox of your background, to be a paradox to your past in order to be free of human past to be the one out of all earth to be free of the compulsions of fear and weakness and doubt which render the rest of us incapable of what you were competent for; that you in your strength would even absolve us of our failure due to our weakness and fears. I dont mean the men out there tonight—' this time the vast hand holding the folded paper made a single rapid clumsy gesture which indicated, seemed to shape somehow in the brilliant insulate room the whole scope of the murmurous and anguished darkness outside and even as far away as the lines themselves—the wire, the ditches dense and, for this time anyway, silent with dormant guns and amazed and incredulous men, waiting, alerted, confused and incredulous with hope '—they dont need you, they are capable of saving themselves, as three thousand of them proved four days ago. They only needed to be defended, protected from you. Not expected to be nor even hope to be: just should have been except that we failed them. Not you this time, who did not even what you would but what you must, since you are you. But I and my few kind, who had rank enough and authority and position enough, as if God Himself had put this warrant in my hand that day against this one three years later, until I failed them and Him and brought it back.' His hand also jerked, flicked, and tossed the folded paper onto the desk in front of the bowl and jug and the still intact morsel, on either side of which the old general's veined and mottled hands lay faintly curled at rest. 'Back to you by hand, as I received it from you. I will have no more of it. I know: by my own token I am too late in returning what I should never have accepted to begin with because even at first I would have known myself incapable of coping with what it was going to entail, if I had only known then what that entailment was going to be. I am responsible. I am responsible, mine is the blame and solely mine; without me and this warrant which you gave me that day three years ago, you could not have done this. By this authority I could have prevented you then, and even afterward I could have stopped it, remanded it. As you—the Commander-in-Chief of all the Allied Armies in France—as Quartermaster General over all embattled Europe west of our and the British and the American wire, I could have decreed that whole zone containing Villeneuve Blanche (or arbitrarily any other point which you might have threatened) at one hundred point one of saturation and forbidden whatever number of men it took to drive those lorries of blank anti-aircraft shells to enter it and even at one hundred absolute of saturation and so forbidden that single supernumerary German one to come out of it. But I didn't. So I was responsible even more than you because you had no choice. You didn't even do what you would but only what you could since you were incapable of else, born and doomed incapable of else. While I did have a choice between could and would, between shall and must and cannot, between must and dare not, between *will do* and *I am afraid to do:* had that choice, and found myself afraid. Oh yes, afraid. But then why shouldn't I be afraid of you, since you are afraid of man?'

'I am not afraid of man,' the old general said. 'Fear implies ignorance. Where ignorance is not, you do not need to fear: only respect. I dont fear man's capacities, I merely respect them.'

'And use them,' the Quartermaster General said.

'Beware of them,' the old general said.

'Which, fear them or not, you should. You someday will. Not I, of course. I'm an old man, finished; I had my chance and failed; who—what—wants or needs me further now? what midden or rubbish heap, least of all that one beside the Seine yonder with its gold hemisphere ravaged from across all of Europe by a lesser one than you since he embroiled himself with all the armies of Europe in order to lose a petty political empire where you have allied all the armies of both hemispheres and finally even the German one too, to lose the world to man.'

'Will you let me speak a moment?' the old general said.

'Of course,' the other said. 'Didn't I tell you I loved you once? Who can control that? All you dare assume mandate over is oath, contract.'

'You say they do not need me to save themselves from me and us since they themselves will save themselves if they are only let alone, only defended and preserved that long from me and us. How do you think we coped with this in time at time and place—at this particular moment in four whole years of moments, at this particular point in that thousand kilometres of regimental fronts? just by being alert? not only alert at this specific spot and moment but prepared to cope and concentrate and nullify at this specific spot and moment with that which every trained soldier has been trained and taught to accept as a factor in war and battle as he must logistics and climate and failure of ammunition; this, in four long years of fateful and vulnerable moments and ten hundred kilometres of fateful and vulnerable spots—spots and moments fateful and vulnerable because as yet we have found nothing better to man them with than man? How do you think we knew in time? Dont you know how? who, since you believe in man's capacities, must certainly know them?'

Now the other had stopped, immobile, looming, vast, his sick and hungry face as though sick anew with foreknowledge and despair. Though his voice was quiet, almost gentle. 'How?' he said.

'One of them told us. One of his own squad. One of his close and familiar own—as always. As that or them or at least one among them for whom man sets in jeopardy what he believes to be his life and assumes to be his liberty or his honor, always does. His name was Polchek. He went on sick parade that Sunday midnight and we should have known about it inside an hour except that apparently a traitor too (by all means call him that if you like) had to outface regimental tape. So we might not have learned in time at all until too late, the division commander being himself already an hour before dawn in a forward observation post where he likewise had no business being, except for a lieutenant (a blatant and unregenerate eccentric whose career very probably ended there also since he held the sanctity of his native soil above that of his divisional channels; he will get a decoration of course but no more, the utmost venerability of his beard can only expose that same lieutenant's insigne) who rang directly through to, and insisted on speaking to someone in authority at, his Army Headquarters. That was how we knew, had even that little time to nullify, get in touch with the enemy and offer him too an alternate to chaos.'

'So I was right,' the other said. 'You were afraid.'

'I respect him as an articulated creature capable of locomotion and vulnerable to self-interest.'

'You were afraid,' the Quartermaster General said. 'Who with two armies which had already been beaten once and a third one not yet blooded to where it was a calculable quantity, had nevertheless managed to stalemate the most powerful and skillful and dedicated force in Europe, yet had had to call upon that enemy for help against the simple unified hope and dream of simple man. No, you are afraid. And so I am well to be. That's why I brought it back. There it lies. Touch it, put your hand on it. Or take my word for it that it's real, the same one, not defiled since the defilement was mine who shirked it in the middle of a battle, and a concomitant of your rank is the right and privilege to obliterate the human instrument of a failure.'

'But can you bring it back here? to me?' the old general said mildly.

'Why not? Weren't you the one who gave it to me?'

'But can you?' the old general said. 'Dare you? ask me to grant you a favor, let alone accept it from me. This favor,' the old general said in that gentle and almost inflectionless voice. 'A man is to die what the world will call the basest and most ignominious of deaths: execution for cowardice while defending his native—anyway adopted—land. That's what the ignorant world will call it, who will not know that he was murdered for that principle which, by your own bitter self-scoriation, you were incapable of risking death and honor for. Yet you dont demand that life. You demand instead merely to be relieved of a commission. A gesture. A martyrdom. Does it match his?'

'He wont accept that life!' the other cried. 'If he does——' and stopped, amazed, aghast, foreknowing and despaired while the gentle voice went on:

'If he does, if he accepts his life, keeps his life, he will have abrogated his own gesture and martyrdom. If I gave him his life tonight, I myself could render null and void what you call the hope and the dream of his sacrifice. By destroying his life tomorrow morning, I will establish forever that he didn't even live in vain, let alone die so. Now tell me who's afraid?'

Now the other began to turn, slowly, a little jerkily, as though he were blind, turning on until he faced the small door again and stopping not as though he saw it but as if he had located its position and direction by some other and lesser and less exact sense, like smell, the old general watching him until he had completely turned before he spoke:

'You've forgotten your paper.'

'Of course,' the other said. 'So I have.' He turned back, jerkily, blinking rapidly; his hand fumbled on the table top for a moment, then it found the folded paper and put it back inside the tunic, and he stood again, blinking rapidly. 'Yes,' he said. 'So I did.' Then he turned again, a little stiffly still but moving almost quickly now, directly anyhow, and went on across the blanched rug, toward the door; at once it opened and the aide entered, carrying the door with him and already turning into rigid attention, holding it while the Quartermaster General walked toward it, a little stiffly and awkwardly, too big too gaunt too alien, then stopped and half-turned his head and said: 'Goodbye.'

'Goodbye,' the old general said. The other went on, to the door now, almost into it, beginning to bow his head a little as though from long habit already too tall for most doors, stopping almost in the door now, his head still bowed a little even after he turned it not quite toward where the old general sat immobile and gaudy as a child's toy behind the untouched bowl and jug and the still uncrumbled bread.

'And something else,' the Quartermaster General said. 'To say. Something else——'

'With God,' the old general said.

'Of course,' the Quartermaster General said. 'That was it. I almost said it.'

† † †

The door clashed open, the sergeant with his slung rifle entered first, followed by a private carrying his unslung one, unbelievably long now with the fixed bayonet, like a hunter dodging through a gap in a fence. They took position one on either side of the door, the thirteen prisoners turning their thirteen heads as one to watch quietly while two more men carried in a long wooden bench-attached mess table and set it in the center of the cell and went back out.

'Going to fatten us up first, huh?' one of the prisoners said. The sergeant didn't answer; he was now working at his front teeth with a gold toothpick.

'If the next thing they bring is a tablecloth, the third will be a priest,' another prisoner said. But he was wrong, although the number of casseroles and pots and dishes (including a small caldron obviously soup) which did come next, followed by a third man carrying a whole basket of bottles and a jumble of utensils and cutlery, was almost as unnerving, the sergeant speaking now though still around, past the toothpick:

'Hold it now. At least let them get their hands and arms out of the way.' Though the prisoners had really not moved yet to rush upon the table, the food: it was merely a shift, semicircular, poised while the third orderly set the wine (there were seven bottles) on the table and then began to place the cups, vessels, whatever anyone wanted to call them—tin cups, pannikins from mess kits, two or three cracked tumblers, two flagons contrived by bisecting laterally one canteen.

'Dont apologise, garçon,' the wit said. 'Just so it's got a bottom at one end and a hole at the other.' Then the one who had brought the wine scuttled back to the door after the two others, and out of it; the private with the bayonet dodged his seven-foot-long implement through it again and turned, holding the door half closed for the sergeant.

'All right, you bastards,' the sergeant said. 'Be pigs.'

'Speak for yourself, *maître*,' the wit said. 'If we must dine in stink, we prefer it to be our own.' Then suddenly, in unpremeditated concert as though they had not even planned it or instigated it, they had not even been warned of it but instead had been overtaken from behind by it like wind, they had all turned on the sergeant, or perhaps not even the sergeant, the human guards, but just the rifles and the bayonets and the steel lockable door, not moving, rushing toward them but just yelling at them—a sound hoarse, loud, without language, not of threat or indictment either: just a hoarse concerted affirmation of invincible repudiation which continued for another moment or so even after the sergeant had passed through the door and it had clashed shut again. Then they stopped. Yet they still didn't rush at the table, still hovering, semicircular, almost diffidently, merely enclosing it, their noses trembling questing like those of rabbits at the odors from it, grimed, filthy, reeking still of the front lines and uncertainty and perhaps despair; unshaven, faces not alarming nor even embittered but harassed—faces of men who had already borne not only more than they expected but than they believed they could and who knew that it was still not over and—with a sort of amazement, even terror—that no matter how much more there would be, they would still bear that too.

'Come on, Corp,' a voice said. 'Let's go.'

'O.K.,' the corporal said. 'Watch it now.' But still there was no stampede, rush. It was just a crowding, a concentration, a jostling itself almost inattentive, not of famishment, hunger but rather of the watchful noncommittance of people still—so far at least—keeping pace with, holding their own still within the fringe of a fading fairy-tale, the cursing itself inattentive and impersonal, not eager: just pressed as they crowded in onto both the fixed benches, five on one side and six on the other facing them until the twelfth man dragged up the cell's one stool to the head of the table for the corporal and then himself took the remaining place at the foot end of the unfilled bench like the Vice to the Chair in a Dickensian tavern's back room—a squat powerful weathered man with the blue eyes and reddish hair and beard of a Breton fisherman, captain say of his own small tough and dauntless boat—laden doubtless with contraband. The corporal filled the bowls while they passed them hand to hand. But still there was no voracity. A leashed quality, but even, almost unimpatient as they sat holding each his upended unsoiled spoon like a boat-crew or a parade.

'This looks bad,' one said.

'It's worse,' another said. 'It's serious.'

'It's a reprieve,' a third said. 'Somebody besides a garage mechanic cooked this. So if they went to all that trouble——' a third began.

'Hold it,' the Breton said. The man opposite him was short and very dark, his jaw wrenched by an old healed wound. He was saying something rapidly in an almost unintelligible Mediterranean dialect—Midi or perhaps Basque. They looked at one another. Suddenly still another spoke. He looked like a scholar, almost like a professor.

'He wants someone to say grace,' he said.

The corporal looked at the Midian. 'Say it then.' Again the other said something rapid and incomprehensible. Again the one who resembled a scholar translated.

'He says he doesn't know one.'

'Does anybody know one?' the corporal said. Again they looked at one another. Then one said to the fourth one:

'You've been to school. Say one.'

'Maybe he went too fast and passed it,' another said.

'Say it then,' the corporal said to the fourth one. The other said rapidly:

'Benedictus. Benedicte. Benedictissimus. Will that do?'

'Will that do, Luluque?' the corporal said to the Midian.

'Yes yes,' the Midian said. They began to eat now. The Breton lifted one of the bottles slightly toward the corporal.

'Okay?' he said.

'Okay,' the corporal said. Six other hands took up the other bottles; they ate and poured and passed the bottles too.

'A reprieve,' the third said. 'They wouldn't dare execute us until we have finished eating this cooking. Our whole nation would rise at that insult to what we consider the first of the arts. How's this for an idea? We stagger this, eat one at a time, one man to each hour, thirteen hours; we'll still be alive at . . . almost noon tomorrow——'

'—when they'll serve us another meal,' another said, 'and we'll stagger that one into dinner and then stagger dinner on through tomorrow night——'

'—and in the end eat ourselves into old age when we cant eat anymore——'

'Let them shoot us then. Who cares?' the third said. 'No. That bastard sergeant will be in here with his firing squad right after the coffee. You watch.'

'Not that quick,' the first said. 'You have forgot what we consider the first of the virtues too. Thrift. They will wait until we have digested this and defecated it.'

'What will they want with that?' the fourth said.

'Fertiliser,' the first said. 'Imagine that corner, that garden-plot manured with the concentrate of this meal——'

'The manure of traitors,' the fourth said. He had the dreamy and furious face of a martyr.

'In that case, wouldn't the maize, the bean, the potato grow upside down, or anyway hide its head even if it couldn't bury it?' the second said.

'Stop it,' the corporal said.

'Or more than just the corner of a plot,' the third said. 'The carrion we'll bequeath France tomorrow——'

'Stop it!' the corporal said.

'Christ assoil us,' the fourth said.

'Aiyiyi,' the third said. 'We can call on him then. He need not fear cadavers.'

'Do you want me to make them shut up, Corp?' the Breton said.

'Come on now,' the corporal said. 'Eat. You'll spend the rest of the night wishing you did have something to clap your jaws on. Save the philosophy for then.'

'The wit too,' the third said.

'Then we will starve,' the first said.

'Or indigest,' the third said. 'If much of what we've heard tonight is wit.'

'Come on now,' the corporal said. 'I've told you twice. Do you want your bellies to say you've had enough, or that sergeant to come back in and say you've finished?' So they ate again, except the man on the corporal's left, who once more stopped his laden knife blade halfway to his mouth.

'Polchek's not eating,' he said suddenly. 'He's not even drinking. What's the matter, Polchek? Afraid yours wont produce anything but nettles and you wont make it to the latrine in time and we'll have to sleep in them?' The man addressed was on the corporal's immediate right. He had a knowing, almost handsome metropolitan or possibly *banlieu* face, bold but not at all arrogant, masked, composed, and only when you caught his eyes unawares did you realise how alert.

'A day of rest at Chaulnesmont wasn't the right pill for that belly of his maybe,' the first said.

'The sergeant-major's *coup de grâce* tomorrow morning will be though,' the fourth said.

'Maybe it'll cure all of you of having to run a fever over what I dont eat and drink,' Polchek said.

'What's the matter?' the corporal said to him. 'You went on sick parade Sunday night before we came out. Haven't you got over it yet?'

'So what?' Polchek said. 'Is it an issue? I had a bad belly Sunday night. I've still got it but it's still mine. I was just sitting here with it, not worrying half as much about what

I dont put in it, as some innocent bystanders do because I dont.'

'Do you want to make an issue of it?' the fourth said.

'Bang on the door,' the corporal said to the Breton. 'Tell the sergeant we want to report a sick man.'

'Who's making an issue of it now?' Polchek said to the corporal before the Breton could move. He picked up his filled glass. 'Come on,' he said to the corporal. 'No heel taps. If my belly dont like wine tonight, as Jean says that sergeant-major's pistol will pump it all out tomorrow morning.' He said to all of them: 'Come on. To peace. Haven't we finally got what we've all been working for for four years now? Come on, up with them!' he said, louder and sharply, with something momentary and almost fierce in his voice, face, look. At once the same excitement, restrained fierceness, seemed to pass through all of them; they raised their glasses too except one—the fourth one of the mountain faces, not quite as tall as the others and with something momentary and anguished in it almost like despair, who suddenly half raised his glass and stopped it and did not drink when the others did and banged the bizarre and incongruous vessels down and reached for the bottles again as, preceded by the sound of the heavy boots, the door clashed open again and the sergeant and his private entered; he now held an unfolded paper in his hand.

'Polchek,' he said. For a second Polchek didn't stir. Then the man who had not drunk gave a convulsive start and although he arrested it at once, when Polchek stood quietly up they both for a moment were in motion, so that the sergeant, about to address Polchek again, paused and looked from one to the other. 'Well?' the sergeant said. 'Which? Dont you even know who you are?' Nobody answered. As one the others except Polchek were looking at the man who had not drunk. 'You,' the sergeant said to the corporal. 'Dont you know your own men?'

'This is Polchek,' the corporal said, indicating Polchek.

'Then what's wrong with him?' the sergeant said. He said to the other man: 'What's your name?'

'I——' the man said; again he glanced rapidly about, at nothing, no one, anguished and despairing.

'His name is——' the corporal said. 'I've got his papers——'

He reached inside his tunic and produced a soiled dog-eared paper, obviously a regimental posting order. 'Pierre Bouc.' He rattled off a number.

'There's no Bouc on this list,' the sergeant said. 'What's he doing here?'

'You tell me,' the corporal said. 'He got mixed in with us somehow Monday morning. None of us know any Pierre Bouc either.'

'Why didn't he say something before this?'

'Who would have listened?' the corporal said.

'Is that right?' the sergeant said to the man. 'You dont belong in this squad?' The man didn't answer.

'Tell him,' the corporal said.

'No,' the man whispered. Then he said loudly: 'No!' He blundered up. 'I dont know them!' he said, blundering, stumbling, half-falling backward over the bench almost as though in flight until the sergeant checked him.

'The major will have to settle this,' the sergeant said. 'Give me that order.' The corporal passed it to him. 'Out with you,' the sergeant said. 'Both of you.' Now those inside the room could see beyond the door another file of armed men, apparently a new one, waiting. The two prisoners passed on through the door and into it, the sergeant then the orderly following; the iron door clashed behind them, against that room and all it contained, signified, portended; beyond it Polchek didn't even lower his voice:

'They promised me brandy. Where is it?'

'Shut up,' the sergeant's voice said. 'You'll get what's coming to you, no bloody fear.'

'I'd better,' Polcheck said. 'If I dont, I might know what to do about it.'

'I've told him once,' the sergeant's voice said. 'If he dont shut up this time, shut him up.'

'With pleasure, sergeant,' another voice said. 'Can do.'

'Take them on,' the sergeant's voice said. Though before the iron clash of the door had ceased the corporal was already speaking, not loud: just prompt, still mild, not peremptory: just firm:

'Eat.' The same man essayed to speak again but again the corporal forestalled him. 'Eat,' he said. 'Next time he will take it out.' But they were spared that. The door opened almost immediately, but this time it was only the sergeant, alone, the eleven heads which remained turning as one to look at him where he faced the corporal down the length of the littered table.

'You,' the sergeant said.

'Me?' the corporal said.

'Yes,' the sergeant said. Still the corporal didn't move. He said again:

'You mean me?'

'Yes,' the sergeant said. 'Come on.' The corporal rose then. He gave one rapid look about at the ten faces now turning from the sergeant to look at him—faces dirty, unshaven, strained, which had slept too little in too long, harassed, but absolute, one in whatever it was—not trust exactly, not dependence: perhaps just one-ness, singleness.

'You're in charge, Paul,' he said to the Breton.

'Right,' the Breton said. 'Till you get back.' But this time the corridor was empty; it was the sergeant himself who closed the door behind them and turned the heavy key and pocketed it. There was no one in sight at all where he—the corporal—had expected to find armed men bristling until they in the white glittering room in the *Hôtel de Ville* sent for them for the last time. Then the sergeant turned from the door and now he—the corporal—realised that they were even hurrying a little: not at all furtive nor even surreptitious: just expedite, walking rapidly back up the corridor which he had already traversed three times—once yesterday morning when the guards had brought them from the lorry to the cell, and twice last night when the guards had taken them to the *Hôtel de Ville* and brought them back, their—his and the sergeant's—heavy boots not ringing because (so recent the factory—when it had been a factory—was) these were not stone but brick, but making instead a dull and heavy sound seeming only the louder because there were only four now instead of twenty-six plus the guards. So to him it was as though there was no other way out of it save that one exit, no destination to go to in it except on, so that he had already begun to pass the small arch with its locked iron gate when the sergeant checked and turned him, nor any other life in or near it so that he didn't even recognise the silhouette of the helmet and the rifle until the man was in the act of unlocking the gate from the outside and swinging it back for them to pass through.

Nor did he see the car at once, the sergeant not quite touching him, just keeping him at that same pace, rapidity, as though by simple juxtaposition, on through the gate into an alley, a blank wall opposite and at the curb-edge the big dark motionless car which he had not noticed yet because of the silence—not the subterrene and cavernous emptiness in which their boots had echoed a moment back but a *cul-de-sac* of it, himself and the sergeant and the two sentries—the one who had unlocked the gate for them and then locked it after them, and his opposite flanking the other side of the gate—not even at parade rest but at ease, their rifles grounded, immobile and remote, as though oblivious to that to which they in their turn were invisible, the four of them set down in a vacuum of silence within the city's distant and indefatigable murmur. Then he saw the car. He didn't stop, it was barely a falter, the sergeant's shoulder barely nudged him before he went on. The driver didn't even move to descend; it was the sergeant who opened the door, the shoulder, a hand too now, firm and urgent against his back because he had stopped now, erect, immobile and immovable even after the voice inside the car said, 'Get in, my child;' then immovable for another second yet before he stooped and entered it, seeing as he did so the pallid glint of braid, a single plane of face above the dark enveloping cloak.

Then the sergeant shut the door, the car already in motion and that was all; only the three of them: the old man who bore far too much rank to carry a lethal weapon even if he were not already too old to use it, and the driver whose hands were full with managing the car even if he had not had his back to him who could not remember in four days anyhow when there had not been one arm or two but from twenty to a thousand already cocked and triggered for his life; out of the alley and still no word—direction or command—from the old man in the braided invincible hat and the night-colored cloak in the corner opposite him, not back to the city but skirting through the fringe of it, faster and faster, pacing its cavernous echoes through the narrow ways of the deserted purlieus, taking the rapid turnings as if the mechanism itself knew their destination, making a long concentric through the city's edge, the ground rising now so that even he began to know where they were probably going, the city itself beginning to tilt toward them as it sank away beneath; nor any word from the old man this time either: the car just stopped, and looking past the fine and delicate profile beneath what should have been the insuperable weight of the barred and braided hat, he could see not the *Place de Ville* itself, they were not that high above the city yet, but rather as though the concentration of its unwearyable and sleepless anxiety had taken on the glow and glare of light.

'Now, my child,' the old general said: not to him this time but to the driver. The car went on and now he did know where they were going because there was nothing else up here but the old Roman citadel. But if he felt any first shock of instinctive and purely physical terror, he didn't show it. And if at the same instant reason was also telling him, *Nonsense. To execute you secretly in a dungeon would undo the very thing which they stopped the war and brought all thirteen of you here to accomplish,* nobody heard that either: he just sat there, erect, a little stiffly who never had sat completely back in the seat, alert but quite calm, rapid watchful and composed, the car in second gear now but still going fast around the final convoluted hairpin turns until at last the stone weight of the citadel itself seemed to lean down and rest upon them like a ponderable shadow, the car making the last *renversement* because now it could go no further, stopping at last and not he nor the driver but the old general himself who opened the door and got out and held the door until he was out and erect again and had begun to turn his head to look until the old general said, 'No, not yet,' and turned on himself, he following, up the final steep and rocky pitch where they would have to walk, the old citadel not looming above them but squatting, not Gothic but Roman: not soaring to the stars out of the aspiration of man's past but a gesture against them of his mortality like a clenched fist or a shield.

'Now turn and look at it,' the old general said. But he already had, was—down the declivity's black pitch to where the city lay trembling and myriad with lights in its bowl of night like a scatter of smoldering autumn leaves in the windy darkness, thicker and denser than the stars in its concentration of anguish and unrepose, as if all of darkness and terror had poured down in one wash, one wave, to lie palpitant and unassuageable in the *Place de Ville*. 'Look at it. Listen to it. Remember it. A moment: then close the window on it. Disregard that anguish. You caused them to fear and suffer but tomorrow you will have discharged them of both and they will only hate you: once for the rage they owe you for giving them the terror, once for the gratitude they will owe you for taking it away, and once for the fact that you are beyond the range of either. So close the window on that, and be yourself discharged. Now look beyond it. The earth, or half of it, full half the earth as far as horizon bounds it. It is dark of course, but only dark from here; its darkness is only that anonymity which a man can close behind him like a curtain on his past, not even when he must in his desperation but when he will for his comfort and simple privacy. Of course he can go only in one direction in it now: west; only one hemisphere of it—the Western—is available to him now. But that is large enough for his privacy for a year because this condition will only last another year, then all earth will be free to him. They will ask for a formal meeting, for terms, sometime this winter; by next year we will even have what we will call peace—for a little while. Not we will request it: they will—the Germans, the best soldiers on earth today or in two thousand years for that matter since even the Romans could not conquer them—the one people out of all the earth who have a passion and dedication not even for glory but for war, who make war not even for conquest and aggrandisement but as an occupation, an avocation, and who will lose this one for that very reason: that they are the best soldiers on earth; not we French and British, who accept war only as a last gambit when everything else has failed, and even enter that final one with no confidence in it either; but they, the Germans, who have not receded one foot since they crossed the Belgian frontier almost four years ago and every decision since has been either nil or theirs and who will not stop now even though they themselves know that one more victory will destroy them; who will win perhaps two or even three more (the number will not matter) and then will have to surrender because the phenomenon of war is its hermaphroditism: the principles of victory and of defeat inhabit the same body and the necessary opponent, enemy, is merely the bed they self-exhaust each other on: a vice only the more terrible and fatal because there is no intervening breast or division between to frustrate them into health by simple normal distance and lack of opportunity for the copulation from which even orgasm cannot free them; the most expensive and fatal vice which man has invented yet, to which the normal ones of lechery and drink and gambling which man fatuously believes are capable of destroying him, stand as does the child's lollypop to the bottle the courtesan and the playing-card. A vice so long ingrained in man as to have become an honorable tenet of his behavior and the national altar for his love of bloodshed and glorious sacrifice. More than that even: a pillar not of his nation's supremacy but of his national survival; you and I have seen war as the last resort of politics; I shant of course but you will—can—see it become the last refuge from bankruptcy; you will—can, provided you will—see the day when a nation insolvent from overpopulation will declare war on whatever richest and most sentimental opponent it can persuade to defeat it quickest, in order to feed its people out of the conqueror's quartermaster stores. But that is not our problem today; and even if it were, by simply being in alliance with the ultimate victor, we—France and Britain—would find ourselves in the happy situation of gaining almost as much from our victory as the German will through his defeat. Our—call it mine if you like—problem is more immediate. There is the earth. You will have half of it now; by New Year's you will very probably have all of it, all the vast scope of it except this minuscule suppuration which men call Europe—and who knows? in time and with a little discretion and care, even that again if you like. Take my car—you can drive one, cant you?'

'Yes,' the corporal said. 'Go?'

'Now,' the old general said. 'Take my car. If you can drive at all, the pennon on its bonnet will carry you anywhere in Europe west of the German wire; if you can drive well, the engine beneath it will take you to the coast—Brest or

Marseilles either—in two days; I have papers ready to pass you aboard any ship you choose there and command its captain. Then South America—Asia—the Pacific islands; close that window fast; lock it forever on that aberrant and futile dream. No no,' he said quickly, 'dont for one second suspect me of that base misreading of your character—you who in five minutes Monday voided that war which the German himself, the best soldier in Europe, in almost four years has never quite nudged from stalemate. Of course you will have money, but only that balance exactly matched to freedom as the eagle or the bandit carry theirs. I dont bribe you with money. I give you liberty.'

'To desert them,' the corporal said.

'Desert whom? Look again.' His hand appeared in a brief rapid gesture toward the wan city unsleeping below them—a gesture not even contemptuous, not anything: just a flick, then gone, already vanished again within the midnight-colored cloak. 'Not them. Where have they been since Monday? Why with their bare hands, since they have enough of them, have they not torn down brick by brick the walls which far fewer hands than theirs sufficed to raise, or torn from its hinges that one door which only one hand sufficed to lock, and set all of you free who had essayed to die for them? Where are the two thousand nine hundred and eighty-seven others you had—or thought you had—at dawn Monday? Why, as soon as you were through the wire, didn't all of them cast down their arms too and simply follow you, if they too believed you were all weaponed and bucklered out of the arsenal of invulnerable human aspiration and hope and belief? why didn't even that mere three thousand then—they would have been enough—erase the bricks and wrench away that door, who believed in you for five minutes anyway enough to risk what you anyway knew you risked—the three thousand that is lacking the twelve who have been locked inside the same incommunicant bricks with you ever since. Where are they even? one of them, your own countryman, blood brother, kinsman probably since you were all blood kin at some time there—one Zsettlani who has denied you, and the other, whether Zsettlani or not or blood kin or not, at least was—or anyway had been accepted into—the brotherhood of your faith and hope—Polchek, who had already betrayed you by midnight Sunday. Do you see? You even have a substitute to your need as on that afternoon God produced the lamb which saved Isaac—if you could call Polchek a lamb. I will take Polchek tomorrow, execute him with rote and fanfare; you will not only have your revenge and discharge the vengeance of the rest of those three thousand whom he betrayed, you will repossess the opprobrium from all that voice down there which cannot even go to bed because of the frantic need to anathemise you. Give me Polchek, and take freedom.'

'There are still ten,' the corporal said.

'Let's try it. We will remain here; I will send the car back with orders to unlock and open that door and then for every man in that building to vanish from it, oblivious of all to which they themselves will be invisible—quietly unlock that door, unlock that gate, and vanish. How long before that ten will have denied you too—betrayed you too, if you can call that choice betrayal?'

'And you see too,' the corporal said. 'In ten minutes there would not be ten but a hundred. In ten hours there would not be ten hundred but ten thousand. And in ten days——'

'Yes,' the old general said. 'I have seen that. Have I not said I dont so basely misread your character? oh yes, let us say it: your threat. Why else have I offered to buy my—our—security with things which most men not only do not want but on the contrary do well to fear and flee from, like liberty and freedom? Oh yes, I can destroy you tomorrow morning and save us—for the time. For the length of my life, in fact. But only for the time. And if I must, I will. Because I believe in man within his capacities and limitations. I not only believe he is capable of enduring and will endure, but that he must endure, at least until he himself invents evolves produces a better tool than he to substitute for himself. Take my car and freedom, and I will give you Polchek. Take the highest of all the ecstasies: compassion, pity: the orgasm of forgiving him who barely escaped doing you a mortal hurt—that glue, that catalyst which your philosophers have trained you to believe holds the earth together. Take the earth.'

'There are still ten,' the corporal said.

'Have I forgotten them?' the old general said. 'Have I not said twice that I have never misread you? You dont need to threaten me; I know that they, not you, are the problem; not you but they are what we are bargaining for. Because for your profit, I must destroy all eleven of you and so compound tenfold the value of your threat and sacrifice. For my profit, I must let them go too, to be witnesses to all the earth that you forsook them; for, talk as much and as loudly and as long as they will, who to believe in the value—value? validity—of the faith they preach when you, its prophet and instigator, elected your liberty to its martyrdom? No no, we are not two Greek or Armenian or Jewish—or for that matter, Norman—peasants swapping a horse: we are two articulations self-elected possibly, anyway elected, anyway postulated, not so much to defend as to test two inimical conditions which, through no fault of ours but through the simple paucity and restrictions of the arena where they meet, must contend and—one of them—perish: I champion of this mundane earth which, whether I like it or not, is, and to which I did not ask to come, yet since I am here, not only must stop but intend to stop during my allotted while; you champion of an esoteric realm of man's baseless hopes and his infinite capacity—no: passion—for unfact. No, they are not inimical really, there is no contest actually; they can even exist side by side together in this one restricted arena, and could and would, had yours not interfered with mine. So once more: take the earth. Now, answer as I know you will: There are still ten.'

'There are still that ten,' the corporal said.

'Then take the world,' the old general said. 'I will acknowledge you as my son; together we will close the window on this aberration and lock it forever. Then I will open another for you on a world such as caesar nor sultan nor khalif ever saw, Tiberius nor Kubla nor all the emperors of the East ever dreamed of—no Rome and Baiae: mere depot for the rapine of ravagers and bagnio for one last exhaustion of the nerve-ends before returning to their gloomy deserts to wrest more of the one or face at home the hired knives of their immediate underlings thirsting to cure them of the need for both; no Cathay: chimaera of poets bearing the same relation to the reality of attainment as the Mahometan's paradise—a symbol of his escape and a justification of its need, from the stinking alleys or fierce sand of his inescapable cradle; nor Kubla's Xanadu which was not even a poet's rounded and completed dream but a drug-sodden English one's lightning-bolt which electrocuted him with the splendor he could not even face long enough to describe it down;—none of these which were but random and momentary constellations in the empyrean of the world's history; but Paris, which is the world as empyrean is the sum of its constellations,—not that Paris in which any man can have all of these—Rome Cathay and Xanadu—provided he is connected a little and does not need to count his money, because you do not want these: have I not said twice now that I have not misread you? but that Paris which only my son can inherit from me—that Paris which I did not at all reject at seventeen but simply held in abeyance for compounding against the day when I should be a father to bequeath it to an heir worthy of that vast and that terrible heritage. A fate, a destiny in it: mine and yours, one and inextricable. Power, matchless and immeasurable; oh no, I have not misread you:—I, already born heir to that power as it stood then, holding that inheritance in escrow to become unchallenged and unchallengeable chief of that confederation which would defeat and subjugate and so destroy the only factor on earth which threatened it; you with the power and gift to persuade three thousand men to accept a sure and immediate death in preference to a problematical one based on tried mathematical percentage, when you had at most only a division of fifteen thousand to work on and your empty hands to work with. What can you not—will you not—do with all the world to work on and the heritage I can give you to work with. A king, an emperor, retaining his light and untensile hold on mankind only until another appears capable of giving them more and bloodier circuses and more and sweeter bread? Bah. You will be God, holding him forever through a far, far stronger ingredient than his simple lusts and appetites: by his triumphant and ineradicable folly, his deathless passion for being led, mystified, and deceived.'

'So we ally—confederate,' the corporal said. 'Are you that afraid of me?'

'I already respect you; I dont need to fear you. I can do without you. I shall; I intend to. Of course, in that case you will not see it—and how sad that commentary: that one last bitterest pill of martyrdom, without which the martyrdom itself could not be since then it would not be martyrdom: even if by some incredible if you shall have been right, you will not even know it—and paradox: only the act of voluntarily relinquishing the privilege of ever knowing you were right, can possibly make you right.—I know, dont say it: if I can do without you, then so can you yourself; to me, your death is but an ace to be finessed, while to you it is the actual ace of trumps. Nor this either: I mentioned the word bribe once; now I have offered it: I am an old man, you a young one; I will be dead in a few years and you can use your inheritance to win the trick tomorrow which today my deuce finessed you of. Because I will take that risk too. Dont even say——' and stopped and raised the hand quickly this time from inside the cloak and said: 'Wait. Dont say it yet.—Then take life. And think well before you answer that. Because the purse is empty now; only one thing else remains in it. Take life. You are young; even after four years of war, the young can still believe in their own invulnerability: that all else may die, but not they. So they dont need to treasure life too highly since they cannot conceive, accept, the possible end of it. But in time you become old, you see death then. Then you realise that nothing—nothing—nothing—not power nor glory nor wealth nor pleasure nor even freedom from pain, is as valuable as simple breathing, simply being alive even with all the regret of having to remember and the anguish of an irreparable wornout body; merely knowing that you are alive—Listen to this. It happened in America, at a remote place called by an Indian name I think: Mississippi: a man who had committed a brutal murder for some base reason—gain or revenge perhaps or perhaps simply to free himself of one woman in order to espouse another; it doesn't matter—who went to his trial still crying his innocence and was convicted and sentenced still crying it and even in the death cell beneath the gallows still crying it, until a priest came to him; not the first time of course nor the second nor perhaps even the third, but presently and in time: the murderer at last confessing his crime against man and so making his peace with God, until presently it was almost as though the murderer and the priest had exchanged places and offices: not the priest now but the murderer the strong one, the calm one, the strong calm steadfast rock not even of tremulous hope but of conviction and unshakable faith, on which the priest himself could now lean for strength and courage; this right up to the very morning of the execution, toward which the murderer now looked with a sort of impatience almost, as though actually fretting a little for the moment when he could doff the sorry ephemeral world which had brought him to this and demanded this expiation and accepted his forgiveness; right up to the gallows itself: which at Mississippi I understand is out-of-doors in the yard of the jail, enclosed temporarily in a high stockade of planks to shield the principal's departure from earth from the merely morbid and curious anyway; though they would come: in their carts and carriages for miles, bringing box lunches: men women children and grandparents, to stand along the tall fence until the bell, clock, whatever it was to mark the passing of the soul, struck and released them to go back home; indeed, able to see even less than the man who stood beneath the noose, already free this whole week now of that sorry and mortal body which was the sorry all which penance could rob him of, standing calm composed and at peace, the trivial noose already fitted to his neck and in his vision one last segment of the sky beyond which his theology had taught him he would presently be translated, and one single branch of an adjacent tree extending over the stockade as though in benison, one last gesture of earth's absolution, with which he had long since severed any frail remaining thread; when suddenly a bird flew onto that bough and stopped and opened its tiny throat and sang—whereupon he who less than a second before had his very foot lifted to step from earth's grief and anguish into eternal peace, cast away heaven, salvation, immortal soul and all, struggling to free his bound hands in order to snatch away the noose, crying, 'Innocent! Innocent! I didn't do it!' even as the trap earth, world and all, fell from under him—all because of one bird, one weightless and ephemeral creature which hawk might stoop at or snare or lime or random pellet of some idle boy destroy before the sun set—except that tomorrow, next year, there would be another bird, another spring, the same bough leafed again and another bird to sing on it, if he is only here to hear it, can only remain—Do you follow me?'

'Yes,' the corporal said.

'Then take that bird. Recant, confess, say you were wrong; that what you led was—led? you led nothing: you simply participated—an attack which failed to advance. Take life from me; ask mercy and accept it. I can give it, even for a military failure. The general commanding your division will—he already has—demand a sacrifice, not in the name of France or of victory, but in that of his blemished record. But it's not he, it's I who wear this hat.'

'There are still ten,' the corporal said.

'Who will hate you—until they forget you. Who will even curse you until they have forgot whom they cursed, and why. No no: close the window upon that baseless dream. Open this other one; perhaps you will—can—see nothing but gray beyond it—except for that bough, always; that one single bough which will be there always waiting and ready for that weightless and ephemeral burden. Take that bird.'

'Dont be afraid,' the corporal said. 'There's nothing to be afraid of. Nothing worth it.'

For a moment the old general didn't seem to have heard the corporal at all, standing a head below the other's high mountain one, beneath the seemingly insuperable weight of the blue-and-scarlet hat cross-barred and dappled with gold braid and heavy golden leaves. Then he said, 'Afraid? No no, it's not I but you who are afraid of man; not I but you who believe that nothing but a death can save him. I know better. I know that he has that in him which will enable him to outlast even his wars; that in him more durable than all his vices, even that last and most fearsome one; to outlast even this next avatar of his servitude which he now faces: his enslavement to the demonic progeny of his own mechanical curiosity, from which he will emancipate himself by that one ancient tried and true method by which slaves have always freed themselves: by inculcating their masters with the slaves' own vices—in this case the vice of war and that other one which is no vice at all but instead is the quality-mark and warrant of man's immortality: his invincible and deathless folly. He has already begun to put wheels under his patio his terrace and his front veranda; even at my age I may see the day when what was once his house has become a storage-place for his bed and stove and razor and spare clothing; you with your youth could (remember that bird) see the day when he will have invented his own private climate and moved it stove bathroom bed clothing kitchen and all into his automobile and what he once called home will have vanished from human lexicon: so that he wont dismount from his automobile at all because he wont need to: the entire earth one unbroken machined de-mountained dis-rivered expanse of concrete paving protuberanceless by tree or bush or house or anything which might constitute a corner or a threat to visibility, and man in his terrapin myriads enclosed clothesless from birth in his individual wheeled and glovelike envelope, with pipes and hoses leading upward from underground reservoirs to charge him with one composite squirt which at one mutual instant will fuel his mobility, pander his lusts, sate his appetites and fire his dreams; peripatetic, unceasing and long since no longer countable, to die at last at the click of an automatic circuit-breaker on a speedometer dial, and, long since freed of bone and organ and gut, leaving nothing for communal scavenging but a rusting and odorless shell—the shell which he does not get out of because he does not need to but which presently for a time he will not emerge from because he does not dare because the shell will be his only protection from the hail-like iron refuse from his wars. Because by that time his wars will have dispossessed him by simple out-distance; his simple frail physique will be no longer able to keep up, bear them, attend them, be present. He will try of course and for a little while he will even hold his own; he will build tanks bigger and faster and more impervious and with more firepower than any before, he will build aircraft bigger and faster and capable of more load and more destruction than any yet; for a little while he will accompany, direct, as he thinks control them, even after he has finally realised that it is not another frail and mortal dissident to his politics or his notions of national boundaries that he is contending with, but the very monster itself which he inhabits. It will not be someone firing bullets at him who for the moment doesn't like him. It will be his own frankenstein which roasts him alive with heat, asphyxiates him with speed, wrenches loose his still living-entrails in the ferocity of its prey-seeking stoop. So he will not be able to go along with it at all, though for a little while longer it will permit him the harmless delusion that he controls it from the ground with buttons. Then that will be gone too; years, decades then centuries will have elapsed since it last answered his voice; he will have even forgotten the very location of its breeding-grounds and his last contact with it will be a day when he will crawl shivering out of his cooling burrow to crouch among the delicate stalks of his dead antennae like a fairy geometry, beneath a clangorous rain of dials and meters and switches and bloodless fragments of metal epidermis, to watch the final two of them engaged in the last gigantic wrestling against the final and dying sky robbed even of darkness and filled with the inflectionless uproar of the two mechanical voices bellowing at each other polysyllabic and verbless patriotic nonsense. Oh yes, he will survive it because he has that in him which will endure even beyond the ultimate worthless tideless rock freezing slowly in the last red and heatless sunset, because already the next star in the blue immensity of space will be already clamorous with the uproar of his debarkation, his puny and inexhaustible and immortal voice still talking, still planning; and there too after the last ding dong of doom has rung and died there will still be one sound more: his voice, planning still to build something higher and faster and louder; more efficient and louder and faster than ever before, yet it too inherent with the same old primordial fault since it too in the end will fail to eradicate him from the earth. I dont fear man. I do better: I respect and admire him. And pride: I am ten times prouder of that immortality which he does possess than ever he of that heavenly one of his delusion. Because man and his folly—'

'Will endure,' the corporal said.

'They will do more,' the old general said proudly. 'They will prevail.—Shall we return?' They went back to the waiting car and descended; they traversed once more the echoing and empty warrens concentric about the distant crowded *Place de Ville*. Then the alley again, the car slowing and stopping once more opposite the small locked gate in front of which, above a struggling group of five men the bayoneted rifles of four of them waved and jerked like furious exclamations. The corporal looked once at the struggling group and said quietly:

'There are eleven now.'

'There are eleven now,' the old general said as quietly; again one arresting gesture of the fine and delicate hand from beneath the cloak. 'Wait. Let us watch this a moment: a man freed of it, now apparently trying to fight his way back into what for all he knows will be his death cell.' So they sat for a moment yet, watching the fifth man (the same one who two hours ago had been taken from the cell by the same guards who came for Polchek) straining stocky and furious in the hands of his four captors apparently not away from the small gate but toward it, until the old general got out of the car, the corporal following, and said, not raising his voice yet either:

'What's wrong here, Sergeant?' The group paused in their straining attitudes. The prisoner looked back then he wrenched free and turned and ran across the pavement toward the old general and the corporal, the four captors following, grasping him again.

'Stand still, you!' the sergeant hissed. 'Attention! His name is Pierre Bouc. He didn't belong in that squad at all, though we didn't discover the mistake until one of them—' he glanced at the corporal '—you—condescended to produce his regimental order. We found him trying to get back in. He denied his name; he wouldn't even produce the order until we took it away from him.' Holding the short and furious man with one hand, he produced the dog-eared paper from his pocket. Immediately the prisoner snatched it from him.

'You lie!' he said to the sergeant. Before they could prevent him he ripped the order to shreds and whirled and flung the shreds in the old general's face. 'You lie!' he shouted at the old general while the bursting gout drifted like a confetti of windless and weightless snow or feathers about the golden and invincible hat, the calm incurious inscrutable face which had looked at everything and believed none of it. 'You lie!' the man shouted again. 'My name is not Pierre Bouc. I am

Piotr—' adding something in a harsh almost musical middle-eastern tongue so full of consonants as to be almost unintelligible. Then he turned to the corporal, going rapidly onto his knees, grasping the corporal's hand and saying something else in the incomprehensible tongue, to which the corporal answered in it though the man still crouched, clinging to the corporal's hand, the corporal speaking again in the tongue, as if he had repeated himself but with a different object, noun perhaps, and then a third time, a third slight alteration in its construction or context or direction, at which the man moved, rose and stood now rigid at attention facing the corporal, who spoke again, and the man turned, a smart military quarter-turn, the four captors moving quickly in again until the corporal said in French:

'You dont need to hold him. Just unlock the gate.' But still the old general didn't move, motionless within the cloak's dark volume, composed, calm, not even bemused: just inscrutable, saying presently in that voice not even recapitulant: not anything:

' "Forgive me, I didn't know what I was doing". And you said, "Be a man", but no move. Then you said "Be a Zsettlani" and no move. Then you said "Be a soldier" and he became one.' Then he turned and got back into the car, the soft voluminous smother of the coat becoming motionless again about him in the corner of the seat; the sergeant came rapidly back across the pavement and stood again just behind the corporal's shoulder; now the old general himself spoke in the rapid unvoweled tongue:

'And became one. No: returned to one. Good night, my child.'

'Goodbye, Father,' the corporal answered him.

'Not goodbye,' the old general said. 'I am durable too; I dont give up easily either. Remember whose blood it is that you defy me with.' Then in French to the driver: 'Let us go home now.' The car went on. Then he and the sergeant turned together, the sergeant once more at and just behind his shoulder, not touching him, back to the iron gate which one of the sentries held open for them to pass through and then closed and locked. Again, so grooved and locked in old assumption, he had begun to turn down the corridor toward the cell when the sergeant once more checked and turned him, this time into a passage only wide enough for one and barely tall enough for any—a one-way secret duct leading as though into the very bowels of incarceration; the sergeant unlocked a solid door this time and closed it between himself and the corporal upon a cell indeed this time, little larger than a big closet containing one endless man-width wooden bench for sleeping and an iron bucket for latrine and two men, all bathed in one fierce glare of light. One of them did have the swaggering face this time, reckless and sardonic, incorrigible and debonair, even to the thin moustache; he even wore the filthy beret and the knotted handkerchief about his throat, even the limp dead cigarette in the corner of his mouth, his hands in his pockets and one foot crossed negligently over the other as he had leaned against the wall of his narrow Montmartre alley, the other shorter man standing beside him with the peaceful and patient fidelity of a blind dog—a squat simian-like man whose tremendous empty and peaceful hands hung almost to his knees as if they were attached to strings inside his sleeves, with a small quite round simian head and a doughy face itself like one single feature, drooling a little at the mouth.

'Pray to enter,' the first said. 'So they tapped you for it, did they? Call me Lapin; anybody in the *Prêfecture* will validate it.' Without removing his hand from the pocket, he indicated the man beside him with a nudge of his elbow. 'This is Cassetête—Horse for short. We're on our way to town, hey, Horse?' The second man made a single hoarse indistinguishable sound. 'Hear that?' the first said. 'He can say "Paris" as good as anybody. Tell him again, Uncle—where we're going tomorrow.' Again the other made the thick wet sound. It was quite true; the corporal could recognise it now.

'What's he doing in that uniform?' the corporal said.

'Ah, the sons of bitches scared him,' the first said. 'I dont mean Germans either. You dont mean they are going to be satisfied to shoot just one of you out of that whole regiment.'

'I dont know,' the corporal said. 'He hasn't always been like this?'

'Got a fag?' the other said. 'I'm out.' The corporal produced a pack of cigarettes. The other spat the stub from his mouth without even moving his head, and took one from the pack. 'Thanks.' The corporal produced a lighter. 'Thanks,' the other said. He took the lighter and snapped it on and lit the cigarette, already—or still—talking, the cigarette bobbing, his arms now crossed in front of him, each hand grasping lightly the opposite elbow. 'What was that you said? Has he always been like this? Naah. A few flies upstairs, but he was all right until—What?' The corporal stood facing him, his hand extended.

'The lighter,' the corporal said.

'I beg pardon?'

'My lighter,' the corporal said. They looked at one another. Lapin made a slight motion with his wrists and up-turned his empty palms. The corporal faced him, his hand extended.

'Jesus,' the other said. 'Dont break my heart. Dont tell me you even saw what I did with it. If you did, then they are right; they just waited one day too late.' He made another rapid movement with one hand; when it opened again, the lighter was in it. The corporal took it.

'Beats hell, dont it?' the other said. 'A man aint even the sum of his vices: just his habits. Here we are, after tomorrow morning neither one of us will have any use for it and until then it wont matter which one of us has it. Yet you've got to have it back just because you are in the habit of owning it, and I have to try to cop it just because that's one of my natural habits too. Maybe that's what all the bother and trouble they're getting ready to go to tomorrow morning is for—parading a whole garrison just to cure three lousy bastards of the bad habit of breathing. Hey, Horse?' he said to the second man.

'Paris,' the second man said hoarsely.

'You bet,' the other said. 'That's the one they're going to cure us of tomorrow: the bad habit of not getting to Paris after working for four years at it. We'll make it this time though; the corporal here is going with us to see that we do.'

'What did he do?' the corporal said.

'That's all right,' the other said. 'Say we. Murder. It was the old dame's fault; all she had to do was just tell us where the money was hidden and then behave herself, keep her mouth shut. Instead she had to lay there in the bed yelling her head off until we had to choke her or we never would have got to Paris——'

'Paris,' the second said in his wet hoarse voice.

'Because that's all we wanted,' the other said. 'All he was trying to do: we were trying to do: just to get to Paris. Only folks kept on steering him wrong, sending him off in the wrong direction, sicking the dogs on him, cops always saying Move on, move on—you know how it is. So when we threw in together that day—that was at Clermont Ferrand in '14—we didn't know how long he had been on the road because we didn't know how old he was. Except that it had been a good while, he hadn't been nothing but a kid then— You found out you were going to have to go to Paris before you even found out you were going to have to have a woman, hey, Horse?'

'Paris,' the second said hoarsely.

'—working a little whenever he could find it, sleeping in stables and hedgerows until they would set the dogs or the police on him again, telling him to move on without even bothering to tell him which way he wanted to go until you would have thought nobody else in France ever heard of Paris, let alone wanted—had—to go there. Hey, Horse?'

'Paris,' the second said hoarsely.

'Then we run into one another that day in Clermont and decided to throw in together and then it was all right, there was a war on then and all you had to do was get yourself inside a government blue suit and you were free of cops and civilians and the whole human race; all you needed was just to know who to salute and do it quick enough. So we took a bottle of brandy to a sergeant I knew——'

'The human race?' the corporal said.

'Sure,' the other said. 'You might not think it to look at him, but he can move in the dark as quiet as a ghost and even see in it like a cat; turn this light off for a second and he will have that lighter out of your pocket and you wont even know it—— So he was in too now——'

'He learned that fast?' the corporal said.

'Of course we had to be a little careful about his hands. He never meant nothing, see: he just didn't know himself how strong they were, like that night last month.'

'So you got along fine then,' the corporal said.

'It was duck soup.—So he was in too now and now he could even ride sometimes, with the government paying for it, getting closer and closer to Paris now; not much over a year and we were all the way up to Verdun, that any boche will tell you is right next door to Paris——'

'And still doing all right,' the corporal said.

'Why not? If you cant trust your money to a bank in peacetime, where else can you put it in a war except up the chimney or under the mattress or inside the clock? Or anywhere else you thought it was hidden for that matter because it didn't matter to us; Horse here has a nose for a ten-franc note like a pig for a truffle. Until that night last month and that was the old dame's fault; all she needed to do was tell us where it was and then lay quiet and keep her mouth shut but that didn't suit her, she had to lay there in the bed hollering her head off until Horse here had to shut her up—you know: no harm intended: just to squeeze her throat a little until we could have a little peace and quiet to hunt for it in. Only we forgot about the hands, and when I got back——'

'Got back?' the corporal said.

'I was downstairs hunting for the money.—got back, it was too late. So they caught us. And you'd have thought that would have satisfied them, especially as they even got the money back——'

'You found the money?' the corporal said.

'Sure. While he was keeping her quiet.—But no, that wasn't enough——'

'You found the money and had got away with it, and then turned around and came back?'

'What?' the other said.

'Why did you change your mind?' the corporal said. After a second the other said:

'Fag me again.' The corporal gave him another cigarette. 'Thanks,' he said. The corporal extended the lighter. 'Thanks,' the other said. He snapped it and lit the cigarette and snuffed the lighter; again his two hands began the rapid and involuted gesture then stopped and in the same motion one of the hands tossed the lighter back to the corporal, the arms crossed again, palms to opposite elbows, the cigarette bobbing while he talked. 'Where was I? oh yes.—But that didn't suit them; just to take us out in a decent and peaceful way and shoot us wasn't enough; they had to take Horse here off in a cellar somewhere and scare the daylights out of him. Justice, see? Protecting our rights. Just catching us wasn't enough; we got to insist we did it. Just me saying so wasn't enough; Horse too has got to holler it to high heaven—whatever that means. But it's all right now. They cant stop us now.' He turned and clapped the second man a hard quick blow on the back: 'Paris tomorrow morning, kid. Fasten on to that.'

The door opened. It was the same sergeant again. He did not enter, saying to the corporal: 'Once more' and then stood and held the door until the corporal had passed him. Then he closed and locked it. This time it was the office of the prison commandant himself and what he—the corporal—assumed to be just another N.C.O. until he saw, arranged on the cleared desk, the utensils for the Last Sacrament—urn ewer stole candles and crucifix—and only then remarked the small embroidered cross on the coat of the man standing beside them, the other sergeant closing that door too between them so that he and the priest were alone, the priest lifting his hand to inscribe into the invisible air the invisible Passion while the corporal paused for a moment just inside the door, not surprised yet either: just once more alert, looking at him: at which moment a third person in the room would have remarked that they were almost of an age.

'Come in, my son,' the priest said.

'Good evening, Sergeant,' the corporal said.

'Cant you say Father?' the priest said.

'Of course,' the corporal said.

'Then say it,' the priest said.

'Of course, Father,' the corporal said. He came on into the room, looking quietly and rapidly again at the sacred implements on the desk while the priest watched him.

'Not that,' the priest said. 'Not yet. I came to offer you life.'

'So he sent you,' the corporal said.

'He?' the priest said. 'What he can you mean, except the Giver of all life? Why should He send me here to offer you what He has already entrusted you with? Because the man you imply, for all his rank and power, can only take it from you. Your life was never his to give you because for all his stars and braid he too before God is just one more pinch of rotten and ephemeral dust. It was neither of them which sent me here: not the One who has already given you life, nor the other who never had yours nor any other life within his gift. It was duty which sent me here. Not this—' for an instant his hand touched the small embroidered cross on his collar '—not my cloth, but my belief in Him; not even as His mouthpiece but as a man——'

'A French man?' the corporal said.

'All right,' the priest said. 'Yes, a Frenchman if you like. —commanded me here to command—not ask, offer: command—you to keep the life which you never had and never will have the refusal of, to save another one.'

'To save another one?' the corporal said.

'The commander of your regiment's division,' the priest said. 'He will die too, for what all the world he knows—the only world he does know because it was the one he dedicated his life to—will call his failure, where you will die for what you anyway will call a victory.'

'So he did send you,' the corporal said. 'For blackmail.'

'Beware,' the priest said.

'Then dont tell me this,' the corporal said. 'Tell him. If I can save Gragnon's life only by not doing something you tell me I already cant and never could do anyway. Tell him then. I dont want to die either.'

'Beware,' the priest said.

'That wasn't who I meant,' the corporal said. 'I meant——'

'I know whom you meant,' the priest said. 'That's why I said Beware. Beware Whom you mock by reading your own mortal's pride into Him Who died two thousand years ago in the postulate that man shall never never never, need never never never, hold suzerainty over another's life and death—absolved you and the man you mean both of that terrible burden: you of the right to and he of the need for, suzerainty over your life; absolved poor mortal man forever of the fear of the oppression, and the anguish of the responsibility, which suzerainty over human fate and destiny would have entailed on him and cursed him with, when He refused in man's name the temptation of that mastery, refused the terrible temptation of that limitless and curbless power when He answered the Tempter: *Render unto caesar the things which are caesar's.*—I know,' he said quickly, before the corporal could have spoken: 'To Chaulnesmont the things which are Chaulnesmont's. Oh yes, you're right; I'm a Frenchman first. And so now you can even cite the record at me, cant you? All right. Do it.'

'The record?' the corporal said.

'The Book,' the priest said. The corporal looked at him. 'You mean you dont even know it?'

'I cant read,' the corporal said.

'Then I'll cite for you, plead for you,' the priest said. 'It wasn't He with His humility and pity and sacrifice that converted the world, it was pagan and bloody Rome which did it with His martyrdom; furious and intractable dreamers had been bringing that same dream out of Asia Minor for three hundred years until at last one found a caesar foolish enough to crucify him. And you are right. But then so is he (I dont mean Him now, I mean the old man in that white room yonder onto whose shoulders you are trying to slough and shirk your right and duty for free will and decision). Because only Rome could have done it, accomplished it, and even He (I do mean Him now) knew it, felt and sensed this, furious and intractable dreamer though He was. Because He even said it Himself: *On this rock I found My church,* even while He didn't—and never would—realise the true significance of what He was saying, believing still that He was speaking poetic metaphor, synonym, parable—that *rock* meant unstable inconstant heart, and *church* meant airy faith. It wasn't even His first and favorite sycophant who read that significance, who was also ignorant and intractable like Him and even in the end got himself also electrocuted by the dream's intractable fire, like Him. It was Paul, who was a Roman first and then a man and only then a dreamer and so of all of them was able to read the dream correctly and to realise that, to endure, it could not be a nebulous and airy faith but instead it must be a *church*, an *establishment*, a morality of behavior inside which man could exercise his right and duty for free will and decision, not for a reward resembling the bed-time tale which soothes the child into darkness, but the reward of being able to cope peacefully, hold his own, with the hard durable world in which (whether he would ever know why or not wouldn't matter either because now he could cope with that too) he found himself. Not *snared* in that frail web of hopes and fears and aspirations which man calls his heart, but *fixed*, *established*, to endure, on that *rock* whose synonym was the seeded capital of that hard durable enduring earth which man must cope with somehow, by some means, or perish. So you see, he is right. It wasn't He nor Peter, but Paul who, being only one-third dreamer, was two-thirds man and half of that a Roman, could cope with Rome. Who did more; who, rendering unto caesar, conquered Rome. More: destroyed it, because where is that Rome now? until what remains but that *rock*, that citadel. Render unto Chaulnesmont. Why should you die?'

'Tell him that,' the corporal said.

'To save another life, which your dream will electrocute,' the priest said.

'Tell him that,' the corporal said.

'Remember—' the priest said. 'No, you cant remember, you dont know it, you cant read. So I'll have to be both again: defender and advocate. *Change these stones to bread, and all men will follow Thee*. And He answered, *Man cannot live by bread alone*. Because He knew that too, intractable and furious dreamer though He was: that He was tempted to tempt and lead man not with the *bread*, but with the *miracle* of that bread, the deception, the illusion, the delusion of that bread; tempted to believe that man was not only capable and willing but even eager for that deception, that even when the illusion of that miracle had led him to the point where the bread would revert once more to stone in his very belly and destroy him, his own children would be panting for the opportunity to grasp into their hands in their turn the delusion of that miracle which would destroy them. No no, listen to Paul, who needed no miracle, required no martyrdom. Save that life. *Thou shalt not kill*.'

'Tell him that,' the corporal said.

'Take your own tomorrow, if you must,' the priest said. 'But save his now.'

'Tell him that,' the corporal said.

'Power,' the priest said. 'Not just power over the mere earth offered by that temptation of simple miracle, but that more terrible one over the universe itself—that terrible power over the whole universe which that mastery over man's mortal fate and destiny would have given Him had He not cast back into the Temptor's very teeth that third and most terrible temptation of immortality: which if He had faltered or succumbed would have destroyed His Father's kingdom not only on the earth but in heaven too because that would have destroyed heaven since what value in the scale of man's hope and aspiration or what tensile hold or claim on man himself could that heaven own which could be gained by that base means—blackmail: man in his turn by no more warrant than one single precedent casting himself from the nearest precipice the moment he wearied of the burden of his free will and decision, the right to the one and the duty of the other, saying to, challenging his Creator: *Let me fall—if You dare*?'

'Tell him that,' the corporal said.

'Save that other life. Grant that the right of free will is in your own death. But your duty to choose is not yours. It's his. It's General Gragnon's death.'

'Tell him that,' the corporal said. They looked at one another. Then the priest seemed to make a terrible faint and convulsive effort, whether to speak or not to speak was still not clear even when he said, like a sort of gesture, a valedictory not to defeat nor despair nor even desperation, but as though to abnegation itself:

'Remember that bird.'

'So he did send you here,' the corporal said.

'Yes,' the priest said. 'He sent for me. To render unto caesar—' He said: 'But he came back.'

'Came back?' the corporal said. 'He?'

'The one who denied you,' the priest said. 'That turned his back on you. Freed himself of you. But he came back. And now there are eleven of them again.' He moved until he was facing the corporal. 'Save me too,' he said. Then he was on his knees before the corporal, his hands clasped fist into fist at his breast. 'Save me,' he said.

'Get up, Father,' the corporal said.

'No,' the priest said. He fumbled a moment inside the

breast of his coat and produced his prayer-book, dog-eared and stained too from the front lines; it seemed to open automatically on the narrow purple ribbon of its marker as the priest reversed it and extended it upward. 'Read it to me then,' he said. The corporal took the book.

'What?' he said.

'The office for the dying,' the priest said. 'But you cant read, can you?' he said. He took the book back and now clasped it closed between his hands at his breast, his head bowed still. 'Save me then,' he said.

'Get up,' the corporal said, reaching down to grasp the priest's arm, though the priest had already begun to rise, standing now, fumbling a little clumsily as he put the book back inside his coat; as he turned, stiffly and clumsily still, he seemed to stumble slightly and was apparently about to fall even, though again he had recovered himself before the corporal touched him, going toward the door now, one hand already lifted toward it or toward the wall or perhaps just lifted, as though he were blind too, the corporal watching him, until the corporal said: 'You've forgotten your gear.'

The priest stopped, though he didn't turn yet. 'Yes,' he said. 'So I did.' Then he said, 'So I have.' Then he turned and went back to the desk and gathered the articles up—basin ewer stole and crucifix—and huddled them clumsily into or onto one arm and extended his hand toward the candles and then stopped again, the corporal watching him.

'You can send back for them,' the corporal said.

'Yes,' the priest said. 'I can send back for them,' and turned and went again to the door and stopped again and after a moment began to raise his hand toward it, though the corporal now had already passed him, to strike two or three rapping blows with his knuckles on the wood, which a moment later swung open and back, revealing the sergeant, the priest standing again for a second or two clasping to his breast the huddled symbols of his mystery. Then he roused. 'Yes,' he said, 'I can send back for them,' and passed through the door; and this time he didn't pause even when the sergeant overtook him and said:

'Shall I take them to the chapel, Father?'

'Thank you,' the priest said, relinquishing them: and now

he was free, walking on; and now he was even safe: outside, out of doors with only the spring darkness, the spring night soft and myriad above the blank and lightless walls and between them too, filling the empty topless passage, alley, at the end of which he could see a section of the distant wire fence and the catwalk spaced by the rigid down-glare of the lights, these spaced in their turn by the red eyes of the Senegalese sentries' cigarettes; and beyond that the dark plain, and beyond the plain in turn the faint unsleeping glow of the sleepless city; and now he could remember when he had seen them first, finally seen them, overtook them at last, two winters ago up near the Chemin des Dames—behind Combles, Souchez, he couldn't remember—the cobbled *Place* in the mild evening (no: mild evening, it was only autumn yet, a little while still before there would begin at Verdun that final winter of the doomed and accursed race of man) already empty again because again he had just missed them by minutes, the arms the hands pointing to show him, the helpful and contradictory voices giving him directions, too many of them in fact, too many helpful voices and too many directions, until at last one man walked with him to the edge of the village to show him the exact route and even point out to him the distant huddle of the farm itself—a walled yard enclosing house byre and all, twilight now and he saw them, eight of them at first standing quietly about the kitchen stoop until he saw two more of them, the corporal and another, sitting on the stoop in baize or oilcloth aprons, the corporal cleaning a fowl, a chicken, the other peeling potatoes into a bowl while beside, above them stood the farmwife with a pitcher and a child, a girl of ten or so, with both hands full of mugs and tumblers; then while he watched, the other three came out of the byre with the farmer himself and crossed the yard carrying the pails of milk.

Nor did he approach nor even make his presence known: just watching while the woman and the child exchanged the pitcher and the drinking vessels for the fowl and bowl and the pails of milk and carried the food on into the house and the farmer filled from the pitcher the mugs and tumblers which the corporal held and passed in turn and then they drank in ritual salutation—to peaceful work, to the peaceful end of day, to anticipation of the peaceful lamplit meal, whatever it was—and then it was dark, night, night indeed because the second time was at Verdun which was the freezing night of France and of man too since France was the cradle of the liberty of the human spirit, in the actual ruins of Verdun itself, within actual hearing range of the anguish of Gaud and Valaumont; not approaching this time either but only to stand from a distance watching, walled by the filth- and anguish-stained backs from where the thirteen would be standing in the circle's center, talking or not, haranguing or not, he would never know, dared not know; thinking *Yes, even then I durst not;* even if they did not need to talk or harangue since simply to believe was enough; thinking, *Yes, there were thirteen then and even now there are still twelve*; thinking, *Even if there were only one, only he, would be enough, more than enough*, thinking *Just that one to stand between me and safety, me and security, between me and peace;* and although he knew the compound and its environs well, for a moment he was dis-oriented as sometimes happens when you enter a strange building in darkness or by one door and then emerge from it in light or by another even though this was not the case here, thinking in a sort of quiet unamazement *Yes, I probably knew from the moment he sent for me what door I should have to emerge from, the only exit left for me.* So it only lasted for a moment or two or possibly even less than that: one infinitesimal vertiginous lurch and wall stone and brick resumed once more its ordered and forever repudiated place; one corner, one turn, and the sentry was where he had remembered he would be, not even pacing his beat but just standing at ease with his grounded rifle beside the small iron gate.

'Good evening, my son,' the priest said.

'Good evening, Father,' the man said.

'I wonder if I might borrow your bayonet?' the priest said.

'My what?' the man said.

'Your bayonet,' the priest said, extending his hand.

'I cant do that,' the man said. 'I'm on parade—on post. The corporal will—— The Officer of the Day himself might come along——'

'Tell them I took it,' the priest said.

'Took it?' the man said.

'Demanded it,' the priest said, his hand still steadily out.

'Come.' Then the hand moved, not fast, and drew the bayonet from the man's belt. 'Tell them I took it,' the priest said, already turning. 'Good night.' Or perhaps the man even answered; perhaps even in the silent and empty alley again one last fading echo of one last warm and human voice speaking in warm and human protest or amazement or simple unquestioning defence of an *is* simply because it *is*; and then no more, thinking *It was a spear, so I should have taken the rifle too,* and then no more: thinking *The left side, and I'm right handed,* thinking *But at least He wasn't wearing an infantryman's overcoat and a* Magasin du Louvre *shirt and so at least I can do that,* opening the coat and throwing it back and then opening the shirt until he could feel the blade's cold minuscule point against his flesh and then the cold sharp whisper of the blade itself entering, beginning to make a sort of thin audible cry as though of astonishment at its own swiftness yet when he looked down at it barely the point itself had disappeared and he said aloud, quietly: 'Now what?' *But He was not standing either,* he thought *He was nailed there and He will forgive me* and cast himself sideways and downward, steadying the bayonet so that the end of the hilt should strike the bricks first, and turned a little until his cheek lay against the still-warm bricks and now he began to make a thin sweet crying of frustration and despair until the pinch of his hand between the bayonet's cross guard and his own flesh told him better and so he could stop the crying now—the sweet thick warm murmur of it pouring suddenly from his mouth.

† † †

Beeping its horn steadily—not pettishly nor fretfully nor even irritatedly but in fact with a sort of unwearyable blasé Gallic detachment—the French staff-car crept through the *Place de Ville* as though patting the massed crowd gently and firmly to either side with the horn itself to make room for its passage. It was not a big car. It flew no general's pennon nor in fact any insignia of any kind; it was just a small indubitable French army motor car driven by a French soldier and containing three more soldiers, three American privates who until they met in the Blois orderly room where the French car had picked them up four hours ago had never laid eyes on one another before, who sat two in the back and one in front with the driver while the car bleated its snaillike passage through the massed spent wan and sleepless faces.

One of the two Americans in the back seat was leaning out of the car, looking eagerly about, not at the faces but at the adjacent buildings which enclosed the *Place*. He held a big much-folded and -unfolded and -refolded map open between his hands. He was quite young, with brown eyes as trustful and unalarmed as those of a cow, in an open reliant invincibly and incorrigibly bucolic face—a farmer's face fated to love his peaceful agrarian heritage (his father, as he would after him, raised hogs in Iowa and rich corn to feed and fatten them for market on) for the simple reason that to the end of his eupeptic days (what was going to happen to him inside the next thirty minutes would haunt him of course from time to time but only in dreams, as nightmares haunt) it would never occur to him that he could possibly have found anything more worthy to be loved—leaning eagerly out of the car and completely ignoring the massed faces through which he crept, saying eagerly:

'Which one is it? Which one is it?'

'Which one is what?' the American beside the driver said.

'The Headquarters,' he said. 'The Ho-tel de Villy.'

'Wait till you get inside,' the other said. 'That's what you volunteered to look at.'

'I want to see it from the outside too,' the first said. 'That's why I volunteered for this what-ever-it-is. Ask him,' he said, indicating the driver. 'You can speak Frog.'

'Not this time,' the other said. 'My French dont use this kind of a house.' But it wasn't necessary anyway because at the same moment they both saw the three sentries—American French and British—flanking the door, and in the next one the car turned through the gates and now they saw the whole courtyard cluttered and massed with motorcycles and staff-cars bearing the three different devices. The car didn't stop there though. Darting its way among the other vehicles at a really headlong speed, now that its gambits were its own durable peers instead of frail untriumphable human flesh, it dashed on around to the extreme rear of the baroque and awesome pile ('Now what?' the one in the front seat said to the Iowan who was still leaning out toward the building's dizzy crenellated wheel. 'Did you expect them to invite us in by the front?'

'It's all right,' the Iowan said. 'That's how I thought it would look.') to where an American military policeman standing beside a sort of basement areaway was signalling them with a flashlight. The car shot up beside him and stopped. He opened the door, though since the Iowan was now engaged in trying to refold his map, the American private in the front seat was the first to get out. His name was Buchwald. His grandfather had been rabbi of a Minsk synagogue until a Cossack sergeant beat his brains out with the shod hooves of a horse. His father was a tailor; he himself was born on the fourth floor of a walk-up, cold-water Brooklyn tenement. Within two years after the passage of the American prohibition law, with nothing in his bare hands but a converted army-surplus Lewis machine gun, he himself was to become czar of a million-dollar empire covering the entire Atlantic coast from Canada to whatever Florida cove or sandspit they were using that night. He had pale, almost colorless eyes; he was hard and slender too now though one day a few months less than ten years from now, lying in his ten-thousand-dollar casket banked with half that much more in cut flowers, he would look plump, almost fat. The military policeman leaned into the back of the car.

'Come on, come on,' he said. The Iowan emerged, carrying the clumsily-folded map in one hand and slapping at his pocket with the other. He feinted past Buchwald like a football halfback and darted to the front of the car and held the map into the light of one of the headlamps, still slapping at his pocket.

'Durn!' he said. 'I've lost my pencil.' The third American private was now out of the car. He was a Negro, of a complete and unrelieved black. He emerged with a sort of ballet dancer elegance, not mincing, not foppish, not maidenly but rather at once masculine and girlish or perhaps better, epicene, and stood not quite studied while the Iowan spun and feinted this time through all three of them—Buchwald, the policeman, and the Negro—and carrying his now rapidly disintegrating map plunged his upper body back into the car, saying to the policeman: 'Lend me your flashlight. I must have dropped it on the floor.'

'Sweet crap,' Buchwald said. 'Come on.'

'It's my pencil,' the Iowan said. 'I had it at that last big town we passed—what was the name of it?'

'I can call a sergeant,' the policeman said. 'Am I going to have to?'

'Nah,' Buchwald said. He said to the Iowan: 'Come on. They've probably got a pencil inside. They can read and write here too.' The Iowan backed out of the car and stood up. He began to refold his map. Following the policeman, they crossed to the areaway and descended into it, the Iowan following with his eyes the building's soaring upward swoop.

'Yes,' he said. 'It sure does.' They descended steps, through a door; they were in a narrow stone passage; the policeman opened a door and they entered an anteroom; the policeman closed the door behind them. The room contained a cot, a desk, a telephone, a chair. The Iowan went to the desk and began to shift the papers on it.

'You can remember you were here without having to check it off, cant you?' Buchwald said.

'It aint for me,' the Iowan said, tumbling the papers through. 'It's for the girl I'm engaged to. I promised her——'

'Does she like pigs too?' Buchwald said.

'—what?' the Iowan said. He stopped and turned his head; still half stooped over the desk, he gave Buchwald his mild open reliant and alarmless look. 'Why not?' he said. 'What's wrong with pigs?'

'Okay,' Buchwald said. 'So you promised her.'

'That's right,' the Iowan said. 'When we found out I was coming to France I promised to take a map and mark off on it all the places I went to, especially the ones you always hear about, like Paris. I got Blois, and Brest, and I'll get Paris for volunteering for this, and now I'm even going to have Chaulnesmont, the Grand Headquarterters of the whole shebang as soon as I can find a pencil.' He began to search the desk again.

'What you going to do with it?' Buchwald said. 'The map. When you get it back home?'

'Frame it and hang it on the wall,' the Iowan said. 'What did you think I was going to do with it?'

'Are you sure you're going to want this one marked on it?' Buchwald said.

'What?' the Iowan said. Then he said, 'Why?'

'Dont you know what you volunteered for?' Buchwald said.

'Sure,' the Iowan said. 'For a chance to visit Chaulnesmont.'

'I mean, didn't anybody tell you what you were going to do here?' Buchwald said.

'You haven't been in the army very long, have you?' the Iowan said. 'In the army, you dont ask what you are going to do: you just do it. In fact, the way to get along in any army is never even to wonder why they want something done or what they are going to do with it after it's finished, but just do it and then get out of sight so that they cant just happen to see you by accident and then think up something for you to do, but instead they will have to have thought up something to be done, and then hunt for somebody to do it. Durn it, I dont believe they have a pencil here either.'

'Maybe Sambo's got one,' Buchwald said. He looked at the Negro. 'What did you volunteer for this for besides a three-day Paris pass? To see Chaulnesmont too?'

'What did you call me?' the Negro said.

'Sambo,' Buchwald said. 'You no like?'

'My name's Philip Manigault Beauchamp,' the Negro said.

'Go on,' Buchwald said.

'It's spelled Manigault but you pronounce it Mannygo,' the Negro said.

'Oh hush,' Buchwald said.

'You got a pencil, buddy?' the Iowan said to the Negro.

'No,' the Negro said. He didn't even look at the Iowan. He was still looking at Buchwald. 'You want to make something of it?'

'Me?' Buchwald said. 'What part of Texas you from?'

'Texas,' the Negro said with a sort of bemused contempt. He glanced at the nails of his right hand, then rubbed them briskly against his flank. 'Mississippi. Going to live in Chicago soon as this crap's over. Be an undertaker, if you're interested.'

'An undertaker?' Buchwald said. 'You like dead people, huh?'

'Hasn't anybody in this whole durn war got a pencil?' the Iowan said.

'Yes,' the Negro said. He stood, tall, slender, not studied: just poised; suddenly he gave Buchwald a look feminine and defiant. 'I like the work. So what?'

'So you know what you volunteered for, do you?'

'Maybe I do and maybe I dont,' the Negro said. 'Why did you volunteer for it? Besides a three-day pass in Paris?'

'Because I love Wilson,' Buchwald said.

'Wilson?' the Iowan said. 'Do you know Sergeant Wilson? He's the best sergeant in the army.'

'Then I dont know him,' Buchwald said without looking at the Iowan. 'All the N.C.O.'s I know are sons of bitches.' He said to the Negro, 'Did they tell you, or didn't they?' Now the Iowan had begun to look from one to the other of them.

'What is going on here?' he said. The door opened. It was an American sergeant-major. He entered rapidly and looked rapidly at them. He was carrying an attaché case.

'Who's in charge?' he said. He looked at Buchwald. 'You.' He opened the attaché case and took something from it which he extended to Buchwald. It was a pistol.

'That's a German pistol,' the Iowan said. Buchwald took it. The sergeant-major reached into the attaché case again; this time it was a key, a door key; he extended it to Buchwald.

'Why?' Buchwald said.

'Take it,' the sergeant-major said. 'You dont want privacy to last forever, do you?' Buchwald took the key and put it and the pistol into his pocket.

'Why in hell didn't you bastards do it yourselves?' he said.

'So we had to send all the way to Blois to find somebody for a midnight argument,' the sergeant-major said. 'Come on,' he said. 'Get it over with.' He started to turn. This time the Iowan spoke quite loudly:

'Look here,' he said. 'What is this?' The sergeant-major

paused and looked at the Iowan, then the Negro. He said to Buchwald:

'So they're already going coy on you.'

'Oh, coy,' Buchwald said. 'Dont let that worry you. The smoke cant help it, coy is a part of what you might say one of his habits or customs or pastimes. The other one dont even know what coy means yet.'

'Okay,' the sergeant-major said. 'It's your monkey. You ready?'

'Wait,' Buchwald said. He didn't look back to where the other two stood near the desk, watching him and the sergeant-major. 'What is it?'

'I thought they told you,' the sergeant-major said.

'Let's hear yours,' Buchwald said.

'They had a little trouble with him,' the sergeant-major said. 'It's got to be done from in front, for his own sake, let alone everybody else's. But they cant seem to make him see it. He's got to be killed from in front, by a Kraut bullet—see? You get it now? he was killed in that attack Monday morning; they're giving him all the benefit: out there that morning where he had no business being—a major general, safe for the rest of his life to stay behind and say Give 'em hell, men. But no. He was out there himself, leading the whole business to victory for France and fatherland. They're even going to give him a new medal, but he still wont see it.'

'What's his gripe?' Buchwald said. 'He knows he's for it, dont he?'

'Oh sure,' the sergeant-major said. 'He knows he's gone. That aint the question. He aint kicking about that. He just refuses to let them do it that way—swears he's going to make them shoot him not in the front but in the back, like any top-sergeant or shave-tail that thinks he's too tough to be scared and too hard to be hurt. You know: make the whole world see that not the enemy but his own men did it.'

'Why didn't they just hold him and do it?' Buchwald said.

'Now now,' the sergeant-major said. 'You dont just hold a French major-general and shoot him in the face.'

'Then how are we supposed to do it?' Buchwald said. The sergeant-major looked at him. 'Oh,' Buchwald said. 'Maybe I get it now. *French* soldiers dont. Maybe next time it will be an

American general and three Frogs will get a trip to New York.'

'Yeah,' the sergeant-major said. 'If they just let me pick the general. You ready now?'

'Yes,' Buchwald said. But he didn't move. He said: 'Yeah. Why us, anyway? If he's a Frog general, why didn't the Frogs do it? Why did it have to be us?'

'Maybe because an American doughfoot is the only bastard they could bribe with a trip to Paris,' the sergeant-major said. 'Come on.'

But still Buchwald didn't move, his pale hard eyes thoughtful and steady. 'Come on,' he said. 'Give.'

'If you're going to back out, why didn't you do it before you left Blois?' the sergeant-major said.

Buchwald said something unprintable. 'Give,' he said. 'Let's get it over with.'

'Right,' the sergeant-major said. 'They rationed it. The Frogs will have to shoot that Frog regiment, because it's Frog. They had to bring a Kraut general over here Wednesday to explain why they were going to shoot the Frog regiment, and the Limeys won that. Now they got to shoot this Frog general to explain why they brought the Kraut general over here, and we won that. Maybe they drew straws. All right now?'

'Yes,' Buchwald said, suddenly and harshly. He cursed. 'Yes. Let's get it over with.'

'Wait!' the Iowan said. 'No! I——'

'Dont forget your map,' Buchwald said. 'We wont be back here.'

'I haven't,' the Iowan said. 'What you think I been holding onto it this long for?'

'Good,' Buchwald said. 'Then when they send you back home to prison for mutiny, you can mark Leavenworth on it too.' They returned to the corridor and followed it. It was empty, lighted by spaced weak electric bulbs. They had seen no other sign of life and suddenly it was as though they apparently were not going to until they were out of it again. The narrow corridor had not descended, there were no more steps. It was as if the earth it tunnelled through had sunk as an elevator sinks, holding the corridor itself intact, immune, empty of any life or sound save that of their boots, the whitewashed stone sweating in furious immobility beneath the whole concentrated weight of history, stratum upon stratum of dead tradition impounded by the *Hôtel* above them—monarchy revolution empire and republic, duke farmer-general and sans culotte, levee tribunal and guillotine, liberty fraternity equality and death and the people the People always to endure and prevail, the group, the clump, huddled now, going quite fast until the Iowan cried again:

'No, I tell you! I aint——' until Buchwald stopped, stopping them all, and turned and said to the Iowan in a calm and furious murmur:

'Beat it.'

'What?' the Iowan cried. 'I cant! Where would I go?'

'How the hell do I know?' Buchwald said. 'I aint the one that's dissatisfied here.'

'Come on,' the sergeant-major said. They went on. They reached a door; it was locked. The sergeant-major unlocked and opened it.

'Do we report?' Buchwald said.

'Not to me,' the sergeant-major said. 'You can even keep the pistol for a souvenir. The car'll be waiting where you got out of it,' and was about to close the door until Buchwald after one rapid glance into the room turned and put his foot against the door and said again in that harsh calm furious controlled voice:

'Christ, cant the sons of bitches even get a priest for him?'

'They're still trying,' the sergeant-major said. 'Somebody sent for the priest out at the compound two hours ago and he aint got back yet. They cant seem to find him.'

'So we're supposed to wait for him,' Buchwald said in that tone of harsh calm unbearable outrage.

'Supposed by who?' the sergeant-major said. 'Move your foot.' Buchwald did, the door closed, the lock clashed behind them and the three of them were in a cell, a cubicle fierce with whitewash and containing the single unshaded electric light and a three-legged stool like a farmer's milking stool, and the French general. That is, it was a French face and by its expression and cast it had been used to enough rank long enough to be a general's, besides the insignia and the dense splash of ribbons and the Sam Browne belt and the leather putties, though the uniform which bore them were the plain G.I. tunic and trousers which a cavalry sergeant would have worn, standing now, erect and rigid now and rather as though enclosed by the fading aura of the convulsive movement which had brought him to his feet, who said sharply in French:

'Attention there!'

'What?' Buchwald said to the Negro beside him. 'What did he say?'

'How in hell do I know?' the Negro said. 'Quick!' he said in a panting voice. 'That Ioway bastard. Do something about him quick.'

'Right,' Buchwald said, turning. 'Grab him then,' and turned on to meet the Iowan.

'No, I tell you!' the Iowan cried. 'I aint going to—' Buchwald struck him skilfully, the blow seeming not to travel at all before the Iowan catapulted backward into the wall then slid down it to the floor, Buchwald turning again in time to see the Negro grasp at the French general and the French general turn sharply face-to and against the wall, his head turned cheek against it, saying over his shoulder in French as Buchwald snapped the safety off the pistol:

'Shoot now, you whorehouse scum. I will not turn.'

'Jerk him around,' Buchwald said.

'Put that damn safety back on!' the Negro panted, glaring back at him. 'You want to shoot me too? Come on. It will take both of us.' Buchwald closed the safety though he still held the pistol in his hand while they struggled, all three of them or two of them to drag the French general far enough from the wall to turn him. 'Hit him a little,' the Negro panted. 'We got to knock him out.'

'How in hell can you knock out a man that's already dead?' Buchwald panted.

'Come on,' the Negro panted. 'Just a little. Hurry.' Buchwald struck, trying to gauge the blow, and he was right: the body collapsed until the Negro was supporting it but not out, the eyes open, looking up at Buchwald then watching the pistol as Buchwald raised it and snapped the safety off again, the eyes not afraid, not even despaired: just incorrigibly alert and rational, so alert in fact as apparently to have seen the squeeze of Buchwald's hand as it started, so that the sudden and furious movement turned not only the face but the whole body away with the explosion so that the round hole was actually behind the ear when the corpse reached the floor. Buchwald and the Negro stood over it, panting, the barrel of the pistol warm against Buchwald's leg.

'Son of a bitch,' Buchwald said to the Negro. 'Why didn't you hold him?'

'He slipped!' the Negro panted.

'Slipped my crap,' Buchwald said. 'You didn't hold him.'

'Son of a bitch yourself!' the Negro panted. 'Me stand there holding him for that bullet to come on through hunting me next?'

'All right, all right,' Buchwald said. 'Now we got to plug that one up and shoot him again.'

'Plug it up?' the Negro said.

'Yes,' Buchwald said. 'What the hell sort of undertaker will you make if you dont know how to plug up a hole in a bastard that got shot in the wrong place? Wax will do it. Get a candle.'

'Where'm I going to get a candle?' the Negro said.

'Go out in the hall and yell,' Buchwald said, swapping hands with the pistol and taking the door key from his pocket and handing it to the Negro. 'Keep on yelling until you find a Frog. They must have candles. They must have at least one thing in this . . . .ing country we never had to bring two thousand miles over here and give to them.'

Friday
Saturday
Sunday

It bade fair to be another bright and perennial lark-filled vernal morning; the gaudy uniforms and arms and jangling accoutrements and even the ebon faces too of the Senegalese regiment seemed to gleam in it as, to the cryptic tribal equatorial cries of its noncoms, it filed onto the parade ground and formed three sides of a hollow square facing the three freshly-planted posts set in a symmetric row on the edge of a long pit or ditch, almost filled and obliterated now by four years of war's refuse—tin cans, bottles, old messkits, worn-out cooking utensils, boots, inextricable coils of rusting and useless wire—from which the dirt had been excavated to form the railroad embankment running across the end of the parade, which would serve as a backstop for what bullets neither flesh nor wood absorbed. They came into position then at rest and grounded arms and stood at ease and then easy, whereupon there rose a steady unemphatic gabble, not festive: just gregarious, like people waiting for the opening of a market-place; the pallid perennial almost invisible lighters winked and flared from perennial cigarette to cigarette among the babble of voices, the ebon and gleaming faces not even watching the working party of white soldiers while they tamped the last earth about the posts and took up their tools and departed in a disorderly straggle like a company of reapers leaving a field of hay.

Then a distant bugle cried once or twice, the Senegalese

N.C.O.'s shouted, the gaudy ranks doused the cigarettes without haste and with a sort of negligent, almost inattentive deliberation came to alert and *at ease* as the sergeant-major of the city garrison, a holstered pistol strapped outside his long buttoned-back coat, came into the vacant side of the square before the three posts and stopped and stood as, to the harsh abrupt ejaculations of the new N.C.O.'s, the mutinied regiment filed into the empty rectangle and huddled, pariahs still, hatless and unarmed, still unshaven, alien, stained still with Aisne and Oise and Marne mud so that against the gaudy arras of the Senegalese they looked like harassed and harried and homeless refugees from another planet, moiling a little though quiet and even orderly or at least decorous until suddenly a handful of them, eleven it was, broke suddenly out and ran in a ragged clump toward the three posts and had knelt facing the posts in the same ragged clump by the time the sergeant-major had shouted something and an N.C.O.'s voice took it up and a file of Senegalese came rapidly out and around and across the empty parade and surrounded the kneeling men and pulled them, not at all roughly, back onto their feet and turned them and herded them back among their companions like drovers behind a small band of temporarily strayed sheep.

Now a small party of horsemen rode rapidly up from the rear and stopped just outside the square, behind it; they were the town major, his adjutant, the provost marshal adjutant and three orderlies. The sergeant-major shouted, the parade (save for the pariah regiment) came to attention in one long metallic clash, the sergeant-major wheeled and saluted the town major across the rigid palisade of Senegalese heads, the town major accepted the parade and stood it at ease then back to attention again and returned it to the sergeant-major who in his turn stood it at ease again and turned to face the three posts as, abruptly and apparently from nowhere, a sergeant and file came up with the three hatless prisoners interspersed among them, whom they bound quickly to the three posts— the man who had called himself Lapin, then the corporal, then the simian-like creature whom Lapin had called Cassetête or Horse—leaving them facing in to the hollow of the square though they couldn't see it now because at the moment there filed between them and it another squad of some twenty men with a sergeant, who halted and quarter-turned and stood them at ease with their backs to the three doomed ones, whom the sergeant-major now approached in turn, to examine rapidly the cord which bound Lapin to his post, then on to the corporal, already extending his (the sergeant-major's) hand to the *Médaille Militaire* on the corporal's coat, saying in a rapid murmur:

'You dont want to keep this.'

'No,' the corporal said. 'No use to spoil it.' The sergeant-major wrenched it off the coat, not savagely: just rapidly, already moving on.

'I know who to give it to,' he said, moving on to the third man, who said, drooling a little, not alarmed, not even urgent: just diffident and promptive, as you address someone, a stranger, on whom your urgent need depends but who may have temporarily forgotten your need or forgotten you:

'Paris.'

'Right,' the sergeant-major said. Then he was gone too; now the three bound men could have seen nothing save the backs of the twenty men in front of them though they could still have heard the sergeant-major's voice as he brought the parade to attention again and drew from somewhere inside his coat a folded paper and a worn leather spectacle case and unfolded the paper and put the spectacles on and read aloud from the paper, holding it now in both hands against the light flutter of the morning breeze, his voice sounding clear and thin and curiously forlorn in the sunny lark-filled emptiness among the dead redundant forensic verbiage talking in pompous and airy delusion of an end of man. 'By order of the president of the court,' the sergeant-major chanted wanly and refolded the paper and removed the spectacles and folded them back into the case and stowed them both away; command, the twenty men about-turned to face the three posts; Lapin was now straining outward against his cord, trying to see past the corporal to the third man.

'Look,' Lapin said anxiously to the corporal.

Load!

'Paris,' the third man said, hoarse and wet and urgent.

'Say something to him,' Lapin said. 'Quick.'

Aim!

'Paris,' the third man said again.

'It's all right,' the corporal said. 'We're going to wait. We wont go without you.'

The corporal's post may have been flawed or even rotten because, although the volley merely cut cleanly the cords binding Lapin and the third man to theirs, so that their bodies slumped at the foot of each post, the corporal's body, post bonds and all, went over backward as one intact unit, onto the edge of the rubbish-filled trench behind it; when the sergeant-major, the pistol still smoking faintly in his hand, moved from Lapin to the corporal, he found that the plunge of the post had jammed it and its burden too into a tangled mass of old barbed wire, a strand of which had looped up and around the top of the post and the man's head as though to assoil them both on in one unbroken continuation of the fall, into the anonymity of the earth. The wire was rusted and pitted and would not have deflected the bullet anyway, nevertheless the sergeant-major flicked it carefully away with his toe before setting the pistol's muzzle against the ear.

As soon as the parade ground was empty (before in fact; the end of the Senegalese column had not yet vanished into the company street) the fatigue party came up with a hand-drawn barrow containing their tools and a folded tarpaulin. The corporal in charge took a wire-cutter from the barrow and approached the sergeant-major, who had already cut the corporal's body free from the broken post. 'Here,' he said, handing the sergeant-major the wire-cutter. 'You're not going to waste a ground-sheet on one of them, are you?'

'Get those posts out,' the sergeant-major said. 'Let me have two men and the ground sheet.'

'Right,' the corporal said. The corporal went away. The sergeant-major cut off a section about six feet long of the rusted wire. When he rose, the two men with the folded tarpaulin were standing behind him, watching him.

'Spread it out,' he said, pointing. They did so. 'Put him in it,' he said. They took up the dead corporal's body, the one at the head a little finicking because of the blood, and laid it on the tarpaulin. 'Go on,' the sergeant-major said. 'Roll it up. Then put it in the barrow,' and followed them, the fatigue-party corporal suddenly not watching him too, the other men suddenly immersed again in freeing the planted posts from the earth. Nor did the sergeant-major speak again. He simply gestured the two men to take up the handles and, himself at the rear, established the direction by holding one corner as a pivot and pushing against the other and then pushing ahead on both, the laden barrow now crossing the parade ground at a long slant toward the point where the wire fence died in a sharp right angle against the old factory wall. Nor did he (the sergeant-major) look back either, the two men carrying the handles almost trotting now to keep the barrow from running over them, on toward the corner where at some point they too must have seen beyond the fence the high two-wheeled farm cart with a heavy farm horse in the shafts and the two women and the three men beside it, the sergeant-major stopping the barrow just as he had started it: by stopping himself and pivoting the barrow by its two rear corners into the angle of the fence, then himself went and stood at the fence—a man of more than fifty and now looking all of it—until the taller of the two women—the one with the high dark strong and handsome face as a man's face is handsome—approached the other side of the wire. The second woman had not moved, the shorter, dumpier, softer one. But she was watching the two at the fence and listening, her face quite empty for the moment but with something incipient and tranquilly promising about it like a clean though not-yet-lighted lamp on a kitchen bureau.

'Where did you say your husband's farm is?' the sergeant-major said.

'I told you,' the woman said.

'Tell me again,' the sergeant-major said.

'Beyond Chalons,' the woman said.

'How far beyond Chalons?' the sergeant-major said. 'All right,' he said. 'How far from Verdun?'

'It's near Vienne-la-pucelle,' the woman said. 'Beyond St Mihiel,' she said.

'St Mihiel,' the sergeant-major said. 'In the army zone. Worse. In the battle zone. With Germans on one side of it and Americans on the other. Americans.'

'Should American soldiers be more terrible than other

soldiers?' the woman said. 'Because they are fresher at it? Is that it?'

'No, Sister,' the other woman said. 'That's wrong. It's because the Americans have been here so young. It will be easy for them.' The two at the fence paid no attention to her. They looked at one another through the wire. Then the woman said:

'The war is over.'

'Ah,' the sergeant-major said.

The woman made no movement, no gesture. 'What else can this mean? What else explain it? justify it? No, not even justify it: plead compassion, plead pity, plead despair for it?' She looked at the sergeant-major, cold, griefless, impersonal. 'Plead exculpation for it?'

'Bah,' the sergeant-major said. 'Did I ask you? Did anyone?' He gestured behind him with the wire-cutter. One of the men released the handle of the barrow and came and took it. 'Cut the bottom strand,' the sergeant-major said.

'Cut?' the man said.

'It, species of a species!' the sergeant-major said. The man started to stoop but the sergeant-major had already snatched the wire-cutter back from him and stooped himself; the taut bottom-most strand sprang with a thin almost musical sound, recoiling. 'Get it out of the barrow,' the sergeant-major said. 'Lively.' They understood now. They lifted the long tarpaulin-wrapped object from the barrow and lowered it to the ground. The woman had moved aside and the three men now waited at the fence, to draw, drag the long object along the ground and through the wire's vacancy, then up and into the cart. 'Wait,' the sergeant-major said. The woman paused. The sergeant-major fumbled inside his coat and produced a folded paper which he passed through the fence to her. She opened it and looked at it for a moment, with no expression whatever.

'Yes,' she said. 'It must be over, since you receive a diploma now with your execution. What shall I do with it? frame it on the parlor wall?' The sergeant-major reached through the wire and snatched the paper from between her hands, his other hand fumbling out the worn spectacle case again, then with both hands, still holding the opened paper, he got the spectacle on his nose and glanced at the paper a moment then with a violent gesture crumpled the paper into his side pocket and produced another folded one from inside his coat and extended it through the wire, shaking it violently open before the woman could touch it, saying in a repressed and seething voice: 'Say you dont need this one then. Look at the signature on it.' The woman did so. She had never seen it before, the thin delicate faint cryptic indecipherable scrawl which few other people had ever seen either but which anyone in that half of Europe on that day competent to challenge a signature would have recognised at once.

'So he knows where his son's half-sister's husband's farm is too,' she said.

'Pah,' the sergeant-major said. 'Further than St Mihiel even. If at any place on the way you should be faced with a pearled and golden gate, that will pass you through it too.—This too,' he said, his hand coming out of his pocket and through the wire again, opening on the dull bronze of the small emblem and the bright splash of its ribbon, the woman immobile again, not touching it yet, tall, looking down at the sergeant-major's open palm, until he felt the other woman looking at him and met the tranquil and incipient gaze; whereupon she said:

'He's really quite handsome, Sister. He's not so old either.'

'Pah!' the sergeant-major said again. 'Here!' he said, thrusting, fumbling the medal into the taller woman's hand until she had to take it, then snatching his own hand quickly back through the wire. 'Begone!' he said. 'Get on with you! Get out of here!' breathing a little hard now, irascible, almost raging, who was too old for this, feeling the second woman's eyes again though he did not meet them yet, flinging his head up to shout at the taller one's back: 'There were three of you. Where is the other one—his *poule*, whatever she is—was?' Then he had to meet the second woman's eyes, the face no longer incipient now but boundless with promise, giving him a sweet and tender smile, saying:

'It's all right. Dont be afraid. Goodbye.' Then they were gone, the five of them, the horse and the cart: rapidly; he turned and took the section of rusted wire from the barrow and flung it down beside the severed bottom strand.

'Tie it back,' he said.

'Isn't the war over?' one of the men said. The sergeant-major turned almost savagely.

'But not the army,' he said. 'How do you expect peace to put an end to an army when even war cant?'

† † †

When they passed through the old eastern city gate this time they were all riding, Marthe with the lines at one end of the high seat and the sister opposite with the girl between them. They were quite high, not in the city's dense and creeping outflux but above it, not a part of it but on it like a boat, the three of them riding out of the city as on a float in a carnival procession, fluxed out of the anguished city on the fading diffusion on the anguish as on a leg-less and wheel-less effigy of a horse and cart as though borne on the massed shoulders in a kind of triumph; borne along so high in fact that they had almost reached the old gate before the owners of the shoulders even appeared or thought to raise their eyes or their attention high enough to remark what they carried and to assume, divine or simply recoil from, what the cart contained.

It was not a recoil, a shrinking, but rather an effacement, a recession: a suddenly widening ring of empty space beginning to enclose the moving cart as water recedes from a float, leaving the float to realise, discover only then that it was not maritime but terrestrial and not supported by a medium but attached to earth by legs and wheels; a recession, as though the shoulders which for a time had borne it were effacing not only the support but the cognizance too of the weight and presence of the burden, the crowd pressing steadily away from the cart and even transmitting on ahead as though by osmosis the warning of its coming, until presently the path was already opening before the cart itself ever reached it, the cart now moving faster than the crowd, the faces in the crowd not even looking toward it until the second sister, Marya, began to call down to them from her end of the high seat, not peremptory, not admonitory: just insistent and serene as if she were speaking to children: 'Come. You owe him no obligation; you dont need to hate. You haven't injured him; why should you be afraid?'

'Marya,' the other sister said.

'Nor ashamed either,' Marya said.

'Hush, Marya,' the other sister said. Marya sat back into the seat.

'All right, Sister,' she said. 'I didn't mean to frighten them: only to comfort them.' But she continued to watch them, bright and serene, the cart going on, the cleared space moving steadily before it as if the emptiness itself cleared its own advancing vacancy, so that when they came to the old gate the archway was completely vacant, the crowd now halted and banked on either side of it for the cart to pass; when suddenly a man in the crowd removed his hat, then one or two more, so that when the cart passed beneath the arch it was as though it had quit the city enclosed in a faint visible soundless rustling. 'You see, Sister?' Marya said with serene and peaceful triumph: 'Only to comfort them.'

Now they were out of the city, the long straight roads diverging away, radiating away like spokes from a hub; above them slowly crawled the intermittent small clouds of dust within which, singly, in groups, sometimes in carts also, the city emptied itself; the parents and kin of the revolted regiment who had hurried toward it in amazement and terror, to compound between the old walls vituperation and anguish, now fled it almost as though in something not quite of relief but shame.

They didn't look back at it though for a while yet it remained, squatting above the flat plain, supreme still, gray and crowned by the ancient Roman citadel and slowly fading until in time it was gone though they still had not looked once back to know it, going on themselves behind the strong slow heavy deliberate unhurryable farm-horse. They had food with them so they didn't need to stop save for a little while at noon in a wood to feed and water the horse. So they only passed through the villages—the silent arrested faces, that same faint visible soundless rustling as the hats and caps came off, almost as though they had an outrider or courier to presage them, the girl crouching in her shawl between the two older women, Marthe iron-faced, looking straight ahead and only the other sister, Marya, to look about them, serene and tranquil, never astonished, never surprised while the heavy shaggy feet of the horse rang the slow cobbles until that one too was behind.

Just before dark they reached Chalons. They were in an army zone now and approaching what five days ago had been a battle zone though there was peace now or at least quiet; still an army zone anyway because suddenly a French and an American sergeant stood at the horse's head, stopping him. 'I have the paper,' Marthe said, producing and extending it. 'Here.'

'Keep it,' the French sergeant said. 'You wont need it here. It is all arranged.' Then she saw something else: six French soldiers carrying a cheap wood coffin approaching the rear of the cart and even as she turned on the seat they had already set the coffin down and were drawing the tarpaulin-swaddled body from the cart.

'Wait,' Marthe said in her harsh strong tearless voice.

'It is arranged, I tell you,' the French sergeant said. 'You go to St Mihiel by train.'

'By train?' Marthe said.

'Why, Sister!' Marya said. 'In the train!'

'Restrain yourself,' the French sergeant said to Marthe. 'You wont have to pay. It's arranged, I tell you.'

'This cart is not mine,' Marthe said. 'I borrowed it.'

'We know that,' the French sergeant said. 'It will be returned.'

'But I must still carry him from St Mihiel to Vienne-la-pucelle—You said St Mihiel, didn't you?'

'Why do you argue with me?' the French sergeant said. 'Have I not told you one million times it is all arranged? Your husband will meet you at St Mihiel with your own cart and horse. Get down. All of you. Just because the war has stopped, do you think the army has nothing else to do but cajole civilians? Come along now. You're holding up your train; it has a little more to do than this too.'

Then they saw the train. They had not noticed it before though the tracks were almost beside them. It was a locomotive and a single van of the type known as forty-and-eight.

They got down from the cart; it was dusk now. The French soldiers finished fastening down the lid of the coffin; they took it up and the three women and the two sergeants followed to the van and stopped again while the soldiers lifted the coffin into the open door, then climbed in themselves and took up the coffin again and carried it forward out of sight and then reappeared and dropped one by one to the ground again.

'In with you,' the French sergeant said. 'And dont complain because you dont have seats. There's plenty of clean straw. And here.' It was an army blanket. None of the three of them knew where he had got it from. That is, they had not noticed it before either. Then the American sergeant said something to the French one, in his own language without doubt since it meant nothing to them, not even when the French sergeant said, '*Attendez*'; they just stood in the slow and failing light until the American sergeant returned carrying a wooden packing-case stencilled with the cryptic symbols of ordnance or supply, that didn't matter either, the American sergeant setting the box in place before the door and now they knew why, with a little of surprise perhaps, climbing in turn onto the box and then into the van, into almost complete darkness with only one pale shapeless gleam from the coffin's unpainted wood to break it. They found the straw. Marthe spread the blanket on it and they sat down; at that moment someone else sprang, vaulted into the van—a man, a soldier, by his silhouette in the door where there was still a little light, an American soldier, carrying something in both hands they smelled the coffee, the American sergeant looming over them now, saying, very loud:

'*Ici café. Café,*' fumbling the three mugs down until Marthe took them and distributed them, feeling in her turn the man's hard hand gripping her hand and the mug both while he guided the spout of the coffee pot into the mug; he even seemed to anticipate the jerk, crying 'Watch it!' in his own language a second or two before the shrill peanut-parcher whistle which did not presage the lurch but rather accompanied it, bracing himself against the wall as the van seemed to rush from immobility into a sort of frantic celerity with no transition whatever; a gout of burning coffee leapt from the mug in her hand onto her lap. Then the three of them managed to brace themselves back against the wall too, the whistle shrieking again shrill as friction, as though it actually were friction: not a warning of approach but a sound of protest and insensate anguish and indictment of the hard dark earth it rushed over, the vast weight of dark sky it burrowed frantically beneath, the constant and inviolable horizon it steadily clove.

This time the American sergeant knelt, braced still, using both hands again to fill the mugs, but only half full now so that, sitting against the wall, they drank by installments the hot sweet comforting coffee, the van rushing on through darkness, themselves invisible even to one another in darkness, even the gleam of the coffin at the other end of the van gone now and, their own inert bodies now matched and reconciled with the van's speed, it was as though there were no motion at all if it had not been for the springless vibration and the anguished shrieks from the engine from time to time.

When light returned, the van had stopped. It would be St Mihiel; they had told her St Mihiel and this would be it, even if there had not been that sixth sense, even after almost four years, that tells people when they are nearing home. So as soon as the van stopped, she had started to get up, saying to the American sergeant: 'St Mihiel?' because at least he should understand that, then in a sort of despair of urgency she even said, began, *'Mon homme à moi—mon mari'* before she stopped, the sergeant speaking himself now, using one or two more of the few other words which were his French vocabulary:

'No no no. *Attention. Attention,*' even in the van's darkness motioning downward at her with his hands as a trainer commands a dog to sit. Then he was gone, silhouetted for another instant against the paler door, and they waited, huddled together now for warmth in the cold spring dawn, the girl between them, whether asleep or not, whether she had ever slept during the night or not, Marthe could not tell though by her breathing Marya, the other sister, was. It was full light when the sergeant returned; they were all three awake now, who had slept or not slept; they could see the first of Saturday's sun and hear the eternal and perennial larks. He had more coffee, the pot filled again, and this time he had bread too, saying, very loud: 'Monjay. Monjay' and they—she—could see him now—a young man with a hard drafted face and with something else in it—impatience or commiseration, she anyway could not tell which. Nor did she care, thinking again to try once more to communicate with him except that the French sergeant at Chalons had said that it was all arranged, and suddenly it was not that she could trust the American sergeant because he must know what he was doing since he had obviously come along with them under orders, but because she—they—could do little else.

So they ate the bread and drank the hot sweet coffee again. The sergeant was gone again and they waited; she had no way to mark or gauge how long. Then the sergeant sprang or vaulted into the van again and she knew that the moment was here. This time the six soldiers who followed him were Americans; the three of them rose and stood and waited again while the six soldiers slid the coffin to the door then dropped to the ground, invisible to them now, so that the coffin itself seemed to flee suddenly through the door and vanish, the three of them following to the door while the sergeant dropped through the door; there was another box beneath the door for them to descend by, into another bright morning, blinking a little after the darkness in the sixth bright morning of that week during which there had been no rain nor adumbration at all. Then she saw the cart, her own or theirs, her husband standing beside the horse's head while the six American soldiers slid the coffin into the cart, and she turned to the American sergeant and said 'Thank you' in French and suddenly and a little awkwardly he removed his hat and shook her hand, quick and hard, then the other sister's and put his hat back on without once looking at or offering to touch the girl, and she went on around the cart to where her husband stood—a broad strong man in corduroy, not as tall as she and definitely older. They embraced, then all four of them turned to the cart, huddling for a moment in that indecision, as people will. But not for long; there would not be room for all four of them on the seat but the girl had already solved that, climbing up over the shafts and the seat and into the body of the cart, to crouch, huddle beside the coffin, huddled into the shawl, her face worn and sleepless and definitely needing soap and water now.

'Why, yes, Sister,' Marya, the older sister said in her voice of happy astonishment, almost of pleasure as though at so simple a solution: 'I'll ride back there too.' So the husband helped her up onto the shaft then over the seat, where she sat also on the opposite side of the coffin. Then Marthe mounted strongly and without assistance to the seat, the husband following with the lines.

They were already on the edge of the city, so they did not need to pass through it, merely around it. Though actually there was no city, no boundaries enclosing and postulating a city from a countryside because this was not even a war zone: it was a battle zone, city and countryside annealed and indistinguishable one from the other beneath one vast concentration of troops, American and French, not poised but rather as though transfixed, suspended beneath, within that vast silence and cessation—all the clutter of battle in a state of arrestment like hypnosis: motionless and silent transport, dumps of ammunition and supplies, and soon they began to pass the guns squatting in batteries, facing eastward, still manned but not poised either, not waiting: just silent, following the now silent line of the old stubborn four-year salient so that now they were seeing war or what six days ago had been war—the shell-pocked fields, the topless trees some of which this spring had put out a few green and stubborn shoots from the blasted trunks—the familiar land which they had not seen in almost four years but which was familiar still, as though even war had failed to efface completely that old verity of peaceful human occupation. But they were skirting the rubble of what had been Vienne-la-pucelle before it seemed to occur to her that there still might be dread and fear; it was only then that she said to the husband in a voice that did not even reach the two others in the body of the cart: 'The house.'

'The house was not damaged,' the husband said. 'I dont know why. But the fields, the land. Ruined. Ruined. It will take years. And they wont even let me start now. When they gave me permission to come back yesterday, they forbade me to work them until they have gone over them to locate the shells which might not have exploded.'

And the husband was right because here was the farm, the land pitted (not too severely; some of the trees had not even been topped) with shell craters where she herself had worked beside her husband in the tense seasons and which had been the life of the brother in the cheap coffin behind her in the cart and which was to have been his some day whom she had brought back to sleep in it. Then the house; the husband had been right; it was unmarked save for a pock a ragged gout of small holes in one wall which was probably a machine-gun burst, the husband not even looking at the house but getting down from the cart (a little stiffly; she remarked for the first time how his arthritis seemed to have increased) to go and stand looking out over his ruined land. Nor did she enter the house either, calling him by name; then she said:

'Come now. Let's finish this first.' So he returned and entered the house; apparently he had brought some of the tools back with him yesterday too because he reappeared at once with a spade and mounted the cart again. Though this time she had the lines, as though she knew exactly where she wanted to go, the cart moving again, crossing the field now rank with weeds and wild poppies, skirting the occasional craters, on for perhaps half a kilometre to a bank beneath an ancient beech tree which also had escaped the shells.

The digging was easier here, into the bank, all of them taking turns, the girl too though Marthe tried once to dissuade her. 'No,' she said. 'Let me. Let me be doing something.' Though even then it took them a long time until the excavation was deep enough into the bank to contain the coffin, the four of them now shoving and sliding the box back into the cave they had made.

'The medal,' the husband said. 'You dont want to put that in too? I can open the box.' But Marthe didn't even answer, taking the shovel herself first until the husband relieved her of it and at last the bank was smooth again save for the shovel marks; afternoon then and almost evening when they returned to the house and (the three women) entered it while the husband went on to the stable to put the horse up for the night. She had not seen it in almost four years, nor did she pause to examine it now. She crossed the room and dropped, almost tossed, the medal onto the vacant mantel and then turned, not really examining the room now. The house had not been damaged: merely eviscerated. They had moved out what the cart would carry that day in 1914, and the husband had fetched that back with him yesterday—enough dishes and bedding, the objects of no value which she had insisted on saving at the expense of things they would actually need when they returned; she could not even remember now what she had felt, thought, then: whether they would ever return or not, if perhaps that anguished day had not been the actual end of home and hope. Nor did she try to remember now, going on to the kitchen; the husband had brought food and fuel for the stove and Marya and the girl were already starting a fire in the stove; again she said to the girl:

'Why dont you rest?'

'No,' the girl said again. 'Let me be doing something.' The lamp was lighted now; it was that near to darkness before she noticed that the husband had not yet come in from the stable. She knew at once where he would be: motionless, almost invisible in the faint last of light, looking at his ruined land. This time she approached and touched him.

'Come now,' she said. 'Supper is ready,' checking him again with her hand at the open lamplit door until he had seen the older sister and the girl moving between the stove and the table. 'Look at her,' she said. 'She has nothing left. She was not even kin to him. She only loved him.'

But he seemed incapable of remembering or grieving over anything but his land; they had eaten the meal and he and she lay again in the familiar bed between the familiar walls beneath the familiar rafters; he had gone to sleep at once though even as she lay rigid and sleepless beside him he flung his head suddenly and muttered, cried, 'The farm. The land:' waking himself. 'What?' he said. 'What is it?'

'It's all right,' she said. 'Go back to sleep.' Because suddenly she knew that he was right. Stefan was gone; all that was over, done, finished, never to be recalled. He had been her brother but she had been his mother too, who knew now that she would have no children of her own and who had raised him from infancy; France, England, America too by now probably, were full of women who had given the lives of their sons to defend their countries and preserve justice and right; who was she to demand uniqueness for grieving? He was right: it was the farm, the land which was immune even to the blast and sear of war. It would take work of course, it might even take years of work, but the four of them were capable of work. More: their palliation and their luck was the work they faced, since work is the only anesthetic to which grief is vulnerable. More still: restoring the land would not only palliate the grief, the minuscule integer of the farm would affirm that he had not died for nothing and that it was not for an outrage that they grieved, but for simple grief: the only alternative to which was nothing, and between grief and nothing only the coward takes nothing.

So she even slept at last, dreamless; so dreamless that she did not know she had been asleep until someone was shaking her. It was the older sister; behind her the girl stood with her worn dirty sleepwalker's face which might be pretty again with a little soap and water and a week of proper food. It was dawn and then she, Marthe, heard the sound too even before the older sister cried: 'Listen, Sister!', the husband waking too, to lie for an instant, then surging upright among the tumbled bedclothing.

'The guns!' he cried, 'the guns!' the four of them transfixed for another ten or fifteen seconds like a tableau while the uproar of the barrage seemed to be rolling directly toward them; transfixed still even after they began to hear above or beneath the steady roar of explosions, the whistle of the shells passing over the house itself. Then the husband moved. 'We must get out of here,' he said, lurching, plunging out of the bed, where he would have fallen if she had not caught and held him up, the four of them in their night clothing running across the room and then out of the house, quitting one roof, one ceiling only to run stumbling on their bare feet beneath that other one filled with thunder and demonic whistling, not realising yet that the barrage was missing the house by two or three hundred metres, the three women following the husband, who seemed to know where he was going.

He did know: a tremendous crater in the field which must have been from a big howitzer, the four of them running, stumbling among the dew-heavy weeds and blood-red poppies, down into the crater, the husband pressing the three women against the wall beneath the lip facing the barrage where they crouched, their heads bowed almost as though in prayer, the husband crying steadily in a voice as thin and constant as a cicada's: 'The land. The land. The land.'

That is, all of them except Marthe. She had not even stooped, erect, tall, watching across the lip of the crater the barrage as it missed the house, skirting the house and the farm buildings as neatly and apparently as intentionally as a scythe skirts a rosebush, rolling on eastward across the field in one vast pall of dust filled with red flashes, the dust still hanging in the air after the flashes of the shell-bursts had winked and blinked rapidly on, to disappear beyond the field's edge like a furious migration of gigantic daylight-haunting fireflies, leaving behind only the thunder of their passing, it too already beginning to diminish.

Then Marthe began to climb out of the crater. She climbed rapid and strong, agile as a goat, kicking backward at the husband as he grasped at the hem of her nightdress and then at her bare feet, up and out of the crater, running strongly through the weeds and poppies, dodging the sparse old craters until she reached the swathe of the barrage, where the three still crouched in the crater could see her actually leaping across and among the thick new ones. Then the field was full of running men—a ragged line of French and American troops which overtook and passed her; they saw one, either an officer or a sergeant, pause and gesticulate at her, his mouth open and soundless with yelling for a moment before he too turned and ran on with the rest of the charge, the three of them out of the crater too now, running and stumbling into the new craters and the fading dust and the fierce and fading stink of cordite.

At first they couldn't even find the bank. And when they did at last, the beech tree had vanished: no mark, nothing remained to orient by. 'It was here, Sister!' the older sister cried, but Marthe didn't answer, running strongly on, they following until they too saw what she had apparently seen—the splinters and fragments, whole limbs still intact with leaves, scattered for a hundred metres; when they overtook her, she was holding in her hand a shard of the pale new unpainted wood which had been the coffin; she spoke to the husband by name, quite gently:

'You'll have to go back and get the shovel.' But before he could turn, the girl had already passed him, running, frantic yet unerring, deer-light among the craters and what remained of the weeds and the quenchless poppies, getting smaller and smaller yet still running, back toward the house. That was Sunday. When the girl returned with the shovel, still running, they took turns with it, all that day until it was too dark to see. They found a few more shards and fragments of the coffin, but the body itself was gone.

Tomorrow

Once more there were twelve of them though this time they were led by a sergeant. The carriage was a special one though it was still third class; the seats had been removed from the forward compartment and on the floor of it rested a new empty military coffin. The thirteen of them had left Paris at midnight and by the time they reached St Mihiel they were already fairly drunk. Because the job, mission, was going to be an unpleasant one, now that peace and victory had really come to western Europe in November (six months after the false armistice in May, that curious week's holiday which the war had taken which had been so false that they remembered it only as phenomena) and a man, even though still in uniform, might have thought himself free, at least until they started the next one, of yesterday's cadavers. So they had been issued an extra wine and brandy ration to compensate for this, in charge of the sergeant who was to have doled it out to them at need. But the sergeant, who had not wanted the assignment either, was a dour introvert who had secluded himself in an empty compartment forward with a pornographic magazine as soon as the train left Paris. But, alert for the opportunity, when the sergeant quitted his compartment at Chalons (they didn't know why nor bother: perhaps to find a urinal; possibly it was merely official) two of them (one had been a fairly successful picklock in civilian life before 1914 and planned to resume that vocation as soon as he was permitted to doff his uniform) entered the compartment and opened the sergeant's valise and extracted two bottles of brandy from it.

So when the Bar-le-Duc express dropped their carriage at St Mihiel, where the local for Verdun would engage it, they (except the sergeant) were a shade better than fairly drunk; and when, shortly after daylight, the local set the carriage on a repaired siding in the rubble of Verdun, they were even another shade better than that; by that time also the sergeant had discovered the ravishing of his valise and counted the remaining bottles and, what with the consequent uproar of his outraged and angry denunciation, plus their own condition, they did not even notice the old woman at first; only then to remark that there had been something almost like a committee waiting for them, as though word of the time of their arrival and their purpose too had preceded them—a clump, a huddle, a small group, all men save one, of laborers from the town and peasants from the adjacent countryside, watching them quietly while the sergeant (carrying the valise) snarled and cursed at them, out of which that one, the old woman, had darted at once and was now tugging at the sergeant's sleeve—a peasant woman older in appearance than in years when seen close, with a worn lined face which looked as though she too had not slept much lately, but which was now tense and even alight with a sort of frantic eagerness and hope.

'Eh?' the sergeant said at last. 'What? What is it you want?'

'You are going out to the forts,' she said. 'We know why. Take me with you.'

'You?' the sergeant said; now they were all listening. 'What for?'

'It's Theodule,' she said. 'My son. They told me he was killed there in 1916 but they didn't send him back home and they wont let me go out there and find him.'

'Find him?' the sergeant said. 'After three years?'

'I will know him,' she said. 'Only let me go and look. I will know him. You have a mother; think how she would grieve for you if you had died and they had not sent you home. Take me with you. I will know him, I tell you. I will know him at once. Come now.' She was clinging to his arm now while he tried to shake her loose.

'Let go!' he said. 'I cant take you out there without an

order, even if I would. We've got a job to do; you would be in the way. Let go!'

But she still clung to the sergeant's arm, looking about at the other faces watching her, her own face eager and unconvinced. 'Boys—children,' she said. 'You have mothers too—some of you——'

'Let go!' the sergeant said, swapping the valise to the other hand and jerking himself free this time. 'Gwan! Beat it:' taking her by the shoulders, the valise pressed against her back, and turning her and propelling her across the platform toward the quiet group which had been watching too. 'There aint nothing out there anymore by now but rotten meat; you couldn't find him even if you went.'

'I can,' she said. 'I know I can. I sold the farm, I tell you. I have money. I can pay you——'

'Not me,' the sergeant said. 'Not but that if I had my way, you could go out there and find yours and bring another one back for us, and we would wait for you here. But you aint going.' He released her, speaking almost gently. 'You go on back home and forget about this. Is your husband with you?'

'He is dead too. We lived in the Morbihan. When the war was over, I sold the farm and came here to find Theodule.'

'Then go on back to wherever it is you are living now. Because you cant go with us.'

But she went no further than the group she had emerged from, to turn and stand again, watching, the worn sleepless face still eager, unconvinced, indomitable, while the sergeant turned back to his squad and stopped and gave them another scathing and introverted look. 'All right,' he said at last. 'All of you that aint seeing double, let's go. Because I dont want to mess around out there long enough to get one stinking carcass, let alone two.'

'How about a drink first?' one said.

'Try and get it.'

'Want me to carry your grip, Sarge?' another said. The sergeant's answer was simple, brief and obscene. He turned, they followed raggedly. A lorry, a closed van, was waiting for them, with a driver and a corporal. They drew the empty coffin from its compartment and carried it to the van and slid it inside and got in themselves. There was straw for them to sit on; the sergeant himself sat on the coffin, the valise in his lap and one hand still gripping the handle as if he expected one or maybe all of them to try to snatch it from him. The lorry moved.

'Dont we get any breakfast?' one said.

'You drank yours,' the sergeant said. 'After you stole it first.' But there was breakfast: bread and coffee at a zinc bar in a tiny bistro for some inscrutable reason untouched by the shelling except that it had a new American-made sheet-iron roof, which stuck upward from the tumbled masses of collapsed walls surrounding and enclosing it. That was arranged too; the meal was already paid for from Paris.

'Christ,' one said. 'The army sure wants this corpse bad if they have started buying grub from civilians.' The sergeant ate with the valise on the bar before him, between his arms. Then they were in the lorry again, the sergeant gripping the valise on his lap; now, through the open rear door of the lorry as it crept between the piles of rubble and the old craters, they were able to see something of the ruined city—the mountains and hills of shattered masonry which men were already at work clearing away and out of which there rose already an astonishing number of the American-made iron roofs to glint like silver in the morning sun; maybe the Americans had not fought all the war but at least they were paying for the restoration of its devastation.

That is, the sergeant could have seen it because almost at once his men had entered a state resembling coma, even before they had crossed the Meuse bridge and reached the corner, where in time the five heroic-sized figures would stare steadily and indomitably eastward in bas-relief from the symbolical section of stone bastion which would frame and contain them. Or rather, the sergeant could have been able to, sitting with the valise huddled between his arms on his lap like a mother with a sick baby, watching them intently for perhaps another ten minutes where they lay sprawled against one another in the straw, the lorry well out of the city now. Then he rose, still carrying the valise; there was a small sliding panel in the lorry's front wall. He opened it and spoke rapidly and quietly for a moment with the corporal beside the driver, then he unlocked the valise and took all the bottles save one of brandy out of it and passed them to the corporal and locked the valise on the single remaining bottle and returned and sat on the coffin again, the valise huddled again on his lap.

So now, as the lorry climbed the repaired road to follow the curve of the Meuse Heights, the sergeant at least could watch beyond the open door the ruined and slain land unfold—the corpse of earth, some of which, its soil soured forever with cordite and human blood and anguish, would never live again, as though not only abandoned by man but repudiated forever by God Himself: the craters, the old trenches and rusted wire, the stripped and blasted trees, the little villages and farms like shattered skulls no longer even recognisable as skulls, already beginning to vanish beneath a fierce rank colorless growth of nourishmentless grass coming not tenderly out of the earth's surface but as though miles and leagues up from Hell itself, as if the Devil himself were trying to hide what man had done to the earth which was his mother.

Then the battered fort which nevertheless had endured, steadfast still even though France, civilization no longer needed it; steadfast still even if only to taint the air not only more than two years after the battle had ended and the mass rotting should have annealed itself, but more than twice that many months after the war itself had stopped. Because as soon as the sergeant, standing now and clasping the valise to his breast, roused them with the side of his boot, they were already smelling it: who had not thought they would have to begin that until they were actually inside the fort; though once the sergeant had kicked and cursed the last of them out of the lorry, they saw why—a midden of white bones and skulls and some still partly covered with strips and patches of what looked like brown or black leather, and boots and stained uniforms and now and then what would be an intact body wrapped in a fragment of tarpaulin, beside one of the low entrances in the stone wall; while they watched two more soldiers in butchers' aprons and with pieces of cloth bound over their nostrils and lower faces, emerged from the low entrance carrying between them a two-man wheel-less barrow heaped with more scraps and fragments of the fort's old 1916 defenders. In time there would be a vast towered chapel, an ossuary, visible for miles across the Heights like the faintly futuristic effigy of a gigantic gray goose or an iguanodon created out of gray stone not by a sculptor but by expert masons—a long tremendous nave enclosed by niches in each of which a light would burn always, the entrance to each arched with the carven names taken not from identity discs but from regimental lists since there would be nothing to match them with—squatting over the vast deep pit into which the now clean inextricable anonymous bones of what had been man, men, would be shoveled and sealed; facing it would be the slope white with the orderly parade of Christian crosses bearing the names and regimental designations of the bones which could be identified; and beyond it, that other slope ranked not with crosses but with rounded headstones set faintly but intractably oblique to face where Mecca was, set with a consistent and almost formal awryness and carved in cryptic and indecipherable hieroglyph because the bones here had been identifiable too which had once been men come this far from their hot sun and sand, this far from home and all familiar things, to make this last sacrifice in the northern rain and mud and cold, for what cause unless their leaders, ignorant too, could have explained some of it, a little of it to them in their own tongue. But now there only the dun-colored battered and enduring walls of the fortress, flanked by the rounded sunken concrete domes of machine-gun placements like giant mushrooms, and the midden and the two soldiers in butchers' aprons dumping their barrow onto it then turning with the empty barrow to look at them for a moment above the taut rags over their nostrils and mouths with the fixed exhaustless unseeing unrecognising glares of sleepwalkers in nightmares before descending the steps again; and over all, permeant and invincible, the odor, the smell, as though, victims of man and therefore quit of him, they had bequeathed him that which had already been invulnerable to him for three years and would still be for thirty more or even three hundred more, so that all that remained to him was to abandon it, flee it.

They looked at the midden, then at the low orifice in the

dun stone through which the two soldiers with the barrow had seemed to plunge, drop as though into the bowels of the earth; they did not know yet that in their eyes too now was that fixed assuageless glare of nightmares. 'Christ,' one said. 'Let's grab one off that dump there and get the hell out of here.'

'No,' the sergeant said; there was something behind his voice not vindictiveness so much as repressed gleeful anticipation—if they had known it. He had worn his uniform ever since September 1914 without ever having become a soldier; he could remain in it for another decade and still would not be one. He was an office man, meticulous and reliable; his files were never out of order, his returns never late. He neither drank nor smoked; he had never heard a gun fired in his life save the amateur sportsmen banging away at whatever moved on Sunday morning around the little Loire village where he had been born and lived until his motherland demanded him. Perhaps all this was why he had been given this assignment. 'No,' he said. 'The order says, Proceed to Verdun and thence with expedition and despatch to the catacombs beneath the Fort of Valaumont and extricate therefrom one complete cadaver of one French soldier unidentified and unidentifiable either by name regiment or rank, and return with it. And that's what we're going to do. Get on with you: forward.'

'Let's have a drink first,' one said.

'No,' the sergeant said. 'Afterward. Get it loaded into the lorry first.'

'Come on, Sarge,' another said. 'Think what that stink will be down that hole.'

'No, I tell you!' the sergeant said. 'Get on there! Forward!' He didn't lead them; he drove, herded them, to bow their heads one by one into the stone tunnel, to drop, plunge in their turn down the steep pitch of the stone stairs as though into the bowels of the earth, into damp and darkness, though presently, from beyond where the stairs flattened at last into a tunnel, they could see a faint unsteady red gleam not of electricity, it was too red and unsteady, but from torches. They were torches; there was one fastened to the wall beside the first doorless opening in the wall and now they could see one another binding across their nostrils and lower faces what soiled handkerchiefs and filthy scraps of rag which they found on themselves (one who apparently had neither was holding the collar of his coat across his face), huddling and then halting here because an officer, his face swatched to the eyes in a silk one, had emerged from the opening; huddling back against the wall of the narrow tunnel while the sergeant with his valise came forward and saluted and presented his order to the officer, who opened it and glanced briefly at it, then turned his head and spoke back into the room behind him, and a corporal carrying an electric torch and a folded stretcher came out; he had a gas-mask slung about his neck.

Then, the corporal with his torch leading now and the foremost man carrying the stretcher, they went on again between the sweating walls, the floor itself beneath the feet viscous and greasy so that there was a tendency to slip, passing the doorless orifices in the walls beyond which they could see the tiered bunks in which in time during those five months in 1916 men had actually learned to sleep beneath the muted thunder and the trembling of the earth, the smell which above ground had had a sort of vividness, as though even yet partaking invincibly still of something of that motion which is life, not increasing so much as becoming familiar—an old stale dead and worn accustomedness which man would never eradicate and so in time would even get used to and even cease to smell it—a smell subterrene and claustrophobe and doomed to darkness, not alone of putrefaction but of fear and old sweat and old excrement and endurance; fear attenuated to that point where it must choose between coma and madness and in the intermittent coma no longer feared but merely stank.

More soldiers in pairs with masked faces and heaped barrows or stretchers passed them; suddenly more sweating and viscid stairs plunged away beneath them; at the foot of the stairs the tunnel made a sharp angle, no longer floored and walled and roofed with concrete; and, turning the corner behind the corporal, it was no longer a tunnel even but an excavation a cavern a cave a great niche dug out of one wall in which during the height of the battle, when there had been no other way to dispose of them, the bodies which had merely been killed and the ones which had been killed and dismembered too in the fort or the connecting machine-gun pits had been tumbled and covered with earth, the tunnel itself continuing on beyond it: a timber-shored burrow not even high enough for a man to stand erect in, through or beyond which they now saw a steady white glare which would have to be electricity, from which as they watched two more hooded and aproned soldiers emerged, carrying a stretcher with what would be an intact body this time.

'Wait here,' the corporal said.

'My orders say——' the sergeant said.

'. . . . your orders,' the corporal said. 'We got a system here. We do things our way. Down here, you're on active service, pal. Just give me two of your men and the stretcher. Though you can come too, if you think nothing less will keep your nose clean.'

'That's what I intend to do,' the sergeant said. 'My orders say——' But the corporal didn't wait, going on, the two with the stretcher, the sergeant stooping last to enter the further tunnel, the valise still clasped against his breast like a sick child. It did not take them long, as if there were plenty in the next traverse to choose from; almost at once, it seemed to the remaining ten, they saw the sergeant come stooping out of the burrow, still clasping the valise, followed by the two men with the burdened stretcher at a sort of stumbling run, then last the corporal who didn't even pause, walking around the stretcher where the two bearers had dropped it, already going on toward the stairs until the sergeant stopped him. 'Wait,' the sergeant said, the valise now clasped under one arm while he produced his order and a pencil from inside his coat and shook the folded order open. 'We got systems in Paris too. It's a Frenchman.'

'Right,' the corporal said.

'It's all here. Nothing missing.'

'Right,' the corporal said.

'No identification of name regiment or rank.'

'Right,' the corporal said.

'Then sign it,' the sergeant said, holding out the pencil as the corporal approached. 'You,' he said to the nearest man.

'About face and bend over.' Which the man did, the sergeant holding the paper flat on his bowed back while the corporal signed. 'Your lieutenant will have to sign too,' the sergeant said, taking the pencil from the corporal. 'You might go on ahead and tell him.'

'Right,' the corporal said, going on again.

'All right,' the sergeant said to the stretcher bearers. 'Get it out of here.'

'Not yet,' the first stretcher bearer said. 'We're going to have that drink first.'

'No,' the sergeant said. 'When we get it into the lorry.' He had not wanted the assignment and indeed he did not belong here because this time they simply took the valise away from him in one concerted move of the whole twelve of them, not viciously, savagely, just rapidly: with no heat at all but almost impersonal, almost inattentive, as you might rip a last year's calendar from the wall to kindle a fire with it; the ex-picklock didn't even pretend to conceal his action this time, producing his instrument in plain view, the others crowding around him as he opened the valise. Or they thought the rapidity and ease of the valise's rape had been because they were too many for the sergeant, staring down at the single bottle it contained with shock then outrage and then with something like terror while the sergeant stood back and over them, laughing steadily down at them with a sort of vindictive and triumphant pleasure.

'Where's the rest of it?' one said.

'I threw it away,' the sergeant said. 'Poured it out.'

'Poured it out, hell,' another said. 'He sold it.'

'When?' another said. 'When did he have a chance to? Or pour it out either.'

'While we were all asleep in the lorry coming out here.'

'I wasn't asleep,' the second said.

'All right, all right,' the ex-picklock said. 'What does it matter what he did with it? It's gone. We'll drink this one. Where's your corkscrew?' he said to a third one. But the man already had the corkscrew out, opening the bottle. 'Okay,' the ex-picklock said to the sergeant, 'you go on and report to the officer and we'll take it up and be putting it into the coffin.'

'Right,' the sergeant said, taking up the empty valise. 'I want to get out of here too. I dont even need to want a drink to prove I dont like this.' He went on. They emptied the bottle rapidly, passing it from one to another, and flung it away.

'All right,' the ex-picklock said. 'Grab that thing up and let's get out of here.' Because already he was the leader, none to say or know or even care when it had happened. Because they were not drunk now, not inebriates but madmen, the last brandy lying in their stomachs cold and solid as balls of ice as they almost ran with the stretcher up the steep stairs.

'Where is it, then?' the one pressing behind the ex-picklock said.

'He gave it to that corporal riding up front,' the ex-picklock said. 'Through that panel while we were asleep.' They burst out into the air, the world, earth and sweet air again where the lorry waited, the driver and the corporal standing with a group of men some distance away. They had all heard the ex-picklock and dropped the stretcher without even pausing and were rushing toward the lorry until the ex-picklock stopped them. 'Hold it,' he said. 'I'll do it.' But the missing bottles were nowhere in the lorry. The ex-picklock returned to the stretcher.

'Call that corporal over here,' one said. 'I know how to make him tell where it is.'

'Fool,' the ex-picklock said. 'If we start something now, dont you know what'll happen? He'll call the M.P.'s and put us all under arrest and get a new guard from the adjutant in Verdun. We cant do anything here. We've got to wait till we get back to Verdun.'

'What'll we do in Verdun?' another said. 'Buy some liquor? With what? You couldn't get one franc out of the whole lot of us with a suction pump.'

'Morache can sell his watch,' a fourth said.

'But will he?' a fifth said. They all looked at Morache.

'Forget that now,' Morache said. 'Picklock's right; the first thing to do is to get back to Verdun. Come up. Let's get this thing into that box.' They carried the stretcher to the lorry and lifted the sheeted body into it. The lid of the coffin had not been fastened down; a hammer and nails were inside the coffin. They tumbled the body into it, whether face-up or face-down they didn't know and didn't bother, and replaced the top and caught the nails enough to hold it shut. Then the sergeant with his now empty valise climbed through the rear door and sat again on the coffin; the corporal and the driver obviously had returned too because at once the lorry moved, the twelve men sitting on the straw against the walls, quiet now, outwardly as decorous as well-behaved children but actually temporarily insane, capable of anything, talking occasionally among themselves, peacefully, idle and extraneous while the lorry returned to Verdun, until they were actually in the city again and the lorry had stopped before a door beside which a sentry stood: obviously the commandant's headquarters: and the sergeant began to get up from the coffin. Then Picklock made one last effort:

'I understood orders said we were to have brandy not just to go to Valaumont and get the body out, but to get it back to Paris. Or am I wrong?'

'If you are, who made you wrong?' the sergeant said. He looked down at Picklock a moment longer. Then he turned toward the door; it was as though he too had recognised Picklock as their leader: 'I'll have to sign some bumf here. Take it on to the station and load it into the carriage and wait for me there. Then we'll have lunch.'

'Right,' Picklock said. The sergeant dropped to the ground and vanished; at once, even before the lorry had begun to move again, their whole air, atmosphere changed, as if their very characters and personalities had altered, or not altered but rather as if they had shed masks or cloaks; their very speech was short, rapid, succinct, cryptic, at times even verbless, as if they did not need to communicate but merely to prompt one another in one mutual prescient cognizance.

'Morache's watch,' one said.

'Hold it,' Picklock said. 'The station first.'

'Tell him to hurry then,' another said. 'I'll do it,' he said, starting to get up.

'Hold it, I said,' Picklock said, gripping him. 'Do you want M.P.'s?' So they stopped talking and just sat, immobile and in motion, furious in immobility like men strained against a pyramid, as if they were straining at the back of the moving lorry itself with the urgency of their passion and need. The lorry stopped. They were already getting out of it, the first ones dropping to the ground before it had stopped moving, their hands already on the coffin. The platform was empty now, or so they thought, would have thought if they had noticed, which they didn't, not even looking that way as they dragged the coffin out of the lorry, almost running again across the platform with it toward where the carriage waited on the siding; not until a hand began to tug at Picklock's sleeve, an urgent voice at his elbow saying:

'Mister Corporal! Mister Corporal!' Picklock looked down. It was the old woman of the morning whose son had died in the Verdun battle.

'Beat it, grandma,' Picklock said, twitching his arm free. 'Come on. Get that door open.'

But the old woman still clung to him, speaking still with that terrible urgency: 'You've got one. It might be Theodule. I will know. Let me look at him.'

'Beat it, I tell you!' Picklock said. 'We're busy.' So it was not Picklock at all, leader though he was, but one of the others who said suddenly and sharply, hissing it:

'Wait.' Though in the next second the same idea seemed to occur to them all, one end of the box resting now on the floor of the carriage and four of them braced to shove it the rest of the way, all of them paused now looking back while the speaker continued: 'You said something this morning about selling a farm.'

'Selling my farm?' the woman said.

'Money!' the other said in his hissing undertone.

'Yes! Yes!' the old woman said, fumbling under her shawl and producing an aged reticule almost as large as the sergeant's valise. Now Picklock did take charge.

'Hold it,' he said over his shoulder, then to the old woman: 'If we let you look at him, will you buy two bottles of brandy?'

'Make it three,' a third said.

'And in advance,' a fourth said. 'She cant tell anything from what's in that box now.'

'I can!' she said. 'I will know! Just let me look.'

'All right,' Picklock said. 'Go and get two bottles of brandy, and you can look at him. Hurry now, before the sergeant gets back.'

'Yes yes,' she said and turned, running, stiffly and awkwardly, clutching the reticule, back across the platform.

'All right,' Picklock said. 'Get it inside. One of you get the hammer out of the lorry.' Luckily their orders had been not to drive the nails home but merely to secure the lid temporarily (apparently the body was to be transferred to something a little more elegant or anyway commensurate with its purpose when it reached Paris) so they could draw them without difficulty. Which they did and removed the lid and then recoiled from the thin burst, gout of odor which rushed up at them almost visibly, like thin smoke—one last faint thin valedictory of corruption and mortality, as if the corpse itself had hoarded it for three years against this moment or any similar one with the gleeful demonic sentience of a small boy. Then the old woman returned, clasping two bottles against her breast, still running or at least trotting, panting now, shaking, almost as though from physical exhaustion because she couldn't even climb the steps when she reached the door, so that two of them dropped to the ground and lifted her bodily into the carriage. A third one took the bottles from her, though she didn't seem to notice it. For a second or so she couldn't even seem to see the coffin. Then she saw it and half knelt half collapsed at the head of it and turned the tarpaulin back from what had been a face. They—the speaker—had been right; she could have told nothing from the face because it was no longer man. Then they knew that she was not even looking at it: just kneeling there, one hand resting on what had been the face and the other caressing what remained of its hair. She said:

'Yes. Yes. This is Theodule. This is my son.' Suddenly she rose, strongly now, and faced them, pressing back against the coffin, looking rapidly from face to face until she found Picklock; her voice was calm and strong too. 'I must have him.'

'You said just to look at him,' Picklock said.

'He is my son. He must go home. I have money. I will buy you a hundred bottles of brandy. Or the money itself, if you want it.'

'How much will you give?' Picklock said. She didn't even hesitate. She handed him the unopened reticule.

'Count it yourself,' she said.

'But how are you going to get it—him away from here? You cant carry it.'

'I have a horse and cart. It's been behind the station yonder ever since we heard yesterday what you were coming for.'

'Heard how?' Picklock said. 'This is official business.'

'Does that matter?' she said, almost impatiently. 'Count it.'

But Picklock didn't open the reticule yet. He turned to Morache. 'Go with her and get the cart. Bring it up to the window on the other side. Make it snappy. Landry'll be back any minute now.' It didn't take long. They got the window up; almost immediately Morache brought the cart up, the big farm-horse going at a heavy and astonished gallop. Morache snatched it to a halt; already the others in the carriage had the sheeted body balanced on the window sill. Morache handed the lines to the old woman on the seat beside him and vaulted over the seat and snatched the body down into the cart and vaulted to the ground beside it; at that moment Picklock inside the carriage tossed the reticule through the window, into the cart.

'Go on,' Morache said to the old woman. 'Get the hell out of here. Quick.' Then she was gone. Morache re-entered the carriage. 'How much was it?' he said to Picklock.

'I took a hundred francs,' Picklock said.

'A hundred francs?' another said with incredulous amazement.

'Yes,' Picklock said. 'And tomorrow I'll be ashamed I took even that much. But that will be a bottle apiece.' He handed the money to the man who had spoken last. 'Go and get it.' Then to the others: 'Get that lid back on. What are you waiting for, anyway: for Landry to help you?' They replaced the coffin lid and set the nails in the old holes. The absolute minimum of prudence would have dictated or at least suggested a weight of some kind, any kind in the coffin first, but they were not concerned with prudence. The ganymede returned, clasping a frayed wicker basket to his breast; they snatched it from him before he could even get into the carriage, the owner of the corkscrew opening the bottles rapidly as they were passed to him.

'He said to bring the basket back,' the ganymede said.

'Take it back then,' Picklock said: and then no more of that either; the hands snatching at the bottles almost before the corks were out, so that when the sergeant returned about an hour later, his outrage—not rage: outrage—knew no bounds. But this time he was impotent because they were indeed in coma now, sprawled and snoring in one inextricable filth of straw and urine and vomit and spilled brandy and empty bottles, invulnerable and immune in that nepenthe when toward the end of the afternoon an engine coupled onto the carriage and took it back to St Mihiel and set it off on another siding, and waking them only because of the glare of yellow light which now filled the carriage through the windows, and the sound of hammers against the outside of it, which roused Picklock.

Clasping his throbbing head and shutting his eyes quickly against that unbearable glare, it seemed to him that there had never been so fierce a sunrise. It was almost like electricity; he didn't see how he could move beneath it to rise, and even on his feet, staggering until he braced himself, he didn't see how he had accomplished the feat, bracing himself against the wall while he kicked the others one by one into sentience or anyway consciousness. 'Get up,' he said. 'Get up. We've got to get out of here.'

'Where are we?' one said.

'Paris,' Picklock said. 'It's already tomorrow.'

'Oh Christ,' a voice said. Because they were all awake now, waking not into remembering, since even comatose they had not really forgotten, but into simple realisation like sleepwalkers waking to find themselves standing on the outside of forty-storey window ledges. They were not drunk now. They didn't even have time to be sick. 'Christ yes,' the voice said. They got up, staggering for balance, shaking and trembling, and stumbled through the door and huddled, blinking against the fierce glare until they could bear it. Except that it was electricity; it was still last night (or perhaps tomorrow night, for all they knew or for the moment cared even): two searchlights such as anti aircraft batteries had used against night-flying aeroplanes during the war, trained on the carriage and in the glare of which men on ladders were nailing long strips of black and funereal bunting along the eaves of the carriage: to whom—which—they paid no attention. Nor was it Paris either.

'We're still in Verdun,' another said.

'Then they've moved the station around to the other side of the tracks,' Picklock said.

'Anyway it's not Paris,' a third said. 'I've got to have a drink.'

'No,' Picklock said. 'You'll take coffee and something to eat.' He turned to the ganymede. 'How much money have you got left?'

'I gave it to you,' the ganymede said.

'Damn that,' Picklock said, extending his hand. 'Come on with it.' The ganymede fumbled out a small wad of paper notes and coins. Picklock took and counted it rapidly. 'It might do,' he said. 'Come on.' There was a small bistro opposite the station. He led the way to it and inside—a small zinc bar at which a single man stood in a countryman's corduroy coat, and two tables where other men in the rough clothes of farmers or laborers sat with glasses of coffee or wine, playing dominoes, all of them turning to look as Picklock led his party in and up to the bar, where a tremendous woman in black said,

'Messieurs?'

'Coffee, Madame, and bread if you have it,' Picklock said.

'I dont want coffee,' the third said. 'I want a drink.'

'Sure,' Picklock said in a calm and furious voice, even lowering it a little: 'Stick around here until somebody comes and lifts that box, let alone opens it. I hear they always give you a drink before you climb the steps.'

'Maybe we could find another—' a fourth began.

'Shut up,' Picklock said. 'Drink that coffee. I've got to think.' Then a new voice spoke.

'What's the matter?' it said. 'You boys in trouble?' It was the man who had been standing at the bar when they entered. They looked at him now—a solid stocky man, obviously a farmer, not quite as old as they had thought, with a round hard ungullible head and a ribbon in the lapel of the coat—

not one of the best ones but still a good one, matching in fact one which Picklock himself wore; possibly that was why he spoke to them, he and Picklock watching one another for a moment.

'Where'd you get it?' Picklock said.

'Combles,' the stranger said.

'So was I,' Picklock said.

'You in a jam of some sort?' the stranger said.

'What makes you think that?' Picklock said.

'Look, Buster,' the stranger said. 'Maybe you were under sealed orders when you left Paris, but there hasn't been much secret about it since your sergeant got out of that carriage this afternoon. What is he, anyway? some kind of a reformist preacher, like they say they have in England and America? He was sure in a state. He didn't seem to care a damn that you were drunk. What seemed to fry him was, how you managed to get twelve more bottles of brandy without him knowing how you did it.'

'This afternoon?' Picklock said. 'You mean it's still today? Where are we?'

'St Mihiel. You lay over here tonight while they finish nailing enough black cloth on your carriage to make it look like a hearse. Tomorrow morning a special train will pick you up and take you on to Paris. What's wrong? Did something happen?'

Suddenly Picklock turned. 'Come on back here,' he said. The stranger followed. They stood slightly apart from the others now, in the angle of the bar and the rear wall. Picklock spoke rapidly yet completely, telling it all, the stranger listening quietly.

'What you need is another body,' the stranger said.

'You're telling me?' Picklock said.

'Why not? I've got one. In my field. I found it the first time I plowed. I reported it, but they haven't done anything about it yet. I've got a horse and cart here; it will take about four hours to go and come.' They looked at one another. 'You've got all night—that is, now.'

'All right,' Picklock said. 'How much?'

'You'll have to say. You're the one that knows how bad you need it.'

'We haven't got any money.'

'You break my heart,' the stranger said. They looked at one another. Without removing his eyes, Picklock raised his voice a little. 'Morache.' Morache came up. 'The watch,' Picklock said.

'Wait now,' Morache said. It was a Swiss movement, in gold; he had wanted one ever since he saw one first, finding it at last on the wrist of a German officer lying wounded in a shell crater one night after he, Morache, had got separated from a patrol sent out to try for a live prisoner or at least one still alive enough to speak. He even saw the watch first, before he saw who owned it, having hurled himself into the crater just in time before a flare went up, seeing the glint of the watch first in the corpse-glare of the magnesium before he saw the man—a colonel, apparently shot through the spine since he seemed to be merely paralysed, quite conscious and not even in much pain; he would have been exactly what they had been sent out to find, except for the watch. So Morache murdered him with his trench knife (a shot here now would probably have brought a whole barrage down on him) and took the watch and lay just outside his own wire until the patrol came back (empty-handed) and found him. Though for a day or so he couldn't seem to bring himself to wear the watch nor even look at it until he remembered that his face had been blackened at the time and the German could not have told what he was even, let alone who; besides that, the man was dead now. 'Wait,' he said. 'Wait, now.'

'Sure,' Picklock said. 'Wait in that carriage yonder until they come for that box. I dont know what they'll do to you then, but I do know what they'll do if you run because that will be desertion.' He held out his hand. 'The watch.' Morache unstrapped the watch and handed it to Picklock.

'At least get some brandy too,' he said. The stranger reached for the watch in Picklock's hand.

'Whoa, look at it from there,' Picklock said, holding the watch on his raised open palm.

'Sure you can have brandy,' the stranger said. Picklock closed his hand over the watch and let the hand drop.

'How much?' he said.

'Fifty francs,' the stranger said.

'Two hundred,' Picklock said.

'A hundred francs.'

'Two hundred,' Picklock said.

'Where's the watch?' the stranger said.

'Where's the cart?' Picklock said. It took them a little over four hours ('You'd have to wait anyhow until they finish nailing up that black cloth and get away from the carriage,' the stranger said) and there were four of them ('Two more will be enough,' the stranger said. 'We can drive right up to it.')—himself and the stranger on the seat, Morache and another behind them in the cart, north and eastward out of the town into the country darkness, the horse itself taking the right road without guidance, knowing that it was going home, in the darkness the steady jounce of jogging horse and the thump and rattle of the cart a sound and a vibration instead of a progress, so that it was the roadside trees which seemed to move, wheeling up out of the darkness to rush slowly backward past them against the sky. But they were moving, even though it did seem (to Picklock) forever, the roadside trees ravelling suddenly into a straggle of posts, the horse, still without guidance, swinging sharply to the left.

'Sector, huh?' Picklock said.

'Yeah,' the stranger said. 'The Americans broke it in September. Vienne-la-pucelle yonder,' he said, pointing. 'It caught it. It was right up in the tip. Not long now.' But it was a little longer than that though at last they were there—a farm and its farmyard, lightless. The stranger stopped the horse and handed Picklock the lines. 'I'll get a shovel. I'm going to throw in a ground-sheet too.' He was not long, passing the shovel and the folded ground-sheet to the two in the back and mounting the seat again and took the lines, the horse lurching forward and making a determined effort to turn in the farmyard gate until the stranger reined it sharply away. Then a gate in a hedgerow; Morache got down and opened it for the cart to pass. 'Leave it open,' the stranger said. 'We'll close it when we come out.' Which Morache did and swung up and into the cart as it passed him; they were in a field now, soft from plowing, the unguided horse still choosing its own unerring way, no longer a straight course now but weaving, at times almost doubling on itself though

Picklock could still see nothing. 'Dud shells,' the stranger explained. 'Fenced off with flags until they finish getting them out. We just plow circles around them. According to the women and the old men who were here then, the whole war started up again after that recess they took last May, right in that field yonder. It belongs to some people named Demont. The man died that same summer; I guess two wars on his land only a week apart was too much for him. His widow works it now with a hired man. Not that she needs him; she can run a plow as good as he can. There's another one, her sister. She does the cooking. She has flies up here.' He was standing now, peering ahead; in silhouette against the sky he tapped the side of his head. Suddenly he swung the horse sharply away and presently stopped it. 'Here we are,' he said. 'About fifty metres yonder on that bank dividing us, there used to be the finest beech tree in this country. My grandfather said that even his grandfather couldn't remember when it was a sapling. It probably went that same day too. All right,' he said. 'Let's get him up. You dont want to waste any time here either.'

He showed them where his plow had first exposed the corpse and he had covered it again and marked the place. It was not deep and they could see nothing and after this length of time or perhaps because it was only one, there was little odor either, the long inextricable mass of light bones and cloth soon up and out and on and then into the folds of the ground-sheet and then in the cart itself, the horse thinking that this time surely it was destined for its stall, trying even in the soft earth of the plowing to resume its heavy muscle-bound jog, Morache closing the hedge gate and having to run now to catch the cart again because the horse was now going at a heavy canter even against the lines, trying again to swing into the farmyard until the stranger sawed it away, using the whip now until he got it straightened out on the road back to St Mihiel.

A little more than four hours but perhaps it should have been. The town was dark now, and the bistro they had started from, a clump of shadow detaching itself from a greater mass of shadow and itself breaking into separate shapes as the nine others surrounded the cart, the cart itself not stopping but going steadily on toward where the carriage in its black pall of bunting had vanished completely into the night. But it was there; the ones who had remained in town had even drawn the nails again so that all necessary was to lift off the top and drag the ground-sheeted bundle through the window and dump it in and set the nails again. 'Drive them in,' Picklock said. 'Who cares about noise now? Where is the brandy?'

'It's all right,' a voice said.

'How many bottles did you open?'

'One,' a voice said.

'Counting from where?'

'Why should we lie when all you've got to do to prove it is to count the others?' the voice said.

'All right,' Picklock said. 'Get out of here now and shut the window.' Then they were on the ground again. The stranger had never quitted his cart and this time surely the horse was going home. But they didn't wait for that departure. They turned as one, already running, clotting and jostling a little at the carriage door, but plunging at last back into their lightless catafalque as into the womb itself. They were safe now. They had a body, and drink to take care of the night. There was tomorrow and Paris of course, but God could take care of that.

† † †

Carrying the gather of eggs in the loop of her apron, Marya, the elder sister, crossed the yard toward the house as though borne on a soft and tender cloud of white geese. They surrounded and enclosed her as though with a tender and eager yearning; two of them, one on either side, kept absolute pace with her, pressed against her skirts, their long undulant necks laid flat against her moving flanks, their heads tilted upward, the hard yellow beaks open slightly like mouths, the hard insentient eyes filmed over as with a sort of ecstasy: right up to the stoop itself when she mounted it and opened the door and stepped quickly through and closed it, the geese swarming and jostling around and over and onto the stoop itself to press against the door's blank wood, their necks extended and the heads fallen a little back as though on the brink of swoons, making with their hoarse harsh unmusical voices faint tender cries of anguish and bereavement and unassuageable grief.

This was the kitchen, already strong with the approaching mid-day's soup. She didn't even stop: putting the eggs away, lifting for a moment the lid of the simmering pot on the stove, then placed rapidly on the wooden table a bottle of wine, a glass, a soup bowl, a loaf, a napkin and spoon, then on through the house and out the front door giving onto the lane and the field beyond it where she could already see them—the horse and harrow and the man guiding them, the hired man they had had since the death of her sister's husband four years ago, and the sister herself moving across the land's panorama like a ritual, her hand and arm plunging into the sack slung from her shoulder, to emerge in that long sweep which is the second oldest of man's immemorial gestures or acts, she—Marya—running now, skirting among the old craters picketed off by tiny stakes bearing scraps of red cloth where the rank and lifeless grass grew above the unexploded shells, already saying, crying in her bright serene and carrying voice: 'Sister! Here is the young Englishman come for the medal. There are two of them, coming up the lane.'

'A friend with him?' the sister said.

'Not a friend,' Marya said. 'This one is looking for a tree.'

'A tree?' the sister said.

'Yes, Sister. Cant you see him?'

And, themselves in the lane now, they could see them both—two men obviously but, even at that distance, one of them moving not quite like a human being and, in time nearer, not like a human being at all beside the other's tall and shambling gait, but at a slow and terrific lurch and heave like some kind of giant insect moving erect and seeming to possess no progress at all even before Marya said: 'He's on crutches:' the single leg swinging metronome and indefatigable yet indomitable too between the rhythmic twin counterstrokes of the crutches; interminable yet indomitable too and indubitably coming nearer until they could see that the arm on that side was gone somewhere near the elbow also, and (quite near now) that what they looked at was not even a whole man since one half of his visible flesh was one furious saffron scar beginning at the ruined homburg hat and dividing his face exactly down the bridge of the nose, across the mouth and chin, to the collar of his shirt. But this seemed to be only outside because the voice was strong and unpitying and the French he addressed them in was fluid and good and it was only the man with him who was sick—a tall thin cadaver of a man, whole to be sure and looking no less like a tramp, but with a sick insolent intolerable face beneath a filthy hat from the band of which there stood a long and raking feather which made him at least eight feet tall.

'Madame Demont?' the first man said.

'Yes,' Marya said with her bright and tender and unpitying smile.

The man with the crutches turned to his companion. 'All right,' he said in French. 'This is them. Go ahead.' But Marya had not waited for him, speaking to the man on crutches in French:

'We were waiting for you. The soup is ready and you must be hungry after your walk from the station.' Then she too turned to the other, speaking not in French now but in the old Balkan tongue of her childhood: 'You too. You will need to eat for a little while longer too.'

'What?' the sister said suddenly and harshly, then to the man with the feather in the same mountain tongue: 'You are Zsettlani?'

'What?' the man with the feather said in French harshly and loudly. 'I speak French. I will take soup too. I can pay for it. See?' he said, thrusting his hand into his pocket. 'Look.'

'We know you have money,' Marya said in French. 'Come into the house.' And, in the kitchen now, they could see the rest of the first man: the saffron-colored scar not stopping at the hat's line but dividing the skull too into one furious and seared rigidity, no eye, no ear on that side of it, the corner of the mouth seized into rigidity as if it was not even the same face which talked and presently would chew and swallow; the filthy shirt held together at the throat by the frayed and faded stripes of what they did not know was a British regimental tie; the stained and soiled dinner jacket from the left breast of which two medals hung from their gaudy ribbons; the battered and filthy tweed trousers one leg of which was doubled back and up and fastened below the thigh with a piece of wire, the Englishman propped on the crutches for a moment yet in the center of the kitchen, looking about the room with that alert calm unpitying eye while his companion stood just inside the door behind him with his ravaged insolent peaceless face, still wearing the hat whose feather now almost touched the ceiling, as though he were suspended from it.

'So this is where he lived,' the man with the crutches said.

'Yes,' Marthe said. 'How did you know? How did you know where to find us?'

'Now, Sister,' Marya said. 'How could he have come for the medal if he didn't know where we were?'

'The medal?' the Englishman said.

'Yes,' Marya said. 'But have your soup first. You are hungry.'

'Thanks,' the Englishman said. He jerked his head toward the man behind him. 'He too? Is he invited too?'

'Of course,' Marya said. She took two of the bowls from the table and went to the stove, not offering to help him, nor could the sister, Marthe, have moved fast or quickly enough to help him as he swung the one leg over the wooden bench and propped the crutches beside him and was already uncorking the wine before the whole man at the door had even moved, Marya lifting the lid from the pot and half-turning to look back at the second man, saying in French this time: 'Sit down. You can eat too. Nobody minds any more.'

'Minds what?' the man with the feather said harshly.

'We have forgotten it,' Marya said. 'Take off your hat first.'

'I can pay you,' the man with the feather said. 'You cant give me anything, see?' He reached into his pocket and jerked his hand out already scattering the coins, flinging them toward and onto and past the table, scattering and clinking across the floor as he approached and flung himself onto the backless bench opposite the Englishman and reached for the wine bottle and a tumbler in one voracious motion.

'Pick up your money,' Marya said.

'Pick it up yourself, if you dont want it there,' the man said, filling the tumbler, splashing the wine into it until it was overfull, already raising the tumbler toward his mouth.

'Leave it now,' Marthe said. 'Give him his soup.' She had moved, not quite enough to stand behind the Englishman but rather over him, her hands resting one in the other, her high severe mountain face which would have been bold and handsome as a man's looking down at him while he reached and poured from the bottle and set the bottle down and raised his glass until he was looking at her across it.

'Health, Madame,' he said.

'But how did you know?' Marthe said. 'When did you know him?'

'I never knew him. I never saw him. I heard about him—them—when I came back out in '16. Then I learned what it was, and so after that I didn't need to see him—only to wait and keep out of his way until he would be ready to do the needing——'

'Bring the soup,' the man with the feather said harshly. 'Haven't I already shown you enough money to buy out your whole house?'

'Yes,' Marya said from the stove. 'Be patient. It wont be long now. I will even pick it up for you.' She brought the two bowls of soup; the man with the feather did not even wait for her to set his down, snatching and wolfing it, glaring across the bowl with his dead intolerant outrageous eyes while Marya stooped about their feet and beneath and around the table, gathering up the scattered coins. 'There are only twenty-nine,' she said. 'There should be one more.' Still holding the tilted bowl to his face, the man with the feather jerked another coin from his pocket and banged it onto the table.

'Does that satisfy you?' he said. 'Fill the bowl again.' She did so, at the stove, and brought the bowl back, while again he splashed the wanton and violent wine into his tumbler.

'Eat too,' she said to the man with the crutches.

'Thanks,' he said, not even looking at her but looking still at the tall cold-faced sister standing over him. 'Only about that time or during that time or at that time or whenever it was afterward that I woke up, I was in a hospital in England so it was next spring before I persuaded them to let me come back to France and go to Chaulnesmont until at last I found that sergeant-major and he told me where you were. Only there were three of you then. There was a girl too. His wife?' The tall woman just looked down at him, cold, calm, absolutely inscrutable. 'His fiancée, maybe?'

'Yes,' Marya said. 'That's it: his fiancée. That's the word. Eat your soup.'

'They were to be married,' Marthe said. 'She was a Marseille whore.'

'I beg pardon?' the Englishman said.

'But not any more,' Marya said. 'She was going to learn to be a farmer's wife. Eat your soup now before it is cold.'

'Yes,' the Englishman said. 'Thanks:' not even looking at her. 'What became of her?'

'She went back home.'

'Home? You mean, back to the—back to Marseilles?'

'Brothel,' the tall woman said. 'Say it. You English. The Americans too. Why did your French boggle at that word, being as good as it is with all the others?—She must live too,' she said.

'Thanks,' the Englishman said. 'But she could have stayed here.'

'Yes,' the woman said.

'But she didn't.'

'No,' the woman said.

'She couldn't, you see,' Marya said. 'She has an old grandmother she must support. I think it's quite admirable.'

'So do I,' the Englishman said. He took up the spoon.

'That's right,' Marya said. 'Eat.' But he was still looking at the sister, the spoon arrested above the bowl. Nor did the man with the feather wait this time to demand to be served, swinging his legs across the bench and carrying the bowl himself to the stove and plunging it, hand and all, into the pot before returning with the dripping and streaming bowl to the table where Marya had made the neat small stack of his coins and where the Englishman was still watching the tall sister, talking:

'You had a husband too then.'

'He died. That same summer.'

'Oh,' the Englishman said. 'The war?'

'The peace,' the tall woman said. 'When they let him come home at last and then the war started again before he could even put a plow in the ground, he probably decided that he could not bear another peace. And so he died. Yes?' she said. He had already taken up a spoon of soup. He stopped the spoon again.

'Yes what?'

'What else do you want of us? To show you his grave?' She just said 'his' but they all knew whom she meant. 'That is, where we think it was?' So did the Englishman merely say 'his'.

'What for?' he said. 'He's finished.'

'Finished?' she said in a harsh stern voice.

'He didn't mean it that way, Sister,' the other woman said. 'He just means that Brother did the best he could, all he could, and now he doesn't need to worry any more. Now all he has to do is rest.' She looked at him, serene and unsurprised and unpitying. 'You like to laugh, dont you?'

He did so, laughing, strong and steady and completely, with that side of his mouth still capable of moving, opening to laugh, the single eye meeting hers—theirs—full and calm and unpitying and laughing too. 'So can you,' he said to Marya. 'Cant you?'

'Why of course,' Marya said. 'Now, Sister,' she said. 'The medal.'

So, in the lane once more, there were three of them now instead of the two he had brought with him—three bits of graved symbolic bronze dangling and glinting from the three candy-striped ribbons bright as carnivals and gaudy as sunsets on the breast of the filthy dinner jacket as, facing them, he braced the two crutches into his armpits and with the hand he still had, removed the ruined homburg in a gesture sweeping and invulnerable and clapped it back on at its raked and almost swaggering angle and turned, the single leg once more strong and steady and tireless between the tireless rhythmic swing and recover of the crutches. But moving: back down the lane toward where he and the man with the feather had appeared, even if the infinitesimal progress was out of all proportion to the tremendous effort of the motion. Moving, unwearyable and durable and persevering, growing smaller and smaller with distance until at last he had lost all semblance of advancement whatever and appeared as though fixed against a panorama in furious progressless unrest, not lonely: just solitary, invincibly single. Then he was gone.

'Yes,' Marya said. 'He can move fast enough. He will be there in plenty of time,' turning then, the two of them, though it was the sister who stopped as though it was only she who had remembered at last the other man, the one with the feather, because Marya said: 'Oh yes, there will be plenty of time for him too.' Because he was not in the house: only the stained table, the bowl and the overturned tumbler where he had fouled and wasted their substance, the stain of the wine and the soup making a little puddle in which sat the neat small stack of coins where Marya had arranged them; all that afternoon while the tall sister went back to the field, the sowing, and Marya cleaned the kitchen and the soiled dishes, wiping the coins neatly off and stacking them again in that mute still pyramidal gleam while the light faded, until dark when they came back into the kitchen and lighted the lamp and he loomed suddenly, cadaverous and tall beneath the raking feather, from the shadows, saying in his harsh intolerable voice:

'What have you got against the money? Go on. Take it——' lifting his hand again to sweep, fling it to the floor, until the tall sister spoke.

'She has picked it up for you once. Dont do it again.'

'Here. Take it. Why wont you take it? I worked for it—sweated for it—the only money in my life I ever earned by honest sweat. I did it just for this—earned it and then went to all the trouble to find you and give it to you, and now you wont take it. Here.' But they only looked at him, alien and composed, cold and composed the one, the other with that bright and pitiless serenity until at last he said with a kind of amazement: 'So you wont take it. You really wont,' and looked at them for a moment longer, then came to the table and took up the coins and put them into his pocket and turned and went to the door.

'That's right,' Marya said in her serene and unpitying voice. 'Go now. It is not much further. You dont have much longer to despair': at which he turned, framed for a moment in the door, his face livid and intolerable, with nothing left now but the insolence, the tall feather in the hat which he had never removed breaking into the line of the lintel as if he actually were hanging on a cord from it against the vacant shape of the spring darkness. Then he was gone too.

'Have you shut up the fowls yet?' the tall sister said.

'Of course, Sister,' Marya said.

† † †

It was a gray day though not a gray year. In fact, time itself had not been gray since that day six years ago when the dead hero whom the quiet uncovered throngs which lined both sides of the Champs Élysées from the Place de la Concorde to the Arch and the dignitaries walking humbly on foot who composed the cortege itself had come to honor, had driven all adumbration from the face of Western Europe and indeed from the whole western world. Only the day was gray, as though in dirge for him to whom it owed (and would forever) for the right and privilege to mourn in peace without terror or concern.

He lay in his splendid casket in full uniform and his medals (the originals, the ones pinned to his breast by the actual hands of the President of his own motherland and the Kings and Presidents of the allied nations whose armies he had led to victory were in the Invalides; these which would return with him to the earth he came from were replicas), the baton of his marshalate lying on his breast beneath his folded hands, on the gun caisson drawn by black-draped and -pompommed horses, beneath the flag to which he in his turn and in its most desperate moment had added glory and eagles; behind him in the slow and measured procession color guards bore the flags of the other nations over whose armies and fates he had been supreme.

But the flags were not first because first behind the caisson walked (doddered rather, in step with nothing as though self-immersed and oblivious of all) the aged batman who had outlived him, in the uniform and the steel helmet still pristine and innocent of war, the rifle through which no shot had ever been fired slung from the bowed shoulder in reverse and as gleaming with tender and meticulous care as a polished serving spoon or drawing-room poker or candelabrum, carrying before him on a black velvet cushion the furled sabre, his head bowed a little over it like an aged acolyte with a fragment of the Cross or the ashes of a saint. Then came the two sergeant-grooms leading the charger, black-caparisoned too, the spurred boots reversed in the irons; and only then the flags and the muffled drums and the unrankable black-banded uniforms of the generals and the robes and mitres and monstrances of the Church and the sombre broadcloth and humble silk hats of the ambassadors, all moving beneath the gray and grieving day to the muffled drums and the minute-spaced thudding of a big gun somewhere in the direction of the Fort of Vincennes, up the broad and grieving avenue, between the half-staffed grieving flags of half the world, in pagan and martial retinue and rite: dead chief and slave and steed and the medal-symbols of his glory and the arms with which he had gained them, escorted back into the earth he came from by the lesser barons of his fiefhold and his magnificence—prince and cardinal, soldier and statesman, the heirs-apparent to the kingdoms and empires and the ambassadors and personal representatives of the republics, the humble and anonymous crowd itself flowing in behind the splendid last of them, escorting, guarding, seeing him too up the avenue toward where the vast and serene and triumphal and enduring Arch crowned the crest, as though into immolation or suttee.

It lifted toward the gray and grieving sky, invincible and impervious, to endure forever not because it was stone nor even because of its rhythm and symmetry but because of its symbolism, crowning the city; on the marble floor, exactly beneath the Arch's soaring center, the small perpetual flame burned above the eternal sleep of the nameless bones brought down five years ago from the Verdun battlefield, the cortege moving on to the Arch, the crowd dividing quietly and humbly behind it to flow away on either side until it had surrounded and enclosed that sacred and dedicated monument, the cortege itself stopping now, shifting, moiling a little until at last hushed protocol once more was discharged and only the caisson moving on until it halted directly before the Arch and the flame, and now there remained only silence and the grieving day and that minute's thud of the distant gun.

Then a single man stepped forward from among the princes and prelates and generals and statesmen, in full dress and medalled too; the first man in France: poet, philosopher, statesman patriot and orator, to stand bareheaded facing the caisson while the distant gun thudded another minute into eternity. Then he spoke:

'Marshal.'

But only the day answered, and the distant gun to mark another interval of its ordered dirge. Then the man spoke again, louder this time, urgent; not peremptory: a cry:

'Marshal!'

But still there was only the dirge of day, the dirge of victorious and grieving France, the dirge of Europe and from beyond the seas too where men had doffed the uniforms in which they had been led through suffering to peace by him who lay now beneath the draped flag on the caisson, and even further than that where people who had never heard his name did not even know that they were still free because of him, the orator's voice ringing now into the grieving circumambience for men everywhere to hear it:

'That's right, great general! Lie always with your face to the east, that the enemies of France shall always see it and beware!'

At which moment there was a sudden movement, surge, in the crowd to one side; the hats and capes and lifted batons of policemen could be seen struggling toward the disturbance. But before they could reach it, something burst suddenly out of the crowd—not a man but a mobile and upright scar, on crutches, he had one arm and one leg, one entire side of his hatless head was one hairless eyeless and earless sear, he wore a filthy dinner jacket from the left breast of which depended on their barber-pole ribbons a British Military Cross and Distinguished Conduct Medal, and a French *Médaille Militaire*: which (the French one) was probably why the French crowd itself had not dared prevent him emerging from it and even now did not dare grasp him and jerk him back as he swung himself with that dreadful animal-like lurch and heave with which men move on crutches, out into the empty space enclosing the Arch, and on until he too faced the caisson. Then he stopped and braced the crutches into his armpits and with his single hand grasped the French decoration on his breast, he too crying in a loud and ringing voice:

'Listen to me too, Marshal! This is yours: take it!' and snatched, ripped from his filthy jacket the medal which was the talisman of his sanctuary and swung his arm up and back to throw it. Apparently he knew himself what was going to happen to him as soon as he released the medal, and defied it; with the medal up-poised in his hand he even stopped and looked back at the crowd which seemed now to crouch almost, leashed and straining for the moment when he would absolve himself of immunity, and laughed, not triumphant: just indomitable, with that side of his ruined face capable of laughing, then turned and flung the medal at the caisson, his voice ringing again in the aghast air as the crowd rushed down upon him: 'You too helped carry the torch of man into that twilight where he shall be no more; these are his epitaphs: They shall not pass. My country right or wrong. Here is a spot which is forever England——'

Then they had him. He vanished as though beneath a wave, a tide of heads and shoulders above which one of the crutches appeared suddenly in a hand which seemed to be trying to strike down at him with it until the converging police (there were dozens of them now, converging from everywhere) jerked it away, other police rapidly forming a cordon of linked arms, gradually forcing the crowd back while, rite and solemnity gone for good now, parade marshals' whistles shrilled and the chief marshal himself grasped the bridles of the horses drawing the caisson and swung them around, shouting to the driver: 'Go on!' the rest of the cortege huddling without order, protocol vanished for the moment too as they hurried after the caisson almost with an air of pell mell, as though in actual flight from the wreckage of the disaster.

The cause of it now lay in the gutter of a small cul-de-sac side street where he had been carried by the two policemen who had rescued him before the mob he had instigated succeeded in killing him, lying on his back, his unconscious face quite peaceful now, bleeding a little at one corner of his mouth, the two policemen standing over him though now that the heat was gone their simple uniforms seemed sufficient to hold back that portion of the crowd which had followed, to stand in a circle looking down at the unconscious and peaceful face.

'Who is he?' a voice said.

'Ah, we know him,' one of the policemen said. 'An Englishman. We've had trouble with him ever since the war; this is not the first time he has insulted our country and disgraced his own.'

'Maybe he will die this time,' another voice said. Then the man in the gutter opened his eyes and began to laugh, or tried to, choking at first, trying to turn his head as though to clear his mouth and throat of what he choked on, when another man thrust through the crowd and approached him—an old man, a gaunt giant of a man with a vast worn sick face with hungry and passionate eyes above a white military moustache, in a dingy black overcoat in the lapel of which were three tiny faded ribbons, who came and knelt beside him and slipped one arm under his head and shoulders and raised him and turned his head a little until he could spit out the blood and shattered teeth and speak. Or laugh rather, which is what he did first, lying in the cradle of the old man's arm, laughing up at the ring of faces enclosing him, then speaking himself in French:

'That's right,' he said: 'Tremble. I'm not going to die. Never.'

'I am not laughing,' the old man bending over him said. 'What you see are tears.'

END

December, 1944
Oxford—New York—Princeton
November, 1953

CHRONOLOGY

NOTE ON THE TEXTS

NOTES

Chronology

1897 Born William Cuthbert Falkner, September 25, in New Albany, northeast Mississippi, first child of Maud Butler Falkner (b. 1871) and Murry Cuthbert Falkner (b. 1870). Father is eldest son of John Wesley Thompson Falkner, eldest son of William Clark Falkner. (Great-grandfather William Clark Falkner, born in Tennessee in 1825, came to Ripley, Mississippi, in his teens and became a lawyer, slave-owning planter, and colonel in the Confederate army. He changed his name, according to family legend, from Faulkner to Falkner to avoid confusion with "some no-account folks," wrote several books, including a successful romance, *The White Rose of Memphis*, was twice acquitted on grounds of self-defense after killing men in quarrels, built a short, narrow-gauge railroad, and was elected to the state legislature. In 1889 he was shot to death by an embittered former partner. Grandfather John Wesley Thompson Falkner, a lawyer and politician, inherited control of the Gulf & Chicago Railroad. Father, Murry Cuthbert Falkner, began working for railroad in 1888 and married Maud Butler in 1896, shortly after becoming general passenger agent for New Albany.)

1898–1901 Father becomes treasurer of railroad in November 1898, and family soon moves to Ripley. Brothers Murry C. Falkner, Jr., (nicknamed "Jack") born June 26, 1899, and John Wesley Thompson Falkner III ("Johncy") born September 24, 1901. William and Murry are dangerously ill with scarlet fever shortly after John's birth.

1902 Grandfather sells railroad and father loses his job. In September family moves forty miles southwest to Oxford, seat of Lafayette County, where grandfather is influential resident of seventeen years. Father begins series of small business ventures and becomes proprietor of a livery stable in November. Maternal grandmother, Lelia Dean Swift Butler ("Damuddy"), moves into family home. Caroline Barr ("Mammy Callie"), born in slavery around 1840, is hired to take care of children. She tells them stories and takes them on long walks in the woods, teaching them to recognize different birds. The Falkner brothers become close to cousin Sallie Murry Wilkins (b. 1899), daughter of aunt Mary Holland Falkner Wilkins.

1903 Meets and occasionally plays with Lida Estelle Oldham (b. 1896), daughter of Republican attorney Lemuel Oldham, when her family moves to Oxford in fall.

1905 Enters first grade. Enjoys drawing and painting with watercolors.

1906 Skips to third grade. Grandmother Sallie Murry Falkner dies December 21.

1907 Grandmother Lelia Butler dies June 1. Third brother, Dean Swift Falkner, born August 15.

1909–13 Begins working in father's livery stable in June. Athletic activities are curtailed in late 1910 when he is put in a tight canvas brace to correct shoulder stoop. Draws, writes stories and poems, and starts to play hooky. Becomes increasingly attracted to Estelle Oldham and shows her his poems. Reads comic magazine *The Arkansas Traveller*, *Pilgrim's Progress*, *Moby-Dick* (telling his brother Murry, "It's one of the best books ever written"), Mark Twain, Joel Chandler Harris, Shakespeare, Fielding, Conrad, Balzac, and Hugo, among others. Shoots his dog accidentally while hunting rabbits in the fall of 1911 and does not hunt again for several years. Becomes active Boy Scout and begins to play high school football in fall 1913.

1914–15 Shows his poetry to law student Phil Stone, four years his senior. Stone becomes close friend, gives him books to read ("Swinburne, Keats and a number of the then moderns, such as Conrad Aiken and the Imagists in verse and Sherwood Anderson and the others in prose," Stone recalls), and introduces him to writer and fellow townsman Stark Young. Helps plan yearbook and does sketches for it. Pitches and plays shortstop on baseball team. Returns to school briefly in fall 1915 to play football, then drops out. Hunts deer and bear at camp of "General" James Stone, Phil's father, near Batesville, in the Mississippi Delta thirty miles west of Oxford.

1916–17 Begins working early in 1916 as clerk at grandfather's bank, the First National, and hates it. Drinks his grandfather's liquor. ("Grandfather thought it was the janitor.") By end of 1916 spends most of his time on campus of University of Mississippi, where he becomes friends with freshman Ben Wasson. Contributes drawings to "Social Activities" section of university yearbook, *Ole Miss*. Continues to write verse influenced by Swinburne and A. E. Housman, among others.

1918 Estelle Oldham tells Falkner she is "ready to elope" with him, despite her engagement to Cornell Franklin, a University of Mississippi graduate now successfully practicing law in Hawaii who is preferred by her family. Falkner insists on getting the Oldhams' consent, but both families oppose marriage, and Estelle's wedding to Franklin is set for April 18. Joins Phil Stone, then studying law at Yale, in New Haven early in April. Meets poets Stephen Vincent Benét and Robert Hillyer. Reads Yeats. Works as ledger clerk at Winchester Repeating Arms Co., where his name is recorded "Faulkner." Determined to join British forces, he and Stone practice English accents and mannerisms. Accepted by Royal Air Force in mid-June. Visits Oxford before reporting to Toronto Recruits' Depot on July 9, where he lists birthplace as Finchley, Middlesex, England, birthdate as May 25, 1898, and spells his name "Faulkner." Brother Murry, serving in the Marines, is wounded in the Argonne on November 1. Faulkner's service is limited to attending ground school. ("The war quit on us before we could do anything about it.") Discharged in December, returns to Oxford wearing newly-purchased officer's uniform and Royal Flying Corps wings and suffering, he claims, from effects of crashing a plane.

1919 Continues to work on poetry. Drinks with friends in gambling houses and brothels in Clarksdale and Charleston, Mississippi, Memphis, and New Orleans. Composes long cycle of poems influenced by classic pastoral tradition and modern poetry, especially T. S. Eliot. Sees Estelle frequently during her four-month visit home from Hawaii with her daughter, Victoria. "L'Apres-Midi d'un Faune," 40-line poem, appears in *The New Republic* August 6. Other poems are not accepted. Registers in September as a special student at University of Mississippi, where father is now assistant secretary of university. Studies French, Spanish, and Shakespeare; publishes poems in campus paper, *The Mississippian*, and Oxford *Eagle*. First published story, "Landing in Luck," appears in *The Mississippian* in November. In December, agrees to be initiated into Sigma Alpha Epsilon fraternity because of family tradition. Given nicknames "Count" and "Count No 'Count" by fellow students, who consider him aloof and affected.

1920 Inscribes *The Lilacs*, 36-page hand-lettered giftbook of poems, to Phil Stone on New Year's Day. Translates four poems by Paul Verlaine that are published in *The Mississippian* in February and March. Contributes drawings to the yearbook. Awarded $10 poetry prize by Professor Calvin S. Brown in June. Does odd jobs and assists with Boy Scout troop. Helps build clay tennis court beside Falkners' university-owned home; becomes a good player. Joins The Marionettes, a new university drama group; finishes one-act play (not produced) and works on stage props and set design. Withdraws from university in November during crackdown on fraternities. Receives commission as honorary second lieutenant in RAF; wears uniform with pips on various occasions. Writes *Marionettes*, an experimental verse play; hand-letters several copies of its 55 pages, adding illustrations influenced by Aubrey Beardsley. Wasson sells five at $5 apiece. The Marionettes decline to produce it.

1921 Favorably reviews *Turns and Movies*, volume of verse by Conrad Aiken, in *The Mississippian*. Paints buildings on campus. Presents Estelle Franklin with 88-page bound typescript volume of poems entitled *Vision in Spring* during her visit home in the summer. Accepts invitation of Stark Young to visit him in New York City in the fall. Revisits New Haven, October–November, then rents rooms in New York City and works as clerk in Lord & Taylor bookstore managed by Stark Young's friend Elizabeth Prall. Returns home in December after Phil Stone and Lemuel Oldham secure him position as postmaster at university post office at salary of $1,500 a year.

1922 Writes while on duty at the post office, neglects customers, is reluctant to sort mail, does not always forward it, and keeps patrons' magazines and periodicals in the office until he and his friends have read them. Praises Edna St. Vincent Millay and Eugene O'Neill in articles published in *The Mississippian*. Grandfather John Wesley Thompson Falkner dies March 13. Faulkner does last drawing for yearbook *Ole Miss*. Plays golf. Writes poems, stories, and criticism. *The Double Dealer*, a New Orleans magazine, publishes his short poem "Portrait." Continues to read widely, including works by Conrad Aiken, Eugene O'Neill, and Elinor Wylie.

1923 Begins driving his own car. Becomes scoutmaster during summer. Submits collection *Orpheus, and Other Poems* to The Four Seas Company of Boston in June. They agree to publish it if Faulkner will pay manufacturing costs; Faulkner declines in November, saying "on re-reading some of the things, I see that they aren't particularly significant."

1924 Receives gift of James Joyce's *Ulysses* from Phil Stone. Reads Voltaire and stories by Thomas Beer, a popular magazine writer of the time. (Faulkner later said that Beer "influenced me a lot.") In May, Four Seas agrees to publish cycle of pastoral poems, *The Marble Faun*, and Faulkner sends $400 to cover publication costs. Phil Stone writes preface and takes active role in negotiations. Continues to write stories and verse, compiling gift volumes for friends. Removed as scoutmaster after local minister denounces his drinking. Faulkner resigns as postmaster October 31. ("I reckon I'll be at the beck and call of folks with money all my life, but thank God I won't ever again have to be at the beck and call of every son of a bitch who's got two cents to buy a stamp.") Visits Elizabeth Prall in New Orleans and meets her husband, Sherwood Anderson, whose work he admires. *The Marble Faun* published in December.

1925 Leaves for New Orleans in January, intending to earn his passage to Europe. Accepts Elizabeth Prall Anderson's invitation to stay in spare room while Sherwood Anderson is away on a lecture tour, then moves into quarters rented from artist William Spratling. Contributes essays, poems, stories, and sketches to the New Orleans *Times-Picayune* and *The Double Dealer*. Meets Anita Loos. Begins work on novel *Mayday*, which Sherwood Anderson, now a close friend, praises. ("We would meet in the afternoons, we'd walk and he'd talk and I'd listen, we'd meet in the evenings and we'd go to a drinking place and we'd sit around till one or two o'clock drinking . . .") Anderson recommends Faulkner's novel to publisher Boni & Liveright. Visits Stone's brother and his family at Pascagoula on Gulf Coast in June; falls in love with Helen Baird (b. 1904), a sculptor he had met in New Orleans. Sails as passenger on a freighter from New Orleans to Genoa with William Spratling July 7; throws mass of manuscript overboard en route. Travels through Italy and Switzerland to Paris, settling on Left Bank. Grows beard. Goes to Louvre and various galleries; writes to mother in August: "went to a very very modernist exhibition the other day—futurist and vorticist. I was talking to a painter, a real one. He wont go to the exhibitions at all. He says its all right to paint the damn things, but as far as looking at them, he'd rather go to the Luxembourg gardens and watch the children sail their boats. And I agree with him." In September writes, "I have spent afternoon after afternoon in the Louvre . . . I have seen Rodin's museum, and 2 private collections of Matisse and Picasso (who are yet alive and painting) as well as numberless young and struggling moderns. And Cezanne! That man dipped his brush in light . . ." Years later, says of James Joyce in Paris: "I would go to some effort to go to the café that he inhabited to look at him. But that was the only literary man that I remember seeing in Europe in those days." Works on articles, poems, and fiction, including two novels, *Mosquito* and *Elmer* (about a young American painter, never finished). Tours France on foot and by train; visits World War I battlefields which still show scars of fighting. Visits England briefly in October, writes of Kent countryside: "Quietest most restful country under the sun. No wonder that Joseph Conrad could write such fine books here." Finds England too expensive and returns to France. Writes his mother, "I am expecting to hear from Liveright when I reach Paris. I waked up yesterday with such a grand feeling that something out of the ordinary has happened to me that I am firmly expecting news of some sort—either very good or very bad." Learns in Paris that novel *Mayday* has been accepted for publication by Boni & Liveright and retitled *Soldiers' Pay*; Faulkner likes new title. Sails to the United States in December. Visits his publishers in New York before returning to Oxford.

1926 Inscribes a hand-lettered, illustrated allegorical tale *Mayday* (the same title originally given novel) to Helen Baird in January. Moves in with Spratling at 632 St. Peter Street, New Orleans, in February, going back to Oxford for brief visits. *Soldiers' Pay* published by Boni & Liveright February 25 in printing of 2,500 copies (sells 2,084 by May). Mother, shocked by sexual material in the novel, says that the best thing he could do is leave the country; father refuses to read it. Reviews are generally favorable—one reviewer notes its "hard intelligence as well as consummate pity." Hand-letters a sequence of poems called *Helen: A Courtship* for Helen Baird in June. Vacations in Pascagoula, where he finishes typescript of novel *Mosquitoes* in early September. Returns to New Orleans in fall. Begins novels *Father Abraham*, about an avaricious Mississippi family named Snopes, and *Flags in the Dust*, depicting four generations of Sartoris family, based on Southern and family lore. Parodies Anderson's style in foreword to *Sherwood Anderson & Other Famous Creoles*, a collection of Spratling's sketches, which they publish themselves in an edition of 400 copies that sells out in a week at $1.50 a copy. Book offends Anderson and causes breach between him and Faulkner. Returns to Oxford at Christmas.

1927 Sees Estelle, who has returned to Oxford after beginning divorce proceedings against Cornell Franklin. Gives her daughter, Victoria, a 47-page tale, *The Wishing Tree*, typed and bound in varicolored paper, in February as a present for her eighth birthday. Helen Baird marries Guy C. Lyman in March. *Mosquitoes* published April 30. Puts *Father Abraham* aside to concentrate on *Flags in the Dust*. Works on it at Pascagoula during summer, and finishes revised typescript in late September. Horace Liveright rejects *Flags in the Dust* in late November and advises Faulkner not to offer it elsewhere.

1928 Begins "Twilight," story about the Compson family, early in the year. ("One day I seemed to shut a door, between me and all publishers' addresses and book lists. I said to myself, Now I can write.") Centered on Caddie Compson, it becomes *The Sound and the Fury*. ("I loved her so much I couldn't decide to give her life just for the duration of a short story. She deserved more than that. So my novel was created, almost in spite of myself.") Sends *Flags in the Dust*, extensively revised, and group of short stories to Ben Wasson, now New York literary agent. Wasson submits *Flags in the Dust* to eleven publishers, all of whom reject it. Faulkner continues to work on new novel. In September, Wasson shows *Flags in the Dust* to Harrison (Hal) Smith, editor at Harcourt, Brace and Company, who writes favorable report. Alfred Harcourt agrees to publish book on condition that it be cut. Faulkner uses $300 advance to go to New York. Dismayed at the cuts Wasson says are necessary, allows him to do most of the cutting. (" 'The trouble is,' he said, 'is that you had about 6 books in here. You were trying to write them all at once.' He showed me what he meant, what he had done, and I realized for the first time that I had done better than I knew . . .") Tries unsuccessfully to sell short stories. Rents a small furnished flat in Greenwich Village and revises and types manuscript of *The Sound and the Fury*. Finishes in October, drinks heavily, and is found unconscious by friends Eric J. (Jim) Devine and Leon Scales, who take care of him in their apartment. Moves in with painter Owen Crump after recovering. Returns to Oxford in December.

1929 *Sartoris* (the cut and retitled *Flags in the Dust*) published by Harcourt, Brace and Company January 31 in first printing of 1,998. Starts writing *Sanctuary*. *The Sound and the Fury* accepted by new firm of Jonathan Cape and Harrison Smith in February; Faulkner receives $200 advance. Estelle's divorce becomes final on April 29. Faulkner receives $200 advance for new novel from Cape & Smith in early May. Completes *Sanctuary* in late May; Smith writes him that it is too shocking to publish. Asks Smith for an additional $500 advance so that he can get married. Marries Estelle in Presbyterian Church in nearby College Hill, June 20. Borrows money from cousin Sallie Murry (Wilkins) Williams and her husband to go to Pascagoula, where he and Estelle have troubled honeymoon. Reads proofs of *The Sound and the Fury*, restoring italicized passages changed by Wasson. Returns to Oxford and takes job on night shift at the university power plant. Visits mother daily. *The Sound and the Fury* published October 7 in printing of 1,789. Reviews are enthusiastic, sales disappointing. Writes *As I Lay Dying* while at work, beginning October 25 and finishing December 11. ("I am going to write a book by which, at a pinch, I can stand or fall if I never touch ink again.")

1930 Finishes typescript of *As I Lay Dying* on January 12. Begins publishing stories in national magazines when *Forum* accepts "A Rose for Emily" for its April issue. Achieves mass-market success when *The Saturday Evening Post* accepts "Thrift" (appears September) and *Scribner's* accepts "Dry September" (published January 1931). April, purchases rundown antebellum house (lacks electricity and plumbing) and four acres of land in Oxford for $6,000 at 6% interest, with no money down. Names it Rowanoak (or Rowan Oak), and begins renovation, doing much of the work himself. Moves into it in June with Estelle and her children, Victoria (born 1919) and Malcolm (born 1923). Household staff includes Caroline Barr and Ned ("Uncle Ned") Barnett, former slave who had been servant of great-grandfather William Clark Falkner. Chatto & Windus publishes *Soldiers' Pay*, with introduction by Richard Hughes, June 20, first of Faulkner's works to appear in England. Sells "Red Leaves" and "Lizards in Jamshyd's Courtyard" to *The Saturday Evening Post* for $750 each (more than he had received for any novel). *As I Lay Dying*, where for the first time in print the Mississippi locale is identified as Yopnapatawpha County, published October 6 by Cape & Smith in printing of 2,522 copies. Harrison Smith now thinks *Sanctuary* may make money for ailing publishing firm, and sends galley proofs in November. Though the resetting costs Faulkner $270, he revises extensively "to make out of it something which would not shame *The Sound and the Fury* and *As I Lay Dying*." Finishes revision in December.

1931 Daughter Alabama, named for Faulkner's great-aunt Alabama, is born prematurely on January 11 and dies after nine days. *Sanctuary*, published February 9 by Cape & Smith, sells 3,519 copies by March 4—more than combined sales of *The Sound and the Fury* and *As I Lay Dying*; elicits high praise and increasing attention for Faulkner abroad. Gallimard acquires the rights to publish *As I Lay Dying* and *Sanctuary* in French. Many in Oxford are shocked by *Sanctuary*; Faulkner's father tells a coed carrying the book that it isn't fit for a nice girl to read, but his mother defends him. Chatto & Windus publishes *The Sound and the Fury* in April. "Spotted Horses" appears in *Scribner's* in June. Begins work on novel tentatively titled *Dark House* in August, developing theme used in rejected short story "Rose of Lebanon." *These 13*, a collection of stories, published by Cape & Smith September 21; sells better than any of his works except *Sanctuary*. Attends Southern Writers' Conference at University of Virginia in Charlottesville on his way to New York in October. Drinks heavily. Wooed by publishers Bennett Cerf and Donald Klopfer of Random House, Harold Guinzberg and George Oppenheimer of Viking, and Alfred A. Knopf. To keep him away from other publishers, Harrison Smith has Milton Abernethy take Faulkner on ship cruise to Jacksonville, Florida, and back to New York. Firm of Cape & Smith is dissolved by Jonathan Cape; Faulkner signs with new firm, Harrison Smith, Inc. Meets his French translator, Princeton professor Maurice Coindreau, banker and future secretary of defense Robert Lovett, Dorothy Parker, H. L. Mencken, Robert Benchley, John O'Hara, John Dos Passos, Frank Sullivan, and Corey Ford (will continue to see some of them on later trips). Spends hours talking and drinking with Dashiell Hammett and Lillian Hellman. Meets Nathanael West. Works on new novel (now called *Light in August*) and stories, one of them—"Turn About"—inspired by war stories told by Lovett (finished in Oxford, and published in *The Saturday Evening Post*, March 1932). Finishes self-deprecatory introduction ("This book . . . is a cheap idea, because it was deliberately conceived to make money") to Random House's Modern Library edition of *Sanctuary* (published 1932). Makes contacts with film studios and writes film treatments. Earns enough money during stay in New York to pay bills at home. Drinks heavily; friends contact Estelle. She arrives early in December, and they return to Oxford before the middle of the month.

Random House publishes story "Idyll in the Desert" in limited edition of 400 copies.

1932 Finishes manuscript of *Light in August* in February and revised typescript in March. Cape's new partnership, Cape & Ballou, goes into receivership in March, owing Faulkner $4,000 in royalties. Goes to work May 7 at Metro-Goldwyn-Mayer studio in Culver City, California, on six-week, $500-per-week contract. Leaves the studio almost immediately, not returning for a week. ("When they took me into a projection room and kept assuring me that it was all going to be very, very easy, I got flustered.") Takes a $30-a-month cottage on Jackson Street near studio and works unsuccessfully on series of treatments and scripts. At the end of contract makes plans to return home, but director-producer Howard Hawks hires him as scriptwriter for film *Today We Live*, based on "Turn About," beginning his longest Hollywood association. Father dies of heart attack August 7, and Faulkner returns home as head of family. "Dad left mother solvent for only about 1 year," he writes Ben Wasson. "Then it is me." Agreement with Hawks allows him to work in Oxford. Takes stepson Malcolm on walks through woods and bottoms, teaching him to distinguish dangerous from harmless snakes. Returns to Hollywood in October for three weeks, taking mother and brother Dean with him. *Light in August* published October 6 by new firm of Harrison Smith and Robert Haas. Paramount buys film rights to *Sanctuary* (released as *The Story of Temple Drake*, May 12, 1933). Faulkner receives $6,000 from sale. Continues working for MGM in Oxford. Spends part of Hollywood earnings on renovation of Rowan Oak.

1933 Begins flying lessons with Captain Vernon Omlie in February, and makes first solo flight April 20 after seventeen hours of dual instruction. *Today We Live* premieres in Oxford, April 12. *A Green Bough*, poems, published April 20 by Smith & Haas. Travels to New Orleans in May to work on film *Louisiana Lou* with director Tod Browning, but refuses to return to Hollywood for revisions; studio terminates contract May 13. Buys more land adjoining Rowan Oak. Works on stories and novel, *The Peasants*, which uses

Snopes characters. Daughter Jill born June 24. Prepares a marked copy (apparently now lost) for a projected Random House limited edition of *The Sound and the Fury* (never published) that would print the Benjy section in three colors, and writes an introduction. ("I wrote this book and learned to read. . . . I discovered that there is actually something to which the shabby term Art not only can, but must, be applied.") Receives $500 for his work on it. Plans novel *Requiem for a Nun*. Buys Omlie's Waco C cabin biplane in fall. Concerned about brother Dean's future, arranges to have Omlie train Dean as a pilot. Flies with Omlie and Dean to New York to meet with publishers early in November, returning in time to go hunting. Earns pilot's license December 14.

1934 Begins new novel *A Dark House* in February, using material from stories "Evangeline" (written 1931) and "Wash" (written 1933). Flies with Omlie to New Orleans for dedication of Shushan Airport February 15. Participates in Mississippi air shows with Omlie, Dean, and others in spring, billed as "William Faulkner's (Famous Author) Air Circus" on one occasion; Faulkner avoids flying aerobatics. *Doctor Martino and Other Stories* published April 16 by Smith & Haas. Pressed for money, writes "Ambuscade," "Retreat," and "Raid," series of Civil War stories centering on Bayard Sartoris and black companion Ringo, hoping to sell them to *The Saturday Evening Post* (they appear in fall). Goes back to work with Hawks in Hollywood for $1,000 a week, from the end of June to late July. Finishes script *Sutter's Gold* in Oxford. Brother Murry is member of FBI team that kills John Dillinger in Chicago, July 22. Writes Smith in August that new novel "is not quite ripe yet," but "I have a title for it which I like, by the way: ABSALOM, ABSALOM; the story is of a man who wanted a son through pride, and got too many of them and they destroyed him." Puts it aside and converts unpublished story "This Kind of Courage" into novel, *Pylon*. Sends first chapter to Harrison Smith in November and finishes it by end of December.

1935 Forms Okatoba Fishing and Hunting Club with R. L. Sullivan and Whitson Cook, receiving hunting and fishing rights to several thousand acres of General Stone's land near Batesville, Mississippi, at eastern edge of the Mississippi Delta. *Pylon* published by Smith & Haas, March 25. Pressed for money, works intensively at writing stories meant to sell. Writes his agent Morton Goldman in April: "What I really need is $10,000.00. With that I could pay my debts, and insurance for two years and really write. I mean, write." Returns to *Absalom, Absalom!* Resumes occasional flying, though the Waco now belongs to Dean. Goes to New York September 23 to negotiate a better contract with Smith & Haas and to sell stories to magazines. Returns home October 15, without gaining much from the trip. Brother Dean and his three passengers are killed when the Waco crashes November 10. Faulkner assists undertaker in futile attempt to prepare Dean's body for open-casket funeral. Distraught and guilt-ridden, assumes responsibility for Dean's pregnant wife, Louise, and stays for several weeks with her and his grieving mother, who feels suicidal. On December 10, goes to Hollywood for five-week, $1,000-per-week assignment with Hawks for Twentieth Century–Fox, taking *Absalom, Absalom!* with him. Works on novel early in the morning before going to the studio. Begins intermittent and sometimes intense fifteen-year affair with Hawks's 28-year-old secretary (later his script supervisor), Mississippi divorcée Meta Doherty Carpenter.

1936 After successful completion of draft of script (*The Road to Glory*), begins to drink heavily. Returns to Oxford on sick leave January 13. Finishes manuscript of *Absalom, Absalom!* January 31. Drinks heavily and is hospitalized in Wright's Sanitarium, small private hospital in Byhalia, Mississippi, fifty miles north of Oxford. Reluctant to delay revision of novel by writing stories to make money, signs new contract with Twentieth Century–Fox (again for $1,000 a week until "employment shall be terminated by either party"). Returns to Hollywood February 26, moving into the Beverly Hills Hotel. Works on several scripts, sees old friends. Dean, daughter of brother Dean Faulkner, born March 22; Faulkner assumes role of surrogate father. Goes boar hunting on Santa Cruz Island with Nathanael West in April. Returns to Oxford early in June and writes to agent when his stories don't sell: "Since last summer I seem to have got out of the habit of writing trash . . ." Draws map of Yoknapatawpha County for *Absalom, Ab-*

salom! Goes back to Hollywood in mid-July (for six-month, $750-per-week contract), taking Estelle, Jill, and two servants with him, and moves into a large house just north of Santa Monica. Captain Omlie dies in crash as passenger on commercial flight August 6. Sees Meta Carpenter, who has decided to marry pianist Wolfgang Rebner. Estelle and Faulkner both drink heavily. *Absalom, Absalom!*, published October 26 by Random House (which has absorbed the firm of Smith & Haas), receives some critical praise, though sales are not enough to allow freedom from script-writing, and Faulkner is unable to sell film rights (had hoped to receive $50,000 for them). Becomes increasingly unproductive at Twentieth Century–Fox and is laid off in December after earning almost $20,000 for the year. Proposes to convert Bayard Sartoris–Ringo stories (now six in number) into novel and is encouraged by Bennett Cerf and Robert Haas. Harrison Smith leaves Random House. Makes final payment on Rowan Oak.

1937 Returns to studio from layoff February 26 at salary of $1,000 a week. Family moves closer to studio. Unhappiness at work and home exacerbates Faulkner's drinking. March to June, works on film script for *Drums Along the Mohawk*, directed by John Ford. Estelle and Jill return to Oxford in late May. Maurice Coindreau stays with Faulkner for week in June to discuss French translation of *The Sound and the Fury*. Writes "An Odor of Verbena," concluding episode in Bayard-Ringo series. Returns to Rowan Oak in late August, having earned over $21,000 for the year working for Twentieth Century–Fox. Begins story "The Wild Palms," then starts to expand it into a novel. Goes to New York in mid-October to prepare the Bayard-Ringo stories for publication with new Random House editor, Saxe Commins. Stays at Algonquin Hotel; sees old friends, including Harrison Smith, Joel Sayre, Eric J. Devine, and Meta Rebner. Renews friendship with Sherwood Anderson ("a giant in an earth populated . . . by pigmies"). Drinks heavily, collapses against steam pipe in hotel room, and suffers palm-sized third-degree burn on his back. Treated by doctor, then cared for by Eric J. Devine. Sherwood Anderson visits him. Returns to Oxford accompanied by Devine. Resumes work on novel, *If I Forget Thee, Jerusalem* (to be published as *The Wild Palms* at publisher's insistence); says the theme of the book is:

"Between grief and nothing I will take grief." Reads Keats and Housman aloud and does crossword puzzles with stepdaughter Victoria after breakup of her first marriage ("He kept me alive," she later says). Intense pain from burn makes sleeping difficult.

1938 *The Unvanquished*, Bayard-Ringo stories reworked with new material into novel, published February 15 by Random House. MGM buys screen rights for $25,000, of which Faulkner receives $19,000 after payment of commissions. Buys 320-acre farm seventeen miles northeast of Oxford and names it Greenfield Farm; insists on raising mules despite brother John's (who is tenant manager) preference for more profitable cattle (later acquires cattle for farm). Despite infection from skin graft performed at the end of February, continues work on *If I Forget Thee, Jerusalem*. Writes to Haas in July: "To me, it was written just as if I had sat on the one side of a wall and the paper was on the other and my hand with the pen thrust through the wall and writing not only on invisible paper but in pitch darkness too . . ." Goes to New York to read proofs of novel, now titled *The Wild Palms*, in late September. Returns to work on Snopes book *The Peasants* and plots out two more volumes, *Rus in Urbe* and *Ilium Falling*, to form trilogy. Takes Harold Ober as new literary agent.

1939 Elected to National Institute of Arts and Letters in January. *The Wild Palms*, published January 19, reviewed in *Time* cover story, sells more than 1,000 copies a week and tops sales of *Sanctuary* by late March. Raises $6,000 (by cashing in life insurance policy and obtaining advance from Random House) to save Phil Stone from financial disaster. Writes stories, hoping to earn money, and works on Snopes trilogy, retitling volumes *The Hamlet*, *The Town*, and *The Mansion*. Helps brother John at Greenfield Farm, sometimes serving tenants in commissary. Influential favorable essays on Faulkner published by George Marion O'Donnell (*Kenyon Review*, summer) and Conrad Aiken (*The Atlantic Monthly*, November). Takes short holidays in New York City in October and December after testifying in Washington, D.C., in plagiarism suit brought against Twentieth Century–Fox by writer who claims (wrongly) to have written *The Road to Glory*. Donates manuscript of *Absalom, Absalom!* to relief fund for Spanish Loyalists. "Barn Burning" wins first O. Henry Memorial Award ($300 prize) for best short story published in an American magazine.

1940 Works on proofs of *The Hamlet*. Caroline Barr, in her mid-nineties, suffers stroke and dies January 31. Faulkner gives eulogy in parlor of Rowan Oak. ("She was born in bondage and with a dark skin and most of her early maturity was passed in a dark and tragic time for the land of her birth. She went through vicissitudes which she had not caused; she assumed cares and griefs which were not even her cares and griefs. She was paid wages for this, but pay is still just money. And she never received very much of that . . .") Writes stories about black families. *The Hamlet*, published by Random House April 1, is reviewed favorably, but sales fall below those of *The Wild Palms*. Faces mounting financial pressure from debts, family obligations, and back taxes, but is reluctant to raise funds by selling property. (Writes Haas in June: "It's probably vanity as much as anything else which makes me want to hold onto it. I own a larger parcel of it than anybody else in town and nobody gave me any of it or loaned me a nickel to buy any of it with and all my relations and fellow townsmen, including the borrowers and frank spongers, all prophesied I'd never be more than a bum.") Appeals to Random House for higher advances against royalties, and proposes to make a novel out of series of stories about related black and white families. Tries to get a job in Hollywood. After unsatisfactory negotiations with Random House, goes to New York late in June to negotiate with Harold Guinzburg of The Viking Press, but Viking cannot substantially improve on the Random House offer. Resumes writing stories (five published in the year).

1941 Wires literary agent Harold Ober on January 16 asking for $100; uses part of it to pay electric bill. Organizes Lafayette County aircraft warning system in late June. Wishing to do more in anticipation of U.S. entry into World War II, thinks about securing military commission and hopes to teach air navigation. "The Bear" accepted by

The Saturday Evening Post for $1,000 in November. Finishes work on series of stories forming novel *Go Down, Moses* in December.

1942 Goes to Washington, D.C., in unsuccessful attempt to secure military or naval commission. *Go Down, Moses and Other Stories*, dedicated to Caroline Barr, published by Random House May 11. (Faulkner considers it a novel; "and Other Stories" added by publisher.) Deeply in debt and unable to sell enough stories to remain solvent, seeks Hollywood work through publishers, agents, and friends. Reports for five-month segment of low-paying ($300 a week), long-term Warner Bros. contract on July 27. Moves into Highland Hotel. Works with producer Robert Buckner on film about Charles de Gaulle until project is dropped. Resumes affair with Meta Carpenter (now divorced from Rebner). Sees other old friends, including Ruth Ford (University of Mississippi alumna who had once dated brother Dean), and Clark Gable and Howard Hawks, with whom he goes fishing and hunting. Becomes friends with writers A. I. ("Buzz") Bezzerides and Jo Pagano. Eats often at favorite restaurant in Hollywood, Musso & Frank Grill. Writes two scenes for *Air Force*, directed by Hawks. Gets month's leave to return to Oxford for Christmas while remaining on payroll.

1943 Returns to Warner Bros. January 16 on a 26-week, $350-per-week contract. Begins working with Hawks in March on *Battle Cry*, film depicting various Allied nations' roles in the war. Sends one of his RAF pips to nephew James Faulkner, who is training to become Marine Corps fighter pilot (pip is lost when nephew is forced to ditch his Corsair off Okinawa in 1945). Warner Bros. picks up 52-week option at $400 a week in late June; Faulkner drinks and collapses. Writes and revises lengthy and complex script for *Battle Cry*. When the film is canceled in August due to its high cost, takes leave of absence without pay to return to Oxford. Receives $1,000 advance from producer William Bacher to work at home on film treatment about the Unknown Soldier of World War I. Describes it in letter to Ober as "a fable, an indictment of war perhaps" and writes 51-page synopsis in fall.

1944 Reports back to Warner Bros. February 14, and moves in with Bezzerides family on Saltair Street, just north of Santa Monica. Begins work for Hawks on film version of Ernest Hemingway's *To Have and Have Not.* Estelle and Jill join him in June, and they move to an apartment in East Hollywood. Works with Hawks and screenwriter Leigh Brackett on film of Raymond Chandler's *The Big Sleep.* Depression, drinking, and periods of hospitalization follow departure of Jill and Estelle in September. Critic Malcolm Cowley writes the first of several essays on Faulkner to "redress the balance between his worth and his reputation," comparing him to Balzac and noting that all his works except for *Sanctuary* are out of print. Works on filmscript for *Mildred Pierce*, directed by Michael Curtiz. Requests leave without pay and returns home December 15, taking with him the script for *The Big Sleep*, which he finishes in Oxford. Offered $5,000 advance to write a nonfiction book on the Mississippi River by Doubleday. Provisionally turns it down, saying: "I am 47. I have 3 more books of my own I want to write. I am like an aging mare, who has three more gestations in her before her time is over, and doesn't want to spend one of them breeding what she considers . . . a mule."

1945 Works on the "fable" about the Unknown Soldier ("writing and rewriting, weighing every word"), hoping to make it into a novel. Returns to Hollywood and Warner Bros. in June, now at $500 a week. Cowley obtains publishers' approval in August to edit a collection of Faulkner's works for the Viking Portable Library series; Faulkner advises him on selections. Works on scripts for *Stallion Road* and briefly with Jean Renoir on *The Southerner.* Continues work on the "fable," rising at 4:00 A.M. and working until 8:00 A.M. before going to the studio. Hollywood agent William Herndon refuses to release him from agent-client agreement and Warner Bros. refuses to release him from exclusive contract. Writes: "I dont like this damn place any better than I ever did. That is one comfort: at least I cant be any sicker tomorrow for Mississippi than I was yesterday." Refusing to assign Warner Bros. film rights to his own writings (including the "fable"), leaves studio without permission September 18. Returns to Rowan Oak, bringing Lady Go-lightly, the mare Jill rode during her stay in California. Redraws map of Yoknapatawpha County and writes "1699–1945 The Compsons" to go with excerpt from *The Sound and the Fury* in Cowley's *Portable Faulkner*; says, "I should have done this when I wrote the book. Then the whole thing would have fallen into pattern like a jigsaw puzzle when the magician's wand touched it." Takes part in annual hunt in November. Short story, "An Error in Chemistry," wins second prize ($250) in *Ellery Queen's Mystery Magazine* contest in December (had received $300 for story itself).

1946 Feels trapped and depressed, drinks heavily. Cerf, Haas, and Ober persuade Jack Warner to give Faulkner leave of absence and release from rights assignment so he can finish his novel. Random House pays immediate advance of $1,000 and $500 a month after that. Faulkner worries that novel will take longer to complete than advances can cover. *The Portable Faulkner* published by Viking April 29. Tells class at University of Mississippi in May that the four greatest influences on his work were the Old Testament, Melville, Dostoevski, and Conrad. European reputation, especially in France, grows as works are translated. Jean-Paul Sartre writes of Faulkner's significance in "American Novelists in French Eyes," in September *Atlantic Monthly*. Sells film rights for stories "Death Drag" and "Honor" to RKO for combined net of $6,600, and "Two Soldiers" to Cagney Productions for $3,750. Random House issues *The Sound and the Fury* (with "1699–1945 The Compsons" retitled "Appendix/Compson: 1699–1945" added as first part) and *As I Lay Dying* together in Modern Library edition in October. Nearly hits trees while landing airplane and does not fly as pilot again. Continues work on "fable" ("I dont write as fast as I used to"). Works secretly, because of exclusive Warner Bros. contract, on film script (unidentified) at home.

1947 Meets in April with six literature classes at University of Mississippi on condition no notes be taken. Ranks Hemingway among top contemporaries, along with Thomas Wolfe, John Dos Passos, and John Steinbeck, but is quoted in wire-service account as saying that Hemingway "has no courage, has never gone out on a limb. He has never used a word where the reader might check his usage in a dictionary." Hemingway is deeply offended, and Faulkner writes apology. ("I have believed for years that the human voice has caused all human ills and I thought I had broken myself of talking. Maybe this will be my valedictory lesson.") Long-time family servant Ned Barnett dies. In November *Partisan Review* refuses excerpt about a horse race from the "fable."

1948 Begins mystery novel in January, based on idea mentioned to Haas in 1940; calls it *Intruder in the Dust*, and finishes it in April. MGM buys film rights for $50,000 before publication. Published by Random House September 27, it is his most commercially successful book, selling over 15,000 copies. Feels free of financial pressure for the first time. Turns down Hamilton Basso's proposal of *New Yorker* profile: "I am working tooth and nail at my lifetime ambition to be the last private individual on earth . . ." Works on short-story collection proposed earlier in the year by Random House. Eager to visit friends, goes to New York for holiday in October and meets Malcolm Cowley for the first time. Collapses after few days and recuperates at Cowley's home in Sherman, Connecticut. Decides to arrange stories in collection by cycles, an idea suggested by Cowley three years earlier. Elected to the American Academy of Arts and Letters November 23.

1949 Director Clarence Brown brings MGM company to Oxford to film *Intruder in the Dust*. Faulkner revises screenplay and helps scout locations, but is not given credit because of legal complications with Warner Bros. Rewrites unpublished 1942 mystery story "Knight's Gambit," expanding it into novella. Buys sloop, which he names *The Ring Dove*, and sails it on Sardis Reservoir, 25 miles northwest of Oxford, during spring and summer. Eudora Welty visits and Faulkner takes her sailing. In August is sought out by 20-year-old Joan Williams, Bard College student and aspiring writer from Memphis, who admires his work. Reluctantly attends world premiere of *Intruder in the Dust* on October 9 at refurbished Lyric Theatre, owned by cousin Sallie Murry Williams and her husband. Event is considered to have caused the most excitement since Union General A. J. Smith burned Oxford in Civil War. "A Courtship" wins O. Henry Award for 1949. Random House publishes *Knight's Gambit*, volume of mystery stories, November 27.

1950 Writes to Joan Williams in January, offering help as a mentor. Goes to New York for ten days in February, staying at Algonquin; sees publishers, old friends (actress Ruth Ford, Joel Sayre, and others), and Joan Williams. Begins sending her notes for a play he hopes they will write together. Writes letter to Memphis *Commercial Appeal* in March protesting failure of Mississippi jury to give death penalty to a white man convicted of murdering three black children. Receives American Academy's William Dean Howells Medal for Fiction in May; does not attend ceremony. Personal involvement with Joan Williams deepens when she returns to Memphis for summer. Gives her manuscript of *The Sound and the Fury*. She is reluctant to rewrite his material for play *Requiem for a Nun*, and their collaboration becomes increasingly difficult. *Collected Stories of William Faulkner* published August 2 by Random House and adopted by Book-of-the-Month Club as alternate fiction selection, receiving generally good reviews. Informed November 10 he will receive 1949 (delayed until 1950) Nobel Prize for Literature. Reluctant to attend, drinks heavily at annual hunt, contracts bad cold, but finally agrees to go to Stockholm with Jill to receive award on December 10. Meets Else Jonsson, widow of Thorsten Jonsson, one of Faulkner's earliest Swedish translators. Gives widely quoted address ("I believe that man will not merely endure: he will prevail"). Afterwards, writes to friend, "I fear that some of my fellow Mississippians will never forgive that 30,000$ that durn foreign country gave me for just sitting on my ass writing stuff that makes my own state ashamed to own me." *The New York Times* reports that 100,000 copies of his books have been sold in Modern Library editions, and that 2.5 million paperback copies are in print.

1951 Takes $5,000 of Nobel Prize money for his own use, establishes "Faulkner Memorial" trust fund with remainder for scholarships and other educational purposes. Goes to Hollywood in February for five weeks scriptwriting on *The Left Hand of God* for Hawks. Earns $14,000, including bonus, for finishing script ahead of schedule (Hawks does not direct film, and Faulkner does not receive writing credit when it is released in 1955). Sees Meta Carpenter for last time. The Levee Press of Greenville, Mississippi, publishes horse-race piece as *Notes on a Horsethief* February 10.

Collected Stories receives National Book Award for Fiction March 6. Releases statement to Memphis *Commercial Appeal* doubting guilt and opposing execution of Willie McGee, a black man convicted of raping a white woman (McGee later executed). Takes three-week trip in April to New York, England, and France, visiting Verdun battlefield, which figures in his "fable." Gives short commencement address at Jill's high school graduation in Oxford May 28. Finishes manuscript of *Requiem for a Nun* in early June. (Writes in letter to Else Jonsson: "I am really tired of writing, the agony and sweat of it. I'll probably never quit though, until I die. But now I feel like nothing would be as peaceful as to break the pencil, throw it away, admit I dont know why, the answers either.") Hears from Ruth Ford that Lemuel Ayers would like to produce *Requiem for a Nun* on stage, and goes to New York for week in July to work on it. Drives Jill to school at Pine Manor Junior College in Wellesley, Massachusetts, with Estelle. *Requiem for a Nun*, with long prose introductions to its three acts, published by Random House October 2. Works on stage version in Cambridge, Massachusetts, in October and November. Becomes officer in the Legion of Honor of the Republic of France at ceremony at French Consulate in New Orleans October 26.

1952 Works on "fable" and trains horse; has two falls in February and March, injuring his back. Attends ceremony commemorating ninetieth anniversary of battle of Shiloh with novelist Shelby Foote, and walks over battlefield with him. Although work now widely taught in colleges, turns down honorary degree of Doctor of Letters from Tulane University, writing: "I feel that for one who did not even graduate from grammar school, to accept an honorary degree representative not only of higher learning but of post-graduate labor in it, would debase and nullify the whole aim of learning." (Later declines all other attempts to award him honorary degrees, often using this same reply.) Attacks "welfare and other bureaus of economic or industrial regimentation" in address delivered May 15 to Delta Council in Cleveland, Mississippi. Takes one-month trip to Europe, though plans to produce his play during Paris cultural festival had fallen through. Collapses in severe pain in Paris; doctors discover two old spinal compression fractures, possibly riding injuries, and advise surgical fusion. Faulkner refuses and visits Harold Raymond of Chatto & Windus in England, still suffering severe pain. Treated near Oslo, Norway, by masseur on advice of Else Jonsson. Returns home feeling better than he has in years, but is not allowed to ride. Helps Joan Williams with her writing, but relationship is increasingly troubled. Injures back in boating accident in August. Hospitalized in Memphis in September for convulsive seizure brought on by drinking and back pain, and again in October, after fall down stairs. X-rays reveal three additional old spinal compression fractures. Wears back brace. Helps Ford Foundation prepare *Omnibus* production of "The Faulkner Story" for television in November. Accepts editor and friend Saxe Commins' invitation to write at his Princeton home. Depression and drinking precipitate collapse and is admitted to private hospital in New York. After discharge stays in New York, working on "fable"; sees Joan Williams. Returns home for Christmas.

1953 Stays in Oxford until Estelle recovers from cataract operation. Returns to New York January 31 for indefinite stay, hoping to finish the "fable." Medical problems continue; has extensive physiological and neurological examinations to determine cause of memory lapses, but nothing new is discovered. Writes semi-autobiographical essay "Mississippi" for *Holiday* (appears April 1954). Returns to Oxford with Jill in late April when Estelle is hospitalized for severe hemorrhage. Goes back to New York May 9, when danger is over. Estelle accompanies him when he gives commencement address at Jill's graduation from Pine Manor. Jill attends University of Mexico in fall, and Estelle goes with her when she leaves in late August. Faulkner stays at Rowan Oak, working on "fable." Hospitalized in September in Memphis and in Wright's Sanitarium in Byhalia. Angered when *Life* magazine publishes two-part article on him, September 28–October 5. Drives to New York with Joan Williams in October; they see Dylan Thomas (whose earlier poetry reading Faulkner had found moving) shortly before Thomas's death in November, and attend subsequent memorial service. Finishes *A Fable* at Commins' house in early November. Leaves for Paris to work with Hawks and screenwriter Harry Kurnitz on film, *Land of the Pharaohs*. Meets 19-year-old admirer, Jean

Stein, in St. Moritz on Christmas Eve. Spends Christmas holidays in Stockholm and sees Else Jonsson.

1954 Stays with Harold Raymond in Biddenden, Kent, England, in early January, and then goes to Switzerland, Paris, and Rome, visiting friends, seeing Jean Stein, and working on film. Arrives in Cairo in mid-February suffering from alcoholic collapse and is taken to Anglo-American Hospital. Continues working on film, but Hawks and Kurnitz do not use most of what he writes. Joan Williams marries Ezra Bowen on March 6. Leaves Egypt March 29. Stays three weeks in Paris, spending one night in hospital. Returns home in late April, after short stay in New York. Writes preface for *A Fable*, but decides not to use it. Works on farm most of May; sells livestock and then rents it out for a year. *A Fable* published by Random House, August 2. At request of U.S. State Department, attends International Writers' Conference in São Paulo, Brazil, stopping off on the way at Lima, Peru. Enjoys trip and offers his services again on return home. Jill marries Paul D. Summers, Jr., August 21, and moves to Charlottesville, Virginia, where Paul attends law school. Faulkner checks into Algonquin Hotel, New York, September 10; divides time between New York and Oxford for next six months. Makes spoken record for Caedmon Records, works on stories and magazine pieces, and feels reassured of ability to earn money. Sees Jean Stein often.

1955 Writes article on hockey game at Madison Square Garden, "An Innocent at Rinkside," for *Sports Illustrated* (appears January 24). Accepts National Book Award for Fiction for *A Fable*, January 25. Works on script for *The Era of Fear*, ABC television program about McCarthyism, but in March angrily rejects contract which includes morals clause and requires membership in unions ABC deals with. Becomes increasingly involved in civil rights issues; writes letters to editors advocating school integration; receives abusive letters and phone calls, and his position angers his brothers. Gives lecture "On Privacy. The American Dream: What Happened to It" at the University of Oregon and University of Montana in April (published in *Harper's*, May). *A Fable* wins Pulitzer Prize in May. Writes article on eighty-first running of Kentucky

Derby for *Sports Illustrated*. Helps publicize *Land of the Pharaohs*. Leaves on State Department trip July 29. Spends three weeks in Japan, visiting Tokyo, Nagano, and Kyoto, and delighting Japanese hosts (remarks from colloquia published as *Faulkner at Nagano*, 1956). Returns to New York by way of Philippines (to visit stepdaughter and family), Italy, France, England, and Iceland, combining State Department appearances and vacation. *Big Woods*, collection of hunting stories with new linking material, illustrated by Edward Shenton, published by Random House, October 14. Rushes to Oxford October 23 when mother, almost eighty-five, suffers cerebral hemorrhage; remains while she recuperates. Speaks against discrimination to integrated audience at Memphis meeting of Southern Historical Association, November 10; receives more threatening letters and phone calls. When Jean Stein visits the South, shows her New Orleans and Gulf Coast; they encounter Helen Baird Lyman on a Pascagoula beach. Begins second Snopes volume (*The Town*) in early December.

1956 Columbia Pictures takes option on *The Sound and the Fury* for $3,500 (film is released by Twentieth Century–Fox in 1959), and Universal buys *Pylon* for $50,000 (released in 1958 as *The Tarnished Angels*, directed by Douglas Sirk). Goes to New York February 8 to discuss finances with Ober: "what to do with money I have, where my kin and friends cant borrow it, against my old age." Worried about imminent violence, writes two articles urging voluntary integration in South to prevent Northern intervention: "On Fear: The South in Labor" (*Harper's*, June), and "A Letter to the North" (*Life*, March). Increasingly alarmed by rising tensions over court-ordered integration of University of Alabama, agrees to interview with *The Reporter* magazine; desperate and drinking, says if South were pushed too hard there would be civil war. Interviewer quotes him as saying that "if it came to fighting I'd fight for Mississippi against the United States even if it meant . . . shooting Negroes." (Later repudiates the interview: "They are statements which no sober man would make, nor it seems to me, any sane man believe.") Does extensive interview with Jean Stein for *The Paris Review*. On return to Oxford, injures back again when he is thrown by horse. Begins vomiting blood March 18; hospitalized in

Memphis. By early April feels well enough to go with Estelle to Charlottesville, Virginia, where first grandson, Paul D. Summers III, is born April 15. Works on *The Town* in Oxford during summer. With P. D. East, starts semiannual satirical paper for Southern moderates, entitled *The Southern Reposure*. First and only issue appears in midsummer. Writes essay for *Ebony*, appealing for moderation and urging blacks to "learn . . . the responsibility of equality." Albert Camus' adaptation of *Requiem for a Nun* successfully staged in Paris. Goes to Washington, D.C., for four days in September as chairman of writers' group in Eisenhower Administration's People-to-People Program. Chooses Harvey Breit of *The New York Times* as co-chairman; attends meeting at Breit's home November 29.

1957 Continues chairman's work into early February. Refuses Estelle's offer of a divorce. Depressed by changing relationship with Jean Stein, suffers collapse. Goes to Charlottesville as University of Virginia's first writer-in-residence February 9; moves into house on Rugby Road. Meets professors Frederick L. Gwynn and Joseph Blotner, who assist him in setting schedules. Arrives in Athens March 17 for two-week visit at invitation of State Department; sees Greek adaptation of *Requiem for a Nun*. Cruises four days on private yacht in the Aegean. Accepts Silver Medal from Greek Academy. *The Town*, published May 1 by Random House, receives mixed reviews. Extensive exhibition of Faulkner materials, including many manuscripts and typescripts, opens at Princeton University on May 10. Presents National Institute of Arts and Letters' Gold Medal for Fiction to John Dos Passos May 22. Concludes successful university semester of classroom and public appearances. Rides with friends and in the Farmington Hunt, and tours Civil War battlefields near Richmond. Returns to Rowan Oak for summer, tends to farm and boat, visits mother. Ignores telegrams from producer Jerry Wald reporting on production of film *The Long Hot Summer*, based on *The Hamlet* (released 1958). Goes to Charlottesville in November, intending to ride and fox-hunt, but falls ill with strep throat. Hunts quail near Oxford in December.

1958 Begins to type first draft of *The Mansion*, third and last of the Snopes trilogy, at Rowan Oak in early January.

Returns to Charlottesville for second term as writer-in-residence, January 30, meeting classes and public groups. (Remarks are published in *Faulkner in the University: Class Conferences at the University of Virginia, 1957–58* in 1959.) At one session presents "A Word to Virginians," an appeal to state to take the lead in teaching blacks "the responsibilities of equality." Goes to Princeton for two weeks, March 1, meeting with students individually and in groups. Returns to Oxford in May. Declines, for political reasons, invitation to visit Soviet Union with group of writers. Saxe Commins dies July 17. Gives away niece Dean Faulkner, daughter of brother Dean, at her wedding November 9, and hosts large reception for her at Rowan Oak. Goes to Princeton for another week of student sessions, and then to New York to work on *The Mansion* with Random House editor Albert Erskine. Returns to Charlottesville and rides in the Keswick and Farmington hunts; is described by a fellow rider as "all nerve." Second grandchild, William Cuthbert Faulkner Summers, born December 2.

1959 Works on *The Mansion* and hunts quail in Oxford. *Requiem for a Nun*, version adapted for the stage by Ruth Ford, opens on Broadway January 30 after successful London run; closes after forty-three performances. Though not reappointed as writer-in-residence for the year, takes position as consultant on contemporary literature to Alderman Library at University of Virginia, and is assigned library study and typewriter. Accepted as outside member in Farmington Hunt and continues riding with Keswick Hunt. Fractures collarbone when horse falls at Farmington hunter trials March 14. Rides again in May at Rowan Oak despite slow and painful recovery; another horse fall causes additional injuries, necessitating use of crutches for two weeks. Works with Albert Erskine in New York on *The Mansion*, eliminating some of the discrepancies between it and *The Hamlet*. Writes preface to *The Mansion* explaining others. Completes purchase of Charlottesville home on Rugby Road, August 21. Attends four-day UNESCO conference in Denver late September. Harold Ober, long-time agent and friend, dies October 31. *The Mansion* published by Random House, November 13. Continues riding and hunting, suffering occasional falls.

1960 Divides time between Oxford and Charlottesville. Hospitalized briefly at Byhalia for collapse brought on by bourbon administered for self-diagnosed pleurisy. Accepts appointment as Balch Lecturer in American Literature at University of Virginia with minimal duties (salary $250 a year) in August. Mother suffers cerebral hemorrhage, dies October 16. Sees Charlottesville friends often, including Joseph and Yvonne Blotner. Becomes full member of Farmington Hunt; writes to Albert Erskine, "I have been awarded a pink coat, a splendor worthy of being photographed in." Establishes William Faulkner Foundation December 28, providing scholarships for black Mississippians and prize for first novels; bequeaths to it the manuscripts he has deposited in the Alderman Library.

1961 Hunts quail in Oxford in January. Reluctantly leaves on two-week State Department trip to Venezuela April 1. Receives the Order of Andrés Bello, Venezuela's highest civilian award; gives speech expressing gratitude in Spanish. Third grandson, A. Burks Summers, born May 30. Shocked by news of Hemingway's suicide, July 2. Returns to Rowan Oak. Begins writing *The Horse Stealers: A Reminiscence*, conceived years earlier as novel about "a sort of Huck Finn"; enjoys work and finishes first draft August 21. Returns to Charlottesville in mid-October. Novel, retitled *The Reivers*, taken by Book-of-the-Month Club eight months before publication. Checks into Algonquin Hotel to work on book with editor Albert Erskine, November 27. Hospitalized in Charlottesville, December 18, suffering from acute respiratory infection, back trouble, and drinking. Leaves after several days, but soon has relapse and is treated at Tucker Neurological and Psychiatric Hospital in Richmond until December 29.

1962 Injured in fall from horse, January 3. Readmitted to Tucker suffering from chest pain, fever, and drinking, January 8. Goes to Rowan Oak to recuperate in mid-January and hunts with nephew James Faulkner. Returns to Charlottesville in early April; intends to make move permanent. Travels to West Point with Estelle, Jill, and Paul, April 19, and reads from *The Reivers*. Turns down President John F. Kennedy's invitation to attend dinner for American Nobel Prize winners. Accepts Gold Medal for

Fiction of National Institute of Arts and Letters, presented by Eudora Welty, May 24. Returns to Oxford. *The Reivers* published by Random House, June 4. Thrown by horse near Rowan Oak, June 17. Endures much pain, but continues to go for walks, and negotiates purchase of Red Acres, 250-acre estate outside Charlottesville, for $200,000. Pain and drinking increase; taken by Estelle and James Faulkner to Wright's Sanitarium at Byhalia, July 5. Dies of heart attack, 1:30 A.M. on July 6. After service at Rowan Oak is buried on July 7 in St. Peter's Cemetery, Oxford, Mississippi.

Note on the Texts

This volume prints the texts of *Go Down, Moses*, *Intruder in the Dust*, *Requiem for a Nun*, and *A Fable* that have been established by Noel Polk. All texts are based on Faulkner's own typescripts, the texts of which have been emended to account for his revisions in proofs, his typing errors, and certain other errors and inconsistencies that clearly demand correction. Underlying typescript and holograph drafts of these typescripts have been consulted regularly throughout the editorial process and have supplied the editor with numerous solutions to problems in Faulkner's final typescripts. By the time these novels were written, Faulkner composed almost exclusively at the typewriter rather than in longhand, which had been his practice up through the third book of *The Hamlet* (1940); although there are holograph drafts of extensive portions of *Requiem for a Nun* and of *A Fable*, most of the editorially significant preliminary materials for the novels in this volume are typescript.

Comparison has been made of all relevant extant forms of these works, published and unpublished, to determine the nature and causes of variants among the texts. The goal of these labors—to discover the forms of these works that Faulkner wanted in print at the time of their original publication—is sometimes elusive. Although thousands of pages of typescript and proof are available to the editor, it is not always clear what Faulkner's final intentions were, or even whether Faulkner had any "final" intentions regarding some of the individual components of his novels.

Copy-texts for all four of these novels are his own ribbon typescript copies (now on deposit at the Alderman Library of the University of Virginia), which were used by the typesetters of the first editions. Faulkner seems to have typed most of these pages himself (clearly some pages of *A Fable* and *Requiem for a Nun* have been typed by somebody else), with different degrees of care; these pages contain both authorial and editorial alterations of varying extent and seriousness. Faulkner was in some ways an extremely consistent writer. He never included apostrophes in the words "dont", "wont", "aint", "cant", or "oclock", and very seldom used an apostrophe to indicate a dropped letter in a spoken dialect word, such as "bout" or "runnin". He never used a period after the titles "Mr", "Mrs", or "Dr". The editors of the first editions generally, but inconsistently, accepted these practices, but compositors often made mistakes, and many periods and apostrophes slipped in. More serious problems also frequently occurred, mostly attendant upon editors' and Faulkner's indifferent proofreading and upon editors' general lack of understanding of what Faulkner was trying to do. Although the editors for these novels did not make the kinds of wholesale alterations that were made in the editing of *Absalom, Absalom!*, for example, or alterations as significant as changing the title of *If I Forget Thee, Jerusalem* to *The Wild Palms*, they did intervene in hundreds of ways that affected the texts of the novels being published. In *Requiem for a Nun*, for instance, Faulkner wrote in one elegiac passage of the effect on Jefferson Negroes of their hangovers after "Juneteenth," a portmanteau word commemorating June nineteenth, the date of emancipation in Texas; the Random House editor, not knowing this, changed "Juneteenth" to "June tenth," in the context a usage not just completely meaningless, but likely to be confusing as well. Likewise, in order to show the unbroken continuity between the prologues and the dramatic portions of *Requiem for a Nun*, Faulkner went to the trouble, at a late stage of composition, to ink out the first two lines of Act I, Scene 1, at the top of typescript page 50, and then to retype a version of those lines at the end of the text of the prologue on typescript page 49: his intention is absolutely clear from the evidence of the typescript, but the editor nevertheless directed the printer to start Scene 1 on a new page. Curiously, the texts of *Go Down, Moses* and *Intruder in the Dust*, novels published in the 1940s, are mostly marked by editorial indifference, and the problems are mostly typographical errors, things that should have been caught by a careful proofreader; the texts of *Requiem for a Nun* and *A Fable*, on the other hand, Faulkner's first two novels after he won the Nobel Prize in 1950, were much more seriously treated by the original editors, though often with cumulatively worse results.

Faulkner's attitude toward such intervention is neither consistent nor entirely clear. Almost from the beginning of his career, he was a supremely confident craftsman; he was at the same time aware of the complexity of the demands his work would make not merely on the reader but also on the publisher, editor, and proofreader. His response, early in his major career, to Ben Wasson's tampering with the Benjy section of *The Sound and the Fury*—that he would rewrite it if publishing were not grown up enough to publish it as he wanted it—reflects both his flexibility toward the realities of publication and his impatience with those mechanical processes of publication beyond his control that might thwart the accomplishment of his artistic goals. He seems to have been indifferent to some types of editorial changes, and he acquiesced to them; he seems not to have cared whether certain words were spelled consistently or not, whether certain of his archaisms were modernized or not, and he seems to have expected his editor to divine from his typescript whether each sentence was punctuated exactly as he wanted it—that is, whether or not a variation from an apparent pattern was in fact a deliberate variation or merely an inadvertency he expected an editor to correct. Thus while some of his marks on galley and page proofs were genuine revisions of his own, many others were clearly attempts to repair damage of one sort or another made by someone else on the typescript setting copy.

With the benefit of decades of intense scholarship, we are now perhaps in a better position to understand Faulkner's intentions, although clearly many of the original editorial problems remain. The Polk texts attempt to reproduce the texts of Faulkner's typescripts as he intended them to be originally published, in so far as that intention can be reconstructed from the evidence. For the most part, only those revisions on typescript or in proof that Faulkner seems to have initiated himself in response to his own text are accepted, and not those he made in response to a revision or a correction suggested or inserted by an editor; this is a very conservative policy that may reject some of Faulkner's proof revisions in favor of his original text. Polk's interventions, then, strive to be minimal, and every effort has been made to preserve Faulkner's idiosyncracies in spelling and punctuation. Nevertheless, certain corrections of unmistakable typing errors and other demonstrable errors in the typescripts have been necessary.

Go Down, Moses is made up of a group of short stories that Faulkner had been writing over a period of several years, and whose relationships with one another he discovered some time around 1940. The book was published on May 11, 1942, under the title *Go Down, Moses and Other Stories*. The editors added "and Other Stories" to the title page, and Faulkner asked them to remove it in 1949 when they proposed to reprint the book in the wake of the success of *Intruder in the Dust*; he wrote to Robert Haas of Random House: "Moses is indeed a novel. . . . Indeed, if you will permit me to say so at this late date, nobody but Random House seemed to labor under the impression that GO DOWN, MOSES should be titled 'and other stories.' I remember the shock (mild) I got when I saw the printed title page. I say, reprint it, call it simply GO DOWN, MOSES, which was the way I sent it in to you 8 years ago."

Go Down, Moses has its general origins in the early 1930s in such short stories as "Red Leaves" and "A Justice," in which Faulkner introduced characters like Issetibbeha and Ikkemotubbe, Mississippi Indians who became land-traders and slave-owners. The novel's specific origins are in a 1935 short story, "Lion," about a dog who tracked a bear. The central character of "Lion," however, is not Isaac McCaslin, but Quentin Compson, who had committed suicide in *The Sound and the Fury* (1929), and whom Faulkner was resurrecting, at the same time he was writing "Lion," for his role in *Absalom, Absalom!* (1936).

In late 1939 Faulkner began writing other stories which he eventually revised and incorporated into *Go Down, Moses*. On October 3 he sent "The Old People," the story of Isaac McCaslin's initiation, to his agent, Harold Ober (it was published in *Harper's*, September 1940). By February 23, 1940, he had completed all three of the stories that he later incorporated into "The Fire and the Hearth," the story of Carothers McCaslin's black descendant, Lucas Beauchamp: "Point of Law" (*Collier's*, June 1940), "Gold Is Not Always" (*American Mercury*, November 1940), and "An Absolution," which was not published in a periodical. On March 18, 1940, he sent Ober the typescript of "Pantaloon in Black" (*Harper's*, October 1940) and on July 24 he sent Ober "Go Down, Moses" (*Collier's*, January 25, 1941), which became the final chapter of the new work, thus completing the materials about the black inheritors of Old Carothers' legacies.

In April 1940 Faulkner wrote to Random House asking for an advance so that he could write two novels, one a "blood and thunder mystery novel" (which would become *Intruder in the Dust* in 1948), and another novel "in method similar to The Unvanquished." By July 1, 1940, he had completed "Almost," an early version of "Was," which remained unpublished until its inclusion in the novel. He sent "Delta Autumn" (*Story*, May–June 1942) to Ober on December 16, 1940. Throughout this period, Faulkner was also apparently working to revise the 1935 story "Lion" into the long and complicated chapter that eventually became "The Bear," though it was still called "Lion" on the typescript he submitted to Random House. In the fall of 1941, needing money as usual, he reduced the narrative materials of "Lion" to a 20-page version (published in *The Saturday Evening Post*, May 4, 1942).

Faulkner then carefully revised each story and sent to Random House a completely revised and retyped typescript, which the editors pushed through to publication with a minimum of intervention that amounted to virtual indifference. They often overlooked problematic passages—like at least one entire line that Faulkner failed to type from a previous version, now lost—that needed editorial query. The typescript submitted by Faulkner is the copy-text for the Polk text.

The years following the publication of *Go Down, Moses* were difficult for Faulkner: he had trouble selling stories to magazines, he got enmeshed in a restrictive contract with a Hollywood agent and movie studio, and he began to write *A Fable* (on which he would work for the next eleven years), taking time out to write "The Compson Appendix" (1946). In increasing financial straits, he put aside work on *A Fable* on January 15, 1948, and began work on the book he had described to Random House nearly seven years earlier, in June 1940, as "a mystery story, original in that the solver is a negro, himself in jail for the murder and is about to be lynched, solves murder in self-defense." He worked very fast and wrote to Robert Haas of Random House on February 22 that he had finished the first draft and was rewriting. By April 27 he had sent the completed work to Random House, and uncharacteristically asked his publishers for help in choosing a title. Faulkner wrote that he wanted "a word, a dignified (or more dignified) synonym for 'shenanigan[']', 'skulduggery[']; maybe a legal-quasi-latin word, for title like this" and he proposed Shenanigan, Skulduggery, and Jugglery, all to be combined with "in the Dust." Haas responded with several other suggestions, all likewise to be combined with "in the Dust": Imposture, Masquerade, Stratagem, Pattern, and Cabal. Faulkner counterproposed Imposter, Intruder, Sleeper, Malfeasance, Substitution, Malaprop, Malpractice, and Trouble. He seems to have settled on "Intruder" by early May. *Intruder in the Dust* was published by Random House on September 27, 1948. Faulkner's typescript is the copy-text for the Polk text.

Faulkner first used the title *Requiem for a Nun* in a letter to his publisher, Harrison Smith, in October 1933, telling him that he had "another bee now, and a good title, I think: REQUIEM FOR A NUN. It will be about a nigger woman. It will be a little on the esoteric side, like I LAY DYING." In December 1933 Faulkner wrote at least three manuscript pages (two different versions of an opening) of a work by that title, though these pages provide inconclusive evidence about whether it was to be a sequel to *Sanctuary* or whether it bears any other relationship to the 1951 novel.

On February 11, 1949, Faulkner began writing *Requiem for a Nun* as a play for his friend Ruth Ford, who had asked him to write a play for her and whose "terrifying determination to be an actress" he had long admired. By this time he had also met an aspiring young writer named Joan Williams, whom he proposed to make a protégé by getting her to collaborate with him. By May 19, 1950, he had reconceived the work as a novel in three acts, each act preceded by a long prose narrative recounting the history of Yoknapatawpha

County and Mississippi. He completed the novel by June 1, 1951, and it was in galleys by June 13.

At Faulkner's instructions, Robert Linscott of Random House sent a set of galleys to Ruth Ford. During the summer of 1951, Faulkner, Ford, and director Albert Marre met in New York and in Cambridge, Massachusetts, to adapt the novel to the stage. As Faulkner worked on the stage version, he made extensive revisions to the galleys of the novel, returning them to Random House with numerous attached carbon typescript sheets containing text that was to replace the text as originally submitted. Thus copy-text for the Polk text of *Requiem for a Nun* is a combination of Faulkner's original typescript and these new sheets from the play script, as they revised the galleys. *Requiem for a Nun* was published on September 7, 1951, in a text marred by a large number of typographical errors and several unfortunate editorial alterations. (The stage version, credited to Faulkner and Ruth Ford, was published by Random House in 1959.)

A Fable was conceived in 1943 during a discussion in wartime Hollywood among Faulkner, producer William Bacher, and director Henry Hathaway about a film on the Unknown Soldier. One proposal was that the Unknown Soldier might have been Jesus Christ returned to earth to give humanity one last chance, an idea Faulkner was enthusiastic about. They never made a film on this theme, but the basic idea was to consume Faulkner for over a decade, with brief stints away from it to work on filmscripts, "The Compson Appendix," *Intruder in the Dust*, the stories that would make up *Knight's Gambit*, and *Requiem for a Nun*. There exist several hundred pages of preliminary typescript and manuscript, some of it dated as early as 1947, and the typescript setting copy is itself composed of typescript pages from several different versions of various passages, typed on at least two different typewriters and clearly representing materials dating from throughout the decade of its composition. Faulkner took the typescript of *A Fable* to Random House on November 5, 1953, and soon after left for four months in Europe, where he visited friends and worked on a film for Howard Hawks. While reading proof in Rome in April 1954, he wired Random House that he had forgotten to include the "Judas Misery" material in the chapter titled "Tomorrow," and he supplied that material when he returned to New York. Random House published the book on August 2, 1954, in a text altered in hundreds of major and minor ways by editorial intervention. Faulkner's typescript is the setting copy for the Polk text reproduced here, except for the "Judas Misery" sequence, for which the first edition is the only extant text.

By preserving his spelling, punctuation, and wording, even when inconsistent or irregular, the Polk texts strive to be as faithful to Faulkner's usage as surviving evidence permits. In this volume, the reader has the results of the most detailed scholarly efforts thus far made to establish the texts of *Go Down, Moses*, *Intruder in the Dust*, *Requiem for a Nun*, and *A Fable*.

Notes

In the notes below, the reference numbers denote page and line of this volume (the line count includes chapter headings). No note is made for material included in standard desk-reference books such as Webster's *Collegiate*, *Biographical*, and *Geographical* dictionaries. For more detailed notes, references to other studies, and further biographical background than is contained in the Chronology, see: Joseph Blotner, *Faulkner, A Biography*, 2 vols. (New York: Random House, 1974); Joseph Blotner, *Faulkner, A Biography, One-Volume Edition* (New York: Random House, 1984); *Selected Letters of William Faulkner* (New York: Random House, 1977), edited by Joseph Blotner; Calvin S. Brown, *A Glossary of Faulkner's South* (New Haven: Yale University Press, 1976); Noel Polk, *Faulkner's Requiem for a Nun, A Critical Study* (Bloomington: Indiana University Press, 1981).

GO DOWN, MOSES

8.29 bitt] Variant spelling of bit.

9.13 soupled out] Stretched out.

10.15 Walker dogs] Foxhounds crossbred from British and American strains.

10.38 to drag his foot] To drag the right foot to a position behind the left while making a ceremonious formal bow.

17.32 road-gaiting] Going an easy pace for distance.

20.1 skun] Raided.

27.20 run] Distillation.

31.16 jimber-jawed] Having a projecting lower jaw.

36.18–19 keeping his . . . and he] Not in Faulkner's typescript. He apparently dropped a line when typing from an earlier draft and the error was not corrected in the first edition or later printings.

123.6 Aramis] One of the title characters in *The Three Musketeers* (1844) by the elder Alexandre Dumas.

169.33–34 Sullivan . . . Tunney.] John L. Sullivan defeated Jake Kilrain in the 75th round of the last bare-knuckle heavyweight championship fight in America, held at Richburg, Mississippi, on July 8, 1889. World heavyweight champion Jack Dempsey lost the title to Gene Tunney at Philadelphia in 1926. In a rematch at Chicago in 1927 he lost a ten-round decision to Tunney, who was given a controversial "long count" after being knocked down in the seventh round.

216.16 A.P.M.] Army Provost Marshal.

220.3–5 *'She . . . fair.'*] John Keats, "Ode on a Grecian Urn," stanza III.

220.36 'Habet] Latin: Has, holds, possesses, used here in the legal sense, as on a writ.

INTRUDER IN THE DUST

303.38 Beat] Survey coordinate designating an administrative district within a county.

308.24 smore] Dense smokiness; smear.

332.34 cosmolined] Coated with cosmoline, a heavy grease distilled from petroleum.

402.22 flag.'] In February 1949 Faulkner sent to Robert Haas at Random House a passage for insertion here in any later printings of the novel. The passage, which was never inserted, reads:

'But what will happen?' he said. 'What will we do and he do, both of us, all of us. What will become of him—Sambo?'

'I just told you,' his uncle said. 'He will disappear. There are not enough of him to resist, to repel, to hold intact his integrity even if he wished to remain a Negro. In time he would have got equity and justice without even asking for it. But by insisting on social equality, what he is actually demanding is racial extinction. Three hundred years ago he didn't exist in America; five hundred years from now he will have vanished and will be no more. Oh, he will still exist now and then as isolate and insulate phenomena, incorrigible, tieless, anachronic and paradox; archaeological and geological expeditions will stumble on him occasionally by individuals and even intact nests in caves in remote Tennessee and Carolina mountain fastnesses or Mississippi and Alabama and Louisiana swamps or, generations ago lost and unrecorded, in the mapless back areas of Detroit or Los Angeles tenement districts; travellers passing through the rotundas of the Croydon or Le Bourget or La Guardia airports or the supra transfer stations of space ships will gape at him intact with banjo and hound and screenless mudchinked cabin and naked pickaninnies playing with empty snuff-bottles in the dust, even to the washpot in the backyard and his bandana-turbaned mate bending over it, as the Union Pacific Railroad used to establish tepees of authentically costumed Blackfoot and Shoshone Indians in the lobby of the Commodore Hotel. But as a race he will be no more; his blood will obtain only in the dusty files of genealogical societies for the members of what will then be the Daughters of Founding Fathers or Lost Causes to wrangle and brag over as the Briton does over his mystic trace of Norman, so that in five hundred years or perhaps even less than that, all America can paraphrase the tag line of a book a novel of about twenty years ago by another Mississippian, the successfully mild little bloke over yonder at Oxford, in which a fictitious Canadian said to a fictitious self-lacerated Southerner in a dormitory room in a not too authentic Harvard: "I who regard you will have also sprung from the loins of African kings".'

404.39 Trigg foxhounds] A strain developed in Kentucky by Colonel Haiden Trigg.

REQUIEM FOR A NUN

476.27–36 Harpes . . . Murrel] The brothers William Micajah "Big" (1768–99) and Wiley "Little" (1770–1804) Harpe, Samuel Mason (1750?–1803), and John Murrel (or Murrell or Murel; 1804?–?1850).

540.3 *(Beginning Was* τὸ ἕν)] Faulkner wrote in a note to his publisher that this was a paraphrase of T. S. Eliot, "Mr. Eliot's Sunday Morning Service": "In the beginning was the Word. / Superfetation of τὸ ἕν" (τὸ ἕν is Greek for "the one").

543.9 Hare] Mississippi outlaw Joseph Thompson Hare.

544.13 p.c.] Post of command.

544.30 Doak's Stand] The Doak's Stand Treaty, signed October 18, 1820, in present-day Madison County, Mississippi, provided for the purchase by the United States of about 5.5 million acres of Choctaw territory in western and central Mississippi.

544.35–38 'Leflore' . . . Rabbit] Greenwood Leflore (1800–65) was one of the Choctaw leaders who signed the treaty of Dancing Rabbit Creek on September 27, 1830. The treaty ceded all remaining Choctaw land east of the Mississippi to the United States in exchange for lands in the western Indian Territory (present Oklahoma). Most of the Choctaw Nation was forced to migrate west between 1831 and 1833, but Leflore remained in Mississippi and became an American citizen.

A FABLE

670.7 *Place de Ville*] Town square.

670.9 *Hôtel*] In full, *Hôtel de Ville*, town hall.

698.16–17 *Comité des Forges*] A national association of iron and steel manufacturers.

698.17 *S.P.A.D.*] *Société Provisoire des Aéroplanes Deperdussin*, a society of aircraft manufacturers.

698.26 expletive . . . legend.] French general Pierre-Jacques Cambronne, commander of the Imperial Guard at Waterloo, was said to have replied "Merde" in response to a British demand for surrender.

708.39 'Gil Blas,'] A picaresque romance by Alain René Lesage (1668–1747).

711.20–21 *Able . . . France*] A play on a well-known palindrome, "Able was I ere I saw Elba."

711.37 *École Militaire*] Military college, then at St. Cyr, for the training of infantry and cavalry officers.

722.24 K.R. and O.] King's Regulations and Orders.

722.29 Sandhurst] Village in England, site of the Royal Military Academy.

722.30–31 Mons . . . bar] The Mons Star medal was given to those who served in France and Belgium before November 23, 1914. The Military Cross is a decoration for bravery awarded to officers; the bar indicates that it has been awarded a second time.

723.9 Cox's] Cox and Co., Bankers and Army Agents.

724.28 R.T.O.] Railway Transport Office.

726.37 A.S.C.] Army Service Corps.

730.19–21 lo . . . dead] Cf. Christopher Marlowe (1564–93), *The Jew of Malta*, IV, 1.

739.38 archie] Anti-aircraft artillery.

742.4–5 *In Christ . . . began*] Cf. 1 Corinthians 15:20–22.

758.2–3 'Change . . . windy] The stock exchange. Windy is slang for afraid, nervous, alarmed (from "got the wind up").

758.11–12 long vac.] The long vacation, as in the Oxford and Cambridge academic year.

759.14 *Gaston de la Tour*] *Gaston de Latour* (1896), unfinished novel by Walter Pater.

759.40 Pip Emma] Signaling code for P.M.

762.34–36 Vickers . . . Lewis] On the S.E. fighter aircraft, a belt-fed Vickers machine gun was mounted on the fuselage in front of the pilot's cockpit and synchronized to fire through the arc of the propeller without hitting its blades. A drum-fed Lewis machine gun was mounted on the top wing; in its normal position it fired forward over the propeller arc, but it could be elevated to fire upwards.

765.23 Aldis] A gun sight.

773.8 napoo] Finished, done, nothing doing, end of argument (from *il n'y a plus*, "it is no more").

773.10 p.b.i.] Poor bloody infantry.

800.21–22 *Les Amis . . . Monde*] Literally, "The Myriad and Anonymous Friends to France of All the World".

802.25 D.C.M.] Distinguished Conduct Medal.

834.36 d'Artagnan] Hero of *The Three Musketeers.*

835.22 espada] Matador.

858.33 p.c.] Signaling code for post of command.

858.39 Ack Emma] A.M.

888.30 Antipas] Herod Antipas (21 B.C.–A.D. 39).

893.6 St Cyr] See note 711.37.

893.29 *banlieu*] Suburbs, outskirts.

916.2 *Der Tag*] The Day.

979.8 No heel taps] A toast, like "Bottoms up!" (from the heel tap shape of the residue of liquor left at the bottom of a glass).

1026.33 his *poule*] His whore.

1031.27 *Mon homme . . . mari*] My man—my husband.

1032.3 'Monjay.] "Eat" (*mangez!*).

CATALOGING INFORMATION

Faulkner, William, 1897–1962.
Novels 1942–1954.
Edited by Joseph Blotner and Noel Polk.

(The Library of America ; 73)
Contents: Go down, Moses—Intruder in the dust—Requiem for a nun—A fable.
I. Title: Go down, Moses. II. Title: Intruder in the dust. III. Title: Requiem for a nun. IV. Title: A fable. V. Series.
PS3511.A86A6 1994 813′.52—dc20 94-2942
ISBN 0-940450-85-2 (acid-free paper)

THE LIBRARY OF AMERICA SERIES

1. Herman Melville, *Typee, Omoo, Mardi* (1982)
2. Nathaniel Hawthorne, *Tales and Sketches* (1982)
3. Walt Whitman, *Poetry and Prose* (1982)
4. Harriet Beecher Stowe, *Three Novels* (1982)
5. Mark Twain, *Mississippi Writings* (1982)
6. Jack London, *Novels and Stories* (1982)
7. Jack London, *Novels and Social Writings* (1982)
8. William Dean Howells, *Novels 1875–1886* (1982)
9. Herman Melville, *Redburn, White-Jacket, Moby-Dick* (1983)
10. Nathaniel Hawthorne, *Novels* (1983)
11. Francis Parkman, *France and England in North America*, vol. I (1983)
12. Francis Parkman, *France and England in North America*, vol. II (1983)
13. Henry James, *Novels 1871–1880* (1983)
14. Henry Adams, *Novels, Mont Saint Michel, The Education* (1983)
15. Ralph Waldo Emerson, *Essays and Lectures* (1983)
16. Washington Irving, *History, Tales and Sketches* (1983)
17. Thomas Jefferson, *Writings* (1984)
18. Stephen Crane, *Prose and Poetry* (1984)
19. Edgar Allan Poe, *Poetry and Tales* (1984)
20. Edgar Allan Poe, *Essays and Reviews* (1984)
21. Mark Twain, *The Innocents Abroad, Roughing It* (1984)
22. Henry James, *Essays, American & English Writers* (1984)
23. Henry James, *European Writers & The Prefaces* (1984)
24. Herman Melville, *Pierre, Israel Potter, The Confidence-Man, Tales & Billy Budd* (1985)
25. William Faulkner, *Novels 1930–1935* (1985)
26. James Fenimore Cooper, *The Leatherstocking Tales*, vol. I (1985)
27. James Fenimore Cooper, *The Leatherstocking Tales*, vol. II (1985)
28. Henry David Thoreau, *A Week, Walden, The Maine Woods, Cape Cod* (1985)
29. Henry James, *Novels 1881–1886* (1985)
30. Edith Wharton, *Novels* (1986)
31. Henry Adams, *History of the United States during the Administrations of Jefferson* (1986)
32. Henry Adams, *History of the United States during the Administrations of Madison* (1986)
33. Frank Norris, *Novels and Essays* (1986)
34. W. E. B. Du Bois, *Writings* (1986)
35. Willa Cather, *Early Novels and Stories* (1987)
36. Theodore Dreiser, *Sister Carrie, Jennie Gerhardt, Twelve Men* (1987)
37. Benjamin Franklin, *Writings* (1987)
38. William James, *Writings 1902–1910* (1987)
39. Flannery O'Connor, *Collected Works* (1988)
40. Eugene O'Neill, *Complete Plays 1913–1920* (1988)
41. Eugene O'Neill, *Complete Plays 1920–1931* (1988)
42. Eugene O'Neill, *Complete Plays 1932–1943* (1988)
43. Henry James, *Novels 1886–1890* (1989)
44. William Dean Howells, *Novels 1886–1888* (1989)
45. Abraham Lincoln, *Speeches and Writings 1832–1858* (1989)
46. Abraham Lincoln, *Speeches and Writings 1859–1865* (1989)
47. Edith Wharton, *Novellas and Other Writings* (1990)
48. William Faulkner, *Novels 1936–1940* (1990)
49. Willa Cather, *Later Novels* (1990)
50. Ulysses S. Grant, *Personal Memoirs and Selected Letters* (1990)
51. William Tecumseh Sherman, *Memoirs* (1990)
52. Washington Irving, *Bracebridge Hall, Tales of a Traveller, The Alhambra* (1991)
53. Francis Parkman, *The Oregon Trail, The Conspiracy of Pontiac* (1991)
54. James Fenimore Cooper, *Sea Tales: The Pilot, The Red Rover* (1991)

55. Richard Wright, *Early Works* (1991)
56. Richard Wright, *Later Works* (1991)
57. Willa Cather, *Stories, Poems, and Other Writings* (1992)
58. William James, *Writings 1878–1899* (1992)
59. Sinclair Lewis, *Main Street & Babbitt* (1992)
60. Mark Twain, *Collected Tales, Sketches, Speeches, & Essays 1852–1890* (1992)
61. Mark Twain, *Collected Tales, Sketches, Speeches, & Essays 1891–1910* (1992)
62. *The Debate on the Constitution: Part One* (1993)
63. *The Debate on the Constitution: Part Two* (1993)
64. Henry James, *Collected Travel Writings: Great Britain & America* (1993)
65. Henry James, *Collected Travel Writings: The Continent* (1993)
66. *American Poetry: The Nineteenth Century,* Vol. 1 (1993)
67. *American Poetry: The Nineteenth Century,* Vol. 2 (1993)
68. Frederick Douglass, *Autobiographies,* (1994)
69. Sarah Orne Jewett, *Novels and Stories* (1994)
70. Ralph Waldo Emerson, *Collected Poems and Translations* (1994)
71. Mark Twain, *Historical Romances* (1994)
72. John Steinbeck, *Novels and Stories 1932–1937* (1994)
73. William Faulkner, *Novels 1942–1954* (1994)

*This book is set in 10 point Linotron Galliard,
a face designed for photocomposition by Matthew Carter
and based on the sixteenth-century face Granjon. The paper is
acid-free Ecusta Nyalite and meets the requirements for permanence
of the American National Standards Institute. The binding
material is Brillianta, a woven rayon cloth made by
Van Heek-Scholco Textielfabrieken, Holland.
The composition is by The Clarinda
Company. Printing and binding by
R. R. Donnelley & Sons Company.
Designed by Bruce Campbell.*

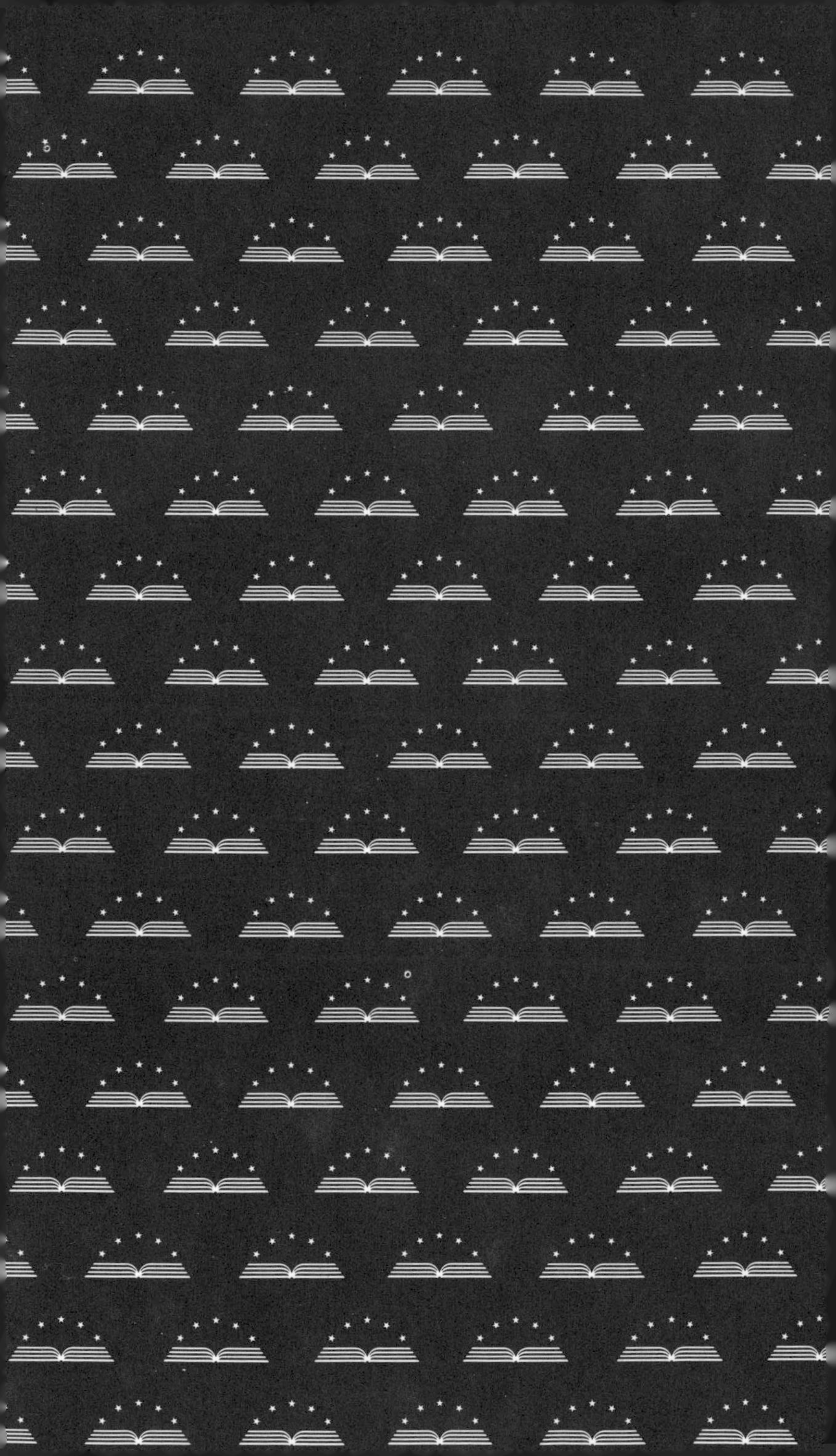